The Virginia Exiles

Books by Elizabeth Gray Vining

THE VIRGINIA EXILES

WINDOWS FOR THE CROWN PRINCE

THE
Virginia Exiles

By *Elizabeth Gray Vining*

J. B. LIPPINCOTT COMPANY
Philadelphia and New York

To V. G. G.
With love

FOREWORD

THE LITTLE-KNOWN EPISODE in American history on which this novel is based is a matter of record. I have taken no liberties with the facts of the arrest, imprisonment, banishment, and return of the twenty Philadelphians. For the purposes of my story, however, I have removed one of the original exiles, Owens Jones, junior, and substituted an imaginary character, Caleb Middleton, junior. A list of the actual exiles is given below.

A note on the "plain language" of the Quakers may be helpful. At the time of the story a transition was taking place from the "thou" of the 17th century to the "thee" which is used by modern Quakers for all cases, subject or object. Even the grammatical older Friends, however, tended to slip into the use of the third person verb with the *thou* instead of the correct second person, as, Thou was, Thou said, Thou has.

THE EXILES

Thomas Affleck, cabinetmaker
Elijah Brown, merchant, father of Charles Brockden Brown, America's first novelist
Henry Drinker, merchant
Charles Eddy, ironmonger
Miers Fisher, lawyer
Samuel Fisher, merchant
Thomas Fisher, merchant
Thomas Gilpin, merchant
John Hunt, merchant
Charles Jervis, merchant
Owen Jones, junior, merchant
Israel Pemberton, merchant

8   FOREWORD

James Pemberton, merchant
John Pemberton, concerned Friend, who lived on inherited income
    and devoted his life to the affairs of the Yearly Meeting
Edward Penington, merchant
Thomas Pike, fencing and dancing master
Samuel Pleasants, merchant
William Smith, broker
William Drewet Smith, apothecary
Thomas Wharton, merchant

The Virginia Exiles

I

THE TWO CALEB MIDDLETONS, father and son, walked together up the hill from the Phoebe Ann Furnace to the Big House. The heart of the son was hot with rebellion. He opened his mouth to protest once more.

"Not now, Caleb," his father anticipated him, raising his hand in the familiar, pompous gesture for silence. "Later, perhaps. But the decision is made. I have told the officer and he has gone. I have told our men."

"Does it make no difference at all what I think?" cried Caleb. "Or what I've heard in the city?"

He had ridden from Philadelphia that day in early August, 1777, full of the news that was pouring through the coffee houses and taverns like water through a sluice. Though he had sent his horse on to the stable by a boy, he was still in his dusty riding clothes, hot and tired, but conscious only of his feelings of outrage and revolt and his swollen thoughts.

"I told thee, I don't want to talk about it any further now. After supper. I have to save my breath to climb the hill, if thou doesn't. These things are not easy at my age."

The old appeal of age to the chivalry of youth! Caleb angrily brushed it aside. But I have had a great blow! he wanted to shout. This is a monstrous thing that has been done! I share in the work of the furnace, I should share in the decisions. I won't sit down under arbitrary pronouncements! The tyranny of the king and the tyranny of his father seemed to be two branches of the same smothering growth and he wanted to resist both. But the knowledge of the respect due to a father lay on him like the lid on a seething pot and kept him silent, scowling and slapping his boot with his riding crop.

He had known soon after he turned off the Great Road that the furnace was out of blast, for where normally he would have begun to hear its intermittent roar he had heard only the chatter of a yellowthroat in the undergrowth, the rustle of the wind in the tall trees overhead, and the other light sounds of the summer afternoon woods. He had been surprised and disappointed but not especially disturbed, since they sometimes had to shut down for a while in the summer when the water in the creek was low.

But when he had come out of the woods into the open valley where the village clustered around the furnace and the Big House on the hill brooded over all, he knew at once that something was wrong. The women who normally would have been off working in the fields at this time gathered around the doors of the tenant houses, talking, while the small children, sensing as children will the trouble of their elders, hung around their skirts instead of playing. Through the open doors of the wheelwright's shop and the smithy men could be seen with their heads together. The furnace at the end of the road was silent and deserted, no wagons hauling ore or charcoal up to the bank, no men running over the bridge to the tunnel-head with baskets and barrows, no voices from the casting shed, no roar from the cold stack.

At the square stone building across the road from the stack, Caleb had dismounted, hailed a passing boy and told him to take Ladybird up to the stable, and had gone inside to find out what had happened, expecting to hear of some serious accident to men or machinery. The store where the workmen and their families came to buy groceries and drygoods and other supplies was empty, but in the office beyond he had found his father and Jacob Heinzel, the iron founder. From them he had learned with shocking abruptness the thing that had been done.

The Phoebe Ann Furnace had been shut down for as long as the war should continue. No more iron would be made there until peace was restored. The forty-odd workmen—founders, keepers, fillers, gutterers, colliers, and the rest—would scatter. The Middletons, as soon as they could get off, would move into Philadelphia, to their house on Third Street. Caleb himself was to devote his time to the store and warehouse in the city and to the management of the real estate that had come into the family with Sarah Leigh Middleton, his stepmother. He had been away a little less than a week, on business for the furnace, and in his absence this high-handed and, to Caleb, unworthy action had been taken.

They climbed a shallow flight of stone steps from the driveway to the broad terrace in front of the house and paused automatically in the usual spot to look at the view. Caleb waited for his father to clear his throat and say, "A fair prospect, a very fair prospect." Although he braced himself for the well-worn words as if for a blow, made irritable by the turmoil within him, he was perversely disappointed when they did not come. His father only sighed and clasped his hands behind his broad back.

It was a fair prospect. Two towering buttonwood trees, left from the original forest, shaded the terrace. They were shedding now, their bark falling away in big flakes, leaving the surface of the upper trunks and limbs pale yellow and smooth as a peeled onion. Below the terrace was the garden which Caleb's own mother had made and loved, enclosed with English box and bright now with pinks and lilies. From the garden the ground fell away to the meadow below, where the creek cut its curves through rich grass, and rose again patterned with fields tawny with wheat stubble or green with corn to the line of plumy woods on the top of the southern hills. To the east, close under the knoll on which the Big House stood and partly hidden by trees, were the massed roofs of furnace and village. Up the hill behind the house and westward, the thousands of acres of woodland upon which the hungry furnace depended for its charcoal supply were a great shawl around the shoulders of the valley.

The Phoebe Ann Furnace, situated on Parson's Creek, a tributary of French Creek, was one of a number of ironworks hidden away among the hills behind the Schuylkill. Each plantation was a little world unto itself. It had its own mine hole and three or four miners to dig the ore out of the ground, its own share of the limestone that lay everywhere under the soil of this country; each had a small troop of woodcutters and colliers to provide the charcoal which was needed in enormous quantities. A furnace the size of the Phoebe Ann devoured the product of an acre or more of woods for every twenty-four hours that it was in blast. Each plantation had its farm and often its gristmill, its gardens and orchards, workshops, barns, store, and millpond. The men lived in the tenant houses in the village; their wives worked in the fields at seedtime and harvest, and in winter carded, spun, and wove the wool from the sheep. Overlooking all was the Big House on the hill, where the ironmaster lived, the feudal lord of his small community. The great wagons drawn by three mule teams that took the pig iron to the forges or over the rutted roads to Philadelphia and its wharves, brought back necessities for the workmen and luxuries for the ironmaster and his family, English china and silver, Turkey carpets, French silks, and India muslins.

Caleb had had other plans for himself than to succeed his father at the Phoebe Ann; but when, five years ago at seventeen, in obedience to Mr. Middleton's demand, he had put aside his desire to become a doctor, he had made a good second best of being an ironmaster. Though he had not chosen the furnace he had grown to love it and the drama of it: the fire against the sky at night, the pulsing roar, the fillers like ants crossing the bridge from the bank to the tunnel-head with their baskets of ore and limestone and charcoal and running back for more, the big water wheel turning slowly and the great bellows forcing the air into the crucible, the tension mounting till the moment came when the decision must be made to tap. Twice a day the climax came, yet it was ever new. A shrill blast on the horn brought the men running, the dam stone was pulled away and the molten iron came pouring forth in a fiery red flood, filling the sand molds of the casting bed, called the sow and pigs, or being ladled into the molds for hollow ware. He liked seeing the wagons go off loaded with pig iron for the forges in the vicinity, Mount Joy and Vincent and Warwick, where it would be reheated and hammered and refined. He liked riding over the wooded hills, inspecting the charcoal pits, deciding which stand of trees to cut next. Hickory made the best charcoal, but oak and chestnut were good too. He enjoyed his association with the men, Jacob Heinzel the chief founder and Mac Murchison his assistant, the Negro freedmen who worked as woodcutters, the Welsh miners, and the others. As Caleb had developed in experience and skill, his father had more and more withdrawn from active work into the office where, warmed on cold days by a ten-plate stove cast on the place, he was busy with orders and accounts and the contents of the wall safe behind the chestnut paneling.

The news that the furnace was to be shut down permanently and that Caleb was to exchange his active life here for all the petty niggling details of a city countinghouse had come like a thunderclap. For the second time he saw the course in life on which he had set his feet threatened by the arbitrary decision of his father, and this time he did not intend to submit tamely.

"The men!" he burst out. "They'll only go to other furnaces, where they'll snap them up. If we let them go now, we'll never get them back. Or," he added pointedly, "they'll enlist in the militia."

His voice betrayed him. What was to have been a cool, ironic thrust came out like the growl of a sulky boy. Though he was almost twenty-three and a man in the eyes of the world, at home he was still a boy under his father's thumb. His smoldering anger turned in upon himself.

"They must follow their own consciences," said Mr. Middleton calmly. "Jacob is a Mennonite—he feels as we do. He'll go back to his father's farm beyond Lancaster. The others will have to follow the light as God gives it to them—if they pay any attention, which I doubt, some of them at least. At any rate I must do what I think is right."

"But what about me?"

"Thou art a Friend, Caleb. Friends do not take part in war or in any work that is preparation for war."

Though his father used the plain language still, he was actually no longer a Friend. Four years ago his Monthly Meeting had disowned him for marrying out of union. Sarah Leigh was an Episcopalian. But still he spoke to his children in the Quaker way, still thought as a Quaker.

"Some Friends," Caleb strove for a voice that should sound reasonable and mature, "have felt it right to resist tyranny." Almost all the other Pennsylvania ironmasters were making iron for the Continental army, and some of them were Quakers. Even if one could not conscientiously make cannon and cannon balls, pig iron was still in demand at the forges, which were turning out necessities for the army. Firebacks and cooking pots and stove-plates might wait for the coming of peace, but salt pans were essential now. "Liberty, thee knows, is also an ancient testimony of Friends."

"There's a great deal of loose talk about tyranny and liberty going around. I told thee, Caleb, I don't want to discuss it now. Shall we go in? I think thy mother is waiting for us."

Caleb pulled a seed pod off a tall spire of dark red hollyhock that grew beside the door and pulled it apart with his thin, sinewy fingers—surgeon's fingers, he had thought once. Sarah Middleton was a good woman, but he would never call her mother.

"I'll be along in a little while," he said. "I want to see if Amos has rubbed down Ladybird properly."

For the first time since they had left the office and started up the hill he looked at his father squarely. His color was bad, almost gray, and the lines that went from his nostrils to the corners of his mouth were deeply etched; his cheeks sagged into his neck. He was sixty-four and he looked older.

"Thee feeling all right?" said Caleb, but the question, or its implications, was only an irritant, and they parted without further words.

As soon as he was inside the stableyard a kind of peace fell upon Caleb, the familiar soothing spell of the place, compounded of the smell of horses and manure, of trampled dirt in the sunshine and mossy stone walls in the shade, the sound of harness jingling, Amos' breathy whistle, the splashing of water into the trough or the whinny of a horse, and partly of the feeling of a safe enclosure that shut out irrelevancies and protected the busy concentrated life that went on within. Perhaps, he thought, as the cords within him loosened and his natural hopefulness asserted itself, perhaps it was too soon to give up. He and his father would talk again after supper, and a way would open. The men had not gone yet. The blowing-in of a furnace after it had been out of blast was tedious, but not much time would be lost.

A girl's laugh, shrill and taunting, cut across the peaceful sounds of the place, followed by a boy's enraged howl.

"I'll smash thy nose, Patty, thee skunk thee!"

From behind the cribhouse Caleb's sister Patty came running, and close behind her, red-faced and furious, his little brother Edward.

"Caleb, save me!" screamed Patty, flinging her arms around his waist and cowering behind him with a show of panic.

He scooped up Edward as he came by, and holding him, kicking and yelling, upside down under his arm, turned to look down at Patty.

"What did thee do to him?" he asked.

"I didn't do *anything*! Did thee hear what he called me? And he said he'd smash my nose!"

"Thee's got a black smudge all across that noble organ. Thee'd better go and wash thy face."

She had their father's Roman nose, china blue eyes, slightly stupid, and an arrogant tilt to her tow-colored head. She was a tall, handsome girl, Caleb thought. She hadn't the kind of beauty that appealed to him, but she'd take some man in some day, and it was to be hoped for his sake that he wouldn't be the thin-skinned kind, for Patty walked where she pleased and she neither knew nor cared whose feelings she was stepping on. Not that that gave Edward license to call her a skunk.

He carried the wriggling small boy to the rain barrel, which was full, and with a swift movement reversed him quickly and dipped him in, giving his posterior a smart spank as he set him on his feet again. "That'll cool thee off—and warm thee up," he said, grinning, and turned to go into the stable.

Wiping his wet face with his sleeve and pushing his hair out of his eyes, Edward followed close on Caleb's heels, pleased on the whole by his big brother's attention.

Caroline Rutter, whom his father admired so much, thought Caleb, was just such another one as Patty, and he didn't like and never would like that fair, florid, Amazonish type, however subtly and persuasively she might be suggested to him. A very different little face, seldom far from his thoughts these days, swam into his mind, so vividly that he could almost see it dancing like the motes in the shaft of sunshine in the dim stable. It was a heart-shaped face, brown-eyed and piquant, with a patch at the corner of the red, moist mouth, calling attention to the pouting lower lip, and a powdered curl against the smooth white neck calling attention to the soft white hills of her bosom. Phyllis. "Phyllis is my only joy . . . Phyllis smiling and beguiling . . ." Phyllis—Pike. Mistress Thomas Pike, the wife of the dancing master.

Ladybird was in her box, eating the oats she had so fully earned. She tossed her head when she saw Caleb and snorted. He ran his hand over her neck. It was dry but he thought she ought to have the thin blanket.

"Amos! A-mos!"

He saw Edward there beside him. "Go find Amos and tell him to put a light blanket on Ladybird."

"Caleb, thee don't know what happened day before yesterday. Some soldiers came and took all the blankets for the army. They took all the ones in the chest, even the best blankets from England, and all the horse blankets."

"Where did they come from?"

"From Reading. How'll we keep warm next winter?"

"Oh, thee can't expect to keep warm. Thee'll have to stay up all night flapping thy arms around thee like the teamsters. There are some old blankets in the harness room. Tell Amos he's to find something."

Whistling the catchy song which had spread through the colonies, "By uniting we stand, by dividing we fall," Caleb crossed the stableyard and went on to the house. His progress as usual took on something of the air of a procession. Horace, the bound boy, ran ahead of him to his room with a brass can of hot water. Hettie, the broad-beamed cook, who had obviously been watching for him, emerged from the kitchen with offers of fresh buttermilk. In the back hall, which was cool and shady, he was met by Sarah Middleton.

She was a markedly homely woman, broad of frame and short of stature, with small eyes, heavy, plain features, and dark hairs on her upper lip and chin. Caleb, to whom beauty in a woman was not an adornment but the indispensable minimum, would have regarded her as a negligible element in the household, had he not been reminded a dozen times a day by the children's acceptance of her that she was the successor to his own lovely mother. That Sarah was strong and warmhearted, generous and quite without conceit, his mind acknowledged, but his heart, sore and jealous because the marriage had come so soon after his mother's death, still was closed against her.

"Caleb, I'm glad you're back," she said. "We've had such a time! I'm anxious about your father. He gets so excited over these people and it's not good for him. Be as soothing as you can, won't you? And Tacy fell down and scraped her knee. It ought to be dressed, but she won't let Sukie or me touch it. She insists you must do it for her."

Tacy, the small sister who had cost his mother her life, was his pet and his darling. He found her upstairs sitting on her nurse's lap, her round face streaked with tears, her brown eyes swimming, her wounded leg stuck out stiffly in front of her.

"Fix it," she commanded regally, with a hiccup.

He bent over and gravely examined the skinned and bloody knee, in which bits of gravel were buried deep. "It's all dirty," he said. "I'll wash it for thee and then I'll give thee a big bandage. How 'bout that?"

She nodded a little apprehensively, and he held out his arms to her. "Come on, let's go out into the hall."

He lifted her up, and she twined her arms tight around his neck, pressed her fat, damp cheek against his and gave him a wet kiss. Kissing the tip of her nose, he blinked his eyes quickly to tickle her face with his eyelashes in the special ritual that they had. She gave a sweet, delighted crow of laughter and he hugged her tight before he set her down carefully on the broad window sill, where the light was good.

The wide, second story hall, which ran the full depth of the house, was furnished with chairs and a sofa and the blanket chest. Between the two windows on the north was a big walnut secretary where stores of medicines were kept.

Mrs. Middleton brought the key and opened the door. On the shelves were jars of manna and senna and rhubarb preparations, opodeldoc and dried roseleaves, camomile and mint, bottles of laudanum and castor oil and Daffy's Elixir, bark both whole and ground, boxes of lint and rolls of old linen, little pots of deer suet and goose grease. Never a day passed on an iron plantation that someone did not come to the mistress for treatment.

It was an important occasion when Caleb officiated. Patty and Edward pressed close to watch, Patty ostentatiously holding her nose as Edward approached. Caleb took off his coat, handing it to Edward to hold, and rolled up his shirt sleeves; he washed his hands carefully in the basin held by Horace, then motioned for him to fill a bowl with fresh water.

"I saw thy nephew in Philadelphia," he told Tacy, dipping a wad of lint in the warm water and gently touching it to the dried blood and gravel on her knee. She whimpered. "Look at what comes off on the lint! He's a fine, big, saucy boy for his age, but he needs thee to teach him manners. Hold still, sweetie, if thee can. I know it stings. I thought it a little remiss of him not to inquire about his Aunt Tacy, but no doubt he will when—that's a good girl, just a little more—no doubt he will when he learns to speak."

For all her woe, this brought a brief flicker of a smile to Tacy's face, and he took advantage of the moment's distraction to swab a raw place that he had not yet dared touch. She shrieked and kicked.

"Shall I hold her?" offered Patty officiously.

They were all reminded of the harrowing time when Tacy had put part of a walnut shell up her nose and three people had had to pinion her while the doctor took it out with a silver hook. The suggestion was an unfortunate one. Tacy howled.

"Certainly not," said Caleb. "Tacy is a brave girl. She'll hold herself." He removed Patty by planting an elbow in her stomach and pushing.

"Come on, Tace, just one more little bit and then I'll put some ointment on and a bandage and give thee the present I brought thee from Philadelphia. Can thee guess what it is?"

He worked swiftly, absorbed in what he was doing. Tall, broad-shouldered, narrow-hipped and muscular, he looked smart even in his travel-worn riding breeches, limp white cambric shirt and rolled-up sleeves. His hair, bright chestnut-brown with a natural wave, was brushed back from his forehead and tied in a fashion symbolic, to strict Quakers, of the gay world. He had brown eyes, deep set and wide apart, a straight nose, flaring at the nostrils, a well-cut mouth, and a firm chin, delicately square. He was capable of great concentration, as now, when he was perhaps at his most attractive, capable also of hot rage and petulance, as well as humor and sudden bursts of gaiety.

"You're moody," his stepmother had said more than once. "It spoils you."

He knew that he never showed his best to her, though some-times, he acknowledged reluctantly, she seemed to see more than she was shown.

"There!" he exclaimed, tucking in the end of an impressive bandage. "Thee's finished. And Sukie can fetch the package out of my saddlebag. . . . John goes to join his regiment next week," he said to Mrs. Middleton over his shoulder as he tidily folded linen and put away the jar of salve, "but first he's going to take Sue and little John to his parents in Lancaster. It seems to be generally expected that Howe will take Philadelphia and that Washington will not be able to prevent him."

She made no answer. They were alone in the hall now, for Edward and Patty had trailed along with Tacy to get the package out of Caleb's bag. "You ought to have been a doctor," she said impulsively. "It's still not too late. I could help you—if you want it."

She had come too close. They both knew it at once. He bowed slightly in the formal way he had picked up somewhere and said, "Thank you, ma'am. I am quite content with being an iron-master."

"Well, never mind," she answered. "Thank you for tending to Tacy."

Frowning, he went into his own room and chased the children out.

"I will not have my son become a man-midwife," his father had declared, and in the end Caleb had yielded, after fruitlessly pointing to Dr. Shippen as an example of a distinguished physician who had saved the life of many an anguished woman without losing either his dignity or other people's respect.

Of the ten children Caleb's mother had borne, five had died in infancy—three little girls hopefully named for her, one after another, and two boys—and of the tenth, who came feet first, she herself had died, in torture. He picked up the miniature which Charlie Peale had painted when he first came back from England, and looked at it. Even then, at forty, a few months before her death, she had still been beautiful. The miniature caught some-thing of the tenderness and humor in her brown eyes, but it was too stiff, too conventionally pretty, too limited by its paint and its ivory, even to suggest the luminous quality of her spirit, which had shone through her worn body as if it had been transparent.

II

After supper Caleb and his father sat on the terrace in the twilight. Mrs. Middleton hovered about protesting that the night vapors were unhealthy and urging them to come into the parlor, but they remained determinedly oblivious to her.

"I might be a fly for all the attention you pay to me," she complained.

She drew up a chair for herself, scraping its legs across the flagstones, and for a time she sat with them, slapping at mosquitoes and inserting cheerful remarks into the conversation, until by an impatient twitch of the shoulder, a loud "harrumph!" and the pointed use of short silences followed by some such phrase as, "I was about to say," or, "To go back to thy observation," her husband made it plain to her that her presence was not required.

She retired in good order, with a mumbled exclamation that gave them to understand she had recollected a duty elsewhere. Restored to politeness once they had won their point, both rose punctiliously when she left, and Caleb went to open the door for her. She mouthed a silent message to him behind his father's back, "Don't keep him up late!" The barrier between son and father thinned a little in the momentary warmth of masculine solidarity as they both felt the relief of having routed the female intrusion.

Caleb knew that his father in his day had changed the direction of his life in obedience to parental wish, and he wondered why the memory of it had not given him more understanding. Or had he accepted long ago and never since examined the premise that the fact of fatherhood endowed a man with a supernatural knowledge of what was best for his children?

Caleb's grandfather, youngest son of a yeoman in Northamptonshire, had come to Philadelphia just before 1700, had won himself a lucky foothold as a merchant, and prospered; he had become a Quaker and married the daughter of an elder in the Bank Meeting. When his third son, Caleb, was old enough, he had been apprenticed to his mother's brother, who had a small fleet of ships in the English trade. He had liked his work, tinged as it was with the drama of the sea; he had had one voyage to London and was looking forward to another, when his father became aware of the profits to be made from the iron industry developing in the Pennsylvania hills and bought a half interest in a furnace newly established on Parson's Creek. Following the fashion of giving women's names to iron furnaces, the owner, Richard Ross, had called it Phoebe for his wife and Ann for his daughter.

The satisfactory business relationship between Mr. Ross and Mr. Middleton resulted in the marriage of Caleb and Ann. Almost at once, in one of those small, sporadic but deadly epidemics of yellow fever, Caleb had lost his wife, his unborn child, and his father-in-law—and acquired the other half of the Phoebe Ann. He had intended to put a manager in to run the furnace which he and his father now owned jointly and to continue in the shipping business which he loved. Instead he found himself headed for the backwoods, with a new trade to master and a wholly new life to live. Whatever anguish of grief and loneliness he endured during those first years on Parson's Creek, he never spoke about it in later life.

He was thirty-seven when, strong, handsome, wearing the cloak of his ironmaster's authority, he went to Philadelphia to the bedside of his dying father and while in the city met Margaret Penington. The seventeen years between them had disappeared in the springing flame of their love, and when he returned to the Phoebe Ann he took his young wife with him. It had been a happy marriage, in spite of the recurrent toll of child-bearing and child-loss. Young Caleb could remember a golden time when there was laughter and tenderness in the house, and his father had seemed to him the embodiment of bravery, goodness, and wisdom.

Looking at his father now, while in the meadow below fireflies rose and gleamed in an endless slow ascension, Caleb felt a softening of his resentment, even as his determination not to be overborne stiffened.

"I've never seen the lightning bugs fly so high as they are doing this year," commented Mr. Middleton, apparently reluctant, even with Sarah safely in the house where she could not interrupt, to open the subject that lay before them.

"Washington was in Philadelphia while I was there," said Caleb. "I caught a glimpse of him going into Robert Morris's. They say he came to meet the young French marquis who is so enthusiastic. Nobody knows exactly where the British fleet is. Every day there's a different rumor. It was seen at the entrance to the Delaware Bay, but some say it went away again. Baltimore may be in danger, but most people think that Philadelphia is the real goal. Many people are evacuating. They are looking for just what we have here, a substantial house in the country off the main roads."

"Why are they all so eager to leave the city?"

"Most patriots don't want to be there when the British troops occupy it."

"I have nothing to fear from the British. On the other hand I have already experienced the depredations of the Continentals. Men who said they were from the Quartermaster General were here day before yesterday requisitioning blankets. They offered money—a ridiculous sum for imported English blankets. I refused to accept it. I'll not sell my blankets for purposes of war."

"So they took them anyhow."

"Yes, but not with my consent. Yesterday two officers came— in military uniform—also from the Quartermaster General. They brought an agreement for me to sign—so many cannons each month, so many balls, so many salt pans. Twenty-five tons a week. We've never cast more than twenty. But I'm to make a prodigious patriotic effort and produce twenty-five. He didn't say where we were to get the charcoal from. It would take six thousand cords of wood a year at that rate. But that's beside the point."

"Thee gave them a final refusal?"

"I did. They offered to argue, but I convinced them it was useless. But there will be more like them, now that they've found the way here and see what we have. That is why I determined to shut down altogether and clear out for the city."

"But, Father, isn't there a middle course? Thee and thy wife and the children go into Philadelphia, while I stay here and run the furnace. Then both of our consciences will be satisfied. I can't think it right to—"

"No, no, it's out of the question. I won't hear to it."

"I understand how thee feels about munitions of war. I don't agree in the circumstances, but if I honor thy scruples, if I make only pig iron and salt pans—no cannon—I think I can satisfy them with that much." He felt rather than saw the upraised hand in the dim light and rushed on. "I can't sit down tamely and do nothing, when the whole question of freedom and oppression is at stake! After all, it was thy wish that I should learn to make iron, and now thee'd prevent me from using that knowledge for my country's benefit."

"Be silent, Caleb. I want to talk to thee about the present commotions. Thou refers, doubtless, to the fact that thou wanted to enroll in the Medical College and I prevailed upon thee to do otherwise. Thou hast in mind, no doubt, whether thou knows it or not, that all fathers are oppressive and that England stands in a father's relation to America. But put aside thy private grievance and consider the facts in the public situation. I agree that the proceedings of the British ministry have been unjust. I am—and have been—willing to join in peaceful legal resistance. But Friends —and in this I am still a Friend—have always been opposed to war and revolution. We cannot give allegiance to a revolutionary government any more than we could assist Britain in her unrighteous methods of conquering the rebellious provinces. I intend to maintain a position of strict neutrality. To supply the Continentals with material directly or indirectly used for war purposes would be to enlist on their side."

"Friends have taken literally Christ's injunction not to resist evil," said Caleb, borrowing an argument from William Penn's secretary a generation earlier, "but they seem to prefer to forget that he also said, Lay not up for yourselves treasures upon earth."

"That line of reasoning implies that if we disobey one of our Lord's commands we must disobey all. It is trivial and foolish, if not downright wicked. There is another, a very practical aspect. I have been to England, thou hast not. Thou hast not seen the might of England. Thou sees Philadelphia, a large and prosperous city, but it is the only one of its proportions on this continent. How can thirteen scattered and feeble colonies, jealous of one another, prevail against the might and power of England?"

"But they *are* united—united in a common hatred of oppression, united by interest and faith, and if thee wants more concrete bonds, by a Continental Congress and a common army."

"My dear boy, Pennsylvania itself is not united. It is torn between the Quaker element in the east, with the Germans in their train, and the self-willed and militant Scotch-Irish frontiersmen in the west. Those violent men of the frontier would change the whole order of civilized life as we have known it—just as they have thrown out the good charter that William Penn gave us and have illegally set up their so-called Constitution with a Supreme Executive Council instead of a governor. But that's not all. They cannot possibly defeat Britain in an armed contest. We have no manufactures—"

"We have iron."

"A mere handful of forges and furnaces. We cannot make cloth for soldiers' uniforms or boots for their feet in quantity sufficient for an army of any size. We have no sea power. We are at the mercy of an army with a fleet that can move at will from Boston to New York to Philadelphia or to Charleston, while Washington wonders helplessly where it will strike next."

He spoke as a man knowing life and the world to an ignorant boy. His tone, kindly in a condescending way, explanatory and slightly amused, galled Caleb into fury. With unsparing eyes, young and scornful and clear, he saw his father moved as much by the fear of being on the wrong side in a losing fight as by conscientious objection to munition-making. Despising caution as the meanest of motives, Caleb had moreover knowledge of the strength of the American cause that his father did not have, a knowledge that was part of his young bones and spirit, the product of the very air of the age in which he lived and to which his mind was open, derived not so much from what he heard his contemporaries say as what he saw and felt in men's gestures and faces and the tone of their voices, that revealed their purpose and their will and their vision.

"So now," he said bitterly, "we are to slink off to Philadelphia and leave the Phoebe Ann shut down behind us. Has thee thought it might be—probably will be—confiscated and that other men will make iron for the American cause if we don't?"

"Perhaps. But in the end, when this is all over, we shall recover it."

Caleb jumped to his feet. "But I shan't stay in Philadelphia," he cried, "because I can't agree to this—"

His father rose too. "Caleb, don't be overhasty—"

His voice trailed off into silence.

For a moment he stood there as if bewildered, before he pitched forward, turning as he fell, to lie stretched full length upon his back. Caleb's first thought as he leaped forward and knelt beside him, was relief that he had fallen on the grass instead of the flagstones. As he bent over his father's inert body, thrusting his hand into the bosom of his shirt in search of the heartbeat, he saw that the right side of the ashen face had slipped, so that it no longer matched the left. But even while his startled mind registered the fact and whispered to him the word "stroke," he saw the twisted features relax and consciousness slowly return. The pale, slightly bloodshot eyes opened and the blue lips moved.

"I'm all right," said his father with reassuring testiness. "Don't make a fuss. Help me up."

Caleb put his arm under his father's shoulders. Strong as he was, he had all he could do to pull the old man to his feet. Breathing hard, both of them, they stood together, swaying a little, at the edge of the terrace. Swiftly a squat figure emerged from the house and took Mr. Middleton's other arm.

"Lean on me, my dear," said Sarah. "Take it slowly. We'll put you to bed in the downstairs chamber."

She gave his son a long look of reproach. "Caleb, I warned you," she said.

III

It took three weeks to move the Middleton household from Parson's Creek to Philadelphia. It was a time of confusion, of nagging details, of endless decisions, many of them petty yet far-reaching in their results as they tied into the network of plans and arrangements in which the future of the family would be caught and held. Mr. Middleton's stroke, if it was a stroke, and the fear that a repetition of it might bring on paralysis or even death, hung over his wife and son like a threatening cloud, seldom mentioned but always there. Because of it, Caleb had promised his stepmother, in a long talk the morning after his father's fall, that he would help with the moving and that until his father was safely established in town he would make—or at least would announce—no drastic decisions of his own.

Mr. Middleton himself, who regarded his loss of consciousness that evening as a momentary upset caused by Caleb's willfulness, had no idea of being ill, now or later. He was, he said at intervals to anyone who would stop to listen to him, as good as ever, though when one was well launched into the sixties one naturally slowed up a little. All he required—and this, he implied, was a trifling matter manifestly due him—was that no one should cross him in any way. This assumption increased the pressure in the house, for he had to know all that was going on and they could never foresee when he would declare that a decision was too insignificant for him to be troubled about and that others should have taken it off his burdened shoulders, and when he would pounce upon some minor arrangement and complain that the disposal of it had been concealed from him with a view to circumventing his wishes.

In addition to all other difficulties, Mrs. Middleton was involved with the servant problem, which, always acute for those who were not willing to own slaves, arose at this moment in a most annoying form. Horace, the bound boy, ran off, and since it was reported that he had gone to offer himself to the army as a drummer boy it appeared useless to try to trace him and bring him back, though Caleb on his father's insistence did insert an advertisement in the *Pennsylvania Gazette*. Then the colored girl, Tess, the daughter of a freed slave, who had been left with the Middletons to be cared for and trained till she was twenty-one, dramatically revealed that she was pregnant. After much questioning and discussion it was decided which of the woodcutters was responsible and Tess was married, hopefully, to him; a disused cabin on the plantation was hastily repaired and furnished, and her husband, Mose, was employed to work under Ambrose Slack, the farmer. As the Middletons had suffered with Tess during the years when she broke everything she touched, nursing her through smallpox and several lesser illnesses and as she was only now at fifteen beginning to be of use to them, Mrs. Middleton was understandably exasperated.

Caleb rode to town twice to make arrangements for opening the house on Third Street and to superintend the wagonloads of supplies that were taken to it: firewood, fodder for the horses and the cow, bacon and hams from the smokehouse and sacks of flour and baskets of apples and vegetables from the farm. Though he was outwardly self-controlled, efficient, and dutiful, inwardly his mind and heart were in a turmoil, caught in the double conflict between his desire to enlist in the cause of liberty, on the one hand, and the Quaker principles in which he was brought up, on the other, between his determination to assert his manhood and make his own decisions and his fear of being responsible for his father's serious illness if he should defy him openly.

While the Phoebe Ann had been running, Caleb had felt confident about the course before him. To make iron acutely needed by the new country in its birth struggle had seemed to him a useful and patriotic action and yet a possible one for a Quaker, since it was not fighting, not engaging in what from his earliest childhood he had heard called "carnal warfare." His knowledge of the Bible was less extensive, since he was a modern Friend with a classical education, than his knowledge of Tacitus or Horace, but there were certain texts that no Quaker child could escape and one of them was, "Put up thy sword into the sheath. . . . My kingdom is not of this world; if my kingdom were of this world, then would my servants fight."

With the Quaker scriptures, the words of Fox and Penn, he was even more familiar. He remembered summer afternoons when his mother, always expecting another baby, would sit sewing on the terrace, while he and Sue, warm from their play, would drop down beside her demanding a story. Even now as he thought of it the scene sprang vividly to his mind; he could see her eyes, warm and tender, feel the slight roughness of her forefinger where the needle had pricked it, hear her vibrant voice. She had a fund of stories, most of them from Quaker history, which was full of adventure: stories of persecutions bravely endured, of shipwrecks and pirates, of threatening Indians who became friendly, of the girl who died on the gallows on Boston Common, of young William Penn in the Tower of London declaring, "My prison shall be my grave before I will budge a jot, for I owe my conscience to no mortal man."

Perhaps oftenest she told the story of George Fox and the jailors at Derby. "They could see he had the build for a soldier," she would say, "for he was tall and broad and strong, and they knew he had courage. So they offered to let him out of prison and make him a captain in the army. And what did he say? He told them, 'I live in the virtue of that life and power that takes away the occasion of all wars.' "

With the Phoebe Ann shut down there were, Caleb thought, two possibilities open to him. He might offer his services to some other furnace. Mark Bird, of the Coventry, had raised a company of militia, equipped it at his own expense, and got a commission as a colonel; he might need a manager to leave behind him. Or he could enlist in the Philadelphia Light Horse. Samuel Morris, the captain of the troop, was a Friend, or had been before he was disowned. Caleb was not happy about either course; both represented a compromise between his desires and his principles.

Early in the morning, when the screech owl quavered through darkness just beginning to turn gray, he would wake up and tussle with his problem. Life, he told himself, thumping his hot pillow, was a matter of compromise at best. One had to decide at what point one would yield and at what point one must stand.

He thought of John Dickinson, who used to come sometimes to the Fourth Street Meeting when Caleb was a student in the College. With his *Letters from a Farmer* he had done more perhaps than anyone else except Sam Adams of Boston to arouse the colonies to resist the injustices of English taxation. He had been an influential member of the Continental Congress, believing firmly in remonstrance and redress by constitutional means. Yet when the Congress, despairing of ever bringing the English ministry to reason, decided to break away and form a new country, Dickinson could not join with them. He voted against the Declaration of Independence and refused to sign it. But after it was passed in spite of him, he felt free, though a Quaker, to fight for the new United States of America. As colonel of a Pennsylvania regiment he had been in action at Princeton and Trenton. The light as he saw it led him to fight for what he could not vote for, while Caleb found himself in the uncomfortable position of endorsing something with his mind and heart which he did not feel free to defend with his body.

At this point he would jump up and pull on breeches and shirt and tiptoe downstairs. Though it might grow hot later in the day the mornings were fresh, with the dew on the grass and the sun still so low that stones in the driveway cast a shadow. He would saddle Ladybird and ride through the orchard and up the wood road to the top of the ridge, to the place where a wide view opened out to the northeast across the valley of the Schuylkill to the hills beyond. There in the morning peace he would decide to go to Meeting the first Sunday they were in town and see whether, in the serenity of that quiet place, in the silence of many seeking hearts, he could find light that would reveal the path that should be uniquely his.

IV

THE MIDDLETONS REACHED PHILADELPHIA on August twenty-second, the day that General Howe with a large force had landed at the Head of Elk on Chesapeake Bay, fifty-five miles from the city. The first possible Sunday on which Caleb might have gone to Meeting was two days later, the twenty-fourth, but that was the day on which General Washington decided to march his brigades through Philadelphia on his way to meet the British, and Caleb went instead to see them pass. He decided that he could get the best view from the windows of Phyllis Pike's lodging.

He had first met Mrs. Pike the previous March, when he had been in town on some errand for the furnace. It had been a cold, glittery day with the merciless sunshine bright on wisps of paper blown against doorsteps and on stray bits of garbage frozen in alley gutters. The wind, flashing off the steely surface of the river, had whipped through bare tree branches and around street corners, carrying the flat city smell of wharf piles and river mud. Caleb had been glad after he had finished his business to turn toward the London Coffee House. He would have a cup of coffee to warm him, read the latest number of the *Pennsylvania Gazette*, and chat with whoever was there before he went to his Cousin Edward Penington's to spend the night.

As he walked up Front Street with his shoulders hunched against the wind at his back, he saw a vessel unloading at the public dock, and he paused for a moment to watch. She was a sloop from South Carolina, someone said, with a cargo evidently of pine products. He lingered idly for a moment, watching the men handling the big barrels with easy skill. He was about to go on again when he saw a little figure moving uncertainly in their midst, in danger of being jostled if not knocked down. It was a girl in a blue mantle with a smart hat perched upon her powdered hair and an ostrich plume which rose and flapped in the wind like a flag on a staff. In her hand she carried a bird cage in which a small, bright bird hopped agitatedly from perch to floor to bar, and on her small, charming face was an expression of woe.

Caleb lost no time in going to her rescue.

"Watch yourself there, fellow," he said sternly to a man with a barrel, and then, in suaver tones, as he stood beside the little lady and looked down at her, "Can I help you?"

The wind swooped again at that moment and blew the end of her plume against his mouth. Having no hand free to take hold of her feather, she swung around, laughing a little, to let the wind blow it back, and the sharpness of the air brought tears to her eyes, which were brown and clear and set about with long, thick lashes. She was, he saw, extremely pretty and, though young, not in the least miss-ish.

"Lord, what a wind! I'm expectin' my husband to meet me," she said in a voice plaintive yet vigorous. "I've come all the way from Charleston."

She handed him the bird cage and the bird became more hysterical than ever. "It's a nonpareil," she said, as if that explained everything.

By the act of handing Caleb the bird cage, she seemed to have handed him her whole problem, and by accepting it he felt he had made himself responsible for her. The transition was swift and easy. He seemed to expand under her confiding gaze. He was a man of the world, handsome, kind, capable, courtly. She was helpless, admiring, grateful, with the almost imperceptible yet comfortable gift of making him understand without words what he might do for her.

He ascertained her name and the address of her husband's lodging, took care of the formalities of arrival at the office of the ship's company near by on Front Street, he saw her modest luggage collected and obtained the services of a boy with a wheelbarrow. Then he suggested that he accompany her to her lodging, which was only three or four squares away, where she could rest and wait for her husband, who no doubt had been detained somewhere.

It was obviously a sensible suggestion, but both seemed reluctant to put it into effect at once. The boy with the wheelbarrow went ahead, with the bird cage perched on top of the boxes and instructions to wait when he reached the lodginghouse. Clouds had blown across the sun and the wind was raw now as well as sharp. The London Coffee House at the corner of Front and High Streets was near at hand. Caleb understood that Mrs. Pike would take heart from a cup of hot coffee and that, although it was a place that ladies seldom ventured into, she would not mind. He found an unoccupied box where they could be unobserved and he ordered two cups of mocha and some queen cakes.

Little Mrs. Pike pulled off her gloves and flexed her stiff fingers. "Cold!" she said, shivering prettily, and her voice, so warm and strong and yet somehow childish, sent pleasant impulses down Caleb's spine. "Feel!" She laid the back of her knuckles lightly against his cheek, and he felt it grow hot under her chilly touch. "This is a monstrous climate. The jessamine is blooming in Carolina now and the air is warm and fragrant."

The log fire blazing on the hearth was reflected on the coffee urn, and cast a glow on the rows of pewter plates and cups and the blue and white Delft ware on the shelves of polished wood. In the warmth and intimacy of the box Mrs. Pike told Caleb how she had romantically met and married Thomas, who was a dancing and fencing master, how he had left her in Charleston at the insistence of her family while he prepared a home for her in Philadelphia, how at last she could bear it no longer and had come to him. She did not say that she was the daughter of a great plantation, but her father, who appeared in her narrative as a towering figure, aristocratically strict and protective, could have belonged only to one of the large establishments, with slaves and gardens and pleasure boats on the river, which Phyllis described so vividly.

"The Delaware is a shocking flat, dull stream, isn't it?" she threw in, and Caleb, startled because he had always understood it to be majestic, felt obliged to set her straight, and he ordered more coffee to occupy them while he explained.

Though the room had been almost empty when they entered, it now was beginning to fill up. The Congress and its committees, as well as the Pennsylvania Assembly, broke up about five, and the members liked to drop in at the coffee house afterward. The sound of footfalls and greetings, of waiters running with trays, increased, but at first Caleb was only vaguely aware of them. Presently, however, he realized that word had got around of a pretty woman in the far box, for men began to drift past casually, glancing in as they went. Two or three acquaintances nodded to him, and he saw in their faces either disapproval or an arch you-gay-dog-you look. The thought that Mrs. Pike might be made uncomfortable roused his anger, and he was casting about for some way of putting an end to the parade, when he caught the look on her face. Not in the least displeased, she might almost be said to bridle. Little sidelong glances, bright and soft, stole from her modestly lowered eyelids, and a conscious smile played around the corners of her warm red mouth.

For the first time it occurred to Caleb that she might be less childlike and even less—he hesitated—virtuous than he had thought her. Somewhat to his surprise he found that this realization did not repel him. On the contrary it made his pulses leap, and he leaned toward her across the table.

Mr. Pike had returned from Wilmington, where he had a regular engagement, just as Caleb delivered Phyllis to Mrs. Duncannon's boardinghouse, and Caleb, loaded down with their thanks, had left them to their reunion. Walking away, he wondered, as interested persons so regularly do, how the man had got the girl. He had recognized Mr. Pike the moment he saw him; he had often seen that conspicuous red coat and laced hat on the street.

He was a thin man, with a thin, rather hatchety profile and light eyes set close together. His manner was too obliging.

It was only polite that before starting for home next morning, Caleb should stop in to inquire for Mrs. Pike, and that it should become habit whenever he was in town after that to pay his respects to her. It had not been difficult to arrange his business trips so that he was in Philadelphia on the days when Mr. Pike was in Wilmington.

On the Sunday morning of August twenty-fourth, Mr. Pike was at home. Not only was he there, in the second story parlor with the windows overlooking Front Street, but a captain and a major, whose brief terms in the militia had already expired, were on hand too, very gay and, Caleb thought disapprovingly, very bumptious.

The day had begun badly, with a downpour at seven. Though the rain soon stopped, still the sky was overcast and the air was cool, damp, and lifeless. People gathered early along the sidewalks to watch the parade and every window on Front Street was filled with spectators. It was generally said that Washington intended to impress the Tories in the city and reassure the patriots by a show of the strength of his army, but the faces of people waiting looked indistinguishably anxious.

In Mrs. Pike's little parlor there was an uneasy air of bonhomie in which Caleb did not join. Mr. Pike, in his scarlet coat with a fresh set of ruffles, was offering wine to the company and proposing toasts to Liberty. The Captain and the Major drained their glasses and smacked their lips and sat down again, sprawling out their legs as if they had been in a tavern—where indeed one of them belonged, behind the bar. Caleb recognized the Major as the one-time barkeeper at the Indian Queen, and he guessed that the Captain, from his general manner and way of talking, had been the driver of a stagecoach. But they were officers now, and gentlemen, under the new dispensation.

Phyllis, charming in a flowered chintz gown with a gauze apron, her unpowdered brown curls escaping from her cap, was mourning the death of her bird and calling for expressions of sympathy.

"I can't be sorry," said Caleb flatly. "I don't like song birds in cages."

She widened her eyes at him reproachfully. "But that one," she said, "was my friend, and he brought me one of my dearest friends."

There was a message for him in her voice and glance as well as in her words, but Caleb's mood was heavy and he could not rise to it. He was put out by the presence of the military, he did not in any case like exchanging soft glances and speeches with double meanings under the hatchet nose of Mr. Pike, and he wished that the parade would hurry up and begin. When the Major, whose sibilants became blurred with his sixth glass of wine, offered to preshent Mistresh Pike with a bigger bird, a better bird, Caleb went to the window and stood looking out in morose silence.

The house was situated on Front Street near Vine, almost at the edge of the Northern Liberties, that region of row houses, shambles, empty lots, and military barracks, where on Saturday nights the butchers from Spring Garden warred wildly with the ship carpenters from Kensington. Beyond West's shipyards across the street the river could be seen, and beyond its pewter-colored breadth, the trees of the Jersey shore rose out of the mist. It was a broad, slow-moving, inexorable and, yes, a majestic river.

"Have you heard," said Phyllis in a low voice at his side, "there's a list circulating of about five hundred people who are to be arrested and banished from the city?"

"What for? What have they done?"

"Nobody seems to know exactly. Inimical to the American cause, or something of the kind. Thomas talked to someone who said he had seen it, but he couldn't find out any of the names from him, though they say they are some of the most respectable citizens."

"Don't worry," said Caleb. "There are certain to be all kinds of rumors with the British army so near."

He looked speculatively at Mr. Pike, who was loudly proposing another toast to Liberty and Down with Tyranny. The dancing master was commonly supposed to be a loyalist.

In the street below a ragged boy raised a shrill cry: "Yonder they come!" and a sharp rat-a-tat of drums almost at the same moment brought everyone in the parlor crowding to the windows.

In another moment the first column was there, and with the approach of marching feet on the brick-paved street began the steady rhythmic beat which was to continue till all of the army had passed before their eyes. The men carried arms, well burnished, and in each man's hat was pinned a sprig of fresh green. "For hope?" Caleb wondered.

From the wild burst of shouts and cheers he knew that Washington must be approaching. He had expected somehow that the general would come later as a climax to the show, but here he was at the head of his troops. Feeling the contagion of emotion, Caleb thrust his head and shoulders out of a window.

He saw, mounted on a fine, high-stepping horse, the tall, stately, grave yet cheerful, already almost legendary man who held in his steady hands the future of the little band of rebellious colonies. He was surrounded by his mounted aides and yet they might all have been invisible, so completely did Washington dominate the scene. As he came directly under the window Caleb's heart beat fast. He had with others complained that the mob made a demi-god of Washington, and yet, this morning, he himself felt an impression of an integrity, a dedication, a largeness of spirit that was superior to the ordinary run of men.

Behind General Washington and his aides came twelve gentlemen of the Philadelphia Light Horse led by Cornet John Dunlap, who in his daily life published the *Pennsylvania Packet*. The troop was well turned out in brown coats, white waistcoats and breeches, and high-topped black boots. Their long cavalrymen's swords, unsheathed, rested against their left arms, their carbines were at their backs, their pistols in brown holsters initialed in white hung at either side of the pommel. On their heads were the visored black hunting caps with a bucktail turned up over the top which they had borrowed from the Gloucester Fox-hunting Club, to which many of them had belonged before the City Troop was founded. Caleb had ridden to hounds with them several times, over the flat fields across the river. He knew that he would be welcomed if he should decide to join the troop. The members were all gentlemen; they armed and equipped themselves; based at Philadelphia, detachments of them went out from time to time on guard or escort duty. Some of them had been in actual fighting last winter in the victories at Trenton and Princeton, but they were not committed to following the army into distant winter quarters or to staying with it during the long frustrating intervals between actions.

The Virginia Cavalry followed, and then after a gap of a hundred yards or so a company of Pioneers in linen hunting shirts belted at the waist, with axes over their shoulders. After another space rode General Nathanael Greene, in whom Caleb felt a particular interest. A Quaker of Rhode Island, the son of a successful iron foundryman, he had applied for a commission in the Rhode Island Kentish Guards, but because he had a stiff knee he had been rejected. Whereupon he had promptly volunteered as a private—and now he was a major general and in people's estimation second only to Washington. The fringe on his gold epaulettes shook as he rode slowly past and his stars gleamed. Caleb looked to see if the struggle with his Quaker heritage had left any traces in his face, but he saw only a large, smooth countenance, open and pleasant, without any subtleties.

"Here comes the Parson," said the Major, digging his elbow into Caleb's ribs as if he had said something roguish.

"What parson? Oh, Muhlenberg, you mean."

The story was well known, how Peter Muhlenberg, minister of a Lutheran church in a little town in Virginia, at the end of his sermon one Sunday had flung open his gown to reveal his blue and buff uniform beneath it, announcing that he was leaving at once to join General Washington. He was now a brigadier, with the men of his regiment marching twelve abreast behind him. They were not quite in step, but their heads were high and they wore their green sprigs at a confident angle.

Behind the artillery, which rumbled noisily over the bricks of the street, came massed drummers and fifers, and the roll of the drums, the shrill notes of a lively tune smartened the steps of the infantry following.

The gay tune faded out, the steady tramping steps came on, column after column, with almost hypnotic effect. Many of the uniforms were shabby, but all were clean and all the guns were polished. Though their hats were cocked at all angles, their faces were set straight ahead and wore a look of common purpose. Here and there one stood out from the rest: a tall, gawky redhead, probably a Scot; a short, slim, swarthy lad who might have been Portuguese; a man with the high cheekbones and reddish skin that revealed Indian blood; a boy so fair and young that he looked like a girl among the others. The Baltimore regiment was composed of farmers in hunting shirts; they had the farmer's weather-beaten features, his dogged mildness and comfortable walk—no nonsense about keeping step or carrying his head as if he wore a check-rein.

There was a flurry in the room when General Stirling rode past at the head of his division. Was he a lord or wasn't he?

"Certainly he's a lord," said Mr. Pike. "He went to court about it in England and won his case."

"Then why ain't he sitting in the House of Lords?" objected the Captain. "We got no use for lords in a republic."

Caleb was conscious of the light pressure of Phyllis's body against his as she leaned forward eagerly to see the lord. He clasped her slender shoulders with his two hands and moved her in front of him, where he could see over her head and smell the fragrance of her hair. "Silly face, hasn't he?" he murmured. "Look at that pretty mouth."

She turned to look at him in surprise, her face so close that he might have snatched a kiss without the others' knowing. "Why, I think he's right handsome," she protested.

"Too soft," said Caleb, amazed, not for the first time, at the kind of man a woman will think good-looking.

Behind the last company of infantry a cavalry troop brought up the rear. Caleb paid more attention to the horses than to the men. Most of them looked thin and hard used. He wondered where the supply wagons were, and tried to estimate the number it must take just to keep the beasts fed.

"That's all," said the Major.

Caleb looked at his watch in surprise. It had been two hours.

"That'll show them—" declared the Captain, "—the Tories and the folks that are afraid of the British. Did you see the Fourth Pennsylvania? They marched good. That was my regiment. After I get a bit of rest I think I'll enlist for another term."

"How long was your first one?"

"Five months, and then I signed on for the rest of the campaign, so it was almost nine altogether." In the pause that followed he must have felt an implied criticism, for he said with a pugnacious thrust of his jaw, "I gotta live, ain't I? I came back to move my family outa the city and make a little money."

Caleb thought of Washington, with an inkling of what it might be to fight a war depending on an army that dissolved under his fingers, against British regulars and Hessian mercenaries, who were disciplined and battle tested, and prevented, furthermore, by the whole width of the Atlantic Ocean from going home for the harvest or a lawsuit or a desire for a rest. The coarse and trifling character of the two specimens with whom he had shared the view from the windows increased his sympathy and heightened his admiration for that lonely and noble figure whose image was still vivid in his mind. He had not seen the British march, but he had a shrewd idea that in comparison with them this two-hour display would seem pathetic and homemade. Yet he found his ardor kindled, and he left the house filled with the idea of joining a regiment of the Continental line under General Washington himself.

Reaction came inevitably.

The next week Caleb spent in the outward activity of his father's business and an inward conflict both distressing and engrossing. The various compromises which he had contemplated between his Quaker principles and his desire to take part in America's struggle for independence now appeared unacceptable to him. Yet the deep tides of his early training and belief, his conviction that war was wrong, arose to check him when he thought of actually enlisting and taking a gun in his hands.

Temperamentally not given to introspection and self-analysis, he yet dimly knew himself capable of two extremes: of being a dedicated and concerned Friend, with none of the latitude which he now allowed himself, or of abandoning altogether the religion of his mother and going the way of many young Friends of his age, who were now captains and majors in the Continental army and whose names had been stricken from the records of their Meetings. The events of the last month had waked him out of his complacent slumber and he felt he must now choose one course or the other.

Moral questions of right and wrong, elements of his long-standing rebellion against his father's domination, the division of loyalty between his inbred conviction of religious truth and his fresh-springing belief in the ideal of a new liberty and justice in a new land, eagerness to take a brave and energetic part, to share the risks and dangers others faced: all this confusion and contradiction of thoughts and impulses, insights and desires, occupied his mind, waking and sleeping. There was no one whose advice he wanted to ask, since he felt that it was his own dilemma, for which he alone must take responsibility. He went to Meeting on Sunday, but the clamor of his own thoughts was so insistent that he could hear no voice from beyond, and the two or three Friends who spoke out of the silence quoted Old Testament texts that did not touch his need.

The week went by without action or decision.

V

LOUD POUNDING ON THE FRONT DOOR sounded through the house. Caleb looked up from the desk in the back parlor, where he was searching for a mislaid document that his father wanted, and listened. The urgency of the knocking made Caleb wonder apprehensively if his father, who, in spite of the muggy heat of the day, had gone to call on a sick friend, might again have collapsed. From the sound of footsteps overhead he knew that his stepmother, probably with the same thought, had gone to the top of the stairs to listen. It was much more probable, he told himself, that some news had come from the armies to the southwest of the city and that the citizens were being aroused, although so far there had been no sound of gunfire.

He heard voices at the front door, indistinguishable at first; then Amos's squeaky tones rose high. "Just a minute, gentlemen," Caleb heard him protest. "If you'll wait in here, please sir, I'll tell him—"

Peremptory footsteps drew near along the hall and the next moment three men strode into the room. Caleb rose, surprised.

He recognized Charles Peale at once. Slight, bright-eyed and handsome, he looked smart in the brown and green uniform of the Philadelphia company of which he was captain. Caleb had come to know him rather well in the days when the young artist, then almost unknown, was painting the miniature of his mother. A genuine pleasure in seeing him again washed out Caleb's momentary annoyance at the abruptness of his entrance.

"It's a long time since I've seen you, Charlie," he said cordially, and turned to the other two, who were strangers. "I believe I've not had the honor—"

Peale said unsmiling, "Mr. Heysham and Mr. Marsh are my associates in the cause of liberty. They accompany me on an errand which I assure you is disagreeable to me."

Stung by the unexpected rebuff, Caleb swept some papers off a chair and dropped them on the desk. "Pray be seated," he said stiffly.

Mr. Marsh, a youngish man, pleasant enough in his appearance, openly leaned over and craned his neck to look at the papers. They were memoranda of agreements, deeds of trust, some bills and personal letters, which had been brought down from the office at the Phoebe Ann. Flushing angrily at the man's rudeness, Caleb deliberately turned up the front of the desk, shutting all the papers inside.

"Hold on!" said Mr. Marsh.

Peale, who was evidently the spokesman, interposed quickly. "I regret very much, Mr. Middleton, the errand that brings me here. I am commanded by the Supreme Executive Council to secure your signature to this document."

Mr. Heysham, a rather short man with a square-jawed, monkey-like face, whipped a sheet of paper out of the portfolio which he carried and presented it to Caleb.

"If you will read that," said Peale, "I think it is self-explanatory."

Wondering, Caleb took the paper and began to read. Flies buzzed around and around the room under the ceiling. Outside in the garden below the window Tacy was playing with her dolls. Her sweet little childish pipe floated into the tense silence of the room. "Will thee have some sugar, my dear? Do have some more of this bohea. It's very fine."

"I——, do promise," read Caleb, "not to depart from my dwelling house——" The first part was so preposterous that he went back and read it again. "——not to depart from my dwelling house and to be ready to appear on demand of the President and Council of Pennsylvania——"

Indignation followed upon bewilderment as he continued: "—— and do engage to refrain from doing anything injurious to the

United States of North America—" He read the final words aloud, slowly, " '—by speaking, writing, or otherwise, and from giving intelligence to the Commander of the British forces or any person whatsoever concerning public affairs.' This has nothing to do with me!" he exclaimed. "There must be some mistake!"

He turned to the three men standing there, Peale embarrassed but determined, Heysham and Marsh staring at him with bold, accusing eyes.

"I can't sign that," said Caleb, tossing it contemptuously onto the table.

"I advise you very strongly to comply," said Captain Peale. "That will relieve you of any further difficulty now, and in the course of time you can straighten yourself out with the Council."

The memory of Phyllis Pike standing by the window and saying that five hundred of the most respectable citizens were to be arrested and banished, returned to him. This visitation, then, must be part of a general gathering up of Tories. Conscious of his own clearness, he said with a smile, "You have the wrong man."

There was no answering smile on Peale's face as he consulted his list. "Caleb Middleton, junior?"

"At your service. But there is no reason for me to be on such a list. I have not the slightest intention of doing anything injurious to the United States of America. On the contrary—" He stopped. It occurred to him that they had confused him with his father. But even his father had done nothing beyond refusing for conscientious reasons to make iron for the army. He had indeed harbored secret doubts about the patriots' chances of success, but a man cannot be condemned to house arrest for his thoughts.

"Then you can have no valid objection to signing this parole," said Captain Peale smoothly.

"It is impossible for me to sign it. The word 'parole' itself implies an admission of guilt."

"In that case I shall have to conduct you to the Freemasons' Hall. Time is short, and I shall have to require you to come at once without further delay."

"On what authority?"

"By virtue of a Resolution of the Congress and by order of Council."

"May I see your orders?"

"I am not permitted to show them to you, but I can tell you that the Congress on Thursday of last week passed a Resolution that the executive authorities of Pennsylvania be requested to cause all notoriously disaffected persons to be apprehended, disarmed, and secured. The Council yesterday determined that the parole which you have just read might be offered to certain ones on the list. I assure you, Mr. Middleton, I am making this as easy for you as possible. There are others who would use more rigor." He smiled almost coaxingly, and for a moment Caleb saw again the young artist whom he had as a boy so much admired.

"No one," said Caleb, "no one at all can say with any truth that I am a disaffected person."

"I am obliged also," said Peale, as if he had not heard, "to make a search for firearms and papers of a political nature."

He nodded, and Heysham stepped forward as if this was what he had been eagerly waiting for, and laid his hand on the desk.

"Those are purely personal and private papers," said Caleb. "They have to do with my father's business affairs. You may take my word for it."

Paying no attention at all, Heysham opened the desk and began to rummage through it, untying bundles of letters, leafing through ledgers, running his fingers deep into pigeonholes, pausing to read anything that interested him. The other man, Marsh, walked around the room looking in the corners and behind the door. Discovering no guns stacked against the walls, he went out into the hall, where he could be heard pulling things about in the closet under the stairs. Caleb stood silent, struggling to control his temper.

"No papers, sir," reported Heysham, turning from a desk now so disordered that it would be a day's work to find anything. A few seconds later Marsh reappeared with the news that he had been unable to discover any firearms.

Sarah Middleton swept into the room after him, with Edward breathing hard in her wake.

"What is all this?" she demanded. "Have you a warrant for searching our house?"

"I have, madam."

"Then show it to me. It is my right to see it."

"I am acting by order of the Supreme Executive Council, madam," said Peale. "I assure you it is disagreeable to me to execute such orders and I do not do it by my own wish. Once more, Mr. Middleton, will you sign the parole?"

"I will not."

"Then I shall have to take you under arrest."

"For mercy's sake!" exclaimed Mrs. Middleton. "On what grounds?"

"On grounds of being suspected of being inimical to the American cause."

"This is a thoroughly arbitrary proceeding!" exclaimed Caleb. "You have no grounds for such a suspicion and no possible right to arrest me without a definite charge."

"You can tell all that to the Council," said Marsh roughly, "when you get to the Masons' Hall."

Caleb caught eagerly at the idea of an immediate hearing. The Freemasons' Hall was not a prison; if the Council were in session there, he would have little difficulty in clearing himself before it. These were, after all, the guardians of American liberty whom he was to meet, not the British oppressors. It occured to him, furthermore, that it would be a good idea to get off before his father came in and said anything injudicious.

"Very well, then," he said evenly. "I am ready to go."

To his stepmother, whose broad face was twisted with distress, he said, "Don't worry. It's all a mistake and will soon be corrected." He rumpled Edward's hair affectionately, and took his hat from Amos's hands. Patty came flying down the front stairs, alight with curiosity, but before she had finished shrieking, "Where's Caleb going?" he was out in the street, preceded by Captain Peale and followed by Heysham and Marsh.

In spite of his consciousness of innocence and his confidence in the fairness of the Council, he felt keenly the indignity of being thus paraded publicly through the streets. People turned to look at him as he passed, and a small boy scrambling over a board fence screeched to another, "Hey, Pete, here's another Tory being taken up!"

At the corner, when they turned to go down Spruce Street, he looked back. Mrs. Middleton and Patty were standing on the steps, while Amos had come out onto the sidewalk and Edward had run halfway to the corner behind him. They all waved when they saw him turn, and Patty threw a kiss.

VI

THE FREEMASONS' HALL was a handsome building in the narrow street called Lodge Alley, which ran west from Second Street between Walnut and Chestnut. It was often used for public concerts and meetings, and the regular dancing assemblies had been held there until the war put an end to them.

As Caleb and his captors turned into the alley, which was lined with rows of posts on both sides to protect the footway, they had to clear a passage through the crowd that had gathered around the entrance to the hall. Among the anxious faces Caleb recognized Karl, the respectable, middle-aged German who was his cousin Edward Penington's devoted servant. The man's heavy face lit up when he saw Caleb, and he made his way through the crowd toward him.

"Is Cousin Edward in there, Karl?" said Caleb.

"*Ja*, Master Caleb. I can't get in to speak with him. Will you ask him, should I fetch his night things? *Ach, es ist schrecklich*! I can bring a pallet. I looked in the window before they drove me off and there's nothing but hard benches and wooden chairs."

"Stand aside there," barked Heysham.

"We'll be away from here before nightfall," said Caleb hastily.

"*Ja, ja,* but chust ask him to come to the window and nod—chust nod and I'll know to bring his things—"

Members of the uniformed City Guard pushed the crowd back as Captain Peale stopped to confer with their commanding officer, Colonel Nicola. Caleb waited, unpleasantly aware of many eyes fastened on him and of the whispering buzz, "Who's that? Who's he?"

Peale turned from Nicola to Heysham and Marsh. "Wait for me here," he said. "I will be with you in a few moments. Now, Mr. Middleton, if you will come this way—"

A guard opened the door of the Lodge and they stepped into the entrance hall, which ran across the front of the building, with a door to the auditorium in the center and stairs on one side leading to the upper floor. Captain Peale drew Caleb into the shadow of the staircase.

"I wanted to have a word with you privately. I have a message from Colonel Matlack. This will be understood to be confidential."

For a moment Caleb was at a loss to understand why Timothy Matlack should send a message to him, until he remembered that Mr. Matlack, apart from being a colonel of militia and a disowned Friend, was the Secretary of the Supreme Executive Council of Pennsylvania, the body responsible for Caleb's arrest. He nodded.

Captain Peale went on in a low voice. "Colonel Matlack is not unforgetful of kindness done to him by your father some years ago when he was in great difficulty. He is aware also that Mr. Middleton, senior, is elderly and infirm. Accordingly when he registered the names of the prisoners, he added 'junior' to that of Caleb Middleton. He trusts that will be satisfactory to both of you. If it is not, will you signify as much immediately through me, so that the mistake can be corrected before any question arises?"

Caleb caught his breath, speechless for a moment in his surprise; then he heard himself saying steadily, "It is entirely satisfactory to me, but I have no doubt that my father would object vigorously if he knew. Will you ask Colonel Matlack to add to his kindness by doing everything in his power to keep my father from finding out what has been done?"

"I will tell him."

"But I regret," said Caleb, unable to suppress the hot words that rose to his lips as the full meaning of Timothy Matlack's message became clear to him, "that a little more kindness did not lead him to omit the name altogether, since his conscience evidently did not prevent him from tampering with the document."

Captain Peale looked at him coldly. "I will tell him that too. Your servant, sir."

He turned on his heel so swiftly that the skirts of his brown and green coat flew out and his sword clanked. The guard opened the front door for him, and then motioned to Caleb to go into the auditorium.

It was a large room with benches down the sides, chairs stacked in the corners and a platform at the far end. Tall, dirty-paned windows, half-open along both sides of the room, let in flies as well as light and the sultry, lifeless air.

Caleb saw perhaps ten or a dozen men in the big room, gathered in little knots of two or three. He turned quickly to the guard. "Where is the Council?"

"Huh?"

"I said, where is the Council? Is it sitting in one of the upstairs rooms, or what?"

"I don't know nothing about no Council. This is where you're to stay."

The door closed behind him.

Caleb would have liked to call Captain Peale back now and unsay that last sarcastic speech of his. It was impolitic, to say the least, and might bring trouble for both Caleb and his father. But more than that, it was ungrateful. He was belatedly aware of Colonel Matlack's real intention of kindness. Though both Caleb and his father were innocent, yet the elder Caleb, having refused to make munitions for the Continental army, was more open to the suspicion of disaffection. Caleb had no doubt of being able to clear himself as soon as he got a hearing. Meanwhile, he could endure a few hours of waiting in the Freemasons' Hall more easily than his choleric parent.

He looked about for his cousin and found him sitting in a chair with his back to the room, reading.

Edward Penington was Caleb's mother's cousin. A prosperous merchant, a man with a dozen public interests and concerns, he achieved a delicate balance between the world and the Meeting. His clothes were "of the best sort, but plain," of the finest broadcloth and linen, the brown coat cut long and without pockets, the fine white shirt made without frills. His graying hair, which was receding at the temples, he wore clubbed at the back. His clean-shaven face had a look of humor and benevolence about the eyes, of stern, almost tight control about the thin, fine lips.

"Cousin Edward—"

Penington looked up, taken by surprise, then smiled. "Well, Caleb," he said, "thou too! I thought thou wert a zealous advocate of independency!"

"I thought so too," said Caleb ruefully.

"Bring up a chair, my boy, and sit down. Thou hast a long wait before thee. I've been here since ten o'clock this morning, and I still do not know either my crime or the sentence."

"Isn't the Council meeting here?"

"No. Why should thou suppose it was?"

"I was told—or at least I was given to understand—that I could talk to the Council here and clear myself."

"Of what? Hast thou been charged with anything?"

"Nothing definite. Something about being inimical to the American cause, which is absurd. Did they show thee their orders? Who brought thee here?"

"No less a person than William Bradford, with some young men who professed great attachment to the cause of liberty. No one is permitted to see their orders. So far as I can tell I am here for having been a friend of Joseph Galloway—who I believe is now with the Royal Army in New York—as if sedition were contagious like the pox. And doubtless also for the crime of being a rich Quaker."

Caleb saw on the other side of the room a slight, dejected figure sitting on the end of a bench with his elbows on his knees and his head in his hands.

"Isn't that Tom Affleck over there?" he said. "He's not a rich Quaker."

"No, poor Tom. He's fairly dazed by the blow. He has four

small children all under six and his wife's poorly. They've nothing to live on but what he makes with his hands. Incidentally, he made this chair I'm sitting on, and it's a very good piece of work, too."

Caleb had known Tom Affleck from the time when, not long come from Aberdeen, he had made the coffin for Caleb's mother. He had used the best mahogany and put it together and polished it with care, as if it were to be on view for a lifetime instead of hidden away in the ground. He had worked all through one night to have it finished in time, and there had been a gentleness about his simple, honest manner that had lingered in Caleb's memory.

"I can't see any reason for arresting a man like him," he said slowly. "His sympathies may be with Britain. It would be natural enough if they were, he's not been here many years. But he's a quiet, hard-working craftsman with a family to support. He'd be a Friend still if he hadn't married out. He won't fight in any case."

His cousin raised an eyebrow. "If thou and others could contemplate fighting for the American cause, possibly other Friends might find it possible to bear arms for Britain—though certainly I have not heard of any who have. But that is their line of reasoning. They are taking the ground that he who is not for them is against them. Sit down, Caleb, sit down. Thou makes me nervous."

Caleb was too restless to sit down. "What's thy book?" He gave a little yelp of laughter when his cousin turned the title page toward him. *"Life of Mahomet* by Prideaux! I thought at least it was Law's *Serious Call to a Devout and Holy Life!"*

Penington looked a little apologetic. "I picked it up in a hurry," he admitted. "I've had it a long time and never read it. I find it very interesting. Mahommet was a more solid character than I realized. Caleb, has thou thought thou might have been taken by mistake for thy father?"

"What makes thee say that?"

"It's obvious. We're all rather weighty people—except Affleck, and he was Governor Penn's protégé. They've escorted the Governor to Fredericksburg, I hear. But thee is young and—thee'll forgive my mentioning it—quite unimportant."

"Please don't express thy thought where any of these captains and majors can overhear thee, or they might take Father up too. He's done nothing, but he might talk rather unwisely. I can easily clear myself."

"If we have a hearing."

"But we must have a hearing! They can't keep us here without giving us a chance to speak in our own defense!" He remembered Karl at the door. "Oh, Karl asked me to find out if thee wants him to bring thy night things. Choost go to the window and nod and he'll understand."

He saw James Pemberton standing with two of the sons of his father's friend, Joshua Fisher, and he went over to speak to them. James was the middle one of the three powerful and important Pemberton brothers. Though he habitually sat at the head of the facing-bench in the Great Meeting on High Street and was a very weighty Friend—in terms of spiritual rather than physical pound-age—Caleb was less in awe of James than of Israel or John, partly because James was rather more human than the other two and partly because his son Phineas had gone to college with Caleb and the two were of the same age, to the day.

"Ah, Caleb," said James Pemberton without preliminary, "wast thou told the Council would hear thee in this place?"

Caleb tried to remember exactly what Marsh had said. "I certainly understood that it would," he said, "but I am not sure of the precise words."

"Thomas Affleck and Charles Eddy came with the same understanding. Charles declares that it was an actual promise. Wast thou on the Congress's list or on that made up by the Council?"

"Why, I don't know, Friend Pemberton. I haven't seen any list at all, and I didn't know there was a distinction."

"The fellow who brought me here showed me—on my insistence—a part of the Resolution of Congress, which spoke of 'apprehending and securing' the persons of certain Friends. I did not see the list, however. There was nothing at all about a hearing. It is my opinion that we are prisoners, and likely to continue so for an indefinite period."

"Prisoners." The word had a shocking sound. The room, which had had a restless, disorganized atmosphere, seemed suddenly to close in upon Caleb, as if this word were what it had been waiting for.

Thomas Fisher, a man about twelve years older than himself, whom he knew through his father's business dealings with the firm of Joshua Fisher and Sons, now turned to him. Caleb admired Thomas. Like his brothers, he had been sent abroad on coming of age to travel in Europe, but he had had the distinction of being captured at sea by a privateer and taken as a prisoner to Spain, whence he had escaped to England after a series of adventures and perils. He had married lively Sarah Logan of Stenton, and their house on Second Street was one of the most elegant and popular in the city.

"Has thy father been taken up?" said Thomas.

"Not yet, at any rate. He went to see thy father this morning and he had not returned when I—left."

"Father is still in bed. He's been ill for several weeks. They came to him early this morning and he gave them a verbal promise not to go out of the house—since he is prevented by the doctor's orders in any case. I left him before thy father got there. I do not understand on what basis people are being apprehended."

Caleb thought he could see why the Fishers might be under suspicion. On the outbreak of the war Joshua and his two older sons had refused to sell supplies to the Continental army, and when their warehouse had been broken into and the goods seized they had refused to accept the paper money issued by the Congress. Samuel, the second son, was outspoken in his loyalty to the English government and unnecessarily antagonistic, even belligerent, in his attitude toward those whose consciences led them to take a different course from his, a curious but not uncommon phenomenon in one who had dedicated his life to peace. Another brother, Jabez Maud, who was in England now, and Miers, the youngest, a lawyer, Caleb knew only by sight.

Assured that Thomas had no information he did not himself possess, Caleb drifted through the door into the hall, to look out from the front window into the alley. At the edge of the crowd that still filled the narrow street, he caught sight of his father in an argument with one of the guard. He could not hear the words, but from the thrust of his father's jaw and the periodic jerk of his head he knew that he was angry. Caleb flung open the window and leaned out.

"Father!" he shouted.

Mr. Middleton turned and in his face the anger cleared away as the sand of a beach is washed smooth by a wave, and his rugged features and his gray eyes in their fleshy hammocks were suffused with anxiety and tenderness.

"Wait there, Caleb," he called. "I'll come to thee."

He began to elbow his way through the milling crowd, which was made up of relatives and servants of the prisoners, mingled with curiosity seekers and the inevitable scuffling small boys and ragged girls. Before he could get near the window he was stopped by a guard, who was clearing a passage for a party approaching from Second Street.

Captain Peale, Caleb saw, was bringing in another captive. He stalked ahead, red faced and resolute, and behind him came Marsh and Heysham, one on each side of the prisoner, whom they held firmly by the arms in such a way as almost to carry him along. Behind, marching in step, came a squad of ten soldiers with muskets. After the soldiers, leaning on the arm of a broad-hatted, gray-clad Friend, was a slender, delicate-looking woman in a dove-colored dress with a white fichu.

A hush came over the crowd as they saw who it was that was being brought in with such a display of force.

John Pemberton, the youngest of the three Pemberton brothers, was well known for his integrity and his kindness. It was still remembered among the poorer people of the city that on the day of his marriage ten years earlier he had ordered provisions sent to all the prisoners in Philadelphia. When he was a young man, no older than Caleb was now, he had withdrawn from the family business and had given himself to the service of religion. His life since then had been filled with preaching missions to England, Ireland, and Holland, arduous travels in the ministry through the backwoods of Pennsylvania and Virginia, tireless effort for friendly relations with the Indians and for the relief of freed slaves, and endless, patient work on the committees of the Yearly Meeting.

Peace was his great concern, peace with Britain, peace within one's own mind. As clerk of the Meeting for Sufferings he had signed—and probably had helped to compose—some "Advices" setting forth the traditional Quaker position against war, urging the young people of the Meeting to refrain from taking part in the present commotions.

Shocked, Caleb watched as John Pemberton was dragged in and taken upstairs. The guards made a motion to prevent his wife from following him, but Hannah Pemberton, still leaning on her companion's arm, looked at them, as a mother quells a child with a long, mild, compelling look, and they stood aside awkwardly to let her pass.

Caleb heard Colonel Nicola say in an undertone to Captain Peale, "May as well let her in. In fact, I don't see any need to keep the families out now. They'll have to bring food and bedding."

Caleb went back to the window to signal to his father, but he had vanished.

In rapid succession more prisoners were brought in, several of whom signed the parole and were released at once; others, according to rumor, were transferred to the New Prison on Walnut Street. Among those who remained to join the group in the auditorium or the room upstairs, Caleb recognized Thomas Gilpin, the brother-in-law and partner of the Fishers, Miers, the lawyer brother, the Reverend Thomas Combe, who was the Rector of Christ Church, and Thomas Wharton, senior, of the firm of Wharton and James.

These were, as Phyllis Pike had said, the most respectable of Philadelphia's citizens. Thomas Wharton, indeed, was a cousin of the man with the same name who was President of the Supreme Executive Council and who was at least partly responsible for the orders that had brought them all here.

With the coming on of twilight the word got around that relatives were being permitted to come in and talk to the prisoners. It was evident now that they would have to spend the night there and that nothing would be done until the next day to clarify their position. A steady stream of wives, mothers, brothers, and servants came trickling in, bearing pillows and bedclothes and covered dishes. Little family groups gathered together in separate clusters over the big room, each one making a small enclosure for itself from chairs and benches. All looked troubled and they talked together in low tones. When candles were lit, mosquitoes and moths came swarming.

Caleb discovered that he was hungry and began to watch the door impatiently, expecting someone to come to his assistance; but the word evidently had not reached home that they would now be admitted. One or two others in the same plight sent to the City Tavern around the corner on Second Street to have supper brought in, but Caleb found that he had come off without any money in his pockets. He was about to borrow some from his cousin when Karl arrived with a big basket containing a teapot wrapped in flannel to keep it hot and a generous supply of cold meat, biscuits, cheese, and pears. Edward and Caleb shared it, drinking in turns out of the one cup.

"Cousin Edward—" said Caleb suddenly, interrupting the older man's anxious account of his wife, Sally, who had taken the children to visit their grandparents in Germantown and who would be immeasurably distressed when she heard what had happened— "has thee ever heard of Father's doing a kindness to Timothy Matlack?"

"Yes, I remember something about it. It was ten or twelve years ago, when Timothy's beer-bottling business in Fourth Street failed. Thy father wrote off the debt owed to him. It didn't save Timothy from ruin, though. He threw in everything he had, poor fellow, and still he couldn't satisfy his creditors, many of whom were Friends. The Meeting disowned him."

"I thought he was disowned for taking part in war. He joined the militia quite early, didn't he, before he became Secretary of the Council?"

"Yes, but that was years after he was disowned. It wasn't only that he failed in business—though certainly Friends are not easy on people who cannot maintain their financial affairs in good order—but he was overfond of cockfighting and horse racing. Friends felt that the company he kept caused him to neglect his business. Besides, he was negligent in attending religious meetings. He was very resentful of censure, and the upshot of it was that he was disowned. He's never forgiven the Meeting, and I think myself that it was unnecessarily harsh. That may be one reason why such a large proportion of the prisoners here are Friends—but no, I don't believe he would be spiteful. Timothy is very hot tempered and he has a long memory for injuries—for favors, too, to do him justice—but I don't believe he is revengeful."

Tag ends of old stories came back to Caleb now, as he reached for another pear.

"He was in debtors' prison, wasn't he?"

"Yes, but not for very long. James Pemberton put up the money and got him released."

"James Pemberton is here. It's odd that Timothy Matlack didn't remember that, when he registered the names—I mean, if he has such a long memory for kindnesses."

"James was like a cow that gave a good bucket of milk and kicked it over. When Timothy first took up the cause of independency and began appearing in the street with his sword dangling by his side, Friends used to stop him and ask what he was doing with that thing. He would always answer grandly, 'I carry it to defend my property and my liberty!' One day he said it to James, and James replied, 'As to thy property, Timothy, thou knows very well thou hasn't any, and as to thy liberty, thou owes it to me.' "

Caleb whistled softly. "It would be hard for anybody to forget that!"

"James didn't mean it unkindly. It's one of those flat-footed things Friends say sometimes. It's true, the Pembertons are a little arrogant, all but John, and even he never forgets that he is a Pemberton. They have many enemies besides Timothy. But I don't suppose Timothy had much to say about who was taken up and who wasn't. He is only the Secretary, after all, and chosen largely for his fine penmanship. He made the official copy of the Declaration of Independence."

They had barely finished eating when Sarah Middleton came with more food, accompanied by Amos carrying a lantern in his hand and a roll of bedding over his shoulder.

Sarah drew Caleb aside. "I've persuaded your father to rest," she said in a whisper. "He's almost beside himself. He thinks it's he they want because of the iron, not you, and I've had all I could do to keep him from giving himself up so that you can go free. But from what I hear, it's some paper the Friends issued advising their members to stay out of war that's behind it all. They say it's seditious. You're a Friend and he isn't. If he gives himself up they'll only keep the two of you. And I've told him he can do more to help you if he stays outside. He's going to see the Council tomorrow. I hear that President Wharton's own cousin is in here—is that true? So it's just for tonight, I think, Caleb. You can stand it for tonight, can't you?"

Reassured, she made up a bed for him on one of the benches, and promising to come in the morning with his breakfast she went off, with fresh lamentations when she learned that the minister of her own church was there among them.

From the front door, to which he accompanied her, Caleb watched her walk down the alley and disappear around the corner. The light of Amos's lantern, bobbing behind her, fell on the gunstock of a guard who stood motionless at the entrance to the alley. Disturbed, bewildered, indignant, but still confident that all would soon be set straight, Caleb turned back to the dim hall, where the prisoners were preparing for the night.

VII

In the morning breakfast of a sort was brought in from a near-by ordinary. Since relatives and friends who gathered anxiously at the door were again shut out, Caleb carried on a highly unsatisfactory conversation with Patty through a window.

"I need money," he told her, "and some clean linen and my razor. We'll probably be out of here by afternoon, but I need those things this morning. Thee run home and send Amos back with them. Don't come thyself."

She was switching her yellow hair over her shoulders and gazing up at him with a die-away, self-conscious display of sisterly devotion in which, he saw with fury, there was not one iota of real attention. It was all for the benefit, no doubt, of some pipsqueak of a boy she had her mind on. He saw Josh Gilpin in the crowd, tall and weedy, with a pretty, babyish profile and a lazy, good-humored assurance which made him irresistible to Patty and her like.

"Tell Mother," he repeated, unaware of using the word he had vowed never to use, "I need money and my razor."

"And some clean linen. I heard thee. It's coming, Mother's getting everything for thee. I didn't wait. I thought thee'd want to know we're all thinking about thee every minute."

"Humph. How's Father?"

"He's very much agitated. But he did say now maybe thee'll learn something at first hand about liberty and tyranny."

"Thee go home!" roared Caleb.

His heated reflections on this ungrateful remark of his father's, which might or might not have been exactly as Patty reported it—

though Caleb could too well imagine the wry chuckle that would accompany it—were diverted by an altercation that was taking place at the next window.

Two of the prisoners had been talking with two men outside and the guard had ordered them to stop. Even while they were reluctantly finishing their sentences, one of the soldiers cocked his gun, aimed it, and threatened to shoot. One prisoner withdrew hastily, but the other, who was Tom Affleck, stood his ground.

"Ye've no rrright to cock yon gun at me," he said, his voice thrilling with indignation and his Scotch r's. "Ah'm unarrmed and ah'm brreaking no law. If ye shoot ye'll have murrrder on your conscience."

Although some bright boy outside called, "He's not that good a shot, Tommy!" there was a general buzz of protest from the people in the alley, and Colonel Nicola sharply ordered the guard away from the window.

The immediate result of the incident was a conference between the prisoners and Colonel Nicola, in which James Pemberton and Miers Fisher acted as spokesmen for the group while the rest stood about and listened. Nicola was a Frenchman, a surveyor and something of a scientist, who dealt in dry goods in a small way for his living and to whom the war had brought opportunities for breaking out of a restricting pattern and moving among men of affairs. With a good deal of originality and enterprise he had organized a corps of invalids, composed of eight companies of a hundred men each, who having been invalided home were still unfit to return to field service but were strong enough for garrison duty. This was the City Guard, of which he was colonel. They were honest, energetic patriots, willing to give of themselves beyond the ordinary call of duty; they loathed Tories and they thought of Quakers only as rich skinflints, Indian-lovers, and probable traitors.

"All I know about your imprisonment," said Colonel Nicola to James Pemberton, "is that the Council ordered me to furnish Colonel Bradford with a guard for the Freemasons' Hall and I have done as they commanded. I have nothing whatever to do with the arrests, and as far as I am concerned there is no reason why your friends should not come in and talk with you. That fellow with the gun was overzealous, and I have reprimanded him."

Having thus transferred his responsibility to William Bradford, Colonel Nicola took his departure, and shortly after that Henry Drinker was brought in.

A severe-looking man, with a heavy nose, long upper lip, firmly compressed, and a long sharp chin, reflected by a second, softer chin beneath it, Henry Drinker was one of the leading Quaker merchants of the city. He had a large brick house and grounds at the corner of Front Street and Drinker's Alley, his own dock on the river, and well-stocked warehouses. His coach was often seen on the road between the city and his country estate at Frankford. In addition, he owned considerable land on the Ohio, and he lent his support to forward movements in manufacturing; he was a member of the American Philosophical Society. Whatever he touched was sound, enlightened, and profitable. He was, in addition, a plain Friend, clerk of the Bank Meeting, and free from all temptations to levity.

In his wake came Charles Jervis, a lesser, lighter figure, and a distant cousin of Henry's charming wife, Elizabeth, whose parents had both been born in Ireland.

The prisoners gathered around the fresh arrivals, eager for news, but Drinker, like the rest, knew only that men had searched his desk for incriminating papers, proffered an unacceptable parole, and brought him here with no prospect of a hearing.

"It is entirely illegal and unprecedented," he said, "and we must make some kind of concerted protest. William Bradford seems to be in charge of the proceedings. He is thy tenant, isn't he, John? Hast thou no influence?"

It was well known that John Pemberton owned the building in which William Bradford conducted the London Coffee House, as well as his print shop next door. John Pemberton's scruples were responsible for the fact that no liquor or tobacco was sold in the Coffee House on Sunday. When Colonel Bradford passed down the alley a little later, it was John Pemberton who called him in and, as an opening, complained of the misbehavior of the guard.

"My dear Mr. Pemberton," said Bradford genially, "I have nothing to do with the guard, who are under the command of Colonel Nicola, and I have no charge over you."

"Then wilt thou be so good as to inform us," said Edward Penington acidly, "by what authority we are confined?"

"By authority of a warrant signed by Mr. George Bryan, Vice-President of the Council, acting upon a recommendation of the Congress."

"We have heard of that warrant," said James Pemberton, "but we have none of us had so much as a glimpse of it."

"I'll read it to you," said Bradford. He took a paper from his inner pocket and unfolded it.

The circle of men waited, silent and intent. Caleb, the youngest, was possibly the only one who had slept well the night before, and even he looked fagged. The suddenness of the attack, the difficulty of getting definite information, the uncertainty as to the future, added a weight of tension to the burden of outrage and injustice that all felt.

There was little in what Colonel Bradford was reading so fast, skimming over the words, that was different from what Caleb had heard from Captain Peale the day before. The phrases rolled on. " 'All persons who have in their general conduct and conversation evinced a disposition inimical to the cause of America . . .' " But a disposition was not action. And why select these few among all the thousands who had thought the Declaration of Independence premature, or who believed that wrongs would be better corrected through remonstrance and discussion than through warfare? " 'Whereas it is necessary for the public safety at this time when a British army has landed in Maryland with a professed design of enslaving this free country and is now advancing toward this city as a principal object of hostility . . .' "

That was it, thought Caleb. That was what they all forgot, John Pemberton and Cousin Edward and Tom Affleck and even Caleb himself—the might of the British army less than fifty miles away and only Washington with his green-sprigged troops to stand between. And if the rebellion failed, not only would a free country be enslaved but its leaders would be hanged as traitors, and no doubt they saw the shadow of the ropes sometimes.

"William, all this is very surprising to us," said John Pemberton in a mild and reasonable tone. "Thou knows our testimony as Friends, and so does the Council, if the Congress does not, being composed mainly of men from other parts where there are few of our persuasion. But in all civilized countries, whatever be the government, men accused of crimes are considered entitled to an opportunity of being heard in their own defense. We should like to know when we shall have this opportunity, and we desire a copy of this warrant which thou hast just folded away so carefully."

"We demand it as our right," interpolated someone at the back of the group.

"If thou wilt leave it with us, we will take a copy and return the original to thee promptly."

"No, no," said Bradford. "I can't do that. But I will report your desire for a hearing to the Council and I will myself make a copy of the warrant for you."

He made his escape, with an air of relief.

Two hours later, when the fiery sun stood overhead and the day seemed already as long as three days together, he was back again. He had just come from the Council, he reported, and they had informed him that since they still had not arrested all the persons on the list, it would not be proper to give a copy of the warrant now. Council had nothing to say about the possibility of a hearing.

The guard was instructed to admit friends of the prisoners, and there was the relief of diversion as people poured in with food and other comforts. Sarah Middleton came herself with the things that Caleb had asked for. She had little news. His father had been out all morning, besieging everyone of influence whom he knew, but the doors of the Council and of the Congress had been closed to him. He had been to see Magistrate Paschall, however, and he had promised to look into the matter. Sarah had persuaded her husband to lie down for a little while after dinner, for his face was as red as a beet and she was afraid he would have an apoplexy.

"I'm surprised they haven't brought in Israel Pemberton," said Sarah. " 'The King of the Quakers'! They say John Adams can't abide the sight of him—says he is Jesuitical." She liked a bit of gossip; she found it distracting and relaxing even—or perhaps especially—in the midst of anxiety. "I saw Mrs. Miers Fisher— now she's a bright, amiable young woman, I wish we could find a wife like that for you. I think Caroline Rutter is a nice girl enough, but she's too open about wanting her own way, and you'd never be able to stand that. Anyhow, Mrs. Fisher told me the Congress had appointed a committee of Mr. Adams and Mr. Duer and Mr. Lee to get up this fine Resolution of theirs, and Mr. Adams would never leave Israel Pemberton off any such list. Mrs. Fisher can't see why he included Miers, though. He—Mr. Adams—came to their house for dinner two-three years ago, and they all got along famously. Mr. Adams paid her many compliments about her hospitality. Oh, well, I mustn't rattle on. This is a tiring, comfortless place for you to be, Caleb, and the worst of it is we don't know how long."

After she had gone Caleb occupied himself with making a list of his fellow prisoners, trying to see some thread of reason in the selection. Sixteen were now confined in the Lodge. Of them, Miers Fisher was a lawyer, Thomas Combe a minister, Tom Affleck a cabinetmaker, Drewet Smith an apothecary, Charles Eddy an iron-monger, John Pemberton a Yearly Meeting Friend, Caleb himself an iron manufacturer; the rest were Quaker merchants. It was natural that the merchants should oppose war for more than religious reasons; their prosperity and indeed their livelihood were tied up with trade with England. Yet many of them had openly opposed British policy for years. Offhand he could count eight or nine who had signed the non-importation agreement and stuck to it, in spite of heavy losses, until merchants in Baltimore and New

York had privately traded with England and undermined the whole movement. He had often heard it discussed, both at home and at the Peningtons'. Cousin Edward had been a member of the Committee of Correspondence which brought the first Continental Congress into being. Thomas Wharton was known to be a friend of Benjamin Franklin's—who was now in France—and he was on so many of the same committees as his cousin Thomas Wharton, the President of the Council, that people called them Senior and Junior to distinguish them.

About three o'clock, Benjamin Paschall, Justice of the Peace, accompanied by Caleb's father, came walking into the big hall. He addressed himself to the man nearest the door, who happened to be William Smith, a wholesale and retail merchant who liked to call himself a broker.

"I am come as a magistrate of this city to know what you are confined here for."

His voice, a little prim and pedantic, sounded through the hot, languid room where flies buzzed in angular circles, and the bored and dispirited men who sat dozing or meditating, conversing in low voices or merely enduring the hot hours, sprang to attention, as if animated by new life.

"We are waiting to know that ourselves," replied William Smith firmly. "We were sent here and detained by a military force, in direct violation of civil procedures, and our cause is the cause of every free man in Pennsylvania!"

He was a Yorkshireman in his thirties, forthright, red-faced, and stoutly built. Caleb was surprised by his modest eloquence.

"Then who is confining you?"

James Pemberton stepped forward. "We do not know that either. But we have been told it is in pursuance of a recommendation of Congress and a resolve of the Council."

"Have you had a hearing?" persisted Mr. Paschall, and was answered by a chorus of "No!"

"Then if you do not know what you are confined for, it is my business as a magistrate to find out."

At this pronouncement several faces brightened. Caleb had a moment for a few words with his father before Mr. Middleton left with the magistrate.

"Don't lose heart, Caleb. It is an outrage, entirely without precedent, and Mr. Paschall is determined to get justice for you. I am going with him now to see these great men of the Council. Keep thy chin up!"

Mr. Middleton was in confident spirits when he used this homely phrase, with which he had been wont to exhort Caleb when he was a little boy. It came out now as an expression of tenderness, and Caleb understood it as such. A little cheered, in spite of his overwhelming ennui, he drifted over to his cousin Edward and sat down.

"I hope they may not be clouds without rain and wind without water," said Edward skeptically.

With the lengthening of the shadows a little breeze sprang up, bringing with it the sound of Christ Church bells ringing five, and as the last note died away Mr. Paschal returned with a heavy step. Failure rode on his sagging shoulders and downcast face.

The Council meeting had broken up before he got there and its members, of whom only five or six were still in town, had scattered. Vice-President Bryan was the only one he had been able to talk with.

"We learned from Mr. Bryan," said Paschall flatly, "that you are to be sent to Virginia, without a hearing."

The words fell in the room with the effect of an explosion. The angry, the bored, the hopeful, the reasonable, the scornful, the fearful, all heard and were stunned.

"Your father, Mr. Middleton," said Mr. Paschall aside to Caleb, "has gone in his chaise to Walnut Grove, where there is some reason to believe that President Wharton has retired. There is no possibility of moving Mr. Bryan. His mind is set, and I regret to say it, but I fear he is indelibly prejudiced against the Society of Friends."

"Bryan is Irish," said Edward Penington, who had a kindly tolerance for everyone, Indians, Negroes, Roman Catholics, Jews, Turks, and Bostonians—everyone but the Irish.

"Where in Virginia are we to be banished?" inquired Thomas Gilpin.

"Staunton was mentioned," replied Mr. Paschall unhappily.

"Staunton! But that is nearly three hundred miles away—in the backwoods!"

"Anywhere in Virginia is outside the jurisdiction of the Council of Pennsylvania," said James Pemberton.

"It is an extraordinary stretch of arbitrary power," said Miers Fisher, "and we must consider how best to meet it. There are legal recourses. Article Nine of the Pennsylvania Constitution guarantees the right to trial by jury, and Article Ten has to do with freedom from search or seizure."

"The public should be informed," suggested Henry Drinker. "It is an alarming precedent. The citizens for their own sakes, if not for ours, would take an interest if they knew what was happening."

They drew chairs into a circle and sat down, with Mr. Paschall in the center. He was doubtless, Caleb thought, a conscientious magistrate, careful about details, but his personality was narrowly intellectual, fussy, and weak. He heard each speaker sympathetically, agreed and tut-tutted, becoming visibly more shocked and burdened as each opinion was added, but he had no vigorous course of action to suggest.

It was decided that a written Remonstrance was the most effective protest open to them, and a committee was named to write a draft. Caleb, sitting on the periphery beside Tom Affleck, made no contribution to the discussion. He had moved away from his cousin Edward, whose mixture of irony and temper, usually amusing to him, now set his teeth on edge.

Caleb's easy assumption of his father's place on the list of prisoners had, he was beginning to realize, placed him in a far more serious position than he had foreseen. It was no longer a matter of a few days' imprisonment, with a hearing at the end of it and swift exoneration. It was now clearly possible, even probable, that he would be sent three hundred miles away, with a company of older men, to some backwoods stockade where the chances of being heard would be small indeed. He was thankful that he could spare his father an experience which would almost certainly bring on another stroke, but the event that called forth the substitution, the arrest on suspicion of sober and responsible citizens and their sentence without a chance to defend themselves, filled Caleb with a deep and smoldering anger. He could free himself, no doubt, by declaring his devotion to the cause of liberty and offering to enlist at once in a regiment of the Continental line, but he no longer wanted to enlist. This was not the kind of liberty for which he could think of sacrificing his Quaker principles.

VIII

TWO MORE PRISONERS WERE brought in before bedtime.

With surprise Caleb recognized Dr. Phineas Bond. The younger brother of Dr. Thomas Bond, the founder of the Pennsylvania Hospital, Phineas was the physician in whose office Caleb would have started his medical career, had he been permitted to have one. Dr. Bond's enchanting daughter, Nancy, was the first girl Caleb had loved. As he now, half incredulous, watched Nancy's father, spare and fastidious, enter the cluttered auditorium, Caleb's wound, which had been a deep one, reopened. He had lost Nancy twice, first by her preference for another man, and then by her death at nineteen.

The ever-present specter of illness and early death rose to confront him. The doctors bled and blistered and applied leeches, they prescribed purges and emetics and febrifuges, and still the bloody fluxes and the fevers and the coughs and putrid sore throats went on, the mothers and the babies died, and women who had lost two husbands married men who had had three wives before them. Even Dr. Bond with all his skill and knowledge had not been able to save his adored daughter. It was presumptuous of Caleb to think that he, given the training and opportunity, might be able to cure when other men could not, and yet, surely, the urge to learn and practice new ways of healing indicated at least a possibility of latent power.

He had yielded too easily. With the cooler perspective that five years had given him, he realized that his father might have thought him more influenced by love and grief than by a real vocation for medicine. He should have stood firm. Self-contempt, the bitter, hot, unsparing flame by which the young see their transient failures and weaknesses fused with their enduring selves, poured over him in a searing flood.

To escape the discomfort of his thoughts, he jumped to his feet and started toward Dr. Bond. Then he saw the second new prisoner.

Hesitating in the doorway, his powdered wig neatly curled in a roll over each ear, his tricorne under his arm, his narrow eyes darting here and there, his scarlet coat garish even in the half-light, stood Thomas Pike, the dancing master.

Amused at seeing him like a bright tropical bird among the sober sparrows and disposed to hear news of Phyllis, Caleb made his way down the hall to greet Mr. Pike.

"Who are these gentlemen?" said Pike. "I recognize Mr. Wharton and Mr. James Pemberton, but who is the tall gentleman in the corner?"

"My cousin, Edward Penington."

"Oh, indeed? I have heard of him. Isn't that Mr. Thomas Fisher —and Mr. Drinker? And who is the gentleman sitting with his eyes closed?"

"John Pemberton," said Caleb shortly. He sought for a way to introduce the subject of Phyllis. Where was she and what would she do while her husband was away?

"Is Mr. Israel Pemberton here too—King Wampum, as they say?"

"He is still at large."

"At any rate," said Mr. Pike, settling the ruffles at his wrists, "I am in very good company."

Caleb opened his mouth to speak and shut it quickly, biting off the scornful words that pressed against his lips. "It looks," he said mildly after a moment, "as if you would have plenty of time to enjoy it."

The next day, which was Thursday, September fourth, Israel Pemberton himself, disrespectfully known as the "King of the Quakers," joined the company at the Masons' Hall.

Israel, Samuel Pleasants, his son-in-law, and John Hunt, an

English Friend who had married and settled in Germantown, came in a body. The three had been together in Israel's house when the soldiers first came for them on Tuesday, and they had acted in concert. Their refusal to budge without a copy of the warrant had been so convincing—or perhaps the amplitude of Israel's mansion on Chestnut Street and his formal gardens sloping down to Dock Creek had been so awe-inspiring—that the soldiers had returned to headquarters without them. During the two days that it took the Council to issue a special order for the arrest of the three, Israel Pemberton had summoned his lawyers to help him write a letter of protest to the President and Council. Thus fortified, the three Friends went with their counsel to the State House and demanded a hearing. It availed them nothing, however, and they were marched to the Lodge by Colonel Nicola himself at the head of a squad of soldiers. They arrived in time to take part in the discussion of the Remonstrance which had been prepared by the committee appointed to draw up a draft.

The Remonstrance was addressed to the President and Council of Pennsylvania. Miers Fisher and Thomas Wharton had been among its authors, and their legal knowledge and mastery of the trenchant phrase were evident in its composition. The paper began by recapitulating the history of the arrest and imprisonment of the subscribers, and went on to claim "the liberties and privileges to which we are entitled, by the fundamental rules of justice, by our birthright and inheritance, by the laws of the land, and by the express provision of the present Constitution under which your board derives its power." It proceeded then to quote in full the pertinent articles of the Constitution and to demonstrate clause by clause how they had been violated: by the vagueness of the charge; the unprecedentedly general nature of the warrant; the authorization of the agents who made the arrests to break into and search private desks for papers indefinitely "political" in nature, without limiting the search to any particular houses; the appointment of unqualified men, who held no civil office, to make the arrests and the search; and the fact that no limit was named for the duration of the imprisonment and no provision made for a hearing.

Such a precedent, it was pointed out, other and more colorful pens now taking their turn at the writing, would establish a system of arbitrary power comparable only to the Inquisition or the despotic courts of the East. They reminded the members of the Council how bitterly they themselves had criticized the British Parliament for condemning the town of Boston unheard, and inquired pointedly how they reconciled their own present conduct with their former declarations in favor of liberty.

The essay closed by committing to the Righteous Judge of all the earth the integrity of the prisoners' hearts and the unparalleled tyranny of the measures of the President and Council.

After some minor corrections and improvements, all the prisoners signed the document except Samuel Fisher, who, never having approved the new government of Pennsylvania, believing it to have been formed without sufficient legal basis after the Declaration of Independence, felt that to address a Remonstrance to it would be tantamount to recognizing it.

John Reynall, a prominent Quaker merchant, and Caleb Middleton, senior, both of whom happened to be visiting the Lodge at the moment, volunteered to take the Remonstrance to the Council, although Edward Penington pointed out to them that they did so at some risk of being themselves arrested, since they were as open to suspicion as any of the men now confined.

The messengers returned safely, however, an hour later, with the report that the Council had already adjourned when they got there. They had been fortunate to find the President, Thomas Wharton, junior, still there; he had read the Remonstrance and had appeared to be somewhat affected by it.

"He blamed you, though," said Mr. Middleton, "for not having accepted the terms of the parole first and then remonstrating. But I think he is in error there. Your position would be very much less strong if you had made what would amount to an acknowledgment of guilt by accepting parole. At all events, he promised to lay it before Council, and thinks he can send you an answer by ten o'clock tomorrow."

The hopes aroused by this prospect were soon dashed by a visit from a Quaker teamster, who came to tell them that he had been ordered to procure wagons for their removal by next Saturday. As Thursday afternoon was already well along, this news threw the company into a fever of agitation.

"Friends!" cried Israel Pemberton, shouting above the babel of voices, "I have a suggestion to make!" A man of sixty-two, tall and still erect, his brown hair streaked with white, his blue eyes fading to gray, his chin sharpening as his lips folded over the gap left by the loss of his front teeth, he was an impressive figure still, a man accustomed to authority, strong-willed, kind and generous, impatient of opposition.

In the lull that followed he continued: "In the light of the unprecedented strides Council is making in the abolition of liberty, would it not be prudent for us to acquaint our fellow citizens with the hardships we are likely to suffer? Men will do things hastily and in the dark which they are ashamed or afraid to do with deliberation in the full daylight. I cannot believe that the people of Philadelphia would countenance this injustice if they knew about it."

The force of this suggestion was immediately felt. There was a murmur of agreement throughout the group.

Henry Drinker raised his voice. "I was saying exactly that last evening, Israel, before thee came. The public should be informed. The citizens would take an interest for their own sakes, if not for ours, if they knew about what is happening."

"How do you propose going about letting them know?" asked Dr. Bond. "Is there time to get an account of the whole affair into Saturday's *Packet?*"

"Would John Dunlap consent to publish such a statement?" queried Miers Fisher. "He is hand-in-glove with the more violent members of the Council."

"We have two papers already written containing both history and argument:" said Israel Pemberton, "the protest that John Hunt and Samuel Pleasants and I drew up, and this Remonstrance which we have all signed and sent to Council. My thought would be to publish both in a handbill and get our friends outside to distribute copies as widely as possible."

This procedure was agreed upon and, since the previous messengers had some time ago departed, full of satisfaction in their efforts and ignorant of the new blow, Edward Penington's Karl was dispatched to the printer's shop on Third Street to summon Robert Bell.

Bell was a Scotsman who had come to Philadelphia eleven years earlier. He had a well-stocked bookstore next to St. Paul's Church, and a print shop at the back where he reprinted a variety of books, from Blackstone's *Commentaries on English Law* to the latest romantic drama, as well as a stream of pamphlets, mostly republican in nature.

Bell came and agreed to get their Remonstrances out at once, on a single sheet printed on both sides, which would be cheap, quickly read, and easily distributed.

By that time it was past eight o'clock. All visitors had departed; the hall was dimly lit by tallow candles here and there. Most of the prisoners were ready to go to bed for lack of anything better to do, and the family groups congregated in little circles, like bobwhites in a November field. Israel Pemberton alone sat on the platform at a table on which a three-branched candlestick blazed with light, and wrote letter after letter dated "from the place of my unjust imprisonment."

The following day, Friday, Elijah Brown was slipped in almost as an afterthought. He was a gentle, reflective man in his early thirties, very much a father and full of talk about his little son, Charles Brockden, who had just got his first pair of breeches.

The prisoners now numbered twenty-two, of whom all but five were members of the Society of Friends.

IX

"FRIENDS, THE ANSWER TO our Remonstrance has come."

All day they had waited for this. The sun had gone down on their hopes deferred, their speculations, their frayed nerves. Now, gathered in one of the smaller rooms upstairs, they were discussing the draft of a proposed "Address to the Inhabitants of Pennsylvania" when a messenger came with a letter which he handed to James Pemberton, who was acting as clerk of the meeting.

Caleb, who had been slouching in a chair at the back of the room, dejected and irritable, sat up with a jerk and folded his arms across his chest. His confidence in the free new government of Pennsylvania, worn theadbare by four days in the Masons' Hall, renewed itself with a surge. The Remonstrance had been a strong one, and if the members of the Council gave any thought to it at all—and evidently they had, since they were answering it— there was but one possible outcome. Nothing further had been heard about their leaving on Saturday, tomorrow, and that in itself gave room for hope.

James Pemberton, having fumbled with his spectacles, opened the letter and held it close to the candle on the table. In the shadowy room, twenty-two men waited expectantly.

There was a long pause, while James Pemberton read the paper, turned it over, read it again.

"It is not addressed to us," he said finally. Disappointment and dismay were written in all the drooping lines of his tired, kindly face. "It is a letter from Timothy Matlack, Secretary of the

Council, to Colonel William Bradford, dated September 5, 1777 —today, that is. I will read it in toto.

> "Sir,
>
> A remonstrance, signed by the gentlemen confined at the Masons' Lodge, having been presented to Council and read, the Council took the same into consideration, and asked the advice of Congress thereupon, which being received, Council thereupon passed the following resolve, which they beg the favor of you to communicate to the aforesaid gentlemen."

"They *asked the advice* of Congress!" interpolated Thomas Wharton indignantly. "What! Are unaccused citizens of Pennsylvania demanding their inherent rights to be delayed a hearing until Congress can be consulted! The Congress from the beginning has been engaged not to interfere in the internal affairs of the governments."

"Let us hear the rest of it," urged the dry voice of Henry Drinker.

> "*Resolved,* That such of the persons now confined in the Lodge as shall take and subscribe the oath or affirmation required by law in this commonwealth, or that shall take and subscribe the following oath or affirmation, to wit:
> " 'I do swear (or affirm) that I will be faithful and bear true allegiance to the Commonwealth of Pennsylvania as a free and independent state' shall be discharged."

James Pemberton paused for a moment, then, heavily, finished the letter. " 'I am respectfully, Your very humble servant, Timothy Matlack, Secretary.' "

There was a stunned, incredulous silence.

"Will the clerk please read it again?" said Dr. Combe.

"All of it?"

"Just the resolution of the Council will be enough."

It was read, and another silence ensued.

Samuel Pleasants rose. His eyes looked very large and dark in the candlelight, and the qualities of innocence and good nature that led his intimates to call him Sammy spoke in his slow, soft voice. "Since there is nothing in that letter about a hearing," he said, "I wonder if it *is* an answer to our Remonstrance, or just an independent communication, in which case we may look for an answer to our document at some future time?"

"The letter begins with a reference to our Remonstrance and to their consideration of it, so that I think we must regard this as their answer."

"In any case," said Israel Pemberton impatiently, with snapping eyes and jutting chin, "it is a very improper proposition to make to men in our situation. First they deprive us of our liberty, on one pretext, and then when they find they cannot justify that, they waive it and require, as a condition before setting us free, that we take this test oath. By taking it under these circumstances, we should confess ourselves to be suspicious characters."

Edward Penington and Charles Jervis stood up at the same moment and Charles Jervis hastily sat down again. "Friends," said Edward, "this is nothing new in history. We have all been brought up on stories of the sufferings of the early Friends. Probably there are few of us here who have not at least one ancestor who was dragged before a magistrate for refusing to take off his hat to someone in authority or for attending a meeting for worship in defiance of the Conventicle Act, and then afterward was offered a test oath which he could not conscientiously take as the only condition on which he could be set free. The pages of history in both old and new England are stained with such accounts. But I should not have expected that these examples would be followed by men professing to be reformers devoted to civil and religious liberty."

"*I* should not have expected," said Israel Pemberton, "that the haven which Friends established in Pennsylvania for the persecuted of all religions would ever become a place of danger to Friends themselves."

Caleb put his elbows on his knees and his head in his hands, running his fingers through his hair, wishing that he could shut out the speeches that people were making. He had no objection to the substance of the oath or affirmation, but how could he take it when it was put to him in this way, at the point of a gun, so to speak, so that the taking of it would not be the act of a free man offering his loyalty but a prisoner's craven grasping at anything for release?

He heard the Scotch voice of Tom Affleck and raised his head to listen.

"If they think we are so dangerous that we must be sent three hundred miles away, out of their jurisdiction altogether, then what difference do they suppose an oath could make? Everybody knows that bad men will swear to anything."

Caleb grinned at him and lowered his head into his hands again. As one after another expressed himself to the same effect, Caleb sighed long, gusty sighs, flung himself back in his chair and stared up at the ceiling, slewed around in his seat with his arm over the back of it and watched a mosquito which had settled itself on his knuckle visibly swell. He felt no desire to add to the spate of words himself; it had all been said, six times over, and there was nothing to say anyhow. He would have given ten years of his life to be able to mount Ladybird and ride up over the hill behind the furnace. The crickets and the katydids would be singing, the air would be as soft as velvet, and the whole enormous star-studded sky would be wheeling slowly overhead.

"It is plainly the sense of the meeting," said James Pemberton, "that we should refuse this proposal. How do you wish to go about it?"

"I think we should draw up a statement refusing the test oath or affirmation, giving the reasons which have already been expressed here," said Thomas Fisher. "We should declare our innocence once more and repeat our demand to be informed of the cause of our commitment and to have a hearing by which we can be acquitted or condemned by our fellow men."

There was a murmur of approval: "I unite with that." "I hope that will be done."

"I should like to see a *small* committee appointed to draw up such a statement," suggested Henry Drinker, who had worked on the Remonstrance. "Six are too many."

"Would three be a suitable number?"

"Two would be still better. Enough has been said here tonight to give them all they need to work on."

Nobody objecting to that, the clerk called for two names.

"Miers Fisher."

"Thomas Wharton."

"If these Friends are willing to serve, I have no doubt they will be open to suggestions from others."

The meeting was winding itself up according to the usual ritual and would soon close "with a few moments of silence." Caleb groaned inwardly when his cousin Edward began to speak.

"The making of a fair copy of such a statement is a task in itself, and I think those who have the arduous labor of composition should not be burdened with copying. Caleb Middleton has a rapid and legible—though scarcely an elegant—hand, and I suggest that he be added to the committee as amanuensis."

Somebody obligingly hoped that would be done, James Pemberton looked at Caleb to see if he had any objections, and Caleb nodded a little self-consciously, pleased on the whole at the idea. It would at least be something to do.

X

AGAINST THE PROTESTS OF his wife, who was sure that he was overtiring himself, Mr. Middleton set forth on Sunday morning to visit his son in the Masons' Hall. Already the day was warm and oppressive, with the September sun magnified by the mist, and the leaves of trees, grown overlarge in the damp summer heat, acting as a roof to keep out any breeze there might be. A brooding air of impending crisis hung over the city, and the people whom he passed looked troubled and restless. Men in uniform were everywhere, and there was none of the usual cheerful Sunday atmosphere of churchgoing and roast chicken.

To his surprise the guard at the Masons' Hall refused to let him in.

"What's this?" he demanded. "Some new measure of the Council's?"

"No, sir. It's the request of the prisoners themselves. They're having their religious services and they don't want to be disturbed."

He felt curiously rejected as he tramped away, leaning rather heavily on his stick. He might have known, he told himself, that they would be holding meeting for worship. That could be held anywhere; no church or altar was needed. If he had got there earlier, he might have joined them.

He had missed the Meeting comparatively little since his disownment, though occasionally, as now, he felt a sharp longing to be part of that waiting stillness. There was nothing to keep him, of course, from attending Meeting in Pine Street as he used to do. More than one disowned Friend continued placidly to appear at meetings for worship, even though he could no longer take part in meetings for business or other activities. But that would not be satisfactory to Mr. Middleton. He could not worship where he had been denied membership.

Sarah was always after him to go to church with her, but he was still too much of a Quaker to feel comfortable at Christ Church. He did not like all that restless jumping up and down, the singing, the repetition of formal prayers. For the most part, he stayed home quite contentedly and caught up with his reading. In the country they were too far away from either Church or Meeting to go often in any case.

He did not regret his marriage, he reflected, waiting for a chaise to pass before he crossed Third Street, even though it had cost him his membership in the Meeting and to some extent the confidence of his son. Sarah was a good woman and a comfort to him in every way. She had been a real mother to the younger children and they gave her the love they would have given their own mother. Her coming into the family had freed Sue to marry young Mercer instead of being sacrificed to the necessity of taking care of her younger brother and sisters, and the property that Sarah brought with her would not be amiss when it came to providing for the younger ones. Caleb of course would have his inheritance from his mother's father in another year or so.

Caleb alone had not welcomed his stepmother. It seemed as if the boy were determined to oppose his father in everything. All that fever to be a doctor, when he was needed at the furnace and a brilliant future lay before him there! If he had wanted to be a lawyer, Mr. Middleton reflected, it might have been different. But doctoring was a messy, morbid sort of business; it put one on too intimate terms with all kinds of people. "I'll not have a man-midwife in the family," he had declared firmly, and in the end the boy had come round. He had thrown himself into the manufacture of iron with a vim and capability that proved how right he, the father, had been. It hadn't taken young Caleb long to adopt the manner and style of an ironmaster, and he plainly enjoyed all the deference and attention that went with his position. Mr. Middleton smiled reminiscently. He had liked to see Caleb taking his proper place, had been proud of him.

It was strange—but just like Caleb's contrariness—that after making such a fuss about going into the iron business, he should be so hotly opposed to closing down the furnace when it was obviously the sensible thing to do. Well, he was getting a dose of "liberty" now—perhaps not a bad thing if it opened his eyes. But it had gone on too long already, and Mr. Middleton meant to get his son out of the Lodge if it was humanly possible.

He would have liked to get Caleb's approval of his plan of action, but since the boy wasn't available he would just have to go ahead with it anyhow. He did not like—turning down Fourth Street past the Meeting House and the school—to remind a man of past favors, and he would not. All that was over and done; it belonged to the past. He would not so much as hint at it. But it *had* been a considerable sum and he doubted if Timothy Matlack had entirely forgotten. Matlack had never been financially able to offer to repay it, but since he had embraced the cause of the colonies his political advancement had been noteworthy and he was in a position now to make a return in a different coin. That was one more thing Mr. Middleton had against the new government of Pennsylvania: the way people who could not stay solvent in business or were not received in the better houses could scramble up the political ladder to places of power and trust.

He came to the Matlack house, a modest brick dwelling in a row, and tapped briskly with the knocker.

The door was opened by Timothy's wife, Ellen, who looked disappointed for a moment but quickly rallied. "I thought it was Timothy come home," she explained. "It's Mr. Middleton, isn't it? Won't you come in, sir?"

"Timothy's not here?"

"No, he had to go back to the State House. The Council's meeting again this morning, even though it's Sunday. They had so much business yesterday they couldn't finish. He said he thought it wouldn't be long. Will you come in and wait for him?"

"No, thank you. I think I'll walk around to the State House and catch him there." He fished in his memory for the subject of a kind inquiry. "How are the little boys?" he found.

"They're not little any longer. Billy is a sergeant in Colonel Bradford's batallion and Mordecai has gone to sea as a midshipman. He seems young for it, though he's turned fourteen."

"Dear me, I'd no idea. You must miss them. Thank you, Madam, and good morning."

He went up Walnut Street to the new prison and crossed the State House yard. The prison was a very fine, large, stone building and Philadelphia was proud of it. Mr. Middleton thought it was perhaps not a bad thing to have the gaol so clearly visible from the back windows of the State House—it might remind the legislators that they too were not above the law and its penalties.

The Congress, which on weekdays shared the building with the state bodies, was not meeting this morning, nor was the Pennsylvania Assembly. Only the Council was carrying on its business behind closed doors. The hallway had the unswept, hard-used, shabby look of public buildings, and Mr. Middleton dusted off a bench with his handkerchief before he sat down to wait for the Council meeting to break up.

He was glad to sit down, for the sudden exhaustion that came so quickly these days swept over him, bringing a hot wave of dizziness with it. He folded his hands over the ivory head of his stick and closed his eyes.

As the clock struck eleven a door opened upstairs, followed by the sound of voices and footsteps. Six men came down the stairs, President Wharton in front, talking with a Mr. Scott, whom Mr. Middleton knew only by sight. They were followed by three who were strangers to him, upcountry men probably, and then Timothy Matlack, the Secretary, brought up the rear.

President Wharton pretended to be so engrossed in his conversation that he did not see Mr. Middleton sitting there on the bench, and he whisked his companion out the back door before there was any chance of his being approached. The others went through the front door onto Chestnut Street. Matlack stopped to speak to the janitor, who had come up from the cellar.

"That's all for today, John. You can lock up now. Ah, good morning, Mr. Middleton. You were waiting for me?"

"Timothy, how are you? I'd like to have a word with you. It's rather a private matter. I thought we might just have a few minutes in one of the rooms here."

"Come to the Coach and Horses Inn with me across the street. There's seldom anybody there when the State House is closed, and I don't like to keep our janitor any longer than necessary."

The small, old, hip-roofed tavern, which at certain hours on weekdays overflowed with politicians, was deserted now. The two men went in under the swinging sign with its somewhat faded picture of a coach and horses, and sitting down at a table in the far corner, ordered coffee.

"You are very busy, I know. I'll be brief."

"We are extremely busy. The Council was so much occupied yesterday with political affairs that there was no time to finish the most pressing military matter, the calling out of the entire Pennsylvania militia to meet the emergency. We met this morning to complete the arrangements."

"Yes, yes." Mr. Middleton brushed aside the city's danger, eager to get on with his business before the other man could finish his coffee and escape. "Timothy, we are old friends. We have been through certain difficulties. We have both been disowned by our Meetings. There is a certain bond between us. That is why I come to you now. Extricate my boy from this unreasonable imprisonment. They're talking about banishment now."

Colonel Matlack's brows drew together in a frown and there was an odd expression in his eyes, Mr. Middleton thought, as Timothy looked at him and then looked away, staring out through the small-paned window at the straggly asters in the vacant lot next to the tavern. The Colonel was a large man, not much over forty, with graying hair, a big, egg-shaped face, a long, heavy nose, and rather small, thin-lipped mouth. It was not easy to read his face, except when it was contorted with anger, as it not infrequently was. But he was not angry now.

"Your boy can free himself quite easily," he said after a long silence, "simply by taking the oath of allegiance. He doesn't even need to swear; he can affirm."

"He won't do that. They won't any of them take an oath— or affirmation—of allegiance now. They say they were taken up on suspicion and given no chance to clear themselves. Now they're offered a test oath as the price of freedom. They won't take it. It isn't a question of loyalty, it's a matter of principle. Caleb's no traitor to the American cause. To say the truth, he's troubled me because he embraces it too uncritically."

"Then why doesn't he join the militia? Both my sons are in the service of their country, and they are much younger than yours."

"Caleb is a Friend."

"So was I. So were Anthony and Sam Morris and about a fifth of all young men members of the Philadelphia Meetings. No, I'm sorry, Mr. Middleton, there's nothing I can do for your son unless he cares to do the simple and obvious thing for himself. Both the Congress and the Council spent hours on the case yesterday, and that in the midst of the most pressing and vital affairs. Do you realize that the British army is within fifty miles of Philadelphia on the west and that the British navy has been reported at the mouth of the Delaware heading for the city?"

"It would take no more than a few minutes to release a score of innocent gentlemen—if you haven't time to give them a hearing."

"How do you know they are all innocent? They are notoriously disaffected. The British army marches toward Philadelphia over country largely inhabited by Quaker farmers, who are likely to be very much influenced by those same innocent gentlemen in the Masons' Lodge. They won't oppose the British—and they may go over to them altogether. Any government has the right in an hour of crisis to arrest and secure persons suspected of giving aid to the enemy or injuring the patriot cause. The crowd in the

Masons' Hall can take the oath or affirmation of allegiance and go free. Or they can go to Staunton as prisoners. They have their choice. The Congress and the Council will not go back on that. And no argument and no handbills will move them now. I'm going to give you, Mr. Middleton, the same advice I have already given Mr. Reynell and Mr. Paschall. Stop running around with remonstrances and protests and appeals, and stay quietly in your homes. I mean it kindly."

"The prisoners are not all Quakers. Five are Church of England."

"They are separate cases. They can take the oath too, and they haven't the peculiarly tender consciences Friends have in such matters."

"On what basis have these men been taken up? Why my son, for instance, and not myself? Why Israel Pemberton and not John Reynell? Why Miers Fisher and not Nicholas Waln?"

Timothy gulped the last of his coffee and rose from the table. "I must leave you now," he said. "I cannot linger any longer."

As he spoke a boy came in with a pile of newspapers and put them down on a table. Matlack picked one up and scanned it with interest. After a second's hesitation Mr. Middleton possessed himself of another.

It was a supplement to the weekly *Pennsylvania Packet* and it contained a series of "Papers Published by the Order of Congress." Mr. Middleton, as he took in their content, uttered a cry of outrage and reached out to seize the skirt of Matlack's coat to prevent him from leaving.

"Look at this!" he exclaimed. "What do you know about this? *Spanktown Yearly Meeting*!"

He passed over four or five statements issued by various Quaker bodies between 1775 and 1777, advising their members to hold fast to the ancient Quaker testimony against war and rebellion, and pointed to one headed, "Extract of a letter from General Sullivan to Congress, August 25, 1777."

"Among the baggage taken on Staten Island," the letter ran,

"the 22nd instant, I find a number of important papers. A copy of three I enclose for the perusal of Congress. The one from the Yearly Meeting at Spanktown, held the 19th instant, I think worthy the attention of Congress."

Then came a list of eight questions concerning military matters, beginning with, "Where is Washington? What number of men or cannon?" and ending, "Be very particular about time and place."

Following that were the answers, described as "Information from Jersey," dated August nineteenth. "It is said Howe landed near the head of Chesapeake Bay but cannot learn the particular spot now when. Washington lays in Pennsylvania, about 12 miles from Coryell's ferry. Sullivan lays about 6 miles northwestward of Morristown, with about 2000 men. *Spanktown Yearly Meeting.*" Another, headed "Intelligence from Jersey July 28, 1777," dealt with troop movements near Morristown and was unsigned.

"You know very well," exclaimed Mr. Middleton, "that there is no Spanktown Yearly Meeting. Even if there were such a body, any official paper would be signed by the clerk for the Meeting. This is a patent forgery, designed to put the prisoners in the worst possible light!"

Colonel Matlack looked uneasy. "I myself have never heard of a Meeting at Spanktown—"

"The very name of Spanktown is an obvious fiction!"

"But the papers were published by the order of Congress, not of Council. The greater part of them are Philadelphia Yearly Meeting Epistles and Advices. They call on their members to be neutral at a time when there can be no neutrality. To us, anyone who is neutral is actually supporting the enemy. I must go, Mr. Middleton. But I'll tell you this—" he was angry now; his temples throbbed and his cheek twitched and two deep lines like exclamation marks had sprung up between his eyebrows—"the prisoners brought the publication of these papers on themselves. When they printed their Remonstrance and it became clear they meant to raise a ferment, then the Congress decided to give its account of this transaction to the public. The Congress has had these papers two weeks or more and would not have published them unless they had felt it to be necessary. I bid you good-day, sir."

Mr. Middleton plumped down again and ordered another cup of coffee. When it came, he was too much agitated to drink it, but sat swishing it round and round in the cup, staring at the table. Caleb would go, then, as a prisoner and unheard, to some remote spot on the Virginia frontier. In an undefinable yet disturbing way he felt responsible for this disaster that had come upon his son. His own decision to close the furnace was, he felt sure, behind it. They had taken the young man, caring nothing for the injustice of it, casting aside the old one as used up and negligible.

He felt a hand on his shoulder and lifted his eyes to see Dr. Hutchinson looking down at him in kindly concern.

"Thee looks tired, Friend Middleton. Ought thee to have come out this morning?"

He had seen the young Quaker physician often during the past few days, for he too had been busy carrying messages and running errands for the prisoners. Already portly at twenty-five, pink-cheeked, kind, and indefatigable, James Hutchinson was, though a birthright Friend and a nephew by marriage of Israel Pemberton, an outspoken republican who went further than many of the radicals in his opposition to wealth and privilege. Family loyalty and frank disapproval of what he called "Star-Chamber methods" had led him to take a conspicuous part in trying to obtain a hearing for the prisoners.

"So thee's seen the supplement to the *Packet*," said Dr. Hutchinson. "An unpleasant affair. I cannot see any justification whatever for printing that."

"Sit down, won't thee, James, and join me in a cup of coffee? Boy! Another cup of mocha. Thou'rt a Whig. Can thee explain to me why the members of the Congress would so lower themselves as to publish a palpable forgery like this—these '*Spanktown*' papers?"

"I find it difficult to understand. Perhaps those actually responsible for their publication believed them to be genuine.

Friends' ways are totally incomprehensible to many non-Friends."

"Anyone who took the slightest trouble to compare the genuine Advices and Epistles with the Spanktown papers could see at a glance the difference in both content and form. These Spanktown papers were written by someone ignorant of the common usages of English grammar. Washington *lays*—Sullivan *lays*—as if they were hens! Did one of the members of Congress himself invent them? Who did it?"

"I think there is no doubt that they were taken from captured prisoners by officers of General Sullivan's army. My own conjecture would be that the papers were the work of a genuine spy—though not a very skillful one—and that someone hostile to Quakers, possibly one of the officers themselves, added the signature, 'Spanktown Yearly Meeting,' either as a joke or with the intention of discrediting the whole Society of Friends. General Sullivan himself obviously believed it to be genuine and so did some of the members of Congress though certainly not all of them."

"Thou'rt very calm about this disgraceful affair."

"I deplore it, I assure thee, and I regret very much that the Congress and Council have thought it necessary to arrest those now in the Lodge. It makes many of us in the patriot cause uneasy. But when a city is threatened with invasion by an approaching enemy, things are done that would not be done under ordinary circumstances. I still have a hope that reason will prevail. Our friends in the Lodge are engaged in writing another Remonstrance to the Council and one to the Congress, and I wish they may have an effect. If I may make a suggestion to thee, Friend Middleton, I think thee would be wise to go home and go to bed. Thee has done all for thy son that thee can do at present, and now thee ought to conserve thy strength."

Mr. Middleton struggled up from his seat at the table and the high-backed settee behind him heaved with his efforts. "I had intended to return to the Lodge to see my son—their Meeting is surely over by now—but perhaps thou'rt right." His breath came in little gasps. "Perhaps I had better go home."

It was only a matter of six squares, but home seemed suddenly a long distance away.

"I have my chaise outside. I had to make a call in the Northern Liberties earlier. I'll just drive thee home."

The young doctor's smooth, round, healthy face was full of kindness and sympathy as he helped Mr. Middleton into the shabby chaise and went to unhitch his apathetic horse. It was a pity, thought Caleb Middleton, that young Hutchinson had thrown himself so deeply into the Continental cause, though certainly he was not following the leaders blindly or uncritically. He was sound in his attitude to both the Spanktown papers and the imprisonment of Caleb and the rest. No doubt young Hutchinson was another of those who, like Timothy Matlack, saw opportunities for advancement in a republican government that they would not have in a royal government. In spite of having married Israel Pemberton's niece, Hutchinson was still the son of a stone mason and might find it more difficult in a settled society to rise above his origin.

But he was showing courage in standing by Israel Pemberton now. Mr. Middleton smoothed out the copy of the *Packet* which he still carried crumpled in his hand and folded it carefully, as they moved slowly over the cobblestones on Chestnut Street past Israel Pemberton's big mansion. Israel had enemies, social, religious, political, who no doubt were rejoicing in his downfall.

"Fear and malice," he said aloud, as the chaise pulled up at the cross-street to let a squad of men in uniform march past, "make a bad combination."

XI

CALEB PUT DOWN HIS QUILL and pressed his flattened forefinger back into shape. It was midday on Monday and he had been writing all morning, copying the prisoners' answer to the offer of the Council to free those who would take the oath or affirmation of allegiance.

It was a long document, written by Thomas Wharton and Miers Fisher and incorporating suggestions made by others. The first draft had been much shorter, but while they were discussing it the afternoon before, a supplement to the *Pennsylvania Packet* had been brought in, containing papers purporting to be from Spanktown Yearly Meeting. Indignation had run high within the Masons' Lodge and there had been many useless speculations as to who had perpetrated this outrage. When they returned to the consideration of their answer to the Council, their attitude had hardened and their words became sharper and tinged with sarcasm.

They had been united in refusing to take the oath or affirmation of allegiance. The five members of the Church of England, although the papers in the *Packet*, directed wholly against Friends, did not incriminate them, stood firm with the rest.

"We have none of us," said Mr. Combe, speaking for the five, "directly or indirectly communicated any intelligence to the British forces, and we would quite cheerfully engage not to hold any correspondence in future, if the demand had not been coupled with ignominious and illegal restrictions. Our consciousness of our own innocence forbids us to accede under the circumstances."

It would have been better, Caleb thought, to make the answer a brief and strong refusal to take the oath, without going over once more all the arguments dealing with their imprisonment, but he was much the youngest among them and his opinions were not solicited.

John Hunt, the oldest of the group, complained that the document was lacking in expressions of conciliating love, but Israel Pemberton declared himself satisfied that "We shall send them such a Remonstrance as they have not before read!" and it was decided to make no further changes in the draft, except for the addition of a pronouncement by Lord Halifax on the subject of test oaths after the Revolution of 1688. "As there is no real security to any state by oaths, so no private person, much less statesman, would ever order his affairs as relying on it; for no man would ever sleep with open doors or unlocked-up treasure, should all the town be sworn not to rob." This quotation was supplied by Elijah Brown, who kept a commonplace book from which apparently he was never separated.

Caleb had copied the Remonstrance in his best hand, and it now lay on the table ready for their twenty-two signatures. Even Samuel Fisher was now willing to concede that recognition did not necessarily signify approval and had promised to sign this protest. Dr. James Hutchinson offered to carry it to the Council.

"Thy father is remaining in bed today, on my advice," he told Caleb, "though he was very anxious to come and see thee. He sent his love to thee."

Caleb thanked him, rather relieved than otherwise that he would not have to hear the lamentations and fulminations of his aroused parent. He was feeling very low in spirits and almost intolerably irked by the fact of imprisonment. The enclosing walls, the dingy windows with their oblongs of cloudy sky, the pressure of other and older men's inescapable presence, the irregular and unappetising meals, the endless conversations, rumors, speculations, denunciations, mingled with the admonitions of the more pious to avoid "murmuring" and to submit to the will of God, fretted his spirit as the rebellion of his young muscles and nerves against the enforced inactivity tortured his body. Despite his anger at the officials of the Congress and Council, he could still see that beyond the fears and suspicions and petty animosities of the stuffy rooms in the State House, there was taking place under the open sky a struggle for true freedom from which he was now debarred. He had no hope that their remonstrances and protests would avail them anything now. Congress would not have published the Spanktown forgery if it had not already made up its mind to banish the prisoners. The only prospect of change from the Masons' Hall that he saw ahead of him was some gaol in the depths of the Virginia mountains, where their voices could not be heard and where they might lie forgotten till they moldered away. Once they were out of sight and sound, who would remember them again, in the midst of a war to be fought against appaling odds?

The afternoon passed somehow. Dr. Hutchinson, round and perspiring in the muggy gray heat of the day, returned with a note from Timothy Matlack saying that the Remonstrance had been read in Council and their business referred to Congress. The prisoners sent him hurrying back to Colonel Matlack to request a copy of the minute of referral and to ask whose prisoners the Council considered them to be, the Council's or the Congress's.

It was late when he returned, without the minute but with the retort from Timothy Matlack that their question was "artful and insidious" and that he was not authorized to answer it.

Pouncing on this evasion like a cat on the tip of a tail disappearing into a mousehole, the prisoners early the next morning, which was Tuesday the ninth of September, sent the same request in writing to the President of the Council. They got no answer but they learned how awkward a question it was. Neither Council nor Congress, Dr. Hutchinson told them, wished to take responsibility for holding them.

"On Seventh Day last, the Congress advised the Council to give you a hearing," he said. "The Council answered that it had no time in the present alarming crisis and requested the Congress to dispose of you. Thomas Wharton, junior, told me he thought you should have a hearing, but others were opposed. They are still debating."

Since there was yet a faint chance that the Council might be moved by reasons, the prisoners wrote another protest, their fourth. Caleb, copying it, thought it was the clearest and strongest of all.

"You condemn us to banishment unheard. . . . You determine matters concerning us which we could have disproved, had our right to a hearing been granted. . . . The charge against us of 'refusing to promise to *refrain* from corresponding with the enemy' insinuates that we have already held such correspondence, *which we utterly and solemnly deny*."

Caleb had also to copy an "Address to the Inhabitants of Pennsylvania," which contained the entire history of their imprisonment, the general warrant for their arrest, all their remonstrances, a protest on their behalf signed by one hundred and thirteen Friends, and the various communications from the Council. This was to be printed in a pamphlet and distributed as widely as possible.

At half past four that afternoon the axe fell.

A messenger came from the Council with the Resolution that had ended the debate. It named the twenty-two "apprehended as persons who have uniformly manifested by their general conduct and conversation a disposition highly inimical to the cause of America," declared that they had renounced all the privileges of citizenship, and ordered that they be "without further delay removed to Staunton in Virginia, there to be treated according to their characters and stations as far as may be consistent with the security of their persons."

Some further delay there was, however—caused by the difficulty of procuring wagons at a time when every available vehicle was needed for carrying stores out of the threatened city, for transporting people who were fleeing before the British advance, and for the demands of Washington's army, now reported to be marching to intercept the British in the valley of the Brandywine.

All Wednesday agents of the Council combed the town for wagons, and those prisoners who had horses or chaises of their own were urged to use them. In the afternoon they were told that they might go home to make their final arrangements for departure on Thursday; if they wished, they might even stay overnight.

"It is the early Quakers all over again," said Edward Penington. "They imprison us unjustly, with every reason for us to feel morally justified in absconding, and then they trust us to go home for the night unattended. My own great-grandfather and others were allowed to transfer themselves from Bridewell to Newgate prison without a guard. It is our influence they fear, not our actions."

XII

BORED AND DISGUSTED THOUGH he was with life in the Masons' Hall, Caleb went home without pleasure. His brown eyes under the level brows were clouded, his lips set and his chin defiant as he walked along the dusty street, where buttonwood leaves, curled and dry, had already fallen. For the moment he was free under the blue September sky, but there was no lift in his heart. What he had seen bearing down upon him like a black storm cloud or a runaway horse was actually coming to pass. He would be sent to Virginia as a disaffected and dangerous person.

He was not looking forward to seeing his father. Too much lay unresolved between them. He could not master the resentment that rose from the conviction that if only they had stayed in the country as he himself had wished and kept the Phoebe Ann going, none of this would have happened. His father had made the decision without consulting him and then, by falling ill, had bound him to it. The report that Patty had brought of the parental humor—now perhaps he'll learn something at first hand about liberty and tyranny—rankled. Like an infection it spread to inflame the wound which his enthusiasm for the American cause had suffered. The consciousness of his sacrifice in taking his father's place as a prisoner brought him none of the consolations of virtue, since he had merely acquiesced in the substitution, not initiated it. Divided and torn within himself, he wanted to escape, not to go back to the place which he held responsible for his pain.

He would do his duty and no more. He would pay his respects to his father and Sarah, see the children, get his things for the journey, and he might as well have a decent meal, but he would not spend the night under his father's roof. He would give Amos instructions about bringing Ladybird to the Lodge next day. The one ray of light in the gloom was that he would be allowed to ride his own mare.

Tacy, playing on the doorstep, was the first to see him. She gave a shriek of joy and came running toward him with her arms spread wide. He stood still to meet the impact and she climbed up his legs like a monkey on a stick, till he caught her up in his arms and lifted her to his shoulders, where she rode in triumph, clutching his forehead with sticky hands. Edward was next, and Amos grinned broadly as he opened the door. Patty had gone to see a classmate, and Mrs. Middleton was upstairs with Caleb's father.

"He's not so good, Master Caleb," said Amos in a low voice. "Dr. Hutchinson's been twice. He say he'll git over it if he rest, but all this runnin' aroun' in the heat afussin' himself ain' done him any good."

The house was cool and elegant, with the shifting shadows of the trees on the pale, papered walls, the reflection of asters in a silver bowl on a polished table. He could look down the dim hall and see the door open upon the sunny garden beyond and smell the faint fragrance of beeswax and the spiced rose petals in the blue and white jars on the mantel.

His stepmother met him at the top of the stairs.

"I'm so thankful you could come, Caleb. I can hardly keep your father in bed. He's been determined to get up and go to meet you. He has overdone, that's all. He'll be all right if he stays quiet. All this running back and forth to the Council and the Congress, trying to see Mr. Hancock and Mr. Wharton and anybody else he thinks of has been almost too much for him. Be careful what you say and don't get him excited. He has really suffered over all this."

Caleb went into the front bedroom where his father lay propped against pillows in the big tester bed. He looked better than he had when Caleb last saw him, as people so often do in bed, surrounded by expanses of white linen, rested, and wearing an expression of welcome for the visitor.

"I brought thee a copy of our 'Address to the Inhabitants,' " said Caleb, wrenching a pamphlet out of his coat pocket. "It came from the printer at noon. We are each to have twenty-five copies to distribute. I thought I'd leave mine with thee. Amos can get them when he takes my things to the Lodge."

Mr. Middleton took the pamphlet in his hands and examined the title page.

"Printed by Robert Bell, I see. I thought he was on the other side of the fence. That clerk of his—what was his name? Paine?— was a rabid republican, with his *Crisis*. Called the Quakers 'fallen, cringing, and Pemberton-ridden people,' I remember distinctly."

"A printer doesn't necessarily believe everything he prints," said Caleb. "Bell has courage. Benjamin Towne refused to print our Remonstrance. He said openly he was afraid of being taken up as a disaffected person and having his press stopped. William Sellers said he would consult a friend about it, but he hasn't been back since."

"This is well put," said Mr. Middleton, riffling through the pages: " 'Nor can any man think himself safe if a precedent of so extraordinary a nature be established by a tame acquiescence with the present wrong.' That's a very revolutionary statement—too revolutionary for even the new rebel government, I should think. Most governments prefer a tame acquiescence on the part of the governed."

Caleb tilted his chair back on two legs, clasped his hands behind his head and yawned. The words of the Address were almost meaningless to him now. He had heard them read and reread, the succeeding drafts discussed and corrected, a word substituted here, a phrase cut there; he had copied one after another six separate remonstrances and protests and the final "Address to the Inhabitants." He was unspeakably weary of what one of the documents called the "peaceable though firm assertion of the inalienable rights of free men," and his hands twitched for action, preferably violent.

"They are right," his father said, "to resist this outrage, even to banishment. But, Caleb, I don't want thee to do it. Thou'rt young. Thou'rt entangled in this through no fault or wish of thy own. Thy sympathies are all on the American side and have been. I saw Dr. Smith the other day. He told me he had been on their list. No, no, not the apothecary—Provost Smith. He was in town earlier, he's gone now to the Falls. He took the test oath, he said. He advised thee to."

Caleb had a good deal of respect for the President of the College of Philadelphia. He would have liked to talk with him about the whole question of oaths of allegiance, for he was conscious of painful confusions in his own mind, but he did not want Dr. Smith's opinions filtered through his father's commands. "No, I can't do it, Father. I won't even think about it."

The older man sighed.

Caleb let the front legs of his chair down to the floor with a thud, and buried his head in his hands. The new government of Pennsylvania, to which the oath or affirmation promised allegiance, had ceased to be for him a noble abstraction and had become instead a personal entity. Thomas Wharton, junior, self-righteous and evasive, George Bryan, the Irishman, who hated everything that was English and noisily identified himself with the people against the well-born, Timothy Matlack, born a Friend, knowing what Friends stood for, accepting as valid papers which he could not help knowing were forged: there they were, mouthing all the slogans about liberty, calling on men to die for it, and in their actions denying the first essentials of it. If he could promise allegiance to what General Washington stood for, that would be one thing, but to swear, or affirm, his faith in Messrs. Wharton, Bryan, Matlack and company, no thanks. Nor was he going to dance when his father pulled the strings.

"I hear that there has been no appropriation for your expenses," his father was saying.

"Council will pay our expenses on the road and then Congress will be applied to, to consider our support during our absence. We got that much from Nicola this morning. But they still won't say whose prisoners we are."

"Who will have custody of you when you get to Virginia?"

"The Governor of Virginia, according to Nicola. Who *is* the Governor of Virginia anyhow?"

"Mr. Henry, I believe. Give him liberty or give him death."

Caleb swore.

"No, no, Caleb, don't swear! That was too bad of me to say that! What I'm getting at, my boy, is that I have foreseen that thou wilt need funds. In the top drawer of the chest, in the right-hand corner, there is a money-belt which I want thee to take. There are twenty gold half-joes in it, and I'll find a way to get more to thee if thou needs it. Thou'll have to change them for Continental bills, but get the best rate thou can."

Caleb took the belt, heavy with coins, and fastened it around his waist inside his shirt. He felt a kind of strength and even a sense of release coming to him from the touch and weight of that belt, which seemed to permeate his viscera directly without passing through his brain.

"I wonder what some of the others will do," he commented, after thanking his father. "Tom Affleck, for instance. He's nearly frantic about his wife and children. And Mr. Pike won't be giving any more lessons in dancing or fencing. If there's any sewing to be done in our house, I wish Mrs. Pike could be employed." She had been a seamstress in Charleston; her husband had let that out one evening. It made no difference to Caleb, but why had she concealed it?

"Speak to thy mother about it."

A faintness in his voice warned Caleb that his father was feeling the sudden devastating fatigue of his condition. He patted the old man's knee, which felt thin and knobby under the sheet, and went off to his own room, where he found his stepmother bent over an open portmanteau. It was the same one that he had used when he came to the city to college, boarding at Mrs. Graydon's until the family moved to town for the winter months; on its shabby lid were his initials in brass-headed tacks.

"I've put your greatcoat in, in case it turns cold in the moun-tains before you can get home, and your leather breeches, and your nankeen jacket and breeches, and two pairs of flannel drawers and two flannel shirts as well as cambric shirts and underwear. I put in half a dozen fine linen shirts and I hope there will be some way to get them properly laundered. Plenty of worsted and thread stockings. Now what I want to know is, should I put in one of your good suits and silk stockings? I suppose I'd better. You never know."

"I'm not making the grand tour of Europe. I'll need some salt. It's getting scarce, and the food from the tavern has been tasteless."

"Yes, that's another thing. I've got tea and chocolate and sugar, and a little bag of raisins, and coffee. And I put in four napkins and a tablecloth, too."

"I'm not going to set up housekeeping out there!"

"No, but you're used to having things nice, and it might make a difference. I put in the plum-colored damask morning-gown with the green baize lining, because that one is warmer than your others. You're a bit of a dandy, Caleb. I never saw such a collection of neckcloths. You go through them and decide which you want to take."

He opened the drawer of the chest and tossed out four or five at random, then carefully selected handkerchiefs, the blue and white silk, the dark green silk, the yellow silk, and a pile of linen ones.

"I'm putting in a quantity of writing paper and your brass ink pot. Be sure to send us word as you can. Have they said anything about letters?"

Caleb made a wry face as he quoted, "Correspondence to be allowed by open letters through the hands of the Continental Secretary of War."

"Who is he?"

"Dick Peters."

"That smart, satirical young sprig! Well, be careful what you write."

"Oh, I don't suppose he'll read the letters personally."

"Somebody will. Just say if you are well, and tell us anything you need, and I'll find a way of sending it somehow."

"Leave some room for books." He took *Tom Jones* from the table by the window, and saw that the sash was propped up with a stick. The weights had been taken to make bullets.

Supper was delicious. The dining-room was in the extension of the house that ran back into the yard, where a few late roses were blooming and a red apple fell now and then from the tree by the well. Sarah had remembered his favorite dishes and had provided cold beef and duck, Indian corn pudding, delicate hot biscuits with sweet butter and gooseberry jam, frothy syllabub, and clear, strong coffee. Patty had come home full of the afternoon spent with her bosom friend, Betty Pleasants.

"Betty is the genteelest girl in town," she pronounced, "and no wonder, because her mother and father are exceedingly genteel. I should think it would do thee good, Caleb, to be associated with Mr. Pleasants. His manners are positively courtly, which can't be said of thine. He stood up when I came into the room. *He* isn't a wet Quaker, either."

"I stand up for ladies," replied Caleb blandly, and flicked a few drops of water with his teaspoon at Patty. "Furthermore, I'm not wet, only a little damp."

"Wet Quaker" was the slang term for those fashionable Friends who walked the top of the wall between the world and the Meeting, sometimes tumbling over the edge altogether and landing in the baptismal font at St. Peter's.

They had scarcely finished supper when a long succession of calls from sympathizing friends began, which lasted all evening. Caleb, senior, upstairs in bed began to feel neglected and rang his little bell furiously; Tacy had a nightmare and awoke screaming; Edward, having begged to stay up because it was Caleb's last night, fell asleep with his head heavy against his brother's arm. Finally the last caller left, and Caleb, having never consciously made the decision to stay all night, went thankfully to his own bed for the first time in nine days and the last for who could say how long?

XIII

IN THE MORNING AMOS trundled Caleb's portmanteau in a wheelbarrow to the Lodge and brought back word that the wagons would not be ready till late afternoon. At three, when Caleb was saying good-by to his family, Patty clinging to him with wet eyes in a sudden belated realization, the sound of firing began. It came from the southwest, the ominous, angry thunder of cannon. They knew without being told that the battle for Philadelphia had started and that in any separation of families now, none could prophesy who would be the fortunate ones or when they would be reunited.

As Caleb walked through the streets he found the city pulsing with excitement. A man went ahead of him up Third Street clanging a handbell and shouting, "Shut up your houses! All men who can carry a gun are ordered to appear on the Commons!" The corporal of a squad of militia marching up Spruce Street stopped Caleb and demanded to know why he was not with his regiment, but when he replied that he was on his way to the Masons' Hall under orders of Council, they went on without further ado. Some wagons rumbled past, piled high with household goods, obviously on their way out of the city. Three carpenters under the direction of a colonel in uniform were at work on St. Paul's Church taking down the bell. Women peered with distraught white faces out of doorways and whisked inside again when anyone approached. Again and again the distant cannon boomed, now faint, now louder, as the light breeze rose or died away. Once Caleb heard the crisp, sharp rattle of drums beating to arms from a street corner, and his scalp prickled.

At the Lodge the first person he met was Miers Fisher.

"Ah, Caleb, I'm glad to see thee back. Dr. Combe last night gave his parole. It is a great surprise to us, after all his protestations."

"Did he take the test oath?"

"No, it was some sort of patched-up arrangement, I understand. What he really wants, it seems, is to get to England, and I believe he is to be sent as a prisoner of war to the West Indies for exchange. And Dr. Bond has been in difficulties."

Dr. Bond, it developed, had attempted to give a parole of his own devising and thought at first that it would be accepted. When, however, he was offered only the same oath that he had refused before, he returned to the Lodge, determined to go on with the others. Colonel Nicola, by this time exasperated, declared that he had already struck the doctor off the list and that he would have to remain in Philadelphia under custody.

The prisoners now numbered twenty, seventeen of whom were Friends.

Miers Fisher had suggested the day before that writs of habeas corpus might be applied for, and after some discussion it had been decided that those who felt inclined to do so were free to proceed. Ten of them, including Caleb, now signed an application and it was taken away to be delivered to Chief Justice M'Kean.

Two members of the Philadelphia Light Horse, as well as a detachment of the City Guard, had been assigned to escort the prisoners as far as Reading. Both Alexander Nesbitt and Samuel Caldwell would have much preferred going with the rest of the troop to the assistance of Washington to escorting a number of their fathers' richest friends and acquaintances out of town in disgrace, and Sam Caldwell, who was in command, was in a towering bad temper.

So many citizens had taken flight that it had been difficult to procure enough vehicles for the prisoners and even to get horses for the members of the City Guard. The baggage wagons proved to be entirely inadequate for the number of portmanteaus and bales that the gentlemen thought necessary, and there was considerable altercation before a promise was extracted that more wagons would be found and sent after them.

The endless delays and adjustments and changes of mind involved in organizing such a cavalcade stretched out the time of departure until the tempers of all were at the snapping point. The large and sober crowd that gathered to bid the prisoners farewell or simply to watch their departure further impeded operations. They offered no resistance, but they got in the way, scores of silent, somber people, moving docilely when they were asked to, flattening themselves against the walls of the houses opposite, but still filling the sidewalks with their bodies, spilling over into the street, so that it was difficult to move a wagon when it was filled or to bring up another horse. They were a mixed group of people interested for one reason or another. Many of them were freed Negroes who had been helped to start their new life by John Pemberton, and they wept aloud when they saw their benefactor led out and boosted into a wagon with a backless bench for a seat.

John Hunt came next. Both he and John Pemberton took the extreme position that they could not co-operate with wrong even to the extent of climbing voluntarily into the wagon, but whereas John Pemberton admitted a symbol of force in the two men who assisted him, one at each elbow, John Hunt had to be lifted up bodily and carried. He did not resist, but he was a dead weight and it took three of the guards to do it. In going through the door they brushed his hat off and it rolled on its round brim to Caleb's feet. He followed and handed it up to John after he was seated, a quaint little figure, with his collarless coat, his gentle and serene countenance, his white hair.

"Thank thee, Caleb," said John, with a flicker of a smile that, like a door opened and quickly shut, revealed the glint of humor within.

"Would you mind stepping aside, Mr. Middleton?" said Caldwell, drawing with visible effort on his last stores of patience.

The wagons as they were filled passed out of the alley and lined up in Second Street. Those who were to ride their own horses or drive their own carriages would come next, and finally as much of the baggage as could be piled onto the two shaky wagons.

"Mr. Affleck, Mr. Brown," shouted Caldwell. "Mr. Pike—"

Caleb looked for Phyllis, but like most of the wives and mothers she had said her farewells in the privacy of home. He had written a note to her earlier and sent it by Amos. It was brief and he was not satisfied with it, but he had had no time to rewrite it. "I cannot leave without sending you a word," he had written. "I shall be thinking of you, alone and unprotected. If you are looking for sewing, please go to my mother. Don't be troubled about us who are in exile. I cannot think it will be for long. I am, Your most humble servant, C.M. Jr."

"Mr. Wharton!"

Thomas Wharton came slowly and ponderously forward and paused on the steps with a look of distaste directed equally at the wagon and the perspiring guard who stood ready to help him up. Something about his deliberation, his disdain, and his consciousness of his own worth irritated the guard beyond control.

"Get in there, you damned Tory!" he snarled, and put his hand on Wharton's shoulder to hustle him.

Out from the crowd of passive bystanders leaped a plain working man, a very angry man, who struck down the soldier's hand, drove him back against the wagon, and towered over him, threatening.

"Dare to abuse a prisoner," he roared, "and I'll thrust my hands down your throat and pull out your heart!"

A murmur of approval went through the crowd.

Thomas Wharton put his hand lightly on the man's arm. "Never mind, Murdoch," he said soothingly. "Thou'rt a good friend, but violence solves nothing. Give me thy hand and help me into this chariot."

The soldier wiped his forehead with his sleeve and signaled to the driver of the next wagon to move up.

After the wagons came Edward Penington's chaise, driven by Karl, and Charles Eddy driving his own sulky with James Pemberton on the seat beside him. Israel Pemberton's man Martin brought up his four-wheeled chaise, and Mr. Caldwell, very taut now and very brisk, read out, "Mr. I. Pemberton."

Israel, like most of the others, had been home the previous night and he showed the benefits of it. Freshly shaven, his hair dressed by a barber, he wore an immaculate gray suit and fresh white neck-cloth, silk stockings and polished shoes with silver buckles. His thin, high-nosed aristocratic face expressed a calm self-control. He nodded to Martin, who had got out of the chaise to stand beside the step, the very embodiment of a well-trained, respectful English coachman ready to take his employer on some conventional outing.

"Friend Caldwell," said Israel, "before I get into the chaise I should like to see thy orders."

"Mr. Pemberton, you are holding up the line. There is no necessity for you to see my orders."

"If thou wilt not show them to me, I must ask that thou at least read them to me."

"No, sir, I will not. Please move along."

"It is plainly our right to have a certified copy of our commitment to the authorities in Virginia and of the orders accompanying it, so that we may know in what light we are being represented to them and in what manner we are to be treated."

Caleb, who was now behind Israel, could not see his face, but he heard his voice, calm and reasonable but commanding, and he saw Caldwell's eyes fall.

"Mr. Nesbitt and I, with some of the City Guards, will accompany you to Reading. From there on you will be in charge of the lieutenants of the counties through which you pass. That is all I can tell you. It is late. Make haste, sir."

His dignity unruffled, Mr. Pemberton stepped into his chaise and was driven out of Lodge Alley.

Amos brought up Ladybird, with a saddlebag in which Sarah Middleton had carefully packed necessities for the journey. Amos's honest face was eloquent with affection and distress as

Caleb leaned down from the saddle to shake his hand in farewell.

"Did thee deliver the note? Directly into her hand?"

"Yes, sir."

"Any answer?"

Amos looked reproachful. "I'd have guv it right to you, Master Caleb."

The Fishers and Sammy Pleasants were riding too. Horses' hooves grated on the cobblestones as they moved at last, a little before six o'clock, out of the alley and into Second Street. Behind them came the two baggage wagons and six members of the City Guard mounted on a motley assortment of nags. Caldwell and Nesbitt, riding their own fine pacers, went to the head of the column, and the first of the wagons moved slowly forward. The crowd in the alley came surging after. From somewhere a fife and drum appeared, and the mocking strains of "Yankee Doodle" followed them up Second Street as far as Vine.

Out of the crowd, spreading to the guard in the rear and from the guard to the prisoners, like fire licking through a field of dry grass, came news.

"What is it?" said Caleb. "What's happened?"

"Something about a battle," said Sammy Pleasants. "Things are going badly and General Lafayette has been wounded."

XIV

IT WAS DARK WHEN they reached Palmer's Tavern at the Falls of Schuylkill and there was not room for all of them in that small and rather primitive inn. Word had gone out, however, of their coming, and hospitable friends in the neighborhood opened their homes to the overflow. A messenger from Dr. William Smith, Provost of the College of Philadelphia, was waiting with an invitation for Caleb and Edward Penington and Thomas and Miers Fisher. One of the guards rode with them up the steep hill to the Smith place and was accommodated in a humbler house near by.

The official residence of the Provost was situated in Fourth Street opposite the Friends' burying ground, but Dr. Smith had built himself a country retreat high above the Schuylkill with a superb view of the river. It was a simple enough stone house, plastered over and whitewashed, but its inaccessibility and the wildness of the surrounding woods had given rise to its name, "Smith's Folly." Here, after an excellent supper presided over by the provost's old-maid sister, Isabella, who remained with him after his wife and children had gone to his father-in-law at Moore Hall, the six men sat on the porch and talked late into the night.

The cordial and genial Dr. Smith, it was rather maliciously whispered, had long cherished hopes of a "pair of lawn sleeves" and people assumed that his "Letters of Cato" opposing independence had been written in the belief that a bishopric would come to him more surely from His Majesty's government than from any new republic; but of late he had expressed his support of the American cause and ten days ago had taken the oath of allegiance. Though he belonged to the Church of England party which opposed the Society of Friends at many points, he still had many friends among the Quakers, and he offered his hospitality tonight as if it were an ordinary social opportunity instead of a possibly incriminating act of kindness to people under a political cloud.

Conscious of being the youngest and least important, Caleb sat silent while the rest talked, looking out over the rough, steep lawn, the tops of the forest trees below, the dark, gunmetal coils of the river, watching the moon slowly fall down the sky toward the hills on the other side. The conversation ranged with jerks and silences over a variety of subjects, the career of Benjamin West, the Philadelphia artist now fashionable in London, whom both Edward Penington and Dr. Smith had assisted in his unknown, farm-boy youth, the inferior men lately elected to the Continental Congress, the probable outcome of today's battle reported to have been near the Brandywine, and came to rest on the question of oaths of allegiance.

"Granted," said Dr. Smith, "that there is no security in the oath of an unscrupulous man—what was it your own Penn said, something about the man that fears to tell untruth not needing to swear because he will not lie, while he that does not fear untruth, what is his oath worth?—granted all that, I am still at a loss to understand why Friends refuse an affirmation of loyalty where they honestly feel it."

"It is partly because history has proved the uselessness of oaths," said Edward Penington. "Oaths have never yet prevented a revolution. The Long Parliament swore allegiance to Charles the First —and beheaded him. General Monk and his army took all the test oaths the Commonwealth imposed—and proceeded to restore Charles the Second to the throne. Oaths only oppress the virtuous element of the people."

Miers Fisher tapped his pipe against the sole of his shoe. Caleb could not see his square, keen, mobile face in the shadows, but he could imagine how it lit up as the young lawyer launched into the subject on which Caleb had already heard him several times hold forth with passionate conviction. Caleb admired and liked Miers more than any of his fellow prisoners. His quick intelligence, his knowledge of the law, his attractive personality and his faithfulness to Friends' principles combined to make him in Caleb's eyes an ideal combination of the Quaker and the man of the world.

"More than that," said Miers, "oaths are actually dangerous to the principle of liberty in a free government. Men who feel free and secure under a government will support it because it is to their interest to do so. You can get no surer safeguard for a government than that. But if the ruling party forces people to swear to whatever arbitrary laws it may enact, then civil liberty disappears and religious liberty with it."

"In a time of crisis," objected Dr. Smith, "when the very life of the state is threatened, then it seems to me the state must have some way of dealing with suspected persons, or all liberty may be lost."

"But some cause of suspicion should be proved against a man before he is publicly stigmatized by being singled out to take an oath which the unsuspected need not subscribe to. If proper legal process proves him disloyal, then suitable action can be taken against him."

"There is another aspect to it," said Thomas Fisher slowly. "I wish John Pemberton were here, for he can express the moral and religious implications better than I can, but it is this, as best I can put it. The body may be subject to compulsion, the mind is not. But if, to make life easier for the body, to avoid imprisonment, to keep one's employment, to win advancement, the mind assents to something it considers wrong, then it suffers a wound from which it does not easily recover. It loses strength for the next encounter, so that a test act in the end is subversive of the morality of the inhabitants."

Now he was invading, with a layman's vocabulary and a Quaker's assurance, the field in which William Smith, D.D., might be supposed to speak as a professional. Caleb turned from watching the round dark shape of a small animal—probably an opossum—

crossing the grass at the edge of the trees, and looked at the theologian.

Dr. Smith made a slight soothing gesture with his hands, and spoke smoothly with something of the unction of his pulpit voice. "I wonder if that isn't taking it a little too seriously. Most people, I think, regard such an oath as a sort of formality, an open and forthright statement of where their loyalties are placed, a sign of a willingness to stand forth and be counted. I have always understood that it was Friends' policy to submit peaceably to all government and to effect change if necessary only by peaceful means and not by violence, so that I should think Friends of all people could subscribe with a clear conscience to such an affirmation of loyalty. Then those who are disaffected or who subscribe dishonestly as a cover, can be easily apprehended by the government as perjurers."

"Thou'rt quite right, Friends are not revolutionaries, but on the other hand we do not acknowledge government as the highest authority. We must obey God rather than man, and where laws of men are at variance with the laws of God we must follow our conscience—as in refusing to take part in warfare. If I commit myself by an oath to act or think in a particular way in the future according to the dictates of a government, then where is my religious liberty? How can I then follow the leadings of the Spirit?"

Dr. Smith shook his head slightly. "I can understand your point and honor your sincerity, sitting here high above the turmoil and out of earshot of the guns. But I can also understand that a political group burdened with many decisions, carrying on war for its very existence in the face of present military defeat and invasion, might have difficulty in grasping your somewhat fine-spun theories."

"They do not have to understand our fine-spun theories," said Miers crisply. "They have only to stand by their own definitely enunciated principles in regard to certain fundamental rights of man, which are, not to be arrested without charge, to be heard in his own defense, and to be presumed innocent until proved guilty."

Caleb suppressed a yawn and wondered what time it was. He had wanted to talk with the Provost about oaths of allegiance, but he found in the conversation no clearing of his own confusions.

You did what you had to do, he thought, pushed by some voiceless force within you and pulled by outside circumstances beyond your control, and sometimes you did not know what your answer would be until you heard the "yes" or "no" emerging from your own throat. He yawned again, almost overcome with sleep, and lost the thread of what they were saying. Through his mind drifted fragmentary memories, no more than shadows and entirely disconnected: his father falling full length on the terrace at the Phoebe Ann, the two militia officers in Phyllis's sitting room the day that Washington rode past, John Hunt being lifted into the wagon in the alley, his father's face as he gave him the money-belt.

He and Miers shared a room that night. As they were undressing Miers said suddenly in a voice so sharp with pain that Caleb scarcely recognized it, "Our little Tommy is only eleven months old, headstrong already and hard to handle, and there will be another child this winter. Sarah's not yet twenty-two. I ought to be there with her."

"There are still the writs of habeas corpus," said Caleb, to comfort him. "They'll reach us at Reading, at the latest."

XV

THE GROUP REASSEMBLED NEXT MORNING at Palmer's Tavern, some coming from the Vanderins' house and some from Joseph Warner's. The contingent from Dr. Smith's came hurrying up last of all, late, apologetic, but fortified with a most satisfactory breakfast. There was a change in the order of march, so that those who rode horseback went first, leaving the slower wagons to follow.

The road, after they passed through the ford at the Wissahickon Creek, was appallingly bad, full of stones and ruts, treacherous soft spots and gaping holes. Caleb was sorry for those in the springless wagons, who were tossed against one another continually by the jolting and lurching. Up they toiled to the ridge above the Schuylkill, through the little village of Barren Hill, past fields where the stumps of trees still marched in untidy ranks, past whitewashed taverns that catered to a trade of drovers and wagoners, through stretches of woodland where squirrels chattered.

Ladybird was fresh and lively, the morning was cool. Caleb was not unaware of the troubles and anxieties which weighed upon the spirits of his companions, but for himself, decision was past and out of his control and he was away from the Masons' Hall.

They stopped at Thompson's Tavern for a dinner of boiled mutton and kidney beans, for which they paid five shillings, and went on again without lingering. In the afternoon the wind veered around to the northwest and blew out as cold and raw as if it had been November. They expected to spend the night at Widow Lloyd's tavern, thirty miles from Philadelphia, but when they reached there at sunset they found it already crowded with refugees from the city.

"Washington has been routed," the word was passed down the line. "Birmingham Meetinghouse is filled with the wounded. Bands of soldiers are running leaderless about the countryside, dropping their blankets and muskets on the road."

Pottsgrove, seven miles farther on, was the next possible stop. Weary now and chilled through and through by the sharp wind, they pressed on.

Here again, as at the Falls, word of their coming had somehow preceded them, and when they reached the little tavern on the wide, grass-bordered street, they found friends waiting to welcome them to their homes. Pottsgrove, a settlement of perhaps twenty brick or stone houses, was the stronghold of the Potts family, a large and varied clan, most of whom were engaged in the manufacture of iron for the Continental army, though a few were Tories and a still smaller number were Quaker objectors to war. Old John Potts, who was dead now, had been a friend and adviser of Caleb's father when he was a young man, and so Caleb was not surprised to find himself invited to the Mansion, where the Widow Potts lived with her eldest son, Thomas, now a colonel in the Continental army, and her unmarried daughters.

The parlor in the great house was big and comfortable, with a fire blazing on the hearth, servants bringing hot drinks, and the pleasant sounds overhead of housewifely bustle with sheets and blankets. A lump of ore gleaming with iron pyrites on the mantelpiece, the elaborately decorated iron fireback, and the diagram of a furnace stack pinned to the wall made Caleb feel himself once more in an ironmaster's house, and he leaned back in his chair sipping his hot spiced cider with a feeling of deep content.

Presently Ruth Potts came into the room to say that the bedrooms were ready whenever the travelers wished to retire. The youngest daughter of John Potts and thirteenth child, Ruth was famous in a small way for having said out loud that she had no intention of marrying until she was too old to bear children. Caleb, who in his imagination had endowed her with the figure and features of his sister Patty, saw instead a slight, vivid, charming young thing with an air of elegance. Charles Eddy, who seemed to know her well, persuaded her to play for them, and she sat down at the spinet and in a fresh sweet voice sang a gay little French song. Her accent was pronounced by Caleb, without knowing very much about it, as truly Parisian.

The next day those prisoners whose baggage had been left behind asked that the group be permitted to wait in Pottsgrove until the extra wagons which had been promised should catch up with them. The weather continued unseasonably cold and they were shivering in summer clothing; some of them had no clean shirts to put on. The gentlemen of the Light Horse assented.

Caleb, whose portmanteau, thanks to Amos's efforts, had got into the first wagon, extracted from it his leather breeches and brown homespun coat and some of the flannels, which he lent to Charles Eddy, his roommate at the Mansion. Charles was a trader in iron, whom Caleb had known through business dealings and also as a member of the Pine Street Meeting. Why Charles should have been arrested and his brother Thomas left free, nobody knew, but as Charles was a bachelor it was less of a hardship for him. He was older than Caleb by ten years at least, a plain, hearty man with a long chin.

Caleb spent most of the day chatting with him, hoping to see Ruth again, and watching the wagons, coaches and chaises that passed in a steady stream along the road, all fleeing from the doomed city. Caleb knew that his own family would stay where they were, confident of good treatment from the British army, which his father apparently believed was composed entirely of gentlemen; but Caleb wondered, since Americans had proved themselves so little able to discriminate between friend and foe, if the English would be very much more discerning.

In the late afternoon in search of diversion he walked down the road to the tavern. To his surprise he found it surrounded by armed men, twenty or more of the local militia, all speaking German and sounding angry and excited. He passed through them without being stopped, nodded to the familiar guards at the door, and went inside. He found the taproom crowded and the atmosphere tense. A number of his fellow prisoners stood massed together, listening with varying expressions of dismay and incredulity to the harangue of a pugnacious young man wearing a captain's insignia.

"I know what is behind this," he was shouting. "I have been warned of your perfidy! But you shall not succeed in it. If you will not come peaceably, then you must come by force. My men are outside. I will give you half an hour to get ready."

James Pemberton spoke for the group. "Friend," he said quietly, "we are peaceable people. Thou needs no threats. But it is not possible for us to collect ourselves and our belongings in half an hour. It is now past four o'clock. Even if we leave here at five, it will be dark long before we could reach Reading. Consider what thou'rt asking. Thou knows the state of the roads. We should run the risk of lamed horses, broken wagons, possibly serious injuries to men old and unaccustomed to rough travel at night."

"You should have thought of that before you dug your heels in and refused to budge."

"We have remained here with the permission of our guard."

"Then you have deceived them. We have had reliable word that you expect to be rescued here by a British force. We intend to forestall that by removing you to Reading immediately. Is that clear?"

"Someone has misrepresented us!" cried Caleb. "There is not one of us who has had any communication with the British."

Nesbitt and Caldwell, who were housed at David Potts', now came in and made themselves known to the Captain, drawing him aside for a low-voiced consultation. Mr. Pike, conspicuous in his red coat, summoned the barkeeper, who had vanished during the shouting, and persuaded him to produce drinks for the military, while the prisoners took stock of their situation. The outlook was not encouraging.

The Germans who made up the greater part of the population hereabouts were not the gentle pietists from the Rhineland who had followed William Penn, but a harder, more aggressive people who came later for economic rather than religious reasons. They could hardly be expected to understand the Quaker position. "If the German translation of our 'Address to the Inhabitants' were only ready," said Israel Pemberton, "this is exactly the situation in which it would be useful."

The upshot of the conference between the gentlemen of the Light Horse and the captain of the militia was that the prisoners were permitted to stay that night in Pottsgrove but they must be ready, baggage or no baggage, to leave at seven the next morning.

They were all on hand even a little before the hour, but before they got under way a messenger, who had ridden most of the night, came with the ten writs of habeas corpus that had been applied for the day they left Philadelphia. They had been allowed by Chief Justice M'Kean and were in good order.

The ten promptly served their writs on Alexander Nesbitt and Samuel Caldwell, who without hesitation refused to touch them.

"We have orders to deliver you to Reading," said Caldwell. "After that we have no further responsibility. You can try your writs then on somebody else."

In spite of this refusal the very fact that the writs had been allowed was evidence that justice still lived, and the spirits of the prisoners rose accordingly. The ten who had not before applied for writs now decided to do so, and a young man who lived in Pottsgrove offered to ride to Philadelphia at once with the new applications.

All this delayed their departure and it was nine o'clock before the cavalcade set off once more. All their friends in Pottsgrove, including the pretty Ruth, were out to wave them off, and Caleb had a warm sense of the sympathy and even approbation of people who understood their position even though they might not share it.

At the edge of the village the company of militia fell in sullenly behind them.

During the ensuing hours Caleb was aware of those steadily tramping feet. In spite of the satisfaction of being able to ride

Ladybird, in spite of the glow created by the Pottses' good will, and the relief which he felt from the possession of the writ of habeas corpus, he tasted, following the slow plodding pace of the wagons in front and hearing the militia behind, the peculiar bitterness of being a prisoner, of knowing himself to be an object of fear, hatred, and contempt.

One small incident lit up for him the temper of the people of the region, their ignorance and their passion.

The cavalcade had stopped to rest the horses, and Caleb, seeing behind a small, mean house a woman drawing water from a well, rode over to ask her for a drink. She was Irish, from the look of her, with bold blue eyes, white skin sown with freckles, and coarse dark hair springing off her forehead with a life of its own. She handed him a gourdful of water and stood waiting, her arms akimbo, for him to drink.

"What's the news from the camp?" she demanded.

"None that I know of. Which camp?"

"Where are those Tories that are to be banished?"

"Why, I suppose I am one of them."

"No, go on. You can't be. You're a gentleman."

"But I am—and you'll see the rest like me. Over there. Look for yourself."

"I don't believe you. If I thought you were telling the truth," she threw back her head and screeched fiercely, "I'd take a gun and shoot you through myself!"

Caleb laughed and handed back the gourd. "No, you wouldn't," he said. "You're too kind. Thanks for the water."

But he was sober as he rejoined the group.

It was a beautiful country through which they rode that bright, cold, windy Sunday morning. The road rose over rib-like hills and dipped to cross the sparkling brooks that cut little valleys to the river, turning as they went the mill-wheels, paper, saw, grist, oil, that ground out prosperity for all the region. Already leaves were beginning to scurry along the road and rustle at the feet of goldenrod and asters in the ditches; here and there a swamp maple flung a flaming branch against the predominant green, or a sweet gum spread out its five-fingered leaves touched with scarlet at the tips.

Now the hills on the other side of the river began to show blue in the distance, and at last the pointed, forest-clad hill called Mt. Penn loomed up ahead of them. A little after two they rode into Reading.

It lay on a slight eminence half encircled by the winding Schuylkill, a comparatively new city, now in the throes of wartime activity. A repository for essential stores which had been moved out of Philadelphia, a center for refugees, a meeting place for Continental officers, it was the vital link, with Philadelphia as good as captured, between the northern and the southern states. Every house and inn was bulging. Most of the indigenous population was German and so ardently pro-American that they saw Tories everywhere, even among those who had fled from Philadelphia to get away from the British.

The streets were full of people returning from church, and the faces turned toward the prisoners as they entered the town were not friendly. Dark looks, shrugs, clenched fists, and a volley of flung stones and clods greeted them; a few men spat contemptuously.

The inn kept by the Widow Withington had been assigned to them. It was a large, bare building near the jail and offered few amenities. The sheriff of the county, Daniel Levan, who was there waiting for them, seemed to be a civil, decent sort of man, sober and short in his manner, but he like the captain of the militia believed that they had refused to leave Pottsgrove in the hope of armed intervention, and they soon saw that he was going to take no risk of their escaping. The guards who had come from Philadelphia were dismissed and German-speaking soldiers posted at all the doors of the inn. Friends who came to inquire or to offer their services were peremptorily ordered away.

In Reading, Caleb saw at once, there would be no pleasant hospitality, no pretty girls singing French songs in a firelit parlor or genial talk over a bountiful breakfast. With Charles Eddy, John Hunt, and Thomas Gilpin, he was assigned to a small room with two beds and a chair that was apparently attached to the wall by a cobweb. Leaving his saddlebag on the floor in a corner, Caleb went downstairs again to see what chance there was of getting something to eat.

The parlor was a plain room with a sanded floor, scarred pine tables and benches, some pewter mugs and wooden plates on shelves, and a fireplace black and sour with old smoke. He found Thomas Pike in the kitchen eloquently describing their hunger to the Widow Withington.

"I was told to provide beds for you," she said, "and beds you'll have. I did not engage to give you meals. It's Sunday and this is a God-fearing house. I've let my servants off. I'm not agoing to turn in and cook a meal for twenty Tories and that is all there is to that and you can put it in your pipe and smoke it."

She opened a door which gave on a stairway, and slammed it behind her.

The fire on the big hearth had been banked, but a kettle on the crane still gave off a thin spiral of steam.

"I think, Mr. Middleton," said Pike, "we could at least make ourselves tea, if we could get at the wagons. There is cheese in one of them, too, and some bread."

A shadow passed across the window. It was one of the guards, marching back and forth with his musket over his shoulder. Caleb went to the back door and opened it. Another guard blocked his way.

"I only want to get some food out of one of the wagons."

The guard said something in German, of which all that Caleb could understand was "nicht."

"Essen," said Caleb. "Ich bin hungry. Let me go get some stuff out of the wagon. I won't run away. *Essen*. You ought to understand that. You look as if you did plenty of it. Come on, that's a good fellow."

The guard remained blank, unyielding.

Hearing shouts from the other side of the house, Caleb turned away, letting the door close behind him, and went to find out what was going on.

Through the big front door, which stood open, came the confused noise of a scuffle. Caleb got there in time to see a soldier lay rough hands on an old man, pull him back from the doorway, and fling him off with such force that he would have gone sprawling into the street if he had not fallen against a younger man behind him. There were shouts from a crowd that had gathered outside, and the next moment stones thudded against the side of the house. One crashed across the floor and Caleb moved just in time. A heavy stone struck the old man on the shoulder and another smaller one hit his cheek. With a little grunt of pain he put his hand up to his face, and looked at it with a dazed air when it came away covered with blood.

Sickened, Caleb recognized the old man as Isaac Zane, a venerable Friend of Philadelphia, John Pemberton's father-in-law. The younger man behind him he did not know by name, but he had seen him in the gallery of the Great Meetinghouse. The next moment a guard slammed the door in Caleb's face.

With the prisoners inside he crowded to a window. Old Isaac Zane, with his handkerchief pressed to his cheek, was being assisted down the street, while an urchin ran after him to fling a handful of gravel at his back. The shouting in the street grew louder, and the faces of the massed men and boys took on the evil and dangerous look of a crowd that is becoming a mob.

"Come away from the window," said the quiet voice of John Hunt. "They see us and we are only exciting them."

John Pemberton sat down heavily on the nearest bench.

"He came out of kindness to inquire for us," he said brokenly. "That such a thing could happen in Pennsylvania!"

XVI

They spent a week in Reading.

The hostility that greeted them on their arrival was not again manifested in so sharp a form. The captain of the Light Horse, Samuel Morris, newly arrived from the battle at the Brandywine, sent in to them that first night a dinner complete with wine and decreed that they were to be allowed to see their friends freely. A birthright Quaker who had been disowned for taking part in war, he had family connections among the prisoners, which gave him an understanding of their point of view and a personal sympathy for them.

Although Isaac Zane returned to Philadelphia without making any further attempt to see them, a number of Friends of Reading and the near-by communities of Exeter and Maiden Creek visited the inn to offer their sympathy and to bring provisions. Some of them were refugees from Philadelphia, but most were country people, dressed in homespun, sober, forthright, plain, and deeply religious. Their respect for the prisoners was based not on outward marks of eminence, which they tended to distrust and disapprove, but upon the solid consideration of their courage and faith in resisting all temptations to compromise. This feeling was not expressed in open approbation, but it emerged in the times of "retirement," when the whole group would sit together in silence in the Quaker way, seeking to experience the presence of God. Out of the silence might come a prayer that the banished Friends be strengthened to endure and upheld in their service for Truth. That they were making a stand for civil and religious liberty and in so doing were rendering their country as definite a service as if they fought for it, was the conviction of the majority of the prisoners. The recognition by their fellow Quakers of the greatness of the issues and the degree of the sacrifice that might be required was as invigorating to the spirits of the prisoners as the fresh country butter and eggs and chickens which the visitors brought were comforting to their bodies.

Caleb, though he was too divided in his own mind, too torn by his private conflict, too restless, to sit through many of these periods of retirement, still saw their effect in the increased steadiness and peace of mind which was shown by the others. Through the indignity and injustice of their confinement, the delays, the discomforts, the anxiety about their families left behind, the exiled Quakers moved as men united in a high purpose and sustained by a sense of divine assistance.

Feeling sometimes a little set apart from the group by his youth, Caleb had a sympathy for the three who were not Friends and sought them out.

Thomas Pike was busy with the problems of catering, making himself a sort of major-domo for the company. He enlisted the services of Richard, Martin, and Karl, the servants of the Pembertons and Edward Penington, persuaded the Widow Withington to co-operate, found tactful ways of letting the visiting Friends know what was needed, and saw to it that Mr. Pemberton, Mr. Wharton, Mr. Drinker, Mr. Penington got the kind of wine they liked before the supply ran out. Caleb, despising the snobbery that lay behind all this solicitude, still enjoyed talking with Friend Pike, as the grateful gentlemen called him, especially when he could steer the conversation around to Phyllis.

That she had been a seamstress he already knew. Now he learned that she had lived in a little house in a little court in Charleston, supporting a father who pretended to be a gentleman but who in his cups, as he usually was, revealed a knowledge of sleight of hand with cards and a familiarity with the interior arrangements of Newgate prison that were probably not unconnected. Phyllis's fingers had been rough with needle pricks, but she had known how to dance—how she could dance!—and Thomas and Phyllis had danced together for exhibition. The pupils had come crowding until, they said, why not make a partnership of it, and so they had married and Thomas had moved into the little house. But that had not been happy. The father had been difficult. Thomas had come to Philadelphia, where he taught fencing as well as dancing, and Phyllis later had followed him. The father? Mr. Pike was vague about the father. He was drunk most of the time. He scarcely knew what was happening.

Tom Affleck, in contrast to Mr. Pike, was unpretentious, plain, uncompromisingly independent. He was one of the small, dark Scots, quiet, intense, and gentle. He was also a very unhappy man, distraught with worry about his young wife, Isabella, left at home to fend for herself and the four small children.

"We have some good furniture she can sell. That will take care of them for a time. Then I'll just have to get back. They can't keep me away."

"You could have got out of this quite easily, you know," said Caleb, curious to see what he would answer, "if you'd only made a few promises."

"And so could everyone else that's here, including yoursel'. No, I couldna do it, and I think Isabella understands. I explained it to her this way: Suppose someone cam' to me and said, 'Noo, ye must promise to stop beating your wife.' I've never beat my wife and I never would, but what kind of a man would I be to make a promise put like that? I didna come to America to knuckle under to test oaths and such goings-on."

"I can't see why they took you up anyhow. You're not responsible for anything the Yearly Meeting says—even if you were still a Friend, and you're not. You were just going along quietly making furniture, so far as I can see. You haven't any particular British connections now, have you?"

"I was in and out of Governor Penn's house, making furniture for him before they sent him away. He brought me to this country in the first place. He's been kind to me, I'd never turn against him. I don't hold with overthrowing our lawful rulers any more than our Lord did—and He was a carpenter too. Render . . . unto Caesar the things that are Caesar's and unto God the things that are God's. That's what our Lord said and that's what I believe. I never made a secret of it. Perhaps the Council didna like that. But it's a fine thing to put a man in prison for his thoughts, is it no'?"

With Drewet Smith, a slender, active man with an odd nervous trick of twisting and screwing his face as he talked, Caleb discussed horses and hunting. Smith, like Nesbitt and Caldwell, had been a member of the Gloucester Fox-hunting Club, though Caleb had never met him on those rare occasions when he rode with the club. They talked too of the drugs that Smith sold in his shop on Chestnut Street, and Smith was rather free in his comments on the doctors and their methods. He was himself practically as good as a doctor, he said, and he could bleed a patient more skillfully than most of them. He had his lancets with him, and he showed Caleb a neat little case with a new device called a thumb-lancet, that worked with a spring, so that the patient could not see the blade or know just when the cut would come.

When John Pemberton came down with a bad cold, a fever, and a pain in his chest, Smith rummaged in his baggage and brought out remedies. For a little while all of the group were worried about John, who seemed to be sinking and who himself took a serious enough view of his condition to declare his forgiveness of his persecutors (together with a not unnatural wish that they might be "humbled before the Lord"); but between Dr. Smith's doses of camomile tea and Peruvian bark and the tender care of Israel and James, who waited on their younger brother and nursed him as if he were a beloved child, he began, before the week was out, to mend.

The most oppressive element in the confinement at the Widow Withington's was the lack of privacy. Four bedrooms and two small parlors were little space for twenty men. They had no place to go to escape the pressure of other personalities, the actual

physical nearness of other bodies, the sound of voices in endless
conversations, or, at night, of snores and coughs and sighs, the
sight of little mannerisms, unnoticed in ordinary times, which
became in this tense crowded atmosphere a painful cause of irritation. Caleb, who had never been unduly squeamish, now found
his nerves rubbed raw by no more than a way of sitting down, of
using a handkerchief, of scratching a head, of pursing the lips and
blowing out the cheeks, and the knowledge that he too would one
day be old and would blow his nose and creak his false teeth or
mumble his sunken lips, smote him with such bitterness of disgust
and depression that he longed for death tomorrow, or perhaps the
next day. Certainly he would not willingly linger on into senility
after his fortieth birthday.

The weather contributed its share to the dreariness of their
situation. On the sixteenth the wind swung round to the northeast
and the rain poured down, dashing against the windows in furious
pelting gusts. Shutters banged, wet logs hissed in the fireplace
and the fire sulked, damp spots appeared on the plastered walls,
and a penetrating chill crept out of every crack.

On the evening of the seventeenth, the second day of restless
wind and lashing rain, a messenger came from Philadelphia with
letters for some of the prisoners. Caleb, having discovered that
there was nothing for him, with the depressing conviction of being
neglected and outcast that comes to those who are passed over
when the mail comes, retreated to a bench against the wall, where
he sat yawning and squirming, changing his position so often and
so convulsively that one after another those who thought to share
the bench with him got up and moved.

Among the letters was a printed bill. Israel Pemberton read
it first through his small square spectacles, uttered a sharp exclamation, and handed it to his brother James. From James it went
to Thomas Wharton, and then the heads of the three Fishers bent
over it together.

"Oh my God," thought Caleb, "now we'll have some more
remonstrances and protests."

The room was buzzing. Thomas Wharton raised his hand. "Friends, this concerns us all. Are we all here?"

John Pemberton was in bed above; two or three others were missing; the rest turned with an apprehensive expectancy toward Wharton, who held the paper at arm's length to the light of a cluster of candles.

"It is a bill," he explained, "introduced into the House of Assembly on the fifteenth and passed on the sixteenth, that is, yesterday. It suspends the Habeas Corpus Act. Now we shall have no chance of a trial."

Edward Penington spoke from the shadows on the far side of the room. His voice was calm and reasoning with the familiar overtone of irony. "This may deprive future dangerous persons like ourselves of their rights, Thomas, but our writs were allowed well before the sixteenth."

"The intention to include us is clear. The bill mentions the taking up of several persons who have refused to take the oath of allegiance."

They argued late as to whether such an act could be made retroactive or not. In the morning the answer came. Samuel Morris arrived to inform them that orders had come that the writs of habeas corpus were to be disregarded and that they would be dispatched within a day or two to Winchester, Virginia.

Caleb, who had scarcely heard of a writ of habeas corpus before he himself applied for one, had fastened upon it then with a faith compounded partly of the urgency of his desire for freedom and partly of his respect for his own newly acquired legal knowledge. He turned his back on the room and stood by the window, looking out and scowling.

The storm had passed. The fresh sunny air had the new tang of fall in it. The stableyard was strewn with leaves and twigs; the horse trough and the puddles caught and held the deep blue of the sky.

Behind Caleb voices rose and fell in question, complaint, demand. The baggage wagons. Stores for the journey were on the way from Philadelphia. Clothing was on the way. They could not go till it came. The two baggage wagons that had come with them from Philadelphia had been taken away. Two of the traveling wagons had gone. The third was so dilapidated that it was all but useless. Four wagons they must have at least, four more wagons.

We lose our freedom, thought Caleb, we are driven out of Pennsylvania like cattle, and we clamor and whine about baggage wagons.

The words changed and with them the voices. Now a note of pleading entered. John Pemberton was ill. He was in no condition for a long and difficult journey. He was old. Several were old. They were infirm.

The legal voices took over. The writs of habeas corpus had been served before witnesses. They antedated the bill suspending the Habeas Corpus Act. The voices charged Samuel Morris and the lieutenant of Berks County on their peril to remove the prisoners from Reading; they must, the legal voices said, pay due regard to the writs.

Caleb turned from the window. Captain Morris looked harassed. His temper was rising.

"I have a new warrant," he said sharply, "dated the sixteenth. This supersedes all previous orders."

"Be so good as to read it to us."

" 'Whereas Israel Pemberton, James Pemberton, John Pemberton . . .' " began Morris promptly, and plowed through the whole list. Caleb heard his own name near the end, with the "junior" still firmly attached. What did they think he had done, the donkeys? " '. . . have been arrested by the Supreme Executive Council of Pennsylvania as persons whose uniform conduct and conversation has evidenced that they are highly inimical to the thirteen United States of North America.' "

So there it was, hearsay and suspicion stated as certainty.

"Sam Morris, I've done nothing and I've said nothing inimical to the United States," shouted Caleb, tearing the charged but decorous silence into pieces.

"Mr. Middleton, you may free yourself at any time by taking the oath of allegiance," said Morris coldly.

John Hunt slipped around two or three and came to stand beside Caleb. He said nothing, but his eyes were bright with affection and his touch on Caleb's arm was light and quieting.

"Shall I continue?" said Captain Morris huffily.

There was nothing new in it, except the substitution of Winchester for Staunton as their destination.

Winchester was almost a hundred miles nearer to Philadelphia. There were Friends in Winchester. Isaac Zane, junior, who with his ironworks and his mills was in high favor with the Whigs, had his plantation only a few miles south of the town. Winchester was better, much better. For a time an actual cheerfulness prevailed.

The two missing baggage wagons rumbled into the yard that afternoon, laden with portmanteaus and bales, with stores of food sent by anxious families in Philadelphia. During the next three days while the final arrangements were made for their departure the prisoners wrote letters. Messengers dashed back and forth between Reading and Philadelphia. Israel Pemberton sent for his Bible and a book called *British Liberty,* his gloves, and his best plush breeches. John Pemberton wanted two pairs of hose and a Testament with larger print than the one he had brought. Miers Fisher, on behalf of them all, wrote a letter to Chief Justice M'Kean, thanking him for the futile writs and, "as thou hast done thy part," sending him the established fees for them, which amounted to seventeen pounds and ten shillings.

With the letters and messages came rumors from the armies which now prowled around the outskirts of Philadelphia, maneuvering for position, warily estimating each other's strength. For several days Washington, crossing and recrossing the Schuylkill, had moved between Howe's army and the city. Then they heard that in the torrents of rain during the storm, the cartridge boxes of the Americans had proved to be so badly made that their powder had got wet and tens of thousands of rounds of ammunition had been ruined. The Continental brigades, drawn up at a favorable spot to attack the marching red-coats, could not fire a shot. Later they heard that Howe was with his army at Swede's Ford with a clear road before him to Philadelphia if he cared to take it. The next day, so it was said, Reading was full of members of the Congress and of the Pennsylvania Assembly who had left Philadelphia in a great hurry. The report went around with a snicker that the delegate from New Hampshire had not even waited for his horse to be saddled but had galloped off bareback.

All through the week in Reading Caleb shared a bed with John Hunt.

"We are the oldest and the youngest," said John. "If we add our ages together and divide by two, we shall find that the mean age of our company is about forty-five, which appears old to thee, doubtless, but still rather young to me."

Caleb made a quick calculation and discovered John Hunt to be about sixty-six. Short and spare and quick, he moved almost with the ease of a young man; his white hair stood up around his face like a halo; his fine, transparent skin, flushed at the cheeks with a pattern of tiny veins, seemed to let out an inward shining; and his clear blue eyes as they looked at Caleb were lit with humor and even tenderness.

"Thee doesn't look so old as some of the others," said Caleb awkwardly, knowing that he was being awkward and that John Hunt knew it and still not feeling uncomfortable.

"I have less to carry than some of them," said John. He might have added that he still had his teeth.

At first Caleb tried so hard not to take more than his share of the bed that he balanced precariously on the extreme edge, but later he forgot.

"Thou rolled completely over on me last night," said John one morning, folding his arms behind his head and smiling benignly. "But I shoved thee back. I find I am able to hold my own even with such a powerful young giant as thou. It gives me some satisfaction."

Caleb turned his betraying face away, to hide his foolish pleasure in being called a powerful young giant.

Sometimes as they lay in bed waiting for the other two in the room to dress, since there was not space for all four to move about at once, John reminisced about his youth.

"I am a convinced Friend," he said once. "It is not the same as being a birthright Friend. A convinced Friend is often a little excessive, proving to himself and others that he has had good reasons for his choice, whereas a birthright Friend wears his Quakerism as naturally—and sometimes as thoughtlessly—as he wears his skin. I grew up in Ipswich and joined the Meeting there, mostly, I think, because of one man who lived his religion in every act of his daily life. I might have found such a man within the Church, but it just happened that I did not. I had seen too much of pulpit religion, of ritual that never went beyond the church door."

"When did thee first come to Pennsylvania?"

"Almost forty years ago, the first time. I had a leading, while I was riding home from a Meeting near London, to visit Friends in America."

"Three years older than I am now."

"Yes. I don't know why they let me come. I am not sure, today, that I should be able to distinguish between a genuine leading in a young, convinced Friend, and a desire to see the world. But the Meeting heard me out, they gave me a traveling minute, and some of them helped me with funds. So I came. I thought I was led to minister to the Americans, and I uttered many safe, correct discourses, no doubt, but in reality it was they who ministered to me. It was on that trip I first met John Woolman. After knowing him I became converted as well as convinced."

"And the next time thee came, thee stayed?"

"No, not the next time. I made another visit in 1756, when there was all the trouble with the Indian war and the Meeting for Sufferings was established. I went back after that, and returned in sixty-nine. I met my dear Rachel, we were married, and I stayed."

"And then this war started. What does thee think will come out of it all?"

"I think America will win her independence. The British are fighting across three thousand miles of sea, and the French, who have never been averse to striking a blow when it suits, are a threat at their back. But whether the United States will destroy their own freedom by the means they use to win it, is another question. It is a time of great sifting and testing, Caleb."

XVII

ONCE AGAIN THEY SET OFF on a Sunday morning. Israel Pemberton, having made a private arrangement, got into Charles Eddy's sulky, with a guard to drive it, and sped off before the rest were ready. Charles Eddy and John Pemberton rode in Israel's chaise. Edward Penington, having found his own chaise, which was a light one, miserably uncomfortable on the rough roads, sent it back to the city with Karl, and himself climbed into one of the wagons and sat down beside Thomas Wharton. He had wanted to send his man back anyhow, because he was anxious about his wife and children and would feel easier if the faithful Karl were with them. Israel Pemberton's Martin was also returning to Philadelphia, for he was an indentured servant and his time would be completed the following month. That left James's Richard the only servant now with the group. He rode a tall, raw-boned horse and fell discreetly behind the seven prisoners on horseback.

They got off at ten, with six new guards from the local militia commanded by Daniel Levan, Sheriff of Berks County, very much occupied with the portfolio of papers which he carried. The gentlemen of the Light Horse, having completed their responsibility in the matter, bade them farewell with genial politeness and obvious relief.

Fording the Schuylkill a few miles beyond Reading, they rode through the rich German farmland, where apples hung bright on the silver-leaved trees, barns were painted red, and the four-horse teams pulling the great blue wagons piled high with yellow corn wore tinkling bells on the collars of their harness. They dined in the village of Womelsdorf and reached Lebanon before dark. There some of them were lodged at the inn and others in private houses. Caleb saw that Israel Pemberton, by going ahead, had managed to get the best room in the inn for himself and his brothers. This proved, as the days went on, to be his regular practice. He was quite open about it and seemed to feel no occasion for apology or shame; he was accustomed to having the best.

In Lebanon a well-known ironmaster, acting as the deputy of the Lieutenant of Lancaster County, met them with real kindness, going about from house to house in the evening to make sure that they had everything they needed and that no one was offering them any rudeness or hostility.

"I know your father, Mr. Middleton," he said to Caleb. "I am sorry indeed to see his son in such circumstances. You have my entire sympathy, I assure you. If the authorities in Philadelphia had not been under such stress—you knew the Council and Assembly are in the process of moving to Lancaster, the Congress to York?—I feel sure this miscarriage of justice would never have occurred."

Caleb wondered that he dared to speak so openly, but he did more. He took a number of copies of their "Address to the Inhabitants," promising to distribute them.

On the way out of Lebanon next day they passed a camp where six hundred Hessian prisoners of war taken at Trenton the previous Christmas were being held. Three hundred more had been marched to Winchester. Caleb gloomily pictured Winchester as one large prison stockade.

That night they spent at Harris's Ferry, where in a barn-like stone building they slept fitfully on makeshift beds neither clean nor comfortable. Caleb in the wakeful hours tried to estimate how far they were from Lancaster. Perhaps twenty-five or thirty miles, he thought. If they had taken the other road from Reading, he might be sleeping tonight in the Mercers' big comfortable house in Lancaster, where his sister Sue and her baby were now staying with her husband's parents. At any rate he could have seen Sue and talked with her. He wondered if she had heard anything about what had happened to him. Now that the Council had moved to Lancaster, perhaps Sue might meet some of them and put in a good word for him. With a husband in the Continental army she should be in good standing—or, on the other hand, he thought, twisting on the bumpy pallet, having a brother exiled to Virginia might cast suspicion on her.

Next morning they crossed the Susquehanna. The river was about a mile wide, not much more than three feet deep at the ford, but swift. The four baggage wagons went first, lurching and swaying while the water swirled around them. After the wagons the sulky and the chaise went carefully into the water, followed by those who rode horseback, Ladybird picking her way daintily over the stony bottom.

It was considered safer to bring those who traveled in the wagons over the river in canoes. After they had landed, the light wagons splashed across, their floors awash. The guards on horseback came last of all. It was eleven o'clock before all were over and assembled on the other side. Even then, just as they were about to start, they were delayed by an old Quaker of the neighborhood, who came hurrying up with a present of six large rockfish.

Five hours later they were in Carlisle, where they had a friendly reception. White's Tavern was crowded, but Caleb with Edward Penington and John Hunt spent the night in a neighboring home where they were kindly entertained. The word that the British army was marching on Philadelphia came into town with the post and flew from house to house.

They stayed two days in Carlisle, for the men with the wagons refused to go any farther and more wagons had to be procured. Everywhere, people said, there was the same difficulty in finding wagons. Supplies of food and clothing intended for Washington's army were piling up in the towns for lack of means to transport them.

When they left the little town at eight o'clock on Friday

morning, a detachment of soldiers on their way to camp met them with abusive language, faces contorted with hate and anger, and some threatening display of guns. The reason for this hostility became clear when they reached Shippensburg that afternoon and found that the Epistles of the Meeting for Sufferings and the Spanktown forgery had been reprinted in a handbill and widely distributed. Dark and in some cases frightened looks followed them as they rode along the wide, grass-bordered street to the inn. This was large enough to provide comfortable quarters for all, and they had a time of silence together before supper.

They expected to get dinner next day at Chamberstown, but there was none to be had, whether through hostility or genuine lack they could not tell. The doors of the houses were shut; the inn refused them entrance. In the end they went beyond the town and fed the horses from stores in the wagons and watered them in a brook. They stayed their own stomachs with bread and cheese, which they ate sitting in a meadow looking off to the blue hills ahead.

They found no town in which to lodge that night. It was a region of forests and lonely farms. Back from the road a hospitable house, prosperous but small, received the three Pembertons. The others scattered and found what they could. Caleb with Miers Fisher and Drewet Smith slept on straw before the hearth in a log cabin, with homespun blankets spread over them. The young farmer and his wife and two children were in the loft above. In the morning the guests moved their beds, and the pale, stringy-haired little wife, whose teeth were a row of black stumps, gave them a breakfast of corn-meal mush and apple sauce sweetened with honey.

The company met at the appointed place next morning. It was Sunday again, the fourth since they had been imprisoned. Now the party spread out, for the road was rough and stony and the wagons made slow progress. It was pleasanter riding this way, and gave almost a sense of freedom. In a wild and lonely place Caleb and Miers met two Friends on their way to the Yearly Meeting scheduled to be held in Philadelphia in a week's time. They stopped to exchange names and news and the two Friends promised to see the families of the exiles and report that they were well.

It had been agreed that all should stop for dinner at Watkins' Ferry on the Potomac. The innkeeper on the north side, however, refused to take them in, and even the miserable little tavern on the south side of the river was closed against them. Seeing the dirt, the squalor, the idiot child with slavered chin peering out of a window, Caleb decided it had little to offer anyhow. But he was hungry, and there was nothing at the next house or the next. The wagons were now too far behind to dip into the stores that they carried. The afternoon was closing in, with the suddenness of late September, when at length they reached a tavern called the Red House.

Beer and bread and cheese were forthcoming immediately, in a room cool and shadowy with the last fingers of sunshine on the window sills, and a dinner of fried chicken was promised. Not long afterward the first of the light wagons came up, with the news that John Pemberton and others had made a formal protest before witnesses against crossing the state line from Pennsylvania into Maryland, and again at the Virginia line.

This, the last night on the road, Caleb slept in a bed, which he shared with Elijah Brown. Most of the party were at the Red House, with the overflow in two houses near by owned by Quaker farmers.

"There are a good many Friends in Winchester—" said Elijah, "Winchester and round about, that is. Most of them came from Chester County originally. They still belong to Philadelphia Yearly Meeting. I've no doubt that Friends will do what they can for us, but it is going to be tedious, very tedious."

In the morning a boy was found willing to ride ahead to and beyond the town to the Marlboro Iron Works, to inform Isaac Zane, junior, that the exiles were on the way. The innkeeper at the Red House told them that Mr. Zane had returned two or three days earlier from Philadelphia. He was well known throughout the countryside, he and his lively younger sister, Sally, who often visited him. His ironworks, his mill, his yellow coach, his wide acquaintance with every sort of important or conspicuous figure, his patriotism: all had a kind of flamboyance. His father and his elder sister, Hannah, who had married John Pemberton, were Philadelphians and plain Friends; young Isaac and Sarah were of the Viriginia frontier.

All that day the exiles rode up the Valley of Virginia, with the Alleghenies on the right and the Blue Ridge on the left. The valley was wide at this end, and so far Caleb had not even had a glimpse of the famous Shenandoah. The rocks that scratched their way through the surface of the fields were pale limestone; the trees were oak and hickory and beech. Now and then a large fuzzy brown caterpillar hustled across the road in front of them; killdeer flew overhead crying, and in the woods acorns pattered on the ground.

The occasional houses they passed were built of squared logs or of limestone, tall and narrow at the gables. Caleb thought the proportion awkward, after the great square brick piles of eastern Pennsylvania with huge double chimneys or the older stone houses with the roof line on two levels and the hooded doorways.

The sun had set when they reached Winchester, a raw little town of new streets and vacant lots and scattered modest buildings. They met a cow being led home from pasture by a tousle-headed boy, a two-wheeled cart piled high with cornstalks, a gentleman on a handsome horse, a colored woman with a basket of laundry on her head, as they jogged slowly down the valley road, which had become the main street of the town. Lighted windows, woodsmoke in the air, the chill of evening, the voice of a mother calling her children, told of suppertime.

A man appeared out of the shadows and spoke to Mr. Levan, who rode at the head of the cavalcade. They all stopped. The horses hung their heads, blew, pawed the ground wearily. The exiles shifted in their saddles and looked around them. In the light wagons the older men were gray with fatigue and dust, their faces deeply creased and drooping in heavy lines. People passing eyed them with curiosity. After a few moments of conference among the guards they moved on again through the dusk.

A large stone building with rows of lighted windows loomed up on their right behind a screen of young willow trees. Over the door hung a sign with a crudely painted deer and the words, "The Golden Buck." A swarm of boys came running to the horses' heads and a large man with rolled-up sleeves and a big apron appeared on the front steps.

Caleb dismounted stiffly. So. This was the end of the journey.

XVIII

CALEB STOOD BY THE WINDOW of the Golden Buck, looking out at the road and an empty lot opposite, through which the Town Run took its meandering course. Between the willow trees he saw something that shot through his whole listless being with sudden vitality. Wandering alone down the road, unself-conscious and unconcerned, was the prettiest girl he had ever seen.

She was a child of the backwoods. Her slim, lissom little body was clothed in gray linsey-woolsey which clung in soft folds without any of the hoops or panniers by which city girls disguised their shape. With her white fichu, white cap, red-gold curls gleaming in the sun and her milky skin she looked as clean and fresh as if she had just been dipped in dew. He had a glimpse of a wide mouth, a short, straight nose, and gray eyes thickly fringed with black, before she stooped suddenly to pick up a walnut that had fallen to the ground from the big tree on the other side of the road. Absorbed as a child, she rubbed off the green outer shell, and looked about for another. Then, as if becoming suddenly aware of Caleb's steady gaze, she glanced up at the window, straightened her little backbone till it was as erect as a daffodil's stalk, dusted her hands together briskly, and made off down a narrow lane that passed through the field to the south of the inn. Before she disappeared Caleb had time to approve her walk, which was of a piece with the rest of her, free, graceful, and surefooted as a fawn's.

He reached for his hat on the peg by the window and was about to set off after her when John Hunt's gentle, amused voice halted him.

"There's a guard at the door, my boy."

Feeling himself flush hotly, Caleb put his hat back and smoothed down his hair with his hand. Then he grinned. "Eheu fugaces!" he said lightly, while his mind raced on after the girl.

She was very young, not more than sixteen at the most, and as natural and innocent as a yellow chick just out of its shell. Although obviously not a young lady in the accepted sense, he reflected, she had a flower-like delicacy which suggested an innate refinement independent of her station in life. She might be an indentured servant in one of the larger houses of the town, or the daughter of an artisan. But she was like a nymph—Daphne vanishing among the forest trees—and he must somehow manage to see her again. She had passed the inn once; perhaps she had regular errands that took her this way. Or if the prisoners could get permission to take exercise in the village, which appeared to be only the minimum of humanity and decency, he could walk systematically up one street and down another until he found her.

Behind him the parlor was filling up with the exiles, who came in looking expectant and serious. Caleb remembered that a meeting of the group with the Lieutenant of the county had been set for eleven o'clock this morning. In the confusion of their arrival the evening before, of getting supper and being assigned to bedrooms, they had been visited by Isaac Zane, junior, and several local officials. All that had come out of it, however, had been the assertion that the papers of their banishment were very confused and irregular, that the Lieutenant of Frederick County was doubtful whether he had any jurisdiction over them and was in favor of sending them back to Carlisle or on to Staunton. Since it was late, decision had been postponed until the morning.

The older men filled the chairs and benches, the younger ones standing at the back. Caleb himself lounged on the wide window sill, where he could keep an eye on the road in case the girl came back.

What he saw, however, put the girl out of his mind altogether. A company of about thirty men in hunting shirts, armed with muskets, came marching up the road past Caleb's window and drew up before the front door. Behind them swarmed citizens of the town. There was something threatening about the purposeful way they approached and the angry scowls on their faces; the clamor of voices in the crowd following had a sinister sound.

"There's one of 'em!" came a hoarse shout from a man who waved his arm toward the window where Caleb sat.

A gun barked sharply.

It must have been fired into the air, for a moment later some leafy twigs drifted out of the willows, but the effect of it was to bring everyone in the inn parlor to his feet in alarm.

The front door opened and the young guard outside, who was a schoolmaster in private life, skipped in and slammed the door behind him. He stuck an agitated face into the parlor. "Where's Mr. Levan?" The next moment he vanished and they heard his feet pounding up the stairs.

Now fists began battering on the door and separate voices rose out of the angry roar.

"We don't want no Tories here!"

"Run 'em out of town!"

"Tar and feather 'em!"

The gentlemen from Philadelphia exchanged quick glances and turned pale. The threat of tar and feathers was not an idle one. Less than a year before in Philadelphia itself the respectable Dr. Kearsley had been seized by the militia at his own door, bundled into a cart, and paraded through the streets to the tune of the "Rogue's March." He had suffered a bayonet wound and barely escaped being plunged into hot tar.

Caleb sprang to close the door from the parlor into the hall and stand with his back braced against it. The others moved hastily away from the windows as grimacing faces were pressed against the panes outside.

John Hunt walked quietly across the room. "Step aside, Caleb," he said gently. "I will speak with them."

"No, John, don't!" cried John Pemberton, "It's folly! They are in no state to listen to reason!"

"I am small and inoffensive," said Hunt.

Smiling a little he opened the door of the parlor and the heavy front door. Several men on the step, taken by surprise, fell back, their mouths dropping slightly.

"Friends," said John Hunt in a clear, cheerful voice, "we were no more eager to come here than you are to have us! We are peaceable people, and we—"

There was no telling what would have happened next if Lieutenant Smith had not come riding up at that moment.

"Hold on!" he shouted. He was mounted on a big handsome horse, a dark dappled gray with a white face, and he rode across the front yard of the inn and into the crowd of armed men, who moved awkwardly back out of range of the horse's heels, as men will. "What's going on here? You, Hauck, you seem to be the leader. What's all this?"

Caleb, who had come to the door behind John Hunt, was stricken with an agony of shame and self-disgust. The Lieutenant of Frederick County was a young man not much older than he was, a fiery young man on a fine horse, acting with authority and vigor, while he, Caleb Middleton, was a helpless prisoner.

"We don't want no Tories in Winchester," answered the man called Hauck. "They've got to go back where they came from."

"Send 'em on to Staunton. They've got plenty Tories there, in stockades."

"That's right."

"We don't want 'em here."

"They are here under orders from the Board of War," answered Smith in a voice that carried to the last man on the outskirts of the crowd. "We must deal with this matter in a legal, orderly way!"

"Virginia's a free state! We don't have to take the sweepings of Pennsylvania!"

"Virginia has not spoken yet. I shall write to Williamsburg and get my orders from there. Go home now and wait till we hear from Governor Henry."

"They ought to be in jail!"

"Send 'em back to Spanktown!"

"Send the fellow in the red coat to the other lobsterbacks—on a rail!"

"You know the size of our jail. It wouldn't hold a fourth of their number. This inn will be as good as a jail. No person who is not authorized will be allowed to go in or out."

"How'll you prevent it?"

"I'll put my own guards at the door. These are quiet, harmless gentlemen; they'll not make trouble. It will be only for a few days anyhow, till we hear from the Governor. You, Hauck, and you, Noakes, will you do guard duty today?"

He knew how to handle men, thought Caleb. The temper of the crowd had cooled, and Hauck and Noakes, faced with some personal effort, backed off.

"No, I can't, sir. I've got work to do."

"Get some of those fellows off the farms."

"Go back to your work now, all of you. You've made your protest, you've done all you can do for the present. I will inform the Governor of your action."

Muttering, they began to withdraw in little knots of two and three. Lieutenant Smith dismounted, turned his horse over to a boy, and came into the inn. Busch, the innkeeper, met him at the door and they went off together. A quarter of an hour later Smith came into the parlor, wearing that reminiscent look of a satisfactory interview just concluded.

"Good morning, gentlemen," he said genially. "I regret that rather unpleasant episode, but I think there is no more to fear from that quarter for the present. I shall have to require you to make no attempt to leave these premises, even for a short walk."

Thomas Wharton, as spokesman for the group, rose to his feet. "Friend Smith," he said, "we are thankful to thee for thy handling of the matter, especially if thou had nothing to do with spreading the reports of us which aroused the people." This insinuation was not lost on Smith, who stiffened and looked grim. Mr. Wharton continued, "Now, not to take any more of thy time than necessary, we have the following questions to ask of thee, and we request that thou give us the answers in writing."

"If you will give me your questions in writing, I will examine them at my leisure and make such answers as I feel free to give at some later time."

"Thou hast seen the papers delivered last night to thee by the Sheriff of Berks County," continued Wharton as if he had not heard. "We desire to know: first, are we the prisoners of Congress or of the Council of Pennsylvania, or are we prisoners of war? Second, in any case do these papers give thee the authority to take charge of us? And finally, if thou consider that thou hast such authority, wilt thou provide for our accommodation at Winchester at the public expense?"

"As I said last night, the papers are confused. I do not consider myself obliged to obey orders either of Congress or of the Council of Pennsylvania unless I have the sanction of the government of Virginia. The proper action for me to take, I believe, is to write at once both to the Congress and to the Governor of Virginia for further directions concerning you."

"Have you any objection," said Miers Fisher, abandoning as the younger Friends did the plain language when talking to people of the world, "to our also writing letters to the same authorities, to be enclosed with yours?"

"No, I think not. I should have to read your letters, of course."

"And we, in return, may see yours before they are sent?"

"I agree to that."

"In the meantime," said Thomas Wharton, "Thou wilt be in charge of us, and responsible for our accommodation at the public expense?"

"No, I cannot engage to do that. These papers give me no such authority. There is no direct order even to hold you at Winchester. There is a letter from Mr. Thomas Wharton—but surely that is a mistake. Are you not Mr. Wharton?"

"My cousin, of the same name. President of the Supreme Executive Council of Pennsylvania."

"Oh, I see. Thomas Wharton, junior. Somewhat unusual, is it

not? A letter from Mr. Thomas Wharton, junior, to Mr. John Hancock, President of the Congress, says: 'Congress fixed on Staunton. They doubtless have their reasons; but if it now appears proper to stop them at Winchester, directions from your Board of War can dispose matters accordingly, for it is a matter of indifference to Council.' Then there is a note addressed to the Lieutenant of Frederick County, signed by Mr. John Adams, Chairman of the Board of War, saying that that body *consents* to the prisoners' being stopped at Winchester. Now there is nothing in that which makes it mandatory on me to hold you here, and there is nothing whatsoever in any of these papers relative to your accommodation here at public expense, and I have no power to commit the government of Virginia to any such undertaking."

The exiles were silent, dismayed. Disagreeable as Winchester might be, with the populace inflamed against them, they were certain that it was much to be preferred to Staunton.

Mr. Levan, the Sheriff of Berks County, who had entered the room behind Lieutenant Smith, now spoke up.

"Someone will have to take charge of these prisoners. I have brought them here from Reading, and I must return at once to Reading and take my men with me. I can't go back without some kind of paper discharging me from my responsibility in the matter. I have delivered them to you as I was commanded to do, and now they are your charge."

Smith's voice rose in annoyance. "You can't deliver them to me because the papers are not in order. Furthermore, the inhabitants of Winchester are dangerously aroused and I can't answer for the safety of these prisoners."

"The town of Winchester has three hundred or more Hessian war prisoners. I can't see why they object to twenty quiet Quaker gentlemen."

"The town of Winchester has a record of unsullied loyalty to the patriot cause. We have some Quakers in our population but so far they have not been Tories. Put a company like this who won't guarantee to hold their tongues into the midst of them and who

knows what they will stir up, not only in town but among the
Quakers of Frederick and Loudon counties as well. I had three
Quaker farmers at my house this morning interceding for these
people, and Busch tells me he turned away a steady stream of them
all last evening. The loyal people of the town don't like it. They've
got sons and fathers with Morgan's division; they're making sacrifices for liberty. You saw that demonstration out there a little
while ago. Those people are hungry. They're violent men. Some
of them are Irish and some are Germans who left Pennsylvania
just because they wanted to get away from Quaker appeasement
of the Indians. They don't want a score of Quaker Tory leaders
here fomenting sedition."

"Well, I can't take them back. You can't send them on to Staunton in the face of that letter from Mr. Adams. No doubt you'll
hear from Congress and the Governor of Virginia in a few days.
You give me some kind of a receipt saying you'll hold them till
further orders come, and let me be off for home. Meanwhile they'll
have to pay their own charges for food and lodging. You can post
a guard to protect them from the population."

"I suppose we shall have to do something of the sort. But it
must be made clear that I am accepting only a conditional charge
over them."

After the lieutenant and the sheriff had gone, the innkeeper
came to establish the rates for food and lodging.

Philip Busch was a German who had been twenty or thirty years
in America. He was among the earliest settlers of Winchester and
his word had weight on the various councils of town and county.
The exiles had learned already that he was a staunch Whig and that
he had consented to lodge them at his inn only at the urgent request of Mr. Zane, whom he appeared to respect highly.

"Now, chentlemen," he began, "we must haf an understandink.
You will stay in my house and I will get my pay from you. Lodgink
is five shillinks a night, breakfast five shillinks, dinner five shillinks, supper three shillinks. Dot is very cheap. You must find
your own cider, wines, tea, coffee, sugar, vinegar, and so on.

Horses can be kept in my stables for ten shillinks a week. If I get into trouble with the townspipple for havink you here, den you will haf to go and no arguments."

"I don't call that cheap," muttered Tom Affleck beside Caleb. "I call it highway robbery. And what's more, I can't pay it. What will they do about that?"

Caleb was grateful to his father for the heavy belt about his waist. "I can let you have what you need for the present," he said. "They will surely make some provision for us later."

In the afternoon new guards, local men, appeared at front and back doors. They were unsmiling and hostile, and in comparison the men who had ridden from Reading seemed like old friends. Caleb got permission to go out to the stable to look after Ladybird, and there he found the Pennsylvania guards helping Richard and the wagoners to unload the stores and carry in the baggage.

The stables were large but badly built, with wide chinks between the logs, and they were dirty. Ladybird nickered a welcome when Caleb appeared. He got hold of a stable boy, a skinny little fellow with big, transparent ears and pale, wary eyes, tipped him well, and stood over him while he cleaned the stall and brought fresh straw.

The schoolmaster guard came to talk to Caleb.

"We're leaving first thing in the morning," he said. "I hope you'll be all right here. Someone sent ahead a lot of those handbills about the Spanktown Yearly Meeting, and the townspeople are excited. I've been with you ten days, and I must say I've never heard anything seditious from any of you. Seems as if government's government, whichever side it's on, and the less of it the better." He hesitated, then went on with a rush. "You've got to pay for yourselves, and that's a hardship for some of the prisoners, I guess. But then so have the men that drive the wagons. They've got to turn around and go back to Carlisle and buy food along the way for themselves and their horses. Mr. Levan's just turning them loose. He says the money the Council appropriated for the journey will barely get him and us guards back."

Caleb thought of the teamsters who worked for the Phoebe Ann. They were a rough, honest, hard-working lot. They owned and maintained their wagons and their teams, lived with their families in stark little fieldstone houses pressed against the hillside, and spent most of their time lurching and heaving over the rough roads, loading and unloading their wagons, coping with broken axles and lamed horses, their only pleasure a mug of beer in one of the plainer taverns that catered to wagoners. The profit on a single trip was small, a trip that did not make expenses was disaster. The Middletons had always taken care of their wagoners at the Phoebe Ann, as they had all of their workmen, and the irresponsible attitude of the Sheriff of Berks infuriated Caleb.

He walked over to the wagon shed where he found one of the teamsters patiently mending a frayed rope harness.

"Look here," he said abruptly, "I've been told you're being sent back without any pay for your trip. Is that true?"

"It's Gawd's truth, sir. They say we may get it from the Congress some time. Huh." He spat.

"That's not fair. Here are a couple of half joes. You ought to be able to get at least thirty-six shillings apiece for them. Divide it among the four of you. It won't be much for each one, but it will help at the taverns."

"I don't like to take it, sir, not from a prisoner, like." His hand went out, nevertheless, and a slow, pleased smile spread over his knotty face. "Thank you kindly, sir. It's Gawd's truth, sir, from what I've seen lately of Whigs and Tories, I'll take Tories."

"I'm not a Tory, you donkey. I'm for a free America." The man looked so surprised that Caleb laughed and clapped him on the shoulder. "It's people like you and me that have to stand fast and make it what we want it to be."

And that, he thought, a little surprised himself as he went back into the inn, is Gawd's truth.

XIX

THE NEW GUARDS WERE FARMERS pressed into service, who grumbled because it was seeding-time for winter wheat and they were needed at home. Caleb talked a good deal to one of them, who, it happened, was just a little younger than he was himself, a lanky, redheaded youth as angular and tough as a young hickory tree blown and stripped by winter winds.

"I've served my time in the army," he said. "Ten months in the Fifth Virginians under General Adam Stephen, and three of them in hospital. Don't know how I come out of that alive. Tain't the guns that's so dangerous, it's the hospitals."

"What's the matter with them? Aren't the doctors any good?"

"Sure, they're good, I reckon. But they ain't got anything to work with. I wasn't so bad off when I went in, I had a flesh wound that healed up after a while, but I got a fever in the hospital that I like to died of. There was twenty of us in one room, lying on straw jammed up together, with the same shirts we was wearing God knows how long before we went in, and maybe one buggy blanket apiece, and nothing to eat but bread and stringy beef. I never want to see beef again 's long's I live. I saw twelve men carted out of that room dead—maybe more, I was out of my head part of the time."

Caleb was horrified. "But what were the surgeons doing all this time? Didn't you have any medical care?"

"Two of the surgeons got sick themselves and one died. Nurses was only men too old to fight. They couldn't even keep that room clean. I don't mean clean the way a room at home is clean, I mean decent. My time run out and I got up and come home. I was so weak I couldn't hardly stand."

"But didn't anybody stop you?"

"Oh, they didn't notice. Anybody who could move at all was in and out all the time, going to the necessary and so on. Some of them sold their guns or blankets and bought rum—there was always somebody hanging around with something to sell—and then they'd get into fights with the other men. So I walked out. Took me three weeks to get home. Rode partway in a wagon with shoes for the army, only they didn't get to the army. They went into a storehouse in Lancaster—to ripen, I reckon, till the price gets higher."

"You must have been more dead than alive when you got home."

"My mother, she took one look at me and she wouldn't let me into the house. Made me strip off all my rags in the yard and she brought buckets from the well and like to drowned me. Lucky it was spring by that time and almost warm. Then I went to bed, between sheets, and she brought me food. Lord, it tasted good. Thing I wanted more than anything else was a roasted potato, hot from the ashes, with new butter and salt."

"It's hard to believe, in this day and age. I don't mean I don't believe you, but it's incredible that conditions like that could be allowed. Were you wounded at Trenton?"

"Skirmish, afterward. My mother, she hasn't any use for officers. One day—I was still in bed in the little room off the kitchen—three captains from Nevill's company came riding up, called her out and ordered her to get dinner for them. No please or would you kindly, but just bring it out and be quick. She did, too. Then they heard a noise in the cellar and wanted to know what it was. Our dog had pups down there, and nothing would do but they must see them. So down she goes through the trap door and hands them up to the officers, one by one. 'What's his name?' says one of them when he takes the first puppy in his hand. 'Captain,' says my mother. Then the second comes up. 'What's this 'un's name?' 'Captain.' And when he asks her the same question about the third and she says that one's Captain too, he wants to know, why does she give all her pups the same name. You'd think anybody'd have more sense 'n to walk into a trap like that, wouldn't you? 'Oh,' says my mother, 'nowadays any puppy dog can get to be a captain.' I like to died laughing. I had to smother my head with the bedclothes."

"Do you know any of the girls around here?"

"Round here? Winchester? Winchester's a big town—it's got a population of eight hundred and there's a good few girls. I know some of 'em."

"I mean a girl that went walking past here on Tuesday morning and turned into the lane."

"What did she look like?"

"She was a little slim thing, young, and she had gold curls under a white cap."

"There's Katie Bason, but she's black-haired and she isn't so little. There's Miss Sally Haines, her hair's sort of light-colored, but she isn't so young. There's the McGuire twins, but they wouldn't hardly go walking by like that, they're too uppity. Their father keeps the McGuire House—twice as big as this place—and they think they're royalty. Can't tell what color their hair is, it's always powdered and dressed up like a wedding cake."

"I'd like to see this girl again. She must be in Winchester somewhere."

"You could go look for her for all of me, but the captain would kill me. I stayed home after I got well because my dad died last year and my mother needs me on the farm, but if I've got to do guard duty over Tories, I might's well be fightin'. They're most of 'em too old to need a guard anyhow, except you and the lawyer and that fellow in the red coat. Why don't you join up with Howe or Cornwallis if you're Tories?"

"I'm not a Tory," said Caleb. Flushing at the quick, incredulous look of the guard, he went on, "But even if I were I wouldn't fight. I'm a Quaker. Friends don't believe in war and violence."

"I don't like war either, and I reckon I know more about it

than you do, mister, but what do you do when they march in and start shootin'?"

"You have to begin earlier, with your protests and negotiation, before the shooting starts, and I suppose you have to be willing, if necessary, to be shot at and not shoot back." But was he really, himself? And might he not have joined the Continental army, after Washington's march through Philadelphia, if he had not been taken prisoner? He saw the closed look on the hollow, freckled face of the guard, and he went on, "What I'd really like to do is be a doctor and help to relieve some of the suffering in the hospitals. Only I didn't get started in time."

Another of the guards, Caleb discovered later, was a Quaker himself. He had been gathered up from his farm five miles away and ordered to take his stand at one of the side doors of the inn. The musket that was issued to him he leaned up against the wall, refusing to touch it.

"The prisoners can leave any time they want," he said defiantly in the hearing of the other guards. "I won't stop them."

When the exiles held their meetings for worship on Sunday morning and afternoon in the inn parlor, that guard and two or three others joined them. Caleb saw his own especial friend standing outside the window looking in, along with Philip Busch and his wife and some of the townspeople, both white and colored. Lieutenant Smith came to the afternoon Meeting, probably just to make sure that they were not conspiring when they sat there in silence, but he behaved very courteously and even reverently.

The next day the exiles were permitted to take short walks about the town attended by a guard, on the condition that they speak to no one along the way. Caleb, whose restlessness indoors had got on everybody's nerves, was urged by the others to go with the first group of six that set out.

It had rained all morning, but in the afternoon it blew out blue and gold and chilly, with the sun glistening on the wet, black trunks of trees and on red and yellow leaves plastered flat on fences and doorsteps. The last rags of clouds were being blown out of the sky above the wall of the Blue Ridge, which stood up higher and nearer than they had yet seen it.

They walked to the Shawnee Spring, named for the tribe that first owned this part of the country, and drank thirstily of the clear cold water, for the well water that they got at the Golden Buck was cloudy and ill-tasting. All along the way Caleb looked for the girl in the gray dress. Each house he passed he examined carefully, hoping for a slim figure in a doorway, or crossing the yard. The little post-office, the blacksmith shop, the big stone building where, their guard told them, some of the Hessian prisoners were confined, the pond and the stony hill above it, the public well where housewives gathered: he raked each one with his eyes, inventing some reason why she might be there.

The girl whom he had so briefly seen haunted his thoughts and his dreams. While the other exiles discussed the changes in the new Essay they were writing—should not "pursued" be substituted for "manifested" in one sentence, and "just cause of" be inserted before "offense" in another?—Caleb imagined scenes in which he met the girl. She came to the inn bringing something from her mistress to Mrs. Busch. Or the inn got on fire and they all rushed out, and Caleb was brilliantly reckless and daring in fighting the flames. Out of the watching crowd stepped Daphne. She had a wet cloth in her hand, she wiped his throbbing, smoke-blackened (but not painful) face, he caught her hand and pressed it to his lips. Or he walked out with the guard—as he was doing now—they passed a little shop, and Daphne came out, having been sent upon an errand . . .

As they crossed a rutted lane the guard nodded toward a low stone building away to the left. "Washington's headquarters," he said, "back in 1755, after Braddock's defeat. Major he was then. Lot of folks in town remember him."

Back again at the Golden Buck, after what Caleb considered so short a walk that it was only tantalizing, though Thomas Wharton commented with satisfaction that they must have gone at least two miles, the guard, a plain, middle-aged man, said to them with a burst of friendliness:

"I wouldn't begrudge ten pounds out of my own pocket to have you gentlemen set at liberty. It's my belief you've been wronged."

Two or three days later this man threw up his job. He was going home, he said, to his own work. There was no sense in guarding these folks. When the harassed captain warned him that he would be fined if he left without permission, he replied calmly, "I can afford it," and off he went, to the amusement of the exiles, who made no public comment but wrote it down in their diaries.

XX

HERE, AS IN READING, Caleb shared a bed with John Hunt. The other bed in the room, a larger one with shabby curtains, was occupied by Edward Penington and Thomas Wharton. Caleb found it rather oppressive to be the young and negligible one in such a weighty group, but there was no help for it unless he shared an attic cell with Mr. Pike, a fate which he regarded with horror. Miers Fisher, the one of the exiles who was nearest his own age and whom he would have liked to know better, was always with his two brothers Thomas and Samuel, and his brother-in-law, Thomas Gilpin. Edward Penington was kind to his young cousin in an elderly, sometimes irascible sort of way, and Thomas Wharton was rather ponderously affable when he remembered to notice him at all; John Hunt, the oldest and the most religious, was by far the easiest to be with, and Caleb found himself growing very fond of his elderly bed-fellow.

One afternoon, when they had been about ten days in Winchester, Caleb was lying on his bed reading *Tom Jones* for the third or fourth time. His roommates were in the parlor below, conferring with visitors from the town. They were attempting, Caleb knew, to get permission for the exiles to go about freely in Winchester, to attend the meeting for worship held at the Hollingsworth house, and even, if possible, to ride beyond the town to look for places where they could board their horses for less than Busch charged. The daily walks to the spring had by now lost the first charm of novelty and were so monotonous and restricting as to be an exasperation. Even more than the others Caleb was galled by them, and as the endless slow days followed one another with no prospect of change, he sought escape by lying on his bed and reading.

One knee was cocked up and the other balanced on it, his free foot jigging steadily. He was eating an apple, one of the yellow York Imperials grown on the high ground west of the town called Apple Pie Ridge. As he took an enormous bite, observing with interest the noise it made as the firm gleaming flesh parted under his strong teeth and licking up neatly with his tongue the juice that ran over the edges of the tough skin, John Hunt came into the room, a little smile on his face.

Caleb grinned and laid his book face down on the homespun bedspread. "Thee looks very pleased with thyself," he remarked with affectionate impudence. "What has thee been and gone and done, as Tacy would say?"

"I am. I have done something for thee that I think thou wilt like. Thou shouldst have been downstairs. Lieutenant Smith was there and with him the Commissary of Prisoners, Joseph Holmes, and a young lawyer of Winchester named Alexander White. They are much concerned about the sickness that has broken out among the Hessian and Brunswick prisoners who are quartered here. It seems that the only physician, Dr. Macky, is away with the militia. They had heard that Drewet Smith is an apothecary and had brought some medicine with him, and they came to ask him to attend the sick prisoners and do what he can for them."

"What kind of sickness?"

"Dysentery and colds and such-like; some inflammation of the lungs, I believe; accidents. What they are afraid of, of course, is camp fever."

"Where are all these prisoners? We've heard about them, but I haven't seen more than a handful. That stone barrack on the Valley Road wouldn't house more than fifty at the most."

"There's a stockade about four miles west of the town, and then they are hired out to farmers all around. Some are working for Isaac Zane. There will be no bounds on Drewet Smith; he will be free to ride wherever he is needed—and I have arranged for thee to go with him as his assistant."

Caleb sat up and swung his legs off the bed in a single lithe movement. "*What?*" he exclaimed.

John sat down on the room's one chair and folded his hands on his knee. "It occurred to me that Dr. Smith might well have an assistant on his rounds, and I put it to the Commissary of Prisoners, who made no objection at all."

Caleb stretched his arms wide above his head and drew a long breath. "Lord!" he said, feeling the bands about his heart already easing as he thought of Ladybird and the road and the hills under the sky. "Thee can't conceive what this means to me!"

John smiled serenely. "And to me. It is partly self-defense. Now I shall be very much obliged to thee if thou wilt refrain from contracting any unpleasant diseases thyself. It is a risk, I suppose, but less of a risk than having thee batter thy spirit to pieces in rebellion against confinement."

"Is Drewet Smith downstairs? I think I had better see him immediately. Does thee think I can really assist him—or is it just a means of getting me out? Which, heaven knows, is a worthy purpose! But I'd like to justify myself, if only to be kept on in the position. How soon do we start, does thee know?"

"I don't know what thee can do. Hold the basin, I suppose, and wrap bandages. I don't really know what Drewet Smith can do. He is not a doctor, and I hope he won't try to go beyond the little he knows about salves and purges. He is skilful in blood-letting, I believe, but whether he has solid judgment as to when to bleed and when not to is another question. But this I do know, Caleb: kindness is often a better medicine than drugs. If thee and Drewet Smith can take these poor prisoners a feeling of friendliness and true concern, you will minister to their souls and perhaps through their souls to their bodies."

Caleb looked down at him curiously. "They are soldiers," he said, "and mercenaries at that. I didn't know thee cared so much about those who engage in carnal warfare."

"They are sinners and exiles from their home—and so are we all. All exiles."

Caleb threw off his damask gown with the warm baize lining, which he had been wearing because the room was chilly, and took down his coat from a peg behind the door. John Hunt had opened his Testament. Caleb put a hand lightly on his shoulder.

"Anyhow," he said, "thank thee very much."

What he meant by that "anyhow" he could not easily have said. He had some unformulated feeling that the older man had given him a gift of obvious value on terms which were not yet clear to him.

John Hunt looked up at him with clear blue eyes in which austerity and tenderness were mingled. The little wrinkles at the corners of his eyes deepened as he answered, "Anyhow, my boy, thee is entirely welcome."

Every day after that Caleb rode out with Drewet Smith. The stable boy brought the horses, Ladybird dancing, Smith's Brownie hanging his head and heaving his gaunt hips, around to the front door. The bag with the lancets, bandages, bottles, packets, and jars, was fastened to Caleb's saddle. Smith climbed up stiffly on the mounting-block, Caleb swung himself lightly into the saddle, and they moved off.

Usually messages had been left at the inn. "Tell the doctor a man in the new stockade has a cough and a fever." "Ask the doctor to stop at Hentzel's farm on the northwest road; one of the prisoners fell out of the barn loft." At each place they visited they would hear of other cases, and sometimes it was late afternoon before they returned to the inn.

The longer the ride, the better pleased Caleb was. The country was beautiful in the crisp October days, with the bright leaves flying and the bare shapes of trees emerging as from a veil. The blue of the distant mountains deepened in moving patterns as the clouds trailed shadows over them. Cedars in the folds of the hills looked greener as the fields faded and dead leaves drifted in piles in all the hollows. Water cress embroidered the edges of little runs with emerald, and the clear water gave back the blue of the sky above it.

There were more prisoners in the region than Caleb had realized. Besides the three hundred Hessians who had left Lebanon before the exiles, there were Scotch and Irish prisoners taken at Pittsburgh. Most of these were held in stockades to the west and south of the town. Some of the Germans had been hired out to farmers at seven dollars and a half a month. Many of them were skilled masons and woodworkers and they were put to quarrying stones for the mansions that were to replace the log houses as soon as possible. Often brutal in victory, these men were docile prisoners, hardworking and phlegmatic. Speaking little or no English, they held no communication with the people of the Valley and no fear was felt of their poisoning the minds of patriotic citizens, as it was thought the highly articulate exiles from Pennsylvania might do.

Those who worked on the farms suffered injuries, falling from ladders, letting axes slip and lay open a foot, being gored by bulls. In the flimsy wood and canvas huts in the crowded stockades, there were putrid sore throats, fevers, stomach disorders. There the men, suffering the languors and despairs of imprisonment, were often dull and sullen, ready to be sick because they got no benefit from being well. Fed on an allowance of seventeen cents a day, they were undernourished and hungry.

Caleb's sleeping desire to be a doctor awoke, and in spite of his ignorance and resulting frustration, in spite of his distrust of Drewet Smith, who, he saw the first day, had no real knowledge of the art of healing and only a superficial acquaintance with the drugs he carried, still Caleb felt deep within him that he was, however inadequately, engaged in the work for which he had come into the world. John Hunt's advice stayed in his mind, and when he could do nothing else he showed his interest and sympathy in a light pat, a smile, the tone of his voice. After a time it came to him that this was hollow and could soon become mechanical and meaningless, and he looked more humbly for some actual service to perform, even though it might be a menial and unpleasant one.

Some of the places where they went were so filthy, so degraded that he had all he could do to fight the nausea of loathing within himself. Some of the men whom he and Dr. Smith tried to help cursed them for the ignorant blunderers that they were, and the hate that was palpable in the stinking hut, together with Caleb's own feeling of guilt, made his attempts to express good will seem clumsy and hypocritical. But to some they did bring relief, and on a second visit they would find a response and a welcome in the haggard and suffering faces.

After the first few days Caleb began to keep a record, in a note-book which he begged from Elijah Brown, who had a supply of little blank books, of the cases which he saw and the treatment they received. He studied it at night by the inn fire, absorbed and serious, not asking himself of what use it could be, thankful only to have found something to fill his mind and satisfy his need for a purpose in his days.

When they first began to go out he looked in each house for the girl whom he called Daphne and hoped at each new place to find her, but gradually he ceased to think of her, or remembered only at the end of the day to comment to himself that once more he had been disappointed.

It had begun to rain one day when they turned back toward Winchester early in the afternoon. The mountains behind them were blotted out, and a thick belt of dripping woods lay between them and the comfort of a fire and dry clothes. The horses, know-ing that they were headed for the stable, became more animated, and the two men rode along in silence. Caleb wondered, as he wondered each day turning toward the inn, whether he would find there some word from home or some news from Williams-burg or York about the decisions which were presumably being made. Now that they had settled down into a fairly comfortable existence at the Golden Buck and he had his daily rides with Drewet Smith to occupy him, he was anxious that they be per-mitted to remain in Winchester until they should be released. Any move to Staunton now would be a great blow, and yet it was a possibility which hung over them like a dark cloud.

At the ford of the Opequon Creek a man was standing. Caleb saw first a figure under a tree, and felt a little start of surprise at meeting someone in this lonely country. As the man stepped forward obviously intending to speak to them, Caleb realized that it was an Indian, more from the swift and economical movement of the body than from any peculiarity of costume or color. He did have his hair screwed up in a sort of topknot with a feather thrust through it, and his skin was dark and ruddy, though not much more than that of a farmer who has been tanned through hours of work in the sun; he wore a sort of leather tunic, and he was unarmed. The striking thing about him was his tall, lean, muscular body and the easy command in which he held it.

Caleb had seen Indians in Philadelphia in full regalia, come to make a protest or ask for favors or celebrate a treaty anniversary; he had employed half-breeds at the furnace; he had seen occasional little bands of men and squaws making their way along the road with something to sell; but this was the first time he had come face to face with an Indian of the forest. Though there was a long history of friendship between the Quakers and the Indians and no Indian had ever knowingly attacked a Quaker, still the massacres on the frontier and the stories of Indian raids and kidnappings reminded people that the Indians were savages still, and dangerous. Caleb felt a little thrill of excitement.

The Indian raised his hand gravely. "How," he said. "Tenskatawa."

There was no way of knowing whether the second word—if it was a word and not a whole sentence—was a name or a greeting. Dr. Smith replied with a "How!" and Caleb ventured on "Tenskatawa."

"You doctor?"

"Yes."

"Man sick. Come with me."

"I don't know whether we can come or not. It is late, and we're on our way back to town. Where is he?"

"I lead. You follow."

Smith turned to Caleb, drew down the corners of his mouth, raised his eyebrows, shrugged his shoulders. Caleb nodded. The Indian, interpreting their expressions as consent, set off at a swift pace along a narrow trail on the west side of the creek. Caleb followed next, since his horse was livelier and he himself more interested. Smith plodded behind, sighing audibly.

It was evidently a short cut they were taking, following the loops and curves of the creek among the low growth at the water's edge. Presently they came upon a cornfield, the stalks standing dry and brown with ears of corn still hanging like flags at a masthead. At home, thought Caleb, the ears would be in yellow piles, with here and there a red ear, and the stalks stacked in tepees. Beyond was a wheat field, half plowed, and then a grove of tall forest trees and a house and outbuildings. The place was neat but bare, and in the steadily falling rain it looked meager and dreary.

They followed the Indian around the corner of the barn to what seemed to be a combination of woodshed and storehouse. There an old-looking young man with thin, stooped shoulders, evidently the farmer, met them.

"Thanks, Tenskatawa," he said. The Indian nodded and walked away without another look at Smith and Caleb. "It's good of you to come. My name's Preston—Edward Preston. You are Dr. Smith?"

"At your service, and this is my assistant, Mr. Middleton."

"We're in a lot of trouble here. I'll take care of your beasts. You go right on into the shedroom there. I've a German prisoner —name is Fritz—and he's been sick ever since I got him. He's got so bad last two-three days, I'm worried. Friend from Winchester told me about you."

There was no window in the shedroom where the sick man lay on straw on a rough wooden bed. He was breathing hoarsely and though his eyes were open he made no sign of seeing them as they went in. The odor in that dark, dank little hole was sickening.

"Ask Mr. Preston to bring a candle," said Dr. Smith, looking around for something to sit on, and finding a rough stool made of a section of a tree trunk.

Caleb was glad for an excuse to escape into the fresh air. He delivered the message to the farmer, who went hurrying off, and then lingered for a moment in the barn door, looking with idle curiosity toward the house.

It was built, like most of the houses of this region, of squared logs chinked with clay. There was a big stone chimney at each narrow end and rows of windows back and front. There were stone steps to the front door and a vine with scarlet leaves crept up the wall beside the door. It was not a large house, but it had evidently been built with hopes that had not yet materialized. As he turned to go back to the sick man in the shed Caleb caught sight of someone looking from a front window, and recognized in a flash the slim figure and piquant little face of the girl in the gray dress.

He lowered his head into the rain, spilling water out of the folds of his hat as he did so, and plunged across the yard.

She came to the front door to meet him. She was wearing the same linsey-woolsey dress with the white kerchief and a little white apron. Her golden hair fell over her shoulders in curls. Her forehead, he saw, was white and round like a child's, and her eyes under delicately arched dark brows were gray and clear, with extravagant black lashes.

"Oh, come right in out of the wet," she said with a little gasp, swinging the door wide open. Her voice was low and surprisingly rich for anyone so young and slight. "I'm so glad Mr. Preston decided to send you right over." She chuckled—a little silver bell of a laugh. "He was going to wait and see how you did with poor Fritz before he let you into the house! Mrs. Preston and the baby are sick upstairs, but it's little Ned I'm really worried about."

Mr. Preston, Mrs. Preston. Then she was not the daughter of the house, an orphan, perhaps, from some decent family, earning her way.

"Neddie's in here," she said, and led the way to a room at the left.

Caleb could hear a child whimpering and even in his bemused state of mind he knew that it was a child in pain, and weak.

The sanded floor gritted under his feet as he crossed the big square room to look down at the child in the wide bed. He saw a pale, pinched little face with dull, almost colorless eyes and parted lips, which were cracked and dry. The limp little hand which he took in his was alarmingly hot. The little boy moved his head restlessly from side to side and cried in feeble anguish.

Daphne picked up a bowl of milk from the table by the bed, dipped a little wad of linen into it, and touched it to the child's lips. He could not swallow, and only cried a little more sharply as she gently wiped away the drops that trickled down his chin.

"I'm so afraid it's putrid sore throat," she whispered, turning a troubled face to Caleb.

"I'll have to go for Dr. Smith. I'm only his assistant. I'm not a doctor—I'd give anything if I were."

She walked to the door with him, and he made the most of the moment.

"Were you in Winchester a fortnight or so ago?"

"Yes, I was. But how did you know?"

"I saw you pass the inn. I thought you were the prettiest girl I'd ever seen. I would have started out after you at once, but then I remembered I was a prisoner."

"The rain is slackening a little. I think you won't get wet if you run. But you're dreadfully wet already, aren't you?"

It seemed important to make her understand what kind of prisoner he was. "They really meant to take my father," he confided, turning back, one foot on the step, his hand on the door-jamb, "but he is old and his heart is not strong, so I am here in his place."

Her gray eyes widened, and for the first time she seemed to be really seeing him. "But that was noble of you!" she exclaimed.

She was so little that she did not even come up to his shoulder.

He would have to lift her up—he could do it so easily with a hand under each of her elbows—to kiss her. Her mouth was wide and sweet, soft and delicately shaped as a flower.

"It was the only thing to do," he said, shamelessly modest. "I am young and strong. That day I saw you, I called you Daphne to myself, because you are like a nymph. I've been looking for you ever since."

"I must go back to Neddie—"

As she turned away a voice floated down from upstairs. "Loveday! Loveday! I want you a minute."

Caleb stepped out vigorously into the rain. So her name was Loveday. It was a quaint, old-fashioned name; it suited her.

He went back to the dark little room in the shed and made himself useful, finding a place to fasten the candle so that it would give light without dripping tallow on the patient, washing the man's arm and holding it still while Dr. Smith opened the vein, catching the blood in the pewter basin which they carried with them in the saddlebag.

"Congestion of the lungs?" he said to Dr. Smith, and Smith answered, "Unquestionably."

Edward Preston stood just outside the door, listening and watching. When Smith had finished with the prisoner, the farmer said hesitantly, "If you don't mind, I'd like you to look at my little boy, in the house."

"I want to get this place cleaned up a little first, and this man made more comfortable. The bed needs fresh straw, and can't you find another shirt for him? If you burned some herbs in a pan, it would sweeten the air. He's pretty ill, you know."

"Yes, I've been remiss, I realize. Perhaps Mr. Middleton would help me, while you go ahead and see the boy. Loveday—that's the girl who's taking care of him—will show you."

While Drewet Smith went off to the house, Caleb and the farmer worked together, the man apologizing with nervous volubility.

"I'm sorry to ask you to do this sort of thing. It had got worse than I realized. If my wife were well, she'd have seen that things were right. I've been short-handed. The two men I had working for me were taken for the militia. Now, that's better, isn't it? What kind of herbs, would you think? My wife has some drying up garret. I'll ask Loveday about it."

When they reached the house, Dr. Smith had already, with Loveday's assistance, finished bleeding the little boy, who lay more bleached and fragile than ever, his pitiful moan thinned to a thread. The apothecary had also visited Mrs. Preston and the baby upstairs, had decided, perhaps because he was tired, not to bleed the woman but to give her a purge instead. Mr. Preston invited Dr. Smith and Caleb into the "other room" for a glass of cider before they started back to Winchester, and Loveday went to fetch it. Caleb followed her to the kitchen in the yard, and stood beside her as she poured the cider into mugs from a big stone jug.

Teasingly he took one of her ringlets in his fingers and drew it out straight. It was warm and dry and silky, almost like something alive, and when he let it go it sprang back softly into the curl again, golden and shining.

A shade passed over the girl's face and she moved her hair out of reach of his hand. She did not toss her head, she moved it, gently, as if she wanted him not to notice and be hurt or embarrassed, yet definitely, as if she were quite sure that she did not want a repetition of the liberty he had taken.

For a moment he was vexed. She was acting miss-ish, and he had no word of severer condemnation. He thought how he disliked Caroline Rutter and her trick of courting attention and then primly disdaining it, like other young ladies of her class and circle who expected a show of reverence from a man as if it were their due as creatures of a superior plane and finer clay. If you wanted warmth and reality and laughter in a girl, he thought, you had to look for it on a different social level, and for a moment Phyllis Pike's heart-shaped face and soft white bosom swam before his eyes. It was tiresome of Daphne—Loveday—to turn miss-ish. But perhaps after all, she was only shy. There had been certainly no provocation in the gesture, which was so quiet that it might even have been unintentional after all.

A colored woman came into the kitchen with a bucket of milk. Caleb looked about for the Indian, but he had vanished.

Loveday added a plate of seed cakes to the tray with the cider and thrust it into Caleb's hands. "If you will carry that into the parlor," she said, "I'll run up garret and look for the herbs that Dr. Smith wanted."

She smiled up at him, and he saw the fine transparency of her white skin over the slender bridge of her nose, the cameo-like flare of her nostrils, the pearly shadow in the little indentation in her short upper lip, the bright color blooming in her cheeks. The next moment he saw her skirts flowing around her slender limbs and her curls bobbing against her straight little back as she skimmed across the yard. Suddenly her shadow sprang onto the wet ground, and he saw that the sun had come out, shedding a yellow glow beneath the dark clouds.

Even after they had finished their cider in the room sparsely furnished with a wooden settee, a chair or two, and a table, Loveday did not reappear, and they had to leave without Caleb's seeing her again.

It was nearly a week before he could persuade Dr. Smith to return for a second visit, and when they did come, the prisoner Fritz was up and sitting in the sunshine, though still weak, and the child had died. Loveday was nowhere to be seen. When Caleb asked about her, he was told that she had gone home.

"She doesn't live here?"

"Oh, no, she was just here to help. My wife's on her feet again now, and little Ned's gone."

"Where does she live then?"

"Over near the Shenandoah toward Williams' Gap."

"You don't say. What is her last name?"

"Parry. Loveday Parry. She's a great hand at nursing, for all she's so young. Seems as if she had magic in her touch—but even she couldn't save Neddie for us. He was such a bright, happy little fellow. I wish you could've seen him before he took sick."

Caleb thought of the small, wracked body in the big bed, so pitifully white and weak after the treatment that was to cure him, and he wondered sorrowfully if it might not have been better for Neddie after all if the Indian had not found them that day.

And what was Loveday thinking of the doctor and his assistant? The child was doomed anyhow, he tried to tell himself, but he carried a weight of remorse on his heart that he knew was irrational and yet obscurely justified. Ignorance was not innocence.

XXI

THE FIRST VISITOR TO bring the exiles news of their families at home was Elizabeth Joliffe, a widow of substance who lived near Hopewell Meeting, about four miles north of Winchester. With her friend Rachel Hollingsworth, also a widow, she had ridden all the way to Philadelphia to the Yearly Meeting. While there she had visited many of the families of the exiles, collected news of others, accepted letters for some of them, and the next day after her return to Hopewell had come riding into town to the Golden Buck to report.

She ate dinner with them in the parlor, and afterward, when the table had been cleared away, she sat in the center of the circle, her plump hands clasped in her green silk lap, her feet set firmly side by side upon the floor, and talked, vivacious and voluble.

"I saw thy wife, John Pemberton. She was sitting on her front porch on Market Street smoking her pipe and she looked as well as I've ever seen her. She sent her dear love and a letter to thee. She has had three letters from thee."

"I have sent her seventeen," murmured John Pemberton.

"There's no doubt about it, the letters are not getting through as they might. Thy wife, Thomas Wharton, says that she has had no word at all from thee since Reading. Thy son Phineas, James Pemberton, has returned to town from Evergreen. He is as thin as a rail, but he was in good spirits and full of sound reflections upon the present commotions."

Did she know, Caleb wondered, that Phinny Pemberton was dying of ulcers on his back and knee that gave him constant and excruciating pain? Caleb thought he saw a look of pity in her bright brown eyes. Perhaps she did know. How better could she comfort James, who loved his only son almost idolatrously, and who might never see him again, than to talk of Phineas as matter-of-factly as she might speak of any other young man?

"Did thee see my wife?" asked Thomas Fisher.

"Yes, I went to thy house especially, since she is very near her time and is not going out now. These days are hard for her, but she keeps up her courage. Thy little son is a fine rascal. He is into everything and keeps that young colored girl busy just following after him. And Miers, thy little Tommy is just beginning to stagger about. He says Ma-ma and Bow for the dog."

It was no use, Caleb knew, to ask about his family, since none of them went near Yearly Meeting now, but he saw no reason why this occasion should be allowed to degenerate into ecstasies over everybody's fine two-year-olds and three-year-olds. "What about the British?" he asked, to turn the conversation. "How are they behaving?"

"Oh, as badly as possible. One might think they were deliberately trying to lose the best friends they have in this country. The commanding officers, it is true, have laid down strict rules about plundering, but the common soldiers are irresponsible and idle and they take what they want. First thing they did was to break up fences for firewood. I am sorry to tell thee, Israel Pemberton, that the Light Dragoons stationed near thy plantation broke into thy wine cellar and made off with six dozen bottles—to say nothing of thy silver spoons."

Was she indulging a private amusement at the expense of Friend Pemberton? Her face was serious and smooth, but her voice, Caleb decided, was a trace too innocent. Even concerned country Friends drank wine, but six dozen bottles and silver spoons in sufficient quantity to have some in every house one owned, even when, as Israel did, one owned four or five, must be accounted worldly. Safely out of range himself of Israel's chilly, all-seeing blue eyes, Caleb grinned openly and was rewarded by the sight of a quirk at the corner of Elizabeth Joliffe's mouth.

"That must be the 'sixty-seven Madeira," said Israel calmly. "Now how did they get the key? Six dozen. Humph."

"General Knyphausen is quartered at Cadwaladers' in Second Street—the Hessian general. He speaks no English at all. They say he spreads his butter on his bread with his thumbnail."

John Hunt looked pained. "What can thee tell us of the sessions of the Yearly Meeting?" he inquired gently. "Were they fairly well attended, in spite of the difficulties?"

"Yes, Friend Hunt, actually they were. None of the New Jersey Friends could come, for the Governor of that state has ordered the river closed, but Pennsylvania Friends were there in good numbers. Nobody seemed to interfere with them on the roads. There was much expression of loving concern about the Friends in exile. A committee of six was appointed to visit the commanding generals of both armies and explain to them Friends' neutrality and our objection to war. When they went to General Washington they were instructed to intercede for you. It was easy enough to see General Howe, for he was in Germantown, but General Washington has his headquarters twenty miles out on Skippack Creek, and the committee had not returned when I left. I don't know how they made out."

"Didst thou hear anything of my wife and children in Germantown?" said Edward Penington.

"No, but I think I should have if anything had gone wrong with them. There was a big battle in Germantown the day the Yearly Meeting concluded. The Americans marched in from White Marsh to surprise the British early on Seventh Day morning. The attack was very well planned, it was said, and might have succeeded, but there was a thick fog that morning and they could hardly see in front of their faces. Some of them even fired on other Americans, thinking they were the enemy. British soldiers made a fortress of Benjamin Chew's big stone mansion, shooting cannon out the windows, and held it against attack. There was a report that General Stephen, who lives not twenty-five miles away from here, got drunk and retreated into somebody's barn. They say he'll be cashiered, if that's the word. Altogether in the end the Americans had to withdraw."

"Were there many wounded?" asked Caleb.

"Hundreds. More than two hundred, taking both sides together, were killed! It was shocking. They cared for some of the wounded in Germantown, but the most of them were brought all the way into city in wagons. They say the Germantown Road is one of the worst in the country and the poor men suffered tortures from the jolting. The groans and cries were enough to break your heart. I saw one wagonload myself. They put the Americans in the State House and the British in the Hospital and the Presbyterian Church and the Playhouse. Thy stepson, James Pemberton, went to see an amputation and came back full of it. What the young people these days will do! He said he watched Dr. John Foulke saw through a leg bone in twenty minutes, just half the time it took the military surgeons."

She took out her handkerchief and blew her nose vigorously. Soft-hearted, Caleb thought, and interested in everything. If she wasn't at the State House watching the amputation, she certainly wasted no time in getting the details from Bob Morton afterward and crying over the poor sufferers. He could imagine her retailing it all to the Friends at each house where she stopped for the night on the long road home from Philadelphia.

"Eliza Drinker," she went on, "sent two men around to the State House and the Playhouse with coffee and wine-whey for the poor wounded men. People said that was just like her, sending something really good and comforting and plenty of it. Both sides, too. I hadn't met her before, but Catharine Greenleaf took me to call on her. Thy son Billy has been poorly, Henry Drinker, but he was much better when I left. Eliza is sorely worried lest she have officers quartered on her; she thinks it would be so bad for the children, let alone the trouble to her. That reminds me, Edward Penington, thy house at Race and Crown has been taken over by Colonel Sir Henry Johnson. And which of you is Caleb Middleton, junior? I didn't meet any of thy family, but I was told that a major has taken a room in thy house and that thy father has gone to bed."

She nodded when she identified Caleb and gave him a motherly little smile.

"The soldiers are all over the place," she went on. "Scotch Highlanders in Chestnut Street near dear Anthony Benezet's making dreadful noises with their bagpipes! They're all, Scotch and English and Hessian, well dressed and well shod and well fed. They say food will be scarce in Philadelphia this winter, but mark my words the British will have all they need."

More questions arose as each in turn inquired about his own family. Only Thomas Pike, his small eyes hard and his mouth pressed into a bitter line, had nothing to say.

"What about Mrs. Pike at Mrs. Duncannon's boardinghouse?" said Caleb hardily.

Mrs. Joliffe shook her head. "I don't know. I haven't heard. But all the lodginghouses and inns are filled with officers or men."

"Are you fairly comfortable here?" said Elizabeth Joliffe when at length, after four hours, she gathered up her bag and cloak. "I can let you have chickens now and then, if P. Busch can't get them for you, and if you can ever get permission to move into private houses I could lodge four easily, and you would not be crowded all into one room either."

She beamed on them, benevolent, cordial, her good will fairly bursting the seams of her dress.

"Yes, Edmund, I'm coming!" she called, as her son, a well-grown boy of fourteen or fifteen, peered somewhat disconsolately in at the window, and off she bustled, her stiff green silk skirts swishing pleasantly.

After that scarcely a day passed without visitors. The local Friends and Friends from Fairfax Meeting across the Blue Ridge in Loudon County came to bring presents of food and to discuss the situation of the country and of Quakers in the present crisis. Virginia officials called to appraise these unusual prisoners who had been inflicted upon the town.

Caleb was usually away with Dr. Smith when they came, but at the end of the day he would hear that Mr. John Harvie, the member of Congress who had his home in Winchester, had been at the inn and had expressed sympathy, that Colonel John Augustus Washington, brother of the General, had stopped to see them and had been most friendly in his conversation, that Colonel Francis Peyton had offered to take letters for their families as far as Lancaster.

The long-awaited decisions from York and Williamsburg came at length, brought by Isaac Zane, junior. The Board of War directed that the mode of their treatment was to be regulated by their behavior and that they were to be supplied with every necessity—at their own expense. The Governor of Virginia recommended them to the care of the Lieutenant of Frederick County "until orders may be given hereafter for their removal." Inconclusive and unsatisfactory as these decrees were, they relieved the immediate fear of being transported to Staunton and resulted in the relaxation of some of the restrictions that had irked them. The guards disappeared and the prisoners were permitted to walk or ride freely in the daytime within a radius of six miles around the town.

Toward the end of the month the news came that General Burgoyne and all his army had been captured in a battle at Saratoga, and that nearly six thousand British prisoners had been sent to Connecticut. Winchester exploded with joy. Inhabitants marched up and down the streets singing, to the accompaniment of fife and drum, and a *feu-de-joie* was fired by the cannon in the public square. At night almost every window was illuminated, and a huge bonfire in the empty lot across from the Golden Buck blazed, roaring and crackling to the sky, dimming the frosty stars. No hostility was offered to the exiles, who stayed quietly within doors during the celebrations, but a local Friend had the windows which he declined to illumine smashed by patriotic stones.

The first Sunday in November Caleb rode to Meeting at Hopewell. On that clear autumn morning the Blue Ridge stood out sharp against the sky and all the gaps showed like nicks in a saw: Chester Gap and Manassas Gap, Williams' Gap, Key's Gap, Harpers Ferry Gap. To the west was Pumpkin Ridge and Apple Pie Ridge behind it; still farther west, visible now that the leaves were off the trees, the line of the Alleghenies. Hopewell Meetinghouse crouched on rising ground above a spring; built of limestone with a roof of white pine shingles, it was comely in its simplicity. It was more than forty years old now and outgrown; the members were talking about building an addition to it. Even the new stable built six years ago was too small now to shelter all the horses that brought Friends to Meeting from farms round about.

The benches inside were filled, mostly with young married people and bright-eyed, restless children, peeping at each other from behind their fingers or over the backs of benches, occasionally ruffling the silence with an audible yawn or a muffled giggle. Caleb looked for a slim, straight figure with red-gold curls, but she was not to be seen.

Elizabeth Joliffe, when he asked her after Meeting, replied vaguely that the Parry farm was near the Shenandoah and thought that the family went to Meeting, if at all, over the Blue Ridge to Crooked Run. She invited Caleb to come home to dinner and meet her young people.

The Joliffe house was a handsome stone house half a mile or so from the Meeting on the Valley Road. There were five children, ranging from Edmund to nine-year-old Elizabeth. They crowded around Caleb, who searched his mind for anecdotes about Patty and Edward and Tacy.

Caleb was happy in the atmosphere here, finding Mrs. Joliffe comfortable and jolly, like her name, and the spaciousness and dignity of the house reminiscent of his own home. They drank tea out of china cups, and stray leaves were carefully skimmed out with a silver mote-spoon with holes in the bowl. By the pride with which twelve-year-old Lydia pointed out the treasure to him Caleb realized that such appointments were rare in this new country far from the eastern cities.

He wished that Mrs. Joliffe's offer might be accepted and that four of the exiles might come to stay with her. It would not only be pleasanter and less crowded than the inn but less expensive as well. Mrs. Joliffe offered them board at a rate that was actually nominal, a fraction of what Philip Busch charged them.

Caleb was beginning to worry about money. His supply of gold was dwindling alarmingly. Prices in Winchester were high and the rate of exchange low. He had made cautious inquiries as to where he could get the most Continental bills for his half-joes and learned that the rate was nearly twice as good in York and Lancaster. He thought of his sister Sue in Lancaster and he resolved to send some money to her to change as soon as he could find a dependable messenger, but in the meantime he was looking for ways of reducing his expenses.

When he broached to his cousin Edward and John Hunt the possibility of moving to Mrs. Joliffe's, they raised the question in one of the regular house meetings of the group. It seemed that others also found the inn too expensive for them. Elijah Brown and Thomas Affleck were anxious to move into the house of Isaac and Sarah Brown, Friends who lived as far south of Winchester as Hopewell was north. The Pembertons and the Fishers, however, thought it would be unwise to separate the group, and so after a day or two of ferment, they all settled down again to the routine as it had established itself.

It was not an uncomfortable routine: a quiet, detached life spent in writing letters, reading, composing the latest Essay, correcting and copying the official diary of the group, taking long walks and visiting Friends in the neighborhood. On Sundays they held meetings for worship morning and afternoon in the parlor. So many of the townspeople, Friends and others, attended—sometimes as many as a hundred in a single meeting—that the Presbyterian minister came to John Pemberton and offered the use of his church for the afternoon Meeting. The animosity which had alarmed them when they first came to Winchester had melted away, and they enjoyed a mild sort of vogue.

John Hunt shook his head. "When everybody speaks well of Friends," he observed, "then it is time to feel uneasy. It is my settled opinion that we are in a more wholesome state, within if not without, when people are berating us."

XXII

WHEN THE BANK AT Isaac Zane's furnace caved in and two men were injured, Dr. Smith was summoned in haste and Caleb went with him. Caleb had been eager to see the Marlboro Ironworks, but as they lay two or three miles outside the six-mile limit this was his first opportunity.

One of the men had died before they got there; the other was in great pain from crushed ribs and what seemed to be a broken pelvis. He screamed if he was moved, and all that Smith could do for him was to give him laudanum to dull his agony for a time.

"I'll sit by him for a while and watch the effect of this stuff," said Dr. Smith.

Caleb was glad to escape from the sight of helpless pain and to walk about with Isaac Zane, inspecting the furnace and the other buildings of the settlement. The Marlboro Furnace was smaller than the Phoebe Ann, but it employed some new methods and its products were acquiring a reputation for toughness.

"We can cast our pots and other utensils thinner than most," explained Zane, leading the way into the casting shed, "and yet they are so tough that they can safely be thrown in and out of the wagons in which they are transported."

The brittleness of cast iron was one of the perennial problems of its manufacture. Caleb looked about him with interest at the forms for the sow and pigs, the molds for hollow ware, and noted the bulletin board on which were chalked the specifications for the latest charge and a direction about a new order. The shape of the now cold crucible swelled out and thinned again to the stack that rose above them to the smoke-stained beams high and dim overhead.

When they went outside again they saw men already at work digging away the debris of the fallen bank. When Zane appeared they worked a little harder, thrusting their shovels smartly into the mass of earth and stones, turning the laden wheelbarrows with quick mastery. The chief founder came to follow Zane, to be at his elbow in case he should want to ask a question or order something to be fetched. The ironmaster was a baron on his plantation, and when he appeared an air of excitement pervaded the place. Caleb recognized the familiar stir and felt nostalgic for the Phoebe Ann. He asked a question about the rate of production.

"We make four tons of pig iron and two tons of castings a week when we're in blast. Not much compared to the Pennsylvania furnaces, but the quality is good. I was getting ready to build another furnace down the creek a bit when the bank fell in."

For a little while they stood looking at the mess and confusion of the cave-in and the men, patient and busy as ants, chipping away the pile. Zane outlined his plan for rebuilding and reinforcing the bank and Caleb nodded.

They went on to the other buildings. Cedar Creek cut a deep gash in the hills, providing power for the bellows of the furnace and the big mill wheel. From a quarry near by stone was cut for all the buildings that clustered along the creek and climbed the steep slopes on both sides: the store, the charcoal house, the distillery, where a fiery liquor was made from Indian corn, the warehouse, and above it, overlooking all, the stone mansion house. The wagon sheds were primitive. Caleb saw three wagons standing out in the open, loaded with the long shapes of cannon under canvas covers and with cannon balls like black dumplings.

"Now let us go up to the house. I want to show thee what I am doing there."

Isaac went ahead, up the stone steps cut into the hillside. He was rather below average height, stockily built, his head, with its broad forehead and deep-set restless eyes, a little large for his body. The energy and vitality which fathered so many schemes and projects spoke in every line of his body and in the quick movements of his hands as he flung them out this way and that to point out some fresh beginning.

Everything was in process of creation, nothing finished. Piles of stones here indicated that a terrace or a wall would be built where now there was a lumpy expanse of red clay strewn with rocks and weeds, or a stack of lumber there foreshadowed a porch where now were only crude steps without even a handrail.

The Big House loomed up on a shelf in the hillside, well built but stark, with bare earth around it. Caleb thought it too near the warehouse, the roof of which obstructed the view of valley and creek.

"There will be a driveway there, so that the coach can go right to the side door," said Isaac, waving his arm. "The front entrance is here. I shall have it leveled and terraced, with rose beds edged with box on both sides of the path."

When they went inside Caleb found a solid masculine comfort. Beyond the sparsely furnished parlor was a small room with a fire on the hearth, broad-based, comfortable chairs, woolen hangings at the windows, even a red-patterned rug on the wide-planked floor. The mantel was a pleasant jumble of pipes and tobacco and spills, small ornaments and spare nails, an inkwell, a brass candlestick and snuffer. Books overflowed the shelves along the wall into piles in the corners of the room.

"Sit down," said Isaac cordially, pulling a chair forward, giving the smoldering logs on the hearth a kick. "It's a nasty, raw day, not so cold really, but the damp is penetrating."

His housekeeper, a middle-aged mulatto woman, brought a tray with two glasses, a decanter of wine, and a plate of biscuits.

"We'll need another glass. Dr. Smith will be here presently. Thee can see what I've got here. Plenty of water power—Cedar Creek is never dry, or even very low—twenty-five thousand acres of land and I'm buying more all the time. Charcoal's the problem, of course—not the wood, for I've good stands of hickory that have never been touched, but the burners. I've twenty-one slaves. I've put it in my will that they're to be gradually emancipated after my death, but as long as I live I can count on them."

He spoke apparently without embarrassment, though slave-owning was a cause for disownment in Philadelphia Yearly Meeting, and Caleb had so far met no Friends in or about Winchester who held Negroes in bondage.

"Thee's casting cannon, I see," said Caleb, wondering if the denial of one of Friends' testimonies led to an insensitiveness to all of them. "Could thee have refused the cannon and balls and still have satisfied the government with pig iron and salt pans?"

"Thee means, from conscientious scruples against making munitions of war? I don't know. Possibly. I didn't try. I've no objection to making cannon. I'm a Quaker for the times, Caleb. I feel there are worse things than war, and when we win our independence and freedom, then we can look forward to living in peace with all men according to our Quaker principles." He lit his pipe and drew on it slowly. "I was a member of the convention at Williamsburg that passed the Virginia Resolutions a year ago last spring. There wouldn't have been any Declaration of Independence without that convention. I saw Patrick Henry then and had a drink with him in the Raleigh Tavern, and I said to him, 'Patrick,' I said—"

Isaac knew all the famous men of the day. One after another they drifted casually through the slow puffs of his pipe. Caleb listened, impressed in spite of himself.

"Friends ought not to be too other-worldly," Isaac concluded. "It was a great mistake, for instance, all of the Quakers resigning from the Pennsylvania Assembly in 'fifty-six because they weren't willing to go to war against the Indians. What happened? The war went on just the same and Friends lost all control of the government. They might have compromised and stayed in, and prevented or at least mitigated some of the mistakes that have been made since then. If Israel Pemberton hadn't led his flock out of government then, he mightn't be a prisoner in Winchester today."

"John Hunt says," remarked Caleb, "that while Friends may claim a divine source for their spiritual insights, their political judgments are not necessarily so inspired. But of course," he added, "William Penn thought that government and religion go together."

"I've got Penn's collected works over there on the shelf—a handsome edition I imported from London—" Isaac changed the subject abruptly. "I'm going to have a fine library here. I'm negotiating with Mary Byrd—Mary Willing that was—for William Byrd's library. I've made her an offer of fifteen hundred pounds for it, and I think likely she'll take two thousand. If I can get it for that, I will. She's having quite a time settling William's estate. It's an excellent library. The catalogue's a small folio bound in red morocco—over a hundred pages—very nice piece of work. I'm going to build a wing on to this house for it. Paneled walls. I can get a really skilled woodworker from the Hessian prisoners. Thee knows, Caleb, I see this place as another Westover, a sort of Valley Westover, a place of good books, good food, good wines, and good company—the only place of its kind west of the Blue Ridge."

Caleb took advantage of a pause in the flow to put in a word for Tom Affleck, who was desperately anxious to earn a little money.

"If thee needs some fine furniture," he suggested, "why not have Tom Affleck make it for thee while he's here? He's one of the best cabinetmakers in Philadelphia, and he's been spending his time making three-legged stools and cake paddles for Philip Busch."

"I hadn't thought of that. I've some fine walnut put away drying for three-four years now. Thee thinks he's really skillful?"

"Governor Penn thought him good enough to bring him out from Aberdeen, and he's made things for other people too. Ask the Pembertons. Classical style mostly, I believe."

"I'll talk to him. I need a highboy right now to keep linens and silver in. And other things too, of course. Chairs, a small table—"

Riding back to Winchester in the late afternoon Caleb was silent, thinking of the Marlboro Furnace, of ironmaster Zane and all his interests. He knew now that it was Isaac Zane, junior, who had intervened with the Congress to keep the exiles in Winchester instead of sending them on to Staunton, who had persuaded Philip Busch to accommodate them, who had put in a word for them in Williamsburg, and would again. He saw in Isaac what he himself might have been on the way to becoming, if things had been different. And the Phoebe Ann was a much better furnace than the unfinished Marlboro. He wished that he had tried to find out what method they used here to achieve that toughness.

That night, sitting on the edge of the bed they shared, he told John Hunt about his day.

"A Quaker for the times?" said John dryly. "I could wish he would direct his mind more toward eternity."

"The same applies to me, I suppose?"

"Thou'rt young, Caleb; younger even than thy years. I am confident thou wilt find thy true way—when once thou really sets out to look for it."

XXIII

THE THIRD MONTH OF THEIR imprisonment and banishment ground to its close and the fourth began, and still the exiles were no nearer to a hearing. On the contrary it seemed that the Congress and the Council, having got them out of the state, were now able to forget their existence.

In the middle of November Caleb, with Edward Penington, Thomas Wharton, and John Hunt, had moved to Elizabeth Joliffe's. At the same time Tom Affleck, Elijah Brown and two others got permission to go to the Browns' house, seven or eight miles south of the town. The extortionate charges at the inn, with the growing surliness of the landlord himself, made the move necessary. To hold the group together they decided to meet every Wednesday at the inn for a meeting for worship in the morning and, after dinner together, a meeting for business in the afternoon.

Four of them were at work on a new Essay to be called "Observations on the Charges Made Against Us in the Several Resolves of Congress" and on two succeeding Wednesdays the draft was read and discussed and corrected with what Caleb impatiently considered picayune changes in the wording. Not quite daring to express himself in the meeting, he grumbled on the way back to Hopewell, and his cousin Edward answered:

"It is essential, Caleb, that those who cannot agree with the majority make their position clear by every means open to them. People who put their faith in change by negotiation rather than violence must be prepared to spend time on discussion and persuasion. And no amount of time spent on finding and stating truth is too much."

Caleb's rides with Drewet Smith came to an end with the return of the Winchester physician, Dr. Macky, from the army and his resumption of his practice. Limited again to the six-mile radius Caleb missed the longer rides and his interest in the patients; he turned to the affairs of Hopewell Meeting.

Hopewell Friends were in the grip of a concern about the Indians who had originally owned the land upon which they lived. When they first settled there they had bought their land from the government of Virginia and no payment had been made to the Shawnees, who had moved westward out of the path of the white men. As early as 1738 an English Friend, Thomas Chalkley, had raised the question of whether they had unjustly dispossessed the Indians, and at intervals since then committees had been appointed to consider the matter, but nothing had been done. Now the Pembertons had come among them and the concern had been revived. The three brothers, founders of the Friendly Association for Helping the Indians, into which at the time of the Indian wars Quakers had poured the money they refused to pay in taxes for war, felt a proprietary interest in the Indians. It took only a few pointed questions from them to bring the whole matter to the boiling point. The winter lull had come to the farms and the local Friends had some leisure; the exiles from Philadelphia, bereft of their customary public activities, moved in with the eagerness of the starved. Meetings were held, a committee appointed, a subscription list circulated. Israel himself headed the list with thirty pounds. Caleb modestly pledged three pounds when he should get his money from Lancaster. A cousin of his sister's husband had come through Winchester and Caleb had entrusted him with letters and gold; he was daily expecting a supply of Continental money.

After several hundred pounds had been collected the question arose as to how the descendants of the original Indians were to be found and reimbursed. Though there had been rumors of scalping parties in the country to the west—a woman killed as she went to the well, a child kidnapped while picking berries on a hillside— no Indians had been seen in the Valley near Winchester.

"If it is impossible to find the direct descendants of the tribes whose land we hold," proposed a Friend, "could we not properly assign the money to the Meeting for Sufferings in Philadelphia to be used for the benefit of any Indians who are in need?"

It was late in the afternoon, and shadows were settling into the room, blanketing bodies and etching hollows under cheekbones and eyes, underscoring the lines of fatigue and patience written into the faces of men and women whose only recreation was to ride for several miles to a cold little Meetinghouse and wrestle with problems of conscience. A murmur of assent passed through the room. "I hope that will be done." "I unite with that."

Another Friend stood up and Caleb groaned inwardly. He was cold and hungry and he wanted the meeting to end.

"I don't wish to prolong this meeting unduly," said the Friend, "but before we send these funds to Philadelphia, I think we should make every effort to find the descendants ourselves. Perhaps Tenskatawa could tell us something of the Shawnees who lived hereabouts forty or fifty years ago."

At the mention of Tenskatawa Caleb sat up.

"He's gone, I believe," said another. "But he will probably return in the spring. I agree that he should be consulted when the way opens."

Under cover of the discussion that followed Caleb whispered to the man next to him, "Who *is* Tenskatawa?"

"He's a Shawnee, a sort of chief in a small way. Found the little Parry girl years ago when she toddled off into the woods and brought her home. He took a great fancy to her, and he still comes to see her twice a year, they say, spring and fall. His tribe has gone the other side of the Alleghenies now."

"Was that Loveday Parry—the baby, I mean?"

"Yes, it was. Thee know her?"

"I've met her. Where is the Parry farm?"

"Oh, it's fifteen-twenty miles away. Near Williams' Gap."

"Can thee tell me how to get there?"

The clerk was looking at them somewhat sternly. "Later," whispered Caleb, realizing that the meeting was settling into its closing few minutes of silence. He folded his arms across his chest to contain the pounding of his heart, and bent his gaze upon his boots as one deep in spiritual meditation.

As soon as the silence was broken and Friends turned to their neighbors for farewells and cheerfully secular talk, Caleb got specific directions for reaching the Parry farm. It was far beyond the present limit, but there might be a change in the rules or he might get special permission. Anything could happen, and in the meantime he had taken a step toward finding the girl again.

Jubilant, he came out of the Meetinghouse into the frosty dusk to find all of the sky to the north lit with a swaying curtain of color. He caught his breath. Unearthly, cold, crimson, the light shimmered and pulsed, fading, changing, swept by a wind that never blew, parting to show the stars behind it. Slowly the crimson was succeeded by the green of clear water, and a mist-white followed the green.

Caleb and John Hunt, watching in silence, turned at length toward the Joliffe house, where the light in the windows was warm and yellow.

"I have never seen the aurora more beautiful," said John. "I wonder if they are seeing it in Philadelphia now."

Caleb wondered if a girl had left the fireside in a farmhouse twenty miles away and run out into the yard to look.

At Elizabeth Joliffe's, where a fire blazed on the hearth and the children were helping to carry bowls of steaming hominy and platters of ham and eggs to the table, they found the group excited and troubled. Edward Penington had returned from Winchester with the news that Drewet Smith had not been seen for three days.

"He left on Sixth Day saying that he was going to Lewis Neale's to get some wild ducks. They expected him back at suppertime, and when he didn't come they decided he must have spent the night there. Yesterday afternoon Thomas Pike rode over to Neale's to inquire, and they said he had not been there at all. It is feared that he has eloped."

"What about his things? Did he take anything with him?"

"Evidently he took a saddlebag with necessities for the journey and his medical kit. I think it is plain that he is not intending to return."

There was a silence in the room as each thought how this might affect the group.

"Has he ever said anything to thee, Caleb, about decamping?"

"Only once that he thought the County Lieutenant didn't care whether we stayed or not."

"We have never given an actual parole, of course," said Thomas Wharton, "but it has been well understood among us that we are bound not to go beyond six miles. I think this will be regarded —and justly—by our keepers as a reflection upon the honor of us all."

"Friends were discussing that aspect of it when I left," said Edward. "They notified Joseph Holmes, since Lieutenant Smith has gone to Williamsburg, and he came to dine with them today. He said he must report it to Congress but agreed to wait until tomorrow. It is most unfortunate. It seems that there has again been some murmuring about us, anyhow among the local patriots. Some of the farmers prefer to barter rather than accept money whose value is changing so rapidly. It is convenient to blame us for it."

"I wish him safe home to Philadelphia," said John Hunt with a sigh. "He has been of some service to the poor prisoners here. I have no doubt we shall be strengthened to meet whatever sufferings may come upon us. Meanwhile I think we should keep as much as possible from repeating—or even hearing—rumors, for they will be frequent and they tend to weaken us."

The color had faded out of the sky when Caleb went to bed. Late the next day snow began to fall, hissing at first against the windows and then dropping into a velvet silence that covered house and yard, barn and stable and fence and the curve of the hill beyond. When at length it ceased to fall, there was a white blanket fifteen inches deep over all the visible world. The road had disappeared, and the air was incredibly pure and light.

XXIV

BEFORE THE SNOW HAD melted away from the hollows and the shady places under the hemlocks, two visitors came from Philadelphia. Friends of the Pembertons, they had ridden by way of Baltimore, and they brought with them in their saddlebags something for almost everybody: a roll of Continental bills for Henry Drinker wrapped up in a pair of worsted stockings, woolen underwear for Israel Pemberton, reeds for John Pemberton's steel pipe, the welcome report of a little daughter to Thomas Fisher, born three weeks earlier, letters for others.

They brought news of the burning of Fairhill by the British and of the increasing arrogance of the occupation forces, the high prices in the city, the cockfights and the balls, the suffering among the poor, the sickening way that lighter elements in the population rushed to curry favor with the officers.

Caleb had two letters from home. He read Sarah Middleton's first.

MY DEAR CALEB:—The two letters we have received from you have been most welcome, though I doubt not you have written others that have not reached us. A whole packet of letters from Winchester was delayed ten days in Wilmington waiting for someone to bring them on to Philadelphia. It is a great relief to know you are well and that you have been able to get some exercise and change of scene.

I can report all well here, except your father of course has his ups and downs. Your letters are a great help to him for he is always troubled about you.

We have had the stove put up in the back parlor and are now very comfortable. Food is scarce and excessively expensive, though the report that we are eating rats at five shillings apiece is not true. Candles are two and six each, so that no one reads very much of nights. Brown sugar six shillings a pound and butter twelve shillings. I tell you the worst to make it more interesting.

The British officers are holding balls every Saturday night in the City Tavern. Patty has been invited and she is wild to go, but your father and I maintain that she is too young. She is now become very grown-up in her manners. Edward with some other boys in his school got into a fight with some British drummer boys and came home with a black eye. Your Tacy is going to a dame school on Society Hill and is happy as a lark, though she still misses you and speaks of you often.

I saw Caroline Rutter yesterday and she had on the highest and most ridiculous headdress I have yet seen. She is smit, I think, with the major who stays at our house. He sleeps in thy room and uses the front parlor to entertain his guests. He has three servants and a Hessian orderly. They cook for him in our kitchen. Our stable is full of his livestock—three horses, three cows, two sheep, two turkeys and several fowls.

I hope whoever reads this along the way will not think I have written anything seditious. Our thoughts and our prayers are with you. All send love. I am

Your most affectionate

SARAH MIDDLETON

The other letter, written in the same hand, had been dictated by Tacy.

DEAR BROTHER CALEB:—I am very hearty and go to school every day if it don't rain. I play with Molly Pemberton.

I was so frightened last Friday morning with the roaring of cannon. Mother and Edward and Patty and I went up on the roof to see where it was. We counted nine ships all afire by Gloucester Point.

Fairhill House was burnt down today and a great many other houses up that road.

I miss thee very much. Amos sends his love and so does Hettie.

Thy loving little sister,

TACY

Nine ships afire! That meant that the blockade of Philadelphia that had been maintained by the Delaware forts, the chevaux-de-frise and American ships, was now being broken. The British would soon have the river as well as the city.

XXV

CALEB SKIPPED THE MEETING for worship at the inn on Wednesday morning the seventeenth of December, and was almost late for dinner besides. He had stopped at Goldsmith Chandlee's shop to order a little gold pin in the shape of a love knot. Some day he would see Loveday again and he wanted to have a gift all ready for her. He was in funds again, for forty-eight pounds Continental had come to him from his sister in Lancaster.

Goldsmith Chandlee was a Quaker and not much interested in making love knots. He was famous for his clocks and watches and surveyor's quadrants. He looked at the design that Caleb drew and pulled his mouth down disapprovingly at the corners; he had no gold for such frivolities, he said. But when Caleb gave him his last coins to melt down, he agreed, and Caleb went off to the Golden Buck in high fettle.

He found the exiles already at dinner, leaving a place empty beside Mr. Pike. Three and a half months of close association with the dancing master had brought Caleb's dislike of the man to such a pitch that he could barely give him a curt greeting. Pike, apparently unaware of his feelings, welcomed Caleb with a specious air of assuming that they two, being men of the world, had a special understanding between them.

"I've had very good news of the Congress," he said in a confidential undertone. "It happened some time ago, I believe, but I have just learned of it—we are so out of things here. Mr. Hancock has resigned from the presidency and Mr. Henry Laurens of South Carolina has been elected to the office in his place."

"Indeed," said Caleb indifferently. "I understand most of the delegates have gone home anyhow."

"Mr. Laurens is a very high-minded gentleman. I knew him well in Charleston. Indeed, I might even claim to have some influence with him. I am confident that even if he should not find it possible to release the whole group, he will see to it that I am discharged—since I am not a Quaker."

"Are you in communication with him?"

"Not at present. But a fresh Memorial to Congress has been prepared and we are all to sign it. I've no doubt that he will take note of my name there."

When dinner was over and the table cleared, the group considered the final draft of the new Memorial. Caleb moved his chair beside Tom Affleck's. Tom was now staying at a house only a short distance from the Marlboro Furnace, of which Caleb wanted the latest news.

"Isaac Zane has gone to Williamsburg," Affleck reported. "I am working on a table for him. He's got a nice piece of Pennsylvania marble he wants set into the top."

They fell silent as Miers Fisher rose to read the paper in his hand. Before he could clear his throat there was a sharp rap at the door. Elijah Brown, who was nearest, went to open it and they heard a brief murmur of voices outside. Elijah turned, looking rather white, and said:

"Major Holmes is here. He has fresh instructions to communicate concerning us." He stood aside, holding the door wide, and Major Joseph Holmes walked in.

Holmes was a merchant of Stevens City, a few miles south of Winchester, an ordinary, ambitious, energetic man with no distinguishing features, who acquired through the war emergency the title of major and the post of commissary of prisoners for Frederick County. In the absence of Lieutenant Smith he was responsible for the Philadelphia prisoners. Usually affable, he wore now an expression of great sternness and portentousness. He bowed abstractedly in response to the greetings of the group and ignored the chair offered him.

"Gentlemen," he began, "I regret very much the necessity which brings me here today. I have received a new order from the Board of War. With your permission I will read it to you." He cleared his throat. " 'The Board of War having had sundry intercepted letters laid before them from several of the Quakers, prisoners stationed at Winchester, in the State of Virginia, by which it appears that they have kept up a correspondence with several others of that Society, without previously showing their letters to the American Commissary of Prisoners, or to any other proper officer at that place. . . .' " He paused for breath. His voice was always a little squeaky and thin.

The exiles sat tense, listening with growing indignation. On their arrival in Winchester they had offered their letters to Lieutenant Smith to inspect, but he had courteously declined, saying that he was confident that they would transmit no news of interest to the enemy.

Major Holmes continued: " 'In the course of which correspondence it also appears that a certain Caleb Middleton, junior, one of the said prisoners—' "

Caleb jumped as if he had been pricked with a pin, and the others turned to look at him in alarm and surprise.

" '—is carrying on with sundry persons in the town of Lancaster a traffic highly injurious to the credit of the Continental currency, by exchanging gold at a most extravagant premium for paper money.' "

Caleb felt himself reddening to the roots of his hair. He had certainly sent his gold to Lancaster, but that it would have the slightest effect on the credit of the Continental currency or that anyone could possibly object to his getting the best value he could for it, had not once occurred to him.

" 'And whereas it is represented to this Board, that since the presence of the above-mentioned prisoners at Winchester, the confidence of the inhabitants in that quarter in the currency of these States has been greatly diminished, especially among the persons of the same Society with themselves—' "

But that was nonsense. Commodities were scarce, prices were high, money bought less. The farmers preferred barter. How could that be the fault of the exiles? The voice went on, pressing to the climax:

" 'Ordered, that Caleb Middleton, junior, be forthwith removed under guard to Staunton, in the County of Augusta, there to be closely confined to jail, and debarred the use of pen, ink and paper.' "

Caleb started to his feet. A hand pulled him down. Major Holmes went on reading.

" 'That the remainder of the prisoners sent from the State of Pennsylvania be removed under the same guard to Staunton and delivered to the County Lieutenant of Augusta, who is hereby directed to require of them a parole or affirmation that they will not directly or indirectly do or say anything tending to the prejudice of these States, agreeably to the form herewith transmitted; and in case of refusal, the said County Lieutenant is hereby requested to confine the said persons in some secure building under proper guards and subject to the same restrictions with Caleb Middleton, junior, before mentioned.' "

They sat stunned, slow to grasp the fact that the blow that they had so long warded off had now fallen.

The letter continued to the bitter end. " 'That copies of these orders, together with the intercepted letters from Caleb Middleton, junior, be transmitted to Mr. Joseph Holmes and the County Lieutenant of Augusta; who are desired to carry the above measures into immediate execution.' Mr. Middleton, I have copies here of two letters from you. Will you identify them?"

Caleb looked them over. They were written in a vile hand, with misspellings, but there was no doubt that they were copies of his letters, one to his sister asking her to get her brother-in-law to change the money for him, one to Richard Mercer, thanking him for the service done.

"Yes, I wrote such letters," said Caleb. "My father gave me gold before I left home. I wanted it changed so as to pay my expenses here. I heard the rate was better in Lancaster and so I asked my sister to attend to it for me. I had no thought of doing anything illegal or wrong in any way. My money was running out pretty fast and I wanted to get as much as I could."

"I have also," said Mr. Holmes, "a deposition taken at York, which I am required to read to you. To cut short the legal verbiage, the deponent says: 'That being last week at Winchester, he heard several of the inhabitants complain heavily that since the Tories of the Quaker Society from Philadelphia had been enlarged and permitted to reside at the Quaker houses in the vicinity of the town, the inhabitants of the Society, who are numerous in that part of the country, have very generally refused to take Continental money.' "

Caleb boiled with sudden hot fury. The room was suffocating. If he didn't get out of there, he thought desperately, he would knock Holmes down, or drive his fist into that silly, solemn, self-important face. The calm of the other exiles, sitting there like rabbits, twitching their noses, added to his rage. Clawing at his neckcloth to loosen it, he made for the door and fresh air.

But when he reached the big front door and flung it open, he found a man standing there, who barred his way with a thrust of his arm. Caleb stared at him, incredulous. "My God," he roared, "it's you again!"

The guard, one of those whom they had come to know well during the first part of October, raised his musket to his shoulder. "Yes, it's me again," he said, and jerked his head backward to indicate that Caleb was to return to the parlor.

John Hunt appeared in the doorway behind him. "Caleb, art thou all right?"

"Stop where you are," ordered the guard. "Caleb's all right," he added in a mocking falsetto, "and he's coming right in."

John Hunt's hand, affectionate and firm, on his arm brought Caleb to his senses. Together they returned to the parlor.

"I cannot understand," Miers Fisher was saying, "why the Board of War should be concerned with our case. We were not found in arms nor charged with any measures tending to war. If we are to be removed from here, it should be done on the order of the Governor of Virginia or of the Council of Pennsylvania."

"The Board of War is the instrument of Congress," said Major Holmes in a tired voice.

Caleb, who thought that Miers tended to rely too much on narrow legal interpretations, broke in vehemently:

"If I have done something wrong and am sentenced to go to Staunton—though I consider it most unjust and unwarranted—but if that is the sentence, then send me alone under guard. It is both unjust and cruel to send the whole body of prisoners. The roads are almost impassable at best—and this is winter. We had fifteen inches of snow last week! There are no proper inns along the way. Have you no compassion, Mr. Holmes?"

"I told you I regretted this business very much, but I am acting upon orders of the Congress. I am already under censure for having permitted some of you to lodge with friends in the country."

"Thou hast done nothing seriously amiss, Caleb," said Edward Penington. "This is merely an excuse for striking at all of us. We have made too many friends in Winchester."

"I have no choice in the matter," continued Holmes, "but to act immediately. I have ordered four wagons and they will be here tomorrow. You will accordingly gather your possessions together at once."

There was an outburst of protest. "Friend Holmes, I ask thee to reflect—" "Such precipitancy is unreasonable—"

Israel Pemberton's voice, measured, authoritative, confident of being heard, dominated the rest. "When thou came in, Joseph Holmes, we were at that very moment concluding a Memorial to Congress which we hoped that one of our own members might be permitted to carry to York. Surely our departure for Staunton can appropriately be delayed until Congress has seen and considered this Memorial."

"Allow one of you to go to York with a paper of arguments? You must know, sir, even if I could have agreed to such a thing last week, it would be impossible now!"

"Well, then," suggested Samuel Pleasants, "allow us to prepare an answer to the present charges and take it thyself to Congress."

"It's out of the question."

There was no possibility of persuading Holmes to disregard the orders; delay was the most they could hope for, and they pressed the point determinedly, watching the Major's face, quick to follow up any argument which brought into the stubborn countenance even the most fleeting look of wavering. It was Thomas Fisher who in the end found an acceptable formula.

"Several of the most respected gentlemen of Winchester have shown interest in our case. If one of them should be willing to go to the Congress with our Memorial as our representative, wouldst thou not be willing to await their further determination concerning us?"

There was no doubt in anybody's mind as to whom he was referring. Alexander White, a young lawyer and son-in-law of James Wood, the founder of the town, had found in some of the exiles interesting and stimulating companionship. There had been an exchange of courtesies; he had dined with them at the inn, and Miers and Thomas Fisher, Samuel Pleasants, and Henry Drinker had more than once dined at White's house; he had at various times openly expressed his opinion that they had been unjustly treated. He might be induced to go to the Congress on behalf of the exiles.

"I'll give you till tomorrow afternoon," said Joseph Holmes slowly. "If you can get some respectable citizen to represent you to the Congress, I will delay your departure—at least until I have further orders. The guards will remain for the present. Those who lodge in the country may go back for tonight, but they must return here tomorrow morning." He stood up. "Your servant, gentlemen," he said in conventional leave-taking, with no thought of irony.

As soon as he had gone, the exiles went to work. A note was written and despatched to Alexander White by James Pemberton's man, Richard. The older men, with the Fishers and Samuel Pleasants, withdrew into the Pembertons' big room upstairs for further consultation.

Though they all made a point of indicating kindly to Caleb by word or gesture that they did not hold him responsible for this new threat of disaster, he felt oppressed by their very forbearance, and burdened with guilt. The thought of riding back to Hopewell and pouring it all out to Elizabeth Joliffe brought some relief.

He was taking his cloak from the row of pegs in the hall when Thomas Pike came up to him.

"The Quaker gentlemen," he said disagreeably, "have been at pains to tell you they don't blame you for this new outrage. You needn't think that includes me. I have my own opinion of people who have money and don't care what harm they do if they can only get more money."

Caleb glared at him. "Never mind," he said sarcastically, "you can get your friend Laurens to let you off."

XXVI

SARAH MIDDLETON SIGHED. A little of her pent-up exasperation escaped with that breath, that faintly hissing sound as of steam, but she closed her lips quickly, pressing them firmly together. She put out a hand to impose quiet on Edward, who was scowling and squirming beside her at the breakfast table. Tacy on the other side leaned back in her chair and kicked her feet rhythmically against the legs. All three of them had stopped eating and were listening to the sounds that issued from the kitchen.

A quarrel was in progress between Hettie, the Middletons' cook, and the three servants of Major Cranborne, who now lived in the Middletons' house. The Camel, Sarah called him, because like the beast in the old story, he had first inserted his head into the tent, politely and deprecatingly, then his shoulders, then, politeness and deprecation abandoned because no longer necessary, his whole ungainly body. All he had wanted, at first, was a quiet place to sleep. He would get his meals at the tavern. He had looked at Caleb's room and found it spacious, commodious, and quiet. He would cause no trouble at all, he had assured them. The Middletons had even welcomed him, attracted by his gentlemanly manners and appearance, and by the idea that his presence in their house would save them from the necessity to billet someone more demanding, a Hessian general or a Scotch colonel. Soon he had taken the front parlor, to entertain his friends, and the study behind it, for his records and letters. His servants invaded the kitchen, first a Hessian orderly who kept his rooms and his clothes in order, then two colored men who cooked and served his meals. Since food was hard to get, the Major's servants convinced him that he should have his own supply of hens and chickens, and that there was plenty of room in the stable for a cow and horse as well. A third servant was added to take care of the livestock and he too was fed from the kitchen. Hettie and Sukie and Amos, all that remained of the Middletons' servants, resented the intrusion bitterly, and clashes like the present one, marked by the banging of pot lids, a scuffling of bodies, and voices raised in anger and taunting laughter, were becoming increasingly frequent.

Mrs. Middleton, who did her best to have the family breakfast finished and out of the way before the Major, who was a late sleeper, called for his, sighed in exasperation. "If you'd got up when I called you," she said sharply to Edward, "that wouldn't have happened. Drink your milk. You'll be late for school."

"It's sour," said Edward in a whining voice.

Sarah took a sip from his glass and had to acknowledge that it had indeed turned. The Camel had fresh milk from his cow, which ate Middleton hay in the Middleton stable, but their cow had gone dry and they had been unable to get another. They bought inferior and expensive milk from a man out Prune Street.

"Don't drink it," said Sarah, "and don't drink yours, Tacy. We'll make cottage cheese out of it. Eat your mush."

"I don't like mush."

"Don't say you don't like good food, when it is so hard to get. There are plenty of children in this city who would be overjoyed to have your nice, hot mush."

Edward took a large spoonful and sat with his cheek bulging, and did not swallow.

Sarah reminded herself that the children had been kept awake late last night while the Major and eight or ten friends, having dined well, entertained themselves by singing songs from the *Beggar's Opera* to the accompaniment of a particularly shrill flute played by the Camel himself. The children were tired this morning as well as late, and correspondingly cross and difficult.

The door from the kitchen burst open with such suddenness that it swung back against the wall, shivering. What seemed like a procession but was actually only two men with trays marched through. One of the unpleasant features of this invasion of the house was the fact that the dining room had become a passageway for the Camel's servants. From the trays came a delectable, tantalizing aroma, and both children rose in their chairs and craned their necks in indignant curiosity to see what the Major was going to have for breakfast. Sarah herself could not forbear a swift glance at the big pitcher of milk, the smaller one of cream, the pile of white bread slices that would be toasted at the parlor fire, the two fried eggs on one of her best china plates and the mound of yellow butter on another. In her nostrils was the fragrance of tea and of sizzling ham.

"Leave your mush, then," she said gently to Edward, "and eat some bread."

"Please pass the butter."

Butter was fifteen shillings a pound and hard to get at any price. Sarah measured off a small piece and Edward spread it over a thick slice of rye bread. Tacy slid down from her high chair and trotted toward the door.

"Come back, Tacy. You haven't finished your breakfast."

"I'm just going to see Major Cranborne. I haven't seen him this morning, and he's my *friend*!"

Edward uttered a howl. "She'll go in there and he'll give her buttered toast and jam and little pieces of ham *from his plate*! You aren't going to let her go?"

The little silver bell tinkled violently upstairs.

"Tacy, run up and tell Dada I'll have his breakfast there in just a minute. Make haste, dear. Don't stop to speak to Major Cranborne now. Edward, you must go or you will be late."

Rising from the table she looked down at the boy with a pang of tenderness. A dark lock of hair fell over his forehead and there were buttery crumbs on his lips. He was pale and much too thin; his brown eyes had grown too big for his face and they had an expression of strain that worried her. Patty had been sent to stay with the Chase cousins near Wilmington, to get her out of the way of the young British officers and the demoralizing effect they had on the girls. Perhaps it would have been better to have sent Edward there too, but there had been school to consider. It mattered very little if a girl's education was interrupted, but a boy was different. Edward was doing well at the Academy, even though along with his Latin he was acquiring a hatred of the British that was becoming awkward, with a major in the house.

"Go right along now, Edward. You'll have to run all the way."

She pulled Tacy's chair back from the table and set it against the wall. It was a charming chair, mahogany like the rest, with a carved back; it looked just like any other chair, except that it was a little narrower and the seat was a good deal higher. It was one that Tom Affleck had made, and she had bought it from Isabella Affleck, who was selling what she could in order to keep her little family afloat. She had been so grateful for the money which Sarah had paid her that Sarah suspected she was pretty well strapped. That had been a month ago. She must go see her again, thought Sarah.

Now she must get Tacy off to her dame school around the corner, supervise Caleb's tray and send Amos upstairs with it, soothe Hettie and confer with her about the day's meals and try to find ways of circumventing the Major's servants; but still she lingered in the cold dining room, looking out of the window at the packed gray earth of the path, mica-spangled in the glittery January sunshine, and the brown and wispy grass under the leafless branches of the apple tree.

The weight of war and anxiety lay heavy on her heart. It seemed to her that if only peace came to settle upon the land, all weariness and sorrow and irritation would cease, even though she knew quite well that in peacetime, too, beloved people fell ill, servants were unsatisfactory, children quarreled and sulked and refused to follow the straight path before them, the milk soured. She was a great gaby, she scolded herself, to stand mooning at the window when there was so much to be done.

In her philosophy, when you felt depressed, then you went out and did something for somebody else, something outside your ordinary line of duty. She would go to see Isabella Affleck this very morning, she decided, and she would begin to put in motion that idea she had had all week about young Caleb.

When she started out an hour later with a basket on her arm, her thoughts were centered about young Caleb. Here it was almost the end of January and they still did not know where he was. The word had come just after New Year's that he was locked up in solitary confinement without pen or paper. Then that they were all to be transferred to Staunton. Then silence. But silence roiled by rumors, as the silence of sleep is roiled by distressing dreams. The word came that they were all set free and were coming home, but when it was investigated it proved to have emanated from someone in Reading who knew nothing whatever about it. Then it was reported that John Pemberton had died, and the families of the prisoners were drawn together in grief and apprehension, for if John Pemberton died, who else might not die too? This rumor had been canceled out by a report from a Wilmington Friend that his cousin in Winchester had written of seeing John Pemberton at Hopewell Meeting early in the month. From this it was assumed that the exiles were still in Winchester, though of course the group might have been divided and Caleb, alone or with others, sent on to Staunton. No one had had a letter for weeks. A packet of mail which had been sent from Winchester to Baltimore had been stolen from the Friend who was bringing it up from Baltimore, at night as he lay at an inn with two strange bedfellows. The Friend could not remember all the people to whom the letters had been addressed. There were two for Hannah Pemberton, he knew, and one for Eliza Drinker, one for Polly Pleasants, half a dozen or more others, he could not say exactly. It made them all nervous to think what might have been in the stolen letters, since Caleb's intercepted letters about his money had done so much harm, but no doubt the exiles were all doubly cautious now in what they said.

Sarah stopped at the corner of Chestnut Street to wait for a big yellow coach to lumber past. She tried to get a glimpse of the man inside, but saw only a coat sleeve and a foam of lace. She liked to have something amusing to tell Caleb when she went home after being out, and it would have been a nice titbit to recount that she had seen General Howe riding in the coach which he had commandeered from Mrs. Israel Pemberton.

On an impulse she stopped at the apothecary Drewet Smith's to get some hoarhound drops for the Affleck children. She had a jar of soup in her basket and half a pound of butter and some corn meal, but there was nothing in that to delight children. The hoarhound drops were sweet and would help their throats. Poor little things, they always seemed to be snuffling and coughing.

The shop was warm and cheerful, with a little fire on the hearth, and redolent of herbs and drugs. Two red-coat officers were demanding a British preparation for toothache and accepting with disdain the bottle of Dr. Storck's Tincture which Drewet recommended. Sarah suppressed an un-Christian satisfaction that the British teeth were aching. There was, actually, nothing wrong about the behavior of those two, yet she found herself resenting them, perhaps only for their unconscious assumption of superiority. They had looked at her, found her middle-aged and homely, and forgot her. Drewet Smith might not have had any existence at all, except as a phantom conjured up to serve their immediate need. They were aware only of themselves and each other, for whom they appeared to be playing a part. They were very smart, she thought; their uniforms new, clean, well fitting, their boots gleaming, their buttons bright. Their voices were crisp and clear, their words spoken as if to an unseen audience. One was short and square and ruddy; the other tall and thin and pale; the symmetry of his face was marred by a swelling in his cheek.

" 'There was never yet philosopher,' " said the thin one, wryly but with a kind of flourish, as if he were reciting, " 'that could endure the toothache patiently.' "

"You will find this tincture soothing, I think, sir," said Dr. Smith, screwing up his face in an expression of sympathy. He was a colorless man, with grayish skin and mouse-colored eyes; it was the way he used his face that marked him out from other people. He could not make the simplest statement without raising his eyebrows, twitching his nose, pulling his mouth down on one side. It gave an emphasis to his prescriptions that perhaps impressed the uncritical.

Sarah hoped that Caleb, associating so much with him in the care of the Hessian prisoners as he had done, had not picked up any of his facial mannerisms. Those things could be contagious, and Caleb was so good-looking it would be a pity for him to start twitching his chiseled nose or pulling his fine, molded mouth out of shape. But how absurd to worry about such trifles, when poor Caleb might be immured in some damp cell somewhere, eating out his heart in rebellion and despair.

When the officers had flung down some bills on the counter and stamped out, not troubling to shut the door behind them, Sarah turned to Dr. Smith with more cordiality than she actually felt. She disapproved strongly of his having broken his parole and come home, and she thought that his doing so might have made things more difficult for the prisoners who remained.

"Did you see the coach pass?" she asked him. "Was that General Howe in it?"

He knew General Howe. When he first arrived back from Winchester, he had been summoned before the General for an interview.

"I didn't see," he answered. "He's a very tall gentleman, very affable and at the same time dignified. You can't but admire him." He measured out the hoarhound drops. "Have you heard anything from Caleb?"

"Not a word. Have you had any news from Winchester?"

He raised his eyebrows and drew down both corners of his mouth. "They don't write to me."

"I thought you might hear something. People talk in a shop."

She left with a feeling of disappointment, which was quite unreasonable, since she had had no real expectation of hearing anything there. But there was always the chance.

She thought of Sue Mercer as she went on again, past the entrance to Orianna Court, where the popular and handsome young Major André occupied Dr. Franklin's sober house. They had not heard from Sue since early December. She had written with innocent satisfaction that she had been able to get her brother's money changed for him advantageously, but that was before the money made so much trouble for Caleb. Sarah had wanted to try to get a letter to Sue, asking whether anything was known in Lancaster about Caleb's fate, but father Caleb had refused to allow it, declaring that Sue might be in difficulties just as Caleb was and that any communication with Philadelphia, if it became known, would only make matters worse.

As soon as she entered the front room of the Afflecks' little house on Second Street, Sarah knew that trouble had moved in since she had last been there. The little room was bare, except for a plain chair or two and the green-painted paneling which gave it a certain cheerful charm, empty as it was. Sarah noticed at once that the beautiful tallboy which she had coveted was gone, and so was the table and the comb-back Windsor chair that used to stand beside the fireplace. The hearth was empty even of ashes, and the room was icy. Most ominous of all, there was the dank, thin, sour odor of sickness and poverty.

"Come away into the kitchen," said Isabella Affleck quickly. "It's warmer there."

Thomas Affleck's wife was a young Scottish girl still in her early twenties. She was not pretty, with her unruly sandy hair escaping from under her clean mobcap, her rather small, pale eyes, her long nose which rose aspiringly at the tip, her wide mouth; but her teeth were white and even, her skin had the color and texture of apple blossoms, and even though she looked this morning thin and tired and anxious, there was about her an air of unquenchable buoyancy that brought the words, "blithe" and "bonny," which were not in Sarah's daily vocabulary, into her mind.

The kitchen was a large, cheerful room and a good fire burned in the big fireplace. A hooded cradle rocked slightly by the hearth and two small children with runny noses, very much bundled up, sat on a braided rug pulling a cornstalk doll apart.

"Whisht!" said Mrs. Affleck, wiping their noses, hoisting them to their feet, and whisking away their employment with a single long sweeping motion like a breeze in a pile of leaves. The younger one promptly sat down again with an angry bellow, while the older stood sucking his thumb and scowling at Mrs. Middleton.

Sarah, taking the chair her hostess drew up for her, noticed that the younger child had a bad fever sore on his lip, that the older one had a croupy cough, and that a wail which was much too feeble was issuing from the cradle. She said nothing, but opened up her little poke of hoarhound drops, and as the children crept forward, shy but irresistibly drawn, she sent a swift glance around the room and saw the bare shelves, the empty rafters from which hung no more than some bunches of herbs and a few ears of popcorn.

"Isabella," she said, "what's happened?"

Isabella, sitting on a stool with her foot on the rocker of the cradle, flushed to the roots of her hair.

"I've sold the tallboy, and we've eaten it up." Her Scottish inflections changed the vowels slightly and made what she said even more poignant. "I've sold the Marlboro table and paid the rent and bought medicine. And noo I've nothing more to sell but the beds and with all the bairns sick most of the time I can't sell them!"

"But isn't there anybody to help you? What about the Meeting?"

"I could never go to the Meeting. Tammas was disowned when he married me. Governor Penn would help if he was here. He brought Tammas out from England to make his furniture and he was always kind. But he's been banished himself, poor man, he's got troubles of his own, no doubt. I'm a Presbyterian and all the bairns were christened in the Second Church, but that has been taken by the British army for a hospital, and most of the members are gone to the country or to Reading. We've no family here, and there's nobody that has a duty to help us. I'm too proud to beg but I'm not too proud to work—only I can't leave the bairns."

She poured it all out, as if she had said it many times over to herself.

"It's Jeanie I'm anxious about," she went on, and Sarah saw that her blue eyes were swimming in tears. "Would ye juist come upstairs and look at her, Mistress Middleton?"

They went out into the cold again and up the narrow, boxed-in staircase to the second floor. Jeanie, who at five was the eldest, lay in the big walnut bed in the front room. She was asleep. Sarah, looking down at her, saw the limp hair spread out over the pillow, the thin little body that scarcely made any thickness under the covers, the open lips, parched and colorless, the shadow of the lashes on the hollow cheeks. Her breath came noisily with a wheeze.

"She looks sick to me. Have you had the doctor?"

Isabella shook her head. "I haven't liked to leave the house to go after him—and I don't know who to go for anyhow."

"Dr. Bond is practicing again. The Council put him in prison, but they left him behind when they went and the British let him out. He's kind and very able, and he wouldn't expect to be paid now. I'll see that he comes."

They tiptoed out of the room and down the stairs again.

"Now, Isabella," said Sarah firmly, "I've left a basket of little things in the kitchen, but it doesn't amount to anything. It won't do more than help you with one meal. What you need is money. You take this now, and I'll see you get more later. It isn't charity, it's a loan. When Thomas comes home—and he shall come home —he can make me a tallboy like the one you sold. Don't cry, child. You've been a brave girl, but you can't do everything by yourself."

It was time to go home, but as the front door closed behind her Sarah turned resolutely in the opposite direction and set out again. A half-formed purpose which she had been turning over in her mind for a week or more had now crystallized. When she said, Thomas *shall* come home, she meant all that was implied by the use of "shall" instead of "will." She was going to do something about it herself. They should all come home, not only Thomas, but Caleb and the rest.

She could not act alone, of course, she would have to have help. Men had tried and failed. This was a business for women. She would go to Mrs. Drinker first and enlist her support, because she knew Mrs. Drinker a little better than the other wives and mothers. Mrs. Drinker also seemed to her a stronger and more positive sort of character than some of the others.

As she marched along the sidewalk with so much vigor that her cheeks shook, she rehearsed the arguments that they would use, she and Mrs. Drinker and whoever else, not more than two or three, should go with them. The injustice and illegality she put aside as undeniable but irrelevant. Men could always talk you down with abstractions, but when it came to young wives left without means of support and little children sick and hungry, then men were helpless before really roused and determined women.

Fifteen minutes later Mrs. Middleton sat in Mrs. Drinker's well-furnished parlor where a Pennsylvania iron stove with polished brass knobs gave out a delicious pervading warmth.

"I'm sorry to entertain thee in the back parlor," said Eliza Drinker, "but our British guest has taken the front parlor."

With some difficulty Sarah resisted the temptation to compare notes on British guests, but she knew that if they got off on that subject there would be no time left for the thing that had brought her here.

"My idea is this," she said: "for four or five of us wives and mothers—four would fit into a coach better—to go directly to General Washington himself at his headquarters at the Valley Forge and lay the whole thing before him. He is humane, everyone says so, and he has the power to act."

She watched Eliza Drinker's face eagerly for her reaction. It was a strong, sweet, serene face, framed in the Quaker cap, but it was not an immediately revealing one. There was a long pause. Finally Mrs. Drinker spoke.

"My own heart has been full of some such thing," she said, "but I don't see the way clear yet. It has not occurred to me to go to George Washington. He is, after all, though a general, in the employment of the Congress. I had thought that a delegation of women might go to York directly, to the Congress itself."

"And to Lancaster, too, to the Council," cried Sarah, catching fire. This was a much larger undertaking. It was three or four times as long a journey as it would be to go to the Valley Forge. But she could see Sue in Lancaster, stay with her at the Mercers' house, no doubt. And Mrs. Drinker was right, it was a matter for ultimate authority. "We shall probably have to see the General too," said Sarah, "to get permission to go through the lines."

But she was progressing too fast for Mrs. Drinker.

"It was only a thought. I have not discussed it with anyone. We should have to consult the Monthly Meeting. And there is another thing. Isaac Zane—the old one, not the son—has gone with some Friends from Pipe Creek Meeting to appeal to Congress. If they are successful, our trip would not be necessary. In any case, we should have to wait till they returned."

Though she was eight or ten years older than Eliza, Sarah felt oddly young and impulsive as she listened to Mrs. Drinker's calm, unhurried voice. Sarah was ready to start off for Winchester itself, if necessary, before the week was out. She had no faith in the success of any committee headed by old Mr. Zane. To wait till those old men tottered off and said their say and tottered back again seemed to her an appalling and possibly a fatal waste of time. Quakers! she thought impatiently.

She felt a gentle touch on her hand.

"Let us keep an open mind," said Eliza Drinker, "and proceed as the way opens."

XXVII

CALEB WAS CHOPPING WOOD, splitting logs for Elizabeth Joliffe's fireplaces to work off his energy and the fret in his mind. Six weeks had passed since the decree that they were to be moved to Staunton, and the exiles were still in Winchester, still uncertain of their fate.

The pleasant popularity which they had enjoyed for a short time in the autumn had vanished utterly. The townspeople had objected to their use of the Presbyterian Church on Sunday afternoons, and now no visitors came to their meetings for worship in the inn. Because of the storm of disapproval resulting from Drewet Smith's departure, they rode abroad no more than was necessary for their regular gatherings on Wednesday at the Golden Buck. Rumors circulated about them, blaming them for high prices, for the scarcity of food, and the refusal of some Quaker millers to grind grain for distilling spirits. Twice the Commissary for Prisoners had come, displaying letters from the Governor of Virginia ordering them to pack up for immediate departure to Staunton, and twice they had wrested a reluctant reprieve from him on the ground that Congressional action was pending.

Alexander White had consented to go to Congress on their behalf, and had actually spent three weeks in York and Lancaster, where he presented their Memorials and delivered a strong plea for them in his own words, urging that they be set free on grounds of humanity, justice, and expediency. All that he had achieved, however, had been a statement from the Council that it considered the exiles the prisoners of Congress. From individual members of Congress he got so many expressions of personal opinion to the effect that no good purpose was served by continuing to hold the prisoners that he believed if it came to a vote they would be released. Some members, however, indelibly prejudiced against Quakers, were strong enough to postpone action on the question. Mr. White had returned to Winchester the second week in January empty-handed but expressing the belief that he had set forces in motion which would yet bring results. At least Caleb's letter explaining his financial transactions in detail had been accepted and though he received no answer there had been no further complaints against him as distinct from the rest of the group.

After White's return Thomas Gilpin's brother George, a colonel in the Fairfax Militia who lived in Alexandria and was a personal friend of several members of Congress, had made a visit to York for the exiles. He was still there. A delegation of concerned Friends from Pipe Creek Meeting in Maryland, joined by Isaac Zane, senior, had also gone to plead for them.

They were not forgotten, there were men working for them, there was hope. Meanwhile the winter was cold, their supplies of tea and coffee and chocolate and wine, those comfortable beverages that lift the spirits as they warm the body, were exhausted. Some of the exiles had no warm clothes and none could be bought at any price. One after another they were falling ill, and they had no medicines. Even vinegar, so essential for health and hygiene, was not to be had.

It was cold this Monday morning, with a blustery wind out of the northwest whipping the bare trees, blowing chips along the ground, flinging gritty dust into Caleb's eyes. As he worked his thoughts moved jerkily, weaving together bits he had heard from here and there, from letters, from talks at the inn, where an occasional traveler brought news, from the *Pennsylvania Packet,* which John Dunlap was printing now in Lancaster, an occasional copy of which reached Winchester, to be passed around until it was as soft as a rag and the print was worn off on the creases.

In the cities, in spite of the war, there were balls. In Philadelphia, in York, in Lancaster, fiddlers played gay music, cold collations of wine and sweet cakes were set out on polished tables in the candlelight, and girls in their high silly headdresses danced with officers in smart uniforms. It made no difference, seemingly, whether the soldiers wore scarlet coats or blue and buff—Caleb tossed a chip of wood at a hen that came jerking her neck and spreading her toes, and the creature fled squawking—but soldiers they must have to dance with and no others would do.

There was no dancing for the men in winter quarters on the hills above the Valley Forge. George Gilpin had told them about that, when he stopped on his way to York. The men in Washington's army were in need of everything, breeches, shoes, stockings, blankets, flour—though barrels of flour were spoiling on the banks of the Susquehanna for lack of boats and wagons. On Christmas night the soldiers in their tents shouted to each other across the snow till the cry echoed back and forth from hill to hill, "No meat! No meat!" Isaac Potts had come on Washington praying. They were using Isaac's big house to bake bread for the soldiers, when they could find the flour.

The forge itself had been burned earlier by the British. What was happening to the Phoebe Ann? Caleb straightened up to rest his back, and leaned the axe against the chopping block. The Phoebe Ann was no farther from the Valley Forge than he was now from Isaac Zane's ironworks.

The charcoal had given out at Zane's, and the furnace was out of blast again. The Phoebe Ann had never had to shut down for lack of charcoal, even though they had less than half the acres of woodland that Zane had. But they had cut wisely, they had replanted, they had hired good men as cutters and colliers and treated them well. They had stayed on the job—until last August. I. Zane, junior, was off again, gone to Westover no doubt to dicker for his books.

Caleb spat on his hands and took up the axe again. For all his big ideas, Isaac, junior, was not half the man his father was. Caleb thought of old Isaac as he had seen him in Reading that day in September, with the blood running down his cheek where the stone had hit him, and the hurt, astonished look in his hooded eyes.

He would like to go to York himself, he, Caleb Middleton, junior. Ride off without telling anybody, not to Philadelphia to escape, as Drewet Smith had done, but to York, to face the men who would not grant him a hearing. His axe hit a knot and the blow shivered up his arm to his shoulder. He would like to stride into the inn where they met, pound on the door of the room where they sat deliberating, the few of them who were still there. Some had gone home. Mr. Adams was in France. Mr. Harvie in Winchester and some others had gone to the camp to investigate Washington, to find out if he was a suitable Commander-in-Chief. Some snake had whispered that no man was more a gentleman than Washington or appeared to more advantage at his dinner table, but that his military talents were despicable. A new Board of War had been appointed with General Gates, fresh from his victory at Saratoga, at its head, and an investigating committee had gone to the Valley Forge.

Or perhaps Caleb would go to Lancaster and confront the Council, because this was a matter for the state after all. He would say to them—a piece of wood split suddenly and the halves bounced away—"You would not be in Pennsylvania today if Quakers a hundred years ago had not refused to take oaths of allegiance to the King. Those early Friends could have freed themselves from the charge of being secret Catholics, when a Catholic was considered as dangerous as a Tory is today, but they had a bone-deep knowledge that taking an oath of allegiance at the command of an official, to avoid trouble for themselves, was an offense against liberty as well as against God. They refused and went to jail, and then they founded a colony where there would be no test oaths because there would be civil and religious liberty for everyone. Now what are you doing to their colony? We can't take your test oath," he would tell them, "but we're serving liberty just the same, if you could only see it."

The dinner bell rang and he hung his axe on the wall of the shed. He was in Winchester, not in Lancaster.

That afternoon, as the Monthly Meeting at Hopewell was about to conclude, John Hunt rose to speak. His face was white and still, his blue eyes had a look of exaltation. His voice when it came was harsh and rhythmic. Caleb felt alarmed. Was he going to have a seizure?

"I have heard with my inward ear and have seen with my inward eye," he intoned, "and now I am free to express to you. The night is far spent; the day is at hand. All about me in this sorrowful time I see people indulging themselves in pleasures, pride and dissipation, notwithstanding the calamities prevailing in the land."

It was not a seizure. He was saying again what he said so often sitting before the fire in the evening, the Friends had gone far from their original simplicity and their vision of a life based on the Sermon on the Mount, that they lived instead in conformity with the world, seeking wealth, luxuriating in fine furniture, rich food, expensive clothes and equipages; but he was speaking, not quietly, calmly, half-humorously, but prophetically, as if he were in the grip of some force outside himself.

"Desolation from the east, desolation from the west, desolation from the north and from the south, even the sword . . . except the inhabitants of America repent and mend their ways . . . I have spoken," he finished, suddenly reverting to his normal gentle tone but with a solemnity that deepened the silence in the room almost to breathlessness, "under a weighty concern and exercise of mind, apprehending that I shall not have a public opportunity again."

He sat down. For an endless time, it seemed to Caleb, there was no slightest sound in the Meetinghouse. Then gradually there came a breath, a cough, a rustle.

The final word from Congress was brought three days later by old Isaac Zane. The rest of the committee from Pipe Creek had returned to their homes, but he made the long detour around by Winchester to take the word to the exiles and to visit his son. He rode into town on Thursday and asked that all the group be called to the inn that evening, so that he could speak to them together. He would spend that night at the Golden Buck and go on next morning to Marlboro. Isaac, junior, had come back the day before.

Thomas Wharton was well enough after his illness to ride to town, but John Hunt was down now with pain and fever. Only two were able to come from the Browns' and at the inn three were confined to bed. February, everyone said, was always a sickly month, but this was worse than usual.

Isaac Zane sat in the big chair by the fire, and the firelight falling on his thin face and rugged features made him look like some ancient bird of prey. His voice, though it had a quality of sadness, was strong and clear and he showed no great fatigue after his long ride.

He told his story in his own way, not willing to be hurried by questions or persuaded to reveal the end before he had gone through all the preliminary stages. He and the five Friends from Pipe Creek, whom he named, had had many conferences with the delegates, both together and separately. They had corrected many false reports. At length the Congress had appointed a committee of three to confer with them.

"They admitted to us," he said, "that they had no other accusation against you than the several Epistles of Advice which had been published by the Meeting for Sufferings in Philadelphia, exciting the members of our religious society to maintain conduct consistent with our religious principles."

In that case, thought Caleb, surely they must see the injustice of imprisoning and banishing seventeen members at random out of a membership of thousands.

"The committee reported back to Congress, recommending that you be either set free or that Congress hear you in your own defense."

"And what action did the Congress take?" demanded Miers Fisher impatiently.

But Caleb knew with a sharp foreboding that had it been one or the other they would have been told before now. Good news bursts out in the first few minutes.

"They debated several days more, and then they passed a Resolution, of which they gave our committee a copy. I have it here and you may keep it for your records. You will be discharged from your confinement and banishment—upon taking the oath or affirmation of allegiance."

There was a bitter silence in the room. No one spoke. No comment was necessary.

XXVIII

Spring spoke through a crack in the wall of February. It was in the shadows that lay along the brown earth, delicate and precise; in the sudden chuckling sound of the brook where ice was melting; in the innocent blue of the sky; in the long, sad call of the white-throated sparrow in the cedars.

Caleb said nothing of his intentions in the house where John Hunt was still in bed racked with fever and the ache in his head, and Edward Penington sat with a book in his hand, the pages unturned, refusing to admit the pain that crept on him. He passed the axe hanging on the wall in the woodshed without a glance.

He saddled Ladybird and rode into Winchester and out again, on the road that led east to the Opequon and the Shenandoah, the Blue Ridge and ultimately Baltimore. He would go, he told himself, to the Opequon and no farther. He would go to the end of the six-mile chain that tethered him like a dog to its kennel.

He rode without joy and without thought, a body driven by inner compulsions, a spirit held in desperate suspense, seeking a release the terms of which were not spelled out even in the secret recesses of his heart. Though the chain that bound him was not of his own forging, he had accepted it. Whether it would snap when he pulled it taut or jerk him to the ground upon his back, he did not try to know; he only rode blindly, pursued by malevolent phantoms of his own being, driven to lose himself through escape or exhaustion.

He came to the ford of the Opequon where he and Drewet Smith had found Tenskatawa waiting for them that day. The leaves were off the bushes now; there was a rim of white ice at the edge of the stream; but he recognized the trail and the great buttonwood tree in the field, spreading its white limbs against the sky, patterning the clouds with its dancing brown balls. Beyond the creek the muddy rutted wagon tracks that were the main road to Baltimore stretched east toward the mountains, where a series of gaps nicked the clear blue line.

He let Ladybird drink, shifting in his saddle as she lowered her head to the water.

It came to him that he might turn and follow the trail along the creek to the house where Loveday had been that day. He might go and see how that family was getting along, the bent-shouldered, young-old man, the young wife with the baby and the gaping hole in her heart where the little boy had been, that little wisp of child they had tried to cure and perhaps had killed. The Prestons would welcome him. People who lived so far away and alone welcomed anyone, and he had news of the world: of the changes in the Board of War, the murmurings against Washington, the extravagances of the British army in Philadelphia, the suffering of the poor there, the conditions in the Walnut Street prison where a brute named Cunningham mistreated American prisoners of war. He had no hope that Loveday would be there. She would be in her home, where the hidden Shenandoah moved near Williams' Gap.

Ladybird raised her head and shook it, water flying in drops from her mouth. Caleb sat irresolute, half wanting to turn to the safe distraction of the farm on the creek, yet resisting a solution so tame and futile, so inadequate an outlet for the pressure within him.

He heard hooves on the road behind him and turned to catch a glimpse over the little rise in the ground of a familiar red coat. He pulled Ladybird around and waited for Pike to come near.

The red coat was dingy now but the ruffles on the shirt beneath it, though badly frayed, had been starched and ironed. Pike's greatcoat lay folded across his saddle bow and his worn valise was fastened on behind. More than these, his expression of dismay and anger on seeing Caleb betrayed the fact that he was riding away from Winchester with no intention of returning.

The mounting dislike which Caleb had held in uneasy control for the last five months rose now to an angry flood.

"Where are you going?" he demanded peremptorily.

"I resent both your question and the manner in which it is put."

"You don't need to answer. I know where you're going. You're decamping." His righteous indignation was all the hotter for the impulses that lay unacknowledged at the bottom of his own mind.

Mr. Pike's small, pale, too close-set eyes narrowed to slits; he answered in venomous fury: "I am not a Quaker. I had nothing to do with the Advices of the Meeting."

Caleb silently admitted that there was justice in this. He tried to be more conciliatory. "You are aware of the damage to the reputation of the group caused by Drewet Smith's sneaking off as he did. You have suffered from it yourself. Can you elope now without a thought for the fate of those you leave behind?"

"The rich and important Pembertons and Fishers and Pleasants' —and Mr. Middleton, of course—will be able to take care of themselves."

"Do you imagine that they will believe you when you take the oath of allegiance?"

"I have no idea of taking the oath of allegiance. I have no faith in the rebel government. I am going to Philadelphia. My wife is there without support or protection. There are opportunities for a dancing and fencing master in Philadelphia today such as there have never been before—and I am not bound by pious hypocrisy."

"Nor, apparently, by any vestiges of honor."

"If I had my sword I would defend my honor now—though it would be small satisfaction to run through a Quaker and a coward."

"Get down off your horse and I'll fight you with bare fists!"

For answer Pike plunged his horse into the ford. A moment later, splashing, he was out on the other side and off at a gallop down the rough road ahead.

Caleb wheeled and urged Ladybird after him, but even while the cold water of the creek swirled around him he knew that it was no use to follow. Overtake him he might, pull him off his horse and tie him up with his own reins and drag him back to Winchester, but what then? Such a violent and possibly bloody act would only bring scandal and ridicule upon them all.

Even as Ladybird scrambled up out of the creek Caleb knew he was defeated. He watched the red coat grow smaller in the distance. At a curve in the road Pike turned and waved mockingly before he disappeared.

Barring mishaps he would be in Baltimore in three days, in Philadelphia before the week was out. He would be with his Phyllis.

Primitive jealousy seized Caleb, hot and suffocating, and shook him fiercely. When the moment passed he squared his shoulders, tucked in his elbows, and spurred Ladybird forward, faster, recklessly, and faster, burying the thoughts that stung and goaded him under the clatter of hooves.

As he rode his mind slowly cleared. When the road forked he turned unhesitatingly to the right into a wood beside a holly thicket. He knew now where he was going, where he had intended to go all along. This was the way to the Parry farm.

He reached the place he had been told about, where the road forked again at a big rock, and took the narrower lane, pressing deeper into the woods. Once he passed a cabin in a clearing and asked the way of a woman there. It was past dinnertime now, but he had no thought of hunger.

A wide field of winter wheat with stubborn stumps still standing in the vivid green told him that he was approaching the farm. Presently the road he followed came to an end in a pair of whitewashed gates and a long lane lined with cedar trees on both sides. The formality of the dark green, cone-shaped trees marching toward a hidden house surprised him. He rode slowly along, accompanied by the crisp chip-chip of a redbird flying from one tree to another beside him.

The house, which was built of stone, stood at the end of the lane, framed by the cedars. Mounds of English box, shining and fragrant in the sun, flanked the doorway. The lane curved to the left around the house.

Caleb might have been expected, so promptly did a servant appear to take his horse, a neat, respectful colored boy such as Caleb had not encountered in many a long day. As Ladybird was led off, Caleb turned to mount the white painted steps to the front door, where gleamed the kind of brass knocker common enough at home but rare in this frontier country. As he lifted it and let it fall, he was suddenly conscious of his dusty boots, his shabby leather breeches and old green broadcloth coat. A little nervously he adjusted his neckcloth, which had been clean that morning.

The door was opened by a colored man-servant. Behind him a middle-aged, moon-faced woman came hurrying forward with outstretched hand.

"Oh," she said, her expression of smiling welcome turning swiftly and rather comically to uncertainty, "it isn't—I was expecting someone else."

"I am Caleb Middleton, junior. I came to see—" he stumbled, "is this where—" he decided to use the Quaker form—"Loveday Parry lives?"

"Yes. Come in. I am Loveday's aunt, Mary Freame."

She led the way to a parlor, where a fire burned brightly. It was not what he had expected at all. He must look strange and wild, he thought, and tried to adjust his countenance to a polite, conventional look, to hide all the confusion and frenzy of the day's emotions.

"Thou art one of the exiled Friends from Philadelphia? Pray sit down. I will call Loveday and my brother. We have very few visitors here—and now today, two. Good things come in bunches, don't they?"

Too restless to sit down, he went to one of the windows and looked out between the brown and white hangings, which had a French-like pattern. There was a garden, the beds marked out with box hardly larger than sprigs and neatly tucked in with a covering of dead leaves. The redbird hopped about on the path, crested and elegant.

Caleb heard the click of the door-latch and a light step, and turned quickly. Loveday was there.

He had been expecting the gray linsey-woolsey dress, but she was all in blue. It made her eyes, which had been gray, as blue as the sea. Her hair was done up on top of her head, so that the line of her neck showed in all its young purity, and the exquisite modeling of her little jaw and chin. It was like meeting a stranger, a stranger who reminded him almost too poignantly of the girl he loved.

For three months she had dwelt in his thoughts, young and slim, gray-eyed, gray-gowned, pliant to his will; now he found her looking altogether different, ensconced in a house with a door knocker and French hangings and guarded by an aunt and a father. His little nymph of the wilderness, product of two glimpses and his romantic dreams, had turned out to be the daughter of a country squire, set about with a palisade of conventions of thought and behavior, of which he had already broken several.

He bowed. "I am afraid I intrude," he apologized. "You were expecting someone?"

"We are expecting my—he's my second cousin, actually— Griffith Parry. But I knew he couldn't get here so soon."

Even in silk, with her hair up, she had that enchanting look of freshness and cleanliness, that young gentleness and innocence that had held his imagination captive these long months. The expression of concern which she had worn when she was with the sick child was gone, and in its place was a glow that delighted Caleb even while it removed her indefinably but perceptibly from his reach.

The aunt came bustling back and competently got them seated, Caleb in an armchair across the room from the stiff little sofa where she placed herself and Loveday.

"Richard Parry will be here directly," she said. "Thou must be thirsty after thy ride—hungry too. I am having a little refreshment brought to thee."

"This is the Caleb Middleton I told thee about, Aunt Mary, who came with Dr. Smith to the Prestons' when little Ned was so sick. He died," she turned to Caleb, "did thee know?—in spite of everything."

What was it the farmer had said of her? Caleb searched his memory. "She's a great hand at nursing, for all she's so young. . . . Seems as if she had magic in her fingers. . . ." They looked like capable little hands, folded and quiet against the little flowered apron that she wore with her silk dress. This was pioneer country, and anyone with the gift of nursing would be called upon to help in cases of illness far and wide.

"Yes, I was so sorry," said Caleb slowly. "We went back later, but the little boy had died, and thee was gone. The Hessian prisoner, at least, recovered."

The scene in the Prestons' kitchen flashed into his mind, the familiar way he had played with her curl and the tenor of his thoughts and impulses as he stood so close to her and fingered her hair. His face flushed hot. The sudden shame he felt was not so much because he had thought her then a serving maid, though there was a little of that, for he should have known from looking at her what she was; it came rather from the insight into himself which the shock of this knowledge gave him. He had met innocence that day and he would have taken advantage of it if he could, forgetting that it was his duty—any decent man's duty—to protect innocence wherever he met it.

The door opened again, and Richard Parry entered. Even without Mrs. Freame's introduction, Caleb would have recognized him as Loveday's father. A man of medium height, both benign and shrewd, he had something of her look of cleanliness. His eyes under a box-like brow were gray and keen, his nose short and straight, his mouth wide, his chin square. There was little of the farmer about his dark gray broadcloth suit and buckled shoes, but the weatherbeaten neck beneath his neat wig and the sinewy scrubbed hands told of hours in the open air.

"I remember hearing thou was of service to poor Edward Preston," he said cordially, fitting himself into a chair. "Dr. Smith later took French leave, I hear?"

"Yes. He— and Mr. Pike too—did not consider themselves bound in the same way as the rest of us. Dr. Macky has returned to Winchester now and resumed his practice."

They must be wondering why he had come, Caleb thought uncomfortably, for all they sat there so polite and friendly. He looked from Richard Parry to Loveday.

There she sat on the sofa in her blue dress, with her eyes shining, beautiful, capable of compassionate and humble and loving service, more desirable than ever and more difficult to attain. Difficult, but not impossible. He would have to ask this father's permission to address his daughter, and before that put himself into a favorable light with the father. But no doubt he knew all about the exiles from Philadelphia; as a Quaker he would feel respect and sympathy for them. A feeling of extraordinary happiness swept through Caleb. That he should have come all this distance, through such anguish of mind, such discouragement and futility, such weight of injustice, and then find, in this unfamiliar wilderness, the girl of all girls in the world, whom he could love and protect and cherish all his life! It made him feel that there was something in the idea of destiny after all and in the mysterious workings of God's purposes.

"I thought when I heard thy horse in the lane," Richard Parry was saying, "that it was Griffith Parry. He's riding up from Alexandria. Where my great-grandfather settled. Where I grew up. We are one of the few families to come to Frederick County over the Blue Ridge. Most of the people hereabouts came up the Valley from Pennsylvania. Griffith and my daughter Loveday will be married this summer—perhaps she told thee?"

"No," said Caleb, while the earth fell away beneath his feet and the sky crashed on his head. "No, I didn't know."

Fool. Imbecile. Idiot. Triple-dyed fool that he was. How was he to get himself out of this before he betrayed his folly?

"Mr. Griffith is to be vastly congratulated," he said between stiff lips, and realized at once that he had got the name wrong and made himself more ridiculous than ever.

The aunt spoke, idly, garrulously, to fill a pause, as women will, and put the cap upon his humiliation.

"How did thee find thy way here?" she asked. "Isn't thee a good bit beyond the six miles, or whatever it is they allow you?"

Caleb ran his finger inside his neckcloth and pulled at it to prevent himself from suffocating and stood up abruptly.

"It is," he said wildly. "Far beyond. I am out of bounds—in every way. I must bid you good day. Servant, sir, madam."

He did not look at Loveday again, or speak to her, but strode from the room, all but knocking down at the door the butler, who was bringing a tray of light refreshment for him. Outside he found his way around the house to the stable, shouted for the boy to bring his horse, tossed him a five shilling note, and galloped off down the lane between the cedar trees.

XXIX

Hot-eyed and tormented, Caleb lay flat on his back in a darkened room. His head was a hollow vessel made of some heated metal, on which blows were struck that reverberated down his spine. His joints ached with an intensity that left him panting. Fever mounted hour by hour, as the locust's shrill rasp in July days screws upward to the breaking point.

It was the same pain, the same fever, that had assailed Thomas Wharton and John Hunt, the same for which Drewet Smith had treated the German prisoners in the stockades. Dr. Macky came from Winchester with his lancet and his doses. He was a thin, dark, sallow young man with coffee-colored eyes. He said he had never known Winchester to be as sickly as it was this winter. He would not agree that Caleb had camp fever. It was quite different from what he had seen in the army, he insisted. Mrs. Joliffe was a good nurse, he said. Caleb would be well in no time.

The hours stretched endless and confused, broken by voices and faces, by bitter draughts held to his mouth and trickling down his neck, by hands on his forehead, cool and heavy or cool and light. He slept fitfully during the daytime, woke with a start to see the sunshine on the floor or to hear rain spattering against the window, slept again and woke at night in the dark, lonely and stricken with irrational fears.

Sleeping or waking, he dreamed. He thought he was the guard at the Golden Buck, sick in an army hospital, and he struggled to get away, to walk out of the hospital and leave it all behind. Hands held him down, fastened the bedclothes tight over him, like a shroud. He was not dead, he tried to tell them, but the words would not issue from his throat, and when he fought against the restricting hands, they turned into Thomas Pike and he shouted aloud at him to prevent him from leaving. Once the hand on his forehead was so light and gentle that he thought it must be Loveday's, but when he spoke to her it was John Hunt's voice that answered, "Lie still, Caleb," and he was quiet, dreadfully tired but clearheaded for a time.

People came into the room. He could not talk to them, but they talked to each other and he heard them, sometimes through a mist, from a long distance, sometimes clearly and sharply, as they said things not intended for him, which he remembered and thought about afterward.

"A sum of five hundred pounds has been subscribed at Hopewell for the Indians."

But the Indians were all gone. Tenskatawa had found a little girl lost in the woods and carried her home. What had Loveday been like as a baby? Curly-haired and confiding, with no fear of the tall savage who picked her up in his arms. The thought of Loveday was a stab at his heart and a heaviness afterward and he could not think why, until he remembered the last time he had seen her and all the mortification of that day came back. The faces of Loveday and her aunt and her father floated before him, and they were all smiling—smiling at him and the way he had behaved. He groaned.

Two letters came for him. He took them in his hand, but he could not read them.

Later John Hunt read them to him and Thomas Wharton came to listen. Edward Penington was sick in the next room and out of his head. They could hear him crying out and Elizabeth Joliffe soothing him.

They all wanted to know what was in Caleb's letters. Everybody's letters were pressed and squeezed for news, like lemons for juice, but they were all dry. No one dared write anything but moral sentiments lest the letters be intercepted and they be accused of giving intelligence to the enemy.

Caleb's father kept his room and fretted much about his son. Tacy had been inoculated for the smallpox and her little arm was a mass of sores, but it was better than having them later on her face perhaps. Edward was well and sent his love. Patty was still with the Chase cousins. The Center Woods had all been cut down for firewood.

The Center Woods cut down. The ringing of the axe sounded in Caleb's ears and mingled with the pain in his head. That would be the British. They had burned all the fences and some of the great houses like Fairhill and Peel Hall. Caleb's father would not like that. "Caleb can learn something about liberty at first hand," he had mocked. Well now, thought Caleb, moving in the bed to ease his blazing, aching body, his father could learn something about tyranny.

Someone brought him milk to drink, and he slept.

When he woke, he discovered that though he was weak he was without pain.

The relief was a joy in itself, so fresh, so light, so keen that he wondered if life could hold any greater bliss than this. With an effort he turned his head and smiled.

Dr. Macky was there again, and John Hunt, looking angelic with the sun behind his fluff of white hair, and Elizabeth Joliffe, substantial and motherly.

"Feeling better, aren't you?" said the doctor.

"Yes." Caleb heard his own voice, distant and faint. He made a further effort. "Hungry," he said, pleased with his achievement.

The broth which Mrs. Joliffe brought and fed to him as if he had been a baby was good. The room was big and peaceful, and so bright that it seemed to glisten and dance. He saw a rim of white on the muntins of the windowpane, and beyond were the balls of the buttonwood tree, topped each one with a little white hat. Snow, that's what it was. That was why the house was wrapped in a velvet silence and the sun sparkled and the air that seeped through the cracks around the windows had a different smell.

Reaction came later when he tested his returning strength trying to get up, and found himself much weaker than he expected. Half dressed, he lay down on the bed again, his feet trailing over the side, and pulled the covers over him. Discouragement sifted like blowing sand into all the crevices of his spirit.

Not only his own humiliations and failures lay like a weight on his chest, but the woes of his country, torn by civil war, by suspicion and fear, overrun by foreign troops and ruled by bunglers who betrayed the very principles of liberty and justice for which their ragged Continentals were starving and dying of sickness, not of wounds. "No meat! No meat!" those poor devils shouted across the hills at Valley Forge. They might as well cry, all of them, himself included, "No hope! No hope!" for where would it all end?

As if in answer to his need John Hunt came in and sat down in the tall-backed chair by Caleb's bed.

"Thou'rt looking better," he said. "Thomas Wharton is himself again, and I am well. Edward Penington is still bad. He is lightheaded, as thou was, only his talk is all of oppressed Indians and thieving clerks, not lovely girls like thine."

"Did I say anything about Loveday Parry?"

"Thou did mention her."

"I suppose I made myself more ridiculous than ever," said Caleb bitterly. "I broke my parole," he went on with a rush, "for that's what it amounted to, even if we have given no formal promises. I went to see Loveday and I made a complete fool of myself. She is engaged to somebody from Alexandria." It was a relief to say it. He swung his feet up on the bed and doubled his pillow under his head so that he could see John Hunt more comfortably. There was a great deal that he would like to say about himself to an understanding and interested listener.

"If we repented our sins," remarked John, "as heartily as we repent our ineptitudes, we should all be considerably farther along the road to perfection than we are."

"Perfection! What do I care about perfection? I want just two things—not to make a fool of myself in front of Loveday Parry and to get out of here and go home." He saw John Hunt's face, which wore an expression of patience, and he felt ashamed of his vehemence and the crude simplicity of his desires. "Or not home," he qualified, "to the Congress. To face them and make them hear us." He paused. The moment for talking about himself and his private troubles was lost. "Where do we stand now?" he asked.

"The Congress has postponed action again, but we are evidently not to be sent to Staunton, at least not at present. Some of us thought Friend Pike's departure might have an adverse effect upon our situation, but apparently it has made little if any difference. Major Holmes sent an express to the Board of War about it. I don't know what he said, but they are apparently not going to take any action because of that."

"But is nothing being done? Are we to molder here indefinitely?"

"George Gilpin was in Winchester day before yesterday on his way home from York. He reported that some of the members of Congress told him privately that if the Council of Pennsylvania asked for our discharge they thought the Congress would acquiesce."

"Did he go to the Council then?"

"No, he thought that would not be prudent. He is, after all, a Virginian. But he reported that a committee from Western Quarterly Meeting is in Lancaster applying to the Council for our release. They are not there for us alone, but also for four Friends imprisoned in Lancaster for refusing to bear arms, and I believe they are bringing up the whole question of test oaths as well."

"Another committee!" Western Quarterly Meeting. That would be Friends from the country Meetings of New Garden, Kennett, West Grove, London Grove. The delegation from Pike Creek headed by old Isaac Zane had failed; Alexander White had failed; Colonel Gilpin had failed; why should these do any better? Especially if they were scattering their efforts on several issues instead of concentrating upon the exiled Friends.

"But Colonel Gilpin did say that some members spoke to him

privately?" pursued Caleb as hope squeezed up again through the one crack left open. "Did he say who they were?"

"Not to me. They spoke in confidence."

"But what are we going to do now?"

"Do?" said John. "The only thing we can. Wait."

XXX

When Caleb was up and about again, James Pemberton rode out from Winchester to see the little group at Hopewell. He ate dinner with them and afterward the five exiles sat around the fire and talked. Edward Penington was downstairs for the first time, looking so thin and old that everyone was shocked.

The talk was hardly cheering, composed as it was of anxiety for their families in Philadelphia, illness in Winchester, and uncertainty about their own future. Samuel Pleasants was down sick, and fretting about his wife and children at home, all of whom, he heard, had been stricken with fever. Henry Drinker had succumbed to fever and Thomas Gilpin had been ill two weeks or more with a heavy cold upon his chest.

"Thomas is a little better," added James. "At least, his brother George felt easy to leave him on Second Day. But this morning he had Miers making some changes in his will."

"My wife," said Thomas Wharton with a chuckle, "says that I believe myself on the point of death if I have so much as a sore toe, but even I have not as yet called in my lawyer to alter my last will and testament."

"Perhaps thy lawyer was not so readily available as Miers. Dear me, we are become a poor weak set of people," said James with an attempt at lightness that missed fire. He sat hunched in the big wing chair; his large, kindly, rugged face drooped in folds, and at the tip of his bulbous nose a drop hung but did not fall. "Israel is very low. John seems to be the only one of the Pembertons who retains his spirits, and his physical strength has actually increased." He sighed. "John has inner resources that Israel and I lack."

"Also he is childless, and his wife is with her father. He hasn't your worries," Edward Penington pointed out. "Hast thou heard anything of thy son Phineas?"

"Very little. He suffers constantly. His handwriting shows a loss of vigor. I wonder sometimes if I shall see him again in this life."

"Has there been any word from Lancaster?" said Thomas Wharton.

James made a wry face. "Only that they have had a very fine ball at the inn, with a Hessian band and cards at a hundred dollars a game for those who did not dance. Thy cousin Thomas was present, it seems."

"The British have a ball every Saturday night in Philadelphia," said Caleb quickly.

"It is not necessary for the Americans to follow the bad example of the British in everything," commented John Hunt mildly.

"Congress like Pilate has washed its hands of us," said Edward, bringing out a handkerchief from his pocket with a tremulous hand and touching the tip of his own nose as an example to James. "They have thrown us back upon the Council and the Council is too occupied with dancing and gambling to consider our case."

"A letter came from my son-in-law, Tom Parke, a day or so ago via Baltimore. He writes rather more freely than the rest."

"What did he say about the Hospital?"

Thomas Parke was one of Philadelphia's most promising younger doctors, and four of the managers of the Hospital were there in Winchester, James and Israel Pemberton, Thomas Wharton and Edward Penington. Caleb looked up, his attention caught as always by any mention of the world of doctors and medicine.

"The British have a firm grasp on it. A few of our sick are still in the new house and garret, but the big wards are filled with their sick and wounded. They have emptied the lunatic wards completely, and no one seems to know where the poor creatures have gone. The managers have lost most of their authority."

When the fresh news from Dr. Parke's letter was exhausted, less recent items of intelligence from the city were retold, re-examined and deplored. General Howe had commandeered Mary Pemberton's coach and rode out in it daily. A certain Lord Murray who was occupying James Pemberton's plantation near Gray's Ferry had been so destructive and had behaved so outrageously to the people in the tenant house that Phoebe Pemberton, a worrying, timid woman accustomed to let her husband stand between her and the world, had screwed herself up to the point of going to General Howe to protest.

"The sorrowful Howe says such things are unavoidable," said James with a touch of sarcasm.

After the American vessels blockading the Delaware had been destroyed by the British, ships had come in freely from Virginia loaded with Tory shopkeepers and Scots from North Carolina, who had swarmed into the shops left empty by those who had fled the city. They had taken over the stock already there and added merchandise from the West Indies, so that though food was scarce and expensive, all kinds of imported luxuries were plentiful. William Smith, "broker," who had felt comparatively easy about his wife, believing that she could carry on his store on Third Street for some time without adding to the stock that he had, now was anxious lest she had not been able to hold on to the store at all. She had no other resources, and there was a boy of six and a younger girl to provide for. He had had no word from her for over a month.

"There's another thing," said James. "We at the inn are likely to be turned out of our lodging. Our landlord has been openly tiring of us for some time, in spite of the exorbitant board we pay. But lately he has become actually abusive and he has said that we must look for another place to live. I don't know just what we shall do. There isn't another inn in the town that would take us."

"I suppose some of the townspeople are getting after Busch," said Thomas Wharton morosely, "impugning his patriotism, no doubt."

"In the first part of our banishment," said John Hunt, "we were aware of the gracious dealings of the Lord and tasted of the cup of consolation, but lately we have experienced a season of drought and poverty. I hope we may learn from this and not grow slack, but rather more attentive and watchful, humbly waiting till the Lord is pleased to knock again at our hearts."

A silence followed his words, deepening perceptibly into the living silence of the meeting for worship. When, half an hour or so later, someone stirred and the stillness was broken, the older men looked less troubled, as if some measure of comfort had been given them, but to Caleb, caught in the grip of a black depression, the cup was bitter and tasted only of failure.

"I wonder just what good we are doing," he said to John Hunt that night as they were undressing, "rotting out in this back country."

"We have taken a public stand against injustice and oppression, and I assume that is a useful thing to do. Yet we are a mixed company and we may have acted from a variety of motives. I think it is important that we inquire, each one of us, into the true ground and spring of our action."

"Does that matter, if the act itself is good?"

"I think it is of primary importance. Do, for instance, human considerations chiefly concern us—the prospect of reputation and honor among men?"

Caleb flung himself into a chair, his neckcloth dangling from his hand. "We may possibly win reputation and honor among Friends, but among men at large, no. They consider us not merely Tories but shrewd and devious as well."

"With some of us, only the opinion of Friends counts. But while such approbation may fortify us to endure suffering for a time, if that is all, if there is not some firmer basis, we may shrink and fail if severer hardships should come."

Self-examination and the analysis of motives were disagreeable to Caleb. He was a stranger to himself, except as he met himself in the mirror of other men's minds, where he appeared some times young and strong and lovable, as in John Hunt's clear soul, some-times distorted and willful, as in his father's mind, sometimes—and the memory of that day at the Parry's flooded him with a hot bitterness that made him wince—absurd and ridiculous. He kicked off his shoe with unnecessary vigor.

"What motive ought we to have, then? I came because it seemed to be the only thing to do. I was like a boy sliding down a haymow. After he gets started there isn't any way to stop."

"Thou dost thyself an injustice. There is a deeper strength and purpose in thee than that. But of this I feel sure, Caleb: when a man undertakes to stand out against the massed convictions of his fellow men—in our case against two governments, for neutralism is an affront to both sides—he must be sure his motives are pure. A true love of liberty and justice, or true devotion to the testi-monies of the Society of Friends may be enough, but we are really supported, I think, only if we know ourselves to be carrying out the will of God."

Walking across the room to get his night cap from the peg, he stumbled suddenly, as if his leg had given way. He bent down and ran his hand over his left foot and ankle.

"Curious," he said. "It's numb. I can't feel a thing."

Caleb jumped up and helped him into the chair. Dropping down on one knee before the older man, he removed his slipper and chafed the foot and ankle with his hands.

"Thee still doesn't feel anything?"

"No." John pressed his fingers into the flesh and pinched it. "It's as if it weren't there. Most peculiar."

Later the pain came, sharp and agonizing. Caleb woke in the night to find John sitting up in bed, breathing hard, like a man who had been running. "Don't disturb anyone," he said. "I am sorry to have roused thee. It's inflammatory rheumatism, I think. I have had it before."

"Can't I get something for thee? A hot fomentation?"

"No, let it alone. I don't want to drive it upward. I'll just wait, and no doubt it will pass over."

But in the morning it was no better. The pain was acute, he admitted, and he felt an intense heat in his foot. Caleb, examining it, saw on the instep and the ankle ominous spots.

"I'll call Elizabeth Joliffe," he said, stuffing his shirt into his breeches.

Before he went downstairs he placed a pillow so as to take the weight of the bedclothes off the foot. John's face, drained of color and etched with deep lines around his firmly compressed lips, was eloquent of suffering.

The big kitchen was warm and crowded. Lydia, the twelve-year-old, sat on a stool in front of the fire with a stocking around her throat and her little red nose dripping. There was a fine smell of sizzling ham as the colored woman held a long grill over the coals. Hoe cakes browned in a row at the edge of the hearth. Elizabeth Joliffe with her sleeves rolled up to her elbows, revealing arms suprisingly round and white and young, was stirring a big pan of fried potatoes with a long spoon.

"Dear me," she said, when Caleb had finished, "that sounds bad. What next!"

Caleb backed up to the fire between the two women and parting his coattails enjoyed the warmth on his rear.

"Thee's had a good deal of trouble with us and our illnesses," he said sympathetically.

"No, no, I didn't mean that. But I'd hate to have anything happen to dear John Hunt. Here, Lyddy, blow thy nose and take this spoon for a few minutes while I go see about Friend Hunt."

When Mrs. Joliffe had taken a quick look at John Hunt's face and a longer one at his foot, she said, "I think we'll just send into town and ask Dr. Macky to stop by and see thee. Shall I send Edmund, Caleb, or does thee feel equal to the ride?"

Downstairs she turned an anxious face to Caleb and whispered, "Make sure he comes, and as quickly as possible. I don't know— I've only seen it once before—but those spots look like gangrene."

"Gangrene! But he hasn't had an injury—"

"I know. But it comes sometimes with older people. Thee sure thee feels able to go? Wrap thyself up well, it's cold. I shouldn't be surprised if we had more snow."

In spite of his concern for John, Caleb's spirits lifted as he went out of the house into the clean, raw air, which had in it a tang of the stable, a dampness from the patches of snow in the shady spots, and an acrid curl of wood smoke. Ladybird was fresh and frisky. He rode off under the gray featherbed of the low-hung sky, thankful to have horseflesh between his knees again and the wide valley before him, stretching gray and dun and black to the purple hills on both sides. It was the first of March. They had been here, thought Caleb, for five months, imprisoned for six months.

He went first to Dr. Macky's house on Piccadilly Street, but the doctor was not there. His wife told Caleb to go on to Busch's inn.

"He was sent for, two hours ago," she said, "for Mr. Gilpin. They say he's dying."

XXXI

THOMAS GILPIN'S DEATH WAS a shock to them all. Caleb, who had liked him without ever having known him well, was surprised now to learn how distinguished a man the others considered him. Though he had been an able partner in the firm of Joshua Fisher and Sons, his real interests had been scientific, and the *Transactions* of the American Philosophical Society were full of his studies and surveys.

"It was largely owing to Thomas's work on the silkworm and mulberry tree," said Edward Penington, "that we formed the Silk Society. I grant thee, that was rather an abortive effort, but it was one of several attempts to stimulate domestic manufactures and so to free ourselves from English domination. I wonder sometimes at the ignorance of these new men who are so angry with the merchants and so certain that they themselves are the only true patriots. They seem to have no understanding of the groundwork done by those who signed the non-importation agreement—it was Joshua Fisher who drafted that, by the way—and advanced the economic independence of the American colonies. A political accommodation redressing the wrongs done us by Britain—and none of us denies there were wrongs—could have been built peacefully upon the economic foundations we were laying, and all this internecine strife could have been avoided."

"It was too slow, Cousin Edward," said Caleb. "Life goes by quickly and people can't wait forever."

"Growth is always slow, but it is steady and safe."

"But, on the other hand, the pains of labor are swift and birth is sudden and bloody."

Edward shrugged away Caleb's metaphor with an expression of distaste and returned to the subject of Thomas Gilpin. "His studies of the wheat-fly, the seventeen-year locust, the coal deposits of Pennsylvania and the like are the best that have been done and of very practical worth in the development of this country. Three or four years ago he designed a chain suspension bridge for the Schuylkill. The powers that be pronounced it too expensive, but in the long run I think it would have proved cheap and we shall someday have it. And then he made plans for a canal to connect the Chesapeake Bay with the Delaware River and so prevent Baltimore from getting all Philadelphia's back-country trade, and someday we shall have that. This man," said Edward bitterly, "who was not quite fifty, had in him years of service to his country intrinsically more valuable than any mere general's—and what has the new government done? They have tossed him aside and killed him."

"His spirit was singularly gentle and pure," said John Hunt, shifting his position in bed to ease his leg. "What was it thou told me about his will, Caleb? The doctor was busy with me and I was not entirely attentive."

"When he realized he was dying he asked Miers to draft a codicil to his will. Miers had put in it something about his being unjustly banished with a number of others and he told him to take that out. He said it might cast a reflection upon persons who had caused it. They say," Caleb added, "that he never expressed any complaint during his illness."

"I have known him many years," said Thomas Wharton thoughtfully, "in the affairs of the Hospital—he was a manager at one time—in the Philosophical Society and on Meeting committees, and I found him always steady in maintaining his own opinions but with care not to give offense to others. He was liberal and I think as free from bigotry as a man can be. It is a great loss. He will be missed in many quarters and especially at home. He has a young family."

Caleb remembered Josh Gilpin in the crowd at Lodge Alley so many months ago. "How many children are there?"

"Three living, I think. Two died. The youngest is a mere babe. Materially they will be well provided for, but nothing can take a father's place."

Thomas Gilpin was buried at Hopewell on the third of March. Snow fell all the day before and continued throughout the night. By Tuesday morning it had stopped, but the blanket was three feet deep and the roads had not been broken. The friends who accompanied the wagon with the coffin from Winchester were three hours on the way.

Caleb thought it unwise for his cousin Edward to venture out so soon after his illness and tried to dissuade him, but Edward, testily declaring that Caleb for all his airs and pretensions was no doctor, put on most of the clothes he possessed and labored through the snowdrifts to stand in the wind at the grave and sit for two hours in the chilly Meetinghouse afterward.

He leaned heavily on Caleb's arm on the way back. "Now our original twenty is reduced to seventeen," he said. "I think it will be sixteen before long. Dr. Macky is careful not to commit himself, but our friend John Hunt does not look right to me."

Caleb saw a redbird fly out of a cedar by the buried fence, skim across the snow in a bright flash, and disappear into another evergreen. It brought back the redbird that had followed him up the lane to the Parrys' house that day, and he closed his mind hastily upon the memory of Loveday. He tried to shut out as well the idea of losing John Hunt, but Edward's somber words stuck in his heart like a barb.

Dr. Macky, though he came regularly, could do nothing for John's leg. The mortification crept steadily upward and with it came fever, pain, and great weakness. After he had made five deep scarifications in the calf with his knife and John had felt nothing, the doctor shook his head. Later, away from the sickroom, he said to those gathering anxiously around him, "I see no hope of recovery. The gangrene will rise higher in his body and he will die. It is only a question of time and of making him as comfortable as possible."

"But in such cases is not an amputation in order?" said Thomas Wharton.

"An amputation might save a younger man. Mr. Hunt is old and very weak. It is a most painful operation. I should be sorry to inflict such agony upon him and then see it unavailing anyhow. Besides," the young man paused, flushing, "I would not hesitate in an emergency involving a healthy young person, but in such a case as this I do not feel competent. I have assisted in more than one amputation, but I have never actually performed the operation myself."

"Isn't there anyone else we could call in?" said Caleb. "Surely there must be an experienced surgeon somewhere in this part of the country."

"There's Dr. General Stephen. He's a good twenty-five miles away near the Packhorse Ford of the Potomac. He's out of the army now, and he's a good surgeon, whatever else you may think of him."

From the look that passed between Mrs. Joliffe and Dr. Macky Caleb understood that both knew something further about Dr. Stephen and that it was not to his credit.

"Would not his advice be useful?" said Thomas Wharton. "A consultation can do no harm, surely, and might bring forth something valuable."

"He got his training at Edinburgh," Dr. Macky conceded. "I would trust him to operate, if in his judgment it was the right measure. Suppose we wait and see how Mr. Hunt is tomorrow. Now I had better visit our other patient."

Edward Penington was ill again and his life too hung in the balance. Elizabeth Joliffe, exhausted by more than a month of nursing and with ailing children of her own upon her hands, had pressed Sidney Wright, a member of Hopewell Meeting, into service. A strong, plain, hearty young woman, Sidney was a capable if somewhat brusque nurse. She divided her time during the day between Edward and John, and at night she slept on a trundle bed in Edward's room, ready to jump up and attend to him when necessary. Caleb, whose touch was lighter and surer, cared for John Hunt during the night.

After Dr. Macky's cuts upon his leg he slept little and his mind was restless. He complained of strange imaginations and unsettled fancies.

"They have not let me know," he said once, "how ill they think me. I am aware that my situation is critical."

The morning after the first mention of Dr. Stephen John Pemberton came to sit with John Hunt. He had come a long way, now that he, with his brothers and Samuel Pleasants, had moved from Philip Busch's to a house south of Winchester. A young Quaker couple with five children under ten years old and a sixth on the way had hospitably offered a home to them when the landlord of the Golden Buck refused to harbor them any longer. The three Fishers were moving to another Quaker home on the Opequon as soon as Miers, who was ill with fever, should be well enough.

Caleb, leaving the two old friends together, sitting in silence or talking reminiscently about John Woolman, whom both had loved, sought out Elizabeth Joliffe to ask her point-blank what was wrong with Dr. Stephen.

"He's that Adam Stephen," she said, as if that explained everything. When Caleb still looked inquiring, she went on, pushing her cap into place with the back of her hand, "They say he's a good surgeon, but he's really more of a soldier than a doctor. He fought with Braddock and they gave him five thousand acres of land near the Potomac for that. He built himself a big house and he was Sheriff for a while. That's all right and nothing to criticize. But there've been things that haven't sounded just right. He was elected to the convention three years ago and then they wouldn't let him take his seat because there was some scandal about the election. He took his old soldiers to the polls to see that people voted the way he wanted or something of the kind. But he was made a general anyhow in the Continental army and he fought well at Trenton—or said he did, he seems to have got most of his praise from himself—and then after the engagement at Germantown last Tenth Month—thee must have heard people talking about it, it made a great stir here—he was tried for unofficer-like conduct and dismissed. Drunkenness, some say it was, though I never heard that that was particularly unofficer-like."

"I remember now. That one. But is he really a surgeon?"

"He was trained at Edinburgh, and I suppose there isn't anything better. He operated on a member of our Meeting about fifteen years ago and he's been as well as most people ever since."

"I can't see that it could do any harm to call him in for consultation."

The odor of gangrene was now a problem to everyone. It pervaded the house and added to the misery of John Hunt himself. On his evening visit Dr. Macky decided abruptly that if Dr. Stephen was ever to be summoned, it must be done immediately.

"If someone were to ride tonight," he said, "we could get Dr. Stephen here by midday tomorrow.

"I'll go," said Caleb promptly, thankful for action at last. "Tell me where to find him."

The directions were simple: to ride north on the Valley Road almost to the Packhorse Ford. Before he reached the river there would be a road to the left, and on that road, on the right, would be the gate to Stephen's farm, marked by stone pillars and a long lane under an avenue of maples.

"You can inquire when you get near. Anyone can tell you."

"What about the six-mile limit?" said Caleb, suddenly remembering that he was a prisoner.

"I'll take responsibility for that. In a case of life and death nobody could object."

It was after midnight when Caleb mounted Ladybird and rode off. The weather was mild and the gibbous moon was high in the sky. In spite of the seriousness of his errand, he could not help feeling a certain elation at being set free to ride so far. The darkness of the woods and fields, the sound of Ladybird's hooves in the night, the sudden sight of a pair of green animal eyes shining out of the blackness of the roadside bushes, the possibility of meeting Indians or highwaymen or militia on the way, combined to give him a feeling of excitement that was pleasant after the long doldrums of illness and confinement.

As the time went past without incident he had to fight against sleepiness, and he sang, to keep himself awake, the "Liberty Song," snatches from the popular "World Turned Upside Down," and bits from hymns which he had heard Sarah Middleton sing.

The moon was halfway down the western sky when Caleb saw a dim light from the open door of a stable and found a tired farmer tending a cow in labor. The man told him how to reach General Stephen's house, but would not let him go till he had the outlines of the emergency that brought Caleb in search of the surgeon at this time in the morning. He shook his head and clicked his tongue in sympathy, but was obviously cheered by the drama of it.

Half an hour later Caleb was pounding on the door of a big stone house.

The General, who came to the door himself, was a big man in his late forties, rugged of feature, with the swollen and pitted red nose of the habitual drinker. In gown and nightcap, with an untidy pigtail down his back and a candle in his hand, he looked more like a Dutch farmer than either a surgeon or a general, but his response to the challenge of need was quick and decisive.

"I'll just get into some clothes and we'll have a bite to eat and I'll be off at once."

He shouted for "Jed" to come and take Caleb's horse and for "Marthy" to get up and make breakfast, and within minutes there was a stir through the house and a light moving in the stable. A tiny, toothless, colored woman drove a boy to rake the ashes from the kitchen hearth and build up the sleeping fire, and soon the copper pots hanging from the ceiling winked back at the flames. Someone showed Caleb where to wash. When he returned to the kitchen a rich fragrance of coffee filled the air. It was weeks since Caleb had tasted coffee and he sniffed the aroma eagerly.

"You'd better snatch a bit of sleep before you start back," said the surgeon, pulling on his coat as he came in, "and give your mount a rest. I'll go ahead. But first we'll eat."

Caleb had seen paneled doors closed upon the wide hallway by which he had entered, but evidently the kitchen was the room that was used. They sat at a well-scrubbed pine table before the fire and ate the bacon and scrambled eggs that the woman named Marthy brought steaming from the iron frying pan. While he ate, Dr. Stephen asked questions about John Hunt's condition and Caleb answered them briefly and as exactly as he could.

"You talk like a physician yourself," said Dr. Stephen, offering him bread on the point of a knife.

"I'd like to be one," said Caleb, "but it's too late now."

"Too late? It's never too late to do something you want to do. Who are you, anyhow? One of that crowd of seditious prisoners they've got down there in Winchester?"

For a moment Caleb wondered if he would refuse to attend anyone whom he considered a Tory.

"We are members of the Society of Friends, which has been opposed to warfare and fighting for a century and a quarter, and we can't take part in the present commotions on either side. But we are not seditious, sir."

"The rebels don't know who are their enemies and who aren't. If it hadn't been for me and my Fifth Virginians at Trenton the war would be over now and certain high and mighty patriots would be in British prisons—if they weren't hanging from British gibbets. But did that keep them from making a scapegoat of me when my division and Greene's got tangled in the fog at Germantown? Now that Frenchman, Lafayette, has got my division, and Greene's been made Commissary General, but here I am, a country doctor, getting up before daylight to ride across the country to try and save the life of some poor old Quaker that the Congress decides is seditious. It's a crazy quilt of a world, and anyone who looks for gratitude, or even justice, is defeated before he starts. Jed, fetch my bag of instruments out of the surgery and be sure the saw is in it, the big one. I'll be off. You finish your breakfast, Mr. Middleton, and then take a nap on the sofa over there. It's comfortable and it's warm. I've had many a snooze there."

He drank the last of his coffee and set the cup on the table with a thud, wiped his mouth with a damask napkin, and tramped down the hall, shouting directions to Jed.

Caleb followed him to the front steps. Dawn had come, and in the gray light from an overcast sky Caleb saw mist rising from the fields beyond the line of maples. A tall, powerful bay horse pawed the ground beside a mounting block made of a mammoth tree stump.

The surgeon checked the contents of his bag before it was fastened to the saddle and sent Jed scurrying back for a pot of ointment and a roll of bandages. Another Negro held the horse's head, and while he waited for Jed Stephen tested the saddle girth. Dressed and seen by daylight he was rather an impressive figure of a man, with his height, his broad shoulders, and straight back. His massive red nose and three-day growth of beard detracted from the elegance of his appearance but took nothing from his look of power.

"Get yourself a nap," he called to Caleb as Jed came running with the last things for the bag. "Good for your horse too."

He mounted, wheeled, and was off down the lane, mud splattering up behind the bay's hooves.

Caleb went back to the kitchen and sat down on the edge of the old and battered sofa. Marthy came to pull off his boots.

"You're asleep on your feet," she said. "Now you jus' rest you'se'f."

"I mustn't sleep more than a couple of hours," said Caleb, finding a hollow that fitted his body.

"No, sir. I'll call you. Lift your foot so's I can free this blanket and spread it over you. Miss Ann knitted it herse'f before she ma'ied Captain Alexander Spottswood Dandridge. Master sure do miss her."

When Caleb got back to Mrs. Joliffe's early that afternoon, the conference between Dr. Macky and General Stephen was over. The General advised an amputation in spite of the risk, and John Hunt, facing all the possibilities, felt, he said, "Free to it." It would be done the following morning.

The night was restless and disturbed for everyone, with the shadow of that great trial hanging over all. Edward Penington, who was on the mend but still very low, felt the unease in the house and demanded to know what had happened. His distress for his friend put an end to sleep for both himself and his nurse Sidney. John Pemberton had stayed over to be with John Hunt and slept in Caleb's bed. Since the doctors were in the spare room, Caleb crawled into bed with Edmund, who kicked, and ten-year-old Amos Joliffe, who ground his teeth, and he thought with longing of the bumpy sofa in the General's kitchen.

When morning came and Dr. Stephen looked again at John Hunt's leg, he said nothing, but stood tapping his lower lip with a blunt forefinger. Then he nodded to Dr. Macky and they left the room, followed closely by Caleb.

"The mortification has increased during the night. I am afraid that the blood vessels will be so relapsed that we should not be able to stop the bleeding. For him to bleed to death that way would be very affecting and the pain of the operation wasted. Under the circumstances I am not willing to amputate. But I don't want to be the one to tell him, after raising his hopes. You do it, Macky, you know him better."

"Let's ask Mr. Pemberton to open the subject, and then we can continue. Would you be so good, sir? He would take it easier from an old friend like you."

A few minutes later John Pemberton came out of the room. "He said at once that from your withdrawing he understood that you were discouraged."

They all went back again into the sickroom, Caleb silently scornful of their estimate of John Hunt. He would meet death—death by torture, if necessary—with all the courage and manliness that any soldier could show, and with good will as well.

In spite of the odor, which was almost overwhelming, there was a look of freshness and sweetness about the man who lay propped up in bed under the sentence of death. His fine fluffy white hair, his white skin with the flush of fever on his sunken cheeks, his deep-set blue eyes with their unquenchably youthful expression, even the sharp bony structure of brow and nose and chin, seemed translucent, revealing the strong and loving spirit within.

Dr. Stephen, making his harsh voice unaccustomedly gentle, repeated what he had said outside.

"I understand," said John. "But I would like to ask, how long dost thou think I am likely to be continued? I am afraid I may be too heavy a burden upon my friends."

"It is impossible to say exactly, sir. There are several factors, the natural strength of your constitution, and so forth."

"Shall I continue the use of the bark?"

"I recommend it, sir. It will protract the time."

"That's hardly what I desire. But I should like to be a little sweeter—"

"The bark will help. I hope—" the General cleared his throat and said in the stiff, determined tone of one who feels obliged to attempt a foreign language to a person whose native tongue it is— "I hope, sir, you will be resigned to the Lord's will."

"I hope I am," said John meekly.

Dr. Stephen took John Hunt's thin hand in his and held it, patting it affectionately. "It's a fine thing to be in such a state of mind," he said warmly and naturally, and a little enviously.

When he got out of the room and before he departed, "I wish I could do something for that fine old gentleman," he said. "Call me again if you need me. You don't need to send a messenger. The post comes twice a week."

Less than a week later he was back again. John Hunt had been sleeping better; the fever was less; the gangrene had ceased to move upward. There seemed to be a very good chance that an operation might be successful and his life might be saved. Once more the doctors met and conferred.

This time they were united in the decision to proceed with the amputation.

"I'll need two assistants," said Dr. Stephen, and turned to Caleb. "Would you be willing to lend a hand, sir?"

XXXII

IT WAS SUNDAY MORNING, the twenty-second of March. A spring rain lashed against the windows and a robin sang over and over his amiable, insensitive refrain. Thomas Wharton plodded off down the muddy lane to Meeting, taking with him the five Joliffe children, while their mother sat with Edward Penington to keep him company and to be within call in case she was needed by the doctors. Sidney Wright had been taken sick with the fever and had gone home the day before.

In John Hunt's room everything was in readiness. A big table had been brought up from the kitchen and placed between the windows where there was most light. On a round table beside it, spread out on a towel, were the implements which the surgeon would use. Caleb picked them up one after another and looked at them curiously: two knives, a larger and a smaller, a saw, so much like an ordinary carpenter's saw that it made him shudder, a slender, sharp-pointed hook attached to a handle, called a tenaculum; a pair of nippers, a pair of shears, a pot of a stiff kind of ointment, a strip of thin leather, a reel of coarse black thread, an assortment of bandages, and a wad of lint. There was also a china dish with a sponge on it, and a pitcher of warm water. Underneath the table, unobtrusive but sinister, stood a bucket.

Dr. Stephen, wearing the same purple broadcloth coat in which he had ridden from his home the day before, looked over the array.

"Everything there but the tourniquet," he said. "We wouldn't get far without that."

Dr. Macky hurriedly dived into the satchel behind the door.

Caleb turned to the fireplace in the corner of the room and

poked up the apple logs to a brighter flame. His own hands were clammy with nervousness. What silent torment must John Hunt be enduring now, as he lay there so quietly in bed, his eyes fixed on what far vision?

"It won't be long now, sir," said Caleb in a low voice. "Half an hour, perhaps, and it will be over."

"Well, gentlemen," said Dr. Stephen heartily. "We're ready to begin. We'll all have a dram, to stiffen our hearts and steady our hands."

He poured whiskey liberally from a bottle on the chest of drawers into four glasses and offered the first to John Hunt, who smiled faintly and shook his head.

"My best advice to you, sir, as your physician, is to take it. You'll find it helps you."

John continued firm in declining, and after a moment's hesitation Caleb too refused. The two doctors tossed off their glasses in a matter-of-fact way and swallowed a small chaser of water. Dr. Stephen took off his coat and rolled up his shirt sleeves. Then, as if a curtain fell, or a door opened, or a clock struck, the very climate of the room changed; time stopped as the serious business of the day began. Caleb forgot his clammy palms, his beating heart; his whole being flowed into a listening ear, a watchful eye, an obedient hand.

With Dr. Macky he lifted John, who proved to be unexpectedly heavy, and placed him gently on the bare table, uncovered the diseased leg.

"Do you wish me to apply a tape first, sir, as a guide?" said Dr. Macky.

"No, I don't use a guide. It isn't necessary. The tourniquet, as near the groin as you can get it. Some operators who don't wish to take the time to fasten a tape will draw a line on the skin or use a thread dipped in ink," said Dr. Stephen, addressing himself to Caleb as if he were lecturing to a class of students, "but I think that merely causes a delay when speed is of the essence."

He took his stand on the left side of the table—"If it were

the right leg, d'you see, I'd stand on the other side, in order to give my left hand more command of the upper thigh"—and motioned Caleb to the end of the table. "Your task, Mr. Middleton, is to hold the leg steady and firm—wrap that towel around it—until I tell you otherwise."

He tested the tourniquet and picked up the larger of the knives. "Now, Dr. Macky—"

Dr. Macky grasped John Hunt's thigh below the tourniquet with both hands and pulled the skin upward as tensely as possible. Caleb, feeling the motion in the lower leg, tightened his hold, concentrating on keeping the leg motionless a little above the surface of the table.

The surgeon laid the sharp edge of the knife against the outside of the leg, paused for a fraction of a second, estimating with his eye the course of the incision, then made a swift cut directed obliquely upward, carrying the knife carefully around the limb in the same direction. There was a muffled cry from John Hunt, and the muscles of his leg retracted sharply.

"The first incision goes through the integuments only. Watch carefully. Give me the other knife."

Avoiding, after one brief glance, the sight of the bitten lips, the clenched fist, the drops of sweat on the victim's forehead, Caleb fixed his eyes on Dr. Stephen's left thumb and forefinger, turning back the skin, while his right hand with the smaller knife carefully freed skin and membranes from the muscles beneath. Dr. Macky drew up the flap thus formed and held it out of the way. A short, sharp groan forced itself between John Hunt's white lips.

"The other knife. No, no, boy, the *knife!*"

Again the long blade, laid close to the under edge of the turned-back skin, cut obliquely inward through the muscle to the bone in a swift circular motion.

"The retractor—that leather piece. It goes around the bone, d'you see, against the soft parts, to prevent their being injured by the saw." He handed the end of the retractor to Dr. Macky. "Careful, dammit, don't pull on it like that! No use in tearing the muscles from the bone. The last thing we want is exfoliation. Some authorities recommend scraping the periosteum from the bone, but I don't hold with that at all. The saw. Now, gentlemen, you can't be too steady."

Caleb braced himself. This part would be less painful, he knew, than the first cutting of the skin, but it seemed nevertheless the most dreadful stage.

The saw met the bone squarely; the strokes were light, careful, short. The hideous, unforgettable, grinding noise of saw on living bone went on as if it would never cease. John Hunt moaned and moved his hands convulsively, the bloody muscles shivered.

The sound of the saw changed, then stopped, and in the same instant the living leg in Caleb's hands became a dead and severed weight. Fighting down a wave of nausea, he dropped it, towel and all, into the bucket under the table.

"The bone nippers. The sponge. Squeeze it out in warm water."

The rough points at the edge of the bone were pinched off, the bone gently wiped with the sponge to clear away the small particles that followed the saw. Caleb's part was finished. He watched the other two at their work of tying the arteries, absorbed and silent. Dr. Stephen forgot to lecture now. His fingers, which appeared so big and blunt, moved with unexpected delicacy and precision, gently drawing out the end of the femoral artery with the tenaculum, tying it with the well-waxed strands of shoemaker's thread.

"The tourniquet. Only a little."

Dr. Macky slackened the pressure of the screw. The big artery pulsed but the ligature held.

"All right. Let it go."

With all pressure removed, the blood spurted from several smaller arteries, and oozed from the whole surface of the stump, even from the bone.

"Put your finger on it, wherever you see an artery spurting, and press—not hard, moderately, regularly. Your finger, sir—"

"Do you mean me, sir?"

"Yes, you. Who else? We need three pairs of hands. Only a

little, just enough to restrain the blood. Some of them will stop of themselves. The others we'll tie."

Dr. Stephen and Dr. Macky, working together, tied four more of the smaller arteries and stopped. Caleb's finger was no longer needed. He wiped the blood away on the sponge, which he washed and squeezed out again with warm water just in time to put it into Dr. Stephen's hand for the final cleansing of the stump.

Now Dr. Macky, encircling the thigh again with both his hands, pressed the collar of integuments and muscles down to cover the end of the bone. The bandaging was begun, with a strip of cotton starting at the top of the thigh wound spirally downward close to the lip of the wound.

"We've almost finished now, sir," said Dr. Stephen, speaking for the first time to the patient. "We've only a little more to do. We're going to move you back to bed for the last part. It will be easier so."

Caleb hastily prepared the bed, pulling the sheet taut and placing across it a pad of old linen four layers thick, before they laid John gently on it, on his side as Dr. Stephen directed, with the stump underneath and the good leg bent and resting on a pillow.

"The most important thing is to keep the body relaxed and easy. You'll suffer less and the stump will be a better one. Now, Dr. Macky, if you'll raise that stump a little I'll slide this bandage underneath. It's a many-tailed bandage, sir, a modern invention that saves the patient considerable discomfort."

The blood that flowed again because of the moving from table to bed was washed away, the ends of the ligatures were carefully drawn to one side or the other and cut to an even length with the shears. Dr. Stephen sat on a chair facing the bed and swiftly, skillfully, drew the lips of the skin over the muscles, pressing the upper edge over the lower in a straight line, covering it with thick pledgets of lint spread with an ointment made of wax and oil. Over the whole he spread lint compresses, which he held in place with the tails of the bandage deftly woven and fastened.

It was finished. John lay in bed, white, exhausted, but able to manage the ghost of a smile. Already Dr. Macky had wiped the instruments and stowed them away in the bag. Caleb had summoned the servants to carry away the table and the bloody cloths and the thing in the bucket. He heard the rain again on the windowpane and the robin still singing. Answering a tap on the door, he found Elizabeth Joliffe anxious on the other side and told her that everything was all right. The amputation was a success.

"I won't come in now," she whispered. "Just let me know when I can do something for him."

Caleb took out his watch and looked at it. A century had been encompassed in less than fifty minutes for everything. He went to sit beside the bed. John's eyes lifted to him affectionately.

"It has been—" Caleb bent over to hear the faint voice which was scarcely more than a breath—"a very practical lesson—in surgery—for a prospective doctor."

Dr. Stephen grasped his hand. "Sir, you have borne it like a hero!" he exclaimed.

"I hope—I have borne it—like a Christian," said John, and he closed his eyes as his muscles twitched and a whip of pain lashed at him.

"I'll give you an opiate now and leave another for tonight, if needed. Dr. Macky will be in to see you early tomorrow, sir, and I shall be back again on Tuesday or Wednesday for the first dressing. I hope you will endeavor to lie as still as possible. Keep the muscles relaxed and the mind serene and we shall avoid spasms and hemorrhage."

Both doctors left after dinner, having given Caleb careful instructions as to what symptoms to watch for, what to do to make the patient comfortable. Thomas Wharton, returning from Meeting, reported that he had mentioned their need of a nurse to Friends there and that one of those present had promised to go immediately and put the situation before a young person whose competence and tender devotion he praised very highly. It would be late in the day before this person could be there, if she consented to come at all. Everyone was deeply concerned about dear

John Hunt, and even before dinner was over the stream of friends bringing dishes of calf's-foot jelly, custard, and chicken broth had already begun.

Caleb sat in the room all afternoon while John slept under the influence of the opiate. Rain fell steadily; the fire sank to embers. Caleb dozed.

A little commotion outside the closed door and a murmur of voices roused him at length. The next moment the door was opened and Elizabeth Joliffe was saying, "Mercy! it's dark and chilly in here! I declare, if they're not both asleep!"

Caleb rose to his feet, automatically running his hand over his hair. The nurse had come, at last.

Mrs. Joliffe crossed to the hearth, laid a log on the coals, and applied the small bellows briskly. In the flare of firelight Caleb saw the little figure that had followed her into the room: the gray dress, white-aproned, the lissom body, the nimbus of shining hair, the little flower face.

"Loveday!" he exclaimed incredulously.

"Sh-h!" she whispered. "Thee'll wake my patient!"

XXXIII

THE DAYS THAT FOLLOWED were for Caleb days of intense yet airy happiness, a sequestered time filled with bright, insubstantial beauty, like the golden light that brings to vivid color the undersides of leaves and the shadows of flowers while the unwatched clouds gather silently overhead. All his life Caleb was to remember the strange, enchanted quality of those days and the way his unreasoning heart soared.

John Hunt was better. Almost free of fever, he slept well; his appetite was good; though he spoke little, he was cheerful and even lively in his gentle way. There was a persistent rumor that the Pennsylvania Council had asked the Congress to return the exiles to its jurisdiction, which could only mean that it had determined to take action at last. And Loveday was there.

Caleb slept in the room with John and cared for him at night. He performed during the daytime the offices that were too heavy or unsuitable for a young girl. But Loveday had taken command. She knew a dozen ways to make the sick man comfortable, to ease the weariness and ache of the long lying in one position, to soothe and refresh and encourage. Under her hand the room took on new order and serenity. The clutter disappeared from the mantelpiece, the curtains hung straight and kept the light from the patient's eyes, there was a little vase of fragrant arbutus on the table by the bed, the pillow slips were smooth and cool, and the rag rugs lay straight on the floor. Loveday moved softly about the room, her step light, her voice low; she had no fussy ways.

Working closely with her, both young people held in the bond of their reverent affection for John Hunt, Caleb fell more deeply in love with her with every hour. It was not a blind, bemused infatuation that he felt. Like one surprised by a stroke of good fortune he counted the separate items of his treasure, or as a lapidarist holds his gems to the light to enjoy their color, the perfection of their shape, and their flawless purity, he was soberly aware of every facet of her character that made her different from all the other girls in the world.

Her beauty satisfied him completely, and he found fresh loveliness each hour as, unobserved, he watched her moving with slender grace about her tasks, wearing the simple gray dress in which he had first seen her. But almost more than her beauty he valued her attitude toward it, one that had not been part of his experience so far: an acceptance of it without either underestimating it or putting a false value upon it. He liked girls to know they were pretty and to expect the deference that was beauty's due—he felt it took some edge from it if they were wholly unconscious—but it bored him when they were constantly aware of it, estimating its effect or using it to provoke attentions.

But Loveday's beauty, he hold himself, was only the beginning, and he must have loved her without it, if it were possible to imagine her plain and awkward. He considered that question for a time, while his voice went on reading at John Hunt's request from John Woolman's *Journal*, pronouncing the words without the slightest impression of their meaning. She could never be plain or awkward, because the greatness of her heart must widen and deepen even the smallest and most pig-like eyes, and her tenderness express itself in the curve of even a small and thin-lipped mouth. Inward grace such as hers must inform the movements of even stiff and angular limbs.

It had been her freshness and innocence, her look of dewy cleanliness that had first attracted him so that he remembered so vividly his first sight of her walking lightly down the road in front of Philip Busch's. Even that, he saw now, was more lovable because with it went a womanliness that gave it depth and meaning, and in conjunction with her youth added a piquancy that made his heart overflow with tenderness at the thought of her. His imagination ran away, picturing her presiding at a breakfast table or holding a baby in her arms.

She had intelligence enough for a woman, he thought, and in its best form—a robust common sense combined with sensitive awareness of other people's ideas. Experience of life, and a husband's kindly tutelage, would expand it into wisdom. He thought he detected spirit and fire in the angle at which she carried her head and the willow-wand straightness of her back, but he had not yet seen her under circumstances that brought it out. He would like to put her to the test, and he busied himself happily picturing appropriate occasions.

There was humor there too, but buried. Her fault—if she had a fault—was that she took herself so seriously. She was young, she was an only child, she lived with an adoring father and aunt, and she was known and valued throughout this part of the Valley as a skillful nurse who would come to the rescue in time of need. No doubt, too, that second cousin of hers was a solemn, pompous owl who would quench any budding impulses toward humor that might venture to expose themselves. What she needed, Caleb decided, was to be teased a little, and how delighted he would be to do it.

He had a serene and unblemished confidence that her engagement to the pompous cousin would wither away and drop off like a useless and premature twig on a tree, and that he, Caleb Middleton, was the man for whom she was destined. Why else had fate brought her here to Elizabeth Joliffe's at this time?

He tried to put a curb on his voice, on his hands, on his thoughts, to remember always that John Hunt's care and comfort during these critical days were his first duty and commanded all his energy and loyalty. He succeeded in being discreet, sober, tirelessly helpful, but he could not control, because he was not aware of it, the light in his brown eyes, which danced and gleamed and followed Loveday's every motion when she was in the room, accompanied her to the door when she left, and watched eagerly its every opening, looking for her return. He could not subdue the elation in his heart.

He saw her one morning from the window, coming across the corner of the meadow with sprays of pussywillow in her hands. She was wearing a blue cape with the hood thrown back, and the morning sun played with all the lights in her red-gold curls. Behind her, her shadow moved on the awakening green of the grass, sharp and delicate as shadows are in spring. Just before she disappeared from Caleb's sight she gave a little skip and broke into a run, as if the life and joy in her could not be contained in a walk.

"I saw thee," he told her later, when they met in the wide hallway downstairs, "capering out under the trees like a spring lamb."

"Capering? I wasn't capering. I was walking with dignity."

"Dignity? Who's he? Some suitor of thine I don't know about?" He exploded into laughter at sight of her reproving face and proceeded to elaborate on the theme. "I must look out for this fellow Dignity."

"Don't be so simple, Caleb. Thee isn't funny."

She was so enchanting when she was ruffled that he revived the feeble jest in the scattered moments when they were alone, for the pleasure of seeing the color mount in her cheeks and her eyes darken with severity.

"The one I'm jealous of is that Mr. Dignity," he would say, or, politely, "How is thy friend Dignity this afternoon?" Until at length she broke down and laughed, and he had to fold his arms across his chest to keep them from going round her.

Dr. Macky came every day and on the fourth day Dr. Stephen arrived at the same time to change the dressing of the wound. It was a painful business for John Hunt, but he endured it without complaint. The wound had suppurated, though not excessively, and the bandages were hard and dry and stuck fast to the stump. When it was all over and the fresh bandages were in place, both doctors declared themselves satisfied that the patient was doing well.

They moved him into the other bed, which had been made up with clean sheets, and then sat for a time talking and watching him covertly to see how he was taking the shock of the dressing. Caleb lounged against the fireplace, resting his elbow on the mantel, and Loveday stood quiet and attentive at the foot of the bed.

"I think our young friend here has the makings of a physician," said Dr. Stephen. "He seems to think it is too late, but I tell him that it is never too late to do what you want to do. I'd be glad to have him as an apprentice—though my practice these days is not very extensive."

"That's very good of you, sir. But I am a prisoner in Winchester, and it is doubtful if the Congress would permit me to move twenty-five miles away from the rest of the company."

"If you ever get back to Philadelphia—or I might better say, when you get back to Philadelphia," Dr. Macky corrected himself hastily, "you might combine apprenticeship with lectures at the Medical College there."

"I have thought of that," said Caleb. "Even with some of the best lecturers, such as Dr. Rush, away, the courses continue, I hear, with Dr. Shippen and Dr. Parke and others."

He was grateful for Dr. Stephen's interest and encouragement, but had no desire to be apprenticed to him. James Pemberton's son-in-law, Dr. Parke, would be his choice, with the hope of an ultimate year or two in Edinburgh, when the war should be over. The rumor that the Council was again taking an interest in them had set him to speculating on what he would do if freedom should come at last.

John Hunt spoke from his bed. "Would thy father still oppose thy wish to become a doctor?"

"I don't know, sir. I rather think not, now. Sometimes I think he might not have continued firm even then, if I had persisted, that perhaps I yielded a little too soon. But even if he should—" he looked at John Hunt but he was speaking now to Loveday—"it would not be insuperable. This fall I shall have my twenty-fourth birthday and then I come into the property that my mother's father willed to me. I shall be financially independent, and I can set up my own home any time I am ready."

"Ho, ho," said Dr. Stephen jovially, "under those circumstances, why work at all?"

"Unless," said Dr. Macky sourly, "the Congress decides to confiscate all Loyalist property. Revolutions are expensive, and the money must come from somewhere."

"Their prisoners don't cost them anything at any rate," said Caleb shortly.

"Keep an open mind," said John Hunt, "and proceed as the way opens."

His voice sounded weary, and the two doctors, prescribing rest, prepared to leave. Caleb went off to see about their horses.

The next afternoon John felt so much better that he urged his nurses to go out for a breath of air.

"I'll just lie here quietly and rest," he assured them. "I promise you I'll not get up and dance a jig or commit any other rash and unseemly act. Youth needs light and sunshine, and you are both beginning to look too pale for my taste."

The air off the mountains was keen and pure. Plowing had begun and the newly turned earth had a clean, hopeful smell.

"Let's walk over to the woodlot and see what wildflowers we can find," said Loveday.

"My mother always watched for the first wildflowers. The woods around the Phoebe Ann were full of them. The white lady's-slippers were her favorite."

They broke twigs of flowering spice bush and chewed the ends, which held the whole tangy taste of spring. They mocked a squirrel that scolded them from the branch of a hickory, counted nine cedar waxwings perched on a bare bough, and stood long listening to a mockingbird which sang so near them that they could see its throat pulsing and swelling.

Inevitably he kissed her there in the woods, out of sight of the house. He took her by surprise, but she ceased to struggle when he pressed his mouth firmly down on hers. Her lips were even sweeter than he had thought they would be.

He was not prepared for her anger when he released her. Her little hand, swift as a kitten's paw but surprisingly hard, flew out and delivered a stinging slap upon his cheek.

"Caleb, thee had no right to do that! I trusted thee and thee took advantage of me. Thee knows very well I am engaged to Griffith."

He stood looking down at her, half abashed, half inclined to laugh. He had wanted to test her spirit, he thought exultantly. Now he had done it. He knew better than to apologize. In a solicitous, gingerly way he felt his cheek and allowed a hurt, reproachful look to appear on his face.

"Oh," she said uncertainly. "I've never done such a thing. Did —did I hurt thee?"

"No. No, not seriously. Just knocked a tooth out, I think."

He had gone too far. She knew he was laughing at her and her eyes flashed fury.

"This was a nice walk but it has been completely spoiled. I'm going back now, but I don't want thee to come with me."

"May I walk behind thee? Very respectfully?"

She deigned no reply to that, but turned on her heel and marched off. Caleb followed after, loving every line of her erect, indignant little person. He was not troubled by her displeasure, though he had no doubt that it was genuine. He had shocked and startled her—but she had kissed him back.

That night there came a change in John Hunt. He had been so much better that Caleb had ceased to sit up in the chair watching him, but had gone to sleep in his own bed, with his mind set as a mother's is for the least sound of distress from the other side of the room. He awoke suddenly, aware that his name had been spoken.

"Yes? I'm right here. Can I get something for thee?"

"Is there any water? I am—very—thirsty."

Caleb lit the candle and saw even as he held the cup to the dry lips that the tide which they had thought was coming in had now started to ebb.

"Is thee in pain?"

"No, very little." He spoke with an obvious effort. "Weak."

Fear mounted to Caleb's throat as he stood holding the candle and looking down upon his friend. He saw a sharper line about the nose, a transparency at the temple.

"Dear John," he said, "don't talk. Just hold on to all thy strength. I'm going to put some clothes on. Don't pay any attention to me."

Making as little stir as possible, as one might move who feared by some unregarded motion to jar the petals of a rose, Caleb pulled on shirt and breeches, stepped into his shoes, and took his jacket off the peg.

"Caleb." The voice was so low that he had to bend over the bed to hear it. "I have never had—a son—but if I had—he could not be any dearer to me—than thou—hast become."

Unable to speak, Caleb kissed John Hunt's cheek and tiptoed out of the room.

He knocked softly and steadily on Loveday's door until a sleepy voice within said, "Umm. What is it?"

He opened the door and stuck his head in. "He's worse," he whispered. "Can thee go to him right away? I'm going for Dr. Macky."

He feared as he galloped toward Winchester that John Hunt would be gone before he got back, but after all he lingered nearly two days longer.

He made no dying speeches. His eyes rested affectionately on those who tended him or came to sit with him. He was, he said once, quite composed. For several hours before his spirit finally slipped its moorings, he was unconscious. On Tuesday evening a week and two days after his operation, he died.

"The amputation was successful," Dr. Macky said. "It was his heart that failed."

Caleb helped Mrs. Joliffe to perform the last services for the body, and then he went into the empty silent parlor and cried.

Loveday, stealing into the room without a candle, found him. He felt her light hand on his shoulder before he knew she was there and turned as if she had struck him. Ashamed of his tears he was thankful for the dark.

"I am so sorry, Caleb. I can imagine what this means to thee. Even as little as I knew him, I loved him."

"I've never known anyone else like him. He was so human and understanding, and yet he was so good. I think he was the only person I've ever known—except perhaps my mother and I was too young to realize what it meant then—who actually experienced God. Other people say they believe and have faith and so on, but it was real to him."

"He loved thee very much. And thee was very good to him. I should think that might comfort thee."

"Yes. Perhaps. Thank thee, Loveday."

She slipped away as quietly as she had come. He went to the window and looked out at the shadowy garden. A weight of depression settled down upon him. It was the thirty-first of March. Seven full months had passed since he had been taken prisoner. Here they were, still in Winchester, still with no definite charges against them and only a rumored prospect of a chance to defend themselves. Two of the group had died, one of them the man who had been closer to Caleb than his own father, who had given him as no one else had ever done an inkling of the reality of the unseen, a sense of the abiding power of love. If John Hunt had only lived longer, or if only, Caleb thought with the remorse that accompanies the fresh wound of death, he had paid more attention to his words, had asked him more, he might have grasped firmly the understanding which already was receding from him.

John would be buried on Thursday at Hopewell, and after that Loveday would vanish. She would go back to her home near the Shenandoah and to the plans for her marriage, and because Caleb was tethered to Winchester by his six-mile chain he could not go after her, could not see her again until, most likely, it would be too late.

It was Loveday that he thought of that night during the hours when he could not sleep. He knew now that he loved her with heart and mind and body; that there had come to him the single opportunity of a lifetime—one given to but few people, for most make do with what chance or propinquity or interest sends them—of a marriage in which there could be such complete union that one would not know where flesh stopped and spirit began, or even what was man and what was woman. It was almost within his reach, such happiness, and yet about to recede from him merely because of obstacles imposed by his imprisonment. He composed long pleading speeches to Loveday, to her father, to Major Holmes of Winchester, to the Congress and the Council, until at length, exhausted, he flung himself without undressing upon his bed and slept.

All the next day, which was clear, cold, and windy, the house was filled with people coming and going, with messengers and arrangements. John Pemberton was the first to arrive. He had ridden out to see John Hunt, expecting to find the improvement of the previous days continuing smoothly.

Haggard with shock and grief, he sat beside the body for a time in the parlor where they had laid it. "Dear me," he kept repeating, "dear me. Poor Rachel, this will be a bitter blow to her." He turned to Caleb. "It is hard for thee too, my boy. I know how it is, because when I was young I enjoyed—under different circumstances—a somewhat similar friendship with an older Friend whom I revered. I was just thy age when I traveled in England and Scotland with John Churchman. Perhaps the name means little to young Friends now. He was an English Friend, a great spiritual leader, and his influence changed the whole direction of my life. After his death I felt for a time almost rudderless. It is men like John Churchman—John Woolman—John Hunt, who light the brand and pass it along to those who come after. Or perhaps they *are* the brand." Silent for a moment, he added, almost as an afterthought, "The spirit of man is a candle of the Lord."

The news which John Pemberton had brought with him, expecting to cheer John Hunt with it, he forgot to mention to anyone else. Miers Fisher told it a little later, riding over from Lewis Neale's in a state of excitement.

"A gentleman in Winchester had word direct from Mr. Harvie, the Winchester Congressman, that the Congress have ordered the Board of War to deliver us to the State of Pennsylvania, who will send for us shortly and bring us to trial."

John Pemberton, restored to the present, admitted that he and his brothers had had the word the day before, from the same source, and had spent the evening discussing its implications. No one had any further information than just what was contained in the bare statement from Mr. Harvie's letter.

Caleb carried the news to his cousin Edward, who still kept his bed in the mornings. Thomas Wharton joined them.

"So we shall be brought to trial," said Edward dryly. "On what charges?"

"Whatever the charge, we can clear ourselves easily enough," cried Caleb. "It is something clear and definite at last!"

"What assurance have we that they will not merely put the test oath to us once more?"

"They know that would be useless. At the worst we shall be in Pennsylvania again, facing our accusers—not in this twilight imprisonment here, away from all touch with the people who claim jurisdiction over us."

To Penington, who under the long strain had lost his ironic imperturbability and had sunk into pessimism and bitterness, the news represented only a mirage and a quagmire. To Caleb it was the first step to vindication and freedom. It removed one great barrier between himself and his love. He went in search of Loveday.

She was in the kitchen, helping Mrs. Joliffe to organize her preparations for the next day.

"With the funeral in the morning, we are certain to have a large party here for dinner afterward. Ham at one end of the table and fried chicken at the other. Dilly can make the biscuits in the morning, but we should get the ham boiled this afternoon and the chickens plucked. We'll need at least two big cakes, and custards or jellies of some sort as well."

"I can make a syllabub."

Caleb left them. It was not the time to pour out his heart to Loveday. That afternoon he got her alone in the small parlor.

"Loveday, I know this is not a suitable time to say what I am going to say to thee, but it's the only chance I shall have. Tomorrow will be even worse and then thee will be gone."

"Then don't say it, Caleb, whatever it is. Don't. Some things are better unsaid."

"But I must. I can't let thee go without a word. Thee needn't answer now, if thee doesn't want to. But thee must know—I love thee with all my heart and soul. I want to marry thee as soon as I am free, and I shall be free before very long now. There will never be anybody else for me but thee. Thee needn't say yes now if thee isn't ready. Only say that thee won't marry that cousin of thine. Just promise me that, my darling, and I won't ask thee anything more now. As soon as I'm free I'll go and ask thy father properly, and then I'll claim thy love."

She drew back, the color draining from her cheeks. "I asked thee not to say it. Thee only gives pain to thyself and me. Thee is so determined, Caleb, and so headstrong—and so handsome— thee *confuses* me. But I do love Griffith."

Caleb's vanity gave a leap when she conceded that he was handsome, but his mind suppressed it quickly, divining that to her, the innocent, serious, stubborn little angel that she was, any physical attraction he might have for her would be only a disadvantage to him, a stimulus to her loyalty to Griffith.

"And besides, the date for our wedding is all set."

"When?"

"The twenty-first of Sixth Month."

"Is thee sure thee does love him?"

"I know I do. I always have, since I was a little child and he used to come to visit—seeming very grown up and important to me—and bring me sweetmeats. And I've promised."

The note of finality in her soft voice was unmistakable. Caleb searched her face for some sign of yielding but found none. Her eyes met his, clear and unfaltering; the sudden tears that blurred their gray-blue depths he was obliged to put down to compassion.

"So thee'll go back to the Shenandoah and I'll go to Lancaster and on to Philadelphia, and thee'll be married before I ever have a chance to try to confuse thee further. Thee couldn't postpone the wedding, just till fall?"

She shook her head.

He took her unresisting hand in his, looked at it, turned it over, and kissed the palm.

"If thee should ever change thy mind," he said, "let me know."

He went out into the yard and for as long as it was light enough to see he chopped wood for tomorrow's kitchen fire. He heard voices now and then from the house. From time to time Bob, the colored boy, brought a visitor's horse to the stable or led one back to the front steps. Lydia wandered out to look at the growing pile of split logs and the scattering of chips and demanded shrilly, "Do we need all that wood?" but in a moment her mother called, "Lyddy, I want thee," and she ran off. No one else came to interrupt him. When at length he hung the axe on the wall of the dim shed and turned toward the house, the realization swept over him afresh that the only person to whom he might have talked about his pain and who could have found some ease if not an answer for it had passed beyond the final and irrevocable door.

It was raining early on the morning of the funeral, but by the time that the lines of people on foot and on horseback, the wagons and the scattering of sulkies converged upon the little stone Meetinghouse, the sun was shining on the puddles, glistening in every drop that lingered on blades of grass or rolled down twigs. Trunks of trees were black with wet, but the sky was a deep clear blue and the only clouds that remained were puffs of white moving toward the faint blue of the eastern hills.

All of the Quaker community was there, from Hopewell and Center Meetings, from Crooked Run and even from distant Fairfax, as well as many people who were not Friends. In accordance with custom the interment took place in the graveyard before everybody gathered in the Meetinghouse for an hour or more of silence broken by messages. There was not room for all to sit down, and some stood at the back.

Caleb sat on the men's side of the house between his cousin Edward and Miers Fisher. Out of the corner of his eye he could see Loveday across the aisle, motionless and remote. Her hair was hidden under a bonnet and she was wearing a sober brown stuff dress and cloak which her aunt had brought her when she and Richard Parry arrived that morning, to attend the funeral and to take Loveday home afterward.

From the facing-benches, from the body of the Meeting, and even from the back where James Pemberton's man, Richard, and some of the other servants stood in the doorway, came an outpouring of expressions of love and respect for John Hunt. Even Caleb, who had been so close to him, was amazed by the number and variety of people who had been affected by the quality of his life. Many referred to the last time he had come to Monthly Meeting and his prophetic outburst then.

When dinner at Elizabeth Joliffe's was over, Caleb with a crowd of others saw the Parrys into their chariot. Except for Isaac Zane's it was the only four-wheeled carriage in the countryside and many of the gaping children had never seen such a marvel before. The roads were so bad that the occupants would probably have been far more comfortable on horseback, but it was generally felt to be a mark of respect both to the dead and to himself that Friend Parry had brought out his coach for this occasion.

If either Loveday's father or her aunt remembered Caleb's ridiculous behavior that humiliating day that now seemed so long ago, they gave no sign of it. They greeted him with impersonal kindliness and said a brief good-by. Loveday, who had avoided his eyes throughout the day, gave him at parting her full gaze and put a cold and tremulous little hand in his.

"Farewell, Caleb," she said. "I—I won't forget thee."

XXXIV

ON THE FOURTH DAY after leaving Winchester the cavalcade of the exiles approached York. Edward Penington, whom the months of banishment and his severe illness had turned into a broken old man, yellow and haggard of face and tremulous of hand, rode with Charles Eddy in his sulky; Israel and John Pemberton rode in Israel's chaise. The rest were all on horseback, their own or borrowed mounts. The baggage, which had filled four wagons on the way from Philadelphia, required only one wagon for the return. Much of it had been used up and worn out, much left behind to be sold or given away.

Caleb rode in silence beside one of the two officers sent by the Council to escort the group. The young man, who happened to be a cousin of his sister Sue's husband, had manifested from the beginning an attitude of reserve and disapproval, which had not been dispelled by the turn-out of Quakers all along the way to greet and congratulate the returning exiles, to welcome them into their houses and entertain them with a tender and admiring respect that might suitably be offered to a cross between sainted martyrs and victorious generals. The young officers, who detested neutrals even more than Tories and who regarded Quakers as tight-fisted and Jesuitical relics from former dark ages, were outraged. Lieutenant Lang had chosen to ride by Caleb, evidently regarding him, because of his respectable relations by marriage, as less sunk in darkness than the others, but even with Caleb he was stiff and silent. For his part Caleb, though he knew he could have won the young man over with the expenditure of a little effort, did not feel like taking the trouble. His heart was heavy and his thoughts were somber.

Except for a perfunctory question or two he did not even talk about Sue and the Mercers. He knew that he·would be seeing his sister in Lancaster and probably spending two or three days with her. He would find his stepmother there too. With Mrs. James Pemberton, Mrs. Pleasants, and Mrs. Drinker, Sarah Middleton had driven from Philadelphia with an "Address to the Congress and Council" and supplies of food, medicine and clothing for the exiles. They had intended to demand permission to go all the way to Winchester but when they had reached Lancaster, finding that the prisoners were already on the point of starting home, they settled down there to wait for them, applying themselves meanwhile to working for better terms of release for them. Caleb had had a triumphant letter from his stepmother and he was looking forward to seeing her with all the enthusiasm of which his sore heart was at the moment capable and much more than he would have thought possible a year ago.

They rode through the wide rich country with the blue bulk of the South Mountain behind them and all the glory of spring at its height spread out around them. The apple trees were in full bloom and dogwoods were greenish white with promise at the edge of the woods. Birds sang on fence posts or swooped across the road under the horses' noses in all the busy purpose of the mating season.

Every step of the way through the bridal world was taking Caleb farther from Loveday. During the final week in Winchester, when they were packing up and waiting for their escort to arrive, riding about to say their farewells to friends in town, to Isaac Zane, junior, to the Meeting families, the restrictions of the six-mile limit had been forgotten. Caleb had ridden to the Parrys' house in an attempt to see Loveday once more, only to find that all the family had gone to Alexandria for a visit. The butler, recognizing Caleb, had invited him in to rest himself and had brought him a dish of tea. He sat in the room where he had sat before, looked out of the window on to the box-bordered garden where yellow cowslips and tall white narcissi were in bloom, and squirmed at the memory of that ludicrous and painful previous visit.

He had left with the butler a small package for Loveday, containing the gold love knot which he had had Goldsmith Chandlee make for him out of two of his unfortunate half-joes. He had put the pretty bauble away in his portmanteau and forgotten it until he took everything out to repack. It had been intended for Loveday from the beginning, and though he had not planned to give it to her as a gift upon her marriage to someone else, he certainly was not going to give it to any other girl. So he left the little box with the butler, wondering if Loveday would ever see it and what she would think if she did. It was a last gesture and, he had thought, riding away, it had fizzled out as flatly as every other effort in his relationship with Loveday. As flatly, in fact, he thought now, riding through the rich Pennsylvania farmland, as every other effort in all of his life. He looked back upon his twenty-three years and saw them as a futile groping in the dark, a series of failures and lost turnings. "We are all exiles," John Hunt had said once, "trying to get back to our true home."

He missed John Hunt and thought it an added turn of the screw that he should have died just before their release came—like Moses barred from the Promised Land. Although, Caleb reminded himself, they had no idea, really, what lay ahead of them: a trial and the opportunity to clear themselves, or only the test oath and renewed imprisonment, or perhaps a nominal release and the confiscation of their property.

The first report, in the letter from Mr. Harvie, had said they were to be brought to trial. The next, a Resolution of the Council dated April eighth, ordered that they be brought to Shippensburg "and there enlarged," at the same time being informed of a law recently passed by which persons going into British-held Philadelphia "on any pretense whatsoever" without obtaining written permission from General Washington, the Congress, or the Council, were liable to fine and imprisonment. Furthermore, the Council ordered that the whole expense of arresting and confining the prisoners, the expenses of their journey to Virginia and all other incidental charges were to be paid by the said prisoners. This blast was followed several days later by a letter from Timothy Matlack, the Secretary of the Council, friendly in tone, saying that at the request of Phoebe Pemberton, Sarah Middleton, Mary Pleasants, and Eliza Drinker, the place of their release had been changed from Shippensburg to Lancaster, which, he pointed out, was greatly in their favor.

The fact that the four women had had a chance to present their Address and that it had had some result was a good omen, and Caleb, turning away from the past as he saw the spire of a church pricking into the sky above the trees ahead, began to look forward to the future with some feeling of pleasure.

York, which had been a pleasant and flourishing village a few years earlier, had grown overnight into a hobbledehoy of a town, with the influx of Congressmen, their wives, and all the men who follow a Congress in search of favors or the hope of a good stroke of business. As they crossed the bridge over Codorus Creek, Lieutenant Lang pointed out the house where Tom Paine lived and a little later, at the corner of Market and Beaver Streets, the building where Mr. Franklin's press printed the Continental bills. Caleb looked with some interest at the source of the money the value of which he had been accused of attempting to depreciate by having his half-joes changed in Lancaster instead of Winchester. He would have been grateful if they had printed an extra roll for him now. When he had paid Elizabeth Joliffe's almost painfully moderate charges for himself and his mare during all the months of warm and generous hospitality, small as the sum was it left almost nothing in his pocket. He hoped that his stepmother had come well provided.

They reached George Updegraff's ordinary and rode into the yard. Caleb dismounted and led Ladybird into the stable, where he unsaddled, fed, and watered her himself, since there were not enough stableboys to take care of so many horses at once. He went into the house, which was large and cool, dim after the bright light outside, and hunted up a place to wash his hands and brush his coat. When he came downstairs again he found the rest of his party receiving a caller in the parlor. From the stir in the room he knew that their guest was a man of some consequence, but even when the group parted and he saw a tall genial man in a Continental uniform with a general's epaulets he had no idea who it was.

"Friend Gates," said Edward Penington, obstinately Quaker to the last ditch, "I should like to present my cousin, Caleb Middleton, junior."

Caleb met the hero of Saratoga and the President of the Board of War with interest. There had been much talk and rumor about him during the winter, which had drifted even as far as Quaker circles in Winchester. He was known to have criticized Washington bitterly for slackness and inaction and it was widely inferred that he considered himself a suitable person to take over Washington's job. The committee sent to Valley Forge to investigate the Commander-in-Chief had, however, brought back a favorable report. But Gates's position as President of the Board of War with permission to serve in the field, so that he was Washington's superior and yet at the same time under his command, must have been a severe trial to Washington. Caleb, who had been deeply impressed by the nobility of General Washington's person and bearing that day of the march-through last August, regarded Horatio Gates with reserve and wondered just why he was going out of his way now to conciliate the Quaker exiles from Philadelphia.

"If I had been in Philadelphia at the time of your being arrested and sent into exile," he said suavely, "I should have prevented it."

Then why, Caleb asked silently, didn't you exert your influence this winter to bring us to trial? That was all we asked.

"We have just had intelligence from London," the General continued, "that will no doubt be pleasing to you who have the peace as well as the prosperity of this country so much at heart. The Parliament of Great Britain has passed Resolutions, by which they will repeal several of the Acts oppressive to America. They have appointed commissioners to come to this country to treat with us and settle the unhappy contest." He stopped, as if waiting for a burst of joy and approval.

"This is indeed good news," said Israel Pemberton cautiously, "if all is as favorable as it appears to be. I should like to know more—what Acts the Parliament is ready to repeal, how much power to negotiate will be given to the commissioners, and with what disposition the Congress is prepared to receive them."

"I think that this time Great Britain has agreed to all that the Americans have hitherto asked or contended for, but of course we have had only a preliminary report. We shall have to await further intelligence from the commissioners themselves. But I thought you would find it heartening. I hope that the conditions of your exile have not been too severe."

"We have had much to be thankful for," said John Pemberton, "especially when I think of the sufferings of the primitive Friends, who were beaten and branded and imprisoned in foul dungeons with not even straw to lie upon. We have indeed been favored by divine support and on the whole preserved from murmuring."

"My dear sir," the General waved his hand deprecatingly, "those persecutions you mention were more than a century ago. Even in England such things are unheard of today, and this is America. Was your journey hither made without mishap or inconvenience?"

"It was very comfortable, thank thee." Samuel Pleasants now took up the thread of the conversation. "We have come to York on our way to Lancaster, and most of us intend to spend tonight here, to rest our horses. But some would like to press on today without waiting for the guard to accompany them, if thou approves of it. I do not know if we require a pass for that purpose?"

"It might perhaps be just as well to have one, in case you encounter some overzealous militia." The General turned to the desk, where he found a sheet of paper and a quill of which he complained humorously. He scratched a line or two, sanded it, and gave it to Sammy. "That will get you past any scouting parties or the like. There is another matter. The wind has been very high at the Susquehanna ferry. I'll have my aide give you an order to Major Eyre, who is commanding officer there, to assist you over, if that should be necessary." With a further cheerful assurance of good will, he departed, and a little later a messenger came from his headquarters next door with a note for Major Eyre at Wright's Ferry.

Since the day was already half spent and Lancaster was twenty-four miles away with a wind-blown river to cross, most of the group decided to remain where they were for the night. Caleb with Sammy Pleasants and James Pemberton, whose wives were waiting for them in Lancaster, decided to go on immediately after dinner.

They were grateful for General Gates's letter when they reached the ferry, for the wind was high and the public boats all hugged the opposite shore. Four ship carpenters, who were building boats for the American service, put them across, and Major Eyre, on the far side, sent the ferryboat back for their horses. The whole process took close to two hours, and it was after suppertime when at length the three reached the town which had been the Pennsylvania capital for the last six months. Caleb's companions parted from him at the main street. Their wives were lodging with a Quaker family on the Sadsbury Road beyond the town and they rode on eagerly.

The sun had set and candles were lit when Caleb reached the house under the big oaks where Sarah Middleton was staying with Sue and her parents-in-law. The sound of horses' hooves brought all the family to the door, and Caleb, seeing their joy and feeling the genuine warmth of their affection, was happy for the first time since he started on his homeward trip.

Sue with her lusty son on her arm and another baby already expected was the embodiment of happy and fruitful young womanhood. She was tall, with flashing brown eyes, more nose than chin, and a loud, cheerful voice.

Caleb kissed her and kissed the soft fluff on the top of the baby's head, and turned to his stepmother, who embraced him, crying, "Caleb, I can hardly believe we've really got you at last! It seems too good to be true!"

Square, squat, hairy, almost bursting out of her fashionable silk gown, she beamed at him in self-forgetting delight. For the first time he saw beyond her homely exterior to the robust beauty within.

"It was good of thee to come, Mother. How's Father?"

"Better. Very eager to see you. He can hardly wait. This winter has been a great trial to him, but he has been remarkably patient— all things considered. Let me look at you, Caleb. You're thinner— more mature—but I do believe that you're taller and handsomer than ever. How far have you ridden today? You must be tired and hungry and I keep you standing here. Come in, come in."

Sue's husband was with Washington at Valley Forge. His father was a prosperous lawyer, his mother the daughter of a New York merchant. Their house in Lancaster had all the comforts and ele- gancies of city living. There were plenty of well-trained servants. A neat nursemaid came to take the baby after his uncle had ad- mired him sufficiently, a man in dark livery brought Caleb supper in the big dining room where candlelight winked on glass prisms and on china with small prim flowers and gold borders, and the paneled walls were painted a cool green.

After Caleb had eaten his fill, he and Sarah and Sue sat in what was called the Blue Parlor talking till late.

Sarah was jubilant over the success of the ladies' mission. "If it hadn't been for us," she pointed out, "you'd have been turned loose in Shippensburg to find your way home without passes, liable to be taken up and imprisoned and fined at any time. You still haven't got passes, but you're in Lancaster where you can attend to that."

"What we want is to hear the charges and speak in our own defense."

"You'll have to arrange that for yourselves! We've done all we could!"

"You've done a great deal and we're all thankful to you. How did it come about?"

"It was my idea in the first place. I thought of it way back in January when we didn't know where you were. I thought we would just go to General Washington and plead with him for your freedom. I went to Mrs. Drinker about it and she thought we ought to go to Congress, but that we'd better wait. So we waited—*and* waited—till we got word that you were sick and Edward and others and that your stores of tea and medicines were all used up and then we thought we'd go all the way to Winchester. We had a number of meetings with other wives in various houses. Then we heard that Mr. Gilpin died—wasn't that too bad, such a good man, and three young children! The weighty Friends had to sit on it—you know how it is—and in the end the four of us came in Polly Pleasants' coach. Mrs. Israel Pemberton would have liked to come, but she is seventy-four—did you know that? Twelve years older than her husband! She doesn't look it. Where was I? Oh, Mr. Israel Morris accompanied us on horseback. We felt rather doubtful about him, especially Eliza. She was determined that he was not to do our talking for us with the Council. But he has really been very helpful."

"But how did you get through the American lines?"

"Oh, we went straight to headquarters at Valley Forge and asked General Washington for permission."

"Did you see the General himself?"

"We certainly did. He invited us to dinner, and we had an elegant dinner with him and General Lee and General Greene and fifteen other officers. Mrs. Washington was there too. She's a pretty, sociable kind of woman. General Washington gave us a pass to go through the lines and a letter to President Wharton saying we wanted permission to go to Winchester and protection for the coach, and then he wrote, *'Humanity itself pleads in their behalf.'* He couldn't have written much more strongly than that, could he?"

"It takes a big man to take time for the troubles of people who aren't of any importance to him," said Caleb thoughtfully.

"It took us four days to get here. We spent the nights with Quaker families along the way. How you Friends do rally round each other! It is like belonging to an enormous family with a very strong sense of family duty and unity. I don't think other churches are like that. I shouldn't expect strangers to lodge and feed me just because I am an Episcopalian. The roads were unspeakable. The armies marching over them have cut them up and then the rains added to the mess. We didn't see the sun for a week. We were out of the coach almost as much as we were in it. In one place we climbed three fences to get around the mud. And when we forded Conestoga Creek the water came right into the coach and wet our feet. I thought we should be caught in the coach and drowned like rats."

"I think they were very brave," said Sue. "I should have been terrified."

"They *were* brave. The whole thing was brave. Did you have any trouble seeing the Council when you got here?"

"Wait till you hear about that! We went straight to Mr. Wharton's door. We were admitted right away, but there were a number of others present, so we asked to see him alone, but he said he was just going out to coffee. He was wearing his sword. They say he wears it all the time, morning, noon, and night, isn't that ridiculous? So we had to wait till the next day. Timothy Matlack came to see us and advise us. He appears very obliging, but I fear it is from the teeth outward. He has that brick house you passed before you turned the corner to come here. We had a dish of tea with his wife, who seemed very glad to see us. She and Polly Pleasants are old friends. One of the members of the Council lives with the Matlacks and we talked to him and two others. Mr. Matlack took our Address to the Council meeting and said he would come back for us. We waited an hour and then he came and said our presence was not necessary. Not necessary! Just putting us off. I was real cross because I thought we should do better if we talked to them ourselves. But they did change the

orders from Shippensburg to Lancaster. We knew by that time, of
course, that you were going to be released and there was no need
for us to go to Winchester."

"What was in your Address? Did you keep a copy of it?"

"Yes. Sue, what did I do with it? We wrote it in Philadelphia
before we left. Everybody had a hand in it. Such a to-do you can't
imagine. All the ministers and elders or whatever you call them
had to look at it and the time they spent haggling over a word
here and a word there! But we stuck to our own ideas and said
what we wanted to say ourselves. We all signed it, all the wives
of the prisoners and three mothers and the Fishers' sister Esther.
Thank you, dear. Here, Caleb, read it for yourself."

"It's shorter than the ones we write," commented Caleb, running his eye down the page. " 'The melancholy account we have
lately received of the indisposition of our beloved husbands and
children, and that the awful messenger—death—has made an
inroad on one of their number—' That was Thomas Gilpin, I
suppose. Haven't you heard about John Hunt?"

"Not till after we got here. That was very sad. You liked him
especially, didn't you?"

"He was the best of us all. This is a good point. 'This application to you is entirely an act of our own. We have not consulted
our absent friends.' " He read it to the end, folded it, and returned
it to Sarah. "It's a very strong appeal, better than most of ours.
Have you heard anything about peace Resolutions in the British
Parliament and the commissioners who are to come over to treat
with America? General Gates was full of it when we saw him today
in York."

"Oh, that's been all over the town these two days. There's
nothing to it. The British will grant everything—they say—except
independence, and the Congress will not yield on that, especially
now that the French have made an alliance with us and recognized
Mr. Franklin as the ambassador from a free country. Hadn't you
heard that? It has been common property for a week or more.

They are waiting for some final official word before it is to be publicly celebrated throughout the land."

Caleb heard this with excitement. Recognition, and a promise of help from a powerful ally! It marked a point from which there could be no going back, no possibility of accommodation with Great Britain now. The struggle for independence would be carried through to its conclusion and to—it must be—ultimate victory. The feeble, scattered little army, the discredited Congress, the divided people were committed before the world to make a reality of the nationhood which they had assumed. They could no longer return like a child to its father's tyrannical but protective care; they must win their way through to independent life, however bitter the suffering.

The rest of the exiles came to Lancaster the following morning, which was Saturday, and the group found a central and convenient meeting place in the Mercers' parlor. They appointed a committee consisting of Israel Pemberton, Henry Drinker, and, to his own surprise, Caleb Middleton, junior, to go to President Thomas Wharton. Thomas Wharton, senior, was at first named but he declined saying that his relations with his cousin would in no way be conducive to the success of the mission.

The three waited on Thomas Wharton, junior, after dinner. They found him alone, wearing, Caleb noted with amusement, his sword. He did not look well; his eyes were dull and his complexion had a gray cast; he seemed to be hearing and seeing them from a long distance. Though he had known Israel Pemberton and Henry Drinker well over long years of association, he greeted them impersonally.

Israel Pemberton spoke first. "We have come to acquaint thee with the fact of our being come to Lancaster, agreeably to the appointment of Council."

"So I have been informed by Mr. Matlack. Pray be seated."

"We should like to have an interview with the Council," said Henry Drinker. "We are ready to answer any charges that they have against us—and presumably they have some reason why they felt justified in depriving us of our liberty and keeping us in exile for so long."

"The Council has adjourned until Monday morning. I will deliver your message to them when they meet, but I recommend to you that you put in writing whatever you think necessary to say to them. I know that they will not grant you a personal interview."

He spoke civilly enough, but there was nothing further to be said. Heavily they made their farewells and went down the street under a shower of tassels falling from oak trees in blossom.

After Meeting for worship the next morning in the Meetinghouse, they got a word with Timothy Matlack, who, to the surprise of local Friends, had attended Meeting for the first time in years.

"The Council won't see you," he said. "It's no use expecting it. But I'll see that your Memorial is read, if it's short."

They composed their final appeal to the Council that afternoon, the last of a long line of Remonstrances, Addresses, and Memorials. This one at least was short, whittled down to the bare minimum. For the last time Caleb made a fair copy and they all signed it, sixteen now instead of twenty.

> TO THE PRESIDENT AND COUNCIL OF PENNSYLVANIA:
> We, the subscribers, inhabitants of the city of Philadelphia, having been there arrested and banished to Winchester in Virginia by your authority, upon groundless suspicions, without any offense being laid to our charge; and being now brought to this place by your messenger after a captivity of near eight months, think it our duty to apply to you to be reinstated in the full enjoyment of the liberty of which we have been so long deprived. We are your real friends, THOMAS FISHER, etc.

The committee took the Memorial to the inn where the Council met and having delivered it to the secretary sat down in an anteroom to wait, on the chance that they might even yet be admitted to face their accusers. At the end of two hours Colonel Matlack appeared.

"The subject matter of your Memorial has been debated," he reported, "and the Council has ordered that you be sent to Potts-grove and there discharged from confinement. You will be fur-nished with a copy of the Resolution, which will be deemed a discharge, and also with a pass for each one of you permitting you to pass unmolested into the County of Philadelphia. This will complete the matter. I must add emphatically that any further application on the subject is unnecessary. The Council will not hear you."

A moment of incredulous silence followed.

"But this," exclaimed Israel Pemberton indignantly, "is mani-festly unjust and unreasonable. This order is to be *deemed* a dis-charge. It contains no acknowledgment of our innocence, no state-ment restoring us to full liberty. You have violently separated us from our families, unjustly detained us in exile, and now at the end, as in the beginning, you refuse to hear us in our own de-fense!"

"I can only repeat, sir, any further application will be useless. I beg of you not to attempt it. It would only take your time to no purpose and that of the Council, who have affairs of public im-portance to attend to."

"There is nothing we can say that will move you?"

"Nothing. The passes will be delivered to you at your lodgings. The escort is ready to accompany you to Pottsgrove."

It was freedom at last, thought Caleb, but what a shabby free-dom.

"Colonel Matlack," he said, detaining him as he prepared to return to the Council room, "the government of Pennsylvania and of the United States is based upon principles of freedom and re-sistance to tyranny and oppression, is it not?"

"I think it is not necessary for me to answer that, Mr. Middle-ton."

They looked at one another squarely. It crossed Caleb's mind that Timothy Matlack eight months earlier had done him the favor of substituting his name for his father's and perhaps now expected some acknowledgment. He let the thought slip past, intent on what he had in his mind to say. Long ago he had ceased to think of himself as his father's substitute, so completely had he identified himself with the others and with the fundamental truths on which they had taken their stand.

"How do you reconcile these principles of liberty and justice with the treatment that has been accorded us?"

"Mr. Middleton, in an internecine struggle for existence there can be no neutrals."

"You should know—and Thomas Wharton, junior, and others who are or have been Friends—that since Quakers cannot conscientiously fight for you they are equally debarred from fighting against you. But there is a principle at stake more important than what happens to a handful of Quakers, and that is whether a government based upon freedom can live if it does not guarantee to its citizens freedom of conscience and protection against imprisonment without the chance of defending themselves."

Timothy Matlack, who was known for the violence of his temper, made a quick gesture with his hand indicating that he had heard all this before and that his patience was nearing an end.

"No, please, let me finish. This is of the utmost importance to me because I have vital decisions to make. We have been standing out for eight months for a principle, the basic principle of civil and religious liberty. Two of our group have died. I have thought that the government of the United States was based upon the same principle, but if the Congress and the Council do not recognize that it even enters into our case, what am I to think of the future of our country?"

The look of anger on Matlack's long, heavy face softened to one of understanding and even sympathy for Caleb's passionate earnestness.

"I understand what you are driving at. You are young, Mr. Middleton, and idealistic, but you must not expect perfection of men and politicians under great stress. An open and free statement of error in a private person is becoming. It is otherwise when governments make mistakes; you must not expect an apology. Governments, though they must appear infallible, are made up after all of ordinary, faulty, harassed men who are in the main striving to do their best for their country. If the result is a little more than half good, that is perhaps as much as we can expect. The only way to increase the proportion is for more men of vision and devotion to offer their services to their country. But this I will tell you for your enlightenment and comfort: when the Council decided to ask the Congress to return the Virginia exiles to our jurisdiction in order to release them, it did so because—and this is spread upon the records of the Congress—'the dangerous example which their longer continuance in banishment may afford on future occasions has already given uneasiness to some good friends to the independency of these States.' Does that remove any of your doubts?"

"I see," said Caleb soberly. "Thank you."

It was not very much, not what he had expected. But as he turned over in his mind this inadequate, elliptical, almost casual expression of the reason for the Council's decision, upon which the Congress had acted, he came to feel that it was of value, that it was perhaps all that he ought to have expected, and enough to go on with. It represented an action taken for a particular occasion, to avoid a bad precedent, rather than a statement of an enduring principle. Yet perhaps it was only by particular acts that general principles could ever be established, and then not once but over and over again. And in the building and preserving of a nation's freedom both kinds of citizens had their essential part: individuals determined to follow their consciences at cost to themselves and against the drift of public opinion, without expecting exoneration and praise at the end; and faulty, harassed men in government striving in the main to serve their country's interests, correcting mistakes as best they could as they went along.

XXXV

LOVEDAY CLOSED HER BEDROOM door carefully and pressed against it until the latch caught with a little click. She was home again. She had said good-night to her father and Aunt Mary; she had thanked Nannie for unpacking her portmanteau and shooed her out of the room. She was alone for the first time in more than two weeks.

Visiting, you are never alone. In Alexandria, at Cousin Anna and Cousin John's, she had shared a room with Aunt Mary, and in the daytime Griffith was always with her. He had so much to show her and to tell her and to teach her, for he was twelve years older than she, that he filled every minute with a flow of talk. "If thee's got a minute, Loveday," he said over and over, like a refrain, "I want thee to see the secretary that Father had made for me when I was fourteen. I wrote my first brief at that desk." Or, "Don't run away. Thee has plenty of time to dress for Meeting. We have a minute now, and I want to explain to thee how a lawyer's wife can help him—"

The only time she was alone in that house, thought Loveday with a little gulp of laughter, was when she was in the necessary. It was a very splendid one, of brick, with a little fan doorway, but one couldn't stay there forever.

Her room looked simple and country-like after the house in Alexandria, the mantel unadorned, the floor bare, with only a little braided mat by the bed, the bed-curtains of white muslin, hemmed, without fringe, the chest of drawers made of cherry wood from their own trees by an itinerant cabinetmaker, gleaming softly in the candlelight but with none of the carvings or the shiny brass handles of the chest-on-chest in Cousin Anna's spare bedroom. But Nannie had put a spray of apple blossom in the blue vase on the table and its delicate fragrance mingled with the faint spicy odor of the pomander hanging on the bedpost; the bed had been turned down and her nightgown and slippers laid out; the room was welcoming and spacious and suddenly so dear that she did not want to leave it, ever.

The three days in the coach, bumped and jolted and tossed over rough roads, fell away, and the two weeks of visiting, of company manners and of endless appreciation, of paying attention to everything Griffith said, fell away too. Griffith was a great talker, much more than she had realized. Or perhaps it was only because he felt he had to make her understand everything about him before they were married, and there was so little time. He talked so much and so fast—she took off her dress, the brown one she had worn to dear John Hunt's funeral, and laid it thoughtfully over a chair —and he seemed to get so excited over it, that he was just a little bit exhausting.

She had wanted to tell him about dear John Hunt, for though she was young and there was very little in her life that was interesting, she had known—had nursed—had loved a rare and beautiful character, and had sat beside him when he died. She had, being close to him, undergone some change, some enlargement of her own spirit, and all her life something of John Hunt would shape her words and thoughts. Perhaps it was because of him and the sorrow that she felt for him that she carried a heaviness of heart like a stone inside her, and not all the plans for the wedding or for the home they would build could lift its weight from her. She had tried several times to tell Griffith about John Hunt, but always he had interrupted her, intent on expressing some thought of his own.

"Griffith, if thee has a minute," she had said at last, playfully but with determination adopting his own favorite phrase, "I want to tell thee about John Hunt. Oh, I *wish* thee could have known him. He was so gentle but so—so penetrating—"

"Thee mustn't be morbid," he had said, kissing her. "When we are married thee is not to nurse anybody but me—and of course our children."

He was always kissing her. She poured water from the flowered pitcher into the basin and washed her face, which was suddenly heated by the memory of Griffith's kisses. She felt ashamed. His lips were so soft and so wet—squashy. (Caleb's lips were hard and searching and piercingly sweet. But she must not think of that.)

She scrubbed her face dry with the towel. Yes, she thought with a rebellious rush, and Caleb was lean and lithe, while Griffith already had a settled look. Oh, he was a fine, tall, well-favored man, of course, but he spent too much of his time sitting, and when he walked his coattails bulged rhythmically.

But she was going to marry Griffith. They were going to have the whole second floor of the ell in Cousin Anna and Cousin John's house, with Griffith's secretary in the sitting room and Griffith's wing chair and his books and his diploma from William and Mary and his maps and his charts and the instruments that he explained to her over and over and she still couldn't understand. He knew a great deal about ships and navigation and he was going to specialize in maritime law. In the fall they would begin to build their own house on a lot which his father had given him, which had a fine view of the Potomac River.

The ponderous wheels of a Quaker marriage had already begun to turn. They had "passed Meeting" once. They had written to the Monthly Meeting at Crooked Run declaring their intention to marry. Griffith's parents and Loveday's father had written letters conveying their consent. A committee had been appointed to visit both and ascertain their "clearness." At the next Monthly Meeting the committee would make its report, and overseers would be appointed to have charge over the wedding itself. The date was tentatively set for Sixth Month twenty-first.

The soft cambric folds of her nightgown descended over her head and fell around her slim body. She pulled her blue wool dressing gown around her, for the spring evening was chilly. She was not ready to go to bed yet. She would brush her hair a hundred times and she would say her prayers properly. How could anyone say her prayers right with Aunt Mary in the room, reading a chapter of the Bible and shutting the book with a slap, plumping down on her knees, and beginning to talk about closing the window and blowing out the candle almost before she opened her eyes and heaved herself, gasping, to her feet again?

What was "clearness," exactly? To the committee it meant, evidently, that they had not given promises to anyone else. So that she was "clear" as to Griffith but obviously not clear for Caleb. And she had told him so and he was to forget her and she was to forget him. She was not to think of his deep-set brown eyes gleaming with laughter or clouded with pain, or of his thin, skillful, long-fingered hands (Griffith's fingers were short and stubby) or of his tenderness and strength as he lifted John Hunt, or— She was not to think of Caleb.

But she did think of Caleb. If it were not for her constant, vigilant control of her thoughts she would be thinking of him all the time, and wasn't that also a sin against clearness, the more deadly because it was secret and hidden?

There was a tap at the door and before Loveday could say, "Come in," Aunt Mary in her gray dressing gown with her nightcap tied under her chin, had swept into the room. She had a cup in one hand and a teaspoon in the other.

"Loveday, isn't thee in bed yet?"

"No, I'm brushing my hair."

"I've brought thee a dose of sulphur and molasses. Thy father and I both think thee looks peakèd, and there's nothing like sulphur and molasses for clearing the blood in the spring. Now don't make a fuss, dear, just take it right down, and thee'll feel better tomorrow."

The gritty stuff, sweet in a nasty way, stuck to Loveday's lips and tongue as she obediently spooned it from the cup and swallowed it. She got some water from the washstand to take the taste away and handed the cup and spoon back to Aunt Mary, smiling at her affectionately—and pityingly. Poor Aunt Mary, she thought, forty at least. Once she had married and loved, or thought she had, and had a little baby that never lived, and lost her husband, all so long ago that she had forgotten it and now thought there was nothing like sulphur and molasses.

"Hop into bed, Loveday, and I'll tuck thee in."

Loveday wielded her hairbrush. "Sixty-seven, sixty-eight, sixty-nine," she counted, choosing numbers large enough to suggest that she had brushed enough already to make it worth while to continue to the hundred mark, yet small enough to make it desirable for her to get on with the job if it was not to take all night.

"Thy hair's very well as it is, it's thy face that needs help. Thee has dark shadows under thy eyes and thee's had no color in thy cheeks for days. Thee needs a good night's sleep now. Is anything worrying thee?"

"Seventy, seventy-one, seventy-two," continued Loveday, sweetly obstinate, as she could be.

"Well, if thee's going to be like that, there's nothing more for me to say."

Loveday flung the brush on the bed and ran to hug her aunt, fairly strangling her in a fiercely affectionate, silent embrace.

"Mercy!" said Mary Freame, returning it as well as she could, impeded by the cup and spoon. "Girls!" she muttered helplessly, finding herself on the other side of the door. "I'm certainly thankful I don't have to go through being young again."

Gathering her robe around her and abandoning the brush and the prayers, Loveday swung herself up onto the broad sill of the west window and clasped her arms around her knees. It was raining outside, a gentle spring rain falling on the leaves of the ivy, splashing a little now and then on the sill. She could see the wet gleam of the branches of the big oak, still bare, though there was a softening pattern of tassels and swelling leaves against the cloudy sky.

There were none of the town sounds that she had grown accustomed to: the footsteps on the sidewalk, the creak of a wheel, the sound of voices. She heard only the patter of the rain and a familiar, half-forgotten, almost mechanical noise, as of a saw cutting through wood or a clock being wound in the distance, over and over, with pauses in between. The monkey-faced owls were bringing up their young in the big oak again.

If only, thought Loveday, drawing her knees up close under her chin, she could recapture the feeling she had had when she and Griffith were first engaged, go back over the months to that time which had seemed so magical and which now appeared remote and unreal.

They had gone to Grandfather's plantation near Alexandria at Christmastime, she and Father and Aunt Mary, and Griffith had been there, part of a big family gathering. Friends did not pay very much attention to Christmas as a general rule, but last Twelfth Month twenty-sixth was Grandfather's seventieth birthday, and all the relatives had rallied round. There were swarms of children always on the run, from the hay barn to the attic, the big ones ahead, the little ones puffing behind, but for the first time Loveday had not been with them. Everyone had had something to say about Loveday's having grown up. She moved sedately in a whole new world, suddenly on the same level with Cousin Griffith, who had always seemed to her a superior being.

He was tall and fair-haired and substantial, not only in his person but in his mind and in his position in the world. He had been to the college at Williamsburg, he had traveled for a year in England and France, he had read law in Alexandria, and he had won his first case. But still he was a plain Friend, sober in his dress and speech, beginning to take a part in the Monthly Meeting. On First Day at Meeting for worship, he had risen to give a message and he had spoken modestly, as became a young man, yet with the assurance of one who spoke not in his own voice but as a channel for the Spirit.

Thinking of him now, recalling him as she saw him then, Loveday could remember her feeling of awe and excitement when he spoke to her after Meeting, gravely yet urgently, and asked her if she would take a walk with him after dinner.

It had been a mild winter day, with a little color lingering in the leaves that still clung to the oaks and a few sweet limp roses still in the garden. They had taken the favorite First Day afternoon walk of courting couples, down to the creek and across the bridge, and back through the woods and over the west field to the end of the garden. There were a few chestnuts in brown burrs on the ground, and blue jays and redbirds flashed their brilliant way among the bushes in the garden.

Speaking slowly and in a hushed sort of voice that made the occasion very solemn, Griffith told her that he had loved her ever since she was a little girl of ten with her golden curls flying as he pushed her in the swing that used to hang from the big maple tree—did she remember? He had known then that she was the only girl for him and he had vowed to wait for her to grow up. Now she was sixteen and old enough to be married. Did she think she could care for him?

The wonder of it! Cousin Griffith, so important, so respected, so wise and good, noticing little Loveday Parry from the other side of the Blue Ridge, waiting six long years for her, asking her so tenderly and so humbly if she could care for him!

He had kissed her, reverently, gently, lightly as if a kitten's paw had touched her lips—not at all as he kissed her now—and they had gone at once to talk to Father.

Father had not been surprised. He had long thought something of the kind might happen. He was fond of Griffith, he thought it eminently suitable. True, Griffith was twelve years older than Loveday, but he himself had been ten years older than Loveday's mother, and no marriage could have been happier than theirs. His only objection was that Loveday was too young. "I counted on having my little girl a few years more."

At the thought of leaving Father lonely and deserted, Loveday was ready to abjure marriage altogether, but Griffith began to speak, in his persuasive, reasoning voice. He had waited six years already, he was twenty-eight, it was time he established himself in life.

Father had promised to reconsider after Loveday had had a little more time to think it over, but somehow before the day was out everybody knew that Loveday and Griffith were to be married in Sixth Month, and the joyful interest in their engagement had almost put Grandfather's seventieth birthday in the shade.

She could remember how it felt, every minute of it, her happiness, her admiring love for Griffith, her humble and wondering gratefulness because he had chosen her and had waited all those years when she was so unconscious and careless—but she could not feel it again. She could only feel that odd heaviness inside, as if she had eaten some sad pastry. It was as if a veil hung between those happy, innocent days and now, a veil made of her sense of guilt because she had begun to pick flaws in Griffith, who was just as splendid as he had been before, and because she could not forget Caleb, who had laughed at her and teased her, who for a week had been almost a part of herself as they together loved and served dear John Hunt.

Feeling cramped and chilly and a little drowsy, she thought that now she might be able to go to sleep. But as soon as she got into bed she was wide awake again, and her thoughts were racing.

Marriage, she knew, was not all new houses and kisses and passing Meeting. It was also bed, where something happened which was indelicate if thought about beforehand but sacred when the right time came. She would die of embarrassment, getting into bed with Griffith!

She rolled over and the happy realization came to her that for the first time in over two weeks she had her bed to herself, without Aunt Mary. The thought was so exhilarating that she stretched herself crosswise in the wide bed and let her head hang over the side, her hair falling down to the floor behind her. The rain kept dripping outside and the monkey-faced owls continued to grind out their peculiar, sad, mysterious noises.

What she must do, she thought with sudden energy, resuming

her normal position in bed, was to see Caleb again. Today was Fifth Day. They must go to Meeting at Hopewell on First Day. There had been some talk, she remembered of the prisoners' being released, or promised a chance to defend themselves, but it had been quite vague; it would take time before they could really get away.

She would see him again, and then she would know.

So now she could go to sleep.

She straightened her nightgown, thumped the pillows, pulled the covers up to her chin, and closed her eyes. Downstairs the big clock struck twelve.

The first time she had seen Caleb, the very first, was that day at Edward Preston's, before little Neddie died. It was raining then too. She had gone to the door to let the doctor in, and Caleb had been standing there. That picture of Caleb was quite different from all the others in her mind, because it was the first, and so a little separate, and very distinct. She had seen someone young and tall, with broad shoulders, brown eyes intent and shining but not glittery as some brown eyes were, soft, with depth, and a straight nose and smiling mouth, a square-cut chin, very clean and firm.

"I'm not a doctor," he had said, "I'd give anything if I were."

She had felt his sorrow.

Out in the kitchen, when she fetched the cider, he had taken liberties with her curls, and so she had not come down again after Catherine Preston had called up upstairs. But that was his way, teasing, admiring. No one had teased her before. She had to learn how to take it. Even when John Hunt was so ill, Caleb had teased her.

John Hunt loved Caleb. It was in his eyes and his voice, in his veined, transparent, trembling hand as he lifted it to touch Caleb's arm.

But she was going too fast. That was much later. She had seen Caleb at the Prestons', and then that day he had come here to see her, that *funny* time—

The clock struck again, but whether it was twelve-thirty or one or one-thirty, she did not know. She heard it strike two and three and four. She was afloat now on a broad stream and she had no wish to pull herself to land. When she had recalled every time she had seen Caleb and everything he said, every look and gesture, then she began to dream other times of seeing him, imagining what he said and what she said, up to the moment when his arms went around her. Some of the scenes she went over twice, they were so lovely. Some she improved on the second run. Once she pictured a beautiful scene of renunciation and sacrifice, when she told Caleb farewell and returned to Griffith, but that was too painful and she revised it, with Griffith simply non-existent, in the comfortable way of fantasy.

All the time, as the hours and the half-hours ticked away, her body was light and taut and vibrant, like a violin string. She was not in the least tired and had no need of sleep.

Sleep she did, though, just as the night turned gray, and when she awoke the sunlight was brilliant in squares on the dark honey-colored floor and Aunt Mary was calling her to breakfast.

She was tired now, she thought, as she hurried into her clothes, so tired that she ached and felt cross. She could tell by their quick looks of surprise and concern as she slipped into her place a few minutes later, that Father and Aunt Mary were quite aware of the turmoil within her. They had waited "silence" for her, and as she bowed her head her prayer was not one of gratitude for the home food, plentiful and fragrant, on the table, but a plea that they would stop noticing her.

Her prayer was answered. Neither Father nor Aunt Mary seemed to see her at all, and the talk at the table ran cheerfully on the subject of the garden and the wood robins, which had returned and were whistling sweetly on every side.

When breakfast was over they pushed back their chairs a little from the table and Joseph brought the Bible and placed it before Father. Joseph and Nannie and Hess and little Elijah filed in and sat down in a row against the wall. Father opened the Bible and began to read from the Book of Ruth, where they had left off when they went to Alexandria. The names rolled over Loveday's head, Elimelech, Mahlon and Chilion, Orpah and Ruth and Naomi.

" 'And Ruth said, Intreat me not to leave thee, or to return from following after thee; for whither thou goest, I will go; and where thou lodgest, I will lodge; thy people shall be my people, and thy God my God; where thou diest, will I die, and there will I be buried: the Lord do so to me, and more also, if ought but death part thee and me.' "

She knew the words were said by a widow to her mother-in-law, but they struck at her heart as the inevitable promise of a girl to the man she loved, words which she herself could never say to Griffith but would offer to Caleb with her whole being.

The reading was finished, the Bible laid aside, the family settled into the customary few minutes of silence before starting the affairs of the day. Loveday closed her eyes tight, but still the hot tears squeezed under her lids and rolled down her cheeks. She put up a finger hastily to wipe them away, hoping desperately that no one had seen.

The servants rose and went out. Richard Parry nodded to his sister and she too slipped away without a word. He turned to Loveday, who gave him a bright, determined smile.

"Lovey," he said gently, "what's the matter? What is troubling thee?"

She blinked rapidly and swallowed, unable to speak.

"If thee doesn't want to marry Griffith, either now or later, thee doesn't have to, thee knows. I've thought all along thee was too young."

She shook her head violently. She was not too young. That wasn't it, at all.

"What we want above all, thy Aunt Mary and I, is for thee to be happy. But I can't help unless I know what is wrong. Here, take my handkerchief and dry thy eyes and blow thy nose and look at me, Loveday, and tell me—is there anyone else?"

Loveday accepted that most reliable of comforts to a woman, a loving man's big, clean, linen handkerchief, and dabbed at her eyes and gulped. Before she could command her voice, Joseph came back into the room with a little package in his hand and laid it on the table before her.

"Mist' Middleton left this," he explained, "after you all went to Alexandria. He expected to see thee, and when thee wasn't here he asked for paper and a pen and he wrote something inside. It altogether slip' my mind to give it to thee last night."

Wondering, Loveday opened the little box and lifted the bit of paper inside. There on a bed of cotton wool she saw a bit of gleaming gold, a pin in the shape of a bow knot. Her heart beating and her hands trembling, she unfolded the paper and read,

"I am sorry to miss thee. This must say farewell for me. We leave for York and Lancaster in a day or two, and Philadelphia after that. C.M. Jr."

She raised a stricken face to her father.

"He's gone!" she cried.

XXXVI

CALEB AND HIS FATHER sat together in Mr. Middleton's bedroom. Through the open window came a warm breeze and sunshine filtered through the new green leaves of the buttonwoods outside.

"This is the only room we have left to sit in," complained Mr. Middleton. "That puppy has absorbed most of the house, like the camel that got into the tent. Thy mother calls him the Camel."

Caleb had been home two days. He was already weary of the subject of the British occupation of Philadelphia. He had seen for himself the devastated outskirts of the city, the fields despoiled of their fences, open to wandering cattle, the charred ruins of houses and barns, the general look of desolation. He had been shocked by the filth in the streets of the city itself and the shabbiness of buildings that had been neat and well-kept, the broken windows mended with paper, scarred doors where a stick or the butt of a gun had been used instead of the knocker, the front-door settles defaced with carved initials, all the evidence of the senseless and idle abuse of property by irresponsible men. He had met the British soldiers everywhere, arrogant and careless, with the "frail women," who used to ply their trade on Water Street at night, walking openly beside them in full daylight.

He had heard over and over about the sins of the Major who was ensconced in his own room, so that he had to share a bed with Edward. Not only had Major Cranborne spread out over most of the house, but he gave dinners almost every night for eight, ten, or twelve officers, or else he was out till all hours, coming in at three or four o'clock, drunk and noisy, waking everybody up.

Caleb felt some amusement over Patty, exiled to Wilmington

after she and Caroline Rutter had engaged in an unusual contest for the attention of the Major.

"She always managed to be on the porch or the stairway when he went in or out," complained Patty's father, "and she was bent and determined that he should invite her to a dance at the coffee house!"

Edward had tagged after a band of town-boys who made their headquarters at Morris's brew-house and fought with the British drummer boys, until one of the drummer boys was killed. Edward had come home once with a broken head and another time with a black eye. Tacy fortunately was too young to be much affected by any of it, though she was a great favorite with the Major and his friends and they encouraged her to be forward.

"I got the coach out of the way," said Mr. Middleton with satisfaction, "before any of the red-coated gentry realized I had one. That monster of rapine, Howe, is riding about in Israel Pemberton's coach, and several others have been taken, but mine is well hidden in the Water Street warehouse and the horses are in Wilmington."

At first secretly amused by the change in his father's attitude toward the British on better acquaintance, Caleb rapidly grew weary of the repeated accounts of their depredations.

"They assume such extraordinarily superior airs, Caleb, walking about the streets of Philadelphia—which is after all a metropolis second only to London—scornful and arrogant, forcing respectable citizens off the sidewalks. Their social affairs are all-important; they stuff themselves with food and drink, no matter what prices are or how many go without. And they have a trail of sycophants following after them, obsequious and eager to please—and to make a profit. Anyone who maintains his self-respect they condemn as a rebel. But it's the wanton destruction that is the worst. They burned the house where Colonel Reid lived, they destroyed Thompson's tavern, they went into Colonel Bayard's and cut his books to pieces with their bayonets, emptied the featherbeds, mixed up a mess of paint and linseed oil and dumped the feathers into it!"

Tacy came and climbed onto Caleb's knee and leaned back contentedly against his chest, her thumb in her mouth. He took it out gently, but as soon as he released it she popped it back in again and tipped her head back to smile up at him challengingly.

"I suppose I've said enough about all this," said Mr. Middleton. "Sarah tells me I harp on it too much, that this is war, and what can we expect. It isn't what I intended to talk to thee about."

"Yes, Father?" He put Tacy down, suggesting that perhaps she could find a four-leaf clover for him in the garden. The child trotted out and Caleb turned his full attention to his father.

In spite of all the annoyances and anxieties of the winter, the older Caleb was looking well. The folds of flesh in chin and neck were a little fuller and softer, the pouches under his eyes deeper, his shoulders rounder, the veins in his hands knottier, but he was vigorous as he had not been in the autumn, and his voice was round and full.

"The Phoebe Ann, as I told thee, has been confiscated by the Americans. Thee said it would be, I remember. Thee was right. But they've kept Jacob to run it."

"Jacob! But I thought he was going home to his father's farm!"

"Well, he didn't. I expected him to, but it seems he thought differently. He's lost his wife, by the way. Very sad. They've built an army hospital at Yellow Springs, and Gertrude took milk and eggs and such-like to the patients every week, till she caught a malignant fever and died of it. Perhaps the same kind of fever thee and Edward Penington had. It's a miracle to me that you both escaped."

"Poor Jacob, he must be lost without his Trüdchen. I suppose the oldest girl is able to cook for him and care for the younger children."

"All of the furnaces and forges in the region have been making munitions for Washington's army." Mr. Middleton lowered his voice. "Jacob sent me word through some spy or other coming into the city. A colored man sold us some country eggs and there was a note in one of them. There's a good deal more communication than might be supposed. Jacob's done his best, but he's had trouble keeping colliers and one thing and another, and he hasn't produced nearly as much as they want and expect—an average of only eight or ten tons a week. But it isn't only difficulties with colliers, he's had some failures. Jacob's a good man but his judgment is not all it might be. In spite of thy youth thee had a surer sense of mixing and timing. Now. All that by way of preliminary."

Mr. Middleton pulled himself erect in his chair, rolling a little, stretching the corners of his mouth till the cords stood out in his neck, and leaning forward toward Caleb, went on in a voice so low that it was almost a whisper,

"Thou wanted last August to go on with the furnace and make iron for the use of the Americans and I overrode thee. I don't like to eat crow any better than anyone else, but I believe thou was right." He leaned back in his chair, expansively, as one who has made a world-shaking statement and awaits recognition of his courage, candor, and generosity.

Caleb looked down at the palms of his hands as if he expected to read something there. "It's very good of thee to say that. I don't know. One can only do what one thinks best at the time."

"Yes, yes, of course. The point is this. They need more iron than they are getting from Jacob. They are using him to run the furnace but so far as I can tell they haven't sold it or transferred the title to anyone else yet. I believe if thou went to them and offered to increase production, thou could get the furnace back and go on with the work thou wanted to do."

Caleb, in his turn, leaned back in his chair, clasping his hands behind his head and looking out of the window. In all his plans for the future, the conversations which he had imagined with his father, he had not foreseen that they would take this turn. He had his own plans. Why could his father not have asked what they were, instead of laying before him a ready-made outline?

"Well, why don't thou say something? What's the matter?"

"Thee's changed during the winter, Father. So have I."

His father directed at him a long, keen, shrewd look, and then burst out laughing. The sound was shocking in that already tense room and Caleb winced. Mr. Middleton, sober the next instant, spoke with an undertone of bitterness. "I've seen too much of the British and thou's had too much of the Americans. Armies are much the same, no matter which side they are on, and so too, no doubt, are governments. But this is our country, Caleb, the hills and fields and creeks and the iron in the ground. We live here. The English don't."

"It's not that. Thee doesn't understand. I've become more of an American this winter, not less, in spite of the Congress and Council. I think our army under Washington is different from the British army and certainly different from the Hessians. I think our people are set on freedom as well as independence. But I've become more of a Friend as well. I thought once I could make munitions. I even thought I could fight. But now I cannot."

"I am not suggesting that thou fight. I am offering thee an opportunity to do just what thou proposed last August—to make pig iron and salt pans."

"I should have to make cannon and cannon balls if I undertook to run the furnace now, and I can't see that there is any essential difference between making munitions to kill people and killing them with one's own gun. In fact it's worse because there's no personal risk in it. A soldier may be killed himself, but the munition-maker is safe—and he is making a good profit too."

Seeing his father's troubled and bewildered expression, he tried to explain further. "I used to talk to Isaac Zane, junior, sometimes in Winchester. I'll tell thee all about it sometime." He hurried on, wishing to avoid having to give all the technical details of the Marlboro Ironworks. "He is making cannon. He says he's a Quaker for the times. He's very prosperous, buying books and furniture and building a big house, and his plantation will be a fine one when it is finished." For a moment the memory of the Phoebe Ann swept over Caleb, the big, elegant house, the wide acres of meadow and woodland, the fires against the sky at night, the village where the workmen lived, and the excitement when the ironmaster walked abroad. He felt a pang of homesickness.

"Well? What's the matter with that?"

"I don't want to be a Quaker for the times."

"Caleb, sometimes I think thou opposes me just for the sake of opposing me. I thought that surely in this at least we would be in agreement."

Caleb looked at his exasperated parent with a sinking heart and the familiar feeling which he thought he had conquered or out-grown, the emotional paralysis which so often had made him un-able to express his thoughts fully or defend his desires, and he felt the tide of inarticulate resentment slowly rise and with it the undertow of self-contempt and futility.

"No," he said slowly, trying to think how he would put it if John Hunt were there before him instead of his father. "I don't mean to do that. But I have another plan, which I have thought of a great deal, riding from Winchester."

"Well, what is it?"

"Medicine is my real vocation. I have come to realize that more fully than ever. At first I thought I should apply to Dr. Parke to be his apprentice as soon as I should return to Philadelphia, and then enroll for the courses in the Medical College in the fall. I thought I could combine the medical courses with the apprentice-ship and then later, when travel becomes possible again, finish with a year or two of study in Edinburgh. But more recently, after being in Lancaster and coming to a clearer understanding of the nature of the struggle for independence, I realized that I could not after all embark on a selfish enterprise of my own, but that I must throw in my lot with my country—"

"Then why not take up my suggestion about the Phoebe Ann for the present, and go to Edinburgh later, if thou still wishes to?"

"I want to save life rather than destroy it. So I have decided," continued Caleb hastily before his father could speak again, "to go to Dr. Hutchinson. He is Israel Pemberton's nephew. He was very helpful to us in September, and since then he has gone into the army as a surgeon—"

"I heard all about that. At twenty-two shillings a day."

"He is at Valley Forge now. I have decided to seek him out and offer him my services as an assistant or an apprentice or any way at all that I can be useful. One of our guards in Winchester—a good-hearted young lad from the country—had been in an army hospital and from what he told me I understand that they can use almost any kind of help. I have had a little experience this winter, and I know that I could be useful. I should be doing something that would harmonize with both my inclination and my conscience and yet—" he hesitated, feeling himself flush, "not too easy."

"I don't like it, Caleb. It seems to me a waste of thy talents and resources. Those army hospitals are full of fevers—look at Jacob's wife, just visiting one. If thou got sick thou'd only be an additional burden instead of a help. It postpones thy establishing thyself in life. And though it seems not to mean anything to thee, it would in all probability result in our losing the Phoebe Ann entirely."

"Yes, it might. I should be sorry for that."

"It doesn't alter thy decision?"

"No."

They looked into each other's eyes. The father's gaze shifted first.

"If that is what thou hast made up thy mind to do, I have nothing more to say. It is thy life and thy decision. I can point out the hazards in the road, but I cannot stop thee from flinging thyself upon them. When dost thou think of going?"

"In a very few days, as soon as I can collect the things I need, talk to some people, and so on. I wanted to see thee and the children first."

"Yes. Umm. Well." His father made a series of noises in his throat indicative of a philosophic acceptance of the inevitable. "Don't hurry away now. Tell me more about thy experiences. I went into Dr. Smith's shop for some elixir one day last winter, and he told me how thou had been his assistant, attending the Hessian prisoners. I told him," he chuckled, "that that might increase the hazards of imprisonment for some of those poor devils. He got quite huffy. He's no sense of humor at all."

"Speaking of Smith makes me think of Pike. Has thee heard anything of him?"

"He's gone to England, he and his wife. He came to see us after he got back from Winchester to bring us word about thee. Very obliging of him. Thy letters were coming very irregularly and very few of them. He was quite unabashed about taking French leave the way he did. He was worried about his wife, alone in the city without resources. I had some sympathy with him."

"It was decent of him to visit you. We parted not very amicably."

"Thy mother had had Mrs. Pike make some things for Patty. She's a good little soul, and a very able seamstress, Sarah says. But it seems Pike heard from his father in Bristol and a ship was going, so they packed up and left. Isabella Affleck has had a very hard time. Sarah was able to help her and so did Polly Pleasants as soon as she heard about it. I think of all the cases that was perhaps the most unjust, that and John Hunt—and thee, of course. Well, they all were."

They were still sitting there, exchanging news with a surface interest while each was busy with his own thoughts and a reappraisal of their relationship, when Sarah came bustling into the room.

"There's a colored man downstairs who wants to see you, Caleb," she said. "He says he's come from Winchester with a letter for you, which he must deliver directly into your hands and no other's."

His father chuckled. "A man of affairs!" he said.

Caleb smiled perfunctorily as he rose and left the room. Running down the stairs he tried to think who in Winchester could have anything to write him of so much importance that it required a special messenger. Had anything happened to one of Elizabeth Joliffe's children—or Philip Busch discovered some long-overlooked item for which he could charge him—did Dr. Stephen wish to press his offer of taking Caleb as an apprentice? Could Loveday—but that was impossible.

He did not recognize the man standing in the front hall, silhouetted against the open door, until he turned and spoke. Then Caleb knew him as the Parrys' houseman—wasn't his name Joseph?

"You have a letter for me?"

The man was gray with dust and fatigue. Through the door Caleb could see a horse hitched to the post outside, his head drooping, his flanks lathered.

"You've ridden hard," he observed, while Joseph fumbled in an inner pocket of his coat. "When did you leave the Shenandoah?"

"Las' Friday, Mist' Middleton. I had to go round about a piece, near Wilmington, so's not to meet the militia." He brought out a letter covered with a blue cotton handkerchief. Caleb waited for him to unfold the wrappings, barely able to restrain himself from snatching at it.

When he had it in his hand, breaking the seal with fingers clumsy with eagerness, he thought how strange it was that he had never seen her writing—yet he would have known anywhere that this clear, open, delicate hand was hers.

"Dear Caleb," he read. It was short. It did not cover one side of the sheet. He read it once and scarcely understood its meaning, read it again, and felt happiness and delight pour through him and lift him up on a great surging wave.

He looked up and saw Joseph standing there, tired, patient, but smiling, as if he caught some reflection of joy from Caleb.

"You must rest," said Caleb, "and have something to eat. Amos!" he shouted. And while Amos was coming, Caleb's mind raced among his plans, overturning them and setting them up afresh. He could ride to Wilmington at once and spend the night with the Chases, go as far as he could on the Baltimore Road to-morrow, borrowing a fresh horse at some Friend's farm along the way. He could reach the Shenandoah in four days, or, with luck, a little less.

"Amos, this is Joseph Parry. Take him to the kitchen and see that he gets a good meal. Then make up a bed for him in your

room. And take care of his horse. He's tied outside. And Amos—
wait a minute—saddle Ladybird."

He unfolded the letter and read it again.

DEAR CALEB: Thank thee very much for the pin, which was
waiting for me here when I came home. It is beautiful and I shall
wear it always.

I love it especially because it gives me courage to write thee
now. Thee said to tell thee if I should change my mind. I am not
going to marry Griffith after all.

Thy true friend,

LOVEDAY PARRY

He could reach the Shenandoah in four days, and after that, after
he had seen Loveday and talked with her father, who must be
willing or she could never have sent Joseph with the letter, after
that he would go to Valley Forge without returning to Philadelphia. Joseph, apparently reluctant to go off with Amos, was saying
something. With difficulty Caleb broke away from his thoughts
to listen.

"Miss Loveday, she say for me to come back quick's I can with
an answer."

Caleb clapped him on the shoulder. "I'll take the answer myself," he cried exultantly. "I'll be there before you are."

During the Revolution, a group of Pennsylvanians, most of them members of the Society of Friends, were banished to Virginia because they refused to subscribe to a loyalty oath. Around this little-known episode in American history, Elizabeth Gray Vining has built a story of moral courage which has a deep significance today.

Caleb Middleton, one of the seventeen Friends, was arrested when his father decided to close down his iron furnace until peace should be restored. Though Caleb felt it was right to resist British tyranny, he stood firm with the other Friends.

Without trial, the Friends were exiled to the mountains of Virginia and there, amid the strangeness and unfamiliarity of frontier life, they work out their relationships and discover their destinies.

Caleb meets and falls in love with a Virginia girl. Among the other exiles are the cabinetmaker, Thomas Affleck, who has been wrenched away from his wife and children; Thomas Pike, a fencing and dancing master whose pretty wife had attracted Caleb back in Philadelphia; and John Hunt, oldest of the group, who is called upon to show physical courage equal to his moral fortitude.

The Virginia Exiles is a solid, substantial and continually absorbing novel, which conveys the Quaker quality of quiet and luminous integrity. It is a timely and powerful defense of liberty of conscience and the right of the individual in a free country.

THE OMNIBUS

P. D. JAMES

by P. D. James

COVER HER FACE
A MIND TO MURDER
UNNATURAL CAUSES
SHROUD FOR A NIGHTINGALE
AN UNSUITABLE JOB FOR A WOMAN
THE BLACK TOWER
DEATH OF AN EXPERT WITNESS
INNOCENT BLOOD
THE SKULL BENEATH THE SKIN
A TASTE FOR DEATH
DEVICES AND DESIRES

Non-fiction

THE MAUL AND THE PEAR TREE
(*with T. A. Critchley*)

The Omnibus
P. D. James

An Unsuitable Job for a Woman

Death of an Expert Witness

Innocent Blood

*with an Introduction
by the author*

faber and faber
LONDON · BOSTON

This omnibus edition first published in 1990
by Faber and Faber Limited
3 Queen Square London WC1N 3AU

Photoset by Wilmaset Birkenhead Wirral
Printed in England
by Clays Ltd, St Ives plc

Introduction © P. D. James, 1990
An Unsuitable Job for a Woman © P. D. James, 1972
Death of an Expert Witness © P. D. James, 1977
Innocent Blood © P. D. James, 1980

A CIP record for this book
is available from the British Library
ISBN 0–571–14492–6

CONTENTS

INTRODUCTION

The three novels selected for this, my first Faber Omnibus, are among my personal favourites and it is, therefore, a particular pleasure to see them reissued in a hardback edition. They are printed in the order of writing but are in no way related, not even by a common detective, and are widely different in subject-matter, mood and setting. *An Unsuitable Job for a Woman*, published in 1972, introduces my girl private detective, Cordelia Gray; *Death of an Expert Witness*, which came out in 1977, features Adam Dalgliesh of New Scotland Yard, and *Innocent Blood*, published in 1980, is unique among my books in being a crime novel rather than a detective story, although it does contain clues and I can clearly see in it the influence of my detective fiction.

This distinction between a crime novel and a detective story perhaps requires an explanation. It seems to me that when we speak of crime writing we can be thinking of a wide spectrum of work stretching from the cosy certainties of Mayhem Parva, that fictional village which, despite its above-average homicide rate, never loses its essential peace and innocence, through the works of such novelists as Wilkie Collins, Anthony Trollope, Charles Dickens and Graham Greene to the great Russian novelists and some of the highest works of the human imagination. For me, the detective story is a sub-genre of the crime novel, arguably more limited in scope, potential and intention and written within recognized conventions. What we expect in the detective story is a central mysterious death, a closed circle of suspects each with motive, means and opportunity for the crime, a detective, either amateur or professional, who comes in rather like an avenging deity to solve it and, by the end of the book, a solution to the mystery which the reader should be able to arrive at himself by logical deduction from the clues inserted in the book with deceptive cunning but essential fairness. One of the criticisms of the genre is that this is mere formula-writing, but what I find fascinating is the extraordinary variety of books and talent which this so-called formula can accommodate, and the extent to which many writers find the technical constraints liberating rather than inhibiting of their creative imagination.

For me the initial inspiration for a new novel is nearly always the setting, and with *An Unsuitable Job for a Woman* it was the wish to write about Cambridge in high summer, a town which I love since I grew up there and met my husband while he was at the University. Setting, important in any novel, is particularly so in a crime novel since it creates an atmosphere of menace, foreboding and mystery, influences the plot, reveals character and helps root the often bizarre events of the story in the firm soil of reality and established place. The power of a beautiful setting to heighten horror by contrast is particularly important to me as a writer as it was to W. H. Auden, an *aficionado* of detective fiction, but who could only enjoy a mystery if it was set in a village or small town. In his fascinating essay on the genre, 'The Guilty Vicarage', he writes: 'Nature should reflect its human inhabitants, i.e. it should be the Great Good Place for the more Eden-like it is, the greater the contradiction of murder.' I have evoked this power of contrast in *An Unsuitable Job for a Woman*, where the beauty and ordered peace of the town and the privileged lives of the rich young students who are among my suspects are contrasted with the horrible death of the victim and with my lonely, courageous and unprivileged private eye, Cordelia Gray. Cordelia has inherited an unsuccessful and seedy detective agency after the suicide of its proprietor, Bernie Pryde, and is unexpectedly called in by a wealthy scientist to investigate the suicide in Cambridge of his only son. This is an opportunity for her first success in a job which all Bernie Pryde's acquaintances assure her is an unsuitable one for a woman. The case embroils her not only in personal danger, but in the investigation of a particularly unnatural and evil murder against the background of one of Europe's loveliest cities. 'By what devious routes and for what a strange purpose she had come at last to Cambridge. The city didn't disappoint her. How indeed, she thought, could the heart be indifferent to such a city, where stone and stained glass, water and green lawns, trees and flowers were arranged in such ordered beauty for the service of learning. But, as regretfully she rose to go, brushing the few crumbs from her skirt, a quotation, untraced and unsought came into her mind: "Then saw I that there was a way to Hell even from the gates of Heaven." '

Death of an Expert Witness also began with a place and here, too, we are in East Anglia but in the remote and desolate blacklands of the fen country. The story is set in Hoggatt's forensic science laboratory and the idea which initially excited me was the irony and horror of murder coming into the very heart of an institution dedicated to the maintenance of official law and order. Edwin Lorrimer, the senior biologist, is found dead on the floor of his laboratory, killed with a mallet which he has been examining for bloodstains. This is obviously a case for the professional police not for a private eye, and Adam Dalgliesh arrives by helicopter to take charge of an investigation which will involve him in the tangled lives and motives of the staff of the laboratory and the village in which it is set. Detective writers are fond of closed communities, and with reason. Not only is such a society an interesting micro-cosm of the wider world outside but it limits the stain of suspicion, which must not be allowed to spread too widely if the suspects are to be kept to a manageable number. In the words of W. H. Auden: 'The detective story writer is also wise to choose a society with an elaborate ritual and to describe this in detail. A ritual is a sign of harmony between the aesthetic and the ethical in which body and mind, individual will and general laws are not in conflict. The murderer uses his knowledge of the ritual to commit the crime and can be caught only by someone who acquires an equal or superior familiarity with it.'

Innocent Blood, because it is primarily a crime novel not a detective story, has neither Adam Dalgliesh nor Cordelia Gray. And the genesis of this novel was not the London setting, although this is very important to the story, but two widely different events, a real-life murder as long ago as 1949, and an Act of Parliament, the Children Act 1975. The murderer was a young father, who, after visiting his new-born son and wife in a maternity nursing-home, called on his parents-in-law and savagely battered them to death. He was subsequently arrested, tried, convicted and executed. On the day of the execution my thoughts were less with him or his victims than with the young mother and her baby and I wondered what eventually she would say to her son when he asked about his father and grandparents. If she decided to conceal the appalling truth, how long would this be possible? Might she even consider giving her son for adoption? When the 1975 Act became law and adopted young people aged eighteen were given the power to obtain their original birth certificate and to begin the search for their natural parents, I remembered this case and the real-life murders and an Act of Parliament came together to give me a novel. *Innocent Blood* tells the story of Philippa Palfrey, a highly intelligent but unloving girl who has been adopted by a sociologist and his wife and who has fantasized a highly agreeable picture of her real parentage and early life. Then, when she obtains her birth certificate, she discovers the horrific truth that her background is a dark swamp of rape and murder, and that neither the horror nor the violence is at an end. It is, I hope, an exciting story of the hunting down of a murderess in London, but it is also about guilt, retribution, remorse and the growth of love.

So what is the future for crime writing and in particular for the fascinating genre of the detective story? There is, at present, a huge resurgence of interest in the classical mystery carefully plotted and clued and unambiguously set in its time and place. But we can never return to the cosy certainties of the 1930s British detective story with its deference to hierarchy, its comfortable orthodoxies, its naïve and simplistic view of law and order. Today, the detective story has moved closer to mainstream fiction and in my view this process will continue. What we writers are doing is exploring the response of men and women to the ultimate crime, demonstrating how fragile are the bridges which we construct over the abyss of social and psychological chaos. And although the modern detective story is more violent, more sexually explicit, less confident in its affirmation of law and order, and closer to the novel of social realism it remains, I suggest, a reassuring genre. It distances for us the atavistic fear of death and by fictionalizing and, to some extent, transforming it into an intellectual puzzle, helps us to come to terms with its inevitability. It affirms the sanctity of the individual human life and confirms our belief that we live in a generally benevolent and rational universe and that even the most difficult problem is capable of solution by human intelligence, human courage and human perseverance. It provides us, too, not only with the challenge of a puzzle but with vicarious excitement and danger. To quote *David Copperfield*: 'Other things are all very well in

their way but give me blood . . . We must have blood, you know.'
Certainly we addicts of the detective story expect our measure of
gore but to the discriminating reader blood alone isn't enough;
something more is demanded. I hope that in this Omnibus my
readers will find it.

P. D. James

AN UNSUITABLE JOB
FOR A WOMAN

An Unsuitable Job for a Woman

For Jane and Peter
who kindly allowed two of
my characters to live at
57 Norwich Street.

A crime novelist, by virtue of his unpleasant craft, has the duty to create at least one highly reprehensible character in each book and it is perhaps inevitable that from time to time their sanguinary misdeeds should impinge upon the dwellings of the just. A writer whose characters have chosen to act out their tragicomedy in an ancient university city is in particular difficulty. He can, of course, call it Oxbridge, invent colleges named after improbable saints and send his characters boating on the Camsis, but this timid compromise merely confuses characters, readers and the author alike, with the result that no one knows precisely where he is and two communities are offered opportunities for offence instead of one.

The greater part of this story is unrepentantly set in Cambridge, a city in which, undeniably, there live and work policemen, coroners, doctors, students, college servants, flower sellers, dons, scientists, and even, no doubt, retired majors. None of them, to my knowledge, bears the slightest resemblance to his counterpart in this book. All the characters, even the most unpleasant, are imaginary; the city, happily for us all, is not.

P.D.J.

CHAPTER ONE

On the morning of Bernie Pryde's death – or it may have been the morning after, since Bernie died at his own convenience, nor did he think the estimated time of his departure worth recording – Cordelia was caught in a breakdown of the Bakerloo line outside Lambeth North and was half an hour late at the office. She came up from Oxford Circus Underground into the bright June sunshine, sped past the early-morning shoppers scanning the windows of Dickins and Jones and plunged into the cacophony of Kingly Street, threading her way between the blocked pavement and the shining mass of cars and vans which packed the narrow street. The hurry she knew was irrational, a symptom of her obsession with order and punctuality. There were no appointments booked; no clients to be interviewed; no case outstanding; not even a final report to be written. She and Miss Sparshott, the temporary typist, at Cordelia's suggestion were circulating information about the Agency to all the London solicitors in the hope of attracting custom; Miss Sparshott would probably be busy with it now, eyes straying to her watch, tapping out her staccato irritation at every minute of Cordelia's lateness. She was an unprepossessing woman with lips permanently taut as if to prevent the protruding teeth from springing from her mouth, a receding chin with one coarse hair which grew as quickly as it was plucked, and fair hair set in stiff corrugated waves. That chin and mouth seemed to Cordelia the living refutation that all men are born equal and she tried from time to time to like and sympathize with Miss Sparshott, with a life lived in bedsitting-rooms, measured in the fivepenny pieces fed to the gas stove and circumscribed by fell seams and hand hemming. For Miss Sparshott was a skilled dressmaker, an assiduous attender at the GLC evening classes. Her clothes were beautifully made but so dateless that they were never actually in fashion; straight skirts in grey or black which were exercises in how to sew a pleat or insert a zip fastener; blouses with mannish collars and cuffs in insipid pastel shades on which she distributed without discretion her collection of costume jewellery;

intricately cut dresses with hems at the precise length to emphasize her shapeless legs and thick ankles.

Cordelia had no premonition of tragedy as she pushed open the street door which was kept perpetually on the latch for the convenience of the secretive and mysterious tenants and their equally mysterious visitors. The new bronze plaque to the left of the door gleamed brightly in the sun in incongruous contrast to the faded and dirt-encrusted paint. Cordelia gave it a short glance of approval:

PRYDE'S DETECTIVE AGENCY
(*Props:* Bernard G. Pryde   Cordelia Gray)

It had taken Cordelia some weeks of patient and tactful persuasion to convince Bernie that it would be inappropriate to append the words 'ex-CID Metropolitan Police' to his name or prefix 'Miss' to hers. There had been no other problem over the plaque since Cordelia had brought no qualifications or relevant past experience to the partnership and indeed no capital, except her slight but tough twenty-two-year-old body, a considerable intelligence which Bernie, she suspected, had occasionally found more disconcerting than admirable, and a half exasperated, half pitying affection for Bernie himself. It was obvious very early to Cordelia that in some undramatic but positive way life had turned against him. She recognized the signs. Bernie never got the enviable front left-hand seat in the bus; he couldn't admire the view from the train window without another train promptly obscuring it; the bread he dropped invariably fell buttered side downwards; the Mini, reliable enough when she drove it, stalled for Bernie at the busiest and most inconvenient intersections. She sometimes wondered whether, in accepting his offer of a partnership in a fit of depression or of perverse masochism, she was voluntarily embracing his ill-luck. She certainly never saw herself as powerful enough to change it.

The staircase smelt as always of stale sweat, furniture polish and disinfectant. The walls were dark green and were invariably damp whatever the season as if they secreted a miasma of desperate respectability and defeat. The stairs, with their ornate wrought-iron balustrade, were covered with split and stained linoleum patched by the landlord in various and contrasting colours only when a tenant complained. The Agency was on the third floor. There was no clatter of typewriter keys as Cordelia entered and she saw that Miss

Sparshott was engaged in cleaning her machine, an ancient Imperial which was a constant cause of justified complaint. She looked up, her face blotched with resentment, her back as rigid as the space bar.

'I've been wondering when you would turn up, Miss Gray. I'm concerned about Mr Pryde. I think he must be in the inner office but he's quiet, very quiet, and the door's locked.'

Cordelia, chill at heart, wrenched at the door handle:

'Why didn't you do something?'

'Do what, Miss Gray? I knocked at the door and called out to him. It wasn't my place to do that, I'm only the temporary typist, I've no authority here. I should have been placed in a very embarrassing position if he had answered. After all, he's entitled to use his own office I suppose. Besides, I'm not even sure if he's there.'

'He must be. The door's locked and his hat is here.'

Bernie's trilby, the stained brim turned up all round, a comedian's hat, was hanging on the convoluted hatstand, a symbol of forlorn decrepitude. Cordelia was fumbling in her shoulder bag for her own key. As usual, the object most required had fallen to the bottom of the bag. Miss Sparshott began to clatter on the keys as if to dissociate herself from impending trauma. Above the noise she said defensively: 'There's a note on your desk.'

Cordelia tore it open. It was short and explicit. Bernie had always been able to express himself succinctly when he had something to say:

'I'm sorry, partner, they've told me it's cancer and I'm taking the easy way out. I've seen what the treatment does to people and I'm not having any. I've made my will and it's with my solicitor. You'll find his name in the desk. I've left the business to you. Everything, including *all* the equipment. Good luck and thank you.' Underneath with the inconsiderateness of the doomed he had scribbled a final unfair plea:

'If you find me alive, for God's sake wait before calling help. I rely on you for this, partner. Bernie.'

She unlocked the door of the inner office and went inside, closing the door carefully behind her.

It was a relief to see that there was no need to wait. Bernie was dead. He lay slumped over the desk as if in an extremity of exhaustion. His right hand was half-clenched and an open cut-throat razor had slithered over the desk top leaving a thin trail of blood like a snail's track and had come to rest precariously poised on the extreme edge of the desk. His left wrist, scored with two parallel cuts, lay palm upwards in the enamel bowl which Cordelia used for the washing-up. Bernie had filled it with water but it was now brimfull with a pale pinky liquid smelling sickly sweet, through which the fingers, curved as if in supplication and looking as white and delicate as those of a child, gleamed as smooth as wax. The blood and water had overflowed on to the desk and floor soaking the oblong of garish rug which Bernie had recently bought in the hope of impressing visitors with his status but which Cordelia privately thought had only drawn attention to the shabbiness of the rest of the office. One of the cuts was tentative and superficial but the other had gone deep as the bone and the severed edges of the wound, drained of blood, gaped cleanly like an illustration in an anatomy text book. Cordelia remembered how Bernie had once described the finding of a prospective suicide when he was first on the beat as a young constable. It was an old man huddled into a warehouse doorway who had slashed his wrist with a broken bottle – but who had later been dragged back to reluctant half-life because an immense clot of blood had blocked the severed veins. Bernie, remembering, had taken precautions to ensure that his blood would not clot. He had, she noticed, taken another precaution; there was an empty tea cup, the one in which she served his afternoon tea, on the right of the desk with a grain or two of powder, aspirin perhaps or a barbiturate, staining the rim and side. A dried trickle of mucus, similarly stained, hung from the corner of his mouth. His lips were pursed and half open like those of a sleeping child, petulant and vulnerable. She put her head round the office door and said quietly:

'Mr Pryde is dead; don't come in. I'll ring the police from here.'

The telephone message was taken calmly, someone would come round. Sitting beside the body to wait and feeling that she needed to make some gesture of pity and comfort Cordelia laid her hand gently on Bernie's hair. Death had as yet no power to diminish these cold and nerveless cells and the hair felt roughly and unpleasantly alive like that of an animal. Quickly she took her hand away and tentatively touched the side of his forehead. The skin was clammy and very cold. This was death; this was how Daddy had felt. As with him, the gesture of pity was meaningless and irrelevant. There was no more communication in death than there had been in life.

She wondered when exactly Bernie had died. No one now would ever know. Perhaps Bernie himself had not known. There must, she supposed, have been one measurable second in time in which he had ceased to be Bernie and had become this unimportant but embarrassingly unwieldy weight of flesh and bone. How odd that a moment of time so important to him should pass without his knowledge. Her second foster mother, Mrs Wilkes, would have said that Bernie did know, that there was a moment of indescribable glory, shining towers, limitless singing, skies of triumph. Poor Mrs Wilkes! Widowed, her only son dead in the war, her small house perpetually noisy with the foster children who were her livelihood, she had needed her dreams. She had lived her life by comfortable maxims stored like nuggets of coal against the winter. Cordelia thought of her now for the first time in years and heard again the tired, determinedly cheerful voice: 'If the Lord doesn't call on his way out, He'll call on his way back.' Well, going or coming, He hadn't called on Bernie.

It was odd but somehow typical of Bernie that he should have retained a dogged and invincible optimism about the business even when they had nothing in the cash box but a few coins for the gas meter and yet had given up hope of life without even a struggle. Was it perhaps that he had subconsciously recognized that neither he nor the Agency had any real future and had decided that this way he could yield up both life and livelihood with some honour? He had done it effectively but messily, surprisingly so for an ex-policeman versed in the ways of death. And then she realized why he had chosen the razor and the drugs. The gun. He hadn't really taken the easy way out. He could have used the gun, but he had wanted her to have it; he had bequeathed it to her together with the rickety filing cabinets, the antique typewriter, the scene-of-crime kit, the Mini, his shock-proof and waterproof wrist watch, the blood-soaked rug, the embarrassingly large stock of writing paper with the ornate heading *Pryde's Detective Agency – We take a Pride in our Work. All* the equipment; he had underlined all. He must have meant to remind her about the gun.

She unlocked the small drawer at the base of Bernie's desk to which only she and he had a key and drew it out. It was still in the suede draw-string bag which she had made for it, with three rounds of ammunition packed separately. It was a pistol, a .38 semi-automatic; she had never known how Bernie had come by it but she was certain that he had no licence. She had never seen it as a lethal weapon, perhaps because Bernie's boyishly naive obsession with it had reduced it to the impotence of a child's toy. He had taught her to become – at any rate in theory – a creditable shot. They had driven for practice into the depths of Epping Forest and her memories of the gun were linked with dappled shade and the rich smell of decaying leaves. He had fixed a target to a convenient tree; the gun was loaded with blanks. She could still hear the excited staccato orders. 'Bend your knees slightly. Feet apart. Arm full length. Now place the left hand against the barrel, cradling it. Keep your eyes on the target. Arm straight, partner, arm straight! Good! Not bad; not bad; not bad at all.' 'But, Bernie,' she had said, 'we can never fire it! We haven't a licence.' He had smiled, the sly self-satisfied smile of superior knowledge. 'If we ever fire in anger it will be to save our lives. In such an eventuality the question of a licence is irrelevant.' He had been pleased with this rotund sentence and had repeated it, lifting his heavy face to the sun like a dog. What, she wondered, had he seen in imagination? The two of them crouching behind a boulder on some desolate moor, bullets pinging against the granite, the gun passed smoking from hand to hand?

He had said: 'We'll have to go carefully with the ammunition. Not that I can't get it of course . . .' The smile had become grim, as if at the memory of those mysterious contacts, those ubiquitous and obliging acquaintances whom he had only to summon from their shadow world.

So he had left her the gun. It had been his most prized possession. She slipped it, still shrouded, into the depths of her shoulder bag. It was surely unlikely that the police would examine the drawers of the desk in a case of obvious suicide but it was as well to take no risk. Bernie had meant her to have the gun and she wasn't going to give it up easily. With her bag at her feet she sat down again by the body. She said a brief convent-taught prayer to the God she wasn't sure existed for the soul which Bernie had never believed he possessed and waited quietly for the police.

The first policeman to arrive was efficient but young, not yet experienced enough to hide his shock and distaste at the sight of violent death nor his disapproval that Cordelia should be so calm. He didn't spend long in the inner office. When he came out he meditated upon Bernie's note as if a careful scrutiny could extract some inner meaning from the bald sentence of death. Then he folded it away.

'I'll have to keep this note for the present, miss. What did he get up to here?'

'He didn't get up to anything. This was his office. He was a private detective.'

'And you worked for this Mr Pryde? You were his secretary?'

'I was his partner. It says so in the note. I'm twenty-two. Bernie was the senior partner; he started the business. He used to work for the Metropolitan Police in the CID with Superintendent Dalgliesh.'

As soon as the words were spoken, she regretted them. They were too propitiatory, too naive a defence of poor Bernie. And the name Dalgliesh, she saw meant nothing to him. Why should it? He was just one of the local uniformed branch. He couldn't be expected to know how often she had listened with politely concealed impatience to Bernie's nostalgic reminiscences of his time in the CID before he was invalided out, or to his eulogies on the virtues and wisdom of Adam Dalgliesh. 'The Super – well, he was just an Inspector then – always taught us . . . The Super once described a case . . . If there was one thing the Super couldn't stand . . .'

Sometimes she had wondered whether this paragon had actually existed or whether he had sprung impeccable and omnipotent from Bernie's brain, a necessary hero and mentor. It was with a shock of surprise that she had later seen a newspaper picture of Chief Superintendent Dalgliesh, a dark, sardonic face which, on her closer scrutiny, disintegrated into an ambiguity of patterned microdots, giving nothing away. Not all the wisdom Bernie so glibly recalled was the received gospel. Much, she suspected, was his own philosophy. She in turn had devised a private litany of disdain: supercilious, superior, sarcastic Super; what wisdom, she wondered, would he have to comfort Bernie now.

The policeman had made discreet telephone calls. He now prowled around the outer office, hardly bothering to hide his puzzled contempt at the shabby second-hand furniture, the battered filing cabinet with one drawer half-open to reveal teapot and mugs, the worn linoleum. Miss Sparshott, rigid at an ancient typewriter, gazed at him with fascinated distaste. At last he said:

'Well, suppose you make yourselves a nice cup of tea while I wait for the police surgeon. There is somewhere to make tea?'

'There's a small pantry down the corridor which we share with the other tenants on this floor. But surely you don't need a surgeon? Bernie's dead!'

'He's not officially dead until a qualified medical practitioner says so.' He paused: 'It's just a precaution.'

Against what, Cordelia wondered – judgement, damnation, decay? The policeman went back into the inner office. She followed him and asked softly:

'Couldn't you let Miss Sparshott go? She's from a secretarial agency and we have to pay for her by the hour. She hasn't done any work since I arrived and I doubt whether she will now.'

He was, she saw, a little shocked by the apparent callousness of concerning herself with so mercenary a detail while standing within touching distance of Bernie's body, but he said willingly enough:

'I'll just have a word with her, then she can go. It isn't a nice place for a woman.'

His tone implied that it never had been.

Afterwards, waiting in the outer office, Cordelia answered the inevitable questions.

'No, I don't know whether he was married. I've a feeling that he was divorced; he never talked about a wife. He lived at 15 Cremona Road, SE2. He let me have a bedsitting-room there but we didn't see much of each other.'

'I know Cremona Road; my aunt used to live there when I was a kid – one of those streets near the Imperial War Museum.'

The fact that he knew the road seemed to reassure and humanize him. He ruminated happily for a moment.

'When did you last see Mr Pryde alive?'

'Yesterday at about five o'clock when I left work early to do some shopping.'

'Didn't he come home last night?'

'I heard him moving around but I didn't see him. I have a gas ring in my room and I usually cook there unless I know he's out. I didn't hear him this morning which is unusual, but I thought he might be lying in. He does that occasionally when it's his hospital morning.'

'Was it his hospital morning today?'

'No, he had an appointment last Wednesday but I thought that they might have asked him to come back. He must have left the house very late last night or before I woke early this morning. I didn't hear him.'

It was impossible to describe the almost obsessional delicacy with which they avoided each other, trying not to intrude, preserving the other's privacy, listening for the sound of flushing cisterns, tip-toeing to ascertain whether the kitchen or bathroom was empty. They had taken infinite trouble not to be a nuisance to each other. Living in the same small terraced house they had hardly seen each other outside the office. She wondered whether Bernie had decided to kill himself in his office so that the little house would be uncontaminated and undisturbed.

*

At last the office was empty and she was alone. The police surgeon had closed his bag and departed; Bernie's body had been manoeuvred down the narrow staircase watched by eyes from the half-opened doors of other offices; the last policeman had left. Miss Sparshott had gone for good, violent death being a worse insult than a typewriter which a trained typist ought not to be expected to use or lavatory accommodation which was not at all what she had been accustomed to. Alone in the emptiness and silence Cordelia felt the need of physical action. She began vigorously to clean the inner office, scrubbing the blood stains from desk and chair, mopping the soaked rug.

At one o'clock she walked briskly to their usual pub. It occurred to her that there was no longer any reason to patronize the Golden Pheasant but she walked on unable to bring herself to so early a disloyalty. She had never liked the pub or the landlady and had often wished that Bernie would find a nearer house, preferably one with a large bosomy barmaid with a heart of gold. It was, she suspected, a type commoner in fiction than in real life. The familiar lunch-time crowd was clustered around the bar and, as usual, Mavis presided behind it wearing her slightly minatory smile, her air of extreme respectability. Mavis changed her dress three times a day, her hair style once every year, her smile never. The two women had never liked each other although Bernie had galumphed between them like an affectionate old dog, finding it convenient to believe that they were great mates and unaware of or ignoring the almost physical crackle of antagonism. Mavis reminded Cordelia of a librarian known to her in childhood who had secreted the new books under the counter in case they should be taken out and soiled. Perhaps Mavis's barely suppressed chagrin was because she was forced to display her wares so prominently, compelled to measure out her bounty before watchful eyes. Pushing a half pint of shandy and a Scotch egg across the counter in response to Cordelia's order, she said:

'I hear you've had the police round.'

Watching their avid faces, Cordelia thought, they know about it, of course; they want to hear the details; they may as well hear them. She said:

'Bernie cut his wrists twice. The first time he didn't get to the vein; the second time he did. He put his arm in water to help the bleeding. He had been told that he had cancer and couldn't face the treatment.'

That, she saw, was different. The little group around Mavis glanced at each other, then quickly averted their eyes. Glasses were momentarily checked upon their upward way. Cutting one's wrist was something which other people did but the sinister little crab had his claws of fear into all their minds. Even Mavis looked as if she saw his bright claws lurking among her bottles. She said:

'You'll be looking for a new job, I suppose? After all, you can hardly keep the Agency going on your own. It isn't a suitable job for a woman.'

'No different from working behind a bar; you meet all kinds of people.'

The two women looked at each other and a snatch of unspoken dialogue passed between them clearly heard and understood by both.

'And don't think, now he's dead, that people can go on leaving messages for the Agency here.'

'I wasn't going to ask.'

Mavis began vigorously polishing a glass, her eyes still on Cordelia's face.

'I shouldn't think your mother would approve of you staying on alone.'

'I only had a mother for the first hour of my life, so I don't have to worry about that.'

Cordelia saw at once that the remark had deeply shocked them and wondered again at the capacity of older people to be outraged by simple facts when they seemed capable of accepting any amount of perverse or shocking opinion. But their silence, heavy with censure, at least left her in peace. She carried her shandy and the Scotch egg to a seat against the wall and thought without sentimentality about her mother. Gradually out of a childhood of deprivation she had evolved a philosophy of compensation. In her imagination she had enjoyed a lifetime of love in one hour with no disappointments and no regrets. Her father had never talked about her mother's death and Cordelia had avoided questioning him, fearful of learning that her mother had never held her in her arms, never regained consciousness, never perhaps even known that she had a daughter. This belief in her mother's love was the one fantasy which she could still not entirely risk losing although its indulgence had become less necessary and less real with each passing year. Now, in imagination, she consulted her mother. It was just as she expected: her mother thought it an entirely suitable job for a woman.

The little group at the bar had turned back to their drinks. Between their shoulders she could see her own reflection in the mirror above the bar. Today's face looked no different from yesterday's face; thick, light brown hair framing features which looked as if a giant had placed a hand on her head and the other under her chin and gently squeezed the face together; large eyes, browny-green under a deep fringe of hair; wide cheekbones; a gentle, childish mouth. A cat's face she thought, but calmly decorative among the reflection of coloured bottles and all the bright glitter of Mavis's bar. Despite its look of deceptive youth it could be a secret, uncommunicative face. Cordelia had early learnt stoicism. All her foster parents, kindly and well-meaning in their different ways, had demanded one thing of her – that she should be happy. She had quickly learned that to show unhappiness was to risk the loss of love. Compared with this early discipline of concealment, all subsequent deceits had been easy.

The Snout was edging his way towards her. He settled himself down on the bench, his thick rump in its appalling tweed pressed close to hers. She disliked the Snout although he had been Bernie's only friend. Bernie had explained that the Snout was a police informer and did rather well. And there were other sources of income. Sometimes his friends stole famous pictures or valuable jewellery. Then the Snout, suitably instructed, would hint to the police where the loot could be found. There was a reward for the Snout to be subsequently shared, of course, among the thieves, and a payoff, too, for the detective, who after all had done most of the work. As Bernie had pointed out, the insurance company got off lightly, the owners got their property back intact, the thieves were in no danger from the police and the Snout and the detective got their payoff. It was the system. Cordelia, shocked, had not liked to protest too much. She suspected that Bernie too had done some snouting in his time, although never with such expertise or with such lucrative results.

The Snout's eyes were rheumy, his hand around the glass of whisky was shaking.

'Poor old Bernie, I could see he had it coming to him. He's been losing weight for the last year and he had that grey look to him, the cancer complexion, my dad used to call it.'

At least the Snout had noticed; she hadn't. Bernie had always seemed to her grey and sick-looking. A thick, hot thigh edged closer.

'Never had any luck, poor sod. They chucked him out of the CID. Did he tell you? That was Superintendent Dalgliesh, Inspector at the time. Christ, he could be a proper bastard; no second chance from him, I can tell you.'

'Yes, Bernie told me,' Cordelia lied. She added: 'He didn't seem particularly bitter about it.'

'No use, is there, in being bitter? Take what comes, that's my motto. I suppose you'll be looking for another job?'

He said it wistfully as if her defection would leave the Agency open for his exploitation.

'Not just yet,' said Cordelia. 'I shan't look for a new job just yet.'

She had made two resolutions: she would keep on Bernie's business until there was nothing left with which to pay the rent, and she would never come into the Golden Pheasant again as long as she lived.

*

This resolution to keep the business going survived the next four days – survived discovery of the rent book and agreement which revealed that Bernie hadn't, after all, owned the little house in

Cremona Road and that her tenancy of the bedsitting-room was illegal and certainly limited; survived learning from the bank manager that Bernie's credit balance would barely pay for his funeral and from the garage that the Mini was shortly due for an overhaul; survived the clearing-up of the Cremona Road house. Everywhere was the sad detritus of a solitary and mismanaged life.

The tins of Irish stew and baked beans – had he never eaten anything else? – stacked in a carefully arranged pyramid as if in a grocer's window; large tins of floor and metal polish, half-used, with their contents dried or congealed; a drawer of old rags used as dusters but still with an amalgam of polish and dirt; a laundry basket unemptied; thick woollen combinations felted with machine washing and stained brown about the crotch – how could he have borne to leave those for discovery?

She went daily to the office, cleaning, tidying, rearranging the filing. There were no calls and no clients and yet she seemed always busy. There was the inquest to attend, depressing in its detached almost boring formality, in its inevitable verdict. There was a visit to Bernie's solicitor. He was a dispirited, elderly man with an office inconveniently situated near Mile End Station who took the news of his client's death with lugubrious resignation as if it were a personal affront, and after a brief search found Bernie's will and pored over it with puzzled suspicion, as if it were not the document he himself had recently drawn up. He succeeded in giving Cordelia the impression that he realized that she had been Bernie's mistress – why else should he have left her the business? – but that he was a man of the world and didn't hold the knowledge against her. He took no part in arranging the funeral except to supply Cordelia with the name of a firm of undertakers; she suspected that they probably gave him a commission. She was relieved after a week of depressing solemnity to find that the funeral director was both cheerful and competent. Once he discovered that Cordelia wasn't going to break down in tears or indulge in the more histrionic antics of the bereaved, he was happy to discuss the relative price and the merits of burial and cremation with conspiratorial candour.

'Cremation every time. There's no private insurance, you tell me? Then get it all over as quickly, easily and cheaply as possible. Take my word, that's what the deceased would want nine times out of ten. A grave's an expensive luxury these days – no use to him – no use to you. Dust to dust, ashes to ashes; but what about the process in between? Not nice to think about, is it? So why not get it over as quickly as possible by the most reliable modern methods? Mind you, miss, I'm advising you against my own best interests.'

Cordelia said:

'It's very kind of you. Do you think we ought to have a wreath?'

'Why not, it'll give it a bit of tone. Leave it to me.'

So there had been a cremation and one wreath. The wreath had been a vulgarly inappropriate cushion of lilies and carnations, the flowers already dying and smelling of decay. The cremation service had been spoken by the priest with carefully controlled speed and with a suggestion of apology in his tone as if to assure his hearers that, although he enjoyed a special dispensation, he didn't expect them to believe the unbelievable. Bernie had passed to his burning to the sound of synthetic music and only just on time, to judge by the impatient rustlings of the cortège already waiting to enter the chapel.

Afterwards Cordelia was left standing in the bright sunlight, feeling the heat of the gravel through the soles of her shoes. The air was rich and heavy with the scent of flowers. Swept suddenly with desolation and a defensive anger on Bernie's behalf, she sought a scapegoat and found it in a certain Superintendent of the Yard. He had kicked Bernie out of the only job he had ever wanted to do; hadn't troubled to find out what happened to him later; and, most irrational indictment of all, he hadn't even bothered to come to the funeral. Bernie had needed to be a detective as other men needed to paint, write, drink or fornicate. Surely the CID was large enough to accommodate one man's enthusiasm and inefficiency? For the first time Cordelia wept for Bernie; hot tears blurred and multiplied the long line of waiting hearses with their bright coronets so that they seemed to stretch in an infinity of gleaming chrome and trembling flowers. Untying the black chiffon scarf from her head, her only concession to mourning, Cordelia set off to walk to the tube station.

She was thirsty when she got to Oxford Circus and decided to have tea in the restaurant at Dickins and Jones. This was unusual and an extravagance but it had been an unusual and extravagant day. She lingered long enough to get full value for her bill and it was after a quarter past four when she returned to the office.

She had a visitor. There was a woman waiting, shoulders against the door – a woman who looked cool and incongruous against the dirty paintwork and the greasy walls. Cordelia caught her breath in surprise, her upward rush checked. Her light shoes had made no sound on the stairway and for a few seconds she saw her visitor unobserved. She gained an impression, immediate and vivid, of competence and authority and an intimidating rightness of dress. The woman was wearing a grey suit with a small stand-away collar which showed a narrow band of white cotton at the throat. Her black patent shoes were obviously expensive; a large black bag with patch pockets was slung from her left shoulder. She was tall and her hair, prematurely white, was cut short and moulded to her head like a cap. Her face was pale and long. She was reading *The Times*, the paper folded so that she could hold it in her right hand. After a couple of seconds, she became aware of Cordelia and their eyes met. The woman looked at her wrist watch.

'If you are Cordelia Gray, then you're eighteen minutes late. This notice says that you would return at four o'clock.'

'I know, I'm sorry.' Cordelia hurried up the last few steps and fitted the Yale key into the lock. She opened the door.

'Won't you come in?'

The woman preceded her into the outer office and turned to face her without giving the room even a glance.

'I was hoping to see Mr Pryde. Will he be long?'

'I'm sorry; I've just come back from his cremation. I mean . . . Bernie's dead.'

'Obviously. Our information was that he was alive ten days ago. He must have died with remarkable speed and discretion.'

'Not with discretion. Bernie killed himself.'

'How extraordinary!' The visitor seemed to be struck by its extraordinariness. She pressed her hands together and for a few seconds walked restlessly about the room in a curious pantomime of distress.

'How extraordinary!' she said again. She gave a little snort of laughter. Cordelia didn't speak, but the two women regarded each other gravely. Then the visitor said:

'Well, I seem to have had a wasted journey.'

Cordelia breathed an almost inaudible 'Oh no!' and resisted an absurd impulse to fling her body against the door.

'Please don't go before talking to me. I was Mr Pryde's partner and

I own the business now. I'm sure I could help. Won't you please sit down?'

The visitor took no notice of the offered chair.

'No one can help, no one in the world. However, that is beside the point. There is something which my employer particularly wants to know – some information he requires – and he had decided that Mr Pryde was the person to get it for him. I don't know if he would consider you an effective substitute. Is there a private telephone here?'

'In here, please.'

The woman walked into the inner office, again with no sign that its shabbiness had made any impression on her. She turned to Cordelia.

'I'm sorry, I should have introduced myself. My name is Elizabeth Leaming and my employer is Sir Ronald Callender.'

'The conservationist?'

'I shouldn't let him hear you call him that. He prefers to be called a microbiologist, which is what he is. Please excuse me.'

She shut the door firmly. Cordelia, feeling suddenly weak, sat down at the typewriter. The keys, oddly unfamiliar symbols encircled in black medallions, shifted their pattern before her tired eyes, then at a blink clicked back to normality. She grasped the sides of the machine, cold and clammy to the touch, and talked herself back to calmness. Her heart was thudding.

'I must be calm, must show her that I am tough. This silliness is only the strain of Bernie's funeral and too much standing in the hot sun.'

But hope was traumatic; she was angry with herself for caring so much.

The telephone call took only a couple of minutes. The door of the inner office opened; Miss Leaming was drawing on her gloves.

'Sir Ronald has asked to see you. Can you come now?'

Come where, thought Cordelia, but she didn't ask.

'Yes, shall I need my gear?'

The gear was Bernie's carefully designed and fitted out scene-of-crime case with its tweezers, scissors, fingerprinting equipment, jars to collect specimens; Cordelia had never yet had occasion to use it.

'It depends upon what you mean by your gear, but I shouldn't think so. Sir Ronald wants to see you before deciding whether to offer you the job. It means a train journey to Cambridge but you should get back tonight. Is there anyone you ought to tell?'

'No, there's only me.'

'Perhaps I ought to identify myself.' She opened her handbag. 'Here is an addressed envelope. I'm not a white slaver if they exist and in case you're frightened.'

'I'm frightened of quite a number of things but not of white slavers and if I were, an addressed envelope would hardly reassure me. I'd insist on telephoning Sir Ronald Callender to check.'

'Perhaps you would like to do so?' suggested Miss Leaming without rancour.

'No.'

'Then shall we go?' Miss Leaming led the way to the door. As they went out to the landing and Cordelia turned to lock the office behind her, her visitor indicated the notepad and pencil hanging together from a nail on the wall.

'Hadn't you better change the notice?'

Cordelia tore off her previous message and after a moment's thought wrote: *I am called away to an urgent case. Any messages pushed through the door will receive my immediate and personal attention on return.*

'That,' pronounced Miss Leaming, 'should reassure your clients.' Cordelia wondered if the remark was sarcastic; it was impossible to tell from the detached tone. But she didn't feel that Miss Leaming was laughing at her and was surprised at her own lack of resentment at the way in which her visitor had taken charge of events. Meekly, she followed Miss Leaming down the stairs and into Kingly Street.

They travelled by the Central Line to Liverpool Street and caught the 17.36 train to Cambridge with plenty of time. Miss Leaming bought Cordelia's ticket, collected a portable typewriter and a briefcase of papers from the left-luggage department and led the way to a first-class carriage. She said:

'I shall have to work in the train; have you anything to read?'

'That's all right. I don't like talking when I'm travelling either. I've got Hardy's *Trumpet Major* – I always have a paperback in my bag.'

After Bishop's Stortford they had the compartment to themselves but only once did Miss Leaming look up from her work to question Cordelia.

'How did you come to be working for Mr Pryde?'

'After I left school I went to live with my father on the continent. We travelled around a good deal. He died in Rome last May after a heart attack and I came home. I had taught myself some shorthand and typing so I took a job with a secretarial agency. They sent me to Bernie and after a few weeks he let me help him with one or two of the cases. He decided to train me and I agreed to stay on permanently. Two months ago he made me his partner.'

All that had meant was that Cordelia gave up a regular wage in return for the uncertain rewards of success in the form of an equal share of the profits together with a rent-free bedsitting-room in Bernie's house. He hadn't meant to cheat. The offer of the partnership had been made in the genuine belief that she would recognize it for what it was; not a good-conduct prize but an accolade of trust.

'What was your father?'

'He was an itinerant Marxist poet and an amateur revolutionary.'

'You must have had an interesting childhood.'

Remembering the succession of foster mothers, the unexplained incomprehensible moves from house to house, the changes of school, the concerned faces of Local Authority Welfare Officers and school teachers desperately wondering what to do with her in the holidays, Cordelia replied as she always did to this assertion, gravely and without irony.

'Yes, it was very interesting.'

'And what was this training you received from Mr Pryde?'

'Bernie taught me some of the things he learnt in the CID: how to search the scene of a crime properly, how to collect exhibits, some elementary self-defence, how to detect and lift fingerprints – that kind of thing.'

'Those are skills which I hardly feel you will find appropriate to this case.'

Miss Leaming bent her head over her papers and did not speak again until the train reached Cambridge.

*

Outside the station Miss Leaming briefly surveyed the car park and led the way towards a small black van. Standing beside it rigidly as a uniformed chauffeur was a stockily built young man dressed in an open-necked white shirt, dark breeches and tall boots whom Miss

Leaming introduced casually and without explanation as 'Lunn'. He nodded briefly in acknowledgement of the introduction but did not smile. Cordelia held out her hand. His grip was momentary but remarkably strong, crushing her fingers; suppressing a grimace of pain she saw a flicker in the large mud-brown eyes and wondered if he had hurt her deliberately. The eyes were certainly memorable and beautiful, moist calves' eyes heavily lashed and with the same look of troubled pain at the unpredictability of the world's terrors. But their beauty emphasized rather than redeemed the unattractiveness of the rest of him. He was, she thought, a sinister study in black and white with his thick, short neck and powerful shoulders straining the seams of his shirt. He had a helmet of strong black hair, a pudgy, slightly pock-marked face and a moist, petulant mouth; the face of a ribald cherub. He was a man who sweated profusely; the underarms of his shirt were stained and the cotton stuck to the flesh emphasizing the strong curve of the back and the obtrusive biceps.

Cordelia saw that the three of them were to sit squashed together in the front of the van. Lunn held open the door without apology except to state:

'The Rover's still in dock.'

Miss Leaming hung back so that Cordelia was compelled to get in first and to sit beside him. She thought: 'They don't like each other and he resents me.'

She wondered about his position in Sir Ronald Callender's household. Miss Leaming's place she had already guessed; no ordinary secretary however long in service, however indispensable, had quite that air of authority or talked of 'my employer' in that tone of possessive irony. But she wondered about Lunn. He didn't behave like a subordinate but nor did he strike her as a scientist. True, scientists were alien creatures to her. Sister Mary Magdalen was the only one she had known. Sister had taught what the syllabus dignified as general science, a hotch-potch of elementary physics, chemistry and biology unceremoniously lumped together. Science subjects were in general little regarded at the Convent of the Immaculate Conception, although the arts were well taught. Sister Mary Magdalen had been an elderly and timid nun, eyes puzzled behind her steel-rimmed spectacles, her clumsy fingers permanently stained with chemicals, who had apparently been as surprised as her pupils at the extraordinary explosions and fumes which her activities with test-tube and flask had occasionally produced. She had been more concerned to demonstrate the incomprehensibility of the universe and the inscrutability of God's laws than to reveal scientific principles and in this she had certainly succeeded. Cordelia felt that Sister Mary Magdalen would be no help to her in dealing with Sir Ronald Callender; Sir Ronald who had campaigned in the cause of conservation long before his interest became a popular obsession, who had represented his country at international conferences on ecology and been knighted for his services to conservation. All this Cordelia, like the rest of the country, knew from his television appearances and the Sunday colour supplements. He was the establishment scientist, carefully uncommitted politically, who personified to everyone's reassurance the poor boy who had made good and stayed good. How, Cordelia wondered, had he come to think of employing Bernie Pryde?

Uncertain how far Lunn was in his employer's or Miss Leaming's confidence, she asked carefully:

'How did Sir Ronald hear about Bernie?'

'John Bellinger told him.'

So the Bellinger bonus had arrived at last! Bernie had always expected it. The Bellinger case had been his most lucrative, perhaps his only, success. John Bellinger was the director of a small family firm which manufactured a specialized scientific instruments. The previous year his office had been plagued by an outbreak of obscene letters and, unwilling to call in the police, he had telephoned Bernie. Bernie, taken on the staff at his own suggestion as a messenger, had quickly solved a not very difficult problem. The writer had been Bellinger's middle-aged and highly regarded personal secretary. Bellinger had been grateful. Bernie, after anxious thought and consultation with Cordelia, had sent in a bill the size of which had astounded them both and the bill had been promptly paid. It had kept the Agency going for a month. Bernie had said: 'We'll get a bonus from the Bellinger case, see if we don't. Anything can happen in this job. He only chose us by picking our name from the telephone directory but now he'll recommend us to his friends. This case could be the beginning of something big.'

And now, thought Cordelia, on the day of Bernie's funeral, the Bellinger bonus had arrived.

She asked no more questions and the drive, which took less than thirty minutes, passed in silence. The three of them sat thigh to thigh, but distanced. She saw nothing of the city. At the end of Station Road by the War Memorial the car turned to the left and soon they were in the country. There were wide fields of young corn, the occasional stretch of tree-lined dappled shade, straggling villages of thatched cottages and squat red villas strung along the road, low uplands from which Cordelia could see the towers and spires of the city, shining with deceptive nearness in the evening sun. Finally, there was another village, a thin belt of elms fringing the road, a long curving wall of red brick and the van turned in through open wrought-iron gates. They had arrived.

*

The house was obviously Georgian, not perhaps the best Georgian but solidly built, agreeably proportioned and with the look of all good domestic architecture of having grown naturally out of its site. The mellow brick, festooned with wisteria, gleamed richly in the evening sun so that the green of the creeper glowed and the whole house looked suddenly as artificial and unsubstantial as a film set. It was essentially a family house, a welcoming house. But now a heavy silence lay over it and the rows of elegantly proportioned windows were empty eyes.

Lunn, who had driven fast but skilfully, braked in front of the porch. He stayed in his seat while the two women got out then drove the van round the side of the house. As she slid down from the high seat Cordelia could glimpse a range of low buildings, topped with small ornamental turrets, which she took to be stables or garages. Through the wide-arched gateway she could see that the grounds dropped slowly away to give a far vista of the flat Cambridgeshire countryside, patterned with the gentle greens and fawns of early summer. Miss Leaming said:

'The stable block has been converted into laboratories. Most of the east side is now glass. It was a skilful job by a Swedish architect, functional but attractive.'

For the first time since they had met her voice sounded interested, almost enthusiastic.

The front door was open. Cordelia came into a wide, panelled hall with a staircase curving to the left, a carved stone fireplace to the right. She was aware of a smell of roses and lavender, of carpets gleaming richly against polished wood, of the subdued ticking of a clock.

Miss Leaming led the way to a door immediately across the hall. It led to a study, a room booklined and elegant, one with a view of wide lawns and a shield of trees. In front of the french windows was a Georgian desk and behind the desk sat a man.

Cordelia had seen his photographs in the press and knew what to expect. But he was at once smaller and more impressive than she had imagined. She knew that she was facing a man of authority and high intelligence; his strength came over like a physical force. But as he rose from his seat and waved her to a chair, she saw that he was slighter than his photographs suggested, the heavy shoulders and impressive head making the body look top-heavy. He had a lined, sensitive face with a high-bridged nose, deep-set eyes on which the lids weighed heavily and a mobile, sculptured mouth. His black hair, as yet unflecked with grey, lay heavily across his brow. His face was shadowed with weariness and, as Cordelia came closer, she could detect the twitch of a nerve in his left temple and the almost imperceptible staining of the veins in the irises of the deep-set eyes. But his compact body, taut with energy and latent vigour, made no concession to tiredness. The arrogant head was held high, the eyes were keen and wary under the heavy lids. Above all he looked successful. Cordelia had seen that look before, had recognized it from the back of crowds as, inscrutable, they had watched the famous and notorious pass on their way – that almost physical glow, akin to sexuality and undimmed by weariness or ill health, of men who knew and enjoyed the realities of power.

Miss Leaming said:

'This is all that remains of Pryde's Detective Agency – Miss Cordelia Gray.'

The keen eyes looked into Cordelia's.

'We take a Pride in our Work. Do you?'

Cordelia, tired after her journey at the end of a momentous day, was in no mood for jokes about poor Bernie's pathetic pun. She said:

'Sir Ronald, I have come here because your secretary said that you might want to employ me. If she's wrong, I would be glad to know so that I can get back to London.'

'She isn't my secretary and she isn't wrong. You must forgive my discourtesy; it's a little disconcerting to expect a burly ex-policeman and to get you. I'm not complaining, Miss Gray; you might do very well. What are your fees?'

The question might have sounded offensive but it wasn't; he was completely matter-of-fact. Cordelia told him, a little too quickly, a little too eagerly.

'Five pounds a day and expenses, but we try to keep those as low as possible. For that, of course, you get my sole services. I mean I don't work for any other client until your case is finished.'

'And is there another client?'

'Well, not just at present but there very well could be.' She went on quickly:

'We have a fair-play clause. If I decide at any stage of the investigation that I'd rather not go on with it, you are entitled to any information I have gained up to that point. If I decide to withhold it from you, then I make no charge for the work already done.'

That had been one of Bernie's principles. He had been a great man for principles. Even when there hadn't been a case for a week, he could happily discuss the extent to which they would be justified in telling a client less than the full truth, the point at which the police ought to be brought into an enquiry, the ethics of deception or lying in the service of truth. 'But no bugging,' Bernie would say, 'I set my face firmly against bugging. And we don't touch industrial sabotage.'

The temptation to either wasn't great. They had no bugging equipment and wouldn't have known how to use it if they had, and at no time had Bernie been invited to touch industrial sabotage.

Sir Ronald said:

'That sounds reasonable but I don't think this case will present you with any crisis of conscience. It is comparatively simple. Eighteen days ago my son hanged himself. I want you to find out why. Can you do that?'

'I should like to try, Sir Ronald.'

'I realize that you need certain basic information about Mark. Miss Leaming will type it out for you, then you can read it through and let us know what else you require.'

Cordelia said:

'I should like you to tell me yourself, please.'

'Is that necessary?'

'It would be helpful to me.'

He settled again into his chair and picked up a stub of pencil, twisting it in his hands. After a minute he slipped it absent-mindedly into his pocket. Without looking at her, he began to speak.

'My son Mark was twenty-one on the 25th of April this year. He was at Cambridge reading history at my old college and was in his final year. Five weeks ago and without warning, he left the university and took a job as gardener with a Major Markland, who lives in a house called Summertrees outside Duxford. Mark gave me no explanation of this action either then or later. He lived alone in a cottage in Major Markland's grounds. Eighteen days later he was found by his employer's sister hanging by the neck from a strap knotted to a hook in the sitting-room ceiling. The verdict at the inquest was that he took his life while the balance of his mind was disturbed. I know little of my son's mind but I reject that comfortable euphemism. He was a rational person. He had a reason for his action. I want to know what it was.'

Miss Leaming, who had been looking out of the french windows to the garden, turned and said with sudden vehemence:

'This lust always to know! It's only prying. If he'd wanted us to know, he'd have told us.'

Sir Ronald said:

'I'm not prepared to go on in this uncertainty. My son is dead. *My* son. If I am in some way responsible, I prefer to know. If anyone else is responsible I want to know that too.'

Cordelia looked from one to the other: She asked:

'Did he leave a note?'

'He left a note but not an explanation. It was found in his typewriter.'

Quietly Miss Leaming began to speak:

'Down the winding cavern we groped our tedious way, till a void boundless as the nether sky appeared beneath us, and we held by the roots of trees and hung over this immensity; but I said: if you please we will commit ourselves to this void, and see whether providence is here also.'

The husky, curiously deep voice came to an end. They were silent. Then Sir Ronald said:

'You claim to be a detective, Miss Gray. What do you deduce from that?'

'That your son read William Blake. Isn't it a passage from *The Marriage of Heaven and Hell*?'

Sir Ronald and Miss Leaming glanced at each other. Sir Ronald said:

'So I am told.'

Cordelia thought that Blake's gently unemphatic exhortation, devoid of violence or despair, was more appropriate to suicide by drowning or by poison – a ceremonious floating or sinking into oblivion – than to the trauma of hanging. And yet there was the analogy of falling, of launching oneself into the void. But this speculation was indulgent fantasy. He had chosen Blake: he had chosen hanging. Perhaps other and more gentle means were not to hand; perhaps he had acted upon impulse. What was it that the Super always said? 'Never theorize in advance of your facts.' She would have to look at the cottage.

Sir Ronald said, with a touch of impatience.

'Well, don't you want the job?'

Cordelia looked at Miss Leaming but the woman did not meet her eyes.

'I want it very much. I was wondering whether you really want me to take it.'

'I'm offering it to you. Worry about your own responsibilities, Miss Gray, and I'll look after mine.'

Cordelia said:

'Is there anything else that you can tell me? The ordinary things. Was your son in good health? Did he seem worried about his work or his love affairs? About money?'

'Mark would have inherited a considerable fortune from his maternal grandfather had he reached the age of twenty-five. In the meantime, he received an adequate allowance from me, but from the date of leaving college he transferred the balance back to my own account and instructed his bank manager to deal similarly with any future payments. Presumably he lived on his earnings for the last two weeks of his life. The post-mortem revealed no illness and his tutor testified that his academic work was satisfactory. I, of course, know nothing of his subject. He didn't confide in me about his love affairs – what young man does to his father? If he had any, I would expect them to be heterosexual.'

Miss Leaming turned from her contemplation of the garden. She held out her hands in a gesture which could have been resignation or despair:

'We knew nothing about him, nothing! So why wait until he's dead and then start finding out?'

'And his friends?' asked Cordelia quietly.

'They rarely visited here but there were two I recognized at the inquest and the funeral: Hugo Tilling from his own college and his sister who is a postgraduate student at New Hall, studying philology. Do you remember her name, Eliza?'

'Sophie. Sophia Tilling. Mark brought her here to dinner once or twice.'

'Could you tell me something about your son's early life? Where was he educated?'

'He went to a pre-prep school when he was five and to a prep school subsequently. I couldn't have a child here running unsupervised in and out of the laboratory. Later, at his mother's wish – she died when Mark was nine months old – he went to a Woodard Foundation. My wife was what I believe is called a High Anglican and wanted the boy educated in that tradition. As far as I know, it had no deleterious effect on him.'

'Was he happy at prep school?'

'I expect he was as happy as most eight-year-olds are, which means that he was miserable most of the time, interposed with periods of animal spirits. Is all this relevant?'

'Anything could be. I have to try to get to know him, you see.'

What was it that the supercilious, sapient, superhuman Super had taught? 'Get to know the dead person. Nothing about him is too trivial, too unimportant. Dead men can talk. They can lead you directly to their murderer.' Only this time, of course, there wasn't a murderer. She said:

'It would be helpful if Miss Leaming could type out the information you have given me and add the name of his college and his tutor. And please may I have a note signed by you to authorize me to make enquiries.'

He reached down to a left-hand drawer in the desk, took out a sheet of writing paper and wrote on it; then he passed it to Cordelia.

The printed heading read: From Sir Ronald Callender, FRS, Garforth House, Cambridgeshire. Underneath he had written: *The bearer, Miss Cordelia Gray, is authorized to make enquiries on my behalf into the death on 26th May of my son Mark Callender.* He had signed and dated it. He asked:

'Is there anything else?'

Cordelia said:

'You talked about the possibility of someone else being responsible for your son's death. Do you quarrel with the verdict?'

'The verdict was in accordance with the evidence which is all one can expect of a verdict. A court of law is not constituted to establish the truth. I'm employing you to make an attempt at that. Have you everything you need? I don't think we can help you with any more information.'

'I should like a photograph.' They looked at each other nonplussed. He said to Miss Leaming.

'A photograph. Have we a photograph, Eliza?'

'There is his passport somewhere but I'm not sure where. I have that photograph I took of him in the garden last summer. It shows him fairly clearly, I think. I'll get it.' She went out of the room.

Cordelia said:

'And I should like to see his room, if I may. I assume that he stayed here during his vacations?'

'Only occasionally, but of course he had a room here. I'll show it to you.'

The room was on the second floor and at the back. Once inside, Sir Ronald ignored Cordelia. He walked over to the window and gazed out over the lawns as if neither she nor the room held any interest for him. It told Cordelia nothing about the adult Mark. It was simply furnished, a school boy's sanctum, and looked as if little had been changed in the last ten years. There was a low white cupboard against one wall with the usual row of discarded childhood toys; a teddy bear, his fur scuffed with much cuddling and one beady eye hanging loose; painted wooden trains and trucks; a Noah's Ark, its deck a-tumble with stiff-legged animals topped by a round-faced Noah and his wife; a boat with limp dejected sail; a miniature darts board. Above the toys were two rows of books. Cordelia went over to examine them. Here was the orthodox library of the middle-class child, the approved classics handed down from generation to generation, the traditional lore of Nanny and mother. Cordelia had come to them late as an adult; they had found no place in her Saturday comic and television-dominated childhood. She said:

'What about his present books?'

'They're in boxes in the cellar. He sent them here for storage when he left college and we haven't had time to unpack them yet. There hardly seems any point in it.'

There was a small round table beside the bed and on it a lamp and a bright round stone intricately holed by the sea, a treasure picked up, perhaps, from some holiday beach. Sir Ronald touched it gently with long tentative fingers then began rolling it under his palm over the surface of the table. Then, apparently without thinking, he dropped it into his pocket. 'Well,' he said. 'Shall we go down now?'

They were met at the foot of the stairs by Miss Leaming. She looked up at them as slowly they came down side by side. There was such controlled intensity in her regard that Cordelia waited almost with apprehension for her to speak. But she turned away, her shoulders drooping as if with sudden fatigue, and all she said was:

'I've found the photograph. I should like it back when you've finished with it, please. I've put it in the envelope with the note. There isn't a fast train back to London until nine thirty-seven, so perhaps you would care to stay for dinner?'

*

The dinner party which followed was an interesting but rather odd experience, the meal itself a blend of the formal and casual which Cordelia felt was the result of conscious effort rather than chance. Some effect, she felt, had been aimed at but whether of a dedicated band of co-workers meeting together at the end of a day for a corporate meal, or the ritual imposition of order and ceremony on a diverse company, she wasn't sure. The party numbered ten: Sir Ronald Callender, Miss Leaming, Chris Lunn, a visiting American professor, whose unpronounceable name she forgot as soon as Sir Ronald introduced her, and five of the young scientists. All the men, including Lunn, were in dinner jackets, and Miss Leaming wore a long skirt of patchwork satin below a plain sleeveless top. The rich blues, greens and reds gleamed and changed in the candlelight as she moved, and emphasized the pale silver of her hair and the almost colourless skin. Cordelia had been rather nonplussed when her hostess left her in the drawing-room and went upstairs to change. She wished that she had something more competitive than the fawn skirt and green top, being at an age to value elegance more highly than youth.

She had been shown to Miss Leaming's bedroom to wash and had been intrigued by the elegance and simplicity of the furniture and the contrasting opulence of the adjacent bathroom. Studying her tired face in the mirror and wielding her lipstick, she had wished she had some eye shadow with her. On impulse, and with a sense of guilt, she had pulled open a dressing-table drawer. It was filled with a variety of make-up; old lipsticks in colours long out of date; half-used bottles of foundation cream; eye pencils; moisturizing creams; half-used bottles of scent. She had rummaged, and eventually found, a stick of eye shadow which, in view of the wasteful muddle of discarded items in the drawer, she had had little compunction in using. The effect had been bizarre but striking. She could not compete with Miss Leaming but at least she looked five years older. The disorder in the drawer had surprised her and she had had to resist the temptation to see if the wardrobe and the other drawers were in a similar state of disarray. How inconsistent and how interesting human beings were! She thought it astonishing that such a fastidious and competent woman should be content to live with such a mess.

The dining-room was at the front of the house. Miss Leaming placed Cordelia between herself and Lunn, a seating which held little prospect of pleasurable conversation. The rest of the party sat where they wished. The contrast between simplicity and elegance showed in the table arrangements. There was no artificial light and three silver branched candlesticks were placed at regular intervals down the table. Between them were set four wine carafes made of thick green glass with curved lips, such as Cordelia had often seen in cheap Italian restaurants. The place mats were of plain cork, but the forks and spoons were antique silver. The flowers were set in low bowls, not skilfully arranged but looking as if they were casualties of a garden storm, blooms which had snapped off in the wind and which someone had thought it kind to place in water.

The young men looked incongruous in their dinner jackets, not ill at ease since they enjoyed the essential self-esteem of the clever and successful, but as if they had picked up the suits second-hand or at a fancy-dress costumier and were participating in a charade. Cordelia was surprised at their youth; she guessed that only one was over thirty. Three were untidy, fast-talking, restless young men with loud emphatic voices who took no notice of Cordelia after the first introduction. The other two were quieter and one, a tall black-haired boy with strong irregular features, smiled at her across the table and looked as if he would like to have sat within speaking distance.

The meal was brought in by an Italian manservant and his wife who left the cooked dishes on hot-plates on a side table. The food was plentiful and the smell almost intolerably appetizing to Cordelia, who hadn't realized until then just how hungry she was. There was a dish heaped high with glistening rice, a large casserole of veal in a rich mushroom sauce, a bowl of spinach. Beside it on the cold table was a large ham, a sirloin of beef and an interesting assortment of salads and fruit. The company served themselves, carrying their plates back to the table with whatever combination of food, hot or cold, they fancied. The young scientists piled their plates high and Cordelia followed their example.

She took little interest in the conversation except to notice that it was predominantly about science and that Lunn, although he spoke less than the others, spoke as their equal. He should, she thought, have looked ridiculous in his rather tight dinner jacket but, surprisingly, he looked the most at ease, the second most powerful personality in the room. Cordelia tried to analyse why this was so, but was defeated. He ate slowly, with finicky attention to the arrangement of the food on his plate, and from time to time, smiled secretly into his wine.

At the other end of the table Sir Ronald was peeling an apple and talking to his guest, his head inclined. The green rind slid thinly over his long fingers and curved down towards his plate. Cordelia glanced at Miss Leaming. She was staring at Sir Ronald with such unwavering and speculative concern, that Cordelia uncomfortably felt that every eye present must be irresistibly drawn to that pale disdainful mask. Then Miss Leaming seemed to become aware of her glance. She relaxed and turned to Cordelia:

'When we were travelling here together you were reading Hardy. Do you enjoy him?'

'Very much. But I enjoy Jane Austen more.'

'Then you must try to find an opportunity of visiting the Fitzwilliam Museum in Cambridge. They have a letter written by Jane Austen. I think you'd find it interesting.'

She spoke with the controlled, artificial brightness of a hostess trying to find a subject to interest a difficult guest. Cordelia, her mouth full of veal and mushrooms, wondered how she would manage to get through the rest of the meal. Luckily, however, the American professor had caught the word 'Fitzwilliam' and now called down the table to enquire about the Museum's collection of majolica in which, apparently, he was interested. The conversation became general.

It was Miss Leaming who drove Cordelia to the station, Audley End this time instead of Cambridge; a change for which no reason was given. They didn't speak about the case during the drive. Cordelia was exhausted with tiredness, food and wine and allowed herself to be firmly taken in hand and placed in the train without attempting to gain any further information. She didn't really think she would have got it. As the train drew out, her tired fingers fumbled with the flap of the strong white envelope which Miss Leaming had handed to her and she drew out and read the enclosed note. It was expertly typed and set out, but told her little more than she had already learnt. With it was the photograph. She saw the picture of a laughing boy, his head half-turned towards the camera, one hand shielding his eyes from the sun. He was wearing jeans and a vest and was half-lying on the lawn, a pile of books on the grass beside him. Perhaps he had been working there under the trees when she had come out of the french windows with her camera and called imperiously to him to smile. The photograph told Cordelia nothing except, that for one recorded second at least, he had known how to be happy. She placed it back in the envelope; her hands closed protectively over it. Cordelia slept.

CHAPTER TWO

Next morning Cordelia left Cremona Road before seven o'clock. Despite her tiredness the night before, she had made her major preparations before she went to bed. They hadn't taken long. As Bernie had taught her, she checked systematically the scene-of-crime kit, an unnecessary routine since nothing had been touched since, in celebration of their partnership, he had first set it up for her. She put ready the polaroid camera; sorted into order the road maps from the jumble pushed into the back of his desk; shook out the sleeping bag and rolled it ready; filled a carrier bag with iron rations from Bernie's store of tinned soup and baked beans; considered, and finally decided to take, their copy of Professor Simpson's book on forensic medicine and her own Hacker portable radio; checked the first-aid kit. Finally she found herself a fresh notebook, headed it *Case of Mark Callender* and ruled up the last few pages ready for her expense account. These preliminaries had always been the most satisfying part of a case, before boredom or distaste set in, before anticipation crumbled into disenchantment and failure. Bernie's planning had always been meticulous and successful; it was reality which had let him down.

Finally, she considered her clothes. If this hot weather continued her Jaeger suit, bought from her savings after much careful thought to see her through almost any interview, would be uncomfortably hot, but she might have to interview the head of a college and the dignified professionalism best exemplified by a suit would be the effect to aim at. She decided to travel in her fawn suede skirt with a short-sleeved jumper and pack jeans and warmer jumpers for any field work. Cordelia enjoyed clothes, enjoyed planning and buying them, a pleasure circumscribed less by poverty than by her obsessive need to be able to pack the whole of her wardrobe into one medium-sized suitcase like a refugee perpetually ready for flight.

Once she had shaken free from the tentacles of north London, Cordelia enjoyed the drive. The Mini purred along and Cordelia thought that it had never run so sweetly. She liked the flat East

Anglian countryside, the broad streets of the market towns, the way in which the fields grew unhedged to the edge of the road, the openness and freedom of the far horizons and wide skies. The country matched her mood. She had grieved for Bernie and would grieve for him again, missing his comradeship and his undemanding affection, but this, in a sense, was her first case and she was glad to be tackling it alone. It was one that she thought she could solve. It neither appalled nor disgusted her. Driving in happy anticipation through the sunbathed countryside, the boot of the car carefully packed with her gear, she was filled with the euphoria of hope.

When she finally reached Duxford village she had difficulty at first in finding Summertrees. Major Markland was apparently a man who thought that his importance warranted omitting the name of the road from his address. But the second person she stopped to ask was a villager who was able to point the way, taking infinite trouble over the simple directions as if fearing that a perfunctory answer might have seemed discourteous. Cordelia had to find a suitable place to turn and then drive back a couple of miles, for she had already passed Summertrees.

And this, at last, must be the house. It was a large Victorian edifice of red brick, set well back, with a wide turfed verge between the open wooden gate leading to the drive and the road. Cordelia wondered why anyone should have wanted to build such an intimidatingly ugly house or, having decided to do so, should have set down a suburban monstrosity in the middle of the countryside. Perhaps it had replaced an earlier more agreeable house. She drove the Mini on to the grass but at some distance from the gate and made her way up the drive. The garden suited the house; it was formal to the point of artificiality and too well kept. Even the rock plants burgeoned like morbid excrescences at carefully planned intervals between the terrace paving stones. There were two rectangular beds in the lawn, each planted with red rose trees and edged with alternate bands of lobelia and alyssum. They looked like a patriotic display in a public park. Cordelia felt the lack of a flag pole.

The front door was open, giving a view of a dark, brown-painted hall. Before Cordelia could ring, an elderly woman came round the corner of the house trundling a wheelbarrow full of plants. Despite the heat, she was wearing wellington boots, a jumper and long tweed skirt and had a scarf tied round her head. When she saw Cordelia she dropped the handle of the wheelbarrow and said:

'Oh, good morning. You've come from the church about the jumble, I expect?'

Cordelia said:

'No, not the jumble. I'm from Sir Ronald Callender. It's about his son.'

'Then I expect you've called for his things? We wondered when Sir Ronald was going to send for them. They're all still at the cottage. We haven't been down there since Mark died. We called him Mark, you know. Well, he never told us who he was which was rather naughty of him.'

'It isn't about Mark's things. I want to talk about Mark himself. Sir Ronald has engaged me to try to find out why his son killed himself. My name is Cordelia Gray.'

This news seemed to puzzle rather than disconcert Mrs Markland. She blinked at Cordelia rapidly through troubled, rather stupid, eyes and clutched at the wheelbarrow handle as if for support.

'Cordelia Gray? Then we haven't met before, have we? I don't think I know a Cordelia Gray. Perhaps it would be better if you came into the drawing room and talked to my husband and sister-in-law.'

She abandoned the barrow where it stood in the middle of the path and led the way into the house, pulling off her head scarf and making ineffective pats at her hair. Cordelia followed her through the sparsely furnished hall, smelling of floor polish, with its clutter of walking sticks, umbrellas and mackintoshes draping the heavy oak hatstand, and into a room at the back of the house.

It was a horrible room, ill-proportioned, bookless, furnished not in poor taste but in no taste at all. A huge sofa of repellent design and two armchairs surrounded the fireplace and a heavy mahogany table, ornately carved and lurching on its pedestal, occupied the centre of the room. There was little other furniture. The only pictures were framed groups, pale oblong faces too small to identify posed in straight innominate lines in front of the camera. One was a regimental photograph; the other had a pair of crossed oars above two rows of burly adolescents, all of whom were wearing low peaked caps and striped blazers. Cordelia supposed it to be a school boating club.

Despite the warmth of the day, the room was sunless and cold.

The doors of the french windows were open. On the lawn outside were grouped a large swinging sofa with a fringed canopy, three cane chairs sumptuously cushioned in a garish blue cretonne, each with its footrest, and a wooden slatted table. They looked part of a setting for a play in which the designer had somehow failed to catch the mood. All the garden furniture looked new and unused. Cordelia wondered why the family should bother to sit indoors on a summer morning while the lawn was so much more comfortably furnished.

Mrs Markland introduced Cordelia by sweeping her arm in a wide gesture of abandonment and saying feebly to the company in general:

'Miss Cordelia Gray. It isn't about the church jumble.'

Cordelia was struck by the resemblance that husband and wife and Miss Markland bore to each other. All three reminded her of horses. They had long, bony faces, narrow mouths above strong, square chins, eyes set unattractively close, and grey, coarse-looking hair which the two women wore in thick fringes almost to the eyes. Major Markland was drinking coffee from an immense white cup, much stained about the rim and sides, which had been set on a round tin tray. He held *The Times* in his hands. Miss Markland was knitting, an occupation which Cordelia vaguely felt was inappropriate to a hot summer morning.

The two faces, unwelcoming, only partly curious, regarded her with faint distaste. Miss Markland could knit without looking at the needles, an accomplishment which enabled her to fix Cordelia with sharp, inquisitive eyes. Invited by Major Markland to sit, Cordelia perched on the edge of the sofa, half expecting the smooth cushion to let out a rude noise as it subsided beneath her. She found it, however, unexpectedly hard. She composed her face into the appropriate expression – seriousness combined with efficiency and a touch of propitiatory humility seemed about right, but she wasn't sure that she managed to bring it off. As she sat there, knees demurely together, her shoulder bag at her feet, she was unhappily aware that she probably looked more like an eager seventeen-year-old facing her first interview than a mature business woman, sole proprietor of Pryde's Detective Agency.

She handed over Sir Ronald's note of authority and said:

'Sir Ronald was very distressed on your account, I mean it was awful for you that it should happen on your property when you'd been so kind in finding Mark a job he liked. His father hopes you won't mind talking about it; it's just that he wants to know what made his son kill himself.'

'And he sent you?' Miss Markland's voice was a compound of disbelief, amusement and contempt. Cordelia didn't resent the rudeness. She felt Miss Markland had a point. She gave what she hoped was a credible explanation. It was probably true.

'Sir Ronald thinks that it must have been something to do with Mark's life at university. He left college suddenly, as you may know, and his father was never told why. Sir Ronald thought that I might be more successful in talking to Mark's friends than the more usual type of private detective. He didn't feel that he could trouble the police; after all, this sort of enquiry isn't really their kind of job.'

Miss Markland said grimly:

'I should have thought it was precisely their job; that is, if Sir Ronald thinks there's something odd about his son's death . . .'

Cordelia broke in:

'Oh no, I don't think there's any suggestion of that! He's quite satisfied with the verdict. It's just that he badly wants to know what made him do it.'

Miss Markland said with sudden fierceness:

'He was a drop-out. He dropped out of university, apparently he dropped out of his family obligations, finally he dropped out of life. Literally.'

Her sister-in-law gave a little bleat of protest.

'Oh, Eleanor, is that quite fair? He worked really well here. I liked the boy. I don't think – '

'I don't deny that he earned his money. That doesn't alter the fact that he was neither bred nor educated to be a jobbing gardener. He was, therefore, a drop-out. I don't know the reason and I have no interest in discovering it.'

'How did you come to employ him?' asked Cordelia.

It was Major Markland who answered.

'He saw my advertisement in the *Cambridge Evening News* for a gardener and turned up here one evening on his bicycle. I suppose he cycled all the way from Cambridge. It must have been about five weeks ago, a Tuesday I think.'

Again Miss Markland broke in:

'It was Tuesday, May 9th.'

The Major frowned at her as if irritated that he couldn't fault the information.

'Yes, well, Tuesday the 9th. He said that he had decided to leave university and take a job and that he'd seen my advertisement. He admitted that he didn't know much about gardening but said that he was strong and was willing to learn. His inexperience didn't worry me; we wanted him mostly for the lawns and for the vegetables. He never touched the flower garden; my wife and I see to that ourselves. Anyway, I quite liked the look of the boy and thought I'd give him a chance.'

Miss Markland said:

'You took him because he was the only applicant who was prepared to work for the miserable pittance you were offering.' The Major, so far from showing offence at this frankness, smiled complacently.

'I paid him what he was worth. If more employers were prepared to do that, the country wouldn't be plagued with this inflation.' He spoke as one to whom economics were an open book.

'Didn't you think it was odd, his turning up like that?' asked Cordelia.

'Of course I did, damned odd! I thought he had probably been sent down; drink, drugs, revolution, you know the sort of things they get up to at Cambridge now. But I asked him for the name of his tutor as a referee and rang him, a fellow called Horsfall. He wasn't particularly forthcoming but he did assure me that the boy had left voluntarily and to use his own words, his conduct while in college had been almost boringly irreproachable. I need not fear that the shades of Summertrees would be polluted.'

Miss Markland turned her knitting and broke into her sister-in-law's little cry of 'What can he have meant by that?' with the dry comment:

'A little more boredom of that kind would be welcome from the city of the plains.'

'Did Mr Horsfall tell you why Mark had left college?' asked Cordelia.

'I didn't enquire. That wasn't my business. I asked a plain question and I got a more or less plain answer, as plain as you can expect from those academic types. We certainly had no complaint about the lad while he was here. I speak as I find.'

'When did he move into the cottage?' asked Cordelia.

'Immediately. That wasn't our idea, of course. We never advertised the job as residential. However, he's obviously seen the cottage and taken a fancy to the place and he asked if we'd mind if he camped out there. It wasn't practicable for him to cycle in from Cambridge each day, we could quite see that, and as far as we knew there was no one in the village who could put him up. I can't say I was keen on the idea; the cottage needs a lot doing to it. Actually we have it in mind to apply for a conversion grant and then get rid of the place. It wouldn't do for a family in its present state but the lad seemed keen on roughing it there, so we agreed.'

Cordelia said:

'So he must have inspected the cottage before he came for the job?'

'Inspected? Oh, I don't know. He probably snooped around to see what the property was like before he actually came to the door. I don't know that I blame him, I'd have done the same myself.'

Mrs Markland broke in:

'He was very keen on the cottage, very keen. I pointed out that there was no gas or electricity but he said that that wouldn't worry him; he'd buy a primus stove and manage with lamps. There's water laid on, of course, and the main part of the roof is really quite sound. At least I think it is. We don't go there you know. He seemed to settle in very happily. We never actually visited him, there was no need, but as far as I could see he was looking after himself perfectly well. Of course as my husband said, he was very inexperienced; there were one or two things we had to teach him, like coming up to the kitchen early every morning for the orders. But I liked the boy; he was always working hard when I was in the garden.'

Cordelia said:

'I wonder if I might have a look at the cottage?'

The request disconcerted them. Major Markland looked at his wife. There was an embarrassed silence and for a moment Cordelia feared that the answer would be no. Then Miss Markland stabbed her needles into the ball of wool and got to her feet:

'I'll come with you now,' she said.

The grounds of Summertrees were spacious. First there was the formal rose garden, the bushes closely planted and grouped according to variety and colour like a market garden, the name tags fixed at precisely the same height from the earth. Next was the kitchen garden cut in two by a gravel path with evidence of Mark Callender's work in the weeded rows of lettuce and cabbages, the patches of dug earth. Finally they passed through a gate into a small orchard of old and unpruned apple trees. The scythed grass, smelling richly of hay, lay in thick swathes round the gnarled trunks.

At the furthest end of the orchard was a thick hedge, so overgrown that the wicket gate into the rear garden of the cottage was at first difficult to see. But the grass around it had been trimmed and the gate opened easily to Miss Markland's hand. On the other side was a thick bramble hedge, dark and impenetrable and obviously allowed to grow wild for a generation. Someone had hacked a way through, but Miss Markland and Cordelia had to bend low to avoid catching their hair on its tangled tentacles of thorn.

Once free of this barrier, Cordelia lifted her head and blinked in the bright sunshine. She gave a little exclamation of pleasure. In the short time in which he had lived here Mark Callender had created a little oasis of order and beauty out of chaos and neglect. Old flower beds had been discovered and the surviving plants tended; the stone path had been scraped free of grass and moss; a minute square of lawn to the right of the cottage door had been cut and weeded. On the other side of the path a patch about twelve feet square had been partly dug. The fork was still in the earth, driven deep about two feet from the end of the row.

The cottage was a low, brick building under a slate roof. Bathed in sunshine, and despite its bare, rain-scoured door, its rotted window frames and the glimpse of exposed beams in the roof, it had the gentle melancholy charm of age which hadn't yet degenerated into decay. Just outside the cottage door, dropped casually side by side, was a pair of heavy gardening shoes encrusted with earth.

'His?' asked Cordelia.

'Who else's?'

They stood together for a moment contemplating the dug earth. Neither spoke. Then they moved to the back door. Miss Markland fitted the key into the lock. It turned easily as if the lock had been recently oiled. Cordelia followed her into the sitting-room of the cottage.

The air was cool after the heat of the garden but unfresh, with a taint of contagion. Cordelia saw that the plan of the cottage was simple. There were three doors, one straight ahead obviously led to the front garden but was locked and barred, the joints hung with cobwebs as if it hadn't been opened for generations. One to the right led, as Cordelia guessed, to the kitchen. The third door was ajar and she could glimpse through it an uncarpeted wooden stairway leading to the first floor. In the middle of the room was a wooden-topped table, the surface scarred with much scrubbing, and with two kitchen chairs, one at each end. In the middle of the table a blue rimmed mug held a posy of dead flowers, black brittle stems bearing sad tatters of unidentifiable plants, their pollen staining the surface of the table like golden dust. Shafts of sunlight cut across the still air; in their beams a myriad of motes, specks of dust and infinitesimal life danced grotesquely.

To the right was a fireplace, an old-fashioned iron range with ovens each side of the open fire. Mark had been burning wood and papers; there was a mound of white ash in the grate and a pile of kindling wood and small logs placed ready for the next cool evening. On one side of the fire was a low wooden slatted chair with a faded cushion and on the other a wheel-backed chair with the legs sawn off, perhaps to make it low enough for nursing a child. Cordelia thought that it must have been a beautiful chair before its mutilation.

Two immense beams, blackened with age, ran across the ceiling. In the middle of one was fixed a steel hook, probably once used for hanging bacon. Cordelia and Miss Markland looked at it without speaking; there was no need for question and answer. After a moment they moved, as if by common consent, to the two fireside chairs and sat down. Miss Markland said:

'I was the one who found him. He didn't come up to the kitchen for the day's orders so after breakfast I walked down here to see if he had overslept. It was nine twenty-three exactly. The door was unlocked. I knocked, but there was no reply so I pushed it open. He was hanging from that hook with a leather belt round his neck. He was wearing his blue cotton trousers, the ones he usually worked in, and his feet were bare. That chair was lying on its side on the floor. I touched his chest. He was quite cold.'

'Did you cut him down?'

'No. He was obviously dead and I thought it better to leave the

44

body until the police arrived. But I did pick up the chair and place it so that it supported his feet. That was an irrational action, I know, but I couldn't bear to see him hanging there without releasing the pressure on his throat. It was, as I've said, irrational.'

'I think it was very natural. Did you notice anything else about him, about the room?'

'There was a half-empty mug of what looked like coffee on the table and a great deal of ash in the grate. It looked as if he had been burning papers. His portable typewriter was where you see it now, on that side table; the suicide note was still in the machine. I read it, then I went back to the house, told my brother and sister-in-law what had happened and rang the police. After the police arrived I brought them to this cottage, and confirmed what I had seen. I never came in here again until this moment.'

'Did you, or Major and Mrs Markland, see Mark on the night he died?'

'None of us saw him after he stopped work at about six-thirty. He was a little later that evening because he wanted to finish mowing the front lawn. We all saw him putting the mower away, then walking across the garden towards the orchard. We never saw him alive again. No one was at home at Summertrees that night. We had a dinner party at Trumpington – an old army colleague of my brother. We didn't get home until after midnight. By then, according to the medical evidence, Mark must have been dead about four hours.'

Cordelia said:

'Please tell me about him.'

'What is there to tell? His official hours were eight-thirty to six o'clock, with an hour for lunch and half an hour for tea. In the evenings he would work in the garden here or round the cottage. Sometimes in his lunch hour he would cycle to the village store. I used to meet him there from time to time. He didn't buy much – a loaf of wholemeal bread, butter, the cheapest cut of bacon, tea, coffee – the usual things. I heard him ask about free-range eggs and Mrs Morgan told him that Wilcox at Grange Farm would always sell him half a dozen. We didn't speak when we met, but he would smile. In the evenings once the light had faded, he used to read or type at that table. I could see his head against the lamplight.'

'I thought Major Markland said that you didn't visit the cottage?'

'They don't; it holds certain embarrassing memories for them. I do.' She paused and looked into the dead fire.

'My fiancé and I used to spend a great deal of time here before the war when he was at Cambridge. He was killed in 1937, fighting in Spain for the Republican cause.'

'I'm sorry,' said Cordelia. She felt the inadequacy, the insincerity of her response and yet, what else was there to say? It had all happened nearly forty years ago. She hadn't heard of him before. The spasm of grief, so brief that it was hardly felt, was no more than a transitory inconvenience, a sentimental regret for all lovers who died young, for the inevitability of human loss.

Miss Markland spoke with sudden passion as if the words were being forced out of her:

'I don't like your generation, Miss Gray. I don't like your arrogance, your selfishness, your violence, the curious selectivity of your compassion. You pay for nothing with your own coin, not even for your ideals. You denigrate and destroy and never build. You invite punishment like rebellious children, then scream when you are punished. The men I knew, the men I was brought up with, were not like that.'

Cordelia said gently:

'I don't think Mark Callender was like that either.'

'Perhaps not. At least the violence he practised was on himself.' She looked up at Cordelia searchingly.

'No doubt you'll say I'm jealous of youth. It's a common enough syndrome of my generation.'

'It ought not to be. I can never see why people should be jealous. After all, youth isn't a matter of privilege, we all get the same share of it. Some people may be born at an easier time or be richer or more privileged than others, but that hasn't anything to do with being young. And being young is terrible sometimes. Don't you remember how terrible it could be?'

'Yes, I remember. But I remember other things too.'

Cordelia sat in silence, thinking that the conversation was strange but somehow inevitable and that, for some reason, she didn't resent it. Miss Markland looked up.

'His girlfriend visited him once. At least, I suppose she was his girlfriend or why should she have come? It was about three days after he started work.'

'What was she like?'

'Beautiful. Very fair, with a face like a Botticelli angel – smooth, oval, unintelligent. She was foreign, French, I think. She was also rich.'

'How could you tell that, Miss Markland?' Cordelia was intrigued.

'Because she spoke with a foreign accent; because she arrived driving a white Renault which I took to be her own car; because her clothes, although odd and unsuitable for the country, weren't cheap; because she walked up to the front door and announced that she wanted to see him with the confident arrogance that one associates with the rich.'

'And did he see her?'

'He was working in the orchard at the time, scything the grass. I took her down to him. He greeted her calmly and without embarrassment and took her to sit in the cottage garden until it was time for him to stop work. He seemed pleased enough to see her but not, I thought, either delighted or surprised. He didn't introduce her. I left them together and returned to the house before he had a chance to. I didn't see her again.'

Before Cordelia could speak she said suddenly:

'You're thinking of living here for a time, aren't you?'

'Will they mind? I didn't like to ask in case they said no.'

'They won't know, and if they did, they wouldn't care.'

'But do you mind?'

'No. I shan't worry you and I don't mind.' They were talking in whispers as if in church. Then Miss Markland got up and moved to the door. She turned.

'You've taken on this job for the money, of course. Why not? But if I were you I'd keep it that way. It's unwise to become too personally involved with another human being. When that human being is dead, it can be dangerous as well as unwise.'

*

Miss Markland stumped off down the garden path and disappeared through the wicket gate. Cordelia was glad to see her go. She was fidgeting with impatience to examine the cottage. This was where it had happened; this was where her job really began.

What was it that the Super had said? 'When you're examining a building look at it as you would a country church. Walk round it first. Look at the whole scene inside and out; then make your deductions. Ask yourself what you saw, not what you expected to see or what you hoped to see, but what you saw.'

He must be a man then who liked country churches and that at least was a point in his favour; for this, surely, was genuine Dalgliesh dogma. Bernie's reaction to churches, whether country or town, had been one of half-superstitious wariness. Cordelia decided to follow the advice.

She made her way first to the east side of the cottage. Here, discreetly set back and almost smothered by the hedge, was a wooden privy with its latched stable-like door. Cordelia peeped inside. The privy was very clean and looked as if it had been recently repainted. When she pulled the chain, to her relief, the bowl flushed. There was a roll of lavatory paper hanging by a string from the door and nailed beside it a small plastic bag containing a crumpled collection of orange papers and other soft wrappings. He had been an economical young man. Next to the privy was a large dilapidated shed containing a man's bicycle, old but well cared for, a large tin of white emulsion paint with the lid rammed down hard and a clean brush upended in a jam jar beside it, a tin bath, a few clean sacks, and a collection of gardening tools. All were shining clean and were neatly disposed against the wall or supported on nails.

She moved to the front of the cottage. This was in marked contrast to the southern aspect. Here Mark Callender had made no attempt to tackle the waist-high wilderness of nettles and grass which stifled the small front garden and almost obliterated the path. A thick climbing shrub sprinkled with small white flowers had thrust its black and thorned boughs to bar the two ground-floor windows. The gate leading to the lane had stuck and would open only wide enough for a visitor to squeeze through. On each side a holly tree stood sentinel, its leaves grey with dust. The front hedge of privet was head-high. Cordelia could see that on either side of the path there had once been twin flower beds edged with large round stones which had been painted white. Now most of the stones had sunk out of sight among the encroaching weeds and nothing remained of the beds but a tangle of wild and straggling roses.

As she took a last look at the front garden, her eye caught a flash of colour half trodden among the weeds at the side of the path. It was a crumpled page of an illustrated magazine. She smoothed it open and saw that it was a colour photograph of a female nude. The woman had her back to the camera and was bending forward, gross buttocks splayed above booted thighs. She was smiling saucily over her shoulder in a blatant invitation made more grotesque by the long androgynous face which even tactful lighting couldn't make other than repellent. Cordelia noted the date at the top of the page; it was the May edition. So the magazine, or at least the picture, could have been brought to the cottage while he was there.

She stood with it in her hand trying to analyse the nature of her disgust which seemed to her excessive. The picture was vulgar and salacious but no more offensive or indecent than dozens on view in the side streets of London. But as she folded it away in her bag – for it was evidence of a kind – she felt contaminated and depressed. Had Miss Markland been more percipient than she knew? Was she, Cordelia, in danger of becoming sentimentally obsessed with the dead boy? The picture probably had nothing to do with Mark; it could easily have been dropped by some visitor to the cottage. But she wished that she hadn't seen it.

She passed round to the west of the cottage and made one more discovery. Hidden behind a clump of elder bushes was a small well about four feet in diameter. It had no superstructure but was closely fitted with a domed lid made of strong slatted wood and fitted at the top with an iron hoop. Cordelia saw that the cover was padlocked to the wooden rim of the well and the lock, although rusty with age, held firm at her tug. Someone had taken the trouble to see that there was no danger here to exploring children or visiting tramps.

And now it was time to explore the interior of the cottage. First the kitchen. It was a small room with a window over the sink looking east. It had obviously been recently painted and the large table which took up most of the room had been covered with a red plastic cloth. There was a poky larder containing half a dozen tins of beer, a jar of marmalade, a crock of butter and the mouldy heel of a loaf. It was here in the kitchen that Cordelia found the explanation of the disagreeable smell which had struck her on entering the cottage. On the table was an open bottle of milk about half full, the silver top crumpled beside it. The milk was solid and furred with putrefaction; a bloated fly was sucking at the rim of the bottle and still stuck to its feast as, instinctively, she tried to flick it away. On the other side of the table was a twin-burner paraffin stove with a heavy pot on one burner. Cordelia tugged at the close-fitting lid and it came off suddenly, letting out a rich repulsive smell. She opened the table drawer and stirred the mess with a spoon. It looked like beef stew. Chunks of greenish meat, soapy-looking potatoes and unidentifiable vegetables floated up through the scum like drowned and putrefying flesh. Beside the sink was an orange box placed on one side and used as a vegetable store. The potatoes were green, the onions had shrunk and sprouted, the carrots were wrinkled and limp. So nothing had been cleaned up, nothing had been removed. The police had taken away the body and any evidence they required but no one, neither the Marklands nor the boy's family or friends, had bothered to come back to clean up the pathetic leavings of his young life.

Cordelia went upstairs. A cramped landing led to two bedrooms, one obviously unused for years. Here the window frame had rotted, the ceiling plaster had crumbled and a faded paper patterned with roses was peeling away with the damp. The second and larger room was the one in which he had slept. There was a single iron bed with a hair mattress and on it a sleeping bag and a bolster folded in two to make a high pillow. Beside the bed was an old table with two candles, stuck with their own wax to a cracked plate, and a box of matches. His clothes were hung in the single cupboard; a pair of bright green corduroy trousers, one or two shirts, pullovers and one formal suit. A few underclothes, clean but not ironed, were folded on the ledge above. Cordelia fingered the pullovers. They were hand-knitted in thick wool and intricate patterns and there were four of them. Someone, then, had cared enough about him to take some trouble on his behalf. She wondered who.

She ran her hands over his meagre wardrobe, feeling for pockets. She found nothing except a slim, brown leather wallet in the bottom left-hand pocket of his suit. Excitedly she carried it over to the window hoping that it might contain a clue – a letter, perhaps, a list of names and addresses, a personal note. But the wallet was empty except for a couple of pound notes, his driving licence and a blood donor's card issued by the Cambridge blood transfusion service, which showed his group as B rhesus negative.

The uncurtained window gave a view of the garden. His books were arranged on the window shelf. There were only a few of them:

several volumes of the *Cambridge Modern History*; some Trollope and Hardy; a complete William Blake; school textbook volumes of Wordsworth, Browning and Donne; two paperbacks on gardening. At the end of the row was a white leather-bound book which Cordelia saw was the Book of Common Prayer. It was fitted with a finely wrought brass clasp and looked much used. She was disappointed in the books; they told her little beyond his superficial tastes. If he had come to this solitary life to study, to write or to philosophize he had come singularly ill-equipped.

The most interesting thing in the room was above the bed. It was a small oil painting about nine inches square. Cordelia studied it. It was certainly Italian and probably, she thought, late fifteenth century. It showed a very young tonsured monk reading at a table, his sensitive fingers enleafed between the pages of his book. The long, controlled face was taut with concentration, the heavy-lidded eyes were fixed on the page. Behind him, a view from the open window was a miniature of delight. Cordelia thought that one would never tire of looking at it. It was a Tuscan scene showing a walled city with towers enclosed by cypresses, a river winding like a silver stream, a gaudily clad procession preceded by banners, yoked oxen working in the fields. She saw the picture as a contrast between the worlds of intellect and action and tried to remember where she had seen similar paintings. The comrades – as Cordelia always thought of that ubiquitous band of fellow-revolutionaries who attached themselves to her father – had been very fond of exchanging messages in art galleries and Cordelia had spent hours walking slowly from picture to picture, waiting for the casual visitor to pause beside her and whisper his few words of warning or information. The device had always struck her as a childish and unnecessarily histrionic way of communicating, but at least the galleries were warm and she had enjoyed looking at the pictures. She enjoyed this picture; he had obviously liked it too. Had he also liked that vulgar illustration which she had found in the front garden? Were they both an essential part of his nature?

The tour of inspection over, she made herself coffee using a packet from his store cupboard and boiling the water on the stove. She took a chair from the sitting-room and sat outside the back door with the mug of coffee in her lap, her head stretched back to feel the sun. She was filled with a gentle happiness as she sat there, contented and relaxed, listening to the silence, her half-closed lids impressed with the visage of the sun. But now it was the time to think. She had examined the cottage in accordance with the Super's instructions. What did she now know about the dead boy? What had she seen? What could she deduce?

He had been almost obsessively neat and tidy. His garden tools were wiped after use and carefully put away, his kitchen had been painted and was clean and ordered. Yet he had abandoned his digging less than two feet from the end of a row; had left the uncleaned fork in the earth; had dropped his gardening shoes casually at the back door. He had apparently burnt all his papers before killing himself, yet had left his coffee mug unwashed. He had made himself a stew for his supper which he hadn't touched. The preparation of the vegetables must have been done earlier in the same day, or perhaps the day before, but the stew was clearly intended for supper that night. The pot was still on the stove and was full to the brim. This wasn't a heated-up meal, one left from the evening before. This surely meant that he had only made the decision to kill himself after the stew had been prepared and had been put on the stove to cook. Why should he trouble to prepare a meal that he knew he wouldn't be alive to eat?

But was it likely, she wondered, that a healthy young man coming in from an hour or two of hard digging and with a hot meal waiting should be in that mood of boredom, accidie, anguish or despair which could lead to suicide? Cordelia could remember times of intense unhappiness, but she couldn't recall that they had followed purposeful outdoor exercise in the sun with a meal in prospect. And why the mug of coffee, the one which the police had taken away to analyse? There were tins of beer in the larder; if he had come in thirsty from his digging, why not open one of those? Beer would have been the quickest, the obvious way of quenching thirst. Surely no one, however thirsty, would brew and drink coffee just before a meal. Coffee came after the food.

But suppose someone had visited him that evening. It wasn't likely to have been someone calling with a casual message as he passed by; it was important enough for Mark to break off his digging even within two feet of the end of a row and invite the visitor into the cottage. It was probably a visitor who didn't like or drink beer – could that mean a woman? It was a visitor who wasn't expected to stay for supper but yet was at the cottage long enough to be offered some refreshment. Perhaps it was someone on his way to his own evening meal. Obviously, the visitor hadn't been invited to supper earlier or why would the two of them have begun the meal by drinking coffee and why would Mark have worked so late in the garden instead of coming in to change? So it was an unexpected visitor. But why was there only one mug of coffee? Surely Mark would have shared it with his guest or, if he preferred not to drink coffee, would have opened a tin of beer for himself. But there was no empty beer can in the kitchen and no second mug. Had it perhaps been washed and put away? But why should Mark wash one mug and not the other? Was it to conceal the fact that he'd had a visitor that evening?

The jug of coffee on the kitchen table was almost empty and the bottle of milk only half full. Surely more than one person had taken milk and coffee. But perhaps that was a dangerous and unwarranted deduction; the visitor might well have had his mug refilled.

But suppose it wasn't Mark who had wished to conceal the fact that a visitor had called that night; suppose it wasn't Mark who had washed and put away the second mug; suppose it was the visitor who had wished to conceal the fact of his presence. But why should he bother to do that since he couldn't know that Mark was going to kill himself? Cordelia shook herself impatiently. This, of course, was nonsense. Obviously the visitor wouldn't have washed up the mug if Mark were still there and alive. He would only have obliterated the evidence of his visit if Mark were already dead. And if Mark had been dead, had been strung up on that hook before his visitor left the cottage, then could this really be suicide? A word dancing at the back of Cordelia's mind, an amorphous half-formed jangle of letters, came suddenly into focus and, for the first time, spelt out clearly the blood-stained word. Murder.

*

Cordelia sat on in the sun for another five minutes finishing her coffee, then she washed up the mug and hung it back on a hook in the larder. She walked down the lane to the road to where the Mini was still parked on the grass verge outside Summertrees, glad of the instinct that had led her to leave it out of sight of the house. Letting in the clutch gently, she drove it slowly down the lane looking carefully from side to side for a possible parking place; to leave it outside the cottage would only advertise her presence. It was a pity that Cambridge wasn't closer; she could then have used Mark's bicycle. The Mini was necessary to her task but would be inconveniently conspicuous wherever she left it.

But she was lucky. About fifty yards down the lane was the entrance to a field, a wide grass verge with a small copse at one side. The copse looked damp and sinister. It was impossible to believe that flowers could spring from this tainted earth or bloom among these scarred and misshapen trees. The ground was scattered with old pots and pans, the upended skeleton of a pram, a battered and rusty gas stove. Beside a stunted oak a matted heap of blankets were disintegrating into the earth. But there was space for her to drive the Mini off the road and under cover of a kind. If she locked it carefully it would be better here than outside the cottage and at night, she thought, it would be unobserved.

But now, she drove it back to the cottage and began to unpack. She moved Mark's few underclothes to one side of the shelf and set her own beside them. She laid her sleeping bag on the bed over his, thinking that she would be glad of the extra comfort. There was a red toothbrush and half-used tube of toothpaste in a jamjar on the kitchen window ledge; she placed her yellow brush and her own tube beside them. She hung her towel next to his across the cord which he had fixed between two nails under the kitchen sink. Then she made an inventory of the contents of the larder and a list of the things she would need. It would be better to buy them in Cambridge; she would only draw attention to her presence if she shopped locally. The saucepan of stew and the half bottle of milk were a worry. She couldn't leave them in the kitchen to sour the cottage with the stench of decay but she was reluctant to throw the contents away. She considered whether to photograph them but decided against it; tangible objects were better evidence. In the end she carried them out to the shed and shrouded them thickly with a piece of old sacking.

Last of all, she thought about the gun. It was a heavy object to carry with her all the time but she felt unhappy about parting with it, even temporarily. Although the back door of the cottage could be locked and Miss Markland had left her the key, an intruder would have no difficulty in breaking in through a window. She decided that the best plan would be to secrete the ammunition among her underclothes in the bedroom cupboard but to hide the pistol itself separately in or near the cottage. The exact place cost her a little thought, but then she remembered the thick and twisting limbs of the elder bush by the well; by reaching high, she was able to feel for a convenient hollow near the fork of a branch and could slip the gun, still shrouded in its draw-string bag, among the concealing leaves.

At last she was ready to leave for Cambridge. She looked at her watch; it was half-past ten; she could be in Cambridge by eleven and there would still be two hours of the morning to go. She decided that her best plan would be to visit the newspaper office first and read the account of the inquest, then to see the police; after that she would go in search of Hugo and Sophia Tilling.

She drove away from the cottage with a feeling very like regret, as if she were leaving home. It was, she thought, a curious place, heavy with atmosphere and showing two distinct faces to the world like facets of a human personality; the north, with its dead thorn-barred windows, its encroaching weeds, and its forbidding hedge of privet, was a numinous stage for horror and tragedy. Yet the rear, where he had lived and worked, had cleared and dug the garden and tied up the few flowers, had weeded the path, and opened the windows to the sun, was as peaceful as a sanctuary. Sitting there at the door she had felt that nothing horrible could ever touch her; she was able to contemplate the night there alone without fear. Was it this atmosphere of healing tranquillity, she wondered, that had attracted Mark Callender? Had he sensed it before he took the job, or was it in some mysterious way the result of his transitory and doomed sojourn there? Major Markland had been right; obviously Mark had looked at the cottage before he went up to the house. Had it been the cottage he wanted or the job? Why were the Marklands so reluctant to come to the place, so reluctant that they obviously hadn't visited it even to clean up after his death? And why had Miss Markland spied on him, for surely such close observation was very close to spying? Had she only confided that story about her dead lover to justify her interest in the cottage, her obsessional preoccupation with what the new gardener was doing? And was the story even true? That ageing body heavy with latent strength, that equine expression of perpetual discontent, could she really once have been young, have lain perhaps with her lover on Mark's bed through the long, warm evenings of long-dead summers? How remote, how impossible and grotesque it all seemed.

Cordelia drove down Hills Road, past the vigorous memorial statue of a young 1914 soldier striding to death, past the Roman Catholic church and into the centre of the city. Again she wished that she could have abandoned the car in favour of Mark's bicycle. Everyone else seemed to be riding one and the air tinkled with bells like a festival. In these narrow and crowded streets even the compact Mini was a liability. She decided to park it as soon as she could find a place and set out on foot in search of a telephone. She had decided to vary her programme and see the police first.

But it didn't surprise her when at last she rang the police station to hear that Sergeant Maskell, who had dealt with the Callender case, was tied up all the morning. It was only in fiction that the people one wanted to interview were sitting ready at home or in their office, with time, energy and interest to spare. In real life, they were about their own business and one waited on their convenience, even if, untypically, they welcomed the attention of Pryde's Detective Agency. Usually they didn't. She hardly expected Sergeant Maskell to welcome it. She mentioned Sir Ronald's note of authority to impress her hearer with the authenticity of her business. The name was not without influence. He went away to enquire. After less than a minute he came back to say that Sergeant Maskell could see Miss Gray at two-thirty that afternoon.

So the newspaper office came first after all. Old files were at least accessible and could not object to being consulted. She quickly found what she wanted. The account of the inquest was brief, couched in the usual formal language of a court report. It told her little that was new, but she made a careful note of the main evidence. Sir Ronald Callender testified that he hadn't spoken to his son for over a fortnight before his death, when Mark had telephoned to tell his father of his decision to leave college and to take a job at Summertrees. He hadn't consulted Sir Ronald before making his decision nor had he explained his reasons. Sir Ronald had subsequently spoken to the Master, and the college authorities were prepared to take his son back for the next academic year if he changed his mind. His son had never spoken to him of suicide and had no health or money worries as far as he was aware. Sir Ronald's testimony was followed by a brief reference to other evidence. Miss

Markland described how she had found the body; a forensic pathologist testified that the cause of death was asphyxia due to strangulation; Sergeant Maskell recounted the measures he had thought it proper to take and a report from the forensic science laboratory was submitted which stated that a mug of coffee found on the table had been analysed and found harmless. The verdict was that the deceased died by his own hand while the balance of his mind was disturbed. Closing the heavy file, Cordelia felt depressed. It looked as if the police work had been thorough. Was it really possible that these experienced professionals had overlooked the significance of the unfinished digging, the gardening shoes dropped casually at the back door, the untouched supper?

And now, at midday, she was free until half-past two. She could explore Cambridge. She bought the cheapest guide book she could find from Bowes and Bowes, resisting the temptation to browse among the books, since time was short and pleasure must be rationed. She stuffed her shoulder bag with a pork pie and fruit bought from a market stall and entered St Mary's church to sit quietly and work out her itinerary. Then for an hour and a half she walked about the city and its colleges in a trance of happiness.

She was seeing Cambridge at its loveliest. The sky was an infinity of blue from whose pellucid depths the sun shone in unclouded but gentle radiance. The trees in the college gardens and the avenues leading to the Backs, as yet untouched by the heaviness of high summer, lifted their green tracery against stone and river and sky. Punts shot and curtsied under the bridges, scattering the gaudy water fowl, and by the rise of the new Garret Hostel bridge the willows trailed their pale, laden boughs in the darker green of the Cam.

She included all the special sights in her itinerary. She walked gravely down the length of Trinity Library, visited the Old Schools, sat quietly at the back of King's College Chapel marvelling at the upward surge of John Wastell's great vault spreading into curved fans of delicate white stone. The sunlight poured through the great windows staining the still air, blue, crimson and green. The finely carved Tudor roses, the heraldic beasts supporting the crown, stood out in arrogant pride from the panels. Despite what Milton and Wordsworth had written, surely this chapel had been built to the glory of an earthly sovereign, not to the service of God? But that didn't invalidate its purpose nor blemish its beauty. It was still a supremely religious building. Could a non-believer have planned and executed this superb interior? Was there an essential unity between motive and creation? This was the question which Carl alone among the comrades would have been interested to explore and she thought of him in his Greek prison, trying to shut her mind to what they might be doing to him and wishing his stocky figure at her side.

During her tour she indulged in small particular pleasures. She bought a linen tea cloth printed with a picture of the chapel from the stall near the west door; she lay on her face on the shorn grass above the river by Kings Bridge and let the cold green water eddy round her arms; she wandered among the book stalls in the market place and after careful reckoning bought a small edition of Keats printed on India paper and a cotton kaftan patterned in greens, blues and browns. If this hot weather continued it would be cooler than a shirt or jeans for wear in the evenings.

Finally, she returned to King's College. There was a seat set against the great stone wall which ran from the chapel down to the river bank and she sat there in the sun to eat her lunch. A privileged sparrow hopped across the immaculate lawn and cocked a bright insouciant eye. She threw him scraps from the crust of her pork pie and smiled at his agitated peckings. From the river floated the sound of voices calling across the water, the occasional scrunch of wood on wood, the harsh call of a duckling. Everything about her – the pebbles bright as jewels in the gravel path, the silver shafts of grass at the verge of the lawn, the sparrow's brittle legs – was seen with an extraordinarily and individual intensity as if happiness had cleared her eyes.

Then memory recalled the voices. First her father's:

'Our little fascist was educated by the papists. It accounts for a lot. How on earth did it happen, Delia?'

'You remember, Daddy. They muddled me up with another C. Gray who was a Roman Catholic. We both passed the eleven-plus exam the same year. When they discovered the mistake they wrote to you to ask if you minded my staying on at the Convent because I'd settled there.'

He hadn't in fact replied. Reverend Mother had tried tactfully to conceal that he hadn't bothered to answer and Cordelia had stayed on at the Convent for the six most settled and happy years of her life, insulated by order and ceremony from the mess and muddle of life outside, incorrigibly Protestant, uncoerced, gently pitied as one in invincible ignorance. For the first time she learned that she needn't conceal her intelligence, that cleverness which a succession of foster mothers had somehow seen as a threat. Sister Perpetua had said:

'There shouldn't be any difficulty over your A-levels if you go on as you are at present. That means that we can plan for university entrance in two years' time from this October. Cambridge, I think. We might as well try for Cambridge, and I really don't see why you shouldn't stand a chance of a scholarship.'

Sister Perpetua had herself been at Cambridge before she entered the Convent and she still spoke of the academic life, not with longing or regret, but as if it had been a sacrifice worthy of her vocation. Even the fifteen-year-old Cordelia had recognized that Sister Perpetua was a real scholar and had thought it rather unfair of God to bestow a vocation on one who was so happy and useful as she was. But for Cordelia herself, the future had, for the first time, seemed settled and full of promise. She would go to Cambridge and Sister would visit her there. She had a romantic vision of wide lawns under the sun and the two of them walking in Donne's paradise: 'Rivers of knowledge are there, arts and sciences flow from thence; gardens that are walled in; bottomless depths of unsearchable councils are there.' By the aid of her own brain and Sister's prayers she would win her scholarship. The prayers occasionally worried her. She had absolutely no doubt of their efficacy since God must necessarily listen to one who at such personal cost had listened to Him. And if Sister's influence gave her an unfair advantage over the other candidates – well, that couldn't be helped. In a matter of such importance neither Cordelia nor Sister Perpetua had been disposed to fret over theological niceties.

But this time Daddy had replied to the letter. He had discovered a need for his daughter. There were no A-levels and no scholarship and at sixteen Cordelia finished her formal education and began her wandering life as cook, nurse, messenger and general camp follower to Daddy and the comrades.

But now by what devious routes and for what a strange purpose she had come at last to Cambridge. The city didn't disappoint her. In her wanderings she had seen lovelier places, but none in which she had been happier or more at peace. How indeed, she thought, could the heart be indifferent to such a city where stone and stained glass, water and green lawns, trees and flowers were arranged in such ordered beauty for the service of learning. But as regretfully she rose at last to go, brushing the few crumbs from her skirt, a quotation, untraced and unsought, came into her mind. She heard it with such clarity that the words might have been spoken by a human voice – a young masculine voice, unrecognized and yet mysteriously familiar: 'Then saw I that there was a way to Hell even from the gates of Heaven.'

*

The police headquarters building was modern and functional. It represented authority tempered with discretion; the public were to be impressed but not intimidated. Sergeant Maskell's office and the Sergeant himself conformed to this philosophy. He was surprisingly young and elegantly dressed, with a square, tough face wary with experience and a long but skilfully cut hair style which, Cordelia thought, could only just have satisfied the Force requirements, even for a plain-clothes detective. He was punctiliously polite without being gallant and this reassured her. It wasn't going to be an easy interview, but she had no wish to be treated with the indulgence shown to a pretty but importunate child. Sometimes it helped to play to part of a vulnerable and naive young girl eager for infor- mation – this was a role in which Bernie had frequently sought to cast her – but she sensed that Sergeant Maskell would respond better to an unflirtatious competence. She wanted to appear efficient, but not too efficient. And her secrets must remain her own; she was here to get information, not to give it.

She stated her business concisely and showed him her note of authority from Sir Ronald. He handed it back to her, remarking without rancour:

'Sir Ronald said nothing to me to suggest that he was not satisfied with the verdict.'

'I don't think that's in question. He doesn't suspect foul play. If he did, he would have come to you. I think he has a scientist's curiosity to know what made his son kill himself and he couldn't very well indulge that at public expense. I mean, Mark's private miseries aren't really your problem, are they?'

'They could be if the reasons for his death disclosed a criminal offence – blackmail, intimidation – but there was never any suggestion of that.'

'Are you personally satisfied that he killed himself?'

The Sergeant looked at her with the sudden keen intelligence of a hunting dog on the scent.

'Why should you ask that, Miss Gray?'

'I suppose because of the trouble you took. I've interviewed Miss Markland and read the newspaper report of the inquest. You called in a forensic pathologist; you had the body photographed before it was cut down; you analysed the coffee left in his drinking mug.'

'I treated the case as a suspicious death. That's my usual practice. This time the precautions proved unnecessary, but they might not have been.'

Cordelia said:

'But something worried you, something didn't seem right?'

He said, as if reminiscing:

'Oh, it was straightforward enough to all appearances. Almost the usual story. We get more than our share of suicides. Here is a young man who gave up his university course for no apparent reason and went to live on his own in some discomfort. You get the picture of an introspective, rather solitary student, one who doesn't confide in his family or friends. Within three weeks after leaving college he's found dead. There's no sign of a struggle; no disturbance in the cottage; he leaves a suicide note conveniently in the typewriter, much the kind of suicide note you would expect. Admittedly, he took the trouble to destroy all the papers in the cottage and yet left the garden fork uncleaned and his work half-completed, and bothered to cook himself a supper which he didn't eat. But all that proves nothing. People do behave irrationally, particularly suicides. No, it wasn't any of those things which gave me a bit of worry; it was the knot.'

Suddenly he bent down and rummaged in the left-hand drawer of his desk.

'Here,' he said. 'How would you use this to hang yourself, Miss Gray?'

The strap was about five feet long. It was a little over an inch wide and was made of strong but supple brown leather, darkened in places with age. One end was tapered and pierced with a row of metal-bound eye holes, the other was fitted with a strong brass buckle. Cordelia took it in her hands; Sergeant Maskell said:

'That was what he used. Obviously it's meant as a strap, but Miss Leaming testified that he used to wear it wound two or three times round his waist as a belt. Well, Miss Gray, how would you hang yourself?'

Cordelia ran the strap through her hands.

'First of all, of course, I'd slip the tapered end through the buckle to make a noose. Then, with the noose round my neck, I'd stand on a chair underneath the hook in the ceiling and draw the other end of the strap over the hook. I'd pull it up fairly tight and then make two half-hitches to hold it firm. I'd pull hard on the strap to make sure that the knot didn't slip and that the hook would hold. Then I'd kick away the chair.'

The Sergeant opened the file in front of him and pushed it across the desk.

'Look at that,' he said. 'That's a picture of the knot.'

The police photograph, stark in black and white, showed the knot with admirable clarity. It was a bowline on the end of a low loop and it hung about a foot from the hook.

Sergeant Maskell said:

'I doubt whether he would be able to tie that knot with his hands above his head, no one could. So he must have made the noose first just as you did and then tied the bowline. But that can't be right either. There were only a few inches of strap between the buckle and the knot. If he'd done it that way, he wouldn't have had sufficient play on the strap to get his neck through the noose. There's only one way he could have done it. He made the noose first, pulled it until the strap fitted his neck like a collar and then tied the bowline. Then he got on the chair, placed the loop over the nail and kicked the chair away. Look, this will show you what I mean.'

He turned over a new page of the file and suddenly thrust it towards her.

The photograph, uncompromising, unambiguous, a brutal sur-realism in black and white, would have looked as artificial as a sick joke if the body were not so obviously dead. Cordelia felt her heart hammering against her chest. Beside this horror Bernie's death had been gentle. She bent her head low over the file so that her hair swung forward to shield her face and made herself study the pitiable thing in front of her.

The neck was elongated so that the bare feet, their toes pointed like a dancer's, hung less than a foot from the floor. The stomach muscles were taut. Above them the high rib cage looked as brittle as a bird's. The head lolled grotesquely on the right shoulder like a horrible caricature of a disjointed puppet. The eyes had rolled upwards under half-open lids. The swollen tongue had forced itself between the lips.

Cordelia said calmly:

'I see what you mean. There are barely four inches of strap between the neck and the knot. Where is the buckle?'

'At the back of the neck under the left ear. There's a photograph of the indentation it made in the flesh later in the file.'

Cordelia did not look. Why, she wondered, had he shown her the photograph? It wasn't necessary to prove his argument. Had he hoped to shock her into a realization of what she was meddling in; to punish her for trespassing on his patch; to contrast the brutal reality of his professionalism with her amateurish meddling; to warn her perhaps? But against what? The police had no real suspicion of foul play; the case was closed. Had it, perhaps, been a casual malice, the incipient sadism of a man who couldn't resist the impulse to hurt or shock? Was he even aware of his own motives?

She said:

'I agree he could only have done it in the way you described, if he did it. But suppose someone else pulled the noose tight about his neck, then strung him up. He'd be heavy, a dead weight. Wouldn't it have been easier to make the knot first and then hoist him on to the chair?'

'Having first asked him to hand over his belt?'

'Why use a belt? The murderer could have strangled him with a cord or a tie. Or would that have left a deeper and identifiable mark under the impression of the strap?'

'The pathologist looked for just such a mark. It wasn't there.'

'There are other ways, though; a plastic bag, the thin kind they pack clothes in, dropped over his head and held tight against his face; a thin scarf; a woman's stocking.'

'I can see you would be a resourceful murderess, Miss Gray. It's possible, but it would need a strong man and there would have to be an element of surprise. We found no sign of a struggle.'

'But it could have been done that way?'

'Of course, but there was absolutely no evidence that it was.'

'But if he were first drugged?'

'That possibility did occur to me; that's why I had the coffee analysed. But he wasn't drugged, the PM confirmed it.'

'How much coffee had he drunk?'

'Only about half a mug, according to the PM report and he died immediately afterwards. Some time between seven and nine p.m. was as close as the pathologist could estimate.'

'Wasn't it odd that he drank coffee before his meal?'

'There's no law against it. We don't know when he intended to eat his supper. Anyway, you can't build a murder case on the order in which a man chooses to take his food and drink.'

'What about the note he left? I suppose it isn't possible to raise prints from typewriter keys?'

'Not easily on that type of key. We tried but there was nothing identifiable.'

'So in the end you accepted that it was suicide?'

'In the end I accepted that there was no possibility of proving otherwise.'

'But you had a hunch? My partner's old colleague – he's a Superintendent of the CID – always backed his hunches.'

'Ah, well, that's the Met, they can afford to indulge themselves. If I backed all my hunches I'd get no work done; it isn't what you suspect, it's what you can prove that counts.'

'May I take the suicide note and the strap?'

'Why not, if you sign for them? No one else seems to want them.'

'Could I see the note now, please?'

He extracted it from the file and handed it to her. Cordelia began to read to herself the first half-remembered words:

a void, boundless as the nether sky appeared
beneath us . . .

She was struck, not for the first time, by the importance of the written word, the magic of ordered symbols. Would poetry hold its theurgy if the lines were printed as prose, or prose be so compelling without the pattern and stress of punctuation? Miss Leaming had spoken Blake's passage as if she recognized its beauty yet here, spaced on the page, it exerted an even stronger power.

It was then that two things about the quotation caught at her breath. The first was not something which she intended to share with Sergeant Maskell but there was no reason why she should not comment on the second.

She said:

'Mark Callender must have been an experienced typist. This was done by an expert.'

'I didn't think so. If you look carefully you'll see that one or two of the letters are fainter than the rest. That's always the sign of an amateur.'

'But the faint letters aren't always the same ones. It's usually the keys on the edges of the keyboard which the inexperienced typist hits more lightly. And the spacing here is good until nearly the end of the passage. It looks as if the typist suddenly realized that he ought to disguise his competence but hadn't time to retype the whole passage. And it's strange that the punctuation is so accurate.'

'It was probably copied direct from the printed page. There was a copy of Blake in the boy's bedroom. The quotation is from Blake, you know, the Tyger Tyger burning bright poet.'

'I know. But if he typed it from the book, why bother to return the Blake to his bedroom?'

'He was a tidy lad.'

'But not tidy enough to wash up his coffee mug or clean his garden fork.'

'That proves nothing. As I said, people do behave oddly when they're planning to kill themselves. We know that the typewriter was his and that he'd had it for a year. But we couldn't compare the typing with his work. All his papers had been burnt.'

He glanced at his watch and got to his feet. Cordelia saw that the interview was over. She signed a chit for the suicide note and the leather belt, then shook hands and thanked him formally for his help. As he opened the door for her he said, as if on impulse:

'There's one intriguing detail you may care to know. It looks as if he was with a woman some time during the day on which he died. The pathologist found the merest trace – a thin line only – of purple-red lipstick on his upper lip.'

New Hall, with its Byzantine air, its sunken court and its shining domed hall like a peeled orange, reminded Cordelia of a harem; admittedly one owned by a sultan with liberal views and an odd predilection for clever girls, but a harem nonetheless. The college was surely too distractingly pretty to be conducive to serious study. She wasn't sure, either, whether she approved of the obtrusive femininity of its white brick, the mannered prettiness of the shallow pools where the goldfish slipped like blood-red shadows between the water lilies, its artfully planted saplings. She concentrated on her criticism of the building; it helped to prevent her being intimidated.

She hadn't called at the Lodge to ask for Miss Tilling, afraid that she might be asked her business or refused admission; it seemed prudent just to walk in and chance to luck. Luck was with her. After two fruitless enquiries for Sophia Tilling's room, a hurrying student called back at her: 'She doesn't live in college but she's sitting on the grass over there with her brother.'

Cordelia walked out of the shadow of the court into bright sunlight and over turf as soft as moss towards the little group. There were four of them, stretched out on the warm-smelling grass. The two Tillings were unmistakably brother and sister. Cordelia's first thought was that they reminded her of a couple of pre-Raphaelite portraits with their strong dark heads held high on unusually long necks, and their straight noses above curved, foreshortened upper lips. Beside their bony distinction, the second girl was all softness. If this were the girl who had visited Mark at the cottage, Miss Markland was right to call her beautiful. She had an oval face with a neat slender nose, a small but beautifully formed mouth, and slanted eyes of a strikingly deep blue which gave her whole face an oriental appearance intriguingly at variance with the fairness of her skin and her long blonde hair. She was wearing an ankle-length dress of fine mauve patterned cotton, buttoned high at the waist but with no other fastening. The gathered bodice cupped her full breasts and the skirt fell open to reveal a pair of tight-fitting shorts in the same material. As far as Cordelia could see, she wore nothing else. Her feet were bare and her long, shapely legs were untanned by the sun. Cordelia reflected that those white voluptuous thighs must be more erotic than a whole city of sun-burnt limbs and that the girl knew it. Sophia Tilling's dark good looks were only a foil to this gentler, more entrancing beauty.

At first sight the fourth member of the party was more ordinary. He was a stocky, bearded young man with russet curly hair and a spade-shaped face, and was lying on the grass by the side of Sophie Tilling.

All of them, except the blonde girl, were wearing old jeans and open-necked cotton shirts.

Cordelia had come up to the group and had stood over them for a few seconds before they took any notice of her. She said:

'I'm looking for Hugo and Sophia Tilling. My name is Cordelia Gray.' Hugo Tilling looked up:

'What shall Cordelia do, love and be silent.'

Cordelia said:

'People who feel the need to joke about my name usually enquire after my sisters. It gets very boring.'

'It must do. I'm sorry. I'm Hugo Tilling, this is my sister, this is Isabelle de Lasterie and this is Davie Stevens.'

Davie Stevens sat up like a jack-in-the-box and said an amiable 'Hi.'

He looked at Cordelia with a quizzical intentness. She wondered about Davie. Her first impression of the little group, influenced perhaps by the college architecture, had been of a young sultan taking his ease with two of his favourites and attended by the captain of the guard. But, meeting Davie Stevens's steady intelligent gaze, that impression faded. She suspected that, in this seraglio, it was the captain of the guard who was the dominant personality.

Sophia Tilling nodded and said 'Hullo.'

Isabelle did not speak but a smile beautiful and meaningless spread over her face. Hugo said:

'Won't you sit down, Cordelia Gray, and explain the nature of your necessities?'

Cordelia knelt gingerly, wary of grass stains on the soft suede of her skirt. It was an odd way to interview suspects – only, of course, these people weren't suspects – kneeling like a suppliant in front of them. She said:

'I'm a private detective. Sir Ronald Callender has employed me to find out why his son died.'

The effect of her words was astonishing. The little group, which had been lolling at ease like exhausted warriors, stiffened with instantaneous shock into a rigid tableau as if struck to marble. Then, almost imperceptibly, they relaxed. Cordelia could hear the slow release of held breath. She watched their faces. Davie Stevens was the least concerned. He wore a half-rueful smile, interested but unworried, and gave a quick look at Sophie as if in complicity. The look was not returned; she and Hugo were staring rigidly ahead. Cordelia felt that the two Tillings were carefully avoiding each other's eyes. But it was Isabelle who was the most shaken. She gave a gasp and her hand flew to her face like a second-rate actress simulating shock. Her eyes widened into fathomless depths of violet blue and she turned them on Hugo in desperate appeal. She looked so pale that Cordelia half expected her to faint. She thought:

'If I'm in the middle of a conspiracy, then I know who is its weakest member.'

Hugo Tilling said:

'You're telling us that Ronald Callender has employed you to find out why Mark died?'

'Is that so extraordinary?'

'I find it incredible. He took no particular interest in his son when he was alive, why begin now he's dead?'

'How do you know he took no particular interest?'

'It's just an idea I had.'

Cordelia said:

'Well, he's interested now even if it's only the scientist's urge to discover truth.'

'Then he'd better stick to his microbiology, discovering how to make plastic soluble in salt water, or whatever. Human beings aren't susceptible to his kind of experiment.'

Davie Stevens said with casual unconcern:

'I wonder that you can stomach that arrogant fascist.'

The gibe plucked at too many chords of memory. Wilfully obtuse, Cordelia said:

'I didn't enquire what political party Sir Ronald favours.'

Hugo laughed.

'Davie doesn't mean that. By fascist Davie means that Ronald Callender holds certain untenable opinions. For example, that all men may not be created equal, that universal suffrage may not necessarily add to the general happiness of mankind, that the tyrannies of the left aren't noticeably more liberal or supportable than the tyrannies of the right, that black men killing black men is small improvement on white men killing black men in so far as the victims are concerned and that capitalism may not be responsible for all the ills that flesh is heir to from drug addiction to poor syntax. I don't suggest that Ronald Callender holds all or indeed any of these reprehensible opinions. But Davie thinks that he does.'

Davie threw a book at Hugo and said without rancour:

'Shut up! You talk like the *Daily Telegraph*. And you're boring our visitor.'

Sophie Tilling asked suddenly:

'Was it Sir Ronald who suggested that you should question us?'

'He said that you were Mark's friends; he saw you at the inquest and funeral.'

Hugo laughed:

'For God's sake, is that his idea of friendship?'

Cordelia said:

'But you were there?'

'We went to the inquest – all of us except Isabelle, who, we thought, would have been decorative but unreliable. It was rather dull. There was a great deal of irrelevant medical evidence about the excellent state of Mark's heart, lungs and digestive system. As far as I can see, he would have gone on living for ever if he hadn't put a belt round his neck.'

'And the funeral – were you there too?'

'We were, at the Cambridge Crematorium. A very subdued affair. There were only six of us present in addition to the undertaker's men; we three, Ronald Callender, that secretary/housekeeper of his and an old nanny type dressed in black. She cast rather a gloom over the proceedings, I thought. Actually she looked so exactly like an old family retainer that I suspect she was a policewoman in disguise.'

'Why should she be? Did she look like one?'

'No, but then you don't look like a private eye.'

'You've no idea who she was?'

'No, we weren't introduced; it wasn't a chummy kind of funeral. Now I recall it, not one of us spoke a single word to any of the others. Sir Ronald wore a mask of public grief, the King mourning the Crown Prince.'

'And Miss Leaming?'

'The Queen Consort; she should have had a black veil over her face.'

'I thought that her suffering was real enough,' said Sophie.

'You can't tell. No one can. Define suffering. Define real.'

Suddenly Davie Stevens spoke, rolling over on to his stomach like a playful dog.

'Miss Leaming looked pretty sick to me. Incidentally, the old lady was called Pilbeam; anyway, that was the name of the wreath.'

Sophie laughed:

'That awful cross of roses with the black-edged card? I might have guessed it came from her; but how do you know?'

'I looked, honey. The undertaker's men took the wreath off the coffin and popped it against the wall so I took a quick butcher's. The card read "With sincere sympathy from Nanny Pilbeam".'

Sophie said:

'So you did, I remember now. How beautifully feudal! Poor old nanny, it must have cost her a packet.'

'Did Mark ever talk about a Nanny Pilbeam?' Cordelia asked.

They glanced at each other quickly. Isabelle shook her head. Sophie said, 'Not to me.'

Hugo Tilling replied:

'He never talked about her, but I think I did see her once before the funeral. She called at college about six weeks ago – on Mark's twenty-first birthday actually, and asked to see him. I was in the Porter's Lodge at the time and Robbins asked me if Mark was in college. She went up to his room and they were there together for about an hour. I saw her leaving, but he never mentioned her to me either then or later.'

And soon afterwards, thought Cordelia, he gave up university. Could there be a connection? It was only a tenuous lead, but she would have to follow it.

She asked out of a curiosity that seemed both perverse and irrelevant:

'Were there any other flowers?'

It was Sophie who replied:

'A simple bunch of unwired garden flowers on the coffin. No card. Miss Leaming, I suppose. It was hardly Sir Ronald's style.'

Cordelia said:

'You were his friends. Please tell me about him.'

They looked at each other as if deciding who should speak. Their embarrassment was almost palpable. Sophie Tilling was picking at small blades of grass and rolling them in her hands. Without looking up, she said:

'Mark was a very private person. I'm not sure how far any of us knew him. He was quiet, gentle, self-contained, unambitious. He was intelligent without being clever. He was very kind; he cared about people, but without inflicting them with his concern. He had little self-esteem but it never seemed to worry him. I don't think there is anything else we can say about him.'

Suddenly Isabelle spoke in a voice so low that Cordelia could hardly catch it. She said:

'He was sweet.'

Hugo said with a sudden angry impatience.

'He was sweet and he is dead. There you have it. We can't tell you any more about Mark Callender than that. We none of us saw him after he chucked college. He didn't consult us before he left, and he didn't consult us before he killed himself. He was, as my sister has told you, a very private person. I suggest that you leave him his privacy.'

'Look,' said Cordelia, 'you went to the inquest, you went to the funeral. If you had stopped seeing him, if you were so unconcerned about him, why did you bother?'

'Sophie went out of affection. Davie went because Sophie did. I went out of curiosity and respect; you mustn't be seduced by my air of casual flippancy into thinking that I haven't a heart.'

Cordelia said obstinately:

'Someone visited him at the cottage on the evening he died. Someone had coffee with him. I intend to find out who that person was.'

Was it her fancy that this news surprised them? Sophie Tilling looked as if she were about to ask a question when her brother quickly broke in:

'It wasn't any of us. On the night Mark died we were all in the second row of the dress circle of the Arts Theatre watching Pinter. I don't know that I can prove it. I doubt whether the booking clerk has kept the chart for that particular night, but I booked the seats and she may remember me. If you insist on being tediously meticulous, I can probably introduce you to a friend who knew of my intention to take a party to the play; to another who saw some at least of us in the bar in the interval; and to another with whom I subsequently discussed the performance. None of this will prove anything; my friends are an accommodating bunch. It would be simpler for you to accept that I am telling the truth. Why should I lie? We were all four at the Arts Theatre on the night of 26th May.'

Davie Stevens said gently:

'Why not tell that arrogant bastard Pa Callender to go to hell and leave his son in peace, then find yourself a nice simple case of larceny?'

'Or murder,' said Hugo Tilling.

'Find yourself a nice simple case of murder.'

As if in obedience to some secret code, they began getting up, piling their books together, brushing the grass cuttings from their clothes. Cordelia followed them through the courts and out of college. Still in a silent group they made their way to a white Renault parked in the forecourt.

Cordelia came up to them and spoke directly to Isabelle.

'Did you enjoy the Pinter? Weren't you frightened by that dreadful last scene when Wyatt Gillman is gunned down by the natives?'

It was so easy that Cordelia almost despised herself. The immense violet eyes grew puzzled.

'Oh, no! I did not care about it, I was not frightened. I was with Hugo and the others, you see.'

Cordelia turned to Hugo Tilling.

'Your friend doesn't seem to know the difference between Pinter and Osborne.'

Hugo was settling himself into the driving seat of the car. He twisted round to open the back door for Sophie and Davie. He said calmly:

'My friend, as you choose to call her, is living in Cambridge, inadequately chaperoned I'm happy to say, for the purpose of learning English. So far her progress has been erratic and in some respects disappointing. One can never be certain how much my friend has understood.'

The engine purred into life. The car began to move. It was then that Sophie Tilling thrust her head out of the window and said impulsively:

'I don't mind talking about Mark if you think it will help. It won't, but you can come round to my house this afternoon if you like – 57 Norwich Street. Don't be late; Davie and I are going on the river. You can come too if you feel like it.'

The car accelerated. Cordelia watched it out of sight. Hugo raised his hand in ironic farewell but not one of them turned a head.

*

Cordelia muttered the address to herself until it was safely written down: 57 Norwich Street. Was that the address where Sophie lodged, a hostel perhaps, or did her family live in Cambridge? Well, she would find out soon enough. When ought she to arrive? Too early would look over-eager; too late and they might have set out for the river. Whatever motive had prompted Sophie Tilling to issue that belated invitation, she mustn't lose touch with them now.

They had some guilty knowledge; that had been obvious. Why else had they reacted so strongly to her arrival? They wanted the facts of Mark Callender's death to be left undisturbed. They would try to persuade, cajole, even to shame her into abandoning the case. Would they, she wondered, also threaten? But why? The most likely theory was that they were shielding someone. But again, why? Murder wasn't a matter of climbing late into college, a venial infringement of rules which a friend would automatically condone and conceal. Mark Callender had been their friend; to two of them he might have been more than a friend. Someone whom he knew and trusted had pulled a strap tight round his neck, had watched and listened to his agonized choking, had strung his body on a hook like the carcass of an animal. How could one reconcile that appalling knowledge with Davie Stevens' slightly amused and rueful glance at Sophie, with Hugo's cynical calm, with Sophie's friendly and interested eyes? If they were conspirators, then they were monsters. And Isabelle? If they were shielding anyone, it was most likely to be her. But Isabelle de Lasterie couldn't have murdered Mark. Cordelia remembered those frail sloping shoulders, those ineffective hands almost transparent in the sun, the long nails painted like elegant pink talons. If Isabelle were guilty, she hadn't acted alone. Only a tall and very strong woman could have heaved that inert body on to the chair and up to the hook.

Norwich Street was a one-way thoroughfare and, initially, Cordelia approached it from the wrong direction. It took her some time to find her way back to Hills Road, past the Roman Catholic church and down the fourth turning to the right. The street was terraced with small brick houses, obviously early Victorian. Equally obviously, the road was on its way up. Most of the houses looked well cared for; the paint on the identical front doors was fresh and bright; lined curtains had replaced the draped lace at the single ground-floor windows and the bases of the walls were scarred where a damp course had been installed. Number fifty-seven had a black front door with the house number painted in white behind the glass panel above. Cordelia was relieved to see that there was space to park the Mini. There was no sign of the Renault among the almost continuous row of old cars and battered bicycles which lined the edge of the pavement.

The front door was wide open. Cordelia pressed the bell and stepped tentatively into a narrow white hall. The interior of the house was immediately familiar to her. From her sixth birthday she had lived for two years in just such a Victorian terraced cottage with Mrs Gibson on the outskirts of Romford. She recognized the steep and narrow staircase immediately ahead, the door on the right leading to the front parlour, the second door set aslant which led to the back parlour and through it to the kitchen and yard. She knew that there would be cupboards and a curved alcove on each side of the fireplace; she knew where to find the door under the stairs. Memory was so sharp that it imposed on this clean, sun-scented interior the strong odour of unwashed napkins, cabbage and grease which had permeated the Romford house. She could almost hear the children's voices calling her outlandish name across the rookery of the primary school playground across the road, stamping the asphalt with the ubiquitous wellington boots which they wore in all seasons, flailing their thin jerseyed arms: 'Cor, Cor, Cor!'

The furthest door was ajar and she could glimpse a room painted bright yellow and spilling over with sunlight. Sophie's head appeared.

'Oh, it's you! Come in. Davie has gone to collect some books from college and to buy food for the picnic. Would you like tea now or shall we wait? I'm just finishing the ironing.'

'I'd rather wait, thank you.'

Cordelia sat down and watched while Sophie wound the flex around the iron and folded the cloth. She glanced around the room. It was welcoming and attractive, furnished in no particular style or period, a cosy hotch-potch of the cheap and the valuable, unpretentious and pleasing. There was a sturdy oak table against the wall; four rather ugly dining chairs; a Windsor chair with a plump yellow cushion; an elegant Victorian sofa covered with brown velvet and set under the window; three good Staffordshire figures on the mantel shelf above the hooded wrought-iron grate. One of the walls was almost covered with a notice board in dark cork which displayed posters, cards, *aides-mémoire*, and pictures cut from magazines. Two, Cordelia saw, were beautifully photographed and attractive nudes.

Outside the yellow-curtained window the small walled garden was a riot of greenery. An immense and multi-flowered hollyhock burgeoned against a tatty-looking trellis; there were roses planted in Ali Baba jars and a row of pots of bright red geraniums lined the top of the wall.

Cordelia said:

'I like this house. Is it yours?'

'Yes, I own it. Our grandmother died two years ago and left Hugo and me a small legacy. I used mine for the down payment on this house and got a local authority grant towards the cost of conversion. Hugo spent all of his laying down wine. He was ensuring a happy middle age; I was ensuring a happy present. I suppose that's the difference between us.'

She folded the ironing cloth on the end of the table and stowed it away in one of the cupboards. Sitting opposite to Cordelia, she asked abruptly:

'Do you like my brother?'

'Not very much. I thought he was rather rude to me.'

'He didn't mean to be.'

'I think that's rather worse. Rudeness should always be intentional, otherwise it's insensitivity.'

'Hugo isn't at his most agreeable when he's with Isabelle. She has that effect on him.'

'Was she in love with Mark Callender?'

'You'll have to ask her, Cordelia, but I shouldn't think so. They hardly knew each other. Mark was my lover, not hers. I thought I'd better get you here to tell you myself since someone's bound to sooner or later if you go around Cambridge ferreting out facts about him. He didn't live here with me, of course. He had rooms in college. But we were lovers for almost the whole of last year. It ended just after Christmas when I met Davie.'

'Were you in love?'

'I'm not sure. All sex is a kind of exploitation, isn't it? If you mean, did we explore our own identities through the personality of the other, then I suppose we were in love or thought that we were. Mark needed to believe himself in love. I'm not sure I know what the word means.'

Cordelia felt a surge of sympathy. She wasn't sure either. She thought of her own two lovers; Georges whom she had slept with because he was gentle and unhappy and called her Cordelia, a real name, her name, not Delia, Daddy's little fascist; and Carl who was young and angry and whom she had liked so much that it seemed churlish not to show it in the only way which seemed to him important. She had never thought of virginity as other than a temporary and inconvenient state, part of the general insecurity and vulnerability of being young. Before Georges and Carl she had been lonely and inexperienced. Afterwards she had been lonely and a little less inexperienced. Neither affair had given her the longed-for assurance in dealing with Daddy or the landladies, neither had inconveniently touched her heart. But for Carl she had felt tenderness. It was just as well that he had left Rome before his lovemaking had become too pleasurable and he too important to her. It was intolerable to think that those strange gymnastics might one day become necessary. Lovemaking, she had decided, was overrated, not painful but surprising. The alienation between thought and action was so complete. She said:

'I suppose I only meant were you fond of each other, and did you like going to bed together?'

'Both of those things.'

'Why did it end? Did you quarrel?'

'Nothing so natural or uncivilized. One didn't quarrel with Mark. That was one of the troubles about him. I told him that I didn't want to go on with the affair and he accepted my decision as calmly as if I were just breaking a date for a play at the Arts. He didn't try to argue or dissuade me. And if you're wondering whether the break had anything to do with his death, well you're wrong. I wouldn't rank that high with anyone, particularly not Mark. I was probably fonder of him than he was of me.'

'So why did it end?'

'I felt that I was under moral scrutiny. It wasn't true; Mark wasn't a prig. But that's how I felt, or pretended to myself that I felt. I couldn't live up to him and I didn't even want to. There was Gary Webber, for example. I'd better tell you about him; it explains a lot about Mark. He's an autistic child, one of the uncontrollable, violent ones. Mark met him with his parents and their other two children on Jesus Green about a year ago; the children were playing on the swings there. Mark spoke to Gary and the boy responded to him. Children always did. He took to visiting the family and looking after Gary one evening a week so that the Webbers could get out to the pictures. During his last two vacs he stayed in the house and looked after Gary completely while the whole family went off for a holiday. The Webbers couldn't bear the boy to go to hospital; they'd tried it once and he didn't settle. But they were perfectly happy to leave him with Mark. I used to call in some evenings and see them together. Mark would hold the boy on his lap and rock him backwards and forwards for hours at a time. It was the one way to quieten him. We disagreed about Gary. I thought he would be better dead and I said so. I still think it would be better if he died, better for his parents, better for the rest of the family, better for him. Mark didn't agree. I remember saying:

' "Oh well, if you think it reasonable that children should suffer so that you can enjoy the emotional kick of relieving them – " After that the conversation became boringly metaphysical. Mark said:

"Neither you nor I would be willing to kill Gary. He exists. His family exists. They need help which we can give. It doesn't matter what we feel. Actions are important, feelings aren't." '

Cordelia said:

'But actions arise out of feelings.'

'Oh, Cordelia, don't you start! I've had this particular conversation too many times before. Of course they do!'

They were silent for a moment. Then Cordelia, reluctant to shatter the tenuous confidence and friendship which she sensed was growing between them, made herself ask:

'Why did he kill himself – if he did kill himself?' Sophie's reply was as emphatic as a slammed door.

'He left a note.'

'A note perhaps. But, as his father pointed out, not an explanation. It's a lovely passage of prose – at least I think so – but as a justification for suicide it just isn't convincing.'

'It convinced the jury.'

'It doesn't convince me. Think, Sophie! Surely there are only two reasons for killing oneself. One is either escaping from something or to something. The first is rational. If one is in intolerable pain, despair or mental anguish and there is no reasonable chance of a cure, then it's probably sensible to prefer oblivion. But it isn't sensible to kill oneself in the hope of gaining some better existence or to extend one's sensibilities to include the experience of death. It isn't possible to experience death. I'm not even sure it's possible to experience dying. One can only experience the preparations for death, and even that seems pointless since one can't make use of the experience afterwards. If there's any sort of existence after death we shall all know soon enough. If there isn't, we shan't exist to complain that we've been cheated. People who believe in an afterlife are perfectly reasonable. They're the only ones who are safe from ultimate disillusionment.'

'You've thought it all out, haven't you. I'm not sure that suicides do. The act is probably both impulsive and irrational.'

'Was Mark impulsive and irrational?'

'I didn't know Mark.'

'But you were lovers! You slept with him!'

Sophie looked at her and cried out in angry pain.

'I didn't know him! I thought I did, but I didn't know the first thing about him!'

They sat without speaking for almost two minutes. Then Cordelia asked: 'You went to dinner at Garforth House didn't you? What was it like?'

'The food and the wine were surprisingly good, but I don't suppose that's what you had in mind. The dinner party wasn't otherwise memorable. Sir Ronald was amiable enough when he noticed I was there. Miss Leaming, when she could tear her obsessive attention from the presiding genius, looked me over like a prospective mother-in-law. Mark was rather silent. I think he'd taken me there to prove something to me, or perhaps to himself; I'm not sure what. He never talked about the evening or asked me what I thought. A month later Hugo and I both went to dinner. It was then I met Davie. He was the guest of one of the research biologists and Ronald Callender was angling to get him. Davie did a vac job there in his final year. If you want the inside dope on Garforth House, you should ask him.'

Five minutes later Hugo, Isabelle and Davie arrived. Cordelia had gone upstairs to the bathroom and heard the car stop and the jabber of voices in the hall. Footsteps passed beneath her towards the back parlour. She turned on the hot water. The gas boiler in the kitchen immediately gave forth a roar as if the little house were powered by a dynamo. Cordelia let the tap run, then stepped out of the bathroom, closing the door gently behind her. She stole to the top of the stairs. It was hard luck on Sophie to waste her hot water, she thought guiltily; but worse was the sense of treachery and shabby opportunism as she crept down the first three stairs and listened. The front door had been closed but the door to the back parlour was open. She heard Isabelle's high unemphatic voice:

'But if this man Sir Ronald is paying her to find out about Mark, why cannot I pay her to stop finding out?'

Then Hugo's voice, amused, a little contemptuous:

'Darling Isabelle, when will you learn that not everyone can be bought?'

'She can't, anyway. I like her.'

It was Sophie speaking. Her brother replied:

'We all like her. The question is, how do we get rid of her?'

Then for a few minutes there was a murmur of voices, the words undistinguishable, broken by Isabelle.

'It is not, I think, a suitable job for a woman.'

There was the sound of a chair scraping against the floor, a shuffle of feet. Cordelia darted guiltily back into the bathroom and turned off the tap. She recalled Bernie's complacent admonition when she had asked whether they needed accept a divorce case.

'You can't do our job, partner, and be a gentleman.' She stood watching at the half-open door. Hugo and Isabelle were leaving. She waited until she heard the front door close and the car drive away.

Then she went down to the parlour. Sophie and Davie were together, unpacking a large carrier bag of groceries. Sophie smiled and said:

'Isabelle has a party tonight. She has a house quite close to here in Panton Street. Mark's tutor, Edward Horsfall, will probably be there and we thought it might be useful for you to talk to him about Mark. The party's at eight o'clock but you can call for us here. Just now we're packing a picnic; we thought we'd take a punt on the river for an hour or so. Do come if you'd like to. It's really much the pleasantest way of seeing Cambridge.'

*

Afterwards, Cordelia remembered the river picnic as a series of brief but intensely clear pictures, moments in which sight and sense fused and time seemed momentarily arrested while the sunlit image was impressed on her mind. Sunlight sparkling on the river and gilding the hairs of Davie's chest and forearms; the flesh of his strong upper arms speckled like an egg; Sophie lifting her arm to wipe the sweat from her brow as she rested between thrusts of the punt pole; green-black weeds dragged by the pole from mysterious depths to writhe sinuously below the surface; a bright duck cocking its white tail before disappearing in a flurry of green water. When they had rocked under Silver Street Bridge a friend of Sophie's swam alongside, sleek and snout-nosed like an otter, his black hair lying like blades across his cheeks. He rested his hands on the punt and opened his mouth to be fed chunks of sandwiches by a protesting Sophie. The punts and canoes scraped and jostled each other in the turbulence of white water racing under the bridge. The air rang with laughing voices and the green banks were peopled with half-naked bodies lying supine with their faces to the sun.

Davie punted until they reached the higher level of the river and Cordelia and Sophie stretched out on the cushions at opposite ends of the punt. Thus distanced it was impossible to carry on a private conversation; Cordelia guessed that this was precisely what Sophie had planned. From time to time, she would call out snatches of information as if to emphasize that the outing was strictly educational.

'That wedding cake is John's – we're just passing under Clare Bridge, one of the prettiest, I think. Thomas Grumbald built it in

1639. They say he was only paid three shillings for the design. You know that view, of course; it's a good view of Queen's, though.'

Cordelia's courage failed her at the thought of interrupting this desultory tourist's chat with the brutal demand:

'Did you and your brother kill your lover?'

Here, rocking gently on the sunlit river, the question seemed both indecent and absurd. She was in danger of being lulled into a gentle acceptance of defeat; viewing all her suspicions as a neurotic hankering after drama and notoriety, a need to justify her fee to Sir Ronald. She believed Mark Callender had been murdered because she wanted to believe it. She had identified with him, with his solitariness, his self-sufficiency, his alienation from his father, his lonely childhood. She had even – most dangerous presumption of all – come to see herself as his avenger. When Sophie took over the pole, just past the Garden House Hotel, and Davie edged his way along the gently rocking punt and stretched himself out beside her, she knew that she wouldn't be able to mention Mark's name. It was out of no more than a vague, unintrusive curiosity that she found herself asking:

'Is Sir Ronald Callender a good scientist?' Davie took up a short paddle and began lazily to stir the shining water.

'His science is perfectly respectable, as my dear colleagues would say. Rather more than respectable, in fact. At present the lab is working on ways of expanding the use of biological monitors to assess pollution of the sea and estuaries; that means routine surveys of plants and animals which might serve as indicators. And they did some very useful preliminary work last year on the degradation of plastics. RC isn't so hot himself, but then you can't expect much original science from the over-fifties. But he's a great spotter of talent and he certainly knows how to run a team if you fancy that dedicated, one for all, band of brothers approach. I don't. They even publish their papers as the Callender Research Laboratory, not under individual names. That wouldn't do for me. When I publish, it's strictly for the glory of David Forbes Stevens and, incidentally, for the gratification of Sophie. The Tillings like success.'

'Was that why you didn't want to stay on when he offered you a job?'

'That among other reasons. He pays too generously and he asks too much. I don't like being bought and I've a strong objection to dressing up every night in a dinner jacket like a performing monkey in a zoo. I'm a molecular biologist. I'm not looking for the holy grail. Dad and Mum brought me up as a Methodist and I don't see why I should chuck a perfectly good religion which served me very well for twelve years just to put the great scientific principle or Ronald Callender in its place. I distrust these sacerdotal scientists. It's a bloody wonder that little lot at Garforth House aren't genuflecting three times a day in the direction of the Cavendish.'

'And what about Lunn? How does he fit in?'

'Oh, that boy's a bloody wonder! Ronald Callender found him in a children's home when he was fifteen – don't ask me how – and trained him to be a lab assistant. You couldn't find a better. There isn't an instrument made which Chris Lunn can't learn to understand and care for. He's developed one or two himself and Callender has had them patented. If anyone in that lab is indispensable it's probably Lunn. Certainly Ronald Callender cares a damn sight more for him than he did for his son. And Lunn, as you might guess, regards RC as God almighty, which is very gratifying for them both. It's extraordinary really, all that violence which used to be expressed in street fights and coshing old ladies, harnessed to the service of science. You've got to hand it to Callender. He certainly knows how to pick his slaves.'

'And is Miss Leaming a slave?'

'Well, I wouldn't know just what Eliza Leaming is. She's responsible for the business management and, like Lunn, she's probably indispensable. Lunn and she seem to have a love-hate relationship, or, perhaps, a hate-hate relationship. I'm not very clever at detecting these psychological nuances.'

'But how on earth does Sir Ronald pay for it all?'

'Well, that's the thousand-dollar question, isn't it? It's rumoured that most of the money came from his wife and that he and Elizabeth Leaming between them invested it rather cleverly. They certainly needed to. And then he gets a certain amount from contract work. Even so, it's an expensive hobby. While I was there they were saying that the Wolvington Trust were getting interested. If they come up with something big – and I gather it's below their dignity to come up with anything small – then most of Ronald Callender's troubles should be over. Mark's death must have hit him. Mark was due to come into a pretty substantial fortune in four years' time and he told Sophie that he intended to hand most of it over to Dad.'

'Why on earth should he do that?'

'God knows. Conscience money, perhaps. Anyway, he obviously thought it was something that Sophie ought to know.'

Conscience money for what, Cordelia wondered sleepily. For not loving his father enough? For rejecting his enthusiasms? For being less than the son he had hoped for? And what would happen to Mark's fortune now? Who stood to gain by Mark's death? She supposed that she ought to consult his grandfather's will and find out. But that would mean a trip to London. Was it really worth it?

She stretched back her face to the sun and trailed one hand in the river. A splash of water from the punt pole stung her eyes. She opened them and saw that the punt was gliding close to the bank and under the shade of overhanging trees. Immediately in front of her a torn branch, cleft at the end and thick as a man's body, hung by a thread of bark and turned gently as the punt passed beneath it. She was aware of Davie's voice; he must have been talking for a long time. How odd that she couldn't remember what he'd been saying!

'You don't need reasons for killing yourself; you need reasons for not killing yourself. It was suicide, Cordelia. I should let it go at that.'

Cordelia thought that she must have briefly slept, since he seemed to be answering a question she couldn't remember having asked. But now there were other voices, louder and more insistent. Sir Ronald Callender's: 'My son is dead. *My* son. If I am in some way responsible, I'd prefer to know. If anyone else is responsible, I want to know that too.' Sergeant Maskell's: 'How would you use this to hang yourself, Miss Gray?' The feel of the belt, smooth and sinuous, slipping like a live thing through her fingers.

She sat bolt upright, hands clasped around her knees, with such suddenness that the punt rocked violently and Sophie had to clutch at an overhanging branch to keep her balance. Her dark face, intriguingly foreshortened and patterned with the shadow of leaves, looked down at Cordelia from what seemed an immense height. Their eyes met. In that moment Cordelia knew how close she had come to giving up the case. She had been suborned by the beauty of the day, by sunshine, indolence, the promise of comradeship, even friendship, into forgetting why she was here. The realization horrified her. Davie had said that Sir Ronald was a good picker. Well, he had picked her. This was her first case and nothing and no one was going to hinder her from solving it.

She said formally:

'It was good of you to let me join you, but I don't want to miss the party tonight. I ought to talk to Mark's tutor and there may be other people there who could tell me something. Isn't it time that we thought about turning back?'

Sophie turned her glance to Davie. He gave an almost imperceptible shrug. Without speaking, Sophie drove the pole hard against the bank. The punt began slowly to turn.

*

Isabelle's party was due to begin at eight o'clock but it was nearly nine when Sophie, Davie and Cordelia arrived. They walked to the house which was only five minutes from Norwich Street; Cordelia never discovered the exact address. She liked the look of the house and wondered how much it was costing Isabelle's father in rent. It was a long, white, two-storey villa with tall curved windows and green shutters, set well back from the street, with a semi-basement and a flight of steps to the front door. A similar flight led down from the sitting-room to the long garden.

The sitting-room was already fairly full. Looking at her fellow guests, Cordelia was glad that she had bought the kaftan. Most people seemed to have changed although not necessarily, she thought, into something more attractive. What was aimed at was originality; it was preferable to look spectacular, even bizarre, than to appear nondescript.

The sitting-room was elegantly but unsubstantially furnished and Isabelle had impressed on it her own untidy, impractical and iconoclastic femininity. Cordelia doubted whether the owners had provided the ornate crystal chandelier, far too heavy and large for the room, which hung like a sunburst from the middle of the ceiling, or the many silken cushions and curtains which gave the room's austere proportions something of the ostentatious opulence of a courtesan's boudoir. The pictures too, must surely be Isabelle's. No house owner letting his property would leave pictures of this quality on the walls. One, hanging above the fireplace, was of a young girl hugging a puppy. Cordelia gazed at it in excited pleasure. Surely she couldn't mistake that individual blue of the girl's dress, that marvellous painting of the cheeks and plump young arms, skin which simultaneously absorbed and reflected light – lovely, tangible flesh. She cried out involuntarily so that people turned to look at her: 'But that's a Renoir!'

Hugo was at her elbow. He laughed.

'Yes; but don't sound so shocked, Cordelia. It's only a small Renoir! Isabelle asked Papa for a picture for her sitting-room. You didn't expect him to provide a print of the *Hay Wain* or one of those cheap reproductions of Van Gogh's boring old chair.'

'Would Isabelle have known the difference?'

'Oh, yes. Isabelle knows an expensive object when she sees one.'

Cordelia wondered whether the bitterness, the hard edge of contempt in his voice, was for Isabelle or for himself. They looked across the room to where she stood, smiling at them. Hugo moved towards her like a man in a dream and took her hand. Cordelia watched. Isabelle had dressed her hair in a high cluster of curls, Grecian style. She was wearing an ankle-length dress of cream matt silk, with a very low square neckline and small intricately tucked sleeves. It was obviously a model and should, Cordelia felt, have looked out of place at an informal party. But it didn't. It merely made every other woman's dress look like an improvisation and reduced her own, whose colours had seemed muted and subtle when she bought it, to the status of a gaudy rag.

Cordelia was determined to get Isabelle alone some time during the evening but could see that it wasn't going to be easy. Hugo stuck tenaciously to her side, steering her among her guests with one proprietorial hand on her waist. He seemed to be drinking steadily and Isabelle's glass was always filled. Perhaps as the evening wore on they would get careless and there would be a chance to separate them. In the meantime, Cordelia decided to explore the house, and a more practical matter, to find out before she needed it where the lavatory was. It was the kind of party where guests were left to find out these things for themselves.

She went up to the first floor and making her way down the passage pushed gently open the door of the far room. The smell of whisky met her immediately; it was overpowering and Cordelia instinctively slipped into the room and closed the door behind her, afraid that it might permeate the house. The room, which was in an indescribable state of disarray, wasn't empty. On the bed and half covered by the counterpane a woman was lying; a woman with bright ginger hair splayed over the pillow and wearing a pink silk dressing-gown. Cordelia walked up to the bed and looked down at her. She was insensible with drink. She lay there emitting puffs of foul, whisky-laden breath which rose like invisible balls of smoke from the half-open mouth. Her lower lip and jaw were tense and creased, giving the face a look of stern censoriousness as if she disapproved strongly of her own condition. Her thin lips were thickly painted, the strong purple stain had seeped into the cracks around the mouth so that the body looked parched in an extremity of cold. Her hands, the gnarled fingers brown with nicotine and laden with rings, lay quietly on the counterpane. Two of the talon-like nails were broken and the brick-red varnish on the others was cracked or peeled away.

The window was obstructed by a heavy dressing-table. Averting her eyes from the mess of crumpled tissues, open bottles of face cream, spilt powder and half-drunk cups of what looked like black coffee, Cordelia squeezed behind it and pushed open the window. She gulped in lungfuls of fresh, cleansing air. Below her in the garden pale shapes moved silently over the grass and between the trees like the ghosts of long-dead revellers. She left the window open and went back to the bed. There was nothing here that she could do but she placed the cold hands under the counterpane and, taking a second and warmer gown from the hook on the door, tucked it around the woman's body. That, at least, would compensate for the fresh air blowing across the bed.

That done, Cordelia slipped back into the passage, just in time to see Isabelle coming out of the room next door. She shot out an arm and half dragged the girl back into the bedroom. Isabelle gave a little cry, but Cordelia planted her back firmly against the door and said in a low, urgent whisper:

'Tell me what you know about Mark Callender.'

The violet eyes slewed from door to window as if desperate for escape.

'I wasn't there when he did it.'

'When who did what?'

Isabelle retreated towards the bed as if the inert figure, who was **now groaning stertorously, could offer support. Suddenly the** woman turned on her side and gave a long snort like an animal in pain. Both girls glanced at her in startled alarm. Cordelia reiterated:

'When who did what?'

'When Mark killed himself; I wasn't there.'

The woman on the bed gave a little sigh. Cordelia lowered her voice:

'But you were there some days earlier, weren't you? You called at the house and enquired for him. Miss Markland saw you. Afterwards you sat in the garden and waited until he'd finished work.'

Was it Cordelia's imagination that the girl suddenly seemed more relaxed, that she was relieved at the innocuousness of the question?

'I just called to see Mark. They gave me his address at the college Lodge. I went to visit him.'

'Why?' The harsh question seemed to puzzle her. She replied simply:

'I wanted to be with him. He was my friend.'

'Was he your lover too?' asked Cordelia. This brutal frankness was surely better than asking whether they had slept together, or gone to bed together – stupid euphemisms which Isabelle might not even understand: it was hard to tell from those beautiful but frightened eyes just how much she did understand.

'No, Mark was never my lover. He was working in the garden and I had to wait for him at the cottage. He gave me a chair in the sun and a book until he was free.'

'What book?'

'I don't remember, it was very dull. I was dull too until Mark came. Then we had tea with funny mugs that had a blue band, and after tea we went for a walk and then we had supper. Mark made a salad.'

'And then?'

'I drove home.'

She was perfectly calm now. Cordelia pressed on, aware of the sound of footsteps passing up and down the stairs, of the ring of voices.

'And the time before that? When did you see him before that tea party?'

'It was a few days before Mark left college. We went for a picnic in my car to the seaside. But first we stopped at a town – St Edmunds town, is it? – and Mark saw a doctor.'

'Why? Was he ill?'

'Oh no, he was not ill, and he did not stay long enough for what you call it – an examination. He was in the house a few minutes only. It was a very poor house. I waited for him in the car, but not just outside the house you understand.'

'Did he say why he went there?'

'No, but I do not think he got what he wanted. Afterwards he was sad for a little time, but then we went to the sea and he was happy again.'

She, too, seemed happy now. She smiled at Cordelia, her sweet, unmeaning smile. Cordelia thought: it's just the cottage that terrifies her. She doesn't mind talking about the living Mark, it's his death she can't bear to think about. And yet, this repugnance wasn't born of personal grief. He had been her friend; he was sweet; she liked him. But she was getting on very well without him.

There was a knock at the door. Cordelia stood aside and Hugo came in. He lifted an eyebrow at Isabelle and, ignoring Cordelia, said: 'It's your party, ducky; coming down?'

'Cordelia wanted to talk to me about Mark.'

'No doubt. You told her, I hope, that you spent one day with him motoring to the sea and one afternoon and evening at Summertrees and that you haven't seen him since.'

'She told me,' said Cordelia. 'She was practically word perfect. I think she's safe to be let out on her own now.'

He said easily:

'You shouldn't be sarcastic, Cordelia, it doesn't suit you. Sarcasm is all right for some women, but not for women who are beautiful in the way that you are beautiful.'

They were passing down the stairs together to meet the hubbub in the hall. The compliment irritated Cordelia. She said:

'I suppose that woman on the bed is Isabelle's chaperone. Is she often drunk?'

'Mademoiselle de Congé? Not often as drunk as that, but I admit that she is seldom absolutely sober.'

'Then oughtn't you to do something about it?'

'What should I do? Hand her over to the twentieth-century Inquisition – a psychiatrist like my father? What has she done to us to deserve that? Besides, she is tediously conscientious on the few occasions when she's sober. It happens that her compulsions and my interest coincide.'

Cordelia said severely:

'That may be expedient but I don't think it's very responsible and it isn't kind.'

He stopped in his tracks and turned towards her, smiling directly into her eyes.

'Oh, Cordelia, you talk like the child of progressive parents who has been reared by a nonconformist nanny and educated at a convent school. I do like you!'

He was still smiling as Cordelia slipped away from them and infiltrated into the party. She reflected that his diagnosis hadn't been so very wrong.

She helped herself to a glass of wine, then moved slowly round the room listening unashamedly to scraps of conversation, hoping to hear Mark's name mentioned. She heard it only once. Two girls and a very fair, rather insipid young man were standing behind her. One of the girls said:

'Sophie Tilling seems to have recovered remarkably quickly from Mark Callender's suicide. She and Davie went to the cremation, did you know? Typical of Sophie to take her current lover to see the previous one incinerated. I suppose it gave her some kind of a kick.'

Her companion laughed.

'And little brother takes over Mark's girl. If you can't get beauty, money and brains, settle for the first two. Poor Hugo! He suffers from a sense of inferiority. Not quite handsome enough; not quite clever enough – Sophie's First must have shaken him – not quite rich enough. No wonder he has to rely on sex to give him confidence.'

'And, even there, not quite . . .'

'Darling, you should know.'

They laughed and moved away. Cordelia felt her face burning. Her hand shook, almost spilling her wine. She was surprised to find how much she cared, how much she had come to like Sophie. But that, of course, was part of the plan, that was Tilling strategy. If you can't shame her into giving up the case, suborn her; take her on the river; be nice to her; get her on our side. And it was true, she was on their side, at least against malicious detractors. She comforted herself with the censorious reflection that they were as bitchy as guests at a suburban cocktail party. She had never in her life attended one of those innocuous if boring gatherings for the routine consumption of gossip, gin and canapés but, like her father who had never attended one either, she found no difficulty in believing that they were hotbeds of snobbery, spite and sexual innuendo.

A warm body was pressing against her. She turned and saw Davie. He was carrying three bottles of wine. He had obviously heard at least part of the conversation, as the girls had no doubt intended, but he grinned amiably.

'Funny how Hugo's discarded women always hate him so much. It's quite different with Sophie. Her ex-lovers clutter up Norwich Street with their beastly bicycles and broken-down cars. I'm always finding them in the sitting-room drinking my beer and confiding to her the awful trouble they're having with their present girls.'

'Do you mind?'

'Not if they don't get any further than the sitting-room. Are you enjoying yourself?'

'Not very much.'

'Come and meet a friend of mine. He's been asking who you are.'

'No thank you, Davie. I must keep myself free for Mr Horsfall. I don't want to miss him.'

He smiled at her, rather pityingly she thought, and seemed about to speak. But he changed his mind and moved away, clutching his bottles to his chest and shouting a cheerful warning as he edged himself through the throng.

Cordelia worked her way around the room, watching and listening. She was intrigued by the overt sexuality; she had thought that intellectuals breathed too rarefied air to be much interested in the flesh. Obviously this was a misapprehension. Come to think of it, the comrades, who might have been supposed to live in randy promiscuity, had been remarkably staid. She had sometimes felt that their sexual activities were prompted more by duty than instinct, more a weapon of revolution or a gesture against the bourgeois mores they despised than a response to human need. Their basic energies were all devoted to politics. It was not difficult to see where most of the energies of those present were directed.

She needn't have worried about the success of the kaftan. A number of men showed themselves willing or even eager to detach themselves from their partners for the pleasure of talking to her. **With one particularly, a decorative and ironically amusing young** historian, Cordelia felt that she could have spent an entertaining evening. To enjoy the sole attention of one agreeable man and no attention at all from anyone else was all she ever hoped from a party. She wasn't naturally gregarious and, alienated by the last six years from her own generation, found herself intimidated by the noise, the underlying ruthlessness and the half-understood conventions of these tribal matings. And she told herself firmly that she wasn't here to enjoy herself at Sir Ronald's expense. None of her prospective partners knew Mark Callender or showed any interest in him, dead or alive. She mustn't get herself tied for the evening to people who had no information to give. When this seemed a danger and the talk became too beguiling, she would murmur her excuses and slip away to the bathroom or into the shadows of the garden where little groups were sitting on the grass smoking pot. Cordelia couldn't be mistaken in that evocative smell. They showed no disposition to chat and here, at least, she could stroll in privacy gaining courage for the next foray, for the next artfully casual question, the next inevitable response.

'Mark Callender? Sorry – we never met. Didn't he go off to sample the simple life and end by hanging himself or something?'

Once she took refuge in Mademoiselle de Congé's room, but she saw that the inert figure had been unceremoniously dumped on a cushion of pillows on the carpet and that the bed was being occupied for quite another purpose.

She wondered when Edward Horsfall would arrive or whether he would arrive at all. And if he did, would Hugo remember or bother to introduce her? She couldn't see either of the Tillings in the hot crush of gesticulating bodies which by now had crammed the sitting-room and spilled into the hall and half-way up the stairs. She was beginning to feel that this would be a wasted evening when Hugo's hand fell on her arm. He said:

'Come and meet Edward Horsfall. Edward, this is Cordelia Gray; she wants to talk about Mark Callender.'

Edward Horsfall was another surprise. Cordelia had subconsciously conjured up the picture of an elderly don, a little distrait with the weight of his learning, a benevolent if detached mentor of the young. Horsfall could not have been much over thirty. He was very tall, his hair falling long over one eye, his lean body curved as a melon rind, a comparison reinforced by the pleated yellow shirt front under a jutting bow tie.

Any half acknowledged, half shameful hope which Cordelia may have nourished that he would immediately take to her and be happily ungrudging of his time so long as they were together was quickly dispersed. His eyes were restless, flicking obsessively back to the door. She suspected that he was alone by choice, deliberately keeping himself free from encumbrances until the hoped-for companion arrived. He was so fidgety that it was difficult not to be fretted by his anxiety. She said:

'You don't have to stay with me all the evening you know, I only want some information.'

Her voice recalled him to an awareness of her and to some attempt at civility.

'That wouldn't exactly be a penance. I'm sorry. What do you want to know?'

'Anything you can tell me about Mark. You taught him history didn't you? Was he good at it?'

It wasn't a particularly relevant question but one which she felt all teachers might respond to as a start.

'He was more rewarding to teach than some students I'm afflicted with. I don't know why he chose history. He could very well have read one of the sciences. He had a lively curiosity about physical phenomena. But he decided to read history.'

'Do you think that was to disoblige his father?'

'To disoblige Sir Ronald?' He turned and stretched out an arm for a bottle. 'What are you drinking? There's one thing about Isabelle de Lasterie's parties, the drink is excellent, presumably because Hugo orders it. There's an admirable absence of beer.'

'Doesn't Hugo drink beer then?' asked Cordelia.

'He claims not to. What were we talking about? Oh, yes, disobliging Sir Ronald. Mark said that he chose history because we have no chance of understanding the present without understanding the past. That's the sort of irritating cliché people come out with at interviews, but he may have believed it. Actually, of course, the reverse is true; we interpret the past through our knowledge of the present.'

'Was he any good?' asked Cordelia. 'I mean, would he have got a First?'

A First, she naively believed, was the ultimate in scholastic achievement, the certificate of pronounced intelligence that the recipient carried unchallenged through life. She wanted to hear that Mark was safe for a First.

'Those are two separate and distinct questions. You seem to be confusing merit with achievement. Impossible to predict his class, hardly a First. Mark was capable of extraordinarily good and original work but he limited his material to the number of his original ideas. The result tended to be rather thin. Examiners like originality but you've got to spew up the accepted facts and orthodox opinions first if only to show that you've learnt them. An exceptional memory and fast legible handwriting; that's the secret of a First. Where are you, incidentally?' He noticed Cordelia's brief look of incomprehension.

'At what college?'

'None; I work. I'm a private detective.'

He took this information in his stride.

'My uncle employed one of those once to find out if my aunt was being screwed by their dentist. She was, but he could have found out more easily by the simple expedient of asking them. His way, he lost the services of a wife and of a dentist simultaneously and paid through the nose for information he could have got for nothing. It made quite a stir in the family at the time. I should have thought that the job was – '

Cordelia finished the sentence for him.

'An unsuitable job for a woman?'

'Not at all. Entirely suitable I should have thought, requiring, I imagine, infinite curiosity, infinite pains and a penchant for interfering with other people.' His attention was wandering again. A group near to them were talking and snatches of the conversation came to them.

' – typical of the worst kind of academic writing. Contempt for logic; a generous sprinkling of vogue names; spurious profundity and bloody awful grammar.'

The tutor gave the speakers a second's attention, dismissed their academic chat as beneath his notice and condescended to transfer his attention but not his regard back to Cordelia.

'Why are you so interested in Mark Callender?'

'His father has employed me to find out why he died. I was hoping that you might be able to help. I mean, did he ever give you a hint that he might be unhappy, unhappy enough to kill himself? Did he explain why he gave up college?'

'Not to me. I never felt that I got near him. He made a formal goodbye, thanked me for what he chose to describe as my help, and left. I made the usual noises of regret. We shook hands. I was embarrassed, but not Mark. He wasn't I think, a young man susceptible to embarrassment.'

There was a small commotion at the door and a group of new arrivals pushed themselves noisily into the throng. Amongst them was a tall, dark girl in a flame-coloured frock, open almost to the waist. Cordelia felt the tutor stiffen, saw his eyes fixed on the new arrival with an intense, half anxious, half supplicating look, which she had seen before. Her heart sank. She would be lucky now to get any more information. Desperately trying to recapture his attention, she said:

'I'm not sure that Mark did kill himself. I think it could have been murder.'

He spoke inattentively, his eyes on the newcomers.

'Unlikely, surely. By whom? For what reason? He was a negligible personality. He didn't even provoke a vague dislike except possibly from his father. But Ronald Callender couldn't have done it if that's what you're hoping. He was dining in Hall at High Table on the night Mark died. It was a College Feast night. I sat next to him. His son telephoned him.'

Cordelia said eagerly, almost tugging at his sleeve.

'At what time?'

'Soon after the meal started, I suppose. Benskin, he's one of the college servants, came in and gave him the message. It must have been between eight and eight-fifteen. Callender disappeared for about ten minutes then returned and got on with his soup. The rest of us still hadn't reached the second course.'

'Did he say what Mark wanted? Did he seem disturbed?'

'Neither. We hardly spoke through the meal. Sir Ronald doesn't waste his conversational gifts on non-scientists. Excuse me, will you?'

He was gone, threading his way through the throng towards his prey. Cordelia put down her glass and went in search of Hugo.

'Look,' she said, 'I want to talk to Benskin, a servant at your college. Would he be there tonight?'

Hugo put down the bottle he was holding.

'He may be. He's one of the few who live in college. But I doubt whether you would winkle him out of his lair on your own. If it's all that urgent, I'd better come with you.'

*

The college porter ascertained without curiosity that Benskin was in the college and Benskin was summoned. He arrived after a wait of five minutes during which Hugo chatted to the porter and Cordelia walked outside the Lodge to amuse herself reading the college notices. Benskin arrived, unhurrying, imperturbable. He was a silver-haired, formally dressed old man, his face creased and thick-skinned as an anaemic blood orange, and would, Cordelia thought, have looked like an advertisement for the ideal butler, were it not for an expression of lugubrious and sly disdain.

Cordelia gave him sight of Sir Ronald's note of authority and plunged straight into her questions. There was nothing to be gained by subtlety and since she had enlisted Hugo's help, she had little hope of shaking him off. She said:

'Sir Ronald has asked me to enquire into the circumstances of his son's death.'

'So I see, Miss.'

'I am told that Mr Mark Callender telephoned his father while Sir Ronald was dining at High Table on the night his son died and that you passed the message to Sir Ronald shortly after dinner began?'

'I was under the impression at the time that it was Mr Callender who was ringing, Miss, but I was mistaken.'

'How can you be sure of that, Mr Benskin?'

'Sir Ronald himself told me, Miss, when I saw him in college some few days after his son's death. I've known Sir Ronald since he was an undergraduate and I made bold to express my condolences. During our brief conversation I made reference to the telephone call of 26th May and Sir Ronald told me that I was mistaken, that it was not Mr Callender who had called.'

'Did he say who it was?'

'Sir Ronald informed me that it was his laboratory assistant, Mr Chris Lunn.'

'Did that surprise you – that you were wrong, I mean?'

'I confess that I was somewhat surprised, Miss, but the mistake

95

was perhaps excusable. My subsequent reference to the incident was fortuitous and in the circumstances regrettable.'

'But do you really believe that you misheard the name?'

The obstinate old face did not relax.

'Sir Ronald could have been in no doubt about the person who telephoned him.'

'Was it usual for Mr Callender to ring his father while he was dining in college?'

'I had never previously taken a call from him, but then answering the telephone is not part of my normal duties. It is possible that some of the other college servants may be able to help but I hardly think that an enquiry would be productive or that the news that college servants had been questioned would be gratifying to Sir Ronald.'

'Any enquiry which can help ascertain the truth is likely to be gratifying to Sir Ronald,' said Cordelia. Really, she thought, Benskin's prose style is becoming infectious. She added more naturally:

'Sir Ronald is very anxious to find out everything possible about his son's death. Is there anything that you can tell me, any help that you can give me, Mr Benskin?'

This was perilously close to an appeal but it met with no response.

'Nothing, Miss. Mr Callender was a quiet and pleasant young gentleman who seemed, as far as I was able to observe him, to be in good health and spirits up to the time he left us. His death has been very much felt in the college. Is there anything else, Miss?'

He stood patiently waiting to be dismissed and Cordelia let him go. As she and Hugo left college together and walked back into Trumpington Street she said bitterly:

'He doesn't care, does he?'

'Why should he? Benskin's an old phoney but he's been at college for seventy years and he's seen it all before. A thousand ages in his sight are but an evening gone. I've only known Benskin distressed once over the suicide of an undergraduate and that was a duke's son. Benskin thought that there were some things that the college shouldn't permit to happen.'

'But he wasn't mistaken about Mark's call. You could tell that from his whole manner, at least I could. He knows what he heard. He isn't going to admit it, of course, but he knows in his heart he wasn't mistaken.'

Hugo said lightly:

'He was being the old college servant, very correct, very proper; that's Benskin all over. "The young gentlemen aren't what they were when I first came to college." I should bloody well hope not! They wore side whiskers then and noblemen sported fancy gowns to distinguish them from the plebs. Benskin would bring all that back if he could. He's an anachronism, pottering through the court hand in hand with a statelier past.'

'But he isn't deaf. I deliberately spoke in a soft voice and he heard me perfectly. Do you really believe that he was mistaken?'

'Chris Lunn and his son are very similar sounds.'

'But Lunn doesn't announce himself that way. All the time I was with Sir Ronald and Miss Leaming they just called him Lunn.'

'Look, Cordelia, you can't possibly suspect Ronald Callender of having a hand in his son's death! Be logical. You accept, I suppose, that a rational murderer hopes not to be found out. You admit, no doubt, that Ronald Callender, although a disagreeable bastard, is a rational being. Mark is dead and his body cremated. No one except you has mentioned murder. Then Sir Ronald employs you to stir things up. Why should he if he's got something to hide? He doesn't even need to divert suspicion; there has been no suspicion, there is no suspicion.'

'Of course I don't suspect him of killing his son. He doesn't know how Mark died and he desperately needs to know. That's why he's taken me on. I could tell that at our interview; I couldn't be wrong about that. But I don't understand why he should have lied about the telephone call.'

'If he is lying there could be half a dozen innocent explanations. If Mark did ring the college it must have been something pretty urgent, perhaps something which his father didn't particularly want to make public, something which gives a clue to his son's suicide.'

'Then why employ me to find out why he killed himself?'

'True, wise Cordelia; I'll try again. Mark asked him for help, perhaps an urgent visit which Dad refused. You can imagine his reaction. "Don't be ridiculous, Mark, I'm dining at High Table with the Master. Obviously I can't leave the cutlets and claret just because you telephone in this hysterical way and demand to see me. Pull yourself together." That sort of thing wouldn't sound so good in open court; coroners are notoriously censorious.' Hugo's voice took on a deep magisterial tone. ' "It is not for me to add to Sir Ronald's distress, but it is, perhaps, unfortunate that he chose to ignore what was obviously a cry for help. Had he left his meal immediately and gone to his son's side this brilliant young student might have been saved." Cambridge suicides, so I've noticed, are always brilliant; I'm still waiting to read the report of an inquest where the college authorities testify that the student only just killed himself in time before they kicked him out.'

'But Mark died between seven and nine p.m. That telephone call is Sir Ronald's alibi!'

'He wouldn't see it like that. He doesn't need an alibi. If you know you're not involved and the question of foul play never arises, you don't think in terms of alibis. It's only the guilty who do that.'

'But how did Mark know where to find his father? In his evidence Sir Ronald said that he hadn't spoken to his son for over three weeks.'

'I can see you have a point there. Ask Miss Leaming. Better still, ask Lunn if it was, in fact, he who rang the college. If you're looking for a villain Lunn should suit admirably. I find him absolutely sinister.'

'I didn't know that you knew him.'

'Oh, he's pretty well known in Cambridge. He drives that horrid little closed van around with ferocious dedication as if he were transporting recalcitrant students to the gas chambers. Everyone knows Lunn. Seldom he smiles and smiles in such a way as if he mocked himself and scorned his spirit that could be moved to smile at anything. I should concentrate on Lunn.'

They walked on in silence through the warm scented night while the waters sang in the runnels of Trumpington Street. Lights were shining now in college doorways and in porters' lodges and the far gardens and interconnecting courts, glimpsed as they passed, looked remote and ethereal as in a dream. Cordelia was suddenly oppressed with loneliness and melancholy. If Bernie were alive they would be discussing the case, cosily ensconced in the furthest corner of some Cambridge pub, insulated by noise and smoke and anonymity from the curiosity of their neighbours; talking low-voiced in their own particular jargon. They would be speculating on the personality of a young man who slept under that gentle and intellectual painting, yet who had bought a vulgar magazine of salacious nudes. Or had he? And if not, how had it come to be in the cottage garden? They would be discussing a father who lied about his son's last telephone call; speculating in happy complicity about an uncleaned spade, a row of earth half dug, an unwashed coffee mug, a quotation from Blake meticulously typed. They would be talking about Isabelle who was terrified and Sophie who was surely honest and Hugo who certainly knew something about Mark's death and who was clever but not as clever as he needed to be. For the first time since the case began Cordelia doubted her ability to solve it alone. If only there were someone reliable in whom she could confide, someone who would reinforce her confidence. She thought again of Sophie, but Sophie had been Mark's mistress and was Hugo's sister. They were both involved. She was on her own and that, when she came to think about it, was no different from how essentially it had always been. Ironically, the realization brought her comfort and a return of hope.

At the corner of Panton Street they paused and he said:

'You're coming back to the party?'

'No, thank you, Hugo; I've got work to do.'

'Are you staying in Cambridge?'

Cordelia wondered whether the question was prompted by more than polite interest. Suddenly cautious, she said:

'Only for the next day or two. I've found a very dull but cheap bed and breakfast place near the station.'

He accepted the lie without comment and they said goodnight. She made her way back to Norwich Street. The little car was still outside number fifty-seven, but the house was dark and quiet as if to emphasize her exclusion and the three windows were as blank as dead rejecting eyes.

*

She was tired by the time she got back to the cottage and had parked the Mini on the edge of the copse. The garden gate creaked at her hand. The night was dark and she felt in her bag for her torch and followed its bright pool round the side of the cottage and to the back door. By its light she fitted the key into the lock. She turned it and, dazed with tiredness, stepped into the sitting-room. The torch, still switched on, hung loosely from her hand, making erratic patterns of light on the tiled floor. Then in one involuntary movement it jerked upwards and shone full on the thing that hung from the centre hook of the ceiling. Cordelia gave a cry and clutched at the table. It was the bolster from her bed, the bolster with a cord drawn tight about one end making a grotesque and bulbous head, and the other end stuffed into a pair of Mark's trousers. The legs hung pathetically flat and empty, one lower than the other. As she stared at it in fascinated horror, her heart hammering, a slight breeze wafted in from the open door and it swung slowly round as if twisted by a living hand.

She must have stood there rooted with fear and staring wild-eyed at the bolster for seconds only, yet it seemed minutes before she found the strength to pull out a chair from the table and take the thing down. Even in the moment of repulsion and terror she remembered to look closely at the knot. The cord was attached to the hook by a simple loop and two half-hitches. So, either her secret visitor had chosen not to repeat his former tactics, or he hadn't known how the first knot had been tied. She laid the bolster on the chair and went outside for the gun. In her tiredness she had forgotten it, but now she longed for the reassurance of the hard cold metal in her hand. She stood at the back door and listened. The garden seemed suddenly full of noises, mysterious rustlings, leaves moving in the slight breeze like human sighs, furtive scurryings in the undergrowth, the bat-like squeak of an animal disconcertingly close at hand. The night seemed to be holding its breath as she crept out towards the elder bush. She waited, listening to her own heart, before she found courage to turn her back and stretch up her hand to feel for the gun. It was still there. She sighed audibly with relief and immediately felt better. The gun wasn't loaded but that hardly seemed to matter. She hurried back to the cottage, her terror assuaged.

It was nearly an hour before she finally went to bed. She lit the lamp and, gun in hand, made a search of the whole cottage. Next she examined the window. It was obvious enough how he had got in. The window had no catch and was easy to push open from outside. Cordelia fetched a roll of Scotch tape from her scene-of-crime kit and, as Bernie had shown her, cut two very narrow strips and pasted them across the base of the pane and the wooden frame. She doubted whether the front windows could be opened but she took no chances and sealed them in the same way. It wouldn't stop an intruder but at least she would know next morning that he had gained access. Finally, having washed in the kitchen, she went upstairs to bed. There was no lock on her door but she wedged it slightly open and balanced a saucepan lid on the top of the frame. If anyone did succeed in getting in, he wouldn't take her by surprise. She loaded the gun and placed it on her bedside table, remembering that she was dealing with a killer. She examined the cord. It was a four-foot length of ordinary strong string, obviously not new and frayed at one end. Her heart sank at the hopelessness of trying to identify it. But she labelled it carefully, as Bernie had taught her, and packed it in her scene-of-crime kit. She did the same with the curled strap and the typed passage of Blake, transferring them from the bottom of her shoulder bag to plastic exhibit envelopes. She was so weary that even this routine chore cost her an effort of will. Then she placed the bolster back on the bed, resisting an impulse to sling it on the floor and sleep without it. But, by then, nothing – neither fear nor discomfort – could have kept her awake. She lay for only a few minutes listening to the ticking of her watch before tiredness overcame her and bore her unresisting down the dark tide of sleep.

CHAPTER FOUR

Cordelia was awakened early next morning by the discordant chattering of the birds and the strong clear light of another fine day. She lay for several minutes stretching herself within her sleeping-bag, savouring the smell of a country morning, that subtle and evocative fusion of earth, sweet wet grass and stronger farmyard smell. She washed in the kitchen as Mark had obviously done, standing in the tin bath from the shed and gasping as she poured saucepans of cold tap water over her naked body. There was something about the simple life which disposed one to these austerities. Cordelia thought it unlikely that, in any circumstances, she would willingly have bathed in cold water in London or so much relished the smell of the paraffin stove superimposed on the appetizing sizzle of frying bacon, or the flavour of her first strong mug of tea.

The cottage was filled with sunlight, a warm friendly sanctum from which she could safely venture out to whatever the day held. In the calm peace of a summer morning the little sitting-room seemed untouched by the tragedy of Mark Callender's death. The hook in the ceiling looked as innocuous as if it had never served its dreadful purpose. the horror of that moment when her torch had first picked out the dark swollen shadow of the bolster moving in the night breeze now had the unreality of a dream. Even the memory of the precautions of the night before was embarrassing viewed in the unambiguous light of day. She felt rather foolish as she unloaded the gun, secreted the ammunition among her underclothes, and hid the pistol in the elder bush, watching carefully to see that she wasn't observed. When the washing-up was done and the one teacloth washed through and hung out to dry, she picked a small posy of pansies, cowslips and meadowsweet from the far end of the garden and set them on the table in one of the ribbed mugs.

She had decided that her first task must be to try to trace Nanny Pilbeam. Even if the woman had nothing to tell her about Mark's **death or his reason for leaving college, she would be able to speak** about his childhood and boyhood; she, probably better than anyone, would know what his essential nature had been. She had cared enough about him to attend the funeral and to send an expensive wreath. She had called on him in college on his twenty-first birthday. He had probably kept in touch with her, might even have confided in her. He had no mother and Nanny Pilbeam could have been, in some sense, a substitute.

As she drove into Cambridge Cordelia considered tactics. The probability was that Miss Pilbeam lived somewhere in the district. It was unlikely that she actually lived in the city since Hugo Tilling had only seen her once. From his brief account of her, it sounded as if she were old and probably poor. It was unlikely, therefore, that she would travel far to attend the funeral. It was apparent that she hadn't been one of the official mourners from Garforth House, hadn't been invited by Sir Ronald. According to Hugo, none of the party had even spoken to each other. This hardly suggested that Miss Pilbeam was the elderly and valued retainer of tradition, almost one of the family. Sir Ronald's neglect of her on such an occasion intrigued Cordelia. She wondered just what Miss Pilbeam's position in the family had been.

If the old lady lived near Cambridge, she had probably ordered the wreath at one of the city florists. Villages were very unlikely to provide this kind of service. It had been an ostentatious wreath, which suggested that Miss Pilbeam had been prepared to spend lavishly and had probably gone to one of the larger florists. The likelihood was that she had ordered it personally. Elderly ladies, apart from the fact that they were seldom on the telephone, like to attend to these matters direct, having, Cordelia suspected, a well-founded suspicion that only face-to-face confrontation and the meticulous recital of one's precise requirements extracted the best service. If Miss Pilbeam had come in from her village by train or by bus, she had probably selected a shop somewhere near the centre of the city. Cordelia decided to begin her search by enquiring of passers-by if they could recommend the name of a good florist.

She had already learned that Cambridge was not a city for the cruising motorist. She drew up and consulted the folding map on the back of her guidebook and decided to leave the Mini on the car park next to Parker's Piece. Her search might take some time and would be best done on foot. She daren't risk a parking fine nor the impounding of the car. She checked her watch. It was still only a few minutes after nine o'clock. She had made a good start to the day.

The first hour was disappointing. The people of whom she enquired were anxious to be helpful but their ideas of what constituted a reliable florist somewhere near the centre of the city were peculiar. Cordelia was directed to small greengrocers selling a few bunches of cut flowers as a sideline, to the supplier of gardening equipment who dealt in plants but not in wreaths, and once to a funeral director. The two florists' shops which at first sight seemed possible had never heard of Miss Pilbeam and had provided no wreaths for the Mark Callender funeral. A little weary with much walking and beginning to feel despondent, Cordelia decided that the whole quest had been unreasonably sanguine. Probably Miss Pilbeam had come in from Bury St Edmunds or Newmarket and had bought the wreath in her own town.

But the visit to the undertakers was not wasted. In reply to her enquiry, they recommended the name of a firm which provided 'a very nice class of wreath, miss, really very nice indeed'. The shop was further from the centre of the city than Cordelia had expected. Even from the pavement it smelt of weddings or funerals, as one's mood dictated, and as she pushed open the door Cordelia was welcomed by a gush of sweet warm air which caught at the throat. There were flowers everywhere. Large green buckets lined the walls holding clumps of lilies, irises and lupins; smaller containers were packed tight with wall flowers and marigolds and stocks; there were frigid bundles of tight-budded roses on thornless stems, each flower identical in size and colour and looking as if it had been cultivated in a test tube. Pots of indoor plants, decorated with variegated ribbon, lined the path to the counter like a floral guard of honour.

There was a room at the back of the shop where two assistants were working. Through the open door Cordelia watched them. The younger, a languid blonde with a spotted skin, was assistant executioner, laying out roses and freesias, predestined victims, graded according to type and colour. Her senior, whose status was denoted by a better-fitting overall and an air of authority, was twisting off the flower heads, piercing each mutilated bloom with wire and threading them closely on to a huge bed of moss in the shape of a heart. Cordelia averted her eyes from this horror.

A buxom lady in a pink smock appeared behind the counter

apparently from nowhere. She was as pungently scented as the shop, but had obviously decided that no ordinary floral perfume could compete and that she had better rely on the exotic. She smelt of curry powder and pine so strongly that the effect was practically anaesthetizing.

Cordelia said her prepared speech:

'I'm from Sir Ronald Callender of Garforth House. I wonder whether you can help us? His son was cremated on 3rd of June and their old nurse very kindly sent a wreath, a cross of red roses. Sir Ronald has lost her address and very much wants to write to thank her. The name is Pilbeam.'

'Oh, I don't think we executed any orders of that type for 3rd June.'

'If you would be kind enough to just look in the book – '

Suddenly the young blonde looked up from her work and called out:

'It's Goddard.'

'I beg your pardon, Shirley?' said the buxom lady repressively.

'The name's Goddard. The card on the wreath said Nanny Pilbeam, but the customer was a Mrs Goddard. Another lady came to enquire from Sir Ronald Callender and that was the name she gave. I looked it up for her. Mrs Goddard, Lavender Cottage, Ickleton. One cross, four foot long in red roses. Six pounds. It's there in the book.'

'Thank you very much,' said Cordelia fervently. She smiled her thanks impartially at the three of them and left quickly in case she got embroiled in an argument about the other enquirer from Garforth House. It must have looked odd, she knew, but the three of them would no doubt enjoy themselves discussing it after she had left. Lavender Cottage, Ickleton. She kept repeating the address to herself until she was at a safe distance from the shop and could pause to write it down.

Her tiredness seemed miraculously to have left her as she sped back to the car park. She consulted her map. Ickleton was a village near the Essex border about ten miles from Cambridge. It wasn't far from Duxford so that she would be retracing her steps. She could be there in less than half an hour.

But it took longer than she had expected to thread her way through the Cambridge traffic and it wasn't until thirty-five minutes later that she came to Ickleton's fine flint and pebble church with its broach spire, and drove the Mini close to the church gate. It was a temptation to take a brief look inside, but she resisted it. Mrs Goddard might even now be preparing to catch the Cambridge bus. She went in search of Lavender Cottage.

It wasn't, in fact, a cottage at all but a small semi-detached house of hideous red brick at the end of the High Street. There was only a narrow strip of grass between the front door and the road and neither smell nor sight of lavender. The iron knocker, in the form of a lion's head, fell heavily, shaking the door. The response came, not from Lavender Cottage, but from the next house. An elderly woman appeared, thin, almost toothless and swathed in an immense apron patterned with roses. She had carpet slippers on her feet, a woollen cap decorated with a bobble on her head and an air of lively interest in the world in general.

'You'll be wanting Mrs Goddard, I daresay?'

'Yes. Could you tell me where I could find her?'

'She'll be over at the graveyard, I don't doubt. She usually is this time of a fine morning.'

'I've just come from the church. I didn't see anyone.'

'Bless you, Miss, she's not at the church! They haven't been burying us there for many a year now. Her old man is where they'll be putting her in time, in the cemetery on Hinxton Road. You can't miss it. Just keep straight on.'

'I'll have to go back to the church for my car,' said Cordelia. It was obvious that she was going to be watched out of sight and it seemed necessary to explain why she was departing in the opposite direction to the one indicated. The old woman smiled and nodded and came out to lean on her gate for a better view of Cordelia's progress down the High Street, nodding her head like a marionette so that the bright bobble danced in the sun.

*

The cemetery was easily found. Cordelia parked the Mini on a convenient patch of grass where a signpost pointed the footpath to Duxford and walked the few yards back to the iron gates. There was a small flint chapel of rest with an apse at the east end and beside it an ancient wooden seat green with lichen and spattered with bird **lime which gave a view of the whole burial ground. A wide swathe** of turf ran straight down the middle and on each side were the graves, variously marked with white marble crosses, grey headstones, small rusted circles of iron heeling over towards the smooth turf and bright splashes of flowers patchworked over the newly dug earth. It was very peaceful. The burial ground was surrounded by trees, their leaves scarcely stirring in the calm, hot air. There was little sound except the chirruping of crickets in the grass and from time to time the nearby ringing of a railway level-crossing bell and the swooping horn of a diesel train.

There was only one other person in the graveyard, an elderly woman bending over one of the far graves. Cordelia sat quietly on the seat, arms folded in her lap, before making her way silently down the grass path towards her. She knew with certainty that this interview was going to be crucial yet paradoxically she was in no hurry to begin. She came up to the woman and stood, still unnoticed, at the foot of the grave.

She was a small woman dressed in black whose old-fashioned straw hat, its brim wreathed with faded net, was screwed to her hair with an immense black-bobbed hat pin. She knelt with her back to Cordelia showing the soles of a pair of misshapen shoes from which her thin legs stuck out like sticks. She was weeding the grave; her fingers, darting like a reptile's tongue over the grass, plucked at small, almost undetectable weeds. At her side was a punnet holding a folded newspaper and a gardening trowel. From time to time, she dropped into the punnet her little mush of weeds.

After a couple of minutes, during which Cordelia watched her in silence, she paused satisfied and began smoothing the surface of the grass as if comforting the bones beneath. Cordelia read the inscription carved deep on the headstone. 'Sacred to the memory of Charles Albert Goddard beloved husband of Annie who departed this life 27th August 1962, aged 70 years. At rest.' At rest; the commonest epitaph of a generation to whom rest must have seemed the ultimate luxury, the supreme benediction.

The woman rested back for a second on her heels and contemplated the grave with satisfaction. It was then that she became aware of Cordelia. She turned a bright much-wrinkled face towards her and said without curiosity or resentment at her presence:

'It's a nice stone, isn't it?'

'Yes, it is. I was admiring the lettering.'

'Cut deep that is. It cost a mint of money but it was worth it. That'll last, you see. Half the lettering here won't, it's that shallow. It takes the pleasure out of a cemetery. I like to read the gravestones, like to know who people were and when they died and how long the women lived after they buried their men. It sets you wondering how they managed and whether they were lonely. There's no use in a stone if you can't read the lettering. Of course, this stone looks a bit top-heavy at present. That's because I asked them to leave space for me: "Also to Annie his wife, departed this life, . . ." and then the date: that'll even it up nicely. I've left the money to pay for it.'

'What text were you thinking of having?' enquired Cordelia.

'Oh, no text! At rest will be good enough for the both of us. We shan't be asking more of the good Lord than that.'

Cordelia said:

'That cross of roses you sent to Mark Callender's funeral was beautiful.'

'Oh, did you see it? You weren't at the funeral were you? Yes, I was pleased with it. They made a nice job of it, I thought. Poor boy, he hadn't much else, had he?'

She looked at Cordelia with benign interest:

'So you knew Mr Mark? Would you be his young lady perhaps?'

'No, not that, but I care about him. It's odd that he never talked about you, his old nurse.'

'But I wasn't his nurse, my dear, or at least, only for a month or two. He was a baby then, it meant nothing to him. No, I was nurse to his dear mother.'

'But you visited Mark on his twenty-first birthday?'

'So he told you that, did he? I was glad to see him again after all those years, but I wouldn't have pushed myself on him. It wouldn't have been right, his father feeling as he did. No, I went to give him something from his mother, to do something she had asked me to do when she was dying. Do you know, I hadn't seen Mr Mark for over twenty years – odd, really, considering that we didn't live that far apart – but I knew him at once. He had a great look of his mother about him, poor boy.'

'Could you tell me about it? It's not just curiosity; it's important for me to know.'

Leaning for support on the handle of her basket, Mrs Goddard got laboriously to her feet. She picked at a few short blades of grass adhering to her skirt, felt in her pocket for a pair of grey cotton gloves and put them on. Together they made their way slowly down the path.

'Important, is it? I don't know why it should be. It's all in the past now. She's dead, poor lady, and so is he. All that hope and promise come to nothing. I haven't spoken to anyone else about it, but then who would care to know?'

'Perhaps we could sit on this bench and talk together for a time?'

'I don't see why we shouldn't. There's nothing to hurry home for now. Do you know, my dear, I didn't marry my husband until I was fifty-three and yet I miss him as if we had been childhood sweethearts. People said I was a fool to take on a man at that age but you see I had known his wife for thirty years, we were at school together, and I knew him. If a man's good to one woman, he'll be good to another. That's what I reckoned and I was right.'

They sat side by side on the bench gazing over the green swathe towards the grave. Cordelia said:

'Tell me about Mark's mother.'

'She was a Miss Bottley, Evelyn Bottley. I went to her mother as under-nursemaid before she was born. There was only little Harry then. He was killed in the war on his first raid over Germany. His Dad took it very hard; there was never anyone to match Harry, the sun shone out of his eyes. The master never really cared for Miss Evie, it was all the boy with him. Mrs Bottley died when Evie was born and that may have made a difference. People say that it does, but I've never believed it. I've known fathers who loved a baby even more – poor innocent things, how can they be blamed? If you ask me, it was just an excuse for not taking to the child, that she killed her mother.'

'Yes, I know a father who made it an excuse too. But it isn't their fault. We can't make ourselves love someone just because we want to.'

'More's the pity, my dear, or the world would be an easier place. But his own child, that's not natural!'

'Did she love him?'

'How could she? You won't get love from a child if you don't give love. But she never had the trick of pleasing him, of humouring him – he was a big man, fierce, loud-talking, frightening to a child. He would have done better with a pretty, pert little thing, who wouldn't have been afraid of him.'

'What happened to her? How did she meet Sir Ronald Callender?'

'He wasn't Sir Ronald then, my dear. Oh, dear no! He was Ronny Callender the gardener's son. They lived at Harrogate you see. Oh, such a lovely house they had! When I first went into service there they had three gardeners. That was before the war, of course. Mr Bottley worked in Bradford; he was in the wool trade. Well, you were asking about Ronny Callender. I remember him well, a pugnacious, good-looking lad but one who kept his thoughts to himself. He was clever that one, oh he was clever! He got a scholarship to the grammar school and did very well.'

'And Evelyn Bottley fell in love?'

'She may have done, my dear. What there was between them when they were young, who can tell. But then the war came and he went away. She was wild to do something useful and they took her on as a VAD, though how she passed the medical I'll never know. And then they met again in London as people did in the war and the next thing we knew they were married.'

'And came to live here outside Cambridge?'

'Not until after the war. At first she kept on with her nursing and he was sent overseas. He had what the men call a good war; we'd call it a bad war I dare say, a lot of killing and fighting, imprisonment and escaping. It ought to have made Mr Bottley proud of him and reconciled to the marriage but it didn't. I think he thought that Ronny had his eye on the money, because there was money to come, no doubt about that. He may have been right, but who's to blame the boy? My mother used to say, "Don't marry for money, but marry where money is!" There's no harm in looking for money as long as there's kindness as well.'

'And do you think there was kindness?'

'There was never unkindness that I could see, and she was mad about him. After the war he went up to Cambridge. He'd always wanted to be a scientist and he got a grant because he was ex-service. She had some money from her father and they bought the house he lives in now so that he could live at home when he was studying. It didn't look the same then, of course. He's done a lot to it since. They were quite poor then and Miss Evie managed with practically no one to help, only me. Mr Bottley used to come and stay from time to time. She used to dread his visits, poor darling. He was looking for a grandchild, you see, and one didn't come. And then Mr Callender finished at the university and got a job teaching. He wanted to stay on at college to be a don or something like that, but they wouldn't have him. He used to say it was because he hadn't influence, but I think he may not have been quite clever enough. In Harrogate we thought he was the cleverest boy in the grammar school. But then, Cambridge is full of clever men.'

'And then Mark was born?'

'Yes, on the 25th April 1951, nine years after they were married. He was born in Italy. Mr Bottley was that pleased when she became pregnant that he increased the allowance and they used to spend a lot of holidays in Tuscany. My lady loved Italy, always had, and I think she wanted the child to be born there. Otherwise she wouldn't have gone on holiday in the last month of her pregnancy. I went to visit her about a month after she came home with the baby and I've never seen a woman so happy. Oh, he was a lovely little boy!'

'But why did you visit her; weren't you living and working there?'

'No, my dear. Not for some months. She wasn't well in the early days of her pregnancy. I could see that she was strained and unhappy and then one day Mr Callender sent for me and told me that she had taken against me and that I'd have to leave. I wouldn't have believed it, but when I went to her she just put out her hand and said: "I'm sorry, Nanny, I think it would be better if you went."

'Pregnant women have strange fancies, I know, and the baby was so important to them both. I thought she might have asked me to come back afterwards and so she did, but not living in. I took a bedsitting-room in the village with the postmistress and used to give four mornings a week to my lady and the rest to other ladies in the village. It worked very well, really, but I missed the baby when I wasn't with him. I hadn't seen her often during her pregnancy but once we met in Cambridge. She must have been near the end of her time. She was very heavy, poor dear, dragging herself along. At first she pretended that she hadn't noticed me and then she thought better of it and came across the road. "We're off to Italy next week, Nanny," she said. "Isn't it lovely?" I said: "If you're not careful, my dear, that baby will be a little Italian," and she laughed. It seemed as though she couldn't wait to get back to the sun.'

'**And what happened after she came home?**'

'She died after nine months, my dear. She was never strong, as I said, and she caught influenza. I helped look after her and I'd have done more but Mr Callender took over the nursing himself. He couldn't bear anyone else to be near her. We only had a few minutes together just before she died and it was then that she asked me to give her prayer book to Mark on his twenty-first birthday. I can hear her now: "Give it to Mark when he's twenty-one, Nanny. Wrap it up carefully and take it to him when he comes of age. You won't forget will you?" I said: "I'll not forget, my darling, you know that." Then she said a strange thing. "If you do, or if you die before then, or if he doesn't understand, it won't really matter. It will mean that God wants it that way." '

'What do you think she meant?'

'Who's to say, my dear? She was very religious was Miss Evie, too religious for her own good, I sometimes thought. I believe we should accept our own responsibilities, solve our own problems, not leave it all to God as if He hadn't enough to be thinking about with the world in the state it is. But that's what she said not three hours before she died and that's what I promised. So when Mr Mark was twenty-one, I found out what college he was at and went to see him.'

'What happened?'

'Oh, we had a very happy time together. Do you know, his father had never spoken about his mother. That sometimes happens when a wife dies but I think a son ought to know about his mother. He was full of questions, things that I thought his father would have told him.

'He was glad to get the prayer book. It was a few days later that he came to see me. He asked the name of the doctor who had treated his mother. I told him that it was old Dr Gladwin. Mr Callender and she had never had any other doctor. I used to think it a pity sometimes, Miss Evie being so frail. Dr Gladwin must have been seventy then, and although there were people who wouldn't say a word against him, I never thought much of him myself. Drink, you know, my dear; he was never really reliable. But I expect he's gone to his rest long since, poor man. Anyway, I told Mr Mark the name and he wrote it down. Then we had tea and a little chat and he left. I never saw him again.'

'And no one else knows about the prayer book?'

'No one in the world, my dear. Miss Leaming saw the florist's name on my card and asked them for my address. She came here the day after the funeral to thank me for attending but I could see it was only curiosity. If she and Sir Ronald were so pleased to see me, what was to stop them from coming over and shaking hands? She as good as suggested that I was there without an invitation. An invitation to a funeral! Who ever heard of such a thing?'

'So you told her nothing?' asked Cordelia.

'I've told no one but you, my dear, and I'm not sure why I've told you. But no, I didn't tell her. I never liked her, to tell you the truth. I'm not saying there was anything between her and Sir Ronald, not while Miss Evie was alive anyway. There was never any gossip and she lived in a flat in Cambridge and kept herself to herself, I'll give her that. Mr Callender met her when he was teaching science at one of the village schools. She was the English mistress. It wasn't until after Miss Evie died that he set up his own laboratory.'

'Do you mean that Miss Leaming has a degree in English?'

'Oh, yes, my dear! She wasn't trained as a secretary. Of course she gave up the teaching when she started working for Mr Callender.'

'So you left Garforth House after Mrs Callender died? You didn't stay on to care for the baby?'

'I wasn't wanted. Mr Callender employed one of those new college-trained girls and then, when Mark was still only a baby, he was sent away to school. His father made it plain that he didn't like me to see the child and after all, a father has his rights. I wouldn't have gone on seeing Mr Mark knowing that his father didn't approve. It would have only put the boy in a false position. But now he's dead and we've all lost him. The coroner said that he killed himself, and he may have been right.'

Cordelia said:

'I don't think he killed himself.'

'Don't you, my dear? That's kind of you. But he's dead, isn't he, so what does it matter now? I think it's time for me to go home. If you don't mind, I won't ask you to tea, my dear, I'm a little tired today. But you know where to find me, and if ever you want to see me again, you'll always be welcome.'

They made their way out of the burial ground together. At the gates, they parted. Mrs Goddard patted Cordelia on the shoulder with the clumsy affection she might have shown to an animal, then walked off slowly towards the village.

As Cordelia drove round the curve of the road, the level crossing came into sight. A train had just passed and the barriers were being raised. Three vehicles had been caught at the crossing and the last in line was quickest away, accelerating past the first two cars as they bumped slowly over the rails. Cordelia saw that it was a small black van.

*

Later Cordelia remembered little of the journey back to the cottage. She drove fast, concentrating on the road ahead, trying to control her rising excitement by meticulous attention to gears and brakes. She drove the Mini hard against the front hedge, careless of whether it were seen. The cottage looked and smelt just as she had left it. She had almost expected to find it ransacked and the prayer book gone. Sighing with relief, she saw that the white spine was still there among the taller and darker covers. Cordelia opened it. She hardly knew what she expected to find; an inscription perhaps, or a message, cryptic or plain, a letter folded between the leaves. But the only inscription could have no possible relevance to the case. It was written in a shaky, old-fashioned hand; the steel nib had crawled spider-like over the page. 'To Evelyn Mary on the occasion of her confirmation, with love from her Godmother, 5th August 1934.'

Cordelia shook the book. No slip of paper fluttered out. She skimmed through the pages. Nothing.

She sat on the bed drooping with disappointment. Had it been unreasonable to imagine that there was something significant in the bequest of the prayer book; had she fabricated a promising edifice of conjecture and mystery on an old woman's confused recollections of a perfectly ordinary and understandable action – a devout and dying mother leaving a prayer book to her son? And even if she hadn't been wrong, why should the message still be there? If Mark had found a note from his mother, placed between the leaves, he might well have destroyed it after reading. And if he hadn't destroyed it, someone else might have done so. The note, if it ever existed, was now probably part of the shifting heap of white ash and charred debris in the cottage grate.

She shook herself out of her despondency. There was still a line of enquiry to pursue; she would try to trace Dr Gladwin. After a second's thought she put the prayer book in her bag. Looking at her watch, she saw that it was nearly one o'clock. She decided to have a picnic lunch of cheese and fruit in the garden and then set off again for Cambridge to visit the central library and consult a medical directory.

Less than an hour later she found the information she wanted. There was only one Dr Gladwin still on the register who could have attended Mrs Callender as an old man of over seventy, twenty years ago. He was Emlyn Thomas Gladwin who had qualified at St Thomas's Hospital in 1904. She wrote down the address in her note book: 4 Pratts Way, Ixworth Road, Bury St Edmunds. Edmunds town! The town which Isabelle had said that she and Mark had visited on their way to the sea.

So the day hadn't been wasted after all – she was following in Mark Callender's footsteps. Impatient to consult a map she went over to the atlas section of the library. It was now two-fifteen. If she took the A45 road direct through Newmarket she could be in Bury St Edmunds in about an hour. Allow an hour for the visit to the doctor and another for the return journey. She could be home at the cottage before half past five.

She was driving through the gentle unemphatic countryside just outside Newmarket when she noticed the black van following her. It was too far away to see who was driving but she thought it was Lunn and that he was alone. She accelerated, trying to keep the distance between them, but the van drew a little nearer. There was no reason, of course, why Lunn shouldn't be driving to Newmarket on Sir Ronald Callender's business, but the sight of the squat little van perpetually in her driving mirror was disconcerting. Cordelia decided to throw him off. There were few side turns on the road she was travelling and the country was unfamiliar to her. She decided to wait until she reached Newmarket and seize what opportunity offered.

The main through street of the town was a tangle of traffic and every turn seemed to be blocked. It was only at the second set of traffic lights that Cordelia saw her chance. The black van was caught at the intersection about fifty yards behind. As the light turned green, she accelerated quickly and swung round to the left. There was another turn to the left and she took it, then one to the right. She drove on through unfamiliar streets, then, after about five minutes, stopped at an intersection and waited. The black van did not appear.

It looked as if she had succeeded in shaking him off. She waited for another five minutes, then made her way slowly back to the main road and joined in the flow of eastward traffic. Half an hour later she had passed through Bury St Edmunds and was driving very slowly down the Ixworth Road, watching for Pratts Way. Fifty yards farther on she came to it, a row of six small stucco houses standing back from a lay-by. She stopped the car outside number four remembering Isabelle, biddable and docile, who had obviously been told to drive further on and wait in the car. Was that because Mark thought the white Renault too conspicuous? Even the arrival of the Mini had provoked interest. There were faces at upper windows and a small group of children had mysteriously appeared, clustered around a neighbouring gate and watching her with wide and expressionless eyes.

Number four was a depressing house; the front garden was unweeded and the fence had gaps where the planks had rotted or had been wrenched apart. The external paint had flaked away to the bare wood and the brown front door had peeled and blistered in the sun. But Cordelia saw that the bottom windows were shining and that the white net curtains were clean. Mrs Gladwin was probably a careful housewife, struggling to keep up her standards but too old for the heavy work and too poor to afford help. Cordelia felt benevolently towards her. But the woman who, after some minutes, finally opened to her knock – the bell was out of order – was a disconcerting antidote to her sentimental pity. Compassion died before those hard distrustful eyes, that mouth tight as a trap, the thin arms clasped in a bony barrier across her chest as if to repel human contact. It was difficult to guess her age. Her hair, screwed back into a small tight bun, was still black but her face was deeply lined and the sinews and veins stood out in the thin neck like cords. She was wearing carpet slippers and a gaudy cotton overall. Cordelia said:

'My name is Cordelia Gray. I wondered if I could talk to Dr Gladwin, if he's in. It's about an old patient.'

'He's in, where else would he be? He's in the garden. You'd better go through.'

The house smelt horrible, an amalgam of extreme old age, the sour taint of excreta and stale food, with an overlay of strong disinfectant.

Cordelia went through to the garden, carefully avoiding looking at the hall or kitchen since curiosity might seem impertinent.

Dr Gladwin was sitting in a high Windsor chair placed in the sun. Cordelia had never seen a man so old. He seemed to be wearing a woollen track suit, his swollen legs were encased in immense felt slippers and there was a knitted patchwork shawl across his knees. His two hands hung over the arms of the chair as if too heavy for the frail wrists, hands stained and brittle as autumn leaves which trembled with a gentle insistence. The high-domed skull, spiked with a few grey bristles, looked as small and vulnerable as a child's. The eyes were pale yolks swimming in their glutinous blue-veined whites.

Cordelia went to him and called him gently by his name. There was no response. She knelt on the grass at his feet and looked up into his face.

'Dr Gladwin, I wanted to talk to you about a patient. It was a long time ago. Mrs Callender. Do you remember Mrs Callender of Garforth House?'

There was no reply. Cordelia knew that there wouldn't be. Even to ask again seemed an outrage. Mrs Gladwin was standing beside him as if displaying him to a wondering world.

'Go on, ask him! It's all in his head you know. That's what he used to tell me. "I'm not one for records and notes. It's all in my head." '

Cordelia said:

'What happened to his medical records when he gave up practice? Did anyone take them over?'

'That's what I've just told you. There never were any records. And it's no use asking me. I told the boy that too. The doctor was glad enough to marry me when he wanted a nurse, but he didn't discuss his patients. Oh, dear no! He was drinking all the practice profits away, but he could still talk about medical ethics.'

The bitterness in her voice was horrible. Cordelia could not meet her eyes. Just then she thought she saw the old man's lips move. She bent down her head and caught the one word. 'Cold.'

'I think he's trying to say that he's cold. Is there another shawl perhaps that he could have round his shoulders?'

'Cold! In this sun! He's always cold.'

'But perhaps another blanket would help. Shall I fetch it for you?'

'You let him be, miss. If you want to look after him, then look after him. See how you enjoy keeping him clean like a baby, washing his nappies, changing the bed every morning. I'll get him another shawl, but in two minutes he'll be pushing it off. He doesn't know what he wants.'

'I'm sorry,' said Cordelia helplessly. She wondered whether Mrs Gladwin was getting all the help available, whether the district nurse called, whether she had asked her doctor to try to find a hospital bed. But these were useless questions. Even she could recognize the hopeless rejection of help, the despair which no longer had energy even to look for relief. She said:

'I'm sorry; I won't trouble either of you any further.'

They walked back together through the house. But there was one question Cordelia had to ask. When they reached the front gate she said:

'You talked about a boy who visited. Was his name Mark?'

'Mark Callender. He was asking about his mother. And then about ten days later we get the other one calling.'

'What other one?'

'He was a gentleman all right. Walked in as if he owned the place. He wouldn't give a name but I've seen his face somewhere. He asked to see Dr Gladwin and I showed him in. We were sitting in the back parlour that day as there was a breeze. He went up to the doctor and said "Good afternoon, Gladwin" loudly as if talking to a servant. Then he bent down and looked at him. Eye to eye they were. Then he straightened up, wished me good day and left. Oh, we're getting popular, we are! Any more of you and I'll have to charge for the show.'

They stood together at the gate. Cordelia wondered whether to hold out her hand but sensed that Mrs Gladwin was willing her not to go. Suddenly the woman spoke in a loud and gruff voice, looking straight ahead.

'That friend of yours, the boy who came here. He left his address. He said he wouldn't mind sitting with the doctor on a Sunday if I wanted a break; he said he could get them both a bit of dinner. I have a fancy to see my sister over at Haverhill this Sunday. Tell him he can come if he wants to.'

The capitulation was ungracious, the invitation grudging, but Cordelia could guess what it had cost her to give it. She said impulsively:

'I could come on Sunday instead. I've got a car, I could get here sooner.'

It would be a day lost to Sir Ronald Callender, but she wouldn't charge him. And even a private eye was surely entitled to a day off on Sundays.

'He won't want a slip of a girl. There's things to do for him that need a man. He took to that boy. I could see that. Tell him he can come.'

Cordelia turned to her.

'He would have come, I know he would. But he can't. He's dead.'

Mrs Gladwin did not speak. Cordelia put out a tentative hand and touched her sleeve. There was no response. She whispered:

'I'm sorry. I'll go now.' She nearly added: 'If there's nothing I can do for you,' but stopped herself in time. There was nothing she or anyone could do.

She looked back once as the road bent towards Bury and saw the rigid figure still at the gate.

*

Cordelia wasn't sure what made her decide to stop at Bury and walk for ten minutes in the Abbey gardens. But she felt she couldn't face the drive back to Cambridge without calming her spirits and the glimpse of grass and flowers through the great Norman doorway was irresistible. She parked the Mini on Angel Hill, then walked through the gardens to the river bank. There she sat for five minutes in the sun. She remembered that there was money spent on petrol to be recorded in her notebook and felt for it in her bag. Her hand brought out the white prayer book. She sat quietly thinking. Suppose she had been Mrs Callender and had wanted to leave a message, a message which Mark would find and other searchers might miss. Where would she place it? The answer now seemed childishly simple. Surely somewhere on the page with the collect, gospel and epistle for St Mark's Day. He had been born on April 25th. He had been named after the saint. Quickly she found the place. In the bright sunlight reflected from the water she saw what a quick rustle through the pages had missed. There against Cranmer's gentle petition for grace to withstand the blasts of false doctrine was a small pattern of hieroglyphics so faint that the mark on the paper was little more than a smudge. She saw that it was a group of letters and figures.

E M C
A A
14.1.52

The first three letters, of course, were his mother's initials. The date must be that on which she wrote the message. Hadn't Mrs Goddard said that Mrs Callender had died when her son was about nine months old? But the double A? Cordelia's mind chased after motoring associations before she remembered the card in Mark's wallet. Surely these two letters under an initial could only show one thing, the blood group. Mark had been B. His mother was AA. There was only one reason why she should have wanted him to have that information. The next step was to discover Sir Ronald Callender's group.

She almost cried out with triumph as she ran through the gardens and turned the Mini again towards Cambridge. She hadn't thought out the implications of this discovery, or even whether her arguments were valid. But at least she had something to do, at least she had a lead. She drove fast, desperate to get to the city before the post office closed. There, she seemed to remember, it was possible to get a copy of the Executive Council's list of local doctors. It was handed over. And now for a telephone. She knew only one house in Cambridge where there was a chance of being left in peace to telephone for up to an hour. She drove to 57 Norwich Street.

Sophie and Davie were at home playing chess in the sitting-room, fair head and dark almost touching over the board. They showed no surprise at Cordelia's plea to use the telephone for a series of calls.

'I'll pay, of course. I'll make a note of how many.'

'You'll want the room to yourself, I expect?' said Sophie. 'We'll finish the game in the garden, Davie.'

Blessedly incurious they carried the chess board with care through the kitchen and set it up on the garden table. Cordelia drew a chair to the table and settled down with her list. It was formidably long. There was no clue about where to begin but perhaps those doctors with group practices and addresses near the centre of the city would be the best bet. She would start with them, ticking off their names after each call. She remembered another reported pearl of the Superintendent's wisdom: 'Detection requires a patient persistence which amounts to obstinacy.' She thought of him as she dialled the first number. What an intolerably demanding and irritating boss he must have been! But he was almost certainly old now – forty-five at least. He had probably eased up a bit by now.

But an hour's obstinacy was unfruitful. Her calls were invariably answered; one advantage of ringing a doctor's surgery was that the telephone was at least manned. But the replies, given politely, curtly or in tones of harassed haste by a variety of respondents from the doctors themselves to obliging daily women prepared to convey a message, were the same. Sir Ronald Callender was not a patient of this practice. Cordelia repeated her formula. 'I'm so sorry to have troubled you. I must have misheard the name.'

But after nearly seventy minutes of patient dialling she struck lucky. The doctor's wife answered.

'I'm afraid you've got the wrong practice. Dr Venables looks after Sir Ronald Callender's household.'

This was luck indeed! Dr Venables wasn't on her preliminary list and she wouldn't have reached the V's for at least another hour. She ran her finger quickly down the names and dialled for the last time.

It was Dr Venables' nurse who answered. Cordelia spoke her prepared piece: 'I'm ringing for Miss Leaming from Garforth House. I'm sorry to trouble you but could you please remind us of Sir Ronald Callender's blood group? He wants to know it before the Helsinki Conference next month.'

'Just a minute, please.' There was a brief wait; the sound of footsteps returning.

'Sir Ronald is Group A. I should make a careful note of it if I were you. His son had to ring a month or so ago with the same enquiry.'

'Thank you! Thank you! I'll be careful to make a note.' Cordelia decided to take a risk.

'I'm new here, assisting Miss Leaming, and she did tell me to note it down last time but stupidly I forgot. If she should happen to call, please don't tell her that I had to trouble you again.'

The voice laughed, indulgent to the inefficiency of the young. After all, it wasn't likely to inconvenience her much.

'Don't worry, I shan't tell her. I'm glad she's got herself some help at last. Everyone's well, I hope?'

'Oh, yes! Everyone's fine.'

Cordelia put down the receiver. She looked out of the window and saw that Sophie and Davie were just finishing their game and were putting the pieces back in the box. She had just finished in time. She knew the answer to her query but she still had to verify it. The information was too important to leave to her own vague recollection of the Mendelian rules of inheritance gleaned from the chapter on blood and identity in Bernie's book on forensic medicine. Davie would know, of course. The quickest way would be to ask him now. But she couldn't ask Davie. It would mean going back to the public library, and she would have to hurry if she were to be there before it closed.

But she got there just in time. The librarian, who by now had got used to seeing her, was as helpful as ever. The necessary reference book was quickly produced. Cordelia verified what she had already known. A man and wife both of whose bloods were A could not produce a B-group child.

*

Cordelia was very tired by the time she got back to the cottage. So much had happened during one day; so much had been discovered. It seemed impossible that less than twelve hours previously she had started out on her search for Nanny Pilbeam with only a vague hope that the woman, if she could be found, might provide a clue to Mark Callender's personality, might tell her something about his formative years. She was exhilarated by the success of the day, restless with excitement, but too mentally exhausted to tease out the tangle of conjecture which lay knotted at the back of her mind. At present the facts were disordered; there was no clear pattern, no theory which would at once explain the mystery of Mark's birth, Isabelle's terror, Hugo and Sophie's secret knowledge, Miss Markland's obsessive interest in the cottage, Sergeant Maskell's almost reluctant suspicions, the oddities and unexplained inconsistencies which surrounded Mark's death.

She busied herself about the cottage with the energy of mental overtiredness. She washed the kitchen floor, laid a fire on top of the heap of ash in case the next evening should be chilly, weeded the back flower patch, then made herself a mushroom omelette and ate it sitting, as he must have done, at the simple table. Last of all, she fetched the gun from its hiding-place and set it on the table beside the bed. She locked the back door carefully and drew the curtains across the window, checking once more that the seals were intact. But she didn't balance a saucepan on the top of her door. Tonight that particular precaution seemed childish and unnecessary. She lit her bedside candle then went to the window to choose a book. The night was balmy and windless; the flame of the candle burned steadily in the still air. Outside, darkness had not yet fallen but the garden was very quiet, the peace broken only by the distant crescendo of a car on the main road or the cry of a night bird. And then, seen dimly through the gloaming, she glimpsed a figure at the gate. It was Miss Markland. The woman hesitated, hand on the latch, as if wondering whether to enter the garden. Cordelia slipped to one side, back pressed against the wall. The shadowy figure was so still that it seemed as if she sensed a watching presence and had frozen like an animal surprised. Then, after two minutes, she moved away and was lost among the trees of the orchard. Cordelia relaxed, took a copy of *The Warden* from Mark's row of books, and wriggled into her sleeping-bag. Half an hour later, she blew out the candle and stretched her body comfortably for the slow acquiescent descent into sleep.

She stirred in the early hours and was instantly awake, eyes wide open in the half-darkness. Time lay suspended; the still air was expectant as if the day had been taken by surprise. She could hear the ticking of her wrist watch on the bedside table and could see beside it the crooked, comforting outline of the pistol, the black cylinder of her torch. She lay and listened to the night. One lived so seldom in these still hours, the time most often slept or dreamt away, that one came to them tentative and unpractised like a creature newly born. She wasn't aware of fear, only of an all-embracing peace, a gentle lassitude. Her breathing filled the quiet room, and the still, uncontaminated air seemed to be breathing in unity with her.

Suddenly, she realized what had woken her. Visitors were coming to the cottage. She must subconsciously in some brief phase of uneasy sleep have recognized the sound of a car. Now there was the whine of the gate, the rustle of feet, furtive as an animal in undergrowth, a faint, broken murmur of voices. She wriggled out of her sleeping-bag and stole to the window. Mark hadn't attempted to clean the glass in the front windows; perhaps he hadn't had time, perhaps he welcomed their occluding dirt. Cordelia rubbed her fingers with desperate haste against the gritty accretion of years. But, at last, she felt the cold smooth glass. It squeaked with the friction of her fingers, high and thin like an animal's squeal so that she thought the noise must betray her. She peered through the narrow strip of clear pane into the garden below.

The Renault was almost hidden by the high hedge but she could see the front of the bonnet gleaming by the gate and the two pools of light from the side lamps shining like twin moons on the lane. Isabelle was wearing something long and clinging; her pale figure trembled like a wave against the dark of the hedge. Hugo was only a black shadow at her side. But then he turned and Cordelia saw the flash of a white shirt-front. They were both in evening dress. They came together quietly up the path and conferred briefly at the front door, then moved towards the corner of the cottage.

Snatching up her torch, Cordelia rushed on silent, naked feet down the stairs and threw herself across the sitting-room to unlock the back door. The key turned easily and silently. Hardly daring to breathe she retreated back into the shadows at the foot of the stairs. She was just in time. The door opened, letting in a shaft of paler light. She heard Hugo's voice:

'Just a minute, I'll strike a match.'

The match flared, illuminating in a gentle, momentary light the two grave anticipatory faces, Isabelle's immense and terrified eyes. Then it went out. She heard Hugo's muttered curse followed by the scratch of the second match striking against the box. This time he held it high. It shone on the table, on the mute accusing hook; on the silent watcher at the foot of the stairs. Hugo gasped; his hand jerked and the match went out. Immediately, Isabelle began to scream.

Hugo's voice was sharp.

'What the hell – '

Cordelia switched on her torch and came forward.

'It's only me; Cordelia.'

But Isabelle was beyond hearing. The screams rang out with such piercing intensity that Cordelia half feared that the Marklands must hear. The sound was inhuman, the shriek of animal terror. It was cut short by the swing of Hugo's arm; the sound of a slap; a gasp. It was succeeded by a second of absolute silence, then Isabelle collapsed against Hugo sobbing quietly.

He turned harshly on Cordelia:

'What the hell did you do that for?'

'Do what?'

'You terrified her, lurking there. What are you doing here anyway?'

'I could ask you that.'

'We came to collect the Antonello which Isabelle lent to Mark when she came to supper with him, and to cure her of a certain morbid obsession with this place. We've been to the Pitt Club Ball. It seemed a good idea to call here on our way home. Obviously, it was a bloody stupid idea. Is there any drink in the cottage?'

'Only beer.'

'Oh God, Cordelia, there would be! She needs something stronger.'

'There isn't anything stronger, but I'll make coffee. You set a light to the fire. It's laid.'

She stood the torch upright on the table and lit the table lamp, turning the wick low, then helped Isabelle into one of the fireside chairs.

The girl was trembling. Cordelia fetched one of Mark's heavy sweaters and placed it round her shoulders. The kindling began to flame under Hugo's careful hands. Cordelia went into the kitchen to make coffee, laying her torch on its side at the edge of the window sill so that it shone on the oil stove. She lit the stronger of the two burners and took from the shelf a brown earthenware jug, the two blue-rimmed mugs and a cup for herself. A second and chipped cup held the sugar. It took only a couple of minutes to boil a kettle of water and to pour it over the coffee grains. She could hear Hugo's voice from the sitting-room, low, urgent, consolatory, interposed with Isabelle's monosyllabic replies. Without waiting for the coffee to brew she placed it on the only tray, a bent tin one patterned with a chipped picture of Edinburgh castle, and carried it into the sitting room, setting it down in the hearth. The faggots spluttered and blazed, shooting out a falling shower of bright sparks which patterned Isabelle's dress with stars. Then a stouter brand caught flame and the fire glowed with a stronger, more mellow, heart.

As she bent forward to stir the coffee Cordelia saw a small beetle scurrying in desperate haste along the ridges of one of the small logs. She picked up a twig from the kindling still in the hearth and held it out as a way of escape. But it confused the beetle still more. It turned in panic and raced back towards the flame, then doubled in its tracks and fell finally into a split in the wood. Cordelia pictured its fall into black burning darkness and wondered whether it briefly comprehended its dreadful end. Putting a match to a fire was such a trivial act to cause such agony, such terror.

She handed Isabelle and Hugo their mugs and took her own. The comforting smell of fresh coffee mingled with the resinous tang of the burning wood. The fire threw long shadows over the tiled floor and the oil lamp cast its gentle glow over their faces. Surely, thought Cordelia, no murder suspects could have been interrogated in a cosier setting. Even Isabelle had lost her fears. Whether it was the reassurance of Hugo's arms across her shoulders, the stimulus of the coffee or the homely warmth and crackle of the fire, she seemed almost at ease.

Cordelia said to Hugo:

'You said that Isabelle was morbidly obsessed by this place. Why should she be?'

'Isabelle's very sensitive; she isn't tough like you.'

Cordelia privately thought that all beautiful women were tough – how else could they survive? – and that Isabelle's fibres could compare well for resilience with her own. But nothing would be gained by challenging Hugo's illusions. Beauty was fragile, transitory, vulnerable. Isabelle's sensitivities must be protected. The toughies could look after themselves. She said:

'According to you, she's only been here once before. I know that Mark Callender died in this room, but you hardly expect me to believe that she's grieving over Mark. There's something that both of you know and it would be better if you told me now. If you don't I shall have to report to Sir Ronald Callender that Isabelle, your sister and you are somehow concerned in his son's death and it will be up to him to decide whether to call in the police. I can't see Isabelle standing up to even the mildest police questioning, can you?'

Even to Cordelia it sounded a stilted, sententious little speech, an unsubstantiated accusation backed up by an empty threat. She half expected Hugo to counter it with amused contempt. But he looked at her for a minute as if assessing more than the reality of the danger. Then he said quietly:

'Can't you accept my word that Mark died by his own hand and that if you do call in the police it will cause unhappiness and distress to his father, to his friends and be absolutely no help to anyone?'

'No, Hugo, I can't.'

'Then if we do tell you what we know, will you promise that it won't go any further?'

'How can I, any more than I can promise to believe you?'

Suddenly Isabelle cried: 'Oh, tell her, Hugo! What does it matter?'

Cordelia said:

'I think that you must. I don't think you've any choice.'

'So it seems. All right.' He put his coffee mug down in the hearth and looked into the fire.

'I told you that we went – Sophie, Isabelle, Davie and I – to the Arts Theatre on the night Mark died but that, as you've probably guessed, was only three-quarters true. They had only three seats left when I booked so we allocated them to the three people mostly likely to enjoy the play. Isabelle goes to the theatre to be seen rather than to see and is bored by any show with a cast of less than fifty, so she was the one left out. Thus neglected by her current lover, she very reasonably decided to seek consolation with the next.'

Isabelle said with a secret, anticipatory smile:

'Mark was not my lover, Hugo.'

She spoke without rancour or resentment. It was a matter of putting the record straight.

'I know. Mark was a romantic. He never took a girl to bed – or anywhere else that I could see – until he judged that there was an adequate depth of interpersonal communication, or whatever jargon he used, between them. Actually, that's unfair. It's my father who uses bloody awful meaningless phrases like that. But Mark agreed with the general idea. I doubt whether he could enjoy sex until he'd convinced himself that he and the girl were in love. It was a necessary preliminary – like undressing. I gather that with Isabelle the relationship hadn't reached the necessary depths, hadn't achieved the essential emotional rapport. It was only a matter of time, of course. Where Isabelle was concerned, Mark was as capable of self-deception as the rest of us.'

The high, slightly hesitant voice was edged with jealousy.

Isabelle said, slowly and patiently, like a mother explaining to a wilfully obtuse child:

'Mark never made love to me, Hugo.'

'That's what I'm saying. Poor Mark! He exchanged the substance for the shadow and now he has neither.'

'But what happened that night?'

Cordelia spoke to Isabelle, but it was Hugo who replied.

'Isabelle drove here and arrived shortly after half past seven. The curtains were drawn across the back window, the front one is impenetrable anyway, but the door was open. She came in. Mark was already dead. His body was hanging by the strap from that hook. But he didn't look as he did when Miss Markland found him next morning.'

He turned to Isabelle:

'You tell her.' She hesitated. Hugo bent forward and kissed her lightly on the lips.

'Go on, tell. There are some unpleasantnesses which all Papa's money can't entirely shield you from and this, darling, is one.'

*

Isabelle turned her head and looked intently into the four corners of the room as if satisfying herself that the three of them were really alone. The irises of her remarkable eyes were purple in the firelight. She leaned towards Cordelia with something of the confiding relish of a village gossip about to relate the latest scandal. Cordelia saw that her panic had left her. Isabelle's agonies were elemental, violent but short lived, easily comforted. She would have kept her secret while Hugo instructed her to keep it, but she was glad of his order of release. Probably her instinct told her that the story, once told, would lose the sting of terror. She said:

'I thought I would call to see Mark and, perhaps, that we would have supper together. Mademoiselle de Congé was not well and Hugo and Sophie were at the theatre and I was bored. I came to the back door because Mark had told me that the front door would not open. I thought that I might see him in the garden, but he was not there, only the garden fork in the ground and his shoes at the door. So I pushed open the door. I did not knock because I thought that I would be a surprise for Mark.'

She hesitated and looked down into the mug of coffee, twisting it between her hands.

'And then?' prompted Cordelia.

'And then I saw him. He was hanging there by the belt from that hook in the ceiling and I knew he was dead. Cordelia, it was horrible! He was dressed like a woman in a black bra and black lace panties. Nothing else. And his face! He had painted his lips, all over his lips Cordelia, like a clown! It was terrible but it was funny too. I wanted to laugh and scream at the same time. He didn't look like Mark. He didn't look like a human being at all. And on the table there were three pictures. Not nice pictures Cordelia. Pictures of naked women.'

Her wide eyes stared into Cordelia's, dismayed, uncomprehending. Hugo said:

'Don't look like that, Cordelia. It was horrible for Isabelle at the time and disagreeable to think about now. But it isn't so very uncommon. It does happen. It's probably one of the more innocuous of sexual deviations. He wasn't involving anyone but himself. And he didn't mean to kill himself; that was just bad luck. I imagine that the buckle of the belt slipped and he never had a chance.' Cordelia said:

'I don't believe it.'

'I thought you might not. But it's true, Cordelia. Why not come with us now and ring Sophie? She'll confirm it.'

'I don't need confirmation of Isabelle's story. I already have that. I mean I still don't believe that Mark killed himself.'

As soon as she spoke she knew that it had been a mistake. She shouldn't have revealed her suspicions. But it was too late now and there were questions she had to ask. She saw Hugo's face, his quick impatient frown at her obtuseness, her obstinacy. And then she detected a subtle change of mood; was it irritation, fear, disappointment? She spoke directly to Isabelle.

'You said that the door was open. Did you notice the key?'

'It was in this side of the door. I saw it when I went out.'

'What about the curtains?'

'They were like now, across the window.'

'And where was the lipstick?'

'What lipstick, Cordelia?'

'The one used to paint Mark's lips. It wasn't in the pockets of his jeans or the police would have found it, so where was it? Did you see it on the table?'

'There was nothing on the table except the pictures.'

'What colour was the lipstick?'

'Purple. An old lady's colour. No one would choose such a colour I think.'

'And the underclothes, could you describe them?'

'Oh, yes! They were from M & S. I recognized them.'

'You mean that you recognized those particular ones, that they were yours?'

'Oh, no Cordelia! They were not mine. I never wear black underclothes. I only like white next to my skin. But they were the kind I usually buy. I always get my underclothes from M & S.'

Cordelia reflected that Isabelle was hardly one of the store's best customers, but that no other witness would have been as reliable when it came to details, particularly of clothes. Even in that moment of absolute terror and revulsion, Isabelle had noticed the type of underclothes. And if she said that she hadn't seen the lipstick, then it was because the lipstick hadn't been there to see.

Cordelia went on inexorably:

'Did you touch anything, Mark's body perhaps, to see if he was dead?'

Isabelle was shocked. The facts of life she could take in her stride, but not the facts of death.

'I couldn't touch Mark! I touched nothing. And I knew that he was dead.'

Hugo said: 'A respectable, sensible, law-abiding citizen would have found the nearest telephone and rung the police. Luckily Isabelle is none of these things. Her instinct was to come to me. She waited until the play ended, and then met us outside the theatre. When we came out she was pacing up and down the pavement on the other side of the road. Davie, Sophie and I came back here with her in the Renault. We only stopped briefly at Norwich Street to collect Davie's camera and flash.'

'Why?'

'That was my idea. Obviously, we had no intention of letting the fuzz and Ronald Callender know how Mark had died. Our idea was to fake a suicide. We planned to dress him in his own clothes, clean his face and then leave him for someone else to find. We hadn't it in mind to fake a suicide note; that was a refinement somewhat outside our powers. We collected the camera so that we could photograph him as he was. We didn't know what particular law we were breaking in faking a suicide, but there must have been one. You can't do the simplest service for your friends these days without it being liable to misconstruction by the fuzz. If there were trouble we wanted some evidence of the truth. We were all fond of Mark in our different ways, but not fond enough to risk a murder charge. However, our good intentions were frustrated. Someone else had got here first.'

'Tell me about it.'

'There's nothing to tell. We told the two girls to wait in the car, Isabelle because she had already seen enough and Sophie because Isabelle was too frightened to be left alone. Besides, it seemed only fair to Mark to keep Sophie out of it, to prevent her from seeing him. Don't you find it odd, Cordelia, this concern one has for the susceptibilities of the dead?'

Thinking of her father and Bernie, Cordelia said:

'Perhaps it's only when people are dead that we can safely show how much we cared about them. We know that it's too late then for them to do anything about it.'

'Cynical but true. Anyway, there was nothing for us to do here. We found Mark's body and this room as Miss Markland described them at the inquest. The door was open, the curtains drawn across. Mark was naked except for his blue jeans. There were no magazine pictures on the table and no lipstick on his face. But there was a suicide note in the typewriter and a mound of ash in the grate. It looked as if the visitor had made a thorough job of it. We didn't linger. Someone else – perhaps someone from the house – might have turned up at any minute. Admittedly, it was very late by then but it seemed an evening for people to pop in. Mark must have had more visitors that night than during his whole time at the cottage; first Isabelle; then the unknown Samaritan; then us.'

Cordelia thought that there had been someone before Isabelle. Mark's murderer had been there first. She asked suddenly:

'Someone played a stupid trick on me last night. When I got back here from the party there was a bolster slung from that hook. Did you do that?'

If his surprise were not genuine, then Hugo was a better actor than Cordelia thought possible.

'Of course I didn't! I thought you were living in Cambridge not here. And why on earth should I?'

'To warn me off.'

'But that would be crazy! It wouldn't warn you off, would it? It might scare some women, but not you. We wanted to convince you that there was nothing to investigate about Mark's death. That sort of trick would only convince you that there was. Someone else was trying to scare you. The most likely person is the one who came here after us.'

'I know. Someone took a risk for Mark. He – or she – won't want me ferreting around. But he would have got rid of me more sensibly by telling me the truth.'

'How could he know whether to trust you? What will you do now, Cordelia? Go back to town?'

He was trying to keep his voice casual but she thought she detected the underlying anxiety. She replied.

'I expect so. I'll have to see Sir Ronald first.'

'What will you tell him?'

'I'll think of something. Don't worry.'

Dawn was staining the eastern sky and the first chorus of birds was noisily contradicting the new day before Hugo and Isabelle left. They took the Antonello with them. Cordelia saw it taken down with a pang of regret as if something of Mark were leaving the cottage. Isabelle examined the picture closely with a grave professional eye before tucking it under her arm. Cordelia thought that she was probably generous enough with her possessions, both people and pictures, provided they were on loan only, to be returned promptly on demand and in the same condition as when she parted with them. Cordelia watched from the front gate as the Renault, with Hugo driving, moved out of the shadow of the hedge. She lifted her hand in a formal gesture of farewell like a weary hostess speeding her final guests, then turned back to the cottage.

The sitting-room seemed empty and cold without them. The fire was dying and she pushed in the few remaining sticks from the hearth and blew on them to kindle the flame. She moved restlessly about the little room. She was too lively to go back to bed, but her short and disturbed night had left her edgy with tiredness. But her mind was tormented by something more fundamental than lack of sleep. For the first time she knew that she was afraid. Evil existed – it hadn't needed a convent education to convince her of that reality – and it had been present in this room. Something here had been stronger than wickedness, ruthlessness, cruelty or expedience. Evil. She had no doubt that Mark had been murdered, but with what diabolical cleverness it had been done! If Isabelle told her story, who now would ever believe that he hadn't died accidentally, but by his own hand? Cordelia had no need to refer to her book on forensic medicine to know how it would appear to the police. As Hugo had said, these cases weren't so very uncommon. He, as a psychiatrist's son, would have heard or read of them. Who else would know? Probably any reasonably sophisticated person. But it couldn't have been Hugo. Hugo had an alibi. Her mind revolted at the thought that Davie or Sophie could have participated in such a horror. But how typical that they should have collected the camera. Even their compassion had been overlaid with self-concern. Would Hugo and Davie have stood here, under Mark's grotesque body, calmly discussing distance and exposure before taking the photograph which would, if necessary, exonerate them at his expense?

She went into the kitchen to make tea, glad to be free of the malignant fascination of that hook in the ceiling. Previously it had hardly worried her, now it was an obtrusive as a fetish. It seemed to have grown since the previous night, to be growing still as it drew her eyes compulsively upwards. And the sitting-room itself had surely shrunk; no longer a sanctum but a claustrophobic cell, tawdry and shameful as an execution shed. Even the bright morning air was redolent with evil.

Waiting for the kettle to boil she made herself contemplate the day's activities. It was still too early to theorize; her mind was too preoccupied with horror to deal rationally with its new knowledge. Isabelle's story had complicated, not illumined the case. But there were still relevant facts to be discovered. She would go on with the programme she had already planned. Today she would go to London to examine Mark's grandfather's will.

But there were still two hours to get through before it was time to start out. She had decided to travel to London by train and to leave the car at Cambridge station since this would be both quicker and easier. It was irritating to have to spend a day in town when the heart of the mystery so obviously lay in Cambridgeshire, but for once she wasn't sorry at the prospect of leaving the cottage. Shocked and restless, she wandered aimlessly from room to room and prowled around the garden, fretting to be away. Finally in desperation she took hold of the garden fork and completed the digging of Mark's unfinished row. She wasn't sure that this was wise; Mark's interrupted work was part of the evidence for his murder. But other people, including Sergeant Maskell, had seen it and could testify if necessary, and the sight of the partly-completed job, of the fork still askew in the soil, was unbearably irritating. When the row was completed she felt calmer and she dug on without pausing for another hour before carefully cleaning the fork and placing it with the other tools in the garden shed.

At last it was time to go. The seven o'clock weather forecast had prophesied thundery storms in the south-east so she put on her suit, the heaviest protection she had brought with her. She hadn't worn it since Bernie's death and she discovered that the waistband was uncomfortably loose. She had lost some weight. After a moment's thought, she took Mark's belt from the scene-of-crime kit and wound it twice round her waist. She felt no repugnance as the leather tightened against her. It was impossible to believe that anything he had ever touched or owned could frighten or distress her. The strength and heaviness of the leather so close to her skin was even obscurely comforting and reassuring, as if the belt were a talisman.

CHAPTER FIVE

The storm broke just as Cordelia alighted from the number 11 bus outside Somerset House. There was a jagged flash of lightning and, almost instantaneously, the thunder crashed like a barrage round her ears and she raced across the inner courtyard between the ranks of parked cars through a wall of water while the rain spouted around her ankles as if the paving stones were being raked with bullets. She pushed open the door and stood draining pools of water on the mat and laughing aloud with relief. One or two of the people present glanced up from their perusal of wills and smiled at her, while a motherly-looking woman behind the counter tut-tutted her concern. Cordelia shook her jacket over the mat then hung it on the back of one of the chairs and tried ineffectually to dry her hair with her handkerchief before approaching the counter.

The motherly woman was helpful. Consulted by Cordelia on the correct procedure, she indicated the shelves of heavy, bound volumes in the middle of the hall and explained that the wills were indexed under the surname of the testator and the year in which the document was lodged with Somerset House. It was for Cordelia to trace the catalogue number and bring the volume to the desk. The original will would then be sent for and she could consult it for a fee of 20 pence.

Not knowing when George Bottley had died, Cordelia was in some perplexity where to begin her search. But she deduced that the will must have been made after the birth, or at least the conception, of Mark, since he had been left a fortune by his grandfather. But Mr Bottley had also left money to his daughter and this part of his fortune had come on her death to her husband. The strong probability was that he had died before her, since otherwise he would surely have made a new will. Cordelia decided to begin her search with the year of Mark's birth, 1951.

Her deductions proved correct. George Albert Bottley of Stonegate Lodge, Harrogate, had died on 26th July 1951, exactly three months and one day after the birth of his grandson and only three weeks after making his will. Cordelia wondered whether his death had been sudden and unexpected or whether this was the will of a dying man. She saw that he had left an estate of nearly three quarters of a million pounds. How had he made this, she wondered? Surely not all from wool. She heaved the heavy book across to the counter, the clerk wrote the details on a white form and pointed out the way to the cashier's office. Within a surprisingly few minutes of paying what seemed to her a modest fee, Cordelia was seated under the light at one of the desks near the window with the will in her hands.

She hadn't liked what she had heard about George Bottley from Nanny Pilbeam and she didn't like him any better after reading his will. She had feared that the document might be long, complicated and difficult to understand; it was surprisingly short, simple and intelligible. Mr Bottley directed that all his possessions should be sold, 'since I wish to prevent the usual unseemly wrangling over bric-à-brac'. He left modest sums to servants in his employ at the time of death but there was no mention, Cordelia noticed, of his gardener. He bequeathed half of the residue of his fortune to his daughter, absolutely, 'now that she has demonstrated that she has at least one of the normal attributes of a woman'. The remaining half he left to his grandson Mark Callender on attaining his twenty-fifth birthday, 'by which date, if he hasn't learned the value of money, he will at least be of an age to avoid exploitation'. The income from the capital was left to six Bottley relations, some of them, apparently, only distant kinsmen. The will created a residual trust; as each beneficiary died his share would be distributed among the survivors. The testator was confident that this arrangement would promote in the beneficiaries a lively interest in each other's health and survival while encouraging them to achieve the distinction of longevity, no other distinction being within their reach. If Mark died before his twenty-fifth birthday the family trust would continue until all the beneficiaries were dead and the capital would then be distributed among a formidable list of charities chosen, as far as Cordelia could see, because they were well known and successful rather than because they represented any personal concern or sympathy on the part of the testator. It was as if he had asked his lawyers for a list of the more reliable charities, having no real interest in what happened to his fortune if his own issue were not alive to inherit it.

It was a strange will. Mr Bottley had left nothing to his son-in-law yet had apparently been unworried by the possibility that his daughter, whom he knew not to be strong, might die and leave her fortune to her husband. In some respects it was a gambler's will and Cordelia wondered again how George Bottley had made his fortune. But, despite the cynical unkindness of its comments, the will was neither unfair nor ungenerous. Unlike some very rich men he hadn't attempted to control his great fortune from beyond the grave, obsessively determined that not one penny should ever get into unfavoured hands. His daughter and his grandson had both been left their fortunes absolutely. It was impossible to like Mr Bottley but difficult not to respect him. And the implications of his will were very clear. No one stood to gain by Mark's death except a long list of highly respectable charities.

Cordelia made a note of the main clauses of the will, more because of Bernie's insistence on meticulous documentation than from any fear of forgetting them; slipped the receipt for 20p into the expenses page of her notebook; added the cost of her cheap day return ticket from Cambridge and her bus fare, and returned the will to the counter. The storm had been as short as it was violent. The hot sun was already drying the windows and the puddles lay bright on the rain-washed courtyard. Cordelia decided that she ought to charge Sir Ronald for half a day only and spend the rest of her time in London at the office. There might be post to collect. There might even be another case awaiting her.

But the decision was a mistake. The office seemed even more sordid than when she had left it and the air smelt sour in contrast to the rain-washed streets outside. There was a thick film of dust over the furniture and the bloodstain on the rug had deepened into a brick-brown which looked even more sinister than the original bright red. There was nothing in the letterbox but a final demand from the electricity board and a bill from the stationer. Bernie had paid dearly – or rather, had not paid – for the despised writing paper.

Cordelia wrote a cheque for the electricity bill, dusted the furniture, made one last and unsuccessful attempt to clean the rug.

Then she locked the office and set off to walk to Trafalgar Square. She would seek consolation in the National Gallery.

*

She caught the eighteen-sixteen train from Liverpool Street and it was nearly eight o'clock before she arrived back at the cottage. She parked the Mini in its usual place in the shelter of the copse and made her way round the side of the cottage. She hesitated for a moment wondering whether to collect the gun from its hiding-place, but decided that this could wait until later. She was hungry and the first priority was to get a meal. She had carefully locked the back door and had stuck a thin strip of Scotch tape across the window sill before leaving that morning. If there were any more secret visitors she wanted to be warned. But the tape was still intact. She felt in her shoulder bag for the key and, bending down, fitted it into the lock. She wasn't expecting trouble outside the cottage and the attack took her completely by surprise. There was the half-second of pre-knowledge before the blanket fell but that was too late. There was a cord around her neck pulling the mask of hot stifling wool taut against her mouth and nostrils. She gasped for breath and tasted the dry strong-smelling fibres on her tongue. Then a sharp pain exploded in her chest and she remembered nothing.

The movement of liberation was a miracle and a horror. The blanket was whipped off. She never saw her assailant. There was a second of sweet reviving air, a glimpse, so brief that it was barely comprehended, of blinding sky seen through greenness and then she felt herself falling, falling in helpless astonishment into cold darkness. The fall was a confusion of old nightmares, unbelievable seconds of childhood terrors recalled. Then her body hit the water. Ice-cold hands dragged her into a vortex of horror. Instinctively, she had closed her mouth at the moment of impact and she struggled to the surface through what seemed an eternity of cold encompassing blackness. She shook her head and, through her stinging eyes, she looked up. The black tunnel that stretched above her ended in a moon of blue light. Even as she looked, the well lid was dragged slowly back like the shutter of a camera. The moon became a half moon; then a crescent. At last there was nothing but eight thin slits of light.

Desperately she trod water, reaching tentatively for the bottom.

There was no bottom. Frantically moving hands and feet, willing herself not to panic, she felt around the walls of the well for a possible foothold. There was none. The funnel of bricks, smooth, sweating with moisture, stretched around and above her like a circular tomb. As she gazed upwards they writhed, expanded, swayed and reeled like the belly of a monstrous snake.

And then she felt a saving anger. She wouldn't let herself drown, wouldn't die in this horrible place, alone and terrified. The well was deep but small, the diameter barely three feet. If she kept her head and took time, she could brace her legs and shoulders against the bricks and work her way upwards.

She hadn't bruised or stunned herself against the walls as she fell. Miraculously she was uninjured. The fall had been clean. She was alive and capable of thought. She had always been a survivor. She would survive.

She floated on her back, bracing her shoulders against the cold walls, spreading her arms and digging her elbows into the interstices of the bricks to get a better grip. Shuffling off her shoes, she planted both feet against the opposite wall. Just beneath the surface of the water, she could feel that one of the bricks was slightly unaligned. She curved her toes around it. It gave her a precarious but welcome foothold for the start of the climb. By means of it, she could lift her body out of the water and could relieve for a moment the strain on the muscles of her back and thighs.

Then slowly she began to climb, first shifting her feet, one after the other in tiny sliding steps, then humping up her body inch by painful inch. She kept her eyes fixed on the opposite curve of the wall, willing herself not to look down, nor up, counting progress by the width of each brick. Time passed. She couldn't see Bernie's watch, although its ticking seemed unnaturally loud, a regular obtrusive metronome to the thumping of her heart and the fierce gasping of her breath. The pain in her legs was intense and her shirt was sticking to her back with a warm, almost comforting effusion, which she knew must be blood. She willed herself not to think of the water beneath her or of the thin but widening clefts of light above. If she were to survive, all her energy must be harnessed for the next painful inch.

Once, her legs slipped and she slithered back several yards before her feet, scrabbling ineffectually against the slimy walls, at last found a purchase. The fall had grazed her injured back and left her whimpering with self-pity and disappointment. She scourged her mind into courage and began climbing again. Once she was gripped by cramp and lay stretched as if on a rack until the agony passed and her fixed muscles could move. From time to time her feet found another small foothold and she was able to stretch her legs and rest. The temptation to stay in comparative safety and ease was almost irresistible and she had to will herself to start again on the slow torturous climb.

It seemed that she had been climbing for hours, moving in a parody of a difficult labour towards some desperate birth. Darkness was falling. The light from the well top was wider now but less strong. She told herself that the climb wasn't really difficult. It was only the darkness and loneliness which made it seem so. If this were a fabricated obstacle race, an exercise in the school gymnasium, surely she could have done it easily enough. She filled her mind with the comforting images of rib-stools and vaulting-horses, of the fifth form shouting their encouragement. Sister Perpetua was there. But why wasn't she looking at Cordelia? Why had she turned away? Cordelia called her and the figure turned slowly and smiled at her. But it wasn't Sister after all. It was Miss Leaming, the lean pale face sardonic under the white veil.

And now when she knew that, unaided, she could get no further, Cordelia saw salvation. A few feet above her was the bottom rung of a short wooden ladder fixed to the last few feet of the well. At first she thought that it was an illusion, a phantasm born of exhaustion and despair. She shut her eyes for a few minutes; her lips moved. Then she opened her eyes again. The ladder was still there, seen dimly but comfortingly solid in the fading light. She lifted impotent hands towards it knowing, even as she did so, that it was out of reach. It could save her life and she knew that she hadn't the strength to reach it.

It was then, without conscious thought or scheming, that she remembered the belt. Her hand dropped to her waist feeling for the heavy brass buckle. She undid it and drew the long snake of leather from her body. Carefully she threw the buckled end towards the bottom rung of the ladder. The first three times the metal struck the wood with a sharp crack but didn't fall over the rung; the fourth time it did. She pushed the other end of the belt gently upwards and the buckle dropped towards her until she could stretch out her hand and grasp it. She fastened it to the other end to form a strong loop. Then she pulled, at first very gently and then harder until most of her weight was on the strap. The relief was indescribable. She braced herself against the brickwork, gathering strength for the final triumphant effort. Then it happened. The rung, rotted at its joints, broke loose with a harsh tearing sound and spun past her into darkness, just missing her head. It seemed minutes rather than seconds before the distant splash reverberated round the wall.

She unbuckled the belt and tried again. The next rung was a foot higher and the throw more difficult. Even this small effort was exhausting in her present state and she made herself take time. Every unsuccessful throw made the next more difficult. She didn't count the number of attempts, but at last the buckle fell over the rung and dropped towards her. When it snaked within reach she found that she could only just buckle the strap. The next rung would be too high. If this one broke, it would be the end.

But the rung held. She had no clear memory of the last half-hour of the climb but at last she reached the ladder and strapped herself firmly to the uprights. For the first time she was physically safe. As long as the ladder held she needn't fear falling. She let herself relax into brief unconsciousness. But then the wheels of the mind, which had been spinning blissfully free, took hold again and she began to think. She knew that she had no hope of moving the heavy wooden cover unaided. She stretched out both hands and pushed against it but it didn't shift, and the high concave dome made it impossible for her to brace her shoulders against the wood. She would have to rely on outside help and that wouldn't come till daylight. It might not come even then, but she pushed the thought away. Sooner or later Miss Markland would come to the cottage. Sooner or later someone would come. She could hope to hold on, thus strapped, for several days. Even if she lost consciousness there was a chance that she would be rescued alive. Miss Markland knew that she was at the cottage; her things were still there. Miss Markland would come.

She gave thought to how she could attract attention. There was room to push something between the boards of wood if only she had something sufficiently stiff to push. The edge of the buckle was possible provided she strapped herself more tightly. But that must wait until the morning. There was nothing she could do now. She would relax and sleep and await rescue.

And then the final horror burst upon her. There would be no rescue. Someone would be coming to the well, coming on quiet and stealthy feet under the cover of darkness. But it would be her murderer. He had to return; it was part of his plan. The attack, which at the time had seemed so astonishingly, so brutally stupid, hadn't been stupid at all. It was intended to look like an accident. He would come back that night and remove the well cover again. Then, sometime next day or within the next few days, Miss Markland would blunder through the garden and discover what had happened. No one would ever be able to prove that Cordelia's death wasn't an accident. She recalled the words of Sergeant Maskell: 'It isn't what you suspect; it's what you can prove.' But this time would there even be suspicion? Here was a young, impulsive, over-curious young woman living at the cottage without the owner's authority. She had obviously decided to explore the well. She had smashed the padlock, drawn back the lid with the coil of rope which the killer would leave ready to be found, and tempted by the ladder, had let herself down those few steps until the final rung broke beneath her. Her prints and no one else's would be found on the ladder, if they took the trouble to look. The cottage was utterly deserted; the chance that her murderer would be seen returning was remote. There was nothing she could do but wait until she heard his footsteps, his heavy breathing, and the lid was drawn slowly back to reveal his face.

After the first intensity of terror, Cordelia waited for death without hope and without further struggle. There was even a kind of peace in resignation. Strapped like a victim to the uprights of the ladder she drifted mercifully into brief oblivion and prayed that it might be so when her killer returned, that she might not be conscious at the moment of the final blow. She had no longer any interest in seeing her murderer's face. She wouldn't humiliate herself by pleading for her life, wouldn't beg for mercy from a man who had strung up Mark. She knew that there would be no mercy.

But she was conscious when the well lid began slowly to move. The light came in above her bowed head. The gap widened. And then she heard a voice, a woman's voice, low, urgent and sharp with terror.

'Cordelia!'

She looked up.

Kneeling at the rim of the well, her pale face immense and seeming to float disembodied in space like the phantasm of a nightmare, was Miss Markland. And the eyes which stared into Cordelia's face were as wild with terror as her own.

Ten minutes later Cordelia was lying slumped in the fireside chair. Her whole body ached and she was powerless to control her violent shivering. Her thin shirt was stuck to her wounded back and every shift of movement was pain. Miss Markland had put a light to the kindling and was now making coffee. Cordelia could hear her moving to and fro in the little kitchen and could smell the stove as it was turned high and, soon, the evocative aroma of coffee. These familiar sights and sounds would normally have been reassuring and comforting, but now she was desperate to be alone. The killer would still return. He had to return, and when he did, she wanted to be there to meet him. Miss Markland brought in the two mugs and pressed one into Cordelia's shivering hands. She stumped upstairs and came down with one of Mark's jumpers which she wound round the girl's neck. Her terror had left her, but she was as agitated as a young girl sharing her first half-shameful adventure. Her eyes were wild, her whole body trembled with excitement. She sat down directly in front of Cordelia and fixed her with her sharp inquisitive eyes.

'How did it happen? You must tell me.'

Cordelia had not forgotten how to think.

'I don't know. I can't remember anything that happened before I hit the water. I must have decided to explore the well and lost my balance.'

'But the well lid! The lid was in place!'

'I know. Someone must have replaced it.'

'But why? Who would have come this way?'

'I don't know. But someone must have seen it. Someone must have dragged it back.'

She said more gently:

'You saved my life. How did you notice what had happened?'

'I came to the cottage to see if you were still here. I came earlier today but there was no sign of you. There was a coil of rope – the one that you used, I expect – left in the path and I stumbled over it. Then

I noticed that the well lid wasn't quite in place and that the padlock had been smashed.'

'You saved my life,' said Cordelia again, 'but please go now. Please go. I'm all right, really I am.'

'But you aren't fit to be left alone! And that man – the one who replaced the lid – he might return. I don't like to think of strangers snooping around the cottage and you here alone.'

'I'm perfectly safe. Besides, I have a gun. I only want to be left in peace to rest. Please don't worry about me!'

Cordelia could detect the note of desperation, almost of hysteria, in her own voice.

But Miss Markland seemed not to hear. Suddenly she was on her knees in front of Cordelia and pouring out a spate of high, excited chatter. Without thought and without compassion, she was confiding to the girl her terrible story, a story of her son, the four-year-old child of herself and her lover, who had broken his way through the cottage hedge and fallen into the well to his death. Cordelia tried to shake herself free from the wild eyes. It was surely all a fantasy. The woman must be mad. And if it were true, it was horrible and unthinkable and she could not bear to hear it. Sometime later she would remember it, remember every word, and think of the child, of his last terror, his desperate cry for his mother, the cold suffocating water dragging him to his death. She would live his agony in nightmares as she would relive her own. But not now. Through the spate of words, the self-accusations, the terror recalled, Cordelia recognized the note of liberation. What to her had been horror, to Miss Markland had been release. A life for a life. Suddenly Cordelia could bear it no longer. She said violently:

'I'm sorry! I'm sorry! You've saved my life and I'm grateful. But I can't bear to listen. I don't want you here. For God's sake go!'

All her life she would remember the woman's hurt face, her silent withdrawal. Cordelia didn't hear her go, didn't remember the soft closing of the door. All she knew was that she was alone. The shaking was over now although she still felt very cold. She went upstairs and pulled on her slacks then unwound Mark's jumper from her neck and put it on. It would cover the bloodstains on her shirt and the warmth was immediately comforting. She was moving very quickly. She felt for the ammunition, took her torch and let herself out of the back door of the cottage. The gun was where she had left it, in the fold of the tree. She loaded it and felt its familiar shape and heaviness in her hand. Then she stood back among the bushes and waited.

*

It was too dark to see the dial of her wrist-watch but Cordelia reckoned that she must have waited there immobile in the shadows for nearly half an hour before her ears caught the sound for which she was waiting. A car was approaching down the lane. Cordelia held her breath. The sound of the engine reached a brief crescendo and then faded away. The car had driven on without stopping. It was unusual for a car to pass down the lane after dark and she wondered who it could be. Again she waited, moving deeper into the shelter of the elder bush so that she could rest her back against the bark. She had been clutching the gun so tightly that her right wrist ached and she moved the pistol to her other hand and rotated the wrist slowly, stretching the cramped fingers.

Again she waited. The slow minutes passed. The silence was broken only by the furtive scuffling of some small night prowler in the grass and the sudden wild hoot of an owl. And then once more she heard the sound of an engine. This time the noise was faint and it came no closer. Someone had stopped a car further up the road.

She took the gun in her right hand, cradling the muzzle with her left. Her heart was pounding so loudly that she felt its wild hammering must betray her. She imagined rather than heard the thin whine of the front gate but the sound of feet moving round the cottage was unmistakable and clear. And now he was in sight, a stocky, broad-shouldered figure, black against the light. He moved towards her and she could see her shoulder bag hanging from his left shoulder. The discovery disconcerted her. She had completely forgotten the bag. But now she realized why he had seized it. He had wanted to search it for evidence, but it was important that, finally, it should be discovered with her body in the well.

He came forward gently on tip-toe, his long simian arms held stiffly away from his body like a caricature of a film cowboy ready for the draw. When he got to the rim of the well he waited and the moon struck the white of his eyes as he gazed slowly round. Then he bent down and felt in the grass for the coil of rope. Cordelia had laid it where Miss Markland had found it, but something about it, some slight difference perhaps in the way it was coiled, seemed to strike him. He rose uncertainly and stood for a moment with the rope dangling from his hand. Cordelia tried to control her breathing. It seemed impossible that he should not hear, smell or see her, that he should be so like a predator yet without the beast's instinct for the enemy in the dark. He moved forward. Now he was at the well. He bent and threaded one end of the rope through the iron hoop.

Cordelia moved with one step out of the darkness. She held the gun firmly and straight as Bernie had shown her. This time the target was very close. She knew that she wouldn't fire but, in that moment, she knew too what it was that could make a man kill. She said loudly: 'Good evening, Mr Lunn.'

She never knew whether he saw the gun. But for one unforgettable second, as the clouded moon sailed into the open sky, she saw his face clearly; saw the hate, the despair, the agony and the rictus of terror. He gave one hoarse cry, threw down the shoulder bag and the rope and rushed through the garden in a blind panic. She gave chase, hardly knowing why, or what she hoped to achieve, determined only that he shouldn't get back to Garforth House before her. And still she didn't fire the gun.

But he had an advantage. As she threw herself through the gate she saw that he had parked the van some fifty yards up the road and left the engine running. She chased after him but could see that it was hopeless. Her only hope of catching up with him was to get the Mini. She tore down the lane feeling in her shoulder bag as she ran. The prayer book and her notebook were both gone but her fingers found the car keys. She unlocked the Mini, threw herself in and reversed it violently on to the road. The rear lights of the van were about a hundred yards ahead of her. She didn't know what speed it could do, but doubted whether it could outpace the Mini. She trod on the accelerator and gave pursuit. She turned left out of the lane on to the subsidiary road and now she could see the van still ahead. He was driving fast and was holding the distance. Now the road turned and for a few seconds he was out of sight. He must be getting very close now to the junction with the Cambridge road.

She heard the crash just before she herself reached the junction, an instantaneous explosion of sound which shook the hedges and made the little car tremble. Cordelia's hands tightened momentarily on the wheel and the Mini jerked to a stop. She ran forward round the corner and saw before her the gleaming, headlamp-lit surface of the main Cambridge road. It was peopled with running shapes. The transporter, still upright, was an immense oblong mass blocking the skyline, a barricade slewed across the road. The van had crumpled under its front wheels like a child's toy. There was a smell of petrol, a woman's harsh scream, the squeal of braking tyres. Cordelia walked slowly up to the transporter. The driver was still in his seat, gazing rigidly ahead, his face a mask of dedicated concentration. People were shouting at him, stretching out their arms. He didn't move. Someone – a man in a heavy leather coat and goggles – said:

'It's shock. We'd better drag him clear.'

Three figures moved between Cordelia and the driver. Shoulders heaved in unison. There was a grunt of effort. The driver was lifted out, rigid as a manikin, his knees bent, his clenched hands held out as if still grasping the immense wheel. The shoulders bent over him in secret conclave.

There were other figures standing round the crushed van. Cordelia joined the ring of anonymous faces. Cigarette ends glowed and faded like signals, casting a momentary glow on the shaking hands, the wide, horrified eyes. She asked:

'Is he dead?' The man in goggles replied laconically: 'What do you think?'

There was a girl's voice, tentative, breathless.

'Has anyone called the ambulance?'

'Yeah. Yeah. That chap in the Cortina's gone off to phone.'

The group stood irresolute. The girl and the young man to whom she was clinging began to back away. Another car stopped. A tall figure was pushing his way through the crowd. Cordelia heard a high, authoritative voice.

'I'm a doctor. Has anyone called the ambulance?'

'Yes, sir.'

The reply was deferential. They stood aside to let the expert through. He turned to Cordelia, perhaps because she was nearest.

'If you didn't witness the accident, young woman, you'd better get on your way. And stand back, the rest of you. There's nothing that you can do. And put out those cigarettes!'

Cordelia walked slowly back to the Mini, placing each foot carefully before the other like a convalescent trying her first painful steps. She drove carefully round the accident, bumping the Mini on the grass verge. There was the wail of approaching sirens. As she turned off the main road, her driving mirror glowed suddenly red and she heard a whoosh of sound followed by a low, concerted groan which was broken by a woman's high, single scream. There was a wall of flame across the road. The doctor's warning had been too late. The van was on fire. There was no hope now for Lunn; but then, there never had been.

Cordelia knew that she was driving erratically. Passing cars hooted at her and flashed their lights and one motorist slowed down and shouted angrily. She saw a gate and drew in off the road and switched off the engine. The silence was absolute. Her hands were moist and shaking. She wiped them on her handkerchief and laid them in her lap feeling that they were separate from the rest of her body. She was hardly aware of a car passing and then slowing to a halt. A face appeared at the window. The voice was slurred and nervous but horribly ingratiating. She could smell the drink on his breath.

'Anything wrong, miss?'

'Nothing. I've just stopped for a rest.'

'No point in resting alone – a pretty girl like you.'

His hand was on the door handle. Cordelia felt in her shoulder bag and drew out the gun. She pushed it into his face.

'It's loaded. Go away at once or I'll shoot.'

The menace in her voice struck cold even to her own ears. The pale, moist face disintegrated with surprise, the jaw fell. He backed away.

'Sorry, miss, I'm sure. My mistake. No offence.'

Cordelia waited until his car was out of sight. Then she turned on the engine. But she knew that she couldn't go on. She turned off the engine again. Waves of tiredness flowed over her, an irresistible tide, gentle as a blessing, which neither her exhausted mind nor body had the will to resist. Her head fell forward and Cordelia slept.

CHAPTER SIX

Cordelia slept soundly but briefly. She didn't know what woke her, whether the blinding light of a passing car sweeping across her closed eyes or her own subconscious knowledge that rest must be rationed to a brief half-hour, the minimum necessary to enable her to do what had to be done before she could give herself over to sleep. She eased her body upright, feeling the stab of pain in her strained muscles and the half-pleasurable itch of dried blood on her back. The night air was heavy and odorous with the heat and scents of the day; even the road winding ahead looked tacky in the glare of her headlights. But Cordelia's chilled and aching body was still grateful for the warmth of Mark's jersey. For the first time since she had pulled it over her head she saw that it was dark green. How odd that she hadn't noticed its colour before!

She drove the rest of the journey like a novice, sitting bolt upright, eyes rigidly ahead, hands and feet tense on the controls. And here at last were the gates of Garforth House. They loomed in her headlights far taller and more ornamental than she remembered them, and they were closed. She ran from the Mini praying that they wouldn't be locked. But the iron latch, although heavy, rose to her desperate hands. The gates swung soundlessly back.

There were no other cars in the drive and she parked the Mini some little way from the house. The windows were dark and the only light, gentle and inviting, shone through the open front door. Cordelia took the pistol in her hand and, without ringing, stepped into the hall. She was more exhausted in body than when she had first come to Garforth House, but tonight she saw it with a new intensity, her nerves sensitive to every detail. The hall was empty, the air expectant. It seemed as if the house had waited for her. The same smell met her of roses and lavender, but tonight she saw that the lavender came from a huge Chinese bowl set on a side table. She recalled the insistent ticking of a clock, but now she noticed for the first time the delicate carving of the clock case, the intricate scrolls and whirls on the face. She stood in the middle of the hall, swaying slightly, the pistol held lightly in her drooping right hand, and looked down. The carpet was a formal geometrical design in rich olive greens, pale blues and crimson, each pattern shaped like the shadow of a kneeling man. It seemed to draw her to her knees. Was it perhaps an eastern prayer mat?

She was aware of Miss Leaming coming quietly down the stairs towards her, her long red dressing-gown sweeping round her ankles. The pistol was taken suddenly but firmly from Cordelia's unresisting hand. She knew that it had gone because her hand felt suddenly lighter. It made no difference. She could never defend herself with it, never kill a man. She had learnt that about herself when Lunn had run from her in terror. Miss Leaming said:

'There is no one here you need defend yourself against, Miss Gray.'

Cordelia said:

'I've come to report to Sir Ronald. Where is he?'

'Where he was the last time you came here, in his study.'

As before, he was sitting at his desk. He had been dictating and the machine was at his right hand. When he saw Cordelia, he switched it off, then walked to the wall and pulled the plug from the socket. He walked back to the desk and they sat down opposite each other. He folded his hands in the pool of light from the desk lamp and looked up at Cordelia. She almost cried out with shock. His face reminded her of faces seen grotesquely reflected in grubby train windows at night – cavernous, the bones stripped of flesh, eyes set in fathomless sockets – faces resurrected from the dead.

When he spoke his voice was low, reminiscent.

'Half an hour ago I learned that Chris Lunn was dead. He was the best lab assistant I ever had. I took him out of an orphanage fifteen years ago. He never knew his parents. He was an ugly, difficult boy, already on probation. School had done nothing for him. But Lunn was one of the best natural scientists I've ever known. If he'd had the education, he'd have been as good as I am.'

'Then why didn't you give him his chance, why didn't you educate him?'

'Because he was more useful to me as a lab assistant. I said that he could have been as good as I am. That isn't quite good enough. I can find plenty of scientists as good. I couldn't have found another lab assistant to equal Lunn. He had a marvellous hand with instruments.'

He looked up at Cordelia, but without curiosity, apparently without interest.

'You've come to report, of course. It's very late, Miss Gray, and, as you see, I'm tired. Can't it wait until tomorrow?'

Cordelia thought that this was as close to an appeal as he could ever bring himself. She said:

'No, I'm tired too. But I want to finish the case tonight, now.' He picked up an ebony paper-knife from the desk and, without looking at Cordelia, balanced it on his forefinger.

'Then tell me, why did my son kill himself? I take it that you do have news for me? You would hardly have burst in here at this hour without something to report.'

'Your son didn't kill himself. He was murdered. He was murdered by someone he knew well, someone he didn't hesitate to let into the cottage, someone who came prepared. He was strangled or suffocated, then slung up on that hook by his own belt. Last of all, his murderer painted his lips, dressed him in a woman's underclothes and spread out pictures of nudes on the table in front of him. It was meant to look like accidental death during sexual experiment; such cases aren't so very uncommon.'

There was half a minute of silence. Then he said with perfect calmness:

'And who was responsible, Miss Gray?'

'You were. You killed your son.'

'For what reason?' He might have been an examiner, putting his inexorable questions.

'Because he discovered that your wife wasn't his mother, that the money left to her and to him by his grandfather had come by fraud. Because he had no intention of benefiting by it a moment longer, nor of accepting his legacy in four years' time. You were afraid that he might make this knowledge public. And what about the Wolvington Trust? If the truth came out, that would be the end of their promised grant. The future of your laboratory was at stake. You couldn't take the risk.'

'And who undressed him again, typed out that suicide note, washed the lipstick from his face?'

'I think I know, but I shan't tell you. That's really what you employed me to discover, isn't it? That's what you couldn't bear not to know. But you killed Mark. You even prepared an alibi just in case it was needed. You got Lunn to ring you at college and announce himself as your son. He was the one person you could rely on absolutely. I don't suppose you told him the truth. He was only your lab assistant. He didn't require explanations, he did what you told him. And even if he did guess the truth, he was safe, wasn't he? You prepared an alibi which you dared not use, because you didn't know when Mark's body was first discovered. If someone had found him and faked that suicide before you had claimed to have spoken to him on the telephone, your alibi would have been broken, and a broken alibi is damning. So you made a chance to talk to Benskin and put matters right. You told him the truth; that it was Lunn who had rung you. You could rely on Lunn to back up your story. But it wouldn't really matter, would it, even if he did talk? No one would believe him.'

'No, any more than they will believe you. You've been determined to earn your fee, Miss Gray. Your explanation is ingenious; there is even a certain plausibility about some of the details. But you know, and I know, that no police officer in the world would take it seriously. It's unfortunate for you that you couldn't question Lunn. But Lunn, as I said, is dead. He burnt to death in a road accident.'

'I know, I saw. He tried to kill me tonight. Did you know that? And earlier, he tried to scare me into dropping the case. Was that because he had begun to suspect the truth?'

'If he did try to kill you, he exceeded his instructions. I merely asked him to keep an eye on you. I had contracted for your sole and whole-time services, if you remember; I wanted to be sure I was getting value. I am getting value of a kind. But you mustn't indulge your imagination outside this room. Neither the police nor the courts are sympathetic to slander nor to hysterical nonsense. And what proof have you? None. My wife was cremated. There is nothing alive or dead on this earth to prove that Mark was not her son.'

Cordelia said:

'You visited Dr Gladwin to satisfy yourself that he was too senile to give evidence against you. You needn't have worried. He never did suspect, did he? You chose him as your wife's doctor because he was old and incompetent. But I did have one small piece of evidence. Lunn was bringing it to you.'

'Then you should have looked after it better. Nothing of Lunn except his bones has survived that crash.'

'There are still the female clothes, the black pants and the bra. Someone might remember who bought them, particularly if that person was a man.'

'Men do buy underclothes for their women. But if I were planning such a murder, I don't think buying the accessories would worry me. Would any harassed shop girl at the cash desk of a popular multiple store remember a particular purchase, a purchase paid for with cash, one of a number of innocuous items, all presented together at the busiest time of the day? The man might even have worn a simple disguise. I doubt whether she would even notice his face. Would you really expect her to remember, weeks afterwards, to identify one of thousands of customers and identify him with sufficient certainty to satisfy a jury? And if she did, what would it prove unless you have the clothes in question? Be sure of one thing, Miss Gray, if I needed to kill I should do it efficiently. I should not be found out. If the police ever learn how my son was found, as they well may do since, apparently, someone other than yourself knows it, they will only believe with greater certainty that he killed himself. Mark's death was necessary and, unlike most deaths, it served a purpose. Human beings have an irresistible urge towards self-sacrifice. They die for any reason or none at all, for meaningless abstractions like patriotism, justice, peace; for other men's ideals, for other men's power, for a few feet of earth. You, no doubt, would give your life to save a child or if you were convinced that the sacrifice would find a cure for cancer.'

'I might. I like to think that I would. But I should want the decision to be mine, not yours.'

'Of course. That would provide you with the necessary emotional satisfaction. But it wouldn't alter the fact of your dying nor the result of your death. And don't say that what I'm doing here isn't worth one single human life. Spare me that hypocrisy. You don't know and you're incapable of understanding the value of what I'm doing here. What difference will Mark's death make to you? You'd never heard of him until you came to Garforth House.'

Cordelia said:

'It will make a difference to Gary Webber.'

'Am I expected to lose everything I've worked for here because Gary Webber wants someone to play squash or discuss history with?'

Suddenly he looked Cordelia full in the face. He said sharply:

'What is the matter? Are you ill?'

'No I'm not ill. I knew that I must be right. I knew that what I had reasoned was true. But I can't believe it. I can't believe that a human being could be so evil.'

'If you are capable of imagining it, then I'm capable of doing it. Haven't you yet discovered that about human beings, Miss Gray? It's the key to what you would call the wickedness of man.'

Suddenly Cordelia could no longer bear this cynical antiphony. She cried out in passionate protest.

'But what is the use of making the world more beautiful if the people who live in it can't love one another?'

She had stung him at last into anger.

'Love! The most overused word in the language. Has it any meaning except the particular sentimental connotation which you choose to give it? What do you mean by love? That human beings must learn to live together with a decent concern for each other's welfare? The law enforces that. The greatest good of the greatest number. Beside that fundamental declaration of common sense all other philosophies are metaphysical abstractions. Or do you define love in the Christian sense, caritas? Read history, Miss Gray. See to what horrors, to what violence, hatred and repression the religion of love has led mankind. But perhaps you prefer a more feminine, more individual definition; love as a passionate commitment to another's personality. Intense personal commitment always ends in jealousy and enslavement. Love is more destructive than hate. If you must dedicate your life to something, dedicate it to an idea.'

'I meant love, as a parent loves a child.'

'The worse for them both, perhaps. But if he doesn't love, there is no power on earth which can stimulate or compel him to. And where there is no love, there can be none of the obligations of love.'

'You could have let him live! The money wasn't important to him. He would have understood your needs and kept silent.'

'Would he? How could he – or I – have explained his rejection of a great fortune in four years' time? People at the mercy of what they call their conscience are never safe. My son was a self-righteous prig. How could I put myself and my work in his hands?'

'You are in mine, Sir Ronald.'

'You are mistaken. I am in no one's hands. Unfortunately for you that tape recorder is not working. We have no witnesses. You will repeat nothing that has been said in this room to anyone outside. If you do I shall have to ruin you. I shall make you unemployable, Miss Gray. And first of all I shall bankrupt that pathetic business of yours. From what Miss Leaming told me it shouldn't be difficult. Slander can be a highly expensive indulgence. Remember that if you are ever tempted to talk. Remember this too. You will harm yourself; you will harm Mark's memory; you will not harm me.'

*

Cordelia never knew how long the tall figure in the red dressing-gown had been watching and listening in the shadow of the door. She never knew how much Miss Leaming had heard or at what moment she had stolen quietly away. But now she was aware of the red shadow moving soundlessly over the carpet, eyes on the figure behind the desk, the gun held closely against her breast. Cordelia watched in fascinated horror, not breathing. She knew exactly what was going to happen. It must have taken less than three seconds but they passed as slowly as minutes. Surely there had been time to cry out, time to warn, time to leap forward and wrench the gun from that steady hand? Surely there had been time for him to cry out? But he made no sound. He half rose, incredulous, and gazed at the muzzle in blind disbelief. Then he turned his head towards Cordelia as if in supplication. She would never forget that last look. It was beyond terror, beyond hope. It held nothing but the blank acceptance of defeat.

It was an execution, neat, unhurried, ritually precise. The bullet went in behind the right ear. The body leapt into the air, shoulders humped, softened before Cordelia's eyes as if the bones were melting into wax, and lay discarded at last over the desk. A thing; like Bernie; like her father.

Miss Leaming said:

'He killed my son.'

'Your son?'

'Of course. Mark was my son. His son and mine. I thought you might have guessed.'

She stood with the gun in her hand gazing with expressionless eyes through the open window to the lawn. There was no sound. Nothing moved. Miss Leaming said:

'He was right when he said that no one could touch him. There was no proof.'

Cordelia cried out appalled:

'Then how could you kill him? How could you be so sure?'

Without releasing her hold on the pistol, Miss Leaming put her hand into the pocket of her dressing-gown. The hand moved over the desk top. A small gilt cylinder rolled over the polished wood towards Cordelia, then rocked into stillness. Miss Leaming said:

'The lipstick was mine. I found it a minute ago in the pocket of his dress suit. He hadn't worn that suit since he last dined in Hall on Feast night. He was always a magpie. He put small objects instinctively into his pocket.'

Cordelia had never doubted Sir Ronald's guilt but now every nerve was desperate for reassurance.

'But it could have been planted there! Lunn could have put it there to incriminate him.'

'Lunn didn't kill Mark. He was in bed with me at the time Mark died. He only left my side for five minutes and that was to make a telephone call shortly after eight o'clock.'

'You were in love with Lunn!'

'Don't look at me like that! I only loved one man in my life and he's the one I've just killed. Talk about things you understand. Love had nothing to do with what Lunn and I needed from each other.'

There was a moment's silence. Then Cordelia said:

'Is there anyone in the house?'

'No. The servants are in London. No one is working late at the lab tonight.'

And Lunn was dead. Miss Leaming said with weary resignation:

'Hadn't you better phone the police?'

'Do you want me to?'

'What does it matter?'

'Prison matters. Losing your freedom matters. And do you really want the truth to come out in open court? Do you want everyone to know how your son died and who killed him? Is that what Mark himself would want?'

'No. Mark never believed in punishment. Tell me what I have to do.'

'We've got to work quickly and plan carefully. We have to trust each other and we have to be intelligent.'

'We are intelligent. What must we do?'

Cordelia took out her handkerchief and, dropping it over the gun, took the weapon from Miss Leaming and placed it on the desk. She grasped the woman's thin wrist and pushed her protesting hand against Sir Ronald's palm, pulling against the instinctive recoil, forcing the stiff but living fingers against the soft unresisting hand of the dead.

'There may be firing residue. I don't really know much about that, but the police may test for it. Now wash your hands and get me a pair of thin gloves. Quickly.'

She went without a word. Left alone, Cordelia looked down at the dead scientist. He had fallen with his chin against the desk top and his arms swinging loosely at his sides, an awkward, uncomfortable-looking pose which gave him the appearance of peering malevolently over his desk. Cordelia could not look at his eyes, but she was conscious of feeling nothing, not hatred, or anger, or pity. Between her eyes and the sprawled figure swung an elongated shape, head hideously crooked, toes pathetically pointed. She walked over to the open window and looked out over the garden with the casual curiosity of a guest kept waiting in a strange room. The air was warm and very still. The scent of roses came in waves through the open window, alternately sickening sweet and then as elusive as a half-caught memory.

This curious hiatus of peace and timelessness must have lasted less than half a minute. Then Cordelia began to plan. She thought about the Clandon case. Memory pictured herself and Bernie, sitting astride a fallen log in Epping Forest and eating their picnic lunch. It brought back the yeasty smell of fresh rolls, butter and tangy cheese, the heavy fungoid smell of summer woods. He had rested the pistol on the bark between them and had mumbled at her through the bread and cheese. 'How would you shoot yourself behind the right ear? Go on, Cordelia – show.'

Cordelia had taken the pistol in her right hand, index finger lightly resting on the trigger, and with some difficulty had strained back her arm to place the muzzle of the gun against the base of the skull. 'Like that?' 'You wouldn't, you know. Not if you were used to a gun. That's the little mistake Mrs Clandon made and it nearly hanged her. She shot her husband behind the right ear with his service revolver and then tried to fake a suicide. But she pressed the wrong finger on the trigger. If he'd really shot himself behind the right ear he'd have pressed the trigger with his thumb and held the revolver with his palm round the back of the butt. I remember that case well. It was the first murder I worked on with the Super – Inspector Dalgliesh, as he was then. Mrs Clandon confessed in the end.' 'What happened to her, Bernie?' 'Life. She'd probably have got away with manslaughter if she hadn't tried to fake a suicide. The jury didn't much like what they heard about Major Clandon's little habits.'

But Miss Leaming couldn't get away with manslaughter; not unless she told the whole story of Mark's death.

She was back in the room now. She handed Cordelia a pair of thin cotton gloves. Cordelia said:

'I think you'd better wait outside. What you don't see you won't have the trouble of forgetting. What were you doing when you met me in the hall?'

'I was getting myself a nightcap, a whisky.'

'Then you would have met me again coming out of the study as you took it up to your room. Get it now and leave the glass on the side table in the hall. That's the kind of detail the police are trained to notice.'

Alone again, Cordelia took up the gun. It was astonishing how repulsive she found this inert weight of metal now. How odd that she should ever have seen it as a harmless toy! She rubbed it thoroughly with her handkerchief erasing Miss Leaming's prints. Then she handled it. It was her gun. They would expect to find some of her prints on the butt together with those of the dead man. She placed it again on the desk top and drew on the gloves. This was the more difficult part. She handled the pistol gingerly and took it over to the inert right hand. She pressed his thumb firmly against the trigger, then wound the cold, unresisting hand round the back of the butt. Then she released his fingers and let the gun fall. It struck the carpet with a dull thud. She peeled off the gloves and went out to Miss Leaming in the hall, closing the study door quietly behind her.

'Here, you'd better put these back where you found them. We mustn't leave them lying around for the police to find.'

She was gone only a few seconds. When she returned, Cordelia said:

'Now we must act the rest just as it would have happened. You meet me as I come out of the room. I have been with Sir Ronald about two minutes. You put down your glass of whisky on the hall table and walk with me to the front door. You say – what would you say?'

'Has he paid you?'

'No, I'm to come in the morning for my money. I'm sorry it wasn't a success. I've told Sir Ronald that I don't want to go on with the case.'

'That's your concern, Miss Gray. It was a foolish business in the first place.'

They were walking out of the front door now. Suddenly Miss Leaming turned to Cordelia and said urgently and in her normal voice:

'There's one thing you had better know. It was I who found Mark first and faked the suicide. He'd rung me earlier in the day and asked me to call. I couldn't get away until after nine because of Lunn. I didn't want him to be suspicious.'

'But didn't it occur to you when you found Mark that there might be something odd about the death? The door was unlocked although the curtains were drawn. The lipstick was missing.'

'I suspected nothing until tonight when I stood there in the shadows and heard you talking. We're all sexually sophisticated these days. I believed what I saw. It was all horror but I knew what I had to do. I worked quickly, terrified that someone would come. I cleaned his face with my handkerchief dampened with water from the kitchen sink. It seemed that the lipstick would never come off. I undressed him and pulled on his jeans which had been thrown over the back of a chair. I didn't wait to put on his shoes, that didn't seem important. Typing the note was the worst part. I knew that he would have his Blake with him somewhere in the cottage and that the passage I chose might be more convincing than an ordinary suicide note. The clattering of the typewriter keys sounded unnaturally loud in the quietness; I was terrified that someone would hear. He had been keeping a kind of journal. There wasn't time to read it but I burnt the typescript in the sitting-room grate. Last of all, I bundled up the clothes and the pictures and brought them back here to be burnt in the lab incinerator.'

'You dropped one of the pictures in the garden. And you didn't quite succeed in cleaning the lipstick from his face.'

'So that's how you guessed?'

Cordelia didn't reply immediately. Whatever happened she must keep Isabelle de Lasterie out of the case.

'I wasn't sure if it was you who had been there first but I thought it must have been. There were four things. You didn't want me to investigate Mark's death; you read English at Cambridge and could have known where to find that Blake quotation; you are an experienced typist and I didn't think that the note had been typed by an amateur despite the late attempt to make it look like Mark's work; when I was first at Garforth House and asked about the suicide note you spoke the whole of the Blake quotation; the typed version was ten words short. I first noticed that when I visited the police station and was shown the note. It pointed direct to you. That was the strongest evidence I had.'

They had reached the car now and paused together. Cordelia said:

'We mustn't waste any more time before ringing the police. Someone may have heard the shot.'

'It's not likely. We're some distance from the village. Do we hear it now?'

'Yes. We hear it now.' There was a second's pause then Cordelia said:

'What was that? It sounded like a shot.'

'It couldn't have been. It was probably a car backfiring.'

Miss Leaming spoke like a bad actress, the words were stilted, unconvincing. But she spoke them; she would remember them.

'But there isn't a car passing. And it came from the house.'

They glanced at each other, then ran back together through the open door into the hall. Miss Leaming paused for a moment and looked Cordelia in the face before she opened the study door. Cordelia came in behind her. Miss Leaming said:

'He's been shot! I'd better phone the police.'

Cordelia said:

'You wouldn't say that! Don't ever think like that! You'd go up to the body first and then you'd say:

' "He's shot himself. I'd better phone the police." '

Miss Leaming looked unemotionally at her lover's body, then glanced round the room. Forgetting her role, she asked:

'What have you done in here? What about fingerprints?'

'Never mind. I've looked after that. All you have to remember is that you didn't know I had a gun when I first came to Garforth House; you didn't know Sir Ronald took it from me. You haven't seen that gun until this moment. When I arrived tonight you showed me into the study and met me again when I came out two minutes later. We walked together to the car and spoke as we have just spoken. We heard the shot. We did what we have just done. Forget everything else that has happened. When they question you, don't embroider, don't invent, don't be afraid to say you can't remember. And now – ring the Cambridge police.'

*

Three minutes later they were standing together at the open door waiting for the police to arrive. Miss Leaming said:

'We mustn't talk together once they're here. And, afterwards, we mustn't meet or show any particular interest in each other. They'll know that this can't be murder unless we two are in it together. And why should we conspire together when we've only met once before, when we don't even like each other?'

She was right, thought Cordelia. They didn't even like each other. She didn't really care if Elizabeth Leaming went to prison; she did care if Mark's mother went to prison. She cared, too, that the truth of his death should never be known. The strength of that determination struck her as irrational. It could make no difference to him now and he wasn't a boy who had cared overmuch what people thought of him. But Ronald Callender had desecrated his body after death; had planned to make him an object, at worst of contempt, at best of pity. She had set her face against Ronald Callender. She hadn't wanted him to die; wouldn't have been capable herself of pressing the trigger. But he was dead and she couldn't feel regret, nor could she be an instrument of retribution for his murderer. It was expedient, no more than that, that Miss Leaming shouldn't be punished. Gazing out into the summer night and waiting for the sound of the police cars, Cordelia accepted once and for all the enormity and the justification of what she had done and was still planning to do. She was never afterwards to feel the least tinge of regret or of remorse.

Miss Leaming said:

'There are things you probably want to ask me, things I suppose you've a right to know. We can meet in King's College Chapel after Evensong on the first Sunday after the inquest. I'll go through the screen into the chancel, you stay in the nave. It will seem natural enough for us to meet by chance there, that is if we are both still free.'

Cordelia was interested to see that Miss Leaming was taking charge again. She said:

'We shall be. If we keep our heads this can't go wrong.'

There was a moment's silence. Miss Leaming said:

'They're taking their time. Surely they should be here by now?'

'They won't be much longer.'

Miss Leaming suddenly laughed and said with revealing bitterness:

'What is there to be frightened of? We shall be dealing only with men.'

So they waited quietly together. They heard the approaching cars before the headlamps swept over the drive, illuminating every pebble, picking out the small plants at the edge of the beds, bathing the blue haze of the wistaria with light, dazzling the watchers' eyes. Then the lights were dimmed as the cars rocked gently to a stop in front of the house. Dark shapes emerged and came unhurriedly but resolutely forward. The hall was suddenly filled with large, calm men, some in plain clothes. Cordelia effaced herself against the wall and it was Miss Leaming who stepped forward, spoke to them in a low voice and led them into the study.

Two uniformed men were left in the hall. They stood talking together, taking no notice of Cordelia. Their colleagues were taking their time. They must have used the telephone in the study because more cars and men began to arrive. First the police surgeon, identified by his bag even if he hadn't been greeted with:

'Good evening Doc. In here please.'

How often he must have heard that phrase! He glanced with brief curiosity at Cordelia as he trotted through the hall, a fat, dishevelled little man, his face crumpled and petulant as a child when forcibly woken from sleep. Next came a civilian photographer carrying his

camera, tripod and box of equipment; a fingerprint expert; two other civilians whom Cordelia, instructed in procedure by Bernie, guessed were scene-of-crime officers. So they were treating this as a sus-
-picious death. And why not? It was suspicious.

The head of the household lay dead, but the house itself seemed to have come alive. The police talked, not in whispers, but in confident normal voices unsubdued by death. They were professionals doing their job, working easily to the prescribed routine. They had been initiated into the mysteries of violent death; its victims held no awe for them. They had seen too many bodies: bodies scraped off motorways; loaded piecemeal into ambulances; dragged by hook and net from the depths of rivers; dug putrefying from the clogging earth. Like doctors, they were kind and condescendingly gentle to the uninstructed, keeping inviolate their awful knowledge. This body, while it breathed, had been more important than others. It wasn't important now, but it could still make trouble for them. They would be that much more meticulous, that much more tactful. But it was still only a case.

Cordelia sat alone and waited. She was suddenly overcome with tiredness. She longed for nothing but to put down her head on the hall table and sleep. She was hardly aware of Miss Leaming passing through the hall on her way to the drawing-room, of the tall officer talking to her as they passed. Neither took any notice of the small figure in its immense woollen jersey, sitting against the wall. Cordelia willed herself to stay awake. She knew what she had to say; it was all clear enough in her mind. If only they would come to question her and let her sleep.

It wasn't until the photographer and the print man had finished their work that one of the senior officers came out to her. She was never afterwards able to recall his face but she remembered his voice, a careful, unemphatic voice from which every tinge of emotion had been excluded. He held out the gun towards her. It was resting on his open palm, protected by a handkerchief from the contamination of his hand.

'Do you recognize this weapon, Miss Gray?'

Cordelia thought it odd that he should use the word weapon. Why not just say gun?

'I think so. I think it must be mine.'

'You aren't sure?'

'It must be mine, unless Sir Ronald owned one of the same make. He took it from me when I first came here four days ago. He promised to let me have it back when I called tomorrow morning for my pay.'

'So this is only the second time you've been in this house?'

'Yes.'

'Have you ever met Sir Ronald Callender or Miss Leaming before?'

'No. Not until Sir Ronald sent for me to undertake this case.'

He went away. Cordelia rested her head back against the wall and took short snatches of sleep. Another officer came. This time he had a uniformed man with him, taking notes. There were more questions. Cordelia told her prepared story. They wrote it down without comment and went away.

She must have dozed. She awoke to find a tall, uniformed officer standing over her. He said:

'Miss Leaming is making tea in the kitchen, Miss. Perhaps you would like to give her a hand. It's something to do, isn't it?'

Cordelia thought; they're going to take away the body. She said: 'I don't know where the kitchen is.'

She saw his eyes flicker.

'Oh, don't you, Miss? You're a stranger here, are you? Well, it's this way.'

The kitchen was at the back of the house. It smelt of spice, oil and tomato sauce, bringing back memories of meals in Italy with her father. Miss Leaming was taking down cups from a vast dresser. An electric kettle was already hissing steam. The police officer stayed. So they weren't to be left alone. Cordelia said:

'Can I help?' Miss Leaming did not look at her.

'There are some biscuits in that tin. You can put them out on a tray. The milk is in the fridge.'

Cordelia moved like an automaton. The milk bottle was an icy column in her hands, the biscuit lid resisted her tired fingers and she broke a nail prising it off. She noticed the details of the kitchen – a wall calendar of St Theresa of Avila, the saint's face unnaturally elongated and pale so that she looked like a hallowed Miss Leaming; a china donkey with two panniers of artificial flowers, its melancholy head crowned with a miniature straw hat; an immense blue bowl of brown eggs.

There were two trays. The police constable took the larger from

Miss Leaming and led the way into the hall. Cordelia followed with the second tray, holding it high against her chest like a child, permitted as a privilege to help mother. Police officers gathered round. She took a cup herself and returned to her usual chair.

And now there was the sound of yet another car. A middle-aged woman came in with a uniformed chauffeur at her shoulder. Through the fog of her tiredness, Cordelia heard a high, didactic voice.

'My dear Eliza, this is appalling! You must come back to the Lodge tonight. No, I insist. Is the Chief Constable here?'

'No, Marjorie, but these officers have been very kind.'

'Leave them the key. They'll lock up the house when they've finished. You can't possibly stay here alone tonight.'

There were introductions, hurried consultations with the detectives in which the newcomer's voice was dominant. Miss Leaming went upstairs with her visitor and reappeared five minutes later with a small case, her coat over her arm. They went off together, escorted to the car by the chauffeur and one of the detectives. None of the little party glanced at Cordelia.

Five minutes later the Inspector came up to Cordelia, key in hand.

'We shall lock up the house tonight, Miss Gray. It's time you were getting home. Are you thinking of staying at the cottage?'

'Just for the next few days, if Major Markland will let me.'

'You look very tired. One of my men will drive you in your own car. I should like a written statement from you tomorrow. Can you come to the station as soon as possible after breakfast? You know where it is?'

'Yes, I know.'

One of the police panda cars drove off first and the Mini followed. The police driver drove fast, lurching the little car around the corners. Cordelia's head lolled against the back of the seat and, from time to time, was thrown against the driver's arm. He was wearing shirt sleeves and she was vaguely conscious of the comfort of the warm flesh through the cotton. The car window was open and she was aware of hot night air rushing against her face, of the scudding clouds, of the first unbelievable colours of day staining the eastern sky. The route seemed strange to her and time itself disjointed; she wondered why the car had suddenly stopped and it took a minute for her to recognize the tall hedge bending over the lane like a menacing shadow, the ramshackle gate. She was home. The driver said: 'Is this the place, miss?'

'Yes, this is it. But I usually leave the Mini further down the lane on the right. There's a copse there where you can drive it off the road.'

'Right, miss.'

He got out of the car to consult the other driver. They moved on slowly for the last few yards of the journey. And now, at last, the police car had driven away and she was alone at the gate. It was an effort to push it open against the weight of the weeds and she lurched round the cottage to the back door like a drunken creature. It took some little time to fit the key into the lock, but that was the last problem. There was no longer a gun to hide; there was no longer need to check the tape sealing the windows. Lunn was dead and she was alive. Every night that she had slept at the cottage Cordelia had come home tired, but never before had she been as tired as this. She made her way upstairs as if sleepwalking and, too exhausted even to zip herself into her sleeping-bag, crept underneath it and knew nothing more.

*

And at last – it seemed to Cordelia after months, not days, of waiting – there was another inquest. It was as unhurried, as unostentatiously formal, as Bernie's had been, but there was a difference. Here, instead of a handful of pathetic casuals who had sneaked into the warmth of the back benches to hear Bernie's obsequies, were grave-faced colleagues and friends, muted voices, the whispered preliminaries of lawyers and police, an indefinable sense of occasion. Cordelia guessed that the grey-haired man escorting Miss Leaming must be her lawyer. She watched him at work, affable but not deferential to the senior police, quietly solicitous for his client, exuding a confidence that they were all engaged in a necessary if tedious formality, a ritual as unworrying as Sunday Matins.

Miss Leaming looked very pale. She was wearing the grey suit she had worn when Cordelia first met her but with a small black hat, black gloves and a black chiffon scarf knotted at her throat. The two women did not look at each other. Cordelia found a seat at the end of a bench and sat there, unrepresented and alone. One or two of the younger policemen smiled at her with a reassuring but pitying kindness.

Miss Leaming gave her evidence first in a low, composed voice. She affirmed instead of taking the oath, a decision which caused a brief spasm of distress to pass over her lawyer's face. But she gave him no further cause for concern. She testified that Sir Ronald had been depressed at his son's death and, she thought, had blamed himself for not knowing that something was worrying Mark. He had told her that he intended to call in a private detective, and it had been she who had originally interviewed Miss Gray and had brought her back to Garforth House. Miss Leaming said that she had opposed the suggestion; she had seen no useful purpose in it, and thought that this futile and fruitless enquiry would only remind Sir Ronald of the tragedy. She had not known that Miss Gray possessed a gun nor that Sir Ronald had taken it from her. She had not been present during the whole of their preliminary interview. Sir Ronald had escorted Miss Gray to view his son's room while she, Miss Leaming, had gone in search of a photograph of Mr Callender for which Miss Gray had asked.

The coroner asked her gently about the night of Sir Ronald's death.

Miss Leaming said that Miss Gray had arrived to give her first report shortly after half past ten. She herself had been passing through the front hall when the girl appeared. Miss Leaming had pointed out that it was late, but Miss Gray had said that she had wanted to abandon the case and get back to town. She had showed Miss Gray into the study where Sir Ronald was working. They had been together, she thought, for less than two minutes. Miss Gray had then come out of the study and she had walked with her to her car; they had only talked briefly. Miss Gray said that Sir Ronald had asked her to call back in the morning for her pay. She had made no mention of a gun.

Sir Ronald had, only half an hour before that, received a telephone call from the police to say that his laboratory assistant, Christopher Lunn, had been killed in a road accident. She had not told Miss Gray the news about Lunn before her interview with Sir Ronald; it hadn't occurred to her to do so. The girl had gone almost immediately into the study to see Sir Ronald. Miss Leaming said that they were standing together at the car talking when they heard the shot. At first she had thought it was a car backfiring but then she realized that it had come from the house. They had both rushed into the study and found Sir Ronald lying slumped over his desk. The gun had dropped from his hand to the floor.

No, Sir Ronald had never given her any idea that he contemplated suicide. She thought that he was very distressed about the death of Mr Lunn but it was difficult to tell. Sir Ronald was not a man to show emotion. He had been working very hard recently and had not seemed himself since the death of his son. But Miss Leaming had never for a moment thought that Sir Ronald was a man who would put an end to his life.

She was followed by the police witnesses, deferential, professional, but managing to give an impression that none of this was new to them; they had seen it all before and would see it again.

They were followed by the doctors, including the pathologist, who testified in what the court obviously thought was unnecessary detail to the effect of firing a jacketed hollow-cavity bullet of ninety grains into the human brain. The coroner asked:

'You have heard the police evidence that there was the print of Sir Ronald Callender's thumb on the trigger of the gun and a palm mark smudged around the butt. What would you deduce from that?'

The pathologist looked slightly surprised at being asked to deduce anything but said that it was apparent that Sir Ronald had held the gun with his thumb on the trigger when pointing it against his head. The pathologist thought that it was probably the most comfortable way in which to hold the weapon, indeed the only comfortable way, having regard to the position of the wound of entry.

Lastly, Cordelia was called to the witness-box and took the oath. She had given some thought to the propriety of this and had wondered whether to follow Miss Leaming's example. There were moments, usually on a sunny Easter morning, when she wished that she could with sincerity call herself a Christian; but for the rest of the year she knew herself to be what she was – incurably agnostic but prone to unpredictable relapses into faith. This seemed to her, however, a moment when religious scrupulosity was an indulgence which she couldn't afford. The lies she was about to tell would not be the more heinous because they were tinged with blasphemy.

The coroner let her tell her story without interruption. She sensed that the court was puzzled by her but not unsympathetic. For once, the carefully modulated middle-class accent, which in her six years at the convent she had unconsciously acquired, and which in other people often irritated her as much as her own voice had irritated her father, was proving an advantage. She wore her suit and had bought a black chiffon scarf to cover her head. She remembered that she must call the coroner 'sir'.

After she had briefly confirmed Miss Leaming's story of how she had been called to the case, the coroner said:

'And now, Miss Gray, will you explain to the court what happened on the night Sir Ronald Callender died?'

'I had decided, sir, that I didn't want to go on with the case. I hadn't discovered anything useful and I didn't think there was anything to discover. I had been living in the cottage where Mark Callender had spent the last weeks of his life and I had come to think that what I was doing was wrong, that I was taking money for prying into his private life. I decided on impulse to tell Sir Ronald that I wanted to finish the case. I drove to Garforth House. I got there at about ten-thirty. I knew it was late but I was anxious to go back to London the next morning. I saw Miss Leaming as she was crossing the hall and she showed me straight into the study.'

'Will you please describe to the court how you found Sir Ronald.'

'He seemed to be tired and distracted. I tried to explain why I wanted to give up the case but I'm not sure that he heard me. He said I was to come back next morning for my money and I said that I only proposed to charge expenses, but that I would like to have my gun. He just waved a hand in dismissal and said, "Tomorrow morning, Miss Gray. Tomorrow morning." '

'And then you left him?'

'Yes, sir. Miss Leaming accompanied me back to the car and I was just about to drive away when we heard the shot.'

'You didn't see the gun in Sir Ronald's possession while you were in the study with him?'

'No, sir.'

'He didn't talk to you about Mr Lunn's death or give you any idea that he was contemplating suicide?'

'No, sir.'

The coroner doodled on the pad before him. Without looking at Cordelia, he said:

'And now, Miss Gray, will you please explain to the court how Sir Ronald came to have your gun.'

This was the difficult part, but Cordelia had rehearsed it. The Cambridge police had been very thorough. They had asked the same questions over and over again. She knew exactly how Sir Ronald had come to have the gun. She remembered a piece of Dalgliesh dogma, reported by Bernie, which had seemed to her at the time more appropriate advice for a criminal than a detective. 'Never tell an unnecessary lie; the truth has great authority. The cleverest murderers have been caught, not because they told the one essential lie, but because they continued to lie about unimportant detail when the truth could have done them no harm.'

She said:

'My partner, Mr Pryde, owned the gun and was very proud of it. When he killed himself I knew that he meant me to have it. That was why he cut his wrists instead of shooting himself, which would have been quicker and easier.'

The coroner looked up sharply.

'And were you there when he killed himself?'

'No, sir. But I found the body.'

There was a murmur of sympathy from the court; she could feel their concern.

'Did you know that the gun wasn't licensed?'

'No, sir, but I think I suspected that it might not have been. I brought it with me on this case because I didn't want to leave it in the office and because I found it a comfort. I meant to check up on the licence as soon as I got back. I didn't expect ever to use the gun. I didn't really think of it as a lethal weapon. It's just that this was my first case and Bernie had left it to me and I felt happier having it with me.'

'I see,' said the coroner.

Cordelia thought that he probably did see and so did the court. They were having no difficulty in believing her because she was telling the somewhat improbable truth. Now that she was about to lie, they would go on believing her.

'And now will you please tell the court how Sir Ronald came to take the gun from you?'

'It was on my first visit to Garforth House when Sir Ronald was showing me his son's bedroom. He knew that I was the sole owner of the Agency, and he asked me if it wasn't a difficult and rather frightening job for a woman. I said that I wasn't frightened but that I had Bernie's gun. When he found that I had it with me in my bag he made me hand it over to him. He said that he didn't propose to engage someone who might be a danger to other people or herself. He said that he wouldn't take the responsibility. He took the gun and the ammunition.'

'And what did he do with the gun?'

Cordelia had thought this one out carefully. Obviously he hadn't carried it downstairs in his hand or Miss Leaming would have seen it. She would have liked to have said that he put it into a drawer in Mark's room but she couldn't remember whether the bedside table had had any drawers. She said:

'He took it out of the room with him; he didn't tell me where. He was only away for a moment and then we went downstairs together.'

'And you didn't set eyes on the gun again until you saw it on the floor close to Sir Ronald's hand when you and Miss Leaming found his body?'

'No, sir.'

Cordelia was the last witness. The verdict was quickly given, one that the court obviously felt would have been agreeable to Sir Ronald's scrupulously exact and scientific brain. It was that the deceased had taken his own life but that there was no evidence as to the state of his mind. The coroner delivered at length the obligatory warning about the danger of guns. Guns, the court were informed, could kill people. He managed to convey that unlicensed guns were particularly prone to this danger. He pronounced no strictures on Cordelia personally although it was apparent that this restraint cost him an effort. He rose and the court rose with him.

After the coroner had left the bench the court broke up into little whispering groups. Miss Leaming was quickly surrounded. Cordelia saw her shaking hands, receiving condolences, listening with grave assenting face to the first tentative proposals for a memorial service. Cordelia wondered how she could ever have feared that Miss Leaming would be suspected. She herself stood a little apart, delinquent. She knew that the police would charge her with illegal possession of the gun. They could do no less. True, she would be lightly punished, if punished at all. But for the rest of her life she would be the girl whose carelessness and naïveté had lost England one of her foremost scientists.

As Hugo had said, all Cambridge suicides were brilliant. But about this one there could be little doubt. Sir Ronald's death would probably raise him to the status of genius.

Almost unnoticed, she came alone out of the courtroom on to Market Hill. Hugo must have been waiting; now he fell into step with her.

'How did it go? I must say death seems to follow you around, doesn't it?'

'It went all right. I seem to follow death.'

'I suppose he did shoot himself?'

'Yes. He shot himself.'

'And with your gun?'

'As you will know if you were in court. I didn't see you.'

'I wasn't there, I had a tutorial, but the news did get around. I shouldn't let it worry you. Ronald Callender wasn't as important as some people in Cambridge may choose to believe.'

'You know nothing about him. He was a human being and he's dead. That fact is always important.'

'It isn't, you know, Cordelia. Death is the least important thing about us. Comfort yourself with Joseph Hall. "Death borders upon our birth and our cradle stands in the grave." And he did choose his own weapon, his own time. He'd had enough of himself. Plenty of people had had enough of him.'

They walked together down St Edward's Passage towards King's Parade. Cordelia wasn't sure where they were making for. Her need at present was just to walk, but she didn't find her companion disagreeable.

She asked:

'Where's Isabelle?'

'Isabelle is home in Lyons. Papa turned up unexpectedly yesterday and found that mademoiselle wasn't exactly earning her wages. Papa decided that dear Isabelle was getting less – or it may have been more – out of her Cambridge education than he had expected. I don't think you need worry about her. Isabelle is safe enough now. Even if the police decide that it's worth while going to France to question her – and why on earth should they? – it won't help them.

Papa will surround her with a barrage of lawyers. He's not in a mood to stand any nonsense from Englishmen at present.'

'And what about you? If anyone asks you how Mark died, you'll never tell them the truth?'

'What do you think? Sophie, Davie and I are safe enough. I'm reliable when it comes to essentials.'

For a moment Cordelia wished that he were reliable in less essential matters. She asked:

'Are you sorry about Isabelle leaving?'

'I am rather. Beauty is intellectually confusing; it sabotages common sense. I could never quite accept that Isabelle was what she is: a generous, indolent, over-affectionate and stupid young woman. I thought that any woman as beautiful as she must have an instinct about life, access to some secret wisdom which is beyond cleverness. Every time she opened that delicious mouth I was expecting her to illumine life. I think I could have spent all my life just looking at her and waiting for the oracle. And all she could talk about was clothes.'

'Poor Hugo.'

'Never poor Hugo. I'm not unhappy. The secret of contentment is never to allow yourself to want anything which reason tells you you haven't a chance of getting.'

Cordelia thought that he was young, well-off, clever, even if not clever enough, handsome; there wasn't much that he would have to forgo on that or any other criterion.

She heard him speaking:

'Why not stay in Cambridge for a week or so and let me show you the city? Sophie would let you have her spare room.'

'No thank you, Hugo. I have to get back to town.'

There was nothing in town for her, but with Hugo there would be nothing in Cambridge for her either. There was only one reason for staying in this city. She would remain at the cottage until Sunday and her meeting with Miss Leaming. After that, as far as she was concerned, the case of Mark Callender would be finished for good.

*

Sunday afternoon Evensong was over and the congregation, who had listened in respectful silence to the singing of responses, psalms and anthem by one of the finest choirs in the world, rose and joined with joyous abandon in the final hymn. Cordelia rose and sang with them. She had seated herself at the end of the row close to the richly carved screen. From here she could see into the chancel. The robes of the choristers gleamed scarlet and white; the candles flickered in patterned rows and high circles of golden light; two tall and slender candles stood each side of the softly illuminated Rubens above the high altar, seen dimly as a distant smudge of crimson, blue and gold. The blessing was pronounced, the final amen impeccably sung and the choir began to file decorously out of the chancel. The south door was opened and sunlight flooded into the chapel. The members of the college who had attended divine service strolled out after the Provost and Fellows in casual disarray, their regulation surplices dingy and limp over a cheerful incongruity of corduroy and tweed. The great organ snuffled and groaned like an animal gathering breath, before giving forth its magnificent voice in a Bach fugue. Cordelia sat quietly in her chair, listening and waiting. Now the congregation was moving down the main aisle – small groups in bright summer cottons whispering discreetly, serious young men in sober Sunday black, tourists clutching their illustrated guides and half-embarrassed by their obtrusive cameras, a group of nuns with calm and cheerful faces.

Miss Leaming was one of the last, a tall figure in a grey linen dress and white gloves, her head bare, a white cardigan slung carelessly around her shoulders against the chill of the chapel. She was obviously alone and unwatched and her careful pretence of surprise at recognizing Cordelia was probably an unnecessary precaution. They passed out of the chapel together.

The gravel path outside the doorway was thronged with people. A little party of Japanese, festooned with cameras and accessories, added their high staccato jabber to the muted Sunday afternoon chat. From here the silver stream of the Cam was invisible but the truncated bodies of punters glided against the far bank like puppets in a show, raising their arms above the pole and turning to thrust it backwards as if participating in some ritual dance. The great lawn lay unshadowed in the sun, a quintessence of greenness staining the scented air. A frail and elderly don in gown and mortarboard was limping across the grass; the sleeves of his gown caught a stray breeze and billowed out so that he looked like a winged and monstrous crow struggling to rise. Miss Leaming said, as if Cordelia had asked for an explanation:

'He's a Fellow. The sacred turf is, therefore, uncontaminated by his feet.'

They walked in silence by Gibbs Building. Cordelia wondered when Miss Leaming would speak. When she did, her first question was unexpected.

'Do you think you'll make a success of it?'

Sensing Cordelia's surprise, she added impatiently:

'The Detective Agency. Do you think you'll be able to cope?'

'I shall have to try. It's the only job I know.'

She had no intention of justifying to Miss Leaming her affection and loyalty to Bernie; she would have had some difficulty in explaining it to herself.

'Your overheads are too high.'

It was a pronouncement made with all the authority of a verdict.

'Do you mean the office and the Mini?' asked Cordelia.

'Yes. In your job I don't see how one person in the field can bring in sufficient income to cover expenses. You can't be sitting in the office taking orders and typing letters and be out solving cases at the same time. On the other hand, I don't suppose you can afford help.'

'Not yet. I've been thinking that I might rent a telephone answering service. That will take care of the orders although, of course, clients much prefer to come to the office and discuss their case. If I can only make enough in expenses just to live, then any fees can cover the overheads.'

'If there are any fees.'

There seemed nothing to say to this and they walked on in silence for a few seconds. Then Miss Leaming said:

'There'll be the expenses from this case anyway. That at least should help towards your fine for illegal possession of the gun. I've put the matter in the hands of my solicitor. You should be getting a cheque fairly soon.'

'I don't want to take any money for this case.'

'I can understand that. As you pointed out to Ronald, it falls under your fair deal clause. Strictly speaking you aren't entitled to any. All the same, I think it would look less suspicious if you took your expenses. Would thirty pounds strike you as reasonable?'

'Perfectly, thank you.'

They had reached the corner of the lawn and had turned to walk towards King's Bridge. Miss Leaming said:

'I shall have to be grateful to you for the rest of my life. That for me is an unaccustomed humility and I'm not sure that I like it.'

'Then don't feel it. I was thinking of Mark, not of you.'

'I thought you might have acted in the service of justice or some such abstraction.'

'I wasn't thinking about any abstraction. I was thinking about a person.'

They had reached the bridge now and leaned over it side by side to look down into the bright water. The paths leading up to the bridge were, for a few minutes, empty of people. Miss Leaming said:

'Pregnancy isn't difficult to fake, you know. It only needs a loose corset and judicious stuffing. It's humiliating for the woman, of course, almost indecent if she happens to be barren. But it isn't difficult, particularly if she isn't closely watched. Evelyn wasn't. She had always been a shy, self-contained woman. People expected her to be excessively modest about her pregnancy. Garforth House wasn't filled with friends and relations swopping horror stories about the ante-natal clinic and patting her stomach. We had to get rid of that tedious fool Nanny Pilbeam, of course. Ronald regarded her departure as one of the subsidiary benefits of the pseudo pregnancy. He was tired of being spoken to as if he were still Ronald Callender, the bright grammar-school boy from Harrogate.'

Cordelia said:

'Mrs Goddard told me that Mark had a great look of his mother.'

'She would. She was sentimental as well as stupid.'

Cordelia did not speak. After a few moments' silence Miss Leaming went on:

'I discovered that I was carrying Ronald's child at about the same time as a London specialist confirmed what the three of us already guessed, that Evelyn was most unlikely to conceive. I wanted to have the baby; Ronald desperately wanted a son; Evelyn's father was obsessional about his need for a grandson and was willing to part with half a million to prove it. It was all so easy. I resigned from my teaching job and went off to the safe anonymity of London and Evelyn told her father she was pregnant at last. Neither Ronald nor I had any conscience about defrauding George Bottley. He was an arrogant, brutal, self-satisfied fool who couldn't imagine how the world would continue without his issue to supervise it. He even subsidized his own deceit. The cheques for Evelyn began to arrive, each with a note imploring her to look after her health, to consult the best London doctors, to rest, to take a holiday in the sun. She had always loved Italy, and Italy became part of the plan. The three of us would meet in London every two months and fly together to Pisa. Ronald would rent a small villa outside Florence and, once there, I became Mrs Callender and Evelyn became me. We had only daily servants and there was no need for them to look at our passports. They got used to our visits and so did the local doctor who was called in to supervise my health. The locals thought it flattering that the English lady should be so fond of Italy that she came back month after month, so close to her confinement.'

Cordelia asked:

'But how could she do it, how could she bear to be there with you in the house, watching you with her husband, knowing that you were going to have his child?'

'She did it because she loved Ronald and couldn't bear to lose him. She hadn't been much success as a woman. If she lost her husband, what else was there for her? She couldn't have gone back to her father. Besides, we had a bribe for her. She was to have the child. If she refused, then Ronald would leave her and seek a divorce to marry me.'

'I would rather have left him and gone off to scrub doorsteps.'

'Not everyone has a talent for scrubbing doorsteps and not everyone has your capacity for moral indignation. Evelyn was religious. She was, therefore, practised in self-deception. She convinced herself that what we were doing was best for the child.'

'And her father? Didn't he ever suspect?'

'He despised her for her piety. He always had. Psychologically he could hardly indulge that dislike and at the same time think her capable of deceit. Besides, he desperately needed that grandchild. It wouldn't have entered his mind that the child might not be hers. And he had a doctor's report. After our third visit to Italy we told Doctor Sartori that Mrs Callender's father was concerned about her care. At our request he wrote a reassuring medical report on the progress of the pregnancy. We went to Florence together a fortnight before the baby was due and stayed there until Mark arrived. Luckily he was a day or two before time. We'd had the foresight to put back the expected date of delivery so that it genuinely looked as if Evelyn had been caught unexpectedly by a premature birth. Dr Sartori did what was necessary with perfect competence and the three of us came home with the baby and a birth certificate in the right name.'

Cordelia said:

'And nine months later Mrs Callender was dead.'

'He didn't kill her, if that's what you're thinking. He wasn't really the monster that you imagine, at least, not then. But in a sense we did both destroy her. She should have had a specialist, certainly a better doctor than that incompetent fool Gladwin. But the three of us were desperately afraid that an efficient doctor would know that she hadn't borne a child. She was as worried as we were. She insisted that no other doctor be consulted. She had grown to love the baby, you see. So she died and was cremated and we thought we were safe for ever.'

'She left Mark a note before she died, nothing but a scribbled hieroglyphic in her prayer book. She left him her blood group.'

'We knew that the blood groups were a danger. Ronald took blood from the three of us and made the necessary tests. But after she was dead even that worry ended.'

There was a long silence. Cordelia could see a little group of tourists moving down the path towards the bridge. Miss Leaming said:

'The irony of it is that Ronald never really loved him. Mark's grandfather adored him; there was no difficulty there. He left half his fortune to Evelyn and it came automatically to her husband. Mark was to get the other half on his twenty-fifth birthday. But Ronald never cared for his son. He found that he couldn't love him, and I wasn't allowed to. I watched him grow up and go to school. But I wasn't allowed to love him. I used to knit him endless jerseys. It was almost an obsession. The patterns got more intricate and the wool thicker as he grew older. Poor Mark, he must have thought that I was mad, this strange, discontented woman whom his father couldn't do without but wouldn't marry.'

'There are one or two of the jerseys at the cottage. What would you like me to do with his things?'

'Take them away and give them to anyone who needs them. Unless you think I ought to unpick the wool and knit it up into something new? Would that be a suitable gesture, do you think, symbolic of wasted effort, pathos, futility?'

'I'll find a use for them. And his books?'

'Get rid of them too. I can't go again to the cottage. Get rid of everything if you will.'

The little group of tourists was very close now but they seemed engrossed in their own chatter. Miss Leaming took an envelope out of her pocket and handed it to Cordelia.

'I've written out a brief confession. There's nothing in it about Mark, nothing about how he died or what you discovered. It's just a brief statement that I shot Ronald Callender immediately after you had left Garforth House and coerced you into supporting my story. You'd better put it somewhere safe. One day you may need it.'

Cordelia saw that the envelope was addressed to herself. She didn't open it. She said:

'It's too late now. If you regret what we did, you should have spoken earlier. The case is closed now.'

'I've no regrets. I'm glad that we acted as we did. But the case may not be over yet.'

'But it is over! The inquest has given its verdict.'

'Ronald had a number of very powerful friends. They have influence and, periodically, they like to exercise it if only to prove that they still have it.'

'But they can't get this case reopened! It practically takes an Act of Parliament to change a coroner's verdict.'

'I don't say that they'll try to do that. But they may ask questions. They may have what they describe as a quiet word in the right ear. And the right ears are usually available. That's how they work. That's the sort of people they are.'

Cordelia said suddenly:

'Have you a light?'

Without question or protest Miss Leaming opened her handbag and handed over an elegant silver tube. Cordelia didn't smoke and was unused to lighters. It took three clicks before the wick burst into flame. Then she leaned over the parapet of the bridge and set fire to the corner of the envelope.

The incandescent flame was invisible in the stronger light of the sun. All Cordelia could see was a narrow band of wavering purple light as the flame bit into the paper and the charred edges widened and grew. The pungent smell of burning was wafted away on the breeze. As soon as the flame tinged her fingers, Cordelia dropped the envelope, still burning, and watched it twist and turn as it floated down small and frail as a snowflake to be lost at last in the Cam. She said:

'Your lover shot himself. That is all that either of us need to remember now or ever.'

*

They didn't speak again about Ronald Callender's death, but walked silently along the elm-lined path towards the Backs. At one point Miss Leaming glanced at Cordelia and said in a tone of angry petulance:

'You look surprisingly well!'

Cordelia supposed that this brief outburst was the resentment of the middle-aged at the resilience of the young which could so quickly recover from physical disaster. It had only taken one night of long and deep sleep to return her to the state which Bernie, with irritating coyness, used to describe as bright-eyed and bushy-tailed. Even without the benison of a hot bath the broken skin on her shoulders and back had healed cleanly. Physically, the events of the last fortnight had left her unscathed. She wasn't so sure about Miss Leaming. The sleek platinum hair was still swathed and shaped immaculately to the bones of the head; she still carried her clothes with cool distinction as if it were important to appear the competent and unharassed helpmate of a famous man. But the pale skin was now tinged with grey; her eyes were deeply shadowed, and the incipient lines at the side of the mouth and across the forehead had deepened so that the face, for the first time, looked old and strained.

They passed through King's Gate and turned to the right. Cordelia had found a place and had parked the Mini within a few yards of the gate; Miss Leaming's Rover was further down Queen's Road. She shook hands firmly but briefly with Cordelia and said goodbye as unemotionally as if they were Cambridge acquaintances, parting with unusual formality after an unexpected meeting at Evensong. She didn't smile. Cordelia watched the tall, angular figure striding down the path under the trees towards John's Gate. She didn't look back. Cordelia wondered when, if ever, they would see each other again. It was difficult to believe that they had met only on four occasions. They had nothing in common except their sex, although Cordelia had realized during the days following Ronald Callender's murder the strength of that female allegiance. As Miss Leaming herself had said, they didn't even like each other. Yet each held the other's safety in her hands. There were moments when their secret almost horrified Cordelia by its immensity. But these were few and would get fewer. Time would inevitably diminish its importance. Life would go on. Neither of them would ever forget completely while the brain cells still lived, but she could believe that a day might come when they would glimpse each other across a theatre or restaurant or be borne unprotestingly past on an underground escalator and would wonder whether what they both recalled in the shock of recognition had really once happened. Already, only four days after the inquest, Ronald Callender's murder was beginning to take its place in the landscape of the past.

There was no longer anything to keep her at the cottage. She spent an hour obsessionally cleaning and tidying rooms which no one would enter, probably for weeks. She watered the mugs of cowslips on the sitting-room table. In another three days they would be dead and no one would notice, but she couldn't bear to throw out the still living flowers. She went out to the shed and contemplated the bottle of sour milk and the beef stew. Her first impulse was to take both and empty them down the lavatory. But they were part of the evidence. She wouldn't need that evidence again, but ought it to be completely destroyed? She recalled Bernie's reiterated admonition: 'Never destroy the evidence.' The Super had been full of cautionary tales to emphasize the importance of that maxim. In the end she decided to photograph the exhibits, setting them up on the kitchen table and paying great attention to exposure and light. It seemed a fruitless, somewhat ridiculous, exercise and she was glad when the job was done and the unsavoury contents of bottle and pan could be disposed of. Afterwards she carefully washed them both and left them in the kitchen.

Last of all she packed her bag and stowed her gear in the Mini together with Mark's jerseys and books. Folding the thick wool, she thought of Dr Gladwin sitting in his back garden, his shrunken veins indifferent to the sun. He would find the jerseys useful, but she couldn't take them to him. That kind of gesture might have been accepted from Mark, but not from her.

She locked the door and left the key under a stone. She couldn't face Miss Markland again and had no wish to hand it back to any other member of the family. She would wait until she got to London, then send a brief note to Miss Markland thanking her for her kindness and explaining where the key could be found. She walked for the last time round the garden. She wasn't sure what impulse led her to the well but she came up to it with a shock of surprise. The soil around the rim had been cleared and dug and had been planted with a circle of pansies, daisies and small clumps of alyssum and lobelia, each plant looking well established in its hollow ring of watered earth. It was a bright oasis of colour among the encroaching weeds. The effect was pretty but ridiculous and disquietingly odd. Thus strangely celebrated, the well itself looked obscene, a wooden breast topped by a monstrous nipple. How could she have seen the well cover as a harmless and slightly elegant folly?

Cordelia was torn between pity and revulsion. This must be the work of Miss Markland. The well, which for years had been to her an object of horror, remorse and reluctant fascination, was now to be tended as a shrine. It was ludicrous and pitiable and Cordelia wished that she hadn't seen it. She was suddenly terrified of meeting Miss Markland, of seeing the incipient madness in her eyes. She almost ran out of the garden, pulled the gate shut against the weight of the weeds and drove finally away from the cottage without a backward glance. The case of Mark Callender was finished.

CHAPTER SEVEN

Next morning she went to the Kingly Street office promptly at nine o'clock. The unnaturally hot weather had broken at last and, when she opened the window, a keen breeze shifted the layers of dust on desk and filing cabinet. There was only one letter. This was in a long stiff envelope and was headed with the name and address of Ronald Callender's solicitors. It was very brief.

'Dear Madam, I enclose a cheque for £30.00 being expenses due to you in respect of the investigation which you carried out at the request of the late Sir Ronald Callender into the death of his son Mark Callender. If you agree this sum, I would be grateful if you would sign and return the attached receipt.'

Well, as Miss Leaming had said, it would at least pay part of her fine. She had sufficient money to keep the Agency going for another month. If there were no further case by that time, there was always Miss Feakins and another temporary job. Cordelia thought of the Feakins Secretarial Agency without enthusiasm. Miss Feakins operated, and that was the appropriate word, from a small office as squalid as Cordelia's own, but which had had a desperate gaiety imposed upon it in the form of multi-coloured walls, paper flowers in a variety of urn-like containers, china ornaments and a poster. The poster had always fascinated Cordelia. A curvaceous blonde, clad in brief hot-pants and laughing hysterically, was leap-frogging over her typewriter, a feat she managed to perform with a maximum of exposure while clutching a fistful of five-pound notes in each hand. The caption read:

'Be a Girl Friday and join the fun people. All the best Crusoes are on our books.'

Beneath this poster Miss Feakins, emaciated, indefatigably cheerful and tinselled like a Christmas tree, interviewed a dispirited trail of the old, the ugly and the virtually unemployable. Her milch cows seldom escaped into permanent employment. Miss Feakins would warn against the unspecified dangers of accepting a permanent job much as Victorian mothers warned against sex. But Cordelia liked her. Miss Feakins would welcome her back, her defection to Bernie forgiven, and there would be another of those furtive telephone conversations with the fortunate Crusoe made with one bright eye on Cordelia, a brothel madam recommending her latest recruit to one of her fussier customers. 'Most superior girl – well educated – you'll like her – and a worker!' The emphasis of amazed wonder on the last word was justified. Few of Miss Feakins' temporaries, beguiled by advertisements, seriously expected to have to work. There were other and more efficient agencies but only one Miss Feakins. Bound by pity and an eccentric loyalty, Cordelia had little hope of escaping that glittering eye. A series of temporary jobs with Miss Feakins' Crusoes might, indeed, be all that was left to her. Didn't a conviction for illegal possession of a weapon under Section I of the Firearms Act 1968 count as a criminal record, barring one for life from socially responsible and safe jobs in the civil service and local government?

She settled down at the typewriter, with the yellow telephone directory to hand, to finish sending out the circular letter to the last twenty solicitors on the list. The letter itself embarrassed and depressed her. It had been concocted by Bernie after a dozen preliminary drafts and, at the time, it hadn't seemed too unreasonable. But his death and the Callender case had altered everything. The pompous phrases about a comprehensive professional service, immediate attendance in any part of the country, discreet and experienced operators and moderate fees, struck her as ridiculously, even dangerously, pretentious. Wasn't there something about false representation in the Trades Description Act? But the promise of moderate fees and absolute discretion was valid enough. It was a pity, she thought drily, that she couldn't get a reference from Miss Leaming. Alibis arranged; inquests attended; murders efficiently concealed; perjury at our own special rates.

The raucous burr of the telephone startled her. The office was so quiet and still that she had taken it for granted that no one would call. She stared at the instrument for several seconds, wide-eyed and suddenly afraid, before stretching out her hand.

The voice was calm and assured, polite but in no way deferential. It uttered no threat, yet to Cordelia, every word was explicit with menace.

'Miss Cordelia Gray? This is New Scotland Yard. We wondered

whether you would be back at your office yet. Could you please make it convenient to call here sometime later today? Chief Superintendent Dalgliesh would like to see you.'

*

It was ten days later that Cordelia was called for the third time to New Scotland Yard. The bastion of concrete and glass off Victoria Street was, by now, fairly familiar to her although she still entered it with a sense of temporarily discarding part of her identity, like leaving shoes outside a mosque.

Superintendent Dalgliesh had imposed little of his own personality on his room. The books in the regulation bookcase were obviously textbooks on law, copies of regulations and Acts of Parliament, dictionaries and books of reference. The only picture was a large water-colour of the old Norman Shaw building on the Embankment painted from the river, an agreeable study in greys and soft ochres lit by the bright golden wings of the RAF Memorial. On this visit, as on previous occasions, there was a bowl of roses on his desk, garden roses with sturdy stems and thorns curved like strong beaks, not the etiolated scentless blooms of a West End florist.

Bernie had never described him; had only fathered on him his own obsessive, unheroic, rough-hewn philosophy. Cordelia, bored by his very name, had asked no questions. But the Superintendent she had pictured was very difficult from the tall, austere figure who had risen to shake her hand when she first came into this room and the dichotomy between her private imaginings and the reality had been disconcerting. Irrationally, she had felt a twinge of irritation against Bernie for so putting her at a disadvantage. He was old of course, over forty at least, but not as old as she had expected. He was dark, very tall and loose-limbed where she had expected him to be fair, thickset and stocky. He was serious and spoke to her as if she were a responsible adult, not avuncular and condescending. His face was sensitive without being weak and she liked his hands and his voice and the way she could see the structure of his bones under the skin. He sounded gentle and kind, which was cunning since she knew that he was dangerous and cruel, and she had to keep reminding herself of how he had treated Bernie. At some moments during the interrogation she had actually wondered whether he could be Adam Dalgliesh the poet.

They had never been alone together. On each of her visits a policewoman, introduced as Sergeant Mannering, had been present, seated at the side of the desk with her notebook. Cordelia felt that she knew Sergeant Mannering well having met her at school in the person of the head girl, Teresa Campion-Hook. The two girls could have been sisters. No acne had ever marked their shiningly clean skins; their fair hair curled at precisely the regulation length above their uniformed collars; their voices were calm, authoritarian, determinedly cheerful but never strident; they exuded an ineffable confidence in the justice and logic of the universe and the rightness of their own place in it. Sergeant Mannering had smiled briefly at Cordelia as she came in. The look was open, not overtly friendly since too generous a smile might prejudice the case, but not censorious either. It was a look which disposed Cordelia to imprudence; she disliked looking a fool before that competent gaze.

She had at least had time before her first visit to decide on tactics. There was little advantage and much danger in concealing facts which an intelligent man could easily discover for himself. She would disclose, if asked, that she had discussed Mark Callender with the Tillings and his tutor; that she had traced and interviewed Mrs Goddard; that she had visited Dr Gladwin. She decided to say nothing about the attempt on her life or about her visit to Somerset House. She knew which facts it would be vital to conceal: Ronald Callender's murder; the clue in the prayer book; the actual way in which Mark had died. She told herself firmly that she mustn't be drawn into discussing the case, mustn't talk about herself, her life, her present job, her ambitions. She remembered what Bernie had told her. 'In this country, if people won't talk, there's nothing you can do to make them, more's the pity. Luckily for the police most people just can't keep their mouths shut. The intelligent ones are the worst. They just have to show how clever they are, and once you've got them discussing the case, even discussing it generally, then you've got them.' Cordelia reminded herself of the advice she had given to Elizabeth Leaming: 'Don't embroider, don't invent, don't be afraid to say you can't remember.'

Dalgliesh was speaking:

'Have you thought of consulting a solicitor, Miss Gray?'

'I haven't got a solicitor.'

'The Law Society can give you the names of some very reliable and helpful ones. I should think about it seriously if I were you.'

'But I should have to pay him, shouldn't I? Why should I need a solicitor when I'm telling the truth?'

'It's when people start telling the truth that they most often feel the need of a solicitor.'

'But I've always told the truth. Why should I lie?' The rhetorical question was a mistake. He answered it seriously as if she had really wanted to know.

'Well, it could be to protect yourself – which I don't think likely – or to protect someone else. The motive for that could be love, fear, or a sense of justice. I don't think you've known any of the people in this case long enough to care for them deeply so that rules out love, and I don't think you would be very easy to frighten. So we're left with justice. A very dangerous concept, Miss Gray.'

She had been closely questioned before. The Cambridge police had been very thorough. But this was the first time she had been questioned by someone who knew; knew that she was lying; knew that Mark Callender hadn't killed himself; knew, she felt desperately, all there was to know. She had to force herself to an acceptance of reality. He couldn't possibly be sure. He hadn't any legal proof and he never would have. There was no one alive to tell him the truth except Elizabeth Leaming and herself. And she wasn't going to tell. Dalgliesh could beat against her will with his implacable logic, his curious kindness, his courtesy, his patience. But she wouldn't talk, and in England there was no way in which he could make her.

When she didn't reply, he said cheerfully:

'Well, let's see how far we've got. As a result of your enquiries you suspected that Mark Callender might have been murdered. You haven't admitted that to me but you made your suspicions plain when you visited Sergeant Maskell of the Cambridge police. You subsequently traced his mother's old nurse and learned from her something of his early life, of the Callender marriage, of Mrs Callender's death. Following that visit you went to see Dr Gladwin, the general practitioner who had looked after Mrs Callender before she died. By a simple ruse you ascertained the blood group of Ronald Callender. There would only be point in that if you suspected that Mark wasn't the child of his parents' marriage. You then did what I would have done in your place, visited Somerset House to examine Mr George Bottley's will. That was sensible. If you suspect murder, always consider who stands to gain by it.'

So he had found out about Somerset House and the call to Dr Venables. Well, it was to be expected. He had credited her with his own brand of intelligence. She had behaved as he would have behaved.

She still didn't speak. He said:

'You didn't tell me about your fall down the well. Miss Markland did.'

'That was an accident. I don't remember anything about it, but I must have decided to explore the well and overbalanced. I was always rather intrigued by it.'

'I don't think it was an accident, Miss Gray. You couldn't have pulled the lid free without a rope. Miss Markland tripped over a rope, but it was coiled neatly and half-hidden in the undergrowth. Would you have even troubled to detach it from the hook if you'd only been exploring?'

'I don't know. I can't remember anything that happened before I fell. My first memory is hitting the water. And I don't see what this has to do with Sir Ronald Callender's death.'

'It might have a great deal to do with it. If someone tried to kill you, and I think that they did, that person could have come from Garforth House.'

'Why?'

'Because the attempt on your life was probably connected with your investigation into Mark Callender's death. You had become a danger to someone. Killing is a serious business. The professionals don't like it unless it's absolutely essential and even the amateurs are less happy-go-lucky about murder than you might expect. You must have become a very dangerous woman to someone. Someone replaced that well lid, Miss Gray; you didn't fall through solid wood.'

Cordelia still said nothing. There was silence, then he spoke again:

'Miss Markland told me that after your rescue from the well she was reluctant to leave you alone. But you insisted that she should go. You told her that you weren't afraid to be alone in the cottage because you had a gun.'

Cordelia was surprised how much this small betrayal hurt. Yet, how could she blame Miss Markland? The Superintendent would have known just how to handle her, probably persuaded her that frankness was in Cordelia's own interest. Well, she could at least betray in her turn. And this explanation, at least, would have the authority of truth.

'I wanted to get rid of her. She told me some dreadful story about her illegitimate child falling down the well to his death. I'd only just been rescued myself. I didn't want to hear it, I couldn't bear it just then. I told her a lie about the gun just to make her go. I didn't ask her to confide in me, it wasn't fair. It was only a way of asking for help and I hadn't any to give.'

'And didn't you want to get rid of her for another reason? Didn't you know that your assailant would have to return that night; that the well cover would have to be dragged clear again if your death were to look like an accident?'

'If I'd really thought that I was in any danger I should have begged her to take me with her to Summertrees House. I wouldn't have waited alone in the cottage without my gun.'

'No, Miss Gray, I believe that. You wouldn't have waited there alone in the cottage that night without your gun.'

For the first time Cordelia was desperately afraid. This wasn't a game. It never had been, although at Cambridge the police interrogation had held some of the unreality of a formal contest in which the result was both foreseeable and unworrying since one of the opponents didn't even know he was playing. It was real enough now. If she were tricked, persuaded, coerced into telling him the truth, she would go to prison. She was an accessory after the fact. How many years did one get for helping to conceal murder? She had read somewhere that Holloway smelt. They would take away her clothes. She would be shut up in a claustrophobic cell. There was remission for good conduct but how could one be good in prison? Perhaps they would send her to an open prison. Open. It was a contradiction in terms. And how would she live afterwards? How would she get a job? What real personal freedom could there ever be for those whom society labelled delinquent?

She was terrified for Miss Leaming. Where was she now? She had never dared ask Dalgliesh, and Miss Leaming's name had hardly been mentioned. Was she even now in some other room of New

Scotland Yard being similarly questioned? How reliable would she be under pressure? Were they planning to confront the two conspirators with each other? Would the door suddenly open and Miss Leaming be brought in, apologetic, remorseful, truculent? Wasn't that the usual ploy, to interview conspirators separately until the weaker broke down? And who would prove the weaker?

She heard the Superintendent's voice. She thought he sounded rather sorry for her.

'We have some confirmation that the pistol was in your possession that night. A motorist tells us that he saw a parked car on the road about three miles from Garforth House and when he stopped to enquire if he could help he was threatened by a young woman with a gun.'

Cordelia remembered that moment, the sweetness and silence of the summer night suddenly overlaid by his hot, alcoholic breath.

'He must have been drinking. I suppose the police stopped him for a breath test later that night and now he's decided to come up with this story. I don't know what he expects to gain by it but it isn't true. I wasn't carrying a gun. Sir Ronald took the pistol from me on my first night at Garforth House.'

'The Metropolitan Police stopped him just over the force border. I think he may persist in his story. He was very definite. Of course, he hasn't identified you yet but he was able to describe the car. His story is that he thought you were having trouble with it and stopped to help. You misunderstood his motives and threatened him with a gun.'

'I understood his motives perfectly. But I didn't threaten him with a gun.'

'What did you say, Miss Gray?'

'Leave me alone or I'll kill you.'

'Without a gun, surely that was an empty threat?'

'It would always have been an empty threat. But it made him go.'

'What exactly did happen?'

'I had a spanner in the front pocket of the car and when he shoved his face in at the window I grasped that and threatened him with it. But no one in his right senses could have mistaken a spanner for a gun!'

But he hadn't been in his right senses. The only person who had seen the gun in her possession that night was a motorist who hadn't been sober. This, she knew, was a small victory. She had resisted the momentary temptation to change her story. Bernie had been right. She recalled his advice; the Superintendent's advice; this time she could almost hear it spoken in his deep, slightly husky voice: 'If you're tempted to crime, stick to your original statement. There's nothing that impresses the jury more than consistency. I've seen the most unlikely defence succeed simply because the accused stuck to his story. After all, it's only someone else's word against yours; with a competent counsel that's half-way to a reasonable doubt.'

The Superintendent was speaking again. Cordelia wished that she could concentrate more clearly on what he was saying. She hadn't been sleeping very soundly for the past ten days – perhaps that had something to do with this perpetual tiredness.

'I think that Chris Lunn paid you a visit on the night he died. There's no other reason that I could discover why he should have been on that road. One of the witnesses to the accident said that he came out in the little van from that side road as if all the devils in hell were following him. Someone was following him – you, Miss Gray.'

'We've had this conversation before. I was on my way to see Sir Ronald.'

'At that hour? And in such a hurry?'

'I wanted to see him urgently to tell him that I'd decided to drop the case. I couldn't wait.'

'But you did wait, didn't you? You went to sleep in the car on the side of the road. That's why it was nearly an hour after you'd been seen at the accident before you arrived at Garforth House.'

'I had to stop. I was tired and I knew it wasn't safe to drive on.'

'But you knew, too, that it was safe to sleep. You knew that the person you had most to fear from was dead.'

Cordelia didn't reply. A silence fell on the room but it seemed to her a companionable not an accusing silence. She wished that she wasn't so tired. Most of all, she wished that she had someone to talk to about Ronald Callender's murder. Bernie wouldn't have been any help here. To him the moral dilemma at the heart of the crime would have held no interest, no validity, would have seemed a wilful confusion of straightforward facts. She could imagine his coarse and facile comment on Eliza Leaming's relations with Lunn. But the Superintendent might have understood. She could imagine herself talking to him. She recalled Ronald Callender's words that love was as destructive as hate. Would Dalgliesh assent to that bleak philosophy? She wished that she could ask him. This, she recognized, was her real danger – not the temptation to confess but the longing to confide. Did he know how she felt? Was this too, part of his technique?

There was a knock at the door. A uniformed constable came in and handed a note to Dalgliesh. The room was very quiet while he read it. Cordelia made herself look at his face. It was grave and expressionless and he continued looking at the paper long after he must have assimilated its brief message.

She thought that he was making up his mind to something. After a minute he said:

'This concerns someone you know, Miss Gray. Elizabeth Leaming is dead. She was killed two days ago when the car she was driving went off the coast road south of Amalfi. This note is confirmation of identity.'

Cordelia was swept with relief so immense that she felt physically sick. She clenched her fist and felt the sweat start on her brow. She began to shiver with cold. It never occurred to her that he might be lying. She knew him to be ruthless and clever but she had always taken it for granted that he wouldn't lie to her. She said in a whisper:

'May I go home now?'

'Yes. I don't think there's much point in your staying, do you?'

'She didn't kill Sir Ronald. He took the gun from me. He took the gun – '

Something seemed to have happened in her throat. The words wouldn't come out.

'That's what you've been telling me. I don't think you need trouble to say it again.'

'When do I have to come back?'

'I don't think you need come back unless you decide that there's something you want to tell me. In that well-known phrase, you were asked to help the police. You have helped the police. Thank you.'

She had won. She was free. She was safe, and with Miss Leaming dead, that safety depended only on herself. She needn't come back again to this horrible place. The relief, so unexpected and so unbelievable, was too great to be borne. Cordelia burst into dramatic and uncontrollable crying. She was aware of Sergeant Mannering's low exclamation of concern and of a folded white handkerchief handed to her by the Superintendent. She buried her face in the clean, laundry-smelling linen and blurted out her pent-up misery and anger. Strangely enough – and the oddness of it struck her even in the middle of her anguish – her misery was centred on Bernie. Lifting a face disfigured with tears and no longer caring what he thought of her, she blurted out a final, irrational protest:

'And after you'd sacked him, you never enquired how he got on. You didn't even come to the funeral!'

He had brought a chair over and had seated himself beside her. He handed her a glass of water. The glass was very cold but comforting and she was surprised to find how thirsty she was. She sipped the cold water and sat there hiccuping gently. The hiccups made her want to laugh hysterically but she controlled herself. After a few minutes he said gently:

'I'm sorry about your friend. I didn't realize that your partner was the Bernie Pryde who once worked with me. It's rather worse than that, actually, I'd forgotten all about him. If it's any consolation to you, this case might have ended rather differently if I hadn't.'

'You sacked him. All he ever wanted was to be a detective and you wouldn't give him a chance.'

'The Metropolitan Police hiring and firing regulations aren't quite as simple as that. But it's true that he might still have been a policeman if it hadn't been for me. But he wouldn't have been a detective.'

'He wasn't that bad.'

'Well, he was, you know. But I'm beginning to wonder if I didn't underrate him.'

Cordelia turned to hand him back the glass and met his eyes. They smiled at each other. She wished that Bernie could have heard him.

*

Half an hour later Dalgliesh was seated opposite the Assistant Commissioner in the latter's office. The two men disliked each other but only one of them knew this and he was the one to whom it didn't matter. Dalgliesh made his report, concisely, logically, without referring to his notes. This was his invariable habit. The AC had always thought it unorthodox and conceited and he did so now. Dalgliesh ended:

'As you can imagine, sir, I'm not proposing to commit all that to paper. There's no real evidence and as Bernie Pryde used to tell us, hunch is a good servant but a poor master. God, how that man could churn out his horrible platitudes! He wasn't unintelligent, not totally without judgement, but everything, including ideas, came apart in his hands. He had a mind like a police notebook. Do you remember the Clandon case, homicide by shooting? It was in 1954 I think.'

'Ought I to?'

'No. But it would have been helpful if I had.'

'I don't really know what you're talking about, Adam. But if I understand you aright, you suspect that Ronald Callender killed his son. Ronald Callender is dead. You suspect that Chris Lunn tried to murder Cordelia Gray. Lunn is dead. You suggest that Elizabeth Leaming killed Ronald Callender. Elizabeth Leaming is dead.'

'Yes, it's all conveniently tidy.'

'I suggest we leave it that way. The Commissioner incidentally has had a telephone call from Dr Hugh Tilling, the psychiatrist. He's outraged because his son and daughter have been questioned about Mark Callender's death. I'm prepared to explain his civil duties to Dr Tilling, he's already well aware of his rights, if you really feel it necessary. But will anything be gained by seeing the two Tillings again?'

'I don't think so.'

'Or by bothering the Sûreté about that French girl who Miss Markland claims visited him at the cottage?'

'I think we can spare ourselves that embarrassment. There's only one person now alive who knows the truth of these crimes and she's proof against any interrogation we can use. I can comfort myself with the reason. With most suspects we have an invaluable ally lurking at the back of their minds to betray them. But whatever lies she's been telling, she's absolutely without guilt.'

'Do you think that she's deluded herself that it's all true?'

'I don't think that young woman deludes herself about anything. I took to her, but I'm glad I shan't be encountering her again. I dislike being made to feel during a perfectly ordinary interrogation that I'm corrupting the young.'

'So we can tell the Minister that his chum died by his own hand?'

'You can tell him that we are satisfied that no living finger pressed that trigger. But perhaps not. Even he might be capable of reasoning that one out. Tell him that he can safely accept the verdict of the inquest.'

'It would have saved a great deal of public time if he'd accepted it in the first place.'

The two men were silent for a moment. Then Dalgliesh said:

'Cordelia Gray was right. I ought to have enquired what happened to Bernie Pryde.'

'You couldn't be expected to. That wasn't part of your duties.'

'Of course not. But then one's more serious neglects seldom are part of one's duty. And I find it ironic and oddly satisfying that Pryde took his revenge. Whatever mischief that child was up to in Cambridge, she was working under his direction.'

'You're becoming more philosophical, Adam.'

'Only less obsessive, or perhaps merely older. It's good to be able to feel occasionally that there are some cases which are better left unsolved.'

*

The Kingly Street building looked the same, smelt the same. It always would. But there was one difference. Outside the office a man was waiting, a middle-aged man in a tight blue suit, pig eyes sharp as flint among the fleshy folds of the face.

'Miss Gray? I'd nearly given you up. My name's Freeling. I saw your plate and just came up by chance, don't you know.'

His eyes were avaricious, prurient.

'Well now, you're not quite what I expected, not the usual kind of private eye.'

'Is there anything I can do for you, Mr Freeling?'

He gazed furtively round the landing, seeming to find its sordidness reassuring.

'It's my lady friend. I've reason to suspect that she's getting a bit on the side. Well – a man likes to know where he stands. You get me?'

Cordelia fitted the key into the lock.

'I understand, Mr Freeling. Won't you come in?'

DEATH OF AN EXPERT WITNESS

Death of
an Expert Witness

BOOK ONE
A Call to Murder

BOOK TWO
Death in a White Coat

BOOK THREE
An Experimental Man

BOOK FOUR
Hanged by the Neck

BOOK FIVE
The Clunch Pit

AUTHOR'S NOTE

There is no official forensic science laboratory in East Anglia and, even if there were, it is in the highest degree improbable that it would have anything in common with Hoggatt's Laboratory, whose staff, like all other characters in this story – even the most unpleasant – are purely imaginary and bear no resemblance to any person living or dead.

P.D.J.

BOOK ONE

A Call to Murder

1

The call had come at 6.12 precisely. It was second nature to him now to note the time by the illuminated dial of his electric bedside clock before he had switched on his lamp, a second after he had felt for and silenced the raucous insistence of the telephone. It seldom had to ring more than once, but every time he dreaded that the peal might have woken Nell. The caller was familiar, the summons expected. It was Detective-Inspector Doyle. The voice, with its softly intimidating suggestion of Irish burr, came to him strong and confident, as if Doyle's great bulk loomed over the bed.

'Doc Kerrison?' The interrogation was surely unnecessary. Who else in this half-empty, echoing house would be answering at 6.12 in the morning? He made no reply and the voice went on.

'We've got a body. On the wasteland – a clunch field – a mile north-east of Muddington. A girl. Strangulation by the look of it. It's probably pretty straightforward but as it's close . . .'

'All right. I'll come.'

The voice expressed neither relief nor gratitude. Why should it? Didn't he always come when summoned? He was paid well enough for his availability, but that wasn't the only reason why he was so obsessively conscientious. Doyle, he suspected, would have respected him more if he had occasionally been less accommodating. He would have respected himself more.

'It's the first turn off the A142 after you leave Gibbet's Cross. I'll have a man posted.'

He replaced the receiver, swung his legs out of bed and, reaching for his pencil and pad, noted the details while they were still fresh in his mind. In a clunch field. That probably meant mud, particularly after yesterday's rain. The window was slightly open at the bottom. He pushed it open, wincing at the rasp of the wood, and put out his head. The rich loamy smell of the fen autumn night washed over his face; strong, yet fresh. The rain had stopped and the sky was a tumult of grey clouds through which the moon, now almost full, reeled like a pale demented ghost. His mind stretched out over the deserted fields and the desolate dykes to the wide moon-bleached sands of the Wash and the creeping fringes of the North Sea. He could fancy that he smelt its medicinal tang in the rain-washed air. Somewhere out there in the darkness, surrounded by all the paraphernalia of violent death, was a body. His mind recalled the familiar ambience of his trade; men moving like black shadows behind the glare of the arc-lights, the police cars tidily parked; the flap of the screens, desultory voices conferring as they watched for the first lights of his approaching car. Already they would be consulting their watches, calculating how long it would be before he could make it.

Shutting the window with careful hands, he tugged trousers over his pyjamas and pulled a polo-necked sweater over his head. Then he picked up his torch, switched off the bedside light and made his way downstairs, treading warily and keeping close to the wall to avoid the creaking treads. But there was no sound from Eleanor's room. He let his mind wander down the twenty yards of landing and the three stairs to the back bedroom where his sixteen-year-old daughter lay. She was always a light sleeper, uncannily sensitive even in sleep to the ring of the telephone. But she couldn't possibly have heard. He had no need to worry about three-year-old William. Once asleep, he never woke before morning.

Actions as well as thought were patterned. His routine never varied. He went first to the small washroom near the back door where his wellington boots, the thick red socks protruding like a pair of amputated feet, stood ready at the door. Pushing up his sleeves over the elbow, he swilled cold water over his hands and arms, then bent down and sluiced the whole of his head. He performed this act of almost ceremonial cleansing before and after every case. He had long ago ceased to ask himself why. It had become as comforting and necessary as a religious ritual, the brief preliminary washing which was like a dedication, the final ablution which was both a necessary chore and an absolution, as if by wiping the smell of his job from his body he could cleanse it from his mind. The water splashed heavily against the glass and, rising to fumble for a towel, he saw his face distorted, the mouth hanging, the heavily lidded eyes half-hidden by glistening weeds of black hair like the surfacing visage of a drowned man. The melancholy of the early hours took hold of him. He thought:

'I'm forty-five next week and what have I achieved? This house, two children, a failed marriage, and a job which I'm frightened of losing because it's the only thing I've made a success of.' The Old Rectory, inherited from his father, was unmortgaged, unencumbered. This wasn't true, he thought, of anything else in his anxiety-ridden life. Love, the lack of it, the growing need, the sudden terrifying hope of it, was only a burden. Even his job, the territory where he moved with most assurance, was hedged with anxiety.

As he dried his hands carefully, finger by finger, the old familiar worry returned, heavy as a morbid growth. He hadn't yet been appointed as Home Office Pathologist in succession to old Dr Stoddard and he very much wanted to be. The official appointment wouldn't give him more money. The police already employed him on an item-of-service basis, and paid generously enough for each case. That and the fees for coroner's post-mortems provided an income which was one of the reasons why his professional colleagues in the pathology department of the district general hospital both envied and resented his unpredictable absences on police work, the long days in court, the inevitable publicity.

Yes, the appointment was important to him. If the Home Office looked elsewhere it would be difficult to justify to the Area Health Authority a continuing private arrangement with the local Force. He wasn't even sure that they would want him. He knew himself to be a good forensic pathologist, reliable, more than competent professionally, almost obsessively thorough and painstaking, a convincing and unflappable witness. The Force knew that their meticulously erected edifices of proof wouldn't fall to pieces under cross-examination when he was in the witness-box, although he sometimes suspected that they found him too scrupulous for complete comfort. But he hadn't the easy masculine camaraderie, the blend of cynicism and *machismo* which had bound old Doc Stoddard so strongly to the Force. If they had to do without him he wouldn't be greatly missed, and he doubted whether they would put themselves out to keep him.

The garage light was blinding. The overhead door swung up easily to his touch and the light splayed out over the gravel of the drive and the unkempt verges of silvered grass. But at least the light wouldn't wake Nell. Her bedroom was at the back of the house. Before switching on the engine he studied his maps. Muddington. It was a town on the edge of his area, about seventeen miles to the north-west, less than half an hour's drive each way if he were lucky. If the laboratory scientists were there already – and Lorrimer, the Senior Biologist, never missed a homicide if he could help it – then there mightn't be much for him to do. Allow, say, an hour at the scene, and with luck he would be home again before Nell woke and she need never know that he had been away. He switched off the garage light. Carefully, as if the gentleness of his touch could somehow silence the engine, he turned on the ignition. The Rover moved slowly into the night.

2

Standing motionless behind the curtains on the front landing, her right hand cupped round the pale flicker of her night-light, Eleanor Kerrison watched the sudden red blaze of the Rover's rear lights as the car stopped at the gate before turning left and accelerating out of sight. She waited until the glare of the headlights had finally faded from view. Then she turned and made her way along the corridor to William's room. She knew that he wouldn't have woken. His sleep was a sensuous gluttony of oblivion. And while he slept she knew that he was safe, that she could be free of anxiety. To watch him then was such a mingled joy of yearning and pity that sometimes, frightened of her waking thoughts but more afraid of the nightmares of sleep, she would carry her night-light into his bedroom and crouch by the cot for an hour or more, her eyes fixed on his sleeping face, her restlessness soothed by his peace.

Although she knew that he wouldn't wake, she turned the handle of the door as carefully as if expecting it to explode. The night-light, burning steadily in its saucer, was unnecessary, its yellow gleam extinguished by the moonlight which streamed through the uncur-tained windows. William, bagged in his grubby sleeping-suit, lay as always on his back, both arms flung above his head. His head had flopped to one side and the thin neck, stretched so still that she could see the pulse beat, looked too fragile to bear the weight of his head. His lips were slightly parted, and she could neither see nor hear the thin whisper of breath. As she watched he suddenly opened sightless eyes, rolled them upwards, then closed them with a sigh and fell again into his little semblance of death.

She closed the door softly behind her and went back to her own room next door. Dragging the eiderdown from her bed, she wrapped it round her shoulders and shuffled her way down the landing to the top of the stairs. The heavily studded oak banister curved down into the darkness of the hall from which the tick of the grandfather clock sounded as unnaturally loud and ominous as a time bomb. The atmosphere of the house came up to her nostrils, sour as a stale vacuum flask, redolent with the sad effluent of stodgy clerical dinners. Placing the night-light against the wall she sat down on the top stair, humping the eiderdown high over her shoulders and gazing into the darkness. The stair-carpet was gritty to her bare soles. Miss Willard never vacuumed it, pleading that her heart couldn't stand the strain of lugging the cleaner from step to step, and her father never appeared to notice the drabness or dirtiness of his house. He was, after all, so seldom there. Sitting rigid in the darkness she thought of her father. Perhaps he was already at the scene of crime. It depended how far he had to drive. If it were on the very fringe of his area he might not be back until lunch-time.

But what she hoped was that he would return before breakfast so that he would find her here, crouched lonely and exhausted on the top stair, waiting for him, frightened because he had left her alone. He would put away the car quietly, leaving the garage open in case the thud of the door woke her, then sneak in like a thief at the back door. She would hear the swirl of water from the downstairs washroom, his footsteps on the tessellated floor of the hall. Then he would look up and see her. He would come running up the stairs, torn between anxiety for her and fear of disturbing Miss Willard, his face suddenly old with weariness and concern as he put his arms round her trembling shoulders.

'Nell, darling, how long have you been here? You shouldn't be out of bed. You'll get cold. Come on, old girl, there's nothing to be frightened of now. I'm back. Look, I'll take you back to bed again and you try to get some sleep. I'll see to the breakfast. Suppose I bring it up on a tray in about half an hour. How would you like that?'

And he would guide her back to her room, cajoling, murmuring reassurance, trying to pretend that he wasn't frightened, frightened that she would start to cry for her mother, that Miss Willard would appear, censorious and whining, complaining that she had to get her sleep, that the precarious little household would fall apart and he would be parted from William. It was William he loved, William he couldn't bear to lose. And he could only keep William and stop the court from giving Mummy custody if she were at home to help care for her brother.

She thought about the day ahead. It was Wednesday, a grey day. Not a black day when she wouldn't see her father at all, but not a yellow day like Sunday, when, unless on call, he might be there most of the time. In the morning, immediately after breakfast, he would be at the public mortuary doing the post-mortem. There would be other autopsies too, those who had died in hospital, the old, the suicides, the accident victims. But the body he was probably examining now would be first on the mortuary table. Murder has priority. Wasn't that what they always said at the Lab? She mused, but without real curiosity, on what he might be doing at this very moment to that unknown cadaver, young or old, male or female. Whatever he was doing, the body wouldn't feel it, wouldn't know about it. The dead had nothing to be frightened of any more, and there was nothing to fear from them. It was the living who held the power to hurt. And suddenly two shadows moved in the darkness of the hall, and she heard her mother's voice, pitched high, frighteningly unfamiliar, a strained, cracked, alien voice.

'Always your job! Your bloody job! And my God, no wonder you're good at it. You haven't the guts to be a real doctor. You made one wrong diagnosis early on and that was the end, wasn't it? You couldn't take responsibility for living bodies, blood that can flow, nerves that can actually feel. All you're fit for is messing about with the dead. It makes you feel good, doesn't it, the way they defer to you? The phone calls at all hours of the day and night, the police escort. Never mind that I'm buried alive here in this bloody fen with your children. You don't even see me any more. I'd be more interesting to you if I were dead and laid out on your slab. At least you'd be forced to take some notice of me.'

Then the low defensive mumble of her father's voice, dispirited, abject. She had listened in the darkness and wanted to call out to him:

'Don't answer her like that! Don't sound so defeated! Can't you understand that it only makes her despise you more?'

His words had come to her in snatches, barely audible.

'It's my job. It's what I do best. It's all that I can do.' And then, more clearly. 'It's what keeps us.'

'Not me. Not any longer.'

And then the slam of the door.

The memory was so vivid that for a second she thought she heard the echo of that slam. She stumbled to her feet, clutching the eiderdown around her, and opened her mouth to call to them. But then she saw that the hall was empty. There was nothing but the faint image of the stained glass in the front door where the moonlight streamed through, the ticking of the clock, the bundle of coats hanging from the hallstand. She sank back again on the stair.

And then she remembered. There was something she had to do. Slipping her hand into her dressing-gown pocket she felt the cold slippery plasticine of her model of Dr Lorrimer. Carefully she drew it out through the folds of the eiderdown and held it close to the flame of the night-light. The model was a little misshapen, the face furred with fluff from her pocket, but it was still intact. She straightened the long limbs and pressed the strands of black cotton she had used for hair more firmly into the scalp. The white coat, cut from an old handkerchief, was particularly successful, she thought. It was a pity that she hadn't been able to use one of his handkerchiefs, a strand of his hair. The model represented more than Dr Lorrimer who had been unkind to her and William, who had practically thrown them out of the laboratory. It stood for the whole of Hoggatt's Lab.

And now to kill it. Gently she knocked the head against the baluster. But the plasticine merely flattened, the head lost its identity. She remodelled it with careful fingers, then held it close to the flame. But the smell was disagreeable and she was afraid that the white linen would burst into flame. She dug the nail of her little finger deeply in behind the left ear. The cut was clean and sharp, right through to the brain. That was better. She sighed, satisfied. Holding the dead creature in her right palm she squeezed the pink plasticine, the white coat, the cotton hair into one amorphous lump. Then, huddling deep into the eiderdown, she sat and waited for the dawn.

The car, a green Morris Minor, had been toppled over the edge of a shallow depression in the wasteland, and had lurched to rest on a grassy plateau about ten feet from the ridge like a clumsy animal going to earth. It must have been there for years, abandoned to the plunderers, an illicit plaything for the local children, a welcome shelter for the occasional vagrant like the seventy-year-old alcoholic who had stumbled on the body. The two front wheels had been removed, and the rusted back wheels with their rotting tyres were firmly embedded in the chalky earth, the paintwork was battered and scratched, the interior stripped of instruments and steering wheel. Two mounted arc-lights, one directed downwards from the top of the bank and the other precariously planted on the edge of the plateau, illumined its stark decrepitude. Thus brightly lit it looked, thought Kerrison, like some grotesque and pretentious modern sculpture, symbolically poised on the brink of chaos. The back seat, its padding springing from the slashed plastic, had been ripped out and hurled to one side.

In the front seat rested the body of the girl. Her legs were decorously planted together, the glazed eyes were slyly half-open, the mouth, devoid of lipstick, was fixed in a drool elongated by two small trickles of blood. They gave a face which must have been pretty, or at least childishly vulnerable, the vacuous look of an adult clown. The thin coat, too thin surely for a night in early November, was pulled waist high. She was wearing stockings; and the suspender clips bit into plump white thighs.

Drawing close to the body, under the watchful eyes of Lorrimer and Doyle, he thought, as he often did at such a scene, that it looked unreal, an anomaly, so singularly and ridiculously out of place that he had to stifle a nervous impulse to laugh. He didn't feel this so strongly when a corpse was far advanced in decay. It was then as if the rotting maggot-infested flesh, or the tags of matted clothing, had already become part of the earth which clung to and enclosed them, no more unnatural or frightening than a clump of compost or a drift of decaying leaves. But here, colours and outlines intensified in the glare, the body, still outwardly so human, looked an absurd burlesque, the skin of the pallid cheek as artificial as the stained plastic of the car against which it rested. It seemed ridiculous that she should be beyond help. As always he had to fight the impulse to fasten his mouth over hers and begin resuscitation, to plunge a needle into the still warm heart.

He had been surprised to find Maxim Howarth, newly appointed director of the Forensic Science Laboratory, at the scene, until he remembered Howarth had said something about following through the next murder case. He supposed that he was expected to instruct. Withdrawing his head from the open door he said:

'It's almost certainly a case of manual throttling. The slight bleeding from the mouth is caused by the tongue being caught between the teeth. Manual strangulation is invariably homicidal. She couldn't have done this herself.'

Howarth's voice was carefully controlled.

'I should have expected more bruising of the neck.'

'That's usual, certainly. There's always some damage to the tissues, although the extent of the bruised area depends on the position of the assailant and victim, the way in which the neck is grasped as well as the degree of pressure. I'd expect to find deep-seated internal bruising, but it's possible to get this without many superficial signs. This happens when the murderer has maintained pressure until death; the vessels have been emptied of blood and the heart stops beating before the hands are removed. The cause of death is asphyxia, and one expects to find the usual signs of this. What is so interesting here is the cadaveric spasm. You'll see that she's clutching the bamboo handle of her bag. The muscles are absolutely rigid, proof that the grasp occurred at or about the moment of death. I've never before seen cadaveric spasm in a case of homicidal manual throttling, and it's interesting. She must have died extraordinarily quickly. But you'll get a clearer idea of what exactly happened when you watch the post-mortem.'

Of course, thought Howarth, the post-mortem. He wondered how early Kerrison would expect to get down to that job. He wasn't afraid that his nerve would fail him, only his stomach, but he wished he hadn't said he would be there. There was no privacy for the dead; the most one could hope for was a certain reverence. It now seemed to him monstrous that tomorrow he, a stranger, would be looking unrebuked at her nakedness. But for the present he had seen enough. He could step aside now without loss of face. Turning up the collar of his Burberry against the chill morning air, he climbed up the slope to the rim of the hollow and stood looking down at the car. This must be what shooting a film was like: the brightly lit scene, the ennui of waiting for the chief actors to appear, the brief moments of activity, the concentrated attention to detail. The body could easily be that of an actress simulating death. He half expected one of the police to dart forward and rearrange her hair.

The night was nearly over. Behind him the eastern sky was already brightening, and the wasteland, which had been a formless void of darkness above the lumpy earth, was assuming an identity and a shape. To the west he could see the outline of houses, probably a council estate, a trim row of identical roofs and square slabs of darkness broken by patterned squares of yellow as the early risers switched on their lights. The track along which his car had bumped, rock-strewn and silver, alien as a moonscape in the glare of the headlights, took shape and direction, became ordinary. Nothing was left mysterious. The place was an arid scrubland between the two ends of the town, litter-strewn and edged with sparse trees above a ditch. He knew that the ditch would be dank with nettles and sour with rotting rubbish, the trees wounded by vandals, the trunks carved with initials, the low branches hanging torn from the boughs. Here was an urban no-man's-land, fit territory for murder.

It was a mistake to have come, of course, he should have realized that the role of voyeur was always ignoble. Few things were more demoralizing than to stand uselessly by while other men demonstrated their professional competence; Kerrison, that connoisseur of death, literally sniffing at the body; the photographers, taciturn, preoccupied with lighting and angles; Inspector Doyle, in charge of a murder case at last, impresario of death, tense with the suppressed excitement of a child at Christmas gloating over a new toy. Once, while waiting for Kerrison to arrive, Doyle had actually laughed, a hearty guffaw, filling the hollow. And Lorrimer? Before touching the body he had briefly crossed himself. It was so small and precise a gesture that Howarth could have missed it, except that nothing that Lorrimer did escaped him. The others seemed unsurprised at the eccentricity. Perhaps they were used to it. Domenica hadn't told him that Lorrimer was religious. But then his sister hadn't told him anything about her lover. She hadn't even told him that the affair was over. But he had needed only to look at Lorrimer's face during the past month to know that. Lorrimer's face, Lorrimer's hands.

Odd that he hadn't noticed how long the fingers were or with what apparent gentleness they had taped the plastic bags over the girl's hands to preserve, as he had tonelessly explained, conscientious in his role of instructor, any evidence under the fingernails. He had taken a sample of blood from the plump flaccid arm, feeling for the vein as carefully as if she could still flinch at the needle's prick.

Lorrimer's hands. Howarth thrust the tormenting, brutally explicit images out of his mind. He had never before resented one of Domenica's lovers. He hadn't even been jealous of her dead husband. It had seemed to him perfectly reasonable that she should eventually wish to marry, just as she might choose, in a fit of boredom or acquisitiveness, to buy herself a fur coat or a new item of jewellery. He had even quite liked Charles Schofield. Why was it then that, even from the first moment, the thought of Lorrimer in his sister's bed had been intolerable. Not that he could ever have been in her bed at least, not at Leamings. He wondered yet again where they had managed to meet, how Domenica had contrived to take a new lover without the whole laboratory and the whole village knowing. How could they have met and where?

It had begun, of course, at that disastrous dinner party twelve months ago. At the time it had seemed both natural and civilized to celebrate the taking-up of his directorship with a small private party at his house for the senior staff. They had, he remembered, eaten melon, followed by bœuf stroganoff and a salad. He and Domenica liked good food and, occasionally, she enjoyed cooking it. He had opened the 1961 claret for them because that was the wine he and Dom had chosen to drink and it hadn't occurred to him to offer his guests less. He and Dom had changed because that was their habit. It amused them to dine in some style, formally separating the working day from their evenings together. It hadn't been his fault that Bill Morgan, the vehicle examiner, had chosen to come in open-necked shirt and corduroys; neither he nor Dom had cared a damn what their guests chose to wear. If Bill Morgan felt awkward about these unimportant shibboleths of taste, he should learn either to change his clothes or to develop more social confidence in his sartorial eccentricities.

It had never occurred to Howarth that the six senior staff sitting awkwardly around his table in the candlelight, unmellowed even by the wine, would see the whole occasion as an elaborate gastronomic charade designed to demonstrate his social and intellectual superiority. At least Paul Middlemass, the Principal Scientific Officer Document Examiner, had appreciated the wine, drawing the bottle across the table towards him and refilling his glass, his lazy ironic eyes watching his host. And Lorrimer? Lorrimer had eaten practically nothing, had drunk less, pushing his glass almost petulantly aside and fixing his great smouldering eyes on Domenica as if he had never before seen a woman. And that, presumably, had been the beginning of it. How it had progressed, when and how they had continued to meet, how it had ended, Domenica hadn't confided.

The dinner party had been a private and public fiasco. But what, he wondered, had the senior staff expected? An evening of solid drinking in the private snug in the Moonraker? A free-for-all jollification in the village hall for the whole Laboratory including the cleaner, Mrs Bidwell, and old Scobie, the Laboratory attendant? 'Knees Up Mother Brown' in the public bar? Perhaps they had thought that the first move should have come from their side. But that was to admit that there were two sides. The conventional sophistry was that the Laboratory worked as a team harnessed by a common purpose, reins lightly but firmly in the director's hands. That had worked well enough at Bruche. But there he had directed a research laboratory with a common discipline. How could you direct a team when your staff practised half a dozen different scientific disciplines, used their own methods, were responsible for their own results, stood finally alone to justify and defend them in the only place where the quality of a forensic scientist's work could properly be judged, the witness-box of a court of law? It was one of the loneliest places on earth, and he had never stood there.

Old Dr Mac, his predecessor, had, he knew, taken the occasional case, to keep his hand in as he would say, trotting out to a scene of crime like an old bloodhound happily sniffing after half-forgotten scents, doing the analysis himself, and finally appearing, like a resurrected Old Testament prophet in the witness-box, greeted by the judge with dry judicial compliments, and boisterously welcomed in the bar by counsel like a long-missed old reprobate drinking comrade happily restored to them. But that could never be his way. He had been appointed to manage the Laboratory and he would manage it in his own style. He wondered, morbidly introspective in the cold light of dawn, whether his decision to see the next murder case through from the call to the scene of crime to the trial had really arisen from a desire to learn or merely from a craven wish to impress or, worse, to propitiate, his staff, to show them that he valued their skills, that he wanted to be one of the team. If so, it had been one more error of judgement to add to the bleak arithmetic of failure since he had taken up his new job.

It looked as if they had nearly finished. The girl's rigid fingers had been prised from her handbag and Doyle's hands, gloved, were spreading out its few contents on a plastic sheet laid on the bonnet of the car. Howarth could just make out the shape of what looked like a small purse, a lipstick, a folded sheet of paper. A love letter probably, poor little wretch. Had Lorrimer written letters to Domenica? he wondered. He was always first at the door when the post arrived, and usually brought his sister her letters. Perhaps Lorrimer had known that. But he must have written. There must have been assignations. Lorrimer would hardly have risked telephoning from the Laboratory or from home in the evenings when he, Howarth, might have taken the call.

They were moving the body now. The mortuary van had moved closer to the rim of the hollow and the stretcher was being manoeuvred into place. The police were dragging out the screens from their van, ready to enclose the scene of crime. Soon there would be the little clutch of spectators, the curious children shooed away by the adults, the press photographers. He could see Lorrimer and Kerrison conferring together a little way apart, their backs turned, the two dark heads close together. Doyle was closing his notebook and supervising the removal of the body as if it were a precious exhibit which he was frightened someone would break. The light was strengthening.

He waited while Kerrison climbed up beside him and together they walked towards the parked cars. Howarth's foot struck a beer-can. It clattered across the path and bounced against what looked like the battered frame of an old pram, with a bang like a pistol shot. The noise startled him. He said pettishly:

'What a place to die! Where in God's name are we exactly? I just followed the police cars.'

'It's called the clunch field. That's the local name for the soft chalk they mined here from the Middle Ages onwards. There isn't any hard building stone hereabouts, so they used clunch for most domestic building and even for some church interiors. There's an example in the Lady Chapel at Ely. Most villages had their clunch pits. They're overgrown now. Some are quite pretty in the spring and summer, little oases of wild flowers.'

He gave the information almost tonelessly, like a dutiful guide repeating by rote the official spiel. Suddenly he swayed and reached for the support of his car door. Howarth wondered if he were ill or whether this was the extremity of tiredness. Then the pathologist straightened himself and said, with an attempt at briskness:

'I'll do the PM at nine o'clock tomorrow at St Luke's. The hall porter will direct you. I'll leave a message.'

He nodded a goodbye, forced a smile, then eased himself into his car and slammed the door. The Rover bumped slowly towards the road.

Howarth was aware that Doyle and Lorrimer were beside him. Doyle's excitement was almost palpable. He turned to look across the clunch field to the distant row of houses, their yellow brick walls and mean square windows now plainly visible.

'He's over there somewhere. In bed probably. That is, if he doesn't live alone. It wouldn't do to be up and about too early, would it? No, he'll be lying there wondering how to act ordinary, waiting for the anonymous car, the ring at the door. If he's on his own, it'll be different, of course. He'll be creeping about in the half-dark wondering if he ought to burn his suit, scraping the mud off his shoes. Only he won't be able to get it all off. Not every trace. And he won't have a boiler big enough for the suit. And even if he had, what will he say when we ask for it? So maybe he'll be doing nothing. Just lying there and waiting. He won't be asleep. He didn't sleep last night. And he won't be sleeping again for quite a time.'

Howarth felt slightly sick. He had eaten a small and early dinner and knew himself to be hungry. The sensation of nausea on an empty stomach was peculiarly unpleasant. He controlled his voice, betraying nothing but a casual interest.

'You think it's relatively straightforward then?'

'Domestic murder usually is. And I reckon that this is a domestic murder. Married kid, torn stump of a ticket for the local Oddfellows' hop, letter in her bag threatening her if she doesn't leave another bloke alone. A stranger wouldn't have known about this place. And she wouldn't have come here with him even if he had. By the look of her, they were sitting there cosily together before he got his hands on her throat. It's just a question of whether the two of them set off home together or whether he left early and waited for her.'

'Do you know yet who she is?'

'Not yet. There's no diary in the bag. That kind don't keep diaries. But I shall know in about half an hour.'

He turned to Lorrimer.

'The exhibits should be at the Lab by nine or thereabouts. You'll give this priority?'

Lorrimer's voice was harsh.

'Murder gets priority. You know that.'

Doyle's exultant, self-satisfied bellow jangled Howarth's nerves.

'Thank God something does! You're taking your time over the Gutteridge case. I was in the Biology Department yesterday and Bradley said the report wasn't ready; he was working on a case for the defence. We all know the great fiction that the Lab is independent of the police and I'm happy to go along with it most of the time. But old Hoggatt founded the place as a police lab, and when the chips are down that's what it's all about. So do me a favour. Get moving with this one for me. I want to get chummy and get him quickly.'

He was rocking gently on his heels, his smiling face uplifted to the dawn like a happy dog sniffing at the air, euphoric with the exhilaration of the hunt. It was odd, thought Howarth, that he didn't recognize the cold menace in Lorrimer's voice.

'Hoggatt's does an occasional examination for the defence if they ask us and if the exhibit is packed and submitted in the approved way. That's departmental policy. We're not yet a police lab even if you do walk in and out of the place as if it's your own kitchen. And I decide priorities in my Laboratory. You'll get your report as soon as it's ready. In the meantime, if you want to ask questions, come to me, not to my junior staff. And, unless you're invited, keep out of my Laboratory.'

Without waiting for an answer, he walked over to his car. Doyle looked after him in a kind of angry bewilderment.

'Bloody hell! His Lab! What's wrong with him? Lately he's been as touchy as a bitch on heat. He'll find himself on a brain-shrinker's couch or in the bin if he doesn't get a hold of himself.'

Howarth said coldly:

'He's right, of course. Any enquiry about the work should be made to him, not to a member of his staff. And it's usual to ask permission before walking into a laboratory.'

The rebuke stung. Doyle frowned. His face hardened. Howarth had a disconcerting glimpse of the barely controlled aggression beneath the mask of casual good humour. Doyle said:

'Old Dr Mac used to welcome the police in his lab. He had this odd idea, you see, that helping the police was what it was all about. But if we're not wanted, you'd better talk to the chief. No doubt he'll issue his instructions.'

He turned on his heel and made off towards his car without waiting for a reply. Howarth thought:

'Damn Lorrimer! Everything he touches goes wrong for me.' He felt a spasm of hatred so intense, so physical that it made him retch. If only Lorrimer's body were sprawled at the bottom of the clunch pit. If only it were Lorrimer's cadaver which would be cradled in porcelain on the post-mortem table next day, laid out for ritual evisceration. He knew what was wrong with him. The diagnosis was as simple as it was humiliating: that self-infecting fever of the blood which could lie deceptively dormant, then flare, as now, into torment. Jealousy, he thought, was as physical as fear; the same dryness of the mouth, the thudding heart, the restlessness which destroyed appetite and peace. And he knew now that, this time, the sickness was incurable. It made no difference that the affair was over, that Lorrimer, too, was suffering. Reason couldn't cure it, nor, he suspected, could distance, nor time. It could be ended only by death; Lorrimer's or his own.

4

At half past six, in the front bedroom of 2 Acacia Close, Chevisham, Susan Bradley, wife of the Higher Scientific Officer in the Biology Department of Hoggatt's Laboratory, was welcomed by the faint, plaintive wail of her two-month-old baby, hungry for her first feed of the day. Susan switched on the bedside lamp, a pink glow under its frilled shade, and reaching for her dressing-gown, shuffled sleepily to the bathroom next door, and then to the nursery. It was a small room at the back of the house, little more than a box, but when she pressed down the switch of the low-voltage nursery light she felt again a glow of maternal, proprietorial pride. Even in her sleepy morning daze the first sight of the nursery lifted her heart; the nursing chair with its back decorated with rabbits; the matching changing-table fitted with drawers for the baby's things; the wicker cot in its stand which she had lined with a pink, blue and white flowered cotton to match the curtains; the bright fringe of nursery-rhyme characters which Clifford had pasted round the wall.

With the sound of her footsteps the cries became stronger. She picked up the warm, milky-smelling cocoon and crooned reassurance. Immediately the cries ceased and Debbie's moist mouth, opening and shutting like a fish, sought her breast, the small wrinkled fists, freed from the blanket, unfurled to clutch against her crumpled nightdress. The books said to change baby first, but she could never bear to make Debbie wait. And there was another reason. The walls of the modern house were thin, and she didn't want the sound of crying to wake Cliff.

But suddenly he was at the door, swaying slightly, his pyjama jacket gaping open. Her heart sank. She made her voice sound bright, matter-of-fact.

'I hoped she hadn't woken you, darling. But it's after half-past six. She slept over seven hours. Getting better.'

'I was awake already.'

'Go back to bed, Cliff. You can get in another hour's sleep.'

'I can't sleep.'

He looked round the little nursery with a puzzled frown, as if disconcerted not to find a chair. Susan said:

'Bring in the stool from the bathroom. And put on your dressing-gown. You'll catch cold.'

He placed the stool against the wall and crouched there in sullen misery. Susan raised her cheek from resting against the soft furriness of the baby's head. The small, snub-nosed leech latched on to her breast, fingers splayed in an ecstasy of content. Susan told herself that she must keep calm, mustn't let nerves and muscles knot themselves into the familiar ache of worry. Everyone said that it was bad for the milk. She said quietly:

'What's wrong, darling?'

But she knew what was wrong. She knew what he would say. She felt a new and frightening sense of resentment that she couldn't even feed Debbie in peace. And she wished he would do up his pyjamas. Sitting like that, slumped and half-naked, he looked almost dissolute. She wondered what was happening to her. She had never felt like this about Cliff before Debbie was born.

'I can't go on. I can't go into the Lab today.'

'Are you ill?'

But she knew that he wasn't ill, at least not yet. But he would be ill if something wasn't done about Edwin Lorrimer. The old misery descended on her. People wrote in books about a black weight of worry, and they were right, that was just how it felt, a perpetual physical burden which dragged at the shoulders and the heart, denying joy, even destroying, she thought bitterly, their pleasure in Debbie. Perhaps in the end it would destroy even love. She didn't speak but settled her small, warm burden more comfortably against her arm.

'I've got to give up the job. It's no use, Sue. I can't go on. He's got me in such a state that I'm as useless as he says I am.'

'But Cliff, you know that isn't true. You're a good worker. There were never complaints about you at your last lab.'

'I wasn't an HSO then. Lorrimer thinks I ought never to have been promoted. He's right.'

'He isn't right. Darling, you musn't let him sap your confidence. That's fatal. You're a conscientious, reliable forensic biologist. You mustn't worry if you're not as quick as the others. That isn't important. Dr Mac always said it's accuracy that counts. What does it matter if you take your time? You get the answer right in the end.'

'Not any longer. I can't even do a simple peroxidase test now without fumbling. If he comes within two feet of me my hands start shaking. And he's begun checking all my results. I've just finished examining the stains on the mallet from the suspected Pascoe murder. But he'll work late tonight doing it again. And he'll make sure that the whole Biology Department knows why.'

Cliff couldn't, she knew, stand up to bullying or sarcasm. Perhaps it was because of his father. The old man was paralysed now after a stroke and she supposed that she ought to feel sorry for him lying there in his hospital bed, useless as a felled tree, mouth slavering, only the angry eyes moving in impotent fury from face to watching face. But from what Cliff had let slip he had been a poor father, an unpopular and unsuccessful schoolmaster yet with unreasonable ambitions for his only son. Cliff had been terrified of him. What Cliff needed was encouragement and affection. Who cared if he never rose any higher than HSO? He was kind and loving. He looked after her and Debbie. He was her husband and she loved him. But he mustn't resign. What other job could he get? What else was he suited for? Unemployment was as bad in East Anglia as it was elsewhere. There was the mortgage to pay and the electricity bill for the central heating – they couldn't economize there because of Debbie needing warmth – and the hire-purchase on the bedroom suite to find. Even the nursery furniture wasn't paid for yet. She had wanted everything nice and new for Debbie, but it had taken all their remaining savings. She said:

'Couldn't you apply to Establishment Department for a transfer?'

The despair in his voice tore at her heart.

'No one will want me if Lorrimer says I'm no good. He's probably the best forensic biologist in the service. If he thinks I'm useless, then I'm useless.'

It was this, too, which she was beginning to find irritating, the obsequious respect of the victim for his oppressor. Sometimes, appalled by her disloyalty, she could begin to understand Dr Lorrimer's contempt. She said:

'Why not have a word with the director?'

'I might have done if Dr Mac was still there. But Howarth wouldn't care. He's new. He doesn't want any trouble with the senior staff, particularly now when we're getting ready to move into the new Lab.'

And then she thought of Mr Middlemass. He was the Principal Scientific Officer Document Examiner, and she had worked for him as a young SO before her marriage. It was at Hoggatt's Laboratory that she had met Cliff. Perhaps he could do something, could speak to Howarth for them, could use his influence with Estabs. She wasn't sure how she expected him to help, but the need to confide in someone was overwhelming. They couldn't go on like this. Cliff would have a breakdown. And how would she manage with the baby and Cliff ill and the future uncertain? But surely Mr Middle-mass could do something. She believed in him because she needed to believe. She looked across at Cliff.

'Don't worry, darling, it's going to be all right. We're going to think of something. You go in today and we'll talk about it in the evening.'

'How can we? Your mother's coming to supper.'

'After supper then. She'll be catching the quarter to eight bus. We'll talk then.'

'I can't go on like this, Sue.'

'You won't have to. I'll think of something. It's going to be all right. I promise you, darling. It's going to be all right.'

5

'Mum, did you know that every human being is unique?'

'Of course I did. It stands to reason, doesn't it? There's only one of every person. You're you. I'm me. Pass your Dad the marmalade and keep your sleeve out of that butter.'

Brenda Pridmore, recently appointed Clerical Officer/receptionist at Hoggatt's Laboratory, pushed the marmalade across the breakfast table and began methodically slicing thin strips from the white of her fried egg, postponing, as she had from early childhood, that cataclysmic moment when she would plunge the fork into the glistening yellow dome. But indulgence in this small personal ritual was almost automatic. Her mind was preoccupied with the excitements and discoveries of her wonderful first job.

'I mean biologically unique. Inspector Blakelock, he's the Assistant Police Liaison Officer, told me that every human being has a unique fingerprint and no two types of blood are exactly the same. If the scientists had enough systems they could distinguish them all, the blood types I mean. He thinks that day may come in time. The forensic serologist will be able to say with certainty where the blood came from, even with a dried stain. It's dried blood that's difficult. If the blood is fresh we can do far more with it.'

'Funny job you've got yourself.' Mrs Pridmore refilled the teapot from the kettle on the Aga hob and eased herself back into her chair. The farmhouse kitchen, its flowered cretonne curtains still undrawn, was warm and cosily domestic, smelling of toast, fried bacon and hot strong tea.

'I don't know that I like the idea of you checking in bits of body and bloodstained clothes. I hope you wash your hands properly before you come home.'

'Oh Mum, it's not like that! The exhibits all arrive in plastic bags with identifying tags. We have to be ever so particular that all of them are labelled and properly entered in the book. It's a question of continuity of evidence, what Inspector Blakelock calls the integrity of the sample. And we don't get bits of body.'

Remembering suddenly the sealed bottles of stomach contents, the carefully dissected pieces of liver and intestines, looking when you came to think of it, no more frightening than exhibits in the science laboratory at school, she said quickly:

'Well, not in the way you mean. Dr Kerrison does all the cutting up. He's a forensic pathologist attached to the Laboratory. Of course, some of the organs come to us for analysis.'

Inspector Blakelock, she remembered, had told her that the Laboratory refrigerator had once held a whole head. But that wasn't the kind of thing to tell Mum. She rather wished that the Inspector hadn't told her. The refrigerator, squat and gleaming like a surgical sarcophagus, had held a sinister fascination for her ever since. But Mrs Pridmore had seized gratefully on a familiar name.

'I know who Dr Kerrison is, I should hope. Lives at the Old Rectory at Chevisham alongside the church, doesn't he? His wife ran off with one of the doctors at the hospital, left him and the two kids, that odd-looking daughter and the small boy, poor little fellow. You remember all the talk there was at the time, Arthur?'

Her husband didn't reply, nor did she expect him to. It was an understood convention that Arthur Pridmore left breakfast conversation to his women. Brenda went happily on:

'Forensic science isn't just helping the police to discover who's guilty. We help clear the innocent too. People sometimes forget that. We had a case last month – of course, I can't mention names – when a sixteen-year-old choir-girl accused her vicar of rape. Well, he was innocent.'

'So I should hope! Rape indeed!'

'But it looked very black against him. Only he was lucky. He was a secreter.'

'A what, for goodness sake?'

'He secreted his blood group in all his body fluids. Not everyone does. So the biologist was able to examine his saliva and compare his blood group with the stains on the victim's . . .'

'Not at breakfast time, Brenda, if you don't mind.'

Brenda, her eyes suddenly alighting on a round milk stain on the table-cloth, herself thought that breakfast wasn't perhaps the most suitable time for a display of her recently acquired information about the investigation of rape. She went on to a safer subject.

'Dr Lorrimer – he's the Principal Scientific Officer in charge of the Biology Department – says that I ought to work for an A-level subject and try for a job as an Assistant Scientific Officer. He thinks that I could do better than just a clerical job. And once I got my ASO I'd be on a scientific grade and could work myself up. Some of the most famous forensic scientists have started that way, he said. He's offered to give me a reading list, and he says he doesn't see why I shouldn't use some of the laboratory equipment for my practical work.'

'I didn't know that you worked in the Biology Department.'

'I don't. I'm mainly on Reception with Inspector Blakelock, and sometimes I help out in the general office. But we got talking when I had to spend an afternoon in his laboratory checking reports for courts with his staff, and he was ever so nice. A lot of people don't like him. They say he's too strict; but I think he's just shy. He might have been Director if the Home Office hadn't passed him over and appointed Dr Howarth.'

'He seems to be taking quite an interest in you, this Mr Lorrimer.'

'Dr Lorrimer, Mum.'

'Dr Lorrimer, then. Though why he wants to call himself a doctor beats me. You don't have any patients at the lab.'

'He's a PhD, Mum. Doctor of Philosophy.'

'Oh, is he? I thought he was supposed to be a scientist. Anyway, you'd better watch your step.'

'Oh Mum, don't be daft. He's old. He must be forty or more. Mum, did you know that our Lab is the oldest forensic science lab in the country? There are regional labs covering the whole country but ours was the first. Colonel Hoggatt started it in Chevisham Manor when he was Chief Constable in 1860, then left the manor house to his force when he died. Forensic science was in its infancy then, Inspector Blakelock says, and Colonel Hoggatt was one of the first Chief Constables to see its possibilities. We've got his portrait in the hall. We're the only lab with its founder's name. That's why the Home Office has agreed that the new Laboratory will still be called Hoggatt's. Other police forces send their exhibits to their regional laboratory, North-East or the Metropolitan and so on. But in East Anglia they say "Better send it to Hoggatt's." '

'You'd better send yourself to Hoggatt's if you want to get there by eight-thirty. And I don't want you taking any short cuts through the new Lab. It isn't safe, only half-built, especially these dark mornings. Like as not you'd fall into the foundations or get a brick down on your head. They're not safe, building sites aren't. Look what happened to your Uncle Will.'

'All right, Mum. We're not supposed to go through the new Lab anyway. Besides, I'm going by bike. Are these my sandwiches or Dad's?'

'Yours, of course. You know your dad's home to dinner on Wednesdays. Cheese and tomato this morning, and I've put you in a boiled egg.'

When Brenda had waved goodbye, Mrs Pridmore sat down for her second cup of tea and looked across at her husband.

'I suppose it's all right, this job she's found for herself.'

Arthur Pridmore, when he did condescend to talk at breakfast, talked with the magisterial authority of head of his family, Mr Bowlem's bailiff and People's warden at the village church. He laid down his fork.

'It's a good job, and she was lucky to get it. Plenty of girls from the grammar school after it, weren't they? An established civil servant, isn't she? And look what they're paying her. More than the pigman gets at the farm. Pensionable too. She's a sensible girl and she'll be all right. There aren't many opportunities left locally for girls with good O-levels. And you didn't want her to take a job in London.'

No indeed, Mrs Pridmore hadn't wɑnted Brenda to go to London, a prey to muggers, IRA terrorists anɑ what the Press mysteriously called 'the drug scene'. None of her infrequent, but uneventful and pleasant, visits to the capital on Women's Institute theatre excursions or rare shopping trips had failed to shake her conviction that Liverpool Street Station was the cavernous entry to an urban jungle, where predators armed with bombs and syringes lurked in every Underground station, and seducers laid their snares for innocent provincials in every office. Brenda, thought her mother, was a very pretty girl. Well, no point in denying it, she took after her mother's side of the family for looks even if she had her dad's brains, and Mrs Pridmore had no intention of exposing her to the temptations of London. Brenda was walking out with Gerald Bowlem, younger son of her father's boss, and if that came off there's no denying it would be a very satisfactory marriage. He wouldn't get the main farm, of course, but there was a very nice little property over at Wisbech which would come to him. Mrs Pridmore couldn't see the sense of more examinations and all this talking about a career. This job at the lab would do Brenda very well until she married. But it was a pity that there was all this emphasis on blood.

As if reading her thoughts, her husband said:

'Of course it's exciting for her. It's all new. But I dare say it's no different from other jobs, pretty dull most of the time. I don't reckon anything really frightening will happen to our Brenda at Hoggatt's Lab.'

This conversation about their only child's first job was one they'd had before, a comforting reiteration of mutual reassurance. In imagination Mrs Pridmore followed her daughter as she pedalled vigorously on her way; bumping down the rough farm track between Mr Bowlem's flat fields to Tenpenny Road, past old Mrs Button's cottage where, as a child, she had been given rice-cake and home-made lemonade, by Tenpenny Dyke where she still picked cowslips in summer, then a right turn into Chevisham Road and the straight two miles skirting Captain Massey's land and into Chevisham village. Every yard of it was familiar, reassuring, unmenacing. And even Hoggatt's Laboratory, blood or no blood, had been part of the village for over seventy years, while Chevisham Manor had stood for nearly three times as long. Arthur was right. Nothing frightening could happen to their Brenda at Hoggatt's. Mrs Pridmore, comforted, drew back the curtains and settled down to enjoy her third cup of tea.

6

At ten minutes to nine the post van stopped outside Sprogg's Cottage on the outskirts of Chevisham to deliver a single letter. It was addressed to Miss Stella Mawson, Lavender Cottage, Chevisham, but the postman was a local man and the difference in name caused him no confusion. There had been Sproggs living in the cottage for four generations, and the small triangle of green in front of the gate had been Sprogg's Green for almost as long. The present owner, having improved the cottage by the addition of a small brick garage and a modern bathroom and kitchen, had decided to celebrate the metamorphosis by planting a lavender hedge and renaming the property. But the villagers regarded the new name as no more than a foreigner's eccentric fancy which they were under no obligation either to use or recognize. The lavender hedge, as if in sympathy with their views, failed to survive the first fen winter and Sprogg's Cottage remained Sprogg's.

Angela Foley, the twenty-seven-year-old personal secretary to the Director of Hoggatt's Laboratory, picked up the envelope and guessed at once by the quality of the paper, the expertly typed address and the London postmark what it must be. It was a letter they had been expecting. She took it through to the kitchen where she and her friend were breakfasting and handed it over without speaking, then watched Stella's face as she read. After a minute she asked:

'Well?'

'It's what we feared. He can't wait any longer. He wants a quick sale, and there's a friend of his who thinks he might like it for a weekend cottage. As sitting tenants we get first refusal, but he must know by next Monday whether we're interested.'

She tossed the letter across the table. Angela said bitterly:

'Interested! Of course we're interested! He knows we are. We told him weeks ago that we were writing round trying to get a mortgage.'

'That's just lawyer's jargon. What his solicitor is asking is whether we're able to go ahead. And the answer is that we can't.'

The arithmetic was plain. Neither of them needed to discuss it. The owner wanted sixteen thousand pounds. None of the mortgage societies they had approached would advance them more than ten. Together they had a little over two thousand saved. Four thousand short. And, with no time left, it might just as well be forty.

Angela said:

'I suppose he wouldn't take less?'

'No. We've tried that. And why should he? It's a fully converted, reed-thatched seventeenth-century cottage. And we've improved it. We've made the garden. He'd be a fool to let it go for under sixteen even to a sitting tenant.'

'But, Star, we are sitting tenants! He's got to get us out first.'

'That's the only reason why he's given us as long as he has. He knows we could make it difficult for him. But I'm not prepared to stay on here under sufferance, knowing that we'd have to go in the end. I couldn't write under those conditions.'

'But we can't find four thousand in a week! And, with things as they are, we couldn't hope for a bank loan even if . . .'

'Even if I had a book coming out this year, which I haven't. And what I make from writing barely pays my part of the housekeeping. It was tactful of you not to say so.'

She hadn't been going to say it. Stella wasn't a conveyor-belt writer. You couldn't expect her novels to make money. What was it that last reviewer had said? Fastidious observation wedded to elegantly sensitive and oblique prose. Not surprisingly, Angela could quote all the reviews even if she sometimes wondered what exactly they were trying to say. Wasn't it she who pasted them with meticulous care into the cuttings-book which Stella so affected to despise! She watched while her friend began what they both called her tiger prowl, that compulsive pacing up and down, head lowered, hands sunk in her dressing-gown pockets. Then Stella said:

'It's a pity that cousin of yours is so disagreeable. Otherwise one might not have minded asking him for a loan. He wouldn't miss it.'

'But I've already asked him. Not about the cottage, of course. But I've asked him to lend me some money.'

It was ridiculous that this should be so difficult to say. After all, Edwin was her cousin. She had a right to ask him. And it was her grandmother's money after all. There was really no reason why Star should be cross. There were times when she didn't mind Star's anger, times even when she deliberately provoked it, waiting with half-shameful excitement for the extraordinary outburst of bitterness and despair of which she herself was less a victim than a privileged spectator, relishing even more the inevitable remorse and self-incrimination, the sweetness of reconciliation. But now for the first time she recognized the chill of fear.

'When?'

There was nothing for it now but to go on.

'Last Tuesday evening. It was after you decided that we'd have to cancel our bookings for Venice next March because of the exchange rate. I wanted it to be a birthday present, Venice I mean.'

She had pictured the scene. Herself handing over the tickets and the hotel reservations tucked into one of those extra-large birthday cards. Star trying to hide her surprise and pleasure. Both of them poring over maps and guidebooks, planning the itinerary of every marvellous day. To see for the first time and together that incomparable view of San Marco from the western end of the Piazza. Star had read to her Ruskin's description. 'A multitude of pillars and white domes, clustered into a long low pyramid of coloured light.' To stand together on the Piazzetta in the early morning and look across the shimmering water to San Giorgio Maggiore. It was a dream, as insubstantial as the crumbling city. But the hope of it had been worth steeling herself to ask Edwin for that loan.

'And what did he say?'

There was no chance now of softening that brutal negative, of erasing the whole humiliating episode from her memory.

'He said no.'

'I suppose you told him why you wanted it. It didn't occur to you that we go away from here to be private, that our holidays are our own affair, that it might humiliate me to have Edwin Lorrimer know that I can't afford to take you to Venice, even on a ten-day package tour.'

'I didn't.' She cried out in vehement protest, horrified to hear the crack in her voice, and feel the first hot, gritty tears. It was odd, she thought, that it was she who would cry. Star was the emotional, the vehement one. And yet Star never cried.

'I didn't tell him anything, except that I needed the money.'

'How much?'

She hesitated, wondering whether to lie. But she never lied to Star.

'Five hundred pounds. I thought we might as well do it properly. I just told him that I badly needed five hundred pounds.'

'So, not surprisingly, faced with that irrefutable argument, he declined to hand out. What exactly did he say?'

'Only that grandmother had made her intentions perfectly plain in her will and that he had no intention of upsetting them. Then I said that most of the money would come to me after his death, anyway – I mean, that's what he told me when the will was read – and it would be too late then. I'd be an old lady. I might die first. It was now that was important. But I didn't tell him why I wanted it. I swear that.'

'Swear? Don't be dramatic. You're not in a court of law. And then what did he say?'

If only Star would stop that agitated pacing, would only turn and look at her instead of questioning her in that cold, inquisitorial voice. And the new bit was even harder to tell. She couldn't explain to herself why it should be, but it was something which she had tried to put out of her mind, for the present anyway. One day she would tell Star, the moment when it was right to tell. She had never imagined being forced into confidence with such brutal suddenness.

'He said that I shouldn't rely on getting anything in his will. He said that he might acquire new obligations. Obligations was the word he used. And if he did, the will would no longer stand.'

And now Star swung round and faced her.

'New obligations. Marriage! No, that's too ridiculous. Marriage, that desiccated, pedantic, self-satisfied prude. I doubt whether he ever deliberately touches a human body except his own. Solitary, masochistic, surreptitious vice, that's all he understands. No, not vice, the word's too strong. But marriage! Wouldn't you have thought . . .'

She broke off. Angela said:

'He didn't mention marriage.'

'Why should he? But what else would automatically set aside an existing will unless he made a new one? Marriage cancels a will. Didn't you know that?'

'You mean that as soon as he married I should be disinherited?'

'Yes.'

'But it isn't fair!'

'Since when has life been noted for its fairness? It wasn't fair that your grandmother left her fortune to him instead of sharing it with you just because he's a man and she had an old-fashioned prejudice that women shouldn't own money. It isn't fair that you're only a secretary at Hoggatt's because no one bothered to educate you for anything else. It isn't fair, come to that, that you should have to support me.'

'I don't support you. In every way except the unimportant one, you support me.'

'It's humiliating to be worth more dead than alive. If my heart gave out tonight, then you'd be all right. You could use the life assurance money to buy the place and stay on. The bank would advance the money once they knew you were my legatee.'

'Without you I shouldn't want to stay on.'

'Well, if you do have to leave here, at least it will give you an excuse to live on your own, if that's what you want.'

Angela cried out in vehement protest:

'I shall never live with anyone else but you. I don't want to live anywhere but here, in this cottage. You know that. It's our home.'

It was their home. It was the only real home she'd ever known. She didn't need to look around her to fix with startling clarity each familiar loved possession. She could lie in bed at night and in imagination move confidently around the cottage touching them in a happy exploration of shared memories and reassurance. The two Victorian lustre plant pots on their matching pedestals, found in The Lanes at Brighton one summer weekend. The eighteenth-century oil of Wicken Fen by an artist whose indecipherable signature, peered at through a microscope, had provided so many shared moments of happy conjecture. The French sword in its decorated scabbard, found in a country sale room and now hanging above their fireplace. It wasn't just that their possessions, wood and porcelain, paint and linen, symbolized their joint life. The cottage, their belongings, were their joint life, adorned and gave reality to it just as the bushes and flowers they had planted in the garden staked out their territory of trust.

She had a sudden and terrifying memory of a recurrent night-mare. They were standing facing each other in an empty attic room, bare walls squared with the pale imprints of discarded pictures, floorboards harsh to the feet, two naked strangers in a void, herself trying to reach out her hands to touch Stella's fingers, but unable to lift the heavy monstrous bolsters of flesh that had become her arms. She shivered and then was recalled to the reality of the cold autumn morning by the sound of her friend's voice.

'How much did your grandmother leave? You did tell me, but I've forgotten.'

'About thirty thousand, I think.'

'And he can't have spent any of it, living with his old father in that poky cottage. He hasn't even renovated the windmill. His salary alone must be more than enough for the two of them, apart from the old man's pension. Lorrimer's a senior scientist, isn't he? What does he get?'

'He's a Principal Scientific Officer. The scale goes up to eight thousand.'

'God! More in a year than I could earn from four novels. I suppose if he jibbed at five hundred he'd hardly part with four thousand, not at a rate of interest we could afford. But it wouldn't hurt him. I've a good mind to ask him for it after all.'

Stella was only teasing, of course; but she recognized this too late to control the panic in her voice.

'No, please, Star! No, you mustn't!'

'You really hate him, don't you?'

'Not hate. Indifference. I just don't want to be under an obligation to him.'

'Nor, come to that, do I. And you shan't be.'

Angela went out to the hall and came back pulling on her coat. She said:

'I'll be late at the Lab if I don't hurry. The casserole is in the oven. Try to remember to switch on at half-past five. And don't touch the regulator. I'll turn down the heat when I get back.'

'I think I can just about manage that.'

'I'm taking sandwiches for lunch, so I shan't be back. There's the cold ham and salad in the fridge. Will that be enough, Star?'

'No doubt I'll survive.'

'Yesterday evening's typing is in the folder, but I haven't read it through.'

'How remiss of you.'

Stella followed her friend out to the hall. At the door she said:

'I expect they think at the Lab that I exploit you.'

'They know nothing about you at the Lab. And I don't care what they think.'

'Is that what Edwin Lorrimer thinks, too, that I exploit you? Or what does he think?'

'I don't want to talk about him.'

She folded her scarf over her blonde hair. In the antique mirror with its frame of carved shells she saw both their faces distorted by a defect in the glass; the brown and green of Stella's huge luminous eyes smeared like wet paint into the deep clefts between nostrils and mouth; her own wide brow bulging like that of a hydrocephalic child. She said:

'I wonder what I'd feel if Edwin died this week; a heart attack, a car accident, a brain haemorrhage.'

'Life isn't as convenient as that.'

'Death isn't. Star, shall you reply today to that solicitor?'

'He doesn't expect an answer until Monday. I can ring him at the London office on Monday morning. That's another five days. Anything can happen in five days.'

7

'But they're just like mine! The panties I mean. I've got a pair like that! I bought them from Marks and Spencer's in Cambridge with my first salary cheque.'

It was 10.35 and Brenda Pridmore, at the reception desk at the rear of the main hall of Hoggatt's Laboratory, watched wide-eyed while Inspector Blakelock drew towards him the first labelled bag of exhibits from the clunch-pit murder. She put out a finger and tentatively slid it over the thin plastic through which the knickers, crumpled and stained round the crotch, were clearly visible. The detective-constable who had brought in the exhibits had said that the girl had been to a dance. Funny, thought Brenda, that she hadn't bothered to put on clean underclothes. Perhaps she wasn't fastidious. Or perhaps she had been in too much of a hurry to change. And now the intimate clothes which she had put on so unthinkingly on the day of her death would be smoothed out by strange hands, scrutinized under ultra-violet light, perhaps be handed up, neatly docketed, to the judge and jury in the Crown Court.

Brenda knew that she would never again be able to wear her own panties, their prettiness contaminated for ever by the memory of this dead unknown girl. Perhaps they had even bought them together in the same store, on the same day. She could recall the excitement of spending for the first time money she had actually earned. It had been a Saturday afternoon and there had been a crush round the lingerie counter, eager hands rummaging among the panties. She had liked the pair with the sprays of pink machine-embroidered flowers across the front. So, too, had this unknown girl. Perhaps their hands had touched. She cried:

'Inspector. Isn't death terrible?'

'Murder is. Death isn't; at least, no more than birth is. You couldn't have one without the other or there'd be no room for us all. I reckon I won't worry overmuch when my time comes.'

'But that policeman who brought in the exhibits said that she was only eighteen. That's my age.'

He was making out the folder for the new case, meticulously transferring details from the police form to the file. And his head, with the cropped dry hair which reminded her so of corn-stubble, was bent low over the page so that she could not see his face. Suddenly she remembered being told that he had lost an only daughter, killed by a hit-and-run driver, and she wished the words unsaid. Her face flared and she turned her eyes away. But when he replied his voice was perfectly steady.

'Aye, poor lass. Led him on, I dare say. They never learn. What's that you've got?'

'It's the bag of male clothes, suit, shoes and underwear. Do you think these belong to the chief suspect?'

'They'll be the husband's, likely as not.'

'But what can they prove? She was strangled, wasn't she?'

'No telling for certain until we get Dr Kerrison's report. But they usually examine the chief suspect's clothes. There might be a trace of blood, a grain of sand or earth, paint, minute fibres from the victim's clothes, a trace of her saliva even. Or she could have been raped. All that bundle will go into the Biology Search Room with the victim's clothes.'

'But the policeman didn't say anything about rape! I thought you said this bundle belongs to the husband.'

'You don't want to let it worry you. You have to learn to be like a doctor or a nurse, detached, isn't it?'

'Is that how forensic scientists feel?'

'Likely as not. It's their job. They don't think about victims or suspects. That's for the police. They're only concerned with scientific facts.'

He was right, thought Brenda. She remembered the time only

three days previously when the Senior Scientific Officer of the instrument section had let her look into the giant scanning electron microscope and watch the image of a minute pill of putty burst instantaneously into an exotic incandescent flower. He had explained:

'It's a coccolith, magnified six thousand times.'

'A what?'

'The skeleton of a micro-organism which lived in the ancient seas from which the chalk in the putty was deposited. They're different, depending on where the chalk was quarried. That's how you can differentiate one sample of putty from another.'

She had exclaimed:

'But it's so lovely!'

He had taken her place at the eyepiece of the instrument.

'Yes, nice, isn't it?'

But she had known that, while she looked back in wonder across a million years, his mind was on the minute scrape of putty from the heel of the suspect's shoe, the trace which might prove a man was a rapist or a murderer. And yet, she had thought, he doesn't really mind. All he cares about is getting the answer right. It would have been no use asking him whether he thought there was a unifying purpose in life, whether it could really be chance that an animal so small that it couldn't be seen by the naked eye could die millions of years ago in the depths of the sea and be resurrected by science to prove a man innocent or guilty. It was odd, she thought, that scientists so often weren't religious when their work revealed a world so variously marvellous and yet so mysteriously unified and at one. Dr Lorrimer seemed to be the only member of Hoggatt's who was known to go regularly to church. She wondered if she dared ask him about the coccolith and God. He had been very kind this morning about the murder. He had arrived at the Laboratory over an hour late, at ten o'clock, looking terribly tired because he had been up that night at the scene of the crime, and had come over to the reception desk to collect his personal post. He had said:

'You'll be getting exhibits from your first murder case this morning. Don't let them worry you, Brenda. There's only one death we need to be frightened of, and that's our own.'

It was a strange thing to have said, an odd way to reassure her. But he was right. She was suddenly glad that Inspector Blakelock had done the documentation on the clunch-pit murder. Now, with care, the owner of those stained panties would remain, for her, unknown, anonymous, a number in the biology series on a manila folder. Inspector Blakelock's voice broke into her thoughts:

'Have you got those court reports we checked yesterday ready for the post?'

'Yes, they've been entered in the book. I meant to ask you. Why do all the court statements have "Criminal Justice Act 1967 sections 2 and 9" printed on them?'

'That's the statutory authority for written evidence to be tendered at committal proceedings and the Crown Court. You can look up the sections in the library. Before the 1967 Act the labs had a hard time of it, I can tell you, when all scientific evidence had to be given orally. Mind you, the court-going officers still have to spend a fair amount of time attending trials. The defence doesn't always accept the scientific findings. That's the difficult part of the job, not the analysis but standing alone in the witness-box to defend it under cross-examination. If a man's no good in the box, then all the careful work he does here goes for nothing.'

Brenda suddenly remembered something else that Mrs Mallett had told her, that the motorist who had killed his daughter had been acquitted because the scientist had crumbled under the cross-examination; something to do with the analysis of chips of paint found on the road which matched the suspect's car. It must be terrible to lose an only child; to lose any child. Perhaps that was the worst thing that could happen to a human being. No wonder Inspector Blakelock was often so quiet; that when the police officers came in with their hearty banter he answered only with that slow, gentle smile.

She glanced across at the Laboratory clock. Ten forty-five. Any minute now the Scene of Crime course would be arriving for their lecture on the collection and preservation of scientific evidence, and this brief spell of quiet would be over. She wondered what Colonel Hoggatt would think if he could visit his Laboratory now. Her eyes were drawn, as they so often were, to his portrait hanging just outside the Director's office. Even from her place at the desk she could read the gold lettering on the frame.

Colonel William Makepeace Hoggatt VC
Chief Constable 1894-1912
Founder of Hoggatt's Forensic Science Laboratory.

He was standing in the room which was still used as a library, his ruddy face stern and bewhiskered under the sprouting plumes of his hat, his braided, bemedalled tunic fastened with a row of gilt buttons. One proprietorial hand was laid, light as a priestly blessing, on an old-fashioned microscope in gleaming brass. But the minatory eyes weren't fixed on this latest scientific wonder; they were fixed on Brenda. Under his accusing gaze, recalled to duty, she bent again to her work.

8

By twelve o'clock the meeting of senior scientists in the Director's office to discuss the furniture and equipment for the new Laboratory was over, and Howarth rang for his secretary to clear the conference table. He watched her as she emptied and polished the ashtray (he didn't smoke and the smell of ash offended him), collected together the copies of the Laboratory plans and gathered up the strewn discarded papers. Even from his desk Howarth could see Middlemass's complex geometrical doodles, and the crumpled agenda, ringed with coffee stains, of the Senior Vehicle Examiner, Bill Morgan.

He watched the girl as she moved with quiet competence about the table wondering, as always, what, if anything, was going on behind that extraordinarily wide brow, those slanted enigmatic eyes. He missed his old personal assistant, Marjory Faraker, more than he had expected. It had, he thought ruefully, been good for his self-conceit to find that her devotion didn't, after all, extend to leaving London where, surprisingly, she had been discovered to have a life of her own, to join him in the fens. Like all good secretaries she had acquired, or at least known how to simulate, some of the idealized attributes of wife, mother, mistress, confidante, servant and friend without being, or indeed expecting to be, any of these. She had flattered his self-esteem, protected him from the minor irritations of life, preserved his privacy with maternal pugnacity, had ensured, with infinite tact, that he knew all he needed to know about what was going on in his laboratory.

He couldn't complain about Angela Foley. She was a more than competent shorthand typist and an efficient secretary. Nothing was left undone. It was just that for her, he felt that he hardly existed, that his authority, meekly deferred to, was nevertheless a charade. The fact that she was Lorrimer's cousin was irrelevant. He had never heard her mention his name. He wondered from time to time what sort of a life she led in that remote cottage with her writer friend, how far it had satisfied her. But she told him nothing, not even about the Laboratory. He knew that Hoggatt's had a heartbeat – all institutions did – but the pulse eluded him. He said:

'The Foreign and Commonwealth Office want us to take a Danish biologist for two or three days next month. He's visiting England to look at the service. Fit him in, will you, when I'm free to give him some time. You'd better consult Dr Lorrimer about his diary commitments. Then let the FCO know what days we can offer.'

'Yes, Dr Howarth.'

At least the autopsy was over. It had been worse than he had expected, but he had seen it through and without disgrace. He hadn't expected that the colours of the human body would be so vivid, so exotically beautiful. Now he saw again Kerrison's gloved fingers, sleek as eels, busying themselves at the body's orifices. Explaining, demonstrating, discarding. Presumably he had become as immune to disgust as he obviously was to the sweet-sour smell of his mortuary. And to all the experts in violent death, faced daily with the final disintegration of the personality, pity would be as irrelevant as disgust.

Miss Foley was ready to go now and had come up to the desk to clear his out tray. He said:

'Has Inspector Blakelock worked out last month's average turn-round figures yet?'

'Yes, sir. The average for all exhibits is down to twelve days, and the blood alcohol has fallen to 1.2 days. But the figure for crimes against the person is up again. I'm just typing the figures now.'

'Let me have them as soon as they're ready, please.'

There were memories which, he suspected, would be even more insistent than Kerrison marking out with his cartilage knife on the milk-white body the long line of the primary incision. Doyle, that great black bull, grinning at him in the washroom afterwards as, side by side, they washed their hands. And why, he wondered, had he felt it necessary to wash? His hands hadn't been contaminated.

'The performance was well up to standard. Neat, quick and thorough, that's Doc Kerrison. Sorry we shan't be able to call for you when we're ready to make the arrest. Not allowed. You'll have to imagine that bit. But there'll be the trial to attend, with any luck.'

Angela Foley was standing in front of the desk, looking at him strangely, he thought.

'Yes?'

'Scobie has had to go home, Dr Howarth. He's not at all well. He thinks it may be this two-day flu that's going about. And he says that the incinerator has broken down.'

'Presumably he telephoned for the mechanic before he left.'

'Yes, sir. He says it was all right yesterday morning when Inspector Doyle came with the court orders authorizing the destruction of the cannabis exhibits. It was working then.'

Howarth was irritated. This was one of those minor administrative details which Miss Faraker would never have dreamed of troubling him with. Miss Foley was, he guessed, expecting him to say something sympathetic about Scobie, to enquire whether the old man had been fit to cycle home. Dr MacIntyre had, no doubt, bleated like an anxious sheep when any of the staff were ill. He bent his head over his papers.

But Miss Foley was at the door. It had to be now. He made himself say:

'Ask Dr Lorrimer to come down for a few minutes, will you please?'

He could, perfectly casually, have asked Lorrimer to stay on after the meeting; why hadn't he? Probably because there might have been an echo of the headmaster in so public a request. Perhaps because this was an interview he had been glad to postpone, even temporarily.

Lorrimer came in and stood in front of the desk. Howarth took out Bradley's personal file from his right-hand drawer and said:

'Sit down will you, please. This annual report on Bradley. You've given him an adverse marking. Have you told him?'

Lorrimer remained standing. He said:

'I'm required by the reporting rules to tell him. I saw him in my office at ten-thirty, as soon as I got back from the PM.'

'It seems a bit hard. According to his file, it's the first adverse report he's had. We took him on probation eighteen months ago. Why hasn't he made out?'

'I should have thought that was obvious from my detailed markings. He's been promoted above his capacity.'

'In other words, the Board made a mistake?'

'That's not so unusual. Boards occasionally do. And not only when it comes to promotions.'

The allusion was blatant, a deliberate provocation, yet Howarth decided to ignore it. With an effort he kept his voice level.

'I'm not prepared to countersign this report as it stands. It's too early to judge him fairly.'

'I made that excuse for him last year when he'd been with us six months. But if you disagree with my assessment you'll presumably say so. There's a space provided.'

'I intend to use it. And I suggest that you try the effect of giving the boy some support and encouragement. There are two reasons for an inadequate performance. Some people are capable of doing better and will if judiciously kicked into it. Others aren't. To kick them is not only pointless, it destroys what confidence they have. You run an efficient department. But it might be more efficient and happier if you learned how to understand people. Management is largely a matter of personal relationships.'

He made himself look up. Lorrimer said through lips so stiff that the words sounded cracked:

'I hadn't realized that your family were noted for success in their personal relationships.'

'The fact that you can't take criticism without becoming as personal and spiteful as a neurotic girl is an example of what I mean.'

He never knew what Lorrimer was about to reply. The door opened and his sister came in. She was dressed in slacks and a sheepskin jacket, her blonde hair bound with a scarf. She looked at them both without embarrassment and said easily:

'Sorry, I didn't realize you were engaged. I ought to have asked Inspector Blakelock to ring.'

Without a word, Lorrimer, deathly pale, turned on his heels, walked past her and was gone. Domenica looked after him, smiled and shrugged. She said:

'Sorry if I interrupted something. It's just to say that I'm going to Norwich for a couple of hours to buy some materials. Is there anything you want?'

'Nothing, thank you.'

'I'll be back before dinner, but I think I'll give the village concert a miss. Without Claire Easterbrook the Mozart will be pretty insupportable. Oh, and I'm thinking of going up to London for the best part of next week.'

Her brother didn't reply. She looked at him and said:

'What's wrong?'

'How did Lorrimer know about Gina?'

He didn't need to ask her if it was she who had told him. Whatever else she may have confided, it would not have been that. She went across, ostensibly to study the Stanley Spencer set in the overmantel of the fireplace, and asked lightly:

'Why? He didn't mention your divorce, did he?'

'Not directly, but the allusion was intended.'

She turned to face him.

'He probably took the trouble to find out as much as possible about you when he knew that you were a candidate for the job here. It isn't such a large service after all.'

'But I came from outside it.'

'Even so, there would be contacts, gossip. A failed marriage is one of those unconsidered trifles he might expect to sniff out. And what of it? After all, it's not unusual. I thought forensic scientists were particularly at risk. All those late hours at scenes of crime and the unpredictable court attendances. They ought to be used to marital break-ups.'

He said, knowing that he sounded as petulant as an obstinate child:

'I don't want him in my Lab.'

'Your Lab? It isn't quite as simple as that, is it? I don't think the Stanley Spencer is right over the fireplace. It looks incongruous. It's strange that Father bought it. Not at all his kind of picture I should have said. Did you put it here to shock?'

Miraculously, his anger and misery were assuaged. But then she had always been able to do that for him.

'Merely to disconcert and confuse. It's intended to suggest that I may be a more complex character than they assume.'

'Oh, but you are! I've never needed "Assumption at Cookham" to prove it. Why not the Greuze? It would look good with that carved overmantel.'

'Too pretty.'

She laughed, and was gone. He picked up Clifford Bradley's report and, in the space provided, wrote:

'Mr Bradley's performance has been disappointing, but not all the difficulties are of his making. He lacks confidence and would benefit from more active encouragement and support than he has received. I have corrected the final marking to what I consider a more just assessment and have spoken to the senior biologist about the personnel management in his department.'

If he did finally decide that, after all, this wasn't the job for him, that snide comment should go some way to ensure that Lorrimer stood no chance of succeeding him as Director of Hoggatt's.

9

At one forty-eight precisely Paul Middlemass, the Document Examiner, opened his file on the clunch-pit murder. The Document Examination Room, which occupied the whole of the front of the building immediately under the roof, smelled like a stationer's shop, a pungent amalgam of paper and ink, sharpened by the tang of chemicals. Middlemass breathed it as his native air. He was a tall, rangy, large-featured man with a mobile, wide-mouthed face of agreeable ugliness and iron-grey hair which fell in heavy swathes over parchment-coloured skin. Easy-going and seemingly indolent, he was in fact a prodigious worker with an obsession for his job. Paper in all its manifestations was his passion. Few men, in or outside the forensic science service, knew so much about it. He handled it with joy and with a kind of reverence, gloated over it, knew its provenance almost by its smell. Identification of the sizing and loading of a specimen by spectrographic or X-ray crystallography merely confirmed what touch and sight had already pronounced. The satisfaction of watching the emergence of an obscure watermark under soft X-rays never palled, and the final pattern was as fascinating to his unsurprised eyes as the expected potter's mark to a collector of porcelain.

His father, long dead, had been a dentist, and his son had taken for his own use the old man's inordinately large store of self-designed surgical overalls. They were old-fashioned in cut, waisted and full-skirted as the coat of a Regency buck, and with crested metal buttons fastening high to the side of the throat. Although they were too short in the arm so that his lean wrists protruded like those of an overgrown schoolboy, he wore them with a certain panache, as if this unorthodox working garb, so different from the regulation white coats of the rest of the Laboratory staff, symbolized that unique blend of scientific skill, experience and flair which distinguishes the good Document Examiner.

He had just finished telephoning his wife, having remembered rather belatedly that he was due to help out that evening with the village concert. He liked women, and before his marriage had enjoyed a succession of casual, satisfactory and uncommitted affairs. He had married late, a buxom research scientist from Cambridge twenty years his junior, and drove back to their modern flat on the outskirts of the city each night in his Jaguar – his chief extravagance – frequently late, but seldom too late to bear her off to their local pub. Secure in his job, with a growing international reputation, and uxoriously contented with his comely Sophie, he knew himself to be successful and suspected himself to be happy.

The Document Examination Laboratory with its cabinets and range of monorail cameras took up what some of his colleagues, notably Edwin Lorrimer, regarded as more than its share of room. But the Laboratory, lit by rows of fluorescent lights and with its low ceiling, was stuffy and ill-ventilated, and this afternoon the central heating, unreliable at the best of times, had concentrated all its efforts on the top of the building. Usually he was oblivious of his working conditions, but a sub-tropical temperature was difficult to ignore. He opened the door to the passage. Opposite and a little to the right were the male and female lavatories, and he could hear the occasional feet, light or heavy, hurried or dilatory, of passing members of staff, and hear the swing of the two doors. The sounds didn't worry him. He applied himself to his task.

But the specimen he was now poring over held little mystery. If the crime had been other than murder he would have left it to his

Scientific Officer assistant, not yet returned from a belated lunch. But murder invariably meant a court appearance and cross-examination – the defence seldom let the scientific evidence go unchallenged in this, the gravest of charges – and a court appearance put document examination in general, and Hoggatt's Laboratory in particular, on public trial. He made it a matter of principle always to take the murder cases himself. They were seldom the most interesting. What he most enjoyed were the historical investigations, the satisfaction of demonstrating, as he had only last month, that a document dated 1872 was printed on paper containing chemical wood-pulp which was first used in 1874, a discovery which had initiated a fascinating unravelling of complicated documentary fraud. There was nothing complicated and little of interest about the present job. Yet, only a few years ago, a man's neck could have depended upon his opinion. He seldom thought of the half-dozen men who had been hanged during the twenty years of his forensic experience, primarily because of his evidence, and when he did, it was not the strained but oddly anonymous faces in the dock which he remembered, or their names; but paper and ink, the thickened downward stroke, the peculiar formation of a letter. Now he spread out on his table the note taken from the dead girl's handbag, placing on each side the two specimens of the husband's handwriting which the police had been able to obtain. One was a letter to the suspect's mother written on holiday at Southend – how, he wondered, had they managed to extract that from her? The other was a brief telephoned message about a football match. The note taken from the victim's purse was even briefer.

'You've got your own chap so lay off Barry Taylor or you'll be sorry. It would be a pity to spoil a nice face like yours. Acid isn't pretty. Watch it. A Wellwisher.'

The style, he decided, was derived from a recent television thriller, the writing was obviously disguised. It was possible that the police would be able to provide him with some more samples of the suspect's handwriting when they visited the lad's place of work, but he didn't really need them. The similarities between the threatening note and the samples were unmistakable. The writer had tried to alter the slant of his hand and had changed the shape of the small r. But the lifts of the pen came regularly at every fourth letter – Middlemass had never yet found a forger who remembered to vary the interval at which he lifted pen from paper – and the dot above the i, high and slightly to the left, and the over-emphatic apostrophe were almost a trade-mark. He would analyse the paper sample, photograph and enlarge each individual letter and then mount them on a comparison chart, and the jury would pass it solemnly from hand to hand and wonder why it needed a highly paid expert to come and explain what anyone could see with his own eyes.

The telephone rang. Middlemass stretched out a long arm and held the instrument to his left ear. Susan Bradley's voice, at first apologetic then conspiratorial and finally close to tears, squeaked into his ear in a long monologue of complaint and desperation. He listened, made soft encouraging noises, held the receiver an inch or two from his ear, and meanwhile noted that the writer, poor bastard, hadn't even thought of altering the distinctive cross-bar of his small letter t. Not that it would have done him any good. And he couldn't have known, poor devil, that his effort would feature as an exhibit in his trial for murder.

'All right,' he said. 'Don't worry. Leave it to me.'

'And you won't let him know that I phoned you?'

'Of course not, Susan. Relax. I'll settle it.'

The voice crackled on.

'Then tell him not to be a fool, for God's sake. Hasn't he noticed that we've got one and a half million unemployed? Lorrimer can't sack him. Tell Clifford to hang on to his job and stop being a bloody fool. I'll deal with Lorrimer.'

He replaced the receiver. He had liked Susan Moffat who, for two years, had worked for him as his SO. She had both more brains and more guts than her husband, and he had wondered, without greatly caring, why she had married Bradley. Pity probably, and an over-developed maternal instinct. There were some women who simply had to take the unfortunate literally to their breast. Or perhaps it was just lack of choice, the need for a home of her own and a child. Well, it was too late to try and stop the marriage now, and it certainly hadn't occurred to him to try at the time. And at least she had the home and the kid. She had brought the baby to the Lab to see him only a fortnight ago. The visit of the prune-faced yelling bundle had done nothing to change his own resolution not to produce a child, but certainly Susan herself had seemed happy enough. And she would probably be happy again if something could be done about Lorrimer.

He thought that the time had perhaps come to do something about Lorrimer. And he had, after all, his own private reason for taking on the job. It was a small personal obligation, and to date it hadn't particularly fretted what he supposed other people called conscience. But Susan Bradley's call had reminded him. He listened. The footsteps were familiar. Well, it was a coincidence, but better now than later. Moving to the door he called at the retreating back:

'Lorrimer. I want a word with you.'

Lorrimer came and stood inside the door, tall, unsmiling in his carefully buttoned white coat, and regarded Middlemass with his dark, wary eyes. Middlemass made himself look into them, and then turned his glance away. The irises had seemed to dilate into black pools of despair. It was not an emotion he felt competent to deal with, and he felt discomforted. What on earth was eating the poor devil? He said, carefully casual:

'Look, Lorrimer, lay off Bradley will you? I know he's not exactly God's gift to forensic science, but he's a conscientious plodder and you're not going to stimulate either his brain or his speed by bullying the poor little beast. So cut it out.'

'Are you telling me how to manage my staff?'

Lorrimer's voice was perfectly controlled, but the pulse at the side of his temple had begun to beat visibly. Middlemass found it difficult to fix his eyes on it.

'That's right, mate. This member of your staff anyway. I know damn well what you're up to and I don't like it. So stow it.'

'Is this meant to be some kind of a threat?'

'More a friendly warning, reasonably friendly anyway. I don't pretend to like you, and I wouldn't have served under you if the Home Office had been daft enough to appoint you Director of this Lab. But I admit that what you do in your own department isn't normally my business, only this happens to be an exception. I know what's going on, I don't like it, and I'm making it my business to see that it stops.'

'I didn't realize that you had this tender regard for Bradley. But of course, Susan Bradley must have phoned you. He wouldn't have the guts to speak for himself. Did she telephone you, Middlemass?'

Middlemass ignored the question. He said:

'I haven't any particular regard for Bradley. But I did have a certain regard for Peter Ennalls, if you can remember him.'

'Ennalls drowned himself because his fiancée threw him over and he'd had a mental breakdown. He left a note explaining his action and it was read out at the inquest. Both things happened months after he'd left the Southern Laboratory; neither had anything to do with me.'

'What happened while he was at the Lab had a hell of a lot to do with you. He was a pleasant, rather ordinary lad with two good A-levels and an unaccountable wish to become a forensic biologist when he had the bad luck to begin work under you. As it happens, he was my wife's cousin. I was the one who recommended him to try for the job. So I have a certain interest, you could say a certain responsibility.'

Lorrimer said:

'He never said that he was related to your wife. But I can't see what difference it makes. He was totally unsuited for the job. A forensic biologist who can't work accurately under pressure is no use to me or the Service and he'd better get out. We've no room for passengers. That's what I propose to tell Bradley.'

'Then you'd better have second thoughts.'

'And how are you going to make me?'

It was extraordinary that lips so tight could produce any sound, that Lorrimer's voice, high and distorted, could have forced itself through the vocal cords without splitting them.

'I shall make it plain to Howarth that you and I can't serve in the same Lab. He won't exactly welcome that. Trouble between senior staff is the last complication he wants just now. So he'll suggest to Establishment Department that one of us gets a transfer before we have the added complication of moving into a new Lab. I'm banking on Howarth – and Estabs come to that – concluding that it's easier to find a forensic biologist than a Document Examiner.'

Middlemass surprised himself. None of this rigmarole had occurred to him before he spoke. Not that it was unreasonable. There wasn't another Document Examiner of his calibre in the Service and Howarth knew it. If he categorically refused to work in the same laboratory as Lorrimer, one of them would have to go. The quarrel wouldn't do either of them any good with the Establishment

Department, but he thought he knew which one it would harm most.

Lorrimer said:

'You helped stop me getting the directorship, now you want to drive me out of the Lab.'

'Personally I don't care a damn whether you're here or not. But just lay off bullying Bradley.'

'If I were prepared to take advice about the way I run my department from anyone, it wouldn't be a third-rate paper fetishist with a second-rate degree, who doesn't know the difference between scientific proof and intuition.'

The taunt was too absurd to puncture Middlemass's secure self-esteem. But at least it warranted a retort. He found that he was getting angry. And suddenly he saw light. He said:

'Look, mate, if you can't make it in bed, if she isn't finding you quite up to the mark, don't take your frustration out on the rest of us. Remember Chesterfield's advice. The expense is exorbitant, the position ridiculous, and the pleasure transitory.'

The result astounded him. Lorrimer gave a strangled cry and lunged out. Middlemass's reaction was both instinctive and deeply satisfying. He shot out his right arm and landed a punch on Lorrimer's nose. There was a second's astonished silence in which the two men regarded each other. Then the blood spurted and Lorrimer tottered and fell forward. Middlemass caught him by the shoulders and felt the weight of his head against his chest. He thought: 'My God, he's going to faint.' He was aware of a tangle of emotion, surprise at himself, boyish gratification, pity and an impulse to laugh. He said:

'Are you all right?'

Lorrimer tore himself from his grasp and stood upright. He fumbled for his handkerchief and held it to his nose. The red stain grew. Looking down, Middlemass saw Lorrimer's blood spreading on his white overall, decorative as a rose. He said:

'Since we're engaging in histrionics, I believe your response ought now to be "By God, you swine, you'll pay for this".'

He was astounded by the sudden blaze of hate in the black eyes. Lorrimer's voice came to him muffled by the handkerchief.

'You will pay for it.' And then he was gone.

Middlemass was suddenly aware of Mrs Bidwell, the Laboratory cleaner, standing by the door, eyes large and excited behind her ridiculous upswept diamanté spectacles.

'Nice goings-on, I don't think. Senior staff fighting each other. You ought to be ashamed of yourselves.'

'Oh we are, Mrs Bidwell. We are.' Slowly Middlemass eased his long arms from his overall. He handed it to her.

'Drop this in the soiled linen, will you.'

'Now you know very well, Mr Middlemass, that I don't go into the gents' cloakroom, not in working hours. You put it in the basket yourself. And if you want a clean one now, you know where to find it. I'm putting out no more clean linen until tomorrow. Fighting, indeed. I might have known that Dr Lorrimer would be mixed up in it. But he's not a gentleman you'd expect to find using his fists. Wouldn't have the guts, that would be my view. But he's been odd in his manner these last few weeks, no doubt about that. You heard about that spot of bother in the front hall yesterday, I suppose? He practically pushed those kids of Dr Kerrison's out of the door. All they were doing was waiting for their dad. No harm in that, I suppose. There's a very nasty atmosphere in this Lab recently, and if a certain gentleman doesn't take a hold of himself there'll be a mischief done, you mark my words.'

10

It was nearly five o'clock and dark before Detective-Inspector Doyle got back to his home in the village four miles to the north of Cambridge. He had tried to telephone his wife once, but without success: the line was engaged. Another of her interminable, secretive and expensive telephone calls to one of her old nursing friends, he thought, and, duty satisfied, made no further attempt. The wrought-iron gate, as usual, was open and he parked in front of the house. It wasn't worth garaging the car for a couple of hours, which was all the time he could allow himself.

Scoope House hardly looked its best in the late afternoon of a dark November evening. No wonder that the agents hadn't recently sent anyone to view. It was a bad time of the year. The house was, he thought, a monument to miscalculation. He had bought it for less than seventeen thousand and had spent five thousand on it to date, expecting to sell it for at least forty. But that was before the recession had upset the calculations of more expert speculators than he. Now, with the property market sluggish, there was nothing to do but wait. He could afford to hang on to the house until the market quickened. He wasn't sure that he would be given a chance to hold on to his wife. He wasn't even sure that he wanted to. The marriage, too, had been a miscalculation, but given the circumstances of the time, an understandable one. He wasted no time on regrets.

The two tall oblongs of light from the first-floor drawing-room window should have been a welcoming promise of warmth and comfort. Instead they were vaguely menacing: Maureen was at home. But where else, she would have argued, was there for her to go in this dreary East Anglian village on a dull November evening?

She had finished tea, and the tray was still at her side. The milk bottle, with its crushed top pressed back, a single mug, sliced bread spilling out of its wrapper, a slab of butter on a greasy dish, a bought fruit cake in its unopened carton. He felt the customary surge of irritation, but said nothing. Once when he had remonstrated at her sluttishness she had shrugged:

'Who sees, who cares?'

He saw and he cared, but it had been many months since he had counted with her. He said:

'I'm taking a couple of hours' kip. Wake me at seven, will you?'

'You mean we aren't going to the Chevisham concert?'

'For God's sake, Maureen, you were yelling yesterday that you couldn't be bothered with it. Kids' stuff. Remember?'

'It's not exactly The Talk of the Town, but at least we were going out. Out! Out of this dump. Together for a change. It was something to dress up for. And you said we'd have dinner afterwards at the Chinese restaurant at Ely.'

'Sorry. I couldn't know I'd be on a murder case.'

'When will you be back? If there's any point in asking?'

'God knows. I'm picking up Sergeant Beale. There are still one or two people we've got to see who were at the Muddington dance, notably a lad called Barry Taylor who has some explaining to do. Depending on what we get out of him, I may want to drop in on the husband again.'

'That'll please you, won't it, keeping him in a muck sweat. Is that why you became a cop – because you like frightening people?'

'That's about as stupid as saying you became a nurse because you get a kick out of emptying bed-pans.'

He flung himself in a chair and closed his eyes, giving way to sleep. He saw again the boy's terrified face, smelt again the sweat of fear. But he'd stood up well to that first interview, hindered rather than helped by the presence of his solicitor, who had never seen his client before and had made it painfully apparent that he would prefer never to see him again. He had stuck to his story, that they'd quarrelled at the dance and he had left early. That she hadn't arrived home by one o'clock. That he'd gone out to look for her on the road and across the clunch-pit field, returning alone half an hour later. That he'd seen no one and hadn't been anywhere near the clunch pit or the derelict car. It was a good story, simple, unelaborated, possibly even true except in that one essential. But, with luck, the Lab report on her blood and the stain on his jacket cuff, the minute traces of sandy soil and dust from the car on his shoes, would be ready by Friday. If Lorrimer worked late tonight – and he usually did – the blood analysis might even be available by tomorrow. And then would come the elaborations, the inconsistencies, and finally the truth. She said:

'Who else was at the scene?'

It was something, he thought, that she had bothered to ask. He said sleepily:

'Lorrimer, of course. He never misses a murder scene. Doesn't trust any of us to know our jobs, I suppose. We had the usual half-hour hanging about for Kerrison. That maddened Lorrimer, of course. He's done all the work at the scene – all anyone can do – and then he has to cool his heels with the rest of us, waiting for God's gift to forensic pathology to come screaming up with a police escort and break the news to us that what we all thought was a corpse is – surprise, surprise – indeed a corpse, and that we can safely move the body.'

'The forensic pathologist does more than that.'

'Of course he does. But not all that much more, not at the actual scene. His job comes later.'

He added:

'Sorry I couldn't ring. I did try but you were engaged.'

'I expect that was Daddy. His offer still stands, the job of Security

Officer in the Organization. But he can't wait much longer. If you don't accept by the end of the month, then he'll advertise.'

Oh God, he thought, not that again.

'I wish your dear Daddy wouldn't talk about the Organization. It makes the family business sound like the Mafia. If it were, I might be tempted to join. What Daddy's got are three cheap, shabby shops selling cheap, shabby suits to cheap shabby fools who wouldn't recognize a decent cloth if it were shoved down their throats. I might've considered coming into the business if dear Daddy hadn't already got Big Brother as a co-director, ready to take over from him, and if he didn't make it so plain that he only tolerates me because I'm your husband. But I'm damned if I'm going to fart around like a pansy floor-walker watching that no poor sod nicks the Y-fronts, even if I am dignified with the name security officer. I'm staying here.'

'Where you've got such useful contacts.'

And what exactly, he wondered, did she mean by that? He'd been careful not to tell her anything, but she wasn't altogether a fool. She could have guessed. He said:

'Where I've got a job. You knew what you were taking on when you married me.'

But no one ever does know that, he thought. Not really.

'Don't expect me to be here when you get back.'

That was an old threat. He said easily:

'Suit yourself. But if you're thinking of driving, forget it. I'm taking the Cortina, the clutch is playing up on the Renault. So if you're planning on running home to Mummy before tomorrow morning, you'll have to phone Daddy to call for you, or take a taxi.'

She was speaking, but her voice, peevishly insistent, was coming from far away, no longer coherent words but waves of sound beating against his brain. Two hours. Whether or not she bothered to rouse him, he knew that he would wake almost to the minute. He closed his eyes and slept.

BOOK TWO
Death in a White Coat

1

It was very peaceful in the front hall of Hoggatt's at eight-forty in the morning. Brenda often thought that this was the part of the working day she liked best, the hour before the staff arrived and the work of the Lab got really under way, when she and Inspector Blakelock worked together in the quiet emptiness of the hall, still and solemn as a church, making up a supply of manila folders ready to register the day's new cases, repacking exhibits for collection by the police, making a final check of the Laboratory reports to courts to ensure that the examination was complete, that no relevant detail had been omitted. Immediately on arrival she would put on her white coat, and at once she felt different, no longer young and uncertain, but a professional woman, almost like a scientist, a recognized member of the Lab staff. Then she would go into the kitchen at the back of the house and make tea. After the dignification of the white coat this domestic chore was something of a let-down, and she didn't really need a drink so soon after breakfast. But Inspector Blakelock, who motored from Ely every day, was always ready for his tea, and she didn't mind making it.

'That's the stuff to give the troops,' he would invariably say, curving back moist lips to the mug's brim and gulping the hot liquid down as if his throat were asbestos. 'You make a nice cup of tea, Brenda, I'll say that for you.' And she would reply:

'Mum says the secret is always to warm the pot and let the tea brew for just five minutes.'

This small ritual exchange, so invariable that she could silently mouth his words and had to resist an impulse to giggle, the familiar domestic aroma of the tea, the gradual warmth as she curved her hands around the thick mug, constituted a reassuring and comforting beginning to the working day.

She liked Inspector Blakelock. He spoke seldom, but he was never impatient with her, always kind, a companionable father figure. Even her mother, when she visited the Lab before Brenda took up her post, had been happy about her working alone with him.

Brenda's cheeks still burned with shame when she remembered her mother's insistence that she should visit Hoggatt's to see where her daughter was going to work, although Chief Inspector Martin, the Senior Police Liaison Officer, had apparently thought it perfectly reasonable. He had explained to her mother how it was an innovation for Hoggatt's having a clerical officer on the desk instead of a junior police officer. If she made a success of the job it would mean a permanent saving in police manpower as well as a useful training for her. As Chief Inspector Martin had told her mother: 'The reception desk is the heart of the Laboratory.' At present he was with a party of police officers visiting the United States and Inspector Blakelock was totally in charge doing the two jobs, not only receiving the exhibits, making out the register of court attendances and preparing the statistics, but discussing the cases with the detective in charge, explaining what the Laboratory could hope to do, rejecting those cases where the scientists couldn't help, and checking that the final statements for the court were complete. Brenda guessed that it was a big responsibility for him and was determined not to let him down.

Already, when she had been making the tea, the first exhibit of the day had arrived, brought in no doubt by a detective-constable working on the case. It was another plastic bag of clothes from the clunch-pit murder. As Inspector Blakelock turned it over in his large hands, she glimpsed through the plastic a pair of dark blue trousers with a greasy waistband, a wide-lapelled striped jacket, and a pair of black shoes with pointed toes and ornate buckles. Inspector Blakelock was studying the police report. He said:

'These belong to the boyfriend she was messing about with at the dance. You'll need a new file for the report, but register it to Biology under the Muddington reference with a sub-group number. Then attach one of the red Immediate slips. Murder gets priority.'

'But we might have two or three murders at the same time. Who decides the priority then?'

'The head of the department concerned. It's his job to allocate the work to his staff. After murder and rape, it's usual to give priority to those cases where the accused hasn't been bailed.'

Brenda said:

'I hope you don't mind my asking so many questions. Only I do want to learn. Dr Lorrimer told me that I ought to find out all I can and not just look on this job as routine.'

'You ask away, lass, I don't mind. Only you don't want to listen too much to Dr Lorrimer. He isn't the director here, even if he thinks he is. When you've registered that clobber, the bundle goes on the Biology shelf.'

Brenda entered the exhibit number carefully in the day-book and moved the plastic-shrouded bundle to the shelf of exhibits waiting to go into the Biology Search Room. It was good to be up to date with the entering. She glanced up at the clock. It was nearly eight-fifty. Soon the day's post would be delivered and the desk would be heaped with padded envelopes containing yesterday's blood samples from the drink and driving cases. Then the police cars would start arriving. Uniformed or plain-clothes policemen would bring in large envelopes of documents for Mr Middlemass, the Document Examiner; specially prepared kits issued by the Laboratory for the collection of saliva, blood and semen stains; unwieldy bags of stained and dirty bed-linen and blankets; the ubiquitous blunt instruments; bloodstained knives carefully taped into their boxes.

And at any moment now the first members of staff would be arriving. Mrs Bidwell, the cleaner, should have been with them twenty minutes ago. Perhaps she had caught Scobie's influenza. The first of the scientific staff to arrive would probably be Clifford Bradley, the Higher Scientific Officer in the Biology Department, scurrying through the hall as if he had no right to be there, with his anxious hunted eyes and that stupid, drooping moustache, so preoccupied that he hardly noticed their greeting. Then Miss Foley, the Director's secretary, calm and self-possessed, wearing always that secret smile. Miss Foley reminded Brenda of Mona Rigby at school, who was always chosen to play the Madonna in the Christmas nativity play. She had never liked Mona Rigby – who wouldn't have been chosen twice for the coveted role if the staff had known as much about her as did Brenda – and she wasn't sure that she really liked Miss Foley. Then someone she did like, Mr Middlemass, the Document Examiner, with his jacket slung over his shoulders, leaping up the stairs three steps at a time and calling out a greeting to the desk. After that they would come in almost any order. The hall would become alive with people, rather like a railway terminus, and at the heart of the seeming chaos, controlling and directing, helping and explaining, were the staff of the reception desk.

As if to signal that the working day was about to begin, the telephone rang. Inspector Blakelock's hand enveloped the receiver. He listened in silence for what seemed a longer period than normal, then she heard him speak.

'I don't think he's here, Mr Lorrimer. You say he never came home last night?'

Another silence. Inspector Blakelock half turned away from her and bent his head conspiratorially over the mouthpiece as if listening to a confidence. Then he rested the receiver on the counter and turned to Brenda:

'It's Dr Lorrimer's old dad. He's worried. Apparently Dr Lorrimer didn't take him his early tea this morning and it looks as if he didn't come home last night. His bed hasn't been slept in.'

'Well, he can't be here. I mean, we found the front door locked when we arrived.'

There could be no doubt about that. As she had come round the corner of the house from putting her bicycle in the old stable block, Inspector Blakelock had been standing at the front door almost as if he were waiting for her. Then, when she had joined him, he had shone his torch on the locks and inserted the three keys, first the Yale, and then the Ingersoll, and lastly the security lock which disconnected the electronic warning system from Guy's Marsh police station. Then they had stepped together into the unlighted hall. She had gone to the cloakroom at the back of the building to put on her white coat and he had gone to the box in Chief Inspector Martin's office to switch off the system which protected the inner doors of the main Laboratory rooms.

She giggled and said:

'Mrs Bidwell hasn't turned up to start the cleaning and now Dr Lorrimer's missing. Perhaps they've run away together. The great Hoggatt scandal.'

It wasn't a very funny joke, and she wasn't surprised when Inspector Blakelock didn't laugh. He said:

'The locked door doesn't necessarily signify. Dr Lorrimer has his own keys. And if he did make his bed and then come in extra early this morning, like as not he'd have relocked the door and set the internal alarms.'

'But how would he have got into the Biology Lab, then?'

'He'd have had to have opened the door and then left it open when he reset the alarms. It doesn't seem likely. When he's here alone he usually relies on the Yale.'

He put the receiver again to his ear and said:

'Hold on a moment will you, Mr Lorrimer. I don't think he's here, but I'll just check.'

'I'll go,' said Brenda, anxious to demonstrate helpfulness. Without waiting to lift the flap she slipped under the counter. As she turned she saw him with startling clarity, brightly instantaneous as a camera flash. Inspector Blakelock, with his mouth half-open in remonstrance, his arm flung out towards her in a gesture, stiff and histrionic, of protection or restraint. But now, uncomprehending, she laughed and ran up the wide stairs. The Biology Laboratory was at the back of the first floor, running with its adjoining search room almost the whole length of the building. The door was shut. She turned the knob and pushed it open, feeling along the wall for the light switch. Her fingers found it and she pressed it down. The two long fluorescent tubes suspended from the ceiling blinked, then glimmered, then glowed into steady light.

She saw the body immediately. He was lying in the space between the two large central examination tables, face downwards, his left hand seeming to claw at the floor, his right arm hunched beneath him. His legs were straight. She gave a curious little sound between a cry and a moan and knelt beside him. The hair above his left ear was matted and spiked like her kitten's fur after he had washed, but she couldn't see the blood against the dark hair. But she knew that it was blood. Already it had blackened on the collar of his white coat and a small pool had separated and congealed on the Lab floor. Only his left eye was visible, fixed and dull and retracted, like the eye of a dead calf. Tentatively she felt his cheek. It was cold. But she had known as soon as she had seen that glazed eye that this was death.

She had no memory of closing the Lab door or coming down the stairs. Inspector Blakelock was still behind the counter, rigid as a statue, the telephone receiver in his hand. She wanted to laugh at the sight of his face, he looked so funny. She tried to speak to him, but the words wouldn't come. Her jaw jabbered uncontrollably and her teeth clattered together. She made some kind of gesture. He said something that she couldn't catch, dropped the receiver on the counter and raced upstairs.

She staggered to the heavy Victorian armchair against the wall outside Chief Inspector Martin's office, Colonel Hoggatt's chair. The portrait looked down at her. As she watched, the left eye seemed to grow larger, the lips twisted to a leer.

Her whole body was seized with a terrible cold. Her heart seemed to have grown immense, thudding against the rib-cage. She was breathing in great gulps. but still there wasn't enough air. Then she became aware of the crackling from the telephone. Rising slowly like an automaton, she made her way over to the counter and picked up the receiver. Mr Lorrimer's voice, frail and querulous, was bleating at the other end. She tried to say the accustomed words 'Hoggatt's Laboratory here. Reception speaking.' But the words wouldn't come. She replaced the receiver in its cradle and walked back to her chair.

She had no memory of hearing the long peal of the doorbell, of moving stiffly across the hall to answer it. Suddenly the door crashed open and the hall was full of people, loud with voices. The light seemed to have brightened, which was odd, and she saw them all like actors on a stage, brightly lit, faces made grotesque and heightened by make-up, every word clear and comprehensible as if she were in the front row of the stalls. Mrs Bidwell, the cleaner, in her mackintosh with the imitation fur collar, her eyes bright with indignation, her voice pitched high.

'What the hell's going on here! Some bloody fool phoned my old man and told him that I needn't come in today, that Mrs Schofield wanted me. Who's playing silly buggers?'

Inspector Blakelock was coming down the stairs, slowly and deliberately, the protagonist making his entrance. They stood in a small circle and looked up at him, Dr Howarth, Clifford Bradley, Miss Foley, Mrs Bidwell. The Director stepped forward. He looked as if he were going to faint. He said:

'Well, Blakelock?'

'It's Dr Lorrimer, sir. He's dead. Murdered.'

Surely they couldn't all have repeated that word in unison, turning their faces towards each other, like a Greek chorus. But it seemed to echo in the quiet of the hall, becoming meaningless, a sonorous groan of a word. Murder. Murder. Murder.

She saw Dr Howarth run towards the stairs. Inspector Blakelock turned to accompany him, but the Director said:

'No, you stay here. See that no one gets any further than the hall.

Phone the Chief Constable and Dr Kerrison. Then get me the Home Office.'

Suddenly they seemed to notice Brenda for the first time. Mrs Bidwell came towards her. She said:

'Did you find him then? You poor little bugger!'

And suddenly it wasn't a play any more. The lights went out. The faces became amorphous, ordinary. Brenda gave a little gasp. She felt Mrs Bidwell's arms go round her shoulders. The smell of the mackintosh was pressed into her face. The fur was as soft as her kitten's paw. And, blessedly, Brenda began to cry.

2

In a London teaching hospital close by the river, from which he could in his more masochistic moments glimpse the window of his own office, Dr Charles Freeborn, Controller of the Forensic Science Service, all six foot four of him, lay rigidly in his narrow bed, his nose peaked high above the methodical fold of the sheet, his white hair a haze against the whiter pillow. The bed was too short for him, an inconvenience to which he had accommodated himself by neatly sticking out his toes over the foot board. His bedside locker held the conglomerate of offerings, necessities and minor diversions considered indispensable to a brief spell in hospital. They included a vase of official-looking roses, scentless but florid, through whose funereal and unnatural blooms Commander Adam Dalgliesh glimpsed a face so immobile, upturned eyes fixed on the ceiling, that he was momentarily startled by the illusion that he was visiting the dead. Recalling that Freeborn was recovering from nothing more serious than a successful operation for varicose veins, he approached the bed and said tentatively:

'Hello!'

Freeborn, galvanized from his torpor, sprang up like a jack-in-the box, scattering from his bedside locker a packet of tissues, two copies of the *Journal of the Forensic Science Society* and an open box of chocolates. He shot out a lean speckled arm encircled by the hospital identity bracelet and crushed Dalgliesh's hand.

'Adam! Don't creep up on me like that, damn you! God, am I glad to see you! The only good news I've had this morning is that you'll be in charge. I thought that you might have already left. How long can you spare? How are you getting there?'

Dalgliesh answered the questions in order.

'Ten minutes. By chopper from the Battersea heliport. I'm on my way now. How are you, Charles? Am I being a nuisance?'

'I'm the nuisance. This couldn't have happened at a worse time. And the maddening part of it is that it's my own fault. The op could have waited. Only the pain was getting rather tedious and Meg insisted that I had it done now before I retired, on the theory, I suppose, that better in the Government's time than my own.'

Recalling what he knew of the ardours and achievements of Freeborn's forty-odd years in the Forensic Science Service, the difficult war years, the delayed retirement, the last five years when he had exchanged his directorship for the frustrations of bureaucracy, Dalgliesh said:

'Sensible of her. And there's nothing you could have done at Chevisham.'

'I know. It's ridiculous, this feeling of responsibility because one isn't actually in post when disaster strikes. They rang from the duty office to break the news to me just after nine. Better that than learning it from my visitors or this evening's paper, I suppose they thought. Decent of them. The Chief Constable must have called in the Yard within a few minutes of getting the news. How much do you know?'

'About as much as you, I imagine. I've spoken to the CC and to Howarth. They've given me the main facts. The skull smashed, apparently by a heavy mallet which Lorrimer had been examining. The Lab found properly locked when the Assistant Police Liaison Officer and the young CO arrived at eight-thirty this morning. Lorrimer's keys in his pocket. He often worked late and most of the Lab staff knew that he proposed to do so last night. No sign of a break-in. Four sets of keys. Lorrimer had one set as the Senior PSO and Deputy Security Officer. The Assistant Police Liaison Officer has the second. Lorrimer or one of the Police Liaison Officers were the only people authorized to lock and open up the building. The Director keeps the third set of keys in his security cupboard, and the fourth are in a safe at Guy's Marsh police station in case the alarm rings in the night.'

Freeborn said:

'So either Lorrimer let in his murderer or the murderer had a key.'

There were, thought Dalgliesh, other possibilities, but now was not the time to discuss them. He asked:

'Lorrimer would have let in anyone from the Lab, I suppose?'

'Why not? He'd probably have admitted any of the local police whom he personally knew, particularly if it were a detective concerned with a recent case. Otherwise, I'm not so sure. He may have admitted a friend or relative, although that's even more doubtful. He was a punctilious blighter and I can't see him using the Lab as a convenient place for a rendezvous. And, of course, he would have let in the forensic pathologist.'

'That's a local man, Henry Kerrison, they tell me. The CC said that they called him in to look at the body. Well, they could hardly do anything else. I didn't know you'd found a successor to Death-House Donald.'

'Nor have we. Kerrison is doing it on an item-of-service basis. He's well thought of and we'll probably appoint him if we can get the Area Health Authority to agree. There's the usual difficulty about his hospital responsibilities. I wish to hell we could get the forensic pathology service sorted out before I go. But that's one headache I'll have to leave to my successor.'

Dalgliesh thought without affection of Death-House Donald with his ghoulish schoolboy humour – 'Not that cake-knife, my dear lady. I used it this morning on one of Slash Harry's victims and the edge is rather blunted' – his mania for self-advertisement and his intolerable bucolic laugh, and was grateful that at least he wouldn't be interrogating that redoubtable old phoney. He said:

'Tell me about Lorrimer. What was he like?'

This was the question which lay at the heart of every murder investigation; and yet he knew its absurdity before he asked it. It was the strangest part of a detective's job, this building-up of a relationship with the dead, seen only as a crumpled corpse at the scene of crime or naked on the mortuary table. The victim was central to the mystery of his own death. He died because of what he was. Before the case was finished Dalgliesh would have received a dozen pictures of Lorrimer's personality, transferred like prints from other men's minds. From these amorphous and uncertain images he would create his own imaginings, superimposed and dominant, but essentially just as incomplete, just as distorted – as were the others –

by his own preconceptions, his own personality. But the question had to be asked. And at least he could rely on Freeborn to answer it without initiating a philosophical discussion about the basis of the self. But their minds must for a moment have flowed together, for Freeborn said:

'It's odd how you always have to ask that question, that you'll only see him through other men's eyes. Aged about forty. Looks like John the Baptist without his beard and is about as uncompromising. Single. Lives with an elderly father in a cottage just outside the village. He is – was – an extremely competent forensic biologist, but I doubt whether he would have gone any higher. Obsessional, edgy, uncomfortable to be with. He applied for the job at Hoggatt's, of course, and was runner-up to Howarth.'

'How did he and the Lab take the new appointment?'

'Lorrimer took it pretty hard, I believe. The Lab wouldn't have welcomed his appointment. He was pretty unpopular with most of the senior staff. But there are always one or two who would have preferred a colleague to a stranger even if they hated his guts. And the Union made the expected noises about not appointing a forensic scientist.'

'Why did you appoint Howarth? I take it you were on the Board.'

'Oh yes. I accept a share of the responsibility. That's not to say that I think we made a mistake. Old Doc Mac was one of the really great forensic scientists – we started together – but there's no denying that he'd let the reins slip a bit in recent years. Howarth has already increased the work turnover by ten per cent. And then there's the commissioning of the new Lab. It was a calculated risk to take a man without forensic experience, but we were looking for a manager primarily. At least, most of the Board were and the rest of us were persuaded that it would be no bad thing, without, I confess, being precisely clear what we meant by that blessed word. Management. The new science. We all make obeisance to it. In the old days we got on with the job, jollied staff along if they needed it, kicked the sluggards in the backside, encouraged the unconfident and per-suaded a reluctant and sceptical police force to use us. Oh, and sent in an occasional statistical return to the Home Office just to remind them that we were there. It seemed to work all right. The Service didn't collapse. Have you ever considered what exactly is the difference between administration and management, Adam?'

'Keep it as a question to confound the candidate at your next Board. Howarth was at the Bruche Research Institute wasn't he? Why did he want to leave? He must have taken a cut in pay.'

'Not more than about six hundred a year, and that wouldn't worry him. His father was rich, and it all came to him and his half-sister.'

'But it's a bigger place surely? And he can't be getting the research at Hoggatt's.'

'He gets some, but essentially, of course, it's a service laboratory. That worried us a bit on the Board. But you can hardly set out to persuade your most promising applicant that he's downgrading himself. Scientifically and academically – he's a pure physicist – he was well ahead of the rest of the field. Actually we did press him a bit and he gave the usual reasons. He was getting stale, wanted a new sphere of activity, was anxious to get away from London. Gossip has it that his wife had recently left him and he wanted to make a clean break. That was probably the reason. Thank God he didn't use that blasted word "challenge". If I have to listen to one more candidate telling me he sees the job as a challenge I'll throw up over the boardroom table. Adam, I'm getting old.'

He nodded his head towards the window.

'They're in a bit of a twitch over there, I need hardly say.'

'I know. I've had an exceedingly brief but tactful interview. They're brilliant at implying more than they actually say. But obviously it's important to get it solved quickly. Apart from confidence in the Service, you'll all want to get the Lab back to work.'

'What's happening now? To the staff, I mean.'

'The local CID have locked all the interior doors and they're keeping the staff in the library and the reception area until I arrive. They're occupying themselves writing out an account of their movements since Lorrimer was last seen alive and the local force are getting on with the preliminary checking of alibis. That should save some time. I'm taking one officer, John Massingham, with me. The Met Lab will take on any of the forensic work. They're sending a chap down from Public Relations Branch to handle the publicity, so I won't have that on my plate. It's obliging of that pop group to break up so spectacularly. That and the Government's troubles should keep us off the front page for a day or two.'

Freeborn was looking down at his big toes with mild distaste as if they were errant members whose deficiencies had only now become apparent to him. From time to time he wriggled them, whether in obedience to some medical instruction or for his own private satisfaction, it was impossible to say. After a moment he spoke.

'I started my career at Hoggatt's, you know. That was before the war. All any of us had then was wet chemistry, test-tubes, beakers, solutions. And girls weren't employed because it wasn't decent for them to be concerned with sex cases. Hoggatt's was old-fashioned even for the 1930 service. Not scientifically, though. We had a spectrograph when it was still the new wonder toy. The fens threw up some odd crimes. Do you remember the Mulligan case, old man who chopped up his brother and tied the remains to the Leamings sluice-gates? There was some nice forensic evidence there.'

'Some fifty bloodstains on the pig-sty wall, weren't there? And Mulligan swore it was sow's blood.'

Freeborn's voice grew reminiscent.

'I liked that old villain. And they still drag out those photographs I took of the splashes and use them to illustrate lectures on blood-stains. Odd, the attraction Hoggatt's had – still has for that matter. An unsuitable Palladian mansion in an unexciting East Anglian village on the edge of the black fens. Ten miles to Ely, and that's hardly a centre of riotous activity for the young. Winters to freeze your marrow and a spring wind – the fen blow they call it – which whips up the peat and chokes your lungs like smog. And yet the staff, if they didn't leave after the first month, stayed for ever. Did you know that Hoggatt's has got a small Wren chapel in the Lab grounds? Architecturally it's much superior to the house because old Hoggatt never messed it about. He was almost entirely without aesthetic taste, I believe. He used it as a chemical store once it had been deconsecrated or whatever it is they do to unused churches. Howarth has got a string quartet going at the Lab and they gave a concert there. Apparently he's a noted amateur violinist. At the moment he's probably wishing that he'd stuck to music. This isn't a propitious start for him, poor devil. And it was always such a happy Lab. I suppose it was the isolation that gave us such a feeling of camaraderie.'

Dalgliesh said grimly:

'I doubt whether that will survive an hour of my arrival.'

'No. You chaps usually bring as much trouble with you as you solve. You can't help it. Murder is like that, a contaminating crime.

Oh, you'll solve it, I know. You always do. But I'm wondering at what cost.'

Dalgliesh did not answer. He was both too honest and too fond of Freeborn to make comforting and platitudinous promises. Of course, he would be tactful. That didn't need saying. But he would be at Hoggatt's to solve a murder, and all other considerations would go down before that overriding task. Murder was always solved at a cost, sometimes to himself, more often to others. And Freeborn was right. It was a crime which contaminated everyone whom it touched, innocent and guilty alike. He didn't grudge the ten minutes he had spent with Freeborn. The old man believed, with simple patriotism, that the Service to which he had given the whole of his working life was the best in the world. He had helped to shape it, and he was probably right. Dalgliesh had learned what he had come to learn. But as he shook hands and said goodbye he knew that he left no comfort behind him.

3

The library at Hoggatt's was at the rear of the ground floor. Its three tall windows gave a view of the stone terrace and the double flight of steps going down to what had once been a lawn and formal gardens, but which was now a half-acre of neglected grass, bounded to the west by the brick annexe of the Vehicle Examination Department, and to the east by the old stable block, now converted into garages. The room was one of the few in the house spared by its former owner's transforming zeal. The original bookcases of carved oak still lined the walls, although they now housed the Laboratory's not inconsiderable scientific library, while extra shelf-room for bound copies of national and international journals had been provided by two movable steel units which divided the room into three bays. Under each of the three windows was a working table with four chairs; one table was almost completely covered by a model of the new Laboratory.

It was in this somewhat inadequate space that the staff were congregated. A detective-sergeant from the local CID sat impassively near the door, a reminder of why they were so inconveniently incarcerated. They were allowed out to the ground-floor cloakroom under tactful escort, and had been told they could telephone home from the library. But the rest of the Laboratory was at present out of bounds.

They had all, on arrival, been asked to write a brief account of where they had been, and with whom, the previous evening and night. Patiently, they waited their turn at one of the three tables. The statements had been collected by the sergeant and handed out to his colleague on the reception desk, presumably so that the preliminary checking could begin. Those of the junior staff who could provide a satisfactory alibi were allowed home as soon as it had been checked; one by one and with some reluctance at missing the excitements to come they went their way. The less fortunate, together with those who had arrived first at the Laboratory that morning and all the senior scientists, had been told they must await the arrival of the team from Scotland Yard. The Director had put in only one brief appearance in the library. Earlier he had gone with Angela Foley to break the news of Lorrimer's death to his father. Since his return he had stayed in his own office with Detective-Superintendent Mercer of the local CID. It was rumoured that Dr Kerrison was with them.

The minutes dragged while they listened for the first hum of the approaching helicopter. Inhibited by the presence of the police, by prudence, delicacy or embarrassment from talking about the subject foremost in their minds, they spoke to each other with the wary politeness of uncongenial strangers stranded in an airport lounge. The women were, on the whole, better equipped for the tedium of the wait. Mrs Mallett, the typist from the general office, had brought her knitting to work and fortified by an unshakeable alibi – she had sat between the postmistress and Mr Mason from the general store at the village concert – and with something to occupy her hands, sat clicking away with understandable if irritating complacency until given the order of release. Mrs Bidwell, the Laboratory cleaner, had insisted on visiting her broom cupboard, under escort, and had provided herself with a feather duster and a couple of rags with which she made a vigorous onslaught on the bookshelves. She was unusually silent, but the group of scientists at the tables could hear her muttering to herself as she punished the books at the end of one of the bays.

Brenda Pridmore had been allowed to collect the Exhibits Received book from the counter and, white-faced but outwardly composed, was checking the previous month's figures. The book took more than its share of the available space; but at least she had a legitimate job. Claire Easterbrook, Senior Scientific Officer in the Biology Department and, with Lorrimer's death, the senior biologist, had taken from her briefcase a scientific paper she had prepared on recent advances in blood grouping and had settled down to revise it with as little apparent concern as if murder at Hoggatt's were a routine inconvenience for which, prudently, she was always provided.

The rest of the staff passed the time each in his own way. Those who preferred the pretence of business immersed themselves in a book and, from time to time, made an ostentatious note. The two Vehicle Examiners, who were reputed to have no conversation except about cars, squatted side by side, their backs against the steel book racks, and talked cars together with desperate eagerness. Middlemass had finished *The Times* crossword by quarter to ten and made the rest of the paper last as long as possible. But now even the deaths column was exhausted. He folded the paper and tossed it across the table to eagerly awaiting hands.

It was a relief when Stephen Copley, the Senior Chemist, arrived just before ten, bustling in as usual, his rubicund face with its tonsure and fringe of black curly hair glistening as if he had come in from the sun. Nothing was known to disconcert him, certainly not the death of a man he had disliked. But he was secure in his alibi, having spent the whole of the previous day in the Crown Court and the evening and night with friends at Norwich, only getting back to Chevisham in time for a late start that morning. His colleagues, relieved to find something to talk about, began questioning him about the case. They spoke rather too loudly to be natural. The rest of the company listened with simulated interest as if the conversation were a dramatic dialogue provided for their entertainment.

'Who did they call for the defence?' asked Middlemass.

'Charlie Pollard. He hung his great belly over the box and explained confidentially to the jury that they needn't be frightened of the so-called scientific expert witness because none of us, including himself of course, really know what we're talking about. They were immensely reassured, I need hardly say.'

'Juries hate scientific evidence.'

'They think they won't be able to understand it so naturally they can't understand it. As soon as you step into the box you see a curtain of obstinate incomprehension clanging down over their minds. What they want is certainty. Did this paint particle come from this car body? Answer Yes or No. None of those nasty mathematical probabilities we're so fond of.'

'If they hate scientific evidence they certainly hate arithmetic more. Give them a scientific opinion which depends on the ability to divide a factor by two-thirds and what do you get from counsel? "I'm afraid you'll have to explain yourself more simply, Mr Middlemass. The jury and I haven't got a higher degree in mathematics, you know." Inference: you're an arrogant bastard and the jury would be well advised not to believe a word you say.'

It was the old argument. Brenda had heard it all before when she ate her lunchtime sandwiches in the room, half-way between a kitchen and a sitting-room, which was still called the Junior Mess. But now it seemed terrible that they should be able to talk so naturally while Dr Lorrimer lay there dead upstairs. Suddenly she had a need to speak his name. She looked up and made herself say:

'Dr Lorrimer thought that the service would end up with about three immense laboratories doing the work for the whole country with exhibits coming in by air. He said that he thought all the scientific evidence ought to be agreed by both sides before the trial.'

Middlemass said easily:

'That's an old argument. The police want a local lab nice and handy, and who's to blame them? Besides, three-quarters of forensic scientific work doesn't require all this sophisticated instrumentation. There's more of a case for highly equipped regional laboratories with local out-stations. But who'd want to work in the small labs if the more exciting stuff went elsewhere?'

Miss Easterbrook had apparently finished her revision. She said:

'Lorrimer knew that this idea of the lab as a scientific arbiter wouldn't work, not with the British accusatorial system. Anyway, scientific evidence ought to be tested like any other evidence.'

'But how?' asked Middlemass. 'By an ordinary jury? Suppose you're an expert document examiner outside the service and they call you for the defence. You and I disagree. How can the jury judge between us? They'll probably choose to believe you because you're better-looking.'

'Or you, more likely, because you're a man.'

'Or one of them – the crucial one – will reject me because I remind him of Uncle Ben and all the family know that Ben was the world's champion liar.'

'All right. All right.' Copley spread plump hands in a benediction of appeasement. 'It's the same as democracy. A fallible system but the best we've got.'

Middlemass said:

'It's extraordinary, though, how well it works. You look at the jury, sitting there politely attentive, like children on their best behaviour because they're visitors in an alien country and don't want to make fools of themselves or offend the natives. Yet how often do they come up with a verdict that's manifestly perverse having regard to the evidence?'

Claire Easterbrook said drily:

'Whether it's manifestly perverse having regard to the truth is another matter.'

'A criminal trial isn't a tribunal for eliciting the truth. At least we deal in facts. What about the emotion? Did you love your husband, Mrs B? How can the poor woman explain that, probably like the majority of wives, she loved him most of the time, when he didn't snore in her ear all night or shout at the kids or keep her short of Bingo money.'

Copley said:

'She can't. If she's got any sense and if her counsel has briefed her properly, she'll get out her handkerchief and sob, "Oh yes, sir. A better husband never lived, as God's my witness." It's a game, isn't it? You win if you play by the rules.'

Claire Easterbrook shrugged:

'If you know them. Too often it's a game where the rules are known only to one side. Natural enough when that's the side which makes them up.'

Copley and Middlemass laughed.

Clifford Bradley had half hidden himself from the rest of the company behind the table holding the model of the new Laboratory. He had taken a book from the shelves at random but, for the last ten minutes, hadn't even bothered to turn the page.

They were laughing! They were actually laughing! Getting up from the table he groped his way down the furthest bay and replaced his book in the rack, leaning his forehead against the cold steel. Unobtrusively Middlemass strolled up beside him and, back to the company, reached up to take a book from the shelf. He said:

'Are you all right?'

'I wish to God they'd come.'

'So do we all. But the chopper should be here any minute now.'

'How can they laugh like that? Don't they care?'

'Of course they care. Murder is beastly, embarrassing and inconvenient. But I doubt whether anyone is feeling a purely personal grief. And other people's tragedies, other people's danger, always provoke a certain euphoria as long as one is safe oneself.' He looked at Bradley and said softly:

'There's always manslaughter, you know. Or even justified homicide. Though, come to think of it, one could hardly plead that.'

'You think I killed him, don't you?'

'I don't think anything. Anyway, you've got an alibi. Wasn't your mother-in-law with you yesterday evening?'

'Not all the evening. She caught the seven forty-five bus.'

'Well, with luck, there'll be evidence that he was dead by then.' And why, thought Middlemass, should Bradley assume that he wasn't? Bradley's dark and anxious eyes narrowed with suspicion.

'How did you know that Sue's mother was with us last night?'

'Susan told me. Actually, she telephoned me at the Lab just before two. It was about Lorrimer.' He thought and then said easily, 'She was wondering whether there was a chance he might ask for a transfer now that Howarth has been in post a year. She thought I might have heard something. When you get home, tell her that I don't propose to tell the police about the call unless she does first. Oh, and you'd better reassure her that I didn't bash in his head for him. I'd do a lot for Sue, but a man has to draw the line somewhere.'

Bradley said with a note of resentment:

'Why should you worry? There's nothing wrong with your alibi. Weren't you at the village concert?'

'Not all the evening. And there's a certain slight embarrassment about my alibi even when I was ostensibly there.'

Bradley turned to him and said with sudden vehemence:

'I didn't do it! Oh God, I can't stand this waiting!'

'You've got to stand it. Pull yourself together, Cliff! You won't help yourself or Susan by going to pieces. They're English policemen, remember. We're not expecting the KGB.'

It was then that they heard the long-awaited sound, a distant grinding hum like that of any angry wasp. The desultory voices at the tables fell silent, heads were raised and, together, the company moved towards the windows. Mrs Bidwell rushed for a place of vantage. The red and white helicopter rattled into sight over the top of the trees and hovered, a noisy gadfly, above the terrace. No one spoke. Then Middlemass said:

'The Yard's wonder boy, appropriately, descends from the clouds. Well, let's hope that he works quickly. I want to get into my lab. Someone should tell him that he's not the only one with a murder on his hands.'

4

Detective-Inspector the Honourable John Massingham disliked helicopters, which he regarded as noisy, cramped and frighteningly unsafe. Since his physical courage was beyond question either by himself or anyone else, he would normally have had no objection to saying so. But he knew his chief's dislike of unnecessary chat, and strapped as they were side by side in uncomfortably close proximity in the Enstrom F28, he decided that the Chevisham case would get off to the most propitious start by a policy of disciplined silence. He noted with interest that the cockpit instrument panel was remarkably similar to a car dashboard; even the airspeed was shown in miles per hour instead of knots. He was only sorry that there the resemblance ended. He adjusted his earphones more comfortably and settled down to soothe his nerves by a concentrated study of his maps.

The red-brown tentacles of London's suburbs had at last been shaken off, and the chequered autumn landscape, multi-textured as a cloth collage, unrolled before them in a changing pattern of brown, green and gold, leading them on to Cambridge. The fitful sunshine moved in broad swathes across the neat, segmented villages, the trim municipal parks and open fields. Miniature tin cars, beetle-bright in the sun, pursued each other busily along the roads.

Dalgliesh glanced at his companion, at the strong, pale face, the spatter of freckles over the craggy nose and wide forehead, and the thatch of red hair springing under the headphones, and thought how like the boy was to his father, that redoubtable, thrice-decorated peer, whose courage was equalled only by his obstinacy and naïveté. The marvel of the Massinghams was that a lineage going back five hundred years could have produced so many generations of amiable nonentities. He remembered when he had last seen Lord Dungannon. It had been a debate in the House of Lords on juvenile delinquency, a subject on which His Lordship considered himself an expert since he had, indubitably, once been a boy and had, briefly, helped organize a youth club on his grandfather's estate. His thoughts, when they finally came, had been uttered in all their simplistic banality, in no particular order of logic or relevance, and in a curiously gentle voice punctuated by long pauses in which he had gazed thoughtfully at the throne and appeared to commune happily with some inner presence. Meanwhile, like lemmings who have smelt the sea, the noble lords streamed out of their chamber in a body to appear, as if summoned by telepathy, when Dungannon's speech drew to its close. But if the family had contributed nothing to statesmanship and little to the arts, they had died with spectacular gallantry for orthodox causes in every generation.

And now Dungannon's heir had chosen this far from orthodox job. It would be interesting to see if, for the first time and in so unusual a field, the family achieved distinction. What had led Massingham to choose the police service instead of his family's usual career of the Army as an outlet for his natural combativeness and unfashionable patriotism Dalgliesh had not enquired, partly because he was a respecter of other men's privacy, and partly because he wasn't sure that he wanted to hear the answer. So far Massingham had done exceptionally well. The police were a tolerant body and took the view that a man couldn't help who his father was. They accepted that Massingham had gained his promotion on merit although they were not so naïve as to suppose that being the elder son of a peer did any man harm. They called Massingham the Honjohn behind his back and occasionally to his face, and bore no malice.

Although the family was now impoverished and the estate sold – Lord Dungannon was bringing up his considerable family in a modest villa in Bayswater – the boy had still gone to his father's school. No doubt, thought Dalgliesh, the old warrior was unaware that other schools existed; like every other class, the aristocracy, however poor, could always find the money for the things they really wanted. But he was an odd product of that establishment, having none of the slightly *dégagé* elegance and ironic detachment which characterized its alumni. Dalgliesh, if he hadn't known his history, would have guessed that Massingham was the product of a sound, upper-middle-class family – a doctor or a solicitor, perhaps – and of an old-established grammar school. It was only the second time they had worked together. The first time, Dalgliesh had been impressed by Massingham's intelligence and enormous capacity for work, and by his admirable ability to keep his mouth shut and to sense when his chief wanted to be alone. He had also been struck by a streak of ruthlessness in the boy which, he thought, ought not to have surprised him since he knew that, as with all good detectives, it must be present.

And now the Enstrom was rattling above the towers and spires of Cambridge, and they could see the shining curve of the river, the bright autumnal avenues leading down through green lawns to miniature hump-backed bridges, King's College Chapel upturned and slowly rotating beside its great striped square of green. And, almost immediately, the city was behind them and they saw, like a crinkled ebony sea, the black earth of the fens. Below them were straight roads ridged above the fields, with villages strung along them as if clinging to the security of high ground; isolated farms with their roofs so low that they looked half-submerged in the peat; an occasional church tower standing majestically apart from its village with the gravestones planted round it like crooked teeth. They must be getting close now; already Dalgliesh could see the soaring west tower and pinnacles of Ely Cathedral to the east.

Massingham looked up from his map-reading and peered down. His voice crackled through Dalgliesh's earphones:

'This is it, sir.'

Chevisham was spread beneath them. It lay on a narrow plateau above the fens, the houses strung along the northerly of two converging roads. The tower of the impressive cruciform church was immediately identifiable, as was Chevisham Manor and, behind it, sprawling over the scarred field and linking the two roads, the brick and concrete of the new Laboratory building. They rattled along the main street of what looked like a typical East Anglian village. Dalgliesh glimpsed the ornate red-brick front of the local chapel, one or two prosperous-looking houses with Dutch gables, a small close of recently built, semi-detached boxes with the developer's board still in place, and what looked like the village general store and post office. There were few people about, but the noise of the engines brought figures from shops and houses and pale faces, their eyes shielded, strained up at them.

And now they were turning towards Hoggatt's Laboratory, coming in low over what must be the Wren Chapel. It stood about a quarter of a mile from the house in a triple circle of beech trees, an isolated building so small and perfect that it looked like an architect's model precisely set in a fabricated landscape, or an elegant ecclesiastical folly, justifying itself only by its classical purity, as distanced from religion as it was from life. It was odd that it lay so far from the house. Dalgliesh thought that it had probably been built later, perhaps because the original owner of the mansion had quarrelled with the local parson and, in defiance, had decided to make his own arrangements for spiritual ministrations. Certainly the house hardly looked large enough to support a private chapel. For a few seconds as they descended, he had an unimpeded view through a gap in the trees of the west front of the chapel. He saw a single high arched window with two balancing niches, the four Corinthian pilasters separating the bays, the whole crowned with a large decorated pediment and topped with a hexagonal lantern. The helicopter seemed almost to be brushing the trees. The brittle autumn leaves, shaken by the rush of air, flurried down like a shower of charred paper over the roof and the bright green of the grass.

And then, sickeningly, the helicopter soared, the chapel lurched out of sight and they were poised, engines rattling, ready to land on the wide terrace behind the house. Over its roof he could see the forecourt patterned with parking lots, the police cars tidily aligned and what looked like a mortuary van. A broad drive, bordered with straggling bushes and a few trees, led down to what the map showed as Stoney Piggott's Road. There was no gate to the driveway. Beyond it he could see the bright flag of a bus stop and the bus shelter. Then the helicopter began to descend and only the rear of the house was in view. From a ground-floor window he could see the smudges of watching faces.

There was a reception committee of three, their figures oddly foreshortened, the necks straining upwards. The thrash of the rotor blades had tugged their hair into grotesque shapes, flurried the legs of their trousers and flattened their jackets against their chests. Now, with the stilling of the engines, the sudden silence was so absolute that he saw the three motionless figures as if they were a tableau of dummies in a silent world. He and Massingham unclasped their seat belts and clambered to earth. For about five seconds the two groups stood regarding each other. Then, with a single gesture, the three waiting figures smoothed back their hair and advanced warily to meet him. Simultaneously his ears unblocked and the world again became audible. He turned to thank and speak briefly to the pilot. Then he and Massingham walked forward.

Dalgliesh already knew Superintendent Mercer of the local CID; they had met at a number of police conferences. Even at sixty feet his ox-like shoulders, the round comedian's face with the wide upturned mouth, and the button-bright eyes, had been instantly recognizable. Dalgliesh felt his hand crushed, and then Mercer made the introductions. Dr Howarth; a tall fair man, almost as tall as Dalgliesh himself, with widely spaced eyes of a remarkably deep blue and the lashes so long that they might have looked effeminate on any face less arrogantly male. He could, Dalgliesh thought, have been judged an outstandingly handsome man were it not for a certain incongruity of feature, perhaps the contrast between the fineness of the skin stretched over the flat cheekbones and the strong jutting jaw and uncompromising mouth. Dalgliesh would have known that he was rich. The blue eyes regarded the world with the slightly cynical assurance of a man accustomed to getting what he wanted when he wanted it by the simplest of expedients, that of paying for it. Beside him, Dr Henry Kerrison, although as tall, looked diminished. His creased, anxious face was bleached with weariness and there was a look in the dark, heavily lidded eyes which was uncomfortably close to defeat. He grasped Dalgliesh's hand with a firm, cool grip but didn't speak. Howarth said:

'There's no entrance now to the back of the house; we have to go round to the front. This is the easiest way.'

Carrying their scene-of-crime cases, Dalgliesh and Massingham followed him round the side of the house. The faces at the ground-floor window had disappeared and it was extraordinarily quiet.

Trudging through the leaves which had drifted over the path, sniffing the keen autumnal air with its hint of smokiness, and feeling the sun on his face, Massingham felt a surge of animal well-being. It was good to be out of London. This promised to be the kind of job he most liked. The little group turned the corner of the house and Dalgliesh and Massingham had their first clear view of the façade of Hoggatt's Laboratory.

5

The house was an excellent example of late seventeenth-century domestic architecture, a three-storey brick mansion with a hipped roof and four dormer windows, the centre three-bay projection surmounted by a pediment with a richly carved cornice and medallions. A flight of four wide, curved stone steps led to the doorway, imposing on its pilasters but solidly, unostentatiously, right. Dalgliesh paused momentarily to study the façade. Howarth said:

'Agreeable, isn't it? But wait till you see what the old man did to some of the interior.'

The front door, with its elegant but restrained brass door handle and knocker, was fitted with two security locks, a Chubb and an Ingersoll, in addition to the Yale. At a superficial glance there was no sign of forcing. It was open almost before Howarth had lifted his hand to ring. The man who stood aside, unsmiling, for them to enter, although not in uniform, was immediately recognizable to Dalgliesh as a police officer. Howarth introduced him briefly as Inspector Blakelock, Assistant Police Liaison Officer. He added:

'All three locks were in order when Blakelock arrived this morning. The Chubb connects the electronic warning system to Guy's Marsh police station. The internal protection system is controlled from a panel in the Police Liaison Officer's room.'

Dalgliesh turned to Blakelock.

'And that was in order?'

'Yes, sir.'

'There is no other exit?'

It was Howarth who answered.

'No. My predecessor had the back door and one side door

274

permanently barred. It was too complicated coping with a system of security locks for three doors. Everyone comes in and goes out by the front door.'

'Except possibly one person last night,' thought Dalgliesh.

They passed through the entrance hall which ran almost the whole length of the house, their feet suddenly loud on the marble tessellated floor. Dalgliesh was used to receiving impressions at a glance. The party did not pause on their way to the stairs, but he had a clear impression of the room, the high moulded ceiling, the two elegant pedimented doors to right and left, an oil painting of the Laboratory founder on the right-hand wall, the gleaming wood of the reception counter at the rear. A police officer with a sheaf of papers before him was using the desk telephone, presumably still checking alibis. He went on with his conversation without glancing up.

The staircase was remarkable. The balustrades were carved oak panels decorated with scrolls of acanthus foliage, each newel surmounted by a heavy oak pineapple. There was no carpet and the unpolished wood was heavily scarred. Dr Kerrison and Superintendent Mercer mounted behind Dalgliesh in silence. Howarth, leading the way, seemed to feel the need to talk:

'The ground floor is occupied with Reception and the Exhibits Store, my office, my secretary's room, the general office and the Police Liaison Officer's room. That's all, apart from the domestic quarters at the rear. Chief Inspector Martin is the chief PLO but he's in the USA at the moment and we only have Blakelock on duty. On this floor we have Biology at the back, Criminalistics at the front and the Instrument Section at the end of the corridor. But I've a plan of the Lab in my office for you. I thought you might like to take that over if it's convenient. But I haven't moved any of my things until you've examined the room. This is the Biology Lab.'

He glanced at Superintendent Mercer, who took the key from his pocket and unlocked the door. It was a long room obviously converted from two smaller ones, possibly a sitting-room or small drawing-room. The ceiling carvings had been removed, perhaps because Colonel Hoggatt had thought them inappropriate to a working laboratory, but the scars of the desecration remained. The original windows had been replaced by two long windows occupying almost the whole of the end wall. There was a range of benches and sinks under the windows, and two islands of work-benches in the middle of the room, one fitted with sinks, the other with a number of microscopes. To the left was a small glass-partitioned office, to the right a dark-room. Beside the door was an immense refrigerator.

But the most bizarre objects in the room were a pair of unclothed window-dressers' dummies, one male and one female, standing between the windows. They were unclothed and denuded of their wigs. The pose of the bald egg-shaped heads, the jointed arms stiffly flexed in a parody of benediction, the staring eyes and curved bow-like lips gave them the hieratic look of a couple of painted deities. And at their feet, a white-clad sacrificial victim, was the body.

Howarth stared at the two dummies as if he had never seen them before. He seemed to think that they required explanation. For the first time he had lost some of his assurance. He said:

'That's Liz and Burton. The staff dress them in a suspect's clothes so that they can match up bloodstains or slashes.' He added: 'Do you want me here?'

'For the moment, yes,' answered Dalgliesh.

He knelt by the body. Kerrison moved to stand beside him. Howarth and Mercer stayed one each side of the door.

After two minutes Dalgliesh said:

'Cause of death obvious. It looks as if he was struck by a single blow and died where he fell. There's surprisingly little bleeding.'

Kerrison said:

'That's not unusual. As you know, you can get serious intracranial injury from a simple fracture, particularly if there's extradural or subdural haemorrhage or actual laceration of the brain substance. I agree that he was probably killed by a single blow and that wooden mallet on the table seems the likely weapon. But Blain-Thomson will be able to tell you more when he gets him on the table. He'll be doing the PM this afternoon.'

'Rigor is almost complete. What sort of estimate did you make of the time of death?'

'I saw him just before nine and I thought then that he'd been dead about twelve hours, perhaps a little longer. Say between eight and nine p.m. The window is closed and the temperature pretty steady at sixty-five Fahrenheit. I usually estimate a fall in body temperature in these circumstances of about one and a half degrees Fahrenheit an hour. I took it when I examined the body and, taken with the rigor which was almost fully established then, I'd say it was unlikely that he was alive much after nine p.m. But you know how unreliable these estimates can be. Better say between eight-thirty and midnight.'

Howarth said from the door:

'His father says that Lorrimer rang him at a quarter to nine. I went to see the old man this morning with Angela Foley to break the news to him. She's my secretary. Lorrimer was her cousin. But you'll be seeing the old man, of course. He seemed pretty confident about the time.'

Dalgliesh said to Kerrison:

'It looks as if the blood flowed fairly steadily, but without any preliminary splashing. Would you expect the assailant to be blood-stained?'

'Not necessarily, particularly if I'm right about the mallet being the weapon. It was probably a single swinging blow delivered when Lorrimer had turned his back. The fact that the murderer struck above the left ear doesn't seem particularly significant. He could have been left-handed, but there's no reason to suppose he was.'

'And it wouldn't have required particular force. A child could probably have done it.'

Kerrison hesitated, disconcerted.

'Well, a woman, certainly.'

There was one question which Dalgliesh had formally to ask although, from the position of the body and the flow of the blood, the answer was in little doubt.

'Did he die almost immediately, or is there any possibility that he could have walked about for a time, even locked the door and set the alarms?'

'That's not altogether unknown, of course, but in this case I'd say it was highly unlikely, virtually impossible. I did have a man only a month ago with an axe injury, a seven-inch depressed fracture of the parietal bone and extensive extradural haemorrhage. He went off to a pub, spent half an hour with his mates, and then reported to the casualty department and was dead within a quarter of an hour. Head injuries can be unpredictable, but not this one, I think.'

Dalgliesh turned to Howarth.

'Who found him?'

'Our clerical officer, Brenda Pridmore. She starts work at eight-thirty with Blakelock. Old Mr Lorrimer phoned to say that his son hadn't slept in his bed, so she went up to see if Lorrimer was here. I arrived almost immediately with the cleaner, Mrs Bidwell. Some woman had telephoned her husband early this morning to ask her to come to my house to help my sister, instead of to the Lab. It was a false call. I thought that it was probably some stupid village prank, but that I'd better get in as soon as possible in case something odd was happening. So I put her bicycle in the boot of my car and got here just after nine. My secretary, Angela Foley, and Clifford Bradley, the Higher Scientific Officer in the Biology Department, arrived at about the same time.'

'Who at any time has been alone with the body?'

'Brenda Pridmore, of course, but very briefly, I imagine. Then Inspector Blakelock came up on his own. Then I was here alone for no more than a few seconds. Then I locked the Laboratory door, kept all the staff in the main hall, and waited there until Dr Kerrison arrived. He was here within five minutes and examined the body. I stood by the door. Superintendent Mercer arrived shortly afterwards and I handed over the key of the Biology Lab to him.'

Mercer said:

'Dr Kerrison suggested that I call in Dr Greene – he's the local police surgeon – to confirm his preliminary findings. Dr Greene wasn't alone with the body. After he'd made a quick and fairly superficial examination I locked the door. It wasn't opened again until the photographers and the fingerprint officers arrived. They've taken his dabs and examined the mallet, but we left it at that when we knew the Yard had been called in and you were on the way. The print boys are still here, in the Police Liaison Officer's room, but I let the photographers go.'

Putting on his search gloves, Dalgliesh ran his hands over the body. Under his white coat Lorrimer was wearing grey slacks and a tweed jacket. In the inside pocket was a thin leather wallet containing six pound notes, his driving licence, a book of stamps, and two credit cards. The right outer pocket held a pouch with his car keys and three others, two Yale and a smaller intricate key, probably to a desk top or drawer. There were a couple of ballpoint pens clipped to the top left-hand pocket of his white coat. In the bottom right-hand pocket was a handkerchief, his bunch of Laboratory keys and, not on the bunch, a single heavy key which looked fairly new. There was nothing else on the body.

He went over to study two exhibits lying on the central workbench, the mallet and a man's jacket. The mallet was an unusual weapon, obviously hand-made. The handle of crudely carved oak was about eighteen inches long and might, he thought, have once been part of a heavy walking-stick. The head, which he judged to weigh just over two pounds, was blackened on one side with congealed blood from which one or two coarse grey hairs sprouted like whiskers. It was impossible to detect in the dried slough a darker hair which might have come from Lorrimer's head, or with the naked eye to distinguish his blood. That would be a job for the Metropolitan Police Laboratory when the mallet, carefully packed and with two identifying exhibit tags instead of one, reached the Biology Department later in the day.

He said to the Superintendent:

'No prints?'

'None, except for old Pascoe's. He's the owner of the mallet. They weren't wiped away, so it looks as if this chap wore gloves.'

That, thought Dalgliesh, would point to premeditation, or to the instinctive precaution of a knowledgeable expert. But if he came prepared to kill it was odd that he had relied on seizing the first convenient weapon; unless, of course, he knew the mallet would be ready to hand.

He bent low to study the jacket. It was the top half of a cheap mass-produced suit in a harsh shade of blue with a paler pinstripe, and with wide lapels. The sleeve had been carefully spread out and the cuff bore a trace of what could have been blood. It was apparent that Lorrimer had already begun the analysis. On the bench was the electrophoresis apparatus plugged into its power pack and with two columns of six paired small circles punched in the sheet of agar gel. Beside it was a test-tube holder with a series of blood samples. To the right lay a couple of buff-coloured laboratory files with biology registrations and, beside them, flat open on the bench, a quarto-sized loose-leaf notebook with a ring binding. The left-hand page, dated the previous day, was closely covered in hieroglyphics and formulae in a thin, black, upright hand. Although most of the scientific jottings meant little to him, Dalgliesh could see that the time at which Lorrimer had started and finished each analysis had been carefully noted. The right-hand page was blank.

He said to Howarth:

'Who is the Senior Biologist now that Lorrimer's dead?'

'Claire Easterbrook. Miss Easterbrook, but it's advisable to call her Ms.'

'Is she here?'

'With the others in the library. I believe she has a firm alibi for the whole of yesterday evening, but as she's a senior scientist she was asked to stay. And, of course, she'll want to get back to work as soon as the staff are allowed into the Laboratory. There was a murder two nights ago in a clunch pit at Muddington – that jacket is an exhibit – and she'll want to get on with that as well as coping with the usual heavy load.'

'I'd like to see her first, please, and here. Then Mrs Bidwell. Is there a sheet we could use to cover him?'

Howarth said:

'I imagine there's a dust-sheet or something of the kind in the linen-cupboard. That's on the next floor.'

'I'd be grateful if you'd go with Inspector Massingham and show him. Then if you'd wait in the library or your own office I'll be down to have a word when I've finished here.'

For a second he thought that Howarth was about to demur. He frowned, and the handsome face clouded momentarily, petulant as a child's. But he left with Massingham without a word. Kerrison was still standing by the body, rigid as a guard of honour. He gave a little start as if recalling himself to reality and said:

'If you don't want me any longer I ought to be on my way to the hospital. You can contact me at St Luke's at Ely or here at the Old Rectory. I've given the sergeant an account of my movements last night. I was at home all the evening. At nine o'clock, by arrangement, I rang one of my colleagues at the hospital, Dr J. D. Underwood, about a matter which is coming up at the next medical committee. I think he's already confirmed that we did speak. He hadn't got the information I was waiting for but he rang me back at about a quarter to ten.'

There was as little reason to delay Kerrison as there was at present to suspect him. After he had left, Mercer said:

'I thought of leaving two sergeants, Reynolds and Underhill, and a couple of constables, Cox and Warren, if that will suit you. They're all sound, experienced officers. The Chief said to ask for anyone and anything you need. He's at a meeting in London this morning, but he'll be back tonight. I'll send up the chaps from the mortuary van if you're ready for them to take him away.'

'Yes, I've finished with him. I'll have a word with your men as soon as I've seen Miss Easterbrook. But ask one of the sergeants to come up in ten minutes to pack up the mallet for the Yard lab, will you? The chopper pilot will want to get back.'

They spoke a few more words about the liaison arrangements with the local force, then Mercer left to supervise the removal of the body. He would wait to introduce Dalgliesh to his seconded officers; after that, his responsibility would end. The case was in Dalgliesh's hands.

6

Two minutes later Claire Easterbrook was shown into the laboratory. She entered with an assurance which a less experienced investigator than Dalgliesh might have mistaken for arrogance or insensitivity. She was a thin, long-waisted girl of about thirty, with a bony, intelligent face and cap of dark curling hair which had been layered by an obviously expert, and no doubt expensive, hand to lie in swathes across the forehead and to curl into the nape of her high-arched neck. She was wearing a chestnut-brown sweater in fine wool belted into a black skirt which swung calf-length above high-heeled boots. Her hands, with the nails cut very short, were ringless and her only ornament was a necklace of large wooden beads strung on a silver chain. Even without her white coat the impression she gave – and no doubt intended – was of a slightly intimidating professional competence. Before Dalgliesh had a chance to speak she said, with a trace of belligerence:

'I'm afraid you'll be wasting your time with me. My lover and I dined last night in Cambridge at the Master's Lodge of his college. I was with five other people from eight-thirty until nearly midnight. I've already given their names to the constable in the library.'

Dalgliesh said mildly:

'I'm sorry, Ms Easterbrook, that I had to ask you to come up before we were able to remove Dr Lorrimer's body. And as it seems impertinent to invite you to sit down in your own laboratory, I won't. But this isn't going to take long.'

She flushed, as if he had caught her out in a social solecism. Glancing with reluctant distaste at the shrouded, lumpen shape on the floor, at the stiff protruding ankles, she said:

'He'd look more dignified if you'd left him uncovered. Like this he could be a sack of rubbish. It's a curious superstition, the universal instinct to cover up the recently dead. After all, we're the ones at a disadvantage.'

Massingham said lightly:

'Not, surely, with the Master and his wife to vouch for your alibi?'

Their eyes met, his coolly amused, hers dark with dislike.

Dalgliesh said:

'Dr Howarth tells me you're the senior biologist now. Could you explain to me, please, what Dr Lorrimer was doing here last night? Don't touch anything.'

She went at once over to the table and regarded the two exhibits, the files and the scientific paraphernalia. She said:

'Would you open this file, please?'

Dalgliesh's gloved hands slipped between the covers and flipped it open.

'He rechecked Clifford Bradley's result on the Pascoe case. The mallet belongs to a sixty-four-year-old fen farm labourer called Pascoe whose wife has disappeared. His story is that she's walked out on him, but there are one or two suspicious circumstances. The police sent in the mallet to see if the stains on it are human blood. They aren't. Pascoe says that he used it to put an injured dog out of his misery. Bradley found that the blood reacted to anti-dog serum and Dr Lorrimer has duplicated his result. So the dog it was that died.'

Too mean to waste a bullet or send for a vet, thought Massingham savagely. It struck him as odd that the death of this unknown mongrel should, for a moment, anger him more than the killing of Lorrimer.

Miss Easterbrook moved over to the open notebook. The two men waited. Then she frowned and said, obviously puzzled:

'That's odd. Edwin always noted the time he began and finished an analysis and the procedure he adopted. He's initialled Bradley's result on the Pascoe file, but there's nothing in the book. And it's obvious that he's made a start with the clunch pit-murder; but that isn't noted either. The last reference is five forty-five and the final note is unfinished. Someone must have torn out the right-hand page.'

'Why do you suppose anyone should do that?'

She looked straight into Dalgliesh's eyes and said calmly:

'To destroy the evidence of what he'd been doing, or the result of his analysis, or the time he'd spent on it. The first and second would be rather pointless. It's obvious from the apparatus what he's been doing, and any competent biologist could duplicate the work. So it's probably the last.'

So the appearance of intelligence wasn't misleading. Dalgliesh asked:

'How long would he take checking the Pascoe result?'

'Not long. Actually, he'd started on that before six and I think he'd finished when I left at six-fifteen. I was the last to leave. The junior staff had gone. It isn't usual for them to work after six. I usually stay later, but I had to dress for the dinner party.'

'And the work he's done on the clunch-pit case – how long would that have taken?'

'Difficult to say. I should have thought it would have kept him busy until nine or later. He was grouping a sample of the victim's blood and the blood from the dried stain by the ABO blood group system, and using electrophoresis to identify the haptoglobins and PGM, the enzyme phosphoglucomutase. Electrophoresis is a technique for identifying the protein and enzyme constituents of the blood by placing the samples in a gel of starch or agar and applying an electric current. As you can see, he'd actually started the run.'

Dalgliesh was aware of the scientific principle of electrophoresis, but didn't think it necessary to mention the fact. He opened the clunch-pit file, and said:

'There's nothing on the file.'

'He would write up the result on the file later. But he wouldn't have started the analysis without noting the details in his book.'

There were two pedal-bins against the wall. Massingham opened them. One, plastic-lined, was obviously for laboratory waste and broken glass. The other was for waste paper. He stirred the contents:

paper tissues, a few torn envelopes, a discarded newspaper. There was nothing which resembled the missing page.

Dalgliesh said:

'Tell me about Lorrimer.'

'What do you want to know?'

'Anything which could throw light on why someone disliked him enough to smash in his skull.'

'I can't help you there, I'm afraid. I've no idea.'

'You liked him?'

'Not particularly. It's not a question I've given much thought to. I got on all right with him. He was a perfectionist who didn't suffer fools gladly. But he was all right to work with if you knew your job. I do.'

'So he wouldn't need to check your work. What about those who don't know their jobs?'

'You'd better ask them, Commander.'

'Was he popular with his staff?

'What has popularity to do with it? I don't suppose I'm popular, but I don't go in fear of my life.'

She was silent for a moment, then said in a more conciliatory tone:

'I probably sound obstructive. I don't mean to be. It's just that I can't help. I've no idea who could have killed him or why. I only know that I didn't.'

'Had you noticed any change in him recently?'

'Change? You mean, in his mood or behaviour? Not really. He gave the impression of a man under strain; but then, he was that kind of man, solitary, obsessional, overworked. One rather odd thing. He's been interesting himself in the new CO, Brenda Pridmore. She's a pretty child, but hardly his intellectual level, I should have thought. I don't think there was anything serious, but it caused a certain amount of amusement in the Lab. I think he was probably trying to prove something to someone, or, perhaps, to himself.'

'You've heard about the telephone call to Mrs Bidwell, of course?'

'I imagine the whole Lab knows. It wasn't I who rang her, if that's what you're thinking. In any case, I should have known that it wouldn't work.'

'How do you mean, it wouldn't work?'

'It depended, surely, on old Lorrimer not being at home yesterday. After all, the caller couldn't rely on his not noticing that Edwin hadn't come home last night until he didn't get his early tea brought to him. As it happens, he went off to bed quite happily. But the hoaxer couldn't have known that. Normally, Edwin would have been missed much earlier.'

'Was there any reason to suppose that old Mr Lorrimer wouldn't be at the cottage yesterday?'

'He was supposed to be admitted to Addenbrooke's hospital in the afternoon for treatment of a skin complaint. I think the whole Biology Lab knew. He used to telephone often enough, fretting about the arrangements and whether Edwin would get time off to drive him there. Yesterday, just after ten, he rang to say that the bed wouldn't be available for him after all.'

'Who took the call?'

'I did. It rang in his private office and I took it there. Edwin hadn't returned from the clunch-pit autopsy. I told him as soon as he arrived.'

'Who else did you tell?'

'When I came out of the office I think I said something casually about old Mr Lorrimer not having to go into hospital after all. I'm not sure of the actual words. I don't think anyone made a comment or took much apparent notice.'

'And all the biology staff were in the Lab at the time and heard you?'

Suddenly she lost her composure. She flushed and hesitated, as if realizing for the first time where all this was leading. The two men waited. Then, angry with herself, she burst out, clumsily defensive:

'I'm sorry, but I can't remember. You'll have to ask them. It didn't seem important at the time and I was busy. We were all busy. I think everyone was there, but I can't be certain.'

'Thank you,' said Dalgliesh coolly. 'You've been remarkably helpful.'

8

Mrs Bidwell arrived at the door as the two attendants from the mortuary van were carrying out the body. She seemed to regret its disappearance and looked at the chalk outline marked by Massingham on the floor as if this were a poor substitute for the real thing. Gazing after the covered metal container, she said:

'Poor devil! I never thought to see him carried out of his lab feet first. He were never popular, you know. Still, I don't suppose that's worrying him where he is now. Is that one of my dust-sheets you've had over him?'

She peered suspiciously at the sheet, now folded neatly at the end of one of the benches.

'It came from the laboratory linen-cupboard, yes.'

'Well, as long as it's put back where you found it. Come to that, it had better go straight into the soiled linen. But I don't want any of your chaps taking it away. Laundry disappears fast enough as it is.'

'Why wasn't he popular, Mrs Bidwell?'

'Too particular by half. Mind you, you've got to be these days if you want to get any work done. But from what I hear he was too fussy for his own good. And he'd been getting worse, no doubt about that. And very odd he'd been lately, too. Nervy. You heard about the unpleasantness in the reception hall the day before yesterday, I suppose? Oh well, you will. Ask Inspector Blakelock. Just before lunch it was. Dr Lorrimer had a real old tussle with that barmy daughter of Dr Kerrison's. Nearly pushed her out of the door. Screeching like a banshee, she was. I came into the hall just in time to see it. Her dad isn't going to like that, I said to Inspector Blakelock. He's crazy about those kids. Mark my words, I said, if Dr Lorrimer doesn't take a hold of himself there'll be murder done in this Lab. I said the same to Mr Middlemass.'

'I want you to tell me about the telephone call this morning, Mrs Bidwell. What time was it?'

'It was near enough seven o'clock. We was eating breakfast and I just filled the teapot for second cups. Had the kettle in me hand when it rang.'

'And who answered it?'

'Bidwell. Phone's in the hall and he got up and went out to it. Cursin' he was 'cos he'd just settled down to his kipper. He hates cold kipper, does Bidwell. We always has kippers on Thursday on account of Marshall's fish van coming from Ely Wednesday afternoons.'

'Does your husband usually answer the phone?'

'He always answers the phone. And if he's not in I lets it ring. I can't abide the dratted things. Never could. Wouldn't have it in the house if our Shirley hadn't paid to get it put in. She's married now and lives Mildenhall way and she likes to think we can ring her if we want her. Fat lot of use that is. I can't never hear what anyone says. And the ring is enough to put the fear of God in a soul. Telegrams and phone rings. I hate 'em both.'

'Who at the Lab would know that your husband always answered the phone?'

'Best part of them, more than likely. They knows I won't touch the thing. There's no secret about that. We're all as the good Lord made us and some of us a sight worse. Nothing to be ashamed of.'

'Of course not. Your husband's at work now, I expect?'

'That's right. Yeoman's Farm, Captain Massey's place. Tractor work mostly. Been there twenty years, near enough.'

Dalgliesh nodded almost imperceptibly to Massingham and the Inspector slipped out to have a quiet word with Sergeant Underhill. It would be as well to check with Mr Bidwell while his memory of the call was fresh. Dalgliesh went on:

'What happened then?'

'Bidwell came back. Said that I wasn't to go to the Lab this morning because Mrs Schofield wanted me over at Leamings particular. I was to bike there and she'd run me and the bike home afterwards. Sticking out of the back of that red Jaguar she's got, I suppose. I thought it was a bit of a cheek seeing as I'm due here mornings but I've nothing against Mrs Schofield and if she wanted me I wasn't above obliging. The Lab would just have to wait, I said to Bidwell. I can't be in two places at once, I said. What don't get done today will get done tomorrow.'

'You work here every morning?'

'Except weekends. Gets here as near eight-thirty as makes no odds, and works till about ten. Then back at twelve in case any of the gentlemen wants their lunch cooking. The girls mostly manage for themselves. Afterwards I washes up for them. I reckons to get away by two-thirty most days. Mind you, it's light work. Scobie – he's the Lab attendant – and I sees to the working labs but all the heavy cleaning is supposed to be done by the contractors. They comes on

Mondays and Fridays only, from seven until nine, a whole van full of them from Ely, and does the main hall, the stairs and all the heavy polishing. Inspector Blakelock gets here early those mornings to let them in and Scobie keeps an eye on them. Not that you'd know they'd been most days. No personal interest, you see. Not like the old days when me and two women from the village did the lot.'

'So what would you normally have done as soon as you arrived if this had been an ordinary Thursday? I want you to think carefully, Mrs Bidwell. This may be very important.'

'No need to think. I'd do the same as I does every day.'

'Which is?'

'Take off me hat and coat in the downstairs cloakroom. Put on me overalls. Get cleaning bucket and powder and disinfectant from the broom cupboard. Clean the toilets, male and female. Then check dirty laundry and get it bagged up. Put out clean white coats where wanted. Then dust and tidy Director's office and general office.'

'Right,' said Dalgliesh. 'Let's do the rounds then, shall we?'

Three minutes later a curious little procession made its way up the stairs. Mrs Bidwell, clad now in a navy-blue working overall and carrying a plastic bucket in one hand and a mop in the other, led the way. Dalgliesh and Massingham followed. The two lavatories were on the second floor at the rear opposite the Document Examination Laboratory. They had obviously been converted from what had once been an elegant bedroom. But now a narrow passage leading to the single barred window had been constructed down the middle of the room. A mean-looking door gave entry to the women's cloakroom on the left, and, a few yards down, a similar door led to the men's washroom on the right. Mrs Bidwell led the way into the left-hand room. It was larger than Dalgliesh had expected, but poorly lit from a single round window with pivoting opaque glass set about four feet from the floor. The window was open. There were three lavatory cubicles. The outer room contained two wash-hand basins with a paper-towel dispenser and, to the left of the door, a long Formica-covered counter with a glass above it which apparently served as a dressing-table. To the right was a wall-mounted gas-fired incinerator, a row of clothes-hooks, a large wicker laundry-basket and two rather battered cane chairs.

Dalgliesh said to Mrs Bidwell:

'Is this how you would expect to find it?'

Mrs Bidwell's sharp little eyes peered round. The doors to the three lavatories were open and she gave them a quick inspection.

'No better nor no worse. They're pretty good about the toilets, I'll say that for them.'

'And that window is usually kept open?'

'Winter and summer, except it's bitter cold. That's the only ventilation you see.'

'The incinerator is off. Is that usual?'

'That's right. Last girl to leave turns it off at night, then I puts it on next morning.'

Dalgliesh looked inside. The incinerator was empty except for a trace of carbon ash. He went over to the window. Rain had obviously driven in sometime during the night and dried splashes were clearly visible on the tiled floor. But even the inside pane, where no rain could have splashed, was remarkably clean and there was no discernible dust around the sill. He said:

'Did you clean the window yesterday, Mrs Bidwell?'

'Of course I did. It's like I told you. I cleans the lavatories every morning. And when I cleans, I cleans. Shall I get on with it now?'

'I'm afraid there'll be no cleaning done today. We'll pretend that you've finished in here. Now what happens? What about the laundry?'

The laundry-basket contained only one overall, marked with the initials C.M.E. Mrs Bidwell said:

'I wouldn't expect many dirty coats, not on a Thursday. They usually manages to make them last a week and drop them in here on Friday before they go home. Monday's the busy day for laundry and putting out the new coats. Looks as though Miss Easterbrook spilt her tea yesterday. That's not like her. But she's particular is Miss Easterbrook. You wouldn't find her going round with a dirty coat, no matter what day of the week.'

So there was at least one member of the Biology Department, thought Dalgliesh, who knew that Mrs Bidwell would make an early visit to the lab to put out a clean white coat. It would be interesting to learn who had been present when the fastidious Miss Easterbrook had had her accident with the tea.

The male washroom, apart from the urinal stalls, differed very little from the women's. There was the same round open window, the same absence of any marks on the panes or sill. Dalgliesh carried over one of the chairs and, carefully avoiding any contact with the window or the sill, looked out. There was a drop of about six feet to the top of the window beneath, and an equal drop to that on the first floor. Below them both a paved terrace ran right up to the wall. The absence of soft earth, the rain in the night and Mrs Bidwell's efficient cleaning meant that they would be lucky to find any evidence of a climb. But a reasonably slim and sure-footed man or woman with enough nerve and a head for heights could certainly have got out this way. But if the murderer were a member of the Lab staff, why should he risk his neck when he must have known that the keys were on Lorrimer? And if the murderer were an outsider, then how account for the locked front door, the intact alarm system, and the fact that Lorrimer must have let him in?

He turned his attention to the wash-basins. None was particularly dirty, but near the rim of the one nearest the door there was a smear of porridge-like mucus. He bent his head over the basin and sniffed. His sense of smell was extremely acute and, from the plug-hole, he detected the faint but unmistakably disagreeable smell of human vomit.

Mrs Bidwell, meanwhile, had thrown open the lid of the laundry-basket. She gave an exclamation.

'That's funny. It's empty.'

Dalgliesh and Massingham turned. Dalgliesh asked:

'What were you expecting to find, Mrs Bidwell?'

'Mr Middlemass's white coat, that's what.'

She darted out of the room. Dalgliesh and Massingham followed. She flung open the door of the Document Examination room and glanced inside. Then she closed the door again and stood with her back against it. She said:

'It's gone! It's not hanging on the peg. So where is it? Where's Mr Middlemass's white coat?'

Dalgliesh asked:

'Why did you expect to find it in the laundry-basket?'

Mrs Bidwell's black eyes grew immense. She slewed her eyes furtively from side to side and then said with awed relish:

'Because it had blood on it, that's why. Lorrimer's blood!'

8

Lastly, they went down the main staircase to the Director's office. From the library there was a broken murmur of voices, subdued and spasmodic as a funeral gathering. A detective-constable was standing at the front door with the detached watchfulness of a man paid to endure boredom but ready to leap into action should, unaccountably, the boredom end.

Howarth had left his office unlocked and the key in the door. Dalgliesh was interested that the Director had chosen to wait with the rest of the staff in the library, and wondered whether this was intended to demonstrate solidarity with his colleagues, or was a tactful admission that his office was one of the rooms which had been due to receive Mrs Bidwell's early-morning attention, and must, therefore, be of special interest to Dalgliesh. But that reasoning was surely too subtle. It was difficult to believe that Howarth hadn't entered his room since the discovery of the body. If there was anything to remove, he best of all must have had the chance to do it.

Dalgliesh had expected the room to be impressive, but it still surprised him. The plasterwork of the coved ceiling was splendid, a joyous riot of wreaths, shells, ribbons and trailing vines, ornate and yet disciplined. The fireplace was of white and mottled marble with a finely carved frieze of nymphs and piping shepherds and a classical overmantel with open pediment. He guessed that the agreeably proportioned salon, too small to be partitioned and not large enough for a working laboratory, had escaped the fate of so much of the house more for administrative and scientific convenience than from any sensitivity on Colonel Hoggatt's part to its innate perfection. It was newly furnished in a style guaranteed not to offend, a nice compromise of bureaucratic orthodoxy and modern functionalism. There was a large glass-fronted bookcase to the left of the fireplace, and a personal locker and a coat-stand to the right. A rectangular conference table and four chairs, of a type provided for senior public servants, stood between the tall windows. Next to it was a steel security cupboard fitted with a combination lock. Howarth's desk, a plain contraption in the same wood as the conference table, faced the door. Apart from an inkstained blotter and a pen-stand it held a small wooden bookshelf containing the

Shorter Oxford Dictionary, a dictionary of quotations, *Roget's Thesaurus* and *Fowler's Modern English Usage*. The choice seemed curious for a scientist. There were three metal trays marked 'In', 'Pending' and 'Out'. The 'Out' tray held two manila files, the top labelled 'Chapel – Proposals for Transfer to Department of the Environment', and the second, a large, old and unwieldy file which had been much mended, marked 'New Laboratory – Commissioning.'

Dalgliesh was struck by the emptiness and impersonality of the whole room. It had obviously been recently decorated for Howarth's arrival, and the pale grey-green carpet, with its matching square under the desk, was as yet unmarked, the curtains hung in pristine folds of dark green. There was only one picture, positioned in the overmantel, but this was an original, an early Stanley Spencer showing the Virgin's Assumption. Plump, foreshortened, varicosed thighs in red bloomers floated upwards from a circle of clutching work-worn hands to a reception committee of gaping cherubim. It was, he thought, an eccentric choice for the room, discordant both in date and style. It was the only object, apart from the books, which reflected a personal taste; Dalgliesh hardly supposed that it had been provided by a Government agency. Otherwise the office had the underfurnished, expectant atmosphere of a room refurbished to receive an unknown occupant, and still awaiting the imprint of his taste and personality. It was hard to believe that Howarth had worked here for almost a year. Mrs Bidwell, her tight little mouth pursed and eyes narrowed, regarded it with obvious disapproval. Dalgliesh asked:

'Is this how you would have expected to find it?'

'That's right. Every bloody morning. Nothing for me to do here really is there? Mind you, I dusts and polishes around and runs the Hoover over the carpet. But he's neat and tidy, there's no denying it. Not like old Dr MacIntyre. Oh, he was a lovely man! But messy! You should have seen his desk of a morning. And smoke! You couldn't hardly see across the room sometimes. He had this lovely skull on his desk to keep his pipes in. They dug it up when they was making the trench for the pipes to the new vehicle examination extension. Been in the ground more than two hundred years, Dr Mac said, and he showed me the crack – just like a cracked cup – where his skull had been bashed in. That's one murder they never solved. I miss that skull. Real lovely that used to look. And he had all these pictures of himself and his friends at university with oars crossed above them, and a coloured one of the Highlands with hairy cattle paddling in a lake, and one of his father with his dogs, and such a lovely picture of his wife – dead she was, poor soul – and another big picture of Venice with gondolas and a lot of foreigners in fancy dress, and a cartoon of Dr Mac done by one of his friends, showing the friend lying dead, and Dr Mac in his deerstalker hat looking for clues with his magnifying glass. That was a real laugh that was. Oh, I loved Dr Mac's pictures!' She looked at the Spencer with a marked lack of enthusiasm.

'And there's nothing unusual about the room this morning?'

'I told you, same as usual. Well, look for yourself. Clean as a new pin. It looks different in the day, mind you, when he's working here. But he always leaves it as if he isn't expecting to come back in the morning.'

There was nothing else to be learned from Mrs Bidwell. Dalgliesh thanked her and told her that she could go home as soon as she had checked with Detective-Sergeant Reynolds in the library that he had all the necessary information about where she had spent the previous evening. He explained this with his usual tact, but tact was wasted on Mrs Bidwell. She said cheerfully and without rancour:

'No use trying to pin this on me, or Bidwell come to that. We was together at the village concert. Sat five rows back between Joe Machin – he's the sexton – and Willie Barnes – he's the Rector's warden, and we stayed there until the end of the show. No sneaking out at half-time like some I could mention.'

'Who sneaked out, Mrs Bidwell?'

'Ask him yourself. Sat at the end of the row in front of us, a gentleman whose office we might or might not be standing in at this very moment. Do you want to talk to him? Shall I ask him to step in?' She spoke hopefully and looked towards the door like an eager gun dog, ears pricked for the command to retrieve.

'We'll see to that, thank you, Mrs Bidwell. And if we want to talk to you again we'll get in touch. You've been very helpful.'

'I thought I might make coffee for them all before I go. No harm in that, I suppose?'

There was no point in warning her not to talk to the Lab staff, or, come to that, to the whole village. Dalgliesh had no doubt that his search of the cloakrooms and the missing bloodstained coat would soon be common knowledge. But no great harm would be done. The murderer must know that the police would be immediately alive to the possible significance of that false early morning call to Mrs Bidwell. He was dealing with intelligent men and women, experienced, even if vicariously, in criminal investigation, knowledgeable about police procedure, aware of the rules which governed his every move. He had no doubt that, mentally, most of the group now waiting in the library to be interviewed were following his actions almost to the minute.

And among them, or known to them, was a murderer.

9

Superintendent Mercer had selected his two sergeants with an eye to contrast or, perhaps, with a view to satisfying any prejudices which Dalgliesh might harbour about the age and experience of his subordinates. Sergeant Reynolds was near the end of his service, a stolid, broad-shouldered, slow-speaking officer of the old school and a native of the fens. Sergeant Underhill, recently promoted, looked young enough to be his son. His boyish, open face with its look of disciplined idealism was vaguely familiar to Massingham, who suspected that he might have seen it in a police recruitment pamphlet, but decided in the interest of harmonious co-operation to give Underhill the benefit of the doubt.

The four police officers were sitting at the conference table in the Director's office. Dalgliesh was briefing his team before he started on the preliminary interviews. He was, as always, restlessly aware of time passing. It was already after eleven and he was anxious to finish at the Laboratory and see old Mr Lorrimer. The physical clues to his son's murder might lie in the Laboratory; the clue to the man himself lay elsewhere. But neither his words nor tone betrayed impatience.

'We start by assuming that the telephone call to Mrs Bidwell and Lorrimer's death are connected. That means the call was made by the murderer or an accomplice. We'll keep an open mind about the caller's sex until we get confirmation from Bidwell, but it was probably a woman, probably also someone who knew that old Mr Lorrimer was expected to be in hospital yesterday, and who didn't know that the appointment had been cancelled. If the old man had been home, the ruse could hardly hope to succeed. As Miss Easterbrook has pointed out, no one could rely on his going early to bed last night and not realizing until after the Lab opened this morning that his son hadn't come home.'

Massingham said:

'The killer would have made it his business to get here early this morning, assuming that he didn't know that his plan had misfired. And assuming, of course, the call wasn't a double bluff. It would be a neat ploy, wasting our time, confusing the investigation and diverting suspicion from everyone except the early arrivals.'

'But for one of the suspects, it could have been an even neater ploy,' thought Dalgliesh. It had been Mrs Bidwell's arrival at Howarth's house in obedience to the call which had given the Director himself the excuse for arriving so early. He wondered what time Howarth usually put in an appearance. That would be one of the questions to be asked. He said:

'We'll start by assuming that it wasn't a bluff, that the murderer, or his accomplice, made the call to delay Mrs Bidwell's arrival and the discovery of the body. So what was he hoping to do? Plant evidence or destroy it? Tidy up something which he'd overlooked; wipe the mallet clean; clear up the evidence of whatever it was he was doing here last night; replace the keys on the body? But Blakelock had the best opportunity to do that, and he wouldn't need to have taken them in the first place. The call could have given someone the chance to replace the spare set in the security cupboard here. But that would be perfectly possible without delaying Mrs Bidwell's arrival. And, of course, it may have been done.'

Underhill said:

'But is it really likely, sir, that the call was intended to delay the finding of the body and to give the killer time to replace the keys? Admittedly Mrs Bidwell could be expected to be first in the Biology Department this morning when she put out the clean coats. But the murderer couldn't rely on that. Inspector Blakelock or Brenda Pridmore could easily have had occasion to go there.'

Dalgliesh thought it a risk that the murderer might well have thought worth taking. In his experience the early-morning routine in an institution seldom varied. Unless Blakelock had the early-morning job of checking on Lab security – and this was yet another of the questions to be asked – he and Brenda Pridmore would probably have got on with their normal work at the reception desk. In the ordinary course of events Mrs Bidwell would have been the one to find the body. Any member of staff who went into the Biology Lab before her would have needed a good excuse to explain his presence there, unless, of course, he was a member of the Biology Department.

Massingham said:

'It's odd about the missing white coat, sir. It can hardly have been removed or destroyed to prevent us learning about the fight between Middlemass and Lorrimer. That unedifying but intriguing little episode must have been round the Lab within minutes of its happening. Mrs Bidwell would see to that.'

Both Dalgliesh and Massingham wondered how far Mrs Bidwell's description of the quarrel, given with the maximum dramatic effect, had been accurate. It was obvious that she had come into the laboratory after the blow had been struck, and had in fact seen very little. Dalgliesh had recognized, with foreboding, a familiar phenomenon: the desire of a witness, aware of the paucity of her evidence, to make the most of it lest the police be disappointed, while remaining as far as possible within the confines of truth. Stripped of Mrs Bidwell's embellishments, the core of hard fact had been disappointingly small.

'What they was quarrelling about I couldn't take it on myself to say, except that it was about a lady, and that Dr Lorrimer was upset because she'd telephoned Mr Middlemass. The door was open and I did hear that much when I passed to go in to the ladies' toilet. I dare say she rang him to arrange a date and Dr Lorrimer didn't like it. I never saw a man more white. Like death he looked, with a handkerchief held up against his face all bloodied, and his black eyes glaring over the top of it. And Mr Middlemass was turkey red. Embarrassed, I dare say. Well, it's not what we're used to at Hoggatt's, senior staff knocking each other about. When proper gentlemen start in with the fists there's usually a woman at the bottom of it. Same with this murder if you ask me.'

Dalgliesh said:

'We'll be getting Middlemass's version of the affair. I'd like now to have a word with all the Lab staff in the library and then Inspector Massingham and I will start the preliminary interviews: Howarth, the two women, Angela Foley and Brenda Pridmore, Blakelock, Middlemass and any of the others without a firm alibi. I'd like you, Sergeant, to get on with organizing the usual routine. I shall want one of the senior staff in each department while the search is going on. They're the only ones who can tell whether anything in their lab has changed since yesterday. You'll be looking – admittedly without much hope – for the missing page of Lorrimer's notebook, any evidence of what he was doing here last night apart from working on the clunch-pit murder, any sign of what happened to the missing coat. I want a thorough search of the whole building, particularly possible means of access and exit. The rain last night is a nuisance. You'll probably find the walls washed clean, but there may be some evidence that he got out through one of the lavatory windows.

'You'll need a couple of men on the grounds. The earth is fairly soft after the rain and if the murderer came by car or motorcycle there could be tyre-marks. Any we find can be checked against the tyre index here; we needn't waste time going to the Met Lab for that. There's a bus stop immediately opposite the laboratory entrance. Find out what time the buses pass. There's always the possibility that one of the passengers or crew noticed something. I'd like the Laboratory building checked first, and as quickly as possible so that the staff can get back to work. They've a new murder on their hands and we can't keep the place closed longer than is absolutely necessary. I'd like to give them access by tomorrow morning.

'Then there's the smear of what looks like vomit on the first basin in the men's washroom. The smell from the pipe is still fairly distinct. I want a sample of that to go to the Met Lab urgently. You'll probably have to unscrew the joint to get at the base of the U-bend. We shall need to find out who used the room last yesterday evening and whether he noticed the smear on the basin. If no one admits to having been sick during the day, or can't produce a witness that he was, we shall want to know what they all ate for the evening meal. It could be Lorrimer's vomit, so we'll need some information on his stomach contents. I'd also like a sample of his blood and hair to be left here at the Lab. But Dr Blain-Thomson will be seeing to that.'

Reynolds said:

'We take it that the crucial time is from six-fifteen when he was last seen alive in his lab, until midnight?'

'For the present. When I've seen his father and confirmed that he made that call at eight forty-five we may be able to narrow it down. And we shall get a clearer idea of the time of death when Dr Blain-Thomson has done the PM. But judging from the state of rigor, Dr Kerrison wasn't far out.'

But Kerrison didn't need to be far out, if he were the murderer. Rigor mortis was notoriously unreliable, and if he wanted an alibi for himself, Kerrison could shift the time of death by up to an hour without suspicion. If the timing were tight he might not need even an hour. It had been prudent of him to call in the police surgeon to confirm his estimate of the time of death. But how likely was Dr Greene, experienced as he might be in viewing bodies, to disagree with the opinion of a consultant forensic pathologist unless the latter's judgement was manifestly perverse? If Kerrison was guilty, he had run little risk by calling in Greene.

Dalgliesh got to his feet.

'Right,' he said. 'Let's get on with it, shall we?'

10

Dalgliesh disliked having more than one other officer present with him at his preliminary and informal interview, so Massingham was taking the notes. They were hardly necessary; Dalgliesh, he knew, had almost total recall. But he still found the practice useful. They were sitting together at the conference table in the Director's office, but Howarth, perhaps because he objected to sitting in his own room other than at his desk, preferred to stand. He was leaning casually against the fireplace. From time to time Massingham lifted an unobtrusive eyebrow to glance at the clear-cut, dominant profile outlined against the classical frieze. There were three bunches of keys on the table; the bunch taken from Lorrimer's body, that handed over by Inspector Blakelock, and the set which Dr Howarth, manipulating the security lock, had taken from its box in the cupboard. Each set of keys was identical, one Yale key and two security keys to the front door, and one smaller key on a plain metal ring. None was named, presumably for security reasons. Dalgliesh said:

'And these are the only three sets in existence?'

'Except for the set at Guy's Marsh police station, yes. Naturally, I checked earlier this morning that the police still have their set. The keys are kept in the safe under the control of the station officer, and they haven't been touched. They need a set at the police station in case the alarm goes off. There was no alarm last night.'

Dalgliesh already knew from Mercer that the station keys had been checked. He said:

'And the smallest key?'

'That's the one to the Exhibits Store. The system is for all incoming exhibits, after they've been registered, to be stored there until they're issued to the head of the appropriate department. It's his responsibility to allocate them to a specific officer. In addition, we store the exhibits which have been examined and are awaiting collection by the police, and those which have been presented to the court during the case and are returned to us for destruction. Those are mainly drugs. They're destroyed here in the incinerator and the destruction witnessed by one of the Laboratory staff and the officer in charge of the case. The Exhibits Store is also protected by the electronic alarm system, but, obviously, we need a key for internal security when the system hasn't been set.'

'And all the Laboratory internal doors and your office were protected last night once the internal alarm system was set? That means that an intruder could only have got out undetected through the top-floor lavatory windows. All the others are either barred or fitted with the electronic alarm?'

'That's right. He could have got in that way too, of course, which was what concerned us most. But it wouldn't have been an easy climb, and the alarm would have gone off as soon as he tried to gain access to any of the main rooms in the Laboratory. We did consider extending the alarm system to the lavatory suite soon after I arrived, but it seemed unnecessary. We haven't had a break-in in the seventy-odd years of the Lab's existence.'

'What are the precise arrangements about locking the Laboratory?'

'Only the two Police Liaison Officers and Lorrimer as the Deputy Security Officer were authorized to lock up. He or the Police Liaison Officer on duty was responsible for ensuring that no staff were left on the premises and that all the internal doors were shut before the alarm was set, and the front door finally locked for the night. The alarm system to Guy's Marsh police station is set whether the door is locked on the inside or the out.'

'And these other keys found on the body, the three in this leather pouch and the single key. Do you recognize any of those?'

'Not the three in the pouch. One is obviously his car key, and I take it that the other two are house keys. But the single one looks very like the key to the Wren chapel. If it is, I didn't know that Lorrimer had it. Not that it's important. But as far as I know, there's only one key to the chapel in existence and that's hanging on the board in the Chief Liaison Officer's room. It isn't a security lock and we're not particularly worried about the chapel. There's nothing left there of real value. But occasionally architects and archaeological societies want to view it, so we let them borrow the key and they sign for it in a book in the office. We don't allow them through the Laboratory grounds to get at it. They have to use the back entrance in Guy's Marsh Road. The contract cleaners take it once every two months to clean and check the heating – we have to keep it reasonably warm in winter because the ceiling and carving are rather fine – and Miss Willard goes there from time to time, to do some dusting. When her father was rector of Chevisham, he used occasionally to hold services in the chapel, and I think she has a sentimental regard for the place.'

Massingham went out to Chief Inspector Martin's office and brought in the chapel key. The two matched. The small notebook which he had found hanging with the key showed that it had last been collected by Miss Willard on Monday the twenty-fifth of October. Howarth said:

'We're thinking of transferring the chapel to the Department of the Environment once we occupy the new Laboratory. It's a constant irritation to the Treasury that our funds are used to heat and maintain it. I've set up a string quartet here, and we held a concert on August the twenty-sixth in the chapel, but otherwise it's completely unused. I expect you will want to take a look at it, and it's worth seeing in its own right. It's a very fine specimen of late seventeenth-century church architecture, although, in fact, it isn't by Wren but by Alexander Fort, who was strongly influenced by him.'

Dalgliesh asked suddenly:

'How well did you get on with Lorrimer?'

Howarth replied calmly:

'Not particularly well. I respected him as a biologist, and I certainly had no complaints either about his work or about his co-operation with me as Director. He wasn't an easy man to know, and I didn't find him particularly sympathetic. But he was probably one of the most respected serologists in the service, and we shall miss him. If he had a fault, it was a reluctance to delegate. He had two scientific officer serologists in his department for the grouping of liquid blood and stains, saliva and semen samples, but he invariably took the murder cases himself. Apart from his casework and attendance at trials and at scenes of crime, he did a considerable amount of lecturing to detective training courses, and police familiarization courses.'

Lorrimer's rough notebook was on the desk. Dalgliesh pushed it towards Howarth and said:

'Have you seen this before?'

'His rough notebook? Yes, I think I've noticed it in his department, or when he was carrying it with him. He was obsessively tidy and had a dislike of odd scraps of paper. Anything of importance was noted in that book, and subsequently transferred to the files. Claire Easterbrook tells me that the last page is missing.'

'That's why we're particularly anxious to know what he was doing here last night, apart from working on the clunch-pit murder. He could have got into any of the other laboratories, of course?'

'If he'd switched off the internal alarm, yes. I believe it was his usual practice, when he was last on the premises, to rely on the Yale lock and the bolt on the front door and only check the internal doors and set the security alarm before he finally left. Obviously it's important not to set off the alarm accidentally.'

'Would he have been competent to undertake an examination in another department?'

'It depends on what he was trying to do. Essentially, of course, he was concerned with the identification and grouping of biological material, blood, body stains and the examination of fibres and animal and plant tissues. But he was a competent general scientist and his interests were wide – his scientific interests. Forensic biologists, particularly in the smaller laboratories, which this has been up to now, become pretty versatile. But he wouldn't attempt to use the more sophisticated instruments in the Instrument Section, the mass spectrometer, for example.'

'And you personally have no idea what he could have been doing?'

'None. I do know that he came into this office. I had to look up the name of a consultant surgeon who was giving evidence for the defence in one of our old cases, and I had the medical directory on my desk when I left last night. This morning, it was back in its place in the library. Few things irritated Lorrimer more than people removing books from the library. But if he was in this office last night, I hardly imagine it was merely to check on my carelessness with the reference books.'

Lastly, Dalgliesh asked him about his movements the previous night.

'I played the fiddle at the village concert. The rector had five minutes or so to fill in and asked me if the string quartet would play something which he described as short and cheerful. The players were myself, a chemist, one of the scientific officers from the Document Examination Department, and a typist from the general office. Miss Easterbrook should have been the first cello, but she had a dinner engagement which she regarded as important, and couldn't make it. We played the Mozart Divertimento in D Major and came third on the programme.'

'And you stayed for the rest of the concert?'

'I intended to. Actually, the hall was incredibly stuffy and just before the interval at eight-thirty I slipped out. I stayed out.'

Dalgliesh asked what precisely he'd done.

'Nothing. I sat on one of those flat tombstones for about twenty minutes, then I left.'

'Did you see anyone, or did anyone see you?'

'I saw a hobby-horse – I know now that it must have been Middlemass deputizing for Chief Inspector Martin – come out of the male dressing-room. He pranced around rather happily, I thought, and snapped his jaws at an angel on one of the graves. Then he was joined by the troupe of morris dancers coming through the grave-yard from the Moonraker. It was an extraordinary sight. There was the racing moon and these extraordinary figures with their bells jingling and their hats decked with evergreens moving through the swirl of ground mist out of the darkness towards me. It was like an outré film or a ballet. All it needed was second-rate background music, preferably Stravinsky. I was sitting motionless on the gravestone, some distance away, and I don't think they saw me. I certainly didn't make myself known. The hobby-horse joined them, and they went into the hall. Then I heard the fiddle start up. I suppose I stayed sitting there for about another ten minutes, and then I left. I walked for the rest of the evening along Leamings Dyke and got home about ten o'clock. My half-sister Domenica will be able to confirm the time.'

They spent a little time discussing the administrative arrangements for the investigation. Dr Howarth said that he would move into Miss Foley's room and make his office available to the police. There would be no chance of the Lab opening for the rest of the day, but Dalgliesh said that he hoped it would be possible for work to start again the next morning. Before Howarth left, Dalgliesh said:

'Everyone I've spoken to respected Dr Lorrimer as a forensic biologist. But what was he like as a man? What, for example, did you know about him except that he was a forensic biologist?'

Dr Howarth said coldly:

'Nothing. I wasn't aware there was anything to know, except that he was a forensic biologist. And now, if you've no more immediate questions, I must telephone Establishment Department and make sure that, in the excitement of his somewhat spectacular exit, they're not forgetting to send me a replacement.'

11

With the resilience of youth, Brenda Pridmore had recovered quickly from the shock of finding Lorrimer's body. She had resolutely refused to be taken home, and by the time Dalgliesh was ready to see her she was perfectly calm and, indeed, anxious to tell her story. With her cloud of rich auburn hair and her freckled wind-tanned face she looked the picture of bucolic health. But the grey eyes were intelligent, the mouth sensitive and gentle. She gazed across the desk at Dalgliesh as intently as a docile child and totally without fear. He guessed that all her young life she had been used to receiving an avuncular kindness from men and never doubted that she would receive it, too, from these unknown officers of police. In response to Dalgliesh's questioning, she described exactly what had happened from the moment of her arrival at the Laboratory that morning to the discovery of the body. Dalgliesh asked:

'Did you touch him?'

'Oh no! I knelt down and I think I did put out my hand to feel his cheek. But that was all. I knew that he was dead, you see.'

'And then?'

'I don't remember. I know I rushed downstairs and Inspector Blakelock was standing at the bottom looking up at me. I couldn't speak, but I suppose he saw by my face that something was wrong. Then I remember sitting on the chair outside Chief Inspector Martin's office and looking at Colonel Hoggatt's portrait. Then I don't remember anything until Dr Howarth and Mrs Bidwell arrived.'

'Do you think anyone could have got out of the building past you while you were sitting there?'

'The murderer, you mean? I don't see how he could have. I know I wasn't very alert, but I hadn't fainted or anything silly like that. I'm sure I would have noticed if anyone had come across the hall. And even if he did manage to slip past me, he would have bumped into Dr Howarth, wouldn't he?'

Dalgliesh asked her about her job at Hoggatt's, how well she had known Dr Lorrimer. She prattled away with artless confidence about her life, her colleagues, her fascinating job, Inspector Blakelock who was so good to her and who had lost his own only daughter, telling with every sentence more than she knew. It wasn't that she was stupid, thought Massingham, only honest and ingenuous. For the first time they heard Lorrimer spoken of with affection.

'He was always terribly kind to me, although I didn't work in the Biology Department. Of course, he was a very serious man. He had so many responsibilities. The Biology Department is terribly overworked and he used to work late nearly every night, checking results, catching up with the backlog. I think he was disappointed at not being chosen to succeed Dr Mac. Not that he ever said so to me – well he wouldn't, would he? – I'm far too junior and he was far too loyal.'

Dalgliesh asked:

'Do you think anyone could have misunderstood his interest in you, might have been a little jealous?'

'Jealous of Dr Lorrimer because he stopped sometimes at the desk to talk to me about my work and was kind to me? But he was old! That's just silly!'

Suppressing a grin as he bent over his notebook and penned a few staccato outlines, Massingham thought that it probably was.

Dalgliesh asked:

'It seems there was some trouble the day before he died when Dr Kerrison's children called at the Laboratory. Were you in the hall then?'

'You mean when he pushed Miss Kerrison out of the front hall? Well, he didn't actually push her, but he did speak very sharply. She had come with her small brother and they wanted to wait for Dr Kerrison. Dr Lorrimer looked at them, well, really as if he hated them. It wasn't at all like him. I think he's been under some terrible strain. Perhaps he had a premonition of his death. Do you know what he said to me after the clunch-pit exhibits came in? He said that the only death we had to fear is our own. Don't you think that was an extraordinary remark?'

'Very strange,' agreed Dalgliesh.

'And that reminds me of another thing. You did say that anything might be important. Well, there was a funny kind of letter arrived for Dr Lorrimer yesterday morning. That's why he stopped at the desk, so that I could hand over any personal post. There was just this thin brown envelope with the address printed, printed by hand in capital letters, I mean. And it was just his name, no qualifications after it. Odd, wasn't it?

'Did he receive many private letters here?'

'Oh no, none really. The Lab writing-paper says that all communications have to be addressed to the Director. We deal at the desk with the exhibits received, but all the correspondence goes to the general office for sorting. We only hand over the personal letters, but there aren't many of those.'

In the quick preliminary examination which he and Massingham had made of Lorrimer's meticulously tidy office, Dalgliesh had found no personal correspondence. He asked whether Miss Pridmore knew if Dr Lorrimer had gone home for lunch. She said that he had. So it was possible that he had taken the letter home. It could mean anything, or nothing. It was just one more small fact which would have to be investigated.

He thanked Brenda Pridmore, and reminded her again to come back to him if she remembered anything which could be of importance, however small. Brenda was not used to dissembling. It was obvious that something had occurred to her. She blushed and dropped her eyes. The metamorphosis from happy confidante to guilty schoolgirl was pathetically comic. Dalgliesh said gently:

'Yes?'

She didn't speak, but made herself meet his eyes and shook her head. He waited for a moment, then said:

'The investigation of murder is never agreeable. Like most unpleasant things in life, it sometimes seems easier not to get involved, to keep oneself uncontaminated. But that isn't possible. In a murder investigation, to suppress a truth is sometimes to tell a lie.'

'But suppose one passes on information. Something private, perhaps, which one hasn't any real right to know – and it throws suspicion on the wrong person?'

Dalgliesh said gently:

'You have to trust us. Will you try to do that?'

She nodded, and whispered 'Yes', but she said nothing further. He judged that this was not the time to press her. He let her go, and sent for Angela Foley.

12

In contrast to Brenda Pridmore's artless confiding, Angela Foley presented a bland inscrutable gaze. She was an unusual-looking girl with a heart-shaped face and a wide, exceedingly high forehead from which hair, baby fine, the colour of ripe grain, was strained back and plaited into a tight coil on top of her head. Her eyes were small, slanted, and so deeply set that Dalgliesh found it hard to guess their colour. Her mouth was small, pursed and uncommunicative above the pointed chin. She wore a dress in fine fawn wool, topped with an elaborately patterned, short-sleeved tabard, and short laced boots, a sophisticated and exotic contrast to Brenda's orthodox prettiness and neat, hand-knitted twinset.

If she was distressed by her cousin's violent death, she concealed it admirably. She said that she had worked as Director's secretary for five years, first with Dr MacIntyre and now with Dr Howarth. Before that, she had been a shorthand typist in the general office of the Laboratory, having joined Hoggatt's straight from school. She was twenty-seven. Until two years ago, she lived in a bedsitting-room in Ely, but now shared Sprogg's Cottage with a woman friend. They had spent the whole of the previous evening in each other's company. Edwin Lorrimer and his father had been her only living relatives, but they had seen very little of each other. The family, she explained as if this were the most natural thing in the world, had never been close.

'So you know very little of his private affairs, his will, for example?'

'No, nothing. When my grandmother left him all her money, and we were at the solicitor's office, he said that he would make me his heir. But I think he just felt guilty at the time that I wasn't named in the will. I don't suppose it meant anything. And, of course, he may have changed his mind.'

'Do you remember how much your grandmother left?'

She paused for a moment. Almost, he thought, as if calculating whether ignorance would sound more suspicious than knowledge. Then she said:

'I think about thirty thousand. I don't know how much it is now.'

He took her briefly but carefully through the events of the early morning. She and her friend ran a Mini, but she usually cycled to work. She had done so that morning, arriving at the Laboratory at her usual time, just before nine o'clock, and had been surprised to see Dr Howarth with Mrs Bidwell driving in before her. Brenda Pridmore had opened the door. Inspector Blakelock was coming downstairs and he had broken the news of the murder. They had all stayed in the hall together while Dr Howarth went up to the Biology Lab. Inspector Blakelock had telephoned for the police and for Dr Kerrison. When Dr Howarth returned to the hall he had asked her to go with Inspector Blakelock and check on the keys. She and the Director were the only two members of staff who knew the combination of his security cupboard. He had stayed in the hall, she thought talking to Brenda Pridmore. The keys had been in their box in the cupboard, and she and Inspector Blakelock had left them there. She had reset the combination lock and returned to the hall. Dr Howarth had gone into his office to talk to the Home Office, telling the rest of the staff to wait in the hall. Later, after the police and Dr Kerrison had arrived, Dr Howarth had driven her in his car to break the news to old Mr Lorrimer. Then he had left her with the old man to return to the Laboratory, and she had telephoned for her friend. She and Miss Mawson had been there together until Mrs Swaffield, the rector's wife, and a constable arrived, about an hour later.

'What did you do at Postmill Cottage?'

'I made tea and took it in to my uncle. Miss Mawson stayed in the kitchen most of the time doing the washing-up for him. The kitchen was in a bit of a mess, mostly dirty crockery from the previous day.'

'How did your uncle seem?'

'Worried, and rather cross about having been left alone. I don't think he quite realized Edwin was dead.'

There seemed little else to be learned from her. As far as she knew, her cousin had had no enemies. She had no idea who could have killed him. Her voice, high, rather monotonous, the voice of a small girl, suggested that it was not a matter of much concern to her. She expressed no regret, advanced no theories, answered all his questions composedly in her high, unemphatic voice. He might have been a casual and unimportant visitor gratifying a curiosity about the routine of the working of the Laboratory. He felt an instinctive antipathy towards her. He had no difficulty in concealing it, but it interested him since it was a long time since a murder suspect had provoked in him so immediate and physical a reaction. But he wondered whether it was prejudice that glimpsed in those deep and secretive eyes a flash of disdain, of contempt even, and he would have given a great deal to know what was going on behind that high, rather bumpy forehead.

When she had left, Massingham said:

'It's odd that Dr Howarth sent her and Blakelock to check on the keys. He must have immediately realized their importance. Access to the Lab is fundamental in this case. So why didn't he check on them himself? He knew the combination.'

'Too proud to take a witness, and too intelligent to go without one. And he may have thought it more important to supervise things in the hall. But at least he was careful to protect Angela Foley. He didn't send her alone. Well, let's see what Blakelock has to say about it.'

13

Like Dr Howarth, Inspector Blakelock chose not to sit. He stood at attention, facing Dalgliesh across Howarth's desk like a man on a disciplinary charge. Dalgliesh knew better than to try to get him to relax. Blakelock had first learned the technique of replying to questions in his detective-constable days in the witness-box. He gave the information he was asked for, no more and no less, his eyes fixed on some spot a foot above Dalgliesh's right shoulder. When he gave his name in a firm expressionless voice, Dalgliesh half expected him to reach out his right hand for the Book and take the oath.

In reply to Dalgliesh's questioning he described his movements since leaving his house in Ely to come to the Laboratory. His account of the finding of the body tallied with that of Brenda Pridmore. As soon as he had seen her face as she came down the stairs he had realized that something was wrong and had dashed up to the Biology Lab without waiting for her to speak. The door had been open and the light on. He described the position of the body as precisely as if its rigid contours were imprinted on the mind's retina. He had known at once that Lorrimer was dead. He hadn't touched the body except, instinctively, to slip his hand into the pocket of the white coat and feel that the keys were there.

Dalgliesh asked:

'When you arrived at the Laboratory this morning you waited for Miss Pridmore to catch you up before coming in. Why was that?'

'I saw her coming round the side of the building after having put her bicycle away, and it seemed courteous to wait, sir. And it saved me having to re-open the door to her.'

'And you found the three locks and the internal security system in good order?'

'Yes, sir.'

'Do you make a routine check of the Laboratory as soon as you arrive?'

'No, sir. Of course if I found that any of the locks or the security panel had been tampered with I should check at once. But everything was in order.'

'You said earlier that the telephone call from Mr Lorrimer senior was a surprise to you. Didn't you notice Dr Lorrimer's car when you arrived this morning?'

'No, sir. The senior scientific staff use the end garage.'

'Why did you send Miss Pridmore to see if Dr Lorrimer was here?'

'I didn't, sir. She slipped under the counter before I could stop her.'

'So you sensed that something was wrong?'

'Not really, sir. I didn't expect her to find him. But I think it did briefly occur to me that he might have been taken ill.'

'What sort of a man was Dr Lorrimer, Inspector?

'He was the senior biologist, sir.'

'I know. I'm asking you what he was like as a man and a colleague.'

'I didn't really know him well, sir. He wasn't one for lingering at the reception desk to chat. But I got on all right with him. He was a good forensic scientist.'

'I've been told that he took an interest in Brenda Pridmore. Didn't that mean that he occasionally lingered at the desk?'

'Not for more than a few minutes, sir. He liked to have a word with the girl from time to time. Everyone does. It's nice to have a young thing about the Lab. She's pretty and hard-working and enthusiastic, and I think Dr Lorrimer wanted to encourage her.'

'No more than that, Inspector?'

Blakelock said stolidly;

'No, sir.'

Dalgliesh then asked him about his movements on the previous evening. He said that he and his wife had bought tickets for the village concert, although his wife was reluctant to go because of a bad headache. She suffered from sinus headaches which were occasionally disabling. But they had attended for the first half of the programme and, because her headache was worse, had left at the interval. He had driven back to Ely, arriving home about a quarter to nine. He and his wife lived in a modern bungalow on the outskirts of the city with no near neighbours and he thought it unlikely that anyone would have noticed their return. Dalgliesh said:

'There seems to have been a general reluctance on the part of everyone to stay for the second part of the programme. Why did you bother to go when you knew your wife was unwell?'

'Dr MacIntyre – he's the former Director, sir – liked the Laboratory staff to take part in village activities, and Chief Inspector Martin feels the same. So I'd got the tickets and my wife thought we might as well use them. She hoped that the concert might help her to forget her headache. But the first half was rather rowdy and, in fact, it got worse.'

'Did you go home and fetch her, or did she meet you here?'

'She came out earlier in the afternoon by the bus, sir, and spent the afternoon with Mrs Dean, wife of the minister at the Chapel. She's an old friend. I went round to collect my wife when I left work at six o'clock. We had a fish-and-chip supper there before the concert.'

'That's your normal time for leaving?'

'Yes, sir.'

'And who locks up the Laboratory if the scientists are working after your time for leaving?'

'I always check who's left, sir. If there are junior staff working then I have to stay until they've finished. But that isn't usual. Dr Howarth has a set of keys and would check the alarm system and lock up if he worked late.'

'Did Dr Lorrimer normally work after you had left?'

'About three or four evenings a week, sir. But I had no anxiety about Dr Lorrimer locking up. He was very conscientious.'

'Would he let anyone into the Laboratory if he were here alone?'

'No, sir, not unless they were members of the staff, or of the police force, maybe. But it would have to be an officer he knew. He wouldn't let anyone in who hadn't got proper business here. Dr Lorrimer was very particular about unauthorized people coming into the Laboratory.'

'Was that why he tried forcibly to remove Miss Kerrison the day before yesterday?'

Inspector Blakelock did not lose his composure. He said:

'I wouldn't describe it as a forcible removal, sir. He didn't lay hands on the girl.'

'Would you describe to me exactly what did happen, Inspector?'

'Miss Kerrison and her small brother came to meet their father. Dr Kerrison was lecturing that morning to the Inspectors' training course. I suggested to Miss Kerrison that she sit down on the chair and wait, but Dr Lorrimer came down the stairs at that moment to see if the mallet had arrived for examination. He saw the children and asked rather peremptorily what they were doing there. He said that a forensic science lab wasn't a place for children. Miss Kerrison said that she didn't intend to leave, so he walked towards her as if he intended to put her out. He looked very white, very strange, I thought. He didn't lay a hand on her but I think she was frightened that he was going to. I believe she's very highly strung, sir. She started screeching and screaming "I hate you. I hate you." Dr Lorrimer turned and went back up the stairs and Brenda tried to comfort the girl.'

'And Miss Kerrison and her small brother left without waiting for their father?'

'Yes, sir. Dr Kerrison came down about fifteen minutes later and I told him that the children had come for him but had left.'

'You said nothing about the incident?'

'No, sir.'

'Was this typical of Dr Lorrimer's behaviour?'

'No, sir. But he hadn't been looking well in recent weeks. I think he's been under some strain.'

'And you've no idea what kind of strain?'

'No, sir.'

'Had he enemies?'

'Not to my knowledge, sir.'

'So you've no idea who might have wanted him dead?'

'No, sir.'

'After the discovery of Dr Lorrimer's body, Dr Howarth sent you with Miss Foley to check that his bunch of keys were in the security cupboard. Will you describe exactly what you and she did?'

'Miss Foley opened the cupboard. She and the Director are the only two people who know the combination.'

'And you watched?'

'Yes, sir, but I can't remember the figures. I watched her twisting and setting the dial.'

'And then?'

'She took out the metal cash box and opened it. It wasn't locked. The keys were inside.'

'You were watching her closely all the time, Inspector? Are you absolutely sure that Miss Foley couldn't have replaced the keys in the box without your seeing?'

'No, sir. That would have been quite impossible.'

'One last thing, Inspector. When you went up to the body Miss Pridmore was here alone. She told me that she's virtually certain that no one could have slipped out of the Laboratory during that time. Have you considered that possibility?'

'That he might have been here all night, sir? Yes. But he wasn't hiding in the Chief Liaison Officer's room because I would have seen him when I went to turn off the internal alarm. That's the room closest to the front door. I suppose he could have been in the Director's office, but I don't see how he could have crossed the hall and opened the door without Miss Pridmore noticing even if she were in a state of shock. It isn't as if the door were ajar. He'd have had to turn the Yale lock.'

'And are you absolutely certain that your own set of keys never left your possession last night?'

'I'm certain, sir.'

'Thank you, Inspector. That's all for the present. Would you please ask Mr Middlemass to come in?'

14

The Document Examiner strolled into the office with easy assurance, arranged his long body without invitation in Howarth's armchair, crossed his right ankle over his left knee and raised an interrogatory eyebrow at Dalgliesh like a visitor expecting nothing from his host but boredom, but politely determined not to show it. He was wearing dark brown corduroy slacks, a fawn turtle-necked sweater in fine wool and bright purple socks with leather slip-on shoes. The effect was of a *dégagé* informality, but Dalgliesh noticed that the slacks were tailored, the sweater cashmere, and the shoes hand-made. He glanced down at Middlemass's statement of his movements since seven o'clock the previous evening. Unlike the efforts of his colleagues, it was written with a pen, not a biro, in a fine, high, italic script, which succeeded in being both decorative and virtually illegible. It was not the kind of hand he had expected. He said:

'Before we get down to this, could you tell me about your quarrel with Lorrimer?'

'My version of it, you mean, as opposed to Mrs Bidwell's?'

'The truth, as opposed to speculation.'

'It wasn't a particularly edifying episode, and I can't say I'm proud of it. But it wasn't important. I'd just started on the clunch-pit murder case when I heard Lorrimer coming out of the wash-room. I had a private matter I wanted a word about so I called him in. We talked, quarrelled, he struck out at me and I reacted with a punch to his nose. It bled spectacularly over my overall. I apologized. He left.'

'What was the quarrel about? A woman?'

'Well hardly, Commander, not with Lorrimer. I think Lorrimer knew that there were two sexes but I doubt whether he approved of the arrangement. It was a small private matter, something which happened a couple of years ago. Nothing to do with this Lab.'

'So we have the picture of your settling down to work on an exhibit from a murder case, an important exhibit since you chose to examine it yourself. You are not, however, so absorbed in this task that you can't listen to footsteps passing the door and identify those of Lorrimer. It seems to you a convenient moment to call him in and discuss something which happened two years ago, something which you've apparently been content to forget in the interim, but which now so incenses you both that you end by trying to knock each other down.'

'Put like that, it sounds eccentric.'

'Put like that, it sounds absurd.'

'I suppose it was absurd in a way. It was about a cousin of my wife's, Peter Ennalls. He left school with two A-levels in science and seemed keen on coming into the Service. He came to me for advice and I told him how to go about it. He ended up as an SO under Lorrimer in the Southern Lab. It wasn't a success. I don't suppose it was entirely Lorrimer's fault, but he hasn't got the gift of managing young staff. Ennalls ended up with a failed career, a broken engagement and what is euphemistically described as a nervous breakdown. He drowned himself. We heard rumours about what happened at the Southern. It's a small Service and these things get around. I didn't really know the boy; my wife was fond of him.

'I'm not blaming Lorrimer for Peter's death. A suicide is always ultimately responsible for his own destruction. But my wife believes that Lorrimer could have done more to help him. I telephoned her after lunch yesterday to explain that I'd be late home and our conversation reminded me that I'd always meant to speak to Lorrimer about Peter. By coincidence I heard his footsteps. So I called him in with the result that Mrs Bidwell has no doubt graphically described. Mrs Bidwell, I don't doubt, detects a woman at the bottom of any male quarrel. And if she did talk about a woman or a telephone call, then the woman was my wife and the telephone call was the one I've told you about.'

It sounded plausible, thought Dalgliesh. It might even be the truth. The Peter Ennalls story would have to be checked. It was just another chore when they were already hard-pressed and the truth of it was hardly in doubt. But Middlemass had spoken in the present tense: 'Lorrimer hasn't the gift of managing junior staff.' Were there, perhaps, junior staff closer to home who had suffered at his hands? But he decided to leave it for now. Paul Middlemass was an intelligent man. Before he made a more formal statement he would have time to ponder about the effect on his career of putting his signature to a lie. Dalgliesh said:

'According to this statement you were playing the part of a hobby-horse for the morris dancers at yesterday evening's village concert. Despite this, you say you can't give the name of anyone who could vouch for you. Presumably both the dancers and the audience could see the hobby-horse galumphing around, but not you inside it. But wasn't anyone there when you arrived at the hall, or when you left?'

'No one who saw me to recognize me. It's a nuisance but it can't be helped. It happened rather oddly. I'm not a morris dancer. I don't normally go in for these rustic rites and village concerts aren't my idea of entertainment. It was the Senior Liaison Officer's show, Chief Inspector Martin, but he had the chance of this USA visit unexpectedly and asked me to deputize. We're about the same size and I suppose he thought that the outfit would fit me. He needed someone fairly broad in the shoulders and strong enough to take the weight of the head: I owed him a favour – he had a tactful word with one of his mates on highway patrol when I was caught speeding a month ago – so I couldn't very well not oblige.

'I went to a rehearsal last week and all it amounted to was, as you say, galumphing round the dancers after they'd done their stuff, snapping my jaws at the audience, frisking my tail and generally making a fool of myself. That hardly seemed to matter since no one could recognize me. I'd no intention of spending the whole evening at the concert, so I asked Bob Gotobed, he's the leader of the troupe, to give me a ring from the hall about fifteen minutes before we were due to go on. We were scheduled to appear after the interval and they reckoned that that would be about eight-thirty. The concert, as you've probably been told, started at seven-thirty.'

'And you stayed working in your lab until the call came?'

'That's right. My SO went out and got me a couple of beef and chutney sandwiches and I ate them at my desk. Bob phoned at eight-fifteen to say that they were running a bit ahead of time and that I'd better come over. The lads were dressed and were proposing to have a beer in the Moonraker. The hall hasn't a licence, so all the audience get in the interval is coffee or tea served by the Mothers' Union. I left the Lab at, I suppose, about eight-twenty.'

'You say here that Lorrimer was alive then as far as you know?'

'We know that he was alive twenty-five minutes later, if his dad is right about the telephone call. But actually I think I saw him. I went out of the front door because that's the only exit but I had to go round the back to the garages to get my car. The light was on then in the Biology Department and I saw a figure in a white coat move briefly across the window. I can't swear that it was Lorrimer. I can only say that it never occurred to me at the time that it wasn't. And I knew, of course, that he must be in the building. He was responsible for locking up and he was excessively tedious about security. He wouldn't have left without checking on all the departments, including Document Examination.'

'How was the front door locked?'

'Only with the Yale and a single bolt. That's what I expected. I let myself out.'

'What happened when you got to the hall?'

'To explain that I'll have to describe the architectural oddities of the place. It was put up cheaply five years ago by the village builder and the committee thought they'd save money by not employing an architect. They merely told the chap that they wanted a rectangular hall with a stage and two dressing-rooms and lavatories at one end, and a reception hall, cloakroom and a room for refreshments at the other. It was built by Harry Gotobed and his sons. Harry is a pillar of the Chapel and a model of Nonconformist rectitude. He doesn't hold with the theatre, amateur or otherwise, and I think they had some difficulty in persuading him even to build a stage. But he certainly didn't intend to have any communicating door between the male and female dressing-rooms. As a result what we've got is a stage with two rooms behind, each with its separate lavatory.

There's an exit at each side into the graveyard, and two doors on to the stage, but there's literally no common space behind the stage. As a result the men dress in the right-hand dressing-room and come on to the stage from the prompt side, and the women from the left. Anyone who wants to enter from the opposite side has to leave the dressing-room, scurry in their costume and probably in the rain through the graveyard and, if they don't trip over a gravestone, break their ankle, or fall into an open grave, finally make a triumphant, if damp, appearance on the proper side.'

Suddenly he threw back his head and gave a shout of laughter, then recovered himself and said:

'Sorry, poor taste. It's just that I was remembering last year's performance by the dramatic society. They'd chosen one of those dated domestic comedies where the characters spend most of their time in evening dress making snappy small-talk. Young Bridie Corrigan from the general store played the maid. Scurrying through the churchyard she thought she saw old Maggie Gotobed's ghost. She made her entrance screaming, cap awry, but remembered her part sufficiently to gasp: "Holy Mother of God, dinner is served!" Whereat the cast trooped dutifully off stage, the men to one side and the women to the other. Our hall adds considerably to the interest of the performances, I can tell you.'

'So you went into the right-hand dressing-room?'

'That's right. It was a complete shambles. The cast have to hang up their outdoor coats as well as keeping the costumes there. There's a row of coat-hooks and a bench down the middle of the room, one rather small mirror and space for two people only to make up simultaneously. The single hand-basin is in the lavatory. Well, no doubt you'll be looking at the place for yourself. Last night it was chaotic with outdoor coats, costumes, boxes and props piled on the bench and overflowing on to the floor. The hobby-horse costume was hanging on one of the pegs, so I put it on.'

'There was no one there when you arrived?'

'No one in the room, but I could hear someone in the lavatory. I knew that most of the troupe were over at the Moonraker. When I had got myself into the costume the lavatory door opened and Harry Sprogg, he's a member of the troupe, came out. He was wearing his costume.'

Massingham made a note of the name: Harry Sprogg. Dalgliesh asked:

'Did you speak?'

'I didn't. He said something about being glad I'd made it and that the chaps were over at the Moonraker. He said he was just going to dig them out. He's the only teetotaller of the party so I suppose that's why he didn't go over with them. He left and I followed him out into the cemetery.'

'Without having spoken to him?'

'I can't remember that I said anything. We were only together for about a couple of seconds. I followed him out because the dressing-room was stuffy – actually it stank – and the costume was extraordinarily heavy and hot. I thought I'd wait outside where I could join the boys when they came across from the pub. And that's what I did.'

'Did you see anyone else?'

'No, but that doesn't mean there was no one there. Vision's a bit restricted through the headpiece. If someone had been standing motionless in the graveyard, I could easily have missed him. I wasn't expecting to see anyone.'

'How long were you there?'

'Less than five minutes. I galumphed around a bit and tried a few trial snaps of the jaw and whisks of the tail. It must have looked daft if anyone was watching. There's a particularly repulsive memorial there, a marble angel with an expression of nauseating piety and a hand pointed upwards. I pranced around that once or twice and snapped my jaws at its asinine face. God knows why! Perhaps it was the joint effect of moonlight and the place itself. Then I saw the chaps coming across the graveyard from the Moonraker and I joined up with them.'

'Did you say anything then?'

'I may have said good evening or hello, but I don't think so. They wouldn't have recognized my voice through the headpiece anyway. I raised the front right-hand hoof and made a mock obeisance and then tagged on behind. We went into the dressing-room together. We could hear the audience settling into their seats, and then the stage manager put his head in and said "Right, boys." Then the six dancers went on, and I could hear the violin strike up, the stamping of feet and the jangling of bells. Then the music changed, and that was the signal for me to join them and do my bit. Part of the act was to go down the steps from the stage and frolic among the audience. It seemed to go down well enough to judge by the girlish shrieks, but if you're thinking of asking whether anyone recognized me, I shouldn't bother. I don't see how they could have.'

'But after the performance?'

'No one saw me after the performance. We came tumbling down the steps from the stage into the dressing-room, but the applause went on. Then I realized with considerable horror that some fools in the audience were calling out "encore". The lads in green needed no second invitation and they were up the stairs again like a troop of parched navvies who'd just been told that the bar's open. I took the view that my agreement with Bill Martin covered one performance, not including an encore, and that I'd made enough of a fool of myself for one evening. So when the fiddle struck up and the stamping began I got out of the costume, hung it back on the nail, and made off. As far as I know no one saw me leave and there was no one in the car-park when I unlocked my car. I was at home before ten and my wife can vouch for that if you're interested. But I don't suppose you are.'

'It would be more helpful if you could find someone to vouch for you between eight forty-five and midnight.'

'I know. Maddening, isn't it? If I'd known someone was proposing to murder Lorrimer during the evening I'd have taken good care not to put the headpiece on until the second before we went on stage. It's a pity the beast's head is so large. It's supported, as you'll discover, from the wearer's shoulders and doesn't actually touch the head or face. If it did you might find a hair or some biological evidence that I'd actually worn the thing. And prints are no good. I handled it at the rehearsal and so did a dozen other people. The whole incident is an example to me of the folly of indulging in good nature. If I'd only told old Bill just what he could do with his blasted hobby-horse I should have been home, and, quite literally, dry before eight o'clock with a nice cosy alibi at the Panton Arms for the rest of the evening.'

Dalgliesh ended the interview by asking about the missing white coat.

'It's a fairly distinctive design. Actually I've got half a dozen of them, all inherited from my father. The other five are in the linen-cupboard here, if you want to have a look at them. They're waisted, in very heavy white linen, buttoning high to the neck with crested Royal Army Dental Corps buttons. Oh, and they've got no pockets. The old man thought pockets were unhygienic.'

Massingham thought that a coat already stained with Lorrimer's blood might be seen by a murderer as a particularly useful protective garment. Echoing his thought, Middlemass said:

'If it is found again I don't think I could say with certainty exactly what bloodstains resulted from our punch-up. There was one patch about four inches by two on the right shoulder, but there may have been other splashes. But presumably the serologists would be able to give you some idea of the comparative age of the stains.'

If the coat were ever found, thought Dalgliesh. It wouldn't be an easy thing to destroy completely. But the murderer, if he had taken it, would have had all night to dispose of the evidence. He asked:

'And you dropped this particular coat in the soiled-linen-basket in the men's washroom immediately after the quarrel?'

'I meant to, but then thought better of it. The stain wasn't large and the sleeves were perfectly clean. I put it on again and dropped it in the soiled-linen-basket when I washed before leaving the Lab.'

'Do you remember what wash-basin you used?'

'The first one, nearest the door.'

'Was the basin clean?'

If Middlemass was surprised by the question, he concealed it.

'As clean as it ever is after a day's use. I wash fairly vigorously so it was clean enough when I left it. And so was I.'

The picture came into Massingham's mind with startling clarity; Middlemass in his blood-spattered coat bending low over the wash-basin, both taps running full on, the water swirling and gurgling down the waste-pipe, water stained pink with Lorrimer's blood. But what about the timing? If old Lorrimer really had spoken to his son at eight forty-five then Middlemass must be in the clear, at least for the first part of the evening. And then he pictured another scene; Lorrimer's sprawled body, the raucous ring of the telephone, Middlemass's gloved hand slowly lifting the receiver. But could old Lorrimer really mistake another voice for that of his son?

When the Document Examiner had left Massingham said:

'At least he has one person to corroborate his story. Dr Howarth saw the hobby-horse prancing round the angel memorial in the

churchyard. They've hardly had opportunity this morning to concoct that story together. And I don't see how else Howarth could
have known about it.'

Dalgliesh said:

'Unless they concocted the story in the graveyard last night. Or
unless it was Howarth, not Middlemass, who was inside that hobby-
horse.'

15

'I didn't like him, and I was frightened of him, but I didn't kill him. I
know everyone will think that I did, but it's not true. I couldn't kill
anyone or anything; not an animal, let alone a man.'

Clifford Bradley had stood up fairly well to the long wait for
questioning. He wasn't incoherent. He had tried to behave with
dignity. But he had brought into the room with him the sour
contagion of fear, that most difficult of all emotions to hide. His
whole body twitched with it: the restless hands clasping and
unclasping in his lap, the shuddering mouth, the anxious blinking
eyes. He was not an impressive figure, and fear had made him
pitiable. He would make an ineffective murderer, thought Massingham. Watching him, he felt some of the instinctive shame of the
healthy in the presence of the diseased. It was easy to imagine him
retching over that wash-basin, vomiting up his guilt and terror. It
was less easy to envisage him tearing out the page of the notebook,
destroying the white coat, organizing that early-morning telephone
call to Mrs Bidwell. Dalgliesh said mildly:

'No one is accusing you. You're familiar enough with Judge's
Rules to know that we wouldn't be talking like this if I were about to
caution you. You say that you didn't kill him. Have you any idea
who did?'

'No. Why should I have? I didn't know anything about him. All I
know is that I was at home with my wife last night. My mother-in-
law came to supper and I saw her off on the seven forty-five bus to
Ely. Then I went straight home, and I was home all the evening. My
mother-in-law telephoned about nine o'clock to say that she'd
reached home safely. She didn't speak to me because I was having a

bath. My wife told her that. But Sue can confirm that, except for taking her mother to the bus, I was home all evening.'

Bradley admitted that he hadn't known that old Mr Lorrimer's hospital admission had been postponed. He thought he had been in the washroom when the old man's call came through. But he knew nothing of the early telephone call to Mrs Bidwell, the missing page from Lorrimer's notebook, or Paul Middlemass's missing white coat. Asked about his supper on Wednesday night, he said that they had eaten curry made with tinned beef, together with rice and tinned peas. Afterwards there had been a trifle which, he explained defensively, had been made with stale cake and custard. Massingham suppressed a shudder as he made a careful note of these details. He was glad when Dalgliesh said that Bradley could go. There seemed nothing else of importance to be learned from him in his present state; nothing more to be learned, indeed, from anyone at the Laboratory. He was fretting to see Lorrimer's house, Lorrimer's next of kin.

But before they left, Sergeant Reynolds had something to report. He was finding it difficult to keep the excitement from his voice.

'We've found some tyre-marks, sir, about half-way up the drive among the bushes. They look pretty fresh to me. We've got them protected until the photographer arrives and then we'll get a plaster cast made. It's difficult to be sure until we compare them with a tyre index, but it looks to me as if the two back tyres were a Dunlop and a Semperit. That's a pretty odd combination. It should help us to get the car.'

It was a pity, thought Dalgliesh, that Superintendent Mercer had told the photographers they could go. But it wasn't surprising. Given the present pressure of work on the Force, it was difficult to justify keeping men hanging about indefinitely. And at least the finger-print officers were still here. He said:

'Have you been able to get in touch with Mr Bidwell yet?'

'Captain Massey says he's up on the five-acre raising sugar beet. He'll tell him you want to see him when he comes in for his dockey.'

'His what?'

'His dockey, sir. That's the meal break which we have in these parts at about half-past ten or eleven.'

'I'm relieved that Captain Massey has a proper sense of priority between agriculture and murder.'

'They're a good bit behind with the five-acre, sir, but Captain Massey will see that he calls in at Guy's Marsh station as soon as they've finished work this afternoon.'

'If he doesn't, you'd better dig him out, even if you have to borrow Captain Massey's tractor to do it. That telephone call is important. I'll have a word with the senior scientists in the library now and explain to them that I want them present in the departments when you do the internal search. The rest of them can go home. I'll tell them that we hope to have finished searching by the end of the day. It should be possible for the Lab to open again tomorrow morning. Inspector Massingham and I will be seeing Dr Lorrimer's father at Postmill Cottage. If anything breaks, you can contact us there or through the car radio control from Guy's Marsh.'

Less than ten minutes later, with Massingham at the wheel of the police Rover, they were on their way.

BOOK THREE

An Experimental Man

1

Postmill Cottage lay two miles to the west of the village at the junction of Stoney Piggott's Road and Tenpenny Lane, where the road curved gently upwards, but so imperceptibly that it was difficult for Dalgliesh to believe that he was on slightly higher ground until the car was parked on the grass verge, and turning to close the door he saw the village strung out along the road below him. Under the turbulent painter's sky, with its changing clusters of white, grey and purple cumulus clouds massing against the pale azure blue of the upper air, and the sunlight moving fitfully across the fields and glittering on roofs and windows, it looked like an isolated frontier outpost, but welcoming, prosperous and secure. Violent death might lurk eastwards in the dark fenlands, but surely not under these neat domestic roofs. Hoggatt's Laboratory was hidden by its belt of trees, but the new building was immediately identifiable, its concrete stumps, ditches and half-built walls looking like the orderly excavation of some long-buried city.

The cottage, a low building of brick with a white wood-cladded front and with the rounded top and sails of the windmill visible behind, was separated from the road by a wide ditch. A wooden plank bridge and white-painted gate led to the front path and the latched door. The first impression of melancholy neglect, induced perhaps by the cottage's isolation and the bareness of outer walls and windows, proved on second glance illusory. The front garden had the dishevelled, overgrown look of autumn, but the roses in the two circular beds, one each side of the path, had been properly tended. The gravel path was clear of weeds, the paintwork on door and windows was shining. Twenty feet farther on two wide and sturdy planks bridged the ditch and led to a flagstoned yard and a brick garage.

There was an old and grubby red Mini already parked next to a police car. Dalgliesh deduced from the bundle of parish magazines, a smaller one of what looked like concert programmes and the bunch of shaggy chrysanthemums and autumn foliage on the back seat, that the rector, or more probably his wife, was already at the cottage, probably on her way to help with the church decorations, although Thursday was an unusual day, surely, for this ecclesiastical chore. He had scarcely turned from this scrutiny of the rectory car when the door of the cottage opened and a woman bustled down the path towards them. No one who had been born and bred in a rectory could be in any doubt that here was Mrs Swaffield. She looked indeed like a prototype of a country rector's wife, large-bosomed, cheerful and energetic, exuding the slightly intimidating assurance of a woman adept at recognizing authority and competence at a glance, and making immediate use of them. She was wearing a tweed skirt covered with a flowered cotton apron, a hand-knitted twinset, thick brogues and open-work woollen stockings. A felt hat, shaped like a pork pie, its crown stabbed with a steel hatpin, was jammed uncompromisingly over a broad forehead.

'Good morning. Good morning. You're Commander Dalgliesh and Inspector Massingham. Winifred Swaffield. Come in, won't you. The old gentleman is upstairs changing. He insisted on putting on his suit when he heard you were on the way, although I assured him that it wasn't at all necessary. He'll be down in a minute. In the front parlour would be best I think, don't you? This is Constable Davis, but of course you know all about him. He tells me that he's been sent here to see that no one goes into Dr Lorrimer's room and to stop any visitors from bothering the old gentleman. Well, we haven't had any so far except one reporter and I soon got rid of him, so that's all right. But the constable has really been very helpful to me in the kitchen. I've just been getting some lunch for Mr Lorrimer. It'll only be soup and an omelette, I'm afraid, but there doesn't seem to be much else in the larder except tins and he might be glad of those in the future. One doesn't like to come laden from the rectory like a Victorian do-gooder.

'Simon and I wanted him to come back to the rectory at once but he doesn't seem anxious to leave, and really one mustn't badger people, especially the old. And perhaps it's just as well. Simon's down with this two-day flu – that's why he can't be here – and we don't want the old gentleman to catch it. But we can't let him stay here alone tonight. I thought that he might like to have his niece here, Angela Foley, but he says no. So I'm hoping that Millie Gotobed from the Moonraker will be able to sleep here tonight, and we'll have to think again tomorrow. But I mustn't take up your time with my worries.'

At the end of this speech, Dalgliesh and Massingham found themselves ushered into the front living-room. At the sound of their footsteps in the narrow hall Constable Davis had emerged from what was presumably the kitchen, had sprung to attention, saluted, blushed and given Dalgliesh a glance of mingled appeal and slight desperation before disappearing again. The smell of home-made soup had wafted appetizingly through the door.

The sitting-room, which was stuffy and smelt strongly of tobacco, was adequately furnished, yet gave an impression of cheerless discomfort, a cluttered repository of the mementoes of ageing and its sad solaces. The chimney-breast had been boarded up and an old-fashioned gas fire hissed out an uncomfortably fierce heat over a sofa in cut moquette with two greasy circles marking where innumerable heads had once rested. There was a square oak table with bulbous carved legs and four matching chairs with vinyl seats, and a large dresser set against the wall opposite the window, hung with the cracked remnants of long-smashed teasets. On the dresser were two bottles of Guinness and an unwashed glass. To the right of the fire was a high winged armchair and beside it a wicker table with a ramshackle lamp, a tobacco pouch, an ashtray bearing a picture of Brighton pier, and an open draught-board with the pieces set out, crusted with dried food and accumulated grime. The alcove to the left of the fire was filled with a large television set. Above it were a couple of shelves holding a collection of popular novels in identical sizes and bindings, issued by a book club to which Mr Lorrimer had once apparently briefly belonged. They looked as if they had been gummed together unopened and unread.

Dalgliesh and Massingham sat on the sofa. Mrs Swaffield perched upright on the edge of the armchair and smiled across at them encouragingly, bringing into the room's cheerlessness a reassuring ambience of home-made jam, well-conducted Sunday schools and massed women's choirs singing Blake's 'Jerusalem'. Both men felt immediately at home with her. Both in their different lives had met her kind before. It was not, thought Dalgliesh, that she was unaware of the frayed and ragged edges of life. She would merely iron them out with a firm hand and neatly hem them down.

Dalgliesh asked:

'How is he, Mrs Swaffield?'

'Surprisingly well. He keeps talking about his son in the present tense, which is a little disconcerting, but I think he realizes all right that Edwin is dead. I don't mean to imply that the old gentleman is senile. Not in the least. But it's difficult to know what the very old are feeling sometimes. It must have been a terrible shock, naturally. Appalling, isn't it? I suppose a criminal from one of those London gangs broke in to get his hands on an exhibit. They're saying in the village that there were no signs of a break-in, but a really determined burglar can get in anywhere, I've always been told. I know Father Gregory has had terrible trouble with break-ins at St Mary's at Guy's Marsh. The poor-box has been rifled twice and two pews of kneelers stolen, the ones the Mothers' Union had specially embroidered to celebrate their fiftieth anniversary. Goodness knows why anyone should want to take those. Luckily we've had no trouble of that kind here. Simon would hate to have to lock the church. Chevisham has always been a most law-abiding village, which is why this murder is so shocking.'

Dalgliesh wasn't surprised that the village already knew that there had been no break-in at the Lab. Presumably one of the staff, on the excuse of needing to telephone home and say that he wouldn't be back for luncheon and avid to break the exciting news, had been less than discreet. But it would be pointless to try to trace the culprit. In his experience news percolated through a village community by a process of verbal osmosis, and it would be a bold man who tried to control or stem that mysterious diffusion. Mrs Swaffield, like any proper rector's wife, had undoubtedly been one of the first to know. Dalgliesh said:

'It's a pity that Miss Foley and her uncle don't seem to get on. If he could go to stay temporarily with her that would at least solve your immediate problem. She and her friend were here when you arrived this morning, I take it?'

'Yes, both of them. Dr Howarth came himself with Angela to break the news, which I think was thoughtful of him, then left her here when he went back to the Lab. He wouldn't want to be away for more than a short time, naturally. I think Angela phoned her friend and she came at once. Then the constable arrived and I was here shortly afterwards. There was no point in Angela and Miss Mawson staying on once I'd come, and Dr Howarth was anxious for most of the staff to be actually in the Lab when you arrived.'

'And there are no other relatives and no close friends, as far as you know?'

'None, I think. They kept themselves very much to themselves. Old Mr Lorrimer doesn't come to church or take any part in village affairs, so that Simon and I never really got to know him. I know that people expect the clergy to come round knocking at doors and rooting people out, but Simon doesn't really believe it does much good, and I must say I think he's right. Dr Lorrimer, of course, went to St Mary's at Guy's Marsh. Father Gregory might be able to tell you something about him, although I don't think he took a very active part in church life. He used to pick up Miss Willard from the Old Rectory and drive her over. She might be worth having a word with, although it seems unlikely that they were close. I imagine that he drove her to church because Father Gregory suggested it rather than from inclination. She's an odd woman, not really suitable to look after children, I should have thought. But here comes the one you really want to talk to.'

Death, thought Dalgliesh, obliterates family resemblance as it does personality; there is no affinity between the living and the dead. The man who came into the room, shuffling a little but still upright, had once been as tall as his son, the sparse grey·hair brushed back from a high forehead still showed streaks of the black it had once been; the watery eyes, sunken under the creased lids, were as dark. But there was no kinship with that rigid body on the laboratory floor. Death, in separating them for ever, had robbed them even of their likeness.

Mrs Swaffield made the introductions in a voice of determined encouragement as if they had all suddenly gone deaf. Then she melted tactfully away, murmuring something about soup in the kitchen. Massingham sprang to help the old man to a chair, but Mr Lorrimer, with a stiff chopping motion of the hand, gestured him aside. Eventually, after some hesitation, as if the sitting-room were unfamiliar to him, he lowered himself into what was obviously his usual place, the shabby, high-backed armchair to the right of the fire, from which he regarded Dalgliesh steadily.

Sitting there, bolt upright, in his old-fashioned and badly cut dark blue suit, which smelt strongly of mothballs and now hung loosely on his diminished bones, he looked pathetic, almost grotesque, but not without dignity. Dalgliesh wondered why he had troubled to change. Was it a gesture of respect for his son, the need to formalize grief, a restless urge to find something to do? Or was it some atavistic belief that authority was on its way and should be propitiated by an outward show of deference? Dalgliesh was reminded of the funeral of a young detective-constable killed on duty. What he had found almost unbearably pathetic had not been the sonorous beauty of the burial service, or even the young children walking hand in hand with careful solmnity behind their father's coffin. It had been the reception afterwards in the small police house, the carefully planned home-cooked food and the drink, ill-afforded, which the widow had prepared for the refreshment of her husband's colleagues and friends. Perhaps it had comforted her at the time, or solaced her in memory. Perhaps old Mr Lorrimer, too, felt happier because he had taken trouble.

Settling himself some distance from Dalgliesh on the extraordinarily lumpy sofa, Massingham opened his notebook. Thank God the old man was calm anyway. You could never tell how the relatives were going to take it. Dalgliesh, as he knew, had the reputation of being good with the bereaved. His condolences might be short, almost formal, but at least they sounded sincere. He took it for granted that the family would wish to co-operate with the police, but as a matter of justice, not of retribution. He didn't connive at the extraordinary psychological interdependence by which the detective and the bereaved were often supported, and which it was so fatally easy to exploit. He made no specious promises, never bullied the weak or indulged the sentimental. And yet they seem to like him, thought Massingham. God knows why. At times he's cold enough to be barely human.

He watched Dalgliesh stand up as old Mr Lorrimer came into the room; but he made no move to help the old man to his chair. Massingham had glanced briefly at his chief's face and seen the familiar look of speculative detached interest. What, if anything, he wondered, would move Dalgliesh to spontaneous pity? He remembered the other case they had worked on together a year previously, when he had been a detective-sergeant; the death of a child. Dalgliesh had regarded the parents with just such a look of calm appraisal. But he had worked eighteen hours a day for a month until the case was solved. And his next book of poems had contained that extraordinary one about a murdered child which no one at the Yard, even those who professed to understand it, had had the temerity even to mention to its author. He said now:

'As Mrs Swaffield explained, my name is Dalgliesh and this is Inspector Massingham. I expect Dr Howarth told you that we would be coming. I'm very sorry about your son. Do you feel able to answer some questions?'

Mr Lorrimer nodded towards the kitchen.

'What's she doing in there?'

His voice was surprising; high-timbred and with a trace of the querulousness of age, but extraordinarily strong for an old man.

'Mrs Swaffield? Making soup I think.'

'I suppose she's used the onions and carrots we had in the vegetable rack. I thought I could smell carrots. Edwin knows I don't like carrots in soup.'

'Did he usually cook for you?'

'He does all the cooking if he isn't away at a scene of crime. I don't eat much dinner at midday, but he leaves me something to heat up, a stew from the night before or a bit of fish in sauce, maybe. He didn't leave anything this morning because he wasn't home last night. I had to get my own breakfast. I fancied bacon, but I thought I'd better leave that in case he wants it for tonight. He usually cooks bacon and eggs if he's late home.'

Dalgliesh asked:

'Mr Lorrimer, have you any idea why anyone should want to murder your son? Had he any enemies?'

'Why should he have enemies? He didn't know anyone except at the Lab. Everyone had a great respect for him at the Lab. He told me so himself. Why would anyone want to harm him? Edwin lived for his work.'

He brought out the last sentence as if it were an original expression of which he was rather proud.

'You telephoned him last night at the Laboratory, didn't you? What time was that?'

'It was a quarter to nine. The telly went blank. It didn't blink and go zig-zag like it sometimes does. Edwin showed me how to adjust the knob at the back for that. It went blank with just one little circle of light and then that failed. I couldn't see the nine o'clock news, so I rang Edwin and asked him to send for the TV man. We rent the set, and they're supposed to come at any hour, but there's always some excuse. Last month when I telephoned they didn't come for two days.'

'Can you remember what your son said?'

'He said that it wasn't any use telephoning late at night. He'd do it first thing in the morning before he went to work. But, of course, he hasn't. He didn't come home. It's still broken. I don't like to telephone myself. Edwin always sees to everything like that. Do you think Mrs Swaffield would ring?'

'I'm sure that she would. When you telephoned him did he say anything about expecting a visitor?'

'No. He seemed in a hurry, as if he didn't like it because I phoned. But he always said to ring the Lab up if I was in trouble.'

'And he said nothing else at all except that he'd ring the TV mechanic this morning?'

'What else would he say? He wasn't one for chatting over the telephone.'

'Did you ring him at the Laboratory yesterday about your hospital appointment?'

'That's right. I was supposed to go in to Addenbrooke's yesterday afternoon. Edwin was going to drive me in. It's my leg, you see. It's psoriasis. They're going to try a new treatment.'

He made as if to roll up his trouser leg. Dalgliesh said quickly:

'That's all right, Mr Lorrimer. When did you know that the bed wasn't available after all?'

'About nine o'clock they rang. He'd only just left home. So I phoned the Lab. I know the number of the Biology Department, of course. That's where he works – the Biology Department. Miss Easterbrook answered the phone and said that Edwin was at the hospital attending a post-mortem but she would give him the message when he got in. Addenbrooke's said they'd probably send for me next Tuesday. Who's going to take me now?'

'I expect Mrs Swaffield will arrange something, or perhaps your niece could help. Wouldn't you like her to be with you?'

'No. What can she do? She was here this morning with that friend of hers, the writing woman. Edwin doesn't like either of them. The friend – Miss Mawson, isn't it? – was rummaging around upstairs. I've got very good ears. I could hear her all right. I went out of the door and there she was coming down. She said she'd been to the bathroom. Why was she wearing the washing-up gloves if she was going to the bathroom?'

Why indeed? thought Dalgliesh. He felt a spasm of irritation that Constable Davis hadn't arrived sooner. It was perfectly natural that Howarth should come with Angela Foley to break the news and should leave her with her uncle. Someone had to stay with him, and who more suitable than his only remaining relative? It was probably natural, too, that Angela Foley should send for the support of her friend. Probably both of them were interested in Lorrimer's will. Well, that too was natural enough. Massingham shifted on the sofa. Dalgliesh could sense his anxiety to get upstairs into Lorrimer's room. He shared it. But books and papers, the sad detritus of a dead life, could wait. The living witness might not again be so communicative. He asked:

'What did your son do with himself, Mr Lorrimer?'

'After work, do you mean? He stays in his room mostly. Reading, I suppose. He's got quite a library of books up there. He's a scholar, is Edwin. He doesn't care much about the television, so I sit down here. Sometimes I can hear the record-player. Then there's the garden most weekends, cleaning the car, cooking and shopping. He has quite a full life. And he doesn't get much time. He's at the Lab until seven o'clock most nights, sometimes later.'

'And friends?'

'No. He doesn't go in for friends. We keep ourselves to ourselves.'

'No weekends away?'

'Where would he want to go? And what would happen to me? Besides, there's the shopping. If he isn't on call for a scene-of-crime visit he drives me into Ely Saturday morning, and we go to the supermarket. Then we have lunch in the city. I enjoy that.'

'What telephone calls did he have?'

'From the Lab? Only when the Police Liaison Officer rings up to say that he's wanted at a murder scene. Sometimes that's in the middle of the night. But he never wakes me. There's a telephone extension in his room. He just leaves me a note and he's usually back in time to bring me a cup of tea at seven o'clock. He didn't do that this morning of course. That's why I rang the Lab. I rang his number first but there wasn't any reply. So then I rang the reception desk.

He gave me both numbers in case I couldn't get through to him in an emergency.'

'And no one else has telephoned him recently, no one has come to see him?'

'Who would want to come and see him? And no one has telephoned except that woman.'

Dalgliesh said, very quietly:

'What woman, Mr Lorrimer?'

'I don't know what woman. I only know she rang. Monday of last week it was. Edwin was having a bath and the phone kept on ringing so I thought I'd better answer it.'

'Can you remember exactly what happened and what was said, Mr Lorrimer, from the time you lifted the receiver? Take your time, there's no hurry. This may be very important.'

'There wasn't much to remember. I was going to say our number and ask her to hang on, but she didn't give me any time. She started speaking as soon as I lifted the receiver. She said: "We're right, there is something going on." Then she said something about the can being burned and that she'd got the numbers.'

'That the can had been burned and she'd got the numbers?'

'That's right. It doesn't sound sense now, but it was something like that. Then she gave me the numbers.'

'Can you remember them, Mr Lorrimer?'

'Only the last one, which was 1840. Or it may have been two numbers, 18 and 40. I remembered those because the first house we had after I was married was number 18 and the second was 40. It was quite a coincidence, really. Anyway, those numbers stuck in my mind. But I can't remember the others.'

'How many numbers altogether?'

'Three or four altogether, I think. There were two, and then the 18 and the 40.'

'What did the numbers sound like, Mr Lorrimer? Did you think she was giving you a telephone number or a car registration, for example? Can you remember what impression they made on you at the time?'

'No impression. Why should they? More like a telephone number, I suppose. I don't think it was a car registration. There weren't any letters, you see. It sounded like a date; eighteen forty.'

'Have you any idea who was telephoning?'

'No. I don't think it was anyone at the Lab. It didn't sound like one of the Lab staff.'

'How do you mean, Mr Lorrimer? How did the voice seem?'

The old man sat there, staring straight ahead. His hands, with the long fingers like those of his son, but with their skin dry and stained as withered leaves, hung heavily between his knees, grotesquely large for the brittle wrists. After a moment he spoke. He said:

'Excited.' There was another silence. Both detectives looked at him. Massingham thought that here again was an example of his chief's skill. He would have gone charging upstairs in search of the will and papers. But this evidence, so carefully elicited, was vital. After about a moment the old man spoke again. The word, when it came, was surprising. He said:

'Conspiratorial. That's what she sounded. Conspiratorial.'

They sat, still patiently waiting, but he said nothing else. Then they saw that he was crying. His face didn't change, but a single tear, bright as a pearl, dropped on to the parched hands. He looked at it as if wondering what it could be. Then he said:

'He was a good son to me. Time was, when he first went to college up in London, that we lost touch. He wrote to his mother and me, but he didn't come home. But these last years, since I've been alone, he's taken care of me. I'm not complaining. I dare say he's left me a bit of money, and I've got my pension. But it's hard when the young go first. And who will look after me now?'

Dalgliesh said quietly:

'We need to look at his room, examine his papers. Is the room locked?'

'Locked? Why should it be locked? No one went into it but Edwin.'

Dalgliesh nodded to Massingham, who went out to call Mrs Swaffield. Then they made their way upstairs.

2

It was a long, low-ceilinged room with white walls and a casement window which gave a view of a rectangle of unmown grass, a couple of gnarled apple trees heavy with fruit burnished green and gold in the autumn sun, a straggling hedge beaded with berries and beyond it the windmill. Even in the genial light of afternoon the mill looked a melancholy wreck of its former puissance. The paint was peeling from the walls and the great sails, from which the slats had fallen like rotten teeth, hung heavy with inertia in the restless air. Behind the windmill, the acres of black fenland, newly sliced by the autumn ploughing, stretched in glistening clumps between the dykes.

Dalgliesh turned away from this picture of melancholy peace to examine the room. Massingham was already busy at the desk. Finding the lid unlocked, he rolled it back for a few inches, then let it drop again. Then he tried the drawers. Only the top left-hand one was locked. If he were impatient for Dalgliesh to take Lorrimer's keys from his pocket and open it, he concealed his eagerness. It was known that the older man, who could work faster than any of his colleagues, still liked occasionally to take his time. He was taking it now, regarding the room with his dark sombre eyes, standing very still as if he were picking up invisible waves.

The place held a curious peace. The proportions were right and the furniture fitted where it had been placed. A man might have space to think in this uncluttered sanctum. A single bed, neatly covered with a red and brown blanket, stood against the opposite wall. A long wall shelf above the bed held an adjustable reading-lamp, a radio, a record-player, a clock, a carafe of water and the Book of Common Prayer. In front of the window stood an oak working-table with a wheel-back chair. On the table was a blotter and a brown and blue pottery mug stacked with pencils and biro pens. The only other items of furniture were a shabby winged armchair with a low table beside it, a double wardrobe in oak to the left of the door, and to the right an old-fashioned desk with a roll-top. The telephone was fitted to the wall. There were no pictures and no mirror, no masculine impedimenta, no trivia on desk top or table-ledge. Everything was functional, well used, unadorned. It was a room a man could be at home in.

Dalgliesh walked over to look at the books. He estimated that there must be about four hundred of them, completely covering the wall. There was little fiction, although the nineteenth-century English and Russian novelists were represented. Most of the books were histories or biographies, but there was a shelf of philosophy; Teilhard de Chardin's *Science and Christ*, Jean Paul-Sartre's *Being and Nothingness: a Humanist Outlook*, Simone Weil's *First and Last*, Plato's

Republic, the *Cambridge History of Late Greek and Early Medieval Philosophy*. It looked as if Lorrimer had at one time been trying to teach himself ancient Greek. The shelf held a Greek primer and a dictionary.

Massingham had taken down a book on comparative religion. He said:

'It looks as if he was one of those men who torment themselves trying to discover the meaning of existence.'

Dalgliesh replaced the Sartre he had been studying.

'You find that reprehensible?'

'I find it futile. Metaphysical speculation is about as pointless as a discussion on the meaning of one's lungs. They're for breathing.'

'And life is for living. You find that an adequate personal credo.'

'To maximize one's pleasures and minimize one's pain, yes, sir, I do. And, I suppose, to bear with stoicism those miseries I can't avoid. To be human is to ensure enough of those without inventing them. Anyway, I don't believe you can hope to understand what you can't see or touch or measure.'

'A logical positivist. You're in respectable company. But he spent his life examining what he could see or touch or measure. It doesn't seem to have satisfied him. Well, let's see what his personal papers have to tell.'

He turned his attention to the desk, leaving the locked drawer to the last. He rolled back the top to reveal two small drawers and a number of pigeon-holes. And here, neatly docketed and compart-mentalized, were the minutiae of Lorrimer's solitary life. A drawer with three bills waiting to be paid, and one for receipts. A labelled envelope containing his parents' marriage lines, his own birth and baptismal certificates. His passport, an anonymous face but with the eyes staring as if hypnotized, the neck muscles taut. The lens of the camera might have been the barrel of a gun. A life assurance certificate. Receipted bills for fuel, electricity and gas. The mainten-ance agreement for the central heating. The hire-purchase agree-ment for the television. A wallet with his bank statement. His portfolio of investments, sound, unexciting, orthodox.

There was nothing about his work. Obviously he kept his life as carefully compartmentalized as his filing system. Everything to do with his profession, the journals, the drafts of his scientific papers, were kept in his office at the Lab. They were probably written there.

That might account for some of the late hours. It would certainly have been impossible to guess from the contents of his desk what his job had been.

His will was in a separate labelled envelope together with a brief letter from a firm of Ely solicitors, Messrs Pargeter, Coleby and Hunt. The will was very short and had been made five years earlier. Lorrimer had left Postmill Cottage and £10,000 to his father, and the rest of his estate absolutely to his cousin, Angela Maud Foley. To judge from the portfolio of investments, Miss Foley would inherit a useful capital sum.

Lastly, Dalgliesh took Lorrimer's bunch of keys from his pocket and unlocked the top left-hand drawer. The lock worked very easily. The drawer was crammed with papers covered with Lorrimer's handwriting. Dalgliesh took them over to the table in front of the window and motioned Massingham to draw up the armchair. They sat there together. There were twenty-eight letters in all and they read them through without speaking. Massingham was aware of Dalgliesh's long fingers picking up each sheet, dropping it from his hand then shifting it across the desk towards him, then picking up the next. The clock seemed to him to be ticking unnaturally loudly and his own breathing to have become embarrassingly obtrusive. The letters were a liturgy of the bitter exfoliation of love. It was all here: the inability to accept that desire was no longer returned, the demand for explanations which, if attempted, could only increase the hurt, the excoriating self-pity, the spasms of irrational renewed hope, the petulant outbursts at the obtuseness of the lover unable to see where her happiness lay, the humiliating self-abasement.

'I realize that you won't want to live in the fens. But that needn't be a difficulty, darling. I could get a transfer to the Metropolitan Lab if you prefer London. Or we could find a house in Cambridge or Norwich, a choice of two civilized cities. You once said that you liked to live among the spires. Or if you wished, I could stay on here and we could have a flat in London for you, and I'd join you whenever I could. I ought to be able to make it most Sundays. The week without you would be an eternity, but anything would be bearable if I knew that you belonged to me. You do belong to me. All the books, all the seeking and reading, what does it come to in the end? Until you taught me that the answer was so simple.'

Some of the letters were highly erotic. They were probably the most difficult of all love letters to write successfully, thought Massingham. Didn't the poor devil know that, once desire was dead, they could only disgust? Perhaps those lovers who used a private nursery talk for their most secret acts were the wisest. At least the eroticism was personal. Here the sexual descriptions were either embarrassingly Lawrentian in their intensity, or coldly clinical. He recognized with surprise an emotion that could only be shame. It wasn't just that some of the outpourings were brutally explicit. He was accustomed to perusing the private pornography of murdered lives; but these letters, with their mixture of crude desire and elevated sentiment, were outside his experience. The naked suffering they expressed seemed to him neurotic, irrational. Sex no longer had any power to shock him; love, he decided, obviously could.

He was struck by the contrast between the tranquillity of the man's room and the turbulence of his mind. He thought: at least this job teaches one not to hoard personal debris. Police work was as effective as religion in teaching a man to live each day as if it were his last. And it wasn't only murder that violated privacy. Any sudden death could do as much. If the helicopter had crashed on landing, what sort of a picture would his leavings present to the world? A conformist, right-wing philistine, obsessed with his physical fitness? *Homme moyen sensuel*, and *moyen* everything else for that matter? He thought of Emma, with whom he slept whenever they got the opportunity, and who, he supposed, would eventually become Lady Dungannon unless, as seemed increasingly likely, she found an elder son with better prospects and more time to devote to her. He wondered what Emma, cheerful hedonist with her frank enjoyment of bed, would have made of these self-indulgent, masturbatory fantasies, this humiliating chronicle of the miseries of defeated love.

One half-sheet was covered with a single name. Domenica, Domenica, Domenica. And then Domenica Lorrimer, a clumsy, uneuphonic linking. Perhaps its infelicity had struck him, for he had written it only once. The letters looked laboured, tentative, like those of a young girl practising in secret the hoped-for married name. All the letters were undated, all without superscription and signature. A number were obviously first drafts, a painful seeking after the elusive word, the holograph scored with deletions.

But now Dalgliesh was pushing towards him the final letter. Here there were no alterations, no uncertainties, and if there had been a previous draft, Lorrimer had destroyed it. This was as clear as an affirmation. The words, strongly written in Lorrimer's black upright script, were set out in even lines, neatly as an exercise in calligraphy. Perhaps this was one he had intended to post after all.

'I have been seeking for the words to explain what has happened to me, what you have made happen. You know how difficult this is for me. There have been so many years of writing official reports, the same phrases, the same bleak conclusions. My mind was a computer programmed to death. I was like a man born in darkness, living in a deep cave, crouching for comfort by my small inadequate fire, watching the shadows flickering over the cave drawings and trying to find in their crude outlines some significance, a meaning to existence to help me endure the dark. And then you came and took me by the hand and led me out into the sunlight. And there was the real world, dazzling my eyes with its colour and its beauty. And it needed only your hand and the courage to take a few small steps out of the shadows and imaginings into the light. *Ex umbris et imaginibus in veritatem.*'

Dalgliesh laid the letter down. He said:

' "Lord, let me know mine end, and the number of my days; that I may be certified how long I have to live." Given the choice, Lorrimer would probably have preferred his murder to go unavenged than for any eyes but his to have seen these letters. What do you think of them?'

Massingham was uncertain whether he was expected to comment on their subject matter or their style. He said cautiously:

'The passage about the cave is effective. It looks as if he worked over that one.'

'But not entirely original. An echo of Plato's *Republic*. And like Plato's caveman, the brightness dazzled and the light hurt his eyes. George Orwell wrote somewhere that murder, the unique crime, should result only from strong emotions. Well, here is the strong emotion. But we seem to have the wrong body.'

'Do you think Dr Howarth knew, sir?'

'Almost certainly. The wonder is that no one at the Lab apparently did. It's not the kind of information that Mrs Bidwell, for one, would keep to herself. First, I think, we check with the solicitors that this will still stands, and then we see the lady.'

But this programme was to be changed. The wall telephone rang, shattering the peace of the room. Massingham answered. It was Sergeant Underhill trying, but with small success, to keep the excitement out of his voice.

'There's a Major Hunt of Messrs Pargeter, Coleby and Hunt of Ely wants to see Mr Dalgliesh. He'd prefer not to talk over the telephone. He says could you ring and say when it would be convenient for Mr Dalgliesh to call. And, sir, we've got a witness! He's over at Guy's Marsh police station now. The name's Alfred Goddard. He was a passenger last night passing the Lab in the nine-ten bus.'

3

'Running down drive he were like the devil out of hell.'

'Can you describe him, Mr Goddard?'

'Naw. He weren't old.'

'How young?'

'I never said 'e were young. I never seed 'im near enough to tell. But he didn't run like an old 'un.'

'Running for the bus, perhaps.'

'If 'e were 'e never catched it.'

'He wasn't waving?'

' 'Course he weren't. Driver couldn't see 'im. No point in waving at back of bloody bus.'

Guy's Marsh police station was a red-brick Victorian building with a white wooden pediment, which looked so like an early railway station that Dalgliesh suspected that the nineteenth-century police authority had economized by making use of the same architect and the same set of plans.

Mr Alfred Goddard, waiting comfortably in the interview room with a huge mug of steaming tea before him, looked perfectly at home, neither gratified nor impressed to find himself a key witness in a murder investigation. He was a nut-brown, wrinkled, under-sized countryman who smelt of strong tobacco, alcohol and cow-dung. Dalgliesh recalled that the early fen settlers had been called 'yellow-bellies' by their highland neighbours because they crawled frog-like over their marshy fields, or 'slodgers', splashing web-footed through the mud. Either would have suited Mr Goddard. Dalgliesh noticed with interest that he was wearing what looked like a leather thong bound round his left wrist, and guessed that this was dried eel-skin, the ancient charm to ward off rheumatism. The misshapen fingers stiffly cradling the mug of tea suggested that the talisman had been less than efficacious.

Dalgliesh doubted whether he would have troubled to come forward if Bill Carney, the conductor of the bus, hadn't known him as a regular on the Wednesday evening service travelling from Ely to Stoney Piggott via Chevisham, and had directed the enquiring police to his remote cottage. Having been summarily dug out of his lair, however, he displayed no particular resentment against Bill Carney or the police, and announced that he was prepared to answer questions if, as he explained, they were put to him 'civil-like'. His main grievance in life was the Stoney Piggott bus: its lateness, infrequency, rising fares and, in particular, the stupidity of the recent experiment of using double-deckers on the Stoney Piggott route and his own subsequent banishment each Wednesday to the upper deck because of his pipe.

'But how fortunate for us that you were there,' Massingham had pointed out. Mr Goddard had merely snorted into his tea.

Dalgliesh continued with the questioning:

'Is there anything at all you can remember about him, Mr Goddard? His height, his hair, how he was dressed?'

'Naw. Middling tall and wearing a shortish coat, or mac maybe. Flapping open, maybe.'

'Can you remember the colour?'

'Darkish, maybe. I never seed 'im for more'n a second, see. Then trees got in the way. Bus were moving off when I first set eyes on him.'

Massingham interposed:

'The driver didn't see him, nor did the conductor.'

'More than likely. They was on lower deck. Isn't likely they'd notice. And driver were driving bloody bus.'

Dalgliesh said:

'Mr Goddard, this is very important. Can you remember whether there were any lights on in the Lab?'

'What do you mean, Lab?'

'The house the figure was running from.'

'Lights in the house? If you mean house why not say house?'

Mr Goddard pantomimed the ardours of intensive thought, pursing his lips into a grimace and half closing his eyes. They waited. After a nicely judged interval he announced:

'Faint lights, maybe. Not blazing out, mind you. I reckon I seed some lights from bottom windows.'

Massingham asked:

'You're quite sure it was a man?'

Mr Goddard bestowed on him the glance of mingled reproof and chagrin of a viva-voce candidate faced with what he obviously regards as an unfair question.

'Wearing trousers, wasn't he? If he weren't a man then he ought to have been.'

'But you can't be absolutely sure?'

'Can't be sure of nothing these days. Time was when folk dressed in a decent, God-fearing manner. Man or woman, it were human and it were running. That's all I seed.'

'So it could have been a woman in slacks?'

'Never run like a woman. Daft runners women be, keeping their knees tight together and kicking out ankles like bloody ducks. Pity they don't keep their knees together when they ain't running, I say.'

The deduction was fair enough, thought Dalgliesh. No woman ran precisely like a man. Goddard's first impression had been that of a youngish man running, and that was probably exactly what he had seen. Too much questioning now might only confuse him.

The driver and conductor, summoned from the bus depot and still in uniform, were unable to confirm Goddard's story, but what they were able to add was useful. It was not surprising that neither of them had seen the runner, since the six-foot wall and its overhanging trees cut off a view of the Laboratory from the bottom deck and they could only have glimpsed the house when the bus was passing the open drive and slowing down at the stop. But if Mr Goddard was right and the figure had only appeared when the bus was moving off, they still wouldn't have seen him.

It was helpful that they were both able to confirm that the bus, on that Wednesday evening at least, was running on time. Bill Carney had actually looked at his watch as they moved away. It had shown nine-twelve. The bus had halted at the stop for a couple of seconds. None of the three passengers had made any preliminary moves to get off, but both the driver and the conductor had noticed a woman waiting in the shadow of the bus shelter and had assumed that she would board. However, she hadn't done so, but had turned away and moved back farther into the shadow of the shelter as the bus drew up. The conductor thought it strange that she was waiting there, since there wasn't another bus that night. But it had been raining slightly and he had assumed, without thinking about it very deeply, that she had been sheltering. It wasn't his job, as he reasonably pointed out, to drag passengers on the bus if they didn't want a ride.

Dalgliesh questioned them both closely about the woman, but there was little firm information they could give. Both agreed that she had been wearing a headscarf and that the collar of her coat had been turned up at her ears. The driver thought that she had been wearing slacks and a belted mackintosh. Bill Carney agreed about the slacks but thought that she had been wearing a duffel coat. Their only reason for assuming that the figure was a woman was the headscarf. Neither of them could describe it. They thought it unlikely that any of the three passengers on the lower deck would be able to help. Two of them were elderly regulars, both apparently asleep. The third was unknown to them.

Dalgliesh knew that all three would have to be traced. This was one of those time-consuming jobs which were necessary but which seldom produced any worthwhile information. But it was astonishing how much the most unlikely people did notice. The sleepers might have been jogged awake by the slowing down of the bus and have had a clearer look at the waiting woman than either the conductor or driver. Mr Goddard, not surprisingly, hadn't noticed her. He enquired caustically how a chap was expected to see through the roof of a bloody bus shelter and, in any case, he'd been looking the other way hadn't he, and a good job for them that he had. Dalgliesh hastened to propitiate him and, when his statement was at last completed to the old man's satisfaction, watched him driven back to his cottage, sitting in some style, like a tiny upright manikin, in the back of the police car.

But it was another ten minutes before Dalgliesh and Massingham could set out for Ely. Albert Bidwell had presented himself conveniently if belatedly at the police station, bringing with him a hefty sample of the mud from the five-acre field and an air of sullen grievance. Massingham wondered how he and his wife had originally met and what had brought together two such dissimilar personalities. She, he felt sure, was born a cockney; he a fenman. He was taciturn where she was garrulous, slow-thinking where she was sharp and as incurious as she was avid for gossip and excitement.

He admitted to taking the telephone call. It was a woman and the message was that Mrs Bidwell was to go to Leamings to give Mrs Schofield a hand instead of to the Lab. He couldn't remember if the caller had given her name but didn't think so. He had taken calls from Mrs Schofield once or twice before when she had rung to ask his wife to help with dinner parties or suchlike. Women's business. He couldn't say whether the voice sounded the same. Asked whether he had assumed that the caller was Mrs Schofield, he said that he hadn't assumed anything.

Dalgliesh asked:

'Can you remember whether the caller said that your wife was to come to Leamings or go to Leamings?'

The significance of this question obviously escaped him but he received it with surly suspicion and, after a long pause, said he didn't know. When Massingham asked whether it was possible that the caller hadn't been a woman but a man disguising his voice, he gave him a look of concentrated disgust as if deploring a mind that could imagine such sophisticated villainy. But the answer provoked his longest response. He said, in a tone of finality, that he didn't know whether it was a woman, or a man pretending to be a woman, or, maybe, a lass. All he knew was that he'd been asked to give his wife a message, and he'd given it to her. And if he'd known it would cause all this botheration he wouldn't have answered the phone.

And with that they had to be content.

4

In Dalgliesh's experience, solicitors who practised in cathedral cities were invariably agreeably housed, and the office of Messrs Pargeter, Coleby and Hunt was no exception. It was a well-preserved and maintained Regency house with a view of the Cathedral Green, an imposing front door whose ebony-black paint gleamed as if it were still wet, and whose brass knocker in the shape of a lion's head had been polished almost to whiteness. The door was opened by an elderly and very thin clerk, Dickensian in his old-fashioned black suit and stiff collar, whose appearance of lugubrious resignation brightened somewhat at seeing them, as if cheered by the prospect of trouble. He bowed slightly when Dalgliesh introduced himself and said:

'Major Hunt is, of course, expecting you, sir. He is just concluding his interview with a client. If you will step this way he won't keep you waiting more than a couple of minutes.'

The waiting-room into which they were shown resembled the sitting-room of a man's club in its comfort and air of controlled disorder. The chairs were leather and so wide and deep that it was difficult to imagine anyone over sixty rising from them without difficulty. Despite the heat from the two old-fashioned radiators there was a coke fire burning in the grate. The large, circular mahogany table was spread with magazines devoted to the interests of the landed gentry, most of which looked very old. There was a glass-fronted bookcase packed with bound histories of the county and illustrated volumes on architecture and painting. The oil over the mantelpiece of a phaeton with horses and attendant grooms, looked very like a Stubbs, and, thought Dalgliesh, probably was.

He only had time briefly to inspect the room, and had walked over to the window to look out towards the Lady Chapel of the cathedral when the door opened and the clerk reappeared to usher them into Major Hunt's office. The man who rose from behind his desk to receive them was in appearance the opposite of his clerk. He was a stocky, upright man in late middle age, dressed in a shabby but well-tailored tweed suit, ruddy-faced and balding, his eyes keen under the spiky, restless eyebrows. He gave Dalgliesh a frankly appraising glance as he shook hands, as if deciding where exactly to place him in some private scheme of things, then nodded as if satisfied. He still looked more like a soldier than a solicitor, and Dalgliesh guessed that the voice with which he greeted them had acquired its loud authoritative bark across the parade-grounds and in the messes of the Second World War.

'Good morning, good morning. Please sit down, Commander.

You come on tragic business. I don't think we have ever lost one of our clients by murder before.'

The clerk coughed. It was just such a cough as Dalgliesh would have expected, inoffensive but discreetly minatory and not to be ignored.

'There was Sir James Cummins, sir, in 1923. He was shot by his neighbour, Captain Cartwright, because of the seduction of Mrs Cartwright by Sir James, a grievance aggravated by some unpleasantness over fishing rights.'

'Quite right, Mitching. But that was in my father's time. They hanged poor Cartwright. A pity, my father always thought. He had a good war record – survived the Somme and Arras and ended on the scaffold. Battle-scarred, poor devil. The jury would probably have made a recommendation to mercy if he hadn't cut up the body. He did cut up the body, didn't he, Mitching?'

'Quite right, sir. They found the head buried in the orchard.'

'That's what did for Cartwright. English juries won't stand for cutting up the body. Crippen would be alive today if he'd buried Belle Elmore in one piece.'

'Hardly, sir. Crippen was born in 1860.'

'Well he wouldn't have been long dead. It wouldn't surprise me if he'd reached his century. Only three years older than your father, Mitching, and much the same build, small, pop-eyed and wiry. They live for ever, that type. Ah well, to our muttons. You'll both take coffee, I hope. I can promise you it will be drinkable. Mitching has installed one of those glass retort affairs and we grind our own fresh beans. Coffee then, please Mitching.'

'Miss Makepeace is preparing it now, sir.'

Major Hunt exuded postprandial well-being, and Massingham guessed, with some envy, that his business with his last client had been chiefly done over a good lunch. He and Dalgliesh had snatched a hurried sandwich and beer at a pub between Chevisham and Guy's Marsh. Dalgliesh, known to enjoy food and wine, had an inconvenient habit of ignoring meal-times when in the middle of a case. Massingham wasn't fussy about the quality; it was the quantity he deplored. But, at least, they were to get coffee.

Mitching had stationed himself near the door and showed no inclination to leave. This was apparently perfectly acceptable. Dalgliesh thought that they were like a couple of comedians in the process of perfecting their antiphonal patter, and reluctant to lose any opportunity of practising it. Major Hunt said:

'You want to know about Lorrimer's will, of course.'

'And anything else you can tell us about him.'

'That won't be much, I'm afraid. I've only seen him twice since I dealt with his grandmother's estate. But of course I'll do what I can. When murder comes in at the window privacy goes out of the door. That's so, isn't it, Mitching?'

'There are no secrets, sir, in the fierce light that beats upon the scaffold.'

'I'm not sure that you've got that one right, Mitching. And we don't have scaffolds now. Are you an abolitionist, Commander?'

Dalgliesh said:

'I'm bound to be until the day comes when we can be absolutely sure that we could never under any circumstances make a mistake.'

'That's the orthodox answer, but it begs quite a lot of questions, doesn't it? Still you're not here to discuss capital punishment. Mustn't waste time. Now the will. Where did I put Mr Lorrimer's box, Mitching?'

'It's here, sir.'

'Then bring it over, man. Bring it over.'

The clerk carried the black tin box from a side table and placed it in front of Major Hunt. The Major opened it with some ceremony and took out the will. Dalgliesh said:

'We've found one will in his desk. It's dated the third of May 1971. It looks like the original.'

'So he didn't destroy it? That's interesting. It suggests that he hadn't finally made up his mind.'

'So there's a later will?'

'Oh indeed there is, Commander. Indeed there is. That's what I wanted to talk to you about. Signed by him only last Friday and both the original and the only copy left here with me. I have them here. Perhaps you'd like to read it yourself.'

He handed over the will. It was very short. Lorrimer, in the accepted form, revoked all previous wills, proclaimed himself to be of sound mind and disposed of all his property in less than a dozen lines. Postmill Cottage was left to his father together with a sum of ten thousand pounds. One thousand pounds was left to Brenda Pridmore 'to enable her to buy any books required to further her scientific education'. All the rest of his estate was left to the Academy of Forensic Science to provide an annual cash prize of such amount as the Academy should see fit for an original essay on any aspect of the scientific investigation of crime, the essay to be judged by three judges, selected by the Academy. There was no mention of Angela Foley.

Dalgliesh said:

'Did he give you any explanation why he left his cousin, Angela Foley, out of the will?'

'As a matter of fact he did. I thought it right to point out that in the event of his death his cousin, as his only surviving relative apart from his father, might wish to contest the will. If she did, a legal battle would cost money and might seriously deplete the estate. I didn't feel any obligation to press him to alter his decision. I merely thought it right to point out the possible consequences. You heard what he replied, didn't you, Mitching?'

'Yes indeed, sir. The late Mr Lorrimer expressed his disapprobation of the way in which his cousin chose to live, in particular he deplored the relationship which, he alleged, subsisted between his cousin and the lady with whom I understand she makes her home, and said that he did not wish the said companion to benefit from his estate. If his cousin chose to contest the will, he was prepared to leave the matter to the courts. It would no longer be of any concern to himself. He would have made his wishes clear. He also pointed out, if I remember rightly, sir, that the will was intended to be transitional in its nature. He had it in mind to marry and if he did so the will would, of course, become void. In the meantime he wished to guard against what he saw as the remote contingency of his cousin inheriting absolutely should he die unexpectedly before his personal affairs became clearer.'

'That's right, Mitching, that in effect is what he said. I must say that it reconciled me somewhat to the new will. If he were proposing to get married obviously it would no longer stand and he could think again. Not that I thought it necessarily an unjust or unfair will. A man has the right to dispose of his property as he sees fit, if the state leaves him anything to dispose of. It struck me as a bit odd that, if he were engaged to be married, he didn't mention the lady in the interim will. But I suppose the principle's sound enough. If he'd left her a paltry sum she'd hardly have thanked him, and if he'd left her the lot, she'd probably promptly have married another chap and it would all pass to him.'

Dalgliesh asked:

'He didn't tell you anything about the proposed marriage?'

'Not even the lady's name. And naturally I didn't ask. I'm not even sure that he had anyone particular in mind. It could have been only a general intention, or, perhaps, an excuse for altering the will. I merely congratulated him and pointed out that the new will would be void as soon as the marriage took place. He said that he understood that and would be coming to make a new will in due course. In the meantime this was what he wanted and this was what I drew up. Mitching signed it, with my secretary as a second witness. Ah, here she is with the coffee. You remember signing Mr Lorrimer's will, eh?'

The thin, nervous-looking girl who had brought in the coffee gave a terrified nod in response to the Major's bark and hastened out of the room. Major Hunt said with satisfaction:

'She remembers. She was so terrified that she could hardly sign. But she did sign. It's all there. All correct and in order. I hope we can draw up a valid will, eh, Mitching? But it will be interesting to see if the little woman makes a fight for it.'

Dalgliesh asked how much Angela Foley would be making a fight for.

'The best part of £50,000, I dare say. Not a fortune these days but useful, useful. The original capital was left to him absolutely by old Annie Lorrimer, his paternal grandmother. An extraordinary old woman. Born and bred in the fens. Kept a village store with her husband over at Low Willow. Tom Lorrimer drank himself into a comparatively early grave – couldn't stand the fen winters – and she carried on alone. Not all the money came from the shop, of course, although she sold out at a good time. No, she had a nose for the horses. Extraordinary thing. God knows where she got it from. Never mounted a horse in her life to my knowledge. Shut up the shop and went to Newmarket three times a year. Never lost a penny, so I've heard, and saved every pound she won.'

'What family had she? Was Lorrimer's father her only son?'

'That's right. She had one son and one daughter, Angela Foley's mother. Couldn't bear the sight of either of them, as far as I can see. The daughter got herself in the family way by the village sexton and the old woman cast her off in approved Victorian style. The marriage turned out badly and I don't think Maud Foley saw her mother again. She died of cancer about five years after the girl was born. The old woman wouldn't have her granddaughter back, so she ended up in local authority care. Most of her life's been spent in foster homes, I believe.'

'And the son?'

'Oh, he married the local schoolmistress, and that turned out reasonably well as far as I know. But the family were never close. The old lady wouldn't leave her money to her son, because, she said, it would mean two lots of death duties. She was well over forty when he was born. But I think the real reason was simply that she didn't much like him. I don't think she saw much of the grandson, Edwin, either, but she had to leave the money somewhere and hers was a generation which believes that blood is thicker than charitable soup and male blood thicker than female. Apart from the fact she'd cast off her daughter and never taken any interest in her granddaughter, her generation didn't believe in leaving money outright to women. It only encourages seducers and fortune-hunters so she left it absolutely to her grandson, Edwin Lorrimer. At the time of her death I think he had qualms of conscience about his cousin. As you know, the first will made her his legatee.'

Dalgliesh said:

'Do you know if Lorrimer told her that he intended to change his will?'

The solicitor looked at him sharply.

'He didn't say. In the circumstances it would be convenient for her if she could prove that he did.'

So convenient, thought Dalgliesh, that she would certainly have mentioned the fact when first interviewed. But even if she had believed herself to be her cousin's heir, that didn't necessarily make her a murderess. If she had wanted a share of her grandmother's money, why wait until now to kill for it?

The telephone rang. Major Hunt muttered an apology and reached for the receiver. Holding his palm over the mouthpiece, he said to Dalgliesh:

'It's Miss Foley, ringing from Postmill Cottage. Old Mr Lorrimer wants to have a word with me about the will. She says he's anxious to know whether the cottage now belongs to him. Do you want me to tell him?'

'That is for you. But he's the next of kin; he may as well know the terms of the will now as later. And so may she.'

Major Hunt hesitated. Then he spoke into the receiver.

'All right, Betty. Put Miss Foley on the line.'

He looked up again at Dalgliesh.

'This piece of news is going to put the cat among the pigeons in Chevisham.'

Dalgliesh had a sudden picture of Brenda Pridmore's eager young face shining across Howarth's desk at him.

'Yes,' he said grimly. 'Yes, I'm afraid it is.'

5

Howarth's house, Leamings, was three miles outside Chevisham village on the Cambridge road, a modern building of concrete, wood and glass cantilevered above the flat fenlands, with two white wings like folded sails. Even in the fading light it was impressive. The house stood in uncompromising and splendid isolation, depending for its effect on nothing but perfection of line and artful simplicity. No other building was in sight except a solitary black wooden cottage on stilts, desolate as an execution shed, and, dramatically, an intricate mirage hung above the eastern skyline, the marvellous single tower and octagon of Ely Cathedral. From the rooms at the back one would see an immensity of sky and look out over vast unhedged fields dissected by Leamings dyke, changing with the seasons from black scarred earth, through the spring sowing to the harvest; would hear nothing but the wind and, in summer, the ceaseless susurration of the grain.

The site had been small and the architect had needed ingenuity. There was no garden, nothing but a short drive leading to a paved courtyard and the double garage. Outside the garage, a red Jaguar XJS stood beside Howarth's Triumph. Massingham cast envious eyes on the Jaguar and wondered how Mrs Schofield had managed to get such quick delivery. They drove in and parked beside it. Even before Dalgliesh had switched off the engine, Howarth had strolled out and was quietly waiting for them. He was wearing a butcher's long blue-and-white-striped overall in which he seemed perfectly at ease, evidently seeing no need either to explain or remove it. As they made their way up the open-tread, carved wooden stairs Dalgliesh complimented him on the house. Howarth said:

'It was designed by a Swedish architect who did some of the modern additions at Cambridge. Actually it belongs to a university friend. He and his wife are spending a couple of years' sabbatical at Harvard. If they decide to stay on in the States, they may sell. Anyway, we're settled for the next eighteen months, and can then look around if we have to.'

They were mounting a wide circular wooden staircase rising from the well of the house. Upstairs someone was playing, very loudly, a record of the finale of the third Brandenburg Concerto. The glorious contrapuntal sound beat against the walls and surged through the house; Massingham could almost imagine it taking off on its white wings and rollicking joyously over the fens. Dalgliesh said, above the music:

'Mrs Schofield likes it here?'

Howarth's voice, carefully casual, came down to them. 'Oh, she may have moved on by then. Domenica likes variety. My half-sister suffers from Baudelaire's *horreur de domicile* – she usually prefers to be elsewhere. Her natural habitat is London, but she's with me now because she's illustrating a new limited edition of Crabbe for the Paradine Press.'

The record came to an end. Howarth paused and said with a kind of roughness, as if regretting an impulse to confide:

'I think I ought to tell you that my sister was widowed just over eighteen months ago. Her husband was killed in a car crash. She was driving at the time but she was lucky. At least, I suppose she was lucky. She was scarcely scratched. Charles Schofield died three days later.'

'I'm sorry,' said Dalgliesh. The cynic in him wondered why he had been told. Howarth had struck him as essentially a private man, one not lightly to confide a personal or family tragedy. Was it an appeal to chivalry, a covert plea for him to treat her with special consideration? Or was Howarth warning him that she was still distraught with grief, unpredictable, unbalanced even? He could hardly be implying that, since the tragedy, she had indulged an irresistible impulse to kill her lovers.

They had reached the top of the stairs and were standing on a wide wooden balcony seemingly hung in space. Howarth pushed open a door and said:

'I'll leave you to it. I'm making an early start on cooking dinner tonight. She's in here.' He called:

'This is Commander Dalgliesh and Detective-Inspector Massingham of the Met. The men about the murder. My sister, Domenica Schofield.'

The room was immense, with a triangular window from roof to floor jutting out over the fields like a ship's prow, and a high curved ceiling of pale pine. The furniture was scant and very modern. The room looked, in fact, more like a musician's studio than a sitting-room. Against the wall was a jangle of music stands and violin cases and, mounted above them, a bank of modern and obviously expensive stereo equipment. There was only one picture, a Sidney Nolan oil of Ned Kelly. The faceless metallic mask, with the two anonymous eyes gleaming through the slit, was appropriate to the austerity of the room, the stark blackness of the darkening fens. It was easy to imagine him, a grim latter-day Hereward, striding over the clogging acres.

Domenica Schofield was standing at a drawing desk placed in the middle of the room. She turned, unsmilingly, to look at them with her brother's eyes, and Dalgliesh encountered again those disconcerting pools of blue under the thick, curved brows. As always, in those increasingly rare moments when, unexpectedly, he came face to face with a beautiful woman, his heart jerked. It was a pleasure more sensual than sexual and he was glad that he could still feel it, even in the middle of a murder investigation.

But he wondered how studied was that smooth deliberate turn, that first gaze, remote yet speculative, from the remarkable eyes. In this light, the irises, like those of her brother, were almost purple, the whites stained with a paler blue. She had a pale, honey-coloured skin, with flaxen hair drawn back from the forehead and tied in a clump at the base of her neck. Her blue jeans were pulled tightly over the strong thighs and were topped with an open-necked shirt of chequered blue and green. Dalgliesh judged her to be about ten years younger than her half-brother. When she spoke, her voice was curiously low for a woman, with a hint of gruffness.

'Sit down.' She waved her right hand vaguely towards one of the chrome and leather chairs. 'You don't mind if I go on working?'

'Not if you don't mind being talked to while you do, and if you don't object to my sitting while you stand.'

He swung the chair closer to her easel, from where he could see both her face and her work, and settled himself. The chair was remarkably comfortable. He sensed that already she was regretting her lack of civility. In any confrontation the one standing has a psychological advantage, but not if the adversary is sitting very obviously at his ease in a spot he has himself selected. Massingham, with an almost ostentatious quietness, had lifted a second chair for himself and placed it against the wall to the left of the door. She must have been aware of his presence at her back, but she gave no sign. She could hardly object to a situation she had herself contrived, but, as if sensing that the interview had started unpropitiously, she said:

'I'm sorry to seem so obsessively busy, but I have a deadline to meet. My brother's probably told you that I'm illustrating a new edition of Crabbe's poems for the Paradine Press. This drawing is for "Procrastination" – Dinah among her curious trifles.'

Dalgliesh had known that she must be a competent professional artist to have gained the commission, but he was impressed by the sensitivity and assurance of the line-drawing before him. It was remarkably detailed but unfinicky, a highly decorative and beautifully composed balance of the girl's slender figure and Crabbe's carefully enumerated objects of desire. They were all there, meticulously drawn; the figured wallpaper, the rose carpet, the mounted stag's head and the jewelled, enamelled clock. It was, he thought, a very English illustration of the most English of poets. She was taking trouble with the period details. On the right-hand wall was mounted a cork board on which were pinned what were obviously preliminary sketches; a tree, half-finished interiors, articles of furniture, small impressions of landscape. She said:

'It's as well one doesn't have to like a poet's work to illustrate him competently. Who was it called Crabbe "Pope in worsted stockings"? After twenty lines my brain begins to thud in rhymed couplets. But perhaps you're an Augustan. You write verse, don't you?'

She made it sound as if he collected cigarette cards for a hobby.

Dalgliesh said:

'I've respected Crabbe ever since I read as a boy that Jane Austen said she could have fancied being Mrs Crabbe. When he went to London for the first time he was so poor that he had to pawn all his clothes, and then he spent the money on an edition of Dryden's poems.'

'And you approve of that?'

'I find it appealing.' He quoted:

> ' "Miseries there were, and woes the world around,
> But these had not her pleasant dwelling found;
> She knew that mothers grieved and widows wept
> And she was sorry, said her prayers and slept:
> For she indulged, nor was her heart so small
> That one strong passion should engross it all." '

She gave him a swift elliptical glance.

'In this case there is happily no mother to grieve nor widow to weep. And I gave up saying my prayers when I was nine. Or were you only proving that you could quote Crabbe?'

'That, of course,' replied Dalgliesh. 'Actually I came to talk to you about these.'

He took a bundle of the letters out of his coat pocket, opened one of the pages and held it out towards her. He asked:

'This is Lorrimer's handwriting?'

She glanced dismissively at the page.

'Of course. It's a pity he didn't send them. I should have liked to have read them, but not now perhaps.'

'I don't suppose they're so very different from the ones he did post.'

For a moment he thought that she was about to deny receiving any. He thought: 'She's remembered that we can easily check with the postman.' He watched the blue eyes grow wary. She said:

'That's how love ends, not with a bang, but a whimper.'

'Less a whimper than a cry of pain.'

She wasn't working, but stood still, scrutinizing the drawing. She said:

'It's extraordinary how unattractive misery is. He'd have done better to have tried honesty. "It means a lot to me, it doesn't mean very much to you. So why not be generous? It won't cost you anything except an occasional half-hour of your time." I'd have respected him more.'

'But he wasn't asking for a commercial arrangement.' said Dalgliesh. 'He was asking for love.'

'That's something I didn't have to give, and he had no right to expect.'

None of us, thought Dalgliesh, has a right to expect it. But we do. Irrelevantly a phrase of Plutarch fell into his mind. 'Boys throw stones at frogs in sport. But the frogs do not die in sport, they die in earnest.'

'When did you break it off?' he asked.

She looked surprised for a moment.

'I was going to ask you how you knew I'd done the breaking. But, of course, you've got the letters. I suppose he was whining. I told him that I didn't want to see him again about two months ago. I haven't spoken to him since.'

'Did you give him a reason?'

'No. I'm not sure that there was a reason. Does there have to be? There wasn't another man if that's what you have in mind. What a beautifully simple view you must have of life. I suppose police work produces a card-index mentality. Victim – Edwin Lorrimer. Crime – Murder. Accused – Domenica Schofield. Motive – Sex. Verdict – Guilty. What a pity that you can't any longer finish it off neatly with Sentence – Death. Let's say I was tired of him.'

'When you'd exhausted his possibilities, sexual and emotional?'

'Say intellectual, rather, if you'll forgive the arrogance. I find that one exhausts the physical possibilities fairly soon, don't you? But if a man has wit, intelligence, and his own peculiar enthusiasms, then there's some kind of purpose in the relationship. I knew a man once who was an authority on seventeenth-century church architecture. We used to drive for miles looking at churches. It was fascinating while it lasted, and I now know quite a lot about the late seventeenth century. That's something on the credit side.'

'Whereas Lorrimer's only intellectual enthusiasms were popular philosophy and forensic science.'

'Forensic biology. He was curiously inhibited about discussing it. The Official Secrets Act was probably engraved on what he would have described as his soul. Besides, he could be boring even about his job. Scientists invariably are, I've discovered. My brother is the only scientist I've ever met who doesn't bore me after the first ten minutes of his company.'

'Where did you make love?'

'That's impertinent. And is it relevant?'

'It could be – to the number of people who knew that you were lovers.'

'No one knew. I don't relish my private affairs being giggled over in the women's loo at Hoggatt's.'

'So no one knew except your brother and yourself?'

They must have decided in advance that it would be stupid and dangerous to deny that Howarth had known. She said:

'I hope you're not going to ask whether he approved.'

'No. I took it for granted that he disapproved.'

'Why the hell should you?' The tone was intended to be light, almost bantering, but Dalgliesh could detect the sharp edge of defensive anger. He said mildly:

'I am merely putting myself in his place. If I had just started a new job, and one of some difficulty, my half-sister's affair with a member of my own staff, and one who probably thought he'd been supplanted, would be a complication I'd prefer to do without.'

'Perhaps you lack my brother's confidence. He didn't need Edwin Lorrimer's support to run his Lab effectively.'

'You brought him here?'

'Seducing one of my brother's staff here in his own house? Had I disliked my brother, it might have given the affair extra piquancy. Towards the end I admit it could have done with it. But as I don't, it would merely have been in poor taste. We both have cars, and his is particularly roomy.'

'I thought that was the expedient of randy adolescents. It must have been uncomfortable and cold.'

'Very cold. Which was another reason for deciding to stop it.' She turned to him with sudden vehemence.

'Look, I'm not trying to shock you. I'm trying to be truthful. I hate death and waste and violence. Who doesn't? But I'm not grieving, in case you thought of offering condolences. There's only one man whose death has grieved me, and it isn't Edwin Lorrimer. And I don't feel responsible. Why should I? I'm not responsible. Even if he killed himself I shouldn't feel that it was my fault. As it is, I don't believe his death had anything to do with me. He might, I suppose, have felt like murdering me. I never had the slightest motive for murdering him.'

'Have you any idea who did?'

'A stranger, I imagine. Someone who broke into the Lab either to plant or to destroy some forensic evidence. Perhaps a drunken driver hoping to get his hands on his blood sample. Edwin surprised him and the intruder killed him.'

'The blood alcohol analysis isn't done in the Biology Department.'

'Then it could have been an enemy, someone with a grudge. Someone he'd given evidence against in the past. After all, he's probably well known in the witness box. Death of an expert witness.'

Dalgliesh said:

'There's the difficulty of how his killer got in and out of the Lab.'

'He probably gained entrance during the day and hid after the place was locked up for the night. I leave it to you to discover how he got away. Perhaps he slipped out after the Lab had been opened for the morning during the kerfuffle after that girl – Brenda Pridmore, isn't it? – discovered the body. I don't suppose that anyone was keeping an eye on the front door.'

'And the false telephone call to Mrs Bidwell?'

'Probably no connection, I'd say. Just someone trying to be funny. She's probably too scared now to admit what happened. I should question the junior female staff of the Lab if I were you. It's the kind of joke a rather unintelligent adolescent might find amusing.'

Dalgliesh went on to ask her about her movements on the previous evening. She said that she hadn't accompanied her brother to the concert, having a dislike of rustic junketing, no wish to hear the Mozart indifferently played, and a couple of drawings to complete. They'd had an early supper at about six forty-five, and Howarth had left home at seven-twenty. She had continued working uninterrupted either by a telephone call or a visitor until her brother returned shortly after ten, when he had told her about his evening over a shared nightcap of hot whisky. Both of them had then gone early to bed.

She volunteered without being asked that her brother had seemed perfectly normal on his return, although both of them had been tired. He had attended a murder scene the night before and had lost some hours' sleep. She did occasionally make use of Mrs Bidwell, for example before and after a dinner party she and Howarth had given soon after their arrival, but certainly wouldn't call on her on a day when she was due at the Lab.

Dalgliesh asked:

'Did your brother tell you that he left the concert for a time after the interval?'

'He told me that he sat on a tombstone for about half an hour contemplating mortality. I imagine that, at that stage of the proceedings, he found the dead more entertaining than the living.'

Dalgliesh looked up at the immense curved wooden ceiling. He said:

'This place must be expensive to keep warm in winter. How is it heated?'

Again there was that swift elliptical flash of blue.

'By gas central heating. There isn't an open fire. That's one of the things we miss. So we couldn't have burnt Paul Middlemass's white coat. Actually, we'd have been fools to try. The most sensible plan would be to weigh it down with stones in the pockets and sling it into Leamings sluice. You'd probably dredge it up in the end, but I don't see how that would help you to discover who put it there. That's what I would have done.'

'No you wouldn't,' said Dalgliesh mildly. 'There weren't any pockets.'

She didn't offer to see them out, but Howarth was waiting for them at the foot of the stairs. Dalgliesh said:

'You didn't tell me that your sister was Lorrimer's mistress. Did you really convince yourself that it wasn't relevant?'

'To his death? Why should it be? It may have been relevant to his life. I very much doubt whether it was to hers. And I'm not my sister's keeper. She's capable of speaking for herself, as you've probably discovered.'

He walked with them out to the car, punctilious as a host speeding a couple of unwelcome guests. Dalgliesh said, his hand on the car door:

'Does the number 1840 mean anything to you?'

'In what context?'

'Any you choose.'

Howarth said calmly:

'Whewell published *Philosophy of the Inductive Sciences*;

Tchaikovsky was born; Berlioz composed the *Symphonie Funèbre et Triomphale*. I think that's the limit of my knowledge of an unremarkable year. Or if you want a different context, the ratio of the mass of the proton to the mass of the electron.'

Massingham called from the other side of the Rover:

'I thought that was 1836, unless you're not fussy about rounding up. Goodnight, sir.'

As they turned out of the drive, Dalgliesh asked:

'How do you come to remember that remarkably irrelevant piece of information?'

'From school. We may have been disadvantaged when it came to social mix, but the teaching wasn't bad. It's a figure which sticks in the mind.'

'Not in mine. What did you think of Mrs Schofield?'

'I didn't expect her to be like that.'

'As attractive, as talented, or as arrogant?'

'All three. Her face reminds me of someone, an actress. French I think.'

'Simone Signoret when she was young. I'm surprised that you're old enough to remember.'

'I saw a revival last year of *Casque d'Or*.'

Dalgliesh said: 'She told us at least one small lie.'

Apart, thought Massingham, from the one major lie which she may or may not have told. He was experienced enough to know that it was that central lie, the affirmation of innocence, which was the most difficult to detect; and the small, ingenious fabrications, so often unnecessary, which in the end confused and betrayed.

'Sir?'

'About where she and Lorrimer made love, in the back of his car. I don't believe that. Do you?'

It was rare for Dalgliesh to question a subordinate so directly. Massingham disconcertingly felt himself under test. He gave careful thought before replying.

'Psychologically it could be wrong. She's a fastidious, comfort-loving woman with a high opinion of her own dignity. And she must have watched the body of her husband being pulled from the wreckage of their car after that accident when she'd been driving. Somehow I don't think she'd fancy sex in the back of anyone's car.

Unless, of course, she's trying to exorcise the memory. It could be that.'

Dalgliesh smiled. 'Actually I was thinking on less esoteric lines. A scarlet Jaguar, and the latest model, is hardly the most inconspicuous vehicle for driving round the country with a lover. And old Mr Lorrimer said that his son hardly left home in the evenings or at night, unless to a murder scene. These are unpredictable. On the other hand he was frequently late at the Lab. Not all the lateness could have been work. I think that he and Mrs Schofield had a rendezvous somewhere fairly close.'

'You think it important, sir?'

'Important enough to cause her to lie. Why should she care if we know where they chose to disport themselves? I could understand it if she told us to mind our own business. But why bother to lie? There was another moment, too, when very briefly she lost composure. It was when she talked about seventeenth-century church architecture. I got the impression that there was a small, almost undetectable moment of confusion when she realized that she'd stumbled into saying something indiscreet, or at least something she wished unsaid. When the interviews are out of the way tomorrow, I think we'll take a look at the chapel at Hoggatt's.'

'But Sergeant Reynolds had a look at it this morning, sir, after he'd searched the grounds. It's just a locked, empty chapel. He found nothing.'

'Probably because there's nothing to find. It's just a hunch. Now we'd better get back to Guy's Marsh for that press conference and then I must have a word with the Chief Constable if he's back. After that I'd like to see Brenda Pridmore again; and I want to call later at the Old Rectory for a word with Dr Kerrison. But that can wait until we've seen what Mrs Gotobed at the Moonraker can do about dinner.'

6

Twenty minutes later, in the kitchen at Leamings, an incongruous compromise between a laboratory and rustic domesticity, Howarth was mixing *sauce vinaigrette*. The sickly, pungent smell of the olive oil, curving in a thin golden stream from the bottle, brought back, as always, memories of Italy and of his father, that dilettante collector of trivia, who had spent most of each year in Tuscany or Venice, and whose self-indulgent, hypochondriacal, solitary life had ended, appropriately enough since he affected to dread old age, on his fiftieth birthday. He had been less a stranger to his two motherless children than an enigma, seldom with them in person, always present mysteriously to their minds.

Maxim recalled a memory of his dressing-gowned figure, patterned in mauve and gold, standing at the foot of his bed on that extraordinary night of muted voices, sudden running footsteps, inexplicable silences, in which his step-mother had died. He had been home from prep school for the holidays, eight years old, ignored in the crisis of the illness, frightened and alone. He remembered clearly his father's thin, rather weary voice, already assuming the languors of grief.

'Your step-mother died ten minutes ago, Maxim. Evidently fate does not intend me to be a husband. I shall not again risk such grief. You, my boy, must look after your step-sister. I rely on you.' And then a cold hand casually laid on his shoulder as if conferring a burden. He had accepted it, literally, at eight years old, and had never laid it down. At first the immensity of the trust had appalled him. He remembered how he had lain there, terrified, staring into the darkness. Look after your sister. Domenica was three months old. How could he look after her? What ought he to feed her on? How dress her? What about his prep school? They wouldn't let him stay at home to look after his sister. He smiled wryly, remembering his relief at discovering next morning that her nurse was, after all, to remain. He recalled his first efforts to assume responsibility, resolutely seizing the pram handles and straining to push it up the Broad Walk, struggling to lift Domenica into her high chair.

'Give over, Master Maxim, do. You're more of a hindrance than a help.'

But afterwards the nurse had begun to realize that he was becoming more of a help than a nuisance, that the child could safely be left with him while she and the only other servant pursued their own unsupervised devices. Most of his school holidays had been spent helping to look after Domenica. From Rome, Verona, Florence and Venice his father, through his solicitor, sent instructions about allowances and schools. It was he who helped buy the clothes, took her to school, comforted and advised. He had attempted to support her through the agonies and uncertainties of adolescence, even before he had outgrown his own. He had been her champion against the world. He smiled, remembering the telephone call to Cambridge from her boarding school, asking him to fetch her that very night 'outside the hockey pavilion – gruesome torture house – at midnight. I'll climb down the fire escape. Promise.' And then their private code of defiance and allegiance: 'Contra mundum.'

'Contra mundum.'

His father's arrival from Italy, so little perturbed by the Reverend Mother's insistent summons that it was obvious that he had, in any case, been planning to return.

'Your sister's departure was unnecessarily eccentric, surely. Midnight assignation. Dramatic car drive across half England. Mother Superior seemed particularly pained that she had left her trunk behind, although I can appreciate that it would have been an encumbrance on the fire escape. And you must have been out of college all night. Your tutor can't have liked that.'

'I'm post-graduate now, Father. I took my degree eighteen months ago.'

'Indeed. Time passes so quickly at my age. Physics, wasn't it? A curious choice. Couldn't you have called for her after school in the orthodox way?'

'We wanted to get as far away from the place as possible before they noticed she'd gone and started looking.'

'A reasonable strategy, so far as it goes.'

'Dom hates school, Father. She's utterly miserable there.'

'So was I at school, but it never occurred to me to expect otherwise. Reverend Mother seems a charming woman. A tendency to halitosis when under stress, but I shouldn't have thought that would have troubled your sister. They can hardly have come into intimate contact. She isn't prepared to have Domenica back, by the way.'

'Need Dom go anywhere, Father? She's nearly fifteen. She doesn't have to go to school. And she wants to be a painter.'

'I suppose she could stay at home until she's old enough for art college, if that's what you advise. But it's hardly worth opening the

London house just for one. I shall return to Venice next week. I'm only here to consult Dr Mavers-Brown.'

'Perhaps she could go back to Italy with you for a month or so. She'd love to see the Accademia. And she ought to see Florence.'

'Oh, I don't think that would do, my boy. Quite out of the question. She had much better take a room at Cambridge and you can keep an eye on her. They have some quite agreeable pictures in the Fitzwilliam Museum. Oh dear, what a responsibility children are! It's quite wrong that I should be troubled like this in my state of health. Mavers-Brown was insistent that I avoid anxiety.'

And now he lay coffined in his final self-sufficiency, in that most beautiful of burial grounds, the British Cemetery at Rome. He would have liked that, thought Maxim, if he could have borne the thought of his death at all, as much as he would have resented the over-aggressive Italian driver whose ill-judged acceleration at the junction of the Via Vittoria and the Corso had placed him there.

He heard his sister's steps on the stairs.

'So they've gone.'

'Twenty minutes ago. We had a brief valedictory skirmish. Was Dalgliesh offensive?'

'No more offensive than I to him. Honours even, I should have said. I don't think he liked me.'

'I don't think he likes anyone much. But he's considered highly intelligent. Did you find him attractive?'

She answered the unspoken question.

'It would be like making love to a public hangman.'

She dipped her finger in the vinaigrette dressing.

'Too much vinegar. What have you been doing?'

'Apart from cooking? Thinking about father. Do you know, Dom, when I was eleven I became absolutely convinced that he'd murdered our mothers.'

'Both of them? I mean yours and mine? What an odd idea. How could he have? Yours died of cancer and mine of pneumonia. He couldn't have fixed that.'

'I know. It's just that he seemed such a natural widower. I thought at the time that he'd done it to stop them having any more babies.'

'Well it would do that all right. Were you wondering whether a tendency to murder is inherited?'

'Not really. But so much is. Father's total inability to make relationships, for example. That incredible self-absorption. Do you know, he'd actually put me down for Stonyhurst before he rememberberd that it was your mother, not mine, who'd been RC.'

'A pity he did find out. I should like to have seen what the Jesuits made of you. The trouble with a religious education, if you're a pagan like me, is that you're left all your life feeling that you've lost something, not that it isn't there.'

She walked over to the table and stirred a bowl of mushrooms with her finger.

'I can make relationships. The trouble is that I get bored and they don't last. And I only seem to know one way to be kind. It's as well that we last, isn't it? You'll last for me until the day I die. Shall I change now, or do you want me to see to the wine?'

'You'll last for me until the day I die.' *Contra mundum*. It was too late now to sever that cord even if he wanted to. He remembered Charles Schofield's gauze-cocooned head, the dying eyes still malicious behind two slits in the bandages, the swollen lips painfully moving.

'Congratulations, Giovanni. Remember me in your garden in Parma.'

What had been so astounding was not the lie itself, or that Schofield had believed it, or pretended to believe it, but that he had hated his brother-in-law enough to die with that taunt on his lips. Or had he taken it for granted that a physicist, poor philistine, wouldn't know his Jacobean dramatists? Even his wife, that indefatigable sexual sophisticate, had known better.

'I suppose you'd sleep together if Domenica happened to want it. A spot of incest wouldn't worry her. But you don't need to, do you? You don't need anything as normal as sex to be more to each other than you are. Neither of you wants anyone else. That's why I'm leaving. I'm getting out now while there's still something left of me to get out.'

'Max, what is it?'

Domenica's voice, sharpened with anxiety, recalled him to the present. His mind spun back through a kaleidoscope of spinning years, through superimposed whirling images of childhood and youth, to that last unforgettable image, still, perfectly in focus, patterned for ever in his memory, Lorrimer's dead fingers clawing at the floor of his laboratory, Lorrimer's dull, half-open eye, Lorrimer's blood. He said:

'You get changed. I'll see to the wine.'

7

'What will people say?'

'That's all you ever think of, Mum, what will people say. What does it matter what they say? I haven't done anything to be ashamed of.'

'Of course not. If anyone says different your dad'll soon put them right. But you know what tongues they have in this village. A thousand pounds. I couldn't hardly believe it when that solicitor rang. It's a tidy sum. And by the time Lillie Pearce has passed the news around in the Stars and Plough it'll be ten thousand, more than likely.'

'Who cares about Lillie Pearce, silly old cow.'

'Brenda! I won't have that language. And we have to live in this village.'

'You may have to, I don't. And if that's the kind of minds they've got the sooner I move away the better. Oh, Mum, don't look like that! He only wanted to help me, he wanted to be kind. And he probably did it on impulse.'

'Not very considerate of him, though, was it? He might have talked it over with your dad or me.'

'But he didn't know that he was going to die.'

Brenda and her mother were alone in the farmhouse, Arthur Pridmore having left after supper for the monthly meeting of the Parochial Church Council. The washing-up was finished and the long evening stretched before them. Too restless to settle to the television and too preoccupied with the extraordinary events of the day to take up a book, they sat in the firelight, edgy, half excited and half afraid, missing Arthur Pridmore's reassuring bulk in his high-backed chair. Then Mrs Pridmore shook herself into normality and reached for her sewing basket.

'Well at least it will help towards a nice wedding. If you have to take it, better put it in the Post Office. Then it'll add interest and be there when you want it.'

'I want it now. For books and a microscope like Dr Lorrimer intended. That's why he left it to me and that's what I'm going to do with it. Besides, if people leave money for a special purpose you can't use it for something else. And I don't want to. I'm going to ask Dad to put up a shelf and a work-bench in my bedroom and I'll start working for my science A-levels straight away.'

'He ought not to have thought of you. What about Angela Foley? She's had a terrible life, that girl. She never got a penny from her grandmother's will, and now this.'

'That's not our concern, Mum. It was up to him. Maybe he might have left it to her if they hadn't rowed.'

'How do you mean, rowed? When?'

'Last week sometime. Tuesday it was, I think. It was just before I came home and most of the staff had left. Inspector Blakelock sent me up to Biology with a query on one of the court reports. They were together in Dr Lorrimer's room and I heard them quarrelling. She was asking him for money and he said he wouldn't give her any and then he said something about changing his will.'

'You mean you stood there listening?'

'Well I couldn't help it, could I? They were talking quite loudly. He was saying terrible things about Stella Mawson, you know, that writer Angela Foley lives with. I wasn't eavesdropping on purpose. I didn't want to hear.'

'You could have gone away.'

'And come up again all the way from the front hall? Anyway, I had to ask him about the report for the Munnings case. I couldn't go back and tell Inspector Blakelock that I hadn't got the answer because Dr Lorrimer was having a row with his cousin. Besides, we always listened to secrets at school.'

'You're not at school now. Really, Brenda, you worry me sometimes. One moment you behave like a sensible adult, and the next anyone would think you were back in the fourth form. You're eighteen now, an adult. What has school to do with it?'

'I don't know why you're getting so het up. I didn't tell anyone.'

'Well, you'll have to tell that detective from Scotland Yard.'

'Mum! I can't! It hasn't got anything to do with the murder.'

'Who's to say? You're supposed to tell the police anything that's important. Didn't he tell you that?'

He told her exactly that. Brenda remembered his look, her own guilty blush. He had known that she was keeping something back. She said, with stubborn defiance:

'Well, I can't accuse Angela Foley of murder, or as good as accuse her anyway. Besides,' she proclaimed triumphantly, remembering something Inspector Blakelock had told her, 'it would be hearsay, not proper evidence. He couldn't take any notice of it. And, Mum, there's another thing. Suppose she didn't really expect him to alter the will so soon? That solicitor told you that Dr Lorrimer made the new will last Friday, didn't he? Well that was probably because he had to go to a scene of crime in Ely on Friday morning. The police call only came through at ten o'clock. He must have gone into his solicitor's then.'

'What do you mean?'

'Nothing. Only if people think that I had a motive, then so did she.'

'Of course you didn't have a motive! That's ridiculous. It's wicked! Oh, Brenda, if only you'd come to the concert with Dad and me.'

'No thank you. Miss Spencer singing "Pale Hands I Loved", and the Sunday School kids doing their boring old maypole dance, and the WI with their handbells, and old Mr Matthews bashing away with the acoustic spoons. I've seen it all before.'

'But you'd have had an alibi.'

'So I would if you and Dad had stayed here at home with me.'

'It wouldn't have mattered where you'd been if it weren't for that thousand pounds. Well, let's hope Gerald Bowlem understands.'

'If he doesn't, he knows what he can do! I don't see what it's got to do with Gerald. I'm not married to him, nor engaged for that matter. He'd better not interfere.'

She looked across at her mother and was suddenly appalled. She had only seen her look like this once before, the night when she had had her second miscarriage and had been told by old Dr Greene that there could never now be another baby. Brenda had only been twelve at the time. But her mother's face, suddenly remembered, had looked exactly as it did now, as if an obliterating hand had passed over it, wiping off brightness, blunting the contours of cheek and brow, dulling the eyes, leaving an amorphous mask of desolation.

She remembered and understood what before she had only felt, the anger and resentment that her mother, indestructible and comforting as a great rock in a weary land, should herself be vulnerable to pain. She was there to soothe Brenda's miseries, not to suffer herself, to comfort, not to seek comfort. But now Brenda was older and she was able to understand. She saw her mother clearly, like a stranger newly met. The cheap Crimplene dress, spotlessly clean as always, with the brooch Brenda had given her for her last birthday pinned to the lapel. The ankles thickening above the sensible low-heeled shoes, the pudgy hands speckled with the brown stains of age, the wedding ring of dull gold biting into the flesh, the curly hair that had once been red-gold like her own, still brushed plainly to one side and held in a tortoiseshell slide, the fresh, almost unlined skin. She put her arms round her mother's shoulders.

'Oh, Mum, don't worry. It'll be all right. Commander Dalgliesh will find out who did it and then everything will be back to normal. Look, I'll make you some cocoa. Don't let's wait till Dad's back from the PCC. We'll have it now. Mum, it's all right. Really it is. It's all right.'

Simultaneously their ears caught the hum of the approaching car. They gazed at each other, speechless, guilty as conspirators. This wasn't their ancient Morris. And how could it be? The Parochial Church Council never finished their business before half-past eight.

Brenda went to the window and peered out. The car stopped. She turned to her mother, white-faced.

'It's the police! It's Commander Dalgliesh!'

Without a word, Mrs Pridmore got resolutely to her feet. She placed a hand briefly on her daughter's shoulder, then went out into the passage and opened the door before Massingham had lifted his hand to knock. She said through stiff lips:

'Come in, please. I'm glad that you're here. Brenda has something to tell you, something that I think you ought to know.'

8

The day was nearly over. Sitting in his dressing-gown at the small table in front of the window in his bedroom at the Moonraker, Dalgliesh heard the church clock strike half-past eleven. He liked his room. It was the larger of the two which Mrs Gotobed had been able to offer. The single window looked out over the churchyard towards the village hall and beyond it the clerestory and square flint tower of St Nicholas's Church. There were only three rooms for guests at the inn. The smallest and noisiest, since it was over the public bar, had fallen to Massingham. The main guest-room had already been taken by an American couple touring East Anglia, perhaps in search of family records. They had sat at their table in the dining-parlour, happily occupied with maps and guidebooks, and if they had been told that their newly arrived fellow guests were police officers investigating a murder, they were too well-bred to betray interest. After a brief smile and a good evening in their soft transatlantic voices they had turned their attention again to Mrs Gotobed's excellent casserole of hare in cider.

It was very quiet. The muted voices from the bar had long since been silent. It was over an hour since he had heard the last shouted goodbyes. Massingham, he knew, had spent the evening in the public bar hoping, presumably, to pick up scraps of useful information. Dalgliesh hoped that the beer had been good. He had been born close enough to the fens to know that, otherwise, Massingham would have found it a frustrating evening.

He got up to stretch his legs and shoulders, looking round with approval at the room. The floorboards were of ancient oak, black and stout as ships' timbers. A fire of wood and turf burned in the iron Victorian grate, the pungent smoke curtsying under a decorated hood of wheat-ears and flower-posies tied with ribbons. The large double bed was of brass, high and ornate with four great knobs, large as polished cannonballs, at the corners. Mrs Gotobed had earlier folded back the crocheted cover to reveal a feather mattress shaken to an inviting plumpness. In any four-star hotel he might have enjoyed greater luxury, but hardly such comfort.

He returned to his work. It had been a crowded day of interrogation and renewed interrogation, telephone calls to London, a hurriedly arranged and unsatisfactory press conference, two consultations with the Chief Constable, the gathering of those odd-shaped pieces of information and conjecture which, in the end, would click together to form the completed picture. It might be a trite analogy, this comparison of detection with fitting together a jigsaw. But it was remarkably apt, not least because it was so often that tantalizing elusive piece with the vital segment of a human face that made the picture complete.

He turned the page to the last interview of the day, with Henry Kerrison at the Old Rectory. The smell of the house was still in his nostrils, an evocative smell of stale cooking and furniture polish, reminding him of childhood visits with his parents to over-large, ill-heated country vicarages. Kerrison's housekeeper and children had long been in bed and the house had held a melancholy, brooding silence as if all the tragedies and disappointments of its numerous incumbents still hung in the air.

Kerrison had answered the door himself and had shown him and Massingham into his study where he was occupied in sorting coloured slides of post-mortem injuries to illustrate a lecture he was to give the following week to the Detection Training School. On the desk was a framed photograph of himself as a boy with an older man, obviously his father. They were standing on a crag, climbing-ropes slung round their shoulders. What interested Dalgliesh as much as the photograph itself was the fact that Kerrison hadn't bothered to remove it.

He hadn't appeared to resent his visitors' late arrival. It was possible to believe that he welcomed their company. He had worked on in the light of his desk-lamp, fitting each slide into his viewer, then sorting it into the appropriate heap, intent as a schoolboy with a hobby. He had answered their questions quietly and precisely, but as if his mind were elsewhere. Dalgliesh asked him whether his daughter had talked to him about the incident with Lorrimer.

'Yes, she did tell me. When I got home for lunch from my lecture I found her crying in her room. It seems that Lorrimer was unnecessarily harsh. But Nell is a sensitive child and it's not always possible to know the precise truth of the matter.'

'You didn't talk to him about it?'

'I didn't talk to anyone. I did wonder whether I ought to, but it would have meant questioning Inspector Blakelock and Miss Pridmore, and I didn't wish to involve them. They had to work with Lorrimer. So, for that matter, did I. The effectiveness of an isolated institution like Hoggatt's largely depends on good relationships between the staff. I thought it was best not to take the matter further. That may have been prudence, or it may have been cowardice. I don't know.'

He had smiled sadly, and added:

'I only know that it wasn't a motive for murder.'

A motive for murder. Dalgliesh had discovered enough motives in this crowded but not very satisfactory day. But motive was the least important factor in a murder investigation. He would gladly have exchanged the psychological subtleties of motive for a single, solid, incontrovertible piece of physical evidence linking a suspect with the crime. And, so far, there was none. He still awaited the report from the Metropolitan Laboratory on the mallet and the vomit. The mysterious figure seen by old Goddard fleeing from Hoggatt's remained mysterious; no other person had yet been traced or had come forward to suggest that he wasn't a figment of the old man's imagination. The tyre-marks near the gate, now definitely identified from the tyre index at the laboratory, still hadn't been linked to a car. Not surprisingly, no trace had been found of Middlemass's white coat and no indication whether or how it had been disposed of. An examination of the village hall and hobby-horse costume had produced nothing to disprove Middlemass's account of his evening and it was apparent that the horse, a heavy all-enveloping con- traption of canvas and serge, ensured that its wearer would be unidentifiable even, in Middlemass's case, to his elegant hand-made shoes.

The central mysteries of the case remained. Who was it who had telephoned the message to Lorrimer about the can being burned and the number 1840? Was it the same woman who had rung Mrs Bidwell? What had been written on the missing sheet from Lor- rimer's rough notebook? What had prompted Lorrimer to make that extraordinary will?

Lifting his head from the files, he listened. There was a noise, faintly discernible, like the creeping of a myriad insects. He remem- bered it from his childhood nights, lying awake in the nursery of his father's Norfolk vicarage, a sound he had never heard in the noise of cities, the first gentle sibilant whisper of the night rain. Soon it was followed by a spatter of drops against the window and the rising moan of the wind in the chimney. The fire spluttered and then flared into sudden brightness. There was a violent flurry of rain against the pane and then, as quickly as it had begun, the brief storm was over. He opened the window to savour the smell of the damp night air, and gazed out into a blanket of darkness, black fen earth merging with the paler sky.

As his eyes became accustomed to the night, he could discern the low rectangle of the village hall and, beyond it, the great medieval tower of the church. Then the moon sailed out from behind the clouds and the churchyard became visible, the obelisks and gravestones gleaming pale as if they exuded their own mysterious light. Below him, faintly luminous, lay the gravel path along which, the previous night, the morris dancers, bells jangling, had made their way through the rising mist. Staring out over the churchyard he pictured the hobby-horse pawing the ground to meet them, rearing its grotesque head among the gravestones and snapping the air with its great jaws. And he wondered again who had been inside its skin.

The door beneath his window opened and Mrs Gotobed appeared and crooned into the darkness, enticing in her cat: 'Snowball! Snowball! Good boy now.' There was a flash of white, and the door was closed. Dalgliesh latched his window and decided that he, too, would call it a day.

BOOK FOUR

Hanged by the Neck

1

Sprogg's Cottage, low-built and top-heavy under its low, occluding roof of thatch, wire-netted, strong against the fen winter gales, was almost invisible from the road. It lay about three-quarters of a mile north-east from the village and was fronted by Sprogg's Green, a wide triangular grass verge planted with willows. Pushing open the white wicker gate on which someone had optimistically but fruitlessly substituted the word 'Lavender' for Sprogg's, Dalgliesh and Massingham stepped into a front garden as brightly ordered and conventional as that of a suburban villa. An acacia tree in the middle of the lawn flaunted its autumn glory of red and gold, the yellow climbing roses trained over the door still gleamed with a faint illusion of summer and a massed bed of geraniums, fuchsia and dahlias, supported by stakes and carefully tended, flared in discordant glory against the bronze of the beech hedge. There was a hanging basket of pink geraniums beside the door, now past their best, but still bright with a few tattered blooms. The knocker was a highly polished brass fish, every scale gleaming.

The door was opened by a slight, almost fragile, woman, barefooted and wearing a cotton overblouse, patterned in greens and brown, above her corduroy slacks. She had coarse dark hair strongly streaked with grey and worn in a short bob, with a heavy fringe which curved low to meet her eyebrows. Her eyes were her most remarkable feature, immense, the irises brown speckled with green, translucently clear under the strongly curved brows. Her face was pale and taut, deeply etched with lines across the forehead and running from the widely springing nostrils to the corners of the mouth. It was the face, thought Dalgliesh, of a tortured masochist in a medieval triptych, the muscles bulging and knotted as if they had been racked. But no one coming under the gaze of those remarkable eyes could call it plain or ordinary. Dalgliesh said:

'Miss Mawson? I'm Adam Dalgliesh. This is Inspector Massingham.'

She gave him a direct, impersonal gaze and said without smiling:

'Come through into the study, will you? We don't light the sitting-room fire until the evening. If you want to speak to Angela, I'm afraid she's not here at present. She's over at Postmill Cottage with Mrs Swaffield meeting the Social Security people. They're trying to persuade old Lorrimer to go into an old people's home. Apparently he's being obstinately resistant to the blandishments of bureaucracy. Good luck to him.'

The front door opened directly into a sitting-room with a low, oak-beamed ceiling. The room surprised him. To enter it was like walking into an antique shop, but one where the proprietor had arranged his oddly assorted wares with an eye to the general effect. The mantelshelf and every ledge bore an ornament, three hanging cupboards held a variety of mugs, teapots, painted jugs and Staffordshire figures, and the walls were almost covered with prints, framed old maps, small oil paintings and Victorian silhouettes in oval frames. Above the fireplace was the most spectacular object, a curved sword with a finely wrought scabbard. He wondered whether the room reflected merely an indiscriminate acquisitiveness, or whether these carefully disposed objects served as comforting talismans against the alien, undomesticated spirits of the encroaching fens. A wood fire was laid but not lit in the open hearth. Under the window a polished gate-legged table was already laid for two.

Miss Mawson led the way through to her study. It was a smaller, less cluttered room at the back with a latticed window giving a view of a stone terrace, a lawn with a sundial in the middle, and a wide field of sugar beet, still unharvested. He saw with interest that she wrote by hand. There was a typewriter, but it stood on a table by itself. The working-desk under the window held only a pad of unlined paper, covered with a black upright holograph in an elegant italic. The lines were carefully patterned on the paper, and even the marginal alterations were aligned.

Dalgliesh said:

'I'm sorry if we're interrupting your work.'

'You aren't. Sit down, won't you both. It isn't going well this morning. If it were I should have hung a "don't disturb" notice on the knocker and you wouldn't have got in. Still, it's nearly finished; only one chapter to do now. I suppose you want me to give Angela an alibi. Helping the police, isn't it called? What were we doing on

Wednesday night; and when, and why, and where, and with whom?'

'We would like to ask you some questions, certainly.'

'But that one first, presumably. There's no difficulty. We spent the evening and night together from six-fifteen, which was the time she arrived home.'

'Doing what, Miss Mawson?'

'What we normally do. We separated the day from the evening, me with whisky, Angela with sherry. I asked about her day and she enquired about mine. Then she lit the fire and cooked the meal. We had avocado pear with *sauce vinaigrette*, chicken casserole and cheese and biscuits. We washed up together and then Angela typed my manuscript for me until nine. At nine we turned on the television and watched the news. followed by the play. That brought us to ten forty-five, cocoa for Angela, whisky for me, and bed.'

'Neither of you left the cottage?'

'No.'

Dalgliesh asked how long she had lived in the village.

'Me? Eight years. I was born in the fens – at Soham actually – and spent most of my childhood here. But I went up to London University when I was eighteen, took a second-class degree, and then worked, not particularly successfully, at various jobs in journalism and publishing. I came here eight years ago when I heard that the cottage was to let. That's when I first decided to give up my job and become a full-time writer.'

'And Miss Foley?'

'She came to live here two years ago. I advertised locally for a part-time typist and she replied. She was living in lodgings at Ely then and wasn't particularly happy there, so I suggested that she moved in. She had to depend on the bus to get to work. Living here is obviously much more convenient for the Lab.'

'So you've lived long enough in the village to get to know people?'

'As much as one ever does in the fens. But not well enough to point the finger at a murderer for you.'

'How well did you know Dr Lorrimer?'

'By sight. I wasn't told that Angela was his cousin until she came to live with me. They're not close and he never came here. I've met most of the Lab staff, of course. Dr Howarth started a string quartet soon after he arrived, and last August they gave a concert in the

Wren chapel. Afterwards there was wine and cheese in the vestry. I met a number of the staff then. Actually, I already knew them by sight and name, as one does in a village. We use the same post office and the same pub. But if you're hoping for village and Lab gossip, it's no use coming to me.'

Dalgliesh said:

'Was the concert in the chapel successful?'

'Not particularly. Howarth is a very fine amateur violinist and Claire Easterbrook is a competent cellist, but the other two weren't up to much. He hasn't repeated the experiment. I gather that there was a certain amount of unkind comment about a new arrival who saw it as his duty to civilize the underprivileged natives, and it may have got to his ears. He does rather give the impression that he sees himself as bridging single-handed the culture-gap between the scientist and the artist. Or perhaps he wasn't satisfied with the acoustics. My own view is that the other three didn't want to go on playing with him. As a leader of a quartet he probably behaved with much the same arrogance as he does as Director. The Lab is certainly more efficient; the work output is up twenty per cent. Whether the staff are happy is another matter.'

So she wasn't altogether immune to Lab and village gossip, thought Dalgliesh. He wondered why she was being so frank. Equally frank, he asked bluntly:

'When you were at Postmill Cottage yesterday, did you go upstairs?'

'Fancy the old man telling you that! What did he think I was after, I wonder? I went up to the bathroom to see if there was a tin of scouring powder there to clean the sink. There wasn't.'

'You know about Dr Lorrimer's will, of course?'

'I imagine the whole village does. Actually I was probably the first to know. The old man was getting agitated to know whether there was any money coming, so Angela rang the solicitor. She'd met him at the time her grandmother's will was read. He told her that the cottage was to go to the old man with £10,000, so she was able to put his mind at rest.'

'And Miss Foley herself gets nothing?'

'That's right. And that new clerical officer at the Lab, whom Edwin had apparently taken a fancy to, gets a thousand pounds.'

'A not particularly just will.'

'Have you ever known beneficiaries who thought a will was just? His grandmother's will was worse. Angela lost the money then, when it could have made a difference to her life. Now she doesn't need it. We manage perfectly well here.'

'Presumably it wasn't a shock to her. Didn't he tell her of his intentions?'

'If that's meant to be a tactful way of finding out whether she had a motive for murder, you can ask her yourself. Here she is.'

Angela Foley came through the sitting-room, tugging off her headscarf. Her face darkened at the sight of the visitors and she said with quick defensive annoyance:

'Miss Mawson likes to work in the mornings. You didn't say that you were coming.'

Her friend laughed.

'They haven't worried me. I've been getting a useful insight into police methods. They're effective without being crude. You're back early.'

'The social work department rang to say that they can't get over until after lunch. Uncle doesn't want to see them, but he wants to see me even less. He's having lunch with the Swaffields at the rectory, so I thought I might as well come home.'

Stella Mawson lit a cigarette.

'You've arrived at an opportune time. Mr Dalgliesh was enquiring tactfully whether you had a motive for murdering your cousin; in other words, did Edwin tell you that he was about to alter his will?'

Angela Foley looked at Dalgliesh and said calmly:

'No. He never discussed his affairs with me and I didn't discuss mine with him. I don't think I've spoken to him during the last two years except about Lab business.'

Dalgliesh said:

'It's surprising, surely, that he should want to change a long-standing will without talking to you about it?'

She shrugged, and then explained:

'It was nothing to do with me. He was only my cousin, not my brother. He transferred to Hoggatt's from the Southern Laboratory five years ago to live with his father, not because I was here. He didn't really know me. If he had, I doubt whether he would have liked me. He owed me nothing, not even justice.'

'Did you like him?'

She paused and thought, as if the question was one to which she herself wanted an answer. Stella Mawson, eyes narrowed, regarded her through the cigarette smoke. Then Miss Foley spoke:

'No, I didn't like him. I think I was even a little afraid of him. He was like a man psychologically burdened, unsure of his place in life. Lately the tension and unhappiness were almost palpable. I found it embarrassing and, well, somehow menacing. People who were really secure in their own personalities didn't seem to notice or be bothered by it. But the less secure felt threatened. I think that's why Clifford Bradley was so afraid of him.'

Stella Mawson said:

'Bradley probably reminded Edwin of himself when he was young. He was painfully insecure, even in his job, when he first started. D'you remember how he used to practise his evidence on the night before he went into the box; writing down all the possible questions the opposing counsel might ask, making sure that he was word perfect with the answers, learning all the scientific formulae by heart to impress the jury? He made a mess of one of his first cases, and never forgave himself.'

There was a strange little silence. Angela Foley seemed about to speak, then changed her mind. Her enigmatic gaze was fixed on her friend. Stella Mawson's eyes shifted. She walked over to her desk and stubbed out her cigarette. She said:

'Your aunt told you. She used to have to read out the questions for him over and over again; an evening of tension and incomprehensible boredom. Don't you remember?'

'Yes,' said Angela in her high, dispassionate voice. 'Yes, I remember.' She turned to Dalgliesh.

'If there's nothing else you want to ask me, there are things I need to get on with. Dr Howarth isn't expecting me at the Lab until this afternoon. And Stella will want to work.'

Both women showed them out, standing together in the doorway as if politely speeding departing guests. Dalgliesh almost expected them to wave goodbye. He hadn't questioned Miss Foley about the quarrel with her cousin. The time might come for that, but it wasn't yet. It had interested, but not surprised him, that she had lied. But what had interested him more was Stella Mawson's story of Lorrimer rehearsing his evidence on the night before a trial.

Whoever had told her this, he was fairly certain that it hadn't been Angela Foley.

As they drove away, Massingham said:

'Fifty thousand pounds would change her whole life, give her some independence, get her away from here. What sort of life is it for a young woman, just the two of them, stuck here in this isolated swamp? And she seems little more than a drudge.'

Dalgliesh, unusually, was driving. Massingham glanced at the sombre eyes in the mirror, the long hands laid lightly on the wheel. Dalgliesh said:

'I'm remembering what old George Greenall, the first detective-sergeant I worked under, told me. He'd had twenty-five years in the CID. Nothing about people surprised him, nothing shocked him. He said:

' "They'll tell you that the most destructive force in the world is hate. Don't you believe it, lad. It's love. If you want to make a detective you'd better learn to recognize it when you meet it." '

2

Brenda was over an hour late at the Laboratory on Thursday morning. After the excitement of the previous day she had overslept and her mother had deliberately not called her. She had wanted to go without her breakfast, but Mrs Pridmore had placed the usual plate of bacon and egg before her, and had said firmly that Brenda wouldn't leave the house until it was eaten. Brenda, only too aware that both her parents would be happier if she never set foot in Hoggatt's again, knew better than to argue.

She arrived, breathless and apologetic, to find Inspector Blakelock trying to cope with a two days' intake of exhibits, a steady stream of arrivals and a constantly ringing telephone. She wondered how he would greet her, whether he had learned about the thousand pounds and, if so, whether it would make any difference. But he seemed his usual stolid self. He said:

'As soon as you've taken off your things, you're to go to the Director. He's in Miss Foley's office. The police are using his. Don't bother about making tea. Miss Foley will be out until after lunch. She has to see someone from the local authority social services about her uncle.'

Brenda was glad that she wouldn't have to face Angela Foley yet. Last night's admission to Commander Dalgliesh was too like betrayal to be comfortable. She said:

'Everyone else is in, then?'

'Clifford Bradley hasn't made it. His wife telephoned to say that he's not well. The police have been here since half-past eight. They've been checking all the exhibits, especially the drugs, and they've made another search of the whole Lab. Apparently they've got the idea that there's something odd going on.'

It was unusual for Inspector Blakelock to be so communicative. Brenda asked:

'What do you mean, something odd?'

'They didn't say. But now they want to see every file in the Lab with a number 18 or 40 or 1840 in the registration.'

Brenda's eyes widened.

'Do you mean for this year only, or do we have to go back to those on microfilm?'

'I've got out this year's and last year's to begin with, and Sergeant Underhill and the constable are working on them now. I don't know what they hope to find, and by the look of them, neither do they. Better look nippy. Dr Howarth said that you were to go into him as soon as you arrive.'

'But I can't do shorthand and typing! What do you think he wants me for?'

'He didn't say. Mostly getting out files, I imagine. And I dare say there'll be a bit of telephoning and fetching and carrying.'

'Where's Commander Dalgliesh? Isn't he here?'

'He and Inspector Massingham left about ten minutes ago. Off to interview someone, I dare say. Never mind about them. Our job's here, helping to keep this Lab working smoothly.'

It was as close as Inspector Blakelock ever got to a rebuke. Brenda hurried to Miss Foley's office. It was known that the Director didn't like people to knock on his door, so Brenda entered with what confidence she could muster. She thought, 'I can only do my best. If that's not good enough, he'll have to lump it.' He was sitting at the desk apparently studying a file. He looked up without smiling in response to her good morning, and said:

'Inspector Blakelock has explained to you that I want some help this morning while Miss Foley's away? You can work with Mrs Mallett in the general office.'

'Yes, sir.'

'The police will be needing some more files. They're interested in particular numbers only. But I expect Inspector Blakelock has explained that.'

'Yes, sir.'

'They're working on the 1976 and '75 registrations now, so you'd better start getting out the 1974 series and any earlier years they want.'

He took his eyes from the files and looked directly at her for the first time.

'Dr Lorrimer left you some money, didn't he?'

'Yes, sir. One thousand pounds for books and apparatus.'

'You don't need to call me, sir. Dr Howarth will do. You liked him?'

'Yes. Yes, I did.'

Dr Howarth had lowered his eyes again and was turning over the pages of the file.

'Odd, I shouldn't have thought that he would have appealed to women, or women to him.'

Brenda said resolutely:

'It wasn't like that.'

'What wasn't it like? Do you mean he didn't think of you as a woman?'

'I don't know. I mean, I didn't think he was trying to . . .'

Her voice broke off. Dr Howarth turned a page. He said:

'To seduce you?'

Brenda took courage, helped by a spurt of anger. She said:

'Well, he couldn't, could he? Not here in the Lab. And I never saw him anywhere else. And if you'd known anything about him at all, you wouldn't talk like that.'

She was appalled at her own temerity. But the Director only said, rather sadly she thought:

'I expect you're right. I never knew him at all.'

She struggled to explain.

'He explained to me what science is about.'

'And what is science about?'

'He explained that scientists formulate theories about how the physical world works, and then test them out by experiments. As long as the experiments succeed, then the theories hold. If they fail, the scientists have to find another theory to explain the facts. He said that, with science, there's this exciting paradox, that disillusionment needn't be defeat. It's a step forward.'

'Didn't you do science at school? I thought you'd taken physics and chemistry at O-level.'

'No one ever explained it like that before.'

'No. I suppose they bored you with experiments about magnetism and the properties of carbon dioxide. By the way, Miss Foley has typed a paper on the ratio of staffing to workloads. I want the figures checked – Mrs Mallett will do it with you – and the paper circulated to all Directors before next week's meeting. She'll give you a list of addresses.'

'Yes, sir. Yes, Dr Howarth.'

'And I'd like you to take this file to Miss Easterbrook in the Biology Lab.'

He looked up at her, and she thought for the first time that he looked kind. He said, very gently:

'I know how you feel. I felt the same. But there's only a white outline on the floor, just a smudge of chalk. That's all.'

He handed her the file. It was a dismissal. At the door Brenda paused. The Director said:

'Well?'

'I was just thinking that detection must be like science. The detective formulates a theory, then tests it. If the facts he discovers fit, then the theory holds. If they don't, then he has to find another theory, another suspect.'

Dr Howarth said drily:

'It's a reasonable analogy. But the temptation to select the right facts is probably greater. And the detective is experimenting with human beings. Their properties are complex and not susceptible to accurate analysis.'

An hour later Brenda took her third set of files into Sergeant Underhill in the Director's office. The pleasant-looking detective-constable leaped forward to relieve her of her burden. The telephone rang on Dr Howarth's desk, and Sergeant Underhill went over to answer it. He replaced the receiver and looked across at his companion.

'That's the Met Lab. They've given me the result of the blood analysis. The mallet was the weapon all right. There's Lorrimer's blood on it. And they've analysed the vomit.'

He looked up, suddenly remembering that Brenda was still in the room, and waited until she had left and the door closed. The detective-constable said:

'Well?'

'It's what we thought. Think it out for yourself. A forensic scientist would know that the Lab can't determine a blood group from vomit. The stomach acids destroy the antibodies. What they can hope to say is what was in the food. So all you need to do, if it's your vomit and you're a suspect, is to lie about what you ate for supper. Who could disprove it?'

His companion said:

'Unless . . .'

Sergeant Underhill reached again for the phone.

'Exactly. As I said, think it out for yourself.'

3

After the last few days of intermittent rain and fitful autumn sunlight, the morning was cold but bright, the sun unexpectedly warm against their necks. But even in the mellow light, the Old Rectory, with its bricks the colour of raw liver under the encroaching ivy, and its ponderous porch and carved overhanging eaves, was a depressing house. The open iron gate to the drive, half off its hinges, was embedded in a straggling hedge which bordered the garden. The gravel path needed weeding. The grass of the lawn was pulled and flattened where someone had made an inexpert attempt at mowing it, obviously with a blunt machine, and the two herbaceous borders were a tangle of overgrown chrysanthemums and stunted dahlias half choked with weeds. A child's wooden horse on wheels lay on its side at the edge of the lawn, but this was the only sign of human life.

As they approached the house, however, a girl and a small boy emerged from the porch and stood regarding them. They must, of course, be Kerrison's children, and as Dalgliesh and Massingham approached the likeness became apparent. The girl must, he supposed, be over school age, but she looked barely sixteen except for a certain adult wariness about the eyes. She had straight, dark hair drawn back from a high, spotty forehead into short dishevelled pigtails bound with elastic bands. She wore the ubiquitous faded blue jeans of her generation, topped with a fawn sweater, loose-fitting enough to be her father's. Round her neck Dalgliesh could glimpse what looked like a leather thong. Her grubby feet were bare and palely striped with the pattern of summer sandals.

The child, who moved closer to her at the sight of strangers, was about three or four years old, a stocky, round-faced boy with a wide nose and a gentle, delicate mouth. His face was a softer miniature model of his father's, the brows straight and dark above the heavily lidded eyes. He was wearing a pair of tight blue shorts and an inexpertly knitted striped jumper against which he was clasping a large ball. His sturdy legs were planted in short, red wellington boots. He tightened his hold on his ball and fixed on Dalgliesh an unblinking, disconcertingly judgemental gaze.

Dalgliesh suddenly realized that he knew virtually nothing about children. Most of his friends were childless: those who were not had learned to invite him when their demanding, peace-disturbing, egotistical offspring were away at school. His only son had died, with his mother, just twenty-four hours after birth. Although he could now hardly recall his wife's face except in dreams, the picture of those waxen, doll-like features above the tiny swathed body, the gummed eyelids, the secret look of self-absorbed peace was so clear and immediate that he sometimes wondered whether the image was really that of his child, so briefly but intently regarded, or whether he had taken into himself a prototype of dead childhood. His son would now be older than this child, would be entering the traumatic years of adolescence. He had convinced himself long ago that he was glad to have been spared them.

But now it suddenly occurred to him that there was a whole territory of human experience on which, once repulsed, he had turned his back, and that this rejection somehow diminished him as a man. This transitory ache of loss surprised him by its intensity. He forced himself to consider a sensation so unfamiliar and unwelcome. Suddenly the child smiled at him and held out the ball. The effect was disconcertingly flattering as when a stray cat would stalk towards him, tail erect, and condescend to be stroked. They gazed at each other. Dalgliesh smiled back. Then Massingham sprang forward and whipped the ball from the chubby hands.

'Come on. Football!'

He began dribbling the blue and yellow ball across the lawn. Immediately the sturdy legs followed. The two of them disappeared round the side of the house and Dalgliesh could hear the boy's high, cracked laughter. The girl gazed after them, her face suddenly pinched with loving anxiety. She turned to Dalgliesh.

'I hope he knows not to kick it into the bonfire. It's almost out, but the embers are still very hot. I've been burning rubbish.'

'Don't worry. He's a careful chap. And he's got younger brothers.'

She regarded him carefully for the first time.

'You're Commander Dalgliesh aren't you? We're Nell and William Kerrison. I'm afraid my father isn't here.'

'I know. We've come to see your housekeeper, Miss Willard, isn't it? Is she in?'

'I shouldn't take any notice of anything she says if I were you. She's a dreadful liar. And she steals Daddy's drink. Don't you want to question William and me?'

'A policewoman will be coming with us to talk to you both, sometime, when your father's at home.'

'I won't see her. I don't mind talking to you, but I won't see a policewoman. I don't like social workers.'

'A policewoman isn't a social worker.'

'She's the same. She makes judgements on people, doesn't she? We had a social worker here after my mother left, before the custody case, and she looked at William and me as if we were a public nuisance which someone had left on her doorstep. She went round the house too, poking into things, pretending to admire, making out it was just a social visit.'

'Policewomen – and policemen – never pretend that they're just paying a social visit. No one would believe us, would they?'

They turned and walked together towards the house. The girl said:

'Are you going to discover who killed Dr Lorrimer?'

'I hope so. I expect so.'

'And then what will happen to him, the murderer, I mean?'

'He'll appear before the magistrates. Then, if they think that the evidence is sufficient, they'll commit him to the Crown Court for trial.'

'And then?'

'If he's found guilty of murder, the judge will pass the statutory penalty, imprisonment for life. That means that he'll be in prison for a long time, perhaps ten years or more.'

'But that's silly. That won't put things right. It won't bring Dr Lorrimer back.'

'It won't put anything right, but it isn't silly. Life is precious to nearly all of us. Even people who have little more than life still want to live it to the last natural moment. No one has a right to take it away from them.'

'You talk as if life were like William's ball. If that's taken away he knows what he's lost. Dr Lorrimer doesn't know that he's lost anything.'

'He's lost the years he might have had.'

'That's like taking away the ball that William might have had. It doesn't mean anything. It's just words. Suppose he was going to die next week anyway. Then he'd only have lost seven days. You don't put someone in prison for ten years to repay seven lost days. They might not even have been happy days.'

'Even if he were a very old man with one day left to him, the law says that he has a right to live it. Wilful killing would still be murder.'

The girl said thoughtfully:

'I suppose it was different when people believed in God. Then the murdered person might have died in mortal sin and gone to hell. The seven days could have made a difference then. He might have repented and had time for absolution.'

Dalgliesh said:

'All these problems are easier for people who believe in God. Those of us who don't or can't have to do the best we can. That's what the law is, the best we can do. Human justice is imperfect, but it's the only justice we have.'

'Are you sure you don't want to question me? I know that Daddy didn't kill him. He isn't a murderer. He was at home with William and me when Dr Lorrimer died. We put William to bed together at half past seven and then we stayed with him for twenty minutes and Daddy read Paddington Bear to him. Then I went to bed because I'd got a headache and wasn't feeling well, and Daddy brought me up a mug of cocoa which he'd made specially for me. He sat by me reading poetry from my school anthology until he thought I'd gone to sleep. But I hadn't really. I was just pretending. He crept away just before nine, but I was still awake then. Shall I tell you how I know?'

'If you want to.'

'Because I heard the church clock strike. Then Daddy left me and I lay there in the dark, just thinking. He came back to look in at me again about half an hour later, but I still pretended to be asleep. So that lets Daddy out, doesn't it?'

'We don't know exactly when Dr Lorrimer died but, yes, I think it probably does.'

'Unless I'm telling you a lie.'

'People very often do lie to the police. Are you?'

'No. But I expect I would if I thought it would save Daddy. I don't care about Dr Lorrimer, you see. I'm glad he's dead. He wasn't a nice man. The day before he died William and I went to the Lab to see Daddy. He was lecturing in the morning to the detective training course and we thought we'd call for him before lunch. Inspector Blakelock let us sit in the hall, and that girl who helps him at the desk, the pretty one, smiled at William and offered him an apple from her lunch box. And then Dr Lorrimer came down the stairs and saw us. I know it was he because the Inspector spoke to him by his name and he said: "What are those children doing in here? A lab isn't a place for children." I said: "I'm not a child. I'm Miss Eleanor Kerrison and this is my brother William, and we're waiting for our father." He stared at us as if he hated us, his face white and twitching. He said: "Well, you can't wait here." Then he spoke very unkindly to Inspector Blakelock. After Dr Lorrimer had gone, he said we'd better go but he told William not to mind and took a sweet out of his left ear. Did you know that the Inspector was a conjurer?'

'No. I didn't know that.'

'Would you like to see round the house before I take you to Miss Willard? Do you like seeing houses?'

'Very much, but I think perhaps not now.'

'See the drawing-room anyway. It's much the best room. There now, isn't it lovely?'

The drawing-room was in no sense lovely. It was a sombre, oak-panelled, over-furnished room which looked as if little had changed since the days when the bombazine-clad wife and daughters of the Victorian rector sat there piously occupied with their parish sewing. The mullioned windows, framed by dark red, dirt-encrusted curtains, effectively excluded most of the daylight so that Dalgliesh stepped into a sombre chilliness which the sluggish fire did nothing to dispel. An immense mahogany table, bearing a jam-jar of chrysanthemums, stood against the far wall and the fireplace, an ornate edifice of marble, was almost hidden by two immense, saggy armchairs and a dilapidated sofa. Eleanor said with unexpected formality, as if the room had recalled her to her duty as a hostess:

'I try to keep at least one room nice in case we have visitors. The flowers are pretty, aren't they? William arranged them. Please sit down. Can I get you some coffee?'

'That would be pleasant, but I don't think we ought to wait. We're really here to see Miss Willard.'

Massingham and William appeared in the doorway, flushed with their exercise, William with the ball tucked under his left arm. Eleanor led the way through a brass-studded, green baize door and down a stone passage to the back of the house. William, deserting Massingham, trotted behind her, his plump hand clutching ineffectively at the skin-tight jeans. Pausing outside a door of unpolished oak, she said:

'She's in here. She doesn't like William and me to go in. Anyway, she smells, so we don't.'

And taking William by the hand, she left them.

Dalgliesh knocked. There was a rapid scrabbling noise inside the room, like an animal disturbed in its lair, and then the door was opened slightly and a dark and suspicious eye looked out at them through the narrow aperture. Dalgliesh said:

'Miss Willard? Commander Dalgliesh and Inspector Massingham from the Metropolitan Police. We're investigating Dr Lorrimer's murder. May we come in?'

The eye softened. She gave a short, embarrassed gasp, rather like a snort, and opened the door wide.

'Of course. Of course. What must you think of me? I'm afraid I'm still in what my dear old nurse used to call my disabilly. But I wasn't expecting you, and I usually have a quiet moment to myself about this time of the morning.'

Eleanor was right, the room did smell. A smell, Massingham diagnosed after a cautious sniff, composed of sweet sherry, unfresh body linen and cheap scent. It was very hot. A small blue flame licked the red-hot ovals of coal briquettes banked high in the Victorian grate. The window, which gave a view of the garage and the wilderness which was the back garden, was open for only an inch at the top despite the mildness of the day, and the air in the room pressed down on them, furred and heavy as a soiled blanket. The room itself had a dreadful and perverse femininity. Everything looked moistly soft, the cretonne-covered seats of the two arm-chairs, the plump row of cushions along the back of a Victorian chaise-longue, the imitation fur rug before the fire. The mantelshelf was cluttered with photographs in silver frames, mostly of a cassocked clergyman and his wife, whom Dalgliesh took to be Miss Willard's parents, standing side by side but oddly dissociated outside a variety of rather dull churches. Pride of place was held by a studio photograph of Miss Willard herself, young, toothily coy, the thick hair in corrugated waves. On a wall shelf to the right of the door was a small wood-carving of an armless Madonna with the laughing Child perched on her shoulder. A night-light in a saucer was burning at her feet, casting a soft glow over the tender drooping head and the sightless eyes. Dalgliesh thought that it was probably a copy, and a good one, of a medieval museum piece. Its gentle beauty emphasized the tawdriness of the room, yet dignified it, seeming to say that there was more than one kind of human loneliness, human pain, and that the same mercy embraced them all.

Miss Willard waved them to the chaise-longue.

'My own little den,' she said gaily. 'I like to be private, you know. I explained to Dr Kerrison that I could only consider coming if I had my privacy. It's a rare and beautiful thing, don't you think? The human spirit wilts without it.'

Looking at her hands, Dalgliesh thought that she was probably in her middle forties, although her face looked older. The dark hair, dry and coarse and tightly curled, was at odds with her faded complexion. Two sausages of curls over the brow suggested that she had hurriedly snatched out the rollers when she heard their knock.

But her face was already made up. There was a circle of rouge under each eye and the lipstick had seeped into the creases pursing her mouth. Her small, square, bony jaw was loose as a marionette's. She was not yet fully dressed and a padded dressing-gown of flowered nylon, stained with tea and what looked like egg, was corded over a nylon nightdress in bright blue with a grubby frill round the neck. Massingham was fascinated by a bulbous fold of limp cotton just above her shoes, from which he found it difficult to avert his eyes, until he realized that she had put on her stockings back to front.

She said:

'You want to talk to me about Dr Kerrison's alibi, I expect. Of course, it's quite ridiculous that he should have to provide one, a man so gentle, totally incapable of violence. But I can help you, as it happens. He was certainly at home until after nine, and I saw him again less than an hour later. But all this is just a waste of time. You bring a great reputation with you, Commander, but this is one crime which science can't solve. Not for nothing are they called the black fens. All through the centuries, evil has come out of this dank soil. We can fight evil, Commander, but not with your weapons.'

Massingham said:

'Well, suppose we begin by giving our weapons a chance.'

She looked at him and smiled pityingly.

'But all the doors were locked. All your clever scientific aids were intact. No one broke in, and no one could have got out. And yet he was struck down. That was no human hand, Inspector.'

Dalgliesh said:

'It was almost certainly a blunt weapon, Miss Willard, and I've no doubt there was a human hand at the end of it. It's our job to find out whose, and I hope that you may be able to help us. You housekeep for Dr Kerrison and his daughter, I believe?'

Miss Willard disposed on him a glance in which pity at such ignorance was mixed with gentle reproof.

'I'm not a housekeeper, Commander. Certainly not a house-keeper. Shall we say that I'm a working house-guest. Dr Kerrison needed someone to live in so that the children weren't left alone when he was called out to a murder scene. They're children of a broken marriage, I'm afraid. The old, sad story. You are not married, Commander?'

'No.'

'How wise.' She sighed, conveying in the sibilant release of breath infinite yearning, infinite regret. Dalgliesh persevered:

'So you live completely separately?'

'My own little quarters. This sitting-room and a bedroom next door. My own small kitchenette through this door here. I won't show it to you now because it's not quite as I should like it to be.'

'What precisely are the domestic arrangements, Miss Willard?'

'They get their own breakfast. The Doctor usually lunches at the hospital, of course; Nell and William have something on a tray when she bothers to prepare it, and I look after myself. Then I cook a little something for everyone in the evenings, quite simple, we're none of us large eaters. We eat very early because of William. It's more a high tea really. Nell and her father do all the cooking during the weekend. It really works out quite well.'

Quite well for you, thought Massingham. Certainly William had seemed sturdy and well-nourished enough, but the girl looked as if she ought to be at school, not struggling, almost unaided, with this isolated and cheerless monstrosity of a house. He wondered how she got on with Miss Willard. As if reading his thoughts, Miss Willard said:

'William is a sweet little boy. Absolutely no trouble. I hardly see him really. But Nell is difficult, very difficult. Girls of her age usually are. She needs a mother's firm hand. You know, of course, that Mrs Kerrison walked out on her husband a year ago? She ran away with one of his colleagues at the hospital. It broke him up completely. Now she's trying to get the High Court to reverse the custody order and give her the children when the divorce is heard in a month's time, and I'm sure it'll be a good thing if they do. Children ought to be with their mother. Not that Nell's a child any longer. It's the boy they're fighting over, not Nell. If you ask me, neither of them cares about her. She gives her father a terrible time of it. Nightmares, screaming attacks, asthma. He's going to London next Monday for a three-day conference on forensic pathology. I'm afraid she'll make him pay for that little jaunt when he gets back. Neurotic, you know. Punishing him for loving her brother more, although, of course, he can't see that.'

Dalgliesh wondered by what mental process she had arrived at that glib psychological assessment. Not, he thought, that it was necessarily wrong. He felt profoundly sorry for Kerrison.

Suddenly Massingham felt sick. The warmth and feculent smell of the room overpowered him. A blob of cold sweat dropped on his notebook. Muttering an apology, he strode over to the window and tugged at the frame. It resisted for a moment then slammed down. Great draughts of cool reviving air poured in. The frail light before the carved Madonna flickered and went out.

When he got back to his notebook, Dalgliesh was already asking about the previous evening. Miss Willard said that she had cooked a meal of minced beef, potatoes and frozen peas for supper, with a blancmange to follow. She had washed up alone and had then gone to say goodnight to the family before returning to her sitting-room. They were then in the drawing-room, but Dr Kerrison and Nell were about to take William up to bed. She had seen and heard nothing else of the family until just after nine o'clock when she had gone to check that the front door was bolted. Dr Kerrison was sometimes careless about locking up and didn't always appreciate how nervous she felt, sleeping alone and on the ground floor. One read such terrible stories. She had passed the study door, which was ajar, and had heard Dr Kerrison speaking on the telephone. She had returned to her sitting-room and had switched on the television.

Dr Kerrison had looked in shortly before ten o'clock to talk to her about a small increase in her salary, but they had been interrupted by a telephone call. He had returned ten minutes or so later and they had been together for about half an hour. It had been pleasant to have the opportunity of a private chat without the children butting in. Then he had said goodnight and left her. She had switched on the television again and had watched it until nearly midnight, when she had gone to bed. If Dr Kerrison had taken out the car, she felt fairly sure that she would have heard it since her sitting-room window looked out at the garage which was built at the side of the house. Well, they could see that for themselves.

She had overslept the next morning and hadn't breakfasted until after nine. She had been woken by the telephone ringing, but it hadn't been until Dr Kerrison returned from the Laboratory that she knew about Dr Lorrimer's murder. Dr Kerrison had returned briefly to the house shortly after nine o'clock to tell her and Nell what had happened and to ring the hospital to say that any calls for him should be transferred to the reception desk at the Laboratory.

Dalgliesh said:

'I believe Dr Lorrimer used to drive you to eleven o'clock service at St Mary's at Guy's Marsh. He seems to have been a solitary and not a very happy man. No one seems to have known him well. I was wondering whether he found in you the companionship and friendship he seems to have lacked in his working life.'

Massingham looked up, curious to see her response to this blatant invitation to self-revelation. She hooded her eyes like a bird, while a red blotch spread like a contagion over her throat. She said, with an attempt at archness:

'Now I'm afraid you're teasing me, Commander. It is Commander, isn't it? It seems so odd, just like a naval rank. My late brother-in-law was in the navy, so I know a little of these matters. But you were talking of friendship. That implies confidence. I should like to have helped him, but he wasn't easy to know. And there was the age difference. I'm not so very much older, less than five years, I suppose. But it's a great deal to a comparatively young man. No, I'm afraid we were just two reprobate High Anglicans in this Evangelical swampland. We didn't even sit together in church. I've always sat in the third pew down from the pulpit and he liked to be right at the back.'

Dalgliesh persisted:

'But he must have enjoyed your company. He called for you every Sunday, didn't he?'

'Only because Father Gregory asked him. There is a bus to Guy's Marsh, but I have to wait half an hour and, as Dr Lorrimer drove past the Old Rectory, Father Gregory suggested that it would be a sensible arrangement if we travelled together. He never came in. I was always ready and waiting for him outside the drive. If his father was ill or he himself was out on a case, he'd telephone. Sometimes he wasn't able to let me know, which was inconvenient. But I knew that if he didn't drive up at twenty to eleven he wouldn't be coming, and then I'd set off for the bus. Usually, of course, he came, except during the first six months of this year when he gave up Mass. But he rang early in September to say that he would be stopping for me as he used to. Naturally I never questioned him about the break. One does go through these dark nights of the soul.'

So he had stopped going to Mass when the affair with Domenica Schofield began, and had resumed his churchgoing after the break. Dalgliesh asked:

'Did he take the Sacrament?'

She was unsurprised by the question.

'Not since he started coming to Mass again in mid-September. It worried me a little, I confess. I did wonder whether to suggest to him that if anything was troubling him he should have a talk with Father Gregory. But one is on very delicate ground. And it really wasn't any concern of mine.'

And she wouldn't want to offend him, thought Massingham. Those lifts in the car must have been very convenient. Dalgliesh asked:

'So he did very occasionally telephone you. Have you ever rung him?'

She turned away and fussed herself plumping up a cushion.

'Dear me, no! Why should I? I don't even know his number.'

Massingham said:

'It seems odd that he went to church at Guy's Marsh instead of in the village.'

Miss Willard looked at him severely.

'Not at all. Mr Swaffield is a very worthy man, but he's Low, very Low. The fens have always been strongly Evangelical. When my dear father was rector here, he had constant fights with the Parochial Church Council over Reservation. And then I think that Dr Lorrimer didn't want to get drawn into church and village activities. It's so difficult not to once you're known as a regular member of the congregation. Father Gregory didn't expect that; he realized that Dr Lorrimer had his own father to care for and a very demanding job. Incidentally, I was very distressed that the police didn't call for Father Gregory. Someone should have called a priest to the body.'

Dalgliesh said gently:

'He had been dead some hours when the body was discovered, Miss Willard.'

'Even so, he should have had a priest.'

She stood up as if signifying that the interview was at an end. Dalgliesh was glad enough to go. He said his formal thanks and asked Miss Willard to get in touch with him immediately if anything of interest occurred to her. He and Massingham were at the door when she suddenly called out imperiously:

'Young man!'

The two detectives turned to look at her. She spoke directly to Massingham, like an old-fashioned nurse admonishing a child:

'Would you please shut the window which you so inconsiderately opened, and relight the candle.'

Meekly, as if in obedience to long-forgotten nursery commands, Massingham did so. They were left to find their own way out of the house and saw no one. When they were in the car fastening their seat-belts, Massingham exploded:

'Good God, you'd think Kerrison could find someone more suitable than that old hag to care for his children. She's a slut, a dipsomaniac, and she's half-mad.'

'It's not so simple for Kerrison. A remote village, a large, cold house, and a daughter who can't be easy to cope with. Faced with the choice of that kind of job and the dole, most women today would probably opt for the dole. Did you take a look at the bonfire?'

'Nothing there. It looks as if they're periodically burning a lot of old furniture and garden rubbish which they've got stacked in one of the coach-houses. William said that Nell made a bonfire early this morning.'

'William can talk, then?' Dalgliesh asked.

'Oh William can talk. But I'm not sure that you'd be able to understand him, sir. Did you believe Miss Willard when she gave that alibi for Kerrison?.

'I'm as ready to believe her as I am Mrs Bradley or Mrs Blakelock when they confirmed Bradley's and Blakelock's alibis. Who can tell? We know that Kerrison did ring Dr Collingwood at nine and was here to receive his return call at about ten. If Miss Willard sticks to her story, he's in the clear for that hour, and I've a feeling that it's the crucial hour. But how did he know that? And if he did, why suppose that we should be able to pin down the time of death so precisely? Sitting with his daughter until nine and then calling on Miss Willard just before ten looks very like an attempt to establish that he was at home during the whole of that hour.'

Massingham said:

'He must have been, to take that ten o'clock call. And I don't see how he could have got to Hoggatt's, killed Lorrimer and returned home in less than sixty minutes, not if he went on foot. And Miss Willard seems confident that he didn't take the car. I suppose it would just be possible if he took a short cut through the new Laboratory, but it would be a close thing,'

Just then the car radio bleeped. Dalgliesh took the call. It was from the Guy's Marsh control room to say that Sergeant Reynolds at the Lab wanted to contact them. The Met Lab report had been received.

4

They opened the door together. Mrs Bradley held a sleeping child in her arms. Bradley said:

'Come in. It's about the vomit, isn't it? I've been expecting you.'

They moved into the sitting-room. He gestured Dalgliesh and Massingham to the two chairs and sat down on the sofa opposite them. His wife moved close to him, shifting the baby's weight against her shoulder. Dalgliesh asked:

'Do you want a solicitor?'

'No. Not yet, anyway. I'm ready to tell the whole truth and it can't hurt me. At least, I suppose it can lose me my job. But that's the worst it can do. And I think I'm almost beyond caring.'

Massingham opened his notebook. Dalgliesh said to Susan Bradley:

'Wouldn't you like to put the baby in her pram, Mrs Bradley?'

She gazed at Dalgliesh with blazing eyes, and shook her head vehemently, holding the child more tightly as if she expected them to tear her from her arms. Massingham was grateful that, at least, the child was asleep. But he wished that neither she nor her mother were there. He looked at the baby, bunched in her pink sleeping suit against her mother's shoulder, the fringe of longer hair above the tender hollowed neck, the round bare patch at the back of the head, the close-shut eyes and ridiculous, snubbed nose. The frail mother with her milky bundle was more inhibiting than a whole firm of recalcitrant anti-police lawyers.

There was a lot to be said for bundling a suspect into the back of a police car and taking him off to the station to make his statement in the functional anonymity of the interrogation room. Even the Bradleys' sitting-room provoked in him a mixture of irritation and pity. It still smelt new and unfinished. There was no fireplace, and the television held pride of place above the wall-mounted electric heater with, above it, a popular print of waves dashing against a rocky shore. The wall opposite had been papered to match the flowered curtains, but the other three were bare, the plaster already beginning to crack. There was a metal baby's high chair and, underneath it, a spread of plastic sheeting to protect the carpet. Everything looked new, as if they had brought to their marriage no accumulation of small personal impedimenta, had come spiritually naked into possession of this small, characterless room. Dalgliesh said:

'We'll take it that your previous account of your movements on Wednesday night wasn't true, or was incomplete. So what did happen?'

Massingham wondered for a moment why Dalgliesh wasn't cautioning Bradley; then he thought he knew. Bradley might have had the guts to kill if provoked beyond endurance, but he'd never have had the nerve to drop from that third-floor window. And if he didn't, how did he get out of the Laboratory? Lorrimer's killer had either used the keys or he had made that climb. All their investigations, all their careful and repeated examination of the building had confirmed that hypothesis. There was no other way.

Bradley looked at his wife. She gave him a brief, transforming smile and held out her free hand. He clasped it and they edged closer. He moistened his lips, and then began speaking as if the speech had been long rehearsed.

'On Tuesday Dr Lorrimer finished writing my annual confidential report. He told me he wanted to talk to me about it next day before he passed it to Dr Howarth, and he called me into his private room soon after he arrived in the Lab. He'd given me an adverse report and, according to the rules, he had to explain why. I wanted to defend myself, but I couldn't. And there wasn't any real privacy. I felt that the whole Laboratory knew what was happening and was listening and waiting. Besides, I was so frightened of him. I don't know why exactly. I can't explain it. He had such an effect on me that he'd only have to be working close to me in the Laboratory and I'd start shaking. When he was away at a scene of crime it was like heaven. I could work perfectly well then. The annual confidential report wasn't unjust. I knew that my work had deteriorated. But he was partly the reason why. He seemed to take my inadequacy as a personal denigration of himself. Poor work was intolerable to him.

He was obsessed by my mistakes. And because I was so terrified, I made them all the more.'

He paused for a moment. No one spoke. Then he went on:

'We weren't going to the village concert because we couldn't get a baby-sitter, and anyway, Sue's mother was coming for supper. I got home just before six. After the meal – the curry and rice and peas – I saw her off on the seven forty-five bus. I came straight back here. But I kept thinking of the adverse report, what Dr Howarth would say, what I was going to do if he recommended a move, how we could possibly sell this house. We had to buy when prices were at their peak, and it's almost impossible to find buyers now, except at a loss. Besides, I didn't think another lab would want me. After a time I thought I'd go back to the Laboratory and confront him. I think I had some idea that we might be able to communicate, that I could speak to him as another human being and make him understand how I felt. Anyway, I felt that I would go mad if I stayed indoors. I had to walk somewhere, and I walked towards Hoggatt's. I didn't tell Sue what I was going to do, and she tried to persuade me not to go out. But I went.'

He looked up at Dalgliesh and said:

'Can I have a drink of water?'

Without a word, Massingham got up and went to find the kitchen. He couldn't see the glasses, but there were two washed cups on the draining-board. He filled one with cold water and brought it back to Bradley. Bradley drained it. He drew his hand over his moist mouth and went on:

'I didn't see anyone on the way to the Laboratory. People don't walk out in this village much after dark, and I suppose most of them were at the concert. There was a light on in the hall of the Laboratory. I rang the bell and Lorrimer came. He seemed surprised to see me but I said I wanted to speak to him. He looked at his watch and said he could only spare me five minutes. I followed him up to the Biology Lab.'

He looked across directly at Dalgliesh. He said:

'It was a strange sort of interview. I sensed that he was impatient and wanted to get rid of me, and part of the time I thought that he hardly listened to what I was saying, or even knew that I was there. I didn't make a good job of it. I tried to explain that I wasn't being careless on purpose, that I really liked the work and wanted to make a success of it and be a credit to the Department. I tried to explain the effect he had on me. I don't know whether he was listening. He stood there with his eyes fixed to the floor.

'And then he looked up and began speaking. He didn't really look at me, he was looking through me, almost as if I wasn't there. And he was saying things, terrible things, as if they were words in a play, nothing to do with me. I kept hearing the same words over and over again. Failure. Useless. Hopeless. Inadequate. He even said something about marriage, as if I were a sexual failure too. I think he was mad. I can't explain what it was like, all this hate pouring out, hate, and misery and despair. I stood there shaking with this stream of words pouring over me as if . . . as if it were filth. And then his eyes focused on me and I knew that he was seeing me, me, Clifford Bradley. His voice sounded quite different. He said:

' "You're a third-rate biologist and fourth-rate forensic scientist. That's what you were when you came into this Department and you'll never change. I have two alternatives, to check every one of your results or to risk the Service and this Laboratory being discredited in the courts. Neither is tolerable. So I suggest that you look for another job. And now I've things to do, so please leave."

'He turned his back on me and I went out. I knew that it was impossible. It would have been better not to have come. He'd never told me before exactly what he thought of me, not in those words, anyway. I felt sick and miserable, and I knew I was crying. That made me despise myself the more. I stumbled upstairs to the men's cloakroom and was just able to reach the first basin before I vomited. I don't remember how long I stood there, leaning over the basin, half crying and half vomiting. I suppose it could have been three or four minutes. After a time I put on the cold tap and swilled my face. Then I tried to pull myself together. But I was still shaking, and I still felt sick. I went and sat on one of the lavatory seats and sank my head in my hands.

'I don't know how long I was there. Ten minutes perhaps, but it could have been longer. I knew I could never change his opinion of me, never make him understand. He wasn't like a human being. I realized that he hated me. But now I began to hate him and in a different way. I'd have to leave; I knew he'd see to that. But at least I could tell him what I thought of him. I could behave like a man. So I went down the stairs and into the Biology Laboratory.'

Again he paused. The child stirred in her mother's arms and gave a little cry in her sleep. Susan Bradley began an automatic jogging and crooning, but kept her eyes on her husband. Then Bradley went on:

'He was lying between the two middle examination tables, face downwards. I didn't wait to see whether he was dead. I know that I ought to feel dreadful about that, about the fact that I left him without getting help. But I don't. I can't make myself feel sorry. But at the time I wasn't glad that he was dead. I wasn't aware of any feeling except terror. I hurled myself downstairs and out of the Laboratory as if his murderer were after me. The door was still on the Yale and I know that I must have drawn back the bottom bolt, but I can't remember. I raced down the drive. I think there was a bus passing, but it had started up before I reached the gate. When I got into the road it was disappearing. Then I saw a car approaching and, instinctively, I stood back into the shadows of the walls. The car slowed down and turned into the Laboratory drive. Then I made myself walk slowly and normally. And the next thing I remember was being home.'

Susan Bradley spoke for the first time:

'Clifford told me all about it. But, of course, he had to. He looked so terrible that I knew something awful must have happened. We decided together what we'd better do. We knew that he'd had nothing to do with what had happened to Dr Lorrimer. But who would believe Cliff? Everyone in the Department knew what Dr Lorrimer thought of him. He would be bound to be suspected anyway, and if you found out that he was there, in the Laboratory, and at the very moment it happened, then how could he hope to persuade you that he wasn't guilty? So we decided to say that we'd been together the whole evening. My mother did ring about nine o'clock to say that she'd got safely home, and I told her that Cliff was having a bath. She'd never really liked my marriage and I didn't want to admit to her that he was out. She'd only start criticizing him for leaving me and the baby. So we knew that she could confirm what I'd said, and that might be some help, even though she hadn't spoken to him. And then Cliff remembered about the vomit.'

Her husband went on, almost eagerly now, as if willing them to understand and believe:

'I knew I'd swilled cold water over my face, but I couldn't be certain that the bowl was clean. The more I thought about it, the more sure I was that it was stained with vomit. And I knew how much you could learn from that. I'm a secreter, but that didn't worry me. I knew that the stomach acids would destroy the antibodies and that the Lab wouldn't be able to determine my blood group. But there was the curry powder, the dye in the peas. They'd be able to say enough about that last meal to identify me. And I couldn't lie about what we'd had for supper because Sue's mother had been here sharing it with us.

'So we had this idea of trying to stop Mrs Bidwell going early to the Laboratory. I always get to work before nine, so I would be first on the scene quite naturally. If I went straight to the washroom as I normally would, and cleaned the bowl, then the only evidence that I was in the Lab the previous evening would be gone for ever. No one would ever know.'

Susan Bradley said:

'It was my idea to phone Mrs Bidwell, and I was the one who spoke to her husband. We knew that she wouldn't answer the phone. She never did. But Cliff hadn't realized that old Mr Lorrimer wasn't entering hospital the previous day. He was out of the Department when old Mr Lorrimer rang. So the plan went all wrong. Mr Lorrimer telephoned Inspector Blakelock, and everyone arrived at the Lab almost as soon as Cliff. After that, there was nothing we could do but wait.'

Dalgliesh could imagine how terrible that time of waiting had been. No wonder that Bradley hadn't been able to face going in to the Lab. He asked:

'When you rang the bell at the Laboratory, how long was it before Dr Lorrimer answered?'

'Almost immediately. He couldn't have come down from the Biology Department. He must have been somewhere on the ground floor.'

'Did he say anything at all about expecting a visitor?'

The temptation was obvious. But Bradley said:

'No. He talked about having things to do, but I took it that he meant the analysis he was working on.'

'And when you found the body, you saw and heard nothing of the murderer?'

'No. I didn't wait to look, of course. But I'm sure he was there and very close. I don't know why.'

'Did you notice the position of the mallet, the fact that there was a page torn from Lorrimer's notebook?'

'No. Nothing. All I can remember is Lorrimer, the body and the thin stream of blood.'

'When you were in the washroom, did you hear the doorbell?'

'No, but I don't think I could have heard it, not above the first floor. And I'm sure I wouldn't have heard it while I was being sick.'

'When Dr Lorrimer opened the door to you, did anything strike you as unusual, apart from the fact that he had come so promptly?'

'Nothing, except that he was carrying his notebook.'

'Are you quite sure?'

'Yes, I'm sure. It was folded back.'

So Bradley's arrival had interrupted whatever it was that Lorrimer had been doing. And he had been on the ground floor, the floor with the Director's office, the Records Department, the Exhibits Store.

Dalgliesh said:

'The car which turned into the drive as you left; what sort of car?'

'I didn't see. All I can remember are the headlights. We don't have a car and I'm not clever at recognizing the different models unless I get a clear look.'

'Can you remember how it was driven? Did the driver turn into the drive confidently as if he knew where he was going? Or did he hesitate as if he were looking for a convenient spot to stop and happened to see the open driveway?'

'He just slowed down a little and drove straight in. I think it was someone who knew the place. But I didn't wait to see if he drove up to the Lab. Next day, of course, I knew that it couldn't have been the police from Guy's Marsh or anyone with a key, or the body would have been discovered earlier.'

He looked at Dalgliesh with his anxious eyes.

'What will happen to me now? I can't face them at the Lab.'

'Inspector Massingham will drive you to Guy's Marsh police station so that you can make a formal statement and sign it. I'll explain to Dr Howarth what has happened. Whether you go back to the Lab and when must be for him and your Establishment Department to say. I imagine they may decide to give you special leave until this affair is settled.'

If it ever was settled. If Bradley was telling the truth, they now knew that Lorrimer had died between eight forty-five, when his father had telephoned him, and just before nine-eleven when the Guy's Marsh bus had moved away from the Chevisham stop. The clue of the vomit had fixed for them the time of death, had solved the mystery of the call to Mrs Bidwell. But it hadn't pointed them to a murderer. And if Bradley were innocent, what sort of life would he have, inside or outside the forensic science service, unless the case were solved? He watched Massingham and Bradley on their way, then set out to walk the half-mile back to Hoggatt's, not relishing the prospect of his interview with Howarth. Glancing back, he saw that Susan Bradley was still standing at the doorway looking after him, her baby in her arms.

5

Howarth said:

'I'm not going to trot out the usual platitude about blaming myself. I don't believe in that spurious acceptance of vicarious liability. All the same, I ought to have known that Bradley was near breaking-point. I suspect that old Dr MacIntyre wouldn't have let this happen. And now I'd better telephone the Establishment Department. I expect they'll want him to stay at home for the present. It's particularly inconvenient from the point of view of the work. They need every pair of hands they can get in the Biology Department. Claire Easterbrook is taking on as much of Lorrimer's work as she can manage, but there's a limit to what she can do. At the moment she's busy with the clunch-pit analysis. She's insisting on starting the electrophoresis again. I don't blame her; she's the one who'll have to give evidence. She can only speak for her own results.'

Dalgliesh asked what was likely to happen about Clifford Bradley.

'Oh, there'll be a regulation to cover the circumstances somewhere. There always is. He'll be dealt with by the usual compromise between expediency and humanity; unless, of course, you propose to arrest him for murder, in which case, administratively speaking, the problem will solve itself. By the way, the Public Relations Branch have rung. You probably haven't had time to see today's Press.

Some of the papers are getting rather agitated about lab security. "Are our blood samples safe?" And one of the Sundays has commissioned an article on science in the service of crime. They're sending someone to see me at three o'clock. Public Relations would like a word with you, incidentally. They're hoping to lay on another press conference later this afternoon.'

When Howarth had left, Dalgliesh joined Sergeant Underhill and occupied himself with the four large bundles of files which Brenda Pridmore had provided. It was extraordinary how many of six thousand cases and nearly twenty-five thousand exhibits which the Laboratory dealt with each year, had the numbers 18, 40 or 1840 in their registration. The cases came from all the departments; Biology, Toxicology, Criminalistics, Document Examination, Blood Alcohol Analysis, Vehicle Examination. Nearly every scientist in the Laboratory above the level of Higher Scientific Officer had been concerned in them. All of them seemed perfectly in order. He was still convinced that the mysterious telephone message to Lorrimer held the clue to the mystery of his death. But it seemed increasingly unlikely that the numbers, if old Mr Lorrimer had remembered them correctly, bore any reference to a file registration.

By three o'clock he had decided to put the task on one side and see if physical exercise would stimulate his brain. It was time, he thought, to walk through the grounds and take a look at the Wren chapel. He was reaching for his coat when the telephone rang. It was Massingham from Guy's Marsh station. The car which had parked in Hoggatt's drive on Wednesday night had at last been traced. It was a grey Cortina belonging to a Mrs Maureen Doyle. Mrs Doyle was at present staying with her parents in Ilford in Essex, but she had confirmed that the car was hers and that on the night of the murder it had been driven by her husband, Detective-Inspector Doyle.

6

The interview room at Guy's Marsh police station was small, stuffy and overcrowded. Superintendent Mercer, with his great bulk, was taking up more than his share of space and, it seemed to Massingham, breathing more than his share of the air. Of the five men present, including the shorthand writer, Doyle himself appeared both the most comfortable and the least concerned. Dalgliesh was questioning him. Mercer stood against the mullioned windows.

'You were at Hoggatt's last night. There are fresh tyre-marks in the earth under the trees to the right of the entrance, your tyre-marks. If you want to waste time for both us, you can look at the casts.'

'I admit that they're my tyre-marks. I parked there, briefly, on Monday night.'

'Why?'

The question was so quiet, so reasonable, he might have had a geniune human interest to know.

'I was with someone.' He paused and then added, 'Sir.'

'I hope, for your sake, that you were with someone last night. Even an embarrassing alibi is better than none. You quarrelled with Lorrimer. You're one of the few people he would have let into the Lab. And you parked your car under the trees. If you didn't murder him, why are you trying to persuade us that you did?'

'You don't really believe I killed him. Probably you already suspect or know who did. You can't frighten me, because I know you haven't any evidence. There isn't any to get. I was driving the Cortina because the clutch had gone on the Renault, not because I didn't want to be recognized. I was with Sergeant Beale until eight o'clock. We'd been to interview a man called Barry Taylor at Muddington, and then we went on to see one or two other people who'd been at the dance last Tuesday. From eight o'clock I was driving alone, and where I went was my own business.'

'Not when it's a case of murder. Isn't that what you tell your suspects when they come out with that good old bromide about the sanctity of their private lives? You can do better than that, Doyle.'

'I wasn't at the Lab on Wednesday night. Those tyre-marks were made when I parked there last Monday.'

'The Dunlop on the left-hand back wheel is new. It was fitted on Monday afternoon by Gorringe's garage, and your wife didn't collect the Cortina until ten o'clock on Wednesday morning. If you didn't drive to Hoggatt's to see Lorrimer, then what were you doing there? And if your business was legitimate, then why park just inside the entrance and under the trees?'

'If I'd been there to murder Lorrimer, I'd have parked in one of the garages at the back. That would have been safer than leaving the Cortina in the drive. And I didn't get to Hoggatt's until after nine. I knew that Lorrimer would be working late on the clunch-pit case, but not that late. The Lab was in darkness. The truth, if you must know, is that I'd picked up a woman at the crossroads just outside Manea. I wasn't in any hurry to get home, and I wanted somewhere quiet and secluded to stop. The Lab seemed as good a place as any. We were there from about nine-fifteen until nine-fifty-five. No one left during that time.'

He had taken his time over what was presumably intended to be a quick one-night lay, thought Massingham. Dalgliesh asked:

'Did you trouble to find out who she was, exchange names?'

'I told her that I was Ronny McDowell. It seemed as good a name as any. She said she was Dora Meakin. I don't suppose that more than one of us was lying.'

'And that's all, not where she lived or worked?'

'She said she worked at the sugar-beet factory and lived in a cottage near the ruined engine-house on Hunter's Fen. That's about three miles from Manea. She said she was a widow. Like a little gentleman, I dropped her at the bottom of the lane leading to Hunter's Fen. If she wasn't telling me a yarn, that should be enough to find her.'

Chief Superintendent Mercer said grimly:

'I hope for your sake that it is. You know what this means for you, of course?'

Doyle laughed. It was a surprisingly light-hearted sound.

'Oh I know, all right. But don't let that worry you. I'm handing in my resignation, and from now.'

Dalgliesh asked:

'Are you sure about the lights? The Lab was in darkness?'

'I shouldn't have stopped there if it hadn't been. There wasn't a light to be seen. And although I admit I was somewhat preoccupied for a minute or two, I could swear that no one came down that drive while we were there.'

'Or out of the front door?'

'That would be possible, I suppose. But the drive isn't more than forty yards long, I'd say. I think I'd have noticed, unless he slipped out very quickly. I doubt whether anyone would have risked it, not if he'd seen my headlights and knew that the car was there.'

Dalgliesh looked at Mercer. He said:

'We've got to get back to Chevisham. We'll take in Hunter's Fen on the way.'

7

Leaning over the back of the Victorian chaise-longue, Angela Foley was massaging her friend's neck. The coarse hairs tickled the back of her hands as, firmly and gently, she kneaded the taut muscles, feeling for each separate vertebra under the hot, tense skin. Stella sat, head slumped forward in her hands. Neither spoke. Outside, a light scavenging wind was blowing fitfully over the fens, stirring the fallen leaves on the patio, and gusting the thin, white wood-smoke from the cottage chimney. But inside the sitting-room all was quiet, except for the crackling of the fire, the ticking of the grandfather clock, and the sound of their breathing. The cottage was full of the pungent, resinous aroma of burning apple wood, overlaid with the savoury smell from the kitchen of beef casserole reheated from yesterday's dinner.

After a few minutes Angela Foley said:

'Better? Would you like a cold compress on your forehead?'

'No, that's lovely. Almost gone in fact. Odd that I only get a headache on those days when the book has gone particularly well.'

'Another two minutes, then I'd better see about dinner.'

Angela flexed her fingers and bent again to her task. Stella's voice, muffled in her sweater, suddenly said:

'What was it like as a child, being in local authority care?'

'I'm not sure that I know. I mean, I wasn't in a home or anything like that. They fostered me most of the time.'

'Well, what was that like? You've never really told me.'

'It was all right. No, that's not true. It was like living in a second-rate boarding house where they don't want you and you know that you won't be able to pay the bill. Until I met you and came here I felt like that all the time, not really at home in the world. I suppose my foster-parents were kind. They meant to be. But I wasn't pretty, and I wasn't grateful. It can't be much fun fostering other people's children, and I suppose one does rather look for gratitude. Looking back, I can see that I wasn't much joy for them, plain and surly. I

408

once heard a neighbour say to my third foster-mother that I looked just like a foetus with my bulging forehead and tiny features. I resented the other children because they had mothers and I hadn't. I've never really outgrown that. It's despicable, but I even dislike Brenda Pridmore, the new girl on our reception desk, because she's so obviously a loved child, she's got a proper home.'

'So have you now. But I know what you mean. By the age of five you've either learned that the world is good, that everything and everyone in it stretches out towards you with love. Or you know that you're a reject. No one ever unlearns that first lesson.'

'I have, because of you. Star, don't you think we ought to start looking for another cottage, perhaps nearer Cambridge? There's bound to be a job there for a qualified secretary.'

'We're not going to need another cottage. I telephoned my publishers this afternoon, and I think it's going to be all right.'

'Hearne and Collingwood? But how can it be all right? I thought you said . . .'

'It's going to be all right.'

Suddenly Stella shook herself free of the ministering hands and stood up. She went into the passage and came back, her duffel-coat over her shoulder, her boots in hand. She moved over to the fireside chair and began to pull them on. Angela Foley watched her without speaking. Then Stella took from her jacket pocket a brown opened envelope and tossed it across. It fell on the velvet of the chaise-longue.

'Oh, I meant to show you this.'

Puzzled, Angela took out the single folded sheet. She said:

'Where did you find this?'

'I took it from Edwin's desk when I was rummaging about for the will. I thought at the time that I might have a use for it. Now I've decided that I haven't.'

'But, Star, you should have left it for the police to find! It's a clue. They'll have to know. This was probably what Edwin was doing that night, checking up. It's important. We can't keep it to ourselves.'

'Then you'd better go back to Postmill Cottage and pretend to find it, otherwise it's going to be a bit embarrassing explaining how we came by it.'

'But the police aren't going to believe that; they wouldn't have missed it. I wonder when it arrived at the Lab. It's odd that he took it home with him and didn't even lock it up.'

'Why should he? There was only the one locked drawer in his desk. And I don't suppose anyone, even his father, ever went into that room.'

'But Star, this could explain why he was killed! This could be a motive for murder.'

'Oh, I don't think so. It's just a gratuitous bit of spite, anonymous, proving nothing. Edwin's death was both simpler, and more complicated, than that. Murder usually is. But the police might see it as a motive, and that would be convenient for us. I'm beginning to think I should have left it where it was.'

She had pulled on her boots and was ready to go. Angela Foley said:

'You know who killed him, don't you?'

'Does that shock you, that I haven't rushed to confide in that extraordinarily personable Commander?'

Angela whispered:

'What are you going to do?'

'Nothing. I've no proof. Let the police do the work they're paid for. I might have had more public spirit when we had the death penalty. I'm not afraid of the ghosts of hanged men. They can stand at the four corners of my bed and howl all night if it pleases them. But I couldn't go on living – I couldn't go on working, which amounts to the same thing for me – knowing that I'd put another human being in prison, and for life.'

'Not really for life. About ten years.'

'I couldn't stand it for ten days. I'm going out now. I shan't be long.'

'But, Star, it's nearly seven! We were going to eat.'

'The casserole won't spoil.'

Angela Foley watched silently as her friend went to the door. Then she said:

'Star, how did you know about Edwin practising his evidence the night before he had to go into the box?'

'If you didn't tell me, and you say that you didn't, then I must have invented it. I couldn't have learnt it from anyone else. You'd better put it down to creative imagination.'

Her hand was on the door. Angela cried out:

'Star, don't go out tonight. Stay with me. I'm afraid.'

'For yourself, or for me?'

'For both of us. Please don't go. Not tonight.'

Stella turned. She smiled and spread her hands in what could have been a gesture of resignation or a farewell. There was a howl of wind, a rush of cold air as the front door opened. Then the sound of its closing echoed through the cottage, and Stella was gone.

8

'My God, this is a dreary place!'

Massingham slammed the car door and gazed about in disbelief at the prospect before them. The lane, down which they had bumped in the fading light, had at last ended at a narrow iron bridge over a sluice, running grey and sluggish as oil, between high dykes. On the other bank was a derelict Victorian engine-house, the bricks tumbled in a disorderly heap beside the stagnant stream, the great wheel half-visible through the ruined wall. Beside it were two cottages lying below water-level. Behind them the scarred and sullen acres of the hedgeless fields stretched to the red and purple of the evening sky. The carcase of a petrified tree, a bog-oak, struck by the plough and dredged from the depths of the peat, had been dumped beside the track to dry. It looked like some mutilated prehistoric creature raising its stumps to the uncomprehending sky. Although the last two days had been dry with some sun, the landscape looked saturated by the weeks of rain, the front gardens sour and water-logged, the trunks of the few stunted trees sodden as pulp. It looked a country on which the sun could never shine. As their feet rang on the iron bridge a solitary duck rose with an agitated squawking, but otherwise the silence was absolute.

There was a light behind the drawn curtains of only one of the cottages, and they walked between windblown clumps of faded Michaelmas daisies to the front door. The paint was peeling, the iron knocker so stiff that Dalgliesh raised it with difficulty. For a few minutes after the dull peremptory thud there was silence. Then the door was opened.

They saw a drab, sallow-faced woman, aged about forty, with pale anxious eyes and untidy straw-coloured hair strained back under two combs. She was wearing a brown checked Crimplene dress topped with a bulky cardigan in a harsh shade of blue. As soon as he saw her, Massingham instinctively drew back with an apology, but Dalgliesh said:

'Mrs Meakin? We're police officers. May we come in?'

She didn't trouble to look at his proffered identity card. She hardly seemed surprised even. Without speaking she pressed herself against the wall of the passage and they passed before her into the sitting-room. It was small and very plainly furnished, drearily tidy and uncluttered. The air smelt damp and chill. There was an electric reflector fire with one bar burning, and the single pendant bulb gave a harsh but inadequate light. A plain wooden table stood in the middle of the room, with four chairs. She was obviously about to start her supper. On a tray there was a plate of three fish fingers, a mound of mashed potato and peas. Beside it was an unopened carton containing an apple tart.

Dalgliesh said:

'I'm sorry that we're interrupting your meal. Would you like to take it into the kitchen to keep it warm?' She shook her head and motioned them to sit down. They settled themselves round the table like three card-players, the tray of food between them. The peas were exuding a greenish liquid in which the fish fingers were slowly congealing. It was hard to believe that so small a meal could produce so strong a smell. After a few seconds, as if conscious of it, she pushed the tray to one side. Dalgliesh took out Doyle's photograph and passed it across to her. He said:

'I believe you spent some time yesterday evening with this man.'

'Mr McDowell. He's not in any trouble is he? You're not private detectives? He was kind, a real gentleman, I wouldn't like to get him into trouble.'

Her voice was low and rather toneless, Dalgliesh thought, a countrywoman's voice. He said:

'No, we're not private detectives. He is in some trouble, but not because of you. We're police officers. You can help him best by telling the truth. What we're really interested in is when you first met him and how long you were together.'

She looked across at him.

'You mean, a sort of alibi?'

'That's right. A sort of alibi.'

'He picked me up where I usually stand, at the crossroads, about half a mile from Manea. That must have been about seven. Then we drove to a pub. They nearly always start off by buying me a drink. That's the part I like, having someone to sit with in the pub, watching the people, hearing the voices and the noise. I usually have a sherry, or a port, maybe. If they ask me, I have a second. I never have more than two drinks. Sometimes they're in a hurry to get away so I only get offered the one.'

Dalgliesh asked quietly:

'Where did he take you?'

'I don't know where it was, but it was about thirty minutes' drive. I could see him thinking where to go before he drove off. That's how I know he lives locally. They like to get clear of the district where they're known. I've noticed that, that and the quick look round they give before we go into the pub. The pub was called the Plough. I saw that from the illuminated sign outside. We were in the saloon bar, of course, quite nice really. They had a peat fire and there was a high shelf with a lot of different coloured plates round it and two vases of artificial roses behind the bar, and a black cat in front of the fire. The barman was called Joe. He was ginger-haired.'

'How long did you stay there?'

'Not long. I had two ports and he had two doubles of whisky. Then he said we ought to be going.'

'Where did he take you next, Mrs Meakin?'

'I think it was Chevisham. I glimpsed the signpost at the cross-roads just before we got there. We turned into the drive of this big house and parked under the trees. I asked who lived there, and he said no one, it was just used for Government offices. Then he put out the lights.'

Dalgliesh said gently:

'And you made love in the car. Did you get into the back seat, Mrs Meakin?'

She was neither surprised nor distressed at the question.

'No, we stayed in the front.'

'Mrs Meakin, this is very important. Can you remember how long you were there?'

'Oh yes, I could see the clock on the dashboard. It was nearly quarter past nine when we arrived and we stayed there until just before ten. I know because I was a bit worried wondering whether he'd drop me at the end of the lane. That's all I expected. I wouldn't have wanted him to come to the door. But it can be awkward if I'm just left, miles from home. Sometimes it isn't easy to get back.'

She spoke, thought Massingham, as if she were complaining about the local bus service. Dalgliesh said:

'Did anyone leave the house and come down the drive while you were in the car? Would you have noticed if they had?'

'Oh yes, I think so. I should have seen if they'd gone out through the space where the gate used to be. There's a street-light opposite and it shines on the drive.'

Massingham asked bluntly:

'But would you have noticed? Weren't you a bit occupied?'

Suddenly she laughed, a hoarse, discordant sound which startled them both.

'Do you think I was enjoying myself? Do you suppose I like it?' Then her voice again became toneless, almost subservient. She said obdurately:

'I should have noticed.'

Dalgliesh asked:

'What did you talk about, Mrs Meakin?'

The question brightened her. She turned to Dalgliesh almost eagerly.

'Oh, he's got troubles. Everyone has, haven't they? Sometimes it helps to talk to a stranger, someone you know you won't ever see again. They never do ask to see me again. He didn't. But he was kind, not in a rush to get away. Sometimes they almost push me out of the car. That isn't gentlemanly; it's hurtful. But he seemed glad to talk. It was about his wife really. Not wanting to live in the country. She's a London girl and keeps nagging him to get back there. She wants him to leave his job and go and work for her father. She's at home with her parents now and he doesn't know whether she'll come back.'

'He didn't tell you he was a police officer?'

'Oh no! He said he was a dealer in antiques. He seemed to know quite a lot about them. But I don't take much notice when they tell me about their jobs. Mostly they pretend.'

Dalgliesh said gently:

'Mrs Meakin, what you are doing is terribly risky. You know that, don't you? Some day a man will stop who wants more than hour or so of your time, someone dangerous.'

'I know. Sometimes when the car slows down and I'm standing there waiting at the side of the road, wondering what he'll be like, I can hear my heart thudding. I know then that I'm afraid. But at least I'm feeling something. It's better to be afraid than alone.'

Massingham said:

'It's better to be alone than dead.'

She looked at him.

'You think so, sir? But then you don't know anything about it, do you?'

Five minutes later they left, having explained to Mrs Meakin that a police officer would call for her next day so that she could be taken to make a statement at Guy's Marsh station. She seemed perfectly happy about this, only asking whether anyone at the factory need know. Dalgliesh reassured her.

When they had crossed the bridge, Massingham turned to look back at the cottage. She was still standing at the door, a thin figure silhouetted against the light. He said angrily:

'God, it's all so hopeless. Why doesn't she get out of here, move to a town, Ely or Cambridge, see some life?'

'You sound like one of those professionals whose advice to the lonely is always the same: "Get out and meet people, join a club." Which, come to think of it, is precisely what she's doing.'

'It would help if she got away from this place, found herself a different job.'

'What job? She probably thinks that she's lucky to be employed. And this is at least a home. It takes youth, energy and money to change your whole life. She hasn't any of those. All she can do is to keep sane in the only way she knows.'

'But for what? To end up another corpse dumped in a clunch pit?'

'Perhaps. That's probably what she's subconsciously looking for. There's more than one way of courting death. She would argue that her way at least gives her the consolation of a warm, brightly lit bar and, always, the hope that, next time, it may be different. She isn't going to stop because a couple of intruding policemen tell her that it's dangerous. She knows that. For God's sake let's get out of here.'

As they buckled their seat belts, Massingham said:

'Who'd have thought that Doyle would have bothered with her?

I can imagine him picking her up. As Lord Chesterfield said, all cats are grey in the dark. But to spend the best part of an hour telling her his troubles.'

'They each wanted something from the other. Let's hope they got it.'

'Doyle got something; an alibi. And we haven't done too badly out of their encounter. We know now who killed Lorrimer.'

Dalgliesh said:

'We think we know who and how. We may even think we know why. But we haven't a scintilla of proof and without evidence we can't move another step. At present, we haven't even enough facts to justify applying for a search warrant.'

'What now, sir?'

'Back to Guy's Marsh. When this Doyle affair is settled I want to hear Underhill's report and speak to the Chief Constable. Then back to Hoggatt's. We'll park where Doyle parked. I'd like to check whether it would be possible for someone to sneak down that drive without being seen.'

9

By seven o'clock the work was at last up to date, the last court report had been checked, the last completed exhibit packed for the police to collect, the figures of cases and exhibits received had been calculated and checked. Brenda thought how tired Inspector Blakelock seemed. He had hardly spoken an unnecessary word during the last hour. She didn't feel that he was displeased with her, merely that he hardly knew she was there. She had talked little herself, and then in whispers, afraid to break the silence, eerie and almost palpable, of the empty hall. To her right the great staircase curved upwards into darkness. All day it had echoed to the feet of scientists, policemen, Scene of Crime officers arriving for their lecture. Now it had become as portentous and threatening as the staircase of a haunted house. She tried not to look at it, but it drew her eyes irresistibly. With every fleeting upward glance she half imagined that she could see Lorrimer's white face forming out of the amorphous shadows to hang imprinted on the still air, Lorrimer's black eyes gazing down at her in entreaty or despair.

At seven o'clock Inspector Blakelock said:

'Well, that's about all then. Your mum won't be best pleased that you've been kept late tonight.'

Brenda said with more confidence than she felt:

'Oh, Mum won't mind. She knew I was late starting. I rang her earlier and said not to expect me until half-past.'

They went their separate ways to collect their coats. Then Brenda waited by the door until Inspector Blakelock had set and checked the internal alarm. All the doors of the separate laboratories had been closed and checked earlier in the evening. Lastly they went out by the front door and he turned the two final keys. Brenda's bicycle was kept in a shed by the side of the old stables, where the cars were garaged. Still together, they went round to the back. Inspector Blakelock waited to start his car until she had mounted, then followed her very slowly down the drive. At the gate he gave a valedictory hoot and turned to the left. Brenda waved and set off briskly, pedalling in the opposite direction. She thought she knew why the Inspector had waited so carefully until she was safely off the premises, and she felt grateful. Perhaps, she thought, I remind him of his dead daughter and that's why he's so kind to me.

And then, almost immediately, it happened. The sudden bump and the scrape of metal against the tarmac were unmistakable. The bicycle lurched, almost throwing her into the ditch. Squeezing on both brakes she dismounted and examined the tyres by the light of the heavy torch which she always kept in her bicycle saddle-bag. Both were flat. Her immediate reaction was one of intense irritation. This would happen on a late night! She swept the torchlight over the road behind her, trying to identify the source of the mishap. There must be glass or something sharp on the road somewhere. But she could see nothing, and realized that it wouldn't help if she did. There was no hope of repairing the punctures. The next bus home was the one due to pass the Laboratory just after nine o'clock, and there was no one left at the Lab to give her a lift. She spent very little time in thinking. The best plan was obviously to return the bicycle to its rack and then make her way home through the new Laboratory. It would cut off nearly a couple of miles and, if she walked fast, she could be home just after seven-thirty.

Anger, and ineffective railing against bad luck, is a powerful antidote to fear. So is hunger and the healthy tiredness that longs for its own fireside. Brenda had jerked the bicycle, now reduced to a ridiculously antiquated encumbrance, back into its stand and had walked briskly through the grounds of Hoggatt's and unbolted the wooden gate which led to the new site, before she began to feel afraid. But now, alone in the darkness, the half-superstitious dread which it had seemed safe to stimulate in the Laboratory with Inspector Blakelock so reassuringly by her side, began to prick at her nerves. Before her the black bulk of the half-completed Laboratory loomed like some prehistoric monument, its great slabs blood-stained with ancient sacrifices, rearing upwards towards the implacable gods. The night was fitfully dark with a low ceiling of cloud obscuring the faint stars.

As she hesitated, the clouds parted like ponderous hands to unveil the full moon, frail and transparent as a Communion wafer. Gazing at it she could almost taste the remembered transitory dough, melting against the roof of her mouth. Then the clouds formed again and the darkness closed about her. And the wind was rising.

She held the torch more firmly. It was solidly reassuring and heavy in her hand. Resolutely she picked out her way between the tarpaulin-shrouded piles of bricks, the great girders laid in rows, the two neat huts on stilts which served as the contractor's office, towards the gap in the brickwork which marked the entrance to the main site. Then once again she hesitated. The gap seemed to narrow before her eyes, to become almost symbolically ominous and frightening, an entrance to darkness and the unknown. The fears of childhood not so far distant reasserted themselves. She was tempted to turn back.

Then she admonished herself sternly not to be stupid. There was nothing strange or sinister about a half-completed building, an artefact of brick, concrete and steel, holding no memories of the past, concealing no secret miseries between ancient walls. Besides, she knew the site quite well. The Laboratory staff weren't supposed to take a short cut through the new buildings – Dr Howarth had pinned up a notice on the staff notice board pointing out the dangers – but everyone knew that it was done. Before the building had been started there had been a footpath across Hoggatt's field. It was natural for people to behave as if it were still there. And she was tired and hungry. It was ridiculous to hesitate now.

Then she remembered her parents. No one at home could know about the punctures and her mother would soon begin worrying. She or her father would probably ring the Laboratory and, getting no reply, would know that everyone had left. They would imagine her dead or injured on the road, being lifted unconscious into an ambulance. Worse, they would see her lying crumpled on the floor of the laboratory, a second victim. It had been difficult enough to persuade her parents to let her stay on in the job, and this final anxiety, growing with every minute she was overdue and culminating in the relief and reactive anger of her late appearance, might easily tip them into an unreasoned but obstinate insistence that she should leave. It really was the worst possible time to be late home. She shone her torch steadily on the entrance gap and moved resolutely into the darkness.

She tried to picture the model of the new Laboratory set up in the library. This large vestibule, still unroofed, must be the reception area from which the two main wings diverged. She must bear to the left through what would be the Biology Department for the quickest cut to the Guy's Marsh road. She swept the torch beam over the brick walls, then picked her way carefully across the uneven ground towards the left-hand aperture. The pool of light found another doorway, and then another. The darkness seemed to increase, heavy with the smell of brick-dust and pressed earth. And now the pale haze of the night sky was extinguished and she was in the roofed area of the Laboratory. The silence was absolute.

She found herself creeping forward, breath held, eyes fixed in a stare on the small pool of light at her feet. And suddenly there was nothing, no sky above, no doorway, nothing but black darkness. She swept the torchlight over the walls. They were menacingly close. This room was surely far too small even for an office. She seemed to have stumbled into some kind of cupboard or storeroom. Somewhere, she knew, there must be a gap, the one by which she had entered. But, disorientated in the claustrophobic darkness, she could no longer distinguish the ceiling from the walls. With every sweep of the torch the crude bricks seemed to be closing in on her, the ceiling to descend inexorably like the slowly closing lid of a tomb. Fighting for control, she inched gradually along one wall, telling herself that, soon, she must strike the open doorway.

Suddenly the torch jerked in her hand and the pool of light spilt over the floor. She stopped dead, appalled at her peril. In the middle of the room was a square well protected only by two planks thrown across it. One step in panic and she might have kicked them away, stumbled, and dropped into inky nothingness. In her imagination the well was fathomless, her body would never be found. She would lie there in the mud and darkness, too weak to make herself heard. And all she would hear would be the distant voices of the workmen as, brick on brick, they walled her up alive in her black tomb. And then another and more rational horror struck.

She thought about the punctured tyres. Could that really have been an accident? The tyres had been sound when she had parked the bicycle that morning. Perhaps it hadn't been glass on the road after all. Perhaps someone had done it purposely, someone who knew that she would be late leaving the Lab, that there would be no one left to give her a lift, that she would be bound to walk through the new building. She pictured him in the darkness of the early evening, slipping soundlessly into the bicycle shed, knife in hand, crouching down to the tyres, listening for the hiss of escaping air, calculating how big a rent would cause the tyres to collapse before she had cycled too far on her journey. And now he was waiting for her, knife in hand, somewhere in the darkness. He had smiled, fingering the blade, listening for her every step, watching for the light of her torch. He, too, would have a torch, of course. Soon it would blaze into her face, blinding her eyes, so that she couldn't see the cruel triumphant mouth, the flashing knife. Instinctively she switched off the light and listened, her heart pounding with such a thunder of blood that she felt that even the brick walls must shake.

And then she heard the noise, gentle as a single footfall, soft as the brush of a coat-sleeve against wood. He was coming. He was here. And now there was only panic. Sobbing, she threw herself from side to side against the walls, thudding her bruised palms against the gritty, unyielding brick. Suddenly there was a space. She fell through, tripped, and the torch spun out of her hands. Moaning she lay and waited for death. Then terror swooped with a wild screech of exultation and a thrashing of wings which lifted the hair from her scalp. She screamed, a thin wail of sound which was lost in the bird's cry as the owl found the paneless window and soared into the night.

She didn't know how long she lay there, her sore hands clutching the earth, her mouth choked with dust. But after a while she controlled her sobbing and lifted her head. She saw the window plainly, an immense square of luminous light, pricked with stars. And to the right of it gleamed the doorway. She scrambled to her feet. She didn't wait to search for the torch but made straight for that blessed aperture of light. Beyond it was another. And, suddenly, there were no more walls, only the spangled dome of the sky swinging above her.

Still sobbing, but now with relief, she ran unthinkingly in the moonlight, her hair streaming behind her, her feet hardly seeming to touch the earth. And now there was a belt of trees before her and, gleaming through the autumn branches, the Wren chapel, lit from within, beckoning and holy, shining like a picture on a Christmas card. She ran towards it, palms outstretched, as hundreds of her forebears in the dark fens must have rushed to their altars for sanctuary. The door was ajar and a shaft of light lay like an arrow on the path. She threw herself against the oak, and the great door swung inwards into a glory of light.

At first her mind, shocked into stupor, refused to recognize what her dazzled eyes so clearly saw. Uncomprehending, she put up a tentative hand and stroked the soft corduroy of the slacks, the limp moist hand. Slowly, as if by an act of will, her eyes travelled upwards and she both saw and understood. Stella Mawson's face, dreadful in death, drooped above her, the eyes half-open, the palms disposed outward as if in a mute appeal for pity or for help. Circling her neck was a double cord of blue silk, its tasselled end tied high to a hook on the wall. Beside it, wound on a second hook, was the single bell-rope. There was a low wooden chair upended close to the dangling feet. Brenda seized it. Moaning, she grasped the rope and swung on it three times before it slipped from her loosening hands, and she fainted.

10

Less than a mile away across the field and the grounds of Hoggatt's, Massingham drove the Rover into the Laboratory drive and backed into the bushes. He switched off the car lights. The street-lamp opposite the entrance cast a soft glow over the path, and the door of the Laboratory was plainly visible in the moonlight. He said:

'I'd forgotten, sir, that tonight is the night of the full moon. He'd have had to wait until it moved behind a cloud. Even so, he could surely get out of the house and down the drive unseen if he chose a lucky moment. After all, Doyle had his mind – and not only his mind – on other things.'

'But the murderer wasn't to know that. If he saw the car arriving, I doubt whether he would have risked it. Well, we can at least find out if it's possible even without the co-operation of Mrs Meakin. This reminds me of a childhood game, Grandmother's Footsteps. Will you try first, or shall I?'

But the experiment was destined never to take place. It was at that moment that they heard, faint but unmistakable, the three clear peals of the chapel bell.

11

Massingham drove the car fast on to the grass verge and braked within inches of the hedge. Beyond them the road curved gently between a tattered fringe of windswept bushes, past what looked like a dilapidated barn of blackened wood and on through the naked fens to Guy's Marsh. To the right was the black bulk of the new Laboratory. Massingham's torch picked out a stile and, beyond it, a footpath leading across the field to the distant circle of trees, now no more than a dark smudge against the night sky. He said:

'Odd how remote from the house it is, and how secluded. You wouldn't know it was there. Anyone would think that the original family built it for some secret, necromantic rite.'

'More probably as a family mausoleum. They didn't plan for extinction.'

Neither of them spoke again. They had instinctively driven the mile and a half to the nearest access to the chapel from the Guy's Marsh road. Although less direct, this was quicker and easier than finding their way by foot through the Laboratory grounds and the new building. Their feet quickened and they found they were almost running, driven by some unacknowledged fear, towards the distant trees.

And now they were in the circle of closely planted beeches, dipping their heads under the low branches, their feet scuffling noisily through the crackling drifts of fallen leaves, and could see at last the faintly gleaming windows of the chapel. At the half-open door Massingham instinctively turned as if to hurl his shoulder against it, then drew back with a grin.

'Sorry, I'm forgetting. No sense in precipitating myself in. It's probably only Miss Willard polishing the brass or the rector saying an obligatory prayer to keep the place sanctified.'

Gently, and with a slight flourish, he pushed open the door and stood aside; and Dalgliesh stepped before him into the lighted ante-chapel.

After that there was no speech, no conscious thought, only instinctive action. They moved as one. Massingham grasped and lifted the dangling legs and Dalgliesh, seizing the chair upturned by Brenda's slumping body, slipped the double loop of cord from Stella Mawson's neck and lowered her to the floor. Massingham tore at the fastenings of her duffel jacket, forced back her head and, flinging himself beside her, closed his mouth over hers. The bundle huddled against the wall stirred and moaned, and Dalgliesh knelt beside her. At the touch of his arms on her shoulders she struggled madly for a moment, squealing like a kitten, then opened her eyes and recognized him. Her body relaxed against his. She said faintly:

'The murderer. In the new Lab. He was waiting for me. Has he gone?'

There was a panel of light switches to the left of the door. Dalgliesh clicked them on with a single gesture, and the inner chapel blazed into light. He stepped through the carved organ screen into the chancel. It was empty. The door to the organ loft was ajar. He clattered up the narrow winding stairway into the gallery. It, too, was empty. Then he stood looking down at the quiet emptiness of the chancel, his eyes moving from the exquisite plaster ceiling, the chequered marble floor, the double row of elegantly carved stalls with their high-arched backs set against the north and south walls, the oak table, stripped of its altar-cloth, which stood before the reredos under the eastern window. All it now held were two silver candlesticks, the tall white candles burnt half-down, the wicks blackened. And to the left of the altar, hanging incongruously, was a wooden hymn-board, showing four numbers:

29
10
18
40

He recalled old Mr Lorrimer's voice, 'She said something about the can being burned and that she'd got the numbers.' The last two numbers had been 18 and 40. And what had been burned was not a can, not cannabis, but two altar candles.

12

Forty minutes later, Dalgliesh was alone in the chapel. Dr Greene had been sent for, had briefly pronounced Stella Mawson dead, and had departed. Massingham had left with him to take Brenda Pridmore home and explain to her parents what had happened, to call at Sprogg's Cottage and to summon Dr Howarth. Dr Greene had given Brenda a sedative by injection, but had held out no hope that she would be fit to be questioned before morning. The forensic pathologist had been summoned and was on his way. The voices, the questions, the ringing footsteps, all for the moment were stilled.

Dalgliesh felt extraordinarily alone in the silence of the chapel, more alone because her body lay there, and he had the sense that someone – or something – had recently left, leaving bereft the unencumbered air. This isolation of the spirit was not new to him; he had felt it before in the company of the recently dead. Now he knelt and gazed intently at the dead woman. In life only her eyes had lent distinction to that haggard face. Now they were glazed and gummy as sticky sweetmeats forced under the half-opened lids. It was not a peaceful face. Her features, not yet settled in death, still bore the strain of life's unquietude. He had seen so many dead faces. He had become adept at reading the stigmata of violence. Sometimes they could tell him how, or where, or when. But essentially, as now, they told him nothing.

He lifted the end of the cord still looped loosely around her neck. It was made of woven silk in royal blue, long enough to drape a heavy curtain, and was finished with an ornate silver and blue tassel. There was a five-foot panelled chest against the wall and, putting on his gloves, he lifted the heavy lid. The smell of mothballs came up to him, pungent as an anaesthetic. Inside the chest was a folded pair of faded blue velvet curtains, a starched but crumpled surplice, the black and white of an MA hood, and, lying on top of this assorted bundle, a second tasselled cord. Whoever had put that cord round her neck – herself or another – had known in advance where it could be found.

He began to explore the chapel. He walked softly, yet his feet fell with portentous heaviness on the marble floor. Slowly, he paced between the two rows of splendidly carved stalls towards the altar. In design and furnishing the building reminded him of his college chapel. Even the smell was the same, a scholastic smell, cold, austere, only faintly ecclesiastical. Now that the altar had been denuded of all its furnishing except the two candlesticks, the chapel looked purely secular, unconsecrated. Perhaps it always had. Its formal classicism rejected emotion. It enshrined man, not God; reason, not mystery. This was a place where certain reassuring rituals had been enacted, reaffirming its proprietor's view of the proper order of the universe and his own place in that order. He looked for some memento of that original owner and found it. To the right of the altar was the chapel's only memorial, a carved bust, half draped with a looped marble curtain, of a bewigged eighteenth-century gentleman, with the inscription:

Dieu aye merci de son ame.

This simple petition, unadorned, so out of period, was singularly inapposite to the formal confidence of the memorial, the proud tilt of the head, the self-satisfied smirk on the opulent marble lips. He had built his chapel and set it in a triple circle of trees, and death had not stayed its hand even long enough to give him time to make his carriage-drive.

On either side of the organ-screen and facing the east window were two ornate stalls under carved canopies, each shielded from draughts by a blue velvet curtain similar to those in the chest. The seats were fitted with matching cushions; soft cushions with silver tassels at each corner lay on the book-rests. He climbed into the right-hand stall. On the cushion was a heavy black leather Book of Common Prayer which looked unused. The pages opened stiffly and the bold black and red lettering shone from the page.

'For I am a stranger with thee: and a sojourner, as all my fathers were. O spare me a little, that I may recover my strength: before I go hence, and be no more seen.'

He held the book by its spine and shook it. No paper fluttered from its rigid leaves. But where it had lain, four hairs, one fair and three dark, had adhered to the velvet pile. He took an envelope from his pocket and stuck them to the gummed flap. He knew how little the forensic scientists could hope to do with only four hairs, but it was possible that something could be learned.

The chapel, he thought, must have been ideal for them. Shielded by its trees, isolated, secure, warm even. The fen villagers kept indoors once darkness fell and, even in the evening light, would have a half-superstitious dread of visiting this empty and alien shrine. Even without a key they need fear no casual intruder. She need only watch that she was unobserved when she drove the red Jaguar into Hoggatt's drive to park it out of sight in one of the garages in the stable block. And then what? Wait for the light in the Biology Department to go out at last, for the advancing gleam of light from Lorrimer's torch as he joined her for that walk through the Lab grounds and into the trees. He wondered whether she had dragged the velvet cushions to the sanctuary, whether it had added to the excitement to make love to Lorrimer in front of that denuded altar, the new passion triumphing over the old.

Massingham's flame of hair appeared in the doorway. He said:

'The girl's all right. Her mother got her straight to bed and she's asleep. I called next at Sprogg's Cottage. The door was open and the sitting-room light on, but there's no one there. Howarth was at home when I rang, but not Mrs Schofield. He said he'd be along. Dr Kerrison is at the hospital at a medical committee meeting. His housekeeper said that he left just after seven. I didn't ring the hospital. If he is there, he'll be able to produce plenty of witnesses.'

'And Middlemass?'

'No answer. Out to dinner, or at the local perhaps. No answer either from the Blakelocks' number. Anything here, sir?'

'Nothing, except what we'd expect to find. You've got a man posted to direct Blain-Thomson when he arrives?'

'Yes, sir. And I think he's arriving now.'

13

Dr Reginald Blain-Thomson had a curious habit, before beginning his examination, of mincing round the body, eyes fixed on it with wary intensity as if half afraid that the corpse might spring into life and seize him by the throat. He minced now, immaculate in his grey pinstriped suit, the inevitable rose in its silver holder looking as fresh in his lapel as if it were a June blossom, newly plucked. He was a tall, lean-faced, aristocratic-looking bachelor with a skin as freshly pink and soft as that of a girl. He was never known to put on protective clothing before examining a body, and reminded Dalgliesh of one of those television cooks who prepare a four-course dinner in full evening dress for the pleasure of demonstrating the essential refinement of their craft. It was even rumoured, unjustly, that Blain-Thomson performed his autopsy in a lounge suit.

But, despite these personal idiosyncrasies, he was an excellent forensic pathologist. Juries loved him. When he stood in the box and recited, with slightly world-weary formality and in his actor's voice, the details of his formidable qualifications and experience, they gazed at him with the respectful admiration of men who know a distinguished consultant when they see one, and have no intention of being so disobliging as to disbelieve what he might choose to tell them.

Now he squatted by the body, listened, smelled and touched. He switched off his examination torch and got to his feet. He said:

'Yes, well. Obviously she's dead and it's very recent. Within the last two hours, if you press me. But you must have reached that conclusion yourselves or you wouldn't have cut her down. When did you say you found her? Three minutes after eight. Dead one and a half hours then, say. It's possible. You're going to ask me whether it's suicide or murder. All I can say at the moment is that there's only the double mark encircling the neck and the cord fits. But you can see that for yourselves. There's no sign of manual throttling, and it doesn't look as if the cord were superimposed on a finer ligature. She's a frail woman, little more than seven stone, I'd estimate, so it wouldn't need strength to overpower her. But there's no sign of a struggle and the nails look perfectly clean, so she probably didn't get the chance to scratch. If it is murder, he must have come up behind her very swiftly, dropped the looped cord over her head, and strung her up almost as soon as unconsciousness supervened. As for the cause of death – whether it's strangulation, broken neck or vagal inhibition – well, you'll have to wait until I get her on the table. I can take her away now if you're ready.'

'How soon can you do the PM?'

'Well, it had better be at once, hadn't it? You're keeping me busy, Commander. No questions about my report on Lorrimer, I suppose?'

Dalgliesh answered:

'None, thank you. I did try to get you on the phone.'

'I'm sorry I've been elusive. I've been incarcerated in committees practically all day. When's the Lorrimer inquest?'

'Tomorrow, at two o'clock.'

'I'll be there. They'll adjourn it, I suppose. And I'll give you a ring and a preliminary report as soon as I've got her sewn up.'

He drew on his gloves carefully, finger by finger, then left. They could hear him exchanging a few words with the constable who was waiting outside to light him across the field to his car. One of them laughed. Then the voices faded.

Massingham put his head outside the door. The two dark-uniformed attendants from the mortuary van, anonymous bureaucrats of death, manoeuvred their trolley through the door with nonchalant skill. Stella Mawson's body was lifted with impersonal gentleness. The men turned to trundle the trolley out through the door. But suddenly the way was blocked by two dark shadows, and Howarth and his sister stepped quietly and simultaneously into the light of the chapel. The figures with the trolley paused, stock-still like ancient helots, unseeing, unhearing.

Massingham thought that their entrance seemed as dramatically contrived as that of a couple of film stars arriving at a première. They were dressed identically in slacks and fawn leather jackets, lined with shaggy fur, the collars upturned. And for the first time he was struck by their essential likeness. The impression of a film was reinforced. Gazing at the two pale, arrogant heads framed with fur, he thought that they looked like decadent twins, their fair, handsome profiles theatrically posed against the dark oak panelling. Again simultaneously, their eyes moved to the shrouded lump on the trolley, then fixed themselves on Dalgliesh. He said to Howarth:

'You took your time coming.'

'My sister was out driving and I waited for her to return. You said you wanted both of us. I wasn't given to understand that it was of immediate urgency. What has happened? Inspector Massingham wasn't exactly forthcoming when he peremptorily summoned us.'

'Stella Mawson is dead by hanging.'

He had no doubt that Howarth appreciated the significance of his careful use of words. Their eyes moved from the two hooks on the chapel wall, one with the bell-rope hitched over it, to the blue cord with its dangling tassel held lightly in Dalgliesh's hand. Howarth said:

'I wonder how she knew how to find the cord. And why choose here?'

'You recognize the cord?'

'Isn't it from the chest? There should be two identical cords. We had an idea of hanging the curtains at the entrance to the chancel when we held our concert on the twenty-sixth of August. As it happens, we decided against it. The evening was too hot to worry about draughts. There were two tasselled cords in the chest then.'

'Who could have seen them?'

'Almost anyone who was helping with the preparations: myself, my sister, Miss Foley, Martin, Blakelock. Middlemass gave a hand arranging the hired chairs, and so did a number of people from the Lab. Some of the women helped with the refreshments after the concert and they were fussing about here during the afternoon. The chest isn't locked. Anyone who felt curious could have looked inside. But I don't see how Miss Mawson could have known about the cord. She was at the concert, but she had no hand in the preparations.'

Dalgliesh nodded to the men with the trolley. They pushed it gently forward, and Howarth and Mrs Schofield stood aside to let it pass. Then Dalgliesh asked:

'How many keys are there to this place?'

'I told you yesterday. I know of one only. It's kept on a board in the Chief Liaison Officer's room.'

'And that's the one at present in the lock?' Howarth did not turn his head. He said:

'If it's got the Laboratory plastic tab – yes.'

'Do you know if it was handed out to anyone today?'

'No. That's hardly the kind of detail Blakelock would worry me with.'

Dalgliesh turned to Domenica Schofield:

'And that's the one, presumably, that you borrowed to get extra keys cut when you decided to use the chapel for your meetings with Lorrimer. How many keys?'

She said calmly:

'Two. One you found on his body. This is the second.'

She took it from her jacket pocket and held it out in the palm of her hand in a gesture of dismissive contempt. For a moment it appeared that she was about to tilt her palm and let it clatter on the floor.

'You don't deny that you came here?'

'Why should I? It's not illegal. We were both of age, in our right minds, and free. Not even adultery; merely fornication. You seem fascinated by my sex life, Commander, even in the middle of your more normal preoccupations. Aren't you afraid it's becoming rather an obsession?'

Dalgliesh's voice didn't change. He went on:

'And you didn't ask for the key back when you broke with Lorrimer?'

'Again, why should I? I didn't need it. It wasn't an engagement ring.'

Howarth hadn't looked at his half-sister during this exchange. Suddenly he said harshly:

'Who found her?'

'Brenda Pridmore. She's been taken home. Dr Greene is with her now.'

Domenica Schofield's voice was surprisingly gentle:

'Poor child. She seems to be making a habit of finding bodies, doesn't she? Now that we've explained to you about the keys, is there anything else you want us for tonight?'

'Only to ask you both where you've been since six o'clock.'

Howarth said:

'I left Hoggatt's at about a quarter to six and I've been at home ever since. My sister's been out driving alone since seven o'clock. She likes to do that occasionally.'

Domenica Schofield said:

'I'm not sure if I can give you the precise route, but I did stop at an agreeable pub at Whittlesford for a drink and a meal shortly before eight o'clock. They'll probably remember me. I'm fairly well known there. Why? Are you telling us that this is murder?'

'It's an unexplained death.'

'And a suspicious one, presumably. But haven't you considered that she might have murdered Lorrimer and then taken her own life?'

'Can you give me one good reason why she should have?'

She laughed softly.

'Murdered Edwin? For the best and commonest of reasons, or so I've always read. Because she was once married to him. Hadn't you discovered that for yourself, Commander?'

'How did you know?'

'Because he told me. I'm probably the only person in the world he ever did tell. He said the marriage wasn't consummated and they got an annulment within two years. I suppose that's why he never brought his bride home. It's an embarrassing business, showing off one's new wife to one's parents and the village, particularly when she isn't a wife at all and one suspects that she never will be. I don't think his parents ever did know, so it's really not so surprising if you didn't. But then, one expects you to ferret out everything about people's private concerns.'

Before Dalgliesh could reply, their ears caught, simultaneously, the hurried footfall on the stone step, and Angela Foley stood inside the door. She was flushed with running. Looking wildly from face to face, her body heaving, she gasped:

'Where is she? Where's Star?'

Dalgliesh moved forward, but she backed away as if terrified that he might touch her. She said:

'Those men. Under the trees. Men with a torch. They're wheeling something. What is it? What have you done with Star?'

Without looking at her half-brother, Domenica Schofield put out her hand. His reached out to meet it. They didn't move closer together, but stood, distanced, rigidly linked by those clasped hands. Dalgliesh said:

'I'm sorry, Miss Foley. Your friend is dead.'

Four pairs of eyes watched as her own eyes turned, first to the blue loops of cord dangling from Dalgliesh's hand, then to the twin hooks, lastly to the wooden chair now tidily placed against the wall. She whispered:

'Oh no! Oh no!'

Massingham moved to take her arm, but she shook free. She threw back her head like a howling animal and wailed:

'Star! Star!' Before Massingham could restrain her she had run from the chapel and they could hear her wild, despairing cry borne back to them on the light wind.

Massingham ran after her. She was silent now, weaving through the trees, running fast. But he caught up with her easily before she reached the two distant figures with their dreadful burden. At first she fought madly; but, suddenly, she collapsed in his arms and he was able to lift her and carry her to the car.

When he got back to the chapel, thirty minutes later, Dalgliesh was sitting quietly in one of the stalls, apparently engrossed with the Book of Common Prayer. He put it down and said:

'How is she?'

'Dr Greene's given her a sedative. He's arranged for the district nurse to stay the night. There's no one else he could think of. It looks as if neither she nor Brenda Pridmore will be fit to be questioned before morning.'

He looked at the small heap of numbered cards on the seat beside Dalgliesh. His chief said:

'I found them at the bottom of the chest. I suppose we can test these and those in the board for fingerprints. But we know what we shall find.'

Massingham asked:

'Did you believe Mrs Schofield's story that Lorrimer and Stella Mawson were married?'

'Oh yes, I think so. Why lie when the facts can be so easily checked? And it explains so much; that extraordinary change of will; even the outburst when he was talking to Bradley. That first sexual failure must have gone deep. Even after all these years he couldn't bear to think that she might benefit even indirectly from his will. Or was it the thought that unlike him, she had found happiness – and found it with a woman – that he found so insupportable?'

Massingham said:

'So she and Angela Foley get nothing. But that's not a reason for killing herself. And why here, of all places?'

Dalgliesh got to his feet.

'I don't think she did kill herself. This was murder.'

BOOK FIVE

The Clunch Pit

1

They were at Bowlem's Farm before first light. Mrs Pridmore had begun her baking early. Already two large earthenware bowls covered with humped linen stood on the kitchen table, and the whole cottage was redolent with the warm, fecund smell of yeast. When Dalgliesh and Massingham arrived Dr Greene, a squat broad-shouldered man with the face of a benevolent toad, was folding his stethoscope into the depths of an old-fashioned Gladstone bag. It was less than twelve hours since Dalgliesh and he had last met, since, as police surgeon, he had been the first doctor to be called to Stella Mawson's body. He had examined it briefly and had then pronounced:

'Is she dead? Answer: yes. Cause of death? Answer: hanging. Time of death? About one hour ago. Now you'd better call in the expert and he'll explain to you why the first question is the only one he's at present competent to answer.'

Now he wasted no time on civilities or questions but nodded briefly to the two detectives and continued talking to Mrs Pridmore.

'The lass is fine. She's had a nasty shock but nothing that a good night's sleep hasn't put right. She's young and healthy, and it'll take more than a couple of corpses to turn her into a neurotic wreck, if that's what you're frightened of. My family has been doctoring yours for three generations and there's none of you gone off your heads yet.' He nodded to Dalgliesh. 'You can go up now.'

Arthur Pridmore was standing beside his wife, his hand gripping her shoulder. No one had introduced him to Dalgliesh; nor was there need. He said:

'She hasn't faced the worst yet, has she? This is the second body. What do you think life in this village will be like for her if these two deaths aren't solved?'

Dr Greene was impatient. He snapped shut his bag.

'Good grief, man, no one's going to suspect Brenda! She's lived here all life. I brought her into the world.'

'That's no protection against slander, though, is it? I'm not saying they'll accuse her. But you know the fens. Folk here can be superstitious, unforgetting and unforgiving. There's such a thing as being tainted with bad luck.'

'Not for your pretty Brenda, there isn't. She'll be the local heroine, most likely. Shake off this morbid nonsense, Arthur. And come out to the car with me. I want a word about that business at the Parochial Church Council.' They went out together. Mrs Pridmore looked up at Dalgliesh. He thought that she had been crying. She said:

'And now you're going to question her, make her talk about it, raking it all up again.'

'Don't worry,' said Dalgliesh gently, 'talking about it will help.'

She made no move to accompany them upstairs, a tact for which Dalgliesh was grateful. He could hardly have objected, particularly as there hadn't been time to get a policewoman, but he had an idea that Brenda would be both more relaxed and more communicative in her mother's absence. She called out happily to his knock. The little bedroom with its low beams and its curtains drawn against the morning darkness was full of light and colour, and she was sitting up in bed fresh and bright-eyed, her aureole of hair tumbling around her shoulders. Dalgliesh wondered anew at the resilience of youth. Massingham, halted suddenly in the doorway, thought that she ought to be in the Uffizi, her feet floating above a meadow of spring flowers, the whole sunlit landscape of Italy stretching behind her into infinity.

It was still very much a schoolgirl's room. There were two shelves of schoolbooks, another with a collection of dolls in national costumes, and a cork board with cut-outs from the Sunday supplements and photographs of her friends. There was a wicker chair beside the bed holding a large teddy bear. Dalgliesh removed it and placed it on the bed beside her, then sat down. He said:

'How are you feeling? Better?'

She leaned impulsively towards him. The sleeve of her cream dressing-jacket fell over the freckled arm. She said:

'I'm so glad you've come. No one wants to talk about it. They can't realize that I've got to talk about it sometime and it's much better now while it's fresh in my mind. It was you who found me, wasn't it? I remember being picked up – rather like Marianne Dashwood in *Sense and Sensibility* – and the nice tweedy smell of your jacket. But I can't remember anything after that. I do remember ringing the bell, though.'

'That was clever of you. We were parked in Hoggatt's drive and heard it, otherwise it might have been hours before the body was found.'

'It wasn't clever really. It was just panic. I suppose you realize what happened? I got a puncture in my bike and decided to walk home through the new Lab. Then I got rather lost and panicked. I started thinking about Dr Lorrimer's murderer and imagining that he was lying in wait for me. I even imagined that he might have punctured the tyres on purpose. It seems silly now, but it didn't then.'

Dalgliesh said:

'We've examined the bicycle. There was a lorryload of grit passing the Lab during the afternoon and some of the load was shed. You had a sharp flint in each tyre. But it was a perfectly natural fear. Can you remember whether there really was someone in the building?'

'Not really. I didn't see anyone and I think I imagined most of the sounds I heard. What really frightened me was an owl. Then I got out of the building and rushed in panic across a field straight towards the chapel.'

'Did you get the impression that anyone might be there alive in the chapel?'

'Well, there aren't any pillars to hide behind. It's a funny chapel, isn't it? Not really a holy place. Perhaps it hasn't been prayed in enough. I've only been there once before when Dr Howarth and three of the staff from the Lab gave a concert, so I know what it's like. Do you mean he could have been crouched down in one of the stalls watching me? It's a horrid idea.'

'It is rather. But now that you're safe, could you bear to think about it?'

'I can now you're here.' She paused. 'I don't think he was. I didn't see anyone, and I don't think I heard anyone. But I was so terrified that I probably wouldn't have noticed. All I could see was this bundle of clothes strung up on the wall, and then the face drooping down at me.'

He didn't need to warn her of the importance of his next question.

'Can you remember where you found the chair, its exact position?'

'It was lying overturned just to the right of the body as if she had kicked it away. I think it had fallen backwards, but it might have been on its side.'

'But you're quite sure that it had fallen?'

'Quite sure. I remember turning it upright so that I could stand on it to reach the bell rope.' She looked at him, bright-eyed.

'I shouldn't have done that, should I? Now you won't be able to tell whether any marks or soil on the seat came from my shoes or hers. Was that why Inspector Massingham took away my shoes last night? Mummy told me.'

'Yes, that's why.'

The chair would be tested for prints, then sent for examination to the Metropolitan Laboratory. But this murder, if it were murder, had been premeditated. Dalgliesh doubted whether, this time, the killer would have made any mistakes.

Brenda said:

'One thing has struck me, though. It's odd, isn't it, that the light was on?'

'That's another thing I wanted to ask you. You're quite sure that the chapel was lit? You didn't switch on the light yourself?'

'I'm quite sure I didn't. I saw the lights gleaming through the trees. Rather like the City of God, you know. It would have been more sensible to have run for the road once I'd got clear of the new building. But suddenly I saw the shape of the chapel and the light shining faintly through the windows, and I ran towards it almost by instinct.'

'I expect it was by instinct. Your ancestors did the same. Only they would have run for sanctuary to St Nicholas's.'

'I've been thinking about the lights ever since I woke up. It looks like suicide, doesn't it? I don't suppose people kill themselves in the dark. I know I wouldn't. I can't imagine killing myself at all unless I was desperately ill and lonely and in terrible pain, or someone was torturing me to make me give them vital information. But if I did, I wouldn't switch the lights off. I'd want to see my last of the light before I went into the darkness, wouldn't you? But murderers always want to delay discovery of the body, don't they? So why didn't he turn off the light and lock the door?'

She spoke with happy unconcern. The illness, the loneliness and the pain were as unreal and remote as was the torture. Dalgliesh said:

'Perhaps because he wanted it to look like suicide. Was that your first thought when you found the body, that she'd killed herself?'

'Not at the time. I was too frightened to think at all. But since I've woken up and started considering it all – yes, I suppose I do think it was suicide.'

'But you're not sure why you think that?'

'Perhaps because hanging is such a strange way of killing someone. But suicides often do hang themselves, don't they? Mr Bowlem's previous pigman did – in the tithe-barn. And old Annie Makepeace. I've noticed that, in the fens, people usually shoot themselves or hang themselves. You see, on a farm, there's always a gun or a rope.'

She spoke simply and without fear. She had lived on a farm all her life. There was always birth and death, the birth and death of animals and of humans too. And the long dark nights of the fen winter would bring their own miasma of madness or despair. But not to her. He said:

'You appal me. It sounds like a holocaust.'

'It doesn't happen often, but one remembers when it does. I just associate hanging with suicide. Do you think this time I'm wrong?'

'I think you could be. But we shall find out. You've been very helpful.'

He spent another five minutes talking to her, but there was nothing that she could add. She hadn't gone with Inspector Blakelock to Chief Inspector Martin's office when he set the night alarms, so couldn't say whether or not the key to the chapel was still on its hook. She had only met Stella Mawson once before at the concert in the chapel, when she had sat in the same row as Angela Foley, Stella Mawson, Mrs Schofield and Dr Kerrison and his children.

As Dalgliesh and Massingham were leaving, she said:

'I don't think Mum and Dad will let me go back to the Lab now. In fact I'm sure they won't. They want me to marry Gerald Bowlem. I think I would like to marry Gerald, at least, I've never thought of marrying anyone else, but not just yet. It would be nice to be a scientist and have a proper career first. But Mum won't have an easy moment if I stay at the Lab. She loves me, and I'm all she's got. You can't hurt people when they love you.'

Dalgliesh recognized an appeal for help. He went back and sat again in the chair. Massingham, pretending to look out of the window, was intrigued. He wondered what they would think at the Yard if they could see the old man taking time from a murder investigation to advise on the moral ambiguities of Women's Lib. But he rather wished that she had asked him. Since they had come into the room she had looked only at Dalgliesh. Now he heard him say:

'I suppose a scientific job isn't easy to combine with being a farmer's wife.'

'I don't think it would be very fair to Gerald.'

'I used to think that we can have almost anything we want from life, that it's just a question of organization. But now I'm beginning to think that we have to make a choice more often than we'd like. The important thing is to make sure that it's our choice, no one else's, and that we make it honestly. But one thing I'm sure of is that it's never a good thing to make a decision when you're not absolutely well. Why not wait a little time, until we've solved Dr Lorrimer's murder anyway? Your mother may feel differently then.'

She said:

'I suppose this is what murder does, changes people's lives and spoils them.'

'Changes, yes. But it needn't spoil. You're young and intelligent and brave, so you won't let it spoil yours.'

Downstairs, in the farmhouse kitchen, Mrs Pridmore was sandwiching fried rashers of bacon between generous slices of crusty bread. She said gruffly:

'You both look as if you could do with some breakfast. Up all night, I dare say. It won't hurt you to sit down and take a couple of minutes to eat these. And I've made fresh tea.'

Supper the previous night had been a couple of sandwiches fetched by a constable from the Moonraker and eaten in the antechapel. Not until he smelt the bacon did Massingham realize how hungry he was. He bit gratefully into the warm bread to the oozing saltiness of home-cured bacon, and washed it down with strong, hot tea. He felt cosseted by the warmth and friendliness of the kitchen, this cosy womb-like shelter from the dark fens. Then the telephone rang. Mrs Pridmore went to answer it. She said:

'That was Dr Greene ringing from Sprogg's Cottage. He says to tell you that Angela Foley is well enough to speak to you now.'

Angela Foley came slowly into the room. She was fully dressed and perfectly calm, but both men were shocked by the change in her. She walked stiffly, and her face looked aged and bruised as if she had suffered all night a physical assault of grief. Her small eyes were pale and sunken behind the jutting bones, her cheeks were unhealthily mottled, the delicate mouth was swollen and there was a herpes on the upper lip. Only her voice was unchanged; the childish, unemphatic voice with which she had answered their first questions.

The district nurse, who had spent the night at Sprogg's Cottage, had lit the fire. Angela looked at the crackling wood and said:

'Stella never lit the fire until late in the afternoon. I used to lay it in the morning before I went to the Lab, and she'd put a match to it about half an hour before I was due home.'

Dalgliesh said:

'We found Miss Mawson's house-keys on her body. I'm afraid we had to unlock her desk to examine her papers. You were asleep, so we weren't able to ask you.'

She said, dully:

'It wouldn't have made any difference, would it? You would have looked just the same. You had to.'

'Did you know that your friend once went through a form of marriage with Edwin Lorrimer? There wasn't a divorce; the marriage was annulled after two years because of non-consummation. Did she tell you?'

She turned to look at him, but it was impossible to gauge the expression in those small, pig-like eyes. If her voice held any emotion, it was closer to wry amusement than to surprise.

'Married? She and Edwin? So that's how she knew . . .' She broke off. 'No, she didn't tell me. When I came to live here it was a new beginning for both of us. I didn't want to talk about the past and I don't think she did either. She did sometimes tell me things, about her life at university, her job, odd people she knew. But that was one thing she didn't tell me.'

Dalgliesh asked gently:

'Do you feel able to tell me what happened last night?'

'She said that she was going for a walk. She often did, but usually after supper. That's when she thought about her books, worked out the plot and dialogue, striding along in the darkness on her own.'

'What time did she go?'

'Just before seven.'

'Did she have the key of the chapel with her?'

'She asked me for it yesterday, after lunch, just before I went back to the Lab. She said she wanted to describe a seventeenth-century family chapel for the book, but I didn't know that she meant to visit it so soon. When she hadn't come home at half past ten, I got worried and went to look for her. I walked for nearly an hour before I thought of looking in the chapel.'

Then she spoke directly to Dalgliesh, patiently, as if explaining something to an obtuse child:

'She did it for me. She killed herself so that I could have the money from her life assurance. She told me that I was her only legatee. You see, the owner wants to sell this cottage in a hurry; he needs the cash. We wanted to buy it, but we hadn't enough money for the deposit. Just before she went out, she asked me what it was like to be in local authority care, what it meant to have no real home. When Edwin was killed, we thought that there might be something for me in his will. But there wasn't. That's why she asked me for the key. It wasn't true that she needed to include a description of the chapel in her book, not this book anyway. It's set in London, and it's nearly finished. I know. I've been typing it. I thought at the time that it was odd that she wanted the key, but I learned never to ask Stella questions.

'But now I understand. She wanted to make life safe for me here, where we'd been happy, safe for ever. She knew what she was going to do. She knew she'd never come back. When I was massaging her neck to make her headache better, she knew that I should never touch her again.'

Dalgliesh asked:

'Would any writer, any writer who wasn't mentally ill, choose to kill herself just before a book was finished?'

She said dully:

'I don't know. I don't understand how a writer feels.'

Dalgliesh said:

'Well, I do. And she wouldn't.'

She didn't reply. He went on gently:

'Was she happy, living here with you?

She looked up at him eagerly, and, for the first time, her voice became animated, as if she were willing him to understand.

'She said that she had never been as happy in all her life. She said that was what love is, knowing that you can make just one other person happy, and be made happy by them in return.'

'So why should she kill herself? Could she really have believed that you'd rather have her money than herself? Why should she think that?'

'Stella always underrated herself. She may have thought that I'd forget her in time, but the money and the security would go on for ever. She may even have thought that it was bad for me to be living with her – that the money would somehow set me free. She once said something very like that.'

Dalgliesh looked across at the slim, upright figure, sitting, hands folded in her lap, opposite to him in the high winged chair. He fixed his eyes on her face. Then he said quietly:

'But there isn't going to be any money. The life assurance policy had a suicide clause. If Miss Mawson did kill herself, then you get nothing.'

She hadn't known. He could be certain of that at least. The news surprised her, but it didn't shock. This was no murderess balked of her spoils.

She smiled and said gently:

'It doesn't matter.'

'It matters to this investigation. I've read one of your friend's novels. Miss Mawson was a highly intelligent writer, which means that she was an intelligent woman. Her heart wasn't strong and her life assurance premiums weren't cheap. It can't have been easy to meet them. Do you really think that she didn't know the terms of her policy?'

'What are you trying to tell me?'

'Miss Mawson knew, or thought she knew, who had killed Dr Lorrimer, didn't she?'

'Yes. She said so. But she didn't tell me who it was.'

'Not even whether it was a man or a woman?'

She thought:

'No, nothing. Only that she knew. I'm not sure that she said that, not in so many words. But when I asked her, she didn't deny it.'

She paused, and then went on with more animation:

'You're thinking that she went out to meet the murderer, aren't you? That she tried to blackmail him? But Stella wouldn't do that! Only a fool would run into that kind of danger, and she wasn't a fool. You said so yourself. She wouldn't voluntarily have gone alone to face a killer, not for any money. No sane woman would.'

'Even if the murderer were a woman?'

'Not alone and at night. Star was so small and fragile and her heart wasn't strong. When I put my arms round her it was like holding a bird.' She looked into the fire and said, almost wonderingly:

'I shall never see her again. Never. She sat in this chair and pulled on her boots, just as she always did. I never offered to go with her in the evenings. I knew that she needed to be alone. It was all so ordinary, until she got to the door. And then I was frightened. I begged her not to go. And I shall never see her again. She won't ever speak again, not to me, not to anyone. She'll never write another word. I don't believe it yet. I know that it must be true or you wouldn't be here, but I still don't believe it. How shall I bear it when I do?'

Dalgliesh said:

'Miss Foley, we have to know if she went out on the night Dr Lorrimer was killed.'

She looked up at him.

'I know what you're trying to make me do. If I say that she did go out, then the case is finished for you, isn't it? It's all nicely tied up; means, motive, opportunity. He was her ex-husband and she hated him because of the will. She went to try and persuade him to help us with some money. When he refused, she seized the first weapon to hand and struck him down.'

Dalgliesh said:

'He may have let her into the Laboratory, although it's unlikely. But how did she get out?

'You'll say that I took the keys from Dr Howarth's security safe and lent them to her. Then I put them back next morning.'

'Did you?'

She shook her head.

'You could only have done that if you and Inspector Blakelock were in this together. And what reason has he for wishing Dr

Lorrimer dead? When his only child was killed by a hit-and-run driver, the evidence of the forensic scientist helped secure an acquittal. But that was ten years ago, and the scientist wasn't Dr Lorrimer. When Miss Pridmore told me about the child we checked. That evidence was to do with paint particles, the job of a forensic chemist, not a biologist. Are you telling me that Inspector Blakelock lied when he said that the keys were in the security cupboard?'

'He didn't lie. The keys were there.'

'Then any case we might seek to build against Miss Mawson weakens, doesn't it? Could anyone really believe that she climbed out of a third-floor window? You must believe that we're here to find the truth, not to fabricate an easy solution.'

But she was right, thought Massingham. Once Angela Foley had admitted that her friend had left Sprogg's Cottage that night, it would be difficult to bring home the crime to anyone else. The solution she had propounded was neat enough and, whoever was brought to trial for Lorrimer's murder, the defence would make the most of it. He watched his chief's face. Dalgliesh said:

'I agree that no sane woman would go out alone at night to meet a murderer. That's why I don't think she did. She thought she knew who had killed Edwin Lorrimer, and if she did have an assignation last night, it wasn't with him. Miss Foley, please look at me. You must trust me. I don't know yet whether your friend killed herself or was killed. But if I'm to discover the truth, I'll have to know whether she went out the night Dr Lorrimer died.'

She said dully:

'We were together all the evening. We told you.'

There was a silence. It seemed to Massingham to last for minutes. Then the wood fire flared and there was a crack like a pistol shot. A log rolled out on the hearth. Dalgliesh knelt and with the tongs eased it back into place. The silence went on. Then she said:

'Please tell me the truth first. Do you think Star was murdered?'

'I can't be sure. I may never be able to prove it. But, yes, I do.'

She said: 'Star did go out that night. She was out from half past eight until about half past nine. She didn't tell me where she'd been, and she was perfectly ordinary, perfectly composed, when she got home. She said nothing, but she did go out.'

*

She said at last:

'I'd like you to go now, please.'

'I think you should have someone with you.'

'I'm not a child. I don't want Mrs Swaffield or the district nurse or any of the village do-gooders. And I don't need a policewoman. I haven't committed a crime, so you've no right to force yourselves on me. I've told you everything I know. You've locked her desk, so no one can get at Stella's things. I shan't do anything foolish – that's the expression people use when they're trying to ask tactfully if you're planning to kill yourself, isn't it? Well, I'm not. I'm all right now. I just want to be left alone.'

Dalgliesh said:

'I'm afraid we shall need to force ourselves on you again later.'

'Later is better than now.'

She wasn't trying to be offensive. It was a simple statement of fact. She got up stiffly and walked towards the door, her head held rigidly high as if only the body's discipline could hold intact the fragile integrity of the mind. Dalgliesh and Massingham exchanged glances. She was right. They couldn't force comfort or company where neither was wanted. They had no legal authority either to stay or to compel her to leave. And there were things to do.

She went over to the window and watched from behind the curtains as the car rounded Sprogg's Green and accelerated towards the village. Then she ran into the hall and dragged out the telephone directory from its shelf. It took only a few seconds of feverishly leafing to find the number she wanted. She dialled, waited, and then spoke. Replacing the receiver, she went back into the sitting-room. Slowly, with ceremony, she lifted the French sword from the wall and stood very still, holding out her arms, the weapon resting across her palms. After a few seconds she curled her left hand round the scabbard, and with her right slowly and deliberately withdrew the blade. Then she took her stand just inside the sitting-room door, naked sword in her hand, and measured the room with her eyes, regarding the disposition of furniture and objects, intent as a stranger calculating her chances in some coming trial.

After a few minutes she moved into the study, and again stood silently surveying the room. There was a Victorian button-backed chair beside the fireplace. She dragged it to the study door and hid the naked sword behind it, the tip resting against the floor; then slid the scabbard under the chair. Satisfied that neither could be seen, she returned to the sitting-room. She took her seat beside the fire and sat motionless, waiting for the sound of the approaching car.

3

If Claire Easterbrook was surprised, on her arrival at the Laboratory just before nine o'clock, to be asked by Inspector Blakelock to see Commander Dalgliesh immediately, she concealed it. She changed first into her white coat, but otherwise did not delay in obeying the summons more than was strictly necessary to assert her independence. When she went into the Director's office, she saw the two detectives, the dark head and the red, quietly conferring together at the window almost, she thought, as if their business was ordinary, their presence unremarkable. There was an alien file on Dr Howarth's desk, and a plan of the Laboratory and an Ordnance Survey map of the village laid open on the conference table, but otherwise the room seemed unchanged. Dalgliesh moved to the desk and said:

'Good morning, Miss Easterbrook. You heard what happened last night?'

'No. Should I have? I was at the theatre after dinner, so people couldn't reach me, and I've spoken to no one but Inspector Blakelock. He hasn't told me anything.'

'Stella Mawson, Miss Foley's friend, was found hanged in the chapel.'

She frowned as if the news were personally offensive, and said with no more than polite interest:

'I see. I don't think I've met her. Oh yes, I remember. She was at the concert in the chapel. Grey-haired, with remarkable eyes. What happened? Did she kill herself?'

'That's one of two possibilities. It's unlikely to have been an accident.'

'Who found her?'

'Miss Pridmore.'

She said with surprising gentleness:

'Poor child.'

Dalgliesh opened the file, picked up two transparent exhibit envelopes, and said:

445

'I'd like you to have a look at these four hairs urgently for me. There's no time to get them to the Met Lab. I want to know, if possible, if the dark hairs came from the same head.'

'It's easier to say whether they don't. I can have a look under the microscope but I doubt whether I can help you. Hair identification is never easy, and I can't hope to do much with only three samples. Apart from microscopic examination, we'd normally use mass spectrometry to try to identify differences in the trace elements, but even that isn't possible with three hairs. If these were submitted to me, I'd have to say that I couldn't give an opinion.'

Dalgliesh said:

'I'd be grateful, all the same, if you'd take a look. It's just a hunch and I want to know whether it's worth following up.'

Massingham said:

'I'd like to watch, if you don't mind.'

She gazed at him.

'Would it make any difference if I did?'

Ten minutes later she lifted her head from the comparison microscope and said:

'If we're talking of hunches, mine, for what it's worth, is that they came from different heads. The cuticle, cortex and medulla are all significantly different. But I think they're both male. Look for yourself.'

Massingham bent his head to the eyepiece. He saw what looked like the sections of two logs, patterned and grained. And beside them were two other logs, their barks shredded. But he could see that they were different logs, and that they came from different trees. He said:

'Thank you. I'll let Mr Dalgliesh know.'

4

There was nothing he could put between himself and that shining, razor-sharp blade. He thought wryly that a bullet would have been worse; but then he wondered. To use a gun at least required some skill, a preliminary aim. A bullet could go anywhere, and if her first shot was wide he could at least have ensured that she got no second chance. But she had three feet of cold steel in her hand and, in this confined space, she had only to lunge or slash and he would be cut to the bone. He knew now why she had shown him into the study. There was no room here to manoeuvre; no object within his range of sight which he could seize and hurl. And he knew that he mustn't look round, must keep his eyes firmly and without fear on her face. He tried to keep his voice calm, reasonable; one nervous smile, one hint of hostility or provocation and it might be too late to argue. He said:

'Look, don't you think we ought to talk about this? You've got the wrong man, believe me.'

She said:

'Read that note. The one on the desk behind you. Read it out loud.'

He didn't dare turn his head, but reached back and fumbled on the desk. His hand encountered a single sheet of paper. He read:

'You'd better check on the cannabis exhibits when Detective-Inspector Doyle's around. How do you think he managed to afford his house?'

'Well?'

'Where did you get this?'

'From Edwin Lorrimer's desk. Stella found it and gave it to me. You killed her because she knew, because she tried to blackmail you. She arranged to meet you last night in the Wren chapel and you strangled her.'

He could have laughed at the irony of it, but he knew that laughter would be fatal. And at least they were talking. The longer she waited, the greater his chances.

'Are you saying that your friend thought that I killed Edwin Lorrimer?'

'She knew that you didn't. She was out walking the night he died and I think she saw someone she recognized leaving the Laboratory. She knew that it wasn't you. She wouldn't have risked meeting you alone if she'd thought that you were a murderer. Mr Dalgliesh explained that to me. She went to the chapel thinking that she was safe, that she could come to some arrangement with you. But you killed her. That's why I'm going to kill you. Stella hated the thought of shutting people away in prison. I can't bear the thought of her murderer ever being free. Ten years in exchange for Stella's life. Why should you be alive when she's dead?'

He had no doubt that she meant what she said. He had dealt before with people pushed over the brink of endurance into madness, had seen before that look of dedicated fanaticism. He stood very still, poised on the soles of his feet, his arms held loosely, his eyes watching her eyes, waiting for that first instinctive tightening of the muscles before she struck. He tried to keep his voice low, calm, but with no trace of facetiousness.

'That's a reasonable point of view. Don't think that I'm against it. I've never understood why people are squeamish about killing a convicted murderer instantaneously and resigned to killing him slowly over twenty years. But at least they have been convicted. There's the little matter of a trial. No execution without due process. And believe me, Miss Foley, you've got the wrong man. I didn't kill Lorrimer, and luckily for me I can prove it.'

'I don't care about Edwin Lorrimer. I only care about Stella. And you killed her.'

'I didn't even know that she was dead. But if she was killed yesterday any time between half past three and half past seven, then I'm in the clear. I've got the best possible alibi. I was at Guy's Marsh police station most of the time being interrogated by the Yard. And when Dalgliesh and Massingham left, I was there for another two hours. Ring them. Ask anyone. Look, you can lock me away in a cupboard – somewhere where I can't escape – while you telephone Guy's Marsh. For God's sake, you don't want to make a mistake, do you? You know me. Do you want to kill me, messily, horribly, while the real murderer escapes? An unofficial execution is one thing; murder's another.'

He thought that the hand holding the sword lost some of its tension. But there was no change in the taut, white face. She said:

'And the note.'

'I know who sent the note – my wife. She wanted me to leave the Force, and she knew that there'd be nothing like a little official harassment to push me into resigning. I had a spot of trouble with the Force about two years ago. The disciplinary committee exonerated me, but I damn well nearly resigned then. Can't you recognize feminine spite when you see it? That note proves nothing except that she wanted me disgraced and out of the Force.'

'But you have been stealing cannabis, substituting an inert substance?'

'Ah, that's a different question. But you're not killing me for that. You won't be able to prove it, you know. The last batch of cannabis exhibits I was concerned with had a destruction authorization from the court. I helped burn them myself. Just in time, luckily; the incinerator broke down immediately afterwards.'

'And the court exhibits you burned, were they cannabis?'

'Some of them were. But you'll never prove I made the substitution, even if you decide to make use of that note, not now. But what does it matter? I'm out of the Force. Look, you know I've been working on the clunch-pit murder. Do you really suppose that I'd have been sitting at home at this time of day, free to drive over here as soon as you rang me merely to satisfy my curiosity, if I were on a murder case, if I hadn't been suspended or resigned? I may not be a shining example of probity to the Force, but I'm not a murderer, and I can prove it. Ring Dalgliesh and ask him.'

There was no doubt about it now, her grip on the sword had relaxed. She stood there, very still, no longer looking at him, but with her gaze fixed out of the window. Her face didn't change, but he saw that she was crying. The tears were streaming out of the tight little eyes to roll unimpeded down her cheeks. He moved quietly forward and took the sword from her unresisting hand. He placed an arm on her shoulders. She didn't flinch. He said:

'Look, you've had a shock. You shouldn't have been left here on your own. Isn't it time we had a cup of tea? Show me where the kitchen is and I'll make it. Or better still, have you anything stronger?'

She said dully:

'There's whisky, but we keep that for Stella. I don't drink it.'

'Well, you're going to drink it now. It'll do you good. And, by God, I need it. And then you'd better sit down quietly and tell me all about it.'

She said:

'But if it wasn't you, who did kill Stella?'

'My guess is, the same person who killed Lorrimer. A couple of murderers loose in one small community is too much of a coincidence. But look, you've got to let the police know about that note. It can't hurt me, not now, and it might help them. If your friend found one incriminating piece of information in Lorrimer's desk, then she may have found another. She didn't use that note. She probably knew how little it was worth. But what about the information she did use?'

She said dully:

'You tell them, if you want to. It doesn't matter now.'

But he waited until he had made the tea. The tidiness and good order of the kitchen pleased him, and he took trouble over the tray, setting it in front of her on a low table which he drew up before the fire. He replaced the sword above the fireplace, standing back to make sure that it hung correctly. Then he made up the fire. She had shaken her head when he had offered her the whisky, but he poured himself a generous measure and sat opposite her on the other side of the fire. She didn't attract him. Even in their brief encounters at the Laboratory he had given her no more than a passing dismissive glance. It was unusual for him to put himself out for a woman from whom he wanted nothing, and the sensation of disinterested kindness was unfamiliar but agreeable. Sitting opposite her in silence, the traumas of the day faded, and he felt a curious peace. They had some quite decent stuff in the cottage, he decided, looking around at the cosy, cluttered sitting-room. He wondered whether it was all coming to her.

It was ten minutes before he went out to telephone. When he returned the sight of his face roused her from her benumbed misery.

She said:

'What is it? What did he say?'

He moved into the room, frowning, puzzled. He said:

'He wasn't there. He and Massingham weren't at Guy's Marsh or at the Lab. They're at Muddington. They've gone to the clunch pit.'

5

They drove again over the route they had followed the previous night when they had heard those three clangs from the chapel bell, the mile and a half to the junction of Guy's Marsh road and then right through the main street of the village. Neither spoke. Massingham had taken one look at his chief's face and had decided that silence would be prudent. And it was certainly no time for self-congratulation. They still lacked proof, the one clinching fact that would break the case open. And Massingham wondered if they would ever get it. They were dealing with intelligent men and women who must know that they had only to keep their mouths shut and nothing could be proved.

In the village street, the first Saturday-morning shoppers were making their appearance. The gossiping groups of women turned their heads to glance briefly at the car as it passed. And now the houses were thinning and Hoggatt's field, with the new building, was on their right. Massingham had changed down to turn into the drive of the Old Rectory when it happened. The blue and yellow ball bounced out into the road in front of them, and after it, red wellingtons flashing, ran William. They were driving too slowly for danger, but Massingham cursed as he swerved and braked. And then came two seconds of horror.

Afterwards it seemed to Dalgliesh that time was suspended so that he saw in memory the whole accident like a film run slowly. The red Jaguar leaping and held suspended in the air; a blaze of blue from the terrified eyes; the mouth gaping in a soundless scream; the white knuckles wrenching at the wheel. Instinctively he cradled his head and braced himself for the impact. The Jaguar crashed the rear bumper of the Rover, ripping it away in a scream of torn metal. The car rocked wildly and spun round. There was a second of absolute silence. Then he and Massingham were out of their seat-belts and rushing across to the opposite verge to that small, motionless body. One boot lay in the road, and the ball trickled slowly towards the grass verge.

William had been tossed into a heap of hay left on the verge after the late summer scything. He lay spreadeagled, so relaxed in his perfect stillness that Massingham's first horrified thought was that his neck was broken. In the couple of seconds in which he was resisting the impulse to sweep the boy into his arms, and turning instead to telephone from the car for an ambulance, William recovered his wind and began struggling against the prickling dampness of the straw. Bereft both of dignity and his ball he began to cry. Domenica Schofield, hair streaming across her bleached distraught face, stumbled up to them.

'Is he all right?'

Massingham ran his hands over William's body, then took the boy in his arms.

'I think so. He sounds all right.'

They had reached the drive of the Old Rectory when Eleanor Kerrison came running down the path towards them. She had obviously been washing her hair. It lay now in dank, dripping swathes across her shoulders. William, seeing her, redoubled his crying. As Massingham strode towards the house she ran clumsily beside him, clutching his arm. Drops of water sprayed from her hair to lie like pearls on William's face.

'Daddy's been called to a body. He said he'd take William and me to lunch at Cambridge when he got back. We were going to buy a grown-up bed for William. I was washing my hair specially. I left William with Miss Willard. He's all right, isn't he? Are you sure he's all right? Oughtn't we to take him to the hospital? What happened?'

'We didn't see. I think he was caught and tossed by the front bumper of the Jaguar. Luckily he landed on a heap of straw.'

'He could have been killed. I warned her about the road. He isn't supposed to play in the garden on his own. Are you sure we oughtn't to get Dr Greene?'

Massingham went straight through the house to the drawing-room and laid William on the sofa. He said:

'It might be as well, but I'm sure he's all right. Just listen to him.'

William, as if he understood, cut off his bawling instantaneously and struggled upright on the couch. He began hiccuping loudly but, apparently undistressed by the paroxysms which were jerking his body, he regarded the company with interest, then fixed his stare consideringly on his bootless left foot. Looking up at Dalgliesh he asked sternly:

'Where's Willum's ball?'

'At the edge of the road, presumably,' said Massingham. 'I'll fetch it. And you'll have to do something about fixing a gate for that drive.'

They heard footsteps in the hall, and Miss Willard stood, fluttering uneasily in the doorway. Eleanor had been sitting beside her brother on the sofa. Now she stood up and confronted the woman with a silent contempt so unmistakable that Miss Willard blushed. She glanced round the watching faces and said defensively:

'Quite a little party. I thought I heard voices.'

Then the girl spoke. The voice, thought Massingham, was as arrogant and cruel as that of a Victorian matron dismissing a kitchen maid. The confrontation would have been almost comic if it hadn't been at once pathetic and horrible.

'You can pack up your bags and get out. You're dismissed. I only asked you to watch William while I washed my hair. You couldn't even do that. He might have been killed. You're a useless, ugly, stupid old woman. You drink and you smell and we all hate you. We don't need you any more. So get out. Pack your beastly, horrible things and go. I can look after William and Daddy. He doesn't need anyone but me.'

The silly, ingratiating smile faded on Miss Willard's face. Two red weals appeared across her cheeks and forehead as if the words had been a physical whiplash. Then she was suddenly pale, her whole body shaking. She reached for the back of a chair for support and said, her voice high and distorted with pain:

'You! Do you think he needs you? I may be middle-aged and past my best but at least I'm not half-mad. And if I'm ugly, look at yourself! He only puts up with you because of William. You could leave tomorrow and he wouldn't care. He'd be glad. It's William he loves, not you. I've seen his face, I've heard him and I know. He's thinking of letting you go to your mother. You didn't know that, did you? And there's something else you don't know. What do you think your precious daddy gets up to when he's drugged you into sleep? He sneaks off to the Wren chapel and makes love to her.'

Eleanor turned and looked at Domenica Schofield. Then she spun round and spoke directly to Dalgliesh.

'She's lying! Tell me she's lying! It isn't true.'

There was a silence. It could only have lasted a couple of seconds while Dalgliesh's mind phrased the careful answer. Then, as if impatient to forestall him, not looking at his chief's face, Massingham said clearly:

'Yes, it's true.'

She looked from Dalgliesh to Domenica Schofield. Then she swayed as if she were about to faint. Dalgliesh went towards her, but she backed away. She said in a voice of dull calm:

'I thought he did it for me. I didn't drink the cocoa he made for me. I wasn't asleep when he came back. I went out and watched him in the garden, burning the white coat on the bonfire. I knew that there was blood on it. I thought he'd been to see Dr Lorrimer because he was unkind to William and me. I thought he did it for me, because he loves me.'

Suddenly she gave a high despairing wail like an animal in torment, and yet so human and so adult that Dalgliesh felt his blood run cold.

'Daddy! Daddy! Oh no!'

She put her hands to her throat and, pulling the leather thong from beneath her sweater, struggled with it, twisting like a creature in a trap. And then the knot broke. Over the dark carpet they scattered and rolled, six newly polished brass buttons, bright as crested jewels.

Massingham stooped and carefully gathered them up into his handkerchief. Still no one spoke. William propelled himself off the sofa, trotted over to his sister and fastened his arms around her leg. His lip trembled. Domenica Schofield spoke directly to Dalgliesh.

'My God, yours is a filthy trade.'

Dalgliesh ignored her. He said to Massingham:

'Look after the children. I'll ring for a WPC and we'd better get Mrs Swaffield. There's no one else I can think of. Don't leave her until they both arrive. I'll see to things here.'

Massingham turned to Domenica Schofield.

'Not a trade. Just a job. And are you saying that it's one you don't want done?'

He went up to the girl. She was trembling violently. Dalgliesh thought that she would cringe away from him. But she stood perfectly still. With three words he had destroyed her. But who else had she to turn to? Massingham took off his tweed coat and wrapped it round her. He said gently without touching her:

'Come with me. You show me where we can make some tea. And then you'll have a lie-down and William and I will stay with you. I'll read to William.'

She went with him as meekly as a prisoner with a gaoler, without looking at him, the long coat trailing on the floor. Massingham took William's hand. The door closed after them. Dalgliesh wished never to see Massingham again. But he would see him again and, in time, without even caring or remembering. He never wanted to work with him again; but he knew that he would. He wasn't the man to destroy a subordinate's career simply because he had outraged susceptibilities to which he, Dalgliesh, had no right. What Massingham had done seemed to him now unforgivable. But life had taught him that the unforgivable was usually the most easily forgiven. It was possible to do police work honestly; there was, indeed, no other safe way to do it. But it wasn't possible to do it without giving pain.

Miss Willard had groped her way to the sofa. She muttered, as if trying to explain it to herself:

'I didn't mean it. She made me say it. I didn't mean it. I didn't want to hurt him.'

Domenica Schofield turned to go.

'No, one seldom does.' She said to Dalgliesh:

'If you want me, you know where I'll be.'

'We shall want a statement.'

'Of course. Don't you always? Longing and loneliness, terror and despair, all the human muddle, neatly documented, on one and a half sheets of official paper.'

'No, just the facts.'

He didn't ask her when it had begun. That wasn't really important; and he thought that he didn't need to ask. Brenda Pridmore had told him that she had sat in the same row as Mrs Schofield and Dr Kerrison and his children at the concert in the chapel. That had been held on Thursday the twenty-sixth of August. And early in September, Domenica had broken with Edwin Lorrimer.

At the door she hesitated and turned. Dalgliesh asked:

'Did he telephone you the morning after the murder to let you know that he'd replaced the key on Lorrimer's body?'

'He never telephoned me. Neither of them did, ever. That was our arrangement. And I never rang him.' She paused and then said gruffly:

'I didn't know. I may have suspected, but I didn't know. We weren't – what's your expression? – in it together. I'm not responsible. It wasn't because of me.'

'No.' said Dalgliesh. 'I didn't suppose it was. A motive for murder is seldom so unimportant.'

She fixed on him her unforgettable eyes. She said:

'Why do you dislike me?

The egotism which could ask such a question, and at such a time, astounded him. But it was his own self-knowledge which disgusted him more. He understood only too well what had driven those two men to creep guiltily like randy schoolboys to that rendezvous, to make themselves partners in her erotic, esoteric game. Given the opportunity, he would, he thought bitterly, have done the same.

She was gone. He went over to Miss Willard.

'Did you telephone Dr Lorrimer to tell him about the burnt candles, the numbers on the hymn-board?'

'I chatted to him when he drove me to Mass the Sunday before last. I had to talk about something on the journey; he never did. And I was worried about the altar candles. I first noticed that someone had lit them when I went to the chapel at the end of September. On my last visit they were burnt even lower. I thought that the chapel might be being used by devil-worshippers. I know it's been decon-secrated, but it's still a holy place. And it's so secluded. No one goes there. The fen people don't like to walk out after dark. I wondered if I ought to talk to the rector or consult Father Gregory. Dr Lorrimer asked me to go to the chapel again next day and let him know the numbers on the hymn-board. I thought it was an odd thing to ask, but he seemed to think that it was important. I hadn't even noticed that they'd been altered. I could ask for the key, you see. He didn't like to.'

But he could have taken it without signing for it, thought Dalgliesh. So why hadn't he? Because of the risk that he might be seen? Because it was repugnant to his obsessional, conformist personality to break a Laboratory rule? Or, more likely, because he couldn't bear to enter the chapel again, to see with his own eyes the evidence of betrayal? She hadn't even bothered to change their meeting-place. She had still used the same ingenious code to fix the date of the next assignation. Even the key she had handed to Kerrison had been Lorrimer's key. And none better than he had known the significance of those four numbers. The twenty-ninth day of the tenth month at six-forty. He said:

'And you waited together last Friday in the shelter of the trees?'

'That was his idea. He needed a witness, you see. Oh, he was quite right to be worried. A woman like that, quite unsuitable to be a stepmother to William. One man after another, Dr Lorrimer said. That's why she had to leave London. She couldn't leave men alone. Any man would do. He knew about her, you see. He said the whole Lab knew. She'd even made advances to him once. Horrible. He was going to write to Mrs Kerrison and put a stop to it. I couldn't tell him the address. Dr Kerrison's so secretive about his letters, and I'm not sure that even he knows exactly where his wife is. But we knew that she'd run away with a doctor, and we knew his name. It's quite a common name, but Dr Lorrimer said he could trace them from the Medical Directory.'

The Medical Directory. So that was why he had wanted to consult it, why he had opened the door so quickly when Bradley rang. He had only to come from the Director's office on the ground floor. And he had been carrying his notebook. What was it that Howarth had said? He hated scraps of paper. He used the book to note down anything of importance. And this had been important. The names and addresses of Mrs Kerrison's possible lovers.

Miss Willard looked up at him. Dalgliesh saw that she was crying, the tears streaking her face and dropping unimpeded over the twisting hands. She said:

'What will happen to him? What will you do to him?'

The telephone rang. Dalgliesh strode across the hall and into the study and lifted the receiver. It was Clifford Bradley. His voice sounded as high and excited as a young girl's. He said:

'Commander Dalgliesh? They said at the police station you might be there. I have to tell you at once. It's important. I've just remembered how I knew the murderer was still in the Lab. I heard a sound as I got to the Lab door. I heard the same sound again two minutes ago coming downstairs from the bathroom. Sue had just finished telephoning her mother. What I heard was someone replacing the telephone receiver.'

It was no more than confirmation of what he had long ago suspected. He returned to the drawing-room and said to Miss Willard:

'Why did you tell us that you overheard Dr Kerrison making that nine o'clock telephone call from his study? Did he ask you to lie for him?'

The blotched face, the tear-drained eyes looked up at him.

'Oh no, he'd never do that! All he asked was whether I'd happened to hear him. It was when he came back to the house after he'd been called to the body. I wanted to help him, to make him pleased with me. It was such a little, unimportant lie. And it wasn't really a lie. I thought that perhaps I did hear him. You might have suspected him, and I knew that he couldn't have done it. He's kind, and good and gentle. It seems such a venial sin to protect the innocent. That woman had got him into her clutches, but I knew he could never kill.'

He had probably always intended to telephone the hospital from the Laboratory if he wasn't back home in time. But, with Lorrimer lying dead, it must have taken nerve. He could barely have put down the receiver before he heard the approaching footsteps. And what then? Into the darkroom to watch and wait? That must have been one of his worst moments, standing there rigidly in the darkness, breath held, his heart thudding, wondering who could be arriving at this late hour, how they could have got in. And it could have been Blakelock; Blakelock who would have rung at once for the police, who would have made an immediate search of the Lab.

But it had only been a terrified Bradley. There had been no telephone call, no summons for help, only the echo of panicking feet down the corridor. And now all he had to do was to follow, make his way quietly out of the Lab and home through the new Lab the way he had come. He had put out the light and reached the front door. And then he had seen the headlights of Doyle's car swinging into the drive and backing to park among the bushes. He no longer dared leave by that door. That way was barred. And he couldn't wait for them to drive off. There was Nell at home who might wake and ask for him. There was the return telephone call at ten o'clock. He had to get back.

But he had still kept his head. It had been a clever move to take Lorrimer's key and lock the Laboratory. The police investigation would inevitably concentrate on the four sets of keys and the limited number of people who had access to them. And he knew the one way he could get out and had the skill and nerve to do it. He had put on Middlemass's jacket to protect his clothes; he knew how fatal a torn thread of cloth could be. But there had been no tear. And in the early hours of the morning a light rain had washed away any evidence on walls or windows which could have betrayed him.

He had reached home safely and made an excuse to call in on Miss Willard, establishing his alibi more firmly. No one had telephoned for him; no one had called. And he knew that, next day, he would be among the first to examine the body. Howarth had said that he had stood by the door while Kerrison made his examination. It must have been then that he had slipped the key into Lorrimer's pocket.

But that had been one of his mistakes. Lorrimer carried his keys in a leather pouch, not loose in his pocket.

There was the crunch of tyres on the gravel of the drive. He looked out of the window and saw the police car with Detective-Sergeant Reynolds and two women police constables in the back. The case had broken; except that it was never the case that broke, only the people. And now he and Massingham were free for the last interview, the most difficult of all.

At the edge of the clunch field a boy was flying a red kite. Tugged by the freshening wind it soared and dipped, weaving its convoluted tail against an azure sky as clear and bright as on a summer day. The clunch field was alive with voices and laughter. Even the discarded beer-cans glinted like bright toys and the waste paper bowled along merrily in the wind. The air was keen and smelt of the sea. It was possible to believe that the Saturday shoppers trailing with their children across the scrubland were carrying their picnics to the beach, that the clunch field led on to dunes and marram grass, to the child-loud fringes of the sea. Even the screen, which the police were fighting to erect against the wind, looked no more frightening than a Punch-and-Judy stand with a little group of curious people standing patiently at a distance, waiting for the show to begin.

It was Superintendent Mercer who came first up the slope of the clunch pit towards them. He said:

'It's a messy business; the husband of the girl who was found here on Wednesday. He's a butcher's assistant. Yesterday he took home one of the knives and came here last night to cut his throat. He left a note confessing to her murder, poor devil. It wouldn't have happened if we'd been able to arrest him yesterday. But Lorrimer's death and Doyle's suspension held us up. We only got the blood result late last night. Who is it you want to see?'

'Dr Kerrison.'

Mercer looked at Dalgliesh keenly, but said only:

'He's finished here now. I'll let him know.'

Three minutes later Kerrison's figure appeared over the rim of the clunch pit and he walked towards them. He said:

'It was Nell, wasn't it?'

'Yes.'

He didn't ask how or when. He listened intently as Dalgliesh spoke the words of the caution, as if he hadn't heard them before and wanted to commit them to memory. Then he said, looking at Dalgliesh:

'I'd rather not go to Guy's Marsh police station, not yet. I want to tell you about it now, just you, no one else. There won't be any difficulty. I'll make a full confession. Whatever happens, I don't want Nell to have to give evidence. Can you promise me that?'

'You must know that I can't. But there's no reason why the Crown should call her if you intend to plead guilty.'

Dalgliesh opened the door of the car, but Kerrison shook his head. He said without a trace of self-pity:

'I'd rather stay outside. There'll be so many years of sitting when I shan't be able to walk under the sky. Perhaps for the rest of my life. If it were only Lorrimer's death, I might have hoped for a verdict of manslaughter. His killing wasn't premeditated. But the other was murder.'

Massingham stayed by the car while Dalgliesh and Kerrison walked together round the clunch pit. Kerrison said:

'It started here, at this very spot, only four days ago. It feels like an eternity. Another life, another time. We'd both been called to the clunch-pit murder, and afterwards he drew me to one side and told me to meet him that evening at eight-thirty at the Laboratory. Not asked; told. And he told me, too, what he wanted to talk about. Domenica.'

Dalgliesh asked:

'Did you know that he was her lover before you?'

'Not until I met him that night. She had never talked about him to me, never once mentioned his name. But when he poured out his stream of hate and envy and jealousy, then, of course, I knew. I didn't ask him how he'd found out about me. I think he was mad. Perhaps we were both mad.'

'And he threatened to write to your wife and prevent your getting custody of the children unless you gave her up.'

'He was going to write anyway. He wanted her back, and I think, poor devil, that he actually believed that it might be possible. But he still wanted to punish me. I've only once before known such hate. He was standing there, white-faced, railing at me, taunting me, telling me that I'd lose the children, that I wasn't fit to be a father, that I'd never see them again. And suddenly it wasn't Lorrimer

460

speaking. You see, I'd heard it all before from my wife. It was his voice, but her words. And I knew that I couldn't take any more. I'd been up for most of the night; I'd had a terrible scene with Nell when I got home; and I'd spent the day worrying what Lorrimer might have to tell me.

'It was then that the telephone rang. It was his father complaining about the television. He only spoke briefly, then he put down the receiver. But when he was speaking I saw the mallet. And I knew that I had gloves in my coat pocket. The call to his father seemed to have sobered him. He told me there was nothing else he wanted to say. It was when he turned his back on me dismissively that I seized the mallet and struck. He fell without a sound. I put the mallet back on the table, and it was then that I saw the open notebook with the names and addresses of three doctors. One of them was my wife's lover. I tore out the page and crumpled it in my pocket. Then I went to the telephone and made my call. It was just nine o'clock. The rest, I think, you know.'

They had circled the clunch pit, pacing together, their eyes fixed on the bright grass. Now they turned and retraced their steps. Dalgliesh said:

'I think you'd better tell me.'

But there was nothing new to learn. It had happened just as Dalgliesh had reasoned. When Kerrison had finished describing the burning of the coat and the page from the notebook, Dalgliesh asked:

'And Stella Mawson?'

'She rang me at the hospital and asked me to meet her in the chapel at half past seven yesterday. She gave me an idea what it was about. She said that she had a draft letter which she wanted to discuss with me, one she'd found in a certain desk. I knew what it would say.'

She must have taken it with her to the chapel, thought Dalgliesh. It hadn't been found in her desk, neither the original nor the copy. It seemed to him extraordinary that she had actually risked letting Kerrison know that she had the letter on her. How could he be sure, when he killed her, that she hadn't left a copy? And how could she be sure that he wouldn't overpower her and take it?

Almost as if he knew what was going through Dalgliesh's mind, Kerrison said:

'It wasn't what you're thinking. She wasn't trying to sell me the letter. She wasn't selling anything. She told me that she'd taken it from Lorrimer's desk almost on impulse because she didn't want the police to find it. For some reason which she didn't explain, she hated Lorrimer, and she bore me no ill will. What she said was: "He caused enough misery in his life. Why should he cause misery after his death?" She said another extraordinary thing. "I was his victim once. I don't see why you should be his victim now." She saw herself as on my side, someone who'd done me a service. And now she was asking me for something in return, something quite simple and ordinary. Something she knew that I'd be able to afford.'

Dalgliesh said:

'The cash to buy Sprogg's Cottage, security for herself and Angela Foley.'

'Not even a gift, merely a loan. She wanted four thousand pounds over five years at a rate of interest she could afford. She needed the money desperately, and she had to find it quickly. She explained to me that there was no one else she could ask. She was perfectly ready to have a legal agreement drawn up. She was the gentlest, most reasonable of blackmailers.'

And she had thought that she was dealing with the gentlest, most reasonable of men. She had been totally without fear, until that last hideous moment when he had drawn the cord from his coat pocket and she had realized that she was facing, not a fellow victim, but her murderer. Dalgliesh said:

'You must have had the cord ready. When did you decide she had to die?'

'Even that, like Lorrimer's death, was almost chance. She had got the key from Angela Foley and she arrived at the chapel first. She was sitting in the chancel, in one of the stalls. She had left the door open, and when I went into the antechapel I saw the chest. I knew the cord was inside it. I'd had plenty of time to explore the chapel when I'd been waiting for Domenica. So I took it out and put it in my pocket. Then I went through to her, and we talked. She had the letter with her, in her pocket. She took it out and showed it to me without the least fear. It wasn't the finished letter; just a draft that he'd been working on. He must have enjoyed writing it, must have taken a lot of trouble getting it right.

'She was an extraordinary woman. I said that I'd lend her the money, that I'd have a proper agreement drawn up by my solicitor. There was a Prayer Book in the chapel, and she made me put my hand on it and swear that I'd never tell anyone what had happened between us. I think she was terrified that Angela Foley would get to know. It was when I realized that she, and only she, held this dangerous knowledge, that I decided that she must die.'

He stopped walking. He turned to Dalgliesh and said:

'You see, I couldn't take a chance on her. I'm not trying to justify myself. I'm not even trying to make you understand. You aren't a father, so you never could understand. I couldn't risk giving my wife such a weapon against me when the custody case comes before the High Court. They probably wouldn't worry overmuch that I had a mistress; that wouldn't make me unfit to care for my children. If it did, what chance would most parents have of getting custody? But a secret affair which I'd concealed from the police with a woman whose previous lover was murdered, a murder for which I had only a weak alibi and a strong motive. Wouldn't that tip the balance? My wife is attractive and plausible, outwardly perfectly sane. That's what makes it so impossible. Madness isn't so very difficult to diagnose, neurosis is less dramatic but just as lethal if you have to live with it. She tore us apart, Nell and me. I couldn't let her have William and Nell. When I stood in the chapel and faced Stella Mawson, I knew it was their lives against hers.

'And it was so easy. I slipped the double cord round her neck and pulled tight. She must have died at once. Then I carried her into the antechapel and strung her up on the hook. I remembered to scrape her boots on the chair seat and leave the chair overturned. I walked back across the field to where I'd left my car. I'd parked it where Domenica parks hers when we meet, in the shadow of the old barn on the edge of Guy's Marsh road. Even the timing was right for me. I was due at the hospital for a medical committee meeting, but I'd planned to go into my laboratory first and do some work. Even if someone at the hospital noted the time when I arrived, there was only about twenty minutes unaccounted for. And I could easily have spent an extra twenty minutes on the drive.'

They walked on in silence towards the car. Then Kerrison began speaking again:

'I still don't understand it. She's so beautiful. And it isn't only her beauty. She could have had any man she wanted. It was amazing that, for some extraordinary reason, she wanted me. When we were together, lying by candlelight in the quietness of the chapel, after we'd made love, all the anxieties, all the tensions, all the responsibilities were forgotten. It was easy for us, because of the dark evenings. She would park her car by the barn in safety. No one walks on the Guy's Marsh road at night, and there are only a few cars. I knew it would be more difficult in the spring with the long light evenings. But then, I didn't expect she would want me that long. It was a miracle that she wanted me at all. I never thought beyond the next meeting, the next date on the hymn-board. She wouldn't let me telephone her. I never saw or spoke to her except when we were alone in the chapel. I knew that she didn't love me, but that wasn't important. She gave what she could, and it was enough for me.'

They were back at the car now. Massingham was holding open the door. Kerrison turned to Dalgliesh and said:

'It wasn't love, but it was in its own way a kind of loving. And it was such peace. This is peace, too, knowing that there's nothing else I need do. There's an end to responsibility, an end of worry. A murderer sets himself aside from the whole of humanity for ever. It's a kind of death. I'm like a dying man now, the problems are still there, but I'm moving away from them into a new dimension. I forfeited so many rights when I killed Stella Mawson, even the right to feel pain.'

He got into the back of the car without another word. Dalgliesh closed the door. Then his heart lurched. The blue and yellow ball came bounding across the clunch field towards him and after it, shouting with laughter, his mother calling after him, ran the child. For one dreadful second, Dalgliesh thought that it was William, William's dark fringe of hair, William's laugh, William's red wellingtons flashing in the sun.

INNOCENT BLOOD

Innocent Blood

BOOK ONE
Proof of Identity

BOOK TWO
An Order of Release

BOOK THREE
Act of Violence

BOOK FOUR
Epilogue at Evensong

Proof of Identity

1

The social worker was older than she had expected; perhaps the nameless official who arranged these matters thought that greying hair and menopausal plumpness might induce confidence in the adopted adults who came for their compulsory counselling. After all, they must be in need of reassurance of some kind, these displaced persons whose umbilical cord was a court order, or why had they troubled to travel this bureaucratic road to identity? The social worker smiled her encouraging professional smile. She said, holding out her hand:

'My name is Naomi Henderson and you're Miss Philippa Rose Palfrey. I'm afraid I have to begin by asking you for some proof of identity.'

Philippa nearly replied: 'Philippa Rose Palfrey is what I'm called. I'm here to find out who I am,' but checked herself in time, sensing that such an affectation would be an unpropitious beginning to the interview. They both knew why she was here. And she wanted the session to be a success; wanted it to go her way without being precisely clear what way that was. She unclipped the fastening of her leather shoulder bag and handed over in silence her passport and the newly acquired driving licence.

The attempt at reassuring informality extended to the furnishing of the room. There was an official-looking desk, but Miss Henderson had moved from behind it as soon as Philippa was announced, and had motioned her to one of the two vinyl-covered armchairs on each side of a low table. There were even flowers on the table, a small blue bowl lettered 'a present from Polperro'. It held a mixed bunch of roses. These weren't the scentless, thornless buds of the florist's window. These were garden roses, recognized from the garden at Caldecote Terrace: Peace, Superstar, Albertine, the blossoms over-blown, already peeling with only one or two tightly furled buds, darkening at the lips and destined never to open. Philippa wondered if the social worker had brought them in from her own garden. Perhaps she was retired, living in the country, and had been recruited part-time for this particular job. She could picture her clumping round her rose bed in the brogues and serviceable tweeds she was wearing now, snipping away at roses which were due for culling, might just last out the London day. Someone had watered the flowers over-enthusiastically. A milky bead lay like a pearl between two yellow petals and there was a splash on the table top. But the imitation mahogany wouldn't be stained; it wasn't really wood. The roses gave forth a damp sweetness; but they weren't really fresh. In these easy chairs no visitor had ever sat at ease. The smile which invited her confidence and trust across the table was bestowed by courtesy of section twenty-six of the Children Act 1975.

She had taken trouble with her appearance, but then she always did, presenting herself to the world with self-conscious art, daily remaking herself in her own image. The aim this morning had been to suggest that no trouble had in fact been taken, that this interview had induced no special anxiety, warranted no exceptional care. Her strong corn-coloured hair, bleached by the summer so that no two strands were exactly the same gold, was drawn back from a high forehead and knotted in a single heavy plait. The wide mouth with its strong, curved upper lip and sensuous droop at each corner was devoid of lipstick, but she had applied her eyeshadow with care, emphasizing her most remarkable feature, the luminous, slightly protuberant green eyes. Her honey-coloured skin glistened with sweat. She had lingered too long in the Embankment Gardens, unwilling to arrive early, and in the end had had to hurry. She wore sandals and a pale green open-necked cotton shirt above her corduroy trousers. In contrast to this casual informality, the careful ambiguity about money or social class, were the possessions which she wore like talismans: the slim gold watch, the three heavy Victorian rings, topaz, cornelian, peridot, the leather Italian bag slung from her left shoulder. The contrast was deliberate. The advantage of remembering virtually nothing before her eighth birthday, the knowledge that she was illegitimate, meant that there was no phalanx of the living dead, no pious ancestor worship, no conditioned reflexes of thought to inhibit the creativity with which she presented herself to the world. What she aimed to achieve was singularity, an impression of intelligence, a look that could be spectacular, even eccentric, but never ordinary.

Her file, clean and new, lay open before Miss Henderson. Across the table Philippa could recognize some of the contents: the orange and brown Government information sheet, a copy of which she had obtained from a Citizens' Advice Bureau in north London where there had been no risk that she would be known or recognized; her letter to the Registrar General written five weeks ago, the day after her eighteenth birthday, in which she had requested the application form which was the first document to identity; a copy of the form itself. The letter was tagged on top of the file, stark white against the buff of bureaucracy. Miss Henderson fingered it. Something about it, the address, the quality of the heavy linen-based paper apparent even in a copy, evoked, Philippa thought, a transitory unease. Perhaps it was a recognition that her adoptive father was Maurice Palfrey. Given Maurice's indefatigable self-advertisement, the stream of sociological publications which flowed from his department, it would be odd if a senior social worker hadn't heard of him. She wondered whether Miss Henderson had read his *Theory and Technique in Counselling: A Guide for Practitioners,* and if so, how much she had been helped in bolstering her clients' self-esteem – and what a significant word 'client' was in social-work jargon – by Maurice's lucid exploration of the difference between development counselling and Gestalt therapy.

Miss Henderson said:

'Perhaps I ought to begin by telling you how far I'm able to help you. Some of this you probably already know, but I find it useful to get it straight. The Children Act 1975 made important changes in the law relating to access to birth records. It provides that adopted adults – that is people who are at least eighteen years old – may if they wish apply to the Registrar General for information which will lead them to the original record of their birth. When you were adopted you were given a new birth certificate, and the information which links your present name, Philippa Rose Palfrey, with your original birth certificate is kept by the Registrar General in confidential records. It is this linking information which the law now requires the Registrar General to give you if you want it. The 1975 Act also provides that anyone adopted before the twelfth of November 1975, that is before the Act was passed, must attend an interview with a counsellor before they can be given the information. The reason for this is that Parliament was concerned about making the new arrangements retrospective, since over the years many natural parents gave up their children for adoption and adopters took on the children on the understanding that their natural parentage would remain unknown. So you have come here today so that we can consider together the possible effect of any enquiries you may make about your natural parents, both on yourself and on other people, and so that the information you are now seeking, and to which you have, of course, a legal right, is provided in a helpful and appropriate manner. At the end of our talk, and if you still want it, I shall be able to give you your original name; the name of your natural mother; possibly – but not certainly – the name of your natural father and the name of the court where your adoption order was made. I shall also be able to give you an application form which you can use to apply to the Registrar General for a copy of your original birth certificate.'

She had said it all before. It came out a little too pat. Philippa said:

'And there's a standard charge of two pounds fifty pence for the birth certificate. It seems cheap at the price. I know all that. It's in the orange and brown pamphlet.'

'As long as it's quite clear. I wonder if you'd like to tell me when you first decided to ask for your birth record. I see that you applied as soon as you were eighteen. Was this a sudden decision or had you been thinking about it for some time?'

'I decided when the 1975 Act was going through Parliament. I was fifteen then and taking my O-levels. I don't think I gave it a great deal of thought at the time. I just made up my mind that I'd apply as soon as I was legally able to.'

'Have you spoken to your adoptive parents about it?'

'No. We're not exactly a communicative family.'

Miss Henderson let that pass for the moment.

'And what exactly did you have in mind? Do you want just to know who your natural parents are, or are you hoping to trace them?'

'I'm hoping to find out who I am. I don't see the point of stopping at two names on a birth certificate. There may not even be two names. I know I'm illegitimate. The search may all come to nothing. I know that my mother is dead so I can't trace her, and I may never find my father. But at least if I can find out who my mother was I may get a lead to him. He may be dead too, but I don't think so. Somehow I'm certain that my father is alive.'

Normally she liked her fantasies at least tenuously rooted in reality. Only this one was different, out of time, wildly improbable and yet impossible to relinquish, like an ancient religion whose archaic ceremonies, comfortingly familiar and absurd, somehow witness to an essential truth. She couldn't remember why she had originally set her scene in the nineteenth century, or why, learning so soon that this was a nonsense since she had been born in 1960, she had never updated the persistent self-indulgent imaginings. Her mother, a slim figure dressed as a Victorian parlour-maid, an upswept glory of golden hair under the goffered cap with its two broderie anglaise streamers, ghost-like against the tall hedge which surrounded the rose garden. Her father in full evening dress striding like a god across the terrace, down the broad walk, under the spray of the fountains. The sloping lawn, drenched by the mellow light of the last sun, glittering with peacocks. The two shadows merging into one shadow, the dark head bending to the gold.

'My darling, my darling. I can't let you go. Marry me.'

'I can't. You know I can't.'

It had become a habit to conjure up her favourite scenes in the minutes before she fell asleep. Sleep came in a drift of rose leaves. In the earliest dreams her father had been in uniform, scarlet and gold, his chest beribboned, sword clanking at his side. As she grew older she had edited out these embarrassing embellishments. The soldier, the fearless rider to hounds, had become the aristocrat scholar. But the essential picture remained.

There was a globule of water creeping down the petal of the yellow rose. She watched it, fascinated, willing it not to fall. She had distanced her thoughts from what Miss Henderson had been saying. Now she made an effort to attend. The social worker was asking about her adoptive parents:

'And your mother, what does she do?'

'My adoptive mother cooks.'

'You mean she works as a cook?' The social worker modified this as if conscious that it could imply some derogation, and added: 'She cooks professionally?'

'She cooks for her husband and her guests and me. And she's a juvenile court magistrate but I think she only took that on to please my adoptive father. He believes that a woman should have a job outside the home, provided, of course, that it doesn't interfere with his comfort. But cooking is her enthusiasm. She's good enough at it to cook professionally, although I don't think she was ever properly taught except at evening classes. She was my father's secretary before they married. I mean that cooking is her hobby, her interest.'

'Well, that's nice for your father and you.'

Presumably that hint of encouraging patronage was by now too unconsciously part of her to be easily disciplined. Philippa gazed at the woman stonily, noted it, took strength from it.

'Yes, we're both greedy, my adoptive father and I. We can both eat voraciously without putting on weight.'

That, she supposed, implied something of an appetite for life, not indiscriminate since they were both appreciative of good food; perhaps a reinforcement of their belief that one could indulge without having to pay for indulgence. Greed, unlike sex, involved no commitment except to oneself, no violence except to one's own body. She had always taken comfort from her discernment about food and drink. That, at least, could hardly have been caught from his example. Even Maurice, convinced environmentalist that he was, would hardly claim that a nose for claret could be so easily acquired. Learning to enjoy wine, discovering that she had a palate, had been one more reassuring affirmation of inherited taste. She recalled her seventeenth birthday; the three bottles on the table before them, the labels shrouded. She couldn't recall that Hilda had been with them. Surely she must have been present for a family birthday dinner, but in memory she and Maurice celebrated alone. He had said:

'Now tell me which you prefer. Forget the purple prose of the colour supplements, I want to know what you think in your own words.'

She had tasted them again, holding the wine in her mouth, sipping water between each sampling since she supposed that this was the proper thing to do, watching his bright challenging eyes.

'This one.'

'Why?'

'I don't know. I just like it best.'

But he would expect a more considered judgement than that. She added:

'Perhaps because with this one I can't distinguish taste from smell and from the feel of it in the mouth. They aren't separate sensations, it's a trinity of pleasure.'

She had chosen the right one. There always was a right answer and a wrong answer. This had been one more test successfully passed, one more notch on the scale of approval. He couldn't entirely reject her, couldn't send her back; she knew that. An adoption order couldn't be revoked. That made it the more important that she should justify his choice of her, that she should give value for money. Hilda, who worked for hours in the kitchen preparing their meals, ate and drank little. She would sit, anxious eyes fixed on them as they shovelled in their food. She gave and they took. It was almost too psychologically neat. Miss Henderson asked:

'Do you resent them for adopting you?'

'No, I'm grateful. I was lucky. I don't think I'd have done well with a poor family.'

'Not even if they loved you?'

'I don't see why they should. I'm not particularly lovable.'

She hadn't done well with a poor family, of that at least she could be certain. She hadn't done well with any of her foster parents. Some smells: her own excreta, the rotting waste outside a restaurant, a young child bundled into soiled clothes on its mother's lap pressed against her by the lurch of a bus, these could evoke a momentary panic that had nothing to do with disgust. Memory was like a searchlight sweeping over the lost hinterland of the self, illuminating scenes with total clarity, the colours gaudy as a child's comic, edges of objects hard as blocks, scenes which could lie for months unremembered in that black wasteland, not rooted, as were other childish memories, in time and place, not rooted in love.

'Do you love them, your adoptive parents?'

She considered. Love. One of the most-used words in the language, the most debased. Héloïse and Abelard. Rochester and Jane Eyre. Emma and Mr Knightley. Anna and Count Vronsky. Even within the narrow connotation of heterosexual love it meant exactly what you wanted it to mean.

'No. And I don't think they love me. But we suit each other on the whole. That's more convenient, I imagine, than living with people that you love but don't suit.'

'I can see that it could be. How much were you told about the circumstances of your adoption? About your natural parents?'

'As much, I think, as my adoptive mother could tell me. Maurice never talks about it. My adoptive father's a university lecturer, a sociologist. Maurice Palfrey, the sociologist who can write English. His first wife and their son died in a car crash when the boy was three. She was driving. He married my adoptive mother nine months afterwards. They discovered that she couldn't have children so they found me. I was being fostered at the time so they took over the care of me and after six months applied to the county court and got an adoption order. It was a private arrangement, the kind of thing your new Act would make illegal. I can't think why. It seems to me a perfectly sensible way of going about it. I've certainly nothing to complain of.'

'It worked very well for thousands of children and their adopters, but it had its dangers. We wouldn't want to go back to the days when unwanted babies lay in rows of cots in nurseries so that adoptive parents could just go and pick out the one they fancied.'

'I don't see why not. That seems to me the only sensible way, as long as the children are too young to know what's happening. That's how you'd pick a puppy or a kitten. I imagine that you need to take to a baby, to feel that this is a child that you want to rear, could grow to love. If I needed to adopt, and I never would, the last thing I'd want would be a child selected for me by a social worker. If we didn't take to each other I wouldn't be able to hand it back without the social services department striking me off the books as being one of those neurotic self-indulgent women who want a child for their own satisfaction. And what other possible reason could there be for wanting an adopted child?'

'Perhaps to give that child a better chance.'

'Don't you mean, to have the personal satisfaction of giving that child a better chance? It amounts to the same thing.'

She wouldn't bother to refute that heresy, of course. Social-work theory didn't err. After all, its practitioners were the new priesthood, the ministry of unbelievers. She merely smiled and persevered:

'Did they tell you anything about your background?'

'Only that I'm illegitimate. My adoptive father's first wife came from the aristocracy, an earl's daughter, and was brought up in a Palladian mansion in Wiltshire. I believe that my mother was one of the maids there, who got herself pregnant. She died soon after I was born and no one knew who my father was. Obviously he wasn't a fellow servant; she couldn't have kept that particular secret from the servants' hall. I think he must have been a visitor to the house. There are only two things I can remember clearly about my life before I was eight; one is the rose garden at Pennington, the other is the library. I think that my father, my real father, was there with me. It's possible that one of the upper servants at Pennington put my adoptive father in touch with me after his first wife died. He never speaks about it. I only learned as much as that from my adoptive mother. I suppose Maurice thought that I'd do because I was a girl. He wouldn't want a boy to bear his name unless he were really his son. It would be terribly important to him to know that a son was really his own.'

'That's understandable, isn't it?'

'Of course. That's why I'm here. It's important for me to know that my parents really were my own.'

'Well, let's say that you think it important.'

Her eyes dropped to the file. There was a rustle of papers.

'So you were adopted on the seventh of January 1969. You must have been eight. That's quite old.'

'I suppose they thought it was better than taking a very young baby and having broken nights. And my adoptive father could see that I was all right, physically all right, that I wasn't stupid. There wasn't the same risk as with a young baby. I know that there are stringent medical examinations, but one can never be quite sure, not about intelligence anyway. He couldn't have borne to find himself saddled with a stupid child.'

'Is that what he told you?'

'No, it's what I've thought out for myself.'

One fact she could be sure of; that she came from Pennington. There was a childhood memory more clear even than that of the rose garden: the Wren library. She knew that she had once stood there under that exuberant seventeenth-century stuccoed ceiling with its garlands and cherubs, had stared down that vast room at the Grinling Gibbons carvings richly spilling from the shelves, at the Roubiliac busts set above the bookcases, Homer, Dante, Shakespeare, Milton. In memory she saw herself standing at the great chart table reading from a book. The book had been almost too heavy to hold. She could still recall the ache in her wrists and the fear that she might drop it. And she was certain that her real father had been with her; that she had been reading aloud to him. She was so sure that she belonged at Pennington that sometimes she was tempted to believe that the Earl had been her father. But the fantasy was unacceptable and she rejected it, faithful to the original vision of the visiting aristocrat. The Earl must have known if he had fathered a child on one of his servants, and surely, surely he wouldn't have rejected her totally, left her unsought and unrecognized for eighteen years. She had never been back to the house, and now that the Arabs had bought it and it had become a Muslim fortress she never would. But when she was twelve she had searched in Westminster reference library for a book on Pennington and had read a description of the library. There had been a picture too. The confirmation had jolted her heart. It was all there, the plaster ceiling, the Grinling Gibbons carvings, the busts. But her memory had come first. The child standing beside the chart table holding the book in her aching hands must have existed.

She scarcely heard the rest of the counselling. If it had to be done, she supposed that Miss Henderson was making a good enough job of it. But it was no more than a statutory nuisance, the way in which uneasy legislators had salved their consciences. None of the arguments so conscientiously put forward could shake her resolve to track down her father. And how could their meeting, however delayed, be unwelcome to him? She wouldn't be coming empty-handed. She had her Cambridge scholarship to lay at his feet.

She said, wrenching her mind back to the present:

'I can't see the point of this compulsory counselling. Are you supposed to dissuade me from tracing my father? Either our legislators think I have a right to know, or they don't. To give me the right and at the same time officially try to discourage me from exercising it seems muddled thinking even for Parliament. Or do they just have a bad conscience about retrospective legislation?'

'Parliament wants adopted people to think carefully about the implications of what they're doing, what it could mean for themselves, for their adoptive parents, for their natural parents.'

'I have thought. My mother is dead, so it can't hurt her. I don't propose to embarrass my father. I want to know who he is, or was if he's dead. That's all. If he's still alive, I should like to meet him, but I'm not thinking of bursting in on a family party and announcing that I'm his bastard. And I don't see how any of this concerns my adoptive parents.'

'Wouldn't it be wise, and kinder, to discuss it first with your adoptive parents?'

'What is there to discuss? The law gives me a right. I'm exercising it.'

Thinking back on the counselling session that evening at home, Philippa couldn't remember the precise moment when the information she sought had been handed to her. She supposed that the social worker must have said something: 'Here, then, are the facts you are seeking' was surely too pretentious and theatrical for Miss Henderson's detached professionalism. But some words must have been said, or had she merely taken the General Register Office paper from the file and passed it over in silence?

But here it was at last in her hands. She stared at it in disbelief, her first thought that there had been some bureaucratic muddle. There were two names, not one, on the form. Her natural parents were shown as Mary Ducton and Martin John Ducton. She muttered the words to herself. The names meant nothing to her, stirred no memory, evoked no sense of completeness, of forgotten knowledge resurrected at a word to be recognized and acknowledged. And then she saw what must have happened. She said, hardly realizing that she spoke aloud:

'I suppose they married my mother off when they found out that she was pregnant. Probably to a fellow servant. They must have been making that kind of tactful arrangement for generations at Pennington. But I hadn't realized that I was placed for adoption before my mother died. She must have known that she hadn't long to live and wanted to be sure that I would be all right. And, of course, if she were married before I was born the husband would be registered as my father. Nominally I suppose I'm legitimate. It's helpful that she did have a husband. Martin Ducton must have been told that she was pregnant before he agreed to the marriage. She may even have told him before she died who my real father was. Obviously the next step is to trace Martin Ducton.'

She picked up her shoulder bag and held out her hand to say goodbye. She only half heard Miss Henderson's closing words, the offer of any future help she could give, reiterated advice that Philippa discuss her plans with her adoptive parents, the gently urged suggestion that if she were able to trace her father it should be done through an intermediary. But some words did penetrate her consciousness:

'We all need our fantasies in order to live. Sometimes relinquishing them can be extraordinarily painful, not a rebirth into something exciting and new, but a kind of death.'

They shook hands, and Philippa, looking into her face for the first time with any real interest, seeing her for the first time as a woman, detected there a fleeting look which, had she not known better, she might have mistaken for pity.

2

She posted her application and cheque to the Registrar General that evening, 4 July 1978, enclosing, as she had done previously, a stamped addressed envelope. Neither Maurice nor Hilda was curious about her private correspondence but she didn't want to risk an officially labelled reply falling through the letter-box. She spent the next few days in a state of controlled excitement which, for most of the time, drove her out of the house, afraid that Hilda might wonder at her restlessness. Pacing round the lake in St James's Park, hands deep in her jacket pockets, she calculated when the birth certificate might arrive. Government departments were notoriously slow, but surely this was a simple enough matter. They had only to check their records. And they wouldn't be coping with a rush of applications. The Act had been passed in 1975.

In exactly one week, on Tuesday 11 July, she saw the familiar envelope on the mat. She took it at once to her own room, calling out to Maurice from the stairs that there was no post for him. She carried it over to the window as if her eyes were growing weaker and she needed more light. The birth certificate, new, crisp, so much more imposing than the shortened form which had served her, as an adopted person, for so long, seemed at first reading to have nothing to do with her. It recorded the birth of a female, Rose Ducton, on 22 May 1960 at 41 Bancroft Gardens, Seven Kings, Essex. The father was shown as Martin John Ducton, clerk; the mother as Mary Ducton, housewife.

So they had left Pennington before she was born. That, perhaps, wasn't surprising. What was unexpected was that they should have moved so far from Wiltshire. Perhaps they had wanted to cut themselves off entirely from the old life, from the gossip, from memories. Perhaps someone had found him a job in Essex, or he might have been returning to his home county. She wondered what he was like, this spurious accommodating father, whether he had been kind to her mother. She hoped that she could like or at least respect him. He might still live at 41 Bancroft Gardens, perhaps with a second wife and a child of his own. Eighteen years wasn't such a long time. She used the telephone extension in her room to ring Liverpool Street Station. Seven Kings was on the eastern suburban line and in the rush hour there were trains every ten minutes. She left without waiting for breakfast. If there were time, she would get coffee at the station.

The 9.25 train from Liverpool Street was almost empty. It was still early enough for Philippa to be travelling against the commuter tide. She sat in her corner seat, her eyes moving from side to side as the train racketed through the urban sprawl of the eastern suburbs; rows of drab houses with blackened bricks and patched roofs from which sprang a tangle of television aerials, frail crooked fetishes against the evil eye; layered high-rise flats smudged in a distant drizzle of rain; a yard piled high with the glitter of smashed cars in symbolic proximity to the regimented crosses of a suburban grave-yard; a paint factory, a cluster of gasometers; pyramids of grit and coal piled beside the track; wastelands rank with weeds; a sloping green bank rising to suburban gardens with their washing-lines and tool-sheds and children's swings among the roses and hollyhocks. The eastern suburbs, so euphoniously but inappropriately named, Maryland, Forest Gate, Manor Park, were alien territory to her, as unvisited and remote from the preoccupations of the last ten years as were the outer suburbs of Glasgow and New York. None of her school friends lived east of Bethnal Green, although a number, unvisited, were reputed to have houses in the few unspoilt Georgian squares off the Whitechapel Road, self-conscious enclaves of culture and radical chic among the tower blocks and the industrial waste-land. Yet the grimy, unplanned urban clutter through which the train rocked and clattered struck some dormant memory, was familiar even in its strangeness, unique despite its bleak uniformity. Surely it wasn't because she had been this way before. Perhaps it was just that the scenery flashing by was so predictably dreary, so typical of the grey purlieus of any large city, that forgotten descriptions, old pictures and newsprint, snatches of film jumbled in her imagination to produce this sense of recognition. Perhaps everyone had been here before. This drab no man's land was part of everyone's mental topography.

There were no taxis at Seven Kings Station. She asked the ticket collector the way to Bancroft Gardens. He directed her down the High Street, left down Church Lane, then first on the right. The High Street ran between the railway and the shopping arcade of small businesses with flats above, a launderette, a newsagent, a greengrocer and a supermarket with shoppers already queuing at the check-outs.

There was one scene so vividly recalled, validated by smell and sound and remembered pain which it was impossible to believe she had imagined. A women wheeling a baby in a pram down just such a street. Herself, little more than a toddler, half stumbling beside the pram, clutching at the handle. The square paving stones speckled with light, unrolling beneath the whirling pram wheels, faster and faster. Her warm grip slipping on the moist metal and the desperate fear that she would lose hold, would be left behind, trampled and kicked under the wheels of the bright red buses. Then a shouted curse. The slap stinging her cheek. A jerk which nearly tore her arm from its socket, and the woman's hand fastening her grip once more on the pram handle. She had called the woman auntie. Auntie May. How extraordinary that she should remember the name now. And the child in the pram had worn a red woolly cap. Its face had been smeared with mucus and chocolate. She remembered that she had hated the child. It must have been winter. The street had been a glare of light and there had been a necklace of coloured bulbs swinging above the greengrocer's stall. The woman had stopped to buy fish. She remembered the slab, bright with red-eyed herrings shedding their glistening scales, the strong oleaginous smell of kippers. It could have been this street, only there was no fishmonger here now. She looked down at the paving stones, mottled with rain. Were these the ones over which she had stumbled so desperately? Or was this street, like the terrain each side of the railway, only one more scene from an imagined past?

Turning from the High Street into Church Lane was stepping from drab commercial suburbia into leafy privacy and cosy domesticity. The narrow street, its verge planted with plane trees, curved gently. Perhaps centuries earlier it had indeed been a lane leading to an ancient village church, a building long since demolished or destroyed by bombing in the Second War. All she could see now was a distant stunted spire which looked as if it had been fabricated from slabs of synthetic stone, and topped by a weather-vane instead of a cross because of some understandable confusion about the building's function.

And here at last was Bancroft Gardens. Stretching out of sight on either side of the road were identical semi-detached houses, each with a path running down the side. They might, she thought, be architecturally undistinguished, but at least they were on a human scale. The gates and railings had been removed and the front gardens were bounded with low brick walls. The front bay windows were square and turreted, a long vista of ramparted respectability. But the uniformity of the architecture was broken by the individuality of the residents. Every front garden was different, a riot of massed summer flowers, squares of lawn meticulously cut and shaped, stone slabs set about with urns bearing geraniums and ivy.

When Philippa reached number 41 she stopped, amazed. The house stood out from its neighbours by a garish celebration of eccentric taste. The grey London bricks had been painted a shiny red outlined with white pointing. It looked like a house built with immense toy bricks. The crenellations of the bay were alternately red and blue. The window was curtained with net looped across and caught up with satin bows. The original front door had been replaced by one with an opaque glass panel and was painted bright yellow. In the front patch of garden an artificial pond of glass was surrounded by synthetic rocks, on which three gnomes with expressions of grinning imbecility were perched with fishing rods.

As soon as she had pressed the doorbell – it let out a musical jingle – Philippa sensed that the house was empty. The owners were probably at work. She tried once more, but there was no reply. Resisting the temptation to peer through the letter-box, she decided to try next door. At least they would know whether Ducton still lived at 41 or where he had gone. The house had no bell and the thud of the knocker sounded unnaturally loud and peremptory. There was no reply. She waited a full minute and was lifting her hand again when she heard the shuffle of feet. The door was opened on a chain, and she glimpsed an elderly woman in apron and hairnet who gave her the unwelcoming suspicious stare of someone to whom no morning visitor at the front door bodes other than ill. Philippa said:

'I'm sorry to disturb you, but I wonder if you can help me. I'm looking for a Mr Martin Ducton who lived next door eighteen years ago. There isn't anyone at home there and I thought you might be able to help.'

The woman said nothing, but stood transfixed, one brown clawlike hand still on the door-chain, the only visible eye staring blankly at Philippa's face. Then there were more steps, firmer and heavier but still muffled. A male voice said:

'Who is it, Ma? What's up?'

'It's a girl, she's asking for Martin Ducton.'

The woman's voice was a whisper, sibilant with wonder and a kind of outrage. A chubby male hand released the chain, and the woman stood there, dwarfed by her son. He was wearing slacks topped with a singlet. On his feet were red carpet slippers. Perhaps, thought Philippa, he was a bus driver or conductor relaxing on his rest day. It hadn't been a good time to call. She said apologetically:

'I'm sorry to trouble you, but I'm trying to trace a Mr Martin Ducton. He used to live next door. I wondered whether you might know what happened to him.'

'Ducton? He's dead, isn't he? Been dead best part of nine years. Died in Wandsworth Prison.'

'In prison?'

'Where else would he be, fucking murderer? He raped that kid, and then he and his missus strangled her. What's he to do with you then? You a reporter or something?'

'Nothing. Nothing. It must be the wrong Ducton. Perhaps I've mistaken the name.'

'Someone been having you on more likely. Ducton he was. Martin Ducton. And she was Mary Ducton. Still is.'

'She's alive then?'

'As far as I know. Coming out soon, I shouldn't wonder. Must've done near ten years by now. Not that she'll be coming back next door. Four families have had that place since the Ductons. It always goes cheap, that house. Young couple bought it six months ago. It's not everyone fancies a place where a kid's been done in. Upstairs in the front room it was.'

He nodded his head towards number 41, but his eyes never met Philippa's face. The woman said suddenly:

'They should've been hung.'

Philippa, astonished, heard herself reply:

'Hanged. The word is hanged. They should have been hanged.'

'That's right,' said the man.

He turned to his mother.

'Buried the kid in Epping Forest, didn't they? Isn't that what they did with her, Ma? Buried her in Epping Forest. Twelve years old she was. You remember, Ma?'

Perhaps the woman was deaf. His last words were an impatient shout. She didn't answer. Still staring at Philippa, she said:

'Her name was Julie Scase. I remember now. They killed Julie Scase. But they never got as far as the forest. Caught with the kid's body in the car boot they was. Julie Scase.'

Philippa made herself ask through lips so stiff that she could hardly form the words:

'Did they have any children? Did you know them?'

'No. We weren't here then. We moved here from Romford after they were inside. There was talk of a kid, a girl, weren't it, who was adopted. Best thing for the poor little bugger.'

Philippa said:

'Then it's not the same Ducton. This Ducton had no children. I've been given the wrong address. I'm sorry to have troubled you.'

She walked away from them down the road. Her legs felt swollen and heavy, weighted bolsters which had no connection with the rest of her body, yet which carried her forward. She looked down at the paving stones, using them as a guide like a drunkard under test. She guessed that the woman and her son were still watching her, and when she had gone about twenty yards she made herself turn round and gaze back at them stolidly. Immediately they disappeared.

Alone now in the empty road, no longer under surveillance, she found that she couldn't go on. She stretched her hands towards the brick wall bordering the nearest garden, found it and sat. She felt faint and a little sick, her heart constricted like a hot pulsating ball. But she mustn't faint here, not in this street. Somehow she must get back to the station. She let her head drop between her knees and felt the blood pound back into her forehead. The faintness passed but the nausea was worse. She sat up again, shutting her eyes against the reeling houses, taking deep gulps of the flower-scented air. Then she opened her eyes and made herself concentrate on the things she could touch and feel. She ran her fingers over the roughness of the wall. Once it had been topped with iron railings. She could feel the coarse grain of the cement-filled holes where they had pierced the brickwork. Perhaps the railings had been taken away in the war to be melted down for armaments. She gazed fixedly at the paving stone under her feet. It was pricked with light, set with infinitesimal specks, bright as diamonds. Pollen from the gardens had blown over it and there was a single flattened rose petal like a drop of blood. How extraordinary that a paving stone should be so varied, should reveal under the intensity of her gaze such gleaming wonders. These things at least were real, and she was real – more vulnerable, less durable than bricks and stones but still present, visible, an identity. If people passed, surely they would be able to see her.

A youngish woman came out of the house two doors down and walked towards her, pushing a pram with an older child trotting beside it and holding on to the handle. The woman glanced at Philippa, but the child dragged his steps, then turned and gazed back at her with a wide, incurious gaze. He had let go of the pram handle and she found herself struggling to her feet, holding out her arms towards him in warning or entreaty. Then the mother stopped and called to him and the child ran up to her and grasped the pram again.

She watched them until they turned the corner into the High Street. It was time to go. She couldn't sit here all day fastened to the wall as if it were a refuge, the one solid reality in a shifting world. Some words of Bunyan came into her mind and she found herself speaking them aloud:

' "Some also have wished that the next way to their father's house were here, and that they might be troubled no more with either hills or mountains to go over, but the way is the way, and there is an end." '

She didn't know why the words comforted her. She wasn't particularly fond of Bunyan and she couldn't see why the passage should speak to her confused mind in which disappointment, anguish and fear struggled for mastery. But as she walked back to the station she spoke the passage over and over again as if the words were in their own way as immutable and solid as the pavement on which she trod. 'The way is the way, there is an end.'

3

When he was working, and that was most of the year, Maurice Palfrey used his room at college. The Sociology Department had swelled since his appointment as senior lecturer, borne on the sixties' tide of optimism and secular faith, and had overflown into an agreeable late eighteenth-century house owned by the college in a Bloomsbury square. He shared the house with the Department of Oriental Studies, colleagues notable for their unobtrusiveness and for the number of their visitors. A succession of small, dark, spectacled men and saried women slid daily through the front door and disappeared into an uncanny silence. He seemed always to be encountering them on the narrow stairs; there were steppings back, bowings, slant-eyed smiles; but only an occasional footfall creaked the upper floor. He felt the house to be infected with secret, mice-like busyness.

His room had once been part of the elegant first-floor drawing-room, its three tall windows and wrought-iron balcony overlooking the square gardens, but it had been divided to provide a room for his secretary. The grace of the proportions had been destroyed and the delicately carved overmantel, the George Morland oil which had always hung in the business-room at Pennington and which he had placed above it, the two Regency chairs looked pretentious and spurious. He felt the need to explain to visitors that he hadn't furnished his room with reproductions. And the conversion hadn't been a success. His secretary had to pass through his room to get to hers and the clatter of the typewriter through the thin partition was so irritating a metallic *obbligato* to his meetings that he had to tell Molly to stop working when he had visitors. It was difficult to concentrate during meetings when he was aware that she was sitting next door glowering across her machine in sullen, ostentatious idleness. Elegance and beauty had been sacrificed for a utility which wasn't even efficient. Helena, on her first visit to the room, had merely said: 'I don't like conversions' and hadn't visited again.

Hilda, who hadn't appeared to notice or care about the room's proportions, had left the department after their marriage and had never come back.

The habit of working away from home had begun after his marriage to Helena when she had bought 68 Caldecote Terrace. Walking hand in hand through the empty echoing rooms like exploring children, folding back the shutters so that the sun came through in great shafts and lay in pools on the unpolished boards, the pattern of their future together had been laid down. She had made it plain that there would be no intrusion of his work into their domestic life. When he had suggested that he would need a study she had pointed out that the house was too small, the whole of the top floor was needed for the nursery and the nanny. She was prepared, apparently, to wash and cook with the aid of daily help, but not to look after her child. She had enumerated their necessities: the drawing-room, dining-room, their two bedrooms and the spare bedroom. There had been no study at Pennington; the suggestion seemed to her eccentric. And there could hardly be a library. She had been brought up with the Wren library at Pennington, and to her any other private library was merely a room in which people kept books.

Now, when he had long ago worked through his grief – and how accurately some of his colleagues had described that interestingly painful psychological process – when he could distance himself even from humiliation and pain, he was intrigued by the moral eccentricity which could, apparently without compunction, father on him another man's child, yet which was outraged by the thought of abortion. He recalled their words when she had told him about the child. He had asked:

'What do you want to do about it, have an abortion?'

'Of course not. Don't be so bourgeois, darling.'

'Abortion can be thought of as distasteful, undesirable, dangerous or even morally wrong if you think in those terms. I don't see what's bourgeois about it.'

'It's all those things. Why on earth should you suppose I want an abortion?'

'You might feel that the baby would be a nuisance.'

'My old nanny is a nuisance, so is my father. I don't kill them off.'

'Then what do you want to do?'

'Marry you, of course. You are free, aren't you? You haven't a wife secreted away somewhere?'

'No, I haven't a wife. But my darling love, you can't want to marry me.'

'I never know what I want. I'm only really sure of what I don't want. But I think we'd better marry.'

It had been the commonest, the most obvious of cheats, and he the most gullible of victims. But he had been in love for the first and only time, a state which he now realized didn't conduce to clear thinking. Poets were right to call love a madness. His love had certainly been a kind of insanity in the sense that his thought processes, his perception of external reality, even his physical life, appetite, digestion, sleep, all had been disturbed. Small wonder that he hadn't calculated with what flattering speed she had singled him out during that short holiday at Perugia, how short the time between that first appraising look across the dining-room table to getting him into her bed.

It was true that she only knew what she didn't want. Her needs had seemed to him reassuringly modest, her unwants had all the force of strong desire. He was surprised that they had found the house in Caldecote Terrace so quickly. All districts of London were apparently impossible for her. Hampstead was too trendy, Mayfair too expensive, Bayswater vulgar, Belgravia too smart. And they had been restricted in choice by her refusal to contemplate a mortgage. It was useless for him to point out the advantages of tax relief. A nineteenth-century earl had once mortgaged Pennington, to the embarrassment of his encumbered heirs. A mortgage was bourgeois. In the end they had found Caldecote Terrace in Pimlico and here she had given him, however casual the gift, the four happiest years of his life. Her death, Orlando's death, had taught him all he knew about suffering. He was glad now that no premature knowledge had despoiled those first few months of grief. It hadn't been until two years after his marriage to Hilda, seeking medical advice on their childlessness, that he had learnt the truth; that he could never father a child. That period of mourning for a woman who hadn't existed, for a son who wasn't his son, now seemed to him a debt discharged, not without honour, a secular grace.

He had grieved more for Orlando than for Helena. Helena's death had been the loss of a joy to which he had never felt entitled, which had never seemed quite real, which he had hoped, rather than expected, would last. Some part of his mind had accepted her loss as inevitable; death could not part them more completely than could life. But for Orlando he had mourned with an elemental violence of grief, a wordless scream of anguish. The death of a beautiful, intelligent and happy child had always seemed to him an outrage, and this child had been his son. His grief had seemed to embrace a cosmic fellowship of suffering. He had indulged no inordinate hopes for Orlando, foisted on his child no high ambition, had asked only that he should continue to exist in his beauty, his loving-kindness, his peculiarly uncoordinated grace.

And it was because Orlando had died that he had married Hilda. He knew that their friends found the marriage an enigma. It was easily explained. Hilda was the only one among his friends, his colleagues, who had wept for Orlando. The day after his return from the funeral at Pennington – the depositing of Helena and Orlando in the family vault had symbolized for him the final separation, they lay now with their own kind – Hilda had come into his office with the morning post. He could remember how she had looked, the white schoolgirl's blouse, the skirt which she had pressed that morning – he could see the impress of the iron across the front pleat. She stood there at the door looking at him. All she said was: 'That little boy. That little boy.' He had watched while her face stiffened and then disintegrated with grief. Two tears oozed from her eyes and ran unchecked over her cheeks.

She had only known Orlando briefly on the few occasions when his nurse had brought him into the office. But she had wept for him. His colleagues had written and spoken their condolences, averting their eyes from a grief they could not assuage. Death was in poor taste. They had treated him with sympathetic wariness, as if he were suffering from a slightly embarrassing disease. She only had paid Orlando the tribute of a spontaneous tear.

And that had been the beginning. It had led to the first invitation to dinner, to their theatre dates, to the curious courtship which had merely reinforced their misconceptions about each other. He had persuaded himself that she was teachable, that she had a goodness and simplicity which could meet his complicated needs, that behind the bland gentle face was a mind which only needed the stimulus of his loving concern to break into some kind of flowering – what, he was never precisely sure. And she had been so different from Helena. It had been flattering to give instead of to take, to be the one who was loved instead of the one who loved. And so, with what to some of his colleagues had seemed indecent haste, they had come to that registry office wedding. Poor girl, she had hoped for a white wedding in church. That quiet exchange of contracts could hardly have seemed to her or her parents like a proper marriage. She had got through it in an agony of embarrassment, afraid perhaps that the registrar had thought that she was pregnant.

He was suddenly aware of his restlessness. He walked across to the tall window and looked out over the dishevelled square. Although the slight rain had now stopped, the plane trees were bedraggled and scraps of sodden litter lay unmoving on the spongy grass. This slow dripping-away of the summer matched his mood. He had always disliked the hiatus between academic years when the detritus of the last term had scarcely been cleared away, yet the next was already casting its shadow. He couldn't remember when the conscientious performance of duty had replaced enthusiasm, or when conscientiousness had finally given way to boredom. What worried him now was that he approached each academic term with an emotion more disturbing than boredom, something between irritation and apprehension. He knew that he no longer saw his students as individuals, no longer had any wish to know or communicate except on the level of tutor to student, and even here there was no trust between them. There seemed to have been a reversal of roles, he the student, they the instructors. They sat in the ubiquitous uniform of the young, jeans and sweaters, huge clumpy plimsolls, open-necked shirts topped with denim jackets, and gazed at him with the fixity of inquisitors waiting for any deviation from orthodoxy. He told himself that they were no different from his former students, graceless, not very intelligent, uneducated if education implied the ability to write their own language with elegance and precision, to think clearly, to discriminate or enjoy. They were filled with the barely suppressed anger of those who have grabbed for themselves sufficient privilege to know just how little privilege they would ever achieve. They didn't want to be taught, having already decided what they preferred to believe.

He had become increasingly petty, irritated by details, by the diminishing, for example, of their forenames, Bill, Bert, Mike, Geoff,

Steve. He wanted to enquire peevishly if a commitment to Marxism was incompatible with a disyllabic forename. And their vocabulary provoked him. In his last series of seminars on the juvenile law they had talked always of 'kids'. The mixture of condescension and sycophancy in the world repelled him. He himself had used the words 'children' and 'young people' punctiliously and had sensed that it had annoyed them. He had found himself talking to them like a schoolmaster to the lower third:

'I've corrected some of the grammar and spelling. This may seem bourgeois pedantry, but if you plan to organize revolution you'll have to convince the intelligent and educated as well as the gullible and ignorant. It might be worthwhile trying to develop a prose style which isn't a mixture of sociological jargon and the standard expected from the C stream of a comprehensive school. And 'obscene' means 'lewd', 'indecent', 'filthy' – it can't properly be used to describe Government policy in not implementing the recommendations of the Finer Report on one-parent families, reprehensible as that decision may be.'

Mike Beale, chief instigator of student power, had received back his last essay muttering under his breath. It had sounded like 'fucking bastard' and might indeed have been 'fucking bastard' except that Beale was incapable of an invective which didn't include the word 'fascist'. Beale had just completed his second year. With luck he would graduate next autumn, departing to take a social-work qualification and find himself a job with a local authority, no doubt to teach juvenile delinquents that the occasional minor act of robbery with violence was a natural response of the underprivileged to capitalist tyranny and to promote political awareness among those council-house tenants looking for an excuse not to pay their rents. But he would be replaced by others. The academic machine would grind on, and what was so extraordinary was that essentially he and Beale were on the same side. He had been too publicly committed and for too long to renege now. Socialism and sociology. He felt like an old campaigner who no longer believes in his cause but finds it enough that there is a battle and he knows his own side.

He stuffed into his briefcase the few letters he had found waiting for him in his cubby-hole that morning. One was from a Socialist Member of Parliament enlisting his help with the General Election which he took for granted would come in early October. Would

Maurice talk on one of the television party political broadcasts? He supposed he would accept. The box sanctified, conferred identity. The more familiar the face, the more to be trusted. The other was yet another appeal to him to apply for the chair in social work at a northern university. He could understand the concern among his colleagues about the chair. There had been a number of recent appointments outside the field of social work. But what the protesters couldn't see was that what mattered was the quality of the academic work and of the research, not the discipline of the applicant. With the present competition for chairs sociology needed to demonstrate its academic respectability, not pursue a spurious professionalism. He was becoming increasingly irritated by the sensitivity of colleagues, unsure of themselves, feeling morbidly undervalued, complaining that they were expected to remedy all the ills of society. He only wished that he could cure his own.

He put away the last few papers and locked his desk drawer. He remembered that tonight the Cleghorns were coming to dinner. Cleghorn was one of the trustees of a fund set up to investigate the causes and treatment of juvenile delinquency, and Maurice had a post-graduate student who was looking for a research job for the next couple of years. The advantage of giving regular dinner parties was that when one was angling for a favour an invitation to dine didn't look too blatant a ploy. Closing the door, he wondered without much curiosity where Philippa had been going that morning so early, and whether she would remember the Cleghorns and get home in time to do the dining-room flowers.

4

When she finally got back to Liverpool Street, Philippa spent the rest of the day walking in the City. It was just after six when she returned to Caldecote Terrace. The rain had nearly stopped and was now so fine that it fell against her warm face as a drifting mist needled with cold. But the pavement stones were as tacky as if it had fallen heavily all day, and a few shallow puddles had collected in the gutter into which occasional dollops dropped with heavy portentousness from a sky as thick and grey as curdled milk. Number 68 looked just as it did when she returned from school on any dull summer evening.

This homecoming was outwardly no different from any other. As always the basement kitchen was brightly lit and the rest of the house was in darkness except for a light shining from the hall through the elegant fanlight of the front door.

The kitchen was on the lower ground floor at the front of the house. The dining-room, which was at the back, had french doors to the garden. The whole of the raised ground floor was taken up by the drawing-room; this, too, had access to the garden by a flight of delicately carved and moulded wrought-iron steps. On summer evenings they would carry their coffee down to the patio to the chairs under the fig tree. The walled garden, only thirty feet long, enclosed the scent of roses and white stocks. The patio was set about with white-painted wooden tubs of geraniums glowing blood-red in the peculiarly intense light before the setting of the sun, then bleached as the patio lamps were turned on.

The light was always on in the north-facing kitchen, yet Hilda never drew the curtains. Perhaps she had never realized that, to the upper world, she moved on a lighted stage. She was there now, already starting on the dinner. Philippa crouched down, clutching the railings, and peered through at her. Hilda cooked with a peculiar intensity, moving like a high priestess among the impedimenta of her craft, consulting her recipe book with the keen unblinking scrutiny of an artist examining his model, then briefly laying her hand on each ingredient like a preparatory blessing. She cleaned and tidied the rest of the house obsessively, but as if nothing it contained had anything to do with her; only here in the organized muddle of her kitchen was she at home. This was her habitat. Here she lived doubly caged behind the protecting iron bars on the windows and the spiked railings above, seeing the world pass as a succession of dilatory or hurrying feet. Her pale lank hair which normally fell forward over her face was strained back from her eyes with two plastic combs. In the white apron which she invariably wore she looked very young and defenceless, like a schoolgirl preoccupied with a practical examination, or a newly engaged maid coping with her first dinner party. And it wasn't because she worked in the kitchen that she looked like a servant. All but the wealthiest of the mothers of the girls at school did most of their own cooking. Cookery had become a fashionable craft, almost a cult. Perhaps it was the white apron, the worried eyes which seemed always to expect, almost to invite a rebuke, which made her look like a woman precariously earning her keep.

Philippa had forgotten that the Cleghorns and Gabriel Lomas were coming to dinner. She saw that the meal was to begin with artichokes. Six of them, solidly ornamental, were ranged on the central table ready for the pot. The kitchen, under the glare of the twin fluorescent lights, was as familiar as a picture on a nursery wall. The one wicker chair with its shabby patchwork cushion. It had never been necessary to buy a second since neither Maurice nor Philippa made it a habit to sit in the kitchen chatting with Hilda while she cooked. The shelf of paperback recipe books with their greasy crumpled covers, the calendar hanging beside the wall-mounted telephone with its garish blue picture of Brixham Harbour, the portable television set, black-and-white since the one colour set was in the drawing-room. Philippa couldn't remember ever seeing Hilda sitting alone in the drawing-room. Why should she? It wasn't her drawing-room. Everything in it had been chosen by Maurice or by his first wife.

Philippa had never heard Maurice speak of Helena, but it never occurred to her that this was because he continued to grieve for her or because he was sensitive to Hilda's feelings. She had long ago decided that he was a man who kept his emotions in compartments. That way there could be no messy spillage from one life to another. From time to time she had felt a vague curiosity about Helena Palfrey, glamorized and dignified as she was for ever by an early and dramatic death. Only once had she seen a picture of Maurice's first wife. It had been at a bring-and-buy sale held at school in aid of Oxfam. One of the parents had donated a bundle of glossy society magazines. They had sold well, she remembered. People were happy to give a penny or two for the brief pleasures of nostalgia and recollection. They had flicked through them giggling.

'Look, here's Molly and John at Henley. My dear, did we really wear skirts that length?'

Browsing through a bundle displayed for sale, she had seen with a shock of surprise and recognition, Maurice's face. It was a younger Maurice, strange yet utterly familiar, wearing the startled half-fatuous smile of a man suddenly caught by the camera who hasn't had time to decide what expression to assume. It had been taken at a wedding. The caption said: 'Mr Maurice Palfrey and Lady Helena

Palfrey chatting to Sir George and Lady Scott-Harries'. And there they were, not chatting to anyone, but staring into the lens, champagne glasses in their hands, as if toasting this second of their joint lives ephemerally recorded in microdots. Lady Helena Palfrey, smiling, stood taller than her husband in her wide-brimmed hat and ridiculously short skirt. Dark hair framed a face which looked no longer young; bony, almost ravaged, heavy-browed. Philippa had torn out the cutting and had kept it, secreted in one of her books, for almost a year. From time to time she had taken it over to the light of her bedroom window to peer at it obsessively, willing it to disclose some clue to the woman's character, to their love, if love there had been, to their joint life together. Eventually, frustrated, she had torn it up and flushed it down the lavatory.

And now, with an equal intensity, she peered through the railings at Maurice's living wife. She was bent over the central table, carefully rolling out fillets of veal. It looked as if the dinner guests were to have veal in wine and mushroom sauce. They would praise the meal, of course; the guests invariably did. Philippa remembered having read that it was the last war which had finally killed the English reticence about the quality of a meal. Now most of the women, and sometimes the men, praised, enquired, exchanged recipes. But with Hilda the praise became effusive, strained, almost embarrassingly insincere. It was as if they needed to reassure or propitiate her, to give her worth in her own eyes. For the whole of her marriage her husband's guests had treated her as if cooking were her only interest, the only topic she could talk about. And now perhaps it was.

There were footsteps coming down the street. Philippa scrambled to her feet, wincing at the pain in her cramped legs. She felt suddenly faint and had to grasp at the spikes of the railings for support. She remembered for the first time that she had walked for nearly seven hours through the streets of London, round the parks, in and out of the City churches, along the Embankment, without stopping to eat. Painfully, she made her way up the steps to the front door.

She turned her key in the lock and passed through the inner porch with its twin panels of Burne-Jones stained glass, an allegory of spring and summer, into the pearl-grey quietness of the hall. She smelled the usual faint smell of lavender and fresh paint, so faint that it was almost illusory, a conditioned response to the familiar objects of home. The delicate banister rail in polished pale mahogany supported by elegant balusters unwound from its scroll and curved upwards drawing the eye to the stained glass of the landing window. The two panes were a continuation of the ones in the porch; a garlanded woman with a cornucopia spilling the fruits of autumn, bearded winter with his faggots and stave. By an earlier taste their self-conscious aestheticism and period charm would have been despised; now Maurice, who didn't particularly like them, wouldn't have dreamed of having them removed, probably knowing to a pound the value they added to his property. But the rest of the hall was his taste, his or that of his first wife; the low shelf with his collection of Staffordshire historical groups, bold against the shiny white wood; a pale elongated Nelson dying black-booted in Hardy's arms; Wellington, Field Marshal's baton on his hip, mounted on his charger Copenhagen; Victoria and Albert with their blond idealized children grouped before the Grand Exhibition; a lighthouse rising from a turbulent sea of unchipped waves, with Grace Darling straining on her oars. Above them, in incongruous proximity but looking somehow right since both combined strength with delicacy, were Maurice's three nineteenth-century Japanese prints in their carved rosewood frames; Nobukazu, Kikugawa, Tokohumi. Like the Staffordshire, which as a child she had been allowed to dust, they were part of her childhood, ferocious warriors with their carved swords, pale moons behind delicate blossomed boughs, the soft pinks and greens of the slant-eyed women in their kimonos. Had she really only known them for ten years? Where then had been those other hallways, forgotten except in nightmares, with their dark dados, the lank greasy mackintoshes hanging inside the door, the smell of cabbage and fish, the claustrophobic horror of the black cupboard under the stairs?

Without taking off her coat she went down to the kitchen. Hilda came out of the pantry, a box of eggs in her hand. Without looking at Philippa she said:

'I'm glad you're back. We've got the Cleghorns for dinner. Can you do the table and the flowers, darling?'

Philippa didn't answer. She felt very calm, light-headed with tiredness, her anger spent. She was glad that she had no need to discipline her voice, that she was in complete control. She closed the kitchen door and leaned her back against it as if barring Hilda's escape. She waited until Hilda, getting no answer, looked up at her. Then she said:

'Why didn't you tell me that my mother was a murderess?'

But she needed to discipline herself after all. Hilda looked so ridiculous, stuck there speechless, mouth gaping, eyes wide with fright, the personification of stage horror, that she had to make a conscious effort to stop herself breaking into nervous laughter. She watched while the box of eggs dropped from Hilda's parting hands as if she had willed them to fall. One bounced free and cracked open, spilling an unbroken dome of yellow, shivering in its glutinous pad of white. Instinctively Philippa stepped towards it. Hilda cried out sharply:

'Don't step in it! Don't step in it!'

Moaning, she seized a cloth and dabbed at the yolk. There was a splurge of yellow over the black and white tiles. Still kneeling, she muttered:

'The Cleghorns, they're coming to dinner. I haven't done the table yet. I knew you'd find out! I told him. I always said so. Who told you? Where have you been all day?'

'I applied for a copy of my birth certificate under the Children Act. Then I went to 41 Bancroft Gardens. There was no one in, but a neighbour told me. Then I spent the day walking in the City. After that I came home, I mean I came back here.'

Hilda was still scrubbing at the tiles, smearing the yellow mucus. She said wildly:

'I don't want to talk about it, not now! I've got to get on with dinner. The Cleghorns are coming. It's important to your father.'

'The Cleghorns? How can it be? If they want something from him they'll hardly complain if the food isn't up to expectations. And if he wants something from them, then he's wasting his time if their decision can be swayed by whether the veal is the best they've eaten since they found that intriguing little inn in the Dordogne.'

She explained patiently:

'Look, they don't matter. I matter. Why didn't you tell me?'

'How could we? A thing like that. They killed that girl. Raped and murdered her. She was only twelve! What good would it have done, your knowing? It wasn't your fault. It was nothing to do with you.

I don't want to think about it. It was horrible, horrible! There are things you can't tell a child, ever. It would have been too cruel.'

'More cruel than letting me find out?'

Hilda turned on her with a sudden flash of defensive spirit.

'Yes, cruel and wrong! You don't mind so much now. At least you're grown up. You have your own life, your own personality. It can't destroy you now. You wouldn't be talking like this if you really cared. You're excited and angry, and I suppose you're shocked, but you aren't really hurt. It isn't real to you. You stand outside life and look at it as if you aren't really part of it. You watch people as if they're acting on some kind of stage. That's how you were looking down at me just now. You thought I didn't know you were there, but I did. You don't really care what your mother did to that child. It doesn't touch you. Nothing does.'

Philippa stared at Hilda, disconcerted by this unexpected perci-pience. She cried:

'But I want it to touch me! I want to feel it!'

She thought:

'It's because I don't really believe it yet. All my past is fabrication. This is just a new story, a different angle, to be explored and experienced. Then I shall return to the reality I fabricated for myself, to that unknown father striding across the lawn at Pennington. It is these newcomers, not he, who are the usurpers.'

Hilda was rinsing out the floor-cloth under the tap, muttering above the splash of the water.

'When you came in just now – you knew what you were going to say. I expect you practised it in the train. But you aren't really unhappy. You're not as unhappy as you would have been if you hadn't got your Cambridge scholarship. You're like your father, neither of you can bear to fail.'

'You mean I'm like Maurice. I don't know whether I'm like my father. That's one of the things I mean to find out.'

'It was Parliament, that Act they passed. They had no right. It was breaking faith with adopters. When we took you on we thought that you'd never be able to find out who your parents were.'

'Took you on.' Was that how Hilda had always seen her, as an obligation, a responsibility, a burden? Probably Hilda had never really wanted her. Why should she? A baby adopted from birth, pitiful, dependent, responsive, might have done something for

Hilda's frustrated maternal feelings. But what satisfaction could she have expected from a difficult and resentful eight-year-old whose parents had suddenly been taken from her, had disappeared without explanation? No, it had been Maurice's doing. Maurice had demanded his experimental material. But the idea of adoption must have been Hilda's. She must have been the one who had originally agitated for a child. Maurice wouldn't have cared one way or the other. But if there had to be an adopted child to satisfy Hilda's thwarted maternal instinct, then he would at least ensure that they chose one with intelligence but from the worst possible background. If he couldn't have a child of his own, at least he could rear one for the glory of sociological theory. It was surprising that he hadn't selected a second female, carefully matched for age and intelligence, to monitor their joint progress. After all, every experiment needed a control. How he and Hilda must have enjoyed their secret! Was this what had kept their odd marriage intact, the titillating confederacy of deceit?

She said:

'I could have applied to a court for permission to see my birth certificate once I came of age. That's always been the law, even if people didn't realize it.'

'But you wouldn't have done that, and if you had, at least we'd have been warned. Then we could have told the court and the judge wouldn't have given you permission. But even if he had, it would still have been better than learning it when you were a child.'

'And all those stories? My mother being a servant at Pennington and dying soon after I was born. Did you concoct them together?'

'No, that was me. He just wanted to tell you that we didn't know who your parents were. But I had to tell you something when you asked. The story just grew.'

'And that bit about the letter my mother wrote, the letter to be handed to me when I'm twenty-one?'

Hilda gazed up at her, puzzled.

'I never told you that. What letter? I didn't say anything about a letter.'

So that part must have been her own fabrication. Together she and Hilda, in unconscious collaboration, had created and embellished their joint fantasy, a small detail there, a touch of local colour, snatches of imagined conversation, small descriptions. Sometimes

Hilda had been forced by Philippa's obsessional questions into embarrassed evasions, but Philippa had always put these down to Hilda's embarrassment at any mention of Pennington and Maurice's first wife. But she had done it very cleverly, you had to give her that. The story had hung together without obvious inconsistencies. Philippa's mother had been a parlour-maid at Pennington. She had given birth to an illegitimate child and had died shortly afterwards. The baby had been fostered by people in the village, now dead, and then by foster parents in London. Maurice had heard about her on one of his return visits to Pennington after his first wife's death, and had suggested to Hilda that they should foster the child. The fostering had been successful and had led six months later to adoption. There was no one now to disprove any of it. The present Earl had sold Pennington nine years previously and had taken refuge from taxation and the exigencies of his ex-wives in the south of France. Very few of the original servants lived in Pennington village and none still worked in the house. It had subsequently been sold to an Arab and was now closed to the public. It would have been difficult to disprove the story and Philippa had never had any inclination to try. It had, she realized now, conformed too neatly with her own private imaginings. She had believed it because she had wanted it to be true. And even now, one small part of her mind obstinately refused to relinquish it.

She said bitterly:

'You'd be a good liar in the witness box. I wouldn't have credited you with that much imagination. I knew that it embarrassed you to talk about my mother but I thought that was because she came from Pennington. It must have amused you, fooling me for all these years. I hope it was some compensation for having me foisted on you.'

Hilda cried:

'It wasn't like that! I wanted you! We both wanted you! When I found out I couldn't give Maurice a child . . .'

'You make a baby sound like an orgasm. And if that's all he married you for – and I can't think why else – it's a pity he didn't send you to a gynaecologist for a certificate of fertility before you went off together to the registry office.'

They heard the quiet thud of the front door closing. Hilda said:

'It's your father! Maurice is home!'

She spoke wildly, terrified, like a woman awaiting a drunken husband. Then she dashed to the bottom of the stairs and called:

'Maurice! Maurice! Come here!'

The footsteps hesitated, then came deliberately down the stairs. He stood in the kitchen doorway watching them. Hilda cried:

'She knows! She found out about that clause in the Children Act. I told you she would. She's got her birth certificate. She's been to Bancroft Gardens.'

He said to Philippa:

'How much do you know?'

'How much is there? That I'm the child of a rapist and a murderess.'

She was glad that he didn't love her, that neither of them loved her, that there was no risk that he would come across to her in spontaneous pity and smother all the shock and misery in his arms. He said calmly:

'I'm sorry, Philippa. I suppose this moment was inevitable, but I wish it didn't have to happen.'

'You should have told me.'

He placed his briefcase on the table, calmly moving the artichokes to make room.

'Even if I agree, and I don't, there hasn't been a moment since the adoption when it seemed the right time to tell. What time precisely would you have chosen? When you were adjusting to living here, when you were eleven and taking the examination into the South London Collegiate, when you were coping with adolescence, working for O-levels, A-levels, the Cambridge scholarship? Ten years pass very quickly, particularly when punctuated with the crises of childhood. With some news, the later the better.'

'Where is she now?'

'Your mother? At Melcombe Grange in the pre-release unit. It's an open prison near York. She's due out I believe in about a month's time.'

'You knew that!'

'I've had an interest in her release date, naturally. But that's all. She's not my responsibility. There's nothing I can do about it.'

'But I can. I can write to her and ask her to come to me. I've saved the money for my European trip. I can take a flat in London and look after her, at least for the two months before I go up to Cambridge.'

The idea, spontaneous, surprising even to her own ears, seemed to have come from outside herself, an impulse not subject to her will. And yet she knew even as she spoke the words that this was what she must do, what she had intended to do from that first moment of learning that her mother was alive. She didn't think about her motives; this wasn't the moment for that egotistical indulgence. But her heart told her that they were corrupt, that this histrionic gesture was born, not out of compassion for that unknown mother, but out of her anger against Maurice, her misery, her own complicated half-acknowledged needs.

He had turned away from her and she couldn't see his face. But his voice was suddenly hard. He said:

'The idea is stupid and dangerous, dangerous for both of you. You owe her nothing, not even the conventional obligation of a child to a parent. All that was expunged with the adoption order. And there's nothing that she has that you need, nothing that she can give you.'

'I wasn't thinking of obligations. And there is something I need that she can give me. Information. Knowledge. A past. She can help me to find out who I am. Don't you understand? She's my mother! I can't wipe that out any more than I can wipe out what she did. I can't suddenly learn that she's alive and not want to meet her, get to know her. What do you expect me to do? Go on as if today had never happened? Concoct a new fantasy to live by? Everything you and Hilda have given me is pretence. This is real.'

Hilda gave a small ridiculous sound between a snort and a sob. Maurice turned and slowly lifted his briefcase from the table. Suddenly he looked and sounded very tired. He said:

'We'll talk about it after dinner. It's a nuisance that the Cleghorns are coming, but we can't put them off at less than an hour's notice. As I said, there's never a convenient moment for this kind of news.'

5

She dressed with care. The guests were only to be the Cleghorns and Gabriel Lomas to even up the numbers, but it wasn't for them that she put on her favourite evening skirt of fine pleated wool and the high-necked green-blue tunic; she was dressing for herself. The skirt and top fulfilled what she most demanded of clothes, that they should be dramatic but easy to put on and sensuously agreeable to wear. She took care with her hair, brushing it until her scalp smarted, then winding it in a high top-knot, curling two thin strands with a wetted finger to lie against each cheek. Afterwards she stood and surveyed herself in the full-length glass. This is how I see myself. How do I look to others?

It surprised her that she was so calm; that the long, bony, honey-coloured face, with its high cheekbones, was so clear in its outlines, the eyes so unclouded. She had half expected the image to fudge and quiver like a reflection seen in a distorting mirror. She stretched out her hands, and fingers splayed to meet fingers encountering the cold glass.

She began to pace slowly round the room, looking at it with the appraising eyes of an inquisitive stranger. It stretched the whole length of the house on the top storey where two attics had been converted into one large, low-ceilinged room. Maurice had furnished it for her to her taste when she was twelve. Unlike the rest of the house it was modern, functional, sparsely furnished, giving an impression of airiness, of being suspended in space. It was very light with windows at each end. The southern window gave a view of the small walled garden and York stone patio, of plane trees, of the multitudinous and varied roofs of Pimlico. The furniture was modern, the bed and fitted wall units in pale wood. At this desk she had worked for O- and A-levels and for her Cambridge entrance. On this bed she and Gabriel had groped and twined in that first unsuccessful attempt at making love. The phrase struck her as ridiculous. Whatever they had been making together, it hadn't been love. He had said, gently at first, and then with controlled irritation:

'Stop thinking about yourself. Stop worrying about what you're feeling. Let yourself go.'

But that she had never been able to do. How could you let go of something which you had never felt was yours to relinquish? To let go implied the utter confidence of undisputed possession, the assurance that nothing of oneself could be violated by that transitory, terrifying loss of control.

It surprised her that this initial sexual fiasco hadn't resulted in an estrangement. Like her, he couldn't tolerate failure. And afterwards, unsatisfied and frustrated, she hadn't even managed the expedience of pretence or the grace of generosity. It had been a bad time to recall the warning of his sister; Sarah's voice, cool, amused, a little spiteful:

'My brother seems to look on the upper sixth as his private harem. He's AC/DC by the way. Not that it matters. But it's as well to know these little details before you try to plug in your kettle.'

Pulling on her dressing-gown, she had said:

'Why did you bother? Was it to prove that you can make it with a woman?'

And he had replied:

'What were you trying to prove? That you can make it at all?'

But he had, if anything, been more attentive, more apparently devoted since that disastrous evening, and she suspected that he knew perfectly well why she played her part in their charade. He was high on her list of objects of use and beauty which she planned to take with her to Cambridge. Having the rich and amusing Honourable Gabriel Lomas in tow would do her absolutely no harm with her contemporaries at King's.

Settling down at this desk to write a history essay on the first Saturday morning after the room had been completed, she had learned an early lesson, that undeserved good fortune was resented. Mrs Cooper, Hilda's cleaning woman, had been brought up by Hilda to admire the room. Hilda involved her in any new domestic arrangements, apparently in a desperate attempt to pretend that they liked each other. But Mrs Cooper, unpropitiated, persisted in calling her 'madam' and held aloof as if to demonstrate that ten shillings an hour and a free lunch could buy obsequiousness, but it couldn't buy affection. She had stared round the room before giving her customary unenthusiastic verdict. 'It's very nice, madam, I'm sure.' But she had lingered a few seconds when Hilda left, then coming quickly up to Philippa had pushed her face close to her cheek. The words had come in a hiss of sour breath.

'Bastard. I hope you're grateful. It isn't right. All this for a bastard when decent kids have to make do four in a room. You ought to be in a home.'

Then her voice had again become respectful:

'Coming, madam.'

Philippa could recall still the shock and anger. But she had learned control. There were no tantrums now. Words, she had discovered, were more effective than screams, more hurtful than kicks and blows. She had said coolly:

'You shouldn't breed four children if you can't afford them. And I expect they'll go on living four to a room if they're as ugly and stupid as you.'

After that Mrs Cooper had handed in her notice, but without giving a reason, and Hilda, as Philippa knew, had been left with an added weight of inadequacy and failure.

She walked across to the bookshelves and ran her hand along the spines of the books. Here was the orthodox library of an upper-middle-class student. With these volumes you could pass an A-level in English literature whatever the year or the syllabus; with luck and a good memory you could even achieve a Cambridge entrance. It wasn't easy to deduce the girl's personal taste, except perhaps that she preferred Turgenev to Tolstoy, Proust to Flaubert, Henry James to Dickens. But here were no battered childhood favourites passed from generation to generation. True the accepted upper-middle-class children's classics were present; the *Just So Stories*, *The Wind in the Willows*, Carroll, and Ransome and Nesbit. They looked read, but they looked, also, as if they had been bought new for this privileged child.

Here on these packed shelves was enough knowledge, wisdom, imagination to sustain her for life. For what life? There wasn't a word which she herself had written, yet it was in this accumulation of other men's thoughts and experiences that she had looked for an affirmation of identity. She thought:

'Even putting on the clothes of my choice was only putting on myself. Naked in the bathroom just now, who was I? I can be described, measured, weighed, my physical processes recorded, given a name, real or unreal, for the convenient documentation of a life. But who am I? Whoever I am, nothing of me comes from Maurice and Hilda. How could it? They've done nothing but provide the props for this charade, the clothes, the artefacts. Even this soliloquy is contrived. Some part of me, that part of me which one day will make me a writer, is watching another me choosing the words to think, deciding what emotions are appropriate to feel.'

She opened the immense fitted wardrobe and rattled the hangers along the rail. The swaying skirts and dresses emitted a faint scent which she recognized as familiar. It must be her own. This girl liked expensive clothes. She bought little but she bought with care. She wore only wool and cotton; obviously she disliked synthetics. She smiled at the facile irony.

She moved over to the noticeboard of charcoal-coloured cork fitted to the wall above the desk unit. It was patterned with postcards, obviously bought on holidays or at art galleries, a school timetable, notices cut from newspapers of forthcoming art exhibitions, *aides-mémoire*, two invitations to parties. She examined the postcards. Hans Holbein's delicate portrait of Cicely Heron; Augustus John's etching of W. B. Yeats; a Renoir nude from the Musée du Jeu de Paume; a Farington aquatint of London Bridge in 1799; a George Brecht. How could one deduce this unknown girl's taste in art from such capricious pickings? They told one nothing except which galleries she had visited.

In this room, she had concocted for herself over ten years a whole mythology of identity. It was slipping away from her now, that dead discredited world. She told herself, nothing has changed; I am the same person as I was yesterday. But who was I yesterday? The room reminded her of a designer's room in a furniture store, its carefully chosen objects disposed around to give the illusion of an absent owner, but one who had no reality except in the designer's mind.

She recalled Hilda's face bending over her to tuck her in at night.

'Where am I when I'm asleep?'

'You're still here, in bed.'

'But how do you know?'

'Because I can see you, silly. I can touch you.'

Only, of course, she very seldom did touch. The three of them lived distanced. That hadn't been Hilda's fault. When Philippa was tucked in at night she had lain rigid, rejecting the final, and in the end merely dutiful, kiss, hating that moist encounter of the flesh more than the rough tickle of the blanket which Hilda always drew from under the sheet and tucked against her face.

'But you know you are here because you can see and touch me. When I'm asleep I can't see or touch anyone.'

'No one can when they're asleep. But you're still here in your bed.'

'If I went into hospital and had an anaesthetic, where would I be then? Not my body, where would *I* be?'

'Best ask Daddy.'

'When I am dead where will I be?'

'With Jesus in heaven.'

But Hilda had spoken that heresy against Maurice's atheism without conviction.

She was drawn again to the bookcase. Here, surely, if anywhere, an answer was to be found. And here, ranked together, were the first editions of Maurice's books, all inscribed in his hand with the name he had bestowed on her. It was surprising in view of this industry that no university had offered him a chair. Perhaps others prominent in his discipline detected in him a dilettantism, a less than whole-hearted commitment to his subject. Or was it simpler than that? Perhaps the rebarbative arrogance of some of his public criticisms irritated or repelled them, as she suspected it might do his pupils. But here they were, the most recent fruits of his intellectual preoccupations, elegantly written for a sociologist, impeccable in scholarship and style, or so the critics said, the books which partly explained Maurice. Now, of course, she saw that they explained her too. *Nature and Nurture: Genetic and Environmental Interactions in Language Development. Tackling Disadvantage: Social Class, Language and Intelligence. Genes and Environment: Environmental Influences on the Concept of Object Permanence. Schooled to Fail: Class Poverty and Education in Great Britain.* Had he planned one day to add another? *Adoption: A Case Study in the Interaction of Heredity and Environment.*

Last of all she comforted herself with a long look at her most prized possession, the Henry Walton oil painting of the Reverend Joseph Skinner and family which she had chosen as Maurice's gift for her eighteenth birthday. It was an extraordinarily attractive and competent painting with none of the slightly sentimental charm of some of his later works. Here was all the elegance, the order, the confidence and the formal good manners of her favourite period in English history. The Reverend Skinner and his three sons were mounted, his wife and two daughters were seated in a barouche. Behind them was their solid decent house, before them their carriage drive, their shadowed lawn set with oaks. They could have had no crises of identity. The long Skinner faces, the high-arched Skinner noses proclaimed their lineage. And yet they spoke to her, telling her only that they had lived and suffered, endured and died. And so in her time would she.

6

Harry Cleghorn who, at forty-five and already balding, still managed to retain his reputation as an up-and-coming politician, looked to Philippa so like a successful Tory back-bencher that she supposed his political career to have been inevitable. He was strongly muscled with a smooth, high-coloured skin, hair so black that it looked dyed, and a moist, rather petulant, mouth whose lips, red at the outlines as if lipsticked, revealed when he spoke an under-bleb of soft pale pink. As far as Philippa could see, he and Maurice had nothing in common except their appearance together as members of the same television chat show and their status as television personalities. But what else did they need to have in common? Differences of background, temperament, interests or political philosophy all faded in the unifying glare which the television studio lights shed on the company of the elect.

Nora Cleghorn faced her across the table, her over-made-up face softened by the candlelight. She must have been attractive when she was twenty to those who liked fair doll-like prettiness, but hers was a beauty which faded early, depending as it did on a pert perfection of skin and colouring, and not on bone structure. She was a silly woman, excessively proud of her husband, but few people disliked her, perhaps because there was something endearingly naive about a belief that membership of the House of Commons represented the summit of human aspiration. She was, as usual, overdressed for an informal dinner party, gleamingly metallic in a sequined, sleeveless top over a velvet skirt. As their shoulders brushed in the doorway she smelled to Philippa of hot moist coins which had been steeped in scent.

If Nora Cleghorn were overdressed, so was Gabriel Lomas, since he was the only man wearing a dinner jacket. But with Gabriel one knew that sartorial eccentricity was deliberate. Maurice apparently liked him despite – or could it be because of – his affectation of an extreme right-wing Toryism. Perhaps it made a change from the majority of his students. For his part, Gabriel sometimes seemed to Philippa to be excessively interested in Maurice. It was from Gabriel that she had learnt most of what she knew about Helena Palfrey. Since she had almost total recall of any conversation which really interested her, she could perfectly remember one snatch of conversation.

'Your father is like all rich Socialists, there's Tory inside which he's struggling to keep down.'

She had replied:

'I don't think Maurice qualifies as a rich Socialist. You shouldn't be misled by our life-style. He inherited this house and most of the furniture and pictures from his first wife. Maurice's background is perfectly respectable from the comrades' point of view. Dad was a post-office supervisor, leading light in the union. Maurice hasn't rebelled, merely conformed.'

'He married an earl's daughter. I don't call that conforming. Admittedly an eccentric earl who is somewhat of an embarrassment to his class, but there's nothing suspect about his lineage, no Victorian creation there. Admittedly, too, knowing Lady Helena, people wondered why marriage, until she produced a baby seven months later, the only seven-month prem to weigh in at eight and a half pounds.'

'Gabriel, how on earth do you get to know these things?'

'An addiction to petty gossip acquired during childhood, long summer afternoons in Kensington Gardens listening to Nanny and her cronies. Sarah, grossly overdressed, sitting up in the huge, shabby family pram, me trotting by the side. God, the suffocating boredom of those perambulations round the Round Pond! Be grateful, privileged little bastard that you are, that you were spared them.'

Now as they started on their artichokes, Gabriel was indulging in a minor Maurice tease, pretending to believe that a recent Labour Party political broadcast by a group of Young Socialists had been put out by the Tory Party.

'Naughty of them, although I don't think it will make them any converts. And if they wanted to scare us I think they rather overdid it. Surely even the young comrades don't actually mouth such a risible combination of spurious philosophy, class hatred and discredited economic theory. And where on earth did they find those singularly unattractive actors? Positively scrofulous most of them. I don't think there's been any research to examine the correlation between acne and left-wing opinions. It might be rather an interesting project for one of your post-graduate students, sir?'

Nora Cleghorn said wonderingly:

'But I thought it was supposed to be a Labour broadcast.'

Her husband laughed:

'You'd certainly be well advised, Maurice, to keep the young comrades under wraps until after the election.'

The political discussion was under way as was inevitable. Conversation between Maurice and Harry Cleghorn, thought Philippa, was seldom memorable being usually either a reiteration of their previous television encounter, or a rehearsal for their next. She detached her mind from arguments which she had heard so often before and glanced across the table at Hilda.

Ever since early adolescence, Philippa's reaction to her adoptive mother had been an urge to alter her, to upgrade her, to make her over as she might a dull but still serviceable winter coat. In imagination she applied make-up, as if by the judicious application of colour the face could be given definition, rescued from its pallid inconsequence. She had a half-shameful vision of confronting Maurice with a wife transformed, presented with her compliments for his approval, a procuress of his pleasure. Even now she hardly ever looked at her adoptive mother without mentally changing her hairstyle, her clothes. About a year ago, when Hilda had needed a new evening dress, she had tentatively suggested to Philippa that they should shop for it together. Perhaps the invitation had conjured up for her an idealized relationship of mother and daughter, a feminine excursion, half-frivolous, conspiratorial. It hadn't been a success. Hilda hated all shops other than those which sold food, was embarrassed by the presence of smarter customers, confused by too abundant a choice, over-deferential to the assistants, shy about undressing. The last store to which Philippa in desperation had taken her had had a large communal dressing-room. What inhibitions of the flesh, she wondered, had caused Hilda to shrink desperately into one corner, trying with ridiculous prudery to undress under cover of her coat while all around her girls and women stripped unselfconsciously to their bras and pants. Philippa had foraged out, desperately hunting among the rails. Nothing looked right on Hilda. Nothing could, since she wore it without confidence, without pleasure, a mute uncomplaining victim offering herself to be adorned for some sacrificial dinner party. In the end they had bought the black woollen skirt she was wearing now, topped by an over-fussy and ill-cut Crimplene blouse. It was the last time they had gone out together, the only time that she had tried to be a daughter. She told herself that she was glad that she need never try again.

Harry Cleghorn's slightly hectoring voice – all his utterances had the resonant boom of the hustings – broke into her comforting disparagement of Hilda, Hilda whose only skills were cooking and deceit.

'Your party claims to understand the so-called working class, but most of you haven't a clue about what they're feeling. Take an old woman living south of the river and holed up on the top of one of your tower blocks. If she can't go out to shop or collect her pension because she's afraid of being mugged, she isn't free in any real sense of that word. Freedom to move about safely in your own capital city is a damned sight more fundamental than the abstractions that the civil liberties lobby prates about.'

'If you could explain how longer prison sentences and tougher detention-centre regimes would make it safer.'

Nora Cleghorn licked sauce vinaigrette from her fingers.

'I do think that they ought to hang murderers.'

She spoke in a brightly conversational voice as though, thought Philippa, she were referring to a neighbour's unaccountable omission to hang curtains. There was a moment of complete silence as if she had dropped something precious. In her mind Philippa heard the tinkle of smashing glass. Then Maurice said evenly:

'They? You mean we ought. As it's not a duty I personally would care to perform, I can hardly expect someone else to do it on my behalf.'

'Oh, Harry would do it, wouldn't you darling?'

'There are one or two I can think of I wouldn't exactly flinch at launching into eternity.'

And this led them, as Philippa knew it would, to a discussion of the century's most notorious child murderess, the name which came up whenever people discussed capital punishment, the touchstone by which liberals tested their response to the death penalty. Philippa wondered if her own mother had served for a longer than normal time because her early release might have stimulated agitation on behalf of that other, more notorious child-killer. She glanced across at Hilda, but Hilda's face, half-hidden by the two swathes of hair, was bent low over her plate. Artichokes were a convenient starter to an embarrassing meal. They required careful attention. Cleghorn said:

'Having decided that it is wrong to hang murderers, we are now waking up to the fact that they don't conveniently die in prison or just fade away. We're also waking up to the fact that someone has to look after them and that if we don't pay society's custodians properly for a disagreeable job we won't find anyone willing to do it. But obviously, sooner or later, the woman will have to be paroled. I suggest that it might be later.'

Nora Cleghorn said:

'But isn't she supposed to have got terribly religious? I think I read somewhere that she wants to go into a convent or nurse lepers or something.'

Gabriel laughed.

'Poor lepers! They seem always to be selected as the sacrificial victims of someone's contrition. You'd think they had enough troubles already.'

Cleghorn's moist lips fastened on the succulent heart of his artichoke, like a child's on a dummy. A trickle of sauce ran down the side of his mouth. His voice was half-muffled in his linen napkin.

'I don't mind who she nurses as long as she keeps away from their children.'

His wife said:

'But if she has really reformed, she wouldn't be agitating to get out of prison, would she?'

Cleghorn spoke impatiently. Philippa had noticed before that he was indulgent to his wife's inanities, but became irritated when she spoke sense.

'Of course she wouldn't. That's the last thing she'd be worried about. After all, if she's hankering to do good, a prison is as suitable a place as any. All this talk about contrition is nonsense. She and her lover tortured a child to death. If she ever comes to an understanding of what she's done, I don't see how she could bear to go on living, let alone start planning for a life outside.'

Gabriel said:

'So we must hope for her own sake that she is unrepentant. But why all this public interest in the state of her soul? I suppose that society has a right to punish her to deter others, and to demand what assurances are possible that she's no longer dangerous before letting her out. What we haven't the right to demand is repentance. That's a matter between her and her god.'

Philippa said:

'Of course. It's as arrogant as me, a Gentile, proclaiming that I've forgiven the Nazis for the holocaust. The statement has no meaning.'

Maurice said drily:

'As little meaning as the statement that repentance is between her and her god.'

Cleghorn laughed:

'Now Maurice, leave the theological argument for your encounter with the Bishop. What are they paying you for the new series, by the way?'

The conversation turned to contracts and the foibles of television producers. There was no more talk of murder. The meal dragged on through the veal, the lemon soufflé, and finally to the leisurely coffee and brandy in the garden. It seemed to Philippa that she had never lived through a longer day. She had woken that morning as a bastard; how short but how endless the hours which had legitimized her into horror and disgrace. It was like experiencing birth and death simultaneously, each separately painful yet both part of the same inexorable process. Now she sat, drained, under the patio lamps and willed the Cleghorns to go.

She was beyond tiredness. Her mind was preternaturally clear yet if fastened on unimportant details which it invested with an egregious significance: Nora Cleghorn's bra-strap slipping down a sequined shoulder, her husband's heavy signet ring biting into his little finger, the peach tree gleaming silver under the patio lamp; surely if she stretched out her arm and shook the trunk its leaves would tinkle down in a shower of glistening pellets.

By half-past eleven the talk had become disjointed, perfunctory. Maurice and Cleghorn had completed their academic business and Gabriel, with his half-ironic formality, had taken his leave. But still the Cleghorns lingered in what seemed an obstinate endurance, long after a damp chill had crept across the garden and the purple sky was stained with the arteries of the dying day. It was nearly midnight before they reminded each other that they had a home, said their protracted goodbyes, and made their way through the garden gate to the mews garage and their Jaguar. Philippa was free at last to go to her room.

7

The letter was more difficult to write than even the most challenging of her weekly school essays. It was astonishing that a short passage of English prose should take so long to compose, that even the most ordinary words should carry such a charge of innuendo, condescension or crass insensitivity. The problems began with the superscription. 'Dear Mother' seemed a startling, almost presumptuous beginning; 'Dear Mrs Ducton' was offensively, almost aggressively formal; 'Dear Mary Ducton' was too obviously a trendy compromise, a confession of defeat. In the end she decided on 'Dear Mother'. That, after all, was the relationship between them, the primal, unalterable, biological tie. To admit the fact needn't imply that it was any more than that.

The first sentence was comparatively easy. She wrote: 'I hope that it won't distress you to receive this letter, but I exercised my right under the Children Act 1975 to apply to the Registrar General for a copy of my birth certificate. Afterwards I went to Bancroft Gardens and learned from a neighbour who you were.'

There was no need to say any more. In that last sentence infamy was plucked from the past, briefly held, then dropped. The words were bloodstained. She went on:

'I should very much like to meet you unless you would much rather not; I could come to Melcombe Grange on any visitors' day if you would let me know when it would be convenient.'

She deleted the second 'much' and hesitated over the last five words, but decided on reflection to leave them in. The sentence didn't satisfy her, but at least it was short and the meaning clear. The next part was more difficult. The words 'released', 'paroled', 'licensed' or 'set free' were pejorative but it was extraordinarily difficult to avoid them. Quickly she scribbled an alternative draft:

'I don't want to force myself on you, but if you haven't anywhere to go . . . anywhere to stay . . . if you haven't finally decided on your plans after you leave Melcombe Grange, would you care to come to me?'

But the last seven words sounded as grudging and patronizing as an invitation to an unwelcome guest. She tried again:

'I shall be taking up my Cambridge scholarship in October and hope to find a flat in London for the next couple of months. If you haven't finally decided on your plans after you leave Melcombe Grange and would care to share the flat, that would be agreeable for me, but please don't feel that you have to say yes.'

It occurred to her that her mother might worry about her share of the rent. Presumably she wouldn't leave prison with very much money. She ought to make it plain that no payment was involved. She began to write that the offer was without obligation, but that bleak commercial note was too reminiscent of a sales catalogue. And there would, after all, be obligations. The demands she would be making of her mother couldn't be satisfied with money. In the end she decided the details could await their meeting. She ended the draft:

'It will only be a small flat – a room for each of us and a kitchen and bathroom – but I hope to find one which will be reasonably central and convenient.'

Convenient for what, she wondered. Covent Garden Opera House, the West End shops, the theatres and restaurants? What sort of life was she implying? What was she visualizing for this stranger who would walk into freedom, if licence from a life sentence was ever freedom, carrying the weight of a dead child? She copied out the draft neatly and signed the letter Philippa Palfrey. She read it through carefully. It was, she thought, disingenuous. She wondered whether her mother would see through the careful words to the truth. There was no real choice for her. She was, in effect, being once again hunted down. The meeting between them was inevitable; if not now, it would come later. There was nothing her mother could do to prevent it.

Perhaps it would have been more honest and, since style depended on honesty, more satisfying to have written the brutal truth.

'If you have nowhere satisfactory to go when you're released from prison, would you care to share a flat with me in London until I go up to Cambridge in October? It can't be longer than that; I'm not intending to alter my life for you. I need to know who I am. If you need a room for two months it would seem a fair exchange. Let me know if you'd like me to come up to Melcombe Grange to talk about it.'

She heard two sets of footsteps mounting the stairs. Then there was a knock. That must be Hilda. Maurice – taught perhaps by Helena – would never have knocked. They stood there, side by side, like a deputation, dressing-gowned; Hilda in her flowered quilted nylon, Maurice in his fine scarlet wool, looking diminished and vulnerable, bringing with them a childhood bathtime smell of soap and powder. He said:

'We have to talk, Philippa.'

'I'm too tired. It's after midnight. And what is there to say?'

'At least do nothing until you've seen her, spoken to her.'

'I've already written. I'll post it tomorrow, today I mean. The offer means nothing if it isn't made before we meet. I can't look her over first as if she were goods on approval.'

'You propose then to commit yourself, for weeks, for months, perhaps even for life, to a woman you don't know, who has done nothing for you, who will be nothing but an embarrassment to you, whom you probably won't even like. The fact that she happens to be a murderess is irrelevant. It's quixotic, Philippa. Worse, it's self-indulgent stupidity.'

'I didn't say anything about commitment.'

'Of course it's a commitment. You're not engaging a junior clerk. If she doesn't give satisfaction you can hardly throw her out. What else is it but a commitment?'

'A sensible arrangement to help her over these first two months outside. All I propose to do is to make the offer. She may not even want to see me. If she does it won't necessarily mean that she'll want to share a flat. She's probably made other arrangements. But if she hasn't found anywhere to go, then I'm free for the next few months. At least she'll have a choice.'

'It's not a question of her finding somewhere to go. If she hasn't a family willing to take her back, then the probation service will have found somewhere for her. She won't be homeless. They don't parole lifers unless the after-care arrangements are approved by the Home Office as satisfactory.'

Hilda said nervously:

'Aren't there hostels, places like that? I've heard they're quite nice. She'll probably go to a hostel just until she's sorted herself out, found herself a job.'

She spoke, thought Philippa, as if her mother were a convalescent being discharged prematurely from hospital. Maurice said:

'Or she'll join up with some woman she's met inside. I don't suppose she's spent all those years entirely alone.'

'You mean a lover? A lesbian?'

He said irritably:

'It's not unknown. You know nothing about her. She let you go out of her life, no doubt because she thought it for the best. Now do the same for her. Hasn't it occurred to you that you may be the last person on earth that she wants to see again?'

'Then all she has to do is say so. I shall write first. I'm not proposing to arrive at the prison unannounced. And if she gave me up it's because she had no choice.'

Hilda's voice was a thin wail of protest.

'But you can't just leave! What are people going to think? What can we say to our friends, to Gabriel Lomas?'

'It's nothing to do with Gabriel. Tell them I'm abroad until October. That's what I was going to do anyway.'

'But they're bound to see you in London. They'll see you with her!'

'What if they do? She won't be branded on her forehead with the divine stigma. I'll think of something to tell your friends if that's all you're worried about. And it's only for a couple of months. People do leave home occasionally.'

Maurice came into the room and walked over to the Henry Walton. Studying the picture, his back to her, he said:

'How much have you read about the murder?'

'I haven't read anything. I know that she killed a child called Julie Scase after my father raped her.'

'You haven't consulted the newspaper reports of the crime?'

'No, I haven't the time to grub about in the archives, and I don't want to.'

'Then I suggest that, before you do anything foolish, make any decision, you get hold of the newspaper cuttings and the trial report and learn the facts.'

'I know the facts. They were told to me this morning with brutal explicitness. I'm not going to spy on my mother before I meet her.

If I want any more facts, she can give them to me. And now, please, I'm very tired. I'd like to go to bed.'

8

Two days later, on Friday 14 July, Norman Scase celebrated simultaneously his fifty-seventh birthday and the last day of his career as a local government accounts clerk. He had told his colleagues that he had been left a modest legacy by an uncle, sufficient to enable him to freeze his pension for three years and to take a premature retirement. The lie worried him; he was unpractised in lying. But something had to be said to explain how a middle-grade unqualified clerk who, to their knowledge, had worn the same suit to work for the last five years could afford the indulgence of an early retirement. He could hardly tell them the truth, that the murderess of his child was due to be released from prison in August and that there were arrangements which he had to make, matters to which he must now devote the whole of his time.

Celebration was not a word he would have used either for the birthday or for his last day at the office. He would have been grateful to have been allowed to slip quietly away as he had at the end of every working day for the last eight years; but there were rituals in the treasurer's department from which not even the least sociable and most private member of the staff was exempt. It was the custom for members of staff who were leaving, getting married, being promoted or retiring to mark the occasion with an invitation either to tea or to sherry, depending on their status and habits and the degree of importance which they attached to the impending change. The invitation was typed by courtesy of the typing pool for those too lowly to have a personal secretary, and circulated by the junior clerical assistant with the miscellaneous departmental notes, circulars and periodicals which went the rounds. On its first appearance Miss Millicent Yelland, the senior personal secretary, would start collecting for a present, tripping conspiratorially from room to room with an envelope to receive donations and a greeting card on which contributors would sign their names under variously worded messages of farewell or good wishes. The choice of card was invariably left to Miss Yelland. At fifty-four she had sublimated her maternal instincts by taking upon herself the role of mother of the division, and had for the past fifteen years promoted, without noticeable success, the fiction that they were all one happy family.

She always took a great deal of trouble, browsing along the racks in the Army and Navy Stores and in the Westminster Abbey Bookshop, and even venturing occasionally as far as Oxford Circus. For more senior staff she usually chose a dog. Dogs were always acceptable, evoking in her mind a mixture of vaguely felt emotions and aspirations, loyalty and devotion, rough tweeded masculinity, mysterious upper-class activities on grouse moors and among the heather, a restrained good taste. Since a country cottage, with its suggestion of shared connubial bliss, was unsuitable for a widower, and it was impossible to associate Mr Scase with anything as frivolous as bambis or black cats, she decided on a moorland scene featuring a shaggy dog of indeterminate breed with a pheasant in its mouth.

When she examined the card again in her office she had a qualm of doubt. The pheasant, at least she supposed it was a pheasant, looked so very dead, pathetic really, with its drooping neck and glazed eye. It was hardly what you would call a cheerful card. She hoped that Mr Scase didn't disapprove of blood sports. And when one came to examine it, the expression on the dog's face was really most unpleasant, almost gloating. Well, it would have to do now. She had spent thirty-three pence from the collection of ten pounds – a disappointing sum, but then poor Mr Scase had never particularly put himself out to be popular – and it would be an idiotic waste to buy another card. It was a pity that he was so difficult to choose for. On the death of his wife, eight months ago, about which he had been as reticent as he was about any of his private concerns, she had sent a mourning card on behalf of the division, a silver cross wreathed with violets and forget-me-nots. Afterwards she had wondered whether her choice then had been suitable. He had worked in the division for nearly nine years yet they knew virtually nothing about him except that, like herself, he commuted to Liverpool Street from one of the eastern suburbs. They seldom met on the station and sometimes she wondered if he deliberately avoided her.

Some years previously, emboldened by two glasses of cheap sherry at the office Christmas party, she had asked him whether he had children, and he had replied 'No.' After a few seconds he had added, 'We did have a daughter, but she died young.' Then he had flushed and turned aside as if regretting that brief confidence. She had been made to feel tactless and inquisitive. She had murmured something about being sorry and had moved away, replenishing the outstretched glasses and responding to the office banter. But afterwards she had told herself that to no one else had he spoken about his child, that the confidence, even if involuntary, had been to her alone. She never mentioned it either to him or in the office, but cherished it as a small secret which somehow affirmed her worth in his eyes. And the knowledge of his private tragedy lent him an interest, almost a distinction, which intrigued her. After the death of his wife she found herself indulging a private fantasy. They were both lonely. And he was thoughtful, conscientious. The junior staff didn't appreciate him, just because he insisted on punctuality and a proper standard of work. It took an older woman, a mature woman, to appreciate his qualities. Perhaps here was someone who would be a friend and later, who knew, more than a friend. It wasn't too late for her to make a man happy. She would have someone other than Mother to cook for and care for. But she knew she would have to make the first move.

Inspiration came to her from the advice column of her woman's magazine, where one of the readers wrote that she was interested in a boy in her office, but he had never been more than polite and friendly. There had been no invitation, no date. The answer had been explicit. 'Buy two theatre tickets for something you think he'll like. Then tell him that you've been given the tickets unexpectedly and ask whether he'd care to see the show with you.' It hadn't been an easy ploy for Miss Yelland to put into effect. There had been the difficulty of persuading a neighbour to sit with her mother, the problem of deciding what tickets to buy. In the end, feeling that music was the safest bet, she had queued for two expensive seats for a Brahms concert at the Royal Festival Hall for a Friday night. On the Monday she spoke to him. The few stiff words had been over-rehearsed and her invitation sounded ungracious as well as insincere. He hadn't answered her at first, keeping his eyes on his ledger, and she began to wonder whether he had heard. Then he had got clumsily to his feet, looked briefly into her eyes and murmured:

'It's very kind of you, Miss Yelland, but I never go out in the evenings.'

She had read in his eyes not merely embarrassment, but a kind of panic. Afterwards, scarlet with humiliation since the rejection had been so absolute, she had sought solitude in the ladies' cloakroom. Tearing up the two tickets she flushed them down the lavatory. It was, she knew, a stupidly extravagant gesture. The concert was a popular one; the booking office could almost certainly have disposed of the tickets. But the gesture was some small comfort to her pride. She had never approached him again, and it seemed to her imagination that he became even more reserved, withdrew more completely beneath his carapace of quiet efficiency. And now he was leaving. For nearly nine years he had circumvented her loving-kindness. Now he was escaping for good.

The formal goodbye was arranged for twelve-thirty, and by one o'clock Mr Willcox, the chief accountant in the division, who undertook these ceremonies for staff whose status didn't warrant the personal appearance of the treasurer, was in full flood:

'And if any of you were to ask me, as his senior officer, what I regard as the salient feature of Norman Scase's work in this division, I shouldn't need to hesitate for a single second before giving you my judgement.'

He then hesitated for a nicely judged half-minute, giving the assembled division time to assume expressions of brightly anticipatory interest as if this fascinating question had indeed been on their lips, while the deputy senior accountant cast lugubrious eyes at the ceiling, the junior personal secretary giggled and Miss Yelland smiled encouragingly at Scase across the throng. The smile wasn't returned. He stood there, holding the canteen glass in his hand, half-filled with sweet South African sherry, and stared slightly over their heads. He had taken the usual trouble with his appearance, neither more nor less. The formal blue suit was a little shabby now, the sleeves polished by the friction of desk top and ledger. The shirt collar was crumpled but very clean, and the nondescript tie precisely knotted. Standing there, a little apart, like a man under judgement, he reminded Miss Yelland of someone; a picture, a photograph, a newsreel, not someone known to her. Then she remembered. It was one of the accused in the dock at Nuremberg. The mental image, impious, offensive, shocked her; she flushed and gazed fixedly into her sherry as if detected in a solecism. But the memory remained. She fixed her eyes again resolutely on Mr Willcox.

'It would be expressed in a single word,' he pronounced, and proceeded to use a thesaurus. 'Conscientiousness, attention to detail, methodicalness' – he slipped a little over this and Miss Yelland wondered whether there was such a word – 'complete reliability. Whatever he has put his hand to, that task has been carried through to the end with accuracy, neatness and with complete reliability.'

His deputy, lowering his eyes, swallowed his sherry in one gulp, since it was not a taste voluntarily to let linger on the tongue, and thought that if there were a more bloody boring, damning vale-diction, then he had yet to hear it. He was intrigued by Scase's early retirement. The legacy, of which he had heard rumours, must have been quite a sum if he could afford to go three years early – unless, of course, he had found himself another job and was keeping quiet about it. But that seemed unlikely. Who, these days, would want to take a fifty-seven-year-old chap without qualifications?

And so the self-satisfied rhetoric boomed on. Sly innuendoes about what Scase would do with his retirement; congratulations only half jocular, he couldn't prevent the note of envy from creeping in that he could afford to freeze his pension and retire three years before he was due to go; the final conventional wish that he would enjoy a long, prosperous and happy retirement and that the division's little gift would be used to provide some small luxury which would remind him of their affection and respect. The cheque was handed over, there was a brief outbreak of self-conscious clapping in which Mr Willcox joined with a curiously soundless and rhythmic clasping and releasing of his palms like a half-hearted cheerleader at a revivalist meeting, and all their eyes swivelled and rested on Scase. He blinked at the envelope which had been pressed into his hand, but he didn't open it. One might suppose that he didn't know the convention, that he was supposed to pretend he couldn't find the flap, raise a gratified eyebrow at the size of the cheque, exclaim over the design on the card, and study the inscribed names. But he clutched it in his delicate hands as a child might do, uncertain if it were really his. He said:

'Thank you very much. I shall miss the division in many ways after nearly nine years.'

'Nine years' hard,' someone called out, and laughed.

He didn't smile.

'After nearly nine years,' he repeated. 'I shall buy a pair of binoculars with your kind gift, and they will remind me of old friends and colleagues in local government. Thank you.'

Then he smiled. He had a singularly sweet smile, but it was so transitory that those who saw it were left wondering whether there had indeed been that extraordinary transformation. He put down his unfinished drink, shook hands with one or two closest to him, and left them.

Back in the small room which he shared with two other clerks, he had already packed his few belongings in a plastic carrier bag; his cup and saucer carefully wrapped in yesterday's *Daily Telegraph*; a ready reckoner and dictionary; his toilet bag. He gave a last look round. Nothing remained to be done. Making his way to the lift he wondered what they would have said, how they would have looked, if he had spoken quite simply what was in his mind.

'I have to retire early because there is something I must do in the next few months, a task which will take a great deal of time and planning. I have to find and kill the murderess of my child.'

Would the ring of nervously smiling faces have frozen into stark disbelief, the mouths set in their conventional smirks have broken into embarrassed laughter? Or would they have stood in a surrealist charade, still smiling, still nodding, toasting him in their cheap sherry, as if the dreadful words were as meaningless as Mr Willcox's pompous platitudes? The thought that he might actually hear himself speaking the truth had come to him during the last seconds of Mr Willcox's peroration. He hadn't, of course, been seriously tempted to such folly; but it surprised and slightly offended him that so iconoclastic and so melodramatic a conceit should have entered his mind. He was not given to the grand gesture, either in thought or action. Killing Mary Ducton was a duty which he neither wanted to escape, nor could escape even had he wanted to. Certainly he planned to commit a successful murder, in the sense that he intended to avoid detection. It was justice, not martyrdom, that he sought. But never until this afternoon had it occurred to him to wonder what his colleagues would think of him as a prospective killer, and he felt obscurely denigrated, his serious purpose cheapened into melodrama, that the thought should have occurred to him now.

9

He took his usual way home over Westminster Bridge, across Parliament Square, down Great George Street and into St James's Park. The quicker way to Liverpool Street Station and the eastern suburban line was by Waterloo and the City line, but he preferred to walk each evening over the river and take the Underground from St James's Park. Since Mavis's death he had been in no hurry to get home. There was no hurry now.

St James's Park was crowded, but he managed to find room on a bench beside the lake. Carefully he lowered the holdall with his few belongings and placed it on the path beneath his feet. Staring at the lake through the boughs of a willow, he realized that he had sat in this identical spot eight months previously, in his lunch hour on the day after his wife's death. It had been an unusually cold Friday in November. He could remember a smudged sun high above the lake like a great white moon, and the willow fronds slowly shedding their pale lances on to the water. In these burgeoning rose beds there had been a few tight red buds, blighted by the cold, their stems choked with dead leaves. The lake had been bronzed and wrinkled with, at its centre, a great salver of beaten silver. An old man, surely too old to be employed by the council, had shuffled along the path past him, spearing the sparse litter. The park then had held an air of sad decrepitude, the handrail of the blue bridge worn by tourists' hands, the fountain silent, the tea house closed for the winter. Now the air was loud with the staccato chatter of tourists, the shrieks and laughter of children. Then, he remembered, there had been one solitary child with his mother. The gulls had risen squawking before his harsh, cracked laughter, and he had stretched out his arms, willing their plump bodies to fall into his palms. Under the far trees patches of early snow had lain between the clumps of grass like the discarded litter of the dead summer.

Remembering that day he could almost feel again the November cold. He shut his eyes against the sunlit greenness of the park, the sheen on the lake; blotted out the calling voices of the children and the distant beat of the band, and willed his mind back to the hospital ward in which Mavis had died.

It had been an inconvenient day and time to die, the Thursday of the major operation list, and at four in the afternoon when the trolleys were coming back from the theatre. These things, he had sensed, were better managed at night when the patients were settled or asleep, when there was time for the nursing staff to turn aside from the battle and minister to those who had already lost it. The staff nurse in charge, harassed, had explained that normally they would have moved his wife into a side ward, but the four side wards were occupied. Perhaps tomorrow. There was the unspoken commitment that if she could die more conveniently then she could die with more comfort. He had sat by her bed behind the drawn curtains. Their pattern was forever fixed in his mind, small pink rosebuds on a green background, cosy, domestic, a prettification of death. They were not completely drawn, and he could glimpse and hear the business of the ward, trolleys being wheeled beside the waiting beds with impersonal efficiency, the long-gowned nurses steadying the swinging drip-bottles, voices and passing feet. From time to time a ward orderly put her head round the curtains and asked brightly:

'Tea?'

He took the cup and saucer, thick white china with two lumps of sugar already dissolving in the spill of brown liquid.

Both her arms lay outside the coverlet. He held her left hand, wondering what dreams, if any, peopled the uplands of her valley of the shadow. Surely they couldn't be as tormenting as the nightmares which, in the weeks following Julie's death, had made dreadful her nights so that he would wake to her shrill screams, to the hot sweet smell of sweat and fear. The world she was inhabiting now was surely gentler, or why would she lie so still? The passing expressions of her face, which he watched with detached interest, were the transitory hints of emotions which she could no longer feel: a peevish frown, a sly unconvincing smile which reminded him disconcertingly of Julie as a baby when she had wind, a petulant frown, the illusion of thought. From time to time her eyes flickered and her lips moved. He bent his head to listen.

'Better use a knife. It's more certain. You won't forget?'

'No, I won't forget.'

'You've got the letter?'

'Yes, I've got the letter.'

'Show me.'

He took it from his wallet. Her eyes focused on it with difficulty. She stretched her right hand trembling towards it and touched it as a believer might touch a relic. She tried to fix her eyes on it. Her jaw dropped and began to quiver as if the effort of concentrating on that oblong of creased white paper had released the final disintegration of muscle and flesh. He took her dry hand in his, and pressed it against the envelope. He said:

'I won't forget.'

He remembered when she had written the letter. It had been just one year before, when the cancer had first been diagnosed. They had been sitting together, distanced, on the sofa watching a television programme about the birds of Antarctica. After he switched off she had said:

'If I don't get better you'll have to do it alone. That might not be so easy. You'll need an excuse for finding out where she is. And after she's dead, if they suspect you, you'll have to explain why you traced her. I'll write a letter, a letter of forgiveness. Then you can say that you promised me on my deathbed to deliver it into her hand.'

She must have been planning that, thinking it out all the time they were watching the programme together. He could still remember the sudden jolt of disappointment and fear. Somehow he had believed that her death might release him, that he wouldn't be expected to carry the burden alone. But there was to be no escape. She had written the letter at once, sitting at the kitchen table, and had placed it in an unsealed envelope remembering that he might need to show it to someone, someone in authority, someone who might let him know where the murderess was. He hadn't read it at the time, and he hadn't read it since. He had carried it with him in his wallet. Until this moment, so short a time before her death, she had never mentioned it again.

She sank into unconsciousness. He sat on stiffly beside her, letting the dry hand rest beneath his. A lizard hand, inert, repellent, the loose skin sliding beneath his touch. He told himself that it had cooked for him, worked for him, cleaned his house, washed his clothes. He tried to picture these things, tried to stimulate pity. It meant nothing. He felt pity but it was a diffuse impersonal hopelessness at the inevitability of loss. The ward seemed loud with ineffective activity, meaningless suffering. He knew that if he wept it would be for all of them there, sick and healthy alike, but most of all for himself. He had to make an effort of will not to draw his hand away. He was helped by the thought that the staff nurse might draw back the curtains and would expect to find him sitting thus linked, dispensing the final consolations of the flesh. Love had died. The woman had throttled it to death when she throttled the life out of their child. Perhaps it hadn't been very strong to die so easily and thus vicariously, but it had seemed strong. They had loved, as surely every human being did, each to the limit of his capacity. But they had failed each other at the end. Perhaps she had been the most culpable because the stronger. But somehow he should have been able to help her back to a kind of living. Now there was one way left in which he wouldn't fail her. Their joint purpose must now be his alone. Perhaps the death of the woman would be both an expiation and, for him, a release into some kind of life, a justification of the long, lost years.

She had nourished grief and revenge like a monstrous foetus, every growing but never delivered. Even her general practitioner, wearily drawing his prescription pad towards him and writing yet another letter for a psychiatric outpatient appointment, made it plain that he thought she had grieved long enough. Grief, after all, was an indulgence, having no merit, no social value, rationed out like coins to the deserving poor, a commodity the strong and self-reliant were too proud to need. Perhaps, he thought, the Victorian habit of formal mourning had its uses. At least it defined the accepted limits of public indulgence. A year in black for a widow, he remembered his grandmother had told him, then six months in grey, then in mauve. Those expensive conventions were not, of course, for her but she had observed them with approval in the large town houses in which she had served as a parlour-maid. How long in black, he wondered, for a raped and murdered child. Not long perhaps. In his grandmother's time there would have been a replacement within a year.

How easily humanity subscribed to the universal commercial imperative: business as usual. You have your life to live, they had told Mavis, and she had gazed at them with huge uncomprehending eyes since, so obviously, she no longer had her life to live. You must think of your husband, her doctor had commanded, and indeed she had thought of him. Lying stiffly, speechlessly, side by side in the double bed of that back suburban bedroom, he had stared into the darkness and seen her thoughts, self-reproachful, like a darker cloud against the blackness of the ceiling, or a contagion spreading from her brain to his. Never once had she turned to him. She had occasionally stretched out a hand, but when he had taken it had withdrawn it as if the flesh which had impregnated her had become repulsive. Once, shy and with a sense of betrayal, he had made himself speak to their doctor. The answer, glib and professional, had done nothing to help. 'She associates physical love with grief, with loss. You must be patient.' Well, he had been patient, patient unto death.

She was trying to speak again. He bent down and caught her breath, sour-sweet with intimations of decay, and had to resist the temptation to put his handkerchief to his mouth to shield him from contamination. He held his breath and tried not to swallow. But in the end he had to take her death into himself. It took her several minutes to get out the words, but when they came between the gibbering lips her voice was surprisingly clear, gruff and deep as it had never been in life.

'Strong,' she said. 'Strong.'

He didn't know what she meant by that word. Was it a final exhortation to him to stay strong in resolution? Or did she mean that the murderess was strong, too strong for him to overcome her if he came unweaponed to the kill. Standing there in the dock of the Old Bailey she hadn't struck him as particularly tall or robust; but perhaps that court, so unexpectedly small, so anonymous, panelled in plain oak, diminished all human beings, guilty and innocent alike. Even the judge, scarlet-sashed under the royal coat of arms, had shrunk to a bewigged marionette. But the years in prison wouldn't have made her less strong. They looked after you in prison. You weren't overworked or underfed. When you were sick they gave you the best medical care. They saw that you got your exercise. When he and Mavis had talked together about the killing, they had planned to throttle the woman since that was how Julie had died. But Mavis was right. He was on his own now. He had better use a weapon.

He hadn't wanted her to die like this, in bitterness and hate. This too the murderess had taken from them with so much else. Love, the solace of responsive flesh; companionship, laughter, ambition, hope. And of course Julie. Sometimes to his surprise he almost forgot Julie. And Mavis had lost her God. Like all other believers she had made Him in her own image, a Methodist God, benign, suburban in his tastes, appreciative of cheerful singing and mildly academic sermons, not demanding more than she could give. The Sunday-morning chapel had been more a comfortable routine than an imperative to worship. Mavis had been brought up a Methodist and she was not a woman to reject early orthodoxies. But she had never forgiven God for letting Julie die. Sometimes Scase thought that she had never forgiven him. Love had died chiefly because of guilt; their joint guilt; her blame of him, his blame of himself. She would return to it again and again.

'We shouldn't have let her join the Guides. She only agreed because she knew you were keen, that it would please you.'

'I didn't want her to be lonely. I remember what it was like when I was a child.'

'You should have called for her every Thursday. It wouldn't have happened if you'd called for her.'

'But you know she wouldn't let me. She told us that Sally Meakin always walked home with her across the recreation ground.'

But Sally Meakin hadn't. No one had, and Julie had been too ashamed to ask him to call for her. She had been like him as a child; unattractive, solitary, introspective, coping as best she could with the irrational terrors and uncertainties of childhood. He had guessed why she hadn't taken the short-cut home across the recreation ground. It must have seemed limitless in its dark emptiness, the swings tied up for the night but creaking in the wind, the great upward sweep of the slide gaunt against the sky, the dark recesses of the shelter, smelling of urine, where in the daytime the mothers sat with their prams. So she had walked alone the long way round, down unfamiliar streets, made less frightening because they were so like her own, bordered with cosy, comfortable semi-detached houses with their lighted windows, comforting symbols of security and home. And it was there in one of those dull streets that she had met her murderer. It must have been because the rapist and his house were both so ordinary that he had been able to entice her in. They had warned her punctiliously against speaking to strange men, accepting sweets, going away with them, and they had always thought that her timidity would protect her. But nothing had protected her, neither their warnings nor their love. His guilt was less now. Time didn't heal, but it anaesthetized. The human mind could only feel so much. He had read somewhere that even the tortured reached a point beyond which there was no more pain, only the thud of unregarded blows, a limbo beyond suffering that was almost pleasurable. He remembered the first cup of tea he had drunk after Julie's death. He couldn't have forced himself to swallow food, but suddenly he had been intensely thirsty, and the taste of the strong, sweet tea had been marvellously good. No tea before or since had tasted like that. She had only been dead a matter of hours and already the voracious, the treacherous body was able to experience pleasure.

Now, sitting in the sun with his few belongings on the ground between his feet, he accepted again the burden laid upon him. He would seek out his child's murderess and kill her. He would try to do it without danger to himself since the prospect of prison terrified him, but he would still do it whatever the cost. The strength of this conviction puzzled him. The will for the deed was absolute, yet the justification eluded his questing mind. Surely it wasn't just the need for revenge. That had long ago ceased to motivate him. His grief for Julie, at first almost as lacerating as Mavis's, had long ago faded into a dull acceptance of loss. He could hardly now recall her face. Mavis had destroyed all their photographs of her after the murder. But there were pictures which he kept in his mind, recalling them almost as a duty, an *aide-mémoire* of grief. Taking his daughter into his arms for the first time, the infinitely small cocooned body, the gummed eyelids, the secretive meaningless smile. Julie toddling towards the sea at Southend, clinging tightly to his finger. Julie in her Guide uniform setting the table for dinner with anxious care, qualifying for her hostess badge. Nothing he did to Mary Ducton at whatever cost could bring her back.

Was it the need to keep faith with Mavis? But how could you keep faith with the dead, who by the very act of dying had put themselves for ever beyond the reach of treachery or betrayal? Whatever he did it couldn't touch Mavis, couldn't harm or disappoint her. She wouldn't return a querulous ghost to reproach him with his weakness. No, he wasn't doing it for Mavis. He was doing it for himself. Was it, perhaps, that after nearly fifty-seven years of living he needed to prove himself, nonentity that he was, capable of courage and action, of an act so terrible and irrevocable that, whatever happened to him afterwards, he could never again doubt his identity as a man? He supposed that it might be so, although none of it seemed relevant to him. But surely it was ridiculous, this sense that the act was inescapable, pre-ordained. And yet he knew that it was so.

The sun had gone in. A chill wind moved across the lake, shaking the willows. He felt under the bench for his holdall and made his way slowly to St James's Station and home.

10

On Thursday 20 July, three days after she had received her mother's reply, Philippa took a day return ticket to York and travelled up on the nine o'clock train from King's Cross. The brief information sheet which had been enclosed with her prison visiting order stated that the bus to Melcombe Grange left the York bus station at two o'clock promptly. She was in a state of restless excitement which drove her to action and movement. It would be easier to pass the waiting hours exploring York than to linger in London for a later train.

At the station bookstall at York she bought a guide book, then checked the time of the return train. Then she walked indefatigably down the narrow paved streets of the walled city, Fossgate, Shambles, Petergate, between the timber-framed houses and the elegant Georgian façades, down secret alleyways and in and out of spice-smelling shops, through the eighteenth-century Assembly Rooms, the medieval Merchant Adventurers' Hall, hung with the splendid banners of the Guilds, the portraits of their benefactors, through the remains of the Roman baths and into ancient churches. She walked in a medieval dream in which the varied delights of the city, colour and light, form and sound, imposed themselves on a consciousness which was simultaneously heightened yet detached. And so at last she passed under the statue of St Peter, through the west door and into the cool immensity of the Minster. Here she sat and rested, looking up where the great east window stained the quiet air. She had bought a cheese and tomato roll for her lunch, and found herself suddenly hungry, but was reluctant to offend the susceptibilities of other visitors by eating it there. Instead she fixed her gaze where God the Father sat in majesty among His creation, glorified in the splendour of medieval stained glass. Before him was an open book, *Ego sum alpha et omega*. How simple life must be for those who could both lose and find identity in that magnificent assurance. But for herself that way was closed. Hers was a bleaker and more presumptuous creed; but it was not without its comfort and she had no other. Now with myself I will begin and end.

She arrived early at the bus station and was glad that she hadn't lingered over her lunch since the bus, a double-decker, rapidly filled. She wondered how many of the passengers were visitors to the prison, how often the same people travelled month after month the same route. The destination board made no mention of the prison but stated simply that the bus went to Moxton via Melcombe. Some passengers seemed to know each other and called out a greeting or edged their way down the aisle to sit together. Most of them carried baskets or humped bulging tote bags on to the rack. About half the passengers were men and they too were laden. But it wasn't a gloomy company nor, she thought, oppressed by any sense of stigma. Each might be carrying a private load of anxiety, but this afternoon, travelling through the bright air, each bore it more lightly. The sun burned through the windows, scorching the plastic seats. The bus smelled of hot leather, bodies, newly baked cakes and the strong grass-scented summer breeze. Almost merrily it bore its chattering load through sparse villages, down green shadowed lanes where the laden boughs of the horse chestnuts scraped against the roof, then, with a grind of gears, upwards to a high narrow road which ran between drystone walls. On either side stretched the close-cropped fields, white with sheep.

Only three passengers on the lower deck seemed immune to the general air of cheerful well-being, a middle-aged grey-haired man, dressed with careful formality, who had taken his seat beside Philippa just before the bus moved off and who spent the journey gazing out of the opposite window and restlessly turning a plain gold ring on his third finger, and two middle-aged women who had settled themselves behind her and who talked for most of the journey, one of them in a querulous whine.

'It's want, want, want with her, every bloody month. It's all very well, I said, but I can't do it. I'm keeping your bloody kids on social security, bread 20p a loaf and I can't do it. It's wool this month, if you please. Twenty balls! She's knitting herself one of those jerkin things. George won't visit any more. He won't put up with it, not George.'

Her companion said:

'They got wool in Paggett's sale.'

'That's no bloody good. It has to be that new French wool. Eighty pence an ounce, if you please. And what about the kids? If she wants to knit, Darren could do with a pullover. I've got no bloody time for knitting, I told her, stuck in the house, three kids under eight. Pity they don't let her out to look after them herself. I'm the one who's in prison, I told her. I'm the one who's been bloody well sentenced.'

And through it all the grey-haired man sat staring through the window, pulling on his ring.

From time to time she slipped her hand through the flap of her shoulder bag and touched the envelope containing her mother's letter. It had arrived on Monday 17 July and had been posted two days previously. It was as short and businesslike as Philippa's own and she knew it by heart.

'Thank you for your letter. Your offer is kind, but I think you ought to see me before you decide. I shall understand if you want to change your mind. I think you would be wise to change it. I have applied for a monthly visiting order for you and if you care to come I am of course always here.' It was signed simply Mary Ducton.

The note of sardonic humour in the last line intrigued her. But then, perhaps it had been meant to intrigue. She wondered if it was a self-protective device, a way of lowering in advance the emotional temperature of this first meeting.

Twenty minutes later the bus slowed to turn left down a narrower road into a valley. The signpost said 'Melcombe 2 miles'. They drove through a village of stone houses, past the Melcombe Arms and a general store and post office, over a humped bridge spanning a shallow fast-running stream, then alongside an eight-foot stone wall. The wall was old but in an excellent state of repair, and it seemed to stretch for miles. Then suddenly it ended and the bus shook to a stop outside two immense wrought-iron gates. They stood wide open. On the wall the notice painted black and white was stark. 'HM Prison. Melcombe Grange'.

It was, she thought, a not entirely unsuitable house for use as a prison for all its stolid domestic origins. It was a sixteenth-century brick-built mansion with wide projecting wings at whose junction with the centre block two heavy castellated towers rose like watch-towers. The rows of tall mullioned windows, coruscated by the sun, were secretive, transomed with stone bars. The doorway was formidable, its heavily ornate porch symbolic of strength and security rather than of the grace of hospitality. It was easy to see that the estate had been institutionalized. The sweep to the main door had been widened to provide a marked parking space for half a dozen cars, and to the right of the house she could see a row of prefabricated huts, craft rooms perhaps or extra dormitories. On the lawn to the left of the main path three women wearing bibbed overalls were tinkering, not very energetically, with a recalcitrant lawn-mower. They turned to stare at the stream of approaching visitors without apparent enthusiasm.

The openness, the absence of custodians, the beauty of the house stretching before her in its ageless calm disconcerted and confused her. The bus had gone on its way bearing the last few remaining passengers to the next village. She had forgotten to ask the time of the return journey, and she experienced a moment of irrational panic that, without this information, there could be no return journey, that she was condemned to be stranded here in this prison which was so alarmingly un-prisonlike. The visitors, sure of them-selves, knowing what awaited them for good or ill, were streaming down the wide gravel path towards the house. Their shoulders dragged with the weight of their bags. Even the grey-haired man was carrying a bundle of books bound with a strap. Only she was coming empty-handed. She walked slowly after them, heart thump-ing. One of them, a black girl of about her own age, her hair minutely plaited and decorated with green and yellow beads, glanced back then waited for her. She said:

'You're new, aren't you? Saw you on the bus. Who d'you want?'

'I'm visiting Mrs Ducton. Mrs Mary Ducton.'

'Mary? She's in the stable block with my mate. I'm going there. I'll show you.'

'Oughtn't I to report to someone?'

'You report to the warden's office over at the stables. Got your VO have you?'

Seeing Philippa's look of momentary incomprehension, she said: 'Your VO. Visiting Order.'

'Yes, I've got that.'

Her companion led the way round the side of the house to a set of converted stables, across a cobbled yard and through an open door to a small office. There was a woman prison officer there in uniform. The black girl handed over her visiting order and dumped her bag on the small table. The woman officer rummaged through the contents with brief expertise. She said in a pleasant Scottish accent:

'My word but you're smart today, Ettie. It beats me how you have the patience to thread in all those beads.'

Ettie grinned and shook her neatly decorative head. The beads danced and jangled, red, yellow and blue. The prison officer turned to Philippa. Philippa held out her pass.

'Oh yes, you're Miss Palfrey. This is your first time, isn't it? The Governor thought you'd like some extra privacy so I've put a notice on the sitting-room door. You'll be all right there for an hour at least. You show Miss Palfrey the sitting-room, will you Ettie, there's a good lass, I can't leave the desk just for a moment.'

The room was a little way down the corridor on the right. A cardboard notice with the word 'engaged' was hung on the door. Ettie didn't open it, but gave the door a gentle kick and said:

'Here you are. See you on the bus maybe.' Then she was gone.

Philippa opened the door slowly. The room was empty. She shut the door and leaned against it for a moment, glad of the comforting strength of wood against her back. Like Miss Henderson's office, this room had a spurious comfort. It was a place of transit but without the ostentatious vulgarity of an airport departure lounge; unpretentious, stuffy, overcrowded with furniture which looked as if it had been rejected from a dozen different homes. Nothing it contained was memorable. It was designed to be used and then mercifully forgotten. No transient would look back on this room with regret or be tempted to leave a humming chord of her misery or hope on the bleak air. There were too many chairs, assorted in size or shape, disposed around half a dozen small highly polished tables. The walls were plain and smudged in places, as if someone had cleansed them of graffiti. Over the fireplace was a print of Constable's *Hay Wain* and below it on the mantelshelf a glass vase of artificial flowers. In the middle of the room was set a small octagonal table with two facing chairs. In contrast to the informality of the room they looked as if they had been specially arranged. Perhaps a helpful inmate, instructed to see that the room was tidy, had placed them there, seeing every visit as a formal confrontation across an invisible but impregnable grille.

The waiting minutes seemed to stretch for hours. Occasionally footsteps passed the door. It was as cheerfully noisy as school at mid-morning break. Philippa's mind was a turmoil of emotions: excitement, apprehension, resentment, and finally anger. What was she doing abandoned here in this dreary room where the furniture was too clean, the walls too grubby, the flowers artificial? They had a large enough garden, surely they could at least provide fresh flowers. A cell would have been less disquieting to wait in. At least it didn't pretend to be anything but what it was. And why wasn't her mother here, waiting for her? She knew that she was coming, she must have known the time of the bus. What was she finding to do that was more important than being here? Her mind spun with grotesque images. Hair that had once been golden but was now dry as straw, dancing with threaded beads, her mother's face sagging under the weight of make-up, a cigarette hanging from a slack mouth, hands with painted talons stretched out to her throat. She thought: 'Suppose I don't like her. Suppose she can't stand me. We've got to spend two months together. I can't get out of it now. I can't go back to Caldecote Terrace and tell Maurice I made a mistake.' She walked over to the window and looked out across the cobbled courtyard at the second set of stables. She would make herself think about the architecture. Maurice had taught her how to look at buildings. This stable block was later than the house; it might even be neo-Georgian. But the clock turret with its swinging golden cock looked older. Perhaps they had re-erected it when the original stables were demolished. They had made a good job of the conversion. But where was her mother? Why didn't she come?

The door opened. She turned round. Her first impression, but so fleeting that the thought and its rejection were almost simultaneous, was that her mother had sent a friend to break the news that she had changed her mind, that she didn't want to meet her after all. It was stupid to have expected so much older a woman. And, at first, she looked so ordinary; a slight, attractive figure in a grey pleated skirt with a paler cotton shirt blouse and a green scarf knotted at the neck.

All her grotesque imaginings fled like shrieking demons before a relic. It was like recognizing oneself. It was the beginning of identity. Surely if she had met this woman anywhere in the world she would have known herself to be flesh of her flesh. Instinctively they each slowly took a chair and regarded each other across the table. Her mother said:

'I'm sorry I've kept you waiting. The bus was early. I didn't want to watch out for it in case you didn't come.'

Philippa knew now from which parent she had inherited her corn-gold hair. But her mother's hair, shaped to her head like a cap and cut in a fringe above her eyes, looked finer and lighter, perhaps because it was streaked with silver. The mouth, wider than her own, had the same curved upper lip, but it was more resolute, the delicate droop at each corner less sensual. But here was the pattern of her high cheekbones, her slightly arched nose. Only the eyes were different, a luminous grey faintly streaked with green. They held a look of half-startled wariness, of endurance, like those of a patient facing once more the inescapable and painful probing. Her skin might once have been honey-coloured, but now looked clear, almost bloodless. The impression was of a face still attractive, still young, but from which colour had been drained by a perpetual weariness, of watchful eyes which had seen too much for too long.

They didn't touch each other. Neither stretched a hand across the table. Philippa said:

'What shall I call you?'

'Mother. Isn't that why you're here?'

Philippa didn't reply. She wanted to say that she was sorry to have come empty-handed, but was frightened that her mother might reply, 'But you've brought yourself.' It would be intolerable if their first meeting began with such banality. Her mother said:

'You do understand what I did, why you were adopted?'

'I don't understand, but I do know about it. My father raped a child and you killed her.'

It seemed to Philippa that the air between them had solidified, had become the oscillating medium through which their words flickered and spun. Now it trembled, and her mother's face was for a moment blank as if some tenuous link of perception had been broken. She said:

'Did feloniously and with malice aforethought kill one Julia Mavis

Scase. It's true, except that they don't use those words any more and it wasn't with malice aforethought. It wasn't meant. But she's just as dead as if it had been. And all murderers tell you that anyway. You don't have to believe it. I don't know why I said it. You must excuse me if I seem socially inept. You are my first visitor for nine years.'

'If you tell me, why shouldn't I believe you?'

'But it's irrelevant. You aren't a romantic, are you? You don't look as if you are. You haven't come here with the idea of proving me innocent? You haven't been reading too many crime novels?'

'I don't read crime novels except Dostoevsky and Dickens.'

The noise from outside was louder now, the voices had become strident, feet were pounding down the corridor. Philippa said:

'They're a noisy lot, aren't they? It's rather like a boarding school.'

'Yes, a boarding school with strict discipline where they take difficult girls off their parents' hands. This part is the old stable block converted into a pre-release hostel. Lifers have to live here for nine months before they let us out. We go out to work. There are a few liberal-minded employers in York with an interest in rehabilitating prisoners. After the prison authorities have deducted a contribution towards our keep and paid out pocket money they bank the surplus. I shall have two hundred and thirty pounds forty-eight pence when I leave. I thought – if you still want me – that the money could go towards the rent of the flat.'

'I can pay the rent of the flat. You'll need your two hundred pounds. What do you do? I mean, what kind of job?'

She hoped she didn't sound like a prospective employer. Her mother said:

'I'm a chamber-maid at a hotel. There wasn't much choice of work. Murderers are easier to place than thieves or confidence tricksters, but with unemployment as high as it is the prison has to take what's on offer. But it does mean that I've had my insurance card stamped.'

'Hotel work must be boring.'

'Tiring, but not boring. I'm not afraid of hard work.'

The statement seemed to Philippa out of character, pathetic, almost demeaning. It embarrassed her by its naïveté. It was too close to an appeal, the Victorian kitchen-maid desperate to be taken on. Suddenly she thought of Hilda, bending over the kitchen table. The memory of Hilda at that moment was intrusive and disconcerting. She said:

'Do we have to stay in here? It's lovely in the sun. Can't we go outside?'

'If you'd rather. The warden suggested that we might like to walk round the lawn. Visitors normally have to stay in the house, but she's made an exception for you, for us.'

A gravel path, bordered with lime trees, circled the immense lawn. It was here that they walked. The gravel glinted in the sun and grated like hot cinders under Philippa's feet. In the distance the bleached skeletons of denuded elms, stricken by Dutch elm disease, stood like pale distorted gibbets against the varying green of oak, beech, horse chestnut and silver birch. Occasionally their black shadows were broken by a path of green sward and she could see tantalizing vistas leading to a circular rose garden, a bulbous stone cherub. The skeleton of a dried beech leaf trembled momentarily on the path before being ground to dust under her feet. Even at the height of summer there were always some dead leaves. Someone somewhere was burning them: there was a sweet, pungent smell redolent of autumn. Surely it was early to be burning leaves. No one burnt leaves in the London parks. This was a country smell, raking memory back to forgotten autumns at Pennington, except that she had never lived at Pennington. The hard boughs of horse chestnut and oak, weighted with summer, the dead leaf, the smoky bonfire tang, the transitory spring sweetness of the lime flowers, all produced in her a momentary confusion, a sense of all seasons coming together in a moment out of time. Perhaps these two months, before she went up to Cambridge, would be similarly lived in a new dimension, not counted against her allotted years. Perhaps she would look back at this visit, uncertain whether it had been spring or autumn, remembering only the discordant scent and sounds, the single dead leaf.

They walked in silence. Philippa tried to analyse her emotions. What was she feeling? Embarrassment? Not that. Comradeship? That was too sturdily complacent a word for the tenuous link between them. Fulfilment? Peace? No, not peace. Here was a balance between excitement and apprehension, a euphoria which had nothing to do with the mind's quietude. Contentment, perhaps. Now at least I know who I am. I know the worst, I shall know the best. Above all, a sense that it was right to be here, that this deliberate pacing, carefully distanced so that the first touch should not be casual, was a ritual of immense significance, an end and a beginning.

She thought for the first time since she had heard it: 'I like her voice.' It was low, unpractised, tentative, as if English were a language her mother had learned. Words were symbols formed in the mind and seldom spoken. It was strange, thought Philippa, that she would have found it more difficult to live with a whining or grating voice than with the knowledge that this woman had killed a child. Her mother asked:

'What are you going to do? I mean, what job?' She paused. 'I'm sorry. That's the kind of question a ten-year-old gets asked and hates answering.'

'I've known since I was ten. I'm going to be a writer.'

'Are you gathering material? Is that why you're offering to help me? I don't mind. At least I shall have given you something. There's nothing else I've given you.'

It was matter-of-fact, with no hint of self-pity or of remorse.

'Except my life. Except my life. Except my life.'

'*Hamlet*. It seems strange now, but I hardly knew Shakespeare before I went to prison. I promised myself that I'd read every play and in chronological order. There are twenty-one. I rationed myself to one every six months. That way I could be sure that they would last out the sentence. You can annihilate thought with words.'

The paradox of poetry.

'Yes,' she said. 'I know.'

The gravel path grated Philippa's feet. She said:

'Can't we walk into the garden?'

'We have to keep to this path. Rules. They haven't the staff to hunt people down all over the grounds.'

'But the gate wasn't locked. You could all walk out.'

'Only into another kind of prison.'

Two women, obviously staff, were hurrying across the grass, running gawkily, lurching together. They weren't in uniform, but it was impossible to mistake them for inmates. One had thrown an arm round her companion's shoulder. Their laughter was happy, conspiratorial. Remembering that they mustn't be called warders, Philippa asked:

'The prison officers, how have they treated you?'

'Some like animals, some like recalcitrant children, some like mental patients. I like best those who treat us as prisoners.'

'And those two, running across the grass, who are they?'

'Two friends. They always ask to get posted together. They live together.'

'You mean they're lovers, lesbians? Is there a lot of that in prison?' She remembered Maurice's snide innuendo.

Her mother smiled.

'You make it sound like an infectious disease. Of course it happens. It happens often. People need to be loved. They need to feel that they matter to someone. If you're wondering about me, the answer is no. I wouldn't have had the chance, anyway. In prison or out, people need someone they can despise more than they do themselves. A child-killer is at the bottom of the heap, even here. Learn to be alone. Don't draw attention to yourself. That way my sort survive. Your father didn't.'

'What was he like, father?'

'He was a schoolmaster. He hadn't a university degree. His father, your grandfather, was a clerk with an insurance company. I don't suppose any member of the family has ever been to a university. Your father went to a teacher training college. That was regarded as a great achievement. He taught the senior boys at an inner London comprehensive school until he couldn't stand it any more. Then he took a job as a clerk with the Gas Board.'

'But what was he like? What were his interests?'

Her mother's voice was a harsh grate:

'His interest was little girls.'

Perhaps the bleak reply was meant to shock, to jolt her into a fresh awareness of why they were here, pacing the gravel together. Philippa waited until she could be sure that her voice was calm. She said:

'That isn't an interest. That's an obsession.'

'I'm sorry, I shouldn't have said that. I'm not even sure that it's true. It's just that I don't seem able to give you what you want.'

'I don't want anything. I'm not here because of wanting.'

But it seemed to Philippa that her question had been only the first of a catalogue of wants. I want to know who I am, I want to be approved of, I want to be successful, I want to be loved. The question, 'Then why *are* you here?' hung between them, unasked, unanswerable.

They walked on together in silence. Her mother seemed to be thinking, then she said:

'He liked second-hand books, exploring old churches, roaming city streets, taking a train to Southend for the day and walking to the end of the pier. He liked reading history and biography, never fiction. He lived in his own imagination, not other men's. He disliked his job but hadn't the courage to change it again. He hadn't the courage to change anything. He was one of the meek who are supposed to inherit the earth. He liked you.'

'How did he manage to entice her into the house?'

She disciplined her voice, politely interested, as if the enquiry were about some social trivia. Did he take sugar in his tea? Did he enjoy sports? How did he rape a child?

'He had his right hand bandaged. It was quite genuine. He'd grazed it when he fell over a garden rake and it had become septic. He had just come home from work when he saw her, walking home after her Girl Guide meeting. He told her that he wanted a cup of tea but couldn't manage to fill the kettle.'

Ah, but that had been clever. He had seen a child coming down that suburban street, walking in the dangerous innocence of child-hood. A Girl Guide in uniform. Her good deed for the day. He had used the one ploy that might succeed even with a suspicious or timid child. She hadn't sensed danger where there was a need she could meet, something within her power. She could picture the child carefully filling the kettle at the cold tap, lighting the gas for him, offering to stay and make the tea, setting out his cup and saucer with anxious care. He had made use of what was good and kind in her to destroy her. If evil existed, if those four letters placed in that order had any reality, then surely here was evil.

She was aware of her mother's voice.

'He didn't mean to harm her.'

'Didn't he? Then what did he mean?'

'To talk, perhaps. To kiss her. To fondle her. I don't know. Whatever he had in mind, it wasn't rape. He was gentle, timid, weak. I suppose that's why he was attracted to children. I thought I could help him because I was strong. But he didn't want strength. He couldn't cope with it. What he wanted was childishness, vulnerability. He didn't hurt her, you know, not physically. It was a technical rape, but he wasn't violent. I suppose if I hadn't killed her she and her parents would have claimed later that he'd ruined her life, that she could never make a happy marriage. Perhaps they would have been right. The psychologists say that children never get over an early sexual assault. I didn't leave her any life to be spoiled. I'm not excusing him. Only you mustn't picture it as worse than it was.'

How could it have been worse than it was, Philippa wondered. A child had been raped and murdered. The physical details she could imagine, had imagined. But the horror, the loneliness, the last terrifying moment; it was no more possible to enter into these by an effort of will than it was physically to feel another's pain. Pain and fear. To experience either was to be aware for ever of the loneliness of the self.

Maurice, after all, had warned her, in one of their short bouts of disconnected talk during those four days when she had been waiting for her mother's reply:

'None of us can bear too much reality. No one. We all create for ourselves a world in which it's tolerable for us to live. You've probably created yours with more imagination than most. Having gone to that trouble, why demolish it?'

And she in her arrogant confidence had replied:

'Perhaps I shall find out that it would have been better for me if I'd been content with it. But it's too late now. That world has gone for good. I have to find another. At least this one will be founded on reality.'

'Will it? How do you know that it won't turn out to be just as illusory and far less comfortable.'

'But it must be better to know the facts. You're a scientist – a pseudo-scientist anyway. I thought you held truth to be sacred.'

And he had replied:

' "What is truth?", said jesting Pilate, and would not stay for an answer. Facts are sacred, if you can discover them, and as long as you don't confuse them with values.'

They had circled the lawn once and were back at the Grange. Rejecting it, they turned slowly and began retracing their steps. She said:

'Have I any relations on my father's side of the family?'

'Your father was an only child. He had a cousin, but she and her husband emigrated to Canada about the time of the trial. They didn't want anyone to know about the connection. I suppose they're still alive. They hadn't any children and they were both middle-aged then. About forty, I think.'

'And your side?'

'I did have a brother, Stephen, eight years younger than I, but he was killed in Ireland the first year of the troubles, before he was twenty. He was in the Army.'

'So my only uncle is dead, and there's no one else?'

'No,' she said gravely, unsmiling. 'Only me. I'm your only blood relation.'

They continued their slow pacing. The sun was hot on Philippa's shoulders. Her mother said:

'They provide tea for visitors, if you'd like a cup.'

'I would, but not here. I'll get it in York. How much longer have we?'

'Before the bus? Another thirty minutes.'

'What do I have to do? I mean, can you just come to me when you leave, or are there formalities?'

She was careful to keep her eyes on the path, unwilling to face what she might see in her mother's eyes. It was the moment of final offer and acceptance. When her mother spoke her voice was controlled.

'The present plan is for me to go to a probation hostel for women in Kensington. I hated the thought of another hostel, but there wasn't any choice, at least for the first month. But I don't think there'll be any difficulty about coming to you instead. They'll send someone to check that you've actually got a flat and the arrangements have to be approved by the Home Office. The first stage is for you to write formally to the Chief Welfare Officer here. But hadn't you better take a week or two to think about it?'

'I have thought about it.'

'What would you normally be doing in these next two months?'

'Probably the same, taking a flat in London. I've left school. I got my Cambridge scholarship last year when I was seventeen. This year I've been taking philosophy and adding to my A-levels just to fill in time. I'm hardly the VSO type – Voluntary Service Overseas. I'm not altering my plans for you, if that's what's worrying you.'

Her mother accepted the lie. She said:

'I shall be an embarrassing flatmate. How will you explain me to your friends?'

'We shan't be seeing my friends. If we do run into them, I shall explain that you're my mother. What else do they need to know?'

Her mother said formally:

'Then, thank you Philippa. Just for the first two months I'd be very glad to join you.'

After that they spoke no more of the future, but walked together, each with her thoughts, until it was time for Philippa to join the desultory stream of visitors making their way up the wide sun-scorched path towards the gates and the waiting bus.

11

Neither Maurice nor Hilda asked any questions when she got home shortly after half-past eight. Not to ask questions was part of Maurice's policy of non-interference; usually he managed to convey the impression of not being particularly interested in knowing. Hilda, who looked flushed and rather sulky, kept a resolute and sullen silence, enquiring only if Philippa had had a good journey. She glanced fearfully at Maurice as she asked this seemingly innocuous question, and appeared not to hear Philippa's answer. The tone was forced; she might have been speaking to a newly arrived and not particularly welcome guest. During a late dinner they sat like strangers; but strangers, after all, were what they were. It was a night when company would have been a relief, but they drank their vichyssoise and ate their chicken marengo almost in silence. As she finally pushed her chair from the table, Philippa said:

'My mother seems quite glad to share a flat for the next month or so. I'll start looking tomorrow.'

The words came out unnaturally loudly, belligerent as a challenge. She was angry with herself that they should sound so forced, that despite her silent rehearsal throughout dinner speaking them aloud had been so difficult. She had never been frightened of Maurice. Why should she start being frightened of him now? She was eighteen, officially an adult, responsible to no one but herself.

She was probably as free now as she was ever likely to be. She had no need to justify her actions. Maurice said:

'You won't find it easy to rent a flat at a price you can afford, not in central London anyway. If you need to borrow money, let me know. Don't go to the bank. There's no point in paying interest at the present rate.'

'I can manage on my own. I've got the money I saved for my European trip.'

'In that case, good luck. You'd better keep your key in case you need to come back. And if you are intending to move out permanently, it would be helpful if we could have as much notice as possible. I could probably find a use for your room.'

He made it sound, thought Philippa, as if he were dismissing a recalcitrant paying guest. But that was how he had intended it to sound.

12

On Monday 17 July, shortly after nine o'clock in the morning, Scase rang a number in the city which he had rung every three months for the last six years. But this time the information he requested wasn't given to him. Nor, as usually happened, was it promised for a few days' time. Instead Eli Watkin asked him to call in at the office as soon as was convenient to him. Within half an hour he was on his way to Hallelujah Passage off Ludgate Hill to see a man whom he had last seen six years ago. Then Mavis had been with him; this time he made his way past St Paul's churchyard and into the dark, narrow little alley on his own.

They had waited for three years after the end of the trial before getting in touch with Eli Watkin Investigations Limited. They found the firm's name in the Yellow Pages of the London telephone directory among a list of some dozen private detective agencies, sandwiched between Designers and Diamond Merchants. They spent a day in London visiting each office in turn, trying to assess from the address and outward appearance whether it was efficient and reputable. Mavis had wanted to exclude any agency which accepted divorce cases, but Scase had persuaded her that this was an unnecessary limitation of choice. The task wasn't easy. Mutually supportive and determined as they were, they nevertheless felt themselves on alien and frightening territory. They were intimidated by the smart, impersonal-looking offices of the largest concerns, and repelled by the seediness of some of the smallest. In the end they ventured into Eli Watkin Investigations because they like the name of Hallelujah Passage, the office exuded a Dickensian atmosphere of cheerful amateurism, and Mavis was reassured and cheered by the window box outside the ground-floor window in which the spears of early daffodils were already beginning to show. They were greeted by an elderly typist, then shown upstairs to Mr Eli Watkin himself.

On their entry into his small, claustrophobic office, they had found him squatting before a hissing gas fire, spooning cat food into three saucers while five squalling cats of varied sizes and hues butted against his thin ankles. A matriarchal tabby sat, paws folded, on top of a bookcase, regarding the mêlée with slit-eyed disdain. When the last of the food had been distributed, she jumped lightly down with a switch of her tail and arranged herself at the third bowl. Only then did Eli Watkin stand up to greet them. They had seen a squat, crumple-faced man with a comb of white hair and heavy-lidded eyes. He had a disconcerting habit of appearing to keep them half-closed when speaking, then of suddenly raising them, as if by a conscious effort, to display small but intensely blue eyes. He welcomed them with none of the smarmy condescension which Scase had feared. Nor did he seem at all surprised by their commission. Scase had practised what he intended to say.

'Three years ago a woman, Mary Ducton, was sentenced for life for the murder of our daughter, Julia Mavis Scase. We want to be kept in touch with her. We want to know when she's moved and where, what she's doing, and when she's due to be released. Is that the kind of information you deal in?'

'Well now, it could be. There's no information in the world that you can't get hold of if you're prepared to pay.'

'Would it be expensive?'

'Not that expensive. Where is the lady now? In Holloway? I thought so. Ring me at this number in ten days' time and we'll see what we can do.'

'How do you obtain your information?'

'The way one always gets information, Mr Scase. By paying for it.'

'This is confidential, of course. There's nothing illegal about it, but we don't want other people to know our business.'

'Of course. That is why you pay a little more.'

After that they had telephoned Eli Watkin four times a year. On each occasion he would ring back three days later and tell them what he knew. Within a week a bill would come, 'to professional services rendered'. The amount varied. Sometimes it was as high as twenty pounds, sometimes as low as five. In this way they learned when Mary Ducton came out of her self-imposed isolation and began working in the prison library, when she was moved from Holloway to Durham and from Durham to Melcombe Grange, when she was admitted to the prison hospital for treatment after an assault by three of the other prisoners, when her case was first considered by the Parole Board. Six months ago he had learned from Eli Watkin that she had been given a conditional release date for August 1978.

It was nearly eleven o'clock when he reached Hallelujah Passage. There was still a window box outside Eli Watkin's office, but now it held nothing but caked earth. The door into the passage was open and the ground-floor office, which was empty, was filled with packing cases. The dingy walls had been stripped; there were oblong shapes where once pictures must have hung. The windows were so filthy that the daylight was almost entirely excluded and he had to feel his way across the tattered linoleum to the uncarpeted stairway.

In the upstairs office Eli Watkin awaited him as he had six years ago. The same gas fire hissed away and he recognized the large roll-topped desk and the two battered filing cabinets. There were no cats now, but it seemed to Scase that there hung on the air the sharp, sour reek of their food. But then he wondered whether what he was smelling was mortal sickness. He could recognize Eli Watkin because the bright blue eyes were the same; nothing else was. The hand held out to grasp his was a cluster of loose bones held together by dry flesh. The face was a yellow death's-head from which the eyes blazed with the brilliance of jewels.

Scase said:

'I've called about Mary Ducton. I rang to ask if you'd yet got the actual day of release. You asked me to call.'

'So I did, so I did, Mr Scase. There are some things which are best said face to face. Come in now, will you?'

He went over to the first of the filing cabinets and took from the top drawer a buff folder. The drawer seemed otherwise to be empty. The folder was faded but clean, almost untouched. But then, thought Scase, it had only been handled four times a year. Eli Watkin carried it back to the desk and opened it. Scase saw that it contained copies of his bills and small scraps of paper – notes, perhaps, of telephone conversations. There was nothing else. Watkin said:

'The subject is due to be released from Melcombe Grange Prison on Tuesday the fifteenth of August 1978.'

'To what address?'

'Now that I can't be telling you, Mr Scase. It was to have been to a probation hostel in North Kensington, but there's talk at the prison that the arrangement may be changed.'

'When would you be able to let me know? Could I telephone you next week?'

'I shan't be here next week, Mr Scase. By next month the builders will be in converting this place to a coffee and sandwich bar. A little tucked away, I should have thought, to suit the customers, but that's not my worry. I've been paid well enough for the lease. And if you should telephone in six months' time they'll tell you, if there's anyone still here and if they care, that I'm dead. By August the fifteenth I shall be in Mexico. I've waited all my life, Mr Scase, to see the floating gardens of Xochimilco, and I'm off in three days' time. This is the last information I'll be giving you. And you, Mr Scase, are my last client.'

Scase said:

'I'm sorry.'

There was nothing else that he could think to say. After a moment he asked:

'And you've no idea what town she'll be travelling to?'

'I imagine she'll come to London. They usually do. She lived in Seven Kings in Essex at the time of the murder, didn't she? Likely as not she'll come to London.'

'Do you know what time they'll release her?'

'It's usually in the morning. I should plan for the morning if I were you. The morning of Tuesday the fifteenth of August.'

Had there been a subtle emphasis on the word 'plan'? Scase said:

'It would be helpful to know. I have to see her personally, to hand her a letter from my wife. I promised Mavis to put it into her hand.'

'I've promised myself all my life that I'd see the floating gardens. Do you believe in reincarnation, Mr Scase?'

'I haven't thought about it. I suppose it could be a comfort to people who need to believe in their own importance.'

'But you can believe in your own importance without myths?'

The swollen lids were suddenly raised and the blue eyes stared at him, unfaded, ironic. He said:

'Killing someone isn't easy, Mr Scase. Even the State has had to give it up. And the State had all the conveniences, you might say; a scaffold, a skilled and experienced operator, the condemned person safely to hand. Are you a skilled operator, Mr Scase?'

He wondered why the words, the implied threat, didn't worry him. And then a glance at that skull, marked out like an anatomist's model with its tributaries of blue veins, at the paper-thin membrane stretched over the jutting bones, told him why. Even the mark of death was enough to make a man virtually harmless. He was already moving away from the petty concerns of the living towards his floating gardens. And what difference did suspicion make? When the murderess was dead he must expect to be the chief, perhaps the only suspect. What mattered was that he should give the police no real evidence, no legal proof. Part of him half believed that they might not look for that proof too assiduously. He said calmly:

'If that's what you believe, aren't you going to warn the police?'

'But that would be unethical, Mr Scase. In my profession I don't often speak to the police, although sometimes they like to speak to me. And you and I have had a long and, I think, fruitful professional relationship. You've paid me well over the years for certain information. What you do with it isn't my responsibility. And I have to catch that plane in three days' time.'

Scase said calmly:

'You are mistaken. I have to see the woman, have to hand over a letter, that's all. My wife wanted her to know that we have forgiven her. One can't go on hating for nearly ten years.'

'Very true. Do you read Thomas Mann, Mr Scase? A fine writer. "For the sake of humanity, for the sake of love, let no man's thoughts be ruled by death." I think I have quoted it correctly, but you get the meaning I'm sure. That will be fifty pounds.'

'It's more than I expected. I've only brought forty pounds in cash with me. I've never paid more than thirty before.'

'But this is the final payment, and I think you can say that the information is worth it. But we'll say forty. We don't want any cheques, do we?'

He paid over the eight five-pound notes. Eli Watkin folded them into his wallet. He said:

'I don't think we need trouble this time with a receipt. And now we can add your file to the rest of this rubbish. There are quite a number of secrets and a lot of misery torn up in this sack. Perhaps you'll deal with it. The file cover is rather too stiff for my hands.'

Scase tore up each scrap of paper, then ripped the file cover into small pieces and shook them into the sack in which the debris of Mr Watkin's small business slid in a restless tide of paper. Last of all they shook hands. Watkin's hand was dry and very cold, but his handshake was surprisingly firm; strong enough, surely, to have torn up the file had he chosen. Scase's last sight of him was of him still sitting at his desk, and looking after him with an amused, benignant pity. But his last words were cheerful enough:

'Don't fall over the dustbins, Mr Scase. Wouldn't it be an inconvenient thing now if you were disabled just at this interesting period of your life?'

That afternoon he telephoned the best known of the local estate agents and instructed them to put his house on the market. The firm said that they would try to send round their Mr Wheatley early next morning. By ten o'clock Mr Wheatley had arrived. He was younger than Scase had expected – not more than twenty, surely – with a sharp, unhealthy-looking face, and was dressed with a desperate respectability, presumably to inspire confidence in the efficiency and probity of the firm. The padded shoulders of his cheap, dark blue suit hung loosely on him as if he had chosen it to allow for growth. But he entered with brisk assurance and was hardly through the door before he began surveying the house with a keen appraising eye. He carried a clip-board and measured each room expertly with a spring measuring tape which he used with a flourish. Walking behind him from room to room, Scase saw that he had a small pustule on his neck. It had broken, staining the top of his shirt collar with blood and pus. He found it difficult to take his eyes off it.

'Well, it's a nice little property, sir. Nicely maintained. We shouldn't have much trouble in getting rid of it for you. Mind you, the market isn't quite what it was six months ago. What price were you thinking of?'

'What price do you suggest?'

He wouldn't, Scase knew, put it higher than he needed to. The commission went up with the price, but what really paid was a quick sale and no trouble. And he wouldn't be valuing it himself for all his pursed lips and air of calculation. His firm would have told him exactly what a reasonably well-maintained semi in Alma Road would fetch.

After a couple of minutes spent slowly pacing from hall to sitting-room, from sitting-room to kitchen, he said:

'You might get nineteen and a half if you're lucky. The garden's a bit neglected and these houses haven't got garages. That always brings the price down. People like a garage. We could start at twenty and be prepared to drop.'

'I want a quick sale. I don't mind starting at nineteen and a half.'

'It's up to you, sir. Now, what about viewing? Will you be in this afternoon?'

'No. I'll give you a spare set of keys. I'd like you to show people round. I don't want to see them.'

'That may hold things up a bit, sir. It's a question of staff, you see. We'd have to try and fit a number of viewers in together. Now, if you could arrange to be home early evenings for, say, a couple of weeks . . .'

Scase thought, let them earn their commission.

'I don't want to see anyone. You can hand over the keys if they sign for them and undertake to lock up carefully. There's nothing here for them to steal.'

'Oh, we wouldn't want to do that, sir. Look, if I could tell prospective purchasers that you might take eighteen and a half, or even eighteen at a pinch, I don't think you'll have to wait long.'

'All right. Ask eighteen and a half.'

'There's a young couple on the books who might be interested at eighteen thousand. They've got two kids and you're handy for the school. I'll see if I can get them over this evening.'

'I want a quick sale. Won't they need a mortgage? That takes time.'

'There'll be no difficulty there, sir. They've been saving with a building society. I think you'll find that it will all go very easily if they like the house.'

Taking one last disparaging look at the meanly proportioned front sitting-room, he added:

'Whoever takes it will probably knock that middle wall down and make one large room. Open it up, like. And the kitchen will need remodelling.'

Scase didn't care what they did to it as long as it was quickly sold. He needed the money to finance his enterprise. He and Mavis had always agreed that selling the house might be necessary. He didn't think Mavis had thought beyond the actual deed; at present he wasn't thinking beyond it himself. But the prospect of virtual homelessness, of moving from this snug suburban respectability into an unknown, intimidating world, filled him with a mixture of excitement and apprehension. It would be so easy to hang on, to see the house as a familiar refuge to which he could retreat if the hunt got hard or disappointing. As he followed behind Mr Wheatley, watching the silver measure leap out to record the meagre dimensions of kitchen and hall, the house seemed to him like the lair of some small predator, earth-bound, secret, holding within its brown walls the beast's very smell. In the kitchen he imagined that he could see its spoor on the linoleum, could see under the table a litter of fur and bones.

13

Philippa knew that in her search for a furnished, two-roomed flat in central London at a reasonable rent, she was privileged; appearance, age, voice and colour – although no one was so unwise as to hint at race – all were in her favour. She read the truth of her advantage in the appraising eyes and deference of the receptionists and inter-viewers in the dozen or so flat agencies at which she called. It was an added attraction to them that the lease required was so short – 'only the three months before I go up to Cambridge' – and that she didn't want a joint let. The words, 'just for the two of us, my mother and me, we want to spend some months together in London before I go up to college and she goes abroad', spoken in her confident, educated voice were, as she well knew, a reassuring guarantee of filial duty and respectability. Any of the agents would gladly have let to her if they had had anything suitable to offer. But short-term furnished leases in inner London were exorbitantly priced for the foreign market, and her tentative suggestion of forty to fifty pounds a week was met with incredulous smiles, shakes of the head, and murmurs of the evil effect of the rent restriction acts. She was made to feel guilty of some deception; she had no right to walk in looking so prosperous and admit to such poverty. Losing interest, the agencies took her name and address and promised nothing.

She followed the same daily routine during the first week of her search. She left 68 Caldecote Terrace after breakfast and spent the morning trudging round the agencies. As soon as the lunchtime editions of the evening paper were available, she bought them and marked the possibilities. The next half-hour was spent in a telephone kiosk where, provided with a supply of coins, she began the frustrating task of trying to contact the advertisers on numbers most of which were either continually engaged or unobtainable. Then came the viewing; flats whose grimy windows overlooked deep wells which no sunlight could ever penetrate; shared lavatories and bathrooms remote from the flat itself and in a state to encourage permanent constipation; furnished flats where the furniture consisted of the landlord's broken rejects, wardrobes whose doors swung perpetually open, cookers with chipped enamel and food-encrusted ovens, tables with scorched tops and uneven legs, and filthy lumpy beds; landlords whose advertisement for a female tenant had less to do with the probable greater cleanliness of the kitchen than with other more elemental needs.

She was soon forced to widen the area of her search. She came to know a different London and she saw it through different eyes. The city was all things to all men. It reflected and deepened mood; it did not create it. Here the miserable were more miserable, the lonely more bereft, while the prosperous and happy saw reflected in its river and glittering life the confirmation of their deserved success. In her week of seeking, unsuccessfully, for a flat in which she could bear, even temporarily, to live, Philippa felt increasingly depressed and rejected. Once, from the security of Caldecote Terrace, she would have seen the meaner streets of north Paddington, Kilburn and Earls Court as fascinating outposts of an alien culture, part of the variety and colour of any capital city.

Now with disenchanted and prejudiced eyes she saw only filth and deformity; the bursting bags of uncollected rubbish, the litter which choked the gutters and blew down the passages of the Underground, the walls defaced by the scribbled hate of extremists of the left and right, the crude obscenities with which the platform posters were embellished, the stink of urine overlaid with disinfectant which rose from the stained concrete of the underground walkways, the ugliness of people. Man, fouling his own habitat, couldn't even behave like a good animal. The alien shrouded bodies crouching on the kerbside, watching from the open doors, threatened her with their strangeness; the prevailing smells of curry, of herded bodies, of scented women's hair, emphasized the sense of exclusion, of being unwanted in her own city.

And then on the morning of Friday 28 July, walking down Edgware Road after finding that yet another advertised flat had been taken, she saw down a side road an agency which she hadn't before discovered. The most remarkable thing about the Raterite Accommodation Bureau was that it existed at all, or that, existing, it did any business. If larger, cleaner and more imposing agencies were short of properties to rent or manage, it was strange that this seedy, unprepossessing establishment attracted prospective landlords. The window was patterned with hand-written cards sellotaped to the smeared glass. Most were brown with age; on some the ink had faded to the colour of thin dried blood. The variety of handwriting and eccentricity of spelling suggested a frequent change of staff and no great discrimination in their choosing. The few clean white cards were intrusive patches of hope which was quickly vitiated by the word 'taken' scrawled across those few which, judging from the reasonable rent demanded, had probably never genuinely been on offer.

Philippa pushed open the door and stepped into a small office containing two desks and a row of four chairs against the wall. On one of these an Indian was sitting in patient resignation. Behind the larger of the two desks a flamboyantly dressed woman with red hair and a multitude of clinking bangles sat smoking a cigarette and doing the crossword in the morning paper. She had the look of a woman who has found life recalcitrant since childhood but has finally succeeded, at some cost to herself, in pounding it into shape. At the second desk a younger, blonde woman was listening with careful uninterest to the volubility of a red-faced, bandy-legged man whose suit of checked tweed and natty, feather-trimmed trilby were more appropriate to the Brighton racecourse than to this seedy office.

The blonde shifted her eyes to Philippa, apparently to indicate that she was now prepared to do business. The bandy-legged man, taking the hint, made for the door.

'Well, see you.'

'See you,' the two women chorused together with a marked lack of enthusiasm.

Philippa said her piece. She was looking for a small, partly furnished, two-roomed flat for herself and her mother in central London for about two months.

'Until I go up to university. There's just the two of us. I don't mind doing something to it if it's basically in good order and fairly central.'

'What sort of rent were you thinking of?'

'What sort of rents are there?'

'Depends. Fifty, sixty, eighty, a hundred and more. We don't usually get anything under fifty a week. It's the Rent Act you see. Doesn't pay a landlord to rent when he can't get the tenants out.'

'Yes, I know all about the Rent Act. I could pay cash in advance.'

The woman at the other desk looked up but didn't speak. The blonde went on:

'Two months, you say? Most landlords look for a bit longer.'

'I thought they liked short lets. Isn't that why they let to foreigners because they know they can get them out? I can promise we'll be out by the autumn.'

The red-headed woman spoke.

'We don't take promises. There'd be an agreement. Mr Wade, the solicitor round the corner, draws it up for us. You did say cash?'

Philippa made herself look hard into the calculating eyes.

'For ten per cent discount.'

The blonde laughed: 'Are you kidding? Anything we get to rent furnished we can let without a discount.'

The woman at the other desk said:

'What about that two-roomed place with kitchen and shared bathroom in Delaney Street?'

'It's taken, Mrs Bealing. That young couple with the kid and the baby on the way. They viewed yesterday. I told you.'

'Let's have a look at the card.'

The blonde opened the top left-hand drawer of her desk and flicked through a card index. The card was passed across. The red-headed woman looked at Philippa.

'Three months' cash in advance. He won't let it go for less than three months. He's asking one hundred and ninety a month. Say five hundred and fifty for the three months, cash down, no cheques. And it's what's called a holiday letting. That means that the Rent Act doesn't apply.'

She had just short of one thousand pounds in her bank account saved from birthday presents and holiday jobs. But money, although she never spent it without thought, had never been important to her. She had always believed that she could earn money. Of all her needs, it seemed to her the most easily satisfied. She said with only a moment's hesitation:

'All right. But if it's taken?'

'Please yourself. It's up to you.'

The blonde glanced at Philippa with the amused, slightly contemptuous look of a woman who has long given up expecting people to behave well, but can still gain some satisfaction from watching them behave badly. Philippa nodded. The older woman picked up the telephone and dialled.

'Mr Baker? The Raterite Bureau here about the flat. Yes. Yes. Yes. Well, the fact of the matter is that Mr Coates isn't happy. Yes, I know he's in New York. He rang. He doesn't like the idea of your wife managing those narrow stairs, not in her condition. And he doesn't want a let with children. Yes, I know, but I'm the one who makes the decisions and I wasn't here when you came in. And then there would be the pram in the hall. No, it wouldn't be any good writing to him. I don't know where he'll be for the next month or two. Sorry. Yes, we'll let you know. Up to forty pounds a week. Yes. I know, Mr Baker. Yes, we've got all the details. Yes. Yes. I don't think it's very helpful to take that attitude. After all, nothing has been signed.'

She took up her cigarette again, and returned to her paper. Without looking at Philippa she said:

'You can view it now if you like. Number 12, Delaney Street. It's at the bottom of Mell Street off the Edgware Road just this side of Praed Street. Two rooms and kitchen. Use of bathroom. The bathroom's shared with the lock-up greengrocery on the ground floor. You won't find anything cheaper, not in central London. It's a snip. It'd be twice the price, but Mr Coates went to New York in a hurry and he wants a short let.'

'Is it furnished?'

The blonde said:

'Not so as you'd notice.'

'Well, most people like to bring in their own bits and pieces. But it's a furnished letting.'

'I'd like to view it now, please.'

She signed for the keys, but didn't at once make her way to Delaney Street. It seemed to her that once there the decision would have been made. If she were going to reject the flat she must do so now. She felt the need to stride out vigorously, to co-ordinate thought with action. But the pavement was too crowded; the pressure of bodies, the tangle of pushchairs and trolleys forced her restless feet from the kerb into the stream of traffic. Almost without thinking she turned into a café about a hundred yards down Edgware Road and found a seat at a grubby formica-topped table near the window. A lank-haired waiter in a stained jacket slouched over from the counter and she ordered a coffee. The coffee, when it arrived in a plastic cup, pale, lukewarm and tasteless, was literally undrinkable. Glancing round at her fellow customers who were not only managing to drink it – although with no apparent signs of pleasure – but had actually bought food, overcooked hamburgers, flabby chips, fried eggs curling brown at the edges and swimming in grease, she reflected that one at least of Maurice's axioms was true: The poor always got worse value pound for pound than the rich.

The window was festooned with wicker baskets of dusty artificial flowers and trailing vine-leaves. Against the glittering panorama of the traffic the pavement was heaving with life. From time to time, faces, grey, brown or black, moved momentarily to the glass to study the price list. They seemed to be staring in at her; face succeeded face like a peripatetic jury, mute witnesses of her moral dilemma.

Nothing she could recognize from her past had equipped her to deal with it. She slipped the key ring on her thumb so that the two keys, the Yale which must be for the shared front door, the Chubb for the door to the flat itself, lay cold and heavy against her palm, reinforcing symbolism. Her moral training – indoctrination Maurice would have called it, smiling a self-satisfied acceptance of his own honesty – had been a matter of semantics, of the intellectualization of a comfortable ethical conformity. You behaved reasonably well to other people in the interest of certain abstractions: good public order, a pleasant life, natural justice – whatever that meant – the greatest good of the greatest number. Most of all, you behaved well to others to ensure that they behaved well to you. The implication was that the clever, the witty, the beautiful or the rich had less need of these expedients; it was the more seemly in them to set an example.

She could find no answer in her schooling. The South London Collegiate was nominally a Christian foundation but the fifteen minutes' corporate worship with which the school started the day had always seemed to her no more than a convenient celebration of tradition, a way of ensuring that the whole school was present when the headmistress read out the day's notices. Some of the girls practised a religion. Anglicanism, particularly High Anglicanism, was accepted as a satisfying compromise between reason and myth, justified by the beauty of its liturgy, a celebration of Englishness; but essentially it was the universal religion of liberal humanism laced with ritual to suit each individual taste. She had never supposed that for Gabriel, professed High Anglican, it had ever been more. The small number of Roman Catholics, Christian Scientists and Non-conformists were regarded as eccentrics governed by family tradition. Nothing that any of them professed to believe interfered with the central dogma of the whole school, the supremacy of human intelligence. The girls, like their brothers at Winchester, Westminster and St Paul's, were conditioned from childhood to a fierce intellectual competitiveness. She herself had been so conditioned from the time of her entry to the lower school. They were marked for success as if with invisible stigmata: the blessed company of the redeemed; redeemed from monotony, from poverty, from inconsequence, from failure. The universities they would go to, the professions they would choose, the men they would marry, were ranked in a hierarchy, unstated but subtly understood. She didn't feel that this was the only world in which she could find a place. She was a writer; all worlds were open to her. But it was the world into which Maurice had raised himself, into which she had been adopted, and she had no quarrel with it. After her foragings among the philistines this civilized city would always open its doors to her, not as an alien but as a freeman.

She supposed that Dame Beatrice, who visited the school once a week to teach moral philosophy, would have had an answer to her dilemma: if asking more questions and discussing their relevance, whether they had, in fact, any meaning, was an answer. She recalled the last weekly essay, which was in itself a diploma of superiority since only the upper sixth attended Dame Beatrice's lectures.

'Act only on the maxim through which you can at the same time will that it should become a universal law. Discuss with reference to Hegel's criticism of Kant's system of moral philosophy.'

And what relevance had that to the opposing claims to a cheap flat of an ex-convict who was a murderess and a pregnant wife? Except that the pregnant wife had got there first. There was a notice on the board in the school hall. 'The Chaplain is available to girls in his study by appointment or on Friday from 12.30–2 p.m. and on Wednesday from 4–5.30 p.m.' A spiritual stud. He was a humourless man and the girls had giggled at the infelicitous wording. But he would, she supposed, have had his answer:

'Behold, I give you a new commandment, that you love one another.'

But that wasn't possible by an act of will. Surely the faithful were justified in replying, 'But Lord, show us how'? And He, that itinerant man/God, whom no one would have heard of if he had died sane and in his bed, would have had his answer too: 'I have.'

The café was not the most suitable place for the resolution of a moral dilemma. The noise was appalling and there was a shortage of seats. Harassed women with folded pushchairs and children clutching at their coats were looking for a place. She had sat there long enough. She left a five-pence tip under the saucer of unfinished coffee, dropped the keys in her shoulder bag and set off resolutely down the Edgware Road towards Mell Street.

14

Delaney Street was at the Lisson Grove end of Mell Street, a narrow street with, on the left, a terrace of small shops with living accommodation above. There was a pub at the end, the Grenadier, with a swinging sign of some splendour, then a betting shop, secretive behind painted glass, giving out a low murmur like a hive of angry bees. Then came a hairdresser's, the front of his window strewn with advertisements for hair tonics and lotions, and the back occupied by four dummy heads. The blank dolls' eyes turned upwards in the gaping sockets, and the wigs, dry as straw, gave the heads the look of guillotine victims of some ancient holocaust, needing only a jagged red line around each severed neck to complete the illusion. The door was open, and Philippa could see two customers awaiting their turn, and a wizened old man, comb poised, busying himself with the back of a customer's neck.

A green door with '12' painted in black and a Victorian iron knocker and letter-box was between a junk shop and a greengrocer whose open-fronted shop had once been the ground floor of the house. On the fascia was painted 'Monty's Fruit and Veg'. Both shops had spilled out on to the pavement. The greengrocer's stall, covered with a mat of lurid artificial grass, was piled with fruit and vegetables, displayed with an eye to artistic effect. An intricate pyramid of oranges gleamed against the dimness of the inner shop; bunches of bananas and grapes hung from a rail above the back of the stall and the boxes of burnished apples, the carrots and tomatoes were arranged in a balanced pattern as if for a church harvest festival. A stocky young man with greasy fair hair straggling to his shoulders, a podgy, amiable face and huge hands, was pouring potatoes from the pan of his scales into the outstretched shopping bag held by the mittened hands of an elderly customer, so well-wrapped against the unkind summer that little of his face was visible between the flat cloth cap and the swathed woollen scarves.

Now that she was here she found herself torn between anxiety to see the flat and a curious reluctance to put the key in the door. It was almost as an exercise in self-control as well as a wish to postpone disappointment that she made herself take stock of her surroundings.

The junk shop looked exciting. Outside there was an assortment of old furniture: four bentwood chairs, two more with broken cane seats, a sturdy kitchen table bearing boxes of paperback novels and old magazines, an ancient treadle sewing-machine, an enamel wash-tub filled with assorted crockery, most of it chipped, and a wooden mangle. Victorian prints and amateur water-colours in a variety of frames rested against the table legs. On the pavement was a square cardboard box of linen in which a couple of young women were rummaging happily. In the shop window every inch of space was occupied. Philippa gained an impression of articles jumbled together, irrespective of merit and, presumably, of price. She could see chipped Staffordshire, delicately painted cups and saucers, dishes and bowls, candlesticks and horse brasses, while an antique doll with a delicate china face and straw-filled bulging legs was perched in the pride of place.

She inserted the Yale key in the lock, aware as she did so of the interested glance of the greengrocer, and found herself in a narrow hall. The hall smelled of apples and loam, a strong rich tang which, she guessed, overlaid less agreeable smells. It was very narrow – too narrow for a pram, she told herself – and obstructed by two sacks of potatoes and a meshed bag of onions. To the right an open door led into the shop; a second, with a glass panel, gave sight of a back yard. She decided to explore this later, although the glimpse of it immediately evoked visions of climbing plants and geranium-filled tubs. A flight of steep, drugget-covered stairs led to a back room on a half landing. She opened the door gingerly and saw that this was the bathroom. The large old-fashioned bath was heavily stained round the waste-pipe, but otherwise surprisingly clean. There was a small wash-basin encrusted with grime and with a slimy face-flannel jammed into the soap dish. The lavatory had a heavy mahogany seat, a high cistern and a chain lengthened by string. Another length of string was stretched across the bath. It sagged with the weight of a pair of jeans and two grubby towels.

She went up a further short flight of stairs to the flat door. The key turned in the Chubb lock without difficulty and she passed into a short hall. After the dimness of the stairway the flat seemed full of light, perhaps because the doors of the three rooms were all open. She moved first into the one at the front which she guessed would be the principal room running the whole width of the house. The curtains were drawn back and a single beam of sunlight shone through the dirty window panes so that the air was iridescent with dancing motes of dust. It wasn't large, she judged about fifteen feet by ten, but was pleasantly proportioned with a carved cornice and with two windows facing over the street. On the left-hand wall was a Victorian grate, its hood patterned with a border of scallop shells and decorated with a design of beribboned grapevines; above it was a plain wooden overmantel. The grate was stuffed with brown and brittle old newspapers, and the tiled surround was littered with cigarette butts, but the air held no taint of cigarette smoke, only the faint autumnal smell of vegetables and apples. The room was shabby. The paint on the window frames had chipped and flaked to the bare wood. The carpet was a dull green, splodged and ringed in front of the fire as if the occupier had placed his hot cooking pans on the floor. But the wallpaper, patterned in small posies of rosebuds, had faded to a pleasant pinkish brown, and was surprisingly intact, and although the ceiling obviously hadn't been painted for years, there were no ominous cracks, no hanging swathes of lining paper. A long cord with a single unshaded light bulb on the end had been drawn from the middle of the ceiling and stretched over a hook so that the light was suspended over the single divan bed.

The divan was covered with a woollen blanket made of handknitted squares in different colours. Philippa drew it back and saw with relief that the mattress was clean, so clean that it looked new. There were two pillows, also new, but no other bedclothes. Between the windows was a small but sturdy oak wardrobe with carved doors. It stood firm when she pulled open the door. Inside were two empty hangers and, folded on the floor, three grey army blankets exuding a smell of moth-balls. The only other items of furniture were a wicker chair with a limp fawn cushion, an oblong table with a centre drawer, and a bentwood rocking-chair with a wicker seat.

The windows were curtained in a coarse unlined linen, slung from wooden hooks on an old-fashioned bamboo curtain rail. They had the creased, grubby look of curtains which had been laid aside, unused, but the material was good. Standing behind them she looked out over the narrow street. Opposite but about thirty yards to the left was another pub, the Blind Beggar. It was a high Dutch-fronted building with the date 1896 painted in heavy curved numerals on an oval plaque under the central gable. The swinging sign, which was competently painted and highly sentimental, was almost certainly the original. It showed a bent white-haired man with sightless eyes being led by a golden-haired child. A narrow passage ran down the side of the building, separating it from a wasteland bordered with a high fence of corrugated iron. It looked like a bomb site which had been neglected since the war but, she thought, more probably it had been cleared for some development which had been thwarted for lack of money. It had been concreted, but the surface had cracked and grass and weeds waist-high had burgeoned in the crevices. Three vehicles had been parked there, a van and two saloons. They had the isolated battered look of ramshackle rejects abandoned in a small oasis of decrepitude. Next to the car park was a second-hand bookshop. The window was half shuttered but two trestle tables outside the shop were bright with the green and orange of old paperbacks. Next came a small general store, the window plastered with notices of special offers. On the corner of Delaney Street and Mell Street was a launderette. As she watched, a black woman came out lugging two plastic bags which she humped on to an empty pushchair. But otherwise the road was empty, lapped in a mid-morning lull.

She turned away from the window and looked round the room again with mounting excitement. Something could be made of it. In her mind's eye she saw it transformed, the grate cleaned and polished, the woodwork painted a gleaming white, the curtains washed. Nothing need be done about the walls, she liked that delicate washed-out pink and brown. The floor would be a problem, of course. She turned back a corner of the carpet. Underneath the solid oak boards were dirty but looked undamaged. The most exciting thing to do would be to sand the floor and then polish it so that the natural oak shone with the simplicity and beauty of wood against the darker walls, but she doubted whether that would be possible. Without the use of a car it would be difficult to hire a sanding machine, and there wasn't very much time. She had never realized before just how important a car could be. But the carpet would have to go. She would rip it out, roll it and get rid of it somehow, and replace it with rugs. The room might in the end be bare, but it would have some grace, some individuality. It wouldn't have what her mind's eye pictured as the dreadful compromise between bleakness and claustrophobic cosiness of a prison cell.

She continued her exploration. At the rear were two rooms, a narrow bedroom and the kitchen. Both overlooked the walled yard and, beyond it, the narrow back gardens of the next street. One or two of them had been carefully tended but most were an untidy conglomeration of ramshackle sheds, dismembered motor bikes, broken and discarded children's toys, washing lines and concrete fuel bunkers. But there was a plane tree at the bottom of the garden opposite the bedroom, providing a green light-filled shield for the worst of the clutter, and at least the view had some human interest.

She decided that the small room would have to be hers. It was too like a cell in its proportions to be suitable for her mother. She sat on the single divan bed and assessed the room's possibilities. There was a fitted cupboard on each side of the iron Victorian grate and the walls had been stripped of paper ready for redecoration. She wouldn't need to buy a wardrobe and it would be a simple matter to apply a coat of emulsion. She liked, too, the pine overmantel. Someone had painted it green but the paint was already peeling. It wouldn't be too difficult to strip and polish it. The window sill was wide enough to hold a plant. She could picture the sill gleaming with white paint, reflecting the green and red of a geranium.

Lastly she went into the kitchen. Here she was agreeably surprised. It was a good-sized room with the sink and teak draining board in front of the double window. The owner had started here with his redecoration and the walls had been painted white. There was a wooden-topped table, two wheel-backed chairs, a small refrigerator and what looked like a new gas stove. She turned on the gas tap and found to her relief that the supply hadn't been disconnected. He must have left for America in a hurry.

After her inspection she relocked the front door and went finally to explore the back yard whose worst horrors had been obscured from the upstairs windows by an overhanging bough of the plane tree. The outside lavatory with its wooden seat and stone floor obviously hadn't worked for years. But at least it didn't smell. The yard was a mess. There was a bicycle against one wall and the other two were piled with rubbish; empty paint cans, a rotting roll of old carpet, and what looked like the dismembered parts of an ancient gas stove. Here, too, were two battered and malodorous dustbins. She supposed that they would have to be dragged into the street for the weekly collection. Something, she decided, would have to be done about the yard, but it would have to wait its turn.

She looked at her watch. It was time that she went back to the agency and confirmed that she would definitely take the flat. She had thirty pounds with her in cash. Perhaps they would take that as a deposit until she could get to her bank and draw out the rest of the rent. Whatever happened, she mustn't lose it now. As soon as the agreement had been signed she would move in and start work. But first it might be prudent to make the acquaintance of her neighbour.

He had just finished serving a customer and was carefully repairing his pyramid of oranges. She watched him for a moment, knowing that he was aware of her but was waiting for her to make the first move. She said:

'Good morning. Are you Monty?'

'Naw. Monty was me granddad. Dead twenty years.' He hesitated, then added: 'I'm George.'

'I'm Philippa. Philippa Palfrey. My mother and I have just taken the upstairs flat.'

She held out her hand. After another hesitation he wiped his palm against his side and gripped her knuckles hard. She winced as the bones ground together. He said:

'Marty gone to New York then?'

'He's gone somewhere. I suppose he'll be back. It's only a short-term let for two or three months. I was wondering about the bathroom. They said at the agency that we share it. I thought we'd better settle about the cleaning.'

He looked, she thought, a little nonplussed.

'Marty's birds always did the cleaning.'

'Well, I'm no one's bird. But as there are two of us and only you, I don't mind taking responsibility for the bathroom, if that's all right by you.'

'Suits me.'

'We'll do the passage and the stairs, too. Do you mind if I clear up the yard, I mean, just get rid of the mess? I thought we might have some pots – geraniums perhaps. I don't suppose it gets much sun with that high wall, but something might grow.'

'I keep me bike in the yard.'

'Oh, I didn't mean I'd move your bike. Of course not. I'd just get rid of those old paint cans and bits of iron.'

'That's OK by me. That outside WC doesn't work.'

'So I found. It hardly seems worth mending it; after all my mother and I won't be monopolizing the bathroom. We can bath out of shop hours. We'll try to keep it clear for you if you let us know when you want to use it.'

'Look love, I pee in the bloody place. It's me bog. I can't tell you when I'm going to be took short, not with the amount of beer I drink.'

'I'm sorry. I saw your bath towel there and I thought you might want to bath after you close the shop.'

'That's Marty's towel. I bath at home. There's only two things I want to do up there and I can't tell you when I'll want to do them. OK?'

'Well, that's all right then.'

They looked at each other. He said:

'Marty OK? Doing all right is he?'

'I haven't the least idea. Considering the rent he's asking, he should be doing fine.'

He smiled. Then with the élan of a conjuror his chubby hands picked out four oranges, tossed them into a bag and held it out to her.

'Sample the produce. Monty's best. It's on the house. House-warming present.'

'That's very kind of you. Thank you. I've never had a house-warming present before.'

The action in its generosity and grace disconcerted and touched her. She smiled at him and turned quickly away, afraid that she might cry. She never cried, but it had been a long and exhausting week and she was at the end of her search at last. Perhaps it was only tiredness and the relief of finding somewhere when she had almost given up hope that made her so ridiculously sensitive to a simple act of kindness. The bag was too fragile for the weight of the oranges and she had to support them on her hands. She looked down at their gleaming pock-marked skin and felt their round solidity resting on her palms. She bore them upstairs slowly and carefully as if they might crack, then rested the bag against the wall while she unlocked the flat door. She had found during her inspection a shallow Wedgwood-patterned bowl in the kitchen cupboard among a miscellany of crockery and half-used tins of coffee and cocoa. She set the oranges in it. Then she placed the bowl precisely in the middle of the kitchen table. It seemed to her that with this action she took possession of the flat.

On the following day, Saturday 29 July, Scase took a cheap day return ticket from Victoria to Brighton. He was on his way to buy the knife. He had been born in Brighton, in a small pub near the station, but his return for the first time since his youth had nothing to do with nostalgia. The purchase of the knife seemed to him of immense significance; he had to make the right choice and to make it without risk that his purchase would afterwards be remembered. That meant that he needed to buy it in a large town, preferably some distance from London, and on the busiest shopping day of the week. He would feel at home in Brighton. There were advantages in not having to cope with so important a purchase and at the same time find his way around a strange town.

His first thought was to buy a hunting or sheath knife from a shop which dealt in camping equipment, but when, after anxiously scrutinizing the window, he ventured inside such a shop, there were no knives on display and the thought of actually having to ask for one, and of perhaps being asked by an assistant, anxious to be helpful, for what precise purpose he wanted it, reinforced his feeling that this wasn't the right place. Wandering among the anoraks, the bed-rolls and the camping gear, he did eventually find a selection of jack-knives hanging from a display board, but he thought that the blades might be too short. He was worried, too, that if he had to act in a hurry his fingers might be too weak to get the blade prised open in time. What he wanted was a simpler weapon. But he did find, and buy, at the camping shop another necessary piece of equipment; a strong canvas rucksack in khaki, about fourteen inches by ten with two metal buckles and a shoulder strap.

In the end he found the knife in the kitchen department of a fashionable household store, new since his time. The goods were displayed in racks; stacks of pretty cups and saucers, earthenware casserole dishes, plain, well-designed cutlery and every possible item of equipment for cooking. The store was very busy and he moved with his bloodstained preoccupation among young couples conferring happily over purchases for their homes, families with boisterous children, chattering foreign tourists and the occasional solitary shopper surveying with a discriminating eye the bottles of spices and coffee beans and the jars of preserves. The store seemed to be staffed by pretty girls in summer dresses, much occupied with their own conversations. No one approached him. Customers selected their own items and carried them in the store's baskets to the check-out desk. He would be one of an endless, moving line of people, anonymous, quickly dealt with, not even required to speak.

He took his time at the knife rack, trying them in his hands for weight and balance and for a comfortable feel of the handle in the grasp of his palm. In the end he chose a strong carving knife with a triangular eight-inch blade, very sharp at the point and riveted into a plain wooden handle. The blade, razor-sharp, was protected with a tough cardboard sheath. The sharp point seemed to him important. It was that first deep thrust into her flesh which he imagined might take all his strength and purpose. That done, the final twist and withdrawal would be little more than a reflex action. He had the right money ready, and after standing in a short queue, was through the check-out within seconds.

He had brought with him to Brighton the binoculars which he had bought as his retiring present. He already had at home a street map of London, but there were two other necessities, and both he bought in Brighton. In a chainstore chemist he purchased the small size of the finest protective gloves which they had on display, and, in another large store, a white transparent mackintosh. Here, but without bothering to try it on, he selected the largest size. If he were to be adequately protected against what might be a gushing fountain of blood, he needed a protective coat which would reach almost to the ground. He put the gloves in the pocket of the mackintosh, then rolled it round the binoculars and the sheathed knife. The bundle fitted easily into the bottom of the rucksack and its wide strap fitted comfortably on his shoulder.

He couldn't be sure why, in the end, he decided after all to visit the Goat and Compasses. Perhaps the reasons were a mixture of the simple and complex; he was, after all, in Brighton and was unlikely to visit here again in the near future, the pub was on his way to the station, he was moving into a new sphere of existence which would distance still further those early traumatic years, it would be interesting to see whether the place had changed. Nothing about it had. It still seemed to crouch under the shadow of the railway arches, a low, dark, claustrophobic pub, liked by its regulars but hardly inviting to the casual passer-by. The wooden-walled public bar was still furnished with the same long oak tables and benches, the walls were still hung with the same maple-framed old photographs of Brighton pier, and groups of sou'wester-clad fishermen before their boats. Opposite and seen through the windows the railway arches still gaped like black menacing mouths. In his childhood the arches had been a place of terror, the lair of the spitting monsters with no necks, whose spittle was death. Always he passed on the other side of the road, not running, in case his padding feet drew their attention, but walking in steady haste, his eyes averted. But then, when he was eleven, he made a pact with them. He used to secrete scraps of his meals, a crust from breakfast, the end of a sausage or a piece of potato from supper, and lay them, a propitiatory offering, at the entrance to the first arch. Returning at night, he would look to see if the offering had been accepted. With part of his mind he knew that the seagulls scavenged there, but when he found that the scraps had gone he went home comforted. But the trains never frightened him. He would lie at night mentally timing their visitation, hands clutching the blanket edge, his eyes fixed on the window, waiting for the preparatory whistle, the approaching rumble, which, almost as soon as he heard it, exploded into a climax of clashing metal and flashing lights while his bed shook under the momentary dazzle of the patterned ceiling.

Sitting there, alone, in the dim corner of the saloon bar with his hands clasped round his glass of lager, he recalled the day when he had first learned that he was ugly. He had been ten years and three months old. His Auntie Gladys and Uncle George were setting out the public bar for the first evening customers. His mother was out with Uncle Ted, the latest of the so-called uncles who came and went in his life, and he was playing alone in the dark little passage between the bar and the sitting-room, sprawled on the floor and taxiing his model biplane carefully on to one of the grey squares of the chequered lino. The door to the bar was swinging open and he could hear footsteps, the clink of bottles, chairs being dragged across the floor, and then his uncle's voice:

'Where's Norm? Marge said he wasn't to go out.'

'In his room, I suppose. That kid gives me the willies, George. He's right ugly. He's a proper little Crippen.'

'Oh come off it! He's not that bad, poor little sod. His dad was no oil painting. The kid's no trouble.'

'I grant you that. More healthy if he was. I like a boy with a bit of spirit to him. He creeps around the place like some sodding animal. You got the key to this till, George?'

The voices sank to a murmur. He slid across the floor soundlessly and stole out of the door and up the twisting stairs to his bedroom. There was a rickety oak chest of drawers in front of the window and on top of it an old-fashioned swivel looking-glass, the mirror spotted with age. He hardly ever used it and had to drag the bedside chair across to the chest and stand on it before he saw the thin grubby fingers pressed white against the oak, the toy plane between them, his face rising to confront him, framed in split mahogany. He gazed at himself stolidly, the protuberant eyes behind the cheap crooked spectacles with their steel rims, the straight fringe of dry brown hair, too thin to obscure the rash of spots across his forehead, the unhealthy pallor of his skin. Ugliness. So this was why his mother didn't love him. The realization didn't surprise him. He didn't love himself. The knowledge that he was ugly and therefore beyond the possibilities of love was only the confirmation of something always known but never, until now, acknowledged, taken in with his milk when she thrust the bottle teat between his gums, mirrored in the anxious disappointed face which bent over his, perpetually present in adults' eyes, heard in the whining nag of her voice. It was too inescapably a part of him to be resented or grieved over. It would have been better for him to have been born with one leg or one eye. People might have been impressed by how well he managed, might have been sorry for him. But this deformity of the spirit was beyond pity as it was beyond healing.

When his mother came home, he followed her up to her room.

'Mum, who was Crippen?'

'Crippen? What a question. Why d'you want to know?'

'I heard someone talking about him at school.'

'Pity they couldn't find something better to talk about then. He was a murderer. He killed his wife and cut her up and buried her in the cellar. That was a long time ago. In your granddad's time. Hilldrop Crescent. That's where it happened!' Her voice brightened at the wonder of memory's capricious cleverness, then resumed its normal hectoring tone. 'Crippen indeed!'

'What happened to him?'

'He was hanged, of course, what do you think happened to him? Give over talking about him, will you.'

So he was wicked as well as ugly, and in some mysterious way the ugliness and the wickedness belonged together. When he thought about his boyhood he marvelled at the child's stoical acceptance of this yoked burden of physical and moral repulsion, hardly made more bearable by the knowledge of its arbitrariness, or of his powerlessness to shift the load from his shoulders.

Two things saved him, delinquency and chess. The first had begun in a small way. He had wandered unobserved into the saloon bar early one Saturday morning before opening time. He liked the bar when it was silent and empty: the round tables with their ornate cast-iron legs and stained tops; the wall clock with its swinging pendulum and flower-painted face measuring the silence with ticks which were too soft to be heard except out of opening hours; the smeared glass dome covering the tray holding two of yesterday's sausage rolls, even the smell of beer which permeated the whole house, but which in this smoky brown-clad cabin was strong and potent as a gas; the mysterious dimness behind the counter with its rows of darkly gleaming bottles awaiting the magic moment when the bar lights would be switched on and the liquids would take fire. Venturing behind the bar into this heartland of the forbidden territory, he saw that the till drawer was unlocked and slightly open. Gently he pulled it towards him. And there it was – money; not money in the possession of grown-ups, a symbol of adult power, not a few crumpled notes being stuffed, almost surreptitiously, into his mother's purse in the corner shop, not coins carefully doled out weekly to him to pay for school dinners or his fares. Here was money under his hands, two bundles of notes held together in rubber bands, silver coins, unnaturally bright, looking as heavy as doubloons, coffee-coloured pennies. Afterwards he couldn't recall taking the one-pound note. All he could remember was being back in his own room, terrified, his heart thudding, his back pressed against the door, turning the note over in his hands.

It was never missed, or if it was, he was not suspected. He spent it that morning on a model railway engine, and on Monday brought it out ostentatiously between lessons, and ran it over his desk top. The boy in the next desk looked at it trying to conceal his envy.

'That's the new Hornby, isn't it? Where d'you get it?'

'Bought it.'

'Let's have a look.'

He passed it across, feeling a momentary pang at the loss of its smooth brightness. He said:

'You can keep it if you like.'

'You mean you don't want it?'

He shrugged his shoulders.

'I mean you can have it.'

Thirty pairs of eyes slewed round to witness this marvel. The form bully said:

'Got any more at home?'

'Might have. Why, d'you want one?'

'I don't mind.'

But he did mind. Looking into the face he feared, into the greedy little eyes, Norman rejoiced in the knowledge of just how much he minded.

'I'll bring you one next week. Monday maybe.'

And that was the end of the persecution and the beginning of a year during which he lived at a pitch of inner excitement, of exhilaration and terror, which he had never experienced since. He didn't again steal from the pub takings. Twice more he stole into the saloon bar in hope, but on neither occasion was the till drawer unlocked. Part of him was relieved to be spared the temptation. To risk a second theft would have been too dangerous. But with the beginning of summer and the influx of visitors came other and safer opportunities. In his solitary wanderings after school along the promenade or on the beach, his restlessly blinking eyes, so deceptively mild behind steel-rimmed spectacles, grew adept at spotting his chances; a purse casually laid on top of a beach bag, a wallet stuck into a blazer pocket, loose change from paying the deck-chair attendant dropped into the pocket of a coat slung across the back of the canvas. He grew skilful at picking pockets, the tiny marsupial hands insinuating their way under the jacket, into the back trouser pocket. Afterwards, his tactic was always the same. He would wait to examine the spoils until he could be sure that he was unobserved. Usually he would seek the rank-smelling metallic saltiness of the gloom under the great iron girders of the pier, take out the money, then scuff the purse or wallet under the sand. Apart from coins, he took away only pound notes. To proffer anything larger at a local shop would be to invite suspicion. But, perhaps because he worked alone, was so unremarkable, looked so neat and respectable, there never was suspicion. Only once, during the whole of the year, was he in danger of discovery. He had bought a model of a breakdown van and had been unable to resist playing with it in the hall before school. His mother's eye had been caught by the unexpected brightness.

'That's new isn't it? Where d'you get it?'

'A man gave it to me.'

'What man?' Her voice was sharp, worried.

'Just a man coming out of the bar. A customer.'

'What did you do for it?'

'Nothing. I didn't do anything.'

'Well, what did he ask you to do?'

'Nothing, Mum. He just gave it to me, honest. I didn't do anything.'

'Well don't, that's all! And don't take toys from strangers.'

But in the following autumn, the beginning of his second year at senior school, came Mr Micklewright, a new and enthusiastic young member of staff, with his passion for chess. The school chess club was formed and Norman joined. The game fascinated him. He played every day, needing no opponent since there were published games to work out, strategies which could be developed in secret, books from the public and school library to teach him the subtleties of the various openings. Encouraged by Mr Micklewright's enthusiasm and praise he rapidly became the best player in the school. Then there were the local school competitions, the Southern Championship, and eventually even a photograph in the *Brighton Evening Argus*, a photograph cut out by his aunt and passed from hand to hand round the saloon bar. That established his fame. From then on he lived the rest of his school life without fear. He stopped stealing because it was no longer necessary for him to steal. Even the spitting monsters deserted the railway arches, leaving nothing but their debris of beer cans, screwed-up cigarette cartons and a brown, mildewed pillow leaking damp feathers against the furthest wall.

On his walk back to the station and his homeward train, he wondered what would have happened to him if he had gone on with the stealing. He couldn't have hoped to have evaded detection for ever. And then what? He would have been officially labelled delinquent; processed through the juvenile justice system; become the unprepossessing object of the machinery of bureaucratic caring. There would have been no respectable career in local government, no meeting with Mavis, no Julie. So much in his life seemed to have depended on that moment when Mr Micklewright set out before his fascinated gaze those mythical warriors whose lives, like his, were governed by such unalterable and arbitrary rules.

When at last he reached home he went to his bedroom and tried on his equipment for murder. He looked at himself in the long wardrobe glass. With the unsheathed knife in his hand, the raincoat hanging in glistening folds from his thin shoulders, he looked like a surgeon gowned for some desperate operation or, perhaps, like the member of a more ancient and sinister priesthood garbed for a ritual slaughter. And yet the image was not wholly terrifying. There was something wrong about it, something almost pathetic. The clothes were right, the naked knife showed the keen edge of fear; but the eyes which met his with their look of mild, almost painful resolution, were the eyes, not of an executioner, but of the victim.

16

On 4 August a probation officer came by appointment to look at the flat. Philippa prepared for the visit with excessive care, cleaning and rearranging the sparse furniture and buying a geranium in a pot to sit on the kitchen window. There was still a lot to do to the flat before it was ready to receive her mother, and only another ten days in which to do it, but she was pleased with her efforts so far. She couldn't remember when she had physically worked harder than during the last week, or with more satisfaction. She had concentrated on her mother's room and it was now nearly ready. The worst job had been taking up the carpet and getting rid of it, but George, hearing her coughing with the dust and struggling on the stairs with the discarded roll, had helped carry it down and had bribed or persuaded the dustmen to take it away. Then she had spent two days scrubbing and staining the floor. She had brought nothing with her from Caldecote Terrace except one suitcase of clothes and the Henry Walton oil. She had hung it above the fireplace in her mother's room where, although it was not in period, she thought it looked particularly good above the newly gleaming firehood and the plain but elegant overmantel.

She was glad that she still had some money in reserve. She was surprised how expensive cleaning materials were; how many small items were essential to domestic comfort and how costly they were to buy. The previous owner had left in a box under the sink his set of tools, and after trial and error and much consulting of a book on elementary carpentry borrowed from the Marylebone Road branch of the Westminster Library, she managed to make a reasonable job of putting up extra shelves in the kitchen and a coat rack in the hall. She found in the market a cheap batch of old Victorian tiles and fixed them behind the sink. Some of the jobs she particularly enjoyed: painting the woodwork white, with the sun from the open window warming her arms; searching in the local junk shops and in Church Street market for the extra pieces of furniture they needed. One particularly successful buy was two small cane chairs. They were in perfect condition but painted a particularly repulsive green. After a coat of paint and with new patchwork cushions they added a touch of gaiety to the two rooms. George, if he saw her struggling with items of furniture, would temporarily leave his shop and give her a hand. She liked him. They seldom spoke, except when she bought from him the fruit which she ate each day for lunch, but she was aware that there flowed from him a general goodwill. Once he asked when Mrs Palfrey was expected to arrive. She told him on August the fifteenth, but didn't correct the name.

At night she lay on the narrow bed in the back room in an almost sensuous languor of exhaustion, with the window wide open, listening to the rumble and murmur of London, watching the stain of its night life on the scudding clouds, letting herself be gently shaken into sleep by the shudder of the Underground trains running between Marylebone and Edgware Road.

The probation officer was ten minutes late. When the downstairs bell at last rang Philippa opened the door to a tall, dark-haired woman who looked little older than herself. She was lugging a bulging plastic bag from the Edgware Road supermarket and seemed harassed. She said:

'Philippa Palfrey? I'm Joyce Bungeld. Sorry I'm late. The gasket went. I only got back from holiday this morning and it's been one hell of a day. All the eight O'Briens in court together. They're apparently terrified that I may be made redundant so they go out on a family shop-lifting bash every time I'm away just to prove to the authorities that I'm indispensable. Very pleased with themselves they were, grinning in the box like a row of monkeys, but I could have done without it. You weren't thinking of making tea, were you? I've got a throat like a gravel pit.'

Philippa made the tea, taking down her two new pottery mugs. Her first visitor. She told herself that she mustn't let resentment at the inspection prejudice her enterprise, and was resolved to counter officialdom with at least a show of docility. The probation officer rummaged in her bag and produced a packet of chocolate whole-meal biscuits. She tore open the package and offered it to Philippa. They munched companionably, sipping hot tea, both perched on the kitchen table.

'Your mother has her own room, has she? I see, in here. I like your picture.'

What was she afraid of, thought Philippa – that she and her mother were about to embark on a sophisticated variety of incest? And how could having separate rooms prevent that? She said:

'Don't you want to look at the bathroom? It's on the half landing.'

'No thanks. I'm not a sanitary inspector, thank God. You're here; the flat's here; your mother has someone and some place to come to. That's all I'm interested in. I'll write to the prison CWO tomorrow. You should hear in a day or two. I think they're trying to keep to the original release date, the fifteenth of August.'

'Will it be all right?' Philippa tried to keep the note of anxiety out of her voice.

'I should think so; why not? But it's finally up to the Home Office. Will you be here much? I mean, I suppose you've got a job?'

'Not yet. I thought we'd get one together; hotel work, waitressing, something like that.' She added, with an echo that was only half ironic: 'We're not afraid of hard work.'

'Then you're the only two people in London who aren't. Sorry. I'm feeling a little sour this afternoon. This would be a lovely job if it weren't for the clients. You go up to Cambridge in October, don't you? What had you in mind then?'

'For my mother? Nothing. I imagine she'll look for a cheaper flat if she can't afford to stay on here, or she could take a living-in job, if she can find one. And there's always one of your post-release hostels.'

She thought that the probation officer looked at her a little strangely. Then she said:

'Then she's probably only postponing most of her problems. Still, the first two months are the most difficult for a lifer. That's when they need support. And she did ask to come here. Thanks for the tea.'

The visit had lasted for less than twenty minutes, but Philippa thought that Miss Bungeld had seen all she wanted to see, had asked all the questions which it was necessary to ask. Shutting the street door after her and climbing the stairs she could imagine her report.

'The prisoner's daughter is of full age. She is an intelligent and sensible girl and the accommodation for which three months' rent has been paid in advance appears adequate. The licensee will have her own room and the flat, although small and unpretentious, was clean and tidy when I called. Miss Palfrey intends to find a job working with her mother. I recommend that the arrangements be approved.'

BOOK TWO
An Order of Release

1

On Tuesday 15 August, Scase was at York Station beginning his watch by half-past eight in the morning. He had travelled to York the previous evening and had taken a room in a dull commercial hotel close to the station. He could have been lodged in any provincial city. It never occurred to him to visit the Minster or to stroll through the cobbled streets within the city walls. Nothing the city promised could seduce his mind for an instant from the task in hand. He travelled light, carrying only his rucksack, adding nothing but his pyjamas and toilet bag to the sheathed knife, the rolled plastic mackintosh, the binoculars and the thin gloves. He was never now parted from the knife and the other impedimenta of murder. It was not that he expected to be able to kill her during the journey to London, a crowded train was hardly likely to afford opportunity, but it had become necessary to him to carry the knife. It was no longer an object of fascination or horror, but a familiar and potent extension of himself; the part which, when he closed his hand round it, completed him and made him whole. Now, even at night, he felt bereft without the drag of the rucksack on his shoulder, without being able to slip his hand under the flap and run his fingers along the cardboard sheath.

It was a convenient station in which to keep watch. From the outside hall an arched passage led through to the small concourse. To the right was the women's waiting-room. He could glimpse through the door a heavy mahogany table with carved legs, a lumpy couch and a row of carved chairs against the wall. Above the unlit gas fire was a nondescript modern print; it looked like a row of fishing nets strung out to dry. The waiting-room was empty except for one very old woman huddled in sleep among an assortment of bulging packages. There was only one entrance to the station concourse and the indicator showed him that the London trains went from platform 8. Beyond it the cavernous arched roof rose from the pale milk-grey pillars with their ornate capitals. There lay over the station the freshness of the early morning redolent with the smell of coffee. It waited in what seemed an eerie and portentous calm for the flood of commuter traffic and the chattering throng of the day's first tourists. Scase knew that, loitering alone so early, he would be conspicuous, but he told himself that it didn't matter. No place was more impersonal and anonymous than a railway station, no one would challenge him, and if they did he would say that he was waiting for a friend from London.

The bookstall was open and he bought a *Daily Telegraph*. A paper would be a quick way of hiding his face when she arrived. Then he settled himself on a bench to wait. He never doubted that Eli Watkin had kept faith with him, that this morning was the day of release. But he began to agitate himself with fears that he might not recognize her, that nearly ten years in prison might have changed her fundamentally or so subtly that she would slip past unnoticed. He took from his wallet the one picture that he had of her, cut from the local paper at the time of the trial. She and her husband had been snapped by a commercial photographer on what looked like a promenade at Southend. It was a photograph of two young people laughing, holding hands in the sun. He wondered how the reporter had managed to get hold of it. It told him nothing, and when he held it close to his eyes the image disintegrated into an anonymous pattern of microdots. It was impossible to connect this face with the woman whom he had last seen in the dock at the Old Bailey.

He had sat alone through every day of the three-week trial of his child's murderess, and by the last day nothing had any longer seemed real to him. It was like living in a dream world confined within the clean claustrophobic courtroom in which the ordinary conventions of life had been replaced by a different logic, an alien set of values. In that surrealist limbo no one except the professionals had any reality. All present were actors, but only those gowned or bewigged moved and spoke with assurance or knew their parts. The two accused sat side by side in the dock, yet distanced, not looking at each other, hardly moving their eyes. Perhaps if each had stretched out an arm their fingers might have touched, but their arms did not move. Touching was not in the script. The searing hatred which had infected him like a fever during the first days after Julie's death, which had driven him out into the suburban streets, walking endlessly, pointlessly, unseeing, desperately striding on to prevent himself from beating his head against those neat suburban walls and howling for vengeance like a dog; all that passed when he looked at their dead faces, since how could you hate someone who wasn't there, who was merely a bit-player, selected to sit in the dock so that the play could go on? They were the most important characters, yet they had the least to do, were the least regarded. They had a look of ordinariness which, in some dreadful way, wasn't ordinary at all; they were shells of flesh from which not only the spirit was missing. If they were pricked, they wouldn't bleed. The members of the jury seemed afraid to meet their eyes. The judge ignored them. He felt that the drama, so muted, so desultory, could have gone on even without their presence.

The court was very full, yet the air had no taste to it, no smell. Time stretched out to accommodate the leisurely charade. Counsel for the prosecution spoke with calm deliberation, his fine voice distastefully reducing horror to an orderly recital of facts. From time to time there was a hiatus when no one spoke, when the bewigged lawyers would suddenly perk up and watch the judge, and the judge would appear sunk in a private reverie. And then the moment would pass. The judge's pen would move again. Counsel would begin again his slow peroration. The court, almost imperceptibly, would relax.

There was one woman member of the jury from whom he had found it difficult to avert his eyes. Afterwards, whenever he thought about the trial, it was she who dominated his mind. The images of the accused and the judge faded, hers became clearer with the years. She was a stockily built grey-haired woman, wearing upswept diamanté-trimmed spectacles, dressed in a plaid cloak of red, green and yellow, her rolls of tightly curled hair topped with a matching cap. The brim was set straight across her intimidating brow, the crown was bulbous, as if stuffed with paper, the whole topped with a pom-pom in red wool. Like the other jurors, she sat very still throughout the trial, grim-faced under the ridiculous hat, only turning her head like an automaton, betraying no emotion.

Both the accused had been represented by the same counsel who had attempted in a voice of quiet reasonableness to persuade the jury that rape had been sexual assault, and murder manslaughter. The verdicts, when they came, conveyed no sense of climax or release. The judge pronounced the two sentences of life imprisonment with no more than the customary comment that this was a mandatory sentence provided by law. He rose without fuss and the court rose with him. The spectators shuffled out of the public gallery, casting last looks behind them as if reluctant to believe that the entertainment was over. The lawyers stuffed their papers and books into briefcases and conferred. The clerks bustled about the court, minds already occupied with the next case. It had been as undramatic and ordinary as the ending of a parish council meeting. Once there would have been a black cap – not a proper cap, but a small square of black cloth which the clerk would have placed grotesquely on top of the judge's wig. Once there would have been a gowned chaplain and the sonorous 'Amen' after the sentence of death. He had felt the need of some such bizarre and histrionic end to this formal celebration of reason and retribution. Something memorable should have been said or done, more worthy of the corporate ritual than the foreman's carefully expressionless voice pronouncing the word 'guilty' in response to the clerk's questions, the judge's dispassionate judicial tone. For one wild second he had been tempted to leap to his feet and to cry out that it wasn't over, that it couldn't be over. It had seemed to him that the trial had been less a judicial process than a comforting formality through which all participants except himself had been purged or justified. It was over for them. It was over for the jury and the judge. It was over for Julie. But for him and for Mavis it had just begun.

The station clock jerked away the minutes and the hours. By eleven o'clock he was thirsty and would have liked to buy himself a coffee and a bun at the buffet, but he was afraid to leave his seat, to take his eyes off the entrance. But when at last he saw her, just after eleven-twenty, he wondered how he could ever have doubted that he would know her again. He recognized her at once, and with such a physical shock that he instinctively turned away, terrified that she would feel across the concourse the surging power of his presence. It was impossible to believe that she could be here within yards of him, yet not be struck by the shock waves from that moment of recognition. Surely not even love could so cry out for a response.

He saw that she was carrying a small case, but apart from that he was aware of nothing about her, only of her face. The years dropped away and he was once again in that wood-panelled court gazing fixedly at the dock, but seeing her now with a dreadful knowledge which then he hadn't had; that he could never escape her as she could never escape him, that both of them were victims. He moved behind a rack of paperbacks in front of the station bookstall, bending like a man in a spasm of pain, hugging the rucksack to his body as if his wrapping arms could stifle the potent signals of the knife. Then he became aware that a man carrying an official briefcase was glancing at him with concern. He straightened up and made himself look again at the murderess. It was then that he noticed the girl. In that moment of recognition there was nothing about Mary Ducton that was hidden from him. The girl was a blood relation. He knew with absolute certainty, even without noting the imprint of the murderess on this younger, more glowing face, without consciously deducing that the girl was too young to be her sister and unlikely to be her niece, that this was Mary Ducton's daughter.

The girl proffered one ticket at the barrier together with a slip of paper, perhaps some kind of travel warrant. The murderess stood back, her eyes fixed ahead like an obedient child under escort. He followed them through the gate and on to platform 8. There was a group of about twenty people waiting for the 11.40 train, and the murderess and her daughter walked some fifty yards farther down the platform and stood alone, not speaking. He dared not make himself conspicuous by detaching himself from the main group. Now, with time to spare and nothing to do, they might well notice him. He opened his newspaper and, with his back half-turned towards them, listened for the vibrations of the approaching train. The first part of his plan was simple. He would move unhurriedly and unselfconsciously towards them as the engine drew in, and get into the same compartment. It was important to travel together if he were not to risk losing them at King's Cross. He was glad that the modern inter-city trains had long open carriages. The old-fashioned corridor trains with their single compartments would have been a difficulty. Apart from the fear that the murderess might recall his face even after all these years, the prospect of having to sit opposite them, almost knee to knee, to feel their eyes straying to his face, momentarily intrigued, perhaps, by his ugliness, his isolation, was intolerable.

The train drew in on time. Prudently he stood back to let a family with young children enter before him, but the two corn-coloured heads were plainly in sight. They had moved down the compartment and had seated themselves side by side facing the engine. He slipped into a vacant window seat just inside the door, kept his rucksack on the table in front of him, and took refuge again behind his paper. Once he was seated their faces were out of sight, but, over his paper, he kept a watchful eye on the far door in case they should, after all, decide on a different carriage. But the door was blocked with incoming passengers and they didn't move.

Almost at once he realized that it had been a mistake to take a window seat. Just before the guard blew his whistle, a family of three, a fat, perspiring couple and their moon-faced teenage son, pushed through the door and settled themselves with grunts of satisfaction into the three empty seats. He shifted himself imperceptibly, disagreeably aware of the warm bulk of the woman urging his thighs nearer to the window. As soon as the train got up speed she opened a bulging plastic bag, took out a Thermos flask and three disposable cups and a plastic sandwich box, and began distributing cheese and pickle sandwiches to her husband and son. A powerful reek of vinegar and cheese hung over the table. He had no room to spread his paper, but he folded it small and pretended an interest in the list of births and deaths on the last page. He hoped he wouldn't need to visit the lavatory. The prospect of asking this hulk of a woman to shift herself intimidated him. But worse was the worry that he might be trapped at the end of the journey, that the murderess and her daughter might slip out of their seats and be gone before he could free himself.

He was hardly aware of the passing of time. For the first hour he sat stiffly, half fearing that the woman would hear the thudding of his heart, would sense the excitement that kept him rigid in his seat. For most of the time he stared out of the window at the bleak landscape of the Midlands, the rain-soaked fields and dripping trees, the alien towns with their blackened back-to-back houses, and the villages, like rejected outposts of a deserted civilization, while beside the track the glistening wires rose and fell. After about an hour the rain stopped and the sun came out, hot and bright, drawing from the sodden fields faint puffs of vapour like a crop of thin cotton wool. Once, by a trick of light, the carriage was reflected in the windows, and he saw a row of ghostly travellers borne through the air, sitting immobile as dummies, their faces cavernous and grey as the faces of the dead. Only once was his attention keenly caught. The train stopped momentarily outside Doncaster and in the brief unnatural calm he saw, in the grass verge, tall strong stalks of cow parsley, bearing their delicate white blossoms like a foam. The flowers reminded him of the Methodist Sunday school to which he had been sent every Sunday afternoon, he supposed to get him out of his mother's way. Every August they had held a Sunday-school anniversary service, and the children, by tradition, had decorated the church with wild flowers. It was an ugly Victorian building, its ponderous dark stone eclipsing the fragile beauty of the flowers. He saw again an earthenware jar of buttercups wilting against the pew end, and the cow parsley shedding its white dust over his Sunday-best shoes. He had sat very still, huddled in his seat lest God should notice him, a Crippen sitting among the blessed, distancing himself from what he had no right to share, terrified he might be seeming to claim it. Sunday school had left him with nothing except that, for the rest of his life, at moments of stress and crisis, biblical texts, not always apposite, would slip unbidden into his mind. Remembering those long-drawn-out, anxiety-filled afternoons, it had never seemed to him a fair exchange.

Once during the journey he turned his eyes from the window and saw the girl coming down the compartment. She passed him without glancing at his table and tugged open the door. For the first time he took note of her and wondered how her existence might affect his plans. He wished her no particular harm. She was, he judged, some two to three years younger than Julie would have been. Julie was dead, she was alive. No other comparison between them was important in the face of that irrevocable alienation. But he doubted whether his gentle, timid daughter would have held herself with such assurance, would have surveyed the world with eyes so calmly confident in their own judgement. He took in every detail; the tight corduroy trousers taut over her thighs, the casually worn jacket, the leather and canvas travelling bag slung over her shoulder, the thick pigtail of hair. The sheen of the corduroy curving over her inner thighs, the front zip which emphasized the flatness of the stomach and pointed to the gently swelling mound beneath it, had evoked in him as she passed a small leap of sexuality, so long dormant that the gentle disturbance released for a brief moment all the forgotten uncertainties and half-shameful excitements of adolescence.

The girl puzzled him. Try as he would he couldn't remember ever having heard of her at the time of the trial. But then, neither he nor Mavis had been interested in the members of that family except for the rapist and the murderess. They alone had existed and the fact of their existence was an abomination which would one day be purged. He wondered what had been happening to the daughter in the intervening years. She looked well-nourished, prosperous. There was nothing of deprivation in that proud carriage, that assured walk. She had presumably kept in touch with her mother since they were here together; but they didn't look intimate. During the time he had observed them they had hardly spoken. Perhaps this journey was no more than a filial duty to be gratefully relinquished when the murderess was safely delivered at her final destination. Her unexplained and unexpected presence was a slight complication, but no more. But as she passed him on her return journey to her seat, balancing two covered plastic mugs and a pork pie, he noticed that there was a small identity tag attached by a narrow strap to the end of her travelling bag. It was just large enough to hold a visiting card, but the name was covered by a curling leather flap. Suddenly it occurred to him that if he could get close enough to her without attracting attention, perhaps in the crush when they were leaving the train, it might be possible gently to bend back the tag and get a sight of the name. The thought excited him. He spent the rest of the journey staring sightlessly out of the window imagining how it might be done.

It was two-fifteen when the train drew into King's Cross, one minute late. As soon as it slowed he stood up and picked up his rucksack. The fat woman grudgingly made way for him and he was one of the first out of his seat. He saw that the murderess and her daughter were making for the door closest to them at the other end of the compartment. He edged his way down the carriage, obstructed now by standing passengers reaching for their bags and struggling into their coats. By the time the two women had reached the doorway he was immediately behind them. There was the usual delay as passengers manoeuvred their luggage through the door and clambered down to the platform, and the women patiently waited their turn. Neither of them looked round. It was far easier than he had hoped. He let his rucksack rest for a moment on the floor then bent down and fumbled with his shoelace. As he rose his eyes were on a level with the dangling tag. It was the work of a second to lift the covering flap with his small cunning hands. The light was poor but it didn't matter. The name wasn't in small print on a visiting card but written by hand in an elegant black script. P. R. Palfrey.

He hoped that the next stage wouldn't be by taxi. It would be too risky to stand in the queue immediately behind them and, even if he did, he was unlikely to hear their directions. In the library books he remembered from his boyhood the hero leapt into the next cab shouting to the driver to follow the one in front. He couldn't see himself doing that, nor did it seem a practicable ruse in the tangle of traffic outside a major London terminus. But to his relief, the girl led the way down the steps to the Underground. This was what he had hoped. He followed about twenty feet behind them, feeling in his pocket for his loose change. There must be no delay at the ticket office. With luck he might get close enough to hear their destination. At worst he would be able to watch the machine from which they got their tickets. But as long as he again travelled with them all would be well. He felt a surge of confidence and excitement. So far it had been easier than he had dared to hope.

But suddenly the entrance tunnel was clamorous with shouting and the clatter of rushing feet. Another train must have disgorged its passengers, and a crowd of youths had hurled themselves down the steps and were shouting and jostling their way past him, forcing him against the wall of the tunnel and momentarily obstructing his view. Desperately he pushed his way forward and saw again the two pale bobbing heads. They passed the entrance to the Northern and Piccadilly lines and, walking on, eventually turned right down the wide steps leading to the concourse of the Metropolitan and Circle lines. The crowd had swollen here and there was a long queue at the ticket office. The girl didn't join it, nor did she attempt to press through the jabbering crowd of travellers at the ticket machines. Instead he saw with horror that she had bought two tickets in advance and that she and the murderess were calmly making their way through the barrier. And the ticket collector was meticulously looking at every ticket. There was no chance of forcing his way through and to try would only draw attention to himself. He almost fought his way to the first machine. His tenpenny piece seemed to stick to his fingers. His hand was trembling as he pushed it home. There was a clatter as the coin, rejected, fell into the waiting receptacle. He pushed it in again, and this time the machine delivered his ticket. But the air was already loud with the clatter of an approaching train, and as he pushed his way through the crowd at the barrier, the noise stopped. He dashed to the west bound platform, the one they had taken, just in time to see the doors of the Circle line train close in his face. Apart from two turbaned Indians, and a tramp laid out asleep on a bench, the platform was empty. Even as he looked up, the train moved, the words 'Circle Line' disappeared from the indicator and the Hammersmith train was signalled.

2

Only when he reached Liverpool Street was he aware of hunger. He bought himself a coffee and roll before catching the train home. It was nearly four before he put his key in the latch. The silence of the house received him conspiratorially as if it had been watching for his return and was waiting to share his failure or success. Although it was still early, he felt very weary and his legs ached. But this positive tiredness was a new sensation, different in kind from the lassitude which had dragged his homeward footsteps at the end of each working day, and had made the half-mile trudge from the station a small daily tribulation. He made himself a high tea of sausages and baked beans, followed by a jam tart from a packet of four in the refrigerator. He supposed that he was hungry, certainly he was rapacious for the food. The sausages split and burned under the grill and the gas flared under the saucepan of beans. He ate voraciously, yet he hardly tasted the meal, aware only of a physical need that demanded satisfaction. As he made a pot of tea in the small back kitchen, taking down the blue and white teapot with its patterned band of roses which he and Mavis had bought together on their honeymoon, he felt for the first time some affection for the house, and a tinge of regret that he must leave it. This struck him as odd. Neither he nor Mavis had ever been at home in it. They had bought it because it was the sort of house they were used to at a price they could afford, and because they needed to leave Seven Kings with all its memories and 19 Alma Road had been available. In the suburbs you could buy anonymity by moving three stations down the line, by changing your job. He remembered how they had first been shown over it, Mavis passing listlessly from room to room while the estate agent, desperately trying to evoke some response, had extolled its advantages. At the end of the inspection she had said tonelessly: 'It'll do. We'll take it.' The man must have been amazed at so easy a sale. They had done little to it in the last eight years, some repainting, new paper in the seldom-used front sitting-room, the minimum structural repairs necessary to preserve their small investment in it. Mavis had worked conscientiously, though without interest, but it had always looked clean. Something about it repelled dust and wear as it repelled intimacy, happiness, love. How strange it was that only now was he beginning to feel that he belonged here, that he would leave something of himself behind its prim laurel hedge. The sense of the house's participation in his enterprise grew so strong that he found himself wondering whether he dared leave it, whether the strangers who would unpack their kettles and saucepans in this kitchen would pause in temporary unease and imbibe from the very air some secret knowledge that here murder had been planned. But he knew that he had to go. The quarry was in London, and in London would be run to earth. And he needed to be free, free even of this new sentience between him and the house, free of personal belongings, however meagre, free to begin his search, moving unrecognized and rootless amongst strangers.

And he knew now where he must look. When he had drunk his tea, he opened his map of London and the chart of the Underground and placed them side by side on the table. They had travelled westward on the Circle line. He counted up the stations. St James's Park was about half-way, so that for any station beyond that it would have been more sensible to travel in the opposite direction. Victoria was out. They would have taken the Victoria line direct. Similarly, he could eliminate South Kensington and Gloucester Road since both were on the Piccadilly line and could be reached direct from King's Cross. That meant that they had almost certainly got out at one of the eight stations between King's Cross and High Street Kensington. It was possible, of course, that they had alighted at Baker Street or Paddington and changed lines or taken a British Rail train out of London. But the thought didn't worry him. He didn't believe for one moment they were in the country. It was in the vast anonymity of the capital that the hunted felt most secure. London, which asked no questions, kept its secrets, provided in its hundred urban villages the varied needs of ten million people. And the girl was no provincial. Only a Londoner would have stridden with such confidence through the complexities of King's Cross Underground Station. And she had bought the tickets in advance. That meant, surely, that she had travelled up to York early that morning. No, they were in London all right.

On his larger map he traced the route of the Circle line. Bloomsbury, Marylebone, Bayswater, Kensington. The districts were unfamiliar to him, but he would get to know them. And the day hadn't been unsuccessful after all. He knew now that she had a daughter, and he knew the name of that daughter. She had changed it to Palfrey from Ducton by deed poll, adoption or marriage. But she hadn't, he remembered, been wearing a wedding-ring. He had been thwarted by one small piece of ill-luck, the fact that she had troubled to buy the Underground tickets in advance. Unless they were in a hurry, and they hadn't walked as if they were in a hurry, that could only mean that she wanted to spare her mother the possible trauma of being crushed among crowds while she waited at the ticket office. If so, it suggested a concern that he hadn't expected. And if the girl were concerned for the murderess, then they might stay together, at least for a time. That surely increased his chances of finding them. If all else failed, the daughter might yet lead him to the mother. He wrote the names of the eight stations in his diary in his careful copperplate, then stared at them as if they were a conundrum and he could will the letters to move and shuffle and, at last, click into place and spell out the address he sought.

Tomorrow he would move into the next phase of the enterprise. He would make a direct effort to trace the murderess through her daughter. Even if they weren't still together, to know where the daughter lived would be a definite gain. He went into the hall and dragged out the L–R London telephone directory. There was no Palfrey, P.R., listed, but that wasn't particularly significant. If she had been adopted the number would be shown under her father's initials. The first step would be to telephone all the seven Palfreys listed in the London directory. It was an obvious ploy, more sensible than perpetually riding the Circle line or walking the squares of Bloomsbury or Kensington; but he would have to think of a plausible excuse, a reason for ringing those seven strangers which wouldn't sound suspicious. Suppose the girl herself came to the telephone, what was he to say? It was vital that the murderess shouldn't suspect that she was hunted. If he frightened her into flight, into changing her name, he might spend a lifetime in tracing her only to fail at last. He was twenty years older than she was. Death had robbed Mavis of revenge, it might even rob him.

And then, as he sat in the quietness of the kitchen, his hands cradling the cup of tea, the idea came to him. It fell into his mind like a minor act of creativity, as if it had always existed in its simplicity, its rightness, waiting the moment until it could slip into his mind. The more he examined it, the more faultless it seemed. He was surprised that he hadn't thought of it earlier. He went to bed impatient for the morning.

3

Her mother walked into the room and stood still. She seemed afraid to speak, only her eyes moved. The room seemed to have shrunk since Philippa left it. The newly stained wooden boards, the faded rugs, the unmatched chairs, did they look too makeshift, too cheap a compromise? Had she glorified them in her own eyes?

'You like it?' She was irritated to hear the note of anxiety in her voice. She had done her best with the place. Presumably it was better than a shared room in a hostel. And it was only for two months.

'Very much.' Her mother smiled, a different smile from the one with which she had greeted Philippa that morning. This time it reached her eyes.

'It's lovely. I didn't expect that it would be as attractive as this. You were clever to find it. And you must have worked hard.'

Her voice shook, and Philippa saw that her eyes were too bright. And she looked very tired. The journey, the pressure of people must have been a strain. Terrified that the unshed tears would fall, she said quickly:

'I enjoyed myself. It was fun rummaging around the market. The greengrocer, George, helped me up with some of my finds. The picture is the only thing I've got from Caldecote Terrace, a Henry

Walton. He was an eighteenth-century painter. Some of his work is too sentimental for my taste – almost Victorian – but I like that picture. I thought that it would look good in that light and against the wallpaper. But you don't have to keep it there.'

'I should like it to stay, unless you want it in your room. Where are you?'

'Here, next to the kitchen. I've got the quietest room and the better view. You've got the sun but more noise. We can change if you'd rather.'

They went into the back room. Her mother walked to the window and stared out over the patch of yard and the narrow strips of cluttered gardens. After a few minutes she turned and looked round the room.

'It doesn't seem fair for me to have the larger room. We could spin a coin.'

'But I've had the larger room for the last ten years. It's your turn now.'

She wanted to ask: 'Do you think you can be happy here?' But the question seemed a presumption with its implication that she – Philippa – had happiness within her gift. It was new to her, this carefulness with words, this sensitivity to their power to wound. It should have caused a constraint between them, but it didn't. She said:

'Come and see the kitchen. I've put the television there. We can carry our easy chairs in there if we want to watch.'

Hilda had said, resentfully:

'You'll have to hire a colour telly. She'll have got used to that in prison. Lifers get these extra privileges. She won't be satisfied with black-and-white.'

They went back together into the front room. Philippa said:

'I thought we might take about ten days' holiday before we start thinking of a job. We could look at London, or have some days in the country if you prefer.'

'I'd like both. Only there's one thing. I don't think I'll be much good going about on my own for a week or so. At least not in crowds.'

'You don't have to be on your own.'

'And could we buy some clothes first? I've only got what I'm wearing and one pair of pyjamas. I thought I could spend about fifty pounds of my two hundred. Then I could get rid of these things in the case. I don't want anything here which I had in prison.'

'That'll be fun. I like buying clothes. The sales are still on in Knightsbridge and we might get something good quite cheaply. We can get rid of what you've got in Mell Street market.'

They could get rid of the case there too, although Philippa doubted whether any of the stallkeepers would give more than a few pence for it. Better still, they could chuck it in the canal. It was a cheap fibre case, already scruffy at the corners. Her mother placed it on the floor, then, kneeling, opened it. She took out a pair of white cotton pyjamas and placed them on the bed. The only other objects in the case were a draw-string toilet bag and a manila envelope. She handed it to Philippa, looking up into her face.

'This is the account I wrote in prison of what happened to Julia Scase. Don't read it now, wait a day or two. And I don't want to know when you've read it. While we're living together I know that you've a right to ask questions about the crime, about me, about your past. But I'd rather that you didn't. Not yet, anyway.'

Philippa took the envelope. Maurice had said:

'Lifers, murderers, have to justify themselves. I'm not talking about political murderers, terrorists – they don't have to waste mental energy fabricating excuses. They get their justification like their political philosophy, second-hand and ready-made. I'm talking about the ordinary lifer, and most of them are ordinary. Murder is the one crime for which there can't be any reparation for the victim. We're all conditioned to regard it with particular abhorrence. So murderers, unless they're psychopaths, have to come to terms with what they've done. Some of them persist in claiming that they're innocent, wrongly convicted. Some probably believe it.'

She had said:

'Some may be innocent.'

'Of course. That's the irrefutable argument against capital punishment. A fair number take refuge in religious confession, officially recognized contrition if you like. There's a beautiful simplicity in claiming that you're assured of God's forgiveness, it puts your fellow humans at a moral disadvantage if they obstinately persist in unforgiveness. And of course there are plenty of eminent people happy to assist you in your emotional wallowings. I'd probably opt myself for conversion in the circumstances. Then there are the excuses based on mental instability, provocation, deprived background, drunkenness, the common stuff of any defending counsel's plea in mitigation. A few of the more robust spirits probably claim justifiable homicide, the victim got no more than he deserved. Your mother has survived nine years in prison on the one charge that the other women there can't ever forgive. That means she's tough. She's probably intelligent. Whatever story she decides to tell you will be plausible and, once she's met you, I've no doubt it will be tailored to what she decides are your particular psychological requirements.'

'Nothing she tells me can alter the fact that she's my mother.'

And he had said:

'So long as you remember that that is probably the least important fact about her.'

She put Maurice out of her mind. There was no hurry about questions. She could begin to learn who she was without an inquisition. After all, they were to have two months together. She said:

'I haven't any rights. We're here together because that's what we both want. It suits us both. You're not demanding to know what my life has been during the last ten years.'

She added, with deliberate lightness:

'There are no obligations except those which sharing a flat necessarily implies – cleaning the bath after use, doing one's share of washing-up.'

Her mother smiled.

'From that point of view I'll probably suit. Otherwise I think you could have chosen more wisely.'

But there was no question of choice. While her mother went to wash Philippa took the envelope into her bedroom and shut it in her bedside drawer. She had been asked to wait before reading it. She would wait, but not for long. She felt triumphant, almost exultant. She thought: 'You're here because you're my mother. Nothing in life or death can alter that. It's the only thing about myself I can be sure of. In your uterus I grew. It was your muscles that forced me into the world, your blood which first bathed me, and it was on your belly where I first took my rest.' Her mother liked the room, was glad to be with her. It was going to be a success. She wouldn't have to return to Maurice and confess failure. He would never be able to say 'I told you so.'

The only post next morning was a letter from the house agent to say that the young couple had obtained their mortgage and that contracts were being drawn up. He read its turgid professional jargon without surprise or particular gratification. The house had to go. Apart from the fact that he needed more money than he had been able to save from a modest salary, he couldn't imagine himself returning to it after the murder. There was nothing in the house that he wanted, not even a photograph of Julie. Mavis had destroyed them all after her death. He would take with him enough clothes to fill one suitcase. The rest of his belongings and the furniture he would sell through one of those firms which advertised that they cleared houses. He supposed that they were called in after the deaths of the old and lonely to dispose of the detritus of unregarded lives and to save the executors trouble. It pleased him to think of moving thus unencumbered into his unknown future, so much alone that if he fell under a bus there would be no one in the world with any responsibility for him, no one who need assume the obligations of grief. He would lie, shrouded and docketed in the public mortuary while the police searched for a next of kin, someone to authorize the disposal of this embarrassingly redundant corpse. To move into this nothingness seemed to him a promise of an intoxicating and limitless freedom. As he boiled his breakfast egg and stirred powdered coffee into his cup of hot milk, it occurred to him that he had become more interesting to himself since he had started out on his enterprise. Before Mavis's death he had been like a man treadmilled on a moving staircase, walking but not advancing, while on each side of him bright images of a synthetic world, blown-up photographs, montages of life moved steadily in the opposite direction. As they passed he was programmed to perform certain actions. At daybreak he would get up and dress. At half-past seven he ate breakfast. At eight o'clock he set out to work. At eight-twelve he caught his train. At midday he ate his sandwiches at his desk. Home again in the evening, he would eat his supper in the kitchen with Mavis, then sit watching television while she knitted. Their evenings had been dominated by the television programmes. For some of her favourites through those bleak years, *Upstairs Downstairs*, *Dixon of Dock Green*, *The Forsyte Saga*, she had even taken some trouble with her appearance. She no longer changed to please him or to go out with him, but she put on a different dress and even applied make-up for these bright ephemeral images. On those evenings they would have supper on a tray. It hadn't been an unhappy life. He hadn't felt any emotion as positive as unhappiness. But now, on the shoulders of the dead, he had hoisted himself into a different air, and although it stung his nostrils, at least it gave him the illusion of living.

Sitting in the train as it flashed through the dull, familiar stations of the eastern suburbs, his rucksack on his shoulder, he reflected that it was an odd and interesting quirk of his new character that he should need to make this particular journey at all. His plan stood an equal chance of success if he stayed at home and rang the Palfrey numbers from the anonymity of his front hall. The lie he was proposing to tell wouldn't be more believable because it would be supported by contrived verisimilitude, yet he knew that every detail would have to be right if he were to succeed. No one was going to challenge him, no one would check up on his story, or demand confirmation, yet he was compelled to act as if by meticulous attention to every small part he could somehow confer the authority of truth on the whole.

From Liverpool Street he took the Central line to Tottenham Court Road and walked down Charing Cross Road. He had decided that Foyle's Bookshop would be the best for his purpose because it was the largest. The book he chose had to be valuable enough to be worth taking trouble about, but not so valuable that an honest finder would naturally take it to a police station. Non-fiction, he reasoned, would be more appropriate than fiction, and after some thought he selected from the shelves Pevsner's first volume on the buildings of London. The girl at the cash desk seemed hardly to look at him as she gave him his change.

Then he walked to Shaftesbury Avenue and took a number 14 bus to Piccadilly Circus. He gave the conductor a pound note for his fare since he knew he would need plenty of small change. At Piccadilly he shut himself up in one of the telephone booths. In the address pages of his pocket diary he wrote in pencil the initials and telephone numbers of all the subscribers listed under the name Palfrey, grateful that the girl had such an uncommon name. None of the Palfreys were shown as 'Miss' but that didn't surprise him. He had read somewhere that to advertise that you were a woman was to invite obscene telephone calls. When the eight numbers had been listed he printed in pencil the words 'Miss P. Palfrey' on the bookshop bag. No one would ever see it, yet he took care to form the letters in large uneven strokes, as different as possible from his own hand. Then, before raising the receiver, he rehearsed mentally the words he was to say:

'Excuse me for troubling you, but my name is Yelland. I've found a book left on a bench in St James's Park. It was bought at Foyles and it's got the name "Miss P. Palfrey" written on the bag. I thought it was worth telephoning to try and trace the owner.'

The first call was answered by a gruff male voice which told him peremptorily that there was no Miss Palfrey at that address. 'Drop it in at a police station,' it commanded, and promptly rang off. He knew that this first attempt hadn't been altogether successful; even to his own ears his voice had sounded false and strained. Perhaps the listener had thought that he was a new breed of con man or was hoping for a reward. He put a cross against the name and dialled the second number.

He was almost relieved when there was no reply. He put a query against the number and dialled again.

The third call was answered by a woman, presumably a maid or an au pair, who spoke in a strong foreign accent and told him that 'Madam is shopping at 'arrods.' He explained that he wanted a Miss Palfrey, not Mrs Palfrey, only to be told again: 'Madam is not at 'ome. She is at 'arrods. Please to ring later.' He put a query against this number too, although he had little doubt that it wasn't the one he was seeking.

The next number rang for twenty seconds, and he had almost given up when the receiver was at last lifted, and he heard a harassed female voice raised to make itself heard against the shrieking of a young child. The sound was as piercingly sustained as a train's whistle. Obviously she was holding the child in her arms. He sensed her impatience with his story, and when he was half-way through she broke in to say briefly that her daughter was only six and wasn't yet buying books, let alone leaving them on park benches. 'Nice of you to bother, though,' she added, and hung up.

He dialled the next number. The call was frustrating. It was answered by yet another female voice, but this had the high monotonous pitch and the quaver of extreme old age. It took a long time before she comprehended his message, then he had to hang on, putting in extra coins, while she held a long conversation with her sister who was called Edith and who was presumably deaf since the conversation was carried on in shouts. Edith disclaimed any knowledge of the book, but her sister was reluctant to ring off, feeling, apparently, that she now had some personal responsibility in the matter.

His stock of small change was getting low. The next name was listed as Palfrey, M. S. The address was 68 Caldecote Terrace, SW1. Once again a woman answered. The voice sound tentative, apprehensive even. She repeated the number carefully as if it were unfamiliar. He said his piece and almost at once he knew that this was it. He ended:

'Perhaps I could have a word with Miss Palfrey?'

'She isn't here. I mean, my daughter isn't at home at present.'

This time there could be no doubt of it. The voice held the breathy rising cadence of fear. He felt a surge of confidence, almost of exhilaration. He said:

'If you could give me her address, I could write or telephone.'

'Oh, I couldn't do that! And they're not on the phone. But I'll tell her about the book if I see her. Only I don't think I shall be seeing her. What did you say it was called?'

He repeated the title.

'It sounds like Philippa. I mean, she does like books about buildings. Perhaps you could post it here and I'll send it on. Only there's the postage. I know she would send the money to you if you enclosed your address. But then it may not belong to her.'

There was a silence. After a few seconds he said:

'Perhaps I'd better return it to Foyle's. They may know who it belongs to. And perhaps your daughter will think to enquire there first.'

'Oh yes, yes! That would be best. If Philippa telephones or calls in I'll tell her what you've done. Thank you for taking so much trouble. I think she's probably showing her – her friend – round London. She may need the book. I'll send her a postcard and tell her about your call.'

Relief made her sound suddenly effusive. He replaced the receiver and stood for a moment with his hand pressed down on it.

The feel of the instrument, warm and sticky, conveyed an almost physical certainty. He knew now where her daughter lived. He knew that she was adopted. He knew that they were still together since the woman had used the plural tense. He knew what the girl's name was. Philippa Palfrey. Philippa R. Palfrey. Somehow the fact of knowing the name seemed more significant than anything he had learned so far.

5

His map showed him that Caldecote Terrace lay on the fringes of Pimlico, south-east of Victoria and Eccleston Bridge, and he walked there from Victoria Underground down a side road flanking the main station. In distance it wasn't far from his old office, but it was the other side of the river and could have been a different city. It was a cul-de-sac of converted but unspoilt late eighteenth-century terraced houses which lay off the wider and busier Caldecote Road. He walked into it resolutely, but uneasily aware that this was not a street in which he could safely loiter, that the tall, immaculately curtained windows might conceal watching eyes. He felt like an interloper entering a private precinct of orderliness, culture and comfortable prosperity. He had never lived in such a street and knew no one who did: yet he indulged his preconceptions of how such people lived. They would affect to despise the smartness of Belgravia; would enthuse about the advantages of a socially mixed society, even if the mixing didn't actually extend to sending their children to local schools; would patronize as a duty the small shopkeepers in Caldecote Road, particularly the dairy and the delicatessen; and would haul off their friends to drink at the week-end in the saloon bar of the local pub where they would be heartily affable to the barman and resolutely matey to the other customers.

He made himself walk down one side of the street and then up the other. The sense of being a trespasser was so strong that he felt he walked in an aura of guilt. But no one challenged him, no front door opened, the curtains didn't move. The street struck him as being peculiarly different from others; then he realized that it was because no cars were parked at the kerb and there were no residents' parking signs. So these desirable homes must have garages at the rear where once the mews had stabled horses. Momentarily the thought depressed him. It would be impossible to watch two exits to number 68, and if Mrs Palfrey customarily drove rather than walked or took public transport, he didn't see how he would be able to tail her. He hadn't thought of a car. But optimism reasserted itself. Single-mindedness, he had discovered, brought with it stamina and self-assurance; it also brought luck. He was here. It was right that he should be here. He knew where the girl lived and where her family lived. Sooner or later she or they would lead him to Mary Ducton.

As he gained confidence in his right to be walking down the terrace he observed the houses more closely. The street had an impressive uniformity; the houses were identical except for var-iations in the patterns of the fanlights and in the wrought-iron tracery of the first-floor balconies. The front railings guarding the basements were spiked and ornamented at the ends with pine-apples. The doors, flanked with columns, were thoroughly intimi-dating, the brass letter-boxes and knockers gleamed. Many of the houses were festive with window boxes; geraniums flared in discordant pinks and reds and trails of variegated ivy curled against the stone façades.

He reached the end of the terrace and crossed the road to the even-number houses. Number 68 was at the top end of the street. It was one of the few houses without window boxes or tubs before the door, uncompromising in its elegance. The door was painted black. The basement kitchen was brightly lit. He walked slowly past, glancing down, and saw that it was occupied. A woman was sitting at the table eating her lunch. There was a tray in front of her with a plate of scrambled eggs, and she was glancing as she ate at the flickering image of a black-and-white television set. So the Palfreys had a maid. He wasn't surprised to see her. He would have expected that girl in the train to have come from a home where they kept a maid, to have lived in just such a house as this, that golden girl who had walked past him down the swaying carriage of the train with the arrogant sexuality which spoke to him, to all the old, the poor, the unattractive: 'Look at me, but don't touch. I'm not for you.'

He returned to Caldecote Road, his mind still occupied with the problem of keeping a watch on the Palfreys' house. The road was in marked contrast to the terrace, a disorderly muddle of shops, cafés, pubs and the occasional office, typical of an inner London commercial street from which any glory had long departed. It was a bus route, and small disconsolate groups of shoppers, laden with their baskets and trolleys, waited at the stops on either side of the road, while the number of cars and lorries adding to the congestion suggested that this was a popular route to the Lambeth and Vauxhall bridges. Here, if not in Caldecote Terrace, he could loiter in safety.

Then he noticed the two hotels. They were on the opposite side of the road, facing down the terrace, two large stuccoed Victorian houses which had survived change, war, decay and demolition and now stood alone, shabby, the stucco peeling, but still grandiosely intact between a car salesroom and the vulgarly ostentatious fascia of a supermarket. From any of the front upper windows he would be able to train his binoculars on the door of number 68; here he would be able to sit in comfort to watch and wait. Here he would have time to think and plan his strategy, freed from the fear of discovery, the tedium and exhaustion of perpetually loitering in the street.

The names might have been chosen to emphasize that neither hotel had any connection with the business next door. The left-hand one was called Hotel Casablanca, its neighbour the Windermere Hotel. The first, less reassuringly named, looked the cleaner and more prosperous and would, he judged, give a slightly better view down Caldecote Terrace. The outer door was open and he stepped into a porch with a framed Underground map on the left wall and a mirror advertising ale on the right. He pushed through an inner door, patterned with overblown facsimiles of credit cards, and was met by the concentrated smell of food, cigarettes and furniture polish. There was no one on duty and the hall was empty except for a young woman seated at a small telephone switchboard behind the reception desk. A brown smooth-haired bitch was sleeping at her feet, its slack pimpled belly flopped over the chequered tiles, its paws gently curving. It took no interest in Scase's arrival except to peer at him briefly through a slitted eye before closing it again and nudging its head closer to the girl's chair. A white guide-dog harness was slung on a hook on the side of the switchboard. She turned as soon as she heard the swing of the inner door, and her sightless eyes, blinking rapidly, seemed to search the air above his head. In one socket the eyeball, retracted and upward-turned, was only half-visible under the lid. The other eye was covered with a milky film. She was slight with a gentle eager face, her straight light brown hair drawn back and fastened behind her ears by two circular blue slides. He wondered irrelevantly why she had chosen blue, how such a decision could be made, what it must mean to be deprived of the petty vanities of choice. He said:

'I'm looking for a room. Do you know if there are any vacancies?'

She smiled, but in the absence of any kindling light or warmth from the dead eyes the undirected smile seemed fatuous, meaningless. She said:

'Mr Mario will be here in a moment, if you will ring the bell, please.'

He had seen the push-button bell on the counter, but hadn't liked to press it since she might have thought that he was impatient for a service which she was powerless to give. It gave out a strident ring. A minute later a short swarthy man in a white jacket appeared through the door to the basement stairs. Scase said:

'I wondered if you'd got a vacant room, one at the front. I don't like being at the back. I've retired and I'm selling my house in the suburbs and looking for a flat in this area.'

This explanation was received with total uninterest. Presumably, if he had explained that he was an IRA terrorist looking for a safe hideout there might have been some response. Mario ducked under the counter hatch and flipped open a grease-stained register. After a brief pretence at consulting it, he said in a voice which was almost entirely Cockney:

'There's a top front single. Ten pounds a night, bed and breakfast, payment in advance. Dinner's extra. We don't do lunches.'

'I'll have to go home for my things.'

He had read somewhere that hotels were suspicious of guests who arrived without luggage. He said:

'Could I take it from tomorrow?'

'It'll be gone by then. This is the busy season, see? You're lucky to get a vacancy.'

'Could I see it, please?'

The request was obviously regarded by Mario as eccentric, but he took a key from the board and pressed the lift button. They were slowly carried up together in cranking, claustrophobic proximity to the top floor. He unlocked the door, then left abruptly, saying, 'See you downstairs at the desk, then.'

As soon as the door closed behind him, Scase went over to the window. He saw with relief that the room was ideal for his purpose. The view from a lower floor would have been constantly obstructed by buses and lorries; here at this meanly proportioned window under the eaves he was high enough to look down unimpeded over the traffic into Caldecote Terrace. Mario had taken the key away with him but there was a bolt on the door. He shot it, then took the binoculars from his rucksack. The door of number 68 trembled, opaque as if seen through a heat haze. He steadied his hands, adjusted the focus and the image leaped at him, gleaming, sharp-edged and so close that he felt that he could stretch out his hands and stroke the glistening paintwork. The binoculars ranged over the façade of the house from window to window, each secretive behind the white veil of its drawn curtains. On the balcony there was a twist of paper, blown up, perhaps, from the street. He wondered how long it would lie there before someone found it and swept it away, that single flaw on the house's perfection.

He put away the binoculars and explored the room. He supposed that he ought not to linger too long; it might seem suspicious. Then he told himself that Mario was unlikely to worry. What, after all, was there to steal or damage in this bleak, impersonal, comfortless cell? He didn't wonder that Mario had left him so promptly, avoiding explanation and excuses.

The floor was covered with a scrappy fawn carpet on which all the previous occupants seemed to have deposited their mark; a spatter of tea or coffee by the bed, more-sinister-looking stains under the wash-basin. In one corner a larger area of dampness mirrored a similar stain on the ceiling where the roof must have leaked. The bed had a plain wooden headboard, presumably so that the occupant shouldn't be tempted to strangle himself with his tie from the bedrail. A large wardrobe stood unsteadily against one wall, its door swinging ajar. An oversized dressing-table in veneered walnut with a spotted mirror occupied the darkest corner. There were some compensations. The bed, when he sat on it, was comfortable enough; a glance showed that the sheets, although crumpled, were clean. He turned on the hot tap and after some minutes of gurgling and erratic flow the water spurted hot. These were small bonuses. He was glad of them but they weren't important. He would have slept as well on a hard bed and been happy to wash in cold water. The room had all that he asked, the view from the window.

And then he noticed the bedside locker. It was a sturdy oblong box in polished oak with one shelf and a cupboard underneath and with a wooden roller at one side for a towel. He recognized it. He had seen one before. It was an old hospital locker, probably part of a job lot, sold off by some hospital management committee when the wards were upgraded. What could more appropriately find a place in this room for human rejects, furnished with rejects? When he opened the cupboard the smell of disinfectant rose up strongly, working like a catalyst on memory. His mother, dying at last and knowing that she was dying, twisting her head restlessly on the pillow, the dyed hair, that last vanity, grey at the roots, the sinews of her wasted neck stretched like cords, her fingers sharp as claws scraping the coverlet. He heard again her querulous voice:

'I've had no bloody luck in my life, by God I haven't. No bloody luck at all.'

He had tried to make some gesture of comfort by straightening the pillow, but, impatiently, she had pushed his hand aside. He had known that he was part of the bad luck, and even on her deathbed nothing he did or said could please her. What, he wondered, would she think if she could see him here now, could know why he was here. He could almost hear her scorn.

'Murder! You? You wouldn't have the guts. Don't make me laugh.'

He left the room, closing the door carefully and quietly behind him as if her wasted body, uncomforted, lay there on the bed. He wished that the hotel had provided a different type of bedside locker. But otherwise the room would do very well indeed.

6

Philippa had always thought that if one were forced to share a flat it would be easier with a stranger than with a friend. And this stranger was so orderly, so quiet, so undemanding; was accommodating without being subservient, was capable about the flat without being obsessional. It was extraordinary how easily they established their shared routine. Philippa awoke now to sounds and smells that quickly became so familiar that it was difficult to believe that they were new. Her day began with the soft rustle of her mother's dressing-gown, with a cup of tea silently placed on her bedside table. Maurice had occasionally brought up her morning tea at Caldecote Terrace. But that was in another country and, besides, that wench was dead. She prepared their breakfast of cereal and boiled egg while her mother cleaned the flat, and then they sat together over their coffee, map spread, planning each day's excursions. It was like showing London to a foreign visitor, but one from a different culture, even a different dimension of time; an intelligent, interested tourist whose eyes surveyed the sights presented for her edification with pleasure, sometimes with delight, but who seemed to be looking beyond them, attempting to reconcile each new experience with an alien, half-remembered world. She was a tourist who was wary of the natives; anxious not to draw attention to herself by any solecism of taste; sometimes confused about the currency, mixing the tenpenny and fifty-pence piece; momentarily disconcerted by space and distance.

Watching her, Philippa thought: she's like a woman who suffers simultaneously from claustrophobia and agoraphobia. And she was a visitor whose native country must be thinly populated since she was so frightened of crowds. London was packed with tourists, and although they set out early and avoided the most popular tourist haunts, it was impossible to avoid the crush of bodies at bus stops and tube-station platforms, in shops and subways. Either they lived as hermits, or they contributed to and endured the hot, chattering, polluting pressure of humanity, breathed air which, on the warmer airless days, seemed to have been exhaled from a million lungs.

She discovered that her mother liked and had an instinctive appreciation of pictures; it was a discovery, too, for her mother. It pleased her to believe that her own pleasure in painting was inherited, enhanced by, but not the result of Maurice's careful tutelage. They became almost obsessive tourists during their first week together, setting out early with a packed lunch to be eaten on park seats, on river steamers, on the top deck of a bus, in the secret squares and gardens of the city.

She thought that she knew the exact moment when her mother had voluntarily taken upon herself the burden of happiness. It was the evening of their third day together when they threw the things she had brought with her from Melcombe Grange into the Grand Union Canal. In the morning they had taken a bus to Knightsbridge and had fought their way into one of the sales. Watching her mother's face as the horde of bodies pressed upon them, Philippa surprised in herself an emotion too close to sadism to be comfortable. They could have shopped perfectly well in Marks and Spencer in Edgware Road, getting there at nine-thirty before the crowd of tourists arrived. Had it been entirely because of a wish to see her mother in expensive clothes that she had led them to this mêlée? Hadn't it been in part deliberate, a test of her mother's courage, perhaps even the half-shameful pleasure of observing with detached interest the physical manifestations of pain and endurance? At the worst moment, the crush at the foot of the escalator, looking at her mother's face, she had been suddenly afraid that she was going to faint. She had taken her mother by the elbow and urged her forward; but she hadn't held her hand. Not once, not even in that bleak sitting-room at Melcombe Grange, had there been a touching of each other's fingers, a meeting of flesh.

But she had been pleased with their bargains; a pair of fawn linen trousers, a jacket to match in fine wool, two cotton shirts. Trying them on again once they were home, her mother had turned to her with a curious look, half rueful, half resigned, which seemed to ask: 'Is this what you want? Is this how you see me? I'm attractive, intelligent, still young. I have to live the rest of my life without a husband, without a lover. So what are these clothes for? What am I for?'

Afterwards she had sat on the bed and watched while her mother packed her case. Everything that she had brought with her from prison went in; the suit in which she had travelled to London, her tights, her underclothes, her shoulder bag, even her toilet articles and pyjamas. It was an extravagance thus to relinquish even the small necessities of living, all of which would have to be replaced; but Philippa didn't check her. It was an extravagance necessary to both of them.

They set out for the canal half an hour before the tow-path was due to be closed to the public, and walked in silence, her mother carrying the case, until they reached an unfrequented stretch of the path overshadowed by trees. It was a warm, heavy evening of low cloud. The canal, rich and sluggish as treacle, slipped undisturbed under the low bridges and seeped into the moist fringes of the bank. A crowd of midges danced above the water, and single leaves, dark green, still glossy with the patina of high summer, floated slowly past on the sluggish stream. The air was rich with a rank river smell overlaid with loamy earth and spiced with the drifting scent of lawn cuttings and roses from the high gardens above the canal. The birds were silent now, except for the occasional distant cry, plaintive and alien, from the zoo aviary.

Still without speaking, Philippa took the case from her mother and hurled it into the middle of the stream. She had first glanced each way to make sure that the tow-path was empty, but even so the splash as the case hit the water sounded so like a falling body that they simultaneously glanced at each other, frightened that someone from the road must have heard. But there were no calling voices, no running footsteps. The case rose slowly, slid along the greasy surface of the water, then reared itself like a sinking ship, toppled and was gone. The circle of ripples died.

She heard her mother give a little sigh. Her face, stained by the green shadows, was extraordinarily peaceful. She looked like a woman in a moment of mystical exultation, even of religious ecstasy. Philippa felt an almost physical relief, as if she had flung away something of herself, of her past, not the past which she knew and recognized, but the formless weight of unremembered years, of childhood miseries which were not less acute because they lurked beyond the frontier of memory. They were gone now, gone for ever, sinking slowly into the mud. She needn't bother any more to try to recall them, nor fear that they might leap out of her subconscious to confuse and terrorize her. She wondered what her mother was thinking, she whose past, seared on so many memories, documented between the buff covers of official files, could not so easily be flung away. They stood in silence at the water's edge. Then the spell broke. Her mother turned to her. Her face relaxed into the smile of a woman released from pain into peace. It was almost a grin of pleasure. But all she said was:

'That's done. Let's go home.'

7

That night she decided that she had waited long enough; it was time to read her mother's account of the murder. But now that the moment had come she found herself reluctant to take the manuscript from her drawer. Almost she wished that her mother hadn't handed it to her, that she could have been spared this new moment of decision. She wished it read; yet dreaded to read it. There was nothing to prevent her from destroying it, but that was unthinkable. It was here; she had to know what it said. She asked herself what was holding her back. Her mother had told her the bare facts on that first visit to Melcombe Grange. Nothing in that waiting foolscap envelope could alter those facts, nothing could extenuate or excuse them.

The night was warm and she lay rigidly under a single blanket staring at the pale haze of the open window. Her mother's window must be open too. She could hear the faint rumble of traffic along Lisson Grove and the occasional shouts and laughter of revellers outside the Blind Beggar. Through her own window there wafted a warm summer smell of flowers and earth as if there lay outside all the richness of a country garden.

There was no sound from her mother's room but she waited to put on her bedside light until the last shouts from the pubs had died away and the street was finally quiet. It seemed to her important that she shouldn't begin reading until she could be sure that her mother was asleep. Then she switched on the lamp and slowly drew the envelope from the drawer. The manuscript was written in her mother's firm, upright, but rather difficult hand on heavy, closely lined paper with a red margin. Her mother had written only on alternate lines. The careful handwriting, the official-looking, very clean paper and the red margin gave the manuscript the look of an affidavit or of an examination script. It was written in the third person:

After she had been in Holloway for five years a new prisoner, a woman who had run a prostitution and extortion racket, standing beside her at the library shelf and looking at her with slant-eyed malice, had whispered:

'You're one of the Ductons, aren't you? I read about you in a book I got from the public library: *Fifty Years of Murder 1920–1970*. It was a kind of encyclopaedia of murder, the most notorious cases. You were under D in the Child Killer section. The Ductons.'

It was then that she realized that she wasn't a person any more. She was a Ducton, categorized by crime, partner in an unholy alliance, indissolubly linked by infamy. But she was surprised that the compiler had thought them worth including. They hadn't seemed notorious at the time, only a commonplace pair of bunglers, putting up a particularly poor fight in a trial which hadn't attracted much publicity, hadn't been able to compete with the suicide of a pop star or the sexual indiscretions of a minister of the Crown. The author must have had to scrape the barrel to pad out his chapter on child-killers. She could guess what he had written under their entry. She herself had browsed through just such an encyclopaedia of death.

'Martin and Mary Ducton, who were convicted in May 1969 of the murder of twelve-year-old Julia Mavis Scase both came from respectable, upper-working-class parents. Ducton was a clerk at the time of the murder, and his wife worked as a hospital medical records clerk. She was studying in her spare time for an external university degree and had some pretensions to culture. She is generally considered to have played the leading part in the child's death.'

She had other pretensions too, to happiness, to achievement, to a different life for them both. And it was true that she took the lead. She always took the lead, even in their joint destruction.

After that meeting she decided to write the truth about the crime, except that the truth was as shifting as her feelings, as unreliable as memory. It was like a butterfly. You could catch it and kill it and pin it down on a board with every delicate detail, every nuance of colour displayed. But then it wasn't a butterfly any more. She thought that the imagery was pretentious; but then she had pretensions.

At the trial she had sworn to tell the truth, the whole truth and nothing but the truth. She had nearly added 'So help me God' but that wasn't written on the card. Only in fiction, apparently, did witnesses speak those words. There had been a little pile of holy books on the ledge of the box. The clerk, who was gowned like a verger, had handed her the Bible. She wondered what would happen if he gave her the wrong one, the Koran perhaps. Would she have to give her evidence all over again? The Bible was black and she took it with distaste because it was contaminated with the sweat of murderers' hands and she knew that they hadn't bothered to disinfect it. That was almost all she remembered of the trial. These facts are the truth.

She remembered coming home a little later that evening because the gynaecological clinic at the hospital where she worked had been busier than usual and she wasn't free until after six. It was very cold even for January. A thin fog writhed round the street lamps and crept into the front gardens truncating the trees so that they seemed to move uprooted in majestic inconsequence, surpliced in white mist. As soon as she opened the front door she heard the child crying. It was a high desolate wailing, not loud but continuous and piercing. At first she thought that it was a cat. But that was ridiculous. She was the last woman to mistake the cry of a child.

And then she saw her husband. He was standing half-way up the stairs looking down at her. She could remember everything about that moment, the thin wailing of the child, the warm familiar smell of the hall, the patterned wallpaper and the break at the join where she hadn't managed to match it accurately, her husband's eyes. She remembered most his look of shame. There had been terror there, too, and a desperate appeal. But what she remembered was the shame. She could never afterwards remember what they said. Perhaps they didn't speak. It wasn't, after all, necessary. She knew.

There is no rehearsal for a murder trial. You have to get it right first time. There are no explanations, only deceptively innocent questions to which the most dangerous response can be the truth. She could only recall one question to her in the witness box from the prosecuting counsel and her reply to that had been fatal.

'And what had you in mind when you went upstairs to the child?'

She supposed that she could have said: 'I wanted to see that she was all right. I wanted to tell her that I was there and that I'd take her home. I wanted to comfort her.' None of the jury would have believed her, but some of them might have wished to believe her. Instead she told them the truth.

'I had to stop her crying.'

Childhood is the one prison from which there's no escape, the one sentence from which there's no appeal. We all serve our time. She was eleven when she realized the truth, that her father didn't beat her and her brother because he was drunk; he got drunk because he enjoyed beating them and that was how he found the courage to do it. When he came home at night her brother would begin crying even before they heard his heavy feet on the stairs and she would slide into bed with him trying to stifle the noise in her arms, hearing the lurching feet, her mother's expostulatory whine. She learned at the age of eleven that there was no hope, only endurance. She endured. But for the rest of her life she couldn't bear to hear a child crying.

Murderers often excuse themselves by claiming that they can't remember exactly what happened. Perhaps it's true. Perhaps the mind mercifully erases what it can't bear to recall. But she could remember so much horror. Why then should this particular moment be a blank? She must have tried to shake the child into silence. She must have lost her temper with this wailing stupid girl who hadn't, after all, been seriously hurt, who surely had been warned that she shouldn't go with strange men, who hadn't even the sense to stop crying and get out of the house and keep quiet. At the trial the pathologist described the post-mortem findings. Death had been by throttling; the neck was bruised with the marks of human hands. They must have been her hands. Who else's could they have been? But she couldn't remember touching the child, nor could she remember the moment when what she was shaking was no longer a child.

After that, memory was like a film rolling on with only a few moments when the picture was lost or no longer in focus. Her husband was in the kitchen. She saw that there were two cups and the teapot and milk jug on the kitchen table. For one moment she had a ridiculous thought, that he was restoring them with tea. She said:

'I've killed her. We must get rid of the body.'

He accepted the brutal statement as if he already knew, as if she was telling him the most commonplace of facts. Perhaps he was so petrified by horror that no new horror could touch him.

He whispered:

'But her parents. We mustn't hide her. We can't let them go on hoping, wondering, praying that she's all right.'

'They won't be left hoping for long. We won't take her very far, just to the edge of Epping Forest. The body will be found soon enough. But it mustn't be found here.'

'What are you going to do?'

Fear sharpened her wits. It was like fabricating a plot. All the details had to be right. She considered, discarded, contrived. They would use the car. The body would be put in the boot. But it would have to be wrapped. If they were suspected, the car would be searched by forensic scientists. They would find traces of the child, hair, dust from her shoes, a thread of cloth. A sheet would do to cover her, a clean, ordinary, white Terylene and cotton sheet from her airing cupboard. She always washed them at the launderette. There would be no laundry mark to betray them. But it would be difficult to dispose of a sheet; they would have to bring it back in the car for washing. Plastic would be better, that long plastic bag in which her winter coat had come back from the cleaners. No one would be able to trace it to her, and after they had disposed of the body it could be screwed up and left in any public litter basket. But they would need an alibi for the time of death and that meant speed. They must start now, at once. She said:

'We'll take back our library books. I'll ask for the new Updike; it's still on the reserve list. That means that the girl will remember us if the police check up. Then we'll go to the cinema at Manse Hill. We'll have to do something there to make the box-office girl notice us. I'll find I haven't enough money and ask you for some. We'll argue about it. No, better still, I'll accuse her of cheating me over the change. That means paying with a five-pound note. Have you got one?'

He nodded.

'I think so.'

He tried to take out his wallet. His hands were shaking as if he were palsied. She put her own hand into his jacket pocket and found it. In the note compartment there was a new five-pound note and a couple of crumpled pound notes. She said:

'We'll only stay in the cinema for about half an hour. Once we're through the foyer we'll take our own tickets and separate. If the police do suspect us they'll be asking people if they saw a couple leaving. They won't expect us to be apart. And we'd better sit at the end of different rows, not next to anyone. It shouldn't be difficult. There won't be many people there on a night like this. But you must keep your eyes on me. As soon as I get up to leave slip out after me. We'll go out by the side entrance, the one that leads straight on to the car park. Then we'll drive to the forest.'

He said:

'I don't want to sit away from you. I don't want us to be parted. Don't leave me.'

He was still shaking. She couldn't be sure that he had understood.

She wished that she could do it all alone, that she could help him to bed, tuck him in with a hot-water bottle, cosset him like a grieving child. But that wasn't possible. He, more than she, must have an alibi. She couldn't leave him alone in the house. They had to be seen together. Then she remembered the brandy, the miniature bottle she had won at the hospital Christmas party. She had been saving it for some unspecified emergency. She hurried to the pantry and poured the brandy into a glass. When she smelled it she knew how much she needed it. But there were only a couple of mouthfuls in the bottle, not enough to do good to two of them. She took it to him. She switched on the third bar of the electric fire.

'Drink this, darling. Try to get warm. Stay here, I'll call you when I'm ready.'

She was amazed at how clearly her mind was working. Before she went upstairs she put the front door on the latch. She went outside and unlocked the boot of the car. The road was deserted. The nearest street light, ten yards away, was a yellow haze in the freezing mist. All the curtains of number 39 were drawn; behind them the dark and empty rooms waited for their new owners. At number 43 only the front downstairs room was lit. Here, too, the curtains were drawn but they couldn't muffle the gusts of laughter from the television comedy show. The Hicksons, inveterate viewers, were settled for the evening.

She took the plastic bag from the hanger in the cupboard under the stairs. Her coat still smelled of cleaning fluid. She wondered whether this familiar pungent smell would always be associated for her with this night. Then she thought of gloves. There was a pair of thin washing-up gloves hung over the taps of the kitchen sink. She hated to work in thick gloves. She put them on. Then she went upstairs.

The bedside lamp was on beside the double bed, the curtains were drawn. It was as if she saw the child for the first time. She lay sprawled on the bed, her left arm flung out, the fingers curving. Her blue knickers were down to her knees. She looked very peaceful. Her spectacles had been shaken off and lay separately on the counterpane. They looked ridiculously small, a delicate contraption of glass and wire. The woman picked them up and felt in the pocket of the child's coat for the case. It wasn't there. She felt a moment of panic as if it were vitally important that the spectacles were kept safe. Then she noticed a small black shoulder bag on the floor. She picked it up. It was made of cheap plastic and looked very new. Perhaps it had been bought specially to go with her Guide's uniform. Inside was a handkerchief, still folded, a Girl Guide diary, a pencil, a small purse containing a few coins, and a red spectacle case. The woman folded the spectacles into the case. Then she opened the diary. The hand was childish, printed letters linked with straight lines. Julia Mavis Scase, 104 Magenta Gardens. She wondered why the child had taken this long way home. Surely it would have been quicker to go across the recreation ground. And if she had gone across the recreation ground she wouldn't be lying here dead. They were a full mile from Magenta Gardens. It might be a day or two after the body was found before the police started their door-to-door enquiries here, and every day would make them safer.

She took the child's coat and the Girl Guide beret and placed them on the body. Gently she pulled up the knickers. Then she drew the long plastic bag carefully over the child, twisting it above her head. Seen through the transparent sheeting her face, unspectacled, the lids closed, was transformed, delicate, beautiful even, but unreal. The lips were slightly parted showing the moist gleam of the thin metal brace across her teeth. A blob of saliva hung on it like a pearl. She looked like a doll gift-wrapped for Christmas, a present for a good girl. When the woman lifted the body in her arms she could feel its warmth through the thin plastic.

The child was heavier than she had expected. The weight dragged at her arms and stomach muscles. It would have been easier to have slung the burden over her shoulder. Wasn't that how they taught you to carry an unconscious person from a burning house? But she found she couldn't do it. She had to carry the child in her arms gently, as if this were a sick and sleeping baby who must not be awakened. Words came into her mind. She is not dead, but sleeping. She wanted to pray: 'Oh God, help us, please help us. Please make it all right.' But that wasn't possible. She had put herself beyond the power of prayer. No one, not even God, could make it all right for them ever again.

Their car was a red second-hand Mini. They had only had it for six months. They had been able to save up for it because she worked. Even so, their Sunday trips to the sea with Rosie had had to be rationed. She was an unpractised driver, unused to fog. She drove very slowly, knowing what it could mean if they were in an accident, were stopped by the police. He sat beside her, propped up like a corpse, eyes staring ahead through the windscreen. She had wound his thick scarf round his neck, half obscuring his face; but she couldn't hide his eyes. Neither of them spoke. Sometimes she murmured foolish sibilant reassurances as one might to a fractious horse. From time to time she took her left hand from the wheel and laid it on his. But she had made him wear his gloves and she didn't know whether those stiff wool-encased fingers were aware of her touch.

The lights of the library windows shone through the fog. Although this was a branch she often used, she hadn't driven there before and was unsure where to leave the car. She turned carefully into a side road and saw two cars parked at the kerb. She stopped the Mini carefully behind them. Then she told him what to do. He nodded. She didn't know if he had understood. She pushed open the library door and was met by the familiar warm effluence of books and floor polish underlaid by the sour smell emanating from the adjacent reading-room where the old men, swathed in their decaying overcoats, sat all day slumped over the newspapers, taking refuge from loneliness and the cold. She could see through the glass partition that three of them were still there. She envied them because they were alive and Martin was dead. That was the only moment during the night in which she was for a second disorientated, the child forgotten, thinking that it was his body huddled there in the boot of the car. But he was walking dead at her side.

She went up to the counter with the three books she had brought with her to return. He remembered her instructions and went over to the nearest fiction shelf. She called out to him:

'There's no time to choose new books, darling, if we're going to get there in time for the big film. I'll just put in my card for the Updike.'

He seemed not to have heard. He stood there stiffly facing the shelves like a dummy in a shop window. There was only one person in front of her, a determinedly bright middle-aged woman apparently returning library books for her invalid mother. The girl librarian listened impassively as she sorted out the tickets while the woman gabbled on about the books she was returning, her mother's health, the books she hoped to take out. She must have been a frequent visitor. Perhaps returning library books was the only chance she got of a little freedom. The librarian said 'Thank you, Miss Yelland' as she handed over the three tickets.

And now it was the woman's turn. She asked to be placed on the waiting list for the Updike and filled up the card with her name and address in bold capitals. She was surprised that her hand could be so steady. She took a lot of trouble over forming the letters, bold and black against the white card. If the police did check up, surely no one could believe that these firm letters had been penned by anyone under stress. Then she went over to her husband. He seemed rooted to the ground and she had almost to lead him to the door and out to the car.

And here, again, the film ceased to roll, the pictures were lost. The worst part of the drive must have been circling the roundabout where five roads met at Manse Hill. But she must have managed that without incident because the next thing she remembered was parking the car in front of the cinema. The car park was more crowded than she had expected, but that was a good thing. It meant that the cinema would be fairly full, that their departure would be less likely to be noticed. She was able to find a parking space close to one of the side exits. When she switched off the engine the silence was almost frightening. They sat together in the fog-shrouded car and she told him again what to do. She said: 'Darling, do you understand?' He nodded, but he didn't speak. They got out of the car and she closed his door for him. The fog was thicker now. It rose and fell like a malignant gas, spilling in glutinous dollops from the high street-lamps. They waded through it, knee-deep, to the foyer.

The last programme must have begun. There were only two people in front of them at the box office. When her turn came she asked for two eight-and-sixpennies and handed over the five-pound note. She took her change and propelled him a little ahead of her, letting one of the four one-pound notes drop from her hand. Then she turned and went back to the box office. She said:

'I think I'm a pound short. There are only three here.'

The woman said stolidly:

'I gave you four, madam. You saw me count them out.'

'There are only three here.'

The woman repeated:

'You saw me count them out, madam,' and turned to the next customer.

She moved away from the box office, then said loudly:

'I'm sorry, I must have dropped it. It's here on the floor.'

The whole episode struck her even at the time as unreal, artificial. The woman in the box office shrugged her shoulders. They moved together across the foyer to the entrance to the stalls. She tried to hand him his ticket, but he wouldn't take it, pretending not to notice her nudging hands. But she knew that he couldn't face sitting apart from her. They would have to stay together.

They stepped into what seemed an immensity of warm-scented blackness. Only the screen was alight, blazing with colour and noise. It was a James Bond film and it must just have begun. She followed the pinpoint of light from the usherette's torch down the centre gangway, one hand behind her clutching at his coat. They were shown into two seats at the end of a row. This wouldn't do. She wanted to slip out from the side entrance, not to walk again up the centre aisle. After they had sat for about ten minutes she whispered to him and took his hand. Together they slipped out of their seats and she led him forward towards the screen until her eyes, more accustomed now to the darkness, could discern a sparsely occupied row. There were only three couples, all seated near the central gangway. They pushed their way past them muttering apologies and took their seats at the far end of the row, almost immediately opposite the red exit sign.

She made herself wait nearly half an hour before she gave him the sign. It was an exciting point in the film; the background music was rising to a crescendo, the screen was full of hurling cars and screaming mouths. In the rows in front of her every face was turned to the screen. She gave a pull on his hand and half rose to her feet. He followed her and they were out through the door. There was a short flight of concrete steps, then she was pushing at the bar of the final door, the cold fog swirled in their faces, and they were in the car park. She felt in her coat pocket for the keys. They weren't there. And instantly she knew. She had left them in the car. Clutching his hand she dragged him with her as she raced through the fog to where she had parked the Mini; but she knew what she would find. The two painted white lines enclosed emptiness. The Mini had gone.

And after that the film of memory broke again. They must have walked for three hours, hand in hand, trudging onwards through the fog towards the forest. Her next memory was of a narrow road stretching straight and unlit between the trees.

The night was icy cold and very still. On each side of the road the forest stretched ahead of them, shrouded in mist. She thought she could hear from it a gentle persistent dripping, slow and portentous as drops of blood. In her imagination it stretched for ever, exuding its black miasma, dropping terror from the tangled bushes, the high leafless boughs, oozing a slow contagion from the slimy trunks. She could see their breath, small puffs of white smoke, leading them onwards. There was no other sound, only the endless ring of their feet on the tarmac. Occasionally they would hear the purr of an approaching car. Instinctively they would step into the darkness of the trees until it passed in a sweep of light, carrying ordinary people, perhaps on their way to a party or driving home late after a long day, happy people with nothing to worry about except mortgages and sickness, their children, their marriages, their jobs.

And then, suddenly, he stopped. He said, his voice dull, utterly defeated:

'I'm tired. Come with me into the forest and we'll find somewhere to sleep. I'll cuddle you. You won't feel the cold. We'll be together. We need never wake up ever again.'

But she failed him. She wouldn't go with him. In the end he pleaded, almost cried, but still she refused. She made him turn with her, defeated, and begin the slow trudge home. Ever since earliest childhood she had been terrified of the forest. It wasn't the forest of primary-school fairy tales, the wail of a hunting horn calling through dappled glades, paths regal with stags. This was a mush of corruption, the place where her father had threatened to lose her if she screamed, the dumping ground for murdered bodies. In her childish imagination the sluggish streams ran with blood.

And it wasn't only the terror of the forest. She didn't share – she never had shared – his pessimism. Life for him was fundamentally tragic, a series of days to be somehow got through, not a privilege to be rejoiced in but a burden to be endured. He was always surprised by joy. The thought of death held no anguish for him; it was life which called for courage. But she was different. Nothing but intolerable pain or utter despair could make her kill herself. The heart of her personality was buoyant with optimism, all her life she had been nourished by hope. She hadn't survived the miseries of her childhood to die so easily now. She told herself that all might yet be well. The car thieves might never open the boot; why should they? The car wasn't worth stealing for its own sake. That meant that they wanted it just for the ride and would abandon it when they had finished with it. In time the police would find it and examine it. But tracing the car to them didn't make her a murderess. The rapist – anyone – could have stolen it from outside their door. All they had to do now was to make their way home, wait for the morning, and report it missing.

But in her heart she knew that the hope was false. Once the car was found they would be the chief suspects. They would be asked about their movements that evening; the call at the library, the argument over the cinema tickets. They would be asked how they had travelled to the cinema. There was no direct or easy bus route. And they couldn't reply that their car had been stolen from outside their house. Why then hadn't they reported the theft before they left the house? She knew that Martin wouldn't be able to stand up to this early and probing questioning. She had banked on having several days before the police got around to him and, even then, with nothing to connect them with the crime, it would only have been a routine door-to-door visit. Nothing was known against him. Now everything was changed. The plastic bag would be traced to the local dry-cleaners. Her recent visit there would be discovered.

And so they trudged home together to the waiting police cars standing already outside the house, to the watching eyes from the houses across the road, to the knowledge that, never again, would they be alone together.

The terrors of the forest were imaginary. All the terrors to come would be real. If she had cared enough she could surely have taken his hand and let him lead her into the darkness under the trees. She could have conquered panic in his arms. Always she had been the stronger. It was to her he had looked for support, for comfort, for reassurance. Wasn't that, after all, why she had married him, because he was a man who had none of the qualities which her father had taught her belonged to manliness? Now, and for the first time, he had asked her to trust to him. He had wanted it that way, wanted to lie in the darkness with her, comforting her into death. But because of her childhood terrors she failed him. She withheld from him the right to die with dignity in his own way and in his own time. She condemned him to the trial, the dock, the torture of those eighteen months in prison before death released him. She had heard what prisoners did to child-molesters. She had lived through those eighteen months separated from him, unable to comfort him, unable to tell him that she was sorry. The child's death hadn't been willed; she told herself that she couldn't have prevented that act of violence. The child had been murdered by the child she had once been. But this desertion of him at the end had been voluntary.

I should have died with him that night. He was right, there was nothing else for us to do. That was the real sin, the failure of love. 'Perfect love casteth out fear.' It didn't need a perfect love not to fail him then. It only needed a little kindness, a little courage.

And there the manuscript broke off. When she had finished reading Philippa turned off the light and lay very still, her heart pounding. She felt sick and at the same time faint. She got up and sat on the edge of her bed for a moment then made her way over to the window and leant out, breathing great gulps of the sweet-smelling air. She didn't ask herself how much of the story she believed. She didn't judge it as writing or as description. She couldn't distance herself from it any more than she could distance herself from the woman who had written it. She knew that she wouldn't tell her mother that she had read it and that her mother wouldn't ask. This was all that she would ever be told about the murder, all she would ever know or need to know. After ten minutes of silently gazing at the night sky she put the manuscript back in her drawer and went back to bed. Only then did she wonder where she had been that night.

8

He returned that same evening and took possession of his command post. Next morning he breakfasted as soon as the dining-room was open at half-past seven, and by eight o'clock he had begun his watch. He sat at the window on the one chair, the binoculars resting on the ledge, the door bolted. At his side he placed the open rucksack ready to slip the binoculars inside and to hurry downstairs once Mrs Palfrey was sighted. It would take too long to go down by lift; he would have to move fast if he were to keep her in sight.

At nine-fifteen precisely a tall, dark-haired man carrying a brief-case left number 68. This, presumably, was Mr Palfrey. He had the businesslike air of a man with his morning planned, and Scase didn't believe that it included calling on the murderess or her daughter. His first conviction had never wavered; it was the woman whose frightened voice he had heard over the telephone who would eventually lead him to them.

At nine-forty-five the maid appeared, bumping a shopping trolley up the basement steps. Then no one left or arrived until she returned two hours later, pulling its laden weight after her and manoeuvring it carefully through the garden gate. He went out and lunched on coffee and sandwiches at a coffee bar down a side street within fifty yards of the hotel, and was back at his post at a quarter to two. All the afternoon he kept watch but no one appeared. The man returned home shortly after six and let himself in at the front door.

He broke off his watch again at seven o'clock for dinner, but was back at the window by eight, and stayed there until the light faded, the street lights came on and, at last, it was eleven o'clock and then midnight. The first day was over.

And this was the routine of the next three days. The man left at nine-fifteen precisely in the morning. The maid, usually with her trolley, was out of the house by ten. It was on the following Monday, tempted by the sun, by the need for exercise and by frustration, that he decided to follow her. He had some idea that he might get into conversation, might at least learn whether Mrs Palfrey was at home, might even think of some excuse for asking her where the girl had gone. He didn't know how he would approach her, or what he would say, but the instinct to follow her was suddenly so immedi-ate, so strong, that he was down the stairs and in the street almost as soon as she had reached the corner of Caldecote Terrace.

The first shop she visited was a local newsagent to pay the paper bill. And here the newsagent greeted her by name, and he knew who she was. He was irritated with himself; the facile assumption which had taken her for a maid had wasted three days. Glancing at her as he pretended to hesitate over his choice of newspaper it was difficult to associate this slight, depressed figure, this anxious face, with the confident girl he had seen in the train, or to see her as mistress of number 68. When she had settled the bill, he bought a *Daily Telegraph*, then followed her at a careful distance to her next call, the butcher. Here there was ham on the bone on display in the window, and he decided to buy a quarter of a pound and lunch on it in his room. He joined the queue behind her and waited patiently while she selected a shoulder of lamb. For the first time he saw her animated. The joint was displayed for her inspection and she and the butcher, confederates in expertise, contemplated it with loving care. She asked for it to be boned and he bore it off willingly, leaving his assistant to serve the queue while he obliged this discriminating customer.

After he had bought the ham he followed her through squares of stuccoed Victorian houses to a street market. Here she moved slowly from stall to stall, eyeing the produce with what seemed to him excessive anxiety, surreptitiously pressing the tomatoes and pears. Lastly she visited a delicatessen. He stood on the pavement, pretending an interest in the shrivelled fingers of dried sausages while she bought smoked salmon, watching while the shopkeeper laid his long knife against the pink flesh, and held drooping over the blade the first rich transparent slice for her inspection. Scase had never tasted smoked salmon and the price on the half fish displayed in the refrigerated window appalled him. They ate well, the Palfreys. The Ducton girl had done well for herself. On impulse he followed Mrs Palfrey into the shop and bought two ounces. He would eat them before dinner in his room and discover what this unknown delicacy tasted like, knowing that her tongue would experience the same sensation, that these two slivers of veined flesh would bind them closer together.

And this was the pattern of his life for the next ten days. Pimlico was her village, and it became his, bounded by Victoria Street and Vauxhall Bridge Road, two flowing thoroughfares like unnavigable rivers over which she never ventured to pass. Twice a week she would walk to the Smith Street branch of the Westminster Library to change her books. He would go into the reading-room and pretend to occupy himself with periodicals while he watched her through the glass partition moving from shelf to shelf. He wondered what books she bore back to solace her in that basement kitchen. It seemed to him that she carried with her a climate of anxiety and loneliness, but it didn't affect him. He couldn't recall any recent time in his life more free from strain. She was easy to trail. Her preoccupations were personal and secret; she seemed hardly to notice the life around her except as it related to shopping and food. But he had no sense of hurry or of time wasted. He knew that this was where he was meant to be. In the end, before long, she would lead him to them.

The weather became warmer, the sun less fitful. On these high summer days she would take a sandwich and fruit to eat on one of the benches in the Embankment Gardens where the boughs of the plane trees dragged to sweep the water with their leaves. He had got into the habit of carrying a packed lunch himself, bought from a delicatessen in Caldecote Road, to be eaten either in a park or at the window of his room. They would sit distanced by twenty or thirty yards on their separate benches and he would watch as she stared over the parapet at the gritty fringes of the Thames, plumed with gulls, at the great barges as they grunted upstream, slapping the tide against the embankment wall. After she had eaten she would feed the sparrows, crouching patiently for as long as fifteen or twenty minutes with the crumbs on her outstretched palm. Once he did the same, and smiled when, after a few minutes of patient waiting, the sparrow fluttered down and he felt the commotion of its frantic wings and the scrape of its tiny claws on his palm. One warm turbulent morning when the high tide heaved in the throes of a spent and distant storm, she brought with her a bag of crusts to feed the gulls. He watched while she stood at the parapet, hurling the bread with stiff ungainly jerks of her arm. The rushing air was suddenly white with wings, spiked with beaks and claws, clamorous with high, desolate screams.

He was surprised how quickly he came to feel at home at the Casablanca. The hotel had few comforts, but it had no pretensions. There was a small and overcrowded bar in a room off the dining-room and most evenings he would take a single dry sherry before his dinner. The meals were predictable: eatable, but only just. But occasionally the standard varied. It was as if the cook were engaged in a private game, judging when the customers were on the point of revolt and then confounding them with a dinner of surprising excellence. But usually little cooking had been done. Scase was familiar with the taste of all the soups; he had opened these tins himself. The prawn cocktail consisted of tinned prawns, hard and salty, smothered with the cheapest of bottled dressing and reposing on a limp lettuce leaf; the pâté maison was commercial liver sausage; the potatoes were invariably served mashed since they were reconstituted from a packet. All his senses were sharpened since he had set out on his enterprise; he noticed these things now, but they didn't bother him.

The Mario who had booked him in seemed to run the place. Scase saw no one else in authority. The other staff were part-time, including Fred, an elderly cripple who spent all night dozing in an armchair behind the counter and whose job it was to let in guests who arrived back after twelve-thirty. The regular clientele were mostly commercial travellers. With some of them Mario was friendly, joining them, white-jacketed, at their table for long intimate conferences. Their common interest was apparently betting. Lists and evening papers were consulted and money changed hands. But most of the trade was foreign package-tours from Spain. With the weekly arrival of the morning coach the hotel came alive. Mario, galvanized into frantic activity, immediately became Spanish in speech and gesture; the hall was blocked with luggage and chattering tourists; the lift invariably broke down and Coffee, the bitch, quivered with excitement.

The hotel was ideal for his purpose. No one bothered about him, no one was curious. The only way in which a visitor could attract interest at the Hotel Casablanca was by failing to settle the bill weekly in advance and in cash. If he felt the need for conversation, a brief craving for the sound of a human voice directed at himself, he would stop to chat to the blind girl. He learned that her name was Violet Tetley and that she was an orphan who had been educated in a residential school for the blind and now lived with a widowed aunt in a council flat off the Vauxhall Bridge Road. In exchange he told her nothing about himself except that his wife and only child were dead. She was the only person to whom he felt he could safely talk. Whatever her private imaginings of him might be, he knew that all his secrets, his past, his present purpose, even his ugliness and his pain, were safe from any probing by those sightless eyes.

On Friday morning, 25 August, he was led by Mrs Palfrey across the newly created piazza and into the cool, incense-sweet immensity of Westminster Cathedral. He saw that she didn't dip her fingers in the stoup of holy water; that she hadn't, apparently, come to pray. The visit was just one more way of killing time. He followed her, attaching himself unobtrusively to a party of French-speaking tourists, as she wandered between the great square marble pillars, paused to survey each of the side chapels, bent to stare with repugnant fascination at the silver-encased body of St John Southworth, small as a child in his glass case.

He had never before been in the Cathedral and its red-brick-bounded Byzantine exterior hadn't prepared him for the wonder which lay beyond the west door. The rough unadorned bricks climbed upwards from great pillars of smooth marble, green, yellow, red and grey, to the black curving immensity of the domed roof. It hung suspended above him, darkness and chaos given a form and substance, and he felt that he crawled crab-like beneath its mystery. The completed Lady Chapel, gleaming with gold mosaics, pretty and sentimental, meant nothing to him. Even the smooth beauty of the marble pillars served only to draw the eye upwards to that curving wonder of the roof. He hadn't expected to be so excited by any building. When the act was done, he would come back and walk here again. He would look up at that dark void and find a comfort which he would gain from no lighted candles, no stained glass. There would be other buildings to explore, perhaps even other cities to visit. There could be a life, solitary though it might be, that was more than mere existence. But now even to experience this wonder pricked him with guilt. He remembered the prick of the sparrow on his palm. That, too, had been a moment very close to joy. But to feel joy while Mary Ducton was still alive was a betrayal of the dead. Already he felt that he was being seduced by routine into a complacent lethargy. He would wait for only one more week. If in that time he hadn't been led to the murderess, if the girl Philippa still hadn't returned to Caldecote Terrace, then he would have to think of a plan, however desperate, to trick Mrs Palfrey into betraying to him where they were.

9

When the ten days of freedom which they had promised themselves were up and it was time to look for a job, they avoided the

Government Job Centre in Lisson Grove, which was too intimidatingly a reminder of officialdom, and searched instead in the evening papers and on the display boards outside newsagents. They found the advertisement for kitchen staff/waitresses at Sid's Plaice off Kilburn High Road pinned to a board outside a stationer's shop at the north end of the Edgware Road. The advertisement said helpfully 'take 16 bus and alight Cambridge Avenue'. It added that the wages were one pound an hour plus food. They calculated that if they worked six hours a day for five days their living expenses should be comfortably covered. One free fish meal a day would be a bonus.

Sid's Plaice was a double-fronted fish-and-chip shop with café attached, and looked and smelled reassuringly fresh. Sid himself, whom Philippa had pictured as small, swarthy and greasy, was discovered to be a blond, ruddy-faced, amateur boxer. He himself worked behind the counter, simultaneously directing operations on both sides of his establishment, crashing down the lid of the fish-fryer, plunging the wire baskets of chips into the sizzling fat, joking with customers at the counter as he wrapped their orders in grease-proof and newspaper, bawling demands at the kitchen staff and slapping fish and chips on plates to be shoved at the waitresses who regularly pushed their heads through the serving hatch and yelled out their orders. The din, to which Sid and his staff were apparently impervious, was constant and appalling. Philippa early decided that customers needed strong nerves although not necessarily a strong stomach to dine at Sid's Plaice.

Sid's girls took it in turn to wait at the tables, if taking the plates from the hatch and dumping them in front of the customers at the formica-topped tables could be described as waitress service. The job was preferred to washing-up, since there were the tips. Sid explained that most customers left something, and there was always the hope of unintended generosity from a visitor or recently arrived immigrant confused about the value of English money. This flexible use of his female labour, which saved him the expense of employing two categories of worker, was described by Sid as 'mucking in together like one big happy family'.

He took on Philippa and her mother with alacrity, and if he were surprised that two apparently educated women were actually seeking work in his shop, he didn't show it. Philippa told herself that this was a place of work where she could be in no possible danger of meeting anyone from her past life, and where no questions would be asked. She was wrong in that; questions were perpetually asked by her fellow workers, but no one cared whether the answers were true.

There were three other washers-up on the evening shift: Black Shirl, Marlene and Debbie. Marlene's hair, spiked and dyed bright orange, looked as if it had been hacked off by shears. Two moons of bright red decorated each cheek, but Philippa was relieved to see that she had apparently jibbed at piercing her ear lobes with safety pins. Her forearm was covered with tattoos, two intertwining hearts pierced with an arrow and surrounded by a garland of roses, and a sixteenth-century galleon in full sail. It fascinated Debbie who was happy to wipe up dishes for Marlene all evening so that she could see it sinking and rising in the detergent.

'Make it sink. Go on, Marl! Make it sink,' she would plead, and Marlene would plunge her arms in the detergent foam and let the bubbles froth around the little craft.

In the damp and ill-equipped kitchen behind the café, with its two sinks, they worked in pairs. They talked incessantly, usually about the previous night's television, their boyfriends, shopping up West. They were given to extraordinary swings of mood and terrifying bursts of temper. They walked out frequently, demonstrating a pathetic and fiercely guarded if illusory independence, and walked in again a few days later. They complained about Sid behind his back, and were alternately surly and outrageously flirtatious to his face. They discussed his alleged sexual inadequacies in anatomical detail and at length, although it was obvious to Philippa that all Sid's energies were spent on the business, his occasional amateur boxing bouts, racing his greyhound and keeping Mrs Sid happy. This lady, of a formidable smartness and vulgarity, appeared briefly once a day in the chippie, apparently to remind Sid and warn the others that she existed. Poor Sid, thought Philippa. He would probably have been afraid of his female helots if they had had enough sense to organize a united confrontation. But they waged their war of attrition with cunning and some success. They regularly stole small quantities of food from him, bread, butter, sugar and tea, and he knew they did. Perhaps this was regarded by both sides as one of the perks of the job; but Philippa saw that he took no chances with his till, which was closely guarded.

Debbie, waif-like, with pale transparent skin, looked as if her life were subcutaneously draining away. Her nose and fingers were perpetually pink-tipped, her anxious eyes swam in red pools and even the ridges of her ears, ragged as if they had been nibbled, looked about to ooze blood. She spoke in whispers and crept about the kitchen bestowing indiscriminately her sweetly inane smile. But it was Debbie who was the most violent. Sharing a sink with Philippa, Black Shirl said:

'She knifed her ma when she was twelve.'

'You mean she killed her?'

'Bloody near thing. They put her in care. But she's all right now as long as you don't let her near your feller.'

'You mean she'd knife him?'

Black Shirl roared with laughter.

'Naw. She'd fuck 'im. She's terrible she is. Lord, that girl, she's terrible!'

Mechanically taking plate after plate from Shirl's hands, Philippa thought that if her father had encountered Debbie instead of Julia Scase, he would be alive now. There would have been no rape, no murder, no adoption. His only problem would have been to get rid of her, to stop another visit; but ten shillings and a bag of sweets would probably have done the trick. It was his bad luck to have met instead Julia Scase, that dangerous mixture of innocence and stupidity.

All three treated her mother with wary respect, perhaps because she was older, perhaps because there was something inhibiting about her quiet composure. Unlike Philippa, she seemed undisturbed by the irrational explosions of violence. Once when Debbie, washing a carving knife, suddenly pointed it at Marlene's throat, she succeeded in persuading the girl to hand it over with no more than a quiet, 'Give it to me, Debbie.' But they were curious about her. One night, when her mother was on waitress duty and Marlene and Philippa were sharing a sink, Marlene said:

'Been in the bin, has she, your ma? You know, a mental hospital?'

'Yes, she has. Why did you ask?'

'You can allus tell. My auntie was the same. You can tell by the eyes, see. All right now, is she?'

'Oh yes, she's fine. The doctor said she mustn't be under any strain. That's why we took this job. It isn't exactly stimulating, but at least you can put it behind you when you go home.'

This was accepted in silence. They all had excuses for lowering themselves by condescending to take Sid's job. Black Shirl, sloshing suds at the next sink, said, belligerent, suspicious:

'Why do you speak posh?'

'It's not my fault. My uncle looked after me when I was a kid, after my dad died. He and my aunt were particular. That's why I ran away. That and my uncle trying to get into bed with me.'

Marlene said:

'My uncle did that to me, too. I didn't mind. He was all right. Used to take me up West Saturday nights.'

Black Shirl said:

'Went to a posh school then, did you?'

'I ran away from that too.'

'Got a place have you? You and your ma?'

'Oh yes, just a room. But we won't be stopping there long. My boyfriend is buying a flat for us.'

'What's his name, your boyfriend?'

'Ernest, Ernest Hemingway.'

The name was received in a disparaging silence. Marlene said:

'You wouldn't get me going out with a feller called Ernest. My granddad was Ernest.'

'What's he like?' asked Black Shirl.

'The outdoor type really. He shoots and hunts a lot. And he likes bulls. Actually, he's getting rather a bore.'

She enjoyed fabricating the lies and soon learnt that they were infinitely credulous. Either nothing was to egregious to be unbelievable, or they didn't greatly care. Their own lives were made tolerable by fantasy; they had none of the pettiness which would grudge it to others. What did worry them, as it obviously did Sid, was the fact that she and her mother had presented their National Insurance cards for stamping. All the girls working in the chippie were drawing unemployment benefit. They felt vaguely threatened by this orthodoxy. Philippa found it necessary to explain:

'It's my probation officer. He knows I'm working. I can't put anything across on him.'

They looked at her pityingly. Probation officers were admittedly less gullible than local authority social workers, but this unreasonable docility lowered her in their eyes. Not by such naïveté did one survive in the urban jungle. Often she smiled to herself, remembering that Gabriel believed, or claimed to believe, that the weak, the sick and the ignorant preyed on the strong, the healthy and the intelligent. He could have found evidence enough at Sid's Plaice. But Philippa, bent over the sink, her back aching, her skin sodden with steam, told herself that Gabriel's world could well survive the pathetic depredations of Marlene, Debbie and Black Shirl.

Two vivid and contrasting mental pictures came frequently into her mind: Gabriel calling for her one bright Saturday morning in the summer term, swinging himself out of his Lagonda, running up the steps of number 68, his cashmere sweater slung from his shoulders; Black Shirl humping to a corner of the kitchen the great bag of washing for her five children which she would wheel in a pram to the launderette on her way home. Perhaps Maurice's mind was patterned with equally vivid images, contrasts which had made him a Socialist and which, even now, kept him one, despite the knowledge, which surely he shared, that his creed would merely transfer the Lagonda to an owner equally, if differently, privileged and that there was no economic system in this world which would transfer the Lagonda to Shirl and the washing and the five children to Gabriel.

Once, when walking to the late-night bus, her mother asked:

'You don't think we exploit them?'

'How? Considering we get through twice the washing-up at our sink that they do at theirs, you could argue that they exploit us.'

'I suppose I mean that we pretend to be friendly, to be one of them, but back home we talk and laugh about them as if they're objects, interesting specimens.'

'But they are interesting specimens, more amusing and interesting than any we'd meet in the typical office. If they don't know how we talk about them does it matter?'

'Perhaps not to them. It might to us.'

After a few seconds' silence, she said:

'Are you going to write about them?'

'That hadn't occurred to me. That isn't why we took the job. I suppose I'll file them in the subconscious until I need them.'

She half expected her mother to ask, 'Will you file me there too?'

But she said nothing, and for a little time they walked together in silence.

In the bus, her mother said:

'How long do you suppose we ought to stay at Sid's?'

'As long as we're happy to live on fish and chips. I admit I sometimes wonder if they've any vacancies for washers-up at L'Ecu de France.'

'Is that where you used to eat?'

'Only on special occasions. That and the Gay Hussar and Mon Plaisir are Maurice's favourites. Bertorelli's was for every day. I used to meet him there for lunch sometimes. I love Bertorelli's.'

She wondered whether Maurice still ate there, and if Signor Bertorelli ever asked for her in that other world. Her mother said tentatively:

'We could stay for another week or so, perhaps, if you're not too tired or bored. I don't mind the fish. I rather like it.'

'I'm not in the least bored. And we can change jobs as soon as we are. We've got our cards nicely stamped up, and I suppose Sid would give us a reference if we twisted his arm. He doesn't give many bills, have you noticed? Two-thirds of his business is on a cash, no-tax basis. I dare say we'd only have to whisper that and he'd happily give us a year's pay in lieu of notice.'

'I don't think we ought to do that. He's been decent to us.'

'I was only joking. Anyway, we're free to go when we like. That's the fun of it. Just let me know when you're tired of fish.'

10

Their freedom did, indeed, seem to be limitless, stretching out in concentric waves from those three small rooms above Monty's Fruit and Veg to embrace the whole of London. The freedom of the city: of the lumpy grass under the elms of St James's Park where they would search for a spare length of grass among the knapsacks of the prone tourists, and lie on their backs, staring up through a dazzle of shivering green and silver and listening to the midday band concert. There would be a circle of deck chairs round the bandstand and here the regulars would sit having taken their seats early: large ladies from the suburbs and the provinces with their sandwiches, their summer hats, their plump, ringed fingers guarding bulging hand-bags on comfortable laps. When the drizzle began they would rummage in their bags and spread mackintoshes over their knees, unfold a concertina of thin plastic to cover their hats. Having paid their money for a deck chair, the vagaries of an English summer couldn't cheat them of their forty minutes of crashing brass, the red-braided uniforms, the conductor's brisk salute.

But for Philippa and her mother, despite these almost daily excursions, the core of their joint life lay in Delaney Street and Mell Street. Philippa told herself that she couldn't have found a better part of London in which to be anonymous. The district had a life of its own, but it was one in which the sense of community was fostered by seeing the same familiar faces, not by enquiring into their business. Delaney Street was a quiet cul-de-sac inhabited chiefly by the middle-aged or elderly living above their small family shops. It had something of the atmosphere of a self-sufficient, ancient and sleepy village, a sluggish backwater between the great surging rivers of the Marylebone Road and the Edgware Road. Many of its occupants, like Mr and Mrs Tookes at the junk shop, and the two eccentric Miss Peggs who spent their time perambulating in Mell Street, leading a string of small discouraged dogs, had been born in the street as had their parents before them. They formed a select and secretive coterie, much given to standing in each other's doorways, apparently wordlessly communicating, seeming to huddle themselves against the cold even on the warmest day, and viewing with dispassionate, amused or ironic eyes the casual visitors or newcomers, like natives viewing the arrival of yet another wave of credulous and soon to be disillusioned settlers. Their chief preoccupation was the rumour and threat of a local authority development which would sweep their world away. They stared across at the corrugated fence of the wasteland with hard but troubled eyes. Philippa, always curious, got to know a little about them by casual discreet questions to George. She might have learned more had she and her mother drunk in the Blind Beggar, but they thought it prudent to keep apart: one could not patronize the local pub for long and remain private. But they felt accepted in the street. Their neighbours were always polite and sometimes friendly. They watched, occasionally they smiled, but they asked no questions.

Saturday was market day in Mell Street. By nine o'clock the police van had arrived, the barriers had been dragged out and were in place and the street was closed to through traffic. It was a small, intimate, bustling market, cosmopolitan but at the same time very English. The bargaining was carried out with humour and good nature, and occasionally in the old money. Early in the morning the seller of second-hand rugs and carpets wheeled up his great wooden barrow and patterned the road with his wares. Uninhibited and unrebuked, the shoppers walked over them. The tarmac itself became festive. Later the market took on something of the atmosphere of an eastern souk when the brass-seller arrived to set out his jangling pots, and a Pakistani who sold cheap jewellery hung across his stall a swinging curtain of wooden beads. On the material stall lengths of brightly patterned cloth were spun from the great bales; the vendors of kitchenware, fruit and vegetables, fish and meat, flowers and plants, bawled out their wares; the air was sickly with the smell from the hot-dog stall; and at a corner of the street a thin gentle-faced boy wearing a button, 'Jesus loves me', patiently held out his pamphlets to the unregarding crowd. Cats looped among the wooden trestles, stretched themselves and curled voluptuously on the woollen jumpers which spilled from the second-hand clothes stall while, outside the shops, the bright-eyed dogs quivered with excitement or crouched gently groaning, their eyes half-closed against the sun. Philippa and her mother rummaged among the clothes stalls for hand-knitted woollens, some of them too worn to be used. Her mother would later unpick, then skein and wash the wool. There seemed always to be crinkled loops of wool drooping across the bath to dry. The boxes of odds and ends placed at the sides of the stalls yielded their treasures, including a teacloth of hand-embroidered linen which they mended, washed and starched and used ceremoniously for Saturday afternoon tea.

Behind the stalls were the small shops: the old-fashioned draper where one could still buy woollen combinations and sleeved vests, and where the pink lace-up corsets hung in the window, their strings dangling; the Greek delicatessen smelling of syrup and sharp Mediterranean wine; the small general store, clean, sweet-smelling, perpetually dark, with a bell on the door, where old Mrs Davies shuffled in from the shadows to serve them with milk, butter and tea; the larger of the half-dozen junk shops whose cluttered interior they would penetrate through to a back yard piled with old furniture and fitted along one wall with racks where a miscellany of crockery, pans and pictures offered the chance of a find. Here it was they uncovered two uncracked cups, one early Worcester, one Staffordshire, with chipped but matching saucers, and an agreeably shaped grime-covered dish which, after washing, was revealed as blue and white seventeenth-century Swansea pottery. It was like playing at housekeeping; the re-enactment of the innocent childhood games which neither of them had known.

Philippa had still learned almost nothing of her mother's past. From time to time they would talk briefly about her life in prison, but nothing about the crime and nothing about their earliest and shared years. Philippa asked no questions. She told herself that L. P. Hartley was right; the past was another country and they could choose whether to visit there. Her mother didn't choose and she had no right to compel her, vulnerable as she was, to travel that stony road. She had been give the account of the murder; she told herself that, for the present, it must be enough. She couldn't use her possession of the flat, her companionship, her defence against the noisy intrusions of this new world to purchase a confidence which wasn't freely offered. There was no commitment and that meant no commitment on either side. But she found that she was visualizing less and less a future in which they would be completely apart. She had virtually compelled her mother to share a flat with her because she needed to discover her own identity. She was discovering it, and in ways which she had neither expected nor planned. Discovering her mother's identity was another matter and it could wait. There was no hurry to explore the past; experiencing the present was interesting enough, and they had, after all, their whole lives before them.

11

After a fortnight her mother's probation officer came to the flat. Philippa knew that the visit was inevitable, a condition of her mother's licence, yet she prepared herself to dislike him. He had written to say when he would arrive, and she arranged to take their sheets to the launderette, ostensibly so that her mother and he could talk in private, but really in the hope of avoiding an introduction.

But when she returned and put the key in the lock she could hear her mother's voice, clear, ordinary, even animated. He was in the kitchen, drinking tea from a mug. She found herself shaking hands with a mild-eyed, stocky young man with a russet, tangled beard and balding head. He wore blue jeans and a fawn sweat-shirt. His sandalled feet were brown and surprisingly clean. Everything about him was clean. Some of Maurice's colleagues dressed with just such informality, but with them it was an ostentation, a desire to demonstrate their solidarity with their students. She felt that this man dressed to suit himself. Her mother introduced him but her mind blocked the words from her consciousness. She wanted none of him, not even his name.

He had brought with him an African violet which he had grown himself from a cutting. Watching him help her mother to pot it, she knew that she resented him, resented her mother's docile acceptance of this mild but degrading surveillance, resented his intrusion on their privacy. And she knew herself to be jealous. She was looking after her mother. They were looking after each other. They didn't need the bureaucratic, carefully rationed caring of the State. Later during the visit, when he and her mother had been discussing the pots of herbs growing in the kitchen window, and her mother had gone to find a pencil and paper to write down some of the names, she said:

'Don't you think that after ten years society could leave my mother alone? She isn't a danger to anyone; you must know that.'

He said gently:

'Licence has to be the same for everyone. The law can't make fish of one and fowl of the other.'

'But what good do you hope to do? Not to my mother; I know the answer there. What good do you do for your more ordinary clients? You do call them clients, don't you? I mean, you are a kind of emotional bank manager.'

He ignored the last question and answered the first.

'Not much. It's more a question of not doing them harm, trying to help them not to do themselves harm.'

'But what exactly do you do?'

'The Statute says "advise, assist and befriend".'

'But you can't befriend someone by Act of Parliament. How could anyone, even the most deprived, be satisfied with or deceived by that kind of friendship, a spurious second-best?'

'Second-best is all that most people ever have. People manage with very little; friendship as well as money. I rely on their goodwill more than they do on mine. Your parsley's doing very well. It won't grow for us. Did you start this from seed?'

'No. It's a root we got from the health-food shop in Baker Street.'

She picked a small bunch for him, glad to give an exchange for the violet. That way they needn't feel under an obligation to him. He took the parsley and, washing his handkerchief under the hot tap of the kitchen sink, rinsed it with cold water and folded the leaves carefully inside it. His hands were large, snub-fingered. He used them gently, unfussily. When he bent over the sink his sweat-shirt rode up to reveal a few inches of smooth flesh, brown and speckled as an egg. She felt a sudden desire to touch it, and found herself wondering what he would be like in bed. Gabriel had made love as if he were a ballet dancer, narcissistically preoccupied with his body, every movement an exercise in control. He performed as if thinking, 'This is a necessary, unaesthetic business; but see how I contrive to give it grace.' She thought that this man would be different, gentle but direct, free of pretence, free of guilt. After he had wrapped the parsley, he said:

'Mara will be glad of that. Thanks.'

She supposed that Mara was his wife or girlfriend. She knew that if she had asked he would have told her; but he never volunteered information. He seemed to view himself and his world with common-sense detachment, accepting kindness at its face value, as if kindness was a common currency of life, answering questions simply, as if unaware of the devious motives from which they sprang. Perhaps in his job it was necessary for survival to take people at their face value too. He hadn't reacted to her obvious antagonism, yet he didn't give her the impression that he was exercising any particular control. She thought that his attitude could be summed up: 'We're all of the same blood, and we're in the same shipwreck. Recriminations, explanations, panic are all a waste of time. Safety requires only that we act towards each other with love.'

She was glad when, at the end of the visit, he said to her mother: 'In about a month's time then. Perhaps you'd rather go back to seeing me at the office. I'm out visiting or in court most days, but you'll find me there Tuesdays and Fridays, nine to twelve-thirty.'

She was glad that he wasn't coming back, that the flat would once again be their own. Apart from George, when he had helped her lug up some furniture, and Joyce Bungeld's brief visit, he was the only other person who had set foot in it. She felt, too, that she wasn't ready yet to cope with someone who might – intriguing and unsettling thought – be naturally good.

12

In the evenings at weekends, or on Mondays when they didn't work, they often watched television together, carrying the two basket chairs from their bedrooms into the kitchen. Watching television was something of a novelty for Philippa. Working for her O- and A-levels and the Cambridge scholarship had taken most of her time, and the television at Caldecote Terrace was seldom switched on. Maurice, like a number of pundits who never refused an invitation to appear, affected to despise all but a few minority-taste programmes. Now she and her mother became mildly addicted to the risible awfulness of a family drama series in which the characters, apparently physically and mentally unscathed by the traumas of the last episode, were resurrected weekly, freshly coiffured, their wounds healed and scarless, for yet another emotional and physical bloodbath. Such a convenient ability to live for the moment with its subliminal message that the past could literally be put behind one had much to recommend it. There ought, she thought, to be a word coined to describe the frank enjoyment to be had from the reassuring second-rate. And that was how, switching the set on too early, they caught the last ten minutes of Maurice's encounter with the Bishop.

Maurice looked relaxed, perfectly at home in this his milieu, swivelling gently in the aggressively modern chair of chrome and black leather, one leg thrown lightly over the other. Philippa recognized the pattern of his socks, the discreet arrow pointing the ankle, the gleam of hand-made leather shoes. He was particular about his clothes. The Bishop, stiffly upright in the twin chair, looked less comfortable. He was a large man. His pectoral cross, insignificant in thin silver, rested crookedly against the episcopal purple. She despised him for this timid affirmation of faith. A talisman, if one went in for these things, should be heavy, beautiful and worn with panache. He had obviously been trapped into fighting on his weakest ground and his heavy face wore the embarrassed, slightly ashamed and conciliatory half-smile of a man who knows that he is letting down the side, but hopes that no one but himself will have noticed it.

Maurice was in excellent form. She anticipated each of the well-remembered mannerisms, the sudden twitch of the left shoulder, the lift of the head away from his opponent, the sudden clasp of his bony hands over the right knee and the hunching of the shoulders as if he were bending his mind to the nub of the argument. None of these antics had anything to do with nervousness. They were the extrovert pantomime of the interaction of mind and body, both too restless to be confined within this trendy contraption of steel and leather, the enclosing cardboard walls with their carefully designed title for the series, *Dissent*. His voice was reedier than normal, a pedant's voice.

'Well, let's just recapitulate what you're asking us to believe. That God, whom you say is a spirit, which I take to mean is incorporeal – doesn't one of your creeds say without shape, form or passions? – has created man in His own image. That man has sinned. I won't hold you to that fable of some celestial Kew Garden and forbidden Cox's Orange Pippin – let's use your own words, that he's fallen short of the glory of God. That every child coming into the world is contaminated with this primeval sin through no fault of his own. That God, instead of demanding in expiation a bloody sacrifice from man, sent His only son into the world to be tortured and done to death in the most barbaric fashion in order to propitiate His Father's desire for vengeance and to reconcile man to his creator. That this son was born of a virgin. Incidentally, you told us last week that sex was somehow sacred because ordained by God, and I confess to finding it curious that He despised the orthodox method of pro-creation which He Himself devised and presumably approves. We are asked to believe that this miraculously born God-made-man lived and died without sin to atone for man's first disobedience. Now we may not have a great deal of historical evidence about the life of Jesus of Nazareth, but we do know quite a lot about Roman methods of capital punishment. Neither you nor I, I'm happy to say, has witnessed a crucifixion, but we can agree that as a method of execution it was agonizing, degrading, slow, bestial and bloody. If you or I actually saw a victim being hauled on to that cross and could get him down – provided, of course, that we didn't risk anything by interfering – I don't think we could prevent ourselves from trying to save him. But the God of Love was apparently content to let it happen, indeed, willed it to happen, and to His only son. You can't ask us to believe in a God of Love who behaves less compassionately than would the least of his creatures. I no longer have a son, but that is hardly my idea of parental love.'

Her mother got up and, without speaking, turned down the sound. She said:

'What does he mean, he no longer has a son?'

'He did once, but Orlando was killed in a road accident with his mother. That's why Maurice and Hilda took me on.'

It was the first time that her adoptive parents had been mentioned between them and she waited, curious to see if this was the moment when their silence would be broken, whether her mother would ask about those lost ten years, whether she had been happy at Caldecote Terrace, where she had gone to school, what kind of life she had led. But she only said:

'Is that how he brought you up, as an atheist?'

'Well, he told me when I was about nine that religion was nonsense and that only fools believed it and then made it clear that I must think its tenets out for myself and make up my own mind. I don't think he has ever been a believer.'

'Well, he believes now, or why does he hate God so much? He wouldn't be so vehement if the Bishop were inviting him to believe in pixies or the theories of the flat-earthers. Poor Bishop! He could only win by saying things that he'd be too embarrassed to utter and which neither the BBC nor the viewers – especially the Christians – would in the least wish to hear.'

What things? she wondered. She said:

'Do you believe?'

Her mother answered.

'Oh yes, I believe.' She glanced towards the screen where Maurice, still articulating, had been reduced to a silent and ridiculously posturing cypher. 'The Bishop doesn't know for certain, but loves what he thinks he believes. Your father knows and hates what he knows. I believe, but I can't love any more. He and I are the unlucky ones.'

Philippa wanted to ask: 'What do you believe? What difference does it make?' She felt the mixture of excitement, curiosity and apprehension of someone putting a first tentative foot on dangerous and uncertain ground. She said:

'But you can't believe in hell.'

'You can once you've been in it.'

'But I thought anything is forgivable. I mean, isn't that the whole point of it? You can't place yourself beyond the mercy of God. I thought Christians only had to ask.'

'You have to believe.'

'Well, you do believe, you've just said so. That's lucky for you. I don't.'

'There has to be contrition.'

'What's so difficult about that? Feeling sorry. I should have thought that was the easiest part.'

'Not sorry because you did something and the results have been unpleasant for you. Not just wishing that you hadn't done it. That's easy. Contrition means saying "I did that thing. I was responsible." '

'Well, is that so difficult? It seems a fair exchange if you can get instant forgiveness and eternal life thrown in for good measure.'

'I can't spend ten years explaining to myself that I wasn't responsible, that I couldn't have prevented myself doing what I did, and then when I'm free, as free as I'll ever be, when society thinks I've been punished enough, when everyone has lost interest, then I can't decide that it would be pleasant to have God's forgiveness as well.'

'I don't see why not. Remember Heine's last words: "*Dieu me pardonnera, c'est son métier.*" '

Her mother didn't reply. Her face had the closed withdrawn look of someone who finds the conversation painful or distasteful. Philippa went on:

'Why don't you like talking about religion?'

'You've managed very well without it so far.'

She glanced towards the television set, then suddenly rose and switched it off. The Bishop's benign, embarrassed face dissolved into a diminishing square of light. Then another and more personal thought fell into Philippa's mind. She asked:

'Was I christened?'

'Yes.'

'You never told me.'

'You never asked before.'

'What did you call me?'

'Rose, after your father's mother. Your father called you Rosie. But you know that your name is Rose. It's on your birth certificate. Before your adoption you were Rose Ducton.'

'I'll make the coffee.'

Her mother seemed about to speak, then changed her mind. She went out of the kitchen and into her own room. Philippa took down the two mugs from the kitchen shelf. Her hands were shaking. She put them on the table and tried to fill the kettle. Of course she had known that her name was Rose, had known it as soon as she had opened that innocuous-looking official envelope and had taken out her birth certificate. But then it had been just another label. She had hardly taken it in, except to notice that Maurice, in relegating it to second place, had nevertheless allowed her to retain something from her past. The edge of the kettle rattled against the tap. Carefully she placed it on the draining board and stood bent, clasping the cold edge of the sink as if fighting nausea. Rose Ducton. Rosie Ducton. Philippa Rose Palfrey. A row of books with Rose Ducton on the spine. It was a trisyllabic cypher, having nothing to do with her. I baptize you in the name of the Father and of the Son and of the Holy Ghost. A trickle of water running over her forehead. It could hardly have been of any real importance since Maurice could wipe it away with a stroke of his pen. Where, she wondered, had she been christened; in that dull suburban church in Seven Kings under the stunted travesty of a spire? Rose. It didn't even suit her. It was a name in a catalogue; Peace, Scarlet Wonder, Albertine. She had thought that she had got used to the knowledge that nothing about her was real, not even her name. Why, then, was she so shaken now?

She had control of the trembling now and, careful as a child entrusted with an unfamiliar task, she filled the kettle. Rose. It was strange that her mother hadn't once called her by that name, hadn't once inadvertently let it slip, the name which, after all, she had chosen, or at least had accepted for her baby, the name which she had used for eight years, the name which she must have had in mind during the last ten years of solitude and survival. If she believed in God, that strange eccentricity which she Philippa – she Rose – would have to explore, she must have used that word in her prayers, if she did pray. God bless Rosie. It must have taken a disciplined effort from their first meeting always to remember to call her Philippa. Every time she spoke that new Maurice-bestowed name she was playing a part, being less than honest. No, that wasn't fair. And it was stupid to mind so much. What did it matter? But she wished that her mother had, just once, forgotten to be careful and had called her by her right name.

13

The loneliness descended on him soon after breakfast, as dragging and exhausting as a physical weight. It was the more disturbing because it was so unexpected. Loneliness was a state he had got used to since Mavis's death and he hadn't expected to feel it again as a positive emotion nor to be visited by its sad aftermath of restlessness and boredom. By eleven o'clock Mrs Palfrey hadn't appeared and he thought it now unlikely that she would. It had been the same last Sunday. Perhaps this was the day when they went out together, leaving by car from the carriage road at the back of the terrace which his investigations had shown led to a row of garages. Without her to follow there was little chance of shaking off this weight of ennui. His life had become so linked with hers, his routine tied to her daily perambulations that, when she didn't appear, he felt deprived as if of her actual company.

The hotel was full; a new package-tour of Spaniards had arrived on Saturday evening and service for the rest of the guests was perfunctory. The dining-room was a jabber of excited voices, the hall obstructed with their luggage. Mario gabbled, gesticulated, rushed frantically from reception desk to dining-room. Glad to get away from the crush, Scase had settled himself early at his bedroom window with his binoculars trained on number 68, but with no real hope of seeing her. It was a morning of alternate rain and sunshine. Fierce and sudden squalls slashed at the window, then as suddenly ceased; the nudging clouds parted and the pavement steamed as the sun reappeared, hot and bright. By half-past eleven restlessness got the better of him and he went downstairs in search of coffee. Violet was at the switchboard as usual, the dog at her feet. Needing to hear a human voice, he said something to her about the pleasure of seeing the sun, then stopped appalled at his tactlessness. He should have said feeling the sun. She smiled, her sightless eyes seeking the echo of his voice. Then to his surprise he heard himself say:

'I thought of going to Regent's Park this afternoon to look at the roses. You go off duty at midday on Sunday, don't you? Would you and Coffee care to come?'

'That would be nice. Thank you. We'd both like it.'

Her hand found the dog's head and pressed it. The animal stirred and pricked its ears, bright eyes fixed on her face.

'And would you like to have some dinner first? Lunch I mean?'

She flushed and nodded. She seemed pleased. He saw that, under her fawn woollen cardigan, she was wearing what looked like a new summer dress in blue cotton. After he had spoken she stroked the skirt gently with both hands and smiled as if glad that she had taken the trouble to put it on. He told himself that having committed one folly, he had now embarked on a second. But it was too late now to draw back and he didn't really want to. Then he wondered where he would take her for luncheon. There was a small sandwich bar off Victoria Street which he used occasionally during the week but he wasn't sure whether it would be open on a Sunday. It was very clean but not at all smart. Then he remembered that the shabbiness of its cramped partitions wouldn't matter since she couldn't see them, and was ashamed that the thought had entered his mind. It was wrong to cheat her just because she was blind. He must try to make the occasion special for her. After all, she would be doing more for him than she knew. And she would be the first woman other than Mavis whom he had taken out since the day of his marriage. Admittedly she was blind. But then, if she hadn't been blind, she wouldn't have accepted his invitation. He remembered that there was an Italian restaurant fairly close to the station. Perhaps that would be open on Sunday. At least Coffee wouldn't be any problem. Children, he had noticed, were seldom welcome, but nobody minded a guide-dog.

The day brightened for him. It was time he took a day off, time too that he walked and talked with another human being. He made arrangements with her to call for her at the desk just before twelve and went back to his room. As he unlocked his room door it struck him that there would be little point this morning in taking with him his rucksack with the accoutrements of murder and he wondered whether it would really be safe to leave it in his locked room. But the rucksack had become almost part of him. He felt that he would walk strangely without its familiar weight on his right shoulder. And why shouldn't he take it? It occurred to him that he had by impulse chosen the best possible person as companion on his walk. She wouldn't wonder what he was carrying in the rucksack. She wouldn't ask. And after the killing, if things did go wrong and the police traced him to the Casablanca, she was the one person they wouldn't ask to identify him.

<h1 style="text-align:center">14</h1>

After breakfast, on 27 August, their second Sunday together, her mother said abruptly:

'Do you mind if we go to church?'

Philippa, surprised, managed to respond as if this were the most usual of requests. She had gone through a phase of sermon-tasting and felt herself as well qualified to recommend a church for its service and music as she was to discuss its architecture. She enquired what her mother had in mind: the ordered ceremonial and beautifully balanced choir of Marylebone parish church? High Anglican Mass at All Saints', Margaret Street, in a dazzle of mosaics, gilded saints and stained glass? The Baroque splendours of St Paul's? Her mother said that she would like somewhere quiet and close, so they went to the eleven o'clock Sung Eucharist in the cool, uncluttered interior of Sir Ninian Comper's St Cyprian's where an all-male choir sang the liturgy in plainsong from the balcony, a gentle-voiced priest preached an uncompromisingly Catholic sermon and the incense rose pungent and sweet, clouding the high altar. Philippa sat throughout the prayers, but with her head slightly bowed since she had, after all, chosen to be there and politeness dictated at least a token compliance. They hadn't compelled her in; why make an offensive parade of unbelief when neither belief nor disbelief mattered? And it was, after all, no hardship to listen to Cranmer's prose, or as much of it as the revisers had left unmutilated. From these sonorous, antiphonal cadences Jane Austen, on her deathbed, receiving the sacrament from her brother's hands, had taken comfort. That fact alone was enough to silence irreverence. Watching her mother's bent head and clasped hands, she wondered what communication she was making to her god. Once she thought, Perhaps she's praying for me, and the idea was obscurely gratifying. But although she herself couldn't pray, she liked to sing the hymns. The sound of her soaring voice always surprised her. It was a rich contralto, deeper than her speaking voice, unrecognizable as her own, the expression, it seemed, of a part of her personality unrestrained and unpredictable, only released by poor metric verse and cheerfully nostalgic school-assembly tunes.

Her mother didn't move forward to the altar when the time came for the faithful to eat and drink their god, and she slipped out, Philippa following, during the last hymn. That way, as Philippa realized, there could be no risk that the priest or members of the congregation would introduce themselves, or try to make the strangers feel welcome. Whatever this strange, unsacramental, religious life meant to her mother, it could never include coffee in the parish room, or cosy valedictory gossip in the porch; and for that, at least, she could be grateful. Closing the porch door behind them softly as the last hymn drew to its close, they decided not to bother with cooking lunch, but to stay out as long as possible while the weather was fine. They would find themselves somewhere cheap to eat in Baker Street, then spend the afternoon in Regent's Park.

Although they lived so close, it was the first time that they had visited the park. The early-morning rain had stopped and high sunlit clouds drifted imperceptibly across a sky of clear blue which deepened to mauve over a cluster of distant trees across the lake. The geraniums and ivy planted each side of the metal bridge trailed down to the water and the rowers laughed, rocking their skiffs as the fronds brushed their faces. The park was coming to life after the rain. Deck chairs, stacked under the trees for shelter, were brought out again; their legs sank into the moist grass as little family groups settled into them to contemplate rose beds, distant vistas and the comforting proximity of toilets and the coffee-house. Staid Sunday promenaders paced with their leashed dogs between the lavender and the delphiniums, and the queue at the coffee-house lengthened. In Queen Mary's rose garden the roses, plumped by the rain, held the last drops between delicate streaked petals: pink Harriny, bright yellow Summer Sunshine, Ena Harkness and Peace.

While her mother wandered among the bushes, Philippa sat on one of the benches under a great swag of small white roses and took from her shoulder bag the pocket edition of Donne's poems picked up for ten pence from a stall in the market. The roses swung gently above her head, thick as May blossom, dropping their sweetness and an occasional shower of small white petals and golden stamens on to the clovered grass. The sun was warm on her face, inducing a gentle lethargic melancholy. She couldn't remember when last she had visited Queen Mary's rose garden, perhaps never. Maurice preferred buildings to nature, even nature as disciplined, organized and formally displayed as Regent's Park. There was one rose garden which she could remember, but that had been at Pennington and her imagined father had been there, coming towards her through the enclosing circle of green. Odd that so clear a memory, scent, warmth and mellow afternoon light, recalled with peculiar intensity, almost with pain, should be nothing but a childish fantasy. But this garden, this park were real enough, and Maurice was right about architecture. Nature needed the contrast, the discipline of brick and stone. The colonnades and pediments of John Nash's terraces, the eccentric outline of the zoo, even the technical phallus of the Post Office Tower soaring above the hedges, contributed to the park's beauty, defined it and set its limits. It would, she thought, be intolerable to contemplate this lush perfection stretching to infinity, a never-ending, corrupted Garden of Eden.

She lowered her eyes from contemplating the swinging roses to watch her mother. She was always watching her mother, who had, she supposed, exchanged one kind of surveillance for another. She was smelling an orange-red rose, cupping the flower gently in her hand. Most of the rose-worshippers closed their eyes to savour the scent; she opened hers wider. She had a look of intense concentration, the facial muscles drawn and taut as if racked with pain. She was standing a little apart, quite motionless, oblivious of everything except the rose resting in her palm.

It was then that Philippa saw the man. He had come up the sloping path from the lake, a small, spectacled, grey-haired man, solicitously accompanying a blind woman with a coffee-coloured guide dog. His glance fell on her, their eyes met and instinctively, and out of the lazy pleasure of the moment, she smiled at him. The result was extraordinary. He stood transfixed, eyes widened, in what seemed a second of incredulous terror. Then he turned abruptly away, and taking the woman by the elbow, almost forced her back down the path and towards the lake. Philippa laughed aloud. He was a plain little man, ordinary but not repulsive, and surely not so plain that no woman before had ever spontaneously smiled at him. Perhaps he thought that she was trying to pick him up, a summer temptress lurking under the swinging roses. She watched the odd couple out of sight, wondering about their relationship, whether he was the girl's father, what excuse he was giving her for so abruptly hurrying her away. Then she thought that she might have seen him somewhere before, but the memory was elusive. His, after all, was hardly a memorable face. But the feeling that she ought to have recognized him was frustrating. She bent her eyes again to her book and put him resolutely out of her mind.

15

Violet Tetley said, her voice sharp with anxiety:

'What is it? What happened? Are you all right?'

His grip must have tightened painfully on her elbow. Or was it that she had smelled the sudden reek of excitement and fear? People said that the blind had an extra sense. He slackened his pace.

'I'm sorry. Nothing's wrong. It's just that I saw someone unexpectedly, a man I used to work with in the accounts office. I didn't want to have to talk to him.'

She was silent. It occurred to him that she might think that he was embarrassed to be seen with her, and he added quickly:

'I've never liked him. He was rather officious, a bit of a bully. You know the kind. I didn't want him to see me. I didn't want to have to speak to him.'

She said gently:

'He must have made you very unhappy.'

'Not really. Not too unhappy. But it was a shock seeing him so unexpectedly. I thought that part of my life was behind me for good. There are some rather nice yellow roses in this bed. I'll find the label and tell you what they're called.'

She said:

'They're called Summer Sunshine.'

It had been hard to keep his voice steady. He felt sick with disappointment. They were there together. He had seen the murderess bending over one of the rose bushes in that second as he turned abruptly away. He had found them at last and he was helpless, tied, prevented from following them. And it was an ideal opportunity. Like the girl, he could have found a seat and sat there innocently in the sun watching them. The park was getting more crowded every minute. When at last they decided to leave for home nothing would have been easier than to tail them, one anonymous man among the crowd. He could even have used his binoculars if necessary. Many of the tourists wore them and trained them occasionally on the more exotic waterfowl. Time, place, chance were all in his favour and he had to let them go. For a moment he toyed with the idea of deserting Violet, making some excuse, planting her on a seat and promising to return. But he couldn't do it, and he was ashamed of the impulse. And after all, he had to return to the hotel and so did she. She would expect some explanation of his desertion and there was none he could give. But, worst of all, Philippa Palfrey had seen him, had actually smiled at him, might recall his face if she saw him again.

The smile, in its spontaneity, its openness, its frank sexual comradeship, had appalled him. It had seemed too like an invitation to a shared happiness in the warmth of the day, the scent of the rose-drenched air, the physical joy of living; an acknowledgement of a common humanity, a kinship of pleasure which he repudiated, most of all from her. But had it been as simple as that? As they made their slow way back to the hotel, not speaking, he tried to recall that moment from which he had turned away with such instinctive horror. Surely he couldn't have been mistaken? It had been a smile of spontaneous pleasure, nothing more. She couldn't have known who he was, couldn't have guessed his purpose. Surely it was madness to persuade himself even for a moment that what he had seen had been a smile of complicity, of shared knowledge?

But one thing was certain. It had spoilt the day for Violet Tetley. It had started so well. She had enjoyed her meal and they had been happy together in the park. He had found himself talking to her without strain. But that was over. Even Coffee lurched along beside them, dejected, tail drooping. And he had learned his lesson. From now on he must learn to bear his loneliness. To move, however cautiously, into the ordinary world of friendship, of caring, of shared confidences, could be fatal. He was totally alone and that was how it must be. He must keep himself unencumbered for the task in hand.

16

And then, at last, on Thursday 31 August, she led him to them. The day had started like any other with himself at his room window, binoculars trained on the door of number 68. Mr Palfrey left as usual at quarter-past nine. He noted the time on his wrist-watch. It wasn't important, but he had grown into this habit of timing every move as if he were a fictional spy. Three minutes later he saw the woman. At once it struck him that there was something different about her, and he saw that she wasn't carrying her string shopping bag or trundling the trolley. All she had with her was a large old-fashioned handbag. She wore a fawn-coloured coat, undistinguished in cut, and a little too long for fashion, instead of her usual cardigan, and her face was obscured by an immense headscarf patterned in blue and white. There was only a gentle humming wind and the day wasn't cold; perhaps she wanted to keep her hair tidy. Most surprisingly, she was wearing fawn gloves, a touch of formality which reinforced his impression that this outing was different, that some attempt had been made at smartness.

He grabbed his rucksack and followed quickly. She was only fifty yards ahead and he saw that she was making her way towards Victoria. As he followed her across Eccleston Bridge and down the side of the station he worried in case she intended to join the queue for taxis at the front entrance and was relieved when she turned instead down the entrance to the Underground. She took a ticket from the thirty-five-pence machine. He found that he hadn't a fivepenny piece and there were two young tourists, rucksack-laden, who, pushing ahead of him, had already inserted ten pence and were taking their time over finding the necessary coins. But he had two tenpenny pieces ready in his hand. He inserted them quickly in the next machine and was able to follow a few yards behind her through the barrier and down to the Victoria line.

He kept as close behind her on the escalator as he dared, afraid that she might just catch a train; but he heard with relief a receding rumble before either of them reached the platform. The next came quickly, and the carriage was only half full. He took a seat close to the door, but distanced from her. She sat very still, unrelaxed, her eyes fixed on the opposite advertisements, feet together, gloved hands in her lap. She looked tense, preoccupied. Was it his imagination that she was bracing herself for some ordeal, rigid with the self-absorption of a victim on her way to a dreaded medical examination or a crucial interview?

She changed at Oxford Circus and he followed her on the long trek to the northbound Bakerloo line. Never once did she glance behind her. She got out at Marylebone and he followed her up the escalator clutching the fifty-pence piece in his hand and suddenly worried that the collector might be dilatory in giving him change for the outstanding fare. But all went well. The thirty-five pence were speedily and nonchalantly pressed into his hand and he was through the barrier before she was half-way across the concourse of Marylebone Station. Again, to his relief, she ignored the queue of three or four people at the taxi rank and made her way south towards Marylebone Road.

Here he let himself fall back a little. The crossing lights were against her and a solid stream of vehicles in both directions blocked her way. He guessed that it might be some time before the lights changed and he didn't want to stand close to her, the two of them alone at the crossing signal. But it was important to cross when she did. If he lost the lights there might be several minutes in which she could be lost in the criss-cross of streets south of the great divide of Marylebone Road. But again, all went well. He was only a few yards behind her as they crossed together, but she seemed unaware of his presence. She turned into Seymour Place.

And here was her destination, an imposing stone building with an elaborately carved coat of arms above the cornice. A name-plate told him that this was the Inner London Juvenile Court. Mrs Palfrey disappeared through the open double green door through which there came a babble of childish voices as piercingly discordant as a school playground. He walked on pondering his next move. Obviously she was neither a delinquent nor the mother of one. He knew that she didn't work here. That meant that she must be either a witness or a juvenile magistrate. The latter seemed to him unlikely, but in either case he had no way of knowing when she would emerge. At last he went resolutely inside and asked the policeman on duty if he could watch the proceedings. The answer was a polite no; the general public were not admitted to a juvenile court. He said:

'A friend of mine, a Miss Yelland, is one of the witnesses. I forget the name of the case, but I said I'd meet her here when it was over. When are they likely to finish?'

'Depends on the list, sir. And there's more than one juvenile bench sitting. If it's a defended case she could be here a long time. But they should be through by mid to late afternoon.'

He returned to the Marylebone Road. There was a seat beside the bus stop and he sat there to consider his next step. Would there be any point in killing time until Mrs Palfrey left at the end of the day? On reflection he decided that this was what he must do. After all, if what he believed was true, and the murderess and the girl were living together in this area, somewhere near to Regent's Park, Mrs Palfrey was reasonably close to them for the first time since he had been trailing her. There was always the chance that she would visit them on her way home. He would return in the late afternoon and wait for her to come out. It wouldn't be an easy doorway to keep watch on. There were no convenient bookshops opposite in which he could pretend to browse. He would have to return in good time and then walk slowly up and down Seymour Place, never out of sight of the courtroom entrance, yet never loitering so close that his presence would arouse interest. The slow parade, the need for constant watchfulness, would be tedious, but it shouldn't be too difficult to avoid suspicion. This was no village street with peering eyes behind the curtains. As long as he kept quietly walking, crossing the road from time to time at the traffic lights, it was unlikely that his comings and goings would be noticed. And what if they were? He told himself that he was getting unnecessarily careful. There were only three people from whom he must keep his presence secret and one of them was inside that building. In the meantime he decided to spend a couple of hours in the public library on Marylebone Road – the girl was someone who bought books and might even turn up there – and then walk in Regent's Park and revisit the rose garden. There was sure to be a place in upper Baker Street where he could buy a sandwich and coffee for lunch. He looked at his wrist-watch. It was now nearly ten o'clock. Shifting his rucksack more firmly on his shoulder he turned right towards Baker Street.

17

She had never really wanted to sit on the juvenile Bench, but Maurice had suggested with the persuasive force of a command that she ought to have what he described as 'some interest outside the kitchen', and the wife of one of his colleagues, herself a magistrate, had suggested the juvenile Bench and had put her name forward. Maurice had said:

'You ought to be able to make a useful contribution. The Bench is stolidly upper-middle class, self-perpetuating. They need shaking out of some of their comfortable misconceptions. And most of them haven't an idea what sort of lives their clients lead. You'll bring to the job a different experience.'

He meant, she knew, that she could bring to the job the experience of living in a small terraced house in the poorer part of Ruislip, of a state-school education, of being the only child of working-class parents who hung their window curtains patterned side outward because what determined conduct and comfort was what the neighbours thought, whose highest ambition for her had been a job as a bank clerk, who saved up to take their annual holiday in the same boarding-house at Brighton.

Sitting on the left of the chairman under the royal coat of arms, none of it seemed particularly relevant. Lady Dorothy, with whom she usually sat, brought to the job the experience of living in Eaton Square with weekends in a converted seventeenth-century rectory in Norfolk. Yet Lady Dorothy, if she didn't share the lives of the children and parents who stood before her in varying attitudes of resignation, sullenness or fear, seemed to have no difficulty in sharing their feelings. She dealt with them with a brisk common sense, tempered with more sensitivity than her heavy tweed-clad body and gruff arrogant voice would suggest. Scanning the social enquiry report with its mention of a common-law husband in prison, of too many children and too little of everything else, she would lean forward and say briskly to the mother of the boy before her:

'I see your husband's not at home at present. That must make it hard for you with four boys. And this office-cleaning job you're doing at Holborn; that's a long journey for you. How do you go? On the Central line?'

And the woman, apparently sensing an interest and compassion which the voice certainly didn't convey to Hilda, would crouch forward eagerly on the edge of her chair and pour it all out as if the courtroom had suddenly emptied and there was no one there except herself and Lady Dorothy: how that, yes, it had been hard, and that Wayne was a good boy at home only he missed his dad and had got in with the Billings gang, and how he wouldn't go to school because of the bullying and she'd tried taking him but it meant losing an hour's pay because she was supposed to start work at eight o'clock and, anyway, he only ran off again after the roll had been taken, and how her journey was all right except that she had to change at Oxford Circus and it was expensive because the tube fares had gone up and it was no use going by bus because they weren't all that reliable in the mornings.

Lady Dorothy would nod as if she had spent all her life changing at Oxford Circus to get to her cleaning job at Holborn. But some communication passed between them. An impulse of sympathy, if unspoken, was acknowledged and understood. The woman felt better at the end of it, and so, she supposed, did Lady Dorothy. Hilda remembered having overheard the words of a fellow justice:

'She treats them all as if they were the wives of her father's gamekeepers, but it seems to work.'

But what made every sitting of the juvenile court a long-drawn-out purgatory for Hilda was not her inadequacy as a justice – she was used to inadequacy by now – but her terror of blushing. It was worse some days than others, but she could never hope entirely to escape its anguish. At some stage in the proceedings, early or late, she knew that it was going to happen, that nothing could stop it; not will-power, not desperate prayer, and not the pathetic expedients she had devised to try to conceal it: the hand casually held up to shield her forehead as if in deep thought, the studious examination of her papers so that the hair hung over her cheeks, a paroxysm of simulated coughing, her handkerchief held to her face. She would feel first the clutch of fear at the heart, as physical as pain, and then it would begin, the burning flush spreading over her neck, mottling her face and forehead, a scarlet deformity of shame. She felt that every eye in the courtroom was fixed on her. The child with his parents, fidgeting in his chair, the clerk lifting his head from the court register to stare in wonder, the social workers watching with their pitying professional eyes, the chairman briefly pausing to glance at her before averting his eyes in embarrassment, the attendant police, stolidly gazing at her with their dead, controlled faces. And then the red pulsating tide would recede, leaving her momentarily as cold and cleansed as a wave-scoured beach.

Today she had managed to get through the morning session without too much trauma. The court rose at one and it was then the custom for the three magistrates to lunch together at a small Italian restaurant in Crawford Street. This morning her fellow magistrates were Group Captain Carter and Miss Belling. The Group Captain was a grey-haired, stiff-moving, punctilious man who treated her with an old-fashioned courtesy which she could sometimes mistake for kindness. Miss Belling, forthright and keen-eyed behind her immense horn-rimmed spectacles, was the senior English mistress at one of the outer London comprehensive schools. She made Hilda feel like a not particularly bright fourth-former, but as this accorded with her private view of herself she didn't resent it. Neither of them was particularly frightening and she might almost have enjoyed her lasagne and beaujolais if she hadn't been worried in case the Group Captain, always punctilious in enquiring about her family, should ask what Philippa was doing.

But the first case on the afternoon list had only been in progress for about twenty minutes when she felt the quickening drum of her heart and immediately the scarlet tide surged over her neck and face. She was holding her handkerchief in her lap and now she raised it to smother her mouth and nose, pretending to stifle an irritating spasm of coughing. During the morning session and in the intervals at lunch her restless hands had tangled the handkerchief to a moist rag. Now it smelled rankly of sweat, meat sauce and wine. As she hacked away, the simulated cough sounding unnatural even to her own ears, the social worker giving evidence hesitated, glanced at the Bench, then went on speaking. Miss Belling in the chair, without glancing at Hilda, pushed across the carafe of water. Hilda reached for the glass, her hands shaking. But as the water, stale and lukewarm, slid over her tongue she knew that the worst was over. This had been a mild attack. The scarlet tide was receding. She would be all right now until the session ended, all right until the next time.

Crumpling the handkerchief into her lap, she looked up and found herself staring into a pair of terrified eyes. At first she thought that the girl sitting alone two feet from the bench was the juvenile defendant. Then she remembered. This was a care case based on allegations of ill-treatment and the girl was the baby's mother. She was a wan-faced, lanky teenager with blonde straggling hair and a sharp narrow nose above a mouth whose top lip was full and curved, the lower slack and almost bloodless. She wore no make-up except for a smudged black line round her eyes. The eyes themselves were remarkable: large, grey and widely spaced. They looked into Hilda's with a desperate appeal.

For the first time Hilda noticed the incongruity of her dress. Someone must have advised her to wear a hat to court. Perhaps the wide-brimmed straw with the bunch of cherries with crushed and faded leaves drooping from the side of the brim had originally been bought for her wedding. She wore a faded fawn cotton top, faintly patterned with some slogan which had been washed out, above a short black skirt. On the top was pinned a metal brooch in the shape of a rose. It dragged at the thin cotton. Her legs were bare, the knees scabbed and knobbly as a child's. On her feet she wore sandals with thick cork soles and plastic straps wound round her ankles. She was nursing a bulging black handbag, old-fashioned in shape and very large, clutching it desperately to her chest as if afraid that one of the magistrates might leap from the bench and snatch it from her. And still her eyes gazed unwaveringly at Hilda. The fixed stare conveyed nothing but a wordless cry for help, but Hilda was aware of a more complicated and personal communication, an impulse of painful pity. She yearned to lean over the bench and stretch out her hands to the girl, to get out from her seat and fold the rigid body in her arms. Perhaps in that impossible embrace both of them would receive comfort. She too was under judgement, officially deemed incompetent, bereft of her child. Her lips cracked in an inadmissible smile. It wasn't returned. The girl – she looked little more than a child – was too petrified to respond even to so timid and suspect an attempt at friendship.

She seemed not to be listening as the local authority social worker continued her evidence. Her child, a ten-week-old boy, was now in a home under an interim care order and the local authority were applying for a second interim order while they prepared their case for the final hearing. At the end of the submission Miss Belling turned first to Group Captain Carter and then to Hilda. She whispered:

'We renew the interim care order then, for another twenty-eight days. That should give the local authority time to prepare their case.'

Hilda didn't reply. Miss Belling said again:

'We make an interim care order, then?'

Hilda found herself saying:

'I think we ought to talk about it.'

With no sign of irritation, Miss Belling informed the court that the magistrates would retire. Surprised, the court shuffled to its feet as Miss Belling led her colleagues out.

Hilda knew that there was nothing she could do or say which would make any difference, that this sick confusion of pity and outrage was futile. They had to protect the baby. The machinery of justice – majestic, well-meaning, fallible – would roll inexorably onward and there was nothing that she could do or say to halt it. And if it were stopped, then perhaps the baby might be harmed again, might even die. In the dull claustrophobic retiring-room her fellow justices were patient with her. After all, she hadn't given them any trouble before. Group Captain Carter attempted to explain what she already knew.

'We're only proposing a twenty-eight-day interim care order. The local authority won't be ready with their case for another three or four weeks. We must continue to protect the baby in the meantime. Then it will be for the court to decide what order to make.'

'But they took her baby away from her six weeks ago! Now she's got to wait another four weeks. And suppose they don't let her have him back even then?'

Miss Belling said with surprising gentleness:

'It's the court that will decide that. It's us, not some anonymous they. The child is being protected under an interim care order. That expires tomorrow. I don't think we can just ignore the local authority application for a second interim order; in effect that would mean sending the baby home. It's too big a risk. You heard the medical evidence, the round burns on the inside of the thighs suggestive of cigarette burns, the healed broken rib, the bruises to the buttocks. Those weren't caused accidentally.'

'But the social worker said that the husband had left home. He's walked out on them. If he's the one responsible then the baby will be all right now.'

'But we don't know whether he was the one responsible. We don't know who ill-treated the baby. It isn't our job to establish that in law. We aren't an adult criminal court. It's our job to consider the welfare of the child. We must continue to protect him until the substantive care proceedings.'

'But then she'll lose her baby completely, I know she will. He's only ten weeks old and they've been parted for six weeks. And who's going to talk for her?'

Miss Belling said:

'That's what worries me about these cases. Until the Government implements section sixty-four of the Children Act 1975 there's no chance of a mother in her situation having a lawyer from legal aid to look after her interests. The child gets the lawyer, not the parent. It's a scandal that section sixty-four hasn't been implemented. There ought to be some procedure for looking at Acts of Parliament which are never brought into force, or which are delayed as long as this. But that's not our concern. There's nothing we can do about it. What we have to do now is decide whether there is sufficient evidence to justify us making an interim order. I don't think we have any real choice. We can't prevent the husband from returning home any time he chooses; presumably the girl wants him to come home. And even if she didn't ill-treat the child herself, she was obviously powerless to prevent him from ill-treating it.'

Hilda whispered:

'I wish I could take her and the baby home with me.'

She thought of Philippa's room, so clean and empty. Philippa hadn't wanted it, had rejected it, but the girl would be safe and happy there. They could put the cot under the south window where it would get the sun. The girl looked as if she needed feeding up; it would be lovely to cook for someone who was really hungry. She heard Miss Belling say:

'You must try and remember what you were told when you were trained. The juvenile court isn't a welfare tribunal. The local authority has the job of looking after the child. We must act judiciously, within the law, within the rules.'

When they had resettled themselves on the bench and Miss Belling had briefly announced the expected decision, Hilda didn't again meet the girl's eyes. She was only aware that one moment the skinny figure clutching the outsized bag was standing like a condemned prisoner to receive sentence, and the next moment was gone. For the rest of the afternoon she made herself attend assiduously to every case. They passed before her, the sad procession of the inadequate, the criminal, the dispossessed. She read each social enquiry report with its catalogue of poverty, fecklessness, misery and failure and felt the increasing weight of her own powerlessness, her own inadequacy. After the session had ended, and as she stood alone in the sun outside the court house, she felt a sudden and overwhelming need to find Philippa, to see that she at least was all right. She wanted to speak to her. She knew that this wasn't possible. Philippa had made it plain that the break, however temporary, had to be complete. But she knew where they were, and Delaney Street was so very close. It wouldn't hurt just to have a look at the outside of their flat, find out exactly where they were.

She walked as usual with her eyes down, carefully avoiding the lines between the paving stones. She had known since early childhood that to step on the line was bad luck. She wondered whether this might be an unpropitious time to risk visiting Delaney Street. If they were both working, and surely they were, they might be coming home about now. It would be dreadful if she ran into them. Philippa would think that she was spying. She had been so insistent that she wanted to be private. No one was to be told where they were, no one was to call. She had only given Hilda the address so that her letters could be sent on, and so that they could contact her in an emergency. What kind of emergency, Hilda wondered. How ill would Maurice have to be before that counted as an emergency? She didn't believe that she herself would ever count. She prayed: 'Please God, don't let them see me.' Her life was punctuated by such desperate and irrational petitions. 'Please God, make the crème brûlée a success.' 'Please God, help me to understand Philippa.' 'Please God, don't make me blush this session.' 'Please God, make Maurice love me again.' The crème brûlée was invariably a success, but she could have managed that on her own. The other petitions, those extravagant demands for love, went unheard. It didn't surprise her. She had stopped going to church after her marriage and she could hardly expect her prayers to be answered when it was so apparent that she feared Maurice more than she feared God.

She made her way towards Marylebone Road without noticing the silent watcher about twenty yards down on the opposite pavement who hurried his footsteps so that he caught the traffic lights, crossed the road with her, and followed her at a careful distance past Marylebone Station, across Lisson Grove, and up Mell Street.

18

So he had found them at last. He stood looking down Delaney Street, outwardly composed, the mild eyes blinking behind his spectacles, but he could have reared his arms and shouted in exultation. A part of him, some memory of that boy who had knelt in the Methodist Chapel at Brighton, wanted to kneel now, to feel his knees pressing the hard pavement. He had been right, they were in London. They were here, within yards of where he stood, living in a flat above a greengrocer's shop at number 12. Here less than ten minutes ago he had seen Mrs Palfrey loiter, look up, walk quickly past the shop, retrace her steps, look up again. If she had been an *agent provocateur* paid to lead him to his quarry, she couldn't have improved on that mime of betrayal. After about two minutes of this pacing she had bought two oranges from the stall, her eyes slewing up to the flat windows, afraid perhaps that they might appear. He wondered why she was so nervous. Had the girl perhaps insisted on privacy? What exactly was the relationship between her and her adoptive parents, if adopted she had been? But of course she had been adopted. There could be no doubt that she was the murderess's daughter, and no doubt either that her name was now Palfrey. Perhaps her adoptive parents had disapproved of her leaving home. He felt a surge of fresh excitement when it occurred to him that this tentative visit by Mrs Palfrey might be the first step to a reconciliation. If the girl went back to Caldecote Terrace and abandoned the murderesss to live alone here then his task would be easy.

After buying the oranges she had walked more quickly than usual up Mell Street to the Edgware Road and had stood in the queue for the 26 bus to Victoria. She was on her way home. He need follow no longer. He had almost run back to Delaney Street, terrified that he might miss the sight of them, the confirmation that they were really here. But, standing at the corner of the street and looking down its drab length, he had no doubt. The intoxication of triumph and fear was familiar. He felt again the sick excitement of the ten-year-old boy standing on the wet sands under Brighton pier with the roar of the sea in his ears, holding in his small hands the spoils of his latest theft. Then, as now, he felt no guilt. It was extraordinary that during the years of innocence he had lived under a perpetual burden of guilt; paradoxically, only when he became a thief had that weight lifted. It was the same with Julie's death. He knew that when he drove the knife into Mary Ducton's throat he would drive out guilt from his mind for ever. He had no way of telling if he could free Mavis's spirit; he only knew how he could free his own.

And then they appeared. The sight of them was less traumatic than when he had seen them in Regent's Park, and he was better able to control himself. The girl shut the front door, saying something to her mother, and they both turned towards Mell Street. They were casually dressed, both wearing jeans and jackets; the girl had her travelling bag slung over her shoulder. He turned quickly to the right up Mell Street, judging that they would be on their way to Baker Street and the West End. But, glancing back, he saw that they were taking the same path and were only about forty yards behind him. He turned quickly down a side street and loitered there until he had seen them pass.

Back in Delaney Street he surveyed it like a strategist. Now that he knew they weren't there to observe him he could take his time. The problem was to know where, without attracting attention to himself, he could safely keep watch. The pub, the Blind Beggar, was an obvious possibility, quickly rejected. In a small London pub all the regulars were known to the publican and each other; a new and frequent customer would be noticed. They wouldn't force themselves on him; nowhere would he be safer from intrusion. But when the body was discovered he would be bound to be among the suspects. If he had to kill here on the murderess's home ground, the police would come with their photographs and questions. And depending on whether the publican and his customers had reason to oblige the police, someone sooner or later would talk. Besides, he drank very little and the prospect of sitting there in the fumes of tobacco and beer under the curious glances of the regulars, trying to make his pint last, repelled him. And it wouldn't really do as a vantage point. Like all Victorian pubs, he saw that little could be glimpsed of the interior from outside. Short of standing up and peering over the ornately painted glass, he would see nothing.

The bookshop next to the pub and the junk shop adjacent to the greengrocer's both afforded an opportunity to browse and loiter. But, here again, he would be noticed and remembered if he became too frequent a visitor. Perhaps the launderette was the best bet. The prospect of burdening himself with his small supply of spare clothes for frequent and unnecessary washing was a disadvantage; but then he told himself that he needn't wash anything. Once the launderette was reasonably busy, he had only to sit there patiently like the others with his plastic bag and newspaper, and it would be assumed that his washing was either being pounded in one of the washing machines, or was revolving in a drier. During Mavis's illness he had taken their sheets to the local launderette. He knew that it was common practice for people to come and go, shopping or visiting the pub until their washing was ready. But here too he would have to be careful. It was a less likely place for the police to make their enquiries, but he couldn't sit there day after day. It was a place, though, where the woman herself or her daughter might well come. Surely they would use a launderette so conveniently close.

More and more it seemed to him that he ought to try and get access to the flat. He walked slowly but purposefully down that side of the road and noticed the lock. It was a simple Yale, one of the easiest to force. The greengrocer's shop occupied what had obviously been the front room of the original house. He saw that there was a door at the side of the shop which must lead into the downstairs hall and that this, too, was fitted with a Yale.

He went across to the second-hand booksellers and began to look through the four trays of paperbacks set out on trestles. Suddenly it occurred to him to wonder why he was here, why he hadn't followed the murderess and her daughter. He had his knife with him. What had prevented him from following them and seizing his opportunity? It had been done before. He had read about it in newspapers often enough: the crowded pavement, the press of bodies at the tube station entrance, the silent attacker slipping in his knife and making his escape before the onlookers, embarrassed, then puzzled and finally horrified, realized what had happened. It was partly, he decided, that it had all been too sudden, too unexpected. Psychologically he wasn't yet ready for the kill. His mind had been preoccupied with the problem of tracking them down; he had not yet turned his thoughts to the deed itself. But there was something more important – that wasn't how it was meant to be, a sordid street crime, public, hurried, clumsy, perhaps even botched. That wasn't how he saw it. In his imaginings he and the murderess were alone together. She was lying on a bed asleep, her neck stretched out, the pulse beating. The execution, the plunge of the knife into her throat, would be unhurried, ceremonious, a ritual of justice and expiation.

The bookshop was a good place to loiter. A small part of the window obscured from within by the back of a bookcase acted as a mirror. Lifting his eyes from the grubby copy of *A Farewell to Arms* which he was pretending to study, he saw that the greengrocer was closing his shop, lugging the sacks of onions and potatoes to the back, piling up the boxes of tomatoes and lettuces, demolishing the careful pyramids of apples and oranges, and dragging the green artificial grass from the front trestle table. Scase put down his book and sauntered across the road to the junk shop. Here part of the pavement was piled with the cheaper items, a wood-topped desk with all the drawers missing, two cane-bottomed chairs with the seats sagging and split, a tin bath piled with cracked crockery. On the desk was a cardboard box almost filled with a tangle of old spectacles. He rummaged among them, picking out one or two pairs to hold before his eyes, as if testing the vision. Through a distorted haze he saw the greengrocer take off his fawn working coat and replace it with a blue denim jacket from a peg at the back of the shop. Then he disappeared for a second and came back with a pole with a hook on the end and clanged down the metal front to the shop.

A few seconds later he came out of the front door, shut it firmly behind him and made his way up Delaney Street. So he didn't live above the shop. But he would still need a key to the Yale lock on the front door since the shop-front had been locked from the inside and there was no other way he could get in to open up the premises except through the front door. He would keep the key on him, perhaps on a ring with others, perhaps in the pocket of his jacket. He had been wearing tight-fitting jeans with two back pockets, both lying flat against the curve of the buttocks. There had been no key there. Almost automatically Scase picked up one pair of spectacles after another and turned them over in his hands. Perhaps it might be worth while buying a pair or two if he could find some which weren't too distorting to his vision. A change of spectacles would alter his appearance. He had never before thought of disguise, since it seemed an art beyond his capacity. But there was one skill he knew he had. It was many years since he had exercised it but then it had never once let him down. He didn't think it would let him down now. He could pick pockets.

The exhilaration of knowing that he had found them at last was so intoxicating that he could hardly bear to leave Delaney Street. But the door of number 12 was locked against him, there was nowhere he could safely conceal himself and he needed to get back to the safety and anonymity of his attic room, needed time to rest and think and plan. Before leaving he walked for the last time down the street, surveying the possibilities. It was then that he noticed the narrow passage which led down the side of the Blind Beggar, and which was flanked by the grimy brick wall of the pub and by the corrugated-iron fence about seven feet high which surrounded the acre of weed-infested wasteland. He saw that the panels which faced Delaney Street, rusting, the concrete supports no longer firmly upright, had sagged apart in places producing slits from which it would be possible to keep watch on the street. The problem was to gain access to the wasteland and to check that there were no high windows in surrounding buildings from which the vantage point could be observed.

He glanced quickly up and down the street, then stepped into the passageway. If challenged he would have a credible excuse ready; he would say apologetically that he was looking for a lavatory. He quickly saw that his explanation would have more plausibility than he had realized. The passage led to a small yard smelling strongly of beer and less strongly of urine and coal dust. To the right was the back door of the pub and in front of him an outside coal store, now disused, and a wooden door with a slit at the top and bottom on which the word 'Gents' had been crudely painted.

He darted into the lavatory and shut the bolt. Through the top slit he could see one dingy and heavily curtained upstairs window at the back of the pub, and could examine the fence. Here it was even less secure than in the front, and the gap between two of the panels was, he thought, sufficiently wide to enable a slim man to force his way through. After dark it could probably be done with some safety, despite the old-fashioned lamp which projected on brackets at the corner of the pub wall. But this was late summer, a miserably cold and disappointing summer but the light still lasted well into the evening. Unless there were no upper windows overlooking the wasteland, his time of observation might have to be restricted to the hours of darkness.

The huge wooden seat almost engulfed him. It must have been here as long as the pub itself. He slid his thin buttocks to its edge and crouched there, keen as a cornered animal, all his senses alert. There were no voices from the house. He could hear no footfalls, no shouts from Delaney Street and even the rumble of traffic passing down Mell Street was muted. The reek of disinfectant was pungent as a gas. A thin drizzle had begun to fall and the wind was rising, blowing a mist through the slit of the door, obscuring his spectacles. He took out his handkerchief to wipe them and saw that his hand was shaking. He thought it strange that this particular moment, closeted as he was in safety, unobserved, should be so traumatic. Perhaps it was a delayed reaction to the shock of finding them at last.

It was time to go. Having made up his mind he left the shed swiftly and with his shoulder pressed against the most vulnerable panel of the fence. It gave slightly. With his hand he pulled the second panel forward, aware of the sharp edge of the metal biting into his hand. The gap widened. He slipped through, the rucksack under his arm.

It was like stepping into a garden. As he worked his way round in the shadow of the fence the weeds were almost waist-high. They looked so fragile with their small pink flowers, yet they had forced their way through this impacted earth, in places splitting the concrete. Where they were highest he paused to survey the waste-land. It was better for his purpose than he had dared to hope. There was only one gate. This faced Delaney Street and he could see that it was barred and padlocked. Once there had been a row of houses there, now demolished, he supposed, for redevelopment, and in front of him was a blank windowless wall where the neighbouring house had been sliced away. There were no windows in the side wall of the Blind Beggar and the area was bounded on the fourth side by a glass and concrete building which looked like a school. He might possibly be seen from its upper windows, but the building would be empty after school hours unless, of course, it was used for evening classes. But surely not in summer? He would have to find out.

Then he realized that it might not be necessary. He could be in luck. Two decrepit vehicles, a battered van and the chassis of a car, wheel-less and with its left door hanging loose, had been parked or dumped within a few yards of the Delaney Street boundary. They could shield him from any prying eyes from the school if only they were in the right place, standing against a part of the fence where the panels weren't completely joined. Even so, vision would be restricted. Ideally he needed to be exactly opposite the door to number 12. He worked his way towards them, still keeping close to the iron fence as if its height and corrugated surface could somehow confuse an onlooker and make him invisible.

He quickened his pace as he approached the van, the first of the abandoned vehicles, resisting the urge to run for its comforting cover. When at last he reached it, he stood panting with relief, eyes closed, back pressed against the fence. After a few seconds he made himself open his eyes and look round the wasteland. It was still deserted but more desolate now as the drizzle turned to a slanting rain and the clumps of weeds strained against the fretful, changeable wind. Then he turned to examine the fence. It was as he had hoped; there was a gap just below eye-level. It wasn't exactly opposite the greengrocer's shop, but it was close enough and the gap sufficiently wide to give him an uninterrupted view.

He stood there, legs slightly bent, arms wide, fingers clutching at the curve of the iron, staring at the closed door of number 12, watching and waiting. The rain fell steadily, soaking his shoulders, running in rivulets under his jacket collar. He tried to wipe his streaming spectacles but his handkerchief was quickly soaked. The street lamp at the corner of Delaney Street was switched on, laying a shivering gleam on the wet pavement. Somewhere a church clock struck the quarters, the half-hours, the sonorous chimes of nine, ten and eleven o'clock. The swish of passing cars down Mell Street became less frequent. The noise from the pub grew, became raucous, then faded with a clatter of departing feet and the last valedictory shouts. And still they didn't come. From time to time he stretched himself upright to ease the intolerable ache of shoulders and legs, but bent his eyes again to the gap whenever he heard a footfall. It was half-past eleven before they returned home. He watched them – both, it seemed, drooping a little with tiredness – as the girl felt in her bag for her keys. They spoke together easily, casually, as she pushed the door open. And then they were inside and it closed behind them. A few seconds later the two windows on the first floor became oblongs of pale light. Only then, so cramped that he could hardly move, aware for the first time of hunger, of his jacket and shirt heavy as wet poultice against his back, he forced himself once more through the gap in the fence and made his painful way to Baker Street Station and took the Circle line to Victoria.

19

When Maurice got home late that afternoon the kitchen, although lit, was empty. He found Hilda in the garden. She was standing at the wrought-iron table arranging a cut-glass bowl of roses. It was a shallow, crudely shaped bowl and it took a second or two before he could remember how they had come by it. Her parents had given it to them as a wedding present. He could picture them conferring anxiously over it, spending more money than they could afford. He remembered, too, that his mother had owned one very like it. He had never been trusted to help wash it up. She had made trifle in it for Sunday tea, a layer of bought sponge cakes covered with jelly and topped with thick synthetic custard. This bowl was filled with crumpled wire to hold the roses. As Hilda forced in each stem the wire scraped against the glass, setting his teeth on edge. The roses had been picked too late and over-handled. Surely Philippa, when she did flowers for the drawing-room, always cut them early in the day and left them in the cool, standing in water. These lay in a flabby heap on the table, their heads already drooping, their stems lax.

Suddenly he decided that he didn't like roses. It was a surprising discovery to make at this particular moment and after so many years. They were an over-praised flower, soon blowzy, their beauty dependent on scent and poetic association. One perfect bloom in a specimen vase placed against a plain wall could be a marvel of colour and form, but flowers ought to be judged by how they grew. A rose garden always looked messy, spiky recalcitrant bushes bearing mean leaves. And the roses grew untidily, had such a brief moment of beauty before the petals bleached and peeled in the wind, littering the soil. And the smell was sickly, the stuff of cheap scent. Why had he ever imagined that it gave him pleasure?

Hilda, dissatisfied with her arrangement and pulling out the stems to start again, had pricked herself. There was a bead of blood on her thumb. 'Died of a rose in aromatic pain.' Browning or Tennyson? Philippa would have known. While his mind was tracing the source of the quotation, she said peevishly:

'I miss Philippa doing the flowers. It's too much, cooking the meal and trying to make the table look nice.'

'Yes, Philippa had a pleasant decorative sense. Are those for tonight?'

Immediately she looked up at him, defensive, worried.

'Won't they do?'

'Isn't the arrangement too large? People need to be able to see each other over the flowers. You can't talk to someone you can't see.'

'Oh, talking!'

'Talking is what a dinner party's about. And they smell too strong. We want to smell the food and wine. Roses on the dinner table confuse the senses.'

She said with the note of sulky truculence which he found particularly irritating and which he had heard more frequently since Philippa's departure:

'I don't seem to be able to do anything right.'

'Right? Right for whom?'

'Right for you. I don't know why you married me.'

As soon as the words were out of her mouth she stared at him appalled, or so it seemed to him; as if there were words between which their minds could formulate, but which it would be fatal to speak aloud. He picked up one of the roses. The blossom drooped over his palm. He said, hearing the coldness in his voice:

'I married you because I was fond of you and because I thought we could be happy together. If you aren't happy you must try to tell me what's worrying you.'

It was paradoxical that the truth could sound so false, could be so much less than the truth. If he had loved her enough he could have made himself lie and say, 'Because I loved you.' But if he had loved her enough the lie wouldn't have been necessary. She muttered:

'You needn't talk to me as if I'm one of your students. I know you think I'm stupid, but you don't have to patronize me.'

He didn't reply, but stood watching her as she forced the last rose stem through the crumpled wire, grazing its stem. But the arrangement was top-heavy and the entangled wire keeled over on to the table spilling rose petals, pollen and dollops of water. She gave a little moan and began dabbing at the water with her handkerchief. She said:

'Philippa leaving, you blamed me for that. I know what you thought. I couldn't give you a child of your own and I couldn't even make the adopted one stay with me.'

'That's ridiculous, and you must know that it is. I could have stopped Philippa leaving, but I wasn't prepared to pay the price. Philippa must find her own way back to reality.'

She said, so quietly that he could only just catch the words:

'It would have been different if I'd been able to have a baby.'

He felt a tremor of pity, transitory, but strong enough to make him unwise. He heard himself speaking:

'That reminds me, there's something I meant to tell you. I went to see Dr Patterson last week. There's nothing wrong, it was only a check-up. But he got out my records and confirmed what I half guessed when we saw the specialist together twelve years ago. I'm the one who's infertile. It's nothing to do with you.'

She stared at him, rose in hand. She said:

'But you had Orlando!'

He said sharply:

'It's nothing to do with Orlando. It happened after he was born. The doctor puts it down to an attack of mumps I had when he was six weeks old. These things aren't uncommon. There's nothing to be done about it.'

She stared at him; her full unwinking gaze was unnerving. He wanted to turn away, dismissing the inconsequent detail of his infertility with a nonchalant shrug, a wry smile at the perversity of fate. But his eyes were held by that dumb unwinking stare. He cursed himself for his folly. Because of a bowl of ruined roses, because of a moment of futile compassion, he had blurted it out. Not the whole truth, he had never imagined himself telling that, but a part of the truth, the essential truth. A secret he had kept for twelve years, a part of him which he had become fond of, as one might a slightly disreputable friend, was his no longer. He had reacted to his particular guilty secret as he supposed the majority of his fellow men did to theirs. Most of the time he had been able to forget it, not by any conscious effort of will, but because it was as much a part of him as his digestion, unintrusive unless it gave trouble. Occasionally it would come into his mind and he would cogitate upon it as an interesting and intriguing complication of his personality which repaid study, much as he might cogitate about the complexities of a student's style. Sometimes he had even enjoyed it. A guilty secret is, nevertheless, a secret and can be relished with at least some of the innocence of childhood conspiracies. Sometimes, but increasingly rarely, it had intruded into his waking thoughts and provoked disagreeable sensations of distress and worry, even slight physical manifestations of quickened breath which he would have diagnosed as guilt and shame if those were words which he had ever cared to use. And now it was no longer his secret. He had borne its weight for twelve years and now he would have to shoulder the burden of her reproach, her renewed disappointment. Self-pity took hold of him. Why should she stare at him like that with those amazed unbelieving eyes? He was the one who was entitled to understanding. It was he, not she, who was maimed. She said:

'You've known all the time, haven't you? It isn't true that you've been to Dr Patterson. You knew when we first had those tests, when you said that you didn't want to go on with them any longer, that you'd had enough. And you let me think it was my fault that we couldn't have a child. All those years, you let me think it was me.'

'It's no one's fault. It's not a question of fault.'

He must have been mad to think for one moment that all that was lacking between them was truth. The tragedy of his marriage – except that tragedy was too grand a word for such a commonplace misfortune – was not that she always made the wrong response to his needs; it was that there was no right response which it was within her power to make. She said accusingly:

'I could have had a child if I hadn't married you.'

'You might have had. That supposes that you would have married someone else, that he wanted a child, that both of you were capable of parenthood.'

She had dropped her eyes at last. Clumsily gathering up the roses, she whispered sulkily:

'There were other men that liked me. George Bocock liked me.'

Who in God's name was George Bocock, he wondered. The name struck a chord. Of course, that pimply youth who had been a clerk in the university admissions office. So he had been competing with George Bocock. If that didn't puncture self-esteem, nothing would.

At dinner she was more withdrawn than usual – less, he thought, from her customary shyness, than because she was preoccupied with her private thoughts. It wasn't until they were alone together in the bedroom that they had an opportunity to talk. Then she said, forcing out the words belligerently as if half expecting him to remonstrate:

'I want to give up the juvenile Bench.'

'Resign your commission. Why?'

'I'm not any good at it. I don't help anyone. And I don't like it. I'll finish this three-month stint, but I won't do any more.'

'If you feel like that, then there's no point in going on. You'd better write to the Lord Chancellor's office. But I suggest you try to think of some less childish reason.'

'Not doing any good, not being able to help anyone isn't a childish reason.'

'What will you do with the extra time? Do you want me to talk to Gwen Marshall about the possibility of school-care work? They're always looking for suitable people.'

'Why should I be any better at that? I can fill up my time.'

She paused, and then said:

'I want a dog.'

'In London? Is that fair? It won't be easy to exercise him.'

'There are places, the Embankment Gardens, St James's Park.'

'I should have thought there were enough dogs fouling the public parks. But if you're sure, you'd better decide what breed you want and we'll find some reputable kennels. We could do it this week-end.'

His magnanimity surprised him. And perhaps it wasn't such a bad idea. She and Philippa hadn't exactly been companions, but the house probably seemed empty without her. A dog needn't inconvenience him if the animal were properly trained. They could drive to the kennels that weekend, make an excursion of it.

She said:

'I don't care about the breed. I want a stray from the Battersea Dogs' Home. I want to pick one out for myself.'

He said irritably:

'Really Hilda, if you're determined on a dog, at least get a good-looking animal.'

'I don't care about good looks. You and Philippa do, but I don't. I want a stray, a dog no one has claimed, one who'll have to be destroyed if they can't find it a home.'

She turned from the dressing-table and spoke for the first time with animation, almost pleadingly:

'He won't make a mess in the garden. I know how you feel about the roses. I'll see he doesn't get on the flower beds. I could train him. He can live in a basket in the kitchen. And he won't be expensive. We waste a lot of food he could eat, and Mr Pantley would be obliging with bones for him. I'm a good customer.'

He said:

'It's all right I suppose, as long as you take responsibility for him.'

It was like humouring an importunate child. She said sadly:

'Oh yes, I'll do that. I'll look after him. That's one thing I can do.'

'If, in making your choice, you could contrive to be attracted to one of the smaller and less yapping varieties, you would oblige me.'

She knew then that it was going to be all right. She remembered that Philippa had once said that when Maurice spoke like a character in a Jane Austen novel it meant that he was in a good mood. The literary allusion meant nothing to her, but she had learnt to recognize the tone. She would be able to have her dog. She pictured him bright-eyed, head cocked up at her, tail quivering. It was no good naming him before she'd chosen him. She would have to see what he looked like. But she rather liked the name Scamp. Maurice and Philippa would say that it was too ordinary, too common; but that was the kind of dog she wanted. Lying down in the single bed in which Maurice now so seldom joined her, she felt a surge of confidence, almost of power. She wasn't barren after all. It was his fault, not hers. She needn't spend her life making up to him for a deprivation which was nothing to do with her. And after this three-month stint she need never sit on the Bench again.

BOOK THREE
Act of Violence

1

And now he moved with a mounting sense of excitement away from his settled routine at Pimlico and into a new world, their world. And the act itself was no longer hidden in an unknown future; the time had come to prepare himself physically and mentally for the deed. But he perceived a difference in himself. Shadowing Mrs Palfrey, he, the follower, had nevertheless felt himself to be in control. She led and he shadowed, but the invisible cord between them had reined her to his controlling hands. It seemed to him that he had followed her in a state of gentle euphoria, unstressed by anxiety, certain that in the end she would lead him to his prey. Her loneliness, the sad futility of her life, the inevitability of her betrayal, had even bred in him a sense of pity and comradeship.

It was different now; he was on enemy ground. He was shadowing two women, not one, and the girl had seen him and would recognize him again. He still remembered that moment in the rose garden with a mixture of shame and horror. And she was younger, keener-eyed, swifter, almost certainly more intelligent. His task had become infinitely more difficult and the risk of discovery greater. He would have to take his time, move with more cunning. The first task must be to watch from his hiding-place on the waste ground and try to get some idea of their daily routine.

It took him a week to discover where they went when they set out every evening at five o'clock. For three days he followed them at a distance up Mell Street, then watched from the shelter of a chemist's doorway until they mounted a number 16 bus going north up the Edgware Road. The next day he secreted himself closer to the bus stop until they arrived, then mounted the bus after them. They took seats on the lower deck, so he went quickly up the stairs. He took a ticket to the terminus to avoid giving a destination, then watched from the window at every stop to see where they got off. When at last, after a twenty-minute ride, he saw them alight at Cricklewood Broadway, he made his way down the stairs, jumped off at the first red traffic light, and hurried back. But he was too late, they were nowhere in sight.

The next evening he again took the bus, hurrying out of his hiding-place to join it once they were safely aboard, and again taking a seat on the top deck. But this time he was ready to alight, and he didn't lose them. He was thirty yards behind them as they entered a fish-and-chip restaurant, Sid's Plaice. He strolled past and joined a queue at the next bus stop, waiting to see if they emerged. After about ten minutes he strolled past the shop and looked through the glass window at the rows of formica-topped tables. They were nowhere to be seen. It didn't surprise him; he had hardly supposed they would travel so far for an evening meal. So this was where they worked. The choice surprised him; but then he understood. They needed to take a job where the daughter would be in no danger of meeting people she knew, could be sure that no one would ask questions.

After that he knew that he could relax his watch every evening between five o'clock and eleven. He couldn't kill her during their bus journeys, nor while she was at work. But what about that late lonely walk down Mell Street? He pictured himself waiting for them one night, straining himself against the door to avoid being seen, knife ready. Then the lunge at her throat, the one word 'Julie' spoken so low that only she would hear, the vicious double twist, the tearing flesh as the knife was wrenched free, and then his feet pounding down Delaney Street to the shelter of – where? It wouldn't work; nothing about it rang true. That quick withdrawing knife, suppose it stuck, twisted in her muscles, was caught behind a bone? He would need time to force it out. He couldn't leave the knife in the wound. Surely the blood must flow freely if she were to die. And the girl would be there, younger, stronger, swifter than he. How could he hope to get away?

Never once during the first week of his surveillance did he see them apart. They were together all day and, more important, they stayed together all night. Since he had rejected the idea of an attack on the murderess in the street, his plan depended on knowing when the girl had left her alone in the flat. He would have to find an excuse for calling, particularly after dark, but that shouldn't be difficult. He would say that he had an urgent message from Caldecote Terrace for Philippa Palfrey. The fact that he knew the girl's name and previous address would ensure that the murderess would at least let him in. And that was all he needed. It would be better if he could kill her while she slept; cleaner, more certain, less horrible, more seemly. But all he needed was to come face to face with her in that flat, and alone.

He followed them on their daily excursions; not because he expected an opportunity to kill, but because he was restless when they weren't in sight. It was simple enough to trail them on the Underground. They usually went from Marylebone, the nearest station. He supposed that, on that first journey from King's Cross, the girl had chosen Baker Street or Edgware Road on the Circle line to save them the time and trouble of a change of line. He would walk behind them at a safe distance, linger in the entrance tunnel while they stood on the platform, then enter a different compartment and stand at the door throughout the journey so that he could watch when they got off. After that it became more difficult. Sometimes prudence made him hang back and lose them. Occasionally they walked along the lonelier reaches of the river, through remote Georgian squares in Islington or the City, where any follower would have been conspicuous. Then he would stand and watch them through his binoculars over the parapet of a bridge, or from the shelter of a church porch or shop doorway, motionless until the two golden heads were out of sight.

It had become less important to trail them, to keep them in sight, than to share their lives, to experience vicariously their interests and pleasures. He had become obsessed with them, itchy with restlessness when he was parted from them, terrified, despite the evidence of their settled way of life, that he might arrive one morning at Delaney Street to find them gone. He noted with obsessive concern the small details of their shared life: that it was the girl who seemed to be in control, who organized their lunching arrangements, taking the oblong plastic picnic box from her shoulder bag and handing it, opened, to her mother; that it was the girl who bought the tickets, who carried the map. He no longer thought of them apart and this, when it occurred to him, was worrying. One night he even had a confused nightmare in which it was the girl whom he killed. She was lying on his bed at the Casablanca, naked, and the wound in her throat was bloodless but gaping, like moistly parted lips. He turned round, the dripping knife in his hand, appalled at his mistake, to find his mother and the murderess standing together in the doorway and clutching at each other, screaming with laughter. The terror stayed with him next day and, for the first time since he had found them, it took an effort of will to leave the shelter of his room.

He was bound to them by hate; he was bound to them, too, by envy. He never saw them touch, they didn't often talk together; when they smiled it was the spontaneous smile of two people who laugh at the same things. They were like friends, undemonstrative, companionable, uneffusive, sharing their days because there was, at present, no other person with whom they preferred to be. So might he have walked and smiled and been companionable with his daughter.

He might have gone on like that for weeks, following them during the daytime, returning to the hotel for his dinner, then waiting behind the iron fence at night, until at last he heard their returning footsteps, the door of number 12 close behind them, and saw the twin oblongs of light shine out from their windows. He hardly knew what he was hoping for, crouching there in the darkness. The girl was hardly likely to leave her mother alone in the flat so late at night. But until the light was finally extinguished he could not bear to leave. And then, on the morning of Saturday 9 September, everything changed.

They were shopping in Mell Street market, as they had on the previous Saturday, and he was shadowing them, anonymous in the milling crowd, watching from the shelter of the antique supermarket, from behind the bric-à-brac stalls, stepping back if their heads turned his way to conceal himself among the swinging hangers of cotton shirts, summer dresses and long printed Indian skirts. It was a bright, warm morning after an early mist and Mell Street was crowded. He was standing at the stall which sold mangoes and huge bunches of unripe bananas to the West Indian women, listening to their high staccato jabber and looking across the road to where the murderess and her daughter were rummaging in a cardboard carton of old linen. They seemed to be searching for pieces of lace. On the edge of the stall was an Australian bush-ranger's hat, broad-brimmed, turned up at the side. Suddenly the girl took it and perched it on her head. Her unbraided golden hair was flowing loose, a swinging curtain of gold. The strap of the hat hung under her chin. She turned on her heel towards her mother and tipped back the brim of the hat in a gesture defiant and debonair. Then she began searching in her shoulder bag for the money. She had bought it, that gallant, ridiculous hat. And the murderess laughed! Across the width of the road, above the rich West Indian voices, above the shouts of the hawkers, the hysterical barking of the dogs, he could hear the laughter, a peal of joyous, spontaneous mirth.

She was laughing. Julie was dead, Mavis was dead, and she was laughing. He was shaken not by anger, which he could have borne, but by a terrible grief. Julie was rotting in her grave. Her life had been choked out of her almost before it had begun. This woman was laughing, opening her throat to the sun. He had no child. She had her daughter alive, healthy, exulting in her candescent beauty as if nourished vampire-like by Julie's blood. They walked in freedom. He slunk behind them like a scavenging animal. They sat companionably together in their shared home and smiled, talked, listened to music. He crouched alone in the cold, night after night, peering like a sexual voyeur through that slit in the wall. He heard again the voice of his Auntie Gladys, dead now like his mother, like Mavis, like Julie. She, being dead, yet speaketh: 'That boy gives me the willies. He creeps round the place like a sodding animal.' Is thy servant a dog that he should do this thing? He might as well cock his leg against the door of the derelict car that sheltered him and void his inadequacy, his self-disgust. The voice of his mother, as clear as if the words had once actually been spoken: 'Murder! You! Don't make me laugh.'

He found that he was crying, soundless, wordless, unassuageable tears. They poured over his face, seeped like salty rain into his quavering mouth, splashed over his unavailing hands. He walked on through the crowds, seeing nothing. There was nowhere he could go, nowhere he could hide. There was no place in London where a man could cry in peace. He thought of Julie, anxious eyes behind the steel National Health spectacles, the brace on her teeth, a thin face armoured with metal. He so seldom admitted that shadowy face into his mind. The greatest horror of murder was that it degraded the memory of the dead. If Julie had died in illness, been killed in a road accident, he could have thought of her now with sadness, but with a measure of acceptance and in peace. Now all memories of his child were corrupted by anger, by a half-salacious horror, by hate. All pictures of her childhood had superimposed on them like a faulty print the horror and humiliation of her dreadful end. The murderers had robbed him even of the common tribute which humanity pays to its dead. He seldom remembered, because it was too uncomfortable to remember. If both of them had hanged, would that have cleansed his thoughts or added a new dimension of horror to her death?

He found that he had walked the length of Mell Street and now trembled on the very edge of the pavement where the stream of traffic flowed down the Edgware Road. He found himself longing for what he now thought of as home, that small high room at the Casablanca. But he had made a decision. This was the end of trailing after them like an animal twitching at the end of its string. If nothing could separate them, then he would have to get access to their flat. He would have to creep in at night when the murderess would be sleeping alone. And that meant that the time had come to steal the keys.

<h2 style="text-align:center">2</h2>

Since they had tacitly agreed that it was not yet time to talk about the lost years of their separation, they talked a great deal about books. With the past outlawed and the future uncertain, English literature was at least a shared experience which they could discuss without embarrassment or constraint, the safest of subjects. It was the more ironic that it should be a minute of commonplace literary chat over breakfast on Friday 15 September that led them directly to Gabriel Lomas.

Philippa asked:

'What did you read inside as well as Shakespeare?'

'The Victorian novelists mostly. The library was better than you'd think. There are two main requirements for cell literature: inordinate length and the writer's ability to create a distinctive and alternative world. I'm the prison-service authority on three-volume novels about intelligent, masochistic women who perversely marry the wrong man or no man at all; you know, *Portrait of a Lady*, *Middlemarch*, *The Small House at Allington*.'

Philippa asked:

'Weren't the books spoilt for you, reading them in prison?'

'No, because, while I was reading them, I wasn't in prison. *Middlemarch* kept me sane for six weeks. There are eighty-six chapters and I rationed myself to two a day.'

Middlemarch was first published in 1871. They would have hanged her mother then, but not in public. Surely public executions were stopped three years earlier. Maurice would know. She said:

'I don't think I'd have had that amount of self-control. *Middlemarch* is a marvellous novel.'

'Yes, but it would be more marvellous if the sexual conventions had let George Eliot be more honest. A novel must be flawed if one of its main themes is the story of a marriage and we can't even be told whether the marriage is consummated. Do you think Casaubon was impotent?'

'Yes, don't you? All the evidence is there.'

'But I don't want to have to deduce facts from evidence in a realistic novel. I want to be told. I know that the Victorians couldn't be explicit, but surely they needn't have been quite so timid.'

Philippa said:

'Timidity is about the last adjective I'd associate with George Eliot. But if you're feeling critical about Victorian writing, why not indulge yourself with Victorian art? It might be fun to go to the exhibition of great Victorian paintings at the Royal Academy this morning. I think it closes on the seventeenth. Afterwards we could go on as planned to the Courtauld Institute, if that won't be a surfeit of painting.'

'I don't think I could have a surfeit of anything now, not even of pleasure.'

And so, at last, they met someone from Philippa's past. That didn't, in itself, matter. She had always known that it was inevitable. What did matter was that it should be Gabriel Lomas.

He came up behind them quietly while they were in the inner gallery, standing in front of Alma-Tadema's *The Baths of Caracalla* and studying the catalogue note. He was alone, which was surprising; but it was surprising that he should be there at all. There was no way in which Philippa could have avoided the introduction and she had no intention of trying. She touched her mother's arm and said:

'This is a friend of mine, Gabriel Lomas. Gabriel, my mother. She's in London and we're spending the day together.'

He hid his surprise admirably. For a second – no more – his

arrogant mobile face froze and his hands tightened on the catalogue. Then he said easily:

'How pleasant for you both. But why not tear yourselves away from these glittering eyeballs and recover with lunch at Fortnum and Mason? Afterwards I thought of going to the Tate. The Henry Moore exhibition is finished, but one doesn't need an excuse for visiting the Tate.'

His mouth smiled, his voice held exactly the right mixture of interest and pleasure, but his eyes, carefully avoiding too keen a scrutiny of her mother, were the eyes of an inquisitor. Gazing steadily at his face, Philippa said:

'No thank you, Gabriel. We're going on to the Courtauld Galleries and lunching later. We've planned rather a full day.'

He would, she knew, be both too well bred and too proud to insist or to force his company on them. He said:

'I telephoned your adoptive mother a couple of weeks ago. She told me that you'd gone to earth. She was intriguingly mysterious.'

'She needn't have been. Didn't she explain that I'm spending two months in London on my own? I'm trying to find out if I can support myself in anything approaching the manner Maurice has accustomed me to. And I'm gaining experience for a book.'

That second explanation sounded pretentious and it was one she would have preferred not to make. But unlike the first, it rang true. Half the upper sixth were probably even now picking up experience for a first novel, as if experience lay like litter on the comfortable surface of their lives.

He said:

'What about Paris, Rome, Ravenna? I thought you said you'd been saving to embark on the Grand Tour before Cambridge.'

'Not so grand. The mosaics at Ravenna will wait. I have a lifetime to see them. But this experiment is now or never.'

'Why not take an evening off from it and come to the ballet – both of you?'

The flick of his eyes towards her mother was amused, inquisitive. She said:

'No thank you, Gabriel. I'm seeing no one. The whole thing will lose its point if I see friends whenever I'm lonely or go home as soon as I'm uncomfortable.'

'You don't look at all comfortable now. On the other hand you're obviously not lonely.'

Her mother had moved a little apart, ostensibly studying her catalogue, dissociating herself from them. He glanced at her, this time with overt curiosity and something like contempt. He said:

'Until Cambridge, then.'

'Until Cambridge.'

'Can I drive you up?'

'Oh Gabriel, I don't know! It all seems so far ahead. Perhaps. I'll be in touch.'

'Ah well, *abiit, excessit, evasit, erupit*. Give my love to the Sisley.'

'What Sisley?'

'*Snow at Lucienne*. That is, if you're really on your way to the Courtauld. And good luck with the experiment.'

He raised his eyebrow and made a small rueful grimace which might have been intended to express regret, but in which she thought she detected a hint of complicity. Then he turned and bowed to her mother and was gone. Philippa went up to her and said:

'I'm sorry about that. I thought he was out of London. Actually he's the last person I should have expected to find here and alone. He affects to despise Victorian art. But we were bound to run across someone I knew sooner or later. I don't mind if you don't.'

'I mind your not being able to invite them home.'

Invite them home. The words conjured up suburban tea-time in the front room, home-made scones on doilies, fish-paste sandwiches, the best tea service brought out so that she wouldn't be disgraced by the family in front of this unknown, eligible young man. Since she had never sat in such a room, it was odd that she knew precisely how it would be. She said:

'But I don't want to. We're perfectly cosy on our own. I shall have three years of Gabriel at Cambridge. You're not bored are you?'

'No. Not bored. Never that.'

'What did you think of him?'

'He's very good-looking, isn't he? Good-looking and confident.'

'He can afford to be. Nothing has ever happened to him to dislodge him from the centre of his universe.'

But one small thing had happened. She felt a twinge of anxiety. Had he really accepted that sexual failure philosophically? Wasn't he a man who would need his small revenge? As if echoing her thoughts, her mother said:

'I think he could be dangerous.'

'He'd be flattered to hear you say so; but he's no more dangerous than any other young male animal, and he's not dangerous to us. No one can be.'

Donne's words came into her mind, but she did not speak them aloud: 'Who is so safe as we where none can do Treason to us, except one of we two.'

She wondered whether her mother had read Donne. She said:

'Forget him. He hasn't spoilt the day for you, has he?'

'No, he couldn't do that. No one could.' She paused as if wondering whether to speak, and then added:

'Do you like him?'

'We don't seem able to stay apart from each other for long. But I don't think that what we have in common has anything to do with liking. Forget Gabriel. Let's fight our way into the coffee bar before it gets too crowded, and then go on to the Courtauld. I want to show you some real pictures.'

3

That evening, just after half-past six, the strident ring of the telephone set Hilda's heart jumping. She had never liked answering it and during the day it seldom rang. Most of Maurice's colleagues telephoned him at the university and he or Philippa would answer it when they were at home, taking it for granted, she supposed, that the call wouldn't be for her. But since Philippa had left she had grown to dread that insistent, broken summons. She was tempted to take off the receiver, but then there might be a call from the court about one of her sittings, or Maurice might ring to say that he would be late home or was bringing a colleague back for dinner. She could think of no possible excuse why he should find the number continually engaged.

It was difficult to forget that the telephone was there. The house seemed infected with instruments. There was one on the table in the hall and another by their bed. Maurice had even had an extension fitted to the wall in the kitchen. Occasionally she would let it ring unanswered, standing stock-still, hardly daring to breathe, as if the instrument held its own secret, sinister life and could detect her presence. But the accusing silence after the final ring, the niggling guilt at her own inadequacy and weakness, were harder to bear than the fear of what she might hear. She hardly knew what it was she dreaded. She only knew that some catastrophe lay waiting in the future and that it would be heralded by this imperious ring.

Now she wiped her hands on her apron and took off the receiver and heard, at the other end, the coin being shot home. Her palms were moist and she felt the receiver slipping through her fingers. She steadied it with her other hand and spoke the number. To her relief it was a voice she knew.

'Mrs Palfrey? It's I, Gabriel Lomas.'

As if she knew a dozen Gabriels; and anyone less pedantic would have said 'It's me'. She had always been a little in awe of him. He had taken too much trouble with her, confusing her with his easy charm. Sometimes his eyes had met hers in a mocking conspiracy, as if to say: 'You know that you're not worth bothering about, I know it, so what are we both up to, my dear, delightful, dull Mrs Palfrey?' But at least this was a familiar voice, a lively voice, not the voice of a stranger, mysterious, heavy with imagined malice. She said:

'How are you, Gabriel?'

'Fine. Look, I've seen Philippa and her mother. I met them at the Arts Council exhibition of great Victorian pictures at the Royal Academy. They were looking at those two Abraham Solomon oils *Waiting for the Verdict* and *The Acquittal*. I oughtn't to have been surprised to meet her there. Philippa has always been fascinated by the Victorians. I must say I adore the peculiar awfulness of high Victorian art. Every picture tells a story. And what a story! A positively decadent feast of colour, my dear. Imperial confidence, pathos, Victorian eroticism and dreadful warnings about the horrid fate which awaited unfaithful wives. Have you seen the exhibition?'

'No, not yet.'

He must have known that she didn't go to exhibitions. Maurice fitted in those that he wished to see during his lunch break and on the way home. Philippa went on her own or with her friends. Sometimes she had gone with Gabriel. Only once, in an effort to interest Hilda in art, she had taken her to an exhibition of paintings from the Prado. It hadn't been a success. There had been an uncomfortable crush of people. The pictures had seemed to Hilda very dark. She remembered only the long, gloomy Spanish faces, the dark heavy robes. It had been difficult to simulate interest. None of the pictures had, she felt, any relation to her or to her life. She strained to hear Gabriel's voice which seemed suddenly to have got fainter. Then she heard it:

'It was unnerving. The pictures, I mean, not the encounter. Although that was unnerving too, in its way.'

'How did she seem, Gabriel? Was she happy?'

'Philippa? Who can tell? No one is better at disguising emotion. She wanted to talk, but we only had about five seconds. Her mother moved tactfully away; at least I thought she was being tactful, giving us the chance for a private word, but now I'm not so sure. It may have been embarrassment. Anyway, she moved to the other wall and began rather ostentatiously studying Ford Madox Brown's *The Last of England*. Well, if one had to look at any picture that was the one most worth attention. It's an extraordinary situation, isn't it? Philippa and her mother, I mean.'

Puzzled and confused, Hilda asked:

'Did Philippa tell you?'

'Oh yes, just the essentials. We only had a second. She wants me to visit her on Thursday at their place. Apparently the mother is going out. She said that there were things she wanted to talk over.'

Hilda was aware of transitory pain that Philippa should have confided her secret so casually, after all her careful and insistent instructions that no one was to be told under any circumstances. No one. But perhaps Gabriel was special. She had sometimes felt that he might be. But how much had she told? And what was that he had said earlier about a verdict and acquittal? She said:

'What things? Is she all right?'

'She isn't ill, if that's what you mean. A bit strained, perhaps, but that might have been a touch of the Alma-Tademas. They were on their way out when we met. As I said, there really wasn't time for confidences other than the main one, where her mother had been all these years.'

So she had told him; he did know. Confused, she said:

'She told you that?'

'Well, I more or less guessed. There is a certain wariness about the eyes. I took one look and thought: either hospital or prison. I'm not sure that taking her to view high Victorian art is exactly calculated to adjust her to contemporary London. I did try to lure them to the Tate, but I got the impression from her mother that my company wasn't exactly welcome.'

'How did they seem to you? Are you sure that Philippa's all right?'

'I'm not altogether sure that the experiment is working, if that's what you mean. I take it that that's what she wants to see me about.'

'Gabriel, try to persuade her to come home. I don't mean permanently if she doesn't want to. Just to come and talk to us.'

'That's what I had in mind. It's silly cutting herself off. It's this thing she has about the biological tie. It's completely irrational. You're her mother in any real sense of the word.'

He didn't believe that. She didn't believe it. And it wasn't important anyway. Why should he need to tell her lies? Why did they all lie to her; obvious, commonplace, childish lies which they didn't even take the trouble to make convincing. But at least he had seen Philippa. At least she would be getting some news. Then she heard his voice again.

'I'm supposed to be there next Thursday at six. The trouble is that I've lost the address. I scribbled it down on the back of my catalogue and now I can't lay my hands on it. The name too.'

'Ducton. The name's Ducton. And they're at 12 Delaney Street, north west one. It's off Mell Street.'

'I remembered Mell Street and the number of the house. And, of course, she introduced her mother as Ducton. It was Delaney Street I couldn't remember. Have you any message for her?'

'Just my love. Give her my love. Perhaps you'd better not say that we've spoken, but Gabriel, try to persuade her to come home.'

'Don't worry,' he said. 'She'll come home all right.'

When she had put down the receiver Hilda's heart was lightened. She felt something very like happiness. After all, if they were visiting exhibitions, things couldn't be too bad. They would hardly be looking at pictures together if life were intolerable for them. And at least Philippa had got in touch with a friend, one of her own age-group. Gabriel would ring her back and give her the news. She wouldn't tell Maurice that he had rung. She knew that he was anxious about Philippa, but she knew, too, that it wasn't an anxiety he was willing to discuss. But, after next Thursday, she would get some news. Perhaps Philippa was ready to come home. Perhaps everything was going to be all right after all.

As she rinsed and dried her hands and went back to chopping the onions, she wondered briefly and totally without anxiety why Gabriel had troubled to telephone from a public box.

4

His plan was basically simple, although he knew that carrying it out would be trickier. He would lift the key ring from Monty's jacket pocket while, at the same time, dropping from his hand a bunch of keys roughly equal in size. Monty would be aware, even if only subconsciously, of the weight and jangle of the keys against his thigh. Simply to steal them would mean almost immediate discovery. Once the keys were in his possession he would have to get the two Yales copied as quickly as possible, preferably somewhere close but where there were plenty of customers so that one face might not be particularly remembered. Then the genuine keys would have to be returned and the substitutes recovered. It would mean two appearances at the shop within a comparatively short time. And there would be other customers; he would have to choose his moment carefully. But first he must get a close look at the key ring and the number and weight of the keys.

On the first day, Monday 11 September, he stationed himself at his watching-post on the wasteland at eight forty-five, binoculars at the ready. The greengrocer arrived on his bicycle at three minutes past nine, felt in the pocket of his close-fitting denim jacket and unlocked the door. But his back was firmly towards the street and it was impossible for Scase to get a glance at the keys. Two minutes later the shop front was cranked open and Monty began the business of dragging forward the crates of fruit and vegetables from the back of the shop, and arranging his display. He had exchanged his blue jacket for the shabby fawn working coat which he wore open. It had two large side-pockets, the left-hand one slightly ripped at the seam. The door between the shop and the ground-floor passage of the house was open.

Shortly after ten past nine a small van stopped outside the shop and the driver and a lad clambered down from the cabin and began

687

lugging crates of fruit and vegetables on to the pavement. The street door was closed. Monty's hand went into his left pocket and he pressed something into the boy's palm. Then he began helping the driver to unload while the lad unlocked the door, wedged it open with a net of Spanish onions and began to hump in the crates of fresh produce. For a few seconds the key was left in the door, the bright ring of metal and the pendant keys hanging against the wood. But the driver, carrying a box of apples, moved across obscuring the view. Then the boy's hand fastened on the keys and he tossed them back to Monty. Scase glimpsed nothing but the flash of metal and Monty's hand snatching at the air.

For the next three days the routine was the same. Scase stayed all day at his post, fortified at mid-morning with sandwiches, but was still unable to get a close look at the keys. Monty worked alone. At midday he went over the road to the Blind Beggar and brought back a brimming pint-mug of beer, then dragged an upturned crate from the back of the shop and sat beside the stall drinking the beer and eating an immense roll of what looked like cheese and tomato. Occasionally during the morning he would go over to the pub. When this happened the wizened little man from the junk shop temporarily took over the stall. Scase guessed that they had this arrangement; that Monty would keep an eye on the junk from time to time while his neighbour covered his visits to the Blind Beggar. During the whole of the three days the connecting door between the shop and the rest of the house was left ajar, except when Monty was about to leave when he would firmly close it. Focusing his binoculars with some difficulty through the slit in the fence, Scase was able to confirm that this door, too, had a Yale lock and he guessed that Monty would be equally punctilious about closing this connecting door before leaving at night.

By Friday morning, frustrated, he knew that he must get closer, must be there early in the morning to watch while the door was unlocked. There was no reason why he shouldn't; someone had to be the first customer. It would mean that he was noticed; it added to the risk that he would be remembered. But that couldn't be helped. He would worry about that later when the time came to fabricate an alibi. Now all his thoughts were fixed on getting possession of that bunch of keys.

The timing was tricky. Monty invariably arrived between nine o'clock and nine-five in the morning. The murderess and her daughter left their apartment between nine-fifteen and nine-thirty. Provided Monty were on time and the other two didn't decide to leave early, he should be all right. But he couldn't safely loiter in Delaney Street before nine o'clock. Neither the junk shop nor the second-hand bookshop opened much before half-past nine, and his presence, unoccupied and aimlessly sauntering in the deserted street, might well be noticed from the window of number 12.

That afternoon he bought a canvas shopping basket from Woolworth's in Edgware Road and next morning began walking slowly down Mell Street towards the junction of Delaney Street just before nine o'clock. At two minutes past nine Monty appeared, cycling from the direction of Lisson Grove, and turned into Delaney Street. Scase quickened his steps and caught him up just before he dismounted. He said:

'Good morning. Are you opening up now?'

'That's right. Take about three minutes. You in a hurry?'

'Not really. I'll just pop round the corner to the station bookstall for a newspaper and come back later.'

As he spoke, Monty, still with one hand on the bar of his cycle, inserted a Yale key into the lock. Scase kept his eyes fixed on the key ring, memorizing its size, its probable heaviness, the shape and number of the keys. It was a large ring and there hung on it two Yales, a small flat key about the size of a car key, and one heavier, solid Chubb about two inches long.

He bought his paper at Marylebone Station and sat reading it in the waiting-room, concealing his face behind it until ten o'clock. Then, when he could be sure that the murderess and her daughter would have left Delaney Street, he returned to Monty's stall and bought four oranges, a pound of apples and a bunch of grapes. He could lighten his load by eating them during the day. Then he walked quickly to Woolworth's and bought a large key-ring. It had a tag attached bearing an ornamental initial, but this, without much difficulty, he was able to prise away.

He spent the rest of the morning searching for substitute keys in the junk shops and antique markets of Mell Street and Church Street. His first find was a substitute for the smallest key; this he took from the lock of a battered tea caddy. A Yale was discovered in a tobacco jar containing screws and pipe cleaners. The heavy Chubb proved more elusive and, in the end, he was forced to steal a key similar in weight and size from the top drawer of an old chest which was standing inside one of the shops. It pleased him that his fingers could act with speed and cunning. He found the second Yale in an old tin box of nails, screws, spectacles and broken pieces of electrical equipment stuck under the table outside the junk shop in Delaney Street. By the end of the morning he had succeeded in putting together a key ring which in appearance and weight was as close to Monty's as he could hope to find.

For the rest of the day he walked again the very streets of his childhood, euphoric, borne on a tide of excitement and terror, half pleasurable, wholly familiar. The concrete underpass at Edgware Road echoed with the distant thunder of the sea. He had only to close his eyes against the sun to feel again the gritty sand creeping between his toes, and to see once more the brightly patterned shore. The raucous voices of children calling to each other down the side streets jolted his heart with half-forgotten playground menace and the smell of the pavement after a squall of summer rain was the smell of the sea. Now, as then, he knew exactly what he had to do, knew the necessity, the inevitability of the act. Now, as then, he was torn between the longing to get it over and the half-shameful hope that he still might have a choice, that it was within his power to stop now, to decide that the risk was too great. With part of his mind he wished that he had returned to the stall as soon as his key ring was complete, and had tried his luck then, carried forward on a tide of optimism and success. But he knew that it could have been fatal. He had yet to prove that the old skills remained to him.

He spent the whole of Sunday and Monday practising. He locked his room and hung his jacket over the corner of a chair. He hooked the new key ring over the little finger of his left hand and insinuated his hand under the flap of the pocket. With his thumb he gently lifted his own key ring at the same time as he slid the substitute ring from his finger. He performed the procedure over and over again, sometimes using his thumb, sometimes his middle finger, watching for the slightest movement of the jacket pocket, counting out the seconds to time himself. Speed meant safety. When he felt that he was proficient he started again, only this time using the fingers of his right hand. He had to be ambidextrous in skill. He couldn't be sure until the moment came, until he was close enough to Monty to press his hand against the jacket, which of the pockets would hold the keys. For two days he hardly left his hotel room except to buy sandwiches – hurrying through the hallway, almost oblivious to Violet's greeting as she recognized his footsteps and her dead eyes searched for him – grudging every moment away from his task. And by Monday evening 18 September he felt that he was ready.

5

The next day he collected together two pairs of underclothes and a couple of shirts and stuffed them into a plastic shopping bag. He went first to the Delaney Street launderette, arriving soon after nine o'clock. Once his washing was swirling in the machine he moved to a chair next to the open door from where he could watch number 12. One possibility worried him, that the murderess and her daughter might choose this morning to visit the launderette themselves. But he told himself that the risk of an encounter was small. If they came out with a bag which might contain clothes, he would simply walk out before they arrived and return later to empty his machine.

But all was well. He saw them emerge as usual by nine-thirty, carrying nothing but their shoulder bags. He moved away from the window, but they passed on the other side of the street and without glancing his way. One or two pensioners, always the earliest out in the mornings, had made their way to Monty's door but business was slack, the street had not yet come alive. When the third customer, an elderly woman, had shuffled away with her load of potatoes, he judged that the moment had come. He picked up the empty bag and moved across the road to the stall. His right hand deep in his jacket pocket fingered the dummy set of keys. The metal grew warm and moist under his touch. It irritated him that his hands were sweating with fear until he remembered that the moistness would help, the keys would slip the more easily from his fingers. And at least his hands weren't trembling. Even at the height of childhood delinquency his hands had never trembled.

Monty, temporarily without a customer, was burnishing Cox's Orange Pippins on his sleeve and arranging them in a line across the front of the stall. Pretending to be interested in a carton of avocado pears, Scase brushed past him, his left hand briefly pressing against

Monty's right-hand pocket. It felt padded; something was there, a handkerchief perhaps, or a rag. But he could detect nothing hard or metallic. So the keys, if they were on him at all, must be in the other pocket. He retreated from the back of the stall, and asked for four oranges, holding open his bag. Monty picked them out and dropped them in. Then Scase demanded and received four of the Cox's Orange Pippins. Lastly he asked for two bananas, not too ripe, and pointed to a couple which formed part of a bunch slung from a rail at the back of the stall. It was the most inaccessible bunch, and Monty had to stretch over to reach them, steadying himself by grasping the rail with his left hand. Scase moved close to him, his eyes fixed on the bananas. He hooked his little finger into the bunch of dummy keys, closed his fist round them, then insinuated his hand into Monty's coat pocket and felt with a surge of triumph the hard tangled coldness of the keys. He strengthened his middle finger and lifted the bunch, at the same time gently relinquishing the dummy ring. After the practice of the last few days, and with no occluding pocket-flap to hinder him, the ploy was surprisingly easy. He judged that it took less than three seconds. By the time Monty had straightened himself to tear the two selected bananas from the bunch and had tossed them into the pan of his scales, Scase was standing meekly by his side, stretching wide his shopping bag to receive them.

He made himself walk unhurriedly down Delaney Street, but as soon as he turned the corner into Mell Street, his steps quickened. He was lucky, there were two taxis waiting outside Marylebone Station. He took the first to Selfridges and went to the key-cutting counter in the basement. Even at this early hour there were two people before him, but it was only minutes before he was prising the two Yale keys from Monty's bunch and handing them over. He asked for two copies of each, knowing that sometimes a newly cut Yale would be defective. He left the store by the front entrance and, as he had hoped, had no difficulty in getting a taxi. They were arriving in a steady stream, dropping tourists for their morning shopping. He asked for Marylebone Station and, after paying off the cab, actually walked on to the concourse in case the driver should be watching. Within two minutes he was back in Delaney Street. His plan was to transfer his washing to the drying machine, then to watch the greengrocer's shop from the window until it seemed a propitious moment to change back the keys. But as he approached the stall his heart sank. Monty was no longer wearing the fawn working coat. The day had become hotter, the stall busier and he was serving now wearing nothing but his blue jeans and a singlet. The coat was nowhere to be seen.

He left Delaney Street and sat on a bench in Marylebone Station waiting for the clock to show five minutes to twelve. Monty invariably went across to the Blind Beggar for his beer just after the hour. The thirty-minute wait seemed interminable. He sat in a fever of anxiety and impatience which drove him every few minutes to pace up and down the concourse. It was unlikely that Monty would want the keys until it was time for him to shut up the shop at night. Even then he wouldn't need them; the locks were both Yales and all that was necessary was for him to close both the shop and street doors after him. He might not discover that he had a substitute set of keys until he tried to open the street door next morning. But there would be no possible chance of making the substitution after nightfall. It had to be done now.

He walked back to Delaney Street at eight minutes to twelve and pretended to browse in the bookshop. At twelve o'clock Monty called to his neighbour and, a second or two later, appeared from the back of the shop wearing his denim jacket and went across to the Blind Beggar. The old man from the junk shop settled himself on the upturned crate, lifted his face for a moment to the sun, then opened his newspaper. It had to be now. It might be only a couple of minutes, perhaps less, before Monty reappeared with his beer. And the only hope of success lay in boldness. He walked briskly across the road and into the recesses of the shop, so quickly that the old man hardly had time to raise his eyes as he brushed past. All was well. The fawn working coat hung on a nail above two sacks of potatoes piled against the wall. As his fingers met the smooth metal of the keys his heart leaped in triumph.

The old man was standing in the space between the wall and the counter. Before he could speak Scase said:

'I've left a Marks and Spencer bag somewhere where I've been shopping. I've only been here, over the road at the bookshop and to the dairy in Mell Street and it isn't there. I thought Monty might have found it and put it on one side for me.'

The sharp little eyes were suspicious. But Scase hadn't been anywhere near the cash register. He wasn't helping himself to anything, hadn't been in the shop long enough to steal. What, anyway, was there worth stealing at the back of the counter? He said grumpily:

'Monty? He's not Monty. Been dead twenty year, Monty has. That's George. And he never said nothing to me.'

'It's not at the back, and there's nowhere else he would have put it. It looks as if I must have left it in the launderette and someone's taken it. Thank you.'

He walked briskly away, crossing the road and stepping on to the kerb outside the Blind Beggar just as Monty – it was difficult to think of him as George – emerged, carefully carrying a brimming pint in each hand.

The relief, the excitement, the exultation were greater than any he had experienced in childhood after the lesser, more innocent delinquencies. His heart sang a paean of undirected praise. If the keys had been strung on a ring he would have needed to spin them in a flashing arc, to have tossed and caught them like a toy. But none of this triumph showed in his face. As George passed he smiled at him. There must have been something strange about the smile. As he turned into Mell Street his last memory was of George's astonished face.

6

He had carefully matched the two sets of keys and had strung them on different lengths of string. One set would open the front door, the second the door leading from the hall into the shop. Until he tried them in the lock he couldn't know which was which. He hoped luck would be with him and that he would get it right first time. The longer he lingered or fumbled at the door, the greater the chance that he would be seen. He watched from his usual vantage point on the wasteland until the murderess and her daughter had left for work, then waited another forty minutes in case they should have forgotten something and return unexpectedly. From the narrow slit in the corrugated iron he had a very restricted view of Delaney Street, but he put his ear against it and listened until he could hear no footfalls. Then he edged his way quickly across the wasteland

and slid through the gap in the fence as he had so many times. Delaney Street was deserted. Above the closed shops he could see a row of lit upstairs windows where he could imagine people eating an early supper or settling down to an evening's television. To his left the launderette shone brightly with light, but he could see only one customer, an elderly woman with a basket on wheels dragging her tangled linen from one of the machines.

He took one set of the keys from his pocket and concealed them in his clenched palm, then he walked quickly but deliberately across the street and inserted the key in the lock. It didn't turn. His lips moved. Silently he said to himself: gently, gently, gently. He felt for the second string of keys and this time the key turned without difficulty and he stepped into the hall, closing the door behind him.

And then there came a moment of atavistic horror. The house had shuddered at his entrance. He stood transfixed, holding his breath. Then he relaxed. The vibration was only the rumble of a passing tube train, presumably in the tunnel between Marylebone and Edgware Road. The noise receded, and the house settled into calmness. He closed the door and stood motionless, listening to the silence. The hall held the earthy, heavy smell of potatoes, with a trace of a lighter, sharper scent, perhaps of apples. At the end of the passage he could see a faint haze where a door with two panels of opaque glass led to a garden or back yard. He switched on his torch and followed the pool of light down the passage. The door was bolted, both at the top and at the bottom. That meant that the yard offered no sanctuary, no place to hide. The murderess and her daughter would almost certainly check those locks before they finally went to bed.

He shone his torch on the stairs and made his way up, testing each stair with his foot before he put his full weight on it. There was a small half landing. He paused, then made his way up the second short flight. Their door was on the left. He shone the torch full on it, and the pool of bright light illumined a security lock.

Disappointment rose in his throat like a hard core of bile which he had to resist the temptation to vomit away. He didn't beat his hands against the door in frustration, but he rested his head against it for a moment, fighting down nausea. Then came anger and a sense of self-betrayal. How stupid of him not to have known that the door would be locked. But he had thought of the premises as the single house which once it had been, with one front door, one lock. And this was no Yale lock. Unless he could again steal a set of keys – and how could he? – he could only force his way through this barrier by breaking down the door.

He had intended to explore the flat in detail, to discover where the murderess slept, so that he could go unhesitatingly to her room and make his escape afterwards without blundering through the wrong door. This was now imposssible. He had to change his plan. But there were things that he could do, preparations that he could make. He could begin by familiarizing himself with the house. He knew that the women weren't due back until midnight, but he walked on tiptoe, the torch beam sheltered by his left palm, his ears keen for the slightest sound. Gently and very quietly he pushed open the door to the bathroom, standing to one side as if expecting to find it occupied. The window was wide open at the top, and the air rushed at him, cool and strong as a wind, billowing the curtains. They were drawn back and he dared not switch on his torch, but the garish London sky, streaked with purple and crimson, showed him the outline of the gas boiler, the delicately-linked hanging chain with its bulbous handle, the great white bath. There was no cupboard, no curtained recess, nowhere here where he could conceal himself.

He spent the next five minutes mounting and descending the stairs, testing them for creaks. The fifth and ninth were particularly noisy; he would have to remember not to tread on them. Most of the others creaked under his tread, but it was possible, by keeping close to the wall, to eliminate all but the slightest sound.

Lastly, he took the second set of keys from his pocket and unlocked the door leading into the shop. As he pushed it open, the rich smell of earth, the zest of lemons and oranges, met him so strongly that it caught at his breath. The darkness was absolute. No chink of light from the street lamps shone through the metal shutters, and if there were a window at the rear of the shop it must have been boarded up. No drawn curtains could so effectively exclude the sky. He leaned back against the door, staring into the blackness, breathing freely for the first time since he had entered the house. Even if the women returned early, they would have no key to this room. Here he could be sure of safety. Emboldened, he switched on his torch and swept it slowly over the shop, over the stall of potatoes and fruit, the folded trestle table, the rolled mat of synthetic grass, the piled boxes of tomatoes, apples and lettuces waiting for the morning, the sacks of potatoes and the meshed bags of onions humped against the wall. At the rear and under the shuttered window was an old porcelain sink; one of the taps was missing, from the other a continuous bead of water formed, then fell. He had to resist the urge to turn it off, to stop the regular soft dripping. To one side his torch shone on a wooden table with a formica top on which were a gas ring, a kettle, and a brown stained teapot. Underneath the table was an orange-box turned on its side, containing two blue-rimmed mugs, a tin marked 'sugar' and a tea caddy with a coronation picture of King George V and Queen Mary.

He propped his torch against one of the boxes. Then, illumined by the single beam of light, he put on the long mackintosh and the gloves, drawing them up over the tucked-in cuffs of the sleeves. Lastly he took the knife from the bottom of the rucksack. He squatted against the strong wooden upright at the back of the stall, knees bent under his chin, his thin buttocks hard against the unyielding floor, the sheathed knife between his palms. It wouldn't happen tonight. He knew that with complete certainty, although he was unable to say why. But he felt obscurely that the mackintosh and the gloves were some protection against leaving a trace of himself for Monty to find, and it was right that he should thus formally garb himself for his task, should be prepared in case, by some miracle, the murderess returned alone. He sat on in the darkness, waiting, counting the regular dripping of the tap, smelling the warmth of the plastic mackintosh superimposed on the loamy scent of the shop, holding his white-gloved hands before him, palm to palm, like the hands of a priest.

It was just before midnight when, at last, they returned and he heard the firm closing of the front door. He thought he could detect a low murmur of voices and the creaking of the stairs, but he wasn't sure. But then they were overhead. The house had not been built as two flats and there were only the joists and the wooden floor between them. The timbers creaked loudly as their feet struck them, and occasionally the wood cracked like a shot. Then his heart would leap and he would stare, petrified, at the ceiling, as if afraid that a foot would descend through the boards. He could hear every move. It seemed impossible that his presence, the very smell of him, the warmth of his spent breath, should not penetrate through to them.

He could identify the two sets of footsteps, one lighter than the other. That would be the murderess; the girl was taller and walked with more confidence. Then the footsteps separated; they were moving about in different rooms. The quieter footfalls were in the front of the house; so the murderess must sleep in the bedroom overlooking the street. After about five minutes he heard her footsteps across the ceiling and, a few minues later, there was the flush of the lavatory cistern and the muffled roar of the gas boiler. So the murderess was in the bathroom. This, if all else failed, could give him his chance. But he needed to know whether, with no one in the house at night except another woman, she would bother to lock the door, whether the door to the flat itself was propped open or closed when either of them went to the bathroom. Perhaps it would be instinctive to close both doors. If, in the end, he had to kill her in the bathroom, these were the facts it would be important to know.

By half-past twelve the last sounds had died away, but still he sat on, the wood of the upright hard against his backbone. The loamy smell of freshly turned earth from the sacks of potatoes was stronger than ever. He found himself trying to hold his breath against memory. But it was no use. Suddenly he was standing again with Mavis by the covered heap of red earth at the edge of Julie's grave in that vast east London cemetery, watching the small white coffin jerking slowly downwards into darkness. They had been the only two mourners; Mavis had insisted on a private funeral. They had always kept themselves to themselves; why should they be generous in grief? Why now should they expose themselves to the avid, salacious eyes of their neighbours? Their own minister had been ill and the young substitute had worn unpolished shoes. Mavis had kept her eyes on them throughout the words of committal. Listening to her complaints afterwards he had said:

'But he took the service very nicely dear, I thought he spoke very well.'

And she had replied in the grudging, obstinate voice with which he was to grow so familiar:

'He should have cleaned his shoes.'

He fixed his mind on the murderess sleeping overhead. Within a few days she would be dead. Perhaps he and the girl would be dead too. In that moment it seemed to him not to be important if they also died. There might be a necessity which he couldn't yet foresee or understand, but which, when the time came, he would be powerless to prevent. That the three of them should die together even had a certain rightness, a completion, an avoidance of future complications which he could almost welcome. For himself, he feared death less than he feared imprisonment. Perhaps it was the possibility of his own imminent death, which he faced now for the first time, more than the certainty of hers, which drove his thoughts back to the past. In his mind there clicked a series of bright, disjointed images, like pictures flashed on a screen. The tinsel Christmas tree on the bar of the Goat and Compasses, glimpsed through the open door; the seaweed hanging in swathes from the girders of the pier, moving in slimy tentacles beneath the green onrushing tide, the grating dampness of the sand as he scuffed it over a stolen purse; Mr Micklewright, holding a knight between his first and second fingers and sliding it towards him across the board; Eli Watkin spooning out the cat meat and hissing endearments at his yowling brood; Julie in her new Girl Guide uniform; Julie sleeping in her pram under the apple tree on the lawn of Magenta Gardens; Mavis glancing at him across the scarred desk of the local secondary school where they had first met at evening classes in French. Why, he wondered, had they chosen French? Neither had ever been to France, neither had ever had any particular wish to go. But that had been the beginning. Nothing that had happened between them afterwards had ever persuaded him that he was lovable; only that, by some miracle of chance, Mavis had found him so.

From time to time he dozed, then woke and stretched his cramped legs. At last, before dawn, he got slowly to his feet, took off his gloves and mackintosh and repacked them with the torch and the sheathed knife in his rucksack. His vigil was over; this was a new day. He wouldn't return that evening; it was important to stay at the Casablanca on alternate nights, to ensure that he kept his senses fresh and alert, that he didn't go too short of sleep. But he would come back on Thursday and on alternate nights after that until his chance came. Optimism had been reborn. He knew that the wait wouldn't be long.

He closed the shop door with infinite care, then crept down the few yards of the passage. There was still the front door to shut, but he didn't fear that that quiet click would wake the sleepers overhead. Even if the murderess still lay awake or stirred in her sleep, so small a sound would hardly disturb her. This was an old house; old houses were full of mysterious nocturnal noises. And by the time she switched on the light and got to the window he would be out of sight. The door closed behind him and he set off for Baker Street Station to wait for the first Circle line train.

7

It was mid-afternoon on Thursday 21 September, and Philippa was sitting in the basket chair at the open window of her room. She and her mother had just returned from a visit to Brompton Oratory to see the Mazzuoli Marbles and there was an hour before they needed to set out for work. Her mother had said that she would make the tea. From the kitchen Philippa could hear small noises like the scrapings of a secretive domestic animal, delicate tinklings, an occasional soft footfall. The sounds were extraordinarily pleasurable. The door of her mother's room was open, but Thursday was early-closing day and no sounds came up from the street. The voices which drifted in through her own window seemed far-away shouts of joy from another world. It had been a hot oppressive day with the threat of thunder, but in the last half-hour the sky had lightened and now the room was filled with the strong mellow light which comes before the dusk.

Philippa sat absolutely still in the silence, and there began to flow through her a sense of tingling delight, entrancing in its strangeness. Even the inanimate objects in the room, the air itself, were suffused with this iridescent joy. She fixed her eyes on the geranium on the window sill. Why had she never realized how beautiful it was? She had seen geraniums as the gaudy expedient of municipal gardeners to be planted in park beds, massed on political platforms, a useful pot plant for the house, since it throve with so little attention. But this plant was a miracle of beauty. Each flowerlet was curled like a miniature rosebud on the end of its furred, tender stem. Imperceptibly but inevitably as her own breathing they were opening to the light. The petals were a clear, transparent pink, faintly striped with yellow, and the fan-like leaves, how intricately veined they were, how varied in their greenness, each with its darker penumbra. Some words of William Blake fell into her mind, familiar but new. 'Everything that lives is holy. Life delights in life.' Even her body's flux, which she could feel as a gentle, almost controlled, flow, wasn't the inconvenient and disagreeable monthly discharge of the body's waste. There was no waste. Everything living was part of one great wholeness. To breathe was to take in delight. She wished that she knew how to pray, that there was someone to whom she could say: 'Thank you for this moment of happiness. Help me to make her happy.' And then she thought of other words, familiar but untraceable to their source: 'In whom we live and move and have our being.'

She heard her mother calling her from the front room. There was a smell of cut lemons and freshly brewed China tea, and the pot, with their two special cups, the Worcester and the Staffordshire, was on a papier-mâché tray on the bedside table. Her mother was smiling and holding out to her a tissue-wrapped package. She said:

'I made it for you.'

Philippa took it and shook out from its folds a polo-necked jumper in a variety of soft browns and fawns, and with two oblongs of apple green carefully placed above the right breast and at the back. The jumper had been constructed from every kind of knitting stitch, and the variety of textures between the panels, the subtle blending of colours, gave its basic simplicity such distinction that Philippa, tugging it over her head, exclaimed aloud with pleasure:

'It's lovely! Lovely! You are clever, but when did you knit it?'

'In my room, late at night. I didn't want you to see it until it was finished. It's quite simple really. The sleeves are just oblongs grafted on to the dropped shoulders. Of course, it's too warm to be worn now, but come the autumn in Cambridge you will be glad of it.'

'I'm glad of it now. I'll always be glad of it. It's beautiful. Everyone will wonder where I bought it. I shall like saying that my mother knitted it for me.'

They looked at each other, two faces transformed with pleasure. 'I shall like saying that my mother knitted it for me.' She had spoken the words spontaneously, without embarrassment. She couldn't remember in her private, self-conscious, fabricated life, when she had been able to speak so simply what was in her heart. She tugged her mane of hair out from the rolled collar and shook it free. Stretching both arms widely, she spun round in pleasure. In the oval glass which she had set between the two windows, she watched her spinning image, gold and fawn and brown and flashing green, and behind her the still flushed face of her mother, bright-eyed and alive.

The peal of the front doorbell, strident and peremptory, broke their mood. Philippa stopped spinning and they gazed at each other with surprised and anxious eyes. No one had rung that bell since the probation officer's last visit. Her mother said:

'Perhaps George has come back for something and has forgotten his key.'

Philippa went to the door. She said:

'You stay here. I'll go.'

The bell had rung again before she reached the bottom of the stairs. And with that second ring she knew that this was trouble. She opened the door.

'Miss Palfrey? I'm Terry Brewer.'

The voice was cautious, almost apologetic. He was proffering a card. He must have had it ready in his hands as he heard her coming down the stairs. She didn't look at it. The police had cards too. There was a card for every purpose: warrants, authorizations, identity cards, licences, passes. They said: 'Let me in. I exist. I am authorized, safe, respectable.' She didn't need a card to know what business he was in. She kept her eyes on his face.

'What do you want?'

He was very young, not much older than she was, with strong, tightly curled hair low on his forehead, a heart-shaped face with a neatly cleft chin, jutting cheekbones and a delicate, moistly pouting mouth. His eyes were large and luminous, pale brown speckled with green. She made herself look into them.

'Just a chat. I'm a feature writer, a freelance. I've been asked to do an article for the *Clarion*. About lifers and their readjustment to the world outside prison. Nothing sensational. You know the *Clarion*. They're not interested in morbid sensationalism. What I'm after is the human interest, how you discovered who your mother was, what it's like living together after all these years, how she survived her time in prison. I'd like to interview you both. Of course, the name will be changed. I shan't mention Ducton.'

It was hopeless to try to close the door in his face. Already his foot was jammed against the wood. She said:

'I don't know what you're talking about and I don't want to see you.'

'Oh, but I don't think you've got much choice, have you? Better me than a dozen others. One interview, exclusive, and I leave you strictly alone. No address printed. No names. The others might not be so accommodating. You don't need me to tell you that.'

It was a lie about being a feature writer or a freelance. She doubted whether he were even a reporter. More likely he was a trainee journalist or had some minor job on the *Clarion* and he saw this as his first big chance. But someone must have tipped him off and there could be only one person. She asked:

'How did you find us?'

'I've got friends.'

'One friend particularly. Gabriel Lomas?'

He didn't answer, but she knew at once that the guess had been correct. His muscles were too undisciplined, the face too mobile for dissembling. So Gabriel must have telephoned Caldecote Terrace, choosing his time so that Hilda would be likely to be there alone. Maurice would have sniffed danger and deceit over the line, but Hilda, silly, innocent Hilda, was a predestined victim. She wondered by what guile Gabriel had extracted the truth from her and how much of it he had learned. He would have lied about their meeting, of course; even if it weren't strictly necessary he couldn't have resisted at least one lie. And then he would have done his research. He was to read history at Cambridge. He would have been meticulous about ascertaining the facts. And it wouldn't have been so very difficult. There weren't many crimes for which a woman would be imprisoned for ten years. He would only have had to study the press cuttings for 1968 and '69. She was surprised that it had taken him as long as a week to discover who her mother was. But, then, he might have had more important matters on his mind. Perhaps this small betrayal hadn't been given top priority.

Watching Brewer's predatory, ingratiating smile, she could understand why Gabriel had been attracted. Singularity and strangeness in a face had always drawn him. Why else, at first, had he bothered with her? He picked people over like bric-à-brac on a street stall. She had seen him at parties momentarily entranced by the fall of light on a turning cheek, a flash of unsuspected wit, the confident turn of a head. And, like bric-à-brac, people could be discarded if he made a bad buy. This face would have intrigued him. The farouche good looks, the hint of corruption and danger, the spurious vulnerability. He was trying to look self-deprecating, harmless, but she could almost smell his excitement. He was rather too carefully dressed and not altogether at ease in his clothes. This must be his best suit, kept for job interviews, weddings, seductions, blackmail. It was a little too well cut, the lapels too wide, the cloth, more synthetic than wool, already creasing. It was odd that Gabriel hadn't done something about his clothes. But he held himself well, he fancied himself, this common little pouf with his false, ingratiating smile.

'Look, you'd better let me in. Get it over with. I'll only be back. And I don't want to discuss it here. I don't want to start shouting. After all, someone from the street might hear us. They think your mother is called Palfrey, I suppose? Better keep it that way.'

Her mother had appeared at the top of the stairs. She whispered: 'Let him in.'

Philippa stepped aside and he slid through the door. Her mother was standing at the open door of the flat and he pushed past her and moved into the front room as confidently as if he had been there before. They followed, side by side, and stood in the doorway regarding him. How eagerly he had pranced up those narrow shabby stairs, despising their poverty, their vulnerability! Now he was frankly surveying the room, keen-eyed as a creditor pricing their few possessions, his glance resting at last on the Henry Walton. The picture, which even to Philippa's eyes looked suddenly out of place, seemed momentarily to confuse him.

It was an abomination that he should be there. Anger flowed through her. She was lifted exhilaratingly on a tide of passionate rage in which inspiration and action flowed together.

'Wait,' she said. 'Wait.'

She ran into the kitchen and dragged the toolbox from the cupboard under the sink. Grasping the largest and strongest chisel, she walked past the front room with only a glance at Brewer's face, stupid and vacant with astonishment, then went out shutting the door of the flat behind her. Then she inserted the blade of the chisel in the narrow gap between the lock and the door-jamb and worked away at the lock. She had no energy to waste on wondering what was happening inside the flat; all her strength, all her mind were concentrated on the task in hand. The lock didn't break. It had been made to resist any such crude assaults. But the door itself was more fragile. It had never been intended as a front door and it had been there for over eighty years. She worked away, grunting with effort, and soon she heard the first creaks, saw the first splintering of the wood. After about two minutes it finally cracked and broke away. She gave a little moan and the door burst open under her hands. And now she was in the front room facing him, breathless, the chisel in her hand. When she could speak her voice was perfectly controlled.

'Right. Now get out. If you write a word, I'll complain to your paper and to the Press Council that you forced your way in here, broke down the door and threatened to betray us to everyone in the neighbourhood unless we gave you an exclusive story.'

He backed against the wall, his eyes fixed on the chisel. His voice shook. He said in a hoarse whisper:

'You crazy bitch! Who's going to believe you?'

'More people than will believe you. Can you afford to take the risk? I'm eminently respectable, remember. Are you? And do you think a reputable newspaper will welcome that kind of publicity? My mother may be beyond compassion, but I'm not. I'm the dutiful daughter, risking my future to help her. Cambridge scholar in back-street hideout. 'She's my mother,' says Mary Ducton's daughter. That's the kind of emotional muck you had in mind, isn't it? I qualify for pity. Do you seriously believe that anyone will believe that I broke down the door myself?'

'It isn't my chisel! Why should I come here with a chisel?'

'Why indeed, except perhaps to force open a door. It's a perfectly ordinary chisel. New, as you see. No distinguishing marks. Prove it isn't yours if you can. And remember, it's two against one. You seem to know who my mother is, what she did. Do you suppose a lie would stick in her throat? Not if it's going to destroy your career it won't.'

He said, with a kind of wonder:

'Christ, I believe you'd do it!'

'I'm her daughter. If this didn't succeed and you got away with it, how long do you think I'd let you last?'

There could be no doubt now of his terror. She could smell it, rancid as vomit. He backed towards the door as she advanced, chisel in hand, the point at his throat. Then he was gone and they heard the clatter of his frantic feet on the stairs.

Her mother moved along from the wall, feeling it with outstretched hands like a blind woman. Philippa went to her and led her to the bed. They sat side by side, their shoulders touching. Her mother whispered:

'You frightened him.'

'I did, didn't I? They won't print anything, and he won't write anything. Not yet anyway. Even if he tells, they'll check with their lawyers first.'

'Couldn't we go away? Not for long, just for a few days so that he'll think he's scared us off. We could go to Ventnor, on the Isle of Wight. I went there once for a Sunday-school treat when I was nine. There are cliffs and sand and little Victorian coloured houses. Once he finds we've gone he won't keep coming back.'

'He won't come back at all. He won't dare. He knows that I wasn't bluffing. The *Clarion* is the last paper to print the kind of sentimental muck he had in mind. Even if they did print a story, they wouldn't identify either of us or print the address. They have their liberal conscience to preserve. They won't see it as their business to hunt you down. After all, as a lifer out on licence, in their eyes you're practically a protected species.'

She was surprised that her mother was so shaken. She had seemed so strong when she first came out of prison. But perhaps nothing had mattered very much to her then. Perhaps it was only when she had stood on the canal bank in the green watery twilight, watching that shabby case finally topple out of sight, that she had laid herself open to the pain of living. She moved closer to her mother and put her arm round the shaking shoulders. She laid her cheek against her mother's cheek, flesh against colder flesh. Then she kissed her. It was all so easy, so beautifully easy. Why had it taken her so long to learn that there was nothing to be afraid of in loving? She said:

'It's going to be all right. Nothing dreadful is going to happen. We're together and no one can touch us.'

'But suppose he goes to another paper?'

'He won't, not while he's working for the *Clarion*. And if he does, we'll destroy his career. All you have to do is confirm what I tell them. If you seem frightened – well that would be natural. All it needs is the capacity to lie.'

'I don't think I'd be very good at lying.'

'I don't see why you should worry about lying. Telling the truth didn't do you much good. But you won't have to lie. I tell you, he's not coming back.'

'The door. How can we lock it?'

'I'll buy a bolt tomorrow and we can use that at night until I can get a new lock fixed. That isn't important, it's the least of our worries. He won't come back, and there's nothing worth stealing except the picture. A professional thief wouldn't bother with this kind of place. He certainly wouldn't take the Henry Walton. We were burgled once at Caldecote Terrace. What they like to pick up are the small, easily disposable valuables. There's nothing here that anyone could want.'

She watched her mother's hands restlessly moving together. Her own fingers, long, bony, the nails strong and narrow, but on her mother's hands. Wringing her hands. It wasn't an expression one would ever write, too trite, too imprecise; but apparently it did happen, except that 'wringing' wasn't the right word for this rhythmic pressing together of the palms. The hands seemed to be comforting each other. She was staring fixedly ahead, apparently oblivious of those kneading palms. Perhaps she was recalling the heavy smoothness of a sea-washed stone rolled between her hands, seeing in memory the layered sea, stretching to infinity, the mottled wave curving to crash in shingled foam against her naked feet. Then her eyes blinked again into the present. She said:

'How did he know?'

'Gabriel Lomas told him. Gabriel can smell out scandal, secrets, fear; it's a talent he has. He couldn't resist telling him. I can understand that. It was too important to him. Like me and the pregnant wife. In the end we think of no one but ourselves.'

'What pregnant wife?'

'No one you know. Someone I did down. Someone who needed this flat.'

'He seems a strange friend for Gabriel Lomas, a different class.'

'Oh Gabriel has a personality like a hexagon. People need touch only one side for an illusion of closeness. Forget about him. Perhaps it would be a good idea to get out of London for a time. Ventnor is as good a place as any, but you mustn't expect to find it the same. No place ever is. And we'll need some money. I've something left in the bank but we must keep a small reserve for when this lease runs out.

It won't be easy to find work on the Isle of Wight, not immediately, not at the end of the season.'

Her mother turned to her with the eyes of a pleading child.

'I'm sure you'll like it there. And we needn't be away long.'

Philippa said:

'And you could change your name, you know. It would make things easier.'

Her mother shook her head.

'No, I couldn't do that. That would be defeat. I have to know who I am.'

Philippa got up from the bed.

'We'll go tomorrow, just as soon as I've got the door mended and a new lock fixed. But first I have to go to Caldecote Terrace. I won't be away long, not more than an hour. Will you be all right?'

Her mother nodded. She said, trying to smile:

'I'm sorry I'm being so stupid. Don't worry. I'll be all right.'

Philippa slung her bag over her shoulder and made for the door. Suddenly her mother called her back. She said:

'Rose! You won't take anything that isn't yours?'

'Don't worry,' she answered. 'I shan't take anything that they don't owe us.'

8

The things to take were the silver caddy spoons. They were small, portable, easily disposed of; silver was fetching a high price. Maurice had over a hundred in his collection. About half were kept in the wall safe in his dressing-room and the others on display in an eighteenth-century rosewood cabinet in the drawing-room. The cabinet was always kept locked, but she knew that the key was in the safe, and she knew, too, the combination. From time to time he would change the ones on display although, once they were arranged on the purple velvet, he seldom looked at them again. As a child she had enjoyed helping him to set them out, had liked the feel of their smooth bowls, their delicate balance in her fingers. He had taught her to recognize the hallmarks, handing the spoons to her as he took them from the box and asking her to guess their date and the name of the silversmith. Yes, it was right that she should take the caddy spoons. And it wouldn't be difficult. If Maurice hadn't changed the combination of his wall safe, and she thought this unlikely, there wouldn't even be a need to break the cabinet lock. It was a pretty object. It would have been a hurtful necessity to have had to damage it. It never once occurred to her to make the theft look like a burglary. She would take as many spoons as she needed to sell to keep herself and her mother without working for about a month. Maurice would know that it was she who had taken them, and one day she would tell him why. She knew which were the rarest and which, therefore, the most valuable. Even quite ordinary ones in Church Street market were fetching thirty pounds. She need only take twenty of the best and their immediate problems would be over. There wouldn't be any difficulty in getting rid of them provided she offered them singly and in the right shops. She wouldn't get what they were worth, but she would get enough.

Because she was in a hurry to get the job done and return to her mother, she decided on the extravagance of a cab from Marylebone Station. She paid if off at the corner of Caldecote Road, an instinctive precaution which, as soon as the taxi moved away, struck her as silly and unnecessary. The basement kitchen was in darkness, as she knew it would be. This was Thursday, Hilda would be in court. But she turned the key in the lock and shut the door behind her with extreme care, holding her breath, as if afraid to wake an echo in the white, clean-smelling hall. She was a stranger here, and it seemed to her that the house knew it. Then she ran lightly upstairs to the front bedroom. As she put her hand on the door, the second before she turned the knob, she knew instinctively and with absolute certainty that she wasn't alone. She stopped dead in the doorway, then slowly pushed the door open.

They were both on the bed, Maurice and the girl, half reclining, transfixed by that first sound of her footsteps on the landing. They had finished making love. The rumpled bed, the spread towel, told their own story, and she thought she could sniff in the air the unmistakable, doughy smell of sex. Maurice was wearing only his pants, but the girl was naked. She shoved herself clumsily from the bed and with a little cry began gathering up her clothes from the chair. Philippa stood at the door, half-aware of Maurice's unembarrassed, ironic gaze, while the girl, scarlet-faced, diminished by shame, tried to cover herself with her skirt, and bent in an ungainly display of buttocks to scrabble under the bed for her shoes. Philippa knew that she had met her before, but for a moment she couldn't recall when or where. Absolute nakedness was intrusive, confusing to the senses. Paradoxically it both revealed and diminished identity.

She made herself stare at the girl's face, and then remembered. She was one of Maurice's students. The name came to her a second later. Sheila. Sheila Manning. Eighteen months ago she had come to dinner; it was an evening when Gabriel had also been invited. She had been an uncomfortable guest, voluble in her nervousness, alternately aggressive and aggrieved, treating them to a rehashed version of Maurice's latest seminar on the cycle of deprivation. Gabriel had taken trouble with her, resisting the frequent temptation to wit or sarcasm, steering the conversation from Marxist dogma to such innocuously boring subjects as food and holidays. It hadn't, Philippa thought, been done through kindness. Like most men, he reserved kindness for women who, beautiful or successful, had the least need of it. She had decided that he was acting either to disoblige her, or in obedience to some nursery dictate that it was the responsibility of a guest to attempt to rescue from social disaster even the most unpropitious dinner party. The girl, as had been painfully apparent, was in love with Maurice even then. Had it really taken her eighteen months to get into his bed?

Now they were face to face, and she stood silently to one side to let the girl pass. She was clutching a bundle of clothes to her chest. Encountering Philippa's disparaging stare she dropped her shoes; scarlet-faced she scrabbled for them, letting slip the rest of the bundle. Philippa noticed the strong body, curiously disproportionate to the etiolated neck and the thin face. Her breasts were as heavy as a nursing mother's, the nipples jutting like miniature udders from their brown concave areolas. How could he have chosen to take them into his mouth? She thought complacently of her own high, tight breasts, the delicately furled nipples, only slightly raised. She was glad she approved of her body, even if, as yet, she hadn't taught it how to give her pleasure.

She came into the room and closed the door. She said:

'I would have thought you'd have had more pride than to bring her here, to fuck her on your own bed.'

'Whose bed are you suggesting I should more properly use? Don't be predictable, Philippa. Do you have to react like a character in a second-rate TV soap opera?'

'But it's that kind of situation, isn't it? Commonplace. Farcical.' And so, she thought, is this conversation. Like everything we say to each other, it's contrived.

He sat on the bed, pulling on his shirt. She was surprised that he hadn't first reached for his trousers. To be trouserless was surely to be vulnerable, ridiculous, the stock butt of bedroom farce. His pants were very short, white and narrowly striped with blue. She had seen Hilda pulling them out of the washing machine often enough. A tangle of male clothes. He was fastidious. Everything was clean every day. He said:

'It may seem farcical and commonplace – but doesn't it occur to you that I might be fond of her, might love her?'

'No. You're like me. We don't know how.'

Once she had been afraid that she would never learn, but not now, not any more. She watched him dress. How long had it been going on, she wondered. Weeks, months, years? Had it perhaps started as soon as Hilda was appointed to the Bench? It must have seemed an ideal opportunity; the house free on the same day every week for three months. How many girls? A new one for each academic year? They would have had to avoid arriving together, but that wouldn't be difficult. He could come home through the mews service road leading to the garden door, then open the front door to her ring. The street was very quiet in the afternoon; but it wouldn't greatly matter if she were seen. After all, he was a lecturer, he had students to supervise. She asked:

'Where is she now?'

'I haven't the least idea. In the bathroom, I imagine.'

'As long as she isn't drowning herself. That would take some explaining away.'

'Oh, I don't think she's suicidal. Insecure and emotionally a bit intense, but not suicidal. But you'd better go and find out if you're worried.'

'She's your responsibility, not mine. She's rather wet isn't she? I shouldn't have thought that she was your type. Is she really the best you can find?'

'Don't underrate her.'

'That would be difficult, judging by her dinner conversation. She was so stupid with her talk about property and theft. Second-hand jargon and third-hand ideas. I got tired of waiting for her to make an original or amusing remark. No wonder you're reduced to fucking her. Anything would be less boring than listening to her conversation.'

He had finished dressing now and was putting on his jacket, carefully transferring odd items from the dressing-table into his pockets. He said:

'Oddly enough, it was after that evening that we became lovers. I felt sorry for her. With me that's always dangerous.'

'Is that why you married Hilda?'

As soon as the words were out she regretted them. But all he said was:

'No, that was because she was sorry for me.'

She waited for him to explain, but he said no more. And suddenly, she thought of Orlando. She had never spoken his name to Maurice, but now she was filled with a sympathy which had to find expression. She said:

'I forgot about Orlando. I always do forget. I suppose it's because you've never talked about him, never even shown me a photograph. And I've never told you that I'm sorry he died. Until now I don't think I was particularly sorry. If he hadn't died I wouldn't be here. And I never knew him: if one can ever know a child. But you've lost him more completely than my mother was ever in danger of losing me. At least she'd have known that I was alive somewhere.'

He didn't reply, but his hands ceased their careful busyness with his jacket. She looked at his face. In one second it had become as vacant as the face of a spent actor's in repose, all emotion, even the lines, smoothed away. Then there passed over it a look so momentary that she almost missed it, of pain, regret, of the rueful acceptance of defeat. She had seen that look once before. The picture came vividly to her mind, limed with the colour of blood. The screech of tyres followed immediately by a crash like an explosion. The young motor-cyclist, helmetless, lying on the kerb at the junction of Oxford Street and Charing Cross Road. The wheels of his motor cycle spinning in the air. A second of eerie silence, absolute, the air holding its breath. Then the babble of voices, cries. A woman with a face like lard, a cardigan stretched across her bolster of a chest, yelling in anger and remembered pain.

'He was coming too fast! He was too bloody fast! Oh Christ, those fucking machines!'

He was lying there, dying so publicly, and her railing voice was the last sound he heard on earth. Involuntarily she had stepped towards him and his eyes had met hers. She had seen in them that same look, the rueful acceptance of a terrible knowledge. Afterwards she had hurried home to write it down, an exercise in the creative recollection of trauma. She had torn up the passage. She always did tear up such exercises. Her life was encumbered enough, the wasteland between imagination and reality already too nebulous. But she wished that she hadn't recalled it now. This was a moment of small triumph, a time for planning and action. She hadn't wanted to think about death.

They were simultaneously aware that Sheila Manning had come into the room. She was dressed and was carrying a jacket and a heavy, old-fashioned handbag. Ignoring Philippa, she spoke directly to Maurice:

'You promised that it would be safe. You said no one would be here.'

She was making a brave attempt at dignity, but she couldn't keep from her voice the note of querulous reproach. She sounded, thought Philippa, like Hilda when Maurice was late home for dinner. He wouldn't welcome that peevish reminder of small delinquencies. There was only one way for her to carry off this débâcle successfully, with humour and panache, but these weren't in her armoury. And whatever she said, this would be the end of the affair. The girl was as humiliated and inept as a child caught out in her first sexual experimenting. This room, this moment, most of all this man would be remembered only with self-disgust. She knew that she herself was part of the humiliation, sitting there calmly on the bed by Maurice's side in possession of more than herself.

She said:

'I'm sorry. It was unintentional.'

She sounded insincere to her own ears. She would have despised anyone who believed her, and the girl didn't.

'It doesn't matter. You've done what you wanted to do.'

She turned away. Watching the drooped head, Philippa wondered whether she had started to cry. Maurice at once got up from the bed and went to her. He put an arm round her shoulders and said gently:

'It was horrible for you. I'm so sorry. Please don't worry. These things aren't important, you know. In a few weeks you'll be able to laugh about it.'

'It has never been important, not to you anyway. I shan't come back.'

Perhaps she hoped, pathetically, that the threat would provoke some response from him; pain, anger, reproach. Instead he said, punctilious as a host:

'I'll see you out. Are you sure you've got everything?'

She nodded. They went out together, his arm still round her shoulder, and a minute later Philippa heard the closing thud of the front door. She waited for him in the bedroom, still sitting on the edge of the dishevelled bed. He stood at the door silently regarding her for a moment, then began to pace up and down the room. He said:

'You are enjoying yourself? You look happy and you look well.'

'Yes. Yes I am. I suppose it's the first time in my life that I've been able to feel important to another human being.'

'Indispensable, you mean. There's nothing so intoxicating to the ego as the knowledge that happiness is in one's gift. It's the foundation of every successful marriage. The other person has to be capable of being made happy, of course, and that capacity is rarer than one might imagine. I take it that your mother is?'

'For most of the time, yes.'

'I suppose there are moments when she wonders whether she has the right to live.'

She said:

'Why should she? The world is full of people who've killed a child: a wartime bomb released, a bullet in Belfast which hits the wrong target, a stamp on the car accelerator in a fit of impatience. And what about the drunken drivers, the incompetent doctors? They don't spend their days wondering whether they've a right to live. And she has survived ten years in prison. If anyone has the right to live, she has.'

'And how do you spend your days? I take it you're enjoying the pleasure of patronage, giving her the benefit of your education.'

She thought: 'You should know about that. You enjoyed teaching me.' She said:

'We look at pictures. And I'm showing her London.'

'Didn't she know London already? She and Ducton lived close enough.'

'I don't know. We never talk about the past. She doesn't want to.'

'That's very wise of her. What, incidentally, have you come home for? It wasn't a particularly propitious moment to choose, but I take it that this *démarche* wasn't planned.'

'I came to get some money. The Press have found out where we are. We've got to get away, at least for a time. I don't think they'll be back, but my mother's too upset to stay in Delaney Street. We're going to the Isle of Wight.'

'So the running has started and she's dragging you with her.'

'Not dragging. Never dragging. I'm going because I want to be with her.'

'For God's sake why the Isle of Wight?'

'We think we'd like it there. She went there once as a girl, some kind of Sunday-school treat.'

'There are cheaper bolt holes. I suppose you intended to help yourself from the safe. What I keep in there will just about get you across the Solent.'

'There are other things here I could take and sell. I thought of the caddy spoons. We only want enough cash for the first week or two. Then we can both get a job. That shouldn't be difficult even at the end of the season. We're not fussy what we do.'

'How did the Press discover where you were?'

'We met Gabriel Lomas at the Royal Academy exhibition. I think he put his boyfriend on to us. But first he must have phoned Hilda and got the address out of her. That wouldn't be difficult, not for Gabriel.'

'You might have expected it from the decadent Tory with his high talking and squalid morality. Well, at least you've learned that betrayal isn't the prerogative of the extreme left.'

'I never thought it was.'

'So now you've got a choice between blackmail and theft. Why don't you sell the Henry Walton, by the way? You've got it. It's yours.'

'We like it. We're taking it with us. Besides, you owe us something.'

'Not any longer. You're eighteen, you're of age. When I adopted you I owed you a home, food, education, a reasonable standard of care. I owed you conscientious affection. Anything more isn't within my gift. I don't think there's anything on the slate.'

'I'm not thinking about me. I'm thinking about my mother. You owe her my purchase price. You didn't have to adopt me. You could have fostered me, become my legal guardian. You could have given me a home and education without taking me away from her for ever. The experiment would have been the same – nearly the same anyway. You would still have been able to say: "Look what I've done. Look what I've made of this odd, difficult, uncommunicative child, the daughter of a rapist and a murderer." It's not as if you ever cared about abstractions like justice or retribution. It's not as if you really worried about what she'd done. And you've never had a high regard for criminal justice, have you? Magistrates' courts, the Crown Court; a formal system for ensuring that the poor and incompetent know their place, that the dispossessed don't get their grubby hands on the spoils. The petty thief ends in prison, the financier who makes his fortune dealing in currency ends up in the Lords. I've heard you often enough. Slice through society – you even know the precise socio-economic point at which the cut should be made – and the top half sits in judgement under the royal arms, the bottom half stands in the dock. The rich man in his castle, the poor man at his gate, law makes them high and lowly and orders their estate. So why didn't she qualify for your kind of mercy? She was poor enough, disadvantaged, under-educated, all the things you preach excuse crime. So why not excuse her?'

He said calmly:

'I'm not in the habit of confusing petty recidivism with murder and rape.'

'But you know nothing about her! You don't know what pressures drove her to kill that child. You never bothered to find out. You only knew that she had something you wanted – experimental material – me. Scarce experimental material, no – unique. A child who might have been specially bred for your purpose, to demonstrate that man is the creature of his environment. And there were incidental advantages, a child to keep your wife occupied while you fucked

716

your students. No wonder you had to get your hands on me. But what about my mother? If she'd been hanged, if it had all happened before the death penalty was abolished, the hangman would have been more just. At least he'd have left her something. You were going to take me away for ever. She would have come out of prison and we'd never have known each other, never even have met. By what right did you do that to us? And then you say that you don't owe her anything!'

'Is this what she's told you?'

'No. It's what I've worked out for myself.'

He came over to her, but he didn't sit beside her on the bed. Instead he stood over her, looking down. When he spoke his voice was harder. He said:

'Is that what you've really felt all these last ten years, that you were experimental material? No, don't answer hastily. Think about it. Be honest. Your generation make such a fetish of honesty. The more hurtful it is to others, the more necessary you appear to find it. When Hilda's excellent food slipped down your gullet, did you really see yourself as an experimental animal being fed its nicely calculated ration of protein, vitamins and minerals?'

'Hilda is different. I wish I could love Hilda.'

He said:

'I dare say we both wish that we could love Hilda.' He added: 'She misses you.'

She wanted to cry out: 'But what about you? Do you miss me?' Instead she said:

'I'm sorry, but I'm not coming back.'

'And what about Cambridge?'

'I'm beginning to think that Cambridge isn't as important as I thought it was.'

'Do you mean you'll delay going up, wait a year?'

'Or not go up at all. After all, I'm going to be a novelist. A university education isn't essential for a writer. It could even be a disadvantage. There are better ways of spending the next three years.'

'You mean with her?'

'Yes,' she said simply. 'With her.'

He went across to the window and stood for a minute, parting the net curtains, looking down into the street. What, she wondered, was he expecting to see? What inspiration did he hope for from those brightly painted doors, the elegant fanlights, the brass-bound tubs and window boxes of the opposite terrace? After a moment he turned and began pacing between the two tall windows, eyes on the ground. Neither of them spoke. Then he said:

'There's something I've got to tell you. No, that's not strictly true, I don't have to tell you. Until this afternoon I didn't intend to tell you. But it's time you stopped living in a fantasy world and faced reality.'

She thought: 'He's trying to sound reluctant, concerned, but what he's really feeling is excitement, triumph.' Something of the excitement communicated itself to her, and she felt, too, a spasm of fear. But it passed quickly. There was nothing he could say now which could harm her or her mother. Her eyes followed his careful pacing. Never before had she been so aware of his physical presence, of every breath he drew, of every bone of his head and hands, of every contraction of muscle; the air between them drummed with his heartbeat. And because of this intensity of awareness there was something else she knew, something that she couldn't explain. If now he wanted to hurt her, it had nothing to do with Sheila Manning. How lightly he had taken that humiliation! What had wounded him had been that blurted-out sympathy for the loss of Orlando. This moment was to do with her and him; but it was to do with Orlando too. She waited without speaking for him to begin. If he wanted to make a pretence of embarrassment, of reluctance, she wasn't going to help him. He said:

'You've assumed that Hilda and I adopted you after the murder, that your mother let you go because she was serving a life sentence, had no real choice. I thought when you started living together that she might have told you the truth. Obviously she hasn't. Your adoption order went through exactly two weeks before Julia Scase was killed, and we'd had you as a foster child for six months before then. The truth is quite simple: your mother let you go, because she didn't want you.'

She wished that he'd stop his slow regular pacing, that he'd come over to her, sit beside her, look into her face, do anything except touch her. Instead he glanced at her, an artful, almost conspiratorial glance, so swift that she wondered whether she had imagined that slit-eyed momentary regard. Something, perhaps a speck of dust, was irritating his left eye. He took his handkerchief from his jacket pocket and rubbed it, then stood blinking. Satisfied, he started again on his slow perambulation. He said:

'I don't know what went wrong originally. She was pregnant when she married and it might have been that. I was told that she had a long and painful labour after a difficult pregnancy. That's one of the diagnostic pointers to child abuse. Anyway, there was no bonding of mother and child. I gather that you weren't easy. You were difficult to feed, an unresponsive, perpetually crying baby. She hardly slept at night for your first two years.'

He paused, but she didn't speak. His voice was as cool and controlled as if this were a dissertation before his students, an exposition that he had given so many times before that he knew it by heart. He went on:

'Things didn't improve. The screaming baby became an unloving child. Both of you had violent tempers, but you, of course, were too young to injure her except psychologically. She, unfortunately, could do more damage. One day she struck out at you and gave you a black eye. After that she became frightened. She decided she wasn't cut out for motherhood, so she went back to work and placed you with foster parents. I understand that it was a weekly arrangement; you came home for the weekends. She could stand you for two days a week.'

Philippa said quietly:

'I remember. I remember Auntie May.'

'There were, no doubt, a succession of spurious aunties of various degress of suitability and of responsibility. In June 1968 one of them brought you down to Pennington; it was supposed to be a treat for you, a day in the country. It was just before the house was sold and the woman was visiting her sister who was the pastry cook there. She's retired now, of course. All the old servants have gone. I had to go down to Pennington to arrange about some of Helena's things before the sale, and Hilda and I met you and your foster parent in the garden. Hilda talked to her. She was a relief, I suppose, from the people in the house. And that's how we heard about you. Beddows was her name, Mrs Gladys Beddows. She wanted to stop fostering you – you weren't the easiest of children – but she was worried about letting you go back full time to your parents. She wasn't very bright and she didn't even like you but she had some sense of responsibility.

'After that meeting I couldn't get you out of my mind. The thought of you was like an irritation, something I would rather not have known but wasn't able to forget. I didn't want to get involved. I told myself that you were no concern of mine. I wasn't even thinking then about adopting a child. Hilda had mentioned the possibility, but it wasn't an idea that appealed to me. Certainly I wasn't looking for a child. I told myself that it would do no harm to find out what had happened to you. It was easy enough to trace Mrs Beddows through her sister. She told me that you were back full time with your mother. I nearly left it at that. But I was in the neighbourhood; it would do no harm to call. I didn't even bother to concoct an excuse for the visit, which was unlike me. I don't usually go into new situations unprepared. It was early evening by then and your mother had just come home from work. You weren't there. You had been admitted two days earlier to King George V Hospital, Ilford, with a suspected fracture of the skull. And that was the most dangerous and the last time that your mother lost her temper with you.'

She said through bloated lips, not realizing what tense she was using:

'Is that why the child could never remember anything that happened before she was eight?'

'The amnesia was partly the result of the injury, partly, I imagine, hysterical, the mind's natural reluctance to recall the unbearable. Neither Hilda nor I have ever attempted to cure it. Why should we?'

'And then what happened to her?'

'Your parents agreed that we should foster you when you came out of hospital, with a view to adoption if it worked out all right. There wasn't a prosecution. The hospital apparently accepted your mother's explanation that you'd fallen downstairs and cracked your head on the bottom banister. Those were the days before the Maria Colwell case and the authorities were less ready than now to suspect deliberate ill-treatment. But she told me the truth, she told me everything that June evening. I think she was glad to have someone, a stranger, to whom she could talk. You came to us straight from hospital and six months later we adopted you. Your parents both gave their consent without, I may say, any apparent reluctance. And that is the mother for whom you now propose to give up Cambridge, become a thief, and spend God knows how many years dragging after her from one watering-place to another. The Scase murder, of course, is hardly relevant. She didn't murder you after all, although I gather it was a pretty close thing.'

She didn't cry out in vehement protest that he was lying, that it wasn't true. Maurice only lied about important things, and then only when he could be certain that he wouldn't be found out. This wasn't important to him, and the truth could easily be proved. But she didn't need to check. She knew that it was the truth. She wished that she didn't feel so cold. Her face, her limbs, her fingers, were icy. He ought to have seen that she was shaking. Why didn't he tug a blanket from Hilda's bed and fold it round her? Even her lips were swollen with cold, stiff and numbed as if she had been given a dental injection. It was difficult to form words and her voice, when it came, sounded slurred.

'Why didn't you tell me?'

'I should like to believe that it was because I didn't want to hurt you. Perhaps it was. There are some cruelties which take courage. Mine are on a meaner scale. I did try to warn you. I told you to find out the facts, to read the press accounts of the trial. Those would have told you the date of the murder. You already knew your date of adoption. It might also have struck you as odd that the press reports made no mention of a child. But then, you didn't want to know the facts, didn't want to talk to us about it; it seemed you were wilfully determined to be blind. It's odd that over something so important you never once used your intelligence, you who have always relied on intelligence, have had such a respect for your own mind.'

She wanted to cry out: 'What else have I had to rely on? What else had I on offer?' Instead she said:

'Thank you for telling me now.'

'It needn't make any difference. It's an irrelevance. After all, you're not concerned with conduct or responsibility or nurture. If the blood tie is all that matters to you, well that at least is intact. But I did have you for ten years. I may not be entitled to make any claims on you, but at least I've a right to express a view about your future. And I'm not letting you give up Cambridge without a struggle. The chance of those three years won't come again, not now, not when you're young which is when they matter.'

He added drily:

'I've also the right to my own Georgian silver. If you need money for her, sell the Henry Walton.'

She said as humbly as a servant at the end of an interview:

'Is there anything else you want to tell me before I go?'

'Only that this is your home if you want it. This is where you belong. I've got an adoption order to prove it. And if that legalistic conveyance of possession lacks the emotional charge of the blood tie; hasn't your family had enough of blood?'

At the door she turned and looked back at him. She said:

'But why did you do it? Why me?'

'I told you, I couldn't put you out of my mind. And I was afraid of what might happen to you. I hate waste.'

'But you must have hoped for something: gratitude, diversion, interest, the gratification of patronage, companionship for your old age, the ordinary things?'

'It didn't seem so at the time, but I suppose I did. My demands have always been presumptuous. Perhaps what I hoped for was love.'

Three minutes later he stood at the window watching her leave. There was something different about her, a sense of brightness dulled, of limbs uncoordinated. Perhaps it was the hunch of the shoulders, diminishing height, foreshowing how she might look as an old woman, or the way in which she scurried from the front door, furtive as an interloper surprised. At the end of the terrace she broke into a run, swerving from the pavement into the path of a taxi. He gasped; his heart skidded. When he could bear to open his eyes he saw that she was safe. Even from this distance he could hear the screech of brakes, the shouted abuse. Then, without a backward glance, she had half run, half shambled out of sight.

He wasn't sorry that he had told her, nor was he seriously concerned about her. She had survived those first seven years; she would survive this. And, after all, she wanted to be a writer. Someone had said – he couldn't remember who – that an artist should suffer in childhood as much trauma as could be borne without breaking. And she wouldn't break. Others would break, but not she. There would be tatters and torn flesh enough on the barbed wire guarding that untender heart. But he was aware of a nag of anxiety, irritating because he guessed that it might be difficult to rationalize away, and because, like all his anxieties, it was allied to guilt. He wondered what she would say to her mother. Whatever the nature of the tie between them, he didn't suppose that she loved her mother in any sense in which he understood that ubiquitous word. After all, they had only been together for five weeks. She had lived with him and Hilda for ten years, undisturbed, apparently, by any need to love. He wondered what she would have said, how she would have looked, if, sitting there on the bed in his post-coital depletion, he had spoken at least a part of the truth about Sheila Manning.

'I took her from egotism, boredom, curiosity, sexual conceit, pity, perhaps even from affection. But she's only a substitute. They're all of them substitutes. When she was in my arms I was imagining that she was you.'

He saw that the bedcover was crooked and he smoothed it. That was the kind of detail that Hilda, obsessive housewife that she was, would notice. Then he went into the bathroom to check that Sheila had left no trace of herself there. He needn't worry that there would be an echo of her scent lingering in the bedroom. Before he had brought her to Caldecote Terrace for the first time he had warned her not to wear scent. She had replied:

'I never do.'

He remembered her face, blotched with embarrassment and hurt, that he shouldn't have noticed that. The warning – revealing as it had a calculation of risk, born perhaps of previous embarrassments and discoveries – had denigrated their love in her eyes, reduced their first time together to a commonplace, sordid intrigue. It hadn't been that; but for him it hadn't been much more. Why, he wondered, was he driven into these petty expedients of lust? Boredom? The ennui of the male menopause? A compensation for his sterility? The need to reassure himself that he was still virile, still attractive to younger women? A search, which he knew in advance to be hopeless, for the lost enchantments of love?

He felt physically and emotionally drained. He needed to cosset himself. He fetched a glass, a bottle of Niersteiner and the ice bucket and went to sit in the garden. The air was as heavy and oppressive as a sweaty blanket and he thought he could sniff the far-off metallic smell of thunder. He wished that the blanket would burst and the rain would fall, that he could lift up his face and feel the great cool sheets of it drenching his skin. He wondered why Hilda was so late, then remembered that she had said something at breakfast about late shopping in Oxford Street. He supposed that meant that they were to make do with a cold supper.

He wasn't distressed about Sheila Manning. Hilda was due to give up the juvenile Bench in two weeks' time, and he had planned to use that as an excuse for ending the affair. This evening's fiasco had saved him the protracted and emotionally wearing strategies, the appeals and reproaches, which usually accompanied the death of desire. The problem about wanting women who evoked his pity was that these were precisely the women who were the most difficult to get rid of. He wished he could be like some of his colleagues and take a succession of the guilt-free, experienced and cheerfully randy young who would ask nothing more of him than the occasional good dinner and the brief exchange of pleasure.

He supposed he would have to let Hilda know about Philippa's visit. He would tell the truth, merely editing out Sheila Manning. He could be confident that Philippa would never tell her, and it seemed to him not of immense importance if she did. Philippa would be coming home now and that should please Hilda. Life would go on as it had before. He supposed that that was what he wanted. He let his mind slip free of worry and guilt and closed his eyes. And in that moment of almost disembodied peace, the smell of wine and roses fused and he was back again, walking between the high hedges into the great circular rose garden at Pennington on a June day ten years ago. He was seeing Philippa for the first time.

9

He had never seen a child like her. She stood very still, a little apart from her keeper, a shapeless ungainly woman, querulous in the heat, and regarded him gravely with those extraordinary luminous green eyes under the curving brows. Her skin absorbed the mellow afternoon light, the shadowed green of the high hedge, so that it was like seeing her through water. Her hair was plaited corn drawn across her forehead in a mature, old-fashioned style which added to the contrast between the sixteenth-century Renaissance head held so proudly, and the childish body. He guessed that she was about seven. She was wearing a kilt too heavy for summer and reaching almost to her calves, with an immense safety-pin bunching it on one side. Her pale arms, downy and glinting in the sun, stuck out from a shirt so thin that it clung to her bony chest, brittle as a bird's. He could see her nipples, two pink delicate tags of flesh.

Hilda began talking to the woman, learning that her name was Gladys Beddows, that she was at Pennington to visit her sister. He spoke to the child:

'Isn't it dull for you here? What would you like to do?'

'Have you any books?'

'Lots, in the library. Would you like to see them?'

She nodded and they began walking across the lawn together, the two women following. She walked at his side, but distanced, her hands held in front of her, the palms folded together in a curiously formal, unchildish gesture. A few yards behind them Mrs Beddows seemed to be confiding her difficulties to Hilda. That type of woman usually did. Hilda, herself uncommunicative, gauche, somehow invited confidences, or lacked the assurance and ruthlessness to reject them. Whenever he entered the kitchen on the two days a week when the daily help was there he would find the two women drinking coffee together, Hilda's head docilely bowed under a spate of domestic disgruntlement. Now the whine of resentment came clearly to them, carried on the warm, rose-scented air.

'Not as if they pay much. And I have her all day, some nights as well. She's a difficult child. Never get a thank-you out of her. And talk about temper! Screaming tantrums some of the time. Nightmares too. Not surprised her mother can't cope. Not what you'd call pretty, is she? Odd-looking child. Clever, mind you. Always got her head in a book. Oh, she's sharp, that one! So sharp she'll cut herself one of these days.'

He glanced at the child. She must have heard. How could she help hearing? But she gave no sign. She walked on in her unchildish, hieratic dignity, but carefully, as if holding something precious between the clasped hands.

The woman was right. She wasn't a pretty child. But the fine bone structure of the face, the green eyes, gave promise of a spectacular if eccentric beauty. And she was intelligent, courageous and proud. These were the qualities he respected. Something could be made of such a child. He wanted to say to her: 'I don't think you're plain.

And I like clever children. Never be ashamed of being clever.' But glancing again at her set face he said nothing. Pity would be an impertinence to this proud, self-absorbed child.

The southern aspect of Pennington stretched out before them, golden and serene, the great orangery shooting shafts of light so that his eyes dazzled. This was the view of the house he had seen when he had first visited Pennington with Helena. That, too, had been in high summer; but then he had been in love, intoxicated with the smell of roses and gillyflowers, with the wine they had drunk with their picnic on the drive down, with happiness, with the immensity of his prize. They had been coming to Pennington together to tell her father that they were to be married. Now walking that same lawn, the child's shadow moving with his like a ghost, he could look back almost dispassionately, with pity as well as with contempt, to that poor deluded fool frolicking in a dead summer which now seemed to have held the concentrated sweetness of all summers, invincibly arrogant in the high renaissance of the heart. And so they walked across the lawn together, the child with her pain, he with his.

The library was dark and cool after the glare of the sun. The books had been sold separately from the house, and already the archivists and workmen were there checking and packing the volumes. It should have pleased him that yet another aristocrat was reneging on his responsibilities, that this great house would no longer be the seat of a family, passing from father to son in the primogeniture of privilege, but would become institutionalized, debased. Instead, looking up at the fine stuccoed ceiling, and at the gorgeous Grinling Gibbons carvings on the bookcases, he was aware of a gentle nostalgic melancholy. If this room had belonged to him, he would never have let it go.

The child stood at his side, both of them looking in silence. Then he led her across the room to the chart table where a miscellany of Helena's books had been collected for him.

He said:

'How old are you? Can you read?'

Her voice rebuked him:

'I'm eight. I could read before I was four.'

'Then let's see how you do with this.'

He picked up the Shakespeare, opened it and handed it to her. He was behaving like a pedant with no particular intention. The afternoon was hot, he was bored, the child intrigued him. She took the book into her hands with difficulty and began to read. He had opened it at *King John*.

> 'Grief fills the room up of my absent child,
> Lies in his bed, walks up and down with me,
> Puts on his pretty looks, repeats his words,
> Remembers me of all his gracious parts,
> Stuffs out his vacant garments with his form.'

She read to the end of the speech, faultlessly. She didn't, of course, speak it in the cadence of blank verse. But she knew that it was poetry and she spoke it carefully in her childish, unemphatic voice, wary of unfamiliar words. It was the more poignant. He felt the tears stinging his eyes for the first time since he had learned that Orlando wasn't his son.

And that was how it had begun. It seemed to him that those two moments, so curiously linked by the memory of Orlando, the first in which he had watched the tears start from Hilda's eyes, the second in which the child's clear voice had brought tears to his, had been the only times in his life which had been free from self-regard. The one had resulted in his second marriage; the other in the adoption of Philippa. He wasn't asking himself now if they had led to disappointment. He wasn't sure what his expectations had been. The absence of expectation had been part of the purity of the moments, had brought them close to what he supposed some people might call goodness. He had almost forgotten the anguish of grief. Now it returned to him, less keen but more diffuse, embracing in one nostalgic melancholy the loss of Orlando, the unborn children he could never father, the stripped library at Pennington, and the child in her ridiculous skirt walking with him across the lawn in the mellow sunlight of a dead June day ten years ago.

10

For Philippa the journey from Caldecote Terrace to Delaney Street was a blank. Time was blotted out completely as if her mind was anaesthetized and her body obeying some programmed instructions. She was aware of only one incident; running for the bus at

Victoria and grasping the slippery rail, a moment of panic, and then the jerk of her armpit as a passenger on the platform caught her and hauled her aboard. Delaney Street was very quiet. The rain had begun to fall steadily in slivers of silver against the street lamps, and behind the patterned glass of the Blind Beggar the lights of the bar shone red and green. She turned her key in the Yale lock, closed the front door quietly behind her and walked up the stairs calmly without switching on the light. In the darkness she pushed the flat door, feeling under her palm the sharpness of the splintered wood. Her mother heard her and called out from the kitchen. She must be preparing supper, mixing the salad dressing; there hung on the air the sharp tang of vinegar. It was the same smell that had greeted her on her return to Caldecote Terrace after her visit to Seven Kings and the two moments fused together, the old pain reinforcing the new. Her mother's voice sounded happy, welcoming. Perhaps she had decided that they needn't move after all. She walked into the kitchen. Her mother turned, smiling, to greet her. Then the smile died, and Philippa watched as the face, so different yet so like her own, drained of blood. Her mother whispered:

'What is it? What's happened? What's happened, Philippa?'

She said:

'Why don't you call me Rose? You called me Rose earlier this evening. You had me christened Rose. I was Rose when you nearly killed me. I was Rose when you decided you didn't want me. I was Rose when you gave me away.'

There was a moment of silence. Her mother felt for a chair and sat down. She said:

'I thought you knew. When you first came to Melcombe Grange I asked if you knew about your adoption. You said you did.'

'I thought you meant did I know about the murder. I thought you were reminding me why it was that you had to give me up. You must have known that's what I thought.'

'And I gave you my account of the murder, when she died, the date of my conviction. Even then, you didn't ask any questions.'

'When I read it I wasn't thinking of dates and times. I was thinking of you.'

Her mother went on as if she hadn't spoken:

'And afterwards, because I was so happy here, I said nothing. I told myself that the past wasn't our past. They were two different people in a different story. I thought I might let myself have just these two months. Whatever happened afterwards, I should have something worth remembering. But I meant to tell you. I would have told you in the end.'

'When you could be sure that I'd got used to having a mother. When I didn't want to let you go. My God, you're clever! Maurice warned me that you were clever. At least I've learned one thing about myself, where I get my scheming intelligence. And what about my father? Did he hate me too? Or was he too ineffective to stop you, too timid to do anything except rape a child? What did you do to him that he needed that act to prove his manhood?'

Her mother looked up at her as if there was something which had to be explained, which could be explained.

'You mustn't blame your father. He wanted to keep you. I per-suaded him to let you go. I was the one who thought it was better for you. And it *was* better for you. What had I to give you?'

'Was I such a nuisance, so much trouble? Couldn't you have tried with me a little longer? Oh God, why did I ever find you!'

'I did try. I wanted to love you. I wanted you to love me. But you didn't respond, ever. You cried endlessly. Nothing I could do comforted you. You wouldn't even let me feed you.'

'Are you telling me that it was I who rejected you?'

'No, only that it seemed like it to me.'

'How could I, a new-born child? I had no choice. I had to love you in order to survive.'

He mother asked with a humility which Philippa found almost unbearable:

'Do you want me to leave at once?'

'No, I'll go. I'll find somewhere. It's easier for me. I don't have to go back to Caldecote Terrace. I've got friends in London. You can stay here until the lease runs out. That'll give you time to find another place. I'll send for the picture. You can have the rest.'

She heard her mother's voice. She spoke so softly that Philippa hardly caught the words:

'Is what I did to you so much more difficult to forgive than what I did to that child?'

She didn't reply. She snatched up her shoulder bag and made for the door. Then she turned and spoke to her mother for the last time:

'I don't want to see you ever again. I wish they'd hanged you nine years ago. I wish you were dead.'

11

She controlled her crying until she was out of Delaney Street. Then it burst out in a scream of agony. Hair flying loose, she ran wildly through the rain, her shoulder bag bumping against her side. Instinctively, she turned up Lisson Grove seeking the dark solitude of the canal towpath. But the gate had long since been closed for the night. She pounded against it, but she knew that it wouldn't yield. On she ran, her face streaming with mingled tears and rain, seeing no one, careless now which way she ran, almost howling with pain. Suddenly a spasm of cramp twisted like a knife in her side. Doubled up, she gasped, gulping in the streaming air like a drowning woman. She clutched at some nearby railings, waiting for the pain to pass. Beyond the railings were tall trees and, even through the rain, she could smell the canal. She checked her crying and listened. The night was full of small secretive noises. And then there came a howl, alien and eerie, louder and wilder even than her own misery, answering pain with pain. It was the cry of an animal; she must be close to Regent's Park zoo.

She was calmer now. Her tears were still flowing but in a gentle, unbroken stream. She walked on through the night. The city was streaked with light, bleeding with light. The headlamps of the cars dazzled on the road and the crimson pools of the traffic lights lay on the surface like blood. The rain was falling in a solid wall of water, drenching her clothes, plastering her hair against her face and eyes; she could taste it on her lips as salty as the sea.

It seemed to her that her mind was a black and seething dungeon, too many thoughts fighting for air, pressing each other down, tortuous elongated thoughts writhing in rank darkness. And from that dense confusion rose the thin misery of a child's cry. It wasn't the peevish complaint one heard in supermarkets; this was a desolation of terror and anguish not to be comforted with a packet of sweets at the check-out. She told herself that she mustn't panic; to panic would be to go mad. She must sort out her thoughts, arrange them, impose order on chaos. But first she had to stop that dreadful crying. She put her hands up to her throat and squeezed, strangling the child into silence, and when she released her hands the crying had stopped.

They hadn't, in all their weeks together, once spoken of the dead child. They hadn't talked about the child's parents. How much had they cared? How long had they grieved? Perhaps they now had other children and this long-dead, violated child was only a painful, half-rejected memory. Grief fills the room up of my absent child. The child was dead. That fact had been less important to her than whether her mother had kept the kitchen clean. Her mother had killed a child, had clamped her small hand to a pram and dragged her faster and faster, until she fell under the spinning wheels. But that was a different child, another place. She had killed the child's father, too. He had come across the lawn in the summer sunshine, beautiful as a god, to where they used to meet in the rose garden at Pennington. And now he, too, was dead. She had buried him in the moist drifts of the forest. To lie in cold obstruction and to rot. He was rotting there under the trees. But that was someone else's father. Hers was under quicklime in an anonymous grave in a prison yard. Or was that only how they buried executed murderers? What did they do with the bodies of felons who died in prison? Did they carry them out secretly at night, cheaply coffined, to be disposed of at the nearest crematorium, without any comfortable words, the furnace flaring like the flames of hell? And what did they do with the ashes? That neatly packaged residue of ground bone must have been buried somewhere. She had never thought to ask, and her mother had never told her. Parthenophil is lost, and I would see him for he is like to something I remember a great while since, a long long time ago.

Suddenly there shone before her the glowing sign of Warwick Avenue Underground Station. The wide road, lined with its Italianate houses and stuccoed villas, ran with liquid light. As she half ran, half walked down the deserted pavement, the overhanging bushes in the front gardens rained a shower of white sodden petals and torn leaves over her hair. And here, at last, was the canal and she was standing on the elegant wrought-iron bridge which spanned the dividing waterway. At the corners of the bridge the high nineteenth-century lamps, each on its pedestal, cast a trembling light over the canal basin, the leafy island, the painted narrowboats moored at the canal wall, the long dark length of tree-shadowed water. Where the lamps shone brightest the plane trees seemed to burn with flickering green flames and below her, where the rain spurted from the roof of a narrowboat, there gleamed a brightly painted enamel jug filled with storm-tossed Michaelmas daisies.

Behind her the unceasing wheels of the cars swished past, slicing through the running gutters and hurling fountains of spray against the bridge. There were no pedestrians in sight and the avenues on each side of the canal were deserted. From the houses the lights shone out from balconied windows, illuminating the plane trees and laying a shivering path of light over the sluggish water.

She was still wearing the jumper her mother had knitted for her. It was sodden and weighted with rain, the high collar cold against her neck. She pulled it over her head then, reaching up, she held it out and let it gently drop over the parapet and into the canal. For a minute it lay on the surface of the water illumined by the lamp-light, looking as frail and transparent as gossamer. The two sleeves were stretched out; it could have been a drowning child. Then, almost imperceptibly, it floated out of the path of light, sinking slowly as it moved, until her swollen watching eyes could only imagine its pattern on the dark water.

With the jumper gone she felt a physical sense of release. She was wearing nothing now but her trousers and a thin cotton shirt. The rain drenched it so that it clung to her like a second skin. And so, unencumbered, she walked on, under the great concrete arches of the Westway and south towards Kensington. She had no awareness of time, no sense of direction; all that mattered was that she should keep walking. She hardly noticed when the rain changed to slow, ponderous drops, then finally stopped, when the noisy bus routes gave way to quiet squares.

But at last she walked herself into exhaustion. It hit her suddenly, as unexpected and violent as a body blow. Her legs sagged and she tottered to the side of the pavement and grasped at a row of iron railings which surrounded the garden of a wide square. But the weariness which cramped her body had released her mind; thought was once again coherent, disciplined, rational. She leaned her head against the railings and felt the iron, parallel red-hot rods, branding her forehead. There was a privet hedge behind the railings, its pungent greenness filled her nostrils and spiked her cheeks. The wave of exhaustion flowed through her, leaving in its wake a gentle tiredness which was almost pleasurable.

Consciousness slipped away. She was jerked back to awareness by a high-pitched yell. The night was suddenly loud with running feet and raucous voices. From the far corner a gang of youths erupted into the square and reeled in a disorderly stream across the road to the garden. They were obviously drunk. Two of them, clutched together, were bawling a plaintive, discordant song. The others shouted meaningless staccato chants, slogans and tribal battle cries in a hoarse, broken cacophony of menace. Terrified that they would see her, that her shoulder bag, she herself, would present too easy a spoil, Philippa strained back against the railings. The gang had no clear purpose or direction. It was possible that they would stagger again into the road and miss seeing her.

But the voices grew louder. They were coming her way. One of them flung a toilet roll. It spun over the railings and into the garden, just missing her head. Its pale, undulating tail, transparent as a stream of light, floated and turned on the night breeze then came to rest on the surface of the hedge, light as a cobweb. And still they came, heads bobbing above the privet. She began to walk quickly away from them, still keeping close to the railings, but as soon as she moved they saw her. They gave a great shout, the jarring, unrelated voices raised in the united bellow of triumph.

She broke into a run, but they pounded after her, more purposeful and less drunk than she had expected. She forgot her tiredness in her fear, but she knew that she couldn't sustain the pace for long. She sped across the wide street and down a road of tall, decaying houses. She could hear her feet slapping the pavement, could see from the corner of her eyes the flashing railings, could feel the wild rhythmic drumming of her heart. They were still behind her, shouting less now, reserving energy for the chase. Suddenly she came to another road turning off to the left. She swerved down it and saw with a gasp of relief that a gate in the railings was open. She almost threw herself down the steps and into the dark, evil-smelling area, almost colliding with three battered dustbins. She squeezed herself behind them and crouched in the narrow space under the flight of steps leading to the front door. Bent almost double she folded her arms over her chest, trying to stifle the pounding of her heart. How could they fail to be drawn to that insistent drumming?

But the running feet hesitated, then clattered past, then died. From down the street she heard their bay of frustrated anger. Then they broke again into the disorganized shouts and singing. There was to be no search. They probably thought that she lived in the street and had gained the safety of her own home. More probably they were too drunk to think clearly. Once the quarry had gone to earth their interest died.

She stayed there long after their voices had faded away, crouched under the curve of the brick roof. She felt herself confined in a dark stinking cell, breathing dust and the spent breath of long-dead captives, bereft of the sky; the three malodorous dustbins, their shape imagined rather than seen, blocking her escape as effectively as a bolted door. There came to her in the darkness no blinding revelation, no healing of the spirit, only a measure of painful self-knowledge. From the moment of her counselling she had thought of no one but herself. Not of Hilda, who had so little to give but asked so little in return and needed that little so much. Hilda, who might reasonably have expected a greater return for those difficult years of caring than occasional help with the dining-room flowers. Not of Maurice, as arrogant and self-deceiving as herself, but who had done his best for her, had given with generosity even if he couldn't give with love, had somehow found the kindness to shield her from the worst knowledge. Not of her mother. What had she been but a purveyor of information, the living pattern of her own physical life, the victim of her patronage and self-love? She told herself that she had to learn humility. She was not sure that the lesson lay within her competence, but this stinking corner of the sleeping city into which she had crept like a derelict was as good a place as any in which to begin. She knew, too, that what bound her to her mother was stronger than hate, or disappointment or the pain of rejection. Surely this need to see her again, to be comforted by her, was the beginning of love; and how could she have expected that there could be love without pain?

After a time she eased herself out of the area and again breathed the cool night air and saw the stars. She walked on, almost lightheaded with tiredness, searching for the names of streets. They told her nothing except that she was in the W10 district. She found herself in another square lying quiet and secret under the surging sky. In her mind the city seemed to stretch for ever, a silent half-derelict immensity, palely illumined by the recurrent moon. It was a dead city, plague-ridden and abandoned, from which all life had fled except for that band of scavenging louts. Now they too would have staggered into some filthy area, huddled together in death. She was completely alone. Behind the peeling stucco, the tall balustrades, lay the rotting dead. The stench of the city's decay rose like a miasma from the basement areas.

And then she saw the woman walking quickly but lightly across the square towards her on high-arched elegant feet. She wore a long pale dress and a stole. Her yellow hair was piled high. Everything about her was pale, the floating dress, her hair, her night-bleached skin. As they came abreast, Philippa asked:

'Could you please tell me where I am? I'm trying to get to Marylebone Station.'

The voice that answered her was pleasant, cheerful, cultured.

'You're in Moxford Square. Walk down this street for about a hundred yards. Take the first turning on the left and you'll find yourself at Ladbroke Grove Underground. I think you'll have missed the last train but you might pick up a late-night bus or a taxi.'

Philippa said:

'Thank you. If I can get to Ladbroke Grove I know my way.'

The woman smiled and walked on across the square. The encounter had been so unexpected and yet so ordinary that Philippa found herself wondering whether her tired brain had conjured up an apparition. Who was she and where was she going, this confident walker of the night? What friend or lover had deposited her here, unescorted, in the early hours? From what party had she come or was she escaping? But the woman's directions proved correct. Five minutes later Philippa found herself at Ladbroke Grove and began walking southwards towards home.

Delaney Street was silent and empty, sleeping as quietly as a village street beneath the unthreatening sky. The rain-washed air smelled of the sea. The windows of all the houses were dark except where number 12 showed a faint haze of light behind the drawn curtains. It wasn't bright enough for the ceiling light. Her mother must be still awake, or if she had fallen asleep, must have done so before she remembered to switch off the bedside lamp. She hoped that she would still be awake. She wondered what they would say to each other. She knew that she wouldn't be able to say that she was sorry, not yet; she had never said that in all her life. But perhaps it was a beginning that she could feel it. Perhaps, too, her mother would understand without the need of words. She would hold out the key of the front door to her and say:

'I must have meant all the time to come back. I didn't remember to leave you the key.'

She would stand there in her mother's doorway, and the fact that she was there would be enough. It would say:

'I love you. I need you. I have come home.'

12

The bedside lamp was on and in its pool of softened light her mother lay on her back asleep. But there was someone else in the room. Sitting slumped forward at the foot of the bed, hands between his knees, was a man, white-robed, shimmering with light. He didn't move or look up as she walked over to the bed. Her mother's face was perfectly calm. But something strange had happened to her neck. An animal had her by the throat, a small, white, slug-like beast with its pink snout buried in her flesh. Something was eating her alive, burrowing away, tearing out the sinews, voiding its leavings on her white skin. But still she didn't stir. Philippa turned to the man; and this time she saw in his dangling hands the bloodstained knife. And then she both saw and understood.

He looked so grotesque that her first thought was that he was the creature of delirium born of her exhaustion and the phantasmagoria of the night. But she knew that he was real. His being there by her mother's side was as inevitable as was her death. He was wearing a long raincoat of white transparent plastic, so thin that it clung to him like a film. On his hands were plastic gloves, surgeon's gloves, clinging to the pale flesh. They were too large for his tiny hands. At the end of each finger the plastic had gummed together and hung in pale flaps as if the skin itself were peeling away. Hiroshima hands. She said:

'Take off your gloves, they disgust me. You disgust me.'

Obediently he peeled them off.

He looked up at her. He said, simply as a child craving reassurance:

'She won't bleed. She won't bleed.'

She moved closer to the bed. Her mother's eyes were closed. It was considerate of her to die with her eyes closed, but was that something one could choose to do? She tried to recall the pictured dead. It wasn't difficult; there were so many of them. The minds of her generation were patterned like nursery wallpaper with images of death; violence lay around their cradles. The corpses of Belsen piled like skinned rabbits in ungainly heaps, spike-bellied children of Ethiopia and India carrying their hunger like a monstrous foetus, the denuded bodies of soldiers sprawled in the clumsy dishevelment of death, all open-eyed. 'Tis a fine deceit to pass away in a dream. Indeed I've slept with mine eyes open a great while. But her mother's eyes were closed. Had she gone so gentle into her good night? She turned to the man and said fiercely:

'Have you touched her?'

He didn't reply. He made a movement of his bent head. It could have meant yes or no. There was an envelope propped against a small tablet-bottle on the bedside table. The flap hadn't been stuck down. She read:

'If God can forgive her death then he will forgive mine. These five weeks have been worth every day of the last ten years. Nothing is your fault. Nothing. This is the better way for me, not just for you. I can die happy because you are alive and I love you. Never be afraid.'

She put the note down on the table and looked again at the man. He was sitting on the edge of the bed, head bowed, the knife drooping from his hands. She took it from him and put it on the table. His hands were small, like a child's hands, a hamster's claws. He was beginning to shake and the bed shook with him. Her mother's body might have been shaking with laughter. She was afraid that the barely closed eyes would jolt open and that she would have to look on death. What was so terrible about grief was not grief itself, but that one got over it. It was strange to learn this truth even before the grieving had begun. She said, more gently:

'Come away from her. She won't bleed. The dead don't bleed. I got to her before you.'

She took hold of his shoulder and, half lifting him from the bed, led him over to the basket chair. The two-bar electric fire was off, as if her mother had remembered that they needed to save electricity. She switched on a single bar and turned it towards him. She said:

'I know who you are. I saw you in Regent's Park and somewhere else too, somewhere before that. Did you always plan to kill her?'

'My wife did, from the moment our daughter died.' Then he added: 'We planned it together.'

He seemed to need to explain.

'I came late tonight, but you hadn't left. The light in the front room was still on. I sat in the shop and listened and waited. But you didn't leave. There were no footsteps overhead, no sounds. At midnight I crept upstairs. The door was smashed and open. I thought she was asleep. She looked as if she was asleep. I didn't notice until I drove in the knife that her eyes were open. Her eyes were wide open and she was looking at me.'

She said:

'You'd better go. You did what you came for. It wasn't your fault that she escaped you in the end.' Death of one person can be paid but once and that she hath discharged. What thou wouldst do is done unto thy hand.

She said more loudly, shaking him gently by the shoulder:

'I shall have to call the police. If you don't want to be here when they come you'd better go now. There's no need for you to get involved.'

He didn't move. He was staring at the bar of the fire. He muttered something. She had to bend her head to hear him:

'I didn't know it would be like this. I want to be sick.'

She supported him into the kitchen and held his head while he retched over the sink, surprised that she could touch him without revulsion, could be so aware of the curiously silken texture of his hair, sliding over the hard skull. It seemed to her that her hand experienced simultaneously every single hair and the soft moving mass. She wanted to say: 'She didn't mean to kill. It was a burst of anger which she couldn't control. She never wanted your child dead in the way that you and I wanted her dead, willed her death.' But what was the use? What did it matter? His child was dead. Her mother was dead. Words, explanations, excuses, were an irrelevance. About that final negation there was nothing new to be thought, nothing new to be said, nothing that could be put right.

Everything in the kitchen was the same. As his head shuddered between her hands and the stink of vomit rose to her nostrils, she gazed round at the familiar objects, marvelling that they were unchanged. The teapot and two cups on the round papier-mâché tray; the glistening pellets of coffee beans in their glass jar, how erotically beautiful they were – freshly ground coffee had been one of their extravagances; the row of herbs in their pots on the window ledge. The north-facing window wasn't the best light for them, but still they had thrived. Tomorrow they had planned to snip the first chives for a herb omelette. The dressing her mother had made was still there in a jug on the table, the tang of vinegar still in the air. She wondered if she would be able to smell it in the future without thinking of this moment. She looked at the carefully folded tea towels, the two mugs on their hooks, the saucepans with their handles carefully aligned. How excessively neat they had been, imposing order and permanence on their insubstantial and precarious lives.

He was still retching but now it was only bile. The worst of the sickness was over. She handed him a towel and said:

'The bathroom's on the half landing if you want it.'

'Yes, I know.' He wiped his face and his mild eyes met hers. 'Won't you get into trouble? With the police, I mean.'

'No. She killed herself. The knife wound was made after death. Doctors can prove that. You saw yourself that she didn't bleed. I don't think there is a criminal offence of mutilating the dead. Even if there is, I don't suppose they'll charge me. All anyone will want is to get the whole unsavoury affair neatly tidied up. You see, no one cares about her. No one will mind that she's dead. She doesn't count as a human being. They think that she should have been killed nine years ago. She should have been hanged, that's what they'll all say.'

'But the police might think you killed her.'

'There's a suicide note to prove I didn't.'

'But suppose they think that you forged it.'

How extraordinary that he should get that idea. What a sophistical mind he must have. She looked into the meek, anxious eyes. Behind them a clever little brain must be scheming away. He ought to be writing thrillers. He had the mind of a thriller writer, obsessive, guilt-ridden, preoccupied with trivia. He had lived too long with thoughts of death. She said:

'I can prove that she wrote it. I've got a long specimen of her handwriting, a story she wrote in prison, a story about a rapist and his wife. Look, you'd better go. There's no point in letting the police find you unless you like the idea of seeing your face in all the newspapers. Some people do; is that what you want?'

He shook his head. He said:

'I want to go home.'

'Home?' she asked. She hadn't thought of him as having a home, this nocturnal predator with his finicky hands that could do so much damage, his stink of vomit. She thought he whispered something about Casablanca being home, but that was surely absurd.

He asked:

'Shall we see each other again?'

'I don't suppose so. Why should we? All we have in common is that we both wanted her dead. I don't see that as a basis for social acquaintance.'

'Are you sure you'll be all right?'

'Oh yes,' she said. 'I'll be all right. There'll be plenty of people to make sure that I'm all right.'

There was a rucksack on the floor beside the door. She hadn't noticed it before. He took off his mackintosh, rolled it, and stuffed it inside. It was, she thought, something he had done many times before. But when he reached for the knife, she said:

'Leave it. Leave it where it is. I'll see that it has my fingerprints on it.'

They went down the stairs together as if he were a dilatory visitor whom she was managing to see off at last. He walked quickly up Delaney Street without a backward glance, and she watched him out of sight. She returned to the bedroom. She couldn't look at her mother, but she made herself take up the knife and hold it for a moment in her hand. Then she ran out of the flat to Marylebone Station to telephone Maurice.

The entrance to the concourse was deserted, the row of telephone booths empty, except for one figure. A young man was huddled in the furthest booth. She couldn't tell whether he was drunk or asleep. Perhaps he might even be dead. But she recognized him. She had seen him before, patiently trying to hand out texts in Mell Street market.

She found a tenpenny piece in her purse, dialled the seven familiar digits, then pushed the coin home as Maurice's voice repeated the number. He had answered at once. But then, the telephone was by his bed. She said:

'It's Philippa. Please come. My mother's dead. I wanted her to kill herself and she has.'

He said:

'Are you sure she's dead?'

'I'm sure.'

'Where are you ringing from?'

'Marylebone Station.'

'I'll come straight away. Wait where you are. Don't talk to anyone. Do nothing until I come.'

The streets were almost empty in the calm of the early hours, but, even so, he must have driven very fast. It seemed only a matter of minutes before she heard the Rover.

She walked towards him and into his arms. Suddenly they were round her, fierce and stiff, a clasp of possession not a gesture of comfort. Then, as suddenly, he let her go and she tottered and nearly fell. She felt his fingers gripping her shoulder, propelling her towards the car. He said:

'Show me.'

The Rover slid to a stop outside the door of number 12. He took his time over locking it, looking up and down the street, calm and unhurried as if this were a late social visit and he would prefer on the whole not to be observed. She turned the key in the Yale lock and he followed her upstairs. Their climbing feet echoed in the hall. If he noticed the smashed lock on the flat door, he said nothing. She led the way to her mother's room and stood aside, waiting and watching while he walked over to the bed and looked down. He read the suicide note, his face expressionless. He picked up the empty bottle and studied the label, then tipped out on to his palm the one white bullet-shaped pellet. He said:

'Distalgesic. Considerate of her to have left this. It'll save the analyst time and trouble. I wonder how she got hold of it. Distalgesic is on prescription; you can't just buy it across the counter. Someone must have smuggled it into prison for her, if she didn't steal it from the hospital wing or have it prescribed for her. That's probably something we'll never know. She's not the first person to have mistaken the strength of this stuff. It's got paracetamol in it; but that isn't the danger. It contains an opium-type compound. An overdose kills very quickly. She was planning the usual histrionic gesture and misjudged the strength.'

Philippa wanted to reply: 'She didn't misjudge anything or anyone. She killed herself because she meant to kill herself, because she knew that's what I wanted her to do. You might at least give her the credit of knowing what she did.' But she said nothing. He bent his head slightly and looked at the savaged throat intently, like a doctor. Then he frowned. It was a frown of worried distaste, as if he were faced with a technical problem and had encountered an unexpected snag. He said:

'Who did this?'

'I did. At least I suppose I did.'

'You suppose you did?'

'I can remember wanting to kill her. I can remember going into the kitchen and getting the knife. That's all.'

'When you talk to the police, forget the first sentence. You didn't kill her, so what you intended or wanted isn't relevant. Did you break down the door, too?'

So he had noticed. But of course he had. She said:

'After I got back from Caldecote Terrace we quarrelled. I ran out of the flat. I didn't intend to come back. But then I did come back. We've only one pair of keys and I'd forgotten to take them. I banged on the door but she wouldn't let me in, so I broke it down. I had a chisel with me from the tool chest. I'm not sure why. I think I might have been threatening her with it before I ran out, but I can't remember now.'

He said:

'If you didn't take the keys with you, how did you get in at the street door? Aren't they on the same ring?'

She had forgotten that. She said quickly:

'There's only a Yale there. I slipped the latch up. I got used to doing that if I went out briefly at night.'

'Where is the chisel, the one you used on the door?'

'I put it back in the tool box.'

The inquisition had ended. He moved from the bed and said:

'Come away from here. Is there another room or somewhere comfortable?'

'No, not very comfortable. There's only my room and the kitchen.'

He placed his arm round her shoulders and pushed her gently into the passage. They went into the kitchen. He said:

'I'm going to ring the police now from Marylebone Station. Do you want to come with me, or are you all right here?'

'I'll come with you.'

'Yes, that would be best. Get your coat. It's cold.'

He made her wait in the car while he telephoned. It didn't take long. When he came back to the car he said:

'They'll be here very quickly. When they come just tell them what you told me. You can't remember anything between going to the kitchen drawer for the knife and running out to telephone me.'

The police came quickly too. There seemed a lot of them for so unimportant a death. She was put to wait in her own room. They lit the gas fire. They brought her tea. She wanted to explain that it was the wrong cup, her mother's cup. There was a policewoman with her, blonde, pretty, almost as young as herself. She looked attractive in her dark blue, well-cut uniform. Her face, disciplined of pity, watchful, was carefully neutral. Philippa thought:

'She isn't sure whether she's guarding a victim or a villain. Normally she would have put a consoling hand round my shoulders. But then, there is that slit in my mother's throat.' When the detective came in to question her Maurice was with him, and another man whom she recognized as Maurice's solicitor. He introduced him formally.

'Philippa, I don't know whether you remember Charles Cullinford, my solicitor. This is my daughter.'

She stood up and shook hands. It was as punctilious and ordinary as if they were meeting in the drawing-room at Caldecote Terrace. He kept his eyes rather too carefully from looking round the bleak little bedroom. The police brought in two chairs from her mother's room. They introduced the inspector to her but she didn't take in his name. He was dark and fitted rather too well into his clothes and his eyes had no kindness in them. But he questioned her gently and Maurice was at her side.

'Has anyone else been here this evening?'

'No. Only us.'

'Who broke in the door?'

'I did it. I did it with the chisel in the kitchen drawer.'

'Why did you take the chisel with you when you left the flat?'

'In case she tried to lock me out.'

'Had your mother ever done that before?'

'No.'

'Why did you think she might lock you out tonight?'

'We had a quarrel after my father had told me that she'd given me away.'

'Your father says that you ran out of the flat and walked for about three hours. What happened when you came back?'

'I found that the door was locked and she didn't answer, so I broke in with the chisel.'

'Did you know when you found her that she was dead?'

'I think so. I can't remember what I felt. I can't remember what happened after I broke down the door. I think I wanted to kill her.'

'Where did you get the knife?'

'From the kitchen drawer.'

'But before that? It's new, isn't it?'

'My mother bought it. We wanted a sharp knife. I don't know where she got it.'

They went away again. There was a knock at the door, loud voices, confident feet. Her door was ajar. The policewoman got up and closed it. The feet were moving more slowly now, half-shuffling down the passage. They were taking her mother away. When she realized this she sprang up with a cry, but the policewoman was quicker. She felt her shoulder seized in a surprisingly strong grip and, gently but firmly, she was forced back into her chair.

The blur of voices came through the door, disconnected words, ' . . . clearly dead when she stuck the knife in. You didn't need to pull me out of bed to tell you that. I suppose you've got a charge somewhere which fits the case if you want to find one, but it can't be homicide.'

Maurice's voice:

'This place is pathetic. God knows what these six weeks have been like for her. I couldn't stop her . . . she's of age . . . my fault. I should never have told her that her mother battered and then abandoned her.'

She thought she heard someone say:

'It's all for the best.' But perhaps that was imagination. Perhaps that was only what they were all thinking. Then Maurice was standing over her.

'We're going home now, Philippa. It's going to be all right.'

But of course it would be all right. Maurice would arrange it all. He would dispose of the flat, selling the last few weeks of the lease, get rid of all that was left of their life together. She would never see any of their belongings again. The Henry Walton would be replaced on her wall at Caldecote Terrace. That was too expensive to be discarded. But it was spoilt for her. She would look at it now with different eyes, seeing behind the elegance and order the prison hulks lying off Gravesend, the flogging-block, the public hangman. But there had to be some limit to the indulgence of sensitivity. She would be expected to go on living with the Walton. But everything else would go. The rest would be treated as the rubbish it was. His lawyers would handle the police, would gentle her through the further questioning, the inquest, the publicity. Only there wasn't likely to be much publicity. Maurice would see to that too. Everyone – police, coroner, Press – would be sympathetic. When they remembered that ravaged throat they would fight down repulsion or dislike, remembering whose daughter she was. They would be sorry for her; but they would be a little frightened too. Had she only imagined the inspector's final words, bluff, almost humorous:

'You can take her home now, sir. And for God's sake keep her away from knives.'

Afterwards, he would take her away, perhaps to Italy since an Italian visit had always been his personal therapy. They would see together the cities she had planned one day to see with her mother. How long would it be before he could look into her eyes without wondering whether she was, after all, her mother's daughter, without asking himself whether she would have plunged that knife into a living throat. Perhaps the thought would excite him; people were excited by violence. What, after all, was the sexual act but a voluntarily endured assault, a momentary death?

BOOK FOUR

Epilogue at Evensong

1

Sunday afternoon Evensong was over. The packed congregation, released from their role of silent participants in the music, joined with cheerful abandon in the concluding hymn. The boy choristers, their calm candle-lit faces rising translucent as flowers from their ruffs, had closed their books and were filing from their stalls. Philippa rose from her knees, shook free her hair, twitched the pleated cotton more comfortably on her shoulders and joined the small band of similarly white-gowned members of college who were following the procession out through the carved screen and into the cool, light-filled immensity of the antechapel.

She saw him almost immediately, but then she would have recognized this insignificant little man anywhere in the world. He was standing in his neat over-pressed suit at the end of the first row, diminished under the marvel of Wastell's surging vault, but with his own small human dignity. His hands, those well-remembered hands, were resting on the back of the chair in front of him. As she came within touching distance, the knuckles tightened into shining pebbles. Their eyes met and he looked steadily at her with what she thought was a mute appeal that she shouldn't escape him. It never occurred to her to try; nor did she believe for one moment that this encounter was by chance. After she left the chapel she lingered at the south porch until he came up quietly beside her. They didn't greet each other but turned, as if by mutual consent, and began pacing the sunlit path beside the Gibbs Building. She said:

'How did you find me? But I'd forgotten; you're an expert at tracking people down.'

'It was your book. I read the reviews and two of them said that you were a student at King's. You published it under your name, Philippa Ducton.'

'Ducton's my name. I dropped the Rose. It didn't suit me. I thought I was entitled to one small personal preference of identity. But you didn't come here, surely, to congratulate me on the novel. Did you read it?'

'I asked for it at the library.'

She laughed, and looking at her he flushed and said:

'Is that the wrong thing to say to a writer? I suppose I ought to have bought it.'

'Why should you? And you couldn't have welcomed it – the name Ducton on your shelves. Did you enjoy it?'

She could see from his face that he wasn't sure whether she was teasing him. At last he said, surprisingly:

'It was clever, of course. Some of the critics said that it was brilliant. But I thought that it was harsh, unfeeling.'

'Yes it was. That's just what it was, unfeeling. But you didn't take all this trouble to track me down just so that we could have a literary discussion.'

Looking at his face, she said quickly:

'I'm not sorry to see you. You had to leave suddenly when we last met. I've had that feeling, too, that there's unfinished business between us. I've wondered from time to time about you, what you were doing, where you were.'

She wanted to add: 'And whether you were happier knowing that my mother was dead.' But looking at his calm, untroubled face, that was a question which she didn't need to ask. Perhaps that was why revenge was so satisfying; it worked.

He answered her eagerly, as if he were glad to be telling her.

'I left London after the inquest on your mother and travelled about England and Wales for about two years. I stayed at cheap boarding-houses in the summer and moved into better-class ones in the autumn and winter. You get special rates out of season. I spent my time looking at places, buildings, thinking about myself. I wasn't unhappy. Six months ago I returned to London and went back to the Casablanca. That's the hotel where I took a room when I was tracking you down. I'm not sure why I went back, except that I felt at home there. It was just the same; the blind telephonist, the one you saw me with in Regent's Park, was still there. Her name's Violet Tetley. We started going out together on her free afternoons. We're going to get married.'

So this was why he had come. She said:

'And you don't know how much you ought to tell her?'

'She knows about Julie, of course. And I told her that both the Ductons were dead. But I'm not sure whether I ought to tell her what

I tried to do. There's no one in the world but you I can talk to about it, no one else to consult. I had to find you.'

She said:

'If you're marrying a blind woman, I shouldn't advise you to tell her that you once twisted a knife in another woman's throat. It could be unsettling.'

The shock and the hurt on his face were as palpable as if she had struck him. Even the physical manifestation was the same. He flushed, and then became very pale, except for one scarlet lash on his cheek. She said more gently:

'I'm sorry. I'm not a kind person. I try to be sometimes, but I'm not very good at it yet.' She nearly added: 'And the person who could have taught me how is dead.' She went on:

'It's your bad luck that you're stuck with me as a confidante. But the advice is still sound. We none of us know another human being so well that we can be absolutely sure about him. I can't see what you gain by telling. Why distress her?'

'But I love her. We love each other. Doesn't that mean that I ought to be honest with her?'

She said:

'This conversation between us is honest as far as I can make it so. That doesn't mean that either of us likes it the better. You have the whole of your past life to be honest about. One incident in it isn't important.'

'It was an important incident to me. And it brought us together. I wouldn't have been at the Casablanca, wouldn't have met Violet, if I hadn't tried to kill your mother.'

She could have replied that his child and her mother would both have been alive if he had kept his daughter at home on a foggy January night twelve and a half years ago. But what point was there in tracing back the long concatenation of chance. She said, interested:

'How are you going to manage? Have you a job?'

'I've lived simply during the last three years. I've got about twelve thousand pounds left from the sale of the house. That will be enough to put down on a cottage somewhere. And my local authority pension starts in a few months' time. We should be all right. We don't want a large place, just somewhere with a garden. Violet loves the smell of roses. She became blind when she was eight; before that she could see, so she has some memories, and if I describe things to her carefully, buildings, the sky, flowers, it helps. I have to look at things differently now, more carefully, so that I can remember them. We're so happy together, I can't believe it.'

She wondered if the happiness included going to bed together. Probably it did. He wasn't sexually repulsive, this poor little murderer manqué. And even Crippen had had his Ethel Le Neve. The unlikeliest couples found their way to that irrational joy. She remembered the feel of his hair under her hand, silkier than her own. And his skin was soft, unblemished. Besides, his Violet wouldn't have to see him. It must be strange to be blind, making love always with one's eyes shut. She caught a glance at his smile, secret, reminiscent, almost lubricious. He had come to her with his anxieties, but that wasn't one of them. Remembering the girl she had seen in the park, she wondered whether his Violet was young enough to have a child. As if his mind had flowed with hers, he said:

'She's much younger than I am. If she has a baby I could help look after him. There's nothing we can't manage together.'

He turned to her.

'Do you ever feel that you don't deserve happiness? The time I first went out with her, the day you saw us in the rose garden, I was exploiting her, making use of her blindness. I was lonely and she was the only person I could feel safe with, because she couldn't see.'

How early he must have learned that primeval lesson, the distrust of joy. Touch wood, cross fingers, light a candle, please God don't notice that I'm happy. She wanted to say:

'I used my mother to avenge myself on my adoptive father. We all use each other. Why should you expect to be less corrupt than the rest of us.' Instead she said:

'Why not learn to be gentle with yourself, to accept the possibility of happiness? Forget about my mother and me. That's over.'

'But suppose Violet found out? She'd find it hard to forgive, the deception or what I did.'

'There's nothing for her to forgive. It wasn't her throat. Besides, we can forgive anything as long as it isn't done to us. Haven't you learned that? And how could she find out? You needn't worry about me. I shan't ever tell.'

'But you're a writer; you might want to use it one day.'

She nearly laughed aloud. So that was what was worrying him.

He must have borrowed her novel from the library in trepidation. What, she wondered, had he been expecting? Some lurid Gothic romance with himself as a pathetic Eumenides? But he would hardly be expecting a dissertation on the nature of the creative imagination. She said:

'Some writers can only write about their own direct experience. That's not the kind of writer I am or want to be. I know that we all use each other, but I hope to use people with rather more subtlety than that.'

He said, tentatively, as if venturing on dangerous ground:

'Do they know about your mother here? After all, you do call yourself Ducton.'

'Some of them know and some of them guess. It's hardly a subject that comes up naturally in conversation.'

'And does it make any difference, to you I mean?'

'Only, perhaps, to make them a little afraid of me. For someone who values privacy that's no bad thing.'

They had reached the bridge over the Cam. Philippa paused and gazed down at the shimmering water. He stood beside her, his tiny hands grasping the parapet. And then he asked:

'Do you miss her?'

She thought: 'I shall miss her every day of my life.' But she said:

'Yes. I'm not sure that I really knew her. We only lived together for five weeks. She didn't say very much. But when she was there she was more there than anyone I've ever known. And I was there too.'

He seemed to understand what she meant. They walked on, again in silence, and then he said:

'I've wondered about you. I'm grateful to you for what you did for me. I'm frightened of authority, frightened of being locked up. If you'd called the police that night I know I would never have been able to cope. And I would never have met Violet again. I've wondered many times how things were with you, what happened after I left you, whether your mother – I mean Mrs Palfrey – is well.'

He could have been asking after any casual acquaintance. She said:

'She's very well. She has a dog now. His name is Scamp. And nothing very much happened to me. My adoptive father arranged everything; he's a great fixer. Afterwards he took me on a long holiday to Italy. We went to see the mosaics at Ravenna.'

She didn't add: 'And in Ravenna I went to bed with him.' She wondered how he would have looked, what he would have said, if she had responded to his confidence with that gratuitous news. And it wasn't, after all, important. What, she wondered, had it meant exactly, that gentle, tender, surprisingly uncomplicated coupling; an affirmation, a curiosity satisfied, a test successfully passed, an obstacle ceremoniously moved out of the way so that they could again take up their roles of father and daughter, the excitement of incest without its legal prohibition, without any more guilt than they carried already? That single night together, the windows open to the smell of cypresses, to the warm Italian night, had been necessary, inevitable, but it was no longer important. She said:

'My mother insured her life for five hundred pounds so that she could pay her share of the flat. There wasn't a suicide prohibition in the policy – I don't suppose they bothered with so small a sum – so I got the money. She must have arranged it secretly soon after we started living together, perhaps when she went to see her probation officer. No one knows for certain how she got hold of the Distalgesic but she must have been secreting those tablets away for months. I tell myself that it shows that she was thinking of killing herself even before she came out of prison, that her death had nothing to do with me. There are so many expedients for getting rid of guilt. You'll find one for yourself in time.'

He said nothing more. He seemed satisfied. Suddenly he stopped and held out his hand. She shook it. The gesture seemed to be important to him. Then he walked on alone down the avenue in the spring sunshine, under the tender green of chestnuts, beeches and lime trees, between the bright grass patterned with gold and purple crocuses. Just before he reached a turn in the avenue he paused and looked back, not, she thought, at her, but at the chapel, as if to fix it in his mind. With what pathetic confidence – meagrely equipped, encumbered, but not by failure, not by guilt – he was setting out on his new odyssey. She hoped he would find his patch of rose garden. She stood watching him until he was out of sight. Almost she envied him. If it is only through learning to love that we find identity, then he had found his. She hoped one day to find hers. She wished him well. And perhaps to be able to wish him well with all that she could recognize of her unpractised heart, to say a short untutored prayer for him and his Violet, was in itself a small accession of grace.

1880